THE NAKED GOD

'Offers a perfect opportunity to look at what's starry in British sci-fi just now . . . the Hamilton series is a joy, in the rollicking, whizzbang, cosmic explosions and wonderful weird alien kind of way . . . There is nothing better of this ilk around'

Guardian

'That, for all its inter-galactic sweep, the narrative is so tightly focused and controlled, and that the author manages to bring the entire narrative to a satisfying and transcendent completion is a monumental achievement . . . Peter F. Hamilton has managed to re-energize my sense of wonder, and thus the only fitting word to describe this trilogy must be "masterpiece"'

Interzone

'Unsettling, genuinely original and worthy of comparision to the best hard sci-fi from the likes of Asimov and Clarke, *The Naked God* is a fittingly brilliant conclusion to one of the major works of British sci-fi'

SFX

'The depth and clarity of the future Hamilton envisions is as complex and involving as they come'

Publishers Weekly

by Peter F. Hamilton

Mindstar Rising

A Quantum Murder

The Nano Flower

Fallen Dragon

Misspent Youth

Pandora's Star

Judas Unchained

The Night's Dawn Trilogy

The Reality Dysfunction

The Neutronium Alchemist

The Naked God

The Confederation Handbook
(A Guide to the 'Night's Dawn Trilogy')

. . . and in the same Timeline

A Second Chance at Eden

Peter F. Hamilton

THE NAKED GOD

BOOK THREE OF THE NIGHT'S DAWN TRILOGY

PAN BOOKS

First published 1999 by Macmillan

This edition published 2000 by Pan Books
an imprint of Pan Macmillan Ltd
Pan Macmillan, 20 New Wharf Road, London N1 9RR
Basingstoke and Oxford
Associated companies throughout the world
www.panmacmillan.com

ISBN-13: 978-0-330-35145-4
ISBN-10: 0-330-35145-1

19 18 17 16

A CIP catalogue record for this book is available from
the British Library.

Typeset by SetSystems Ltd, Saffron Walden, Essex
Printed and bound in Great Britain by
Mackays of Chatham plc, Chatham, Kent

Finally, some well-deserved acknowledgements

The 'Night's Dawn' trilogy took me six and a half years to write, during which time I was given support, drinks, love, parties, bad jokes, sympathy, friendship, and exotic e-mails by the following:

John F. Hamilton
Kate Fell
Simon Spanton-Walker
Jane Spanton-Walker
Kate Farquhar-Thomson
Christine Manby
Antony Harwood
Carys Thomas

James Lovegrove
Lou Pitman
Peter Lavery
Betsy Mitchell
Jim Burns
Dave Garnett
Jane Adams
Graham Joyce

Thanks, Chaps.

Peter F. Hamilton
Rutland, April 1999

The Timeline and Cast of Characters are

to be found after the main text

1

Jay Hilton was sound asleep when every electrophorescent strip in the paediatric ward sprang up to full intensity. The simple dream of her mother broke apart like a stained-glass statue shattered by a powerful gust of sharp white light, colourful splinters tumbling off into the glare.

Jay blinked heavily against the rush of light, raising her head in confusion. The familiar scenery of the ward hardened around her. She felt so tired. It certainly wasn't morning yet. A huge yawn forced her mouth open. All around her the other children were waking up in bleary-eyed mystification. Holomorph stickers began reacting to the light, translucent cartoon images rising up to perform their mischievous antics. Animatic dolls cooed sympathetically as children clutched at them for reassurance. Then the doors at the far end of the ward slid open, and the nurses came hurrying in.

One look at the brittle smiles on their faces was all Jay needed. Something was badly wrong. Her heart shivered. Surely not the possessed? Not here?

The nurses began ushering children out of their beds, and along the central aisle towards the doors. Complaints and questions were firmly ignored.

'It's a fire drill,' the senior staff nurse called out. 'Come along, quickly now. I want you out of here and into the lifts. Pronto. Pronto.' He clapped his hands loudly.

Jay shoved the thin duvet back and scuttled down off the bed.

Her long cotton nightie, tangled round her knees, took a moment to straighten. She was about to join the others charging along the aisle when she caught the flickers of motion and light outside the window. Every morning since she'd arrived Jay had sat in front of that window, gazing solemnly out at Mirchusko and its giddy green cloudscape. She'd never seen speckles of light swarming out there before.

Danger.

The silent mental word was spoken so quickly Jay almost didn't catch it, though the feel of Haile was unmistakable. She looked round, expecting to see the Kiint ambling towards her. But there was only the rank of flustered nurses propelling children along.

Knowing full well she wasn't doing what she was supposed to, Jay padded over to the big window and pressed her nose against it. A slim band of tiny blue-white stars had looped itself round Tranquillity. They were all moving, contracting around the habitat. She could see now that they weren't really stars, they were lengthening. Flames. Brilliant, tiny flames. Hundreds of them.

My friend. My friend. Lifeloss anguish.

Now that was definitely Haile, and intimating plenty of distress. Jay took a step back from the window, seeing misty grey swirls where her face and hands had pressed against it. 'What's the matter?' she asked the empty air.

A cascade of new flames burst into existence outside the habitat. Expanding knots blossoming seemingly at random across space. Jay gasped at the sight. There were thousands of them, interlacing and expanding. It was so pretty.

Friend. Friend.

Evacuation procedure initiated.

Jay frowned. The second mental voice came as a faint echo. She thought it was one of the adult Kiint, possibly Lieria. Jay had only encountered Haile's parents a few times. They were awfully intimidating, though they'd been nice enough to her.

Designation. Two.

No. The adult responded forcefully. **Forbidden.**

Designation.

You may not, child. Sorrow felt for all human suffering. But obedience required.

2

No. Friend. My friend. Designation. Two. Confirmed.

Jay had never felt Haile so determined before. It was kind of scary. 'Please?' she asked nervously. 'What's happening?'

A torrent of light burst through the window. It was as if a sun had risen over Mirchusko's horizon. All of space was alive with brilliant efflorescences.

The adult Kiint said: **Evacuation enacted.**

Designated.

Jay felt a wash of guilty triumph rushing out from her friend. She wanted to reach out and comfort her, who she knew from the adult's reaction was in Big Trouble over something. Instead, she concentrated on forming a beaming smile at the heart of her own mind, hoping Haile would pick it up. Then the air around her was crawling as if she was caught in a breeze.

'Jay!' one of the nurses called. 'Come along sweetie, you . . .'

The light around Jay was fading fast, along with the sounds of the ward. She could just hear the nurse's gasp of astonishment. The breeze abruptly turned into a small gale, whipping her nightie around and making her bristly hair stand on end. Some kind of grey fog was forming around her, a perfectly spherical bubble of the stuff, with her at the centre. Except she couldn't feel any dampness in the air. It darkened rapidly, reducing the ward to weak spectral outlines. Then the boundary expanded at a speed so frightening that she screamed. The boundary vanished, and with it any sign of the ward. She was alone in space devoid of stars. And falling.

Jay put her hands to her head and screamed again, as hard as she possibly could. It didn't put a stop to any of the horror. She paused to suck down a huge breath. That was when the boundary reappeared out on the edge of nowhere. Hurtling towards her so fast from every direction that she knew the impact would squash her flat. She jammed her eyes shut. 'MUMMY!'

Something like a stiff feather tickled the soles of her feet, and she was abruptly standing on solid ground. Jay windmilled her arms for balance, pitching forward. She landed hard on some kind of cool floor, her eyes still tight shut. The air she gulped down was warmer than it had been in the ward, and a lot more humid. Funny smell. Rosy light was playing over her eyelids.

Still crouched on all fours, Jay risked a quick peep as she gathered herself to scream again. The sight which greeted her was so incredible that the breath stalled in her throat. 'Oh gosh,' was all she eventually managed to squeak.

*

Joshua initiated the ZTT jump with little enthusiasm. His downbeat mood was one he shared with all the *Lady Mac*'s crew and passengers (those that weren't in zero-tau). To have achieved so much, only to have their final triumph snatched away.

Except ... Once the initial shock of finding Tranquillity had vanished from its orbit had subsided, he wasn't frightened. Not for Ione, or his child. Tranquillity hadn't been destroyed, there was at least that comfort. Which logically meant the habitat had been possessed and snatched out of the universe.

He didn't believe it.

But his intuition was hardly infallible. Perhaps he simply didn't want to believe it. Tranquillity was home. The emotional investment he had in the habitat and its precious contents was enormous. Tell anyone that everything they ever treasured has been erased, and the reaction is always the same. Whatever. His vacillation made him as miserable as the rest of the ship, just for a different reason.

'Jump confirmed,' he said. 'Samuel, you're on.'

Lady Mac had jumped into one of Trafalgar's designated emergence zones, a hundred thousand kilometres above Avon. Her transponder was already blaring out her flight authority codes. Somehow Joshua didn't think that would quite be enough. Not when you barged in unexpected on the Confederation's primary military base in the middle of a crisis like this one.

'I've got distortion fields focusing on us,' Dahybi said drolly. 'Five of them, I think.'

The flight computer alerted Joshua that targeting radars were locking on to the hull. When he accessed the sensors rising out of their recesses, he found three voidhawks and two frigates on interception courses. Trafalgar's Strategic Defence Command was directing a barrage of questions at him. He glanced over at the Edenist as he started to datavise a response. Samuel was lying prone on his acceleration couch, eyes closed as he conversed with other Edenists in the asteroid.

4

Sarha grinned round phlegmatically. 'How many medals do you think they'll give us apiece?'

'Uh oh,' Liol grunted. 'However many it is, we might be getting them posthumously. I think one of the frigates has just realized our antimatter drive is ever so slightly highly radioactive.'

'Great,' she grumbled.

Monica Foulkes didn't like the sound of that; as far as the Confederation Navy was aware, it was only Organization ships who were using antimatter. She hadn't wanted to take Mzu back to Tranquillity, and she certainly hadn't wanted to wind up at Trafalgar. But in the discussion which followed their discovery of Tranquillity's disappearance she didn't exactly have the casting vote. The original agreement between herself and Samuel had just about disintegrated when they rendezvoused with the *Beezling*.

Then Calvert had insisted on the First Admiral being the final arbitrator of what was to be done with Mzu, Adul, and himself. Samuel had agreed. And she couldn't produce any rational argument against it. Silently, she acknowledged that maybe the only true defence against more Alchemists being built was a unified embargo covenant between the major powers. After all, such an agreement almost worked for antimatter.

Not that such angst counted for much right now. Like ninety per cent of her mission to date, the critical deciding factor was outside her control. All she could do was stick close to Mzu, and make sure the prime requirement of technology transfer wasn't violated. Though by allowing it to be deployed against the Organization she'd probably screwed that up too. Her debrief was shaping up to be a bitch.

Monica frowned over at Samuel, who was still silent, his brow creased up in concentration. She added a little prayer of her own to all the unheard babble of communication whirling around *Lady Mac*, for the navy to exercise some enlightenment and tolerance.

Trafalgar's Strategic Defence Command told Joshua to hold his attitude, but refused to grant any approach vector until his status was established. The navy's emergence zone patrol ships approached to within a cautious hundred kilometres, and took up a three-dimensional diamond observation formation. Targeting radars remained locked on.

5

Admiral Lalwani herself talked to Samuel, unable to restrain her incredulity as he explained what had happened. Given that the *Lady Macbeth* contained not only Mzu and others who understood the Alchemist's principles, but a quantity of antimatter as well, the final decision on allowing the ship to dock belonged to the First Admiral himself. It took twenty minutes to arrive, but Joshua eventually received a flight vector from Strategic Defence Command. They were allocated a docking-bay in the asteroid's northern spaceport.

'And Joshua,' Samuel said earnestly, 'don't deviate from it. Please.'

Joshua winked, knowing it was being seen by the hundreds of Edenists who were borrowing the agent's eyes to monitor *Lady Mac*'s bridge. 'What, Lagrange Calvert fly off line?'

The flight to Trafalgar took eighty minutes. The number of antimatter technology specialists waiting for them in the docking-bay was almost as great as the number of marines. On top of that were a large complement of uniformed CNIS officers.

They weren't stormed, exactly. No personal weapons were actually taken out of their holsters. Though once the airlock tube was sealed and pressurized, *Lady Mac*'s crew had little to do except hand over the powerdown codes to a navy maintenance team. Zero-tau pods were opened, and the various bewildered occupants Joshua had accumulated during his pursuit of the Alchemist were ushered off the ship. After a *very* thorough body scan, the polite, steel-faced CNIS officers escorted everyone to a secure barracks deep inside the asteroid. Joshua wound up in a suite that would have done a four-star hotel credit. Ashly and Liol were sharing it with him.

'Well now,' Liol said as the door closed behind them. 'Guilty of carrying antimatter, flung in prison by secret police who've never heard of civil rights, and after we're dead, Al Capone is going to invite us to have a quiet word.' He opened the cherrywood cocktail bar and smiled at the impressive selection of bottles inside. 'It can't get any worse.'

'You forgot Tranquillity being vanquished,' Ashly chided. Liol waved a bottle in apology.

Joshua ignored the suite's ritzy decor, and slumped down into a soft black leather chair in the middle of the lounge. 'It might not get worse for you. Just remember, I know what the Alchemist does, and how. They can't afford to let me go.'

'You might know what it does,' Ashly said. 'But with respect, Captain, I don't think you would be much help to anyone seeking the technical details necessary to construct another.'

'One hint is all it takes,' Joshua muttered. 'One careless comment that'll point researchers in the right direction.'

'Stop worrying, Josh. The Confederation passed that point a long time ago. Besides, the navy owes us big-time, and the Edenists, and the Kulu Kingdom. We pulled their arses out of the fire. You'll fly *Lady Mac* again.'

'Know what I'd do if I was the First Admiral? Put me into a zero-tau pod for the rest of time.'

'I won't let them do that to my little brother.'

Joshua put his hands behind his head, and smiled up at Liol. 'The second thing I'd do would be to put you in the pod next to mine.'

*

Planets sparkled in the twilight sky. Jay could see at least fifteen of them strung out along a curving line. The nearest one appeared a bit smaller than Earth's moon. She thought that was just because it was a long way off. In every other respect it was similar to any of the Confederation's terracompatible planets, with deep blue oceans and emerald continents, the whole globe wrapped in thick tatters of white cloud. The only difference was the lights; cities larger than some of Earth's old nations gleamed with magisterial splendour. Entire weather patterns of cloud smeared across the nightside diffused the urban radiance, soaking the oceans in a perpetual pearl gloaming.

Jay sat back on her heels, staring up delightedly at the magical sky. A high wall ringed the area she was in. She guessed that the line of planets extended beyond those she could see, but the wall blocked her view of the horizon. A star with a necklace of inhabited planets! Thousands would be needed to make up such a circle. None of Jay's didactic memories about solar systems mentioned one with so many planets, not even if you counted gas giant moons.

Friend Jay. Safe. Gleefulness at survival.

Jay blinked, and lowered her gaze. Haile was trying to run towards her. As always when the baby Kiint got overexcited her legs lost most of their coordination. She came very close to tripping with every other step. The sight of her lolloping about chaotically made Jay smile. It faded as she began to take in the scene behind her friend.

She was in some kind of circular arena two hundred metres across, with a marblelike ebony floor. The wall surrounding it was thirty metres high, sealed with a transparent dome. There were horizontal gashes at regular intervals along the vertical surface, windows into brightly lit rooms that seemed to be furnished with large cubes of primary colours. Adult Kiint were moving round inside, although an awful lot of them had stopped what they were doing to look directly at her.

Haile thundered up, half-formed tractamorphic tentacles waving round excitedly. Jay grabbed on to a couple of them, feeling them palpitate wildly inside her fingers.

'Haile! Was that you who did this?'

Two adult Kiint were walking across the arena floor towards her. Jay recognized them as Nang and Lieria. Beyond them, a black star erupted out of thin air. In less than a heartbeat it had expanded to a sphere fifteen metres in diameter, its lower quarter merging with the floor. The surface immediately dissolved to reveal another adult Kiint. Jay stared at the process in fascination. A ZTT jump, but without a starship. She focused hard on her primer-level didactic memory of the Kiint.

I did, Haile confessed. Her tractamorphic flesh writhed in agitation, so Jay just squeezed tighter, offering reassurance. Only we were designated to evacuate the all around at lifeloss moment. I included you in designation, against parental proscription. Much shame. Puzzlement. Haile turned her head to face her parents. Query lifeloss act approval? Many nice friends in the all around.

We do not approve.

Jay flicked a nervous gaze at the two adults, and pressed herself closer against Haile. Nang formshifted his tractamorphic appendage into a flat tentacle, which he laid across his daughter's back. The juvenile Kiint visibly calmed at the gesture of affection. Jay thought there was a mental exchange of some kind involved, too, sensing a hint of compassion and serenity.

Why did we not help? Haile asked.

We must never interfere in the primary events of other species during their evolution towards Omega comprehension. You must learn and obey

8

this law above all else. However, it does not prevent us from grieving at their tragedy.

Jay felt the last bit was included for her benefit. 'Don't be angry with Haile,' she said solemnly. 'I would have done the same for her. And I didn't want to die.'

Lieria reached out a tentacle tip, and touched Jay's shoulder. I thank you for the friendship you have shown Haile. In our hearts we are glad you are with us, for you will be completely safe here. I am sorry we could not do more for your friends. But our law cannot be broken.

A sudden sensation of bleak horror threatened to engulf Jay. 'Did Tranquillity really get blown up?' she wailed.

We do not know. It was under a concerted attack when we left. However, Ione Saldana may have surrendered. There is a high possibility the habitat and its population survived.

'We left,' Jay whispered wondrously to herself. There were eight adult Kiint standing on the arena floor now, all the researchers from Tranquillity's Laymil Project. 'Where are we?' She glanced up at the dusky sky again, and that awesome constellation.

This is our home star system. You are the first true human to visit.

'But . . .' Flashes of didactic memory tumbled through her brain. She looked up at those enticing, bright planets again. 'This isn't Jobis.'

Nang and Lieria looked at each other in what was almost an awkward pause.

No, Jobis is just one of our science mission outposts. It is not in this galaxy.

Jay burst into tears.

*

Right from the start of the possession crisis the Jovian Consensus had always acknowledged that it was a prime target. Its colossal industrial facilities were inevitably destined to produce a torrent of munitions, bolstering the reserve stocks of Adamist navies which thanks to budgetary considerations were not all they should be. The response of the Yosemite Consensus to the Capone Organization had already shown what Edenism was capable of achieving along those lines, and that was with a mere thirty habitats. Jupiter had the resources of four thousand two hundred and fifty at its disposal.

Requests for material support started almost as soon as Trafalgar issued its first warning about the nature of the threat the Confederation was facing. Ambassadors requested and pleaded and called in every favour they thought Edenism owed them to secure a place in production schedules. Payment for the weapons involved loan agreements and fuseodollar transfers on a scale which could have purchased entire stage four star systems.

On top of that, it was Edenism which was providing the critical support for the Mortonridge Liberation in the form of serjeant constructs to act as foot soldiers. The one utterly pivotal psychological campaign waged against the possessed, proving to the Confederation at large that they could be beaten.

Fortunately, the practical aspects of assaulting one or more habitats were extremely difficult. Jupiter already had a superb strategic-defence network; among the possessed only the Organization had a fleet which could hope to mount any sort of large-scale offensive, and the distance between Earth and New California almost certainly precluded that. However, the prospect of a lone ship carrying antimatter on a fanatical suicide flight was a strong one. And then there was the remote possibility that Capone would acquire the Alchemist and use it against them. Although Consensus didn't know how the doomsday device worked, a ship certainly had to jump in to deploy it, which in theory gave the Edenists an interception window to destroy the device before it was deployed.

Preparations to solidify their defences had begun immediately. Fully one-third of the armaments coming out of the industrial stations were incorporated into a massively expanded SD architecture. The five hundred and fifty thousand kilometre orbital band containing the habitats was the most heavily protected, with the number of SD platforms doubled, and seeded with seven hundred thousand combat wasps to act as mines. A further million combat wasps were arranged in concentric shells around the massive planet out to the orbit of Callisto. Flotillas of multi-spectrum sensor satellites were dispersed among them, searching for any anomaly, however small, which pricked the potent energy storms churning through space around the gas giant.

Over fifteen thousand heavily armed patrol voidhawks complemented the static defences, circling the volatile cloudscape in elliptical, high-inclination orbits, ready to interdict any remotely suspicious incoming molecule. The fact that so many voidhawks had been taken off civil cargo flights was actually causing a tiny rise in the price of He$_3$, the first for over two hundred and sixty years.

Consensus considered the economic repercussions to be a worthwhile trade for the security such invulnerable defences provided. No ship, robot, or inert kinetic projectile could get within three million kilometres of Jupiter unless specifically permitted to do so.

Even a lone maniac would acknowledge an attempted attack would be the ultimate in futility.

*

The gravity fluctuation which appeared five hundred and sixty thousand kilometres above Jupiter's equator was detected instantaneously. It registered as an inordinately powerful twist of space-time in the distortion fields of the closest three hundred voidhawks. The intensity was so great that the gravitonic detectors in the local SD sensor array had to be hurriedly recalibrated in order to acquire an accurate fix. Visually it appeared as a ruby star, the gravity field lensing Jupiter's light in every direction. Surrounding dust motes and solar wind particles were sucked in, a cascade of pico-meteorites fizzing brilliant yellow.

Consensus went to condition one alert status. The sheer strength of the space warp ruled out any conventional starship emergence. And the location was provocatively close to the habitats, a hundred thousand kilometres from the nearest designated emergence zone. Affinity commands from Consensus were loaded into the combat wasps drifting inertly among the habitats. Three thousand fusion drives flared briefly, aligning the lethal drones on their new target. The patrol voidhawks formed a sub-Consensus of their own, designating approach vectors and swallow manoeuvres to englobe the invader.

The warp area expanded out to several hundred metres, alarming individual Edenists, though Consensus itself absorbed the fact calmly. It was already far larger than any conceivable voidhawk or blackhawk wormhole terminus. Then it began to flatten out into a perfectly circular two-dimensional fissure in space-time, and the real expansion sequence began. Within five seconds it was over eleven kilometres in diameter. Consensus quickly and concisely reformed its response pattern. Approaching voidhawks performed frantic fifteen-gee parabolas, curving clear then swallowing away. An extra eight thousand combat wasps burst into life, hurtling in towards the Herculean alien menace.

After another three seconds the fissure reached twenty kilometres in diameter, and stabilized. One side collapsed inwards, exposing the wormhole's throat. Three small specks zoomed out of the centre. *Oenone* and the other two voidhawks screamed their identity into the general affinity band, and implored: **HOLD YOUR FIRE!**

For the first time in its five hundred and twenty-one year history, the Jovian Consensus experienced the emotion of shock. Even then, its response wasn't entirely blunted. Specialist perceptual thought routines confirmed the three voidhawks remained unpossessed. A five second lockdown was loaded into the combat wasps.

What is happening? Consensus demanded.

Syrinx simply couldn't resist it. **We have a visitor**, she replied gleefully. Her entire crew was laughing around her on the bridge.

The counter-rotating spaceport was the first part to emerge from the gigantic wormhole terminus. A silver-white disc four and a half kilometres in diameter, docking-bay lights glittering like small towns huddled at the base of metal valleys, red and green strobes winking bright around the rim. Its slender spindle slid up after it, appearing to pull the dark rust-red polyp endcap along.

That was when the other starships began to rampage out of the terminus, voidhawks, blackhawks, and Confederation Navy vessels streaking off in all directions. Jupiter's SD sensors and patrol voidhawk distortion fields tracked them urgently. Consensus fired guidance updates at the incoming combat wasps, determinedly vectoring them away from the unruly incursion.

The habitat's main cylinder started to coast up out of the terminus, a prodigious seventeen kilometres in diameter. After the first thirty-two kilometres were clear, its central band of starscrapers emerged, hundreds of thousands of windows agleam with the radiance of lazy afternoon sunlight. Their bases just cleared the rim of the wormhole. There were no more starships to come after that, only the rest of the cylinder. When the emergence was complete, the wormhole irised shut and space returned to its natural state. The flotilla of patrol voidhawks thronging round detected a capacious distortion field folding back into the broad collar of polyp around the base of the habitat's southern endcap that formed the bed of its circumfluous sea.

Consensus directed a phenomenally restrained burst of curiosity at the newcomer.

Greetings, chorused Tranquillity and Ione Saldana. There was a distinct timbre of smugness in the hail.

*

For nearly ten hours the lift capsule had skimmed down the tower linking Supra-Brazil asteroid with the Govcentral state after which it was named. A smooth, silent ride that barely seemed to be moving at all. The only clue to how fast the lift capsules travelled (three thousand kilometres per hour) would come when they passed each other. But as they clung to rails on the exterior of the tower, and the only windows gave a direct view outward, such events remained out of sight to their passengers. Deliberately so; watching another capsule hurtling towards you at a combined speed of six thousand kilometres per hour was considered an absolute psychological no-go zone by the tower operators.

Just before it entered the upper fringes of the atmosphere, the lift capsule decelerated to subsonic velocity. It reached the stratosphere as dawn broke over South America. On Earth that was no longer an invigorating sight, all the passengers saw was an unbroken murky-grey cloud layer which covered most of the continent and a third of the South Atlantic. Only when the lift capsule was ten kilometres above the frothing upper layer could Quinn see the army of individual streamers from which the gigantic cyclone was composed, flowing around each other at perilous velocities. The seething mass was as compressed as any gas giant storm band, but infinitely drabber.

They descended into the slashing tendrils of cirrus, and the windows immediately reverberated from the barrage of fist-sized raindrops. There was nothing else to see after that, just formless smears of grey. A minute before they reached the ground station, the windows went black as the lift capsule entered the sheath which guarded the bottom of the tower from the worst violence of the planet's rabid weather.

Digits on the Royale Class lounge's touchdown counter reached zero, an event marked by only the slightest tremble as latch clamps closed round the base of the lift capsule. The magnetic rail disengaged, and a transporter rolled it clear of the tower, leaving the reception berth clear for the next capsule. Airlock hatches popped open, revealing long extendable corridors leading into the arrivals complex where treble the usual numbers of customs, immigration, and security officers waited to scan the passengers. Quinn sighed in mild resignation. He'd quite enjoyed the trip down, mellowing out with all the facilities the Royale Class lounge could provide. A welcome period of contemplation, assisted by the Norfolk Tears he'd been drinking.

He had arrived at Earth with one goal: conquest. Now at least he had some notions of how to go about subduing the planet for his Lord. The kind of exponential brute force approach the possessed had used up to now just wasn't an option on Earth. The arcologies were too isolated for that. It was curious, but the more Quinn thought about it, the more he realized that Earth was a representation of the Confederation in miniature, its vast population centres kept separate by an amok nature almost as lethal as the interstellar void. Seeds of his revolution would have to be planted very carefully indeed. If Govcentral security ever suspected an outbreak of possession, the arcology in question would be quarantined. And Quinn knew that even with his energistic powers there would be nothing he could do to escape once the vac-trains had been shut down.

Most of the other passengers had disembarked, and the chief stewardess was glancing in Quinn's direction. He rose from his deep leather seat, stretching the tiredness from his limbs. There was absolutely no way he'd ever get past the immigration desk, let alone security.

He walked towards the airlock hatch, and summoned the energistic power, mentally moulding it into the now familiar pattern. It crawled over his body, needle spears of static penetrating every cell. A swift groan was the only indication he showed of the grotesquery he experienced passing through the gateway into the ghost realm. His heart stopped, his breathing ceased, and the world about him lost its glimmer of substance. The solidity of walls and floors was still present, but ephemeral. Irrelevant if he really pressed.

The chief stewardess watched the last passenger step into the airlock, and turned back to the bar. Secured below the counter were several bottles of the complimentary Norfolk Tears and other expensive spirits and liqueurs which her team had opened. They were careful never to leave much, at most a third, before opening a new bottle. But a third of these drinks was an expensive commodity.

She began inventorying all these bottles as empty in her stock control block. The team would split them later, filling their personal flasks and taking them home. As long as they didn't get too greedy the company supervisor would let it pass. Her block's datavise turned to nonsense. She gave it an annoyed glare, and automatically rapped it against the bar, just as the lights started to flicker. Puzzled now, she frowned up at the ceiling. Electrical systems were failing all over the lounge. The AV pillar projection behind the bar had crashed into rainbow squiggles, the airlock hatch activators were whining loudly, though the hatch itself wasn't moving.

'What—?' she grumbled. Power loss was just about impossible in the lift capsules. Every component had multiple redundancy back-ups. She was about to call the lift capsule's operations officer when the lights steadied, and her stock control block came back on-line. 'Bloody typical,' she grunted. It still bothered her badly. If things could go wrong on the ground, they could certainly go wrong halfway up the tower.

She gave the waiting bottles a forlorn glance, knowing she was giving them up if she logged an official powerdown incident report. The company inspectorate authority would swarm all over the lift capsule. She carefully erased the inventory file she'd started, and datavised the lounge processor for a channel to the operations officer.

The call never got placed. Instead she received a priority datavise from the arrivals complex Security Office ordering her to remain exactly where she was. Outside, an alarm siren started its high-pitched urgent wailing. The sound made her jump, in eleven years of riding the tower she'd only ever heard it during practice drills.

The siren's clamour sounded muffled to Quinn. He'd watched the airlock lights quiver, and sensed the delicate electronic patterns of nearby processors storm wildly as he pushed himself through the gateway. There was nothing he could do about it. It took all of his concentration to marshal his energistic power into the correct pattern. Now it seemed that pattern had an above-average giveaway effect on nearby electronics, though nothing had happened when he'd slipped out of the ghost realm into the Royale Class lounge at the start of the descent. Of course, he wasn't exerting himself then, quite the opposite, he'd actually been reining in the power.

Ah well, something to remember.

Thick security doors were rumbling across the end of the corridor, trapping stragglers among the passengers. Quinn walked past them, and reached the door. It put up a token resistance as he pushed himself through, as if it were nothing more than a vertical sheet of water.

The arrivals complex on the other side was made up of a series of grandiose multi-level reception halls, stitched together by wave stairs and open-shaft lifts. It could cope with seventy passenger lift capsules disembarking at once, a capacity which had been operating at barely twenty-five per cent since the start of the crisis. As Quinn made his way out from the sealed admission chamber at the end of the corridor, his first impression was that the air-conditioning grilles were pumping out adrenalin gas.

Down below on the main concourse, a huge flock of people were running for cover. They didn't know where they were going, the exits were all closed, but they knew where they didn't want to be, and that was anywhere near a lift capsule that was crammed full of possessed. They were damn sure there was no other reason for a security alert of such magnitude.

Up on Quinn's level, badly hyped security guards in bulky kinetic armour were racing for the admission chamber. Officers were screaming orders. All the passengers from the lift capsule were being rounded up at gunpoint and being made to assume the position. Anyone who protested was given a sharp jab with a shock rod. Three stunned bodies were already sprawled on the floor, twitching helplessly. It encouraged healthy cooperation among the remainder.

Quinn went over to the rank of guards who were forming a semicircle around the door to the admission chamber. Eighteen of the stubby rifles were lined up on it. He walked round one guard to get a closer look at the weapon. The guard shivered slightly, as if a chilly breeze was finding its way through the joint overlaps of her armour. Her weapon was some kind of machine-pistol. Quinn knew enough about munitions to recognize it as employing chemical bullets. There were several grenades hanging from her belt.

Even though God's Brother had granted him a much greater energistic strength than the average possessed, he would be very hard-pressed to defend himself against all eighteen of them firing at him. Earth was obviously taking the threat of possession very seriously indeed.

A new group of people had arrived to move methodically among the whimpering passengers. They weren't in uniforms, just ordinary blue business suits, but the security officers deferred to them. Quinn could sense their thoughts, very calm and focused in comparison to everyone else. Intelligence operatives, most likely.

Quinn decided not to wait and find out. He retreated from the semicircle of guards as an officer was ordering them to open the admission chamber door. The wave stair down to the main concourse had been switched off, so he climbed the frozen steps of silicon two at a time.

People huddled round the barricaded exits felt his passage as a swift ripple of cool air, gone almost as it started. On the plaza outside, more squads of security guards were setting up; two groups were busy mounting heavy-calibre Bradfield rifles on tripods. Quinn shook his head in a kind of bemused admiration, then carefully walked round them. The long row of lifts down to the vac-train station was still working, though there were few people left on the arrivals complex storey to use them. He hopped into one with a group of frightened-looking business executives just back from a trip to Cavius city on the Moon.

The lift took them a kilometre and a half straight down, opening into a circular chamber three hundred metres across. The station's floor was divided up by concentric rows of turnstiles, channelling passengers into the cluster of wave stairs occupying the centre. Information columns of jet-black glass formed a picket line around the outside, knots of fluorescent icons twirling around them like electronic fish. Lines of holographic symbols slithered through the air overhead, weaving sinuously around each other as they guided passengers to the wave stair which led down to their platform.

Quinn sauntered idly round the outside of the information columns for a while, watching the contortions of the holograms overhead. The bustling crowd (all averting their eyes from each other), the confined walls and ceiling, wheezing air-conditioners pouring out gritty air, small mechanoids being kicked as they attempted to clean up rubbish – he welcomed them all back into his life. Even though he was going to destroy this world and despoil its people, for a brief interlude it remained the old home. His satisfaction came to a cold halt; the name EDMONTON, in vibrant red letters, trickled over his head, riding along a curving convoy of translucent blue arrowheads towards one of the wave stairs. The vac-train was departing in eleven minutes.

It was so tempting. Banneth, at last. To see that face stricken with fear, then suffering – for a long, *long* time, the suffering – before the final ignominy of empty-headed imbecility. There were so many stages of torment to inflict òn Banneth, so much he wanted to do to her now he had the power; intricate, malicious applications of pain, psychological as well as physical. But the needs of God's Brother came first, even before the near-sexual urgings of his own serpent beast. Quinn turned away from the glowing invitation in disgust, and went to find a vac-train which would take him direct to New York.

People were starting to congregate around the windows of the bars and fast-food outlets making up the perimeter wall of the station. Kids stared with intrigued expressions at the images coming at them from newschannel AV projectors, while adults achieved the blank-faced otherwhereness which showed they were receiving sensevises. As he passed a pasta stall, Quinn caught a brief glimpse of the image inside a holoscreen above the sweating cook. Jupiter's cloudscape formed an effervescent ginger backdrop to a habitat; dozens of spaceships were swirling round it in what could almost be read as a state of high excitement.

It wasn't relevant to him, so he walked on.

*

Ione had gone straight to De Beauvoir Palace after Tranquillity emerged above Jupiter, coordinating the habitat's maintenance crews and making a public sensevise to reassure people and tell them what to do. The formal reception room was a more appropriate setting for such a broadcast than her private apartment. Now, with the immediate crisis over, she was snuggled back in the big chair behind her desk and using Tranquillity's sensitive cells to observe the last of the voidhawks assigned to implement the aid response settle on its docking-ledge pedestal. A procession of vehicles trundled over the polyp towards it, cargo flatbed lorries and heavy-lift trucks eager to unload the large fusion generator clamped awkwardly in the void-hawk's cargo cradles.

The generator had come from one of the industrial stations of the nearest Edenist habitat, Lycoris; hurriedly ferried over by Consensus as soon as Tranquillity's status was established. There were currently fifteen technical crews working on similar generators around the docking-ledge, powering them up and wiring them in to the habitat's power grid.

When she sank her mentality deeper into the neural strata and the autonomic monitor routines which operated there, Ione could feel the electricity flowing back into the starscrapers through the organic conductors, their mechanical systems gradually coming back on-line. The habitat's girdling city had been in emergency powerdown mode since the swallow manoeuvre, along with other non-essential functions. Grandfather Michael's precautions hadn't been perfect after all. She grinned to herself; pretty damn good, though. And even without the Jovian Consensus on hand to help with all its resources, they had the smaller fusion generators in the non-rotating spaceport.

We would have been OK.

Of course we would, Tranquillity said. It managed a mildly chastising tone, surprised at her doubt.

Obviously, nobody had fully thought through the implications of the swallow manoeuvre for Tranquillity. When it entered the wormhole the hundreds of induction cables radiating out from the endcap rims had been sliced off, eliminating nearly all of the habitat's natural energy-generation capability. It would take their extrusion glands several months to grow new ones out to full length.

By which time they might have to move again.

Let's not worry about that right now, Tranquillity said. We're in the safest orbit in the Confederation; even I was surprised by the amount of firepower Consensus has amassed here to protect itself. Be content.

I wasn't complaining.

Nor are our inhabitants.

Ione felt her attention being focused inside the shell.

It was party time in Tranquillity. The whole population had come up out of the starscrapers (using the lifts' emergency power reserves) to wait in the parkland around the lobbies until the electricity was restored. Elderly plutocrats sat on the grass next to students, waitresses shared the queue to the toilets with corporate presidents, Laymil Project researchers mingled with society vacuumheads. Everybody had grabbed a bottle on the way out of their apartment, and the galaxy's biggest mass picnic had erupted spontaneously. Dawn was now five hours late, but the moonlight silver light-tube only enhanced the ambience. People drank, and ran stim programs, and laughed with their neighbour as they told and retold their personal tale of combat-wasp-swarms-I-have-seen-hurtling-towards-me. They thanked God but principally Ione Saldana for rescuing them, and declared their undying love for her, that goddam beautiful, brilliant, canny, gorgeous girl in whose habitat they were blessed to live. And, hey, Capone; how does it feel, loser? Your almighty Confederation-challenging fleet screwed by a single non-military habitat; everything you could throw at us, and we beat you. Still happy you came back to the wonders of this century?

The residents from the two starscrapers closest to De Beauvoir Palace walked over the vales and round the spinneys to pay their respects and voice their gratitude. A huge crowd was singing and chanting outside the gates, calling, pleading for their heroine to appear.

Ione slid the focus over them, smiling when she saw Dominique and Clement in the throng, as well as a wildly drunk Kempster Getchell. There were others she knew, too, directors and managers of multistellar companies and finance institutions, all swept along with a tide of emotion. Red-faced, exhilarated, and calling her name with hoarse throats. She let the focus float back to Clement.

Invite him in, Tranquillity urged warmly.

Maybe.

Survival of dangerous events is a sexual trigger for humans. You should indulge your instincts. He will make you happy, and you deserve that more than anything.

Romantically put.

Romance has nothing to do with this. Enjoy the release he will bring.

What about you? You performed the swallow manoeuvre.

When you are happy, I am happy.

She laughed out loud. 'Oh what the hell, why not.'

That is good. But I think you will have to make a public appearance first. This crowd is good-natured, but quite determined to thank you.

Yes. She sobered. But there is one last official duty.

Indeed. Tranquillity's tone matched her disposition.

Ione felt the mental conversation widen to incorporate the Jovian Consensus. Armira, the Kiint Ambassador to Jupiter, was formally invited to converse with them.

Our swallow manoeuvre has produced an unexpected event, Ione said. We are hopeful that you can clarify it for us.

Armira injected a sensation of stately amusement into the affinity band. I would suggest, Ione Saldana and Tranquillity, that your entire swallow manoeuvre was an unexpected event.

It certainly surprised the Kiint we were host to, she said. They all left, very suddenly.

I see. Armira's thoughts hardened, denying them any hint of his emotional content.

Tranquillity replayed the memory it had from the time of the attack, showing all the Kiint vanishing inside event horizons.

What you have seen demonstrated is an old ability, Armira responded dispassionately. We developed the emergency exodus facility during the era when we were engaged in interstellar travel. It is merely a sophisticated application of your distortion-field systems. My colleagues helping with your Laymil research project would have used it instinctively when they believed they were threatened.

We're sure they would, Consensus said. And who can blame them? That's not the point. The fact that you have this ability is most enlightening to us. We have always regarded as somewhat fanciful your claim that your race's interest in star travel is now over. Although the fact that you had no starships added undeniable weight to the argument. Now we have seen your personal teleport ability, the original claim is exposed as a complete fallacy.

We do not have the same level of interest in travelling to different worlds that you do, Armira said.

Of course not. Our starships are principally concerned with commercial and colonization flights, and an unfortunate amount of military activity. Your technological level would preclude anything as simple as commercial activity. We also believe that you are peaceful, although you must have considerable knowledge of advanced weapons. That leaves colonization and exploration.

A correct analysis.

Are you still conducting these activities?

To some degree.

Why did you not tell us this, why have you hidden your true abilities behind a claim of mysticism and disinterest?

You know the answer to that, Armira said. Humans discovered the Jiciro race three hundred years ago; yet you have still not initiated contact and revealed yourselves to them. Their technology and culture is at a very primitive level, and you know what will happen if they are exposed to the Confederation. All that they have will be supplanted by what they will interpret as futuristic items of convenience, they will cease to develop anything for themselves. Who knows what achievements would be lost to the universe?

That argument is not pertinent here, Consensus said. The Jiciro do not know what the stars are, nor that solid matter is composed of atoms. We do. We acknowledge that our technology is inferior to yours. But equally you know that one day we will achieve your current level. You are denying us knowledge we already know exists, and you have done so twice, in this field and in your understanding of the beyond. This is not an act of fellowship. We have opened ourselves to you in honesty and friendship, we have not hidden our flaws from you; yet you have clearly not reciprocated. Our conclusion is that you are simply studying us. We would now like to know why. As sentient entities we have that right.

Study is a pejorative term. We learn of you, as you do us. Admittedly that process is imbalanced, but given our respective natures, that is inevitable. As to bestowing our technology, that would be interference of the grandest order. If you want something, achieve it for yourselves.

Same argument you gave us concerning the beyond, Ione remarked testily.

Of course, Armira said. Tell me, Ione Saldana, what would your reaction have been if a xenoc race announced that you had an immortal soul, and proved it, and then went on to demonstrate that the beyond awaited, though as Laton said, only for some? Would you have greeted such a revelation with thanks?

No, I don't suppose I would.

We know that our introduction to the concept of the beyond was accidental, Consensus said. Something happened on Lalonde which allowed the souls to come back and possess the living. Something extraneous. This calamity has been inflicted upon us. Surely such circumstances permit you to intervene?

There was a long pause. We will not intervene in this case, Armira

22

said. For two reasons. Whatever happened on Lalonde happened because you went there. There is more to travelling between stars and exploring the universe than the physical act.

You are saying we must accept responsibility for our actions.

Yes, inevitably.

Very well, with reservations we accept that judgement. Though please appreciate we do not like it. What is the second reason?

Understand, there is a faction among my people who have argued that we should intervene in your favour. The possibility was rejected because what we have learned of you so far indicates that your race will come through this time successfully. Edenists especially have the social maturity to face what follows.

I'm not an Edenist, Ione said. What about me, and all the other Adamists, the majority of our race? Are you going to stand back as we perish and fall into the beyond? Does the survival of an elite few, the sophisticates and the intellectuals, justify discarding the rest? Humans have never practised eugenics, we regard it as an abomination, and rightly so. If that's the price of racial improvement, we're not willing to pay it.

If I am any judge, you too will triumph, Ione Saldana.

Nice to know. But what about all the others?

Fate will determine what happens. I can say no more other than to restate our official response: the answer lies within yourselves.

That is not much of a comfort, Consensus remarked.

I understand your frustration. My one piece of advice is that you should not share what you have learned about my race with the Adamists. Believing we have a solution, and piety alone will extract it from us, would weaken their incentive to find that answer.

We will consider your suggestion, Consensus said. But Edenism will not voluntarily face the rest of eternity without our cousins. Ultimately, we are one race, however diverse.

I acknowledge your integrity.

I have a final question, Ione said. Where is Jay Hilton? She was taken from Tranquillity at the same time as your researchers. Why?

Armira's thoughts softened, shading as close to embarrassment as Ione had ever known a Kiint to come. That was an error, the Ambassador said. And I apologize unreservedly for it. However, you should know the error was made in good faith. A young Kiint included Jay Hilton in the emergency exodus against parental guidance. She was simply trying to save her friend.

Haile! Ione laughed delightedly. You wicked girl.

I believe she has been severely reprimanded for the incident.

I hope not, Ione said indignantly. She's only a baby.

Quite.

Well, you can bring Jay back now; Tranquillity isn't as vulnerable as you thought.

I apologize again, but Jay Hilton cannot be returned to you at this time.

Why not?

In effect, she has seen too much. I assure you that she is perfectly safe, and we will of course return her to you immediately your current situation is resolved.

*

The walls of the prison cell were made from some kind of dull-grey composite, not quite cool enough to be metal, but just as hard. Louise had touched them once before sinking down onto the single cot and hugging her legs, knees tucked up under her chin. The gravity was about half that of Norfolk, better than Phobos, at least; though the air was cooler than it had been on the *Jamrana*. She spent some time wondering about Endron, the old systems specialist from the *Far Realm*, thinking he might have betrayed them and alerted High York's authorities. Then decided it really didn't matter. Her one worry now was that she'd been separated from Gen; her sister would be very frightened by what was happening.

And I got her into this mess. Mother will kill me.

Except Mother was in no position to do anything. Louise hugged herself tighter, fighting the way her lips kept trembling.

The door slid open, and two female police officers stepped in. Louise assumed they were police, they wore pale blue uniforms with Govcentral's bronze emblem on their shoulders, depicting a world where continents shaped as hands gripped together.

'OK, Kavanagh,' said the one with sergeant's stripes. 'Let's go.'

Louise straightened her legs, looking cautiously from one to the other. 'Where?'

'Interview.'

'I'd just shove you out the bloody airlock, if it was up to me,' said the other. 'Trying to sneak one of those bastards in here. Bitch.'

'Leave it,' the sergeant ordered.

'I wasn't . . .' Louise started. She pursed her lips helplessly. It was so complicated, and Heaven only knew how many laws she'd broken on the way to High York.

They marched her down a short corridor and into another room. It made her think of hospitals. White walls, everything clean, a table in the middle that was more like a laboratory bench, cheap waiting-room chairs, various processor blocks in a tall rack in one corner, more lying on the table. Brent Roi was sitting behind the table; he'd taken off the customs uniform he'd worn to greet the *Jamrana*, now he was in the same blue suit as the officers escorting her. He waved her into the chair facing him.

Louise sat, hunching her shoulders exactly the way she was always scolding Gen for doing. She waited for a minute with downcast eyes, then glanced up. Brent Roi was giving her a level stare.

'You're not a possessed,' he said. 'The tests prove that.'

Louise pulled nervously at the black one-piece overall she'd been given, the memory of those tests vivid in her mind. Seven armed guards had been pointing their machine-guns at her as the technicians ordered her to strip. They'd put her inside sensor loops, pressed hand-held scanners against her, taken samples. It was a million times worse than any medical examination. Afterwards, the only thing she'd been allowed to keep was the medical nanonic package round her wrist.

'That's good,' she said in a tiny voice.

'So how did he blackmail you?'

'Who?'

'The possessed guy calling himself Fletcher Christian.'

'Um. He didn't blackmail me, he was looking after us.'

'So you rolled over and let him fuck you in return for protection against the other possessed?'

'No.'

Brent Roi shrugged. 'He preferred your little sister?'

'No! Fletcher is a decent man. You shouldn't say such things.'

'Then what the hell are you doing here, Louise? Why did you try and infiltrate a possessed into the O'Neill Halo?'

'I wasn't. It's not like that. We came here to warn you.'

'Warn who?'

'Earth. Govcentral. There's somebody coming here. Somebody terrible.'

'Yeah?' Brent Roi raised a sceptical eyebrow. 'Who's that, then?'

'He's called Quinn Dexter. I've met him, he's worse than any normal possessed. Much worse.'

'In what way?'

'More powerful. And he's full of hate. Fletcher says there's something wrong about him, he's different somehow.'

'Ah, the expert on possession. Well, if anyone is going to know, it'll be him.'

Louise frowned, unsure why the official was being so awkward. 'We came here to warn you,' she insisted. 'Dexter said he was coming to Earth. He wants revenge on someone called Banneth. You have to guard all the spaceports, and make sure he doesn't get down to the surface. It would be a disaster. He'll start the possession down there.'

'And why do you care?'

'I told you. I've met him. I know what he's like.'

'Worse than ordinary possessed; yet you seemed to have survived. How did you manage that, Louise?'

'We were helped.'

'By Fletcher?'

'No . . . I don't know who it was.'

'All right, so you escaped this fate worse than death, and you came here to warn us.'

'Yes.'

'How did you get off Norfolk, Louise?'

'I bought tickets on a starship.'

'I see. And you took Fletcher Christian with you. Were you worried there were possessed among the starship crew?'

'No. That was one place I was sure there wouldn't be any possessed.'

'So although you knew there were no possessed on board, you still took Christian with you as protection. Was that your idea, or his?'

'I . . . It . . . He was with us. He'd been with us since we left home.'

'Where is home, Louise?'

'Cricklade Manor. But Dexter came and possessed everyone. That's when we fled to Norwich.'

'Ah yes, Norfolk's capital. So you brought Christian with you to

Norwich. Then when that started to fall to the possessed, you thought you'd better get offplanet, right?'

'Yes.'

'Did you know Christian was a possessed when you bought the tickets?'

'Yes, of course.'

'And when you bought them, did you also know Dexter wanted to come to Earth?'

'No, that was after.'

'So was it dear old Samaritan Fletcher Christian who suggested coming here to warn us?'

'Yes.'

'And you agreed to help him?'

'Yes.'

'So where were you going to go originally, before Fletcher Christian made you change your mind and come here?'

'Tranquillity.'

Brent Roi nodded in apparent fascination. 'That's a rather strange place for a young lady from Norfolk's landowner class to go. What made you chose that habitat?'

'My fiancé lives there. If anyone can protect us, he can.'

'And who is your fiancé, Louise?'

She smiled sheepishly. 'Joshua Calvert.'

'Joshua Cal . . . You mean *Lagrange* Calvert?'

'No, Joshua.'

'The captain of the *Lady Macbeth*?'

'Yes. Do you know him?'

'Let's say the name rings a bell.' He sat back and folded his arms, regarding Louise with a strangely mystified expression.

'Can I see Genevieve now?' she asked timidly. No one had actually said she was under arrest yet. She felt a lot more confident now the policeman had actually listened to her story.

'In a little while, possibly. We just have to review the information you've provided us with.'

'You do believe me about Quinn Dexter, don't you? You must make sure he doesn't get down to Earth.'

'Oh, I assure you, we will do everything we can to make sure he doesn't get through our security procedures.'

'Thank you.' She glanced awkwardly at the two female officers standing on either side of her chair. 'What's going to happen to Fletcher?'

'I don't know, Louise, that's not my department. But I imagine they'll attempt to flush him out of the body he's stolen.'

'Oh.' She stared at the floor.

'Do you think they're wrong to try that, Louise?'

'No. I suppose not.' The words were troubling to speak; the truth, but not what was right. None of what had happened was right.

'Good.' Brent Roi signalled her escort. 'We'll talk again in a little while.' When the door closed behind her, he couldn't help a grimace of pure disbelief.

'What do you think?' his supervisor datavised.

'I have never heard someone spout quite so much bullshit in a single interview before,' Brent Roi replied. 'Either she's a retard, or we're up against a new type of possessed infiltration.'

'She's not a retard.'

'Then what the hell is she? Nobody is that dumb, it's not possible.'

'I don't believe she's dumb, either. Our problem is, we're so used to dealing with horrendous complexities of subterfuge, we never recognize the simple truth when we see it.'

'Oh, come on, you don't actually believe that story?'

'She is, as you said, from the Norfolk landowner class; that doesn't exactly prepare her for the role of galactic master criminal. And she is travelling with her sister.'

'That's just cover.'

'Brent, you are depressingly cynical.'

'Yes, sir.' He held on to his exasperation, it never made the slightest impression on his supervisor. The anonymous entity who had guided the last twenty years of his life lacked many ordinary human responses. There were times when Brent Roi wondered if he was actually dealing with a xenoc. Not that there was much he could do about that now; whatever branch of whatever agency the supervisor belonged to, it was undoubtedly a considerable power within Govcentral. His own smooth, accelerated promotion through the Halo police force was proof of that.

'There are factors of Miss Kavanagh's story which my colleagues and I find uniquely interesting.'

'Which factors?' Brent asked.

'You know better than that.'

'All right. What do you want me to do with her?'

'Endron has confirmed the Phobos events to the Martian police, however we must establish exactly what happened to Kavanagh on Norfolk. Initiate a direct memory retrieval procedure.'

*

Over the last five hundred years, the whole concept of Downtown had acquired a newish and distinctly literal meaning in New York; naturally enough, so did Uptown. One thing, though, would never change; the arcology still jealously guarded its right to boast the tallest individual building on the planet. While the odd couple of decades per century might see the title stolen away by upstart rivals in Europe or Asia, the trophy always came home eventually.

The arcology now sprawled across more than four thousand square kilometres, housing (officially) three hundred million people. With New Manhattan at the epicentre, fifteen crystalline domes, twenty kilometres in diameter, were clumped together in a semicircle along the eastern seaboard, sheltering entire districts of ordinary skyscrapers (defined as buildings under one kilometre high) from the pummelling heat and winds. Where the domes intersected, gigantic conical megatowers soared up into the contused sky. More than anything, these colossi conformed to the old concept of 'arcology' as a single city-in-a-building. They had apartments, shopping malls, factories, offices, design bureaux, stadiums, universities, parks, police stations, council chambers, hospitals, restaurants, bars, and spaces for every other human activity of the twenty-seventh century. Thousands of their inhabitants were born, lived, and died inside them without ever once leaving.

At five and a half kilometres tall, the Reagan was the current global champion, its kilometre-wide base resting on the bedrock where the town of Ridgewood had stood in the times before the armada storms. An apartment on any of its upper fifty floors cost fifteen million fuseodollars, and the last one was sold twelve years before they were built. Their occupants, the new breed of Uptowners, enjoyed a view as spectacular as it was possible to have on Earth. Although impenetrably dense cloud swathed the arcology for a minimum of two days out of every seven, when it was clear the hot air was very clear indeed. Far below them, under the transparent hexagonal sheets which comprised the roof of the domes, the tide of life ebbed and flowed for their amusement. By day, an exotic hustle as kaleidoscope rivers of vehicles flowed along the elevated 3D web of roads and rails; by night, a shimmering tapestry of neon pixels.

Surrounding the Reagan, streets and skyscrapers fanned out in a radial of deep carbon-concrete canyons, like buttress roots climbing up to support the main tower. The lower levels of these canyons were badly cluttered, where the skyscraper bases were twice as broad as their peaks, and the elevated roads formed a complex intersecting grid for the first hundred and fifty metres above the ground. High expressways throwing off curving slip roads at each junction down to the local traffic lanes; broad freight-only flyovers shaking from the eighty-tonne autotrucks grumbling along them twenty-four hours a day, winding like snakes into tunnels which led to sub-basement loading yards; metro transit carriages gliding along a mesh of rails so labyrinthine that only an AI could run the network. Rents were cheap near the ground, where there was little light but plenty of noise, and the heavy air gusting between dirty vertical walls had been breathed a hundred times before. Entropy in the arcology meant a downward drift. Everything that was worn-out, obsolete, démodé, economically redundant – down it came to settle on the ground, where it could descend no further. People as well as objects.

Limpet-like structures proliferated among the criss-cross of road-support girders bridging the gap between the skyscrapers, shanty igloos woven from salvaged plastic and carbotanium composite, multiplying over the decades until they clotted into their own light-killing roof. Under them, leeched to the streets themselves, were the market stalls and fast-food counters; a souk economy of fifth-hand cast-offs and date-expired sachets shuffled from family to family in an eternal round robin. Crime here was petty and incestuous, gangs ruled their turf, pushers ruled the gangs. Police made token patrols in the day, and went off-shift as the unseen sun sank below the rim of the domes above.

This was Downtown. It was everywhere, but always beneath the feet of ordinary citizens, invisible. Quinn adored it. The people who dwelt here were almost in the ghost realm already; nothing they did ever affected the real world.

He walked up out of the subway onto a gloomy street jammed with canopied stalls and wheelless vans, all with their skirt of goods guarded by vigilant owners. Graffiti struggled with patches of pale mould for space on the skyscraper walls. There were few windows, and those were merely armoured slits revealing little of the mangy shops and bars inside. Metallic thunder from the roads above was as permanent as the air which carried it.

Several looks were quickly thrown Quinn's way before eyes were averted for fear of association. He smiled to himself as he strode confidently among the stalls. As if his attitude wasn't enough to mark him out as an interloper, he had clothed himself in his jet-black priest's robe again.

It was the simplest way. He wanted to find the sect, but he'd never been to New York before. Everybody in Downtown knew about the sect, this was their prime recruiting ground. There would be a coven close by, there always was. He just needed someone who was bound to know the location.

Sure enough, he hadn't got seventy metres from the subway when they saw him. A pair of waster kids busy laughing as they pissed on the woman they'd just beaten unconscious. Her two-year-old kid lay on the sidewalk bawling as blood and urine pooled round its feet. The victim's bag had been ripped apart, scattering its pitiful contents on the ground around her. They put Quinn in mind of Jackson Gael; late adolescence, with pumped bodies, their muscle shape defined by some exercise but mostly tailored hormones. One of them wore a T-shirt with the slogan: CHEMICAL WARFARE MACHINE. The other was more body-proud, favouring a naked torso.

He was the one who saw Quinn first, grunted in amazement, and nudged his partner. They sealed their flies and sauntered over.

Quinn slowly pushed his hood down. Hypersensitive to trouble, the street was depopulating rapidly. Pedestrians, already nervous from the mugging, slipped away behind the forest of support pillars. Market stall shutters were slammed down.

The two waster kids stopped in front of Quinn, who grinned in welcome. 'I haven't had sex for ages,' Quinn said. He looked straight at the one wearing the T-shirt. 'So I think I'll fuck you first tonight.'

The waster kid snarled, and threw a punch with all the strength his inflated muscles could manage. Quinn remained perfectly still. The fist struck his jaw, just to the left of his chin. There was a crunch which could easily be heard above the traffic's clamour. The waster kid bellowed, first in shock, then in agony. His whole body shook as he slowly pulled his hand back. Every knuckle was broken, as if he had punched solid stone. He cradled it with frightened tenderness, whimpering.

'I'd like to say take me to your leader,' Quinn said, as if he hadn't even noticed the punch. 'But organizing yourselves takes brains. So I guess I'm out of luck.'

The second waster kid had paled, shaking his head and taking a couple of steps backward.

'Don't run,' Quinn said, his voice sharp.

The waster kid paused for a second, then turned and bolted. His jeans burst into flames. He screamed, stumbling to a halt, and flailing wildly at the burning fabric. His hands ignited. The shock silenced him for a second as he held them up disbelievingly in front of his face. Then he screamed again, and kept on screaming, staggering about drunkenly. He crashed into one of the flimsy stalls which crumpled, folding about him. The fire was burning deeper into his flesh now, spreading along his arms, and up onto his torso. His screaming became weaker as he bucked about in the smouldering wreckage.

The T-shirted kid raced over to him. But all he could do was look down in a horror of indecision as the flames grew hotter.

'For Christ's sake,' he wailed at Quinn. 'Stop it. Stop it!'

Quinn laughed. 'Your first lesson is that God's Brother cannot be stopped.'

The body was motionless and silent now, a black glistening husk at the centre of the flames. Quinn put a hand on the shoulder of the sobbing waster kid at his side. 'It hurts you, doesn't it? Watching this?'

'Hurts! Hurts? You bastard.' Even with a face screwed up from pain and rage, he didn't dare try to twist free from Quinn's hand.

'I have a question,' Quinn said. 'And I've chosen you to answer it for me.' His hand moved down, caressing the waster kid's chest before it reached his crotch. He tightened his fingers round the kid's balls, aroused by the fear he was inflicting.

'Yes, God, yes. Anything,' the kid snivelled. His eyes were closed, denying what he could of this nightmare.

'Where is the nearest coven of the Light Bringer sect?'

Even with the pain and dread scrambling his thoughts, the waster kid managed to stammer: 'This dome, district seventeen, Eighty-Thirty Street. They got a centre somewhere along there.'

'Good. You see, you've learnt obedience, already. That's very smart of you. I'm almost impressed. Now there's only one lesson left.'

The waster kid quailed. 'What?'

'To love me.'

*

The coven's headquarters had chewed its way, maggot-fashion, into the corner of the Hauck skyscraper on Eighty-Thirty Street. What had once been a simple lattice of cube rooms, arranged by mathematics rather than art, was now a jumbled warren of darkened chambers. Acolytes had knocked holes in some walls, nailed up barricades in the corridors, pulled down ceilings, sealed off stairwells: drones shaping their nest to the design of the magus. From the outside it looked the same, a row of typically shabby Downtown shops along the street, selling goods cheaper than anywhere else – they could afford to, everything was stolen by the acolytes. But above the shops, the slim windows were blacked out, and, according to the building management processors, the rooms unoccupied, and therefore not liable to pay rent.

Inside, the coven members buzzed about industriously twenty-four hours a day. Looked at from a strictly corporate viewpoint, which was how Magus Garth always regarded his coven, it was quite a prosperous operation. Ordinary acolytes, the real sewer-bottom shit of the human race, were sent out boosting from the upper levels; they brought back a constant supply of consumer goodies that were either used by the sect or sold off in the coven-front shops and affiliated street market stalls. Sergeant acolytes were deployed primarily as enforcers to keep the others in line, but also to run a more sophisticated distribution net among the dome's lower-middle classes, competing (violently) with ordinary pushers out in the bars and clubs. Senior acolytes, the ones who actually had a working brain cell, were given didactic memory courses and employed running the pirate factory equipment, bootlegging MF albums, black sensevise programs, and AV activant software, as well as synthesizing an impressive pharmacopoeia of drugs, hormones, and proscribed viral vectors.

In addition to these varied retail enterprises, the coven still engaged in the more traditional activities of crime syndicates. Although sensevise technology had essentially eliminated a lot of prostitution outside of Downtown, that still left protection rackets, extortion, clean-water theft, blackmail, kidnapping, data theft, game-rigging, civic-service fraud, power theft, embezzlement, and vehicle theft, among others.

The coven performed all of them with gusto, if not finesse. Magus Garth was satisfied with their work. They hadn't missed their monthly target in over three years, making the required financial offering to New York's High Magus over in Dome Two. His only worry was that the High Magus would realize how lucrative the coven was, and demand a higher offering. Increased payments would cut into Garth's personal profits, the eight per cent he'd been skimming every month for the last five years.

There were times when Garth wondered why nobody had noticed. But then, looking at Sergeant Acolyte Wener, maybe he shouldn't be all that surprised. Wener was in his thirties, a big man, but rounded rather than wedge-shaped like most of the acolytes. He had a thick beard, dark hair sprouting from his face in almost simian proportions. His head was in keeping with the rest of his body, though Garth suspected the bone thickness would be a lot greater than average. An overhanging forehead and jutting chin gave him a permanently sullen, resentful expression – appropriately enough. You couldn't geneer that quality, it was a demonstration that the incest taboo was finally starting to lose force among Downtown residents. Fifteen years in the sect, and Wener was as far up the hierarchy as he'd ever get.

'They got Tod, and Jay-Dee,' Wener said. He smiled at the memory. 'Tod went down swinging. Hit a couple of cops before they shot him with a fucking nervejam. They started kicking him then. I got out.'

'How come they spotted you?' Garth asked. He'd sent Wener and five others out to steam a mall. Simple enough, two of them bang into a civilian, cut a bag strap, slice trouser pocket fabric. Any protest: you get crushed by a circle of aggressive faces and tough young bodies looking for an excuse to hurt you as bad as they can. Three seconds and it's over. Twenty victims in one place, then the steamers are out, moving on.

Wener shifted some flesh around on top of his shoulders, his way of shrugging. 'Dunno. Cops maybe saw what was going down.'

'Ah, fuck it.' Garth knew. They'd hit a streak and stayed too long, allowed the mall patrols to realize what was happening. 'Did Tod and Jay-Dee have anything on them?'

'Credit disks.'

'Shit.' That was it. The cops would send them straight down to the Justice Hall, walk them past a judge whose assistant's assistant would access the case file and slap them with an Involuntary Transportation sentence. Two more loyal followers lost to some asshole colony. Though Garth had heard that the quarantine was even affecting colony starship flights. Ivet holding pens at every orbital tower station were getting heavily overcrowded, the news companies were hot with rumours of riots.

Wener was shoving his hands in his pockets, pulling out credit disks and other civilian crap: fleks, jewellery, palm-sized blocks ... 'I got this. The steam wasn't a total zero.' He spilt the haul on Garth's desk, and gave the Magus a hopeful look.

'OK, Wener. But you've got to be more careful in future. Fuck it, God's Brother doesn't like failure.'

'Yes, Magus.'

'All right, get the hell out of my sight before I give you to Hot Spot for a night.'

Wener lumbered out of the sanctum, and closed the door. Garth datavised the room's management processor to turn up the lights. Candles and shadowy gloom were the sect's habitual trappings, as standardized as the accessories of a global fast-food franchise. When acolytes were summoned before him, the study conformed to that. A sombre cave lit by a few spluttering red candles in iron candelabra, its walls invisible.

Powerful beams shone down out of the ceiling, revealing a richly furnished den: drinks cabinet filled with a good selection of bottles, extensive AV and sensevise flek library, new-marque Kulu Corporation desktop processor (genuine – not a bootleg), some of the weirder art stuff that was impossible to fence. A homage to his own greed, and devoutness. If you see something you want: take it.

'Kerry!' he yelled.

She came in from his private apartment, butt naked. He hadn't allowed her to wear clothes since the day her brother brought her in. Best-looking girl the coven had acquired in ages. A few tweaks with cosmetic adaptation packages, pandering to his personal tastes, and she was visual perfection.

'Get my fifth invocation robes,' he told her. 'Hurry up. I've got the initiation in ten minutes.'

She bobbed her head apprehensively, and retreated back into the apartment. Garth started picking up the junk Wener had left, reading the flek labels, datavising the blocks for a menu. A gentle gust of cool air wafted across his face. The candles flickered. It broke his concentration for a moment. Air-conditioner screwed up again.

There was nothing of any interest among Wener's haul, no blackmail levers; some of the fleks were company files, but a quick check found no commercially sensitive items. He was indifferent about that. Data was the other offering the coven made to the High Magus, and that on a weekly basis. A gift that never brought any return, other than the invisible umbrella of political protection the sect extended to its senior members. So Garth played along, considering it his insurance premium. The reports were more than a simple summary of what was happening inside the coven; the High Magus insisted on knowing what action was going down on the street, every street. Which gangs were up, why they were up, what they were pushing, new faces, vanished faces, who was trouble, who had a score to settle and why.

Years of being out on the street at the hard edge had taught Garth the value of good intelligence, but this was like a fetish with the High Magus.

Kerry returned with his robes. The fifth invocation set were appropriately flamboyant, black and purple, embroidered with scarlet pentagrams and nonsense runes. But they were a symbol of authority, and the sect was very strict about internal discipline. Kerry helped him into them, then hung a gold chain with an inverted cross round his neck. When he looked into a mirror he was satisfied with what he saw. The body might be sagging slightly these days, but he used weapon implants rather than straight physical violence to assert himself now, while the shaven skull and eyes recessed by cosmetic adaptation packages gave him a suitably ominous appearance.

The temple was at the centre of the headquarters, a cavity three storeys high. Straight rows of severed steel-reinforcement struts poking out of the walls showed where the floors and ceilings used to be. A broad pentagon containing an inverted cross was painted across the rear wall. It was illuminated from below by a triple row of skull candles, great gobs of wax in upturned craniums. Stars, demons, and runes formed a constellation around it, although they were fading under layers of soot. The altar was a long carbon-concrete slab, ripped from the sidewalk outside, and mounted on jagged pillars of carbotanium. Impressively solid, if nothing else. There was a black brazier on top of it, lithe blue flames slithering out of the trash bricks it was filled with, sending up a plume of sweet-stinking smoke. A pair of tall serpent-shaped candlesticks flanked it. Ten iron hoops, sunk into the carbon-concrete, trailed lengths of chain which ended in manacles.

Just over half of the coven's acolytes were waiting obediently when Garth arrived. Standing in rows, wearing their grey robes, with coloured belts denoting seniority. Garth would have preferred more. But they were stretched pretty thin right now. A turf dispute with a gang operating out of Ninety-Ten Street had resulted in several clashes. The gang lord was doubtless thinking it would all be settled with a boundary agreement. Garth was going to cure him of that illusion. God's Brother did not negotiate. Acolytes had the gang under observation, building up a picture of their entire operation. It wasn't something the gang understood or could ever emulate, they didn't have the discipline or the drive. Their only motivation was to claw in enough money to pay for their own stim fixes.

That was what made the sect different, serving God's Brother so rewarding.

In another week Garth would unlock the weapons stash and launch a raid. The High Magus had already arranged for him to take delivery of sequestration nanonics; that would be the fate of the gang's leadership, turned into biological mechanoids. Any attractive youths would be used as bluesense meat after the acolytes had enjoyed their victory orgy. And, inevitably, there would be a sacrifice.

The acolytes bowed to Garth, who went to stand in front of the altar. Five initiates were shackled to it. Three boys and two girls, lured in by the promises and the treachery of friends. One of the boys stood defiantly straight, determined to show he could take whatever the initiation threw at him so he could claim his place, the other two were just surly and subdued. Garth had ordered one of the girls to be tranked after he'd spoken to her earlier. She'd virtually been abducted by an acolyte angry at losing her to an outside rival, and was likely to go into a mental melt-down if she wasn't eased into her new life; she had strong ambitions to better herself and rise out of Downtown.

Garth held up his arms, and made the sign of the inverted cross. 'With flesh we bond in the night,' he intoned.

The acolytes started a low, mournful chanting, swaying softly in unison.

'Pain we love,' Garth told them. 'Pain frees the serpent beast. Pain shows us what we are. Your servants, Lord.'

He was almost in a trance state as he spoke the words, he'd said them so many times before. So many initiations. The coven had a high turnover, arrests, stim burnouts, fights. But never drop-outs.

Indoctrination and discipline helped, but his main weapon of control was belief. Belief in your own vileness, and knowing there was no shame in it. Wanting things to get worse, to destroy and hurt and ruin. The easy way forward . . . once you gave in to your true self, your serpent beast. All that started right here, with the ceremony.

It was a deliberate release of sex and violence, an empowerment of the basest instincts, permitting little resistance. So easy to join, so natural to immerse yourself in the frenzy around you. Indulge the need to belong, to be the same as your brethren family. An act which gave the existing acolytes that fraternity.

As to the initiates, they passed through the eye of the needle. Fear kept them in place at first, fear of knowing how exquisitely ugly the sect really was, how they would be dealt with if they disobeyed or attempted to leave. Then the cycle would turn, and there would be another initiation. Only this time it would be them showing their devotion to God's Brother, revelling in the unchaining of their serpent beast. Doing as they had been done by, and enraptured by the accomplishment.

Whoever had designed the ritual, Garth thought, had really understood basic conditioning psychology. Such elemental barbarism was the only possible way to exert any kind of control over a Downtown savage. And there was no other sort of resident here.

'In darkness we see You, Lord,' Garth recited. 'In darkness we live. In darkness we wait for the true Night that You will bring us. Into that Night we will follow You.' He lowered his arms.

'We will follow You,' the acolytes echoed. Their rustling voices had become hot with expectation.

'When You light the true path of salvation at the end of the world, we will follow You.'

'We will follow You.'

'When Your legions fall upon the angels of the false Lord, we will follow You.'

'We will follow You.'

'When the time—'

'That time is now,' a single clear voice announced.

The acolytes grunted in surprise, while Garth spluttered to a halt, more astonished than outraged at the interruption. They all knew how important he considered the sect's ceremonies, how intolerant of sacrilege. Only true believers can inspire belief in others.

'Who said that?' he demanded.

A figure walked forward from the back of the temple, clad in a midnight-black robe. The opening at the front of the hood seemed to absorb all light, there was no hint of the head it contained. 'I am your new Messiah, and I have come among you to bring our Lord's Night to this planet.'

Garth tried to use his retinal implants to see into the hood, but they couldn't detect any light in there, even infrared was useless. Then his neural nanonics reported innumerable program crashes. He yelled, 'Shit!' and thrust his left hand out at the robed figure, index finger extended. The fire command to his microdart launcher never arrived.

'Join with me,' Quinn ordered. 'Or I will find more worthy owners for your bodies.'

One of the acolytes launched herself at Quinn, booted foot swinging for his kneecap. Two others were right behind her, fists drawn back.

Quinn raised an arm, his sleeve falling to reveal an albino hand with grizzled claw fingers. Three thin streamers of white fire lashed out from the talons, searingly bright in the gloomy, smoke-heavy air. They struck his attackers, who were flung backwards as if they'd been hit by a shotgun blast.

Garth grabbed one of the serpent candlesticks and swung it wildly, aiming to smash it down on Quinn's head. Not even a possessed would be able to survive a mashed brain, the invading soul would be forced out. Air thickened around the candlestick, slowing its momentum until it halted ten centimetres above the apex of Quinn's hood. The serpent's head that held the candle hissed and closed its mouth, biting the rod of wax in half.

'Swamp him!' Garth shouted. 'He can't defeat all of us. Sacrifice yourself, for God's Brother.'

A few of the acolytes edged closer to Quinn, but most stayed where they were. The candlestick began to glow along its entire length. Pain stabbed into Garth's hands. He could hear his skin sizzling. Squirts of greasy smoke puffed out. But he couldn't let go; his fingers wouldn't move. He saw them blister and blacken; bubbling juices ran down his wrists.

'Kill him,' he cried. 'Kill. Kill.' His burning hands made him scream out in agony.

Quinn leant towards him. 'Why?' he asked. 'This is the time of God's Brother. He sent me here to lead you. Obey me.'

Garth fell to his knees, arms shaking, charred hands still clenched round the gleaming candlestick. 'You're a possessed.'

'I was a possessed. I returned. My belief in Him freed me.'

'You'll possess all of us,' the Magus hissed.

'Some of you. But that is what the sect prays for. An army of the damned; loyal followers of our darkest Lord.' He turned to the acolytes and held up his hands. For the first time his face was visible within, pale and deadly intent. 'The waiting is over. I have come, and I bring you victory for eternity. No more pathetic squabbling over black stimulants, no more wasting your life mugging geriatric farts. His true work waits to be done. I know how to bring Night to this planet. Kneel before me, become true warriors of darkness, and together we will rain stone upon this land until it bleeds and dies.'

Garth screamed again. All that was left now of his fingers were black bones soldered to the candlestick. 'Kill him, shitbrains!' he roared. 'Smash the fucker into the bedrock, curse you.' But through eyes blurred with tears he could see the acolytes slowly sinking to the floor in front of Quinn. It was like a wave effect, spreading across the temple. Wener was the closest to Quinn, his simple face alive with admiration and excitement. 'I'm with you,' the lumbering acolyte yelled. 'Let me kill people for you. I want to kill everyone, kill the whole world. I hate them. I hate them real bad.'

Garth groaned in mortification. They believed him! Believed the shit was a real messenger from God's Brother.

Quinn closed his eyes and smiled in joy as he gloried in their adulation. Finally, he was back among his own. 'We will show the Light Bringer we are the worthy ones,' he promised them. 'I will guide you over an ocean of blood to His Empire. And from there we will hear the false Lord weeping at the end of the universe.'

The acolytes cheered and laughed rapturously. This was what they craved; no more of the Magus's tactical restraint, at last they could unleash violence and horror without end, begin the war against the light, their promised destiny.

Quinn turned and glanced down at Magus Garth. 'You: fuckbrain. Grovel, lick the shit off my feet, and I'll allow you to join the crusade as a whore for the soldiers.'

The candlestick clattered to the ground, with the roast remains of Garth's hands still attached. He bared his teeth at the deranged possessor standing over him. 'I serve my Lord alone. You can go to hell.'

'Been there,' Quinn said urbanely. 'Done that. Come back.' His hand descended on Garth's head as if in anointment. 'But you will be of use to me. Your body, anyway.' His needle-sharp talons pierced the skin.

The Magus discovered that the pain of losing his hands was merely the overture to a very long and quite excruciating symphony.

2

It was designated Bureau Seven, which somewhat inevitably for a government organization was acronymed down to B7. To anyone with Govcentral alpha-rated clearance, it was listed as one of the hundreds of bland committees which made up the management hierarchy of the Govcentral Internal Security Directorate. Officially its function was Policy Integration and Resource Allocation, a vital coordination role. The more senior GISD Bureaux produced their requirements for information and actions, and it was B7's job to make sure none of the new objectives clashed with current operations before they designated local arcology offices with carrying out the project and assigned funds. If there was any anomaly to be found with B7, it was that such an important and sensitive responsibility did not have a political appointee assigned to run it. Certainly the chiefs of Bureaux One through Six changed with every new administration, reflecting fresh political priorities; and several hundred minor posts among the lower Bureaux were also up for grabs as a loyalty reward to the new President's retinue. Again, no junior positions were available in B7.

So B7 carried on as it always had, isolated and insular. In fact, just how insular would have come as a great shock to any outsider who investigated the nature of its members – that is, a shock in the brief period left to them before being quietly terminated.

Although the antithesis of democracy, it did take the job of guarding the republic of Earth extremely seriously. Possession was the one threat which had the potential not just to overthrow but actually eliminate Govcentral, a prospect which hadn't arisen for nearly four hundred and fifty years, since the population pressures of the Great Dispersal.

Possession, therefore, was the reason why a full meeting of all sixteen members had been convened for the first time in twelve years. Their sensenviron conference had a standard format, a white infinity-walled room with an oval table in the centre seating their generated representations. There was no seniority among them, each had his or her separate area of responsibility, the majority of which were designated purely on geographical terms, although there was a supervisor for GISD's division dealing in Military Intelligence.

An omnidirectional projection hung over the table, showing a warehouse on Norfolk which was burning with unnatural ferocity. Several museum-piece fire engines were racing towards it, along with men in khaki uniforms.

'It would appear the Kavanagh girl is telling the truth,' said the Central American supervisor.

'I never doubted it,' Western Europe replied.

'She's certainly not possessed,' said Military Intelligence. 'Not now, anyway. But she'd still have those memories if she had been.'

'If she'd been possessed, she would have admitted it,' Western Europe said indolently. 'You're building in complications for us.'

'Do you want a full personality debrief to confirm her authenticity?' Southern Africa asked.

'I don't think we should,' Western Europe said. He absorbed the mildly polite expressions of surprise the representations around the table were directing at him.

'Care to share with us?' South Pacific asked archly.

Western Europe looked at the Military Intelligence supervisor. 'I believe we have crossover from the *Mount's Delta*?'

Military Intelligence gave a perfunctory nod. 'Yes. We confirmed that the starship was carrying two people when it docked at Supra-Brazil. One of them slaughtered the other in an extravagantly gory fashion right after docking was completed, the body was literally exploded. All that we can tell you about the victim is that he was male. We still don't know who he was, there's certainly no correlating DNA profile stored in our memory cores. I've requested that all governments we're in contact with run a search through their records, but I don't hold out much hope.'

'Why not?' South Pacific asked.

'The *Mount's Delta* came from Nyvan; he was probably one of their citizens. None of their nations remains intact.'

'Not relevant, anyway,' said Western Europe.

'Agreed,' Military Intelligence said. 'Once we'd stripped down the *Mount's Delta* we ran extremely thorough forensic tests on the life-support capsule and its environmental systems. Analysis on the faecal residue left in the waste-cycle mechanism identified the other occupant's DNA for us. And this is where the story gets interesting, because we have a very positive match on his DNA.' Military Intelligence datavised the sensevise's controlling processor, and the image above the table changed. Now it showed an image taken from Louise Kavanagh's brain a few minutes before the warehouse was fired; a young man with a pale, stern face, dressed in a jet-black robe. The viewing angle was such that he looked down on the members of B7 with a derisory sneer. 'Quinn Dexter. He was an Ivet shipped to Lalonde last year, sentenced for resisting arrest, the police thought he was running an illegal package into Edmonton. He was, as it happens. Sequestration nanonics.'

'Oh, Christ,' Central America muttered.

'The Kavanagh girl confirms he was on Norfolk, and both she and Fletcher Christian strongly suspect he was the one who took over the frigate *Tantu*. Following that, the *Tantu* made one unsuccessful attempt to penetrate Earth defences, and immediately withdrew, damaging itself in the process.'

Western Europe datavised the sensenviron management processor, and the image above the table changed again. 'Dexter got to Nyvan. One of the surviving asteroids confirmed that the *Tantu* docked at Jesup asteroid. That's when their real troubles started. Ships from Jesup planted the nukes in the abandoned asteroids.' He pointed at the image of Nyvan which had replaced Dexter. It was a world like nothing previously seen in the galaxy, as if a ball of lava had congealed in space, a crinkled black surface crust riddled with contorted fissures of radiant red light. The two atmospheric aspects were in constant conflict, supernatural and supernature boiling against each other with harrowing aggression. For any survivors down on the surface, their environment couldn't even be classified as terracompatible any more.

'Dexter was there on Lalonde at incident one, according to Laton and our Edenist friends,' Western Europe said remorselessly. 'He was on Norfolk, which we now recognize as the major distribution source of infection. He was at Nyvan, which has elevated the crisis to a completely new stage; as far as we can tell one which has proved as hostile to the possessed as it is to the ordinary population. And now we are certain he arrived here at Supra-Brazil.' He looked directly at the South American supervisor.

'There was an alert at the Brazil tower station fifteen hours after the *Mount's Delta* arrived,' South America said tonelessly. 'Just after its descent, one of the lift capsules suffered exactly the kind of electronic glitches known to be inflicted by the possessed. We had the entire arrivals complex sealed and surrounded within ninety seconds. Nothing. No sign of any possessed.'

'But you think he's here?' Eastern Europe pressed.

South America smiled without humour. 'We know he is. After the alert, we hauled in everyone who came down on the lift capsule, passengers and crew. This is what we got from several neural nanonics memory cells.' Nyvan faded away to show a slightly fuzzy two-dimensional picture, indicating a low-grade recording. The figure in the Royale Class lounge wearing a blue silk suit, slumped comfortably in a deep chair, was undoubtedly Dexter.

'Merciful Allah,' North Pacific exclaimed, 'we'll have to shut down the vac-trains. It's our one advantage. I don't care how good he is at eluding our sensors, the little shit can't walk a thousand kilometres along a vacuum tunnel. Isolate the bastard, and hit him with an SD platform strike.'

'I believe even we would have trouble shutting down the vac-trains,' South Pacific said significantly. 'Not without questions being asked.'

'I don't mean we should issue the order,' North Pacific snapped. 'Feed the information up to B3, and make the President's office authorize it.'

'If the public find out there's a possessed on Earth, there will be absolute pandemonium,' North Africa said. 'Even we would have trouble retaining control over the arcologies.'

'Better than being possessed,' North America said. 'Because that's what he'll do to the arcology populations if we don't stop him. Even we would be in danger.'

'I think his objective is more complex than that,' Western Europe said. 'We know what he did to Nyvan, I think we can assume he wants to do the same thing here.'

'Not a chance,' Military Intelligence said. 'Even if he could sneak around up in the Halo, which I doubt, he'd never acquire enough nukes to split an asteroid open. You can't remove one of those beauts from storage without anyone knowing.'

'Maybe, but there's something else. Kavanagh and Fletcher Christian both say that Dexter is here to hunt down Banneth and have his revenge on her. I checked Dexter's file; he used to be a sect member in Edmonton. Banneth was his Magus.'

'So what?' asked North Pacific. 'You know what those crazy brute sect members do to each other when the lights go off. I'm not surprised he wants to beat the crap out of Banneth.'

'You're missing the point,' Western Europe said patiently. 'Why would the soul possessing Quinn Dexter's body care about Dexter's old Magus?' He looked questioningly round the table. 'We're dealing with something new here, something different. An ordinary person who has somehow gained the same powers as the possessed, if not superior ones. His goals are not going to be the same as theirs, this craving they have to flee the universe.'

North America caught it first. 'Shit. He used to be a sect member.'

'And presumably remains so,' Western Europe agreed. 'He was still performing their ceremony on Lalonde; that was incident one, after all. Dexter is a true believer in the Light Bringer teachings.'

'You think he's come back to find his God?'

'It's not a god he worships, it's the Devil. But no, he's not here to find him. My people ran a psychological profile simulation; what they got indicates he's come back to prepare the way for his Lord, the Light Bringer, who glories in war and chaos. He'll try to unleash as much mayhem and destruction on both us and the possessed as it's possible to do. Nyvan was just the warm-up. The real game is going to be played out down here.'

'Well, that settles it, then,' North Pacific said. 'We have to close the vac-trains. It'll mean losing an entire arcology to him; but we can save the rest.'

'Don't be so melodramatic,' Western Europe said. 'Dexter is a problem; a novel one, granted. He's different, and more powerful than all the others B7 has faced over the centuries. But that's what we are here for, ultimately, to solve problems which would defeat conventional government action. We simply have to locate a weakness and use it.'

'An invisible megalomaniac as powerful as a minor god has a weakness?' North Pacific said. 'Allah preserve us, I should like to hear what it is.'

'The Kavanagh girl has escaped him twice. Both times it was due to the intervention of an unknown possessed. We have an ally.'

'On Norfolk! Which has bloody vanished.'

'Nevertheless, Dexter does not command total support from the possessed. He is not invincible. And we have what should be a decisive advantage over him.'

'Which is?'

'We know about him. He knows nothing about us. That can be exploited to trap him.'

'Ah yes,' the Halo supervisor said contentedly. 'Now I understand the reluctance for a personality debrief on the Kavanagh girl.'

'Well, I don't,' South America declared querulously.

'Personality debrief requires a much more invasive procedure,' Western Europe said. 'At the moment Kavanagh is not aware of what has happened to her. That means we can use her ignorance to get very close to Dexter.'

'Close to . . .' South Pacific trailed off. 'My God, you want to use her as a lightning conductor.'

'Exactly. At the moment we have one chance for proximity, and that's Banneth. Unfortunately there is only a limited degree of preparation we can make with her. The possessed, and therefore presumably Dexter, can sense the emotional content of the minds around them. We have to proceed with extreme caution if he is to be lured into a termination option. If he learns someone is hunting him, we could lose several arcologies, if not more. Moving the Kavanagh girl back into the game doubles our chances of engineering an encounter with him.'

'That's goddam risky,' North America said.

'No, I like it,' Halo said. 'It has subtlety; that's more us than closing down the vac-trains and using SD fire to incinerate entire arcology domes.'

'Oh, Heaven forfend we should let our standard of style drop when the whole fucking world is about to go down the can,' South Pacific groused.

'Does anyone have a substantial objection?' Western Europe enquired.

'Your operation,' North Pacific said hotly. 'Your responsibility.'

'Responsibility?' Australia chided lightly.

There were several smiles around the table as North Pacific glowered.

'Naturally I accept the consequences,' Western Europe purred volubly.

'You're always such an arrogant little shit when you're this age, aren't you?' North Pacific said.

Western Europe just laughed.

*

The three Confederation Navy marines were polite, insistent, and resolutely uncommunicative. They escorted Joshua the entire length of Trafalgar. Which, he thought, was a hopeful sign; he was being taken away from the CNIS section. A day and a half of interviews with sour-faced CNIS investigators, cooperating like a good citizen. None of his questions answered in return. Certainly no access to a lawyer – one of the investigators had given him a filthy look when he half-jokingly asked for legal aid. Net processors wouldn't respond to his datavises. He didn't know where the rest of his crew was. Didn't know what was happening to *Lady Mac*. And could make a pretty good guess what kind of report Monica and Samuel were concocting.

From the tube carriage station a lift took them up to a floor which was plainly officer country. A wide corridor, good carpet, discreet lighting, holograms of famous naval events (few he recognized), intent men and women looping from office to office, none of them under the rank of senior lieutenant. Joshua was led into a reception room with two captains sitting at desks. One of them stood, and saluted the marines. 'We'll take him from here.'

'What is this?' Joshua asked. It definitely wasn't a firing squad on the other side of the ornate double doors in front of him, and hopefully not a courtroom either.

'The First Admiral will see you now,' the Captain said.

'Er,' Joshua said lamely. 'OK, then.'

The large circular office had a window overlooking the asteroid's biosphere. It was night outside, the solartubes reduced to a misty oyster glimmer revealing little of the landscape. Big holoscreens on the walls were flashing up external sensor images of Avon and the asteroid's spaceports. Joshua looked for *Lady Mac* among the docking-bays, but couldn't find her.

The Captain beside him saluted. 'Captain Calvert, sir.'

Joshua locked eyes with the man sitting behind the big teak desk in front of him, receiving a mildly intrigued gaze from Samual Aleksandrovich.

'So,' the First Admiral said. 'Lagrange Calvert. You fly some very tight manoeuvres, Captain.'

Joshua narrowed his eyes, unsure just how much irony was being applied here. 'I just do what comes naturally.'

'Indeed you do. I accessed that section of your file, also.' The First Admiral smiled at some internal joke, and waved a hand. 'Please sit down, Captain.'

A blue-steel chair swelled up out of the floor in front of the desk. Alkad Mzu was sitting in the one next to it, body held rigid, staring ahead. On the other side of her, Monica and Samuel had relaxed back into their own chairs. The First Admiral introduced the demure Edenist woman beside them as Admiral Lalwani, the CNIS Chief. Joshua responded with a very nervous twitch of greeting.

'I think I had better start by saying the Confederation Navy would like to thank you for your part in the Nyvan affair, and solving the Alchemist problem for us,' the First Admiral said. 'I do not like to dwell on the consequences had the Capone Organization acquired it.'

'I'm not under arrest?'

'No.'

Joshua let out a hefty breath of relief. 'Jesus!' He grinned at Monica, who responded with a laconic smile.

'Er, so can I go now?' he asked without much hope.

'Not quite,' Lalwani said. 'You're one of the few people who knows how the Alchemist works,' she told him.

Joshua did his best not to glance at Mzu. 'A very brief description.'

'Of the principles,' Mzu said.

'And I believe you told Samuel and Agent Foulkes that you would submit to internal exile in Tranquillity so no one else could obtain the information,' Lalwani said.

'Did I? No.'

Monica pantomimed deep thought. 'Your exact words were: "I'll stay in Tranquillity if we survive this, but I have to know."'

'And you said you'd stay there with me,' Joshua snapped back. He scowled at her. 'Ever heard of Hiroshima?'

'The first time an atomic bomb was used on Earth,' Lalwani said.

'Yeah. At the time the only real secret about an atom bomb was the fact that it was possible to build one that worked. Once it got used, that secret was out.'

'The relevance being?'

'Anyone who visits the location where we deployed Alchemist and sees the result is going to be able to figure out those precious principles of yours. After that, it's just a question of engineering. Besides, the possessed won't build another. They're not geared around that kind of action.'

'Capone's Organization might be able to,' Monica said. 'They certainly thought they could, remember? They wanted Mzu at any price, incarnate or just her soul. And who's going to know where the Alchemist was used unless you and your crew tell them?'

'Jesus, what do you people want from me?'

'Very little,' said the First Admiral. 'I think we've established to everyone's satisfaction that you're trustworthy.' He grinned at Joshua's sour expression. 'Despite what that may do to your reputation. So I'm just going to ask you to agree to a few ground rules. You do not discuss the Alchemist with anyone. And I mean anyone.'

'Easy enough.'

'For the duration of our current crisis you do not put yourself in a position where you will encounter the possessed.'

'I've already encountered them twice, I don't intend to do it again.'

'That effectively means you will not fly anywhere outside the Sol system. Once you get home, you stay there.'

'Right.' Joshua frowned. 'You want me to go to Sol?'

'Yes. You will take Dr Mzu and the *Beezling* survivors there. As you pointed out with your Hiroshima analogy, we cannot push the information genie back into the lamp, but we can certainly initiate damage limitation. The relevant governments have agreed that Dr Mzu can be returned to a neutral nation, where she will not communicate any details of the Alchemist to anyone. The Doctor has consented to that.'

'They'll get it eventually,' Joshua said softly. 'No matter what agreements they sign, governments will try to build Alchemists.'

'No doubt,' Samual Aleksandrovich said. 'But such problems are for the future. And that is going to be a very different place to today, is it not, Captain?'

'If we solve today, then, yeah. It'll be different. Even today is different than yesterday.'

'So. Lagrange Calvert has become a philosopher?'

'Haven't we all, knowing what we do now?'

The First Admiral nodded reluctantly. 'Perhaps it's not such a bad thing. Somebody has to find a solution. The more there are of us searching, the quicker it will be revealed.'

'That's a lot of faith you have there, Admiral.'

'Of course. If I didn't have faith in the human race, I would have no right to sit in this chair.'

Joshua gave him a strong look. The First Admiral wasn't quite what he'd envisaged, the gung-ho military archetype. That made him more confident for the future. Slightly. 'OK, so where do you want me to take the Doc in the Sol system, exactly?'

Samual Aleksandrovich smiled broadly. 'Ah yes, this is one piece of news I shall enjoy imparting.'

*

Friend Jay, please cry not.

Haile's voice was no stronger than the memory of a dream. Jay had closed up her mind as tight as her eyelids. She just lay on the floor, all curled up, sobbing at . . . everything. Ever since that terrible day on Lalonde when the Ivets went mad, she and Mummy had been torn further and further apart. First the cramped house on the savannah. Then Tranquillity, where she'd heard rumours of the possessed taking Lalonde out of the universe – even though the paediatric ward staff had been careful about allowing the refugee kids access to any news. Now this, flying like an angel to another galaxy. Where she'd never get back from. And she'd never see Mummy ever again. Everyone she knew was either dead, or about to be possessed. She wailed louder, so much it hurt her throat.

The back of her head was full of warm whispers, pushing to be let in.

Jay, please restrain yourself.

She is developing cyclic trauma psychosis.

We should impose a thalamic regulator routine.

Humans respond better to chemical suppressors.

Certainty?

Ambiguous context.

Referral to Corpus.

Tractamorphic flesh was slithering round her, rubbing gently. She shook at the touch of it.

Then there was a sharp regular clicking sound, *tac tac tac*, like heels on the cool hard floor. Human heels.

'What in seven heavens' name do you lot think you're doing?' a woman's voice asked sharply. 'Give the poor dear some air, for goodness' sake. Come on, get back. Right back. Move out the way.' There followed the distinctive sound of a human hand being slapped against a Kiint hide.

Jay stopped crying.

'Move! You too, you little terror.'

That causes painfulness, Haile protested.

'Then learn to move quicker.'

Jay smeared some of the tears from her eyes, and peered up just in time to see someone's finger and thumb pinching the crater ridge of skin around Haile's ear, hauling her aside. The baby Kiint's legs were getting all twisted round as she skittled hurriedly out of the way.

The owner of the hand smiled down at Jay. 'Well, well, sweetie, haven't you just caused a stir? And whatever are all these tears for? I suppose you had a bit of shock when they jumped you here. Don't blame you. That stupid leaping through the darkness stunt used to give me the chronic heebie-jeebies every time. I'll take a Model-T over that any day. Now there was a really gracious method of transport. Would you like a hanky, wipe your face a bit?'

'Uh,' Jay said. She'd never seen a woman quite so old before; her brown Mediterranean skin was deeply wrinkled, and her back curved slightly, giving her shoulders a permanent hunch. The dress she wore had come straight out of a history text, lemon-yellow cotton printed with tiny white flowers, complemented by a wide belt and lace collar and cuffs. Thin snow-white hair was permed into a neat beret, and a double loop of large pearls round her neck chittered softly with every movement. It was as if she'd turned age into a statement of pride. But her green eyes were vividly alert.

A frilly lace handkerchief was pulled from her sleeve, and proffered to Jay.

'Thank you,' Jay gulped. She took the hanky, and blew into it heavily. The huge adult Kiint had all backed off, standing several paces behind the small woman, keeping close together in a mutual support group. Haile was pressed against Lieria, who had formshifted a tractamorphic arm to stroke her daughter soothingly.

'So now, sweetie, why don't you start by telling me your name.'

'Jay Hilton.'

'Jay.' The woman's jowls bobbled, as if she was sucking on a particularly hard mint. 'That's nice. Well, Jay, I'm Tracy Dean.'

'Hello. Um, you are real, aren't you?'

Tracy laughed. 'Oh, yes, sweetie, I'm genuine flesh and blood, all right. And before you ask why I'm here, this is my home now. But we'll save the explanations until tomorrow. Because they're very long and complicated, and you're tired and upset. You need to get some sleep now.'

'I don't want to sleep,' Jay stammered. 'Everybody in Tranquillity's dead, and I'm here. And I want Mummy. And she's gone.'

'Oh, Jay, no, sweetie.' Tracy knelt beside the little girl, and hugged her tight. Jay was sniffling again, ready to burst into tears. 'Nobody's dead. Tranquillity swallowed away clean before any of the combat wasps reached it. These silly oafs got it all wrong and panicked. Aren't they stupid?'

'Tranquillity's alive?'

'Yes.'

'And Ione, and Father Horst, and everybody?'

'Yes, all safe and sound. Tranquillity is orbiting Jupiter right this minute. That surprised everybody, let me tell you.'

'But . . . how did it do that?'

'We're not quite sure yet, but it must have an awful lot of energy patterning cells tucked away somewhere inside it.' She gave Jay a sly grin, and winked. 'Tricky people, those Saldanas. And very clever with it, thankfully.'

Jay managed an experimental smile.

'That's better. Now, let's see about finding you that bed for the night.' Tracy rose to her feet, holding Jay's hand.

Jay used her free hand to wipe the handkerchief across her face as she scrambled to her feet. 'Oh, right.' Actually, she thought that talk of explanations sounded quite fascinating now. There was so much about this place she wanted to know. It would be worth staying awake for.

You now have betterness, query? Haile asked anxiously.

Jay nodded enthusiastically at her friend. 'Much better.'

That is good.

I will assume complete Jay Hilton guardian responsibility now.

Jay cocked her head to give Tracy Dean a sideways look. How could she use the Kiint mental voice?

Confirm, Nang said. The words Jay could hear in her head speeded up then, becoming a half-imagined birdsong, but suffused with feeling.

We will venture wide together, Haile said. **See new things. There is muchness here to see.**

'Tomorrow, maybe,' Tracy said. 'We have to get Jay settled in here first.'

Jay shrugged at her friend.

'Now then, Jay, we're going to jump out of here. It'll be the same as before, but this time you know it's happening, and I'll be with you the whole time. All right?'

'Couldn't we just walk, or use a groundcar, or something?'

Tracy smiled sympathetically. 'Not really, sweetie.' She pointed up at the planets arching over the dark sky. 'My home is on one of those.'

'Oh. But I will be seeing Haile while I'm here, won't I?' Jay raised her hand and waved at her friend. Haile formshifted the tip on one of her tractamorphic arms into a human hand, and wriggled the fingers.

We will build the castles of sand again.

'Close your eyes,' Tracy said. 'It's easier that way.' Her arm went round Jay's shoulder. 'Are you ready?'

This time it wasn't so bad. There was that quick breeze ruffling her nightie again, and despite having her eyes shut her stomach was telling her very urgently that she was falling again. A squeak crept out of her lips in spite of her best efforts.

'It's all right, sweetie, we're here now. You can open your eyes again.'

The breeze had vanished, its departure signalling a whole symphony of fresh sound. Hot sunlight tingled her skin; when she breathed in she could taste salt.

Jay opened her eyes. There was a beach in front of her, one which made the little cove on Tranquillity seem quite pallid by comparison. The powder-fine sand was snow-white, stretching out on either side of her for as far as she could see. Wonderfully clear turquoise water lapped against it, languid waves rolling in from a reef several hundred metres out. A beautiful three-masted yacht of some golden wood was anchored halfway between the shore and the reef, undeniably human in design.

Jay grinned at it, then shielded her eyes with a hand and looked round. She was standing on a circle of the same ebony material as before, but this time there was no encircling wall or watching Kiint. The only artefact was a bright orange cylinder, as tall as she was, standing next to the edge. Scatterings of sand were drifting onto the circle.

Behind her, a thick barricade of trees and bushes lined the rear of the beach. Long creeper tendrils had slithered out of them over the hard-packed sand, knitting together in a tough lacework that sprouted blue and pink palm-sized flowers. The only noise was the waves and some kind of honking in the distance, almost like a flock of geese. When she searched the cloudless sky, she could see several birds flapping and gliding about in the distance. The arch of planets was a line of silver discs twinkling away into the horizon.

'Where are we now?' Jay asked.

'Home.' Tracy's face managed to produce even more wrinkles as she sniffed distastefully. 'Not that anywhere is really home after spending two thousand years swanning loyally round Earth and the Confederation planets.'

Jay stared at her in astonishment. 'You're two thousand years old?'

'That's right, sweetie. Why, don't I look it?'

Jay blushed. 'Well . . .'

Tracy laughed, and took hold of her hand. 'Come along, let's find you that bed. I think I'll put you in my guest quarters. That'll be simplest. Never thought I'd ever get to use them.'

They walked off the ebony circle. Up ahead of them, Jay could see some figures lazing on the beach, while others were swimming in the sea. Their strokes were slow and controlled. She realized they were all as old as Tracy. Now Jay was paying attention, she could make out several chalets lurking in the vegetation behind the beach. They were strung out on either side of a white stone building with a red tile roof and a sizeable, well-manicured garden; it looked like some terribly exclusive clubhouse. Still more old people were sitting at iron tables on the lawns, reading, playing what looked like a board game, or just staring out to sea. Mauve-coloured globes, the size of a head, were floating through the air, moving sleekly from table to table. If they found an empty glass or plate they would absorb it straight through their surface. In many cases they would extrude a replacement; the new glasses were full, and the plates piled with sandwiches or biscuit-type snacks.

Jay walked along obediently at Tracy's side, her head swivelling about as she took in the amazing new sights. As they approached the big building, people looked their way and smiled encouragingly, nodding, waving.

'Why are they doing that?' Jay asked. All the excitement and fright had worn off now she knew she was safe, leaving her very tired.

Tracy chuckled. 'Having you here is the biggest event that's happened to this place for a long time. Probably ever.'

Tracy led her towards one of the chalets, a simple wooden structure with a veranda running along the front, on which stood big clay pots full of colourful plants. Jay could only think of the pretty little houses of the Juliffe villages on the day she and her mother had started sailing upriver to Aberdale. She sighed at the recollection. The universe had become very strange since then.

Tracy patted her gently. 'Almost there, sweetie.' They started up the steps to the veranda.

'Hi there,' a man's voice called brightly.

Tracy groaned impatiently. 'Richard, leave her alone. The poor little dear's dead on her feet.'

A young man in scarlet shorts and a white T-shirt was jogging barefoot across the sands towards them. He was tall with an athletic figure, his long blond hair tied back into a ponytail by a flamboyant leather lace. He pouted at the rebuke, then winked playfully at Jay. 'Oh, come on, Trace; just paying my respects to a fellow escapee. Hello, Jay, my name's Richard Keaton.' He gave a bow, and stuck his hand out.

Jay smiled uncertainly at him, and put out her own hand. He shook it formally. His whole attitude put her in mind of Joshua Calvert, which was comforting. 'Did you jump out of Tranquillity as well?' she asked.

'Heavens, no, nothing like that. I was on Nyvan when someone tried to drop a dirty great lump of metal on me. Thought it best I slipped away when no one was looking.'

'Oh.'

'I know everything is real weird for you right now, so I just wanted you to have this.' He produced a doll resembling some kind of animal, a flattish humanoid figure made from badly worn out brown-gold velvet; its mouth and nose were just lines of black stitching, and its eyes were amber glass. One semicircular ear had been torn off, allowing tufts of yellowing stuffing to peek out of the gash.

Jay gave the battered old thing a suspicious look, it wasn't anything like the animatic dolls back in Tranquillity's paediatric ward. In fact, it looked even more primitive than any toy on Lalonde. Which was pretty hard to believe. 'Thank you,' she said awkwardly as he proffered it. 'What is it?'

'This is Prince Dell, my old Teddy bear. Which dates me. But friends like this were all the rage on Earth when I was young. He's the ancestor of all those animatic dolls you kids have these days. If you hold him close at night he keeps troubles away from your dreams. But you have to keep cuddling him tight for him to be able to do that properly. Something to do with earth magic and contact; funny stuff like that. He used to sleep with me until I was a lot older than you. I thought he might be able to help you tonight.'

He sounded so serious and hopeful that Jay took the bear from him and examined it closely. Prince Dell really was very tatty, but she could just picture him in the embrace of a sleeping boy with blond hair. The boy was smiling blissfully.

'All right,' she said. 'I'll hold on to him tonight. Thank you very much.' It seemed a bit silly, but it was kind of him to be so considerate.

Richard Keaton smiled gladly. 'That's good. The Prince hasn't had much to do for a long time. He'll be happy to have a new friend. Make sure you treat him nicely, he's a bit delicate now, poor thing.'

'I will,' Jay promised. 'Are you really old, as well?'

'Older than most people you've ever met, but nothing like as antique as good old Trace, here.'

'Huh,' Tracy sniffed critically. 'If you're quite finished.'

Richard rolled his eyes for Jay's benefit. 'Sweet dreams, Jay. I'll see you tomorrow, we've got lots to talk about.'

'Richard,' Tracy asked reluctantly. 'Did Calvert do it?'

A huge smile flashed over his face. 'Oh yeah. He did it. The Alchemist is neutralized. Just as well, it was a brute of a weapon.'

'Typical. If they'd just devote ten per cent of their military budget and all that ingenuity into developing their social conditions.'

'Preaching to the converted!'

'Are you talking about Joshua?' Jay asked. 'What's he done?'

'Something very good,' Richard said.

'Amazingly,' Tracy muttered drily.

'But . . .'

'Tomorrow, sweetie,' Tracy said firmly. 'Along with everything else. I promise. Right now, you're going to bed. Enough delaying tactics.'

Richard waved, and walked away. Jay held Prince Dell against her tummy as Tracy's hand pressed into her back, propelling her up the steps and into the chalet. She glanced down at the ancient bear again. His dull glass eyes stared right back at her; it was an incredibly melancholic expression.

*

The first hellhawk came flashing out of its wormhole terminus twelve thousand kilometres from Monterey asteroid. New California's gravitonic detector warning satellites immediately datavised an alert to the naval Tactical Operations Centre. The high-pitched audio alarm startled Emmet Mordden, who was the duty officer in the large chamber. At the time he was sitting with his feet up on the commander's console, reading through a four hundred sheet hard-copy guide of a Quantumsoft accountancy program in preparation for his next upgrade to the Treasury computers. With most of the Organization fleet away at Tranquillity, and the planet reasonably stable right now, it was a quiet duty, just right to catch up on his technical work.

Emmet's feet hit the floor as the AI responsible for threat analysis squirted a mass of symbols and vectors up on one of the huge wall-mounted holoscreens. In front of him, the equally surprised SD network operators scrambled to interpret what was happening. There weren't many of them among the eight rows of consoles in the centre, nothing like the full complement which the Organization had needed at the height of the Edenist harassment campaign. Right now, spaceflight traffic was at a minimum, and the contingent of Valisk hellhawks on planetary defence duty had done a superb job of clearing Edenist stealth mines and spy globes from space around the planet.

'What is it?' Emmet asked automatically, by which time another three wormholes had opened. The precariously stacked pile of hard copy avalanched off his console as he determinedly cleared his keyboard ready to respond.

The AI had acquired X-ray laser lock-on for the first four targets, and was requesting fire authority. Another ten wormholes were opening. Jull von Holger, who acted as the go-between for the Valisk hellhawks and the operations centre, leapt to his feet, shouting: 'Don't shoot!' He waved his arms frantically. 'They're ours! They're our hellhawks.'

Emmet hesitated, his fingers hovering over the keys. According to his console displays, over eighty wormholes had now opened to disgorge bitek starships. 'What the fuck do they think they're doing busting in on us like that? Why aren't they with the fleet?' Suspicion flowered among his thoughts, and he didn't care that von Holger could sense it. Hellhawks were dangerously powerful craft, and with the fleet away they could make real trouble. He'd never really trusted Kiera Salter.

Jull von Holger's face went through a wild panoply of emotion-derived contortions as he conducted fast affinity conversations with the unexpected arrivals. 'They're not from the fleet. They've come here directly from Valisk.' He halted for a moment, shocked. 'It's gone. Valisk has gone. We lost to that little prat Dariat.'

*

'Holy shit,' Hudson Proctor gasped.

Kiera stuck her head round the bathroom door as the beautician tried to wrap her sopping wet hair in a huge fluffy purple towel. The Quayle Suite in the Monterey Hilton was a temple to opulence and personal luxury. As Rubra had denied everyone access to the Valisk starscrapers, along with their apartment bathrooms, Kiera had simply groomed herself with energistic power alone. She had forgotten what it was to sprawl in a jacuzzi with a selector that could blend in any of a dozen exotic salts. And as for having her hair styled properly rather than forcing it into shape . . .

'What?' she snapped in annoyance; though the beacon-bright dismay in her associate's mind tempered any real fury at being interrupted.

'The hellhawks are here,' he said. 'All of them. They've come from Valisk. It's . . .' He flinched in trepidation. Delivering bad news to Kiera was always a desperately negative career move. Just because she had the kind of teenage-sweetheart looks which could (and had) suckered in non-possessed kids from right across the Confederation didn't mean her behaviour matched. Quite the opposite – she took a perverse enjoyment from that, too. 'Bonney chased after Dariat, apparently. There was a big fight in one of the starscrapers. Plenty of our people got flung back into the beyond. Then she forced him to ally with Rubra, or something.'

'What happened?'

'They, er . . . Valisk's gone. The two of them took the habitat out of the universe.'

Kiera stared at him, little wisps of steam starting to lick out of her hair. She'd always bitterly regretted that Marie Skibbow didn't have some kind of affinity faculty, its absence had always put at her at a slight disadvantage in Valisk. But she'd coped, the entire worldlet and its formidable starships had belonged to her. She'd been a power to contend with. Even Capone had sought out her help. Now—

Kiera gave the non-possessed beautician girl a blank-eyed glance. 'Get lost.'

'Ma'am.' The girl curtseyed, and almost sprinted for the suite's double doors on the other side of the lounge.

Kiera allowed herself a muted scream of fury when the doors closed. 'That fucking Dariat! I knew it! I fucking knew he was a disaster waiting to happen.'

'We're still in charge of the hellhawks,' Hudson Proctor said. 'That gives us a big chunk of Capone's action, and the Organization is in charge of a couple of star systems, with more on the way. It's not such a loss. If we'd been inside the habitat it would be one hell of a lot worse.'

'If I'd been inside, it would never have happened,' she snapped back. Her hair was abruptly dry, and her towelling robe blurred, running like hot wax until it became a sharp mauve business suit. 'Control,' she murmured almost to herself. 'That's the key here.'

Hudson Proctor could sense her focusing on him, both her eyes and her mind.

'Are you with me?' she asked. 'Or are you going to ask good old Al if you can sign on as one of his lieutenants?'

'Why would I do that?'

'Because if I can't keep control of the hellhawks, I'm nothing to the Organization.' She smiled thinly. 'You and I would have to start right back at the beginning again. With the hellhawks obeying us, we'll still be players.'

He glanced out of the big window, searching space for a sight of the bitek starships. 'We've got no hold on them any more,' he said dejectedly. 'Without the affinity-capable bodies stored in Valisk, there's no way they'll do as they're ordered. And there aren't any more of Rubra's family left for us to replace them with. We've lost.'

Kiera shook her head impatiently. Considering she'd co-opted the ex-general to her council for his ability to think tactically, he was doing a remarkably poor job of it. But then, maybe a politician's instinct was naturally quicker at finding an opponent's weakness. 'There's one thing left which they can't do for themselves.'

'And that is?'

'Eat. The only sources of their nutrient fluid which they'll be able to use are on Organization-held asteroids. Without food, even bitek organisms will wither and die. And we know our energistic power can't magic up genuine food.'

'Then Capone will control them.'

'No.' Kiera could sense his anxiety at the prospect of losing his status, and knew she could rely on him. She closed her eyes, focusing on assignments for the small number of her people she'd brought with her to Monterey. 'Which is the most reliable hellhawk we've got on planetary defence?'

'Reliable?'

'Loyal, idiot. To me.'

'That'll probably be Etchells in the *Stryla*. He's a regular little Nazi, always complaining hellhawks never see enough battle action. Doesn't get on too well with the others, either.'

'Perfect. Call him back to Monterey's docking-ledges and go on board. I want you to visit every Organization asteroid in this system with a nutrient fluid production system. And blow it to shit.'

Hudson gave her an astounded look, trepidation replacing the earlier anxiety. 'The asteroids?'

'No, shithead! Just the production systems. You don't even have to dock, just use an X-ray laser. That'll leave Monterey as their only supply point.' She smiled happily. 'The Organization has enough to do right now without the burden of maintaining all that complicated machinery. I think I'll go down there right now with our experts, and relieve them.'

*

It wasn't dawn which arose over the wolds, inasmuch as there was no sun to slide above the horizon any more, but nonetheless the darkened sky grew radiant in homage to Norfolk's lost diurnal rhythm. Luca Comar felt it developing because he was a part of making it happen. By coming to this place he had freed himself from the clamour of the souls lost within the beyond, their tormented screams and angry pleas. In exchange he had gained an awareness of community.

Born at the tail end of the twenty-first century, he'd grown up in the Amsterdam arcology. It was a time when people still clung to the hope that the planet could be healed, their superb technology employed to turn the clock back to the nevertime of halcyon pastoral days. In his youth, Luca dreamed of the land returned to immense parkland vistas with proud white and gold cities straddling the horizon. A child brought up by some of the last hippies on Earth, his formative years were spent loving the knowledge that together-ness was all. Then he turned eighteen, and for the first time in his existence reality had bitten, and bitten hard; he had to get a job, and an apartment, and pay taxes. Not nice. He resented it until the day his body died.

So now he had stolen a new body, and with the strange powers that theft had bestowed he'd joined with the others of this planet to create their own Gaia. Unity of life was a pervasive, shroudlike presence wrapping itself around the planet, replacing the regimented order of the universe as their provider. Because the new inhabitants of Norfolk wished there to be a dawn, there was one. And as they equally desired night, so the light was banished. He contributed a little of himself to this Gaia, some of his wishes, some of his strength, a constant avowal of thanks to this new phase of his existence.

Luca sat on the edge of the huge bed in the master bedroom to watch the light strengthen outside Cricklade; a silver warmth shining down from the sky, its uniformity leaving few shadows. With it came the sense of anticipation, a new day to be treasured because of the opportunity it might bring.

A dull dawn, bland and boring, just as the days have become. We used to have two suns, and revelled in the contrast of colours they brought, the battle of shadows. They had energy and majesty, they inspired. But this, this . . .

The woman on the bed beside Luca stretched and rolled over, resting her chin in her hand and smiling up at him. 'Morning,' she purred.

He grinned back. Lucy was good company, sharing a lot of his enthusiasms, as well as a wicked sense of humour. A tall woman, great figure, thick chestnut hair worn long, barely into her mid-twenties. He never asked how much of her appearance was hers, and how much belonged to her host. The age of your host had swiftly become taboo. He liked to think himself modern enough so that bedding a ninety-year-old wouldn't bother him, age and looks being different concepts here. He still didn't ask, though. The solid image was good enough.

An image so close to Marjorie it verges on the idolatrous. Did this Lucy see that in my heart?

Luca yawned widely. 'I'd better get going. We have to inspect the mill this morning, and I need to know how much seedcorn we've actually got left in the silos over in the estate's western farms. I don't believe what the residents are telling me. It doesn't correspond with what Grant knows.'

Lucy pulled a dour face. 'One week in heaven, and the four horsemen are already giving us the eye.'

'Alas, this is not heaven, I'm afraid.'

'And don't I know it. Fancy having to work for a living when you're dead. God, the indignity.'

'The wages of sin, lady. We did have one hell of a party to start with, after all.'

She flopped back down on the bed, tongue poised tautly on her upper lip. 'Sure did. You know I was quite repressed back when I was alive first time around. Sexually, that is.'

'Hallelujah, it's a miracle cure.'

She gave a husky chuckle, then sobered. 'I'm supposed to be helping out in the kitchen today. Cooking the workers' lunch, then taking it out to the fields for them. Bugger, it's like some kind of Amish festival. And how come we're reverting to gender stereotypes?'

'What do you mean?'

'It's us girls that are doing all the cooking.'

'Not all of you.'

'The majority. You should work out a better rota for us.'

'Why me?'

'You seem to be taking charge around here. Quite the little baron.'

'OK, I designate you to draw up a proper equitable rota.' He stuck his tongue out at her. 'You should be good at secretarial work.'

The pillow hit him on the side of his head, nearly knocking him off the bed. He caught the next one, and put it out of her reach. 'I didn't do it deliberately,' he said seriously. 'People tell me what they can do, and I shove them at the first matching job. We need to get a list of occupations and skills sorted out.'

She moaned. 'Bureaucracy in heaven, that's worse than sexism.'

'Just think yourself lucky we haven't got round to introducing taxes yet.' He started searching round for his trousers. Luckily, the manor had entire wardrobes of Grant Kavanagh's high-quality clothes. They weren't quite Luca's style, but at least they fitted perfectly. And the outdoor gear was hard-wearing, too. It saved him from having to dream up new stuff. That was harder here, in this realm. Imagined items took a long time to form, but when they did, they had more substance, and persevered longer. Concentrate hard enough and long enough on changing something, and the change would become permanent, requiring no more attention.

But that was inert objects: clothes, stone, wood, even chunks of machinery (not electronics), they could all be fashioned by the mind. Which was fortunate; Norfolk's low-technology infrastructure could be repaired with relative ease. Physical appearance, too, could be governed by a wish, flesh gradually morphing into a new form – inevitably firmer and younger. The majority of possessed were intent on reverting to their original features. As seen through a rose-tinted mirror, Luca suspected. Having quite so many beautiful people emerge in one place together was statistically implausible.

Not that vanity was their real problem. The one intractable difficulty of this new life was food. Energistic power simply could not conjure any into existence, no matter how creative or insistent you were. Oh, you could cover a plate with a mountain of caviar; but cancel the illusion and the glistening black mass would relapse into a pile of leaves, or whatever raw material you were trying to bend to your will.

Irony or mockery, Luca couldn't quite decide what their deliverance had led them to. But whichever it was, eternity tilling the fields was better than eternity in the beyond. He finished dressing, and gave Lucy an expectant, slightly chiding look.

'All right,' she grumbled. 'I'm getting up. I'll pull my communal weight.'

He kissed her. 'Catch you later.'

Lucy waited until the door shut behind him, then pulled the sheets back over her head.

Most of the manor's residents were already awake and bustling about. Luca said a dozen good-mornings as he made his way downstairs. As he walked along the grand corridors, the state of the building gradually registered. Windows left ajar, allowing the nightly sprinkling of rain to stain the carpets and furniture; open doors showed him glimpses of rooms with clothes strewn everywhere, remnants of meals on plates, grey mould growing out of mugs, sheets unwashed since the start of Norfolk's possession. It wasn't apathy, exactly, more like teenage carelessness – the belief that Mum will always be around to clean up after you.

Bloody squalor junkies. Wouldn't have happened in my day, by damn.

There were over thirty people having their breakfast in Cricklade's dining hall, which now served as the community's canteen. The big chamber was three storeys high, with a wooden ceiling supported by skilfully carved rafters. Cascade chandeliers hung on strong chains; their light globes were inoperative, but they bounced plenty of the sky's ambient light around the hall, illuminating the elaborate Earth-woodland frescos painted between every window. A thick blue and cream coloured Chinese carpet silenced Luca's boots as he walked over to the counter and helped himself to scrambled egg from an iron chafing dish.

The plate he used was chipped, the silver cutlery was tarnished, and the polish on the huge central table was scuffed and scratched. He nodded to his companions as he sat, holding back any criticism. Focus on priorities, he told himself. Things are up and running at a basic level, that's what counts. The food was plain but adequate; not rationed exactly, but carefully controlled. They were all reverting to a more civilized state of behaviour.

For a while after Quinn left, Cricklade's new residents had joyfully discarded the sect's loathsome teachings the monster had imposed, and dived into a continual orgy of sex and overconsumption. It was a reaction to the beyond, deliberately immersing themselves in complete sensory-glut. Nothing mattered except feeling, and taste, and smell. Luca had eaten and drunk his way through the manor's extensive cuisine supplies, shagged countless girls with supermodel looks, flung himself into ludicrously dangerous games, persecuted and hounded the non-possessed. Then, with painful slowness, the morning after had finally dawned, bringing the burden of responsibility and even a degree of decency.

It was the day when the bathroom shower nozzle squirted raw sewage over him that Luca started to gather up like-minded people and set about restoring the estate to working order. Pure hedonistic anarchy, it turned out, was not a sustainable environment.

Luca saw Susannah emerge from the door leading to the kitchen. His every movement suddenly became very cautious. She was carrying a fresh bowl of steaming tomatoes, which she plonked down on the self-service counter.

As he had applied himself to getting the farming side of the estate functional again, so she had taken on the manor itself. She was making a good job of providing meals and keeping the place rolling along (even though it wasn't maintained as it had been in the old days). Appropriately enough, for Susannah was possessing Marjorie Kavanagh's body. Naturally, there had been little room for physical improvement; she'd discarded about a decade, and shortened her extravagant landowner hair considerably, but the essential figure and features remained the same.

She picked up the empty bowl and walked back to the kitchen. Their eyes met, and she gave him a slightly confused smile before she disappeared back through the door.

Luca swallowed the mush of egg in his mouth before he choked on it. There had been so much he wanted to cram into that moment. So much to say. And their troubled thoughts had resonated together. She knew what he knew, and he knew . . .

Ridiculous!

Hardly. She belongs with us.

Ridiculous because Susannah had found someone: Austin. They were happy together. And I have Lucy. For convenience. For sex. Not for love.

Luca forked up the last of his eggs, and washed them down with some tea. Impatience boiled through him. I need to be out there, get those damn slackers cracking.

He found Johan sitting at the other end of the table, with the single slice of toast and glass of orange which was his whole meal. 'You ready yet?' he asked curtly.

Johan's rounded face registered an ancient expression of suffering, creasing up into lines so ingrained they must have been there since birth. There was a glint of sweat on his brow. 'Yes, sir; I'm fit for another day.'

Luca could have mouthed the ritual reply in tandem. Johan was possessing Mr Butterworth. The physical transformation from a lumbering, chubby sixty-year-old to virile twenty-something youth was almost complete, though some of the old estate manager's original characteristics seemed to defy modification.

'Come on, then, let's be going.'

He strode out of the hall, directing sharp glances at several of the men around the table as he went. Johan was already rising to his feet to scurry after Luca. Those who had received the visual warning crammed food in their mouths and stood hurriedly, anxious not to be left behind.

Luca had a dozen of them follow him into the stables, where they started to saddle up their horses. The estate's rugged farm ranger vehicles were still functional, but nobody was using them right now. The electricity grid had been damaged during the wild times, and only a couple of possessed in Stoke County owned up to having the knowledge to repair it. Progress was slow; the small amount of power coming from the geothermal cables was reserved for tractors.

It took Luca a couple of minutes to saddle up his horse, buckles and straps fastened into place without needing to think – Grant's knowledge. Then he led the piebald mare out into the courtyard, past the burnt-out ruins of the other stable block. Most of the horses Louise had set free during the fire had come back; they still had over half of the manor's superb herd left. Thank Christ. He knew food had been short for a time. But that was just outright bloody barbarism. Dog, though, dog didn't taste so bad.

He had to ride slower than he liked, allowing the others to keep up. But the freedom of the wolds made up for it. All as it should be. Almost.

Individual farms huddled in the lee of the shallow valleys, stolid stone houses seeking protection against Norfolk's arctic winters; they were scattered about the estate almost at random. Their fields had all been ploughed now, and the tractors were out drilling the second crop. Luca had gone round the storage warehouses himself, selecting the stock of barley, wheat, maize, oats, a dozen varieties of beans, vegetables. Some fields had already started to sprout, dusting the rich dark soil with a gossamer haze of luxuriant emerald. It was going to be a good yield, the nightly rain they conjured up would ensure that.

He was thankful that most of the disruption to the estate had been superficial. It just needed a firm guiding hand to get everything back on track.

As they approached Colsterworth, the farms were closer together, fields forming a continual quilt. Luca led his team round the outskirts. The streets were busy, clotted by the town's residents as they strove for activity and normality. Nearly all of them recognized Luca as he rode past. His influence wasn't quite so great here, though it was his objectives which had been adopted. The town had elected itself a council of sorts, who acknowledged Luca had the right goals in restarting the county's basic infrastructure. A majority of the townsfolk went along with the council, repairing the water pumphouse and the sewage-treatment plant, clearing the burnt carriages and carts from the streets, even attempting to repair the telephone system. But the council's real power came from food distribution, over which it had a monopoly, loyalists mounting a round the clock guard on the warehouses.

Luca spurred his horse over the canal bridge, a wood and iron arch in the Victorian tradition. The structure was another of the council's repair projects. Lengths of genuine fresh timber had been dovetailed into the original seasoned planking; energistic power had been utilized to re-form the iron girders that had been smashed and twisted (somehow they couldn't quite match the blue paint colour, so the new sections were clearly visible).

The Moulin de Hurley was on the other bank, a big mill house which supplied nearly a quarter of Kesteven Island with flour. It had dark red brick walls cut by tall iron-rimmed windows; one end was built over a small stream, which churned excitedly out of a brick arch before emptying into the canal at the end of the wharf. A series of tree-lined reservoir ponds were staggered up the gentle curve of the valley rising away behind the building.

There was a team appointed by the council to help him waiting by the Moulin's gates. Their leader, Marcella Rye, was standing right underneath the metal archway supporting an ornate letter K. Which gave Luca a warm sensation of contentment. After all, he owned the mill. No! The Kavanaghs. The Kavanaghs owned it. Used to own it.

Luca greeted Marcella enthusiastically, hoping the flush of bon-homie would prevent her from sensing his agitation at the lapse. 'I think it'll be relatively easy to get this up and running again,' he said expansively. 'The water powers the large grinder mechanism, and there's a geothermal cable to run the smaller machines. It should still be producing electricity.'

'Glad to hear it. The storage sheds were ransacked, of course.' She pointed at a cluster of large outbuildings. Their big wooden doors had been wrenched open; splintered and scorched, they now hung at a precarious angle. 'But once the food was gone, nobody bothered with the place.'

'Fine, as long as there's no—' Luca broke off, sensing the whirl of alarm in Johan's thoughts. He turned just in time to see the man stumble, his legs giving way to pitch him onto his knees. 'What's—?'

Johan's youthful outline was wavering as he pressed his fists against his forehead; his whole face was contorted in an agony of concentration.

Luca knelt beside him. 'Shit, what is it?'

'Nothing,' Johan hissed. 'Nothing. I'm OK, just dizzy, that's all.' Sweat was glistening all over his face and hands. 'Heat from the ride got to me. I'll be fine.' He clambered to his feet, wheezing heavily.

Luca gave him a confused glance, not understanding at all. How could anyone be ill in a realm in which a single thought had the power of creation? Johan must be severely hung over; a body wasn't flawlessly obedient to the mind's wishes here. They still had to eat, after all. But his deputy didn't normally go in for heroic benders.

Marcella was frowning at them, uncertain. Johan gave a forced *I'm fine* nod. 'We'd best go in,' he said.

Nobody had been in the mill since the day Quinn Dexter had arrived in town. It was cool inside; the power was off, and the tall smoked-glass windows filtered the daylight down to a listless pearl. Luca led the party along the dispenser line. Large, boxy stainless-steel machines stood silent above curving conveyor belts.

'Initial grinding is done at the far end,' he lectured. 'Then these machines blend and refine the flour, and bag it. We used to produce twelve different types in here: plain, self-raising, granary, savoury, strong white – you name it. Sent them all over the island.'

'Very homely,' Marcella drawled.

Luca let it ride. 'I can release new stocks of grain from the estate warehouses. But—' He went over to one of the hulking machines, and tugged a five-pound bag from the feed mechanism below the hopper nozzle; it was made of thick paper, with the Moulin's red and green water wheel logo printed on the front. 'Our first problem is going to be finding a new stock of these to package the flour in. They used to come from a company in Boston.'

'So? Just think them up.'

Luca wondered how she'd wound up with this assignment. Refused to sleep with the council leader? 'Even if we only produce white flour for the bakeries, and package it in sacks, you're looking at a couple of hundred a day,' he explained patiently. 'Then you need flour for pastry and cakes, which people will want to bake at home. That's several thousand bags a day. They'd all have to be thought up individually.'

'All right, so what do you suggest?'

'Actually, we were hoping you might like to come up with a solution. After all, we're supplying the expertise to get the mill going again, and providing you with grain.'

'Gee, thanks.'

'No thanks needed. This isn't a Communist society, we're not giving it away. You'll have to pay for it.'

'It's as much ours as it is yours.' Her voice had risen until it was almost an indignant squeal.

'Possession is nine-tenths of the law.' He grinned mirthlessly. 'Ask your host.' His mind detected his people were sharing his amusement (even Johan's thoughts were lighter). While the townies were highly uncomfortable with the facts being presented.

Marcella regarded him with blatant mistrust. 'How do you propose we pay?'

'Some kind of ledger, I suppose. Work owed to us. After all, we're the ones growing the food for you.'

'And we're running the mill for you, and transporting the stuff all over the county.'

'Good. That's a start, then, isn't it? I'm sure there'll be other useful industries in Colsterworth, too. Our tractors and field machinery will need spares. Now all we need is a decent exchange rate.'

'I'm going to have to go back to the council with this.'

'Naturally.' Luca had reached the wall separating the dispenser line from the chamber housing the main grinder. There were several large electrical distribution boxes forming their own mosaic over the bricks. Each one had an amber light glowing brightly on the front. He started pressing the trip buttons in a confident sequence. The broad tube lights overhead flickered as they came alight, sending down a blue-white radiance almost brighter than they sky outside. Luca smiled in satisfaction at his mental prowess. The circuitry for governing this old island was mapped out in his mind now, percolating up from his host.

His modest feeling of contentment faded, absorbed by a new body of emotion slipping over his perceptual horizon. Around him, the others were reacting in the same fashion. All of them turned instinctively to face the same outer wall, as if trying to stare through the bricks. A group of people were approaching Colsterworth. Dark thoughts sliding through Norfolk's atmosphere of the mind like threatening storm clouds.

'I think we'd better go take a look,' Luca said. There were no dissenters.

*

They used the railway to get about over the island, adapting one of the utilitarian commuter trains which had trundled between the island's towns. A steam-powered ironclad fortress now clanked and hissed its way along the rails, hauling a couple of Orient Express carriages behind it. Several sets of what looked like twin recoilless ack-ack guns had been mounted at both ends of the train, while the barrel of a big tank cannon pointed along the top of the boiler, emerging from the combination turret/driver's cabin.

Just outside Colsterworth, where the rail went over the canal before it got to the station, Luca and Marcella stood side by side on the embankment at the head of their combined teams. More people were emerging from the town, bolstering their numbers. Antibodies responding to an incursive virus, Luca thought. And they were right to do so. People here were made to wear their hearts on their sleeves, visible to everyone else. It saved a lot of bullshitting around. Plain for all to see, those coming down the track were set on just one thing.

The train let out a long annoyed whistle, sending a fountain of steam rocketing up into the sky. Metallic screeches and janglings came pouring out of the engine when its riders realized how committed the townie blockaders were. Its pistons pounded away, reversing the wheel spin.

Luca and Marcella stood their ground as it howled forwards. A thought-smile flashed between them, and they stared down at the tracks, concentrating. The rails just in front of their feet creaked once, then split cleanly. Bolts holding them to the timber sleepers shot into the air, and the rails started to curl up, rolling into huge spirals. Flame spewed out of the train's wheels. The riders had to exert a lot of energistic strength to halt its momentum. It stopped a couple of yards short of the coils. Billows of angry steam jetted out of valves all along the underside, water splattered down onto the tracks. A thick iron door banged open on the side of the driver's cabin. Bruce Spanton jumped down.

He was dressed in antihero black leathers, impenetrable sunglasses pressed tight against his face. Heavy boots crunched on the gravel chippings of the embankment as he stalked towards the huddled townsfolk. A holster with a gold-plated Uzi slapped his leg with every step.

'Hello,' Luca muttered, 'somebody watched way too many bad cable movies when they were younger.'

Marcella subdued a grin as the ersatz Bad Guy halted in front of them.

'You,' Bruce Spanton growled. 'You're in my way, friend. You must feel lucky to try a move like that.'

'What do you boys want here?' Luca asked wearily. The bad vibes emanating from Spanton and the others in the train weren't entirely forged. Not everyone on Norfolk had calmed down after returning from the beyond.

'Me and the guys, just passing through,' Spanton said challengingly. 'No law against that, here, is there?'

'No law, but plenty of wishes,' Luca said. 'This county doesn't want you. I'm sure you'll respect that majority opinion.'

'Tough shit. You got us. What you gonna do, call the cops?'

A big silver Western sheriff's badge mushroomed on the front of Marcella's tunic. 'I am the police in Colsterworth.'

'Listen,' Bruce Spanton said. 'We're just here to check out the town. Have us a bit of fun. Stock up on some food, grab some Norfolk Tears. Then tomorrow we'll be gone. We don't want no trouble; it's not as if we want to stay here. Crappy dump like this, not our scene. Know what I mean?'

'And how are you going to pay for your food?' Marcella asked. Luca did his best not to turn and frown at her.

'Pay for it?' Spanton yelled in astonishment. 'What the fuck are you scoring, sister? We don't pay for anything any more. That got left behind along with all the rest of the lawyers and shit we had to put up with back there.'

'It doesn't work like that,' Luca said. 'It's our food. Not yours.'

'It's not yours, shithead. It belongs to everyone.'

'We've got it. You don't. It's ours. That simple enough for you?'

'Fuck you. We've got to eat. We've got a right to eat.'

'I remember you now,' Luca said. 'You were one of Dexter's people. Real devout arse-licker. Do you miss him?'

Bruce Spanton stabbed a finger at Luca. 'I'm going to remember you, shithead. And you're going to wish I fucking hadn't.'

'Learn the rules when you go abroad,' Luca said forcefully. 'And then live by them. Now either you climb back on your pathetic little cartoon mean machine and leave. Or, you stay and find yourself a useful job, and earn a living like everybody else. Because we're not in the business of supporting worthless parasite scum like you.'

'Get a jo—' Disbelief and rage made Bruce Spanton splutter to a halt. 'What the hell is this?'

'For you, exactly that: hell. Now get out of our county before we run you out.' Luca heard several cheers from behind him.

The sound made Bruce Spanton look up. He glanced round the crowd, sensing their mood, the belligerence and resentment focusing on him. 'You fuckers are crazy. You know that? Crazy! We've just escaped from all this shit. And you're trying to bring it back.'

'All we're doing is building ourselves a life as best we can,' Luca said. 'Join in, or fuck off.'

'Oh we'll be back,' Bruce Spanton said, tight-lipped. 'You'll see. And people will join us, not you. Know why? Because it's easier.' He stomped off back to the train.

Marcella grinned at his back. 'We won. We showed the bastards, eh? Not such a bad combination, you and me. We won't be seeing them again.'

'This is a small island on a small planet,' Luca said, more troubled than he wanted to be by Spanton's parting shot.

3

Sinon's serjeant body had been divested of its last medical package just five hours before the *Catalpa* flew out of its wormhole terminus above Ombey. The voidhawk's crew toroid was overcrowded, carrying thirty-five of the hulking serjeants and their five-strong biomedical supervisory team in addition to the usual crew. Heavy dull-rust coloured bodies stood almost shoulder to shoulder as they performed lumbering callisthenics all around the central corridor, discovering for themselves the parameters of their new physiques.

There was no fatigue in the fashion of a genuinely human body, the tiredness and tingling aches. Instead blood-sugar depletion and muscle-tissue stress registered as mental warning tones within the neural array housing the controlling personality. Sinon thought they must be similar to a neural nanonic display, but grey and characterless rather than the full-spectrum iconographic programs which Adamists enjoyed. Interpreting them was simple enough, thankfully.

He was actually quite satisfied with the body he now possessed (even though it was unable to smile at that particular irony for him). The deep scars of the serjeant's assembly surgery were almost healed. What minimal restriction they imposed on his movements would be gone within a few more days. Even his sensorium was up to the standard of an Edenist body. Michael Saldana certainly hadn't skimped on the design of the bitek construct's genetic sequence.

Acclimatization to his new circumstances had twinned a growing confidence throughout the flight, a psychological boost similar to a patient recovering from his injuries as more and more of the medical packages became redundant. In this case it was shared with all the other serjeant personalities who were going through identical emotional uplifts, the general affinity band merging their emerging gratification into synergistic optimism.

Despite a total lack of hormonal glands, Sinon was hot for the Mortonridge Liberation campaign to begin. He asked the *Catalpa* to share the view provided by its sensor blisters as the wormhole terminus closed behind them. The external image surged into his mind, featuring Ombey as a silver and blue crescent a hundred and twenty thousand kilometres ahead. Several settled asteroids swung along high orbits, grubby brown specks muffled by a fluctuating swirl of silver stardust as their industrial stations deflected spears of raw sunlight. Larger, more regular, motes of light swarmed around *Catalpa*, its cousins emerging from their termini and accelerating in towards the planet.

This particular squadron was comprised of just over three hundred of the bitek starships. It wasn't even the first to arrive at the Kingdom principality today. The Royal Navy's Strategic Defence Centre on Guyana had combined its flight management operations and sensors with civil traffic control to guide the torrent of arriving starships into parking orbits.

The voidhawks headed down towards the planet, merging into a long line as they spiralled into alignment over the equator. They shared the five hundred kilometre orbit with their cousins and Adamist starships from every star system officially allied to the Kingdom. Military and civil transports unloaded their cargo-pods into fleets of flyers and spaceplanes; Confederation Navy assault cruisers had brought an entire battalion of marines, and even the voidhawks were eager to see the huge Kulu Royal Navy *Aquilae*-class starships.

After reaching low orbit, the *Catalpa* had to wait a further eight hours before its spaceplane received clearance to ferry the first batch of serjeants down to Fort Forward. Sinon was on it as the night-shadowed ocean fled past underneath the glowing fuselage. Their little craft had aerobraked down to Mach five when Xingu's western coastline rose over the horizon ahead. The red cloud was just visible to the sensors, a slice of curving red light, as if the fissure between land and sky had been rendered in gleaming neon. Then their altitude dropped, and it sank away.

They must know we're here, Choma said. **With ten thousand spaceship flights hyperbooming across the ocean every day, they'll hear us arriving if nothing else.** In the twenty-fifth century, Choma had been an astroengineering export manager based at Jupiter. Although he'd readily admitted to the other serjeant personalities that his personal knowledge-base of obsolete deep space star-tracker sensors was not very relevant to the Liberation, his main interest was strategy games, combined with the odd bit of role-playing. For himself and his fellow quirky enthusiasts, the kind of simulation arenas available to Edenists through perceptual reality environments were anathema. They wanted authentic mud, forests, rock faces, redoubts, heavy backpacks, heat, costumes, horse riding, marches, aching joints, flagons of ale, making love in the long grass, and songs around the campsite. To the amusement of the other inhabitants, they would take over vast tracts of habitat parkland for their contests; it was quite a faddish activity at the time. All of which made Choma the closest thing Sinon's squad had to an experienced soldier.

A lot of the old strategy game players had come out of the multiplicity to animate serjeant bodies. Slightly surprisingly, very few ex-intelligence agency operatives had joined them, the people whose genuine field operations experience would really have been valuable.

Very likely, Sinon agreed. **Dariat demonstrated his perceptive ability to the Kohistan Consensus; no doubt the combined faculty of the Mortonridge possessed will provide them with some foreknowledge.**

That and the ring of starships overhead. The convoys aren't exactly unobtrusive.

But they are obscured by the red cloud.

Don't count on it.

Does that worry you? Sinon asked.

Not really. Surprise was never going to be our strategic high ground. Best we could hope for is the scale of the Liberation being a nasty shock to Ekelund and her troops.

I wish I had experience of the combat situations we will be facing rather than theoretical memories.

I expect that experience is going to be one thing you'll be collecting plenty of, in a very short timespan.

The *Catalpa*'s spaceplane landed at Fort Forward's new spaceport, racing along one of the three prefabricated runways laid out in parallel. Another was touching down forty-five seconds behind it; that managed to spark a Judeo of concern in Sinon's mind. Even with an AI in charge of slotting the traffic together, margins were being stretched. Ion-field flyers were landing and launching vertically from pads on the other side of the spaceport's control tower at a much faster rate than the runways could handle spaceplanes.

For the moment, the spaceport's principal concern was to offload cargo and send it on to Fort Forward. The hangars were frantically busy, heavy-lift mechanoids and humans combining to keep the flow of pods going; any delay here would have a knock-on effect right back up to orbit. Nearly all of the Liberation's ground vehicles were assigned to carry cargo. Passenger vehicles were still up in orbit.

Sinon and the others were given a static charge test by Royal Marines as they got to the bottom of the spaceplane's stairs. That it was perfunctory was understandable, but Sinon was satisfied to see they did test everybody. As soon as they were cleared the spaceplane taxied away, joining a queue of similar craft waiting to take off. Another one rolled into place, extending its airstair. The marine squad moved forward again.

An Edenist liaison officer they never even saw told them that they were going to have to get to Fort Forward on foot. They were part of a long line of serjeants and marines marching along a road of freshly unrolled micro-mesh composite next to the new six-lane motorway. After they got underway, Sinon realized that it wasn't only Confederation Marines who made up the human contingent of the Liberation's ground forces. He walked over to a boosted mercenary taller than himself. The mercenary's brown skin had exactly the same texture as leather, and long buttress ropes of muscle were clumped round the neck, supporting a nearly globular skull armoured with silicolithium like an all-over helmet. In place of a nose and mouth there was an oval cage grille at the front, and the saucer eyes were set very wide apart, giving little overlap, normal aside from the blue-green irises, which appeared to be multifaceted.

When Sinon asked, she said her name was Elena Duncan. 'Excuse me for enquiring,' he said. 'But what exactly are you doing here?'

'I'm a volunteer,' Elena Duncan replied with an overtly feminine voice. 'We're part of the occupation force. You guys take the ground from those bastards, we'll hold on to it for you. That's the plan. Listen up, I know you Edenists don't approve of my kind. But there aren't enough marines to secure the whole of Mortonridge, so you've got to use us. That, and I had some friends on Lalonde.'

'I don't disapprove. If anything I'm rather glad there's someone here who has actually been under fire before. I wish I had.'

'Yeah? Now, see, that's what I don't get. You're cannon fodder, and you know you're cannon fodder. But it doesn't bother you. Me, I know I'm taking a gamble, that's a life-choice I made a long time ago.'

'It doesn't bother me because I'm not human, just a very sophisticated bitek automaton. I don't have a brain, just a collection of processors.'

'But you got a personality, don'tcha?'

'This is only an edited copy of me.'

'Ha. You must be very confident about that. A life is a life, after all.' She broke off, and tipped her head back, neck muscles flexing like heavy deltoids. 'Now there's a sight which makes all this worthwhile. You can't beat those old warships for blunt spectacle.'

A CK500–090 Thunderbird spaceplane was coming in to land. The giant delta-wing craft was at least twice the size of any of the civil cargo spaceplanes using the runways. Air thundered turbulently in its wake as it slipped round to line up on its approach path, large sections of the trailing edges bending with slow agility to alter the wing camber. Then a bewildering number of hatches were sliding open all across its fuselage belly; twelve sets of undercarriage bogies dropped down. The Thunderbird hit the runway with a roar louder than a sonic boom. Chemical rockets in the nose fired to slow it as dirty ablation smoke poured out of all ninety-six brake drums.

'God damn,' Elena Duncan murmured. 'I never thought I'd ever see an operation like this, never mind be a part of it. A real live land army on the move. I'm centuries after my time, you know, I belong back in the nineteenth and twentieth centuries, marching on Moscow with Napoleon, or struggling across Spain. I was born for war, Sinon.'

'That's stupid. You know you have a soul now. You shouldn't be risking it like this. You have invented a crusade for yourself to follow rather than achieve anything as an individual. That is wrong.'

'It's my soul, and in a way I'm no different to Edenists.'

Sinon felt a rush of real surprise. 'How so?'

'I'm perfectly adjusted to what I am. The fact that my goals are different to those of your society doesn't matter. You know what I think? Edenists don't get caught in the beyond because you're cool enough under pressure to figure your way out. Well, me too, pal. Laton said there was a way out. I believe him. The Kiint found it. Just knowing that it's possible is my ticket to exit. I'll be happy searching because I know it's not pointless, I won't suffer like those dumbasses that wound up trapped. They're losers, they gave up. Not me. That's why I'm signed up on this mad Liberation idea, it's just part of getting ready for the big battle. Good training, is all.'

She gave his shoulder an avuncular pat with a hand whose fingers had been replaced by three big claws, and marched off.

That's an excess of fatalism, Choma remarked. **What a strange psychology.**

She is content, Sinon answered. **I wish her well in that.**

*

A large quantity of love had been invested in constructing the farmhouse. Even the Kulu aristocracy with their expensive showy buildings employed modern materials in their fabric. And Mortonridge was a designated rapid growth area, with government subsidies to help develop the farms. A resolutely middle-class province. Their buildings were substantial, but cheap: assembled from combinations of carbon-concrete, uniform-strength pulpwood planks, bricks made from grains of clay cemented by geneered bacteria, spongesteel structural girders, bonded silicon glass. For all their standardization, such basic components afforded a wealth of diversity to architects.

But this was unmistakable and original. Beautifully crude. A house of stone, quarried from a local outcrop with an industrial fission blade; large cubes made the walls thick enough to repel the equatorial heat and keep the rooms cool without air-conditioning. The floor and roof beams were harandrid timbers, sturdy lengths dovetailed and pegged together as only a master carpenter could manage. Inside, they'd been left uncovered, the gaps between filled with reed and plaster, then whitewashed. It was as historic as any of the illusions favoured by the possessed, not that anyone could mistake something so solid for an ephemeral aspiration.

There was a barn attached at the end, also stone, forming one side of the farmyard. Its big wooden doors were swinging open in the breeze the day the Karmic Crusader pulled up outside. Stephanie Ash had been tired and fed up by the time they pulled off the main road and drove along the unmarked dirt track. Investigating it had been Moyo's idea.

'The road must lead somewhere,' he had insisted. 'This land was settled recently. Nothing's had time to fall into disuse yet.'

She hadn't bothered to argue with him. They'd driven a long way down the M6 after handing the children over, a journey which meant having to pass back through Annette Ekelund's army. This time they'd been pointedly ignored by the troops billeted in Chainbridge. After that they'd zigzagged from coast to coast looking for a refuge, somewhere self-sufficient where they could rest up and wait for the grand events beyond Mortonridge to play themselves out. But the towns in the northern section of the peninsula were still occupied, though there was a steady drift out to farms. They were unwelcome there; the possessed were learning to guard their food stocks. Every unoccupied farm they'd visited had been ransacked for food and livestock. It was a monotonous trend, and finding a functional power supply to recharge the Karmic Crusader was becoming more difficult.

After the joy and accomplishment of evacuating the children, the comedown to excluded refugee status was hard. Stephanie hadn't exactly lost faith, but the narrow road was no different to any of the dozens they'd driven down the last few days. Hope rebutted unfailingly each time.

The road took the bus through a small forest of aboriginal trees, then dipped into a shallow, lightly wooded valley which meandered extravagantly. A stream bubbled along the lush grassy floor, its speed revealing they were actually travelling up at quite an angle. After four kilometres, the valley ended by opening out into a nearly circular basin. It was so regular, Stephanie suspected it was an ancient impact crater. A lacework of silver brooks threaded their way down the sides, feeding a lake at the centre, which was the origin of the valley's stream. The farmhouse stood above the shore, separated from the rippling water by a neatly trimmed lawn. Behind it, someone had converted the north-facing walls of the basin into stepped terraces, making a perfect sun-trap. The levels were cultivated with dozens of terrestrial fruit and vegetable plants, from citrus tree groves to lettuce, avocados to rhubarb. Almost all the aboriginal vegetation had been removed: even the south side looked as if it was covered in terrestrial grass. Goats and sheep were wandering around grazing peacefully.

They all piled out of the Karmic Crusader, smiling like entranced children.

'There's nobody here,' Rana said. 'Can you sense it? This whole place is empty.'

'Oh goodness,' Tina exclaimed nervously. She took the last step off the bus's stairs, her scarlet stilettos sinking awkwardly into the road's loose-packed gravel surface. 'Do you really think so? This is simply paradise. It's just what we all deserve after everything we've done for others. I couldn't bear us being thrown out by someone else claiming they were here first. It would be excruciating.'

'There are no vehicles left,' McPhee grunted. 'The owners probably received the Kingdom's warning and cleared out before Ekelund's people arrived in these parts.'

'Lucky for them,' Rana said.

'More so for us,' Moyo said. 'It's absolutely bloody perfect.'

'I think the irrigation system is screwed,' McPhee said. He was shielding his eyes with a hand as he squinted up at the terraces. 'There, see? There must be channels to divert the brooks so that each level receives a decent supply. But it's spilling over like a waterfall. The plants will drown.'

'No, they won't,' Franklin Quigly said. 'It's not broken. The power's off, and there's no one here to manage it. That's all. We could get it fixed inside of a day. That's if we're staying.'

They all turned to look at Stephanie. She was amused rather than gratified by the compliment. 'Oh, I think so.' She smiled at her ragged little band. 'We're not going to find anywhere better.'

They spent the rest of the day wandering round the farmhouse and the terraces. The basin was an intensive-cultivation market garden; there were no cereal crops on any of the terraces. There were signs of a hurried departure all through the building, drawers pulled out, clothes spilled on the shiny floorboards, a tap left running, two old suitcases abandoned half-packed in one of the bedrooms. But there was a lot of basic foodstuffs left in the pantry, flour, jams, jellied fruit, eggs, whole cheeses, and a big freezer was filled with fish and joints of meat. Whoever the farm belonged to, they didn't believe in modern sachets and ready-made meals.

Tina took one look inside the kitchen with its simple array of shining copper pots and pans, and sniffed with emphatic disapproval. 'You can take the worship of all things rustic too far, you know.'

'It's appropriate to what we are now,' Stephanie told her. 'The consumer convenience society cannot exist in our universe.'

'Well, just don't expect me to give up silk stockings, darling.'

Moyo, Rana, and McPhee scrambled up to the top of the basin to a small building they assumed was a pumphouse for the irrigation system. Stephanie and the rest started clearing out the farmhouse. By the third day, they'd got the terrace irrigation equipment working again. Not perfectly, their presence still glitched some of the management processors; but there was a manual backup control panel in the pumphouse. Even the clouds' gloomy claret illumination had grudgingly brightened as they established themselves and began exerting their influence. It wasn't the pure sunlight which shone upon towns and larger groups of possessed, but the plants gleefully absorbed the increased rain of photons, and perked up accordingly.

A week later Stephanie had every right to be content as she walked out into the relatively cool air of early morning. The right, but not the reality. She opened the iron-framed French doors which led out to the lawn, and stepped barefoot onto the dewy grass.

As usual the red clouds tossed through the sky above, their massive braids strumming the air until it groaned in protest. This time, though, a more subtle resonance was carried by the rancorous vapour. It couldn't be heard, it merely preyed on the mind like a troublesome dream.

She walked down to the shore of the lake, her head turning slowly from side to side as she scanned the sky, questing for some kind of hint. Anything. The nettling sensation had been building for many days now. Whatever the origin, it was too far away for her senses to distinguish, skulking below the horizon like a malevolent moon.

'So you like feel the cosmic blues sounding out, too?' Cochrane said ruefully.

Stephanie jumped, she hadn't noticed him approach. The bells on the ancient hippy's velvet flares were silent as he trod lightly over the grass. An exceptionally large reefer hung from the corner of his mouth. It smelt different than usual, not nearly as sweet.

He caught her puzzlement, and his beard parted to show a smug grin. Fingers with many rings plucked the brown tube from his mouth, and held it vertically. 'Guess what I found growing on some forgotten terrace? This Mr Taxpaying Johnny Appleseed we've taken over from here wasn't quite as straight as his fellow Rotarians believed. Know what this is? Only like genuine *Nicotiana*. And as illegal as hell around these parts. Man, but it feels good, first real drag I've had in centuries.'

Stephanie smiled indulgently as he stuck it back in his mouth. Indulgent was all you could be with Cochrane. Moyo was coming out of the farmhouse, his mind darkened with concern.

'You know it's here, too, don't you?' she asked sadly. 'This must be what Ekelund meant when she told me the Saldana Princess was preparing.'

'And Lieutenant Anver,' Moyo muttered.

'The earth can feel war's coming, that blood's going to be spilt. How very . . . biblical; bad vibes in the ether. I'd so hoped Ekelund was wrong, that she was just trying to justify maintaining her army by claiming phantom enemies were waiting on the other side of the hill.'

'No way,' Cochrane said. 'The bad dude cavalry's like mounting up. They'll charge us soon, guns blazing.'

'Why us?' Stephanie asked. 'Why this planet? We said we wouldn't threaten them. We promised, and we kept it.'

Moyo put his arm round her. 'Being here is a threat to them.'

'But it's so stupid. I just want to be left alone, I want time to come to terms with what's happened. That's all. We've got this beautiful farm, and we're making it work without hurting anybody. It's good here. We can support ourselves, and have enough time left over to think. That doesn't make us a threat or a danger to the Confederation. If we were allowed to carry on we might be able to make some progress towards an answer for this mess.'

'I wish we could be left alone,' Moyo told her sadly. 'I wish they'd listen to us. But they won't. I know what it'll be like out there now. Common sense and reason won't matter. Forcing us out of Morton-ridge is a political goal. Once the Saldanas and other Confederation leaders have declared it, they won't be able to pull back. We're in the path of a proverbial irresistible force.'

'Perhaps if I went back up to the firebreak and spoke to them. They know me. They might listen.'

Alarm at what she was saying made Moyo tighten his grip around her. 'No. I don't want you doing anything crazy like that. Besides, they wouldn't listen. Not them. They'd smile politely for a while, then shove you into zero-tau. I couldn't stand that, I've only just found you.'

She rested her head against him, quietly thankful for his devotion. He'd been there for her since the very first day. More than a lover, a constant source of strength.

'You can't go,' Cochrane said. 'Not you. These cats would like fall apart without you to guide them. We need you here, man. You're our den mother.'

'But we won't last long if we stay here, and the Princess sends her army to find us.'

'A little more time is better than the big zippo. And who knows what our karma's got mapped out for us before the jackboots kick our door down.'

'You're not normally the optimist,' Stephanie teased.

'Face it, babe, I'm not normally alive. That kinda warps your outlook, dig? You gotta have faith these days, man. Some cool happening will come along to like blow our minds away.'

'Groovy,' Moyo deadpanned.

'All right, you win,' Stephanie assured them. 'No noble sacrifices on my part. I'll stay here.'

'Maybe they'll never come,' Moyo said. 'Maybe Ekelund will defeat them.'

'Not a chance,' Stephanie said. 'She's good, and she's mean, which is everything it takes. But she's not that good. Just stop and feel the weight of them building up out there. Ekelund will cause them a whole load of grief when the invasion starts, but she won't stop them.'

'What will you do then, when they reach the farm? Will you fight?'

'I don't think so. I might lash out, that's human nature. But fight? No. What about you? You said you would, once.'

'That was back when I thought it might do some good. I suppose I've grown up since then.'

'But it's still not fair,' she complained bitterly. 'I adore this taste of life. I think going back to the beyond will be worse now. Next time, we'll know that it doesn't have to be permanent, even though it probably will be. It would have been far better if we'd been spared knowing. Why is the universe persecuting us like this?'

'It's karma, man,' Cochrane said. 'Bad karma.'

'I thought karma was paying for your actions. I never hurt anyone badly enough for this.'

'Original sin,' Moyo said. 'Nasty concept.'

'You're wrong,' she said. 'Both of you. If I know anything now, it's that our religions are lies. Horrid, dirty lies. I don't believe in God, or destiny, not any more. There has to be a natural explanation for all this, a cosmological reason.' She sank into Moyo's embrace, too tired even for anger. 'But I'm not smart enough to work it out. I don't think any of us are. We're just going to have to wait until someone clever finds it for us. Damn, I hate that. Why can't I be good at the big things?'

Moyo kissed her brow. 'There are forty kids on the other side of the firebreak who are mighty glad you achieved what you did. I wouldn't call that a small thing.'

Cochrane blew a smoke ring in the direction of the oppressive presence beyond the firebreak. 'Anyhow, nobody's served us an eviction order on these bodies yet. The evil Kingdom's warlords have got to like catch us first. I'm going to make chasing after me tragically expensive to the taxpayers. That always pisses them off big-time.'

*

We really should be doing this in a perceptual reality, Sinon moaned. I mean: actual physical training. It's barbaric. I'm amazed Ralph Hiltch hasn't assigned us a crusty old drill sergeant to knock us into shape. We've got the right scenario.

That morning, the serjeants had been driven out to a training ground ten kilometres east of Fort Forward, a rugged stretch of land with clumps of trees and mock-up buildings. It was one of twenty-five new training zones, their basic facilities thrown up as quickly as

Fort Forward itself. Royal Marines engineers were busy constructing another ten.

Choma half-ignored Sinon's diatribe, concentrating on the bungalow in front of them. The rest of the squad were spread out round the dilapidated building in a semicircle, learning to cling to whatever cover was available. Stupid, really, he thought, considering the possessed can sense us from hundreds of metres. But it added to the feeling of authenticity. The point which Sinon was missing.

Suddenly, one of the small bushes fifty metres away shimmered silver, and metamorphosed into a green-skinned hominoid with bug-eyes. Balls of white light shot away from his pointing hand. The two serjeants swivelled smoothly, lining their machine-guns up on the apparition.

Ours, they told the rest of the squad. Sinon squeezed the trigger down with his right index finger, while his left hand twisted the gun's side grip, selecting the fire rate. The small chemical projectile cases reverberated loudly as they fired, smothering all other sounds. Ripples of static shivered over the end of the barrel as the pellets hammered into their target.

The static gun was the weapon which the Kingdom had developed to arm the serjeants for the Liberation. A simple enough derivative of an ordinary machine-gun, the principal modification was to the bullet. Inert kinetic tips had been replaced by spherical pellets which carried a static charge. Their shape reduced their velocity compared to ordinary bullets (and their accuracy), though they could still inflict a lethal amount of damage on a human target, while their electrical discharge played havoc with the energistic ability of a possessed. Every pellet carried the same level of charge, but the variable rate of fire would allow the serjeants to cope with the different strengths of the individual possessed they encountered; and as the gun's mechanism was mechanical, the possessed couldn't glitch it – in theory.

It took three seconds of concentrated fire on the green monster before it stopped flinging white light back at Sinon and Choma. The image collapsed into an ordinary human male, who pitched forward. A holographic projector lens glinted in the bush behind it.

You were too slow to respond to the target's strength, their supervisor told them, **in a genuine combat situation his white fire would have disabled the pair of you. And, Sinon . . .**

Yes?

Work on improving your aim, that entire first burst you fired was wide.

Acknowledged, Sinon informed the supervisor curtly. He adopted singular-engagement mode to talk to Choma. **Wide shooting, indeed! I was simply bringing the gun round onto the target. Approaching fire can be a large psychological inhibitor.**

Certainly can, Choma replied with strict neutrality. He was scanning the land ahead, alert for new dangers. It would be just like the training ground controllers to hit them immediately again.

I think I am beginning to comprehend the gun's parameters, Sinon declared. **My thought routines are assimilating its handling characteristics at an autonomic level.**

Choma risked a mildly exasperated glance at his squad mate. **That's the whole point of this training. We can hardly accept a tutorial thought routine from a habitat, now can we? The Consensus didn't even know about static guns when we left Saturn. Besides, I always said the best lessons are the ones you learn the hard way.**

You and your atavistic Olympiad philosophy. No wonder it fell out of fashion by the time I was born.

But you're getting the hang of it, aren't you?

I suppose so.

Good. Now come on, we'd better advance to the building or we'll wind up on latrine duty.

At least the serjeant's lips and throat allowed Sinon to sigh plaintively. **Very well.**

*

Princess Kirsten had switched her retinal implants to full resolution so that she could watch the squads advancing over various sections of the training ground. There was an old saying running loose in her mind, as if one file was continually leaking from a memory cell: I don't know about the enemy, but by God they frighten me. This was the first time she'd ever encountered the big bitek constructs outside of a sensevise. Their size and mien combined to make them both impressive and imposing; she was now rather glad Ralph Hiltch had the courage to suggest using them. At the time she'd been only too happy deferring the final choice to Allie. The family does so lack the bravery to make really important decisions, thank God he still has the guts. It was the same even when we were kids, we all waited for his pronouncement.

Several hundred of the dark figures were currently crawling, slithering, and in some cases running through the undergrowth, bushes, and long grass while colourful holographic images popped into existence to waylay them. The sound of gunfire rattled through the air; it was a noise she was becoming very familiar with.

'They're making good progress,' Ralph Hiltch said. He was standing beside the Princess on the roof of the training ground's management centre, which gave them an uninterrupted view over the rumpled section of land which the Liberation army had annexed. Their respective entourages were arranged behind them, officers and Cabinet ministers forming an edgy phalanx. 'It only takes two sessions on average to train up a serjeant. The support troops need a little longer. Don't get me wrong, those marines are excellent troops; I don't just mean the Kingdom's, our allies have sent their best, and the mercs are formidable at the best of times. It's just that they're all way too reliant on their neural nanonic programs for fire control and tactics, so we really discourage their usage. If a possessed does break through the front line, that's the first piece of equipment that's going to glitch.'

'How many serjeants are ready?' Kirsten asked.

'About two hundred and eighty thousand. We're training them up at the rate of thirty thousand a day. And there's another five training grounds opening each day. I'd like the rate increased, but even with the Confederation Navy brigades, I've only got a limited number of engineering corps; I have to balance their assignments. Completing the accommodation sections of Fort Forward is my priority.'

'It would appear as though you have everything under control.'

'Simple enough, we just tell the AI what we want, and it designates for us. This is the first time in history a land army commander doesn't have to worry unduly about logistics.'

'Providing a possessed doesn't get near the AI.'

'Unlikely, ma'am; believe me, unlikely. And even that's in our contingency file.'

'Good, I'd hate us to become overconfident. So when do you think you'll be able to begin the Liberation?'

'Ideally, I'd like to wait another three weeks.' He acknowledged the Princess's raised eyebrow with a grudging smile. They'd spent the best part of two hours that morning under the gaze of rover reporters, inspecting the tremendous flow of *matériel* and personnel surging through Fort Forward's spaceport. To most people it looked as if they already had the military resources to invade a couple of planets. 'Our greatest stretch is going to be the opening assault. We have to ring the entire peninsula, and it's got to be one very solid noose, we can't risk anything less. That'll have to be achieved with inexperienced troops and untested equipment. The more time spent preparing, the greater chance we have for success.'

'I'm aware of that, Ralph. But you were talking about balance a moment ago.' She glanced back at Leonard DeVille, who responded with a reluctant twitch.

'Expectations are running rather high, and not just here on Ombey. We've demanded and received a colossal amount of support from our political allies and the Confederation Navy. I don't need to remind you what the King said.'

'No, ma'am.' His last meeting with Alastair II, the time when he'd received his commission, needed no file. The King had been adamant about the factors at play, the cost of external support, and the public weight of anticipation and belief.

Success. That was what everyone wanted, and expected him to deliver, on many fronts. And I have to give them that. This was all my idea. And my fault.

Unlike the Princess, Ralph didn't have the luxury of glancing round his people for signs of support. He could well imagine Janne Palmer's opinion – she'd be right too.

'We can begin preliminary deployment in another three days,' he said. 'That way we'll be able to start the actual Liberation in eight days' time.'

'All right, Ralph. You have another eight days' grace. No more.'

'Yes, ma'am. Thank you.'

'Have you actually managed to test one of the static guns on a possessed yet?'

'I'm afraid not, ma'am, no.'

'Isn't that taking a bit of a chance? Surely you need to know their effectiveness, if any?'

'They'll either work, or not; and we don't want to give Ekelund's people any advance warning just in case they can devise a counter. We'll know if they're any use within seconds of our first encounter. If they aren't, then the ground troops will revert to ordinary light arms. I just hope to God they don't have to, we'll inflict a hell of a lot of damage on the bodies we're trying to recover. But the theory's perfect, and the machinery's all so beautifully simple as well. Cathal and Dean dreamed up the concept. It should have been obvious from the start. I should have come up with it.'

'I think you've worked enough miracles, Ralph. All the family wants from you now is a mundane little victory.'

He nodded his thanks, and stared out over the training ground again. It was changeover time, hundreds of grubby-red serjeants were on the move, along with a good number of ordinary troops. Though ordinary was a relative term when referring to the boosted mercenaries.

'One question,' Leonard DeVille said; he sounded apologetic, if not terribly sincere about it. 'I know this isn't quite what you want to hear right now, Ralph. But you have allocated room for the rover reporters to observe the action during the assault, haven't you? The AI does know that's a requirement?'

Ralph grinned. This time he gave Palmer a direct look before locking eyes with the Home Office Minister. The Princess was diplomatically focused on the returning serjeants.

'Oh, yes. We're putting them right in the front line for you. You'll get sensevises every bit as hot as the one Kelly Tirrel produced on Lalonde. This is going to be one very public war.'

*

Chainbridge was different now. When Annette Ekelund had first arrived here, she'd transformed it into a simple headquarters and garrison town. Close enough to the firebreak to deploy her irregulars if the Kingdom sent any of its threatened 'punishment' squads over to snatch possessed, far enough away so that it was outside the range of any inquisitive sensors – incidentally making it reasonably safe from SD fire. So she'd gathered her followers to her, and allowed them their illusion of freedom. A genuine rabble army, with a licence to carouse and cavort for ninety per cent of the time, with just a few of her orders to follow the morning after. Something to do, something vaguely exciting and heroic-seeming, gave them a sense of identity and purpose. For that, they stayed together. It made them into a unit for her, however unwieldy and unreliable. That was when Chainbridge resembled a provincial town under occupation by foreign troops with unlimited expense accounts. Not a bad analogy. There were parties and dances every evening, and other people began to hang around, if for no other reason than the army made damn sure they had full access to Mortonridge's dwindling food supplies. It was a happy town kept in good order, Annette even established the hub of Mortonridge's downgraded communication net in the old Town Hall, which was commandeered as her command post. The net allowed her to retain a certain degree of control over the peninsula, keeping her in touch with the councils she'd left in charge of the towns her forces had taken over. There wasn't much she could do to enforce her rule, short of complete overkill and sending in a brigade of her troops, but in the main she'd created a small society which worked. That was before any of the inhabitants really believed that the Kingdom would break its word and invade with the express intention of ripping body from (usurping) soul.

Now Chainbridge's parties had ended. The few inhabited buildings had lost their ornate appearance in favour of a bleakly oppressive, fortress-like solidity. Non-combatants, the good-timers and hangers on, had left, drifting away into the countryside. The town was preparing for war.

From her office window in the Town Hall she could look down on the large cobbled square below. The fountains were off, their basins dry and duned by clumps of litter. Vehicles were parked in neat ranks under the rows of leghorn trees that circled the outer edge of the square. They were mostly manual-drive cars and four-wheel-drive farm rovers, as per her instructions. None of them wore any kind of illusory image. Engineers were working on several of them, readying them for the coming ordeal.

Annette came back to the long table where her ten senior officers were sitting. Devlin and Milne, the two people she relied on the most, had taken the chairs on either side of hers. Devlin claimed to have been an officer in the First World War, while Milne had been an engineer's mate during Earth's steamship era, which made him a wizard with all things mechanical, though he freely admitted to knowing very little about electronics. Beyond them sat Hoi Son, who was a veteran of early twenty-first-century bush wars, an ecological agitator, he called himself. Annette gathered his battles hadn't been fought along national lines, but rather corporate ones. Whatever he wanted to describe himself as, his tactical know-how in the situation they faced was invaluable. The rest of them were just divisional commanders, gaining the loyalty of their troops through personality or reputation. Just how much loyalty was a moot point.

'What are today's figures?' Annette asked.

'Nearly forty deserted last night,' Devlin said. 'Little shits. In my day they would have been shot for that kind of cowardice.'

'Fortunately, we're not in your day,' Hoi Son said. 'When I fought the desecrators who stole my land I had legions of the people who did what they had to because our cause was just. We needed no military police and prisons to enforce the orders of our commanders then, nor do we here. If in their hearts people do not want to fight, then forcing them will not make them good soldiers.'

'God is on the side of the big battalions,' Devlin sneered. 'Owning your claptrap nobility doesn't guarantee victory.'

'We are not going to win.' Hoi Son smiled peacefully. 'You do understand that, don't you?'

'We'll have a damn good try, and to hell with your defeatist talk. I'm surprised you didn't leave with the rest of them.'

'I think that'll do,' Annette said. 'Devlin, you know Hoi Son is right, you've felt what the Kingdom is gathering to fling against us. The King would never commit his forces against us unless he was convinced of the outcome. And he has the backing of the Edenists, who even more than he won't engage in a foolhardy venture. This is a showpiece war; they intend to demonstrate to the Confederation's general public that we are beatable. They cannot afford to lose, no matter what it costs them.'

'So what the hell do you want us to do, then?' Devlin asked.

'Make that cost exorbitant,' Hoi Son said. 'Such people always assign a value to everything in monetary terms. We might not be able to defeat them on Mortonridge, but we can certainly prevent any further Liberation campaigns after this one.'

'Their troops will have reporters with them,' Annette said. 'They'll want to showcase their triumphs. This war will be fought on two fronts, the physical one here, and the emotional one broadcast by the media across the Confederation. That is the important one, the one we have to win. Those reporters must be shown the terrifying price of opposing us. I believe Milne has been making some preparations.'

'Not doing so bad on that front, lass,' Milne said. He sucked on a big clay pipe for emphasis, every inch the solid, reliable NCO. 'I've been training up a few lads, teaching them tricks of the trade, like. We can't use electrical circuits, of course, not our type. So we've gone back to basics. I've come up with a nice little mix of chemicals for an explosive; we're shoving it into booby traps as fast as we can make 'em.'

'What kind of booby traps?' Devlin asked.

'Anti-personnel mines, ground vehicle snares, primed buildings, spiked pits, that kind of thing. Hoi's been showing us what he used to rig up when he were fighting. Right tricky stuff, it is, too. All with mechanical triggers, so their sensors won't pick them up, even if they can get them working under the red cloud. I'd say we're due to give Hiltch's boys a load of grief once they cross the firebreak. We've also rigged bridges to blow, as well as the major junction flyovers along the M6. That ought to slow the buggers down.'

'All very good,' Devlin said. 'But with respect, I don't think a few scraps of rubble will make much difference to their transport. I remember the tanks we used to have, great big brutes, they were. But by Heaven they could crunch across almost every surface; and the engineers have had seven centuries to improve on that.'

'Ruining the road junctions might not make a huge impact, but it will certainly have some effect,' Hoi Son said impassively. 'We know how large this Liberation army is, even in these times that makes it unwieldy. They will use the M6, if not for front-line troops, then certainly for their supplies and auxiliaries. If we delay them even by an hour a day, we add to the cost. Slowing them down will also give us time to respond and retaliate. It is a good tactic.'

'OK, I'm not arguing with you. But these booby traps and blown bridges are a passive response. Come on, man, what've you got that'll allow us to attack them?'

'My lads have found quite a few light engineering factories and the like in Chainbridge,' Milne said. 'The machine tools still work if you switch 'em to manual. Right now, I've got 'em churning out parts for a high-velocity hunting rifle. I don't know what the hell that sparky machine-gun is that the souls have seen Hiltch's boys practising with. But I reckon my rifle's got an easy twice the range of 'em.'

'They'll be wearing armour,' Devlin warned.

'Aye, I know that. But Hoi's told me about kinetic enhanced-impact bullets. Our armourers are doing their best to produce them, you'll have a decent stock in another few days. We'll be able to inflict a lot of damage with them, you see if we don't.'

'Thanks, Milne,' Annette said. 'You've done a great job, considering what you've had to work with, and what we're facing.'

Milne cocked his pipe at her. 'We'll put up a good account of ourselves, lass, no worries.'

'I'm sure.' She gazed round at the rest of her commanders. There was a good range of emotions distributed among them, from clear nerves to stupid overconfidence. 'Now we know roughly what our own capabilities are, we need to start working out how we're going to deploy. Devlin, you're probably the best strategist we have . . .'

'Butt-headed traditionalist,' Hoi Son muttered *sotto voce*.

Annette raised a warning eyebrow and the old guerrilla made a conciliatory shrug. 'What is Hiltch likely to do?' she asked.

'Two things,' Devlin said, ignoring Hoi. 'Firstly, their initial assault is going to be a lulu. He'll throw everything he's got at us, on as many fronts as he can afford to open. We'll be facing massive troop incursions, this wretched space warship bombardment, aircraft carpet bombing, artillery. The aim is to demoralize us right from the start, make it quite clear from the scale of the Liberation that we'll lose, drumming it home in a fashion we can't possibly ignore. I'd recommend that we actually pull back a little way from the borders of the peninsula; don't give him an easy target. Leave it to Milne's booby traps to snarl up his timetable, and stall any immediate visible success he wants to lay on for the reporters.'

'OK, I can cope with that. What's his second likely objective?'

'His target missions. If he's got any sense, he'll go for our population centres first. Our power declines with our numbers, which will make his mopping-up operation a damn sight easier.'

'Population centres!' Annette exclaimed in annoyance. 'What population centres? People are deserting the towns in droves. The councils are reporting we're now down to less than half the numbers we had in urban areas when we took over Mortonridge. They're like our deserters, heading for the hills. Right now we're spread over this land thinner than a pigeon's fart.'

'It's not the hills they're after,' Hoi said, his soft tone a rebuke. 'It's the farms. Which was only to be expected. You are well aware of the food situation across the peninsula. Had your efforts been directed at developing our civil infrastructure instead of our military base, it would be a different story.'

'Is that a criticism?'

His gentle laugh was infuriating, mockingly superior. 'A plea for industrialization, from me? Please! I regard the land and the people as integral. Nature provides us with our true state. It is our towns and cities, with their machines and hunger, which have birthed the corruption that has contaminated human society for millennia. The defence of people who chose to live with the land is paramount.'

'OK, thanks for the party manifesto. But it doesn't alter what I said. We haven't got that many population centres to lure Hiltch's forces into ambush.'

'We will have. I suspect Devlin is correct when he says Hiltch will want to open with a grand gesture. That should work in our favour. As always when a land is invaded, its people pull together. They'll see that as individuals they can offer no resistance to the Liberation forces, and they'll flee their isolation in search of group sanctuary. We will gather ourselves together as a people again. Then the battle will be joined in full.'

Annette's growing smile was a physical demonstration of the satisfaction spreading through her thoughts. 'Remember Stephanie Ash, what I told her about having to decide whose side she was on? That self-righteous cow just stood there smiling politely the whole time, knowing her world view was the real thing, and I'd come round to her way of thinking in the end. Looks like I'll have the last laugh after all – even if it is only a short one. Damn, I'm going to enjoy that almost as much as I am bollixing up my dear old friend Ralph's campaign.'

'You really think we'll be able to start recruiting into the regiments again?' Devlin asked Hoi Son.

'Can you think of nothing but your own position and power? It is not the regiments which will inflict the worst casualties, but the united people. Group ten of us together, and the destructive potential of our energistic power is an order of magnitude greater than any artillery the Liberation forces can bring to bear.'

'Which is less than one per cent of the lowest-powered maser on a strategic-defence platform, and that's before we get into the heavy duty systems like their X-ray lasers,' Annette said, tired of their bickering. 'It's not our numbers that matter, but our ability to communicate and organize. That's what we have to safeguard until the last of us is shoved into zero-tau.'

'I agree,' Devlin said. 'The whole war is going to be an extremely fluid situation from the start. Lightning strikes, hit the bastards and run, are what we should be planning for.'

'Exactly, that's where I expect you two to combine for me. Your overall strategy, Devlin, combined with Hoi's tactics. It's a lethal alliance, the equivalent of the Kingdom and the Edenists.'

'An inspired comparison,' Hoi chuckled.

'My pleasure. All right, let's start looking at the map, and see who we're going to send where.'

*

It was Emmet Mordden, again, who was on duty in the operations centre when the Organization fleet started to emerge above New California. The hellhawks were first, their wormholes opening more or less in the official emergence zone, a hundred thousand kilometres above Monterey. That gave them some warning that the Adamist craft were en route. Emmet quickly called in five more operatives to monitor their rag-tag arrival. They certainly aimed for the emergence zone, but with possessed officers on board aiming and hitting were increasingly separate concepts. Event horizons started to inflate across a vast section of space around the planet; the only thing regular about them was the timing. One every twenty seconds.

The big flight-trajectory holoscreens ringing the centre had to change perspective several times, clicking down through their magnification to encompass space right out to Requa, New California's fourth moonlet. Black icons started to erupt across the screen as if it was being struck by dirty rain.

The AI began to absorb the swarm of information datavised in from the SD sensor platforms, and started plotting the starships' erratic trajectories. Multiple vector lines sprang up on every console display. The operators studied them urgently, opening communication circuits to verify the ships were still under Organization control. Emmet got so carried along by the pandemonium of the first few minutes it took a while before he began to realize something was badly wrong with the whole episode. Firstly, they were too early, Admiral Kolhammer's task force couldn't possibly have arrived at Tranquillity yet. Secondly, there were too many ships. Even if the ambush had been a massive success, some ships would have been lost. Of all Capone's lieutenants, he had the most pragmatic view of just how effective the fleet ships were.

Those two ugly facts were just beginning to register, when he sensed the dismay bubbling up among Jull von Holger's thoughts, as the hellhawk liaison man communicated with his colleagues.

'What the hell is it?' Emmett demanded. 'Why are they back here? Did they lose, chicken out, or what?'

Jull von Holger shook his head in bewilderment, most reluctant to be the messenger of bad news. 'No. No, they didn't lose. Their target . . . Tranquillity jumped away.'

Emmett frowned at him.

'Look, just call Luigi, OK. I don't understand it myself.'

Emmett gave him a long dissatisfied look, then turned to his own console. He ordered it to find the *Salvatore*'s transponder, and open a channel to the flagship. 'What's going on?' he asked when a fuzzy picture of Luigi Balsamo appeared in the corner of his display.

'She tricked us,' Luigi shouted angrily. 'That Saldana bitch ran away. Christ knows how she managed it, but the whole thing vanished down a wormhole. Nobody told us a habitat could do that. You never warned us, did you? You're supposed to be the Organization's technical whizz-kid. Why the fuck didn't you say something?'

'About what? What do you mean, it went down a wormhole? What went down a wormhole?'

'Why don't you *listen*, shitbrain? The habitat! The habitat vanished in front of us!'

Emmett stared at the image, refusing to believe what he'd heard. 'I'm calling Al,' he said eventually.

*

It was the first time Luigi had ever been intimidated by the big double doors of the Nixon Suite. There were a couple of soldiers on duty outside, wearing their standard fawn double-breasted suits, big square-jawed guys with a dark rasp of stubble, glossy Thompson sub-machine-guns held prominently. He could sense several people milling about inside, their familiar thoughts dull and unhappy as they waited for him. He thought of all the punishments and reprimands he'd attended in his own capacity as one of the Organization's elite lieutenants. The omens weren't good.

One of the soldiers opened the doors, a superior in-the-know grin on his face. He didn't say anything, just made a mocking gesture of welcome. Luigi resisted the urge to smash his face to pulp, and walked in.

'What the fuck happened?' Al bellowed.

Luigi glanced round at the semicircle of erstwhile friends as the doors closed behind him. Patricia was there, as was Silvano, Jezzibella, Emmet, Mickey, and that little bitch Kiera. All of them going with the tide that was sweeping him away to drown.

'We were given some very bad information.' He looked pointedly at Patricia. 'Perez sold us a dummy. And you bought it.'

'He didn't,' she snapped. 'He possessed one of the First Admiral's top aides in Trafalgar. Kolhammer was heading straight for Tranquillity.'

'And we would have got him, too. If somebody had just warned me. I mean, Jesus H. Christ, an entire goddam habitat flitting off. Do you have any idea how big that thing was?'

'Who cares?' Al said. 'The habitat wasn't your main target. You were there to blow up Kolhammer's ships.'

'The only way we could do that was if we'd captured the habitat first,' Luigi said angrily. 'Don't try blaming all this on me. I did everything you asked.'

'Who the fuck else am I going to blame?' Al asked. 'You were there, it was your responsibility.'

'Nobody has ever heard of a habitat that can do that before,' Luigi ground out. 'Nobody.' He shoved an accusatory finger at Jezzibella. 'Right?'

For whatever reason, Jezzibella had assumed her impish adolescent girl persona, red ribbons tying her hair into ponytails, a white blouse and grey pleated skirt not really covering her body. She pouted, a gesture which was almost obscenely provocative. It was an act which various judges had been asked to ban when she performed it live on tour. 'Right. But I'm hardly an expert on energy patterning systems, now am I?'

'Christ Almighty. Emmet?' It was almost a plea.

'It is unprecedented,' Emmet said with some sympathy.

'And you.' Luigi glared at Kiera. 'You lived in a habitat. You knew all about how they work, why didn't you tell us?' The attack didn't quite kick up the response he expected. A flash of icy anger twisted Kiera's thoughts, while Al simply sneered scornfully.

'Valisk was not capable of performing a swallow manoeuvre,' she said. 'As far as we know, only Tranquillity has that ability. Certainly none of the Edenist habitats can. I don't know about the other three independent habitats.'

'Didn't stop Valisk from vanishing, though, did it,' Al muttered snidely.

Silvano gave an overloud laugh, while Jezzibella smiled demurely at Kiera's discomfort. Luigi looked from one to the other in puzzlement. 'OK, so are we agreed? It was a shitty situation, sure. But there was nothing I could do about it. That Saldana girl took everyone by surprise.'

'You were the fleet's commander,' Al said. 'I gave you that job because I thought you were smart, man, that you had some flare and imagination. A guy with a few qualities, know what I mean? If all I want is some putz who expects a slap on the back every time he does what he's told I would have given the job to Bernhard Allsop. I expected more from you, Luigi, a lot more.'

'Like what? I mean, come on here, tell me, Al, just what the hell would you have done?

'Stopped it from flying out. Don't you get it, Luigi? You were my man on the ground. I was goddam depending on you to bring the Organization through this OK. Instead, I'm left with shit all over my face. Once you saw what was happening you should have zeroed the place.'

'Christ, why won't any of you *listen*? I was fucking trying to zero it, Al. That's what spooked Saldana; that's what made her scoot the hell out of there. I'd got nearly five thousand of those war rockets chasing after her faster than a coyote with a hornet up its ass, and she got clean away. There was *nothing* we could do. We were damn lucky to cut free ourselves. The explosions from all those war rockets did some damage, too, we were . . .'

'Woah there.' Al held up a hand. 'What explosions? You just said the combat wasps never touched Tranquillity.'

'Yeah, but most of them detonated when they hit the wormhole entrance. I don't understand none too well; the technical boys, they say it's like a solid barrier, but it's made out of nothing. Beats me. Anyway, the first ones started to go off, and . . . hell, you know how powerful antimatter is, they set off the others. The whole lot went off like a string of goddam firecrackers.'

'All of them? Five thousand antimatter-powered combat wasps?'

'That's right. Like I said, we were lucky to get out alive.'

'Sure you were.' Al's voice had dropped to a dangerous monotone. 'You're alive, and I'm out one planet which we postponed invading, I'm down a Confederation Navy task force you were supposed to ambush, and I've also got to replace five thousand combat wasps fuelled up by the goddam rarest substance in the whole fucking universe. Jeez, I'm real glad you're back. Seeing you here smiling away in one piece makes me feel absolutely fucking peachy. You piece of *shit*! Do you have any idea how badly you've screwed up?'

'*It wasn't my fault!*'

'Oh, absolutely. You're right. No way are you to blame for this. And you know what? I bet I now who it was. Yeah. Yeah, now I think about it, I know. It was me. That's right, me. I'm to blame. I'm the asshole here. I made the biggest fucking mistake of my life when I put you in charge.'

'Yeah? Well I didn't hear you whining none when I came back from Arnstadt. Remember that day? I delivered a whole fucking planet on a fucking plate for you, Al. You gave me the keys for the city back then. Parties, girls, you even made Avvy track down a genuine copy of the Clark Gable *Gone With the Wind* for me. Nothing. Nothing was too much trouble. I was loyal to you then, and I'm loyal to you now. I don't deserve any of this. All you lost was a few lousy rockets and some fancy fuel. I put my life on the line for you, Al. And we all know how goddam precious that is now, don't we? Well, do *you* know what? I don't deserve to be treated like this. It ain't right.'

Al scowled, looking round the other lieutenants. They all kept their faces blank, of course, but their minds were boiling. Annoyance and doubt were the predominant emotions. He guessed his own mind would show the same. He was fucking furious with Luigi, it was the first defeat the Organization had been dealt, the news boys would crow about it clear over the Confederation. His image would take a terrible battering, and as Jez always said: image was everything in the modern world. The aura of the Organization's invincibility would be hit badly. Yet at the same time, Luigi was right, he had done his best, right from the start when they'd all walked into City Hall in the ballsiest escapade this side of the Trojan Horse.

'By rights, I ought to fucking fry you, Luigi,' Al said darkly. 'We've been set back weeks thanks to what happened at Tranquillity. I've got to find another planet to invade, I've got to wait until we've built up a decent new stock of antimatter, the reporters will hang me out to dry, everyone's confidence is busted. But I'm not going to. And the only reason I'm not going to is because you came back here like a man. You ain't afraid to admit you made a mistake.'

There was a new flash of anger in Luigi's mind at that. Al waited, mildly intrigued, but it was never voiced. He materialized a Havana, and took a comfortable drag before saying: 'So I'll make you an offer. You can stay with the Organization, but I'm going to bust you right back down to the bottom of the ladder again. You're a private zero class, Luigi. I know the other guys'll go hard on you for a while, but you stay loyal, you keep your nose clean, and you can work your way back up again. I can't be no fairer than that.'

Luigi gawped at Al, struggling with disbelief at what he'd just heard while a strangled choke growled up from his throat. His mind was telegraphing the notion of outright rebellion. Al fixed him with *the look*, all humour eradicated. 'You won't like the alternative.'

'All right, Al,' Luigi said slowly. 'I can live with that. But I'm telling you, I'll be back in charge of the fleet inside of six months.'

Al guffawed, and clapped Luigi's arm. 'That's my boy. I knew I made the right decision with you.' Luigi managed a brief smile, and turned to walk out of the room. Al slumped his shoulders when the doors shut. 'Guess that's one guy we've lost for good.'

Jezzibella rubbed his arm in sympathy. 'You did the right thing, baby. It was honourable. He did fuck up something chronic.'

'I wouldn't have been so generous,' Kiera said. 'You shouldn't show so much kindness. People will see it as a weakness.'

'You're dealing with people, not mechanoids,' Jezzibella said blankly. 'You have to make allowances for the odd mistake. If you shoot every waiter who spills a cup of coffee over your skirt, you wind up with a self-service bar.'

Kiera smiled condescendingly at her. 'What you'll actually wind up with is a group of highly efficient waiters who can do the job effectively.'

'You mean, like the way your team handled things on Valisk?'

'All teams need an effective leader.'

Al was tempted to let them go for it – nothing like a good cat-fight. But one bust-up among his senior lieutenants was enough for today. So instead, he said: 'Speaking of which, Kiera, are the hellhawks going to keep flying for me?'

'Of course they will, Al. I've been busy setting up my new flight coordination office in one of the docking-ledge departure lounges. Close to the action, as it were. They'll do what I tell them to.'

'Uh huh.' He didn't like the implications of that sweetly spoken assurance any more than the unpleasant note of victory rippling through her mind. And judging by the sudden suspicion colouring Jez's thoughts, neither did she.

*

It was one of those absurd left–right, left–right sideways shuffles that seemingly automatically occur when two people try to get out of each other's way simultaneously which finally blew Beth's temper. She'd come out of the washroom at one end of the *Mindori*'s life-support module to find Jed standing outside waiting to use it. He immediately dropped his head so he didn't have to look at her and danced to one side. A move she instinctively matched. They dodged about for a couple of seconds.

The next thing Jed knew was a hand grasping his collar, and hauling him into the washroom. Bright mock-sunbeams poured through the smoked-glass portholes, producing large white ovals on the polished wood floor. Archaic brass plumbing gleamed and sparkled all around the small compartment. Jed's knee banged painfully on the rim of the enamel bath as Beth smoothly slewed his weight round like some kind of ice skater act. The door slammed shut, the lock *snicked* and he was shoved flat against the wall. 'Listen, ball-brain,' she snarled, 'I was not shagging him. OK?'

He risked a sneer, praying she wasn't still carrying the nervejam stick. 'Yeah? So what were you doing in bed with him?'

'Sleeping.' She saw the new expression of derision forming on his face, and twisted his sweatshirt fabric just a fraction tighter. 'Sleeping,' she repeated forcefully. 'Jeeze, mate, the guy's brain is totally zonked. It took a time to get him quietened down, that's all. I dozed off. Big deal. If you hadn't stormed out so bloody fast you would have seen I still had all my clobber on.'

'That's it?'

'What the hell do you expect? The pair of us were working our way through a *Karma Sutra* recording? Is that what you think of me? That I'm going to leap into bed with the first geriatric I meet?'

Jed knew his answer to that question was going to be critical, and possibly close to fatal if he got it wrong. 'No,' he insisted, willing himself to believe it totally. Voice only would never be good enough. He often suspected Beth had some kind of advanced telepathic ability. 'I don't think that of you at all. Um . . . you've got more class that that. I always said so.'

'Hmmm.' Her grip on his sweatshirt loosened slightly. 'You mean you were always miffed I didn't let you shag me.'

'That's not it!' he protested.

'Really?'

Jed thought that gibe was best ignored in its entirety. 'What do you make of this delay?' he asked.

'Bit odd. I don't understand why we didn't dock with Valisk before we went on another rendezvous. I mean, we were already there in the Srinagar system, least that's what I thought.'

'Yeah. I didn't see Valisk, though, just some gas giant. Then the ship swallowed away again. I thought I was going to die. We were *there*.'

'Choi-Ho and Maxim said this new rendezvous was major-league important when I asked them. They clammed up pretty smart when I asked them where it was, though. You think that's important?'

'Course it's important. Question is, why?'

'We might have to dodge some navy patrols to make the new rendezvous. That'll be risky.'

'So why not tell us?'

'There's a lot of kids on board. Could be they don't want to worry them.'

'Makes sense.'

'But you don't reckon?'

'Dunno. It's funny, you know. When we busted our balls to get a flight. Everything we had got left behind, our families, friends, everything. But I didn't have any doubts. Now we're as good as there ... I don't know, it's just such a big thing. Maybe I'm a bit scared. What about you?'

Beth gave him a careful look, unsure just how much she should reveal. He really had invested a lot in the ideal of Valisk and all it promised. 'Jed, I know Gerald's a bit flaky, but he told me something.'

'A *bit* flaky.'

'Jed! He said Kiera is actually called Marie, that she's his daughter. He reckons that Valisk is no different to any other place the possessed have taken over.'

'Crap,' he said angrily. 'That's total crap. Look, Beth. We know Kiera is a possessor, she's never hidden that. But she's only borrowing that girl's body. She said things like that won't matter after Valisk leaves the universe. She can take on her own form again.'

'Yes, but, Jed ... His daughter.'

'Just a weird coincidence, that's all. Mind, it explains why the old fart is so crazy.'

She nodded reluctantly. 'Maybe. But then again it wouldn't do any harm to start thinking the unthinkable, would it?'

He took hold of both her arms, just above the elbows. 'We'll be all right,' he said intently. 'You've accessed Kiera's recording enough times. You know she's telling us the truth. This is like wedding night nerves.'

She gave his hands a curious glance; normally she would have instantly shaken free from such a grip. But this flight was not an ordinary time. 'Yeah. Thanks, mate.' She gave him a timid smile.

Jed returned an equally uncertain flutter. He started to lean forward slowly, bringing his face down towards hers. Her lips parted slightly. He closed his eyes. Then a finger was resting on his chin.

'Not here,' Beth said. 'Not in a dunny.'

*

Beth actually let him hold her hand as they walked along the life-support module's central corridor. Somehow it didn't seem to matter so much now. Back on Koblat it would have meant everyone knowing: Beth and Jed, Jed and Beth. The boys would have smiled and whooped and given Jed the thumbs up. 'Well done, mate. Scored with an ice maiden, nice one. So what does she look like with her kit off? Are they big tits? Is she any good at it? Has she gone down on you yet?' While the girls would have clustered round her and asked if he'd said he loved her. 'Does he devote enough time to you? Are you going to apply for an apartment together?'

It was a horrendous cycle spinning around her, a compendium of everything she hated about Koblat. The loss of any purpose to life. Surrendering to the company and signing on as another of its cheaply produced multi-function biological tools. She knew several girls on her corridor level who were grandmothers at twenty-eight.

Their weakness had given her the strength to strive for at least the hope of something more, to resist almost intolerable peer pressure. Star of her education stream, exceptionally receptive to each didactic memory she received. Applying for every college scholarship and exchange programme she could locate in the asteroid's memory cores. Enduring the jeers and whispers. But it had been hard hard hard. Then along came Kiera, who offered a way out from all that awful pressure. A life that was different and kind. And Beth had believed, because Kiera was the same sort of age, and empowered, and taking control of her own destiny. And because . . . it was easy. For the first time ever.

They stopped outside the cabin she'd been sharing with Gerald, and Jed kissed her before she could turn the handle. Not a very good kiss, he almost missed her lips, and definitely no tongue like there was in all the low-rated blue sensevise recordings she'd accessed. His anxious expression almost made her laugh, as if he was expecting her to deck him. Which, she admitted, she probably would have done three weeks ago if he'd come on fresh with her. She got the door open, and they stumbled inside, not bothering with the lights. Jed kissed her again. A better attempt, this time. When he finished, she asked: 'Will you think of her?'

'Who?' he asked in confusion.

'You know, her, Kiera. Will you think of her when you're doing it with me?'

'No!' Although there was enough of a quaver in his voice to reveal the truth. To her, if no one else. She knew him well enough, growing up together for ten years. It was almost too close.

He had become – not obsessed, that wasn't strong enough – captivated by Kiera and that exquisite beguiling beauty of hers. In dismay Beth knew it wouldn't be her face he saw when he closed his eyes in ecstasy, not her body he could feel below his fingers. For some reason, despite the humiliation, she didn't really care. After all, she had her own reasons for this. She twined a forearm behind his head, and pulled him down to kiss her again. The lights came on. Beth gasped in surprise, and twisted to look at the bunk, expecting to see Gerald there. It was empty, the blankets rumpled.

There was a melodic chime from the dresser, and the small mirror above it shimmered with colour. A man's face appeared on it; he was middle aged, with a Mediterranean complexion and a long chin which pulled his lips downwards, making him appear permanently unhappy.

'Sorry to interrupt,' he said. 'But I think you'll find what I have to say quite important.'

Jed had stiffened the second he appeared, quickly pulling his hands away from Beth. She tried not to show how annoyed she was by that; she'd just made *the* decision –what did he have to be guilty about?

'Who are you?' she asked.

'Rocio Condra; I am the soul possessing this hellhawk.'

'Oh, brother,' she murmured. Jed managed to blush even deeper.

'I was listening to your conversation in the washroom. I believe we can help each other.'

Beth smiled weakly. 'If you're powerful enough to do that, how can we possibly help you? You can do anything.'

'My energistic power gives me a great deal of influence over the local environment, I agree. But there are some things which remain beyond me. Listening to you, for example, I had to use a bitek processor; there's one in every section of the *Mindori*'s life-support module.'

'If you've heard everything we've talked about, then you know about Gerald and Marie,' Beth said.

'Indeed. That is why I chose you to make my offer to. You already know everything is not what it seems.'

Jed peered at Rocio's image. 'What offer?'

'The end requirements haven't yet been finalized. However, if all goes well, I expect I shall require you to perform some physical tasks for me. Nothing too difficult. Just venture into a few places I obviously cannot reach.'

'Such as?'

'That is not yet apparent. We will have to advance this partnership one step at a time. As a gesture of goodwill, I am prepared to impart some information to you. If, based on what you hear, you then wish to continue with this relationship, we can move forward together.'

Beth gave Jed a puzzled glance, not surprised to find he was equally mystified.

'Go on,' she said. 'We'll listen.'

'I am about to swallow into the New California system. We will probably dock at Monterey asteroid, the headquarters of the Capone Organization.'

'No way!' Jed cried.

'There never was a new rendezvous, was there?' Beth asked, somehow unsurprised by the revelation.

'No,' Rocio said. 'We did not dock at Valisk because it is no longer in this universe. There was a battle for control between different factions of possessed inside. The victors subsequently removed it.'

Jed took a couple of paces backwards, and sank down onto the bunk. His face was fragile with dismay. 'Gone?'

'I'm afraid so. And I am genuinely sorry. I know how much hope you had for your future there. Unfortunately, that hope was extremely misplaced.'

'How?' Beth asked through clenched teeth.

'There never was any Deadnight, not really. Kiera Salter simply wanted fresh bodies to possess so that she could expand the habitat's population base. Had you disembarked there, you would have been tortured until you surrendered yourselves to possession.'

'Oh, Jeeze,' Beth whispered. 'And Monterey? What's going to happen to us at Monterey?'

'Much the same, I expect. The Organization does retain professional non-possessed who have specialist fields of expertise. Are you highly qualified in any subject?'

'Us?' Beth barked in consternation. 'You've gotta be bloody joking, mate. The only thing we know how to do proper is mess up. Every bloody time.' She was afraid she was going to start crying.

'I see,' Rocio said. 'Well, in return for your help, I am prepared to hide you on board when we dock at Monterey.'

'What sort of help?' Jed asked.

Beth wheeled round to glare at him. 'Does it bloody matter! *Yes*, we'll help. As much as you want.'

Rocio's image gave a dry smile. 'As I said, my requirements will not be fully established until I have analysed the local situation. It may be that I won't require you to do anything. For the moment, I shall simply hold you in reserve.'

'Why?' Beth asked. 'You're part of them. You're a possessor. What do you want us for?'

'Because I am not part of them. We are not all the same. I was being coerced into helping Kiera. Now I must find out what has happened to the other hellhawks, and decide what to do next. In order to do that, I must keep every conceivable option open. Having allies who are in no position to betray me will provide an excellent advantage.'

'All right,' Beth said. 'What do we have to do?'

'I will swallow into the New California system in another thirty minutes. Even if Kiera and the other hellhawks have left there, the passengers will have to be disembarked. For now, the pair of you must be hidden. I believe I have a place which will put you outside the perception range of Choi-Ho and Maxim Payne.'

'What perception range?' Jed asked.

'All possessed are able to sense the thoughts of other people. The range varies between individuals, of course.'

'You mean they know what I'm thinking?' he hooted.

'No. But they are aware of your presence, and with that your emotions. However, such perception through solid matter is difficult; I believe the fluid in some of my tanks will shield you. We just have to get you at the centre of a suitably large cluster.'

'There had better be room for five of us in this nest of yours,' Beth said brightly.

'I only require two people.'

'Tough, mate. You get yourself a bargain package with us. Gerald and the girls come too.'

'I don't need them.'

She gave his image a cold smile. 'Must have been dead a long time, huh? To forget what it's like to have other people, friends, responsibilities. What? You think we'd leave them behind for Capone? A couple of kids? Come on!'

'The Organization is unlikely to possess the girls. They pride themselves in being altruistic and charitable.'

'Good for them. But it doesn't make any difference. You get all five of us, or none at all.'

'That's right,' Jed said, coming up to stand beside her. 'Gari's my sister. I'm not leaving her with Capone.'

Rocio sighed heavily. 'Very well. But only those three. If you have a flock of second cousins on board, they will have to take their chances with the Organization.'

'No second cousins. What do you want us to do?'

*

It took a lot of nerve to saunter idly into the *Mindori*'s main lounge with a bland expression on his face, knowing what he did. Jed felt he carried it off rather well; his visits to the Blue Fountain in search of sympathetic starship crews had provided a good rehearsal for brazening out awkward moments. There was a big press of Deadnight kids in the lounge, more than usual as the extended flight finally approached its end. All of them gazing eagerly out of the big forward-looking window at the silver-on-black starfield.

Jed let his eyes flick round quickly, confirming Choi-Ho and Maxim Payne weren't anywhere about. Rocio had assured him they were both in their cabin, but he didn't entirely trust everything the hellhawk's soul said.

In this instance, Rocio hadn't lied. The two possessed were nowhere to be seen. Jed walked confidently across the lounge to one of the fitted cupboards on the far side. Its narrow slatted doors were made from rosewood, with small brass handles moulded to resemble rosebuds. As he put his hand round the cool metal, it turned to black plastic below his fingers. A narrow display panel appeared briefly to one side, framing a block of grey alphanumerics which flickered too fast to be read. He waited until he heard a discreet *click* then pulled gently. The door opened a fraction, and he moved closer, covering his actions.

Rocio had told him the bitek processor blocks were on the third shelf from the top. The thin gap allowed him to confirm the slim rectangular units were waiting there. It was obviously some kind of general equipment storage cupboard; he could see tool kits, and test blocks, and sensor modules, as well as several devices he couldn't fathom at all. A rack on the fourth shelf contained five compact laser pistols.

He froze.

It was probably Rocio's final assessment of his suitability. If he could turn his back on the weapons he would be resolute enough to be of use to the hellhawk. If he knew anything about this nebulous deal, whatever help Rocio wanted, it would not be small, not when the exchange price was his own life. But a weapon would offer some security, however feeble. And Beth had her nervejam stick.

Knowing his heated thoughts would be betraying his guilt to Rocio in a way no clandestine visual observation ever could, Jed reached calmly for a pistol, then slid his hand smoothly up to one of the processor blocks. He tucked both of them neatly into his inside jacket pocket, and shut the cupboard door again. The electronic lock vanished instantly beneath a slick ripple of wood grain which lapped over it.

Walking back out of the lounge was the worst part. Some little part of Jed's brain was yelling at him to warn them. All of a sudden, he hated them. Sweetly trusting kids, their eyes happy and shining as they gawped out at the enchanting vista of interstellar space. All that hope suffusing unseen, yet cloying, into the air as they waited for the window to reveal their own special nirvana waiting for them at the end of the next wormhole.

Fools! Blind, stupid, and ridiculously ingenuous. The hatred clarified then. He was looking at multiple reflections of himself.

*

Beth got Gerald to come along with her, which he did unquestioningly. Jed brought Gari and Navar, who were intensely curious, twittering together as they walked down the length of the corridor. Their curiosity turned to hard-edged scepticism as Jed knocked softly on the washroom door.

'You told us this was important,' Navar said accusingly.

'It is,' he assured her. Something in his tone stalled the scornful sniff she was preparing as a retort.

Beth unlocked the washroom door and slid it open. Jed checked the corridor to make sure no one was watching. With only fifteen minutes to go until the swallow manoeuvre, all the other Deadnights were crowding round the observation ports in the forward cabins. The two girls gave Gerald a confused look as they all crowded into the confined space of the cabin. In turn, Gerald barely noticed them. Jed took the bitek processor block from his pocket. One surface shimmered with a moiré holographic pattern, then cleared to show Rocio's face.

'Well done, Jed,' he said. 'Bluffing it out is often the best option.'

'Yeah, all right, now what?'

'Who's that?' Navar asked.

'We'll explain later,' Beth said. 'Right now, we've got to get into position ready for when the ship docks.' She said it to the girls, although she was actually studying Gerald intently. He was in one of his passive moods, unperturbed by what was happening. She just prayed he stayed that way while they were hidden away.

'Aren't we getting off at Valisk?' Gari asked her big brother in a forlorn voice.

'No, doll, sorry. We're not even docking with Valisk.'

'Why not?'

'Guess we got lied to.' The bitter sorrow in his voice silenced her.

'You will need to clear the floor,' Rocio instructed.

Beth and the two girls climbed into the bath, while Gerald sat on the toilet lid. Jed pressed himself back against the door. The floorboards faded away, rich honey colour bleaching to a sanitary grey-green, resilient texture becoming the uncompromising hardness of silicolithium composite. Some residual evidence of the wood illusion remained, little ridges where the planks had lain, dark flecks in the surface a pallid mimicry of the grain pattern. In the centre of the floor was an inspection hatch, with recessed metal locking clips at each corner.

'Turn the clips ninety degrees clockwise, then pull them up,' Rocio said.

Jed knelt down and did as he was told. When the clips were free, the hatch rose ten centimetres with a swift hiss of air. He swung it aside. There was a narrow metal crawlway below it, bordered by foam-insulated pipes and bundled cables. Beth activated the light stick she'd brought along, and held it over the hatch. There was a horizontal T-junction a couple of metres down.

'You will go first, Beth,' Rocio said, 'and light the way. I will supply directions. Jed, you must close the hatch behind you.'

Reluctantly, with the girls pouting and scowling, they all climbed down into the crawlway. Jed tugged the hatch back into place after him, nearly catching his fingers as it guillotined shut. When it was in place, the washroom floor silently and fastidiously sealed over with elegant floorboards again.

4

Dariat wandered along the valley, not really paying much attention to anything. Only the memories pulled at him, bittersweet recollections guiding him towards the sacred places he hadn't dared visit in the flesh for thirty years, not even when he'd roamed through Valisk to avoid Bonney and Kiera.

The wide pool, apparently carved into the grey-brown polyp-rock by the stream's enthusiastic flow, was nature at its most pleasing. Where tufts of soft pink grass lined the edges, strains of violet and amber moss sprawled over the scattering of boulders, and long fronds of water reeds swayed lazily in the current. Last seen when the body of Mersin Columba was drifting up against the bank, blood running from its broken skull. The teenage boy standing above it, face contorted in rage, cudgel slowly lowering. So young, such incredible anger.

The flat expanse of land between the slope of the valley and an ox-bow loop in the stream. An animal track wound through it, curving round invisible obstacles as it led down to a shallow beach where the herds could drink. Apart from that it was untouched, the pink grass which currently dominated the plains was thick and lush here, its tiny mushroom-shaped spoor fringes poised on the verge of ripeness. Nobody had camped here for years, despite its eminent suitability. None of the Starbridge tribes had ever returned. Not after . . .

Here. He walked to one side of the empty tract, the taller stalks of grass swishing straight through his translucent legs. Yes, this was the place. Anastasia's tepee had been pitched here. A sturdy, colourful contraption. Strong enough to take her weight when she tied the rope round her neck. Was the pink grass slightly thinner here? A rough circle where the pyre had been. Her tribe sending her and her few belongings on their way to the Realms (every possession except one, the Thoale stones, which he had kept safe these thirty years). Her body dispersed in fire and smoke, freeing the soul from any final ties with the physical universe.

How had they *known*? Those simple, backward people. Yet their lives contained such astonishing truth. They more than anyone would be prepared for the beyond. Anastasia wouldn't have suffered in the same way as the lost souls he'd encountered during his own fleeting time there. Not her.

Dariat sat on the grass, his toga crumpling around chubby limbs, though never really chafing. If any of her essence had indeed lingered here, it was long gone now. So now what? He looked up at the light-tube, which had become even dimmer than before. The air was cooler, too, nothing like Valisk's usual balmy medium. He was rather surprised that phenomenon registered. How could a ghost sense temperature? But then most aspects of his present state were a mystery.

Dariat?

He shook his head. Hearing things. Just to be certain, he looked around. Nobody, alive or spectral, was in sight. An interesting point though. Would I be able to see another ghost?

Dariat. You are there. We feel you. Answer us.

The voice was like affinity, but much softer. A whisper into the back of his mind. Oh great, a ghost being haunted by another ghost. Thank you again, Thoale. That could only ever happen to me.

Who is this? he asked.

We are Valisk now. Part of us is you.

What is this? What are you?

We are the habitat personality, the combination of yourself and Rubra.

That's crazy. You cannot be me.

But we are. Your memories and personality fused to Rubra's within the neural strata. Remember? The change to us, to the neural strata's thought routines, was corporeal and permanent. We remain intact. You, however,

115

were a possessing soul, you were torn out by the habitat's shift to this realm.

A realm hostile to the possessed, he said rancorously.

Exactly.

Don't I know it. I'm a ghost. That's what the shift did to me. A bloody ghost.

How intriguing. We cannot see you.

I'm in the valley.

Ah.

Dariat could feel the understanding within the personality. It knew which valley he meant. A true affinity.

Can we have access to your sensorium, please. It will allow us to analyse the situation properly.

He couldn't think of a reasonable objection, even though the idea sat uncomfortably. After thirty years of self-imposed mental isolation, sharing came hard. Even with an entity that claimed to be derived from himself.

Very well, he griped. He allowed the affinity link to widen, showing the personality the world through his eyes – or at least what he imagined to be his eyes.

As requested, he looked at his own body for the personality, walked about, demonstrated how he had no material presence.

Yet you persist in interpreting yourself as having human form, the personality said. How strange.

Force of habit, I guess.

More likely to be subconscious reassurance. The pattern is your basic foundation, the origin of quintessential identity. Retention of that is probably critical to your continuation as a valid entity. In other words, you're very set in your ways. But then we know that already, don't we.

I don't believe I'm that self-destructive. So if you wouldn't mind cancelling the insults for a few decades.

As you wish. After all, we do know how to cut the deepest.

Dariat could almost laugh at the impression of déjà vu which the exchange conjured up. He and Rubra had spent days in this same verbal fencing while he was possessing Horgan's body. Was there a reason you wanted to talk to me? Or did you just want to say hello?

This realm is not hostile to souls alone. It is also affecting our viability right down to the atomic level. Large sections of the neural strata have ceased to function, nor are such areas static, they flow through the strata at random, requiring persistent monitoring. Such failures threaten even our homogenized presence. We have to run constant storage replication routines to ensure our core identity is not erased.

That's tough, but unless the failure occurs everywhere simultaneously, you'll be safe.

As may be. But the overall efficiency of our cells is much reduced. The sensitive cell clusters cannot perceive as clearly as before; organ capability is degrading to alarming levels. Muscle membrane response is sluggish. Electrical generation is almost zero. All principal mechanical and electrical systems have shut down. The communication net and most processors are malfunctioning. If this situation continues, we will not be able to retain a working biosphere for more than ten days, a fortnight at most.

I hate to sound negative at a time like this, but what do you expect me to do about it?

The remaining population must be organized to assist us. There are holding procedures which can be enacted to prevent further deterioration.

Physical ones. You'll have to ask the living, not me.

We are attempting to. However, those who have been de-possessed are currently in an extremely disorientated state. Even those we have affinity contact with are unresponsive. As well as undergoing severe psychological trauma, their physiological condition has deteriorated.

So?

There are nearly three hundred of our relatives still in zero-tau. Your idea, remember? Kiera was holding them ready as an incentive for the hellhawk possessors. If they were to be taken out, we would have a functional work force ready to help, one that has a good proportion of qualified technicians among it.

Good idea ... Wait, how come their zero-tau pods are working when everything else has failed?

The zero-tau systems are self-contained and made from military grade components, they are also located in the deep caverns. We assumed that combination affords them some protection from whatever is affecting us.

If all you've got to do is flick one switch, why not just use a servitor?

Their physiological situation is even worse than the humans'. All the animals in the habitat seem to be suffering from a strong form of sleeping sickness. Our affinity instructions cannot rouse them.

Does that include all the xenoc species?

Yes. Their biochemistry is essentially similar to terrestrial creatures. If our cells are affected, so are theirs.

OK. Any idea what the problem is? Something like the energistic glitch which the possessed gave out?

Unlikely. It is probably a fundamental property of this realm. We are speculating that the quantum values of this continuum are substantially different from our universe. After all, we did select it to have a detrimental effect on the energy pattern which is a possessing soul. Consequently, we must assume that mass–energy properties here have been altered, that is bound to affect atomic characteristics. But until we can run a full analysis on our quantum state, we cannot offer further speculation.

Ever considered that the Devil simply doesn't allow electricity in this particular part of hell?

Your thought is our thought. We prefer to concentrate on the rational. That allows us to construct a hypothesis which will ultimately allow us to salvage this shitty situation.

Yeah, I can live with that. So what is it that you want me to do?

See if you can talk to someone called Tolton. He will switch off the zero-tau pods for us.

Why? Who is he?

A street poet, so he claims. He was one of the inhabitants we managed to keep out of Bonney's clutches.

Does he have affinity?

No. But legend has it that humans can see ghosts.

Shit, you're grasping at straws.

You have an alternative?

*

Ghosts can get tired. An unwelcome discovery that made itself quite clear as Dariat trudged over the grassland towards the ring of starscraper lobbies in the middle of the habitat. But then if you have imaginary muscles, they are put under quite a strain carrying your imaginary body across long distances, especially when that body has Dariat's bulk.

This is bloody unfair, he declared to the personality. When souls come back from the beyond, they all see themselves as physically perfect twenty-five-year-olds.

That's simple vanity.

I wish I was vain.

Valisk's parkland was also becoming less attractive. Now he had hiked out of the valley, the vivid pink grass which cloaked the southern half of the cylinder was grading down to a musky grey, an effect he equated to a city smog wrapping itself round the landscape. It couldn't be blamed entirely on the diminished illumination; the slim core of plasma in the axial light-tube was still a valiant neon blue. Instead it seemed to be part of the overall lack of vitality which was such an obvious feature of this realm. The xenoc plant appeared to be past its peak, as if its spore fringes had already ripened and now it was heading back into dormancy.

None of the insects which usually chirped and flittered among the plains had roused themselves. A few times, he came across field mice and their xenoc analogues, which were sleeping fitfully. They'd just curled up where they were, not making any attempt to return to their nests or warrens.

Ordinary chemical reactions must still be working, he suggested. If they weren't, then everything would be dead.

Yes. Although from what we're seeing and experiencing, they must also be inhibited to some degree.

Dariat trudged on. The spiral-springs of grass made the going hard, causing resistance as his legs passed through them. It was as though he was walking along a stream bed where the water was coming halfway up his shins. As his complaints became crabbier, the personality guided him towards one of the narrow animal tracks.

After half an hour of easier walking, and pondering his circumstances, he said: You told me that your electrical generation was almost zero.

Yes.

But not absolute?

No.

So the habitat must be in some kind of magnetic field if the induction cables are producing a current.

Logically, yes.

But?

Some induction cables are producing a current, the majority are not. And those that are do so sporadically. Buggered if we can work out what's going on, boy. Besides, we can't locate any magnetic field outside. There's nothing we can see that could be producing one.

What is out there?

Very little.

Dariat felt the personality gathering the erratic images from clusters of sensitive cells speckling the external polyp shell, and formatting them into a coherent visualization for him. The amount of concentration it took for the personality to fulfil what used to be a profoundly simple task (it was essentially autonomic before) surprised and worried him.

There were no planets. No moons. No stars. No galaxies. Only a murky void.

The eeriest impression he received from the expanded affinity bond was the way Valisk appeared to be in flight. Certainly he was aware of movement of some kind, though it was purely subliminal, impossible to define. The huge cylinder appeared to be gliding through a nebula. Not one recognizable from their universe. This was composed from extraordinarily subtle layers of ebony mist, shifting so slowly they were immensely difficult to distinguish. Had he been seeing it with his own eyes, he would have put it down to overstressed retinas. But there were discernible strands of the smoky substance out there; sparser than atmospheric cloud, denser than whorls of interstellar gas.

Abruptly, a fracture of hoary light shimmered far behind the hub of Valisk's southern endcap, a luminous serpent slithering around the insubstantial billows. Rough tatters of gritty vapour detonated into emerald and turquoise phosphorescence as it twirled past them. The phenomenon was gone inside a second.

Was that lightning? Dariat asked in astonishment.

We have no idea. However, we can't detect any static charge building on our shell. So it probably wasn't electrically based.

Have you seen it before?

That was the third time.

Bloody hell. How far away was it?

That is impossible to determine. We are trying to correlate parallax data from the external sensitive cells. Unfortunately, lack of distinct identifiable reference points within the cloud formations is hampering our endeavour.

You're beginning to sound like an Edenist. Take a guess.

We believe we can see about two hundred kilometres altogether.

Shit. That's all?

Yes.

Anything could be out there, behind that stuff.

You're beginning to catch on, boy.

Can you tell if we're moving? I got the impression we were. But it could just be the way that cloud stuff is shifting round out there.

We have the same notion, but that's all it ever can be. Without a valid reference point, it is impossible to tell. Certainly we're not under acceleration, which would eliminate the possibility we're falling through a gravity field . . . if this realm has gravity, of course.

OK, how about searching round with a radar? Have you tried that? There are plenty of arrays in the counter-rotating spaceport.

The spaceport has radar, it also has several Adamist starships, and over a hundred remote maintenance drones which could be adapted into sensor probes. None of which are functioning right now, boy. We really do need to bring our relatives out of zero-tau.

Yeah, yeah. I'm getting there as quick as I can. You know what, I don't think fusing with my thought routines has made that big an impression on you, has it?

*

According to the personality, Tolton was in the parkland outside the Gonchraov starscraper lobby. Dariat didn't get there on the first attempt. He encountered the other ghosts before he arrived.

The pink grassland gradually gave way to terrestrial grass and trees a couple of kilometres from the starscraper lobbies. It was a lush manicured jungle which boiled round the habitat's midsection, with gravel tracks winding round the thicker clumps of trees and vines. Big stone slabs formed primitive bridges over the rambling brooks, their support boulders grasped by thick coils of flowering creepers. Petals were drooping sadly as Dariat walked over them. As he drew closer to the lobby, he started to encounter the first of the servitor animal corpses, most of them torn by burnt scars, the impact of white fire. Then he noticed the decaying remains of several of their human victims lying in the undergrowth.

Dariat found the sight inordinately depressing. A nasty reminder of the relentless struggle which Rubra and Kiera had fought for dominance of the habitat. 'And who won?' he asked morbidly.

He cleared another of the neolithic bridges. The trees were thinning out now, becoming more ornate and taller as jungle gave way to parkland. There were flashes of movement in front of him coupled with murmurs of conversation, which made him suddenly self-conscious. Was he going to have to jump up and down waving his arms and shouting to get the living to notice him?

Just as he was psyching himself up for the dismaying inevitable, the little group caught sight of him. There were three men and two women. Their clothes should have clued him in. The eldest man was wearing a very long foppish coat of yellow velvet with ruffled lace down the front; one of the women had forced her large fleshy frame into a black leather dominatrix uniform, complete with whip; her mousy middle-aged companion was in a baggy woollen overcoat, so deliberately dowdy it was a human stealth covering; of the remaining two men, one was barely out of his teens, a black youth with panther muscles shown off by a slim red waistcoat, while the other was in his thirties, covered by a baggy mechanic's overall. They made a highly improbable combination, even for Valisk's residents.

Dariat stopped in surprise and with some gratification, raising a hand in moderate greeting. 'Hello, there. Glad you can see me. My name's Dariat.'

They stared at him, already unhappy expressions displaced by belligerent suspicion.

'You the one Bonney had everyone chasing?' the black guy asked.

Dariat grinned modestly. 'That's me.'

'Motherfucker. You did this to us!' he screamed. 'I had a body. I had my life back. You fucked that. You fucked me. You ruined everything. Everything! You brought us here, you and that shit living in the walls.'

Comprehension dawned for Dariat. He could see the faint outlines of branches through the man. 'You're a ghost,' he exclaimed.

'All of us are,' the dominatrix said. 'Thanks to you.'

'Oh, shit,' he whispered in consternation.

There are other ghosts? the personality asked. The affinity band was awash with interest.

What does it bloody look like!

The dominatrix took a step towards him, her whip flicked out, cracking loudly. She grinned viciously. 'I haven't had a chance to use this properly for a long time, dearie. That's a shame, because I know how to use it real bad.'

'Gonna get you plenty of chance to catch up now,' the black guy purred to her.

Dariat stood his ground shakily. 'You can't blame me for this. I'm one of you.'

'Yeah,' said the mechanic. 'And this time you can't get away.' He drew a heavy spanner from his leg pocket.

They must all be here, the personality said. **All the possessing souls. Just great.**

'Can we hurt him?' the mousy woman asked.

'Let's find out,' the dominatrix replied.

'Wait!' Dariat implored. 'We need to work together to get the habitat out of this place. Don't you understand? It's collapsing around us, everything's breaking down. We'll be trapped here.'

The black guy bared his teeth wide. 'We needed you to work with us to beat the habitat back in the real universe.'

Dariat flinched. He turned and ran. They gave chase immediately. That they'd catch him was never in doubt. He was appallingly overweight, and he'd just finished a nine kilometre hike. The whip slashed against the back of his left calf. He wailed, not just from the sharp sting, but from the fact it could sting.

They whooped and cheered behind him, delighted by the knowledge they could inflict injury, pain. Dariat staggered over the end of the bridge, and took a few unsteady steps towards the thicker part of jungle. The whip struck him again, flaying his shoulder and cheek, accompanied by the dominatrix's gleeful laugh. Then the lean black guy caught up with him, and jumped high, kicking him in the small of the back.

Dariat went flying, landing flat on his stomach, arms and legs spread wide. Not a single blade of grass even bent as he struck the ground; his bloated body seemed to be lying on a median height of stalks, while longer stems poked straight through him.

The beating began. Feet kicked savagely into his flanks, his legs, neck. The whip whistled down again and again, landing on his spine each time. Then the mechanic stood on his shoulders, and brought the spanner down on his skull. The battering became rhythmic, horrifyingly relentless. Dariat cried out at every terrifying impact. There was pain, in abundance there was pain, but no blood, nor damage, nor bruising or broken bones. The blaze of hurt had its origin in a concussion of hatred and fury. Each blow reinforcing, emphasizing how much they wanted him ruined.

His cries grew fainter, though they were just as insistent, and tainted with increasing anguish. The spanner, and the whip, and the boots, and the fists began to sink into him, puncturing his intangible boundary. He was sinking deeper into the grass, the hammering propelling his belly into the soil. Coldness swept into him, a wave racing on ahead of the solid surface with which he was merging. His shape was lacking definition now, its outline becoming less substantial. Even his thoughts began to lose their intensity.

Nothing could stop them. Nothing he said. Nothing he begged. Nothing he could pay. None of his prayers. Nothing. He had to endure it all. Not knowing what the outcome would be; terrifyingly, not knowing what it could be.

They let him be, eventually. After how much time not one of them knew. As much as it took to satisfy their hunger for vengeance. To dull the enjoyment of sadism. To experiment with the novel methods of brutality available to ghosts. There wasn't much of his presence left when they finished. A gauzy patch of pearl luminescence loitering amid the grass, the back of his toga barely bobbing above the surface of the soil. Limbs and head were buried.

Laughing, they walked away.

Amid the coldness, darkness, and apathy, a few strands of thought clung together. A weak filigree of suffering and woe. Everything he was. Very little, really.

*

Tolton had a brief knowledge of scenes like this. Second-hand knowledge, old and stale, memories of tales told to him by the denizens of the lowest floors of the starscrapers. Tales of covert combat operations, of squads that had been hit by superior firepower, waiting to be evac-ed out of the front line. Their bloody, battered casualties wound up in places like this, a field hospital triage. It was the latest development in the saga of the habitat population's misfortunes. Lately, studying the parkland had become a form of instant archaeology. Evolving stages of residence were laid out in concentric circles, plain to see.

In the beginning was the starscraper lobby, a pleasing rotunda of stone and glass, blending into the superbly maintained parkland. Then with the arrival of possession the lobby had been smashed up during one of the innumerable firefights between Kiera's followers and Rubra, and a shanty town had sprung up in a ring around it. Tiny Tudor cottages had stood next to Arabian tents, which were pitched alongside shiny Winnebagos; the richness of imagination on display was splendid. That was before Valisk departed the universe.

After that, the illusion of solidity had melted away like pillars of salt in the rain, exposing rickety shacks assembled from scraps of plastic and metal. They leant together precariously, one stacked against another to provide a highly dubious stability. The narrow strips of grass between were reduced to slippery runnels of mud, often used as open sewers.

So now the survivors of Valisk's latest change in fortune had moved again. Repelled from the hovels of their erstwhile possessors, they were simply sprawling uncaringly across the surrounding grass. They lacked the energy and will-power to do anything else. Some lay on their backs, some had curled up, some were sitting against trees, some stumbled about aimlessly. That wasn't so bad, Tolton thought, after what they'd been through a period of stupefaction was under-standable. It was the sound which was getting to him. Wails of distress and muffled sobbing mingling together to poison the air with harrowing dismay. Five thousand people having a bad dream in unison.

And just like a bad dream, you couldn't wake them from it. To begin with, when he'd emerged from his hiding place, he'd moved from one to another. Offering words of sympathy, a comforting arm around the shoulder. He'd persisted valiantly for a couple of hours like that, before finally acknowledging how quite pathetically pointless it all was. Somehow, they would have to get over the psychological trauma by themselves.

It wasn't going to be easy, not with the ghosts as an ever-present reminder of their ordeal. The ex-possessors were still slinking fur-tively through the outlying trees of the nearby jungle. For whatever reason, once they'd been expelled from their host bodies, they wouldn't leave. Immediately after Valisk's strange transformation they had clung longingly to their victims, following them with perverted devotion as they crawled about shaking and vomiting in reaction to their release. Then, as people had gradually started to recover their wits and take notice, the anger had surfaced. It was that massive deluge of communal hatred which had forced the ghosts to retreat, rather than the shouts of abuse and threats of vengeance.

They'd fled into the refuge of the jungle around the parkland, almost bewildered by the response they'd spawned. But they hadn't gone far. Tolton could see them thronging out there amid the funereal trees, their eerie pale radiance casting diaphanous shadows which twisted fluidly amid the branches and trunks.

But the ghosts never went any further than the trees. It was as if the greater depths of the darkling habitat frightened them, too. That was the aspect of this whole affair which worried Tolton the most.

His own wanderings were almost as aimless as anyone in the throws of recovery. Like them, he didn't relish the idea of venturing through the shanty town, he also considered it prudent not to fraternize with the ghosts. Though somewhere at the back of his mind was some ancient piece of folklore about ghosts never actually killing anybody. Whichever prehistory warlock came up with that prophecy had obviously never encountered these particular ghosts.

So he kept moving, avoiding eye contact, searching for . . . well, he'd know what when he saw it. Ironically, the thing he missed most was Rubra, and the wealth of knowledge which came with that contact. But the processor block he'd used to stay in touch with the habitat personality had crashed as soon as the change happened. Since then he'd tried using several other blocks. None of them worked, at most he got a trickle of static. He didn't have enough (actually, any) technical knowledge to understand why.

Nor did he understand the change the habitat had undergone, only the result, the mass exorcism. He assumed it had been imposed by some friendly ally. Except Valisk didn't have any allies. And Rubra had never dropped any hint that this might happen, not in all the weeks he'd kept Tolton hidden from the possessed. There was nothing for it but to keep moving for the delusion of purpose it bestowed, and wait for developments. Whatever they might be.

'Please.' The woman's voice was little more than a whisper, but it was focused enough to make Tolton hesitate and try to see who was speaking.

'Please, I need some help. Please.' The speaker was in her late middle age, huddled up against a tree. He walked over to her, avoiding a couple of people who were stretched out, almost comatose, on the grass.

Details were difficult in this leaden twilight. She was wrapped in a large tartan blanket, clutching it to her chest like a shawl. Long unkempt hair partially obscured her face, glossy Titian roots contrasted sharply with the dirty faded chestnut of the tresses. The features glimpsed through the tangle were delicate, a pert button nose and long cheekbones, implausibly artistic eyebrows. Her skin seemed very tight, almost stretched, as if to emphasize the curves.

'What's wrong?' Tolton asked gently, cursing himself for the stupidity of the question. As he knelt beside her, the light-tube's meagre nimbus glimmered on the tears dribbling down her cheeks.

'I hurt,' she said. 'Now she's gone, I hurt so badly.'

'It'll go. I promise, time will wash it away.'

'She slept with hundreds of men,' the woman cried wretchedly. 'Hundreds. Women, too. I felt the heat in her, she loved it, all of it. That slut, that utter slut. She made my body do things with those animals. Awful, vile things. Things no decent person would ever do.'

He tried to take one of her hands, but she snatched it away, turning from him. 'It wasn't you,' he said. 'You didn't do any of those things.'

'How can you say that? It was done to me. I felt it all, every minute of it. This is my body. Mine! My flesh and blood. She took that from me. She soiled me, ruined me. I'm so corrupt I'm not even human any more.'

'I'm sorry, really I am. But you have to learn not to think like that. If you do, you're letting her win. You've got to put that behind you. It's over, and you've won. She's been exorcized, she's nothing but a neurotic wisp of light. That's all she'll ever be now. I'd call that a victory, wouldn't you?'

'But I hurt,' she persisted. Her voice dropped to a confessional tone. 'How can I forget when I hurt?'

'Look, there are treatments, memory suppressors, all sorts of cures. Just as soon as we get the power turned back on, you can—'

'Not my mind! Not just that.' She had begun to plead. 'It's my body, my body which hurts.'

Tolton started to get a very bad feeling about where the conversation was heading. The woman was shaking persistently, and he was sure some of the moisture glistening on her face had to be perspiration. He flicked an edgy glance back at her unnatural roots. 'Where, exactly, does it hurt?'

'My face,' she mumbled. 'My face aches. It's not me any more. I couldn't see me when she looked in a mirror.'

'They all did that, all imagined themselves to look ridiculously young and pretty. It's an illusion, that's all.'

'No. It became real. I'm not me, not now. She even took my identity away from me. And . . .' her voice started trembling. 'My shape. She stole my body, and still that wasn't enough. Look, look what she's done to me.'

Moving so slowly that Tolton wanted to do it for her, she drew the folds of the blanket apart. For the first time, he actually wished there was less light. To begin with it looked as though someone had badly bungled a cosmetic package adaptation. Her breasts were grossly misshapen. Then he realized that was caused by large bulbs of flesh clinging to the upper surface like skin-coloured leeches. Each one almost doubled the size of the breast, the weight pulling them down heavily. The natural tissue was almost squashed from view.

The worst part of it was they obviously weren't grafts or implants; whatever the tissue was, it had swollen out of the natural mammary gland. Below them, her abdomen was held anorexically flat by a broad oval slab of unyielding skin. It was as though she'd developed a thick callus across the whole area, fake musculature marked out by faint translucent lines.

'See?' the woman asked, staring down at her exposed chest in abject misery. 'Bigger breasts and a flat belly. She really wanted bigger breasts. That was her wish. They'd be more useful to her, more fun, more spectacular. And she could make wishes come true.'

'God preserve us,' Tolton murmured in horror. He didn't know much about human illnesses, but there were some scraps of relevant information flashing up out of his childhood's basic medical didactic memories. Cancer tumours. Almost a lost disease. Geneering had made human bodies massively resistant to the ancient bane. And for the few isolated instances when it did occur, medical nanonics could penetrate and eradicate the sick cells within hours.

'I used to be a nurse,' the woman said, as she shamefully covered herself with the blanket again. 'They're runaways. My breasts are the largest growths, but I must have the same kind of malignant eruptions at every change she instituted.'

'What can I do?' he asked hoarsely.

'I need medical nanonic packages. Do you know how to program them?'

'No. I don't even have neural nanonics. I'm a poet, that's all.'

'Then, please, find me some. My neural nanonics aren't working either, but a processor block might do instead.'

'I . . . Yes, of course.' It would mean a trip into the lifeless, lightless starscraper to find some, but his discomfort at that prospect was nothing compared to her suffering. Somehow, he managed to keep a neutral expression on his face as he stood up, even though he was pretty certain a medical nanonic package wouldn't work in this weird environment. But it might, it just might. And if that slender chance existed, then he would bring one for her, no matter what.

He cast round the dismal sight of people strewn about, holding themselves and moaning. The really terrifying doubt engulfed him then. Suppose the anguish wasn't all psychological? Every possessed he'd seen had changed their appearance to some degree. Suppose every change had born a malignancy, even a small one.

'Oh, fucking hell, Rubra. Where are you? We need help.'

*

As always, there was no warning when the cell door opened. Louise wasn't even sure when it had swung back. She was curled up on the bunk, dozing, only semi-aware of her surroundings. Quite how long she'd been in this state, she didn't know. Somehow, her time sense had got all fouled up. She remembered the interview with Brent Roi, his sarcasm and unconcealed contempt. Then she'd come back here. Then . . . She'd come back here hours ago. Well, a long time had passed . . . She thought.

I must have fallen asleep.

Which was hard to believe; the colossal worry of the situation had kept her mind feverishly active.

The usual two female police officers appeared in the doorway. Louise blinked up at their wavering outlines, and tried to right herself. Bright lights flashed painfully behind her eyes; she had to clamp her mouth shut against the sudden burst of nausea.

What is wrong with me?

'Woah, there, steady on.' One of the police officers was sitting on the bed beside her, holding her up.

Louise shook uncontrollably, cold sweat beading on her skin. Her reaction calmed slightly, though it was still terribly hard to concentrate.

'One minute,' the woman said. 'Let me reprogram your medical package. Try to take some deeper breaths, OK?'

That was simple enough. She gulped down some air, her chest juddering. Another couple of breaths. Her rogue body seemed to be calming. 'Wha . . . What?' she panted.

'Anxiety attack,' said the policewoman. 'We see a lot of them in here. That and worse things.'

Louise nodded urgently, an attempt to convince herself that's all it was. No big deal. Nothing badly amiss. The baby's fine – the medical package would ensure that. Just stay calm.

'OK. I'm OK now. Thank you.' She proffered a small smile at the police officer, only to be greeted with blank-faced indifference.

'Let's go, then,' said the officer standing by the door.

Louise girded herself, and slowly stood on slightly unsteady legs. 'Where are we going?'

'Parole Office.' She sounded disgusted.

'Where's Genevieve? Where's my sister?'

'Don't know. Don't care. Come on.'

Louise was almost shoved out into the corridor. She was improving by the minute, although the headache lingered longer than anything else. A small patch of skin at the back of her skull tingled, as if she'd been stung. Her fingers stroked it absently. Anxiety attack? She hadn't known there was such a thing before. But given everything she currently had to think about, such a malaise was more than likely.

They got into a lift which had to be heading down. The gravity field had risen to almost normal when they got out. This part of the asteroid was different from the cells and interview rooms she'd been kept in until now. Definitely government offices, the standardized furniture and eternally polite personnel with their never-smiling faces were evidence of that. She took a little cheer from the fact these corridors and glimpsed rooms weren't as crushingly bleak as the upper level. Her status had changed for the better. Slightly.

The police officers showed her into a room with a narrow window looking out over High York's biosphere cavern. Not much to see, it was dawn, or dusk, Louise didn't know which. The grassland and trees soaking up the gold-orange light were a brighter, more welcoming green than the cavern in Phobos. Two curving settees had been set up facing each other in the middle of the floor, bracketing an oval table. Genevieve slouched on one of them, hands stuffed into the pockets of her ship-suit, feet swinging just off the floor, looking out of the window. Her expression was a mongrel cross between sullen resentment and utter boredom.

'Gen!' Louise's voice nearly cracked.

Genevieve raced across the room and thudded into her. They hugged each other tightly. 'They wouldn't tell me where you were!' Genevieve protested loudly. 'They wouldn't let me see you. They wouldn't say what was happening.'

Louise stroked her sister's hair. 'I'm here now.'

'It's been for ever. Days!'

'No, no. It just seems like that.'

'Days,' Genevieve insisted.

Louise managed a slightly uncertain smile, wanting for herself the reassurance she was attempting to project. 'Have they been questioning you?'

'Yes,' Genevieve mumbled morosely. 'They kept on and on about what happened in Norwich. I told them a hundred times.'

'Me too.'

'Everybody must be really stupid on Earth. They don't understand anything unless you've explained it five times.'

Louise wanted to laugh at the childish derision in Gen's voice, pitched just perfectly to infuriate any adult.

'And they took my games block away. That's stealing, that is.'

'I haven't seen any of my stuff either.'

'The food's horrid. I suppose they're too thick to cook it properly. And I haven't had any clean clothes.'

'Well, I'll see what I can do.'

Brent Roi hurried into the room, and dismissed the two waiting police officers with a casual wave. 'OK, ladies, take a seat.'

Louise flashed him a resentful look.

'Please?' he entreated without noticeable sincerity.

Holding hands, the sisters sat on the settee opposite him. 'Are we under arrest?' Louise asked.

'No.'

'Then you believe what I told you?'

'To my amazement, I find sections of your story contain the odd nugget of truth.'

Louise frowned. This attitude was completely different to the one he'd shown her during the interview. Not that he was repenting, more like he'd been proved right instead of her.

'So you'll watch out for Quinn Dexter?'

'Most assuredly.'

Genevieve shuddered. 'I hate him.'

'That's all that truly matters,' Louise said. 'He must never be allowed to get down to Earth. If you believe me, then I've won.'

Brent Roi shifted uncomfortably. 'OK, we've been trying to decide what to do with the pair of you. Which I can tell you is not an easy thing, given what you were attempting. You thought you were doing the right thing, bringing Christian here. But believe me, from the legal side of things, you are about as wrong as it's possible to be. The Halo Police Commissioner has spent two days being advised by some of our best legal experts on what the hell to do with you, which hasn't improved his temper any. Ordinarily we'd just walk you past a warm judge and fly you off to a penal colony. There'd be no problem obtaining a guilty verdict.' He gazed at Genevieve. 'Not even your age would get you off.'

Genevieve pushed her shoulders up against her neck, and glowered at him.

'However, there are mitigating circumstances, and these are strange times. Lucky for you, that gives the Halo police force a large amount of discretion right now.'

'So?' Louise asked calmly. For whatever reason she wasn't afraid; if they were due to face a trial none of this would be happening.

'So. Pretty obviously: we don't want you up here after what you've done; plus you don't have the basic technical knowledge necessary to live in an asteroid settlement, which makes you a liability. Unfortunately, there's an interstellar quarantine in force right now, which means we can't send you off to Tranquillity where your fiancé can take care of you. That just leaves us with one option: Earth. You have money, you can afford to stay there for the duration of the crisis.'

Louise glanced at Genevieve, who squashed her lips together with a dismissive lack of interest.

'I'm not going to object,' Louise said.

'I couldn't care less if you did,' Brent Roi told her. 'You have no say in this at all. As well as deporting you, I am officially issuing you with a police caution. You have engaged in an illegal act with the potential of endangering High York, and this will be entered into Govcentral's criminal data memory store with a suspended action designation. Should you at any time in the future be found committing another criminal act of any nature within Govcentral's domain this case will be reactivated and used in your prosecution. Is that clear?'

'Yes,' Louise whispered.

'You cause us one more problem, and they'll throw you out of the arcology and lock the door behind you.'

'What about Fletcher?' Genevieve asked.

'What about him?' Brent Roi said.

'Is he coming down to Earth with us?'

'No, Gen,' Louise said. 'He's not.' She tried to keep the sorrow from her voice. Fletcher had helped her and Gen through so much, she still couldn't think of him as a possessor, one of the enemy. The last image she had was of him being led out of the big airlock chamber where they'd been detained. A smile of forlorn encouragement on his face, directed at her. Even in defeat, he didn't lose his nobility.

'Your big sister's right,' Brent Roi told Genevieve. 'Stop thinking about Fletcher.'

'Have you killed him?'

'Tough to do. He's already dead.'

'Have you?'

'At the moment he's being very cooperative. He's telling us about the beyond, and helping the physics team understand the nature of his energistic power. Once we've learned all we can, then he'll be put into zero-tau. End of story.'

'Can we see him before we go?' Louise asked.

'No.'

*

The two female police officers escorted Louise and Genevieve directly up to the counter-rotating spaceport. They were given a standard class berth on the *Scher*, an inter-orbit passenger ship. The interstellar quarantine hadn't yet bitten into the prodigious Earth–Halo–Moon economic triad; outsystem exports made up barely fifteen per cent of their trade. Civil flights between the three were running close to their usual levels.

They arrived at the departure lounge twelve minutes before the ship was scheduled to leave. The police returned their luggage and passports, with Earth immigration clearance loaded in; they also got their processor blocks back. Finally, they handed Louise her Jovian Bank credit disk.

Louise had her suspicions that the whole procedure was deliberately being rushed to keep them off-balance and complacent. Not that she knew how to kick up a fuss. But there was probably some part of their treatment which a good lawyer could find fault with. She didn't really care.

Scher's life-support capsule had the same lengthy cylindrical layout as the *Jamrana*, except that every deck was full of chairs. A sour stewardess showed them brusquely to their seats, strapped them in, and left to chase other passengers.

'I wanted to change,' Genevieve complained. She was pulling dubiously at her ship-suit. 'I haven't washed for ages. It's all clammy.'

'We'll be able to change when we get to the tower station, I expect.'

'Which tower station? Where are we going?'

'I don't know.' Louise glanced at the stewardess, who was chiding an elderly woman's attempts to fasten her seat straps. 'I think we'll just have to wait and find out.'

'Then what? What do we do when we get there?'

'I'm not sure. Let me think for a minute, all right?'

Louise squirmed her shoulders, letting her muscles relax. Free fall always made her body tense up as it tried to assume more natural gravity-evolved postures. Thankfully, the cabin chairs were almost flat, preventing her from getting stomach twinges.

What to do next hadn't bothered her much while she'd been in custody. Convincing Brent Roi about Dexter was her only concern. Now that had been accomplished, or seemed to have been. She still couldn't quite believe he had taken her warnings particularly seriously; they'd been released far too quickly for that. Dismissed, almost.

The authorities had Fletcher in custody, and he was cooperating with them about possession. That was their true prize, she thought. They were confident their security procedures would spot Dexter. She wasn't. Not at all. And she'd made one solemn promise to Fletcher, which covered exactly this situation.

If I can't help him physically, at least I can honour my promise. If our positions were reversed, he would. Banneth, I said I'd find and warn Banneth. Yes. And I will. The sudden resolution did a lot to warm her again.

Then she was aware of a strangely rhythmic buzzing sound, and blinked her eyes open. Genevieve had activated her processor block; its AV projector lens was shining a conical fan of light directly on her face. Frayed serpents of pastel colour stroked her cheeks and nose, glistening on a mouth parted in an enraptured smile. Her fingers skated with fast dextrous motions over the block's surface, sketching eccentric ideograms.

I'm really going to have to do something about this obsession, Louise thought, *it can't be healthy.*

The stewardess was shouting at a man cradling a crying child. Tackling Gen was probably best delayed until they reached Earth.

*

It wasn't rugged determination, or even victorious self-confidence which brought him back. Instead came the slow, dreadful comprehension that this awful limbo wouldn't end if he did nothing.

Dariat's thoughts hung amid vast clusters of soil molecules, membranous twists of nebula dust webbing the space between stars, insipid, enervated. Completely unable to evaporate, to fade away into blissful non-existence. Instead, they hummed with chilly misery as they conducted pain-soaked memories round and around on a never-ending circuit, humiliation and fear undimmed by time and repetition.

Worse than the beyond. At least in the beyond there were other souls, memories you could raid to bring an echo of sensation. Here there was only yourself; a soul buried alive. Nothing to comfort you but your own life. Screaming from the pain of the blows which battered him down might have stopped, but the internal scream of self-loathing could never cease. Not incarcerated here. He didn't want to go back, not to the dimly sensed light and air above, the vicious brutality of the ghosts waiting there. Every time he emerged they would pummel him down again. That was what all of them wanted. He would go through the same suffering again and again. Yet he couldn't stay here, either.

Dariat moved. He thought of himself, visualized pushing his bulky body up through the soil, as if he was doing some kind of appalling fitness-fad press-up. It wasn't anything like that easy. Imagination couldn't power him as before. Something had happened to him, weakening him. The vitality he owned, even as a ghost, had been leeched out by the matter with which he was entwined. Fantasy muscles trembled as he strained. Finally, along his back, sensation was returning in a paltry trickle. A warmth, but not on his skin. Inside, just below the surface.

It inspired greed, a hunger for more. Nothing else mattered, the warmth was revitalizing, a font of life. It leant to his strength, and he began to rise faster through the soil, sucking in more warmth as he went. Soon, his face cleared the ground, and he was moving at an almost normal speed. Extricating himself from the soil meant discovering just how cold he was. Dariat stood up, teeth chattering, arms crossed over his chest, hugging tight as his hands tried to rub some heat into icy flesh. Only his feet were warm, though that was a relative term.

The grass around his sandals was a sickly yellow-brown, dead and drooping. Each blade was covered in a delicate sprinkle of hoarfrost. They made up a roughly oval patch about two metres long. Body-shaped, in fact. He stared at it, completely bewildered.

Damn, I'm cold!

Dariat? That you, boy?

Yes, it's me. One question – he didn't really want to ask, but had to know: **how long was I . . . out for?**

It's been seventeen hours.

Seventeen years was a figure he could have believed quite easily. Is that all?

Yes. What happened?

They beat me into the ground. Literally. It was . . . Bad. Real bad.

Then why didn't you come out earlier?

You won't understand.

Did you kill the grass?

I don't know. I suppose so.

How? We thought you didn't interact with solid matter.

Don't ask me. There was a kind of warmth as I came out. Or maybe it was just hatred which killed the grass, concentrated hatred. That's what they were giving off. Thoale be damned, but they hated me. I'm cold now. He scanned round, searching through the tree trunks for any sign of the other ghosts. After a moment, he walked away from the patch of dead grass, spooked by the place. The opposite of consecrated ground.

Movement felt good, it was making his legs warm up. When he glanced down, he saw a line of frosted footsteps in the grass trailing back to the burial patch. But he was definitely getting warmer. He started walking again, a meagre lick of heat seeping up from his legs to his torso. It would take a long time to dispel the chill, but he was sure it would happen eventually.

The starscraper is the other way, the personality said.

I know. That's why I'm going back to the valley. I'll be safe there.

For a while.

I'm not risking another encounter.

You have to. Look, forewarned is forearmed. Just take it carefully. If you see any ghosts waiting ahead of you, go around them.

I'm not doing it.

You have to. Our internal status is still decaying. We must have those descendants out of zero-tau. What good will a dead habitat do you? You know they're the only chance of salvation any of us have. You know that. You just showed us how bad entombment here is; that could become permanent if we don't get clear.

Shit! He stopped, standing with his fists clenched. Tendrils of frost slithered out from under his soles to wilt the grass.

It's common sense, Dariat. You won't be giving in to Rubra just by agreeing.

137

That's not—

Ha. Remember what we are.

All right! Bastards. Where's Tolton?

*

Tolton had found the light stick in an emergency equipment locker in the starscraper's lobby. It gave out a lustreless purple-tinged glow, and that emerged at a pitiful percentage of its designated output wattage. But after forty minutes his eyes had acclimatized well. Navigating down through the interior of the starscraper posed few physical problems. Resolution, however, was a different matter. In his other hand he carried a fire axe from the same locker as the light stick. It hardly inspired confidence.

Beyond the bubble of radiance which enveloped him, it was very dark indeed. And silent with it. No light shone in through any of the windows; there wasn't even a dripping tap to break the monotony of his timorous footsteps. Three times since he'd been down here the electrophorescent cells had burst into life, some arcane random surge of power sending shoals of photons skidding along the vestibules and stairwells. The first time it happened, he was petrified. The zips of light appeared from nowhere, racing towards him at high speed. By the time he yelled out and started to cower down they were already gone, behind him and vanishing round some corner. He didn't react much better the next two times, either.

He told himself that he should be relieved that some aspect of Rubra and the habitat was still functioning, however erratically. It wasn't much reassurance; that the stars had vanished from view had been a profound shock. He'd already decided he wasn't going to share that knowledge with the other residents for a while. What he couldn't understand was, where were they? His panicky mind was constantly filling the blank space outside the windows with dreadful imaginings. It wasn't much of a leap to have whatever skulked outside getting in to glide among the opaque shadows of the empty starscraper. Grouping together and conspiring, flowing after him.

The muscle membrane door at the bottom of the stairwell was partially expanded, its edges trembling slightly. He cautiously stuck the light stick through the gap, and peered round at the fifth-floor vestibule. The high ceilings and broad curving archways that were the *mise en scène* of Valisk's starscrapers had always seemed fairly illustrious before; bitek's inalienable majesty. That was back when they were bathed in light and warmth twenty-four hours a day. Now they clustered threateningly round the small area of illumination he projected, swaying with every slight motion of the light stick.

Tolton waited for a moment, nerving himself to step out. This floor was mainly taken up by commercial offices. Most of the mechanical doorways had frozen shut. He walked along, reading the plaques on each one. The eighth belonged to an osteopath specializing in sports injuries. There ought to be some kind of medical nanonics inside. The emergency lock panel was on the top of the frame. He broke it open with the blunt end of the axe, exposing the handle inside. Now the power was off, or at least disabled, the electronic bolts had disengaged. A couple of turns on the handle released the lock entirely, and he prised the door open.

Typical waiting room: not quite expensive chairs, soft drinks dispenser, reproduction artwork, and lush potted plants. The large circular window looked out at nothing, a black mirror. Tolton saw his own reflection staring back, with a fat man in a grubby robe standing behind him. He yelped in shock, and dropped the light stick. Flat planes of light and shadow lurched around him. He turned, raising the axe up ready to swipe down on his adversary. Almost overbalancing from the wild motion.

The fat man was waving his arms frantically, shouting. Tolton could hear nothing more than a gentle murmur of air. He gripped the axe tightly as it wobbled about over his head, ready for the slightest sign of antagonism. None came. In fact, there probably couldn't ever be any. Tolton could just see the door through the fat man. A ghost. That didn't make him any happier.

The ghost had put his hands on his hips, face screwed up in some exasperation. He was saying something slowly and loudly, an adult talking to an idiot child. Again, there was that bantam ruffling of air. Tolton frowned; it corresponded to the movements of the fat ghost's jaw.

In the end, communication became a derivative of lip reading. There was never quite enough sound (if that's what it truly was) to form whole words, rather the faint syllables clued him in.

'Your axe is the wrong way round.'

'Uh.' Tolton glanced up. The blade was pointing backwards. He shifted it round, then sheepishly lowered it. 'Who are you?'

'My name's Dariat.'

'You're wasting your time following me, you can't possess me.'

'I don't want to. I'm here to give you a message.'

'Oh, yeah?'

'Yes. The habitat personality wants you to switch off some zero-tau pods.'

'How the hell do you know that?'

'We're in affinity contact.'

'But you're a . . .'

'Ghost. Yes, I had noticed. Although I think a revenant is a term more applicable in my case.'

'A what?'

'The personality never warned me you were this stupid.'

'I am not . . .' Tolton's outrage spluttered to a halt. He started to laugh.

Dariat gave the alleged street poet a mildly annoyed glare. 'Now what?'

'I've had some weird shit dumped on me in my time, but I think arguing with a ghost over my IQ has got to be the greatest.'

Dariat felt his lips move up in a grin. 'Got a point there.'

'Thank you, my man.'

'So, are you going to help?'

'Of course. Will turning off the pods be of any use?'

'Yeah. That mad bitch Kiera was holding a whole load of my illustrious relatives in stasis. They should be able to get things up and running again.'

'Then we can get out of . . .' Tolton took another look at the window. 'Where are we, exactly?'

'I'm not sure you can call this a place, more like a different state of being. It exists to be hostile to the possessed. Unfortunately, there are a few unexpected side-effects.'

'You sound as though you're talking from a position of knowledge, which I frankly find hard to believe.'

'I played a part in bringing us here,' Dariat admitted. 'I'm not completely sure of the details, though.'

'I see. Well, we'd better get started, then.' He picked up the light stick. 'Ah, wait. I promised a woman I'd try and find some medical nanonic packages for her. She really does need them.'

'There's some in the osteopath's storage cabinet, through there.' Dariat pointed.

'You really are in touch with Rubra, aren't you?'

'He's changed a bit, but, yes.'

'Then I'm curious. Why did the two of you choose me for this task?'

'His decision. But most of the other corporeal residents got whacked out when they were de-possessed. You saw them up in the park. They're no good for anything right now. You're the best we've got left.'

'Oh, bloody hell.'

*

When they emerged into the decrepit lobby, Tolton sat down and tried to get a processor block to work. He'd never had a didactic memory imprint covering their operations and program parameters. Never needed one; all he used them for was recording and playing AV fleks, and communications, plus a few simple commands for medical nanonics (mainly concerned with morning-after blood detoxification).

Dariat started to advise on how to alter the operating program format, essentially dumbing down the unit. Even he had to consult with the personality about which subroutines to delete. Between the three of them, it took twenty minutes to get the little unit on-line with a reliable performance level.

Another fifteen minutes of running diagnostics (far slower than usual), and they knew what medical nanonics could achieve in such an antagonistic environment. It wasn't good news; the filaments which wove into and manipulated human flesh were sophisticated molecular strings, with correspondingly high-order management routines. They could bond the lips of wounds together, and infuse doses of stored biochemicals. But fighting a tumour by eliminating individual cancer cells was no longer possible.

We can't waste any more time on this, the personality protested.

Tolton was hunched up over the block. Dariat waved a hand under his face – the only way to catch his attention. Out here in the park the poet found it even harder to hear him, Dariat suspected his 'voice' was actually some kind of weak telepathy.

'It'll have to do,' Dariat said.

Tolton frowned down once again at the horribly confusing mass of icons eddying across the block's screen. 'Will they be able to cure her?'

'No. The tumours can't be reversed, but the packages should be able to contain them until we get back to the real universe.'

'All right. I suppose that'll do.'

Dariat managed to feel mildly guilty at the sadness in Tolton's voice. The way the street poet could become so anxious and devoted to a stranger he'd only spent five minutes with was touching.

They walked through the moat of decaying shacks and into the surrounding ring of human misery. The loathing directed at Dariat by those that saw him was profound enough to sting. He, a creature now purely of thought, was buffeted by the emanation of raw emotion; his own substance refined against him. It wasn't as strong as the blows inflicted by his fellow ghosts, but the cumulative effect was disturbingly debilitating. When he'd sneaked into the lobby he hadn't attracted such attention, a few glances of sullen resentment at most. But then, he realized, he was still suffering from the effects of the entombment, he'd been weaker, less substantial.

Now, the jeering and catcalls which chased him were building to a crescendo as more and more people realized what the commotion was about and joined in. He started staggering about, groaning at the pain.

'What is it?' Tolton asked.

Dariat shook his head. There was real fear building in him now. If he stumbled and fell here, victim to this wave of hatred, he might never be able to surface from the soil again. At every attempt he would be pressed back by the throng of people above him, dancing on his living grave.

'Going,' he grunted. 'Got to go.' He pressed his hands over his ears (fat lot of good that it did) and tottered as fast as he could out towards the shadowy trees beyond. 'I'll wait for you. Come when you've finished.'

Tolton watched in dismay as the ghost scurried away, becoming all too aware of the animosity which was now focusing on him. Head down, he hurried away in the direction he thought he'd left the woman.

She was still there, propped up against the tree. Dull eyes looked up at him, suffused with dread, hope denied. It was the only part of her which betrayed any emotion. Her stretched-tight face seemed incapable of displaying the slightest expression. 'What was the noise about?' she mumbled.

'I think there was a ghost around here.'

'Did they kill it?'

'I don't know. I don't think you can kill ghosts.'

'Holy water. Use holy water.' Tolton knelt down, and gently eased her clutching hands from the blanket. This time when it parted he was determined not to grimace. It was hard. He placed the nanonic medical packages on her breasts and belly the way Dariat had said, and used the block to activate the preloaded programs. The packages stirred slightly as they started to knit with her skin.

She let out a soft sigh, embodying both relief and happiness.

'It'll be all right,' he told her. 'They'll stop the cancer now.'

Her eyes had closed. 'I don't believe you. But it's nice of you to say it.'

'I mean it.'

'Holy water; that'll burn the bastards.'

'I'll remember.'

*

Tolton found Dariat skulking among the fringes of the trees. The ghost couldn't keep still, nervously searching round for signs of anyone approaching.

'Don't fret, man. The others don't care about you so long as you stay away from them.'

'I intend to,' Dariat grumbled. 'Come on, we've got a way to go.'

He started walking.

Tolton shrugged, and started after him.

'How was the woman?' Dariat asked.

'Perky. She wanted to sprinkle you with holy water.'

'Silly cow,' he snorted with derisive amusement. 'That's for vampires.'

*

Kiera had decreed that the zero-tau pods should be put in the deep chambers around the base of the northern endcap. The polyp in that section was a honeycomb of caverns and tunnels; the chambers used almost exclusively by the astronautics industry to support the docking-ledge infrastructure, stores, workshops, and fabrication plants all dedicated to supplying Magellanic Itg's blackhawk fleet. It was a logical place to use. The equipment was already close to hand. There wasn't as much danger from Rubra's insurgency in the big, unsophisticated caverns as there was in the starscrapers. And if they wanted them set up anywhere else, they'd be facing a troublesome relocation job.

As soon as Dariat told him where the zero-tau pods were, Tolton tried to use one of the rentcop jeeps abandoned around the starscraper lobby. It crawled along barely at walking pace. Stopped. Started. Crawled some more. Stopped.

They walked the whole way to the base of the northern endcap. Several times during the day Tolton caught Dariat studying the path behind them, and asked what he was trying to see.

'Footprints,' the fat ghost replied.

Tolton decided that after what he'd been through Dariat was entitled to a reasonable degree of neurotic paranoia. The light stick grew steadily brighter as they ventured into the cavern levels. Indicator lights began winking on some chunks of machinery. After a while, when they were deep inside the habitat shell, the electrophorescent strips were glowing; not as bright as before, but they remained steady.

Tolton switched the light stick off. 'You know, I even feel better down here.'

Dariat didn't answer. He was aware of the difference himself. An atmosphere reminiscent of those heady days thirty years ago, endless bright summer days when being alive was such a blessing. The personality was right, the otherworldliness of this continuum hadn't fully penetrated down here. Things worked as they were supposed to.

We might manage to salvage something from this yet.

They found the zero-tau pods in a lengthy cavern. At some time, there had been machinery or shelving pinned to the wall; small metal brackets still protruded from the dark-amber polyp. Deep scratches told of their recent hurried removal. Now the cavern was empty except for the row of interstellar-black sarcophagi running the length of the floor. Each of them had been taken from a blackhawk, the crudely severed fittings were proof of that. Thick cables had been grafted on to the interface panels, wiring them into clumps of spherical high-density power cells.

'Where do I start?' Tolton asked.

The processor block he was carrying bleeped before Dariat could begin the usual prolonged process of exaggerated enunciation. 'It doesn't matter. Pick one.'

'Hey.' Tolton grinned. 'You're back.'

'Rumours of my demise have been greatly exaggerated.'

Oh, please, Dariat said.

What's the matter with you? We're back on track. Rejoice.

Dariat was abruptly party to a resurgence of optimism, the sense of a hibernating animal approaching winter's end. Holding his scepticism in check, he watched Tolton go over to the closest zero-tau pod. The personality issued a couple of simple instructions, and Tolton pecked at a keyboard.

Erentz completed her cower as the scene above her switched. One instant a Chinese warlord with a cruel smile, promising that the next thing she would know was the torture leading up to possession, the next a moderately overweight, wide-eyed man with a good ten days' worth of grubby stubble was peering anxiously down at her. The light was dimmer, too. The wail which she'd started before the pod was activated continued, rising in pitch.

It's all right. Calm yourself.

Erentz paused, gathering her breath. *Rubra?* The mental voice which had chivvied her along since before she could remember felt slightly different.

Almost. But don't worry. The possessed have gone. You're safe.

There was a background emotion which sparked a small doubt. But the obvious apprehension and concern of the man staring down at her was a strange, fast-acting tonic. He definitely wasn't possessed.

'Hello,' Tolton said, desperate for some kind of response from the startled young woman.

She nodded slowly, and raised herself gingerly into a sitting position. It didn't help that the first thing she saw was Dariat hanging back by the cavern entrance. She emitted a frightened gasp.

I'm on your side, Dariat told her, earning a twitchy laugh in response.

What is happening here? she demanded.

The personality began to fill her in. Acceptance of her new

situation came amid a rush of relief. Erentz, like all the others released from zero-tau, relied on Rubra to provide a substantial part of their confidence. That he was the one who'd beaten the possessed was a heady boost for them. Fifteen minutes saw the last of the zero-tau pods deactivated. Dariat and Tolton were sidelined to slightly peeved observers as the brigade of Rubra's descendants quickly and efficiently set about releasing their cousins. After that, when they'd come down off the hype, the habitat personality began marshalling them into groups and giving them assignments.

First priority was given to igniting the various fusion generators dotted about the spaceport. They made two attempts to initiate fusion, both of which failed. Microfusion generators, they soon found, worked well in the deep caverns; so they began the arduous process of manoeuvring starship auxiliary tokamaks through the spaceport and down the endcap. When the first one came on-line operating at thirty-eight per cent efficiency, they knew they really did stand a chance.

Schedules were drawn up to install another dozen in the caverns, feeding their energy into the habitat's organic conductors. After two days' unstinting effort, the light-tube began to blaze with early-morning intensity. Noonday brightness was beyond them, but the resumption of near-normal light provided a huge psychological kick for every resident (curiously, that also included the ostracized ghosts). In tandem, the habitat's huge organs began to function again, ingesting and revitalizing the myriad fluids and gases utilized within the polyp.

Confidence guaranteed, the personality and its team set about investigating their continuum. Equipment was ransacked from physics labs and Magellanic Itg research centres and taken down to the caverns, where it was powered up. Crude space probes were prepared from the MSVs, sprouting simple sensor arrays. Outside that hot hive core of activity, the rest of the residents slowly began to gather themselves together mentally and physically. Although that promised to be possibly the longest journey of all.

But after a week, Valisk had regained a considerable amount of its most desired commodity: hope.

*

There was a broad grin smeared across Joshua's face during the entire approach manoeuvre; sometimes it came from admiration, sometimes plain affection. He knew he must look utterly gormless. Simply didn't care. *Lady Mac*'s external sensor array was feeding his neural nanonics a panoramic view of Jupiter's snarled pink and white cloudscape. Tranquillity formed a sharp midnight-black silhouette sailing across the storms.

The massive habitat looked completely undamaged, although its counter-rotating spaceport was darker than usual. The docking-bays, normally the focus of frantic time-pressure maintenance efforts, were shut down and lightless, leaving the curving ebony hulls of Adamist starships half-hidden in their eclipsed metal craters. Only the navigation and warning strobes were still flashing indomitably around the edges of the big silver-white disc.

'It's really here,' Ashly said in a stunned voice from across the bridge. 'That's, that's . . .'

'Outrageous?' Beaulieu suggested.

'Damn right it is,' Dahybi said. 'Nothing that big can be a starship. Nothing.'

Sarha laughed quietly. 'Face it, people; we're living in interesting times.'

Joshua was glad that the Mzu, her compatriots, and the agency operatives were all down in capsule D's lounge. After everything they'd been through, for the crew to show such bewilderment now was almost an admission of weakness, as if they couldn't cope with the rigours of starflight after all.

Jovian Flight Management Authority datavised their final approach vector, and Joshua reduced the fusion drives to a third of a gee as they crossed the invisible boundary where Tranquillity's traffic control centre took over guidance responsibility. Their escort of five voidhawks matched the manoeuvre with consummate elegance, unwilling to show anything other than perfection to Lagrange Calvert, a tribute to the modest debt Edenism owed him for Aethra.

If only they knew, Samuel said. They'd be flying parabolas of joy.

The Jovian sub-Consensus which dealt with classified security matters acknowledged the sentiment with an ironic frisson. Given our culture's fundamental nature, the restriction of knowledge is always a curious paradox to us, it said. However, in the case of the Alchemist, it is fully justified. Every Edenist does not need to know specific details, hence the requirement for my existence. And your job.

Ah yes, my job.

You are tired of it.

Very. As soon as the *Lady Macbeth* had emerged above Jupiter, Samuel had been conversing with the security sub-Consensus. It was the reason there had been relatively little fuss made about their arrival. First Admiral Aleksandrovich's decision had quickly been accepted by Consensus and Tranquillity.

After that, Samuel had immersed his mentality in Consensus, allowing his worries and tension to dissipate among his fellows. Sympathy for Edenists was so much more than a simple expression of compassion; with affinity he could feel it reaching into his mind, warmth and light dispelling the accumulation of icy shadows that were fear's legacy. No longer alone. Floating in a buoyant sea of welcome understanding. His thoughts began to flow in more regular patterns, and with that state achieved his body quietened. A sense of well-being claimed him; sharing himself with Consensus, entwined with the billions living contentedly above Jupiter, sporting with the voidhawks, he became whole again.

Yet this is the time we need you most, sub-Consensus replied. You have proved how valuable you are. Your skills are essential to this crisis.

I know. And if I'm needed for another assignment, I'll go. But I think after this, it's time I found a new career. Fifty-eight years of one thing is enough, even for a low-stress job.

We understand. There is no immediate field assignment awaiting you. We would like you to resume the observation of Dr Mzu for the time being.

I think that's a formality now.

Yes. But it will help to have you there in person. You have proved your worth to Monica Foulkes, she trusts you, and it is her report that will influence the Duke more than anything, and through him, the King. In this affair we must reassure the Kingdom we are playing fair.

Of course. Our alliance is a remarkable achievement, even in these circumstances.

Quite.

I'll stay with Mzu.

Thank you.

Samuel used his affinity to stay in communication with the voidhawk escort, so he could borrow the image of Jupiter from their sensor blisters. It was a much more satisfying view than the AV projection of *Lady Macbeth*'s sensor array. He watched their approach to Tranquillity, awed by the giant habitat, and not a little disconcerted by its star-jumping capability. It was so strange seeing it here, a familiar place, in a familiar location; but the two didn't belong together. He smiled at his own discomfort.

'You look happy,' Monica said gruffly.

They had taken acceleration couches slightly apart from Mzu and the *Beezling* survivors, the two groups still not quite trusting each other. During the flight they'd been formal and polite, nothing more.

Samuel waved at the lounge's AV pillar with its moiré sparkle, which was also showing the approach. 'I rather like the idea of thwarting Capone in such a fashion. A habitat that can perform a swallow manoeuvre! Who'd have thought it? Well, a Saldana did, obviously. I doubt many others would.'

'I didn't mean that,' Monica said. 'You were happy the moment we arrived here, and you've been getting happier ever since. I've been watching you.'

'Coming home is always comforting.'

'It's more than that, it's like you've mellowed out.'

'I have. Communion with my people and Consensus always does that. It's a valuable psychological relief. I don't relish being apart from it for so long.'

'Oh, God, here we go again, more propaganda.'

Samuel laughed. They might not have affinity, but he knew her well enough by now that it almost didn't make any difference. A pleasant revelation when dealing with an Adamist, let alone an ESA operative. 'I'm not trying to convert you, I'm just saying it's good for me. As you noticed.'

Monica grunted. 'You ask me, it's a weakness. You're dependent, and that can't be good in our profession. People should be capable of acting by themselves without any hang-ups. If I get wound up, I just run a stim program.'

'Ah yes, the natural human method of dealing with stress.'

'No worse than yours. Faster and cleaner, too.'

'There are many ways of being human.'

Monica stole a glance over at Mzu and Adul, still resentful at what they'd all been through. 'Inhuman, as well.'

'I think she's realized her folly. That's good. It's a sign of maturity to learn from one's mistakes, especially after living with them for so long. She may yet make a positive contribution to our society.'

'Maybe. But as far as I'm concerned, she'll need watching till the day she dies. And even then I'd be none too sure, she's that tricky. I still think the First Admiral was wrong, we should have zero-taued the lot of them.'

'Well, rest easy; I've already told Consensus I'll continue watching over her. I'm too old and jaded for another active assignment. Once this crisis is concluded I'll move on to something else. I always rather fancied wine growing; fine wine, of course. The kind of vintage that would satisfy the real oenophile. After all, I've tasted enough rubbish while I've travelled round the Confederation. Some of our habitats have superb vineyards, you know.'

Monica gave him a single surprised look, then snorted in amusement. 'Exactly who are you trying to fool?'

*

It certainly wasn't a hero's welcome. Only Collins bothered to report that the *Lady Macbeth* had docked, and they did it in a tone which suggested Joshua was slinking back home.

Five serjeants greeted Mzu and the *Beezling* survivors, escorting them to their new quarters. They weren't under arrest, Tranquillity explained, speaking through the constructs; but it laid down the guidelines for their residence quite austerely. A few friends were waiting for the crew in the bay's reception compartment. Dahybi and Beaulieu vanished off with them, heading for a bar. Sarha and Ashly took a commuter lift together. Two deputy managers from the Pringle Hotel greeted Shea and Kole, ushering them away to their rooms.

That left Joshua with Liol to take care of. He wasn't entirely sure what to do about that. They were still orbiting round each other, though it was a closer orbit now. A hotel was out, too cold, Liol was family after all. He just wished they'd managed to sort out the problem of *Lady Mac* and Liol's gung-ho claim. Though his brother had definitely become more conciliatory as the flight progressed. A good sign. It looked as though Liol would have to share his apartment. Well, at least he'd understand bachelor mess.

But as soon as Joshua air-swam out from their airlock tube, Ione was in front of him, toes pressed with ballerina grace on the compartment's stikpad. Doubts about Liol vanished. She was wearing a simple maroon polka-dot summer dress, ruffed gold-blond hair floating daintily. It made her seem girlish and elegant all at once. The sight of her like that summoned up memories warmer than any neural nanonics catalogued recollections could ever be.

She grinned knavishly, and held out both hands. Joshua caught hold and let her gently secure him. They kissed, a tingle lost somewhere between just good friends and old lovers. 'Well done,' she whispered.

'Thanks, I . . .' He frowned when he saw who was waiting behind her. Dominique. Dressed in a tight sleeveless black leather T-shirt that was tucked into white sports shorts. All curves and blatant athleticism. As overt as Ione was demure.

'Joshua, darling!' Dominique squealed happily. 'My God, you look so divine in a ship-suit. So well packaged. What can those naughty designers have been thinking of?'

'Er, hello, Dominique.'

'Hello?' She pouted with tragic disappointment. 'Come here, gorgeous.'

Arms that were disproportionately strong wrapped round him. Wide lips descended happily, a tongue wriggling into his mouth. Hair and pheromones tickled his nose, making him want to sneeze.

He was too embarrassed to resist. Then she stiffened suddenly. 'Oh *wow*, there's two of you.'

The embrace was broken. Dominique stared hungrily behind him, long fronds of blond hair writhing about.

'Um, this is my brother,' Joshua mumbled.

Liol gave her a languid grin, and bowed. It was a good manoeuvre considering he wasn't anchored to a stikpad. 'Liol Calvert, Josh's bigger brother.'

'Bigger.' Dominique's eyes reflected slivers of light like coquettish diamonds.

In some way he couldn't quite work out, Joshua was no longer between the two of them.

'Welcome to Tranquillity,' Dominique purred.

Liol took a hand gently and kissed her knuckles. 'Nice to be here. It looks spectacular so far.'

A small groan of dismay rumbled up from Joshua's throat.

'There's plenty more to see, and it gets a whole lot better.' Dominique's voice became so husky it was almost bass. 'If you want to risk it, that is.'

'I'm just a simple boy from a provincial asteroid; of course I'm looking forward to the delights of the big bad habitat.'

'Oh, we have several bad things you'll never find in your asteroid.'

'I can believe it.'

She crooked a finger in front of his nose. 'This way.'

The two of them levitated out of the hatch together.

'Hmm.' Ione smiled with sly contentment. 'Eight seconds total; that's pretty fast even for Dominique.'

Joshua looked back from the hatch to her amused blue eyes. He realized they were alone. 'Oh, very neat,' he remarked in admiration.

'Let's just say, I had a premonition they might hit it off.'

'She'll eat him alive. You know that, don't you?'

'You never complained.'

'How did you know about him?'

'While you were on your approach flight I was busy assimilating memories from the serjeants. The two that are left, anyway. You had a hell of a time.'

'Yeah.'

'You'll do all right, you and Liol. Just a bit too similar for comfort at the start, that's all.'

'Could be.' He squirmed uncomfortably.

She rested a hand on each shoulder, smiling softly. 'But not identical.'

There was nothing much said while they rode the commuter lift down the spaceport spindle. Just looks and smiles. Shared knowledge of what was to come when they got back to her apartment. Coming from shared relief that they'd both survived, and maybe wanting a return to times past for the reassurance that would bring. It wouldn't be the same, but it would still be familiar. It wasn't until they got into a tube carriage that they kissed properly. Joshua reached up to stroke her cheek.

'Your hand,' she exclaimed. A whole rush of noxious memories were bubbling forth: the corridor in Ayacucho, Joshua on all fours in the slush, his hand blackened and charred, the two girls clinging together, whimpering, and the furious Arab snarling then horrified as the serjeant opened fire. The roar of bullets and stink of hot blood. Not a sensevise she'd accessed, remote and vaguely unreal; she'd been a genuine witness to the actual event and always would be.

Joshua took his hand away from her face as she gave it a concerned look. A medical nanonic package had formed a thin glove to cover his fingers and palm. 'I'm OK. The navy medics matched and grafted some muscle tissue; they've had a lot of practice with this kind of injury. It'll be fine in another week.'

'Good.' She kissed the tip of his nose.

'You're worried about a couple of fingers; I was scared shitless about Tranquillity. Jesus, Ione, you've no idea what it was like finding you gone. I thought you'd been possessed just like Valisk.'

Her broad freckled face crinkled with mild bafflement. 'Hmm, interesting. I get surprised by other people being surprised. All right, it could have been possession. But you of all people should have worked it out. I as good as told you.'

'When?'

'The very first night we met. I said that Grandfather Michael believed that we would eventually encounter whatever the Laymil had come up against. Of course, back then everyone thought it was an external threat, which was a reasonable enough assumption. Unfortunately, that also meant that Tranquillity was likely to be the first to confront it. Either we'd find it among the Ruin Ring, or it would return to Mirchusko, the last place it had visited. Grandfather knew we probably wouldn't be able to beat it with conventional weapons, he hoped we'd discover what it was so we could develop some kind of defence in time. But just in case . . .'

'He wanted to be able to run,' Joshua concluded.

'Yes. So he ordered a modification to the habitat's genome.'

'And nobody realized? Jesus.'

'Why should they? There's a ring of energy patterning cells around the shell, at the end of the circumfluous sea. If you look at the habitat from the outside, the ridge containing the water is actually a kilometre wider than the sea itself. But who's going to measure?'

'Hidden in plain view.'

'Quite. Michael didn't see any reason to advertise the fact. Our royal cousins know . . . I assume, anyway. The files are stored in the Apollo Palace archives. It gives us the ability to jump away from trouble, a long way away. I chose Jupiter this time, because we considered Jupiter safe. But ultimately Tranquillity could jump across the galaxy in thousand light-year swallows, and the possessed would never be able to follow us. And if the crisis gets that bad, I'll do it.'

'Now I get it. That's how you knew the *Udat*'s wormhole vector.'

'Yes.'

When the tube carriage arrived at Ione's apartment Joshua was feeling comfort as much as excitement. Neither of them took the lead, asking or pressing the other, they simply went to the bedroom because it was what the moment had ordained. They both slipped out of their clothes, admiring each other. Almost dreamily, Joshua tasted her breasts again, regretting how long it had been. Both of them showed off the old skills, knowing precisely what to do to each other's flesh to invigorate and arouse.

Only once, when she knelt in front of him, did Ione speak. 'Don't use your nanonics,' she whispered. Her tongue licked along his cock, teeth closing delicately on one ball. 'Not this time. This should be natural.'

He agreed, complying, making the encounter raw, and relishing every second of their performance. It was new. The big jelly-mattress bed was the same, so were the positions they accomplished. This time, though, they had honesty, openly celebrating the physical power they exerted over each other. It was as emotionally satisfying as it was sensually rewarding.

Afterwards they spent the night sleeping in each other's arms, snuggled up like childhood siblings. The loitering contentment made breakfast a civilized meal. They wrapped themselves in huge house robes to sit at a big old oak table in a room mocked up to resemble a conservatory. Palms, ferns, and delecostas grew out of moss-coated clay pots, their multiplying stems interlaced with broad iron trellises to produce verdant walls. The illusion was almost perfect but for the small neon-bright fish swimming past on the other side of the glass.

House chimps served them scrambled parizzat eggs, with English tea and thick-cut toast. While they ate, they accessed various news broadcasts from Earth and the O'Neill Halo, following the Confederation's response to Capone, the build-up of forces for the Mortonridge Liberation, rumours of the possessed spreading among the asteroids, appearing in star systems previously thought clean.

'Quarantine busters,' Ione said sharply at the item on Koblat being taken out of the universe. 'The idiots in those asteroids are still letting them dock. At this rate the Assembly will have to shut down interplanetary flights as well.'

Joshua looked away from the AV projection. 'It won't make any difference.'

'It will! They have to be isolated.'

He sighed, regretful at how easily the mood had gone. Forgetting everything for a day had been so comfortable. 'You don't understand. It's like saying you'll be safe if Tranquillity jumps across the galaxy where the possessed can't find you. Don't you see, they'll always find you. They are what you become. You, me, everyone.'

'Not everyone, Joshua. Laton mentioned some kind of journey through the afterworld, he didn't believe he'd be trapped in the beyond. The Kiint have as good as admitted we don't all wind up there.'

'Good, build on that. Find out why.'

'How?' She gave him a measured look. 'This isn't like you.'

'I think it is. I think it took that possessed to make me realize.'

'You mean that Arab in Ayacucho?'

'Yeah. No kidding, Ione, I was staring death and what comes after right in the face. Bound to make you stop and wonder. You can't solve everything with direct action. That's what makes this Mortonridge Liberation so ridiculous.'

'Don't I know it. That whole miserable campaign is nothing more than a propaganda exercise.'

'Yeah. Though I expect the people they do de-possess will be grateful enough.'

'Joshua! You can't have it both ways.'

He grinned at her over the rim of a huge tea cup. 'We're going to have to, though, aren't we? There has to be some solution to satisfy both sides.'

'Right,' she said cautiously.

5

In any given month there would be between two and seven armada storms rampaging across Earth's surface, a relentless assault they'd persevered with for over five hundred years. Like so many things, their name had become everyday currency. Few knew or cared its origin.

It had begun with chaos theory: the soundbite assertion that one butterfly flapping its wings in a South American rainforest would start a hurricane in Hong Kong. Then in the twenty-first century came cheap fusion, and mass industrialization; entire continents elevated themselves to Western-style levels of consumerism within two decades. Billions of people found themselves with the credit to buy a multitude of household appliances, cars, exotic holidays; they moved into new, better, bigger homes, adopting lifestyles which amplified their energy consumption by orders of magnitude. Hungry to service their purchasing power, companies built cities of new factories. Consumer and producer alike pumped out vast quantities of waste heat, agitating the atmosphere beyond the worst-case scenarios of most computer models.

It was after the then largest storm in history raged across the eastern Pacific in early 2071 that a tabloid newscable presenter said it must have taken a whole armada of butterflies flapping their wings to start such a brute. The name stuck.

The storm which had swept up from mid-Atlantic to swamp New York was ferocious even by the standards of the twenty-seventh century. Its progress had been under observation for hours by the arcology's anxious weather defence engineers. When it did arrive, their response systems were already on-line. It looked as though a ragged smear of night was sliding across the sky. The clouds were so thick and dense no light could boil through to illuminate their underbelly. That was until the lightning began. Then the rotund tufts could sometimes be distinguished, streaked with leaden grey strata as they undulated overhead at menacing speed. The energy levels contained within would prove fatal for any unprotected building. Consequently, the ability to deflect or withstand the storms was the prime requirement of any design brought before the New York Civil Engineering Review Board for a building permit. It was the one criterion which could never be corroded by backhanders or political pressure.

The tip of every megatower was crowned with high-wattage lasers whose beams were powerful enough to puncture the heart of the heavy clouds. They etched out straight channels of ionized air, cajoling the lightning to discharge directly into the superconductor grids masking the tower structure. Every tower blazed like a conical solar flare above the dome residents, spitting out residual globules of violet plasma.

Amid them fell the rain. Fist-sized drops hurled out by a furious wind to hammer against the domes. Molecular-binding-force generators were switched on to reinforce the transparent hexagons against a kinetic fusillade which had the force to abrade raw steel. At the height of the storm, the volume of water supported by the domes more than quadrupled their weight. With a diameter of twenty kilometres to traverse, an endless procession of waves to rival any found at a surfer's beach rolled down the slopes. At the edges, the surge of water foamed into the intake grilles of impellers which forced it down pipes large enough to qualify as vertical rivers.

The noise from this barrage of elements drummed through the dome to shake the gridwork of carbotanium struts supporting the metro transit rails. Most above-ground traffic had shut down anyway. Right across the arcology, emergency crews were on full standby in case of a breakthrough. Police were alert for nervy criminals. Lighting along the streets and inside buildings was proving slightly erratic. Even the shield of lasers and superconductors was no guarantee against power spikes in such conditions. In such times, sensible people went home or to bars and waited until sharp slivers of pewter light started to carve up the clouds, signalling the end of the deluge. A time when fear was heightened. When more primitive thoughts were brought to the fore.

A good time. Useful.

Quinn looked up at the old building which was home to the High Magus of New York, content with what he saw. Barely eight hundred metres high, the Leicester skyscraper was the kind of graceless affair so idealized by design teams dominated by accountants, where every proposed adornment or hint of originality was scrutinized for cost effectiveness and obediently rejected for the most minor frivolity. Unembellished, a giant tombstone with windows, one of forty cloned tombstones that formed a fence around Hackett Park in Dome Two.

High overhead, sheets of lightning hurtled between the six mega-towers standing guard around the dome, flicking the shadows round in harsh random increments. For a moment, Quinn could believe that the Leicester was actually on the move, sheer walls lurching about. Lights which backlit over half of the thousands of windows were fading in and out as though they were flames caught in a draft rather than modern panel illumination. He gained a curt satisfaction from that, the storm would provide a degree of cover this night.

The sect members were piling out of the vans behind him. Only ten possessed, so far. A manageable number for what he had in mind. The rest, the acolytes and initiates, followed obediently, in awe of the apostles of evil who now commanded them.

Faith, Quinn mused, was a strange power. They had committed their lives to the sect, never questioning its gospels. Yet in all of that time, they had the reassurance of routine, the notion that God's Brother would never actually manifest himself. The bedrock of every religion, that your god is a promise, never to be encountered in this life, this universe.

Now the souls were returning, owning the power to commit dark miracles. The acolytes had fallen into stupefaction rather than terror, the last doubt vanquished. Condemned as the vilest outcasts, they now knew they'd been right all along. That they were going to win. Whatever they were ordered to do, they complied unquestioningly.

Quinn motioned the first team forward. Led by Wener, the three eager acolytes scampered down a set of steps at the base of the wall, and clustered round the disused basement door at the bottom. A codebuster block was applied, then a programmable silicon probe was worked expertly into the crack between the door and the frame. The silicon flexed its way under the ageing manual bolts, then began to reformat its shape, pushing them back. Within thirty seconds, the way in was open. No alarms, and no give-away use of energistic power.

Quinn stepped through.

The difference between the headquarters and the dingy centre on Eighty-Thirty Street surprised even Quinn. At first he even thought he might have the wrong place, but Dobbie, who now possessed Magus Garth's body, reassured him this was indeed where they should be. The corridors and chambers were an inverse mirror of the Vatican's splendour. Rich fittings and extravagant artwork, but sybaritic rather than warmly exquisite, celebrating depravity and pain.

'Fuck, look at this place,' Wener muttered as they marched down one of the corridors. Sculptures took bestiality as their theme, featuring both mythical and xenoc creatures, while paintings showed the saintly and revered from history being violated and sacrificed on the altars of the Light Bringer.

'You should take a good look,' Quinn said. 'It's yours. Those hours ripping off citizens and pushing illegals on the street, that paid for all this. You live in shit, so the High Magus can live like a Christian bishop. Nice, isn't it.'

Wener and the other acolytes glowered round at the perverse grandeur, envious and angry. They split up, as arranged, one of the possessed leading each group of acolytes, securing the exits and strategic areas, the weapons cache. Quinn went straight for the High Magus. Three times he encountered acolytes and priests scurrying along the corridors. They were all given the same simple choice: follow me, or be possessed.

They took one look at the black robe, listening to the voice whispering out of the seemingly empty hood, and capitulated. One of them even gave a mad little laugh of relief, a strong sense of vindication flooding his mind.

The High Magus was taking a bath when Quinn strode into his quarters. It could have been the penthouse of some multistellar corporation president, certainly there was little evidence of idolatrous worship amongst the opulence. Much to Wener's disappointment he didn't even have naked servant girls to wash him. Slimline domestic mechanoids stood quietly among the white and blue furnishings. His one concession to turpitude appeared to be the goblet he was drinking a seventeen-year-old red wine out of, its vulvic influences impossible to ignore. Islands of lime-green bubbles drifted round his round frame, giving off a scent of sweet pine.

He was already frowning as Quinn glided over the gold-flecked marble to the sunken bath, presumably forewarned by the failure of his neural nanonics. His eyes widened at the invasion, then narrowed as the eccentric delegation stared down at him.

'You're a possessed,' he said directly to Quinn.

There was no panic in the mind of the High Magus, which surprised Quinn, if anything the old man appeared curious. 'No, I am the Messiah of our Lord.'

'Really?'

The mocking irony of the tone caused the hem of Quinn's robe to stir. 'You will obey me, or I will have your fat shit body possessed by someone more worthy.'

'More compliant, you mean.'

'Don't fuck with me.'

'I have no intention of fucking with you or anyone else.'

Quinn was puzzled by this whole exchange. The original calmness he could sense in the High Magus was slowly replaced by weariness. The High Magus took another sip of the wine.

'I'm here to bring Night to the Earth as our Lord bids,' Quinn said.

'He *bids* nothing of the sort, you pathetic little prick.'

Quinn's ashen face materialized to thrust out of his hood.

The High Magus laughed out loud at the shock and anger he saw there, and committed suicide. Without any noise or hysterics, his body froze, then slowly slithered down the side of the bath. It rolled to one side, and floated inertly on the surface, white bloated rims of fat bobbing among the green bubbles. The wine goblet sank, a red stain marking where it had vanished.

'What are you doing?' Quinn shouted at the departing soul. He sensed a final sneer as the retreating wisps of energy evaporated amid dimensional folds. His claw hands shot out of the voluminous sleeves, as if to pull the essence of the High Magus back to face judgement. 'Shit!' he gasped. The magus must have been demented.

Nobody, *nobody* went into the beyond, not now they knew for sure what awaited them there.

'Asshole,' Wener grunted. Along with the other acolytes, he was perturbed by the death. Trying not to show it.

Quinn knelt down at the side of the bath, searching the corpse with eyes and eldritch senses for the mechanism of its demise. There were the usual weapons implants, he could perceive those all right, hard splinters among the softer grain of organic matter, even the neural nanonics were discernible. But Quinn's energistic power had nullified them. What then? What instrument could effect an instantaneous and painless suicide? And more curiously, why was the High Magus equipped with it?

He straightened slowly, retracting his head and arms back within his cloak's veil of night. 'It doesn't matter,' he told his agitated followers. 'God's Brother knows how to deal with traitors, the beyond is not a refuge for those who fail Him.'

A dozen heads nodded in eager acceptance before him. 'Now go and bring them to me,' he said.

The acolytes scattered to do his bidding. They rounded up everyone in the headquarters, and herded them into the temple. It was a vaulted chamber nestled at the core of the Leicester, a baroque fabrication of gilded pillars and crudely cut stone blocks. Six giant pentagons were etched on the curving ceiling, emitting a dull crimson glow. The grumble of the storm was just audible, a bass reverberation sneaking through the Leicester to give the floor a faint vibration.

Quinn stood beside the altar as the captives were ushered up to him one at a time. Every time he repeated the simple choice of futures: follow me, or be possessed. Merely claiming they would submit was no use. Quinn interrogated their innermost beliefs and fears before passing his final decree. He wasn't surprised by how many failed. Inevitably, this far up the sect hierarchy, they had grown soft. Still evil, still exploiting the soldiers below them, but not for the right reasons. Maintaining their own status and comforts had evolved into their dominant urge, not a willingness to further the cause of the Light Brother. Traitors.

He made them suffer for their crime. Over thirty were chained to the altar and vanquished. By now he had become proficient in opening a fissure back into the beyond; but more importantly he'd learned how to impose his own presence around the opening, valiantly guarding the gateway from the unworthy. Even in their utter desperation for escape, many souls turned aside from such a custodian. Those who did emerge conformed to Quinn's ideal. Nearly all of them had been sect members while they were alive.

He gathered them together after the ceremony, explaining what God's Brother had decided for them. 'We need more than one arcology to bring Night to this world,' he told them. 'So I'm leaving you this one for yourselves. Don't piss this opportunity away. I want you to take it over, but carefully, not like the way the possessed do on other planets, even Capone. Those dickheads just rush up and head butt every town they come across. And each time, the cops swoop down and pick them off. This time it's gonna be different. You've got the acolytes worshipping the ground you shit on. Use them. Moving around is what lets those fucking AIs sniff you out. You mess with processors and power cables just by being near them. So don't go near them. Stay in the sect centres and get the acolytes to bring people to you.'

'Which people?' Dobbie asked. 'I understand how we don't gotta move about. But, shit, Quinn, there's over three hundred million people in New York. The acolytes can't bring them all to us.'

'They can bring the ones that count, the police captains and technical guys, the ones gonna cause you grief. Or at least knock them out, stop them from reporting that you've arrived in town. That's all I want from you right now. Get yourselves established. There's a sect centre in every dome, take them over and hole up there for a while. Live like a fucking king, I'm not saying don't enjoy yourself. But I want you ready, I want you to build up a coven of possessed in each dome. Loyal ones, you all know how fucking important discipline is. We're going strategic. Learn where the major fusion generators are, hunt down the fresh-water stations and the sewage plants, see which intersections the transport system depends on, track down critical nodes in the communication net. The acolytes will know all this crap, or they can find out. Then when I give the word, you smash each of those sites into lava. You paralyse the whole fucking arcology with terrorism, bring it to its knees. That way the cops won't be able to organize any resistance when we emerge to claim glory for Him. You come out into the open and start possessing others, and you turn them loose. Nobody can run, there's nowhere to go, no outside. Possessed always win on asteroids, this is no different, just bigger, is all.'

'The new possessed, they won't worship God's Brother,' someone said. 'We can chose a few who will to start with, but if we turn them loose, there's no way millions of them is going to do like we say.'

'Of course not,' Quinn said. 'Not at first, anyway. They have to be forced into this, like I did to Nyvan. Haven't you worked it out yet? What's going to happen to an arcology with three hundred million possessed living in it?'

'Nothing,' Dobbie said in puzzlement. 'It won't work.'

'Right,' Quinn purred. 'Nothing's going to work. I'm going to visit as many arcologies as I can, and I'm going to seed all of them with possessed. And they're all going to collapse, because energistic power breaks the machinery. The domes won't be able to hold off the weather any more, there isn't going to be any food, or water. Nothing. Not even forty billion possessed wishing at once are going to be able to change that. They'll shift Earth into another realm, but it still won't make any difference. Just being somewhere else isn't going to put food on the table, won't restart the machines. That's when *it* will happen. The revelation that they have nowhere else to turn. Our Lord will have won their minds.' He lifted his hands, and allowed a pallid smile to show from his hood. 'Forty billion possessors, and the forty billion they possess. Eighty billion souls screaming into the Night for help. Don't you see? It's a cry so strong, so full of anguish and fear, that it will bring Him. Finally, He will emerge from the Night, bringing light to those who have come to love Him.' Quinn laughed at the astonishment on their faces, and dark delight in their minds.

'How long?' Dobbie asked avidly. 'How long we gotta wait?'

'A month, maybe. It'll take me a while to visit all the arcologies. But I'll penetrate them all in the end. Wait for my word.' The silhouette of his robe began to fade. Outlines of the furniture behind him started to show through. Then he was gone. A cold breeze drifted across the chamber, perturbing the shallow gasps of consternation that echoed from the dismayed disciples.

*

The *Mindori* approached Monterey at a steady half-gee acceleration. Two hundred kilometres ahead, the asteroid's features were resolving, crumpled dust-grey rock speared by metallic spires and panels. It was surrounded by a swarm of pearl-white specks that flashed and glinted in the tenacious sunlight. The Organization fleet: over six hundred Adamist warships floating in attendance while small service craft flitted among them. Each one a unique knot in Rocio Condra's distortion field.

Gliding among them were the more subtle interference patterns of other distortion fields. Valisk's hellhawks were here. Rocio called out in welcome. Those who bothered to acknowledge his arrival were subdued. The emotional content simmering within most of his fellows was one of grudging acceptance. Rocio accepted it reluctantly. It was what he'd been expecting.

Glad to see you found your way back to us, Hudson Proctor said. **What have you got?**

The affinity link provided Rocio an opening to the man's eyes. He was in one of the docking-ledge lounges, overlooking the pedestals where several hellhawks were perched. The room had been altered into an executive-style office. Kiera Salter was sitting at a broad desk, her head coming up to give him a hard, enquiring stare.

Deadnight kids, Rocio said. **I haven't told them Valisk has gone.**

Good, good.

'The Organization hasn't got any real use for that kind of waster trash,' Kiera said as Hudson repeated his silent conversation. 'Dock here and disembark them. They'll be dealt with appropriately.'

And what about us? Rocio asked mildly. **What do the hellhawks do now?**

'I'll have you assigned to fleet support duties,' Kiera said impassively. 'Capone is preparing another invasion. The hellhawks are becoming essential to ensure viability.'

I don't wish to fly combat duties any more, thank you. This starship is proving an excellent host for my soul, I have no intention of endangering it, especially now you have no reserve body for me to inherit.

Kiera's answering smile portrayed regret. It wasn't an emotion Hudson relayed via affinity, keeping the exchange scrupulously neutral.

'I'm afraid we're effectively on a war footing,' Kiera said. 'Which means that wasn't a request.'

Are you trying to order me?

'I'm offering you one simple choice. You do as I tell you, or you fuck off back to the Edenists right now. You know why that is? Because we're the only two who can feed you. I am now in full command of the only possessed-owned nutrient supply in this star system. Me, not Capone and the Organization, me. If you want to prevent that excellent host of yours from expiring from malnutrition, you do exactly what I ask, and in return you'll be permitted to dock and ingest as much of that goo as you can hold. No one else can provide you with that, non-possessed asteroids will blow you away with their SD platforms before you get within a hundred kilometres. Only the Edenists can supply you. And they've got their price, too, as I'm sure they've told you. If you cooperate with them, it'll be to help understand the nature of the interface with the beyond. They'll find out how to banish us. You and I will both be zapped back into that infernal oblivion. So decide, Rocio; where your loyalty lies, who you're going to fly for. I'm not asking for you and me to be friends, I want to know if you'll obey, that's all. And you will tell me now.'

Rocio opened his affinity to converse with the other hellhawks. **Is this what she holds over us?**

Yes, they answered. **There is no third alternative that we can see.**

This is monstrous. I'm happy with this form. I don't want to risk it in Capone's egotistical conquests.

Then protect it, you pitiful bastard, Etchells said. **Stop whingeing and fight for what you believe in. Some of you are so pathetic, you don't deserve what you've got.**

Rocio remembered Etchells, always eager to intercept the void-hawks observing Valisk. When Capone had first approached Kiera for help, he'd been excited and anxious to become involved in the conflict.

Piss off, you fascist bigot.

A coward, and a way with words, Etchells retorted. **No wonder you're so insecure.**

Rocio closed his affinity with the offensive hellhawk. **I'll dock at Monterey and offload the passengers,** he told Hudson and Kiera. **What kind of fleet support are you proposing?**

Kiera's smile lacked grace. 'While the fleet is here, all hellhawks are on a rota to interdict the spy globes and stealthed bombs. The voidhawks have just about given up that nonsense, but they're still probing our defences, so we have to remain vigilant. Apart from that, there's also some communication duties, VIP flights and collecting cargo from asteroids. Nothing too demanding.'

And when Capone finds a new planet to invade?

'You fly escort for the fleet, and then you help them eliminate the target world's strategic-defence network.'

Very well. I will be docking in another eight minutes, please have a pedestal ready to receive me. Rocio abandoned Hudson Proctor's mind, and analysed what had been said. The situation was almost what he'd been expecting. Controlling the supply of nutrient fluid was the only practical way of binding the hellhawks to the Organization. What he hadn't predicted was Kiera still being in charge. She'd obviously come to the same conclusion about coercion.

A few queries to a couple of friendlier hellhawks, and he found that Etchells had visited most of the asteroid settlements in the New California system, blasting their nutrient production machinery. Kiera had ordered the flight, and Hudson had been on board to make sure everything ran smoothly. Kiera and the Organization were still separate. She was using her control over the hellhawks to maintain her status as a power player. Scheming little bitch. And it would be the hellhawks who paid for that status.

Rocio's ersatz beak parted slightly. Even though he couldn't manage a modestly contented smile any more, the intent was there. Forced obedience always generated discontent. Allies wouldn't be hard to find. He abandoned his favoured bird-image just as he slipped round Monterey's counter-rotating spaceport. The *Mindori* settled its hull on one of the docking-ledge pedestals, and gratefully received the hose nozzles probing its underbelly. Muscle membranes contracted round the seal rings, and the thick nutrient fluid pulsed its way up into the nearly depleted reserve bladders. The whole process served to emphasize just how vulnerable the giant bitek starship was. After such a long flight, Rocio was enduring a strong subconscious pressure to ingest again, and he had absolutely no control over the substance pumped along the pipes. Kiera could be giving him anything, from water to an elaborate poison. It tasted fine, to his limited internal sense and filter glands, but he could never be quite sure. His plight was intolerable. So what? he asked himself, bitterly. Blackmail, of course, always was.

The rebellion began at once. Rocio ordered his bitek processor array to open a channel into the asteroid's communication network. Access to any defence-critical system was denied; the Organization had protected its electronic architecture as thoroughly as the New California defence force it had usurped. However, that left a lot of civil memory cores and sensors to access. He began to analyse what information he was permitted, and hooked in to various cameras to look round.

A large bus trundled over the rock ledge, its flaccid elephant-trunk airlock tube snuggling up to the *Mindori*'s life-support section. Inside the hellhawk, the Deadnight kids raced through their cabins, snatching up their bags. A long, agitated queue formed outside the main airlock hatch. Choi-Ho and Maxim Payne stood at the end, smiling placidly.

When the hatch swung open amid a hiss of white vapour, the kids let out a collective gasp of delight. Kiera herself was waiting for them. Gorgeous body clad in a small scarlet dress, hair tumbling over her honey-coloured shoulders. And that mesmerizing smile was every bit as bright in real life as it was in the recording. They filed past her in a numb daze, eyes wide with awe as she said hello to each and every one of them. All she got was a few mumbled words in return.

'That was easy enough,' she said to Choi-Ho and Maxim at the end. 'We had a couple of flights end in riots when they realized they weren't at Valisk. For no-hopers, they can be vicious little shits. There was a lot of damage, and it's hard getting replacement components for these life-support modules.'

'So what do we do now?' Maxim asked.

'I always need good officers. Or you can join the Organization if you like. Capone is keen to recruit soldiers to enforce his rule down on the planet. You'll be on the cutting edge of his empire,' she said sweetly.

'I'm good at what I do now,' Choi-Ho said levelly. Maxim quickly agreed.

Kiera observed their minds. There was a tang of resentment, of course, there always was. But they'd capitulated. 'All right, you're in. Now let's get these loser brats into the asteroid. They won't be suspicious if we stay with them.'

She was right. Her presence alone was enough to fool the besotted Deadnights, none of them ever questioning why the bus windows were blanked out. It wasn't until they walked through the next set of airlocks that suspicions started to bubble up. They were all from asteroid settlements, and the equipment here was very similar to what they thought they'd left behind. Habitats were supposed to be different, devoid of this many mechanical contrivances. With the elder ones slightly puzzled now, they trooped into the main arrivals hall. The Organization gangsters were waiting. It only took two acts of violence against the bravest rebels to quell any further resistance. They were quickly segregated and classified according to the charts Leroy and Emmet had provided.

Amid a welter of tearful and frightened crying, individuals were hauled off into the corridors. As the Organization was still very male dominated, the older boys were all taken down to Patricia Mangano and imminent possession by new soldiers. With them went the less attractive girls. Prettier girls were dispatched to the brothel where they would service the Organization's soldiers and non-possessed followers. The children (and definition was difficult, puberty plus a couple of years appeared to be the deciding factor) were flown down to the planet, where Leroy paraded them in front of the rover reporters, claiming their salvation from Deadnight as more humanitarian charity on Al's behalf. The distorted image of a weeping seventeen-year-old girl being shoved along by a machine-gun-toting gangster in a brown pinstripe suit vanished from the processor block's screen in a hail of static.

'I can't find any further working cameras in that section,' Rocio announced. 'Would you like me to return to the arrivals hall?'

Jed had to work hard against his tightening throat muscles. 'No. That's enough.' When the hellhawk possessor had shown them the first pictures snatched from cameras, Jed had wanted to scramble out of their cramped refuge. Kiera was actually on board! A mere thirty metres away from him. He'd suddenly wondered what the hell he was doing, crouched painfully between cold, condensation-smeared tanks with loops of grimy cable wiping his forehead. The sight of her brought back all the old rapture. And she was smiling. Kiera would make the angels envious of her beauty and compassion.

Then he heard bonkers Gerald reciting, 'Monster, monster, monster, monster,' like it was some kind of freaky spell.

Beth was rubbing the old fart's arm, all full of sympathy, saying, 'It's OK, you'll get her back, you will.'

Jed wanted to shout out how barmy the pair of them were. But by then the last of the Deadnights were in the bus, and Kiera's smile was gone. In its place was a hideously alien expression of contempt verging on cruelty. The words which came from her lips were cold and harsh. Rocio had been telling the truth.

Despite the evidence, that lost part of Jed's heart had wanted to believe in his divine savour and her promises of a better world. Now he knew that was gone. Worse than that, it had never existed. Even Digger had been right. Bloody Digger, for Christ's sake! He was just a dumb stupid waster kid trying to score the ultimate escape trip from Koblat. If Beth and the girls hadn't been in there with him, he knew he would have burst into tears. For Jed, not even the scenes in the arrivals hall were as horrific as that final moment when Kiera's smile vanished.

By the time Rocio Condra's face reappeared on the block, the girls were sniffling quietly, arms around each other. Beth made no attempt to hide the tears meandering down her cheeks. Gerald had shrunk back into his usual uncommunicative self.

'I'm sorry,' Rocio said. 'But I did suspect that something like this was going to happen. If it's of any comfort, I am in a similar position.'

'Similar?' Beth grunted. 'Comfort? I knew some of those girls, damn you. How can you compare what they're going to go through with what you've got to do? That's not patronizing, that's sickening.'

'They are being forced to prostitute themselves with men in order to survive. I have to risk my life and that of my host in hostile combat conditions if I wish to continue my existence in this universe. Yes, I have to say there is similarity, whether you see it or not.'

Beth glared at the processor block through her misery. She'd never felt so low before, not even when those men had grabbed her that time when she met Gerald.

'So now what?' Jed asked dolefully.

'I'm not certain,' Rocio answered. 'Obviously, we must find a new source of nutrient fluid for myself and those hellhawks that share my beliefs. I shall have to gather a lot more information before that option opens itself.'

'Do we have to stay in here the whole time?'

'No, of course not. There is no one inside the life-support section, you may come out now.'

It took a hot, aggravating five minutes to wriggle free from the confines of the cramped under-floor service ducts. Jed was the first to extricate himself from the hatch in the washroom floor. He quickly helped the others free. They wandered out into the central corridor, glancing about anxiously, not quite believing Rocio when he said they were alone.

They stood in the big forward lounge, looking out of the long window at the docking-ledge. The row of pedestals stretched away, gradually curving above them, silver mushrooms sprouting from the grizzled rock, each one bathed in a pool of yellow light. But for three other docked hellhawks suckling their nutrient fluid from the hoses, it could have been a post-industrial wasteland. Some technicians were working on the cargo cradles of one craft, but apart from that, nothing moved.

'So we just wait,' Beth said, flopping down into a settee.

Jed pressed his nose to the transparency, trying to see the rock wall at the back of the ledge. 'Guess so.'

'I'm hungry,' Gari complained.

'Then go eat,' Jed said. 'I'm not going to stop you.'

'Come with us.'

He turned from the window, seeing his sister's apprehensive expression, and smiled reassuringly. 'Sure, kid, no problem.'

The galley was one compartment Rocio hadn't tried to modify with his energistic imagination, leaving the contemporary metal and composite surfaces undisturbed. However, they'd plainly been pillaged by some passing barbarian army. A cascade of empty sachets were littering the floor, stuck in place by treacle-like liquids. Storage cabinet doors swung open, revealing empty spaces. The timer on an induction oven bleeped away relentlessly.

A ten minute search turned up five cans of drinking chocolate, a sachet of unhydrated oatmeal cakes, and a serve-three pizza with extra anchovies.

Jed surveyed the cache with dismay. 'Oh, Jeeze, there's nothing left to eat.' He knew what that meant, one of them would have to sneak into the asteroid to find some supplies. Zero guesses who'd get picked for that doozy.

*

Jay woke up in a wonderfully soft bed, wrapped inside a smooth cocoon of clean cotton sheets smelling faintly of lavender. It was that warm drowsy state which always followed a really long, deep sleep. She squirmed round a little, enjoying the contentment of being utterly at peace. Some small object had managed to wedge itself under her shoulder, harder than the luxurious pillow. Her hand closed round it, pulling it out. Coarse fur tickled her fingers. Frowning, squinting she held up the . . . doll. Tatty old thing. She smiled cosily, and put Prince Dell down beside her. Snuggling into the mattress.

Her eyes flipped wide open. A fog of hoary light was curving round a pair of plain navy-blue curtains. It illuminated a neat wooden room, with its sloping ceiling supported by a scaffold of naked A-frame beams. The tight-fitting wall boards had all been painted a silky green, bedecked with picture frames that were mainly landscape watercolours, though there were several sepia photos of people in history-text clothes. A glazed pedestal washbasin with brass taps stood in the corner, a towel hanging beside it. There was a wicker chair at the foot of the bed, with a pair of fat cushions crammed into it. The sound of waves rolling gently onto a beach could just be heard in the background.

Jay flung back the sheet and slithered down off the bed. Her feet touched a warm carpet, and she padded over to the window. She lifted a corner of the curtain, then pulled it wide open. The beach was outside: a fringe of grass blending into white sands, followed by gorgeous turquoise water stretching out to a mild horizon haze. A clear azure sky rose from the other side of the haze, cut in half by that incredible curving line of brilliant silver-white planets. She laughed in amazed delight. It was real, really real.

The bedroom door opened into the chalet's hallway. Jay ran along it, out onto the veranda. The hem of her nightie flapped around bare feet, Prince Dell was clutched in one hand. Outside, the heat and salty humidity gusted over her along with the intense sunlight. She flew down the steps and onto the grass, dancing round and whooping. The sand was hot enough to make her jump up and down before retreating back onto the grass. She gave the glittering water an exasperated look. How lovely it would have been to dive right in. Haile was going to adore this place.

'Good morning to you, young Jay Hilton.'

Jay jumped, and turned round. One of the purple globes she remembered from last night was floating half a metre above her head. Her nose wrinkled up in bemusement. It seemed to be the victim of a talented graffiti artist who'd inflicted two black and white cartoon eyes rimmed with black-line eyebrows; more black lines defined a pug nose, while the mouth was a single curve sealed by smile commas. 'What are you?' she asked.

'Well, waddaya know, my name's Mickey. I'm a universal provider. But I'm a special one, coz I'm all yours.' The mouth jerked up and down in time with its voice.

'Oh yeah?' Jay asked suspiciously. That silly face was far too happy for her liking. 'What does a universal provider do, then?'

'Why, I provide, of course.'

'You're a machine.'

'Guess so,' it said with goofy pleasure.

'I see. So what do you provide?'

'Whatever you want. Any material object, including food.'

'Don't be stupid. You're tiny, what if I wanted a . . . a vac-train carriage.'

'Why would you want one of those?'

Jay sneered at it smugly. 'I just want one. I'm proving a point.'

The face lines squiggled their way into an expression of dozy obedience. 'Oh. Okey-dokey, then. It's going to take about a quarter of an hour to put it together.'

'Sure,' Jay sneered.

'Hey! That's got lots of complicated parts inside, you know.'

'Right.'

'If you'd asked for something simple, I could provide straight away.'

'All right. I want the Diana statue from the Paris arcology. That's just a lump of carved rock.'

'Easy peasy.'

'Uh—' Jay managed to grunt.

Mickey zipped out over the beach, too fast for her to follow. She swivelled, just in time to see it inflating equally fast. At ten metres in diameter, its ridiculous face was suddenly not so pleasant and harmless as it loomed above her. A pair of shoes began to ooze through the bottom. They were as long as Jay was tall. Mickey started to rise up, exposing legs, waist, torso . . .

The full fifteen metre height of the granite statue gazed out serenely across the Kiint ocean. Pigeon droppings scarred its shoulders. Above Diana's head, Mickey shrank to its usual size and floated back down to Jay. Its mouth line shifted up into feline gratification.

'What have you done?' Jay yelled.

'Provided the statue. Wossamatter, wrong one?'

'No! Yes!' She glanced frantically along the beach. There were figures moving round outside the other chalets and big white clubhouse, but fortunately none of them seemed to have noticed. Yet. 'Get rid of it!'

'Oh. Charming.' Mickey inflated out again. Its hurt pout was ominous on such a scale. The statue was swallowed whole. The only memorial: a pair of giant footprints in the sand.

'You're mad,' Jay accused as it shrank once again. 'Utterly mad. They should switch you off.'

'For what?' it wailed.

'For doing that.'

'Just doing what I'm told,' it grumbled. 'I suppose you want to cancel the vac-train as well, now?'

'Yes!'

'You should make up your mind. No wonder they won't hand over my kind of technology to the Confederation. Think of all the statues you'd leave lying round the place.' Its voice changed pitch to a near-hysterical whine. 'Any humans on this planet? Oh, yes, I can see all the obelisks they planted to replace the aboriginal forests.'

'How do you do it?' she asked sharply. 'How do you work? I bet you've never even been to Earth, how do you know what Diana's statue looked like?'

Mickey's voice dropped back down to normal. 'The Kiint have this whopping great central library, see. There's no end of stuff stored in there, including your art encyclopedias. All I've gotta do is find the template memory.'

'And you make it inside you?'

'Small things, no problem. I'm your man, just shout. The bigger stuff, that's gotta be put together in a place like a high-speed factory.

Then when it's done and polished they just ship it in through me. *Simplissimo.*'

'All right. Next question, who decided to give you that silly voice?'

'Whaddya mean, silly? It's *magnifico*.'

'Well, you don't talk like an adult, do you?'

'Ha, hark who's talking. I'll have you know, I'm an appropriate companion personality for a girl your age, young missy. We spent all night ransacking that library to see what I should be like. You got any idea what it's like watching eight million hours of Disney AVs?'

'Thank you for being so considerate, I'm sure.'

'What I'm here for. We're partners, you and me.' Mickey's smile perked up again.

Jay folded her arms and fixed it with a stare. 'OK, *partner*; I want you to provide me with a starship.'

'Is this another of those point thingies?'

'Could be. I don't care what type of starship it is; but I want it to be one I can pilot by myself, and it has to have the range to get me back to the Confederation galaxy.'

Mickey's eyes blinked slowly, as if lethargic shutters were coming down. 'Sorry, Jay,' it said quietly. 'No can do. I would if I could, honest, but the boss says no.'

'Not much of a companion, are you?'

'How about a chocolate and almond ice lolly instead? Big yummy time!'

'Instead of a starship? I don't think so.'

'Aww, go on. You know you want to.'

'Not before breakfast, thank you.' She turned her back on it.

'OK. I know, how about a megalithic strawberry milkshake, with oodles and oodles of—'

'Shut up. And you're not called Mickey, either. So don't pretend you are.' Jay smiled at the silence, imagining it must be contorting its sketched face into hurt dismay. Her name was being called from the chalet.

Tracy Dean stood on the veranda, waving hopefully. She was dressed in a pale lemon dress with a lace collar, its design obsolete but still stylish. Jay walked back, aware that the provider machine was following. 'The face wasn't a good idea, was it?' Tracy said with dry amusement after Jay climbed the steps to the veranda. 'Didn't think so. Not for someone who's seen all you have. But it was worth a try.' She sighed. 'Program discontinued. There, it's just an ordinary provider, now. And it won't talk stupid any more, either.'

Jay glanced up at the purple sphere, which was now completely featureless. 'I don't mean to be awkward.'

'I know, sweetie. Now come and sit down. I've got some breakfast for you.'

A white linen tablecloth had been spread over a small table beside the weather-worn railings. It had Spanish pottery bowls with cereal and fruit, a jug of milk and another of orange juice. There was also a teapot with a battered old strainer.

'Twining's Ceylon tea,' Tracy said happily as they sat down. 'Best you can have for breakfast, in my opinion. I became completely addicted to it in the late nineteenth century, so I brought some back with me once. Now the providers can synthesize the leaves for me. I'd like to be all snobbish and say that I can tell it's not the same, but I can't. We'll let it brew for a while, shall we?'

'Yes,' Jay said earnestly. 'If you like.' There was something deliciously fascinating about this old woman who had Father Horst's compassion and Powel Manani's determination.

'Have you never brewed tea in a pot before, young Jay?'

'No. Mummy always bought it in sachets.'

'Oh dear me. There are some things which the march of progress doesn't improve, you know.'

Jay poured some milk over the cereal bowl, deciding not to ask about the strange-shaped flakes. One thing at a time. 'Do the Kiint live on all these planets?'

'Ah, yes. I did promise I'd explain things today, didn't I, sweetie?'

'Yes!'

'Such impatience. Where to start, though?' Tracy sprinkled some sugar onto her grapefruit, and sank a silver spoon into the soft fruit. 'Yes, the Kiint live on all these planets. They built them, you know. Not all at once, but they have been civilized for a very long time. One planet couldn't possibly accommodate them all any more, just like there are too many humans to live on Earth nowadays. So they learned how to extract matter from their sun and condense it. Quite an achievement, actually, even with their technology. The arc is one of the wonders of this galaxy. Not just physically, culturally, too. All the species who've achieved FTL starflight visit here eventually. Some that haven't, too. It's the greatest information exchange centre we know of. And the Kiint know of a few, believe me.'

'The provider said there was a big library here.'

'It was being modest. You see, when you've got the technology to take care of your every physical requirement, there's not much else you can do but develop your knowledge base. So that's what they do. And it's a big universe to get to know. It keeps them occupied, and fulfils life's basic requirement.'

'What's that?'

'To live is to experience, and experience is living. I had a lovely little chuckle when the first Kiint Ambassador from Jobis told the Confederation they had no interest in starflight. Travel broadens the mind, and heavens do they travel. They have this quite magical society, you see, they spend their whole time developing their intellects. The best way I can put it for you is that wisdom is their equivalent of money, that's what they pursue and hoard. I'm generalizing, of course. A population as large as theirs is bound to have dissidents. Nothing like our Edenist Serpents, of course; their disagreements are mostly philosophical. But there are a few Kiint who turn their backs on their own kind. There's even a couple of planets in the arc they can go to where they're free of the central society.

'Whatever faction they come from, they're all very noble by our standards. And I'll admit it leaves them superbly prepared to face transcendence when their bodies die. But to be honest, that kind of existence is rather boring for humans. I don't think we'll ever go quite so far down that road. Different mental wiring, thankfully. We're too impatient and quarrelsome. Bless us.'

'So you are really human, then?'

'Oh, yes, sweetie. I'm human. All of us living here are.'

'But why are you here?'

'We work for the Kiint, helping them to record human history. All of us take little unobtrusive jobs where we can get a good view of events. In the old days it was as servants of lords and kings, or joining up with nomads. Then when the industrial age started up we moved into the media companies. We weren't front-line investigative reporters, we were the office mundanes; but it meant we had access to an avalanche of information most of which never made it into the official history books. It was perfect for us, and we still mostly work in the information industries today. I'll show you how to use the AV projector later if you want, every broadcast humans make goes into the arc's library. That always tickled me, if those desperate marketing departments only knew just how wide an audience they really have.'

'Are the Kiint really that interested in us?'

'Us, the Tyrathca, the Laymil, xenocs you've never heard of. They're fascinated by sentience, you see. They've witnessed so many self-aware races dwindle away to nothing, or self-destruct. That kind of loss is tragic for the races which succeed and prosper. Everybody's different, you see, sweetie. Life alone is precious, but conscious thought is the greatest gift the universe offers. So they try and study any entities they find; that way if they don't survive their knowledge won't be entirely lost to the rest of us.'

'How did you end up working for them?'

'The Kiint found Earth when they were exploring that galaxy about two and a half thousand years ago. They took DNA specimens from a few people. We were cloned from that base, with a few alterations.'

'What like?' Jay asked eagerly. This was a wonderful story, so many secrets.

'We don't age so quickly, obviously, and we've got a version of affinity; little things like that.'

'Gosh. And you've been on Earth since you were born?'

'Since I grew up, yes. We had to be educated the Kiint way first. Their prime rule in dealing with other species, especially primitive ones, is zero intervention. They were worried that we might become too sympathetic and go native. If we did that, we'd introduce ideas that were wrong for that era; I mean, think what would have happened if the Spanish Armada was equipped with weather-radar. That's why they made us sterile, too; it should help us remain impartial.'

'That's horrid!'

Tracy smiled blankly at the horizon. 'There are compensations. Oh, sweetie, if you'd seen a fraction of what I have. The Imperial Chinese dynasties at their height. Easter Islanders carving their statues. Knights in armour battling for their tiny kingdoms. The Inca cities rising out of jungles. I was a servant girl at Runymede when

King John signed the Magna Carta. Then lived as a grandee noble-woman while Europe was invigorated by the Renaissance. I waved from the harbour when Columbus set sail across the Atlantic; and spat as Nazi tanks rolled into Europe. Then thirty years later I stood on Coco beach and cried when Apollo 11 took off for the Moon I was so proud of what we'd achieved. And there I was in the spaceplane which brought Richard Saldana down to Kulu. You have no idea how blessed my life has been. I know everything, *every*thing, humans are capable of. We are a good species. Not the best, not by Kiint standards, but so much better than most. And wonderfully unique.' She sniffed loudly, and dabbed a handkerchief on her eyes.

'Don't cry,' Jay said quietly. 'Please.'

'I'm sorry. Just having you here, knowing what you could accomplish if you have the chance, makes this hurt so much harder. It's so bloody *unfair*.'

'What do you mean?' Jay asked. Seeing the old woman so upset was making her nervous. 'Aren't the Kiint going to let me go home?'

'It's not that.' Tracy smiled bravely, and patted Jay's hand. 'It's what kind of home will be left for you. This shouldn't have happened, you see. Discovering energistic states and what they mean normally comes a lot later in a society's development. It's a huge adjustment for anybody to make. Human-type psychologies need a lot of preparation for that kind of truth, a generation at least. And that's when they're more sociologically advanced than the Confederation. This breakthrough was a complete accident. I'm terrified the human race won't get through this, not intact. We all are, all the Kiint observers want to help, to point the researchers in the right direction if nothing else. Our original conditioning isn't strong enough to restrict those sort of feelings.'

'Why don't you?'

'Even if they allowed us, I'd be no use. I've been part of all our history, Jay. I've seen us evolve from dirty savages into a civilization that has spread among the stars. More than anybody I know what we could grow into if we just had the chance. And I have the experience to intervene without anyone ever knowing they'd been guided. But at the most crucial time of our social evolution, when that experience is utterly *vital*, I've got to stay here.'

'Why?' Jay pleaded.

Tracy's frail shoulders trembled from repressed emotion. 'Oh, sweetie, haven't you worked out what this dreadful place is yet? It's a bloody retirement home.'

*

The view arrived suddenly. For over twenty minutes Louise had been sitting in one of the lounge's big chairs, its webbing holding her in the deep hollow of cushioning. Her belly muscles were beginning to strain as they were obliged to hold her in a curving posture. Then she felt a slight trembling in the decking as the lift capsule was shunted onto the tower rail. A tone sounded. Thirty seconds later they flashed out of the Skyhigh Kijabe asteroid. There was a quick impression of soured-white metal mountains, but they shrank from sight overhead. Gentle gravity relieved her muscles, and the webbing slackened.

Earth shone with a mild opalescent light below her. It was midday in Africa, at the base of the tower, and the clouds were charging in from the oceans on either side. There seemed to be a lot more of them than there had been on Norfolk, although the *Far Realm* had been orbiting at a much lower altitude. That might account for it. Louise couldn't be bothered to find the correct meteorology files in her processor block and run a comparison program. The sight was there to enjoy not analyse. She could actually see the giant white spirals spinning slowly as they battered against each other. It must be a pretty impressive speed for the movement to be visible from such a height.

Genevieve switched her webbing off and glided over to the lounge window, pressing herself against it. 'It's beautiful,' she said. Her face was flushed as she smiled back at Louise. 'I thought Earth was all rotten.'

Louise glanced about, slightly worried by what the other passengers would think of the little girl's remark. With the quarantine, most of them must be from Earth or the Halo. But nobody was even looking at her. In fact, it seemed as though they were deliberately not looking. She went over to stand beside Gen. 'I guess that's as wrong as everything else in the school books.'

The Halo was visible against the stars, a huge slender thread of stippled light curving behind the planet, like the most tenuous of a gas giant's rings. For five hundred and sixty-five years, companies and finance consortiums had been knocking asteroids into Earth

179

orbit. The process was standardized now; first the large-scale mining of mineral resources, hollowing out the habitation caverns, then the gradual build-up of industrial manufacturing stations as the initial resources were depleted and the population switched to a more sophisticated economy. There were nearly fifteen thousand inhabited asteroids already drifting along in their common cislunar orbit, and new rocks were arriving at the rate of thirty-five a year. Tens of thousands of inter-orbit craft swooped between the spinning rocks, fusion exhausts tangling together in a single scintillating nimbus. Every asteroid formed a tiny bulge in the loop, wrapped behind a delicate haze of industrial stations.

Louise gazed at the ephemeral testament to astroengineering commerce. More fragile than the bridge of heaven in Norfolk's midsummer sky, but at the same time more imposing. The vista inspired a great deal of confidence. Earth was strong, much stronger than she'd realized; it sprang from a wealth which she knew she would never truly comprehend.

If we're safe anywhere, we're safe here. She put her arm round Genevieve. For once, contented.

Below the majesty of the Halo, Earth was almost quiescent by comparison. Only the coastlines of North and South America hinted at the equal amount of human activity and industry on the ancient planet. They remained in darkness, awaiting the dawn terminator sliding over the Atlantic; but the night didn't prevent her from seeing where people were. Arcologies blazed across the land like volcanoes of sunlight.

'Are they the cities?' Genevieve asked excitedly.

'I think so, yes.'

'Gosh! Why is the water that colour?'

Louise switched her attention away from the massive patches of illumination. The ocean was a peculiar shade of grey-green, not at all like the balmy turquoise of Norfolk's seas when they were under Duke's stringent white glare.

'I'm not sure. It doesn't look very clean, does it? I suppose that must be the pollution we hear about.'

A small contrite cough just behind them made both girls start. It was the first time anyone apart from the stewards had even acknowledged they existed. When they turned round they found themselves facing a small man in a dark purple business suit. He'd already got some thin wrinkles on his cheeks, though he didn't seem particularly old. Louise was surprised by his height, she was actually an inch taller than him, and he had a very broad forehead, as if his hair wouldn't grow properly along the top of it.

'I know this is rude,' he said quietly. 'But I believe you're from outsystem?'

Louise wondered what had given them away. She'd bought the pair of them new clothes in Skyhigh Kijabe, one-piece garments like ship-suits but more elaborate, with pronounced pockets and cuffs. Other women were wearing the fashion, so she'd hoped they would blend in.

'Yes,' Louise said. 'From Norfolk, actually.'

'Ah. I'm afraid I've never tasted Norfolk Tears. Too expensive, even with my salary. I was most sorry to hear about its loss.'

'Thank you.' Louise kept her face blank, the way she'd learned to do whenever Daddy started shouting.

The man introduced himself as Aubry Earle. 'So this is your first visit to Earth?' he asked.

'Yes,' Genevieve said. 'We want to go to Tranquillity, but we can't find a flight.'

'I see. Then this is all new to you?'

'Some of it,' Louise said. She wasn't quite sure what Aubry wanted. He didn't seem the type to befriend a pair of young girls. Not from altruism, anyway.

'Then allow me to explain what you are seeing. The oceans aren't polluted, at least not seriously; there was an extensive effort to clean them up at the end of the twenty-first century. Their present colouring comes from algae blooms. It's a geneered variety that floats on the top. I think it looks awful, myself.'

'But it's everywhere,' Genevieve said.

'Alas, yes. That's our carbon sink these days. Earth's lungs, if you like. It performs the job once done by forests and grasslands. The surface vegetation is not what it used to be, so Govcentral introduced the algae to prevent us from suffocating ourselves. Actually, it's a far more successful example of terraforming than Mars. Though I would never be so undiplomatic as to say that to a Lunar citizen. We now have less carbon dioxide in our atmosphere than at any time in the last eight hundred years. You'll be breathing remarkably clean air when you arrive.'

'So why do you all live in the arcologies?' Louise asked.

'Heat,' Aubry said sadly. 'Do you know how much heat a modern industrial civilization of over forty billion people generates?' He gestured down at the globe. 'That much. Enough to melt the polar ice and quicken the clouds. We've taken all the preventative measures we can, of course. That was the original spur to build the orbital towers, to prevent spaceplanes aerobraking and shedding even more heat into the air. But however economic we are, we can't dissipate it at a rate that'll turn the clock back. The old ocean currents have shut down, there's no ozone layer at all. And that kind of ecological retro-engineering is beyond even our ability. We're stuck with the current environment, unfortunately.'

'Is it very bad?' Genevieve asked. What he'd described sounded worse than the beyond, though she thought the man didn't sound terribly upset by the cataclysm.

He smiled fondly at the planet. 'Best damn world in the Confederation. Though I expect everyone says that about their homeworld. Am I right?'

'I like Norfolk,' Louise said.

'Of course you do. But if I might make an observation, this is going to be noisier than anything you've experienced before.'

'I know that.'

'Good. Take care down there. People aren't likely to help you. That's our culture, you see.'

Louise gave him a sideways look. 'Do you mean they don't like foreigners?'

'Oh, no. Nothing like that. It's not racism. Not overtly, anyway. On Earth everybody is a foreigner to their neighbour. It's because we're all squashed up so tight. Privacy is a cherished commodity. In public places, people don't chat to strangers, they avoid eye contact. It's because that's the way they want to be treated. I'm really breaking taboos by talking to you. I doubt any of the other passengers will. But I've been outsystem myself, I know how strange it all is for you.'

'Nobody's going to talk to us?' Genevieve asked apprehensively.

'Not as readily as I.'

'That's fine with me,' Louise said. She couldn't quite bring herself to trust Aubry Earle. At the back of her mind was the worry that he would volunteer to become their guide. It had been bad enough in

Norwich when she'd depended on Aunt Celina; Roberto was family. Earle was a stranger, one prepared to drop Earth's customs in public when it suited him. She gave him a detached smile, and led an unprotesting Gen away from the window. The lift capsule had ten decks, and her standard class ticket allowed her into four of them. They managed to avoid Earle for the rest of the flight. Though she realized he was telling the truth about privacy. Nobody else talked to them.

The isolation might have been safer, but it made the ten hour trip incredibly boring. They spent a long time watching the view through the window as Earth grew larger, and talking idly. Louise even managed to sleep for the last three hours, curling up in one of the big chairs.

She woke to Gen shaking her shoulder. 'They just announced we're about to reach the atmosphere,' her sister said.

Louise combed some strands of hair from her face, and sat up. Other passengers who'd been dozing were now stirring themselves. She took the hair clip off as she reorganized her mane, then fastened it up again. First priority when they were down must be to get it washed. The last time she'd managed properly was back on Phobos. Maybe it was time for a cut, a short style that was more manageable. Though the usual arguments still applied: she'd invested so much time keeping in condition, cutting it was almost a confession of defeat. Of course, back at Cricklade she'd had the time to groom herself every day, and had a maid to help.

Whatever did I do all day back then?

'Louise?' Genevieve asked cautiously.

She raised an eyebrow at the girl's tone. 'What?'

'Promise you won't get mad if I ask?'

'I won't get mad.'

'It's just that you haven't said yet.'

'Said what?'

'Where we're going after we touch down.'

'Oh.' Louise was completely stumped. She hadn't even thought about their destination. Getting away from High York and Brent Roi had been her absolute priority. What she needed to do was find somewhere to stay so she could think about what to do next. And without consulting her block there was really only one city name from her ethnic history classes which she was certain would still exist. 'London,' she told Genevieve. 'We're going to London.'

*

The African orbital tower was the first to be built, a technological achievement declared the equal of the FTL drive by the Govcentral committees and politicians who'd authorized it. Typical self-aggrandizing hyperbole, but acknowledged to be a reasonable comparison nonetheless. As Aubry Earle had said, it was intended to replace spaceplanes and the enormously detrimental effect they were having on Earth's distressed atmosphere. By 2180 when the tower was finally commissioned (eight years late), the Great Dispersal was in full swing, and the volume of spaceplane traffic had become so injurious to the atmosphere that meteorologists were worrying about elevating the armada storms to an even greater level of ferocity.

The question became academic. Once the tower was on-line, its cargo capacity exceeded thirty per cent of the world's spaceplane fleet. Upgrades were being planned before the first lift capsule ran all the way up to Skyhigh Kijabe. Four hundred and thirty years later, the original slender tower of monocarbon fibre was now nothing more than a support element threading up the centre of the African Tower. A thick grey pillar dwindling off up to infinity, immune to the most punishing winds the armada storms could fling at it. The outer surface was lined with forty-seven magnetic rails, the structure's maximum. It was now cheaper to build new towers than expand it any further.

The lower five kilometres were the fattest section, providing an outer sheath of tunnels to protect the lift capsules from the winds, enabling the tower to remain operational in all but the absolutely worst weather conditions. Exactly where the tower ended and the Mount Kenya Station started was no longer certain. With a daily cargo throughput potential of two hundred thousand tonnes, and up to seventy-five thousand passengers, the capsule-handling infrastructure had moulded itself tumescently around the base, a mountain in its own right. Eighty vac-train tunnels intersected in the bedrock underneath it, making it the most important transport nucleus on the continent.

To keep the passengers flowing smoothly, there were eighteen separate arrival halls. All of them followed the same basic layout, a long marble-floored concourse with the exit doors from customs and immigration rooms on one side, and lifts on the other, leading to the subterranean vac-train platforms. Even if an arriving passenger knew exactly which lift cluster they wanted, they first had to negotiate a formidable barricade of retail stalls selling everything from socks to luxury apartments. Keeping track of one individual (or a pair) amid the perpetual scrum occupying the floor wasn't easy, not even with modern equipment.

B7 left nothing to chance. A hundred and twenty GISD field operatives had been pulled off their current assignments to provide saturation coverage. Fifty were allocated to Hall Nine, where the Kavanagh sisters were due to disembark, their movements coordinated by an AI that was hooked into every security sensor in the building. Another fifty were already on their way to London within minutes of Louise saying that was her intended goal. Twenty were held in reserve in case of cock-ups, misdirection, or good old-fashioned acts of God.

The arrangements had caused more arguments among B7; all of the supervisors remained extremely proprietorial when it came to their respective territories. Southern Africa, in whose domain the Mount Kenya Station fell, disputed Western Europe's claim that he should take personal command of the surveillance. Western Europe counterclaimed that as the tower station was just a brief stopover for the sisters, and the whole operation was his anyway, he should have the necessary authority. The other B7 supervisors knew Southern Africa, renowned for the tedious minutiae of procedure worship, was just going through the motions.

Western Europe was given his way over the tower station, as well as gaining concessions to steer the operation through whichever territory the Kavanaghs roamed in their search for Banneth.

Southern Africa acceded to the decision, and withdrew testily from the sensenviron conference. Smiling quietly at his inevitable victory, Western Europe datavised the AI for a full linkage. With the station layout unfolding in his mind, he began to designate positions to the agents. Tied in with that was the lift capsule's arrival time, and the departure times of each scheduled vac-train. The AI computed every possible travel permutation, plotting the routes which the sisters would have to walk across the concourse. It even took into account the types of stalls which might catch their eye. Satisfied the agents were placed to cover every contingency, Western Europe stoked his fire and settled back into a leather armchair with a brandy to wait.

It was probably the ultimate tribute to the fieldcraft of the GISD agents that after all fifty of them took up position in Hall Nine, Simon Bradshaw didn't notice them, not even with his hyper instinct for the way of things on the concourse. Simon was twenty-three years old, though he could easily pass for fifteen. Selected hormone courses kept him short and skinny, with soft ebony skin. His large eyes were moist brown, which people mistook for mournful. Their endearing appeal had salvaged him from trouble countless times in the twelve years he'd been strutting the concourses of the Mount Kenya Station. Local floor-patrol cops had his profile loaded in their neural nanonics, along with hundreds of other regular sneak opportunists. Simon used cosmetic packages every fortnight or so, altering his peripheral features, though his size remained constant. It was the act you had to vary to prevent the cops from putting a comparison program into primary mode. Some days dress smart and act little boy lost, dress casual and act street tough, dress neutral act neutral, pay a cousin to lend you their five-year-old daughter and come over as a protective big brother. But never ever dress poor. Poor people had no business in the station, even the stall vendors had neat franchise uniforms below their shiny franchise smiles.

Today Simon was in a franchise uniform himself: the scarlet and sapphire tunic of Cuppamaica, the coffee café. Being unobtrusive by being mundane. Nobody was suspicious of station workers. He saw the two girls as soon as they emerged through the customs and immigration archway. It was like they had a hologram advert flashing over their heads saying: EASY. He couldn't ever remember seeing such obvious offworlders before. Both of them gawping round at the cavernous hall, delighted and amazed by the place. The little one giggled, pointing up at the transit informatives, baubles of light charging about overhead like insane dragonflies, shepherding passengers towards the right channels.

Simon was off immediately, coming away from the noodle stall he'd been slouching against as if powered by a nuclear pulse. Moving at a fast walk, the luggage cab buzzing incessantly at his heels as its small motors strained to keep up. He was desperately trying not to run, the urgency was so hot. His principal worry now was if the others of his profession saw them. It would be like a feeding frenzy.

Louise couldn't bring her legs to move. Her fellow passengers had swept her and Genevieve out of customs, carrying her along for a few yards before her surroundings exerted a grip on her nerves. The arrivals hall was awesome, a stadium of coloured crystal and marble, saturated with noise and light. There must surely have been more people thronging across its floor than lived in the whole of Kesteven Island. Like her, they all had luggage cabs chasing after them, adding to the bedlam. The squat oblong box had been supplied by the line company operating the lift capsule. Her bags had been dumped inside by the retrieval clerk, who'd promptly handed her a circular card. The cab, he promised, would follow her everywhere as long as she kept the card with her. It was also the key to open it again when they got down to their vac-train platform. 'After that you're on your own,' he said. 'Don't try and take it on the carriage. That's MKS property, that is.'

Louise swore she wouldn't. 'How do we get to London?' Gen asked in a daunted tone. Louise glanced up at the mad swarms of photons above them. They were balls of tightly packed writing, or numbers. Logically, it must be travel information of some kind. She just didn't know how to read it.

'Ticket office,' she gulped. 'They'll tell us. We'll have to buy a ticket for London anyway.'

Genevieve turned a complete circle, trying to scan the hall through the mêlée of bodies and luggage cabs. 'Where's the ticket office?'

Louise pulled the processor block out of her shoulder purse. 'I'll find it,' she said with determination. It was just a question of accessing a local net processor and loading a search program. An operation she'd practised a hundred times with the tutorial. Watching the graphics assemble themselves in the display as she ordered conjured up a welcome feeling of satisfaction.

I've got a problem and I'm solving it. By myself, and for myself. I'm not dependent.

She grinned happily at Gen as the search program interrogated the station information processors. 'We're actually on Earth.' She said it as though she'd only just realized. Which, in a strange way, she had.

'Yes.' Genevieve grinned back. Then she scowled as a scrawny youth in a red and blue uniform barged into her. 'Hey!'

He mumbled a grudging apology, side-stepped round the luggage cab and walked away.

The block bleeped to announce it had located the vac-train ticket dispensers for Hall Nine. There were seventy-eight of them. Without showing any ire, Louise started to redefine the search parameters.

Easy, easy, easy. Simon wanted to yell it out. That jostle with the little kid was the modern equivalent of the shell game. Visually confusing as their respective luggage cabs crossed paths, and allowing his grabber to intercept their tag card code at the same time. He fought the impulse to turn round and check the new luggage cab at his feet. Those girls were in for a hell of a shock when they got to their platform and found only a pile of beefbap wrappers inside it.

Simon headed for the stalls at a brisk pace. There was a staff lift at the middle. Route down to a quieter level, where he could examine his prize. He was ten metres from the front line of stalls when he was aware of two people closing on him. It wasn't an accidental path, either, they were coming at him with all the purpose of combat wasps. Running wasn't going to do any good, he knew that. He pressed the release button on the grabber hidden in his palm. The girls' luggage cab swerved away, no longer following him. Now, if he could just dump the grabber in a waste bin. No proof.

Shit. How could his luck turn like this?

One of the cops (or whoever) went after the luggage cab. Simon hunted round for a bin. Anywhere there was a fast-food bar. He ducked round the first stall, making one last check on his pursuers. That was why he never saw the third GISD agent (or fourth and fifth, for that matter) until the woman bumped right into him. He did feel, briefly, a small sting on his chest. Exactly the same place she was now taking her hand away from. His guts suddenly turned very cold, then that sensation faded to nothing.

Simon looked down at his chest in puzzlement just as his legs faltered, dropping him to his knees. He'd heard of weapons like this, so slim they never left a mark as they punctured your skin; but inside it was like an EE grenade going off. The world was going quiet and dim around him. High above, the woman watched him with a faint sneer of satisfaction on her lips.

'For a couple of bags?' Simon coughed incredulously. But she'd already turned, walking away with a calm he could almost respect. A real pro. Then he was somehow aware of himself finishing the fall to the floor. Blood rushed out of his gaping mouth. After that, the darkness rushed up to drown him. Darkness, but not total night. The world was only the slightest of distances away. And he wasn't alone in observing it from outside. The lost souls converged upon him to devour the font of keen anguish that was his mind.

'That way,' Louise said brightly. The block's little screen was showing a floor layout, which she thought she'd aligned right.

With Genevieve skipping along at her side she negotiated the obstacle course of stalls. They slowed down to window-shop the things on display, not really understanding half of them. She also thought there must be a subtle trick to negotiating the crowd which was eluding her. Twice on the way to the dispenser people banged into her. It wasn't as though she didn't look where she was going.

The block had told her there was neither a ticket office nor an information desk. A result which made her acknowledge she was still thinking along Norfolk lines. All the information she needed was in the station electronics, it just needed the right questions to extract it.

A vac-train journey to London cost twenty-five fuseodollars (fifteen for Gen); a train left every twelve minutes from platform thirty-two; lifts G to J served that level. Once she knew that, even the transit informatives whirling past overhead began to make a kind of sense.

Western Europe accessed an agent's sensevise to watch the sisters puzzle out the ticket dispenser. Enhanced retinas zoomed in on Genevieve, who had started clapping excitedly when a ticket dropped out of the slot.

'Don't they have ticket dispensers on Norfolk, for Heaven's sake?' the Halo supervisor asked querulously. He had maintained executive control over the observation team during the Kavanaghs' trip from High York down to the Mount Kenya Station, anxious that nothing should mar the handover. Now, curiosity had impelled him to tarry. Having initiated a few unorthodox missions in his time, he was nevertheless impressed with Western Europe's chutzpah in dealing with Dexter.

Western Europe smiled at the sensevise overlay of Halo, who appeared to be leaning against the marble fireplace, sipping a brandy. 'I doubt it. Some cheery faced old man in a glass booth would be more their style. Haven't you accessed any recent sensevises of Norfolk? Actually, just any sensevises of the place would do. It hasn't changed much since the founding.'

'Damn backward planet. It's like the medieval section of a theme park. Those English-ethnic morons abused the whole Great Dispersal ethos with that folly.'

'Not really. The ruling Landowner class introduced a stability we're still striving for, and without one per cent of the bloodshed we employ to keep a lid on things down here. In a way, I envy all those pastoral planets.'

'But not enough to emigrate.'

'That's a very cheap shot. Quite beneath you. We're as much products of our environment as the Kavanaghs are of theirs. And at least they're free to leave.'

'Leave, yes. Survive in the real world, no.' He indicated the observation operation's status display. It wasn't a pleasing tally. Five people had been eliminated by the guardian blanket of GISD agents – pickpockets, sneak thieves, a scam jockey – as the sisters made their way across the concourse. Extermination was the quick, no arguments, solution. It was also going to cause an uproar with the local police when the bodies were discovered. 'At this rate, you're going to wind up slaughtering more people than Dexter has to protect them.'

'I always thought station security should be sharper,' Western Europe said casually. 'What kind of advert is it for Govcentral when visitors get ripped off within ten minutes of their arrival on the good old homeworld?'

'Most don't.'

'Those girls aren't *most*. Don't worry, they'll be safer when they reach London and book into a hotel.'

Halo studied Western Europe's handsome young face, amused by the mild expression of preoccupation to be found there. 'You fancy Louise.'

'Don't be absurd.'

'I know your taste in women as well as you know my preferences. She's exactly your type.'

Western Europe swirled the brandy round his three-hundred-year-old snifter, not looking up at the smug overlay image. 'I admit there's something really rather appealing about Louise. Naivety, one supposes. It does always attract, especially when coupled with youthful physical beauty. Earth girls are so ... in your face. She has breeding, manners, and dignity. Also something the natives here lack.'

'That's not naivety, it's pure ignorance.'

'Don't be so uncharitable. You'd be equally adrift on Norfolk. I doubt you could ride to the hunt in pursuit of the cunning hax.'

'Why would anybody, let alone me, want to go to Norfolk?'

Western Europe tilted the snifter back and swallowed the last of the brandy in one go. 'Exactly the answer one expects from someone as jaded and decadent as you. I worry that one day this whole planet will think like us. Why do we bother protecting them?'

'We don't,' Halo chuckled. 'Your memory transfer must have glitched. We protect ourselves. Earth merely is our citadel.'

6

It was as if space had succumbed to a bleak midwinter. Monterey was moving into conjunction with New California, sinking deeper through the penumbra towards the eclipse. Looking through the Nixon Suite's big windows, Al could see the shadows above him expanding into black pools of nothingness. The asteroid's crumpled rock surface was slowly melting from view. Only the small lights decorating the thermal-exchange panels and communication rigs gave him any indication that it hadn't been removed from the universe entirely. Equally, the Organization fleet gathered outside was now invisible save for navigation strobes and the occasional spectral gust of blue ions fired from a thruster.

Beneath his feet, New California slid across the brilliant starscape, a gold-green corona crowning an empty circle. From this altitude there were no city lights, no delicate web of lustrous freeways gripping the continents. Nothing, in fact, to show that the Organization existed at all.

Jezzibella's arms crept round his chest, while her chin came to rest on his shoulder. A mild forest-morning perfume seeped into the air. 'No sign of red clouds,' she said encouragingly.

He lifted one hand to his lips, and kissed the knuckles. 'No. I guess that means I'm still *numero uno* around here.'

'Of course you are.'

'You wouldn't fucking think so, the beefs everyone's got. Not just what they say, either. What they think counts for a whole lot.'

'They'll be all right once the fleet's in action again.'

'Sure,' he snorted. 'And when's that gonna be, huh? Fucking Luigi, I shoulda popped him properly, screwing up like that. It's gonna take another twenty, thirty days to build up our antimatter stocks to anything like a load we can risk another invasion with. So Emmet says. That means six weeks minimum, I know. Goddam! I'm losing it, Jez. I'm fucking losing it.'

Her grip tightened. 'Don't be silly. You were bound to have setbacks.'

'I can't afford one. Not now. Morale's going to shit out there. You've heard what Leroy said. Possessed crew are going down to the surface for funtime and ain't coming back. They think I'm gonna lose control of the planet and they'll be better off down there when it happens.'

'So get Silvano to tighten up.'

'Maybe. You can only be so tough, you know?'

'You sure you can't bring the next invasion forward?'

'No.'

'Then we need something else to keep the soldiers and lieutenants occupied and committed.'

He turned to face her. She was wearing one of those whore's dresses again, just tiny little strips of pale yellow fabric up the front (he had ties wider than that), and a teensy skirt. So much skin tantalizingly revealed; it made him want to tug it off. As if he'd never seen her in the buff before. But then she was always alluring in some new fashion, a mirror hall chameleon.

A sensational piece of ass, no doubt about it. But the way she kept on coming up with ideas for him (just like her never-ending mystique) had become vaguely unnerving of late. It was like he'd become dependent, or something.

'Like what?' he asked flatly.

Jezzibella pouted. 'I don't know. Something which doesn't need the whole fleet, but'll still be effective. Not a propaganda exercise like Kursk; we need to hurt the Confederation.'

'Kingsley Pryor's gonna do that.'

'He might. Although that's a very long shot, remember?'

'OK, OK.' Al wished up one of his prime Havanas, and took a drag. Even they seemed to have lost their bite recently. 'So how do we use some itsy piece of the fleet to piss the Feds?'

'Dunno. Guess you'd better go call Emmet in; see what he can come up with. That's strictly his field.' She gave him a slow wink and sauntered off to the bedroom.

'Where the hell are you going?' he demanded.

A hand waved dismissively. 'This dress is for your eyes only, baby. I know how hot you get when other people see what I've got to offer. And you need to have a clear head when you're talking to Emmet.'

He sighed as the tall doors closed behind her. Right again.

*

When Emmet Mordden arrived fifteen minutes later, Al had returned to the window. There was very little light in the big lounge, just some red jewels glimmering high up on the white and gold walls. With Monterey now fully into the umbra, the window was little more than a slate-grey rectangle, with Al's ebony silhouette in the middle. His youthful face was illuminated by a diminutive orange glimmer coming from the Havana.

Emmet tried not to show too much annoyance at the cigar smoke clogging the room. The Hilton's conditioners never managed to eliminate the cloying smell, and using energistic power to ward it off was too much like overkill. It might just offend Al, too.

Al raised a hand in acknowledgement, but didn't turn away from the window with its empty view. 'Can't see anything out there today,' he said quietly. 'No planet, no sun.'

'They're still there, Al.'

'Yeah, yeah. And now is when you tell me I got responsibilities to them.'

'I'm not going to tell you that, Al. You know the way it is.'

'Know what, and don't tell Jez this, I'd trade in the whole shebang for a trip home to Chicago. I used to have a house in Prairie Avenue. You know? Like, for my family. It was a nice street in a decent neighbourhood, full of regular guys, trees, good lighting. There was never any trouble there. That's where I want to be, Emmet, I wanna be able to walk down Prairie Avenue and open my own front door again. That's all. I just wanna go home.'

'Earth ain't like it used to be, Al. And it hasn't changed for the best. Take it from me, you wouldn't recognize it now.'

'I don't want it now, Emmet. I want to go *home*. Capeesh?'

'Sure, Al.'

'That sound crazy to you?'

'I had a girl before. It was a good thing back then, you know.'

'Right. See, I had this idea. I remember there was this Limey guy, Wells, I think his name was. I never read any of his books, mind. But he wrote about things that are happening today in this crazy world, about Mars men invading and a time machine. Boy, if he's come back, I bet he's having a ball right now. So ... I just wondered; he was thinking stuff like that, a time machine, back in the twentieth century, and the Confederation eggheads, they can build these starships today. Did they ever try to make a time machine?'

'No, Al. Zero-tau can carry ordinary people into the future, but there's no way back. The big theory guys, they say it can't be done. Not in practice. Sorry.'

Al nodded contemplatively. 'That's OK, Emmet. Thought I'd ask.'

'Was that all, Al?'

'Shit, no.' Al smiled reluctantly, and turned from the window. 'How's it going out there?'

'We're holding our own, especially down on the planet. Haven't had to use an SD strike for three days now. Some of the lieutenants have even caught a couple of AWOL starship crew. They're getting shipped back up here tonight. Patricia's going to deal with them. She's talking about setting an example.'

'Good. Maybe now those bastards will learn there ain't no get-out clause when you sign up with me.'

'The voidhawks have stopped dumping their stealth bombs and spyglobes on the fleet. Kiera's hellhawks have done a good job clearing them out.'

'Huh.' Al opened the liquor cabinet, and poured himself a shot of bourbon. The stuff was imported from a planet called Nashville. He couldn't believe they'd called a whole goddam planet after that hick dirt-town. Their booze had a kick, though.

'You remember she moved her people into the rooms along the docking-ledge?' Emmet said. 'I know why she did it, now. They've knocked out all the machinery which makes the nutrient fluid for the hellhawks. And not just here in Monterey, all over the system, too. The *Stryla* visited all the asteroids we run, and layered their nutrient machinery. Her people are guarding the only one left working. If the hellhawks don't do as they're told, they don't get fed. They don't eat, they die. It's that simple.'

'Neat,' Al said. 'Let me guess, if we try to muscle in on the last machine, it gets zapped.'

'Looks like it. They've let slip that it's booby-trapped. I'd hate to risk it.'

'As long as the hellhawks do what I want, she can stay. Barricading herself in like that is dumb. It makes her even more dependent on me for status. She has to support me, she's not important to anyone else.'

'I've put a couple of people on surveying what's left of the machinery she smashed up. We might be able to put a working unit back together eventually, but it'll take time.'

'Time is something which is giving me a fucking headache, Emmet. And I ain't talking about Wells's machine here. I need to get the fleet back into action, soonest.'

'But, Al—' He stopped as Al held up a hand.

'I know. We can't launch no invasion right now. Not enough antimatter. There's gotta be something else they can do. I'm being honest with you here, Emmet, the boys are so antsy they'll mutiny if we keep them kicking their heels in port much longer.'

'I suppose you could launch some fast strike raids. Let people know we've still got some punch.'

'Strike on what? Just blowing things up for the sake of it ain't my style. We have to give the fleet a purpose.'

'There's the Mortonridge Liberation. The Confederation's been beaming propaganda about that to every city on New California, telling us how we're bound to lose eventually. If we hit some of their supply convoys we'd be helping the possessed on Ombey.'

'Yeah,' Al said. The notion didn't really appeal, too few visible returns. 'What I'm looking for is something that'll cause a shitload of trouble for the Confederation each time. Knocking out a couple of ships ain't going to do that.'

'Well . . . This is just an idea, Al. I don't know if it's the kind of thing you're looking for. It depends on how many planets you want to rule over.'

'The Organization has to keep up its momentum to exist. Ruling planets is only a part of that. So talk to me, Emmet.'

*

Kiera could see eight hellhawks out on the ledge below her. They were all sitting on their pedestals, ingesting nutrient fluid. A rotor had been drawn up so the whole flock could feed on the ten metallic mushrooms which remained functional. Studying the huge creatures, so powerful yet utterly dependent, Kiera couldn't avoid the religious analogy. They were like a devout congregation coming to receive mass from their priestess. Each of them abased themselves before her, and if the correct obeisance was performed they received her blessing in return, and were allowed to live.

The *Kerachel* swept in above the ledge, appearing so swiftly out of the umbra it might have just swallowed in. A pointed lozenge shape a hundred metres long, it hardly hesitated as it found its designated pedestal and sank down. Knowing that even though it couldn't see her expression, it could sense her thoughts, she smiled arrogantly down upon it. 'Any problems?' she asked casually.

'Monterey's command centre monitored its patrol flight,' Hudson Proctor replied. 'No deviations. Eight suspect objects destroyed.'

'Well done,' she murmured. A hand waved languid permission to start.

Hudson Proctor picked up a handset, and began speaking into it. Two hundred metres below the departure lounge, her loyal little team opened a valve, and the precious fluid surged along a pipe out to the pedestal. A feeling of contentment strummed the air like background music as *Kerachel* began sucking in its food. Kiera could feel the hellhawk's mood, it mellowed her own.

There were eighty-seven hellhawks based at Monterey now. A formidable flotilla by anyone's standards. Securing them for herself had absorbed all her efforts over the last few days. Now it was time to start thinking ahead again. Her position here was actually a lot stronger than it had been at Valisk. If the habitat was a fiefdom then New California was a kingdom in comparison. One which Capone appeared singularly inept at maintaining. The main reason she'd established herself so easily in the docking-ledges was the apathy spreading through Monterey. Nobody thought to question her.

That simply wouldn't do. In building his Organization, Capone had grasped an instinctive truth. People, possessed or otherwise, needed structure and order in their lives. It was one of the reasons they fell into line so easily, familiarity was a welcome comrade. Give them the kind of nirvana which existed (though she had strong suspicions about that) in the realm where planets shifted to, and the population would sink into a wretched, lotus-eating state. The Siamese twin of unending indulgent leisure. If she was honest with herself, she was terrified of the immortality she'd been given. Life would change beyond comprehension, and that was going to be very hard indeed. For an adaptation of that magnitude, she would no longer be herself.

And that I will not permit.

She enjoyed what she was and what she'd got, the drives and needs. Like this, at least she remained recognizably human. That identity was worth preserving. Worth fighting for.

Capone wouldn't do it. He was weak, controlled by that ingenious trollop Jezzibella, by a non-possessed.

In the Organization, a method of enforcing control over an entire planetary population had been perfected. If she was in charge, it could be used to implement her policies. The possessed would learn to live with their phobia of open skies. In return they would have the normal human existence they craved. There would be no dangerous metamorphosis into an alien state of being. She would remain whole. Herself.

A twitch of motion broke her contemplation. Someone was walking along the docking-ledge, someone in a bulky orange and white spacesuit with a globular helmet. Compared to modern SII suits, the thing was ridiculously old fashioned. The only reason for wearing one was if you didn't have neural nanonics.

'Are there any engineering crews on the ledge?' Kiera asked. She couldn't see any hellhawks receiving maintenance right now.

'A couple,' Hudson Proctor answered. 'The *Foica* is being loaded with combat wasps, and *Varrad*'s main fusion generator needs work on its heat-dump panels.'

'Oh. Where . . .'

'Kiera,' Hudson held up the handset in trepidation. 'Capone's calling all his senior lieutenants. It's an invite to some kind of glam party this evening.'

'Really?' She gave the spacesuited figure one last glance. 'And I haven't a thing to wear. But if our Great and Glorious Leader has summoned me, I'd better not disappoint him.'

*

Back on Koblat, they called these spacesuits ballcrushers. Jed had worn one before for an emergency evacuation drill, and now he was remembering why. Putting it on was easy enough; when they got it out of the locker it was a flaccid sack three times too large for his frame. He'd wriggled into it, standing with arms outstretched and legs apart so the baggy fabric could hang unobstructed off each limb. Then Beth had activated the wrist pad control and the fabric contracted like an all-over tourniquet. Now every part of his body was being squeezed tight. It was the same principle as an SII suit, preventing any loose bubbles of air becoming trapped between his skin and the suit. If a suit contained any sort of gas, it would inflate like a rigid balloon as soon as he stepped out into a vacuum.

This way, he could move about almost unrestricted. Providing he ignored the sharp pincer sensation besetting his crotch at every motion. Not an entirely easy thing to disregard.

But apart from that, the suit was functioning smoothly. He wished his heart would do the same. According to the hazy purple icons projected onto the inside of his helmet, the suit's integral thermal-shunt strips were conducting away a lot of heat. Nerves and an adrenalin high were making the blood pound away in his arteries. His tension wasn't helped by the rank of huge hellhawks he was walking along. He knew they could sense his thoughts and all the guilt cluttering up his skull, which made the torment even worse. A bad case of feedback. Bubbles of plastic and dark metal clung to the underbellies of the bitek starships like mechanical excrescences. Weapons and sensors. He was sure every one of them was tracking him.

'Jed, you're getting worse,' Rocio told him.

'How can you tell?'

'Why are you whispering? You are using a legitimate spacesuit radio frequency. If the Organization is monitoring this, which I doubt, they still have to decrypt the signal, which I also doubt their ability to do. As far as they are concerned you are just one of Kiera's people, while she will think you belong to the Organization. That's the beauty of this in-fighting, nobody knows what anyone else is doing around here.'

'Sorry,' Jed said contritely into the helmet mike.

'I'm monitoring your body functions, and your heart rate is still climbing.'

That brought a shudder which rippled up from Jed's legs to make his chest quiver. 'Oh, Jeeze. I'll come back.'

'No, no, you're doing fine. Only another three hundred metres to the airlock.'

'But the hellhawks are going to know!'

'Only if you don't take precautions. I think it's time we used a little chemical help here.'

'I didn't bring any. We weren't supposed to need that in Valisk.'

'I don't mean your underclass narcotics. The suit medical module will provide what you need.'

Jed hadn't even known the suit had a medical module. Following Rocio's instructions, he tapped out a series of orders on the wrist pad. The air in the helmet changed slightly, becoming cooler, and smelling of mint. For such a small suffusion, its effect was swift. The cold massaged its way in through Jed's muscles, bringing a nearly orgasmic sigh from his throat. It was a hit stronger than anything he'd ever scored in Koblat. His mind was being methodically purged of fright by this balmy tide of well-being. He held up his arms, expecting to see all his anxiety streaming out of his fingertips like liquid light.

'Not bad,' he declared.

'How much did you infuse?' Rocio asked.

The hellhawk's voice came across as brittle and irritating. 'What you said,' Jed retorted in a fashion which demonstrated quite plainly who was occupying the lead role. A couple of the physiology icons were flashing a rather pleasing pink in front of him. Like pretty little flower buds opening, he thought.

'All right, Jed, let's keep going, shall we?'

'Sure thing, mate.'

He started walking forwards again. Even the twinge in his groin was less of an issue now. That medical suffusion was good shit. The hellhawks had stopped radiating their intimidation. With his mind chilling he started to see them in a different context; grounded on their pedestals, sucking desperately at their drink. Not so much different to himself and the girls. He acquired a more confident stride as he passed the last two.

Rocio's voice started issuing directions again, guiding him in towards the airlock. Tall spires of machinery ran up the rock cliff at the back of the ledge, sprouting pipes in a crazed dendritic formation. Several small fountains of thin vapour were jetting out horizontally from junctions and micrometeorite punctures, their presence a testament to Monterey's floundering maintenance programme. Windows were set into the drab, sheared rock, long panoramic rectangles fronting departure lounges and engineering management offices. All but two were dark, reflecting weak outlines of the floodlit hellhawks. The remaining pair revealed nothing but vague shadows moving behind their frosted anti-glare shielding.

Maintenance vehicles, cargo trucks, and crew buses had been left scattered along the base of the cliff. Jed made his way through the maze they formed, thankful of the cover. The airlocks waited for him beyond, unlit tunnels leading into the asteroid. Conduits that would take him directly to the nest of the most feared possessed in the Confederation. His trepidation rose again as he approached them. He stopped on the threshold of a personnel airlock, and used the wrist pad again.

'Careful how much of that trauma suppressor you inhale,' Rocio said lightly. 'It's strong stuff, they designed it to keep you functional after an accident.'

'No worries,' Jed said earnestly. 'I can handle it.'

'Very well. There's no one in the area immediately behind the airlock. Time to go in.'

'Jed?' Beth's voice sounded loud and high in his helmet. 'Jed, can you hear me?'

'Sure, doll.'

'OK. We're watching the screens, too. Rocio is relaying images from the cameras inside, so we'll look out for you, mate. And he's right about the medical module, go easy on it, huh? I want to share some of that suffusion with you when you get back.'

Even in his tranquil state, Jed interpreted that right. He went into the airlock feeling majestic.

He took his helmet off, and took a breath of neutral air. It helped to clear his head a bit, not so much euphoria, but none of the fright, either. Good enough. Rocio gave him a whole string of directions to follow, and he started off cautiously down the corridor.

The storeroom for crew supplies wasn't far from the airlock, naturally enough. Rocio had been keeping a careful watch on things, seeing what happened when other hellhawks came to dock. Several of his bitek comrades still had crew on board. The combat wasps they carried required activation codes, and following standard security procedures Kiera and Capone had split the codes between loyalists. No one person could fire them. It was a significant point that she hadn't asked Rocio to carry any.

Jed found the door Rocio nominated, and pulled back the clamps. Cold air breezed out, turning his breath to foggy streamers. Inside, the room was split into aisles by long free-standing shelves. Despite the Organization's claim that normalizing food production on New California was a priority, there weren't many packs left. Processing food for the space industry was a specialist business; ideally, everything had to be crumb-free, taste-strengthened, and packaged in minimum volume. Leroy Octavius had decided that restarting the kitchen facilities of the relevant companies wasn't cost effective. Consequently, fleet crews had been making do with old stocks and standard pre-packed meals.

'What's there?' Beth asked impatiently. There were no cameras actually in the storeroom, Rocio had to go on what he'd seen being taken in and out.

Jed walked down the aisles, brushing the frost dust off various labels. 'Plenty,' he muttered. Providing you liked yoghurt, mint potato cakes, cheese and tomato flans (dehydrated in sachets that looked like fat biscuits), blackcurrant and apple mousse concentrate complemented with hotfrozen cubes of broccoli, spinach, carrot, and sprouts.

'Oh, bugger.'

'What's the matter?' Rocio asked.

'Nothing. The boxes are heavy, that's all. We're going to have a real party when I get this lot back to the ship.'

'Are there any chocolate oranges?' Gari piped up.

'I'll have a look, sweetheart,' Jed lied. He went back out into the corridor to fetch a trolley which had been abandoned just along from the storeroom. It ought to fit through the airlock, which meant he could use that to transport everything back to the *Mindori*. Then they'd all have to be carried up the stairs to the life-support module's airlock. It was going to be a long hard day.

'Somebody coming,' Rocio announced after Jed had got a dozen boxes out of the storeroom and onto the trolley.

Jed stopped dead, hugging a box of compressed rye chips. 'Who?' he hissed.

'Not sure. Camera image isn't too good. Small guy.'

'Where is he?' Jed dropped the box, wincing at the sound.

'A hundred metres away. But heading your way.'

'Oh, Jeeze. Is he possessed?'

'Unknown.'

Jed shot across the storage room and closed the door. Nothing he could do about the damning trolley outside, though. His heart began yammering as he flattened himself against the wall beside the door – as if that made a difference.

'Still coming,' Rocio announced calmly. 'Seventy metres now.'

Jed's hand crept down to the utility pocket on his hip. Fingers flicked the seal catch, and he dug inside. His hand closed around the cold, reassuring grip of the laser pistol.

'Thirty metres. He's coming to the junction with your corridor.'

Don't look at the bloody trolley, Jed prayed. Christ, please don't.

He drew the laser pistol out, and studied the simple controls for a second. Switched modes to constant beam, full power. Repeater was no good, a possessed would be able to screw with the electrics inside while he was shooting. He was only going to have one chance.

'He's in the corridor. I think he's seen the trolley. Stopping just outside.'

Jed closed his eyes, shaking badly. A possessed would be able to sense his thoughts. They would all be hauled off to face Capone. He would be tortured and Beth would get sent to the brothel.

I should have left the door open, that way I could have sprung out and surprised them.

'Hello?' a voice called. It was very high pitched, almost a girl's.

'Is that them?' he whispered to his suit mike.

'Yes. He's examined the trolley. Now by the door.'

The locking clamp moved, slowly hinging back. Jed stared at it in dread, desperate for one last hit from the suit's medical module.

If the laser doesn't work, I'll kill myself, he decided. Better that . . .

'Hello?' the high voice sounded timid. 'Is someone there?'

The door started to open.

'Hello?'

Jed shouted in fury, and jumped from the wall. Holding the laser pistol in a double-handed grip, he spun round and fired out into the corridor. Webster Pryor was saved by two things: his own diminutive height, and Jed's quite abysmal aim.

The red strand of laserlight was brilliant compared to the corridor lighting. It left Jed squinting against the glare, trying to see what he was shooting at. Blue-white flames and black smoke were squirting out of the corridor wall opposite, tracing a meandering line in the composite. Then the smoke stopped, and a spray of molten metal rained down. He was slicing through a conditioning duct.

He did – just – see a small man dive to the floor at his feet as the laser slashed round in search of a target. There was a yell of panic, and someone was screaming, 'Don't shoot me! Don't shoot me!' in a high-pitched voice.

Jed yelled himself. Confused all to hell by what was happening. Tentatively, he took his finger off the laser's trigger. Metal creaked alarmingly as the duct sagged around the dripping gap in its side. He looked down at the figure in the white jacket and black trousers grovelling on the floor. 'What in Christ's name is going on? Who are you?'

A terrified face was looking up at him. It wasn't a bloke, just a kid. 'Please don't kill me,' Webster pleaded. 'Please. I don't want to be one of them. They're horrible.'

'What's happening?' Rocio asked.

'Not sure,' Jed mumbled. He took a look down the corridor. All clear.

'Was that a laser?'

'Yeah.' He aimed it down at Webster. 'Are you possessed?'

'No. Are you?'

'Course bloody not.'

'Well, I didn't know,' Webster wailed.

'How did you get a weapon?' Rocio asked.

'Shut up! Jeeze, give me a break. I just got one, OK?'

Webster was frowning through his tears. 'What?'

'Nothing.' Jed hesitated, then put the laser pistol back in his utility pocket. The kid looked harmless, though the waiter's jacket with its brass buttons which he wore, along with his oil-slicked hair, was a little odd. But he was more scared than anything else. 'Who are you?'

The story came out in broken sentences, punctuated by sobs. How Webster and his mother had been caught up in Capone's takeover. How they'd been held in one of the asteroid's halls with hundreds of other women and children. How some Organization woman came searching them out from the rest. How he'd been separated from his mother and put to work serving drinks and food for the gangster bosses and a peculiar, very pretty, lady. How he kept hearing Capone and the lady mention his father's name, and then glance in his direction.

'What are you doing down here?' Jed asked.

'They sent me for some food,' Webster said. 'The cook told me to find out if there were any swans left in storage.'

'This is the spacecraft section,' Jed said. 'Didn't you know?'

Webster sniffled loudly. 'Yes. But if I look everywhere, I could stay away from them for a while.'

'Right.' He straightened, and found one of the small camera lenses. 'What do we do?' he asked, flustered by the boy's tale.

'Get rid of him,' Rocio said curtly.

'What do you mean?'

'He's a complication. You've got the laser pistol, haven't you?'

Webster was looking up at him passively, eyes red-rimmed from the tears. All mournful and beat; the way not so long ago Jed had looked at Digger when the pain was at its worst.

'I can't do that!' Jed exclaimed.

'What do you need, a note from your mother? Listen to me, Jed, the second he steps within range of a possessed, they'll know something's happened to him. Then they'll come looking for you. They'll get you, and Beth, and the girls.'

'No way. I can't. I just can't. Not even if I wanted to.'

'So what are you going to do instead?'

'I don't know! Beth? Beth, have you been switched on to all this?'

'Yes, Jed,' she replied. 'You're not to touch that boy. We've got plenty of food, now, so bring him back with you. He can come with us.'

'Really?' Rocio enquired disdainfully. 'And where's his spacesuit? How's he supposed to get out to me?'

Jed looked at Webster, thoroughly disconcerted. This whole situation was just getting worse and worse. 'For Christ's sake, just get me out of this.'

'Stop being an arsehole,' Beth snapped. 'It's bloody obvious, you'll have to steal one of the vehicles. There's plenty of them about. I can see some of them docked to the airlocks close to where you went in. Take one and drive it over to us.'

Jed wanted to curl up into a ball and take a decent hit. A vehicle! In full view of this whole nest of possessed.

'Please, Jed, come back,' Gari entreated. 'I don't like it here without you.'

'All right, doll,' he said, too bushed to kick up an argument. 'On my way.' He rounded on Webster. 'And you'd better not be any trouble.'

'You're going to take me away?' the boy asked in wonder.

'Sort of, yeah.'

Jed didn't bother about collecting any more food from the shelves. He just started pushing the trolley, making sure Webster was in sight the whole time.

Rocio reviewed the camera images and schematic data available to him, and quickly devised a route to one of the docking-ledge vehicles. It meant the two of them taking a lift up to the lounge level, which he didn't like. But previewing enabled him to hurry them past the sections where crews were still working without incident.

The vehicle he'd chosen for them was a small taxi with a five-seater cab. Large enough to take the trolley, and simple enough for Jed to drive. He was back at the *Mindori* three minutes after disengaging from the airlock. It actually took him longer than that to match the taxi's docking tube with the starship's life-support module hatch. Once the tube was locked and pressurized, Beth, Gari, and Navar came rushing in to greet the returning hero. Beth put her hands on either side of his face and gave him a long kiss. 'I'm proud of you,' she said.

That wasn't something she'd ever told him before, and she didn't hand out platitudes, either. Of course, today had been full of not merely the unusual but the positively weird. However, the words left him warm and uncertain. The moment was only slightly spoilt when the two younger girls started reading labels and found out what he'd brought back.

*

It had taken the Monterey Hilton's head chef over three hours to prepare the meal. A dozen or so senior lieutenants and their partners had been invited to an evening with Al and Jezzibella. Pasta with a sauce that was at least as good as they used to make on Earth (supervised by Al), swan stuffed with fish, fresh vegetables boosted up from the planet that afternoon, desserts heavy on chocolate and calories, matured cheeses, the finest wines New California could produce, the fanciest liqueurs. As well as the food, there was a five-piece band, and some showgirls for later. Guests would also receive items of twenty-four carat jewellery (genuine, not energistic baubles), personally selected by Al himself. The evening was intended to be memorable. Nobody left Al Capone's party without a smile on their face. His reputation as a wild and exuberant host had to be preserved, after all.

What Al didn't know was that Leroy had to be taken off Organization administration duties in order to make the arrangements. He'd spent over an hour calling senior Organization personnel to facilitate the ingredients and people necessary to make the party work. That bothered the obese manager. The picture he and Emmet were getting from various lieutenants and city bosses down on the surface was a smooth one, things falling neatly into place, people doing as they were told. But not so long ago, when the fleet left for Arnstadt, Leroy had put together a grand ball in under a week. A time when the planet and high-orbit asteroids had fought for the privilege of supplying Al with the best of anything they had. This party was a fraction of that scale and a multiple of the effort.

However, despite the grudging donations, the Nixon Suite's dining room was an impressive and dramatic example of lavishness when Leroy finally arrived, immaculate tuxedo straining around his huge frame. One of the more lissom girls from the brothel was on his arm, the pair of them a gross example of human glandular divergence. Heads turned to look at him when they arrived together. Silent calculations were quickly performed when a smiling Al greeted them, and handed the girl a diamond necklace which even her cleavage couldn't devour. No snide remarks were ventured, though the mind-tones said it all.

Monterey was out of the umbra again, heading into the light. Outside the broad window New California's green and blue crescent gleamed warmly. It was a sumptuous atmosphere for the pre-dinner drinks, and the atmosphere was suitably relaxed. Waiters circulated with gold and silver trays of canapés, making sure no glass was ever in danger of heading towards half empty. Conversation flowed, and Al circulated with grace, showing no favouritism.

His mood didn't even falter when Kiera showed up an easy fifteen minutes after everyone else. She wore a provocatively simple sleeveless summer dress of some thin mauve fabric, cut to emphasize her figure. On a girl of her body's age it would have been charmingly guileless, on her it was a declaration of all-out fashion war against the other females in the room. Only Jezzibella in the ever-classic little black cocktail number looked snazzier. And by the bright cherub's smile she used to welcome Kiera, she knew it.

'Al, darling.' Kiera's smile was wide and sweltering as she kissed Al's cheek. 'Great party, thanks for the invite.'

For a second, Al worried her teeth might be going for his jugular. Her thoughts bristled with an icy superiority. 'Wouldn't be the same without you,' he told her. Jeeze, and to think he'd once considered her a possible lay. His wang would get so cold inside her it'd snap clean off.

The notion made him shiver. He beckoned to one of the waiters. The guy must have been in his nineties, one of those dignified old coots that were perfect as butlers. Young Webster should have been doing this job, Al thought, it would have made for a cuter image. But he hadn't seen the boy all evening. The old man wobbled forwards obediently, carrying a tray of black velvet with a shimmering sapphire cobweb necklace resting on it.

'For me?' Kiera simpered. 'Oh, how lovely.'

Al took the necklace off the tray and slowly fastened it round her neck, ignoring her lecherous smirk at his proximity.

'It's so nice to see you here,' Jezzibella said, clinging to Al's arm. 'We weren't sure if you could spare the time.'

'I've always got time for Al.'

'That's nice to hear. Keeping the hellhawks in line must take up a big part of your day.'

'I don't have any trouble coping. They know I'm in charge of them.'

'Yeah, you got some interesting moves there,' Al said. 'Emmet was full of praise for what you did. Said it was smart. Coming from him, that's quite a compliment. I'll have to remember them in case I'm ever in a similar situation.'

Kiera removed a champagne flute from one of the waiters, and her gaze searched the room like a targeting laser until she found Emmet. 'You won't be in a similar situation, Al. I'm covering that flank for you. Very thoroughly.'

Jezzibella morphed into her hero-worshipping early-teens persona. 'Covering for Al?' her high girlish voice piped.

'Yes. Who else?'

'Come on, Jez.' Al grinned in mock-rebuke. 'There ain't no one else in the market for hellhawks, you know that.'

'I do.' Jezzibella looked up adoringly at him, and sighed.

'And without me, there's no reason for New California to keep supporting them,' Al said.

Kiera's attention moved back from Emmet. 'Believe me, I'm very aware of everyone's position. And their worth.'

'That's nice,' Jezzibella said blandly.

'Enjoy your drink, babe,' Al said, and patted Kiera's arm. 'I got a small announcement to make before we sit down to eat.' He marched over to Emmet, and signalled the head waiter to bang a gong. The room fell silent, people picking up on the focused excitement in Al's mind. 'This ain't the usual kind of speech to make at table. I ain't got no stag jokes, for a start.'

Faithful smiles switched on all around. Al took another sip of champagne – damn, but he wanted a shot of decent bourbon. 'All right, I ain't gonna bullshit around with you. We got problems with the fleet, on account of it ain't got nowhere to go. You know how it is, we gotta keep momentum going or the boys'll go sour on us. That right, Silvano?'

The brooding lieutenant nodded scrupulously. 'Some of the guys are getting close to the boil, sure, Al. Nothing we can't keep a lid on.'

'I don't wanna keep no fucking lid on nothing. We gotta give the bastards something to do while we build up stocks of antimatter. We can't take over no planet again, not for a while. So we're gonna hit the Confederation from another angle. That's what I got for you, something new. This way we cause them one fuck of a lot of damage, and don't get hurt ourselves. And we got Emmet here to thank for that.' He put his arm round the Organization's reluctant technology expert, and gave him a friendly hug. 'We're gonna launch some raids on other planets, and break through their space-fort defences. Once we've done that, we can sling a whole load of our guys down to the surface. Tell them, Emmet.'

'I've done some preliminary designs for one-man atmospheric entry pods,' Emmet said in a tense voice. 'They're based on standard escape boats, but they can descend in under fifteen minutes. That's high gees for whoever's inside, but with our energistic strength it shouldn't be a problem. And they're simple enough that we shouldn't screw up the guidance electronics. All the fleet has to do is create a window in the SD coverage long enough for them to get down. Once they're on the ground, the good old exponential curve comes into play.'

'Without the fleet firepower to back them up, they'll lose,' Dwight said bluntly. 'The local cops will wipe them out.'

'It depends on how together the planet is, and how many soldiers we can shove down there,' Al said, untroubled. 'Emmet's right about how fast we can expand. That's gonna cause the governments a shitload of grief.'

'But, Al, the Organization can't expand as fast as ordinary possessed. We've got to have time to let Harwood and his guys vet the souls that're coming back. Christ, we've had enough trouble with loyalty on New California, let alone Arnstadt. If we don't have committed lieutenants, the Organization'll fall apart.'

'Who gives a shit?' Al laughed round at the startled expressions. 'Come on, you guys! Just how many goddam planets do you think we can run? Even the King of Kulu's only got half a dozen. If I gave all you dopeheads one apiece to be emperor of, that still leaves hundreds of free ones left out there to screw with us. We gotta start levelling the odds here. I say shoot possessed down to the surface and let the fuckers run loose. We can use all our hotheads from here, all the crap artists who wanna take New California out of the universe, send them, get rid of the assholes permanently. That way we're solving two problems at once. Fewer traitors here, and planets dropping out of the Confederation. You retards grabbed what that'll mean yet? It means less hassle for us. Every planet we hit is gonna scream to the navy for the same kinda help Mortonridge is getting. That'll cost them plenty to provide. Money they can't spend dicking with us.' He looked round the room, knowing he'd won them over. Again. His face reddened with the heat of victory, three tiny white lines proud on his cheek. That reluctant admiration he'd kindled in them proving he was the man with the plan, and the balls to see it through.

Al raised his glass high in triumph. And it was like a room full of Krauts doing their knee-jerk Fascist salute as the others held their own glasses up, fast. Jezzibella winked impishly at him from behind the back row, while Kiera's face was drawn as she considered the implications.

'A toast. Goodbye to that goddam pain in the ass Confederation.'

*

The *Mindori*'s distortion field expanded outwards in a specific pattern of swirls, generating ripples in the fabric of space-time. They pushed against the hull, lifting it from the pedestal in a simple, smooth motion.

Inside the large forward lounge, none of the six passengers noticed even a quiver in the apparent gravity field. They'd just finished their meal of mashed turkey granules, which was the only meat product Beth could hammer into a burger shape. Jed was ignoring the sullen stares that were getting flashed his way. Turkey wasn't so bad after it had been grilled.

Gerald Skibbow looked up at the lounge's big screen as the edge of the docking-ledge slipped towards them. 'Where are we going?' he asked.

Webster twitched in surprise, it was the first time he'd heard Gerald speak. The others stared at him, slightly nervous of what would follow. Even now, after all this time, he was still nutty Gerald to them. Rocio had privately confided to Jed and Beth he couldn't make any sense of Gerald's thoughts at all.

A small picture of Rocio's face appeared in one corner of the screen. 'I've been given a patrol flight vector,' he said. 'It's not a very demanding one, we'll never be more than three million kilometres from New California. I suspect it's a trial to see if I do as I'm told. I have just filled my reserve bladders with nutrient fluid; if I was going to leave, now would be an obvious time.'

'Are you going to?' Beth asked.

'No. The only place to go is the Edenist habitats and the Confederation. The price for their sanctuary would be cooperating with their physicists. As that would ultimately lead to the defeat of the possessed, I told you before: I need to find other options.'

'I don't want to leave Monterey,' Gerald said. The screen was now showing the asteroid's counter-rotating spaceport receding at a considerable speed. 'Please go back and let me disembark.'

'Can't do that, Gerald, mate,' Beth said. 'Them possessed, they'd spot you inside Monterey in a flash. Give the whole game away. We'd all wind up like Marie, that way, and they'd punish Rocio, too.'

'I will assist you with Kiera in whatever way I can,' Rocio said. 'But first, I must establish myself as one of her servile flock.'

Beth reached over and gripped Gerald's arm. 'We can wait that long, eh?'

Gerald considered her words; although he was sure his thoughts were taking longer to form these days. There was a time when he could give an instant reply to any topic or question. That Gerald existed only in his mind now, a memory that was hard to find and difficult to see. 'All right,' he said. It was a tough concession to make. To have been so close to *her*. Just a few hundred metres. And now having to leave, to abandon her. It would probably be days until they could return. Days darling Marie would have to spend enduring the torment of that terrible woman's control. The notions of what she would get up to with her captive flesh were horrible. Marie was a lovely little girl, so pretty. Always had lots of boyfriends, which he'd tried not to get upset and protective over. Back on Lalonde, sex seemed the only thing the possessed were interested in. And like every father since the dawn of civilization, Marie's sexuality was the one thing Gerald never dared dwell upon.

It would be that, he admitted in his dark heart. Night after night, Kiera would allow some man to run his hands over her. Would laugh and groan at the abuse. Would demand hot physical violations. Bodies writhing together in the darkness. Beautiful, strong bodies. Gerald whimpered softly.

'You OK?' Beth asked. Beside her, Jed was frowning.

'Fine,' Gerald whispered. His hands were rubbing his perspiring forehead, trying to massage the pain inside. 'I just want to help her. And if I could just get to her, I know I could. Loren said so, you see.'

'We'll be back there in no time, OK, no worries.'

He nodded lamely, returning to pick at the food they'd given him. He had to get to Marie soon. He was sorry about everyone else's predicament, but what Marie was suffering was unspeakable. Next time they landed at Monterey, he decided, it would be different. No details, but definitely different.

Rocio was aware of Gerald's ardent, fractured anxiety sinking back under calmer emotions. That man's mind was a complete enigma. Not that Rocio actually wanted to be privy to such tortured thoughts. Shame that he couldn't convince Beth and Jed to stay on board by themselves. This entourage of people were making his position more complicated. Ideally, he'd like to winnow the numbers down again.

Now he was clear of the asteroid, he began to accelerate. Modifying the distortion field to generate ever more powerful ripples in space-time. He surfed them at seven gees, a secondary manipulation alleviating the force around the life-support section. As the sense of freedom rose in tandem with his speed, he allowed his dreamform to blossom. Dark wings slowly spread wide, sweeping eagerly, sending motes of interplanetary dust swirling in his wake. He shook his neck, blinking huge red eyes, flexing his talons. In this state, he was perfectly at one with himself and life. It reaffirmed the conviction that Kiera's hold over himself and his comrades must be broken.

He began talking to the other hellhawks, probing for emotional nuances. Building a pattern of those who thought as he did. Of the seventy currently in the New California system, he thought there were possibly nineteen he could count on for open support, another ten would probably side with him if things looked favourable. Several were playing it very coy, while eight or nine, led by Etchells and Cameron Leung, revelled in the prospect of following the Organization fleet into glory. Good enough odds.

Eight hours into his patrol, Hudson Proctor delivered new instructions. **There's an interplanetary ship decelerating towards New California,** Kiera's lieutenant said. **Coming straight in along the south pole, one and** a half million kilometres out. We think it's come from the Almaden asteroid. Can you sense it?

Rocio expanded his distortion field, probing where Proctor indicated. The ship slithered into his perception as a tight kink of mass, alive with energy.

Got it, he acknowledged.

Intercept them, and order them to return.

Are they hostile?

I doubt it. Probably just another bunch of idiots who think they can live where they want instead of where the Organization tells them.

Understood. And if they don't want to return?

Blow them to shit. Any questions?

No.

Rocio changed the distortion field again, concentrating it on a small area just ahead of his beak. Power surged through his patterning cells, and the stress he was applying leapt towards infinite. A wormhole interstice opened, and he shot through, emerging from the terminus less than two seconds later. It folded neatly behind his tail feathers, returning local space-time to its usual consonance.

The interplanetary ship was three kilometres away, a long silk-grey splinter of metal and composite. Standard configuration of barrel-shaped life-support module separated from the drive section by a lattice tower. It was decelerating at two-thirds of a gee, blue-white fusion flame spearing cleanly from its exhaust. Rocio was also aware of another wormhole terminus opening five thousand kilometres away. A hellhawk slid out, deflating its distortion field immediately, and drifting inert. He resisted the temptation to hail it. Shadowing him in such a fashion to monitor his conduct was very unsubtle.

A radar pulse triggered the ship's transponder: according to the code it was called the *Lucky Logorn*. Rocio matched velocities with it, and opened a short-range channel. 'This is the Organization ship *Mindori*,' he told them. 'You're approaching New California's strategic-defence network without clearance. Please identify yourself.'

'This is Deebank, I guess I'm the captain around here. We haven't been advertising our presence in case we attracted those goddam voidhawks. Sorry about that, didn't mean to give you a scare. We'd like clearance to rendezvous with a low-orbit station.'

'Clearance refused. Return to your asteroid.'

214

'Now just a goddam minute, we're loyal members of the Organization here. What gives you the right to order us about?'

Rocio activated a maser cannon on his lower hull, and targeted one of the thermo-dump panels plumbed into *Lucky Logorn*'s equipment bay. 'One. I'm not ordering you, I'm relaying an instruction from the Organization. Two.' He fired.

The blast of coherent maser radiation thumped a half-metre hole into the middle of the thermo-dump panel. Fluorescent orange shards spun away, their glimmer slowly fading to black.

'Fuck you,' Deebank shouted. 'You bastards can't keep us out here for ever.'

'Realign your drive. Now. My second shot will be through your fusion tube. You'll be left drifting out here. The only thing you'll have to occupy yourselves with is a sweepstake. Is your food going to run out first? Or will it be the air? Then again, a voidhawk might pick you up, and you get used as research lab beasts by the Confederation.'

'You piece of shit.'

'I'm waiting.' Rocio slid closer, picking up the resentment and anger boiling through the eight people in the life-support section. There was bitter resignation in there, too.

Sure enough, the fusion drive plume twitched round, sending *Lucky Logorn* on a shallow arc which would ultimately see it heading back to Almaden. Cancelling so much delta-v was a long, energy-expensive business. It would take them hours.

'We're going to remember you,' Deebank promised. 'Time will come when you need to join us. Don't expect it to be easy.'

'Join you where?' Rocio asked, genuinely curious.

'On a planet, dick-for-brains.'

'Is that what this was all about? Your fear of space?'

'What the hell did you think we were doing? Invading?'

'I wasn't told.'

'OK. So now you understand, will you let us through?'

'I can't.'

'Bastard.'

Rocio played for the sympathy angle, marshalling his thoughts into contrite concern. 'I mean it. There's another hellhawk shadowing me, making sure I do what I'm told. They're not certain about my commitment to the cause, you see.'

215

'Hear that splashing sound? That's my heart bleeding.'

'Why doesn't the Organization want you on New California?'

'Because they need the products Almaden makes in its industrial stations. The asteroid has plenty of astroengineering companies who specialize in weapons systems. And we're the poor saps who have to terrorize non-possessed technicians into keeping them running. You got any idea what that's like? It's a crock of shit. I was a soldier when I was alive, I used to fight the kind of fascists who enslaved people like this. I'm telling you, it ain't right. It ain't what I was brought up to do. None of this is.'

'Then why stay in the Organization?'

'If you ain't for Capone, you're against him. That's the way it works. He's been real smart the way he's set things up. Those lieutenants of his will do anything to keep their position. They put the screws on us, and we have to put the screws on the non-possessed. If there's any trouble, if we start to object, or get uppity, they just call on the fleet for back-up. Don't they? You're the enforcers, you make it all hang together for him.'

'We have our own enforcer, she's called Kiera.'

'The Deadnight babe? No shit? I wouldn't mind submitting my poor body to some enforcement by her.' Laughter rumbled across the gap between the ships.

'You wouldn't say that if you'd ever met her.'

'Tough bitch, huh?'

'The worst.'

'You don't sound too happy about that.'

'You and I are in the same situation.'

'Yeah? So listen, maybe we can come to some kind of arrangement? I mean, if we have to go back to Almaden, the lieutenants are going to make us eat shit for pulling this stunt. Why don't you take us back to New California, let us off at a low-orbit station, or if you've got a spaceplane we could use that. If we get down there to the surface, we stay. Believe me. There'd be no comeback.'

'Fine for you.'

'We'll get you a body. A human one, the very best there is. There's millions of non-possessed left on the planet; we'll get one ready for possession and hold it for you. This way you get down there without any of the risk we'll be going through. Listen, you can sense I'm telling the truth. Right?'

'Yes. But it doesn't interest me.'

'What? Why not? Come on! It's the greatest deal in town.'

'Not for me. You people really hate this empty universe, don't you?'

'Oh, like you don't? You were in the beyond. You can hear the beyond. It's always there, just one step away on the other side from night. We have to get away from that.'

'I don't.'

'Crap.'

'But I don't. Really. Certainly I can still hear the lost souls, but it's not as if they can touch me. All they are is a reminder of that nothingness. They're not a threat themselves. Fear is the only thing that drives you to escape. I've got over that. *Mindori* belongs here in the emptiness, this is its perfect milieu. Having this construct as my host has taught me not to be afraid. Perhaps it should be you who try and find blackhawk and voidhawk bodies. Can you imagine that? It would solve everyone's problem, without all this conflict and violence, if after you die you were to be given a voidhawk body to possess. Enough could be grown for the lost souls, I'm sure of it, given time and commitment. Then ultimately, space would become filled with billions of us, the entire human race transformed into dark angels flitting between the stars.'

'Hey, pal, know what? Possessing that monster didn't cure you, it made you take a swan dive over the edge.'

'Perhaps. But which of us is content?'

'You got Kiera to worry about. Remember? How come you don't flap off into the sunset?'

'As you say, Kiera is a problem.'

'Right, so don't come over all superior.'

'I wasn't. Your offer to deal interests me. It may be possible to come to some arrangement. I have a notion, but it'll take some time to check the requirements. Once you're back on Almaden, I'll look you up.'

*

Coming down to the gym in the Hilton's basement always stirred Kiera's darker animal feelings. She rather enjoyed her new role of laid-back vamp, letting her eye wander over the young men being put through their paces by a gruff Malone. Their apprehension was pleasurable as they saw her watching, the nudges and worried glances. It wasn't that she'd never had affairs back on New Munich, she'd taken several lovers during her marriage, both before and after her husband's fall from grace. But they'd all been insipid, cautious encounters. Most of the thrill had come from the concept of having an affair, of cheating and not getting caught. The sex had never been anything special.

Now, though, she was free to explore her sexuality to the full, with no one to disapprove or condemn. Part of her allure came from being a woman in power, she was a challenge to any male; the rest came from Marie Skibbow's gorgeous body. It was the second factor which brought her down here to the non-possessed. Possessed lovers, like poor old Stanyon, were so artificial. Men inevitably gave themselves big penises, could stay erect all night, had Greek-god bodies. Strutting clichés that spoke volumes about their weaknesses and insecurities.

She much preferred the youngsters from the gym for the reality they provided. Unable to hide behind any mental or physical illusion, sex with them was raw and primitive. Dominating them in bed, without a single inhibition, was utterly delicious. And Marie herself had a surprising amount of knowledge which Kiera could extract and experiment with. Despised memories and skill gained during a long river journey spent capitulating to an old man called Len Buchannan. Enduring the nightly humiliation for one reason alone, the freedom which waited at the end of the river. The girl had a single-minded determination which Kiera quite admired. It came close to her own. Even now, captive and tragic, inside her mental prison, Marie clung to the notion of deliverance.

But how? Kiera wondered lightly.

Somehow. One day.

Not with me in command of you.

Nothing lasts for ever. As *you* know.

Kiera dismissed the impudent girl from her thoughts with a derisory mental sneer. Her gaze found a rather delicious nineteen-year-old hammering his fists into a long leather punchbag. The desperate aggression and sweating muscles were highly arousing. He knew she was standing behind him, but refused to turn. Hoping if he avoided eye contact she would pass by. She crooked at finger at Malone, who came over reluctantly.

'What's his name?' she asked huskily.

'Jamie.' The squat trainer's thoughts were full of contempt.

'Are you frightened of me, Jamie?'

He stopped punching, steadying the bag. Gentle grey eyes stared at her levelly. 'You, no. What you can do, yeah.'

She applauded languidly. 'Very good. Don't worry, I'm not going to hurt you.' She glanced down at Malone. 'I'll bring him back to you in the morning.'

Malone took his cap off, and spat on the floor. 'Whatever you say, Kiera.'

She walked right up to Jamie, enjoying his discomfort at her proximity. 'Oh dear, I'm not that bad, am I?' she murmured.

He was a head taller than her. When he looked down, his eyes were drawn to the rich tanned skin revealed by her mauve summer dress. Embarrassment warred with other, more subtle emotions. Kiera grinned in victory. At least something was going right tonight. Capone and his damn sedition plans! She took his big hand in hers, and began to lead him out of the gym like a giant puppy. Before she reached the double doors, they swung open. Luigi barged through, carrying a pile of towels. He caught sight of Kiera, and glared angrily. Commander of the fleet, now running trivial demeaning errands for the nonentity Malone. The resentment twisting him up was almost strong enough to manifest itself as pernicious violence; he was sure she was here simply to witness his humiliation first-hand. The boss's new favourite gloating over her ex-rival's downfall.

'Luigi,' Kiera said brightly. 'Fancy seeing you here. How wonderful.'

'Piss off, bitch.' He elbowed past her, scowling.

'After the towels, will you be going down on your knees to tie up their boots?'

Luigi twisted in mid-step, and marched back to her. He thrust his head forward so their noses were touching. 'You're a whore. A very cheap whore. With only one thing to sell. When the Organization has used up your hellhawks, you'll be nothing. Best thing is, you know it's coming. Your bullshit ice empress routine doesn't fool anyone. This whole damn asteroid is laughing at you.'

'Of course it's coming,' she said serenely. 'But they wouldn't be used up if the fleet was commanded properly.'

Confusion marred his face and his thoughts. 'What?'

That uncertainty was enough for Kiera. She patted Jamie's heavily muscled forearm. 'Why don't you take those heavy towels from Luigi, darling. It looks like I won't be needing you tonight, after all.'

Jamie peered over the pile of towels unexpectedly dumped in his arms, watching the doors close behind Kiera and Luigi. 'I don't get it,' he complained. Part of him had actually been quite looking forward to the sex, despite what the others kept saying about the Deadnight witch.

Malone patted the big lad's shoulder in a paternal fashion. 'Don't worry about it, my boy. You're well off out of that kind of scene.'

*

Given Dr Pierce Gilmore's senior position within the CNIS's scientific staff (Weapons Analysis Division) it was inevitable that a large part of his nature tended towards the bureaucratic. Precise and methodical in his work, he believed strongly in following sanctioned procedures to the letter during his investigations. Such adherence to protocol was something of a joke among his department's junior staff, who accused him of inflexibility and lack of imagination. He endured their behind-his-back humour stoically, while politely and consistently refusing to take short cuts and play up to wild hunches. To his credit, it was exactly the kind of leadership the Weapons Division needed. Eternal patience is a prime requisite in the dismantling of unknown weapons that have been designed illegally (mostly under government patronage) and tend to incorporate elements that actively discourage close examination. In the seven years he'd held his post, the division's safety record was exemplary.

Also to his credit, he didn't indulge in the usual internal empire building so beloved of government employees, especially those who, like him, were essentially unaccountable. As a result, his office was a modest one, roughly equivalent to the entitlement of a middle manager in some multistellar company. There were few personal items, some ornaments and desktop solid images; a shelf of Stanhopea orchids flourished under a slim solaris tube. The furniture was formal, a comfortable reproduction of the flared darkwood Midwest-ethnic style he'd grown up with. Broad holographic windows of Cheyenne's heroically rugged countryside did little to disguise the room's actual location, buried deep inside Trafalgar. In its favour, the electronic suite Gilmore had installed was a top-of-the-range Edenist processor array verging on AI status. Such a system helped facilitate the twice-weekly multi-disciplinary councils he chaired to investigate the capabilities of the possessed.

This was the second time the team heads had met since Jacqueline Couteur had made her bid for freedom in maximum-security Court Three, and the aftermath was still affecting everyone's mood. Professor Nowak, the quantum physicist, was first to arrive, helping himself to some of the coffee from the percolator jug which Gilmore kept going full time. Dr Hemmatu, the energy specialist, and Yusuf, the electronics chief, came in together talking in low tones. They gave Gilmore a perfunctory nod and sat down at the conference desk. Mattox was next, the neurology doctor keeping to himself as usual, choosing a chair one along the desk from Yusuf. Euru completed the group, sitting directly opposite Gilmore. In contrast to the rest of them, the dark-skinned Edenist appeared almost indecently happy.

Gilmore had known his deputy long enough to see it wasn't just the usual contentment which all Edenists shared. 'You have something?' he enquired.

'A voidhawk has just arrived from the Sinagra system. It was carrying an interesting recording.'

Hemmatu perked up. 'From Valisk?' The independent habitat had supplied a large amount of very useful data on the behaviour of the possessed before it vanished.

'Yes, just before Rubra and Dariat took it away,' Euru said, smiling broadly. He instructed his bitek processor block to datavise the file to them.

The sensevise they received was a strange one, lacking the resolution normally associated with full nerve channel input. Conversions from Edenist habitat memories to a standard Adamist electronic format were notoriously quirky, but this was something else again. Nesting within its environment of pastel colours, tenuous scents, and mild tactorials, Gilmore tried bravely to avoid using the connotation *spectral*. He failed dismally.

The memory was of Dariat, while he bobbed about on the surface of some icy water inside a dark polyp-walled tube. The cold was severe enough to penetrate even his energistic protection, judging by the way it was numbing his appropriated limbs, and making him shiver. A plump black woman clung to him, shaking violently inside her strange waistcoat of cushions.

Did you gain any impression of size? the Kohistan Consensus asked Dariat.

Not really, a universe is a universe. How big is this one?

Consensus received his quick recollection of the beyond. His soul had become a feeble flicker of identity adrift in a nowhere at one remove from reality. Nowhere full of similar souls; all of them with the same craving, the sensations available on the other side.

The memory of someone else's memory: if the sensenviron of the Valisk starscraper waste tube was tenuous, this was as insubstantial as a nearly forgotten dream. The beyond, as far as Dariat was concerned, lacked any physical sensation, all that betrayed its presence was a transparent tapestry of emotions. Anguish and yearning flooded through the realm. Souls clustered round, desperately suckling at his memories for the illusion of physical sensation they contained.

Confusion and fear reigned in Dariat's mind. He wanted to flee. He wanted to plunge into the glorious star of sensation burning so bright as Kiera and Stanyon forced open a path into Horgan's body. The beyond withered behind him as he surged along the tear through the barrier between planes of existence.

And how do you control the energistic power? Consensus asked.

Dariat gave them a visualization (perfectly clear this time) of desire overlaying actuality. More handsome features, thicker hair, brighter clothes. Like a hologram projection, but backed up by energy oozing out of the beyond to shore it up, providing solidity. Also, the destructive power, a mental thunderbolt, aimed and thrown amid boiling passion. The rush of energy from the beyond increasing a thousandfold, sizzling through the possessed body like an electric charge.

What about senses? This ESP faculty you have? The world around him altered, shifting to slippery shadows.

There were several more questions and observations on the nature of Dariat's state, which the rebel possessor did his best to answer. In total, the recording amounted to over fifteen minutes.

'Wealth indeed,' Gilmore said when it ended. 'This kind of

clarification is just what we need to pursue a solution. It seemed to me as though Dariat actually had some freedom of movement in the beyond. To my mind, that implies physical dimensions.'

'A strange sort of space,' Nowak said. 'From the way the souls were pressed close enough to overlap, there appeared to be very little of it. I won't call it a place, but it's definitely a unified area. It was almost a closed continuum, yet we know it exists in parallel to our own universe, so it must have infinite depth. That's damn close to being paradoxical.' He shrugged, disturbed by his own reasoning.

'That perception ability Dariat demonstrated interests me,' Euru commented. 'The effect is remarkably similar to a voidhawk's mass-perception sense.'

Gilmore looked across his desk to the tall Edenist, inviting him to continue.

'I'd say the possessed must be interpreting local energy resonances. Whatever type of energy they operate within, we know it pervades our universe, even if we can't distinguish it ourselves yet.'

'If you're right,' Nowak said, 'that's a further indication that our universe is contiguous with this beyond realm, that there is no single interface point.'

'There has to be an identifiable connection,' Euru said. 'Dariat was clearly aware of the lost souls while he occupied Horgan's body. He could hear them – for want of a better phrase. They were pleading with the possessors the whole time, asking to be given bodies. Somewhere there is a connection, a conduit leading back there.'

Gilmore glanced round the desk to see if anyone else wanted to pick up on the point. They were all silent, concentrating on the implications Euru and Nowak raised. 'I've been considering that we might need to approach this from a different angle,' he said. 'After all, we've had a singular lack of success in trying to analyse the quantum signature of the effect, perhaps we should concentrate less on the exact nature of the beast, and more on what it does and implies.'

'In order to deal with it, we have to identify it,' Yusuf said.

'I'm not advocating a brute force and ignorance approach,' Gilmore replied. 'But consider: when this crisis started, we believed we were dealing with an outbreak of some energy virus. I maintain that is essentially what we have here. Our souls are self-contained patterns capable of existence and travel outside the matrix of our bodies. Hemmatu, how would you say they are formed?'

The energy expert stroked his cheek with long fingers, pondering the question. 'Yes, I think I see what you're driving at. The beyond energy is apparently present in all matter, including cells, although the quantity involved must necessarily be extremely tenuous. Therefore, as intelligence arises during life, it imprints itself into this energy somehow.'

'Exactly,' Gilmore said. 'The thought patterns which arise in our neuron structure retain their cohesion once the brain dies. That is our soul. There's nothing spiritual or religious about it, the entire concept is an entirely natural phenomenon, given the nature of the universe.'

'I'm not sure about denying religion,' Nowak said. 'Being inescapably plugged into the universe at such a fundamental level seems somewhat spiritually impressive to me. Being at one with the cosmos, literally, makes us all part of God's creation. Surely?'

Gilmore couldn't quite work out if he was joking. A lot of physicists took to religion as they struggled with the unknowable boundaries of cosmology, almost as many as embraced atheism. 'If we could just put that aside for the moment, please?'

Nowak grinned, waving a hand generously.

'What I'm getting at is that something is responsible for retaining a soul's cohesion. Something glues those thoughts and memories together. When Syrinx interviewed Malva, she was told: *life begets souls.* That it is *the pattern which sentience and self-awareness exerts on the energy within the biological body.*'

'So souls accrue from the reaction of thoughts upon this energy,' Nowak said. 'I'm not disputing the hypothesis. But how can that help us?'

'Because it's only us: humans. Animals don't have souls. Dariat and Laton never mentioned encountering them.'

'They never mentioned encountering alien souls either,' Mattox said. 'But according to the Kiint, they're there.'

'It's a big universe,' Nowak said.

'No,' Gilmore countered. 'That can't apply. Only some souls are trapped in the section we know about, the area near the boundary.

Laton as good as confirmed that. After death, it's possible to embark on the great journey. Again, his words.'

Euru shook his head sadly. 'I wish I could believe him.'

'In this I agree with him, not that it has much bearing on my principal contention.'

'Which is?' Mattox asked.

'I believe I know the glue which holds souls together. It has to be sentience. Consider, an animal like a dog or cat has its individuality as a biological entity, but no soul. Why not? It has a neural structure, it has memories, it has thought processes operating inside that neural structure. Yet when it dies, all that loses coherence. Without a focus, a strong sense of identity, the pattern dissolves. There is no order.'

'The formless void,' Nowak muttered in amusement.

Gilmore disregarded the gibe. 'We know a soul is a coherent entity, and both Couteur and Dariat have confirmed there is a timeflow within the beyond. They suffer entropy just as we do. I am convinced that makes them vulnerable.'

'How?' Mattox asked sharply.

'We can introduce change. Energy, the actual substance of souls, cannot be destroyed, but it can certainly be dissipated or broken up, returned to a primordial state.'

'Ah, yes,' Hemmatu smiled in admiration. 'Now I follow your logic. Indeed, we have to reintroduce some chaos into their lives.'

Euru gave Gilmore a shocked stare. 'Kill them?'

'Acquire the ability to kill them,' Gilmore responded smoothly. 'If they have the ability to leave the part or state of the beyond where they are now, they must clearly be forced to do so. The prospect of death, real *final* death, would provide them with the spur to leave us alone.'

'How?' Euru asked. 'What would be the method?'

'A virus of the mind,' Gilmore said. 'A universal anti-memory that would spread through thought processes, fracturing them as it went. The beauty of it is, the possessed are constantly merging their thoughts with one another to fulfil their quest for sensation. En masse, they are a mental superconductor.'

'You might just be on to something here,' Hemmatu said. 'Are there such things as anti-memory?'

'There are several weapons designed to disable a target's mental processes,' Mattox said. 'Most of them are chemical or biological agents. However, I do know of some that are based upon didactic imprint memories. But so far my colleagues have only produced variants that induce extreme psychotic disorders such as paranoia or schizophrenia.'

'That's all we need,' Nowak grunted. 'Extra-demented lost souls. They're quite barmy enough as it is.'

Gilmore gave him a disapproving glance. 'Would an anti-memory be possible, theoretically?' he asked Mattox.

'I can't think of any immediate show-stoppers.'

'Surely it would just self-destruct?' Yusuf said. 'If it eradicates the mechanism of its own conductivity, how can it sustain itself?'

'We'd need something that rides just ahead of its own destruction wave,' Mattox said. 'Again, it's not a theoretical impossibility.'

'Nobody said the concept wouldn't need considerable development work,' Gilmore said.

'And trials,' Euru said. His handsome face was showing a considerable amount of unease. 'Don't forget that phase. We would need a sentient being to experiment on. Probably several.'

'We have Couteur,' Gilmore muttered. He acknowledged the Edenist's silent censure. 'Sorry: natural thought. She caused us more than her fair share of trouble in Court Three.'

'I'm sure there will be bitek neural systems adequate for the purpose,' Mattox said hurriedly. 'We don't have to use humans at this stage.'

'Very well,' Gilmore said. 'Unless anyone has any objections, I'd like to prioritize this project. The First Admiral has been placing considerable pressure on us for an overall solution for some time. It'll be a relief to report we might be able to finally go on the offensive against the possessed.'

*

Edenist habitats gossiped among themselves. The discovery first surprised then amused Ione and Tranquillity. But then their multiplicity personalities were made up from millions of people, who like all the elderly were keen to see how their young relatives were doing and spread the word among friends. The personalities were also integral to Edenist culture, so naturally they took an avid interest in human affairs for the reaction it would ultimately have upon themselves. The minutiae of political, social, and economic behaviour from the Confederation at large were absorbed, debated, and meditated upon. Knowledge was the right of all Edenists. It was just the method of passing on the more miscellaneous chunks which was delightfully quirky. Manifold sub-groups would form within every personality, with interests as varied as classical literature and xenobiology, early industrial age steam trains and Oort cloud formations. There was nothing formal, nothing ordained about such clusterings of cognate mentalities. It was, simply, the way it was. An informal anarchy.

Observing this, Tranquillity began to consider itself the equivalent of some ageing uncle overseeing a brood of unruly young nephews and nieces. Its own decorum generated a mild feeling of alienation from its contemporaries (which Ione also found amusing). Only when the full Jovian Consensus, with all its solemn nobility, arose from the gabbling minds was there a notion of kinship.

By the time Tranquillity did arrive at Jupiter, there were literally millions of sub-groups convening within the habitat personalities to consider every possible aspect of the possession problem (essentially, Gilmore's committee to the nth degree). Eager to participate in the search for a solution, Tranquillity contributed its memories and conclusions of the crisis to date, information which was eagerly disseminated and deliberated over. Among the groupings who surveyed all matters religious, the most interesting development was the Kiint's curiosity in the Tyrathca Sleeping God. The question of what the Sleeping God might actually be was passed to the cosmology groupings. They didn't have much of an idea, so they queried the xenopsychology field. In turn, they wondered if the enigma would be better served by the xenocultural historians . . .

At which point, two very distinct (and in their different ways, very important) mentalities among the collective personalities became aware of the Sleeping God problem. The sub-Consensus for security and Wing-Tsit Chong together decided the matter was best dealt with by themselves and a few of their own specialists. In collaboration with Ione, of course.

*

Joshua had a bad feeling about Ione calling him to a conference without telling him the reason. There were resonances of being asked to go after Mzu coming into play. It got worse when she told him it was to be convened in De Beauvoir Palace. That meant it was going to be formal, official.

When he arrived at the small tube station which served visitors to the palace, Mzu was climbing the steps ahead of him. He wanted to turn round and go back to supervising *Lady Mac*'s refit. But at least this was as bad as it could possibly get. They made laboured small-talk as they walked along the dark yellow stone path to the classical building. Mzu didn't know why she'd been invited, either.

A horde of servitor chimps were scurrying about on either side of the path, along with specialist agronomy servitors. All of them were busy repairing the once immaculate parkland. Grass had been trampled into mud by thousands of dancing feet, topiary bushes were knocked into odd shapes, with bottles sticking out of unusual crevices. But it was the tomis shrubs which had taken the worst battering; with their blue and gold trumpet-shaped flowers torn from broken branches to form a brown, slippery mat across the path. The servitors were optimistically trying to repair them with adroit pruning and staking, though the smaller ones were simply being replaced. Vandalism on such a scale was unheard of in Tranquillity. Though Joshua did have to smile at the pile of clothes which the chimps had gathered up. It was mostly underwear.

A pair of serjeants were on guard duty outside the basilica's archway entrance. 'The Lord of Ruin is expecting you,' one intoned. It led them along the nave to the audience chamber.

Ione sat in her accustomed place behind the crescent table in the centre. Long, flat streamers of light from the towering windows intersected around her, giving her an almost saintly portrayal. Joshua was hard pressed not to comment on the theatre of the moment when she smiled a welcome, but he played the game and bowed solemnly. Mzu was given a more punctilious nod of recognition. There were six high-backed chairs set up along the convex side of the table, four of them already occupied. Joshua knew Parker Higgens; Samuel was there as well; but he had to run a search through his neural nanonics to name the Laymil Project's chief astronomer, Kempster Getchell. The fourth turned to face him . . .

'You!'

'Hello, Joshua,' Syrinx said. The possibility of a smile teased her lips.

'Oh,' Ione murmured in a suspiciously sweet tone. 'Do you two know each other?'

Joshua gave Ione a punitive look, then went over to Syrinx and gave her a light kiss on the cheek. 'I heard what happened on Pernik. I'm glad you came through it all right.'

She touched the medical nanonic on his hand. 'I'm not the only one who's come through, apparently.'

Joshua returned the smile, and sat next to her.

'There's a file I want you and Dr Mzu to review before we start,' Ione told him.

The miserable scene of Coastuc-RT swamped Joshua's mind; with Waboto-YAU arguing through its translator, and the two menacing soldier-caste Tyrathca standing close to Reza Malin. He'd avoided accessing most of Kelly's recordings when Collins released them. Lalonde was one planet he didn't want to return to by any method. The close presence of the mercenary leader was a short cut to emotions he'd rather leave dormant.

When the recording ended, he looked up to see one of the long glass windows behind Ione had darkened. Instead of emitting strong golden light, it now contained the image on an ancient Oriental man sitting in an antique wheelchair.

'Wing-Tsit Chong will speak for the Jovian Consensus today,' Ione announced.

'Right,' Joshua said. He loaded that name into a search program, ready to run it through his memory files.

Syrinx leant across. 'The founder of Edenism,' she said softly. 'Quite a major historical figure, in fact.'

'Name the inventor of the ZTT drive,' Joshua retorted.

'Julian Wan normally gets the credit. Although technically he was only the head of the New Kong asteroid's stardrive research team; a bureaucrat, basically.'

Joshua frowned in pique.

'Possibly the present would provide us with a more suitable topic for discussion,' Wing-Tsit Chong chided gently.

'The Sleeping God throws up a number of questions,' Ione said. 'Very relevant questions, given the Tyrathca psychology. They believed it would be able to help them against possessed humans. And they don't lie.'

'So far this entity or object has made no appreciable impact upon our situation,' Wing-Tsit Chong said. 'Implying three options. It is a myth, and the Tyrathca were either fooled or mistaken by their encounter with it. It is not capable of assisting them. Or it does exist, it is capable, and it has simply restrained itself, so far.'

'That third implication is the most interesting,' Kempster said. 'It's an assumption that the Sleeping God is sentient, or at least self-aware; which rules out a celestial event.'

'I always agreed with the artefact possibility myself,' Parker Higgens said. 'The arkship Tyrathca would surely recognize a celestial event for what it was. And celestial events don't keep watch. Waboto-YAU was quite insistent about that. The Sleeping God dreams of the universe, it knows everything.'

'I concur,' Wing-Tsit Chong said. 'This entity has been assigned extraordinary perceptive powers by the Tyrathca. Although we can assume the memories of Sireth-AFL's family would become open to degradation down the centuries, the major elements must retain their integrity. Something very unusual is out there.'

'Have you asked the Kiint direct what it is, and what their interest is?' Joshua asked.

'Yes. They claim a total lack of knowledge on the subject. Ambassador Armira simply repeats Lieria's claim that they are interested in the full record of Kelly Tirrel's sojourn on Lalonde so they might understand the nature of human possession.'

'They might be telling the truth.'

'No,' Parker Higgens said forcefully. 'Not them. They've been lying to us since first contact. This is more than coincidence. The Kiint are desperately interested. And I'd love to beat them to it.'

'A race that can teleport?' Joshua said light-heartedly. The old director's vehemence was out of character here.

'Even if the Kiint aren't interested,' Ione said swiftly, 'we certainly are. The Tyrathca believe it to be real and able to assist them. That alone justifies sending a mission to it.'

'Wait—' Joshua said. He couldn't believe he'd been so slow. 'You want me to go after it, don't you?'

'That's why you're here,' Ione answered calmly. 'I believe you said you wanted to make a contribution?'

'Yes, I did.' There was a residue of reluctance in the acknowledgement. Some of the old bravado. I want to originate the solution. Claim all the glory. Shades of the good old days.

He grinned at Ione, wondering if she'd guessed what he was thinking. More than likely. But if there was a chance this xenoc god might have an answer, he wanted in. He owed a lot of people the effort. His dead crew. His unborn child. Louise and the rest of Norfolk. Even himself, now he refused to avoid thinking of death and the mysteries that inaugurated. Facing up to fate in such a fashion might be frightening, but it made living a hell of a lot easier. And, to be honest with himself, so did the prospect of flying again.

'And so, I believe, did Syrinx,' Ione said. The voidhawk captain nodded admission.

'The Kiint stonewalled you, huh?' Joshua asked.

'Malva was very polite about it, but essentially, yes.'

Joshua settled back, gazing up at the domed ceiling. 'Let me see. If a Tyrathca arkship encountered this god, then it has to be a long way off, a very long way. Not too much problem for a voidhawk, but ... ah, now I get it. The antimatter.' *Lady Mac*'s inclusion was obvious now. Her delta-v reserve was currently five or six times greater than most Adamist warships, making her an obvious candidate to surmount the problem of galactic orbital mechanics. For starships, there's a lot more than just distance to the gulf between stars. Ultimately, it is velocity which governs their design and finances.

Earth's sun orbits the galactic centre roughly once every two hundred and thirty million years, giving it an approximate velocity of two hundred and twenty kilometres per second relative to the core. Other stars, of course, have different orbital velocities, depending on their distance from the core, so their velocities relative to each other are also different. Voidhawks can cope with the variance by tailoring their wormhole terminus to match a local star's vector. It's a manoeuvre which uses up an inconvenient amount of energy from the patterning cells; however, because they obtain their energy for free it doesn't affect their commercial performance except in terms of recharging time. But for Adamist starship captains that variance isn't merely inconvenient, it's a positive bane. The ZTT jump might provide a short cut across the interstellar gulf, but it cannot magically change inertia. A starship emerging from a jump has precisely the same vector it had when it started. In order to rendezvous with the planet or asteroid at its destination, its delta-v has to be altered to match. It's a tedious process which uses up plenty of fuel; in other words, it costs money. And the further the stars are away from each other, the greater the velocity difference. For most Adamist starships, a flight right across the longest axis of Confederation space, a distance approaching nine hundred light-years, would use up over ninety per cent of their reaction drive fuel. Several marques would be incapable of the feat anyway. The limit is imposed because they all use fusion drives.

Antimatter, of course, provides a vastly superior delta-v. And the antimatter *Lady Mac* had taken on board from the *Beezling* was still in her confinement chambers. The First Admiral had given Samuel instructions for the secure military facilities at Jupiter to dispose of it. One of the five specialist ships qualified to handle the substance was still en route to Tranquillity.

'There is a high possibility that a long flight will be required to bring this task to a fruitful conclusion,' Wing-Tsit Chong said. 'I congratulate you on your clarity of thought, young Joshua.'

Syrinx and Ione swapped a glance. 'You're going to let him use antimatter?' Mzu asked in surprise.

'A voidhawk and Adamist starship are a good pairing for this kind of assignment,' Syrinx said. 'Both of us have strengths and weaknesses which complement the other. Providing the Adamist ship can manage to keep up with a voidhawk, of course.'

'Outperform, or outsmart?' Joshua asked civilly.

'All right,' Mzu said. 'So why am I here?'

'We believed you might be able to help us analyse the nature of the Sleeping God,' Kempster Getchell said. 'Especially if it turns out to be a high-technology weapon rather than a natural phenomenon, which is my field.'

Alkad glanced round at their faces, depressed when she knew she should have been flattered. 'I had one idea,' she said. 'Once. Thirty years ago.'

'One original insight,' Wing-Tsit Chong said. 'Which is one more than most people have had, or ever will have. You have a mind

232

capable of it. An ability which can innovate on such a level is an asset we cannot overlook.'

'What about Foulkes?' Alkad asked Samuel.

'If you agree to participate, I'll speak with her. The non-contact prohibition placed upon you does not apply in this situation. You will be permitted to fly on this mission. However, I will accompany you along with Monica.'

'I'm flattered.'

'Don't be. And please don't interpret our continued presence with approval for what you did. It so happens, that there are sections of this mission which require the kind of ability which Monica and I specialize in.'

'How very enigmatic. Very well, if you think I'm the right person for the job, I'd be honoured to take part.'

'Good,' Ione said.

'But I'll need Peter with me.'

'This isn't a honeymoon cruise,' Samuel told her, reproachfully.

'We worked as a team putting the Alchemist together. It's a synergistic relationship.'

'Somehow, I doubt that,' Ione said. 'But for argument's sake, I'll permit you to ask him if he wants to accompany you.'

'So where were you thinking of sending us?' Joshua asked.

'Regretfully, you will have to go directly to the source,' Wing-Tsit Chong said. 'Which is one of the reasons this mission is being assembled under the auspices of the Jovian security sub-Consensus. A thorough search of xenology records both at Jupiter and Earth have revealed absolutely no reference to the Sleeping God. The Tyrathca have never mentioned it to us before.'

'The source? Oh, Jesus, you mean Hesperi-LN, the Tyrathca home planet?'

'Initially, yes. Waboto-YAU told us that it was another arkship which encountered the Sleeping God, not Tanjuntic-RI. Therefore, that arkship must have lasered the information to all the other Tyrathca arkships in the exodus fleet. We must hope that a recording of that message is still aboard Tanjuntic-RI. If you can find it, you may be able to establish the approximate location of the encounter.'

'That could be a long way off,' Joshua said. His neural nanonics started to access almanac and Tyrathca history files from memory cells, running them through a navigation program. The result rising into his mind in the form of gold and scarlet icons was both fascinating and alarming. 'Hesperi-LN isn't their genuine home planet, remember. It's just the last colony world Tanjuntic-RI founded. Look, the original Tyrathca star, Mastrit-PJ, the one they escaped from, is on the other side of the Orion Nebula. That puts it *at least* sixteen hundred light-years away. Now if we get real unlucky, and the arkship which found the Sleeping God was going in the opposite direction to Tanjuntic-RI, you're talking twice as far.'

'We are aware of that,' Wing-Tsit Chong said.

Joshua sighed with indubitable regret. To take *Lady Mac* on such a voyage would have been awesome. 'I'm sorry, there isn't that much antimatter left. I can't take the old girl that far.'

'We are aware of your starship's performance capabilities,' Wing-Tsit Chong said. 'However, there is a supply of antimatter which you will be able to use.'

'You keep some here at Jupiter?' Joshua asked in what he figured was a casual voice.

'No,' Syrinx said. 'A CNIS agent called Erick Thakrar located a production station which may be supplying Capone.'

'Thakrar—' Joshua's search program located the appropriate file; he locked eyes with Ione. 'Really? That's . . . helpful.'

'With the 1st Fleet somewhat overstretched, the First Admiral's staff have asked for Jupiter's voidhawks to tackle it,' Samuel said.

'Which they are preparing to do,' Wing-Tsit Chong said. 'However, before the station is finally annihilated, you will be able to take on board as much antimatter as the *Lady Macbeth*'s confinement systems can handle.'

'Three thousand light-years,' Joshua murmured. 'Jesus.'

'Meredith Saldana's task force has a large contingent of Confederation Navy marines assigned to it,' Ione said. 'They'll secure the station for you once the personnel surrender to the voidhawk squadron.'

'What if the station operatives just suicide?' Joshua said. 'They usually do when the navy confronts them.'

'And take as many of us with them as they can,' Syrinx whispered.

'They will be offered a penal planet sentence instead of the usual death penalty,' Samuel said. 'We can only hope that proves attractive enough to them.'

'All right, but even if we load *Lady Mac* with enough antimatter, the Tyrathca have ended communications with the Confederation,' Joshua said. 'Do you really think they'll allow us to search through Tanjuntic-RI's electronic systems?'

'Probably not,' Samuel said. 'But as we don't intend to ask their permission, it doesn't really matter, does it?'

7

You didn't have to be attuned to the land like a possessed to know it was about to happen. Most of Ombey's population was aware the time had come.

Day after day the news companies had been broadcasting sensevises from rover reporters covering the build-up of Liberation forces. Everybody knew somebody who was connected to somebody who was involved in some way; from hauling equipment out to Fort Forward to serving drinks to Edenists (!) in spaceport bars. Speculation on the current affairs programmes was deliberately vague about specific dates and precise numbers, even the communication net gossips were showing restraint in naming the day. Hearsay aside, the evidence was pretty solid.

The types of cargo raining down on the planet had changed. Combat gear was slowly being replaced by heavy-duty civil engineering equipment, ready to repair the expected damage to Mortonridge and provide additional support infrastructure for the occupying forces. The personnel arriving at Fort Forward were also subject to a shift in professions. Just under a million serjeants had been sent from Jupiter, along with nearly a quarter of a million marines and mercenaries from across the Confederation. The Liberation army was essentially complete. So now it was the medical teams being ferried down from orbit, civilian volunteers complementing entire mobile military hospitals. Estimated casualty figures (both military and civilian) were strictly classified. But everyone knew the twelve thousand medical staff were going to suffer a heavy workload. Eighty voidhawks had already been assigned evac duties, spreading the wounded around facilities in the Kingdom and its allies.

Throughout the seventh day following Princess Kirsten's visit, Ralph Hiltch and his command staff studied the figures and displays provided by the AI. The neuroiconic image which accumulated in his mind kept expanding as more information was correlated. By late afternoon, his conscious perception point seemed to be hanging below a supergalaxy of multicoloured stars, which threatened to make him giddy as he tried to examine it in all directions at once. Despite its coherence, what he really wanted was more training time, more transport, more supplies, and definitely more intelligence assessments of the terrain ahead. But, essentially, his army was as ready as it would ever be. He gave the order for final stage deployment to begin.

Over half of the serjeants and their back-up brigades had already left Fort Forward. The previous two days had been spent mustering at their preliminary positions offshore. Nearly a hundred islands around Mortonridge's coast had been taken over as temporary depots; from reefs which barely showed above the waves to resort atolls dotted with luxury hotels. Where there were no convenient scraps of land, huge cargo ships had been hurriedly converted into floating docks and anchored thirty kilometres from the shore.

For the first stage of the coastal assault, the army was scheduled to use boats. They were actually going to storm ashore, wading through the waves and up onto the sand, almost in homage to a great many of the incarnations from the past they were facing. Ralph wasn't prepared to risk flying even the simplest of aircraft into the energistic environment over Mortonridge, not until after they'd dealt with the red cloud at least.

The remainder of the Liberation ground forces emptied out of Fort Forward in massive convoys, spreading out along the firebreak in thousands of multi-terrain vehicles. There was no attempt at secrecy, no hugging the cover behind ridges and hills. The squads drove through the encroaching twilight and into the night, the nimbus of their massed headlight beams creeping like an anaemic dawn along the horizon paralleling the firebreak.

Across Xingu a civil curfew order was enacted once again, with the police put on full alert. Although they were fairly sure no possessed were left outside Mortonridge, the continent's authorities were taking Annette Ekelund's threat of sabotage very seriously. When dawn arrived, no civilian would be allowed out onto the streets. People grumbled and groaned, and datavised protests to local news shows, remembering what a nuisance the curfew had been last time. It was almost a bravado display of defiance. In the main, they just settled back and accessed the show.

High above the planet, the strategic-defence centre on Guyana began coordinating the Royal Navy's part of the assault. Thrusters flared on low-orbit weapons platforms, refining their new orbits. A flotilla of three hundred voidhawks also began to accelerate, synchronizing their distortion fields to rise away from the planet in a long curve.

The psychic pressure mounting against Mortonridge shifted from faint intimation to blatantly unmistakable.

*

To casual observation, Chainbridge was still a busy town. When Annette Ekelund reached a slight ridge a couple of kilometres from the outskirts, she stopped the sturdy country rover she was driving and looked back over her shoulder. Hundreds of lighted windows shone out across the farmland, burning steady against the flickering crimson waves scattered down from the lumbering cloud roof. The buildings were warm, too, warm enough to fool any perfunctory sensor scans into believing they were occupied. But no one was left there, her command group was the last to leave.

'It'll keep the blighters tied up for a while,' Devlin assured her. He was sitting in the passenger seat beside her, clad in his old khaki uniform, a discreet row of scarlet and gold ribbons on his chest.

In the back seat, Hoi Son veiled a sneer. He, too, had reverted to type: dark jungle fatigues and a felt bush-ranger hat. 'For at least a quarter of an hour.'

'Would you like to return to the beyond fifteen minutes early?' Devlin enquired lightly.

'Any time we delay them is good time,' Annette told the pair of them. She took the brake off, and accelerated down the secondary road. They were heading for Cold Overton, a small village eighty kilometres away. Their field command centre; picked virtually at random by Hoi Son, central but not strategically so, adequate road links, surrounded by thick forest. It was as good as any, not that they'd be staying long. Fluid tactics were the key to this campaign.

Hoi Son clapped Devlin on the shoulder. 'And this is our time, eh? You and I both. Onward to death and glory.'

'There is no glory here.' Devlin spoke so quietly, the others could only just hear him against the bass grumble of thunder.

'Don't tell me you're having second thoughts?'

'I heard my men wailing at night,' the old soldier replied emotionlessly. 'The ones left out in no man's land, left behind to drown in puddles of their own blood; the ones that weren't vomiting their lungs up from that devilish gas. Screaming for us to help them, more frightened at being alone than they were of being shot.'

'You Christians, you always take life so personally. We're here by accident, not design. Nothing is ordained, you are only what you make of yourself. You can never go back, the past doesn't change. Stop thinking about it. The only part of history which matters is the future.'

'It broke my heart, not being able to help them. Good, decent men; boys, a lot of them. I swore I'd never get involved in such madness again. They called it total war. But it wasn't, it was total bloody murder. Insanity had become a disease, and we all caught it. Twice in my lifetime my nation sent its youth out to die for a just cause, to protect ourselves and our way of life.' He smiled frigidly at the eco-warrior. 'And now here I am once again. Seven bloody centuries later. Seven hundred years, and nothing has changed. Not one damn thing. I'm fighting to preserve myself and my new life. A righteous war with me on the side of the angels, even though they've become fallen angels. And I can already hear the screams, God help me.'

'All I hear is our victory song,' Hoi Son said. 'The voice of the land is louder and stronger than any human cry. This is our place, we are at one with it. We belong here. We have a right to exist in this universe.'

Devlin closed his eyes and tipped his head back. 'Lord, forgive me, I am such a fool. Here we all are, embarking on a crusade to storm the very gates of heaven itself in our desperation. What a monumental folly. I shall smite at the dark angels massed against us, crying for death, for only in death will we ever find peace. Yet You have already revealed that death is not our destiny, nor ever can be.'

'Wake up, old man. We're not fighting God, we're fighting an unjust universe.'

For the first time since his return from the beyond, Devlin smiled. 'You think there's a difference?'

*

The island was enchanting, its botany and geology combining into the kind of synergistic idyll which was the grail of Edenist habitat designers. Inland, there were craggy rocks hosting long white waterfalls, and thick lush forests choked with sweet-scented flowers. While the edges comprised cove after cove, their pale gold sands gleaming under the azure sky; except for one, where the offshore reef crumbled under the foaming breakers to give the sands an exquisite fairydust coating of pink coral. It appealed to humans on a primal level, urging them to slow down and spend time just soaking in nature. As a reward for their worship, time itself would expand and become almost meaningless.

Even in his current existence, Sinon wished he was staying longer than their eighteen-hour stopover. Five thousand serjeants had descended on this tiny jewel of land glinting in the ocean, along with their equipment and support personnel. Marines were camped ten to a room in the resort hotels, gardens and tennis courts had been requisitioned as landing pads, and the coves were harbours for a hundred of the regiment's landing boats. All day, the boats had taken their turn to nuzzle the shore, extending their forward ramps so that jeeps and light trucks could drive on board. Now, in the evening, the serjeants were finally embarking.

Syrinx would like this place, Sinon told Choma. I must tell her about it. He was two-thirds of the way along a line of serjeants who were wading out to their landing boat. There wasn't enough room on this particular beach to berth more than three boats at a time, so the other eleven were anchored a hundred metres offshore. A column of serjeants snaked out to each one, making slow time through the water. The big constructs were laden with backpacks, carrying their weapons above their heads to stop them getting wet. Groups of Royal Marines milled about on the bluff, watching the process. If all went well, they'd be doing the same thing next morning.

Now there's good healthy optimism, Choma replied.

What do you mean?

I've been working out our probable casualty rate. Would you like to know how many of our squad are likely to survive the entire campaign?

Not particularly. I have no intention of becoming a statistic.

Where have I heard that before? In any case, it's two. Two out of ten.

Thank you very much. Sinon reached the landing boat. It was an ugly, rugged affair, one design serving the entire Liberation armada. A carbosilicon hull mass produced over on Esparta, with power cells and an engine that could have come from any of a dozen industrialized star systems allied to the Kingdom. Hard-pressed navy engineers had plugged the standard components together, completing several hundred each day. The three on the beach were still being worked on by technicians.

Honesty is supposed to be our culture's strength, Choma said, mildly irked by the negative reaction.

We're a long way from Eden now. Sinon slung his rifle high on his shoulder, and started climbing the ladder up the side of the boat. When he reached the top of the gunwale he looked back to shore. The sun was sinking into the sea, leaving a rosy haze above the darkening water. Parodying that, on the opposite horizon, the glow of the red cloud was visible, a narrow fracture separating water and air.

Last chance, Sinon told himself. The other serjeants were all climbing down into the boat, their mind-tones subdued but still resolute. Rationally, he was buying the Confederation time to find a genuine answer. And Consensus itself had approved this course of action. He swung his legs over the rail, and put a hand down to help Choma. **Come on, let's go storm the Dark Lord's citadel.**

*

The Royal Marine ion-field flyer was a lone spark of gold shimmering high in the night sky, brighter than any star. It flew across the top of the Mortonridge peninsula, keeping parallel to the firebreak, twenty-five kilometres to the north, and holding a steady fifteen kilometre altitude.

Ralph Hiltch sat in the flyer's cabin as Cathal Fitzgerald piloted them above the northern end of the mountain range forming the peninsula's spine. Eight hours of neural nanonics enforced sleep had left him feeling fresh, but emotionally dead. His mind had woken immune to the human consequences of the Liberation. Whether it was numb from the torrent of information which had been bullying his brain for weeks, or guilty at the enormity of what he'd organized, he wasn't sure.

It meant that now he was hooked into the flyer's sensor suite he could view the last stages of the deployment with godlike dispassion. Which was probably for the best, he thought. Accepting personal responsibility for every casualty would drive anyone insane within the first two minutes. Even so, he'd wanted this one last overview. To convince himself it was genuine if nothing else. The last insecurity, that all the data and images he'd handled had been transformed to physical reality.

There could be no doubt. The army spread out below him, *his* army, was flowing over the black land in streamers of fluid light, bending and curling round hills and valleys. Individual vehicles were expressed as twinkles of light, barely different to icons blipping their way across a map. Except here there was no colour, just the white headlight beams contrasting the funeral ground.

It was after midnight, and two-thirds of the ground deployment was complete. Both flanks were established, now there was only the centre to set up, the most difficult aspect. His main spearhead was going to drive right along the M6, allowing the huge supply and back-up convoys an easy ride. Using the motorway was a disturbingly obvious strategy, but essential if they were to complete in a minimum timescale.

Ekelund would have sabotaged the road, but bridges could be repaired, blockades shunted aside, and gorges filled. The combat engineering corps were ready for that. At least the possessed didn't have air power. Though occasionally he had images of propeller biplanes roaring overhead and strafing the jeeps. Victory rolls with the pilot's white silk scarf flapping jauntily in the slipstream. Stupid.

Ralph switched the suite's focus to the red cloud. Its edges were still arched down to the ground, sealing the peninsula away from the rest of the planet. Dusky random wave shadows rolled across the pulpy surface. He thought they might be more restless than usual, though that could well be his imagination. Thankfully, there was no sign of that peculiar oval formation which he'd seen once before. The one he absolutely refused to call an eye. All he really wanted was one glimpse through; to reassure himself the peninsula was still there, if nothing else. They'd had no data of any kind from inside since the day Ekelund had brought the cloud down. No links with the net could be established; no non-possessed had managed to sneak out. A final sweep with the flyer's sensors revealed nothing new.

'Take us back,' he told Cathal.

The flyer performed a fast turn, curving round to line up on Fort Forward. Ahead of it, the giant Thunderbirds continued to swoop down out of the western sky, delta heat-shields glowing a dull vermilion against the starfield backdrop. That aspect of the build-up, at least, remained unchanged. Cathal landed them inside the secure command complex, along the southern side of the new city. Ralph trotted down the airstair, ignoring the armed marine escort which fell in around him. The trappings of his position had ceased to register as special some time ago, just another aspect of this extraordinary event.

Brigadier Palmer (the first person Ralph had promoted) was waiting outside the door to the Ops Room. 'Well?' she asked, as they walked in.

'I didn't see anyone waving a white flag.'

'We'd know if they wanted to.' Like a lot of people involved with the Liberation, especially those who'd been on Mortonridge since the start, she considered herself to have a connection with the possessed hidden behind the red cloud, an awareness of attitude. Ralph wasn't convinced, although he acknowledged the possessed exerted some kind of psychic presence.

The Ops Room was a long rectangular chamber with glass walls separating it from innumerable specialist planning offices. Completing electronic systems integration and connecting their architecture with Ombey's military communication circuits was another triumph for the overworked Royal Marine engineering corps, though its rushed nature was evident in the bundled cables hanging between consoles and open ceiling panels, air-conditioning which was too chilly, and raw carbon-concrete corner pillars. Its floor-space was taken up by cheap corporate-style desks holding consoles, AV projectors, and communication gear. Right now, it was full to capacity. Over fifty officers from the Royal Navy were collaborating with an equal number of Edenists; the next largest contingent was the Confederation Navy with twenty, while the remainder were drawn from various participating allies.

They were going to be the coordinators of the Liberation, the human analysis and liaison between the ground forces and the controlling AI back in Pasto. A failsafe against the maxim 'No battle plan survives contact with the enemy'. Every one of them stood up as Ralph Hiltch entered. That, he did notice. Together they had spent the past few weeks planning this together, arguing, pleading, contributing ideas, working miracles. They'd learned to cooperate and coordinate their fields of expertise, putting aside old quarrels so they melded into a unified, dedicated team. He was proud of them and what they'd accomplished.

Their show of respect rekindled several of his suppressed emotions. 'I'll keep this short,' he told the hushed chamber. 'We can't pretend this is going to solve the problem possession poses to the Confederation, but it's a damn sight more important than a propaganda war, which is what some reporters have been calling it. We're fighting to free two million people, and we're battling to bring hope into the lives of an awful lot more. To me, that's more than worthwhile, it's essential. So let's make our contribution a good one.'

Amid scattered applause, he made his way to his office at the far end. His desk gave him a view down the whole length of the Ops Room, providing he craned his neck over the stack of processor block peripherals connected to his main desktop console. While he was datavising the array for strategic updates, his executive command group joined him. As well as Janne Palmer, who was the chief of the occupying forces, there was Acacia, the Edenist liaison, an elderly woman who had served as Ambassador to Ombey for five years. He'd also drafted in Diana Tiernan to act as the army's technical adviser, helping to filter the scientific reports on the possessed which were flooding in from across the Confederation. Cathal completed the gathering, still holding his post as Ralph's assistant, but now with the rank of lieutenant-commander.

When the glass door slid shut, isolating them from the noise from outside, Ralph requested a security level one sensenviron conference. Princess Kirsten and Admiral Farquar joined them around the white bubble room's table. 'The deployment's going remarkably well,' Ralph said. 'All our principal front-line divisions will be in place at zero-hour.'

'My occupation troops are effectively ready,' Janne said. 'There are a few minor hitches, mostly logistical. But given the amount of *matériel* involved, and the different groupings we're attempting to coordinate, I'm happy. We're well within estimated parameters. The AI should have the bugs knocked out by morning.'

'The serjeants are also ready,' Acacia reported. 'Again, there are some hitches, mainly with transport equipment, but we are committed.'

'Admiral Farquar?' Kirsten asked.

'All space-based assets are functional. Platform orbits are synchronized, and the voidhawks are reaching apogee. It looks good.'

'Very well,' Kirsten said. 'God help me for this, but they've left us with no alternative. General Hiltch, you now have full command authority for Ombey's military forces. Engage the enemy, Ralph, evict them from my planet.'

*

Standard military doctrine was, somewhat inevitably, fairly unimaginative. Every kind of tactic and counter-tactic had been attempted, practised, and refined by generals, warlords, and emperors down the centuries until there was little room for mistake. So even though Mortonridge was unique from a philosophical standpoint, it could be defined in military terms as a large-scale hostage/siege scenario. Given that assessment, the method of resolving it was clear cut.

Ralph wanted to isolate the possessed in small groups. They were vulnerable like that, capable of being overwhelmed. To achieve it, their communications should be broken, denying them the ability to regroup and mount any kind of counterattack. Harassment should be constant, wearing them down. And, if possible, he wanted them deprived of the cover provided by their red cloud. In summary: divide and conquer. An ancient principle, but now aided by the kind of firepower only modern technology could provide.

*

Ombey had four and a half thousand low-orbit strategic-defence platforms. Their orbital vectors were orchestrated to provide a constant barrier above the surface, similar to the way electrons pirouetted around their nucleus. For the Liberation, all that had changed. Navy starships had taken over the low-orbit protection duty, leaving the platforms free for an altogether different task. Their elaborate inclinations had been shifted, ion thrusters firing for hours at a time to clump them into flocks of twenty-five. Now they formed a single chain around the planet, with an inclination tilted at just a couple of degrees to the equator. One flock would pass over Mortonridge every thirty seconds.

Sensor satellites had been manoeuvred into the gaps between the platforms, ready to provide the Liberation forces with an unparalleled coverage of the peninsula once the red cloud had been broken apart. Admiral Farquar used them to watch the dawn terminator sliding over the ocean towards the louring band of red cloud. Tactical overlays showed him the positions of the landing boats heading in for the beaches. Far overhead, the flotilla of voidhawks had passed apogee, and were now hurtling downwards, accelerating at eight gees.

In one hour, dawn would reach Mortonridge's eastern seaboard. The Admiral datavised his command authority code to Guyana's SD control centre. 'Fire,' he ordered.

*

Though they never knew it, the Liberation forces very nearly won in the first ninety seconds. The initial flock of SD platforms sent seventy-five electron beams slamming down through the upper atmosphere to strike the red cloud. They were aimed along the north–south axis of the peninsula, and defocused, so that at the point of impact they were over fifty metres across. The intention wasn't to pierce the red cloud, just to pump it full of electrical energy, the possessed's one known Achilles heel. Each beam began scanning from side to side, in gigantic ten-second sweeps that took them from coast to coast.

Then the second flock of platforms slid up over the horizon and into range. Another seventy-five beams speared down. There was a ten-second overlap before the first flock were out of range.

*

Annette Ekelund let out a single shriek of agony, and dropped helplessly to her knees. The pain was incredible. A shaft of blue-star sunlight flung down from a height greater than heaven lanced clean through her skull. It didn't just burn her stolen brain, it set fire to her very thoughts. That part of her spirit which communed so gladly with the others on Mortonridge was the treacherous conductor. The part which created the shield of cloud and gave them all a subliminal sense of community. Her belief in whatever humanity had survived the incarceration of the beyond. And now it was killing her.

She abandoned it in its entirety. Her scream twisting from pain to wretchedness. All around her the other souls were shrinking away from each other, withdrawing into self. The last sob burbled out from her lips, and she flopped limply onto her back. Her body was freezing, shaking in shock. Devlin and Hoi Son were scrabbling in the dirt somewhere nearby, she could hear their whimpers. She couldn't see either of them, the world had gone completely black.

*

Every possessed across the Confederation was instantly aware of the strike. Pain and shock reverberated through the beyond. Wherever they were, whatever they were doing, they felt it.

Al Capone was underneath Jezzibella when it happened, adopting a complicated position so that her breasts were pushed into his face while he could still bend his knees for the leverage to give her a damn good shafting. Her laugh was halfway between a giggle and a moan when the mental impact knocked him with the force of a wild hockey puck. He convulsed, shouting in pained panic.

Jezzibella cried out as his frantic motion twisted her arm, nearly dislocating her shoulder. 'Al! Fuck. That fucking hurts, you fucking dickhead. I told you I don't do that sado shit, fuck you.'

Al grunted in confused dismay, shaking his head to clear the weird dizziness foaming inside. He was so disoriented, he fell off the side of the bed.

For the first time, Jezzibella actually caught a glimpse of Brad Lovegrove's natural features beneath the illusion. Not too different to Al, they could almost be brothers. Her anger faded at the sight of him grimacing, limbs twitching in disarray. 'Al?'

'Fuck,' he gasped. 'What the fuck was that?'

'Al, you OK, baby? What happened?'

'God damn! I don't know.' He looked round the bedroom, expecting to see some kind of bomb damage, G-men storming through the door ... 'I ain't got a clue.'

For Jacqueline Couteur the invisible shockwave almost proved fatal. Strapped onto the examination table in the demon trap she couldn't move when her muscles spasmed. Her vital signs monitor alerted the staff to some kind of seizure, at which point her conscious defence against the electric current they were shunting through her body began to crumble. Fortunately, one of the more alert team members shut the power off before she was genuinely electrocuted. It took her five or six minutes to recover her normal antagonism, and prowess.

On patrol a million kilometres above New California, Rocio Condra lost control of the distortion field, letting it flare and contract wildly. The big hellhawk tumbled crazily, its bird-form imploding in a cloud of dark scintillations. Gravity inside the life-support cabin vanished along with the quaint steamship interior. Jed, Beth, Gerald and the three kids suddenly found themselves in free fall. Then gravity returned in a rush, far too strong, and in the wrong direction, making one of the bulkhead walls the floor. The surface swatted them hard, then the gravity failed again to send them flying across the cabin in a tangle of limbs and screams. Stars gyrated savagely beyond the viewport. Another wash of gravity sucked them down onto the ceiling.

In Quinn Dexter's case, it was his first setback on Earth. He had just arrived at Grand Central Station to take a vac-train to Paris. Not the original station building on Manhattan, the island itself was actually abandoned and flooded; but New Yorkers were sentimental about such things. This was the third such edifice to carry the name. Buried nearly a kilometre below the centre of Dome Five, it formed the hub of the arcology's intercontinental train network.

Once more he had secluded himself within the ghost realm to avoid any risk of detection. That was when he began to notice just how many ghosts haunted the station and other subterranean sections of the vast arcology. Hundreds of them drifted mournfully amid the unseeing streams of commuters. They were drab, despondent figures, staring round at the faces that rushed past. There was so much longing and desperation in their expressions, as if every one of them was searching for some long-lost child. They were aware of Quinn, gazing at him in bewilderment as he strode through the main concourse on his way to the platforms. In turn, he ignored them, worthless creatures incapable of either aiding or hindering his crusade. They really were as good as dead.

He was twenty metres short of the wave elevator for platform fifty-two when the flashback from the Liberation reached him. The impact wasn't actually too great, he'd withstood far worse at Banneth's hands, it was the suddenness of it all which shocked him. Without warning he was yelling as streaks of pain flared out from the centre of his brain to infect his body. Edmund Rigby's captive thoughts writhed in agony, transfixed by the blast of torment.

Quinn panicked, frightened by the unknown. Until this moment he believed he was virtually omnipotent. Now some witchery was attacking him in a method he couldn't fathom. Souls in the beyond were screaming in terror. The ghosts around him began wailing, clasping their hands together in prayer. His control over the energistic power faltered as his thoughts dissolved into chaos.

Bud Johnson never saw where the guy came from. One second he was hurrying to the wave elevator, on his way to catch a San Antonio connection – the next, some man in a weird black robe was kneeling on all fours on the polished marble floor at his feet. That was almost impossible, everyone who grew up on Earth and lived in the arcologies had an instinctive awareness of crowds, the illogical tides and currents of bodies which flowed through them. He always knew where people were in relation to himself, alert to any possible collision. Nobody could just *appear*.

Bud's momentum kept his torso going forwards, while his legs were completely blocked. He went flying, pivoting over the man's back to crash onto the cool marble. His wrist made a nasty snapping sound, firing hot pain up his arm. And his neural nanonics did nothing. Nothing! There were no axon blocks, no medical display. Bud let out a howl of pain, blinking back tears as he looked up.

Those tears might have accounted for two or three of the curious faces peering down at him. Pale and distressed, wearing extremely odd hats. When he blinked the salty fluid clear, they'd gone. He clutched at his injured wrist. 'Sheesh, dear God, that hurts.' A murmur of surprise rattled over his head, a strong contrast to the screams breaking out across the rest of the station. No one seemed particularly concerned about him.

'Hey, my neural nanonics have failed. Someone call me a medic. I think my wrist's broken.'

The man he'd fallen over was now rising to his feet. Bud was acutely conscious of the silence that had closed around him, of people backing away. When he looked up, any thoughts of shouting curses on the clumsy oaf vanished instantly. There was a face inside the large hood, barely visible. Bud was suddenly very thankful for the robe's shadows. The expression of fury and malice projected by the features he could see was quite bad enough. 'Sorry,' he whispered.

Fingers closed around his heart. He could actually feel them, individual joints hinging inwards, fingernails digging into his atriums. The hand twisted savagely. Bud choked silently, his arms flapping wildly. He was just aware of people closing in on him again. This time, they registered concern. Too late, he tried to tell them, far too late. The aloof Devil turned casually and faded from his sight. Then so did the rest of the world.

Quinn observed Bud's soul snake away from his corpse, vanishing into the beyond, adding his screams to the beseeching myriad. There was a big commotion all around, people shoving and jostling to get a good view of whatever was going down. Only a couple of them had gasped as he returned himself to the ghost realm, fading out right in front of them. At least he'd retained enough composure not to use the white fire. Not that it mattered now. He'd been seen, and not just by people with glitched neural nanonics; the station's security sensors would have captured the event.

Govcentral knew he was here.

*

Tucked down in the central hold of the landing boat, Sinon couldn't physically see the rest of the squadron closing on the shore. Affinity made it unnecessary; all the Edenist minds on and orbiting Ombey were linked together, providing him with more information than General Hiltch had available. He was aware of his personal position, as well as that of his comrades, even the Liberation's overall situation was available to him. The voidhawk flotilla revealed the red cloud beneath them. Huge lightning bolts were writhing across the upper surface as the SD platforms continued their electron barrage. At the centre, along the spine of hills, the glow was fading, allowing pools of darkness to ripple outward.

Along with all the other serjeants, Sinon craned forwards for a look. The barrier of red cloud had grown steadily through the night as the boats headed in for the beach. From ten kilometres offshore it stretched right across the water, solid and resolute like the wall at the end of the world.

Small flickers of lightning arose to dance along the bottom, slashing down into the waves. Steam plumes screwed upwards from the discharges. Then the lightning streamers were coming together into massive dazzling rivers, rising up, following the steep curve of the cloud to arch inland. The red glow faded, taking less then five seconds to die completely. Its disappearance startled Sinon and the other serjeants. The victory was too sudden. This was not the epic struggle they'd been preparing for. The crawling webs of lightning more than made up for the absence; blazing bright right across the horizon.

You know, that is actually a very big cloud, Sinon said. The brilliant flashes were near-continuous now, keeping the dark mass illuminated prominently.

You noticed that, Choma retorted.

Yes. Which could be a problem. It was rather nicely contained while the possessed were using it as a shield. As such, we tended to disregard its physical properties; it was, after all, primarily a psychological barrier.

Psychological or not, we can't cruise straight through with all that electrical activity.

Choma wasn't the only one to reach that conclusion. They could already feel the boat slowing as the captain reduced power to the engines. A precaution repeated simultaneously by the entire armada.

*

'Recommendations?' Ralph asked.

'Shut down the SD assault,' Acacia said. 'The landing boats are already slowing. They can't penetrate that kind of lightning storm.'

'Diana?'

'I think so. If the red light is an indication of the possessed's control, then we've already routed them.'

'That's a very big if,' Admiral Farquar protested.

'We don't have a lot of choice,' the elderly technology adviser said. 'The landing boats clearly can't get through, nor can the ground vehicles, for that matter. We have to let the energy discharge itself naturally. If the red light returns when they're inside, we can resume the electron-beam attack until the cloud itself starts to break up.'

'Do it,' Ralph ordered. 'Acacia, get the serjeants as close as they can to the cloud, then as soon as the lightning's finished, I want them through.'

'Yes, General.'

'Diana, how long is it going to take to dissipate that electricity?'

'A good question. We're not sure how deep or dense that cloud is.'

'Answer me.'

'I'm afraid I can't. There are too many variables.'

'Oh, great. Acacia, is the lightning going to affect the harpoons?'

'No. The cloud's too low for that, and they're going too fast. Even if one took a direct hit from a lightning bolt, the trajectory won't be altered by more than a couple of metres at best.'

*

The voidhawk flotilla was only one and a half thousand kilometres from the surface of Ombey. Mortonridge filled their sensor blister coverage, changing from a red smear to a seething mass of blue-white streamers, more alive than ever before. There was just time for one last query.

We're still go, Acacia assured them.

All three hundred voidhawks reached the apex of their trajectory. Their bone-crushing eight-gee acceleration ended briefly. Each one flung a swarm of five thousand kinetic harpoons from its weapons cradles. Then power surged through their patterning cells again, reversing the previous direction of the distortion field. The punishing intensity was unchanged, still eight gees, pushing them desperately away from the planet with its dangerous gravity field.

Far below, the delicate filigree of shimmering lightning vanished beneath an incandescent corona as the upper atmosphere ignited. The plasma wake left by one and a half million kinetic harpoons had merged together into a single photonic shockwave. It hit the top of the cloud, puncturing the churning grey vapour with such speed there was little reaction. At first. Acacia was quite right, the cloud, for all its bulk and animosity, was too little too late to deflect the harpoons from their programmed targets.

No human could draw up that list, it was the AI in Pasto that ultimately designated their impact points. They descended in clumps of three, giving a ninety-seven per cent probability of a successful hit. Mortonridge's communication net was the main target.

Urban legend dictated that modern communication nets were

annihilation-proof. With hundreds of thousands of independent switching nodes spread over an entire planet, and millions of cables linking them, backed up by satellite relays, their anarchistic-homogeneous nature made them immune to any kind of cataclysm. No matter how many nodes were taken out, there was always an alternative route for the data. You'd have to physically wipe out a planet before its data exchange was stalled.

But Mortonridge was finite, its net isolated from the redundancy offered by the rest of the planet. The location of every node was known to within half a metre. Unfortunately, ninety per cent of them were proscribed, because they were inside a built-up urban area. If kinetic harpoons started dropping amid the buildings, the resulting casualties would be horrendous. That left the cables out in the open countryside. A lot of them followed roads, nestled in utility conduits along the side of the carbon-concrete, but many more took off across the land, laid by mechanoids operating by themselves for months at a time, tunnelling through forests and under rivers, with nothing on the surface to indicate their existence.

Long-inactive files of their routes had been accessed and analysed by the AI. Strike coordinates were designated, with the proscription that there should be no habitable structure within three-quarters of a kilometre. Given the possessed's considerable ability to defend themselves on a physical level, it was considered a reasonably safe distance.

*

Stephanie Ash lay quivering on the floor even after her mind had recoiled from the communion with other souls. The loss hurt her more than any pain from the electron-beam attack against the cloud. That simple act of union had given her hope. As long as people went on supporting each other, she knew, despite everything else, they remained human to some small degree. Now even that fragile aspiration had been wrenched from them.

'Stephanie?' Moyo called. His hand was shaking her shoulder gently. 'Stephanie, are you all right?'

The fear and concern in his voice triggered her own guilt. 'God, no.' She opened her eyes. The bedroom was lit solely by a small bluish flame coming from his thumb. Outside the window, blackness covered the whole world. 'What did they do?' She could no longer sense the psychic weight pressing against her from the other side of the firebreak. Only the valley was apparent.

'I don't know. But it's not good.' He helped her to her feet.

'Are the others all right?' She could sense their minds, spread out through the farmhouse, embers of worry and pain.

'Same as us, I guess.' A bright flash from outside silenced him. They both went to the window and peered out. Huge shafts of lightning skidded along the underbelly of the cloud.

Stephanie shivered uncomfortably. What had successfully shielded them from the open sky was now an intimidatingly large mass far too close overhead.

'We're not in charge of it any more,' Moyo said. 'We let go.'

'What's going to happen to it?'

'It'll rain, I guess.' He shot her an anxious look. 'And that's a lot of cloud up there. We just kept adding to it, like a baby's security blanket.'

'Maybe we should get the animals in.'

'Maybe we should get the hell out of here. The Princess's army will be coming.'

She smiled sadly. 'There's nowhere to go. You know that.'

The frequency of the lightning had increased dramatically by the time they rounded up Cochrane, Rana, and Quigley to help chase after the chickens and lambs that normally ambled round inside the farmyard. The first few big drops of water began to patter down.

Moyo stuck his hand out, palm up. As if confirmation was really needed. 'Told you,' he said smugly.

Stephanie turned her cardigan into a cagoule, even though she didn't hold out much hope of staying dry. The drops were larger than any she'd ever known. All the chickens were running through the open gate, the lambs had already vanished into the atrocious night. She was just about to suggest they didn't bother trying to catch them when daylight returned to Mortonridge.

Cochrane gaped up at the sky. The clouds had turned into translucent veils of grey silk, allowing the light to pour through. 'Wow! Who switched the sun back on, man?' The bottom of the clouds detonated into incandescent splinters, searing down through the air. Vivid star-tips pulling down a hurricane cone of violet mist after them. Stephanie had to shield her eyes, they were so bright.

'It's the end of the world, kids,' Cochrane cried gleefully.

All one and a half million harpoons struck the ground within a five-second period. A clump of them were targeted on a cable four kilometres from the farm valley, their terrible velocity translated into a single devastating blast of heat. The radiant orange flash silhouetted the valley rim, lasting just long enough to reveal the debris plume boiling upwards.

'Ho, shit,' Cochrane grunted. 'That Mr Hiltch *really* doesn't like us.'

'What were they?' Stephanie asked. It seemed incredible that they were still in their bodies. Surely that kind of violence would wipe them out?

'Some kind of orbital bombardment,' Moyo said. 'It must have been aimed at Ekelund's troops.' He didn't sound too convinced.

'Aimed? It was everywhere.'

'Then why didn't it hit us?' Rana asked. Moyo just shrugged. That was when the roar of the impact reached them, a drawn-out rumble loud enough to swallow any words.

Stephanie covered her ears, and looked up again. The cloud was in torment, its rumpled underbelly foaming violently. Ghostly billows of luminescent purple air left behind by the harpoons snaked around the tightly packed whorls, the two of them flowing against each other, yet never merging, like liquids with different densities. She frowned, blinking upwards as the light dimmed. A thick slate-grey haze was emerging, oozing out of the cloud to swallow both the lightning and the tattered sheets of ion vapour. It was expanding fast, darkening.

'Inside,' she said in a small voice as the last echoes of the explosion reverberated across the valley. They all turned to look at her. The big drops of rain had returned. A breeze arose to stroke their clothes. 'Get inside. It's going to rain.'

They glanced up at the descending haze, awed and fearful as understanding reached them.

*

'Nothing!' Annette screamed furiously at the processor block. The primitive schematic displayed on its screen proved it was functioning, yet nobody was answering her calls. 'We're cut off.'

Hoi Son studied the display on his block. 'All the lines are down, from what I can see,' he said.

'Don't be absurd, you can't knock out an entire net,' Annette protested. Doubt stung. 'It's not possible.'

'I imagine that was the idea behind the bombardment,' Hoi Son replied, unperturbed. 'It was rather spectacular, after all. They wouldn't expend that much effort for no reason. And we didn't have the whole net functioning in the first place, only the critical links.'

'Damn it, how the hell am I going to organize our resistance now?'

'Everyone has their original orders, and they have no choice but to fight. All this means is that you are no longer in charge of the possessed.'

Even his complacency soured at the look she gave him.

'Oh, really?' she asked dangerously.

The light began to fade outside. Annette strode across to the big front window. She'd taken over a folksy restaurant called the Black Bull in the middle of Cold Overton, giving her a commanding position at the end of the broad main street. Fifty vehicles were parked on the stone slabs of the market square outside, waiting for the troops who'd taken refuge in the nearby shops and cafés. Milne and a few of his engineers were walking about, inspecting the equipment. There didn't seem to be any damage, though several of the harpoons had fallen just outside the village.

'Hoi,' she said, 'take a couple of squads and check the roads. I want to know how quickly we can get out of here.'

'As you wish.' He nodded briskly, and made for the door.

'There's a big group of us in Ketton,' she said, almost to herself. 'That's only ten kilometres west of here. We'll link up with them. Should be able to convince some civilians to join up, too. After that we can move on to the next group.'

'We could use runners to carry messages,' Devlin suggested. 'That's what we did back in my time. Communications were always pretty damn poor close to the front.'

There was very little light left now. Annette saw Milne and the others running. There was no fear in their minds, just urgency. Raindrops splattered against the window. Within seconds the whole of main street was awash. Gutters started to fill up, with small whirlpools forming over the drains.

'I've never seen anything like that before,' Hoi Son exclaimed, raising his voice against the noise. He was standing in the open doorway, a waterproof poncho forming round his shoulders. The drumming sound of the huge drops was easily as loud as the red cloud's thunder had been. 'And we saw some storms round the Pacific in my day, believe me.'

A rivulet of dirty water began to seep in around his feet, trickling round the tables. Annette couldn't see anything outside now, the rain was battering heavily against the glass, producing the kind of spume that normally topped ocean waves. Behind that, there was only blackness.

Devlin moved up beside her to get a better look. 'Nobody's going anywhere in this.'

'Yes,' Annette agreed shakily. 'You'd better wait.'

'How long, though?' Devlin muttered. 'We didn't think about this when we drew the cloud over us.'

'Don't worry,' Hoi Son said. 'Nobody's going to do any fighting for a while. It's just as bad for them. And at least we're inside.'

*

The landing boat surged forwards as soon as the dazzling corona from the kinetic harpoons lit up the sky. Sinon used the voidhawks' vantage point to observe the giant splash of plasma sinking into the dark mantle of cloud.

It's expanding, Acacia announced. Confirm that, we're tracking it.

Vast cyclonic spirals of cloud were stirring across the upper surface. Washed by Ombey's pale moonlight, the movement appeared almost majestic. Primeval forces had awoken. Along the edges of the cloud, gargantuan tornadoes began to spin away, careering off over the sea.

The whole damn thing's breaking up, Choma said.

Sinon shared a shiver of consternation with the other serjeants; not just in his boat. All of them were facing the same onslaught. He stared out over the prow, watching mountains of water on the move. A wind had risen from nowhere to blow straight at him.

We can't turn back, Choma said. It'll catch us on the open water. Best head for shore.

Sinon's hand patted his lifebelt, seeking reassurance. The massif of cloud seemed to be hurtling towards them, a light-absorbing void distending across the ocean.

Keep going was the decision agreed by the rest of the Edenists and

General Hiltch's command group. Every boat in the Liberation armada rammed its engines to full, and met the stormfront head on.

It wasn't rain they faced, not in the ordinary sense. The deluge crashing down over them was like standing under a waterfall. As the clouds rampaged overhead, so the waves rose, as if seeking to bridge the gap. The landing boats were thrown around pitilessly. Sometimes Sinon had to hold himself against a deck that was lifting over thirty degrees to the vertical. The jeeps secured along the centre of the hold strained against their restraint cables as their weight was flung about in directions the designers had never anticipated. Bilge pumps were wailing plaintively, to little effect. Sinon clung to a guard rail as the cold water mounted steadily against his legs, sloshing between the hull walls. He was worried he'd get tossed overboard. He was worried his newly assembled body would split along surgical lines as he strained muscles and tendons to hold on. He was worried that a jeep would break free and crush him. He was worried they wouldn't reach the beach before the rain and waves filled the hold and sunk them.

Not even sharing the anxiety in the Edenist fashion did much to alleviate it. There was way too much distress bubbling through the ether as the armada battled for shore. The Edenists in secondary support roles, safe away from the megastorm, along with the voidhawks and their crews overhead, did their best to offer what reassurance and comfort they could to their beleaguered kinsmen. But they all felt the death toll rising, compounding the alarm. Landing boats collapsed, pitched over, individual serjeants lost their grip to drown amid the monster waves. Voidhawks laboured tirelessly to absorb the fresh memories of the dying serjeant personalities.

*

A nausea-suppression program went primary as an aghast Ralph watched the nightmare unfurling. Neatly tabulated icons blinked up inside his mind, indicating the woeful progress the boats were making. Some were even being driven backwards as the gales howled out from the land. He did what he could. For all it was worth. Ordering the ground forces along the firebreak to stay put and dig in. Putting the medical teams on immediate standby. Designating search patrols for the aircraft, ready for the time when it became feasible to fly.

Diana Tiernan and the AI couldn't give him any estimate of when that would be. There was no way of knowing the true weight of water powering the storm. Radar scans from the SD sensor satellites to discover the depth and density were badly distorted by the tremendous electrical discharges still churning madly over Mortonridge. All they could do was wait.

'We couldn't have known,' Janne Palmer said. 'Dealing with the possessed is one giant unknown.'

'We should have guessed,' Ralph answered bitterly. 'At least considered it.'

'Best information we had was that the cloud was a couple of hundred metres thick,' Diana said. 'That's all it was on Lalonde and every other planet they took over. But this blasted thing, it must be kilometres deep. They must have sucked every gram of water from the air. There may even be some kind of osmotic process involved, siphoning it up out of the sea.'

'Damn those bastards,' Ralph spat.

'They are afraid,' Acacia said calmly. 'They built the thickest, highest wall they could to keep us out. It's human nature.'

Ralph couldn't bring himself to answer the Edenist. It was Acacia's people who were taking the brunt of the calamity. And it was his plan, his orders, which had put them there. Anything he said would be pathetically inadequate.

Outside, the rain had reached Fort Forward, and was doing its best to wash the city's programmable silicon structures into the nearby river. Fast rivulets were gouging the soil away from their base anchors. Ops Room staff glanced round nervously as banshee winds pummelled away at the walls. Fifty minutes after the kinetic harpoon barrage, the landing boats started to reach the beaches.

'They're coming through,' Acacia said. The first strands of confidence were starting to emerge within the combined Edenist psyche as serjeants exported the feeling of sand crunching underfoot. Proof that success was possible, the sense of relief which accompanied it. 'It's going to be OK, we're going to make it.'

'Right,' Ralph croaked. One icon gleamed darkly at the centre of his woeful thoughts: 3,129. The number of dead so far. And we're the only ones shooting.

*

An immense wave smacked the landing craft down on the beach with an almighty crunch. The blow sent Sinon skidding back along the hold on his arse, limbs flailing. Water slowed his momentum quickly. He came to rest in a jumble of other serjeants. All struggling to disentangle themselves. The three at the bottom were completely immersed. Affinity was supremely useful in coordinating their movements, like unpicking a three-dimensional puzzle.

They'd just got free when the next wave clobbered the side of the landing boat. It lacked the brutality of the previous one, simply shoving the hull further up the beach, and twisting them at an angle.

Dry land! Choma cried triumphantly.

Well . . . land, anyway, Sinon acknowledged dutifully as he sloshed forwards up the hold. The rain here was even worse than out at sea. Visibility was down to maybe fifteen metres, and that was with the boat's powerful lights shining down.

Sometimes, I think you have completely the wrong attitude for this.

Sinon sent a smile image at his friend. He carried on searching through the water for pieces of his kit lost during the last portion of the voyage.

The squad began to assess their position. Five had been injured seriously enough to disqualify them from the campaign altogether. Several more had suffered minor cracking in their exoskeletons, which the medical nanonics could cope with. (Surprisingly, the medical nanonics were working reasonably well.) The beach they'd wound up on was three kilometres south of their designated landing point, Billesdon. The truck at the back of the hold was so badly flooded it would require a complete maintenance overhaul. The landing boat was wedged into the shingle, and would need towing off at high tide before it could return to the resort island for the marines.

On the plus side, the forward ramp worked, allowing the three functional jeeps out. Most of their armament was intact. All the other landing boats containing their regiment had made it ashore, though they were spread out along the coast. After a brief discussion with their Ops Room liaison, they agreed to make their way to

Billesdon and regroup there. According to their original plan, the back-up forces and supplies would use the town's harbour as their disembarkation point. But it still had to be secured.

By the time the boat's forward ramp came down it was technically dawn. Hunched down in the almost non-existent shelter provided by the starboard hull, Sinon couldn't notice any difference. The only way he knew the jeeps were lumbering out was by using his affinity to see out through the driver's eyes.

Looks like we're on, Choma said.

They rose to their feet, and checked their kit one last time. Sinon's squad took up position by the second jeep. Intense headlight beams pierced ten metres through the deluge before the grey water defeated them. It was slow going. Their feet sank deep into the saturated shingle. Twice they had to push the jeep when its wide tyres dug themselves into axle-high ruts.

The squad were totally dependent on their guidance blocks. Satellite images taken before the possession provided them with a high-resolution picture of the cove, and the single narrow track leading away from it into the forest at the rear. Inertial guidance designated their position to within ten centimetres. Supposedly. There was no way of checking. Satellite sensors still couldn't penetrate the cloud to give them a verified location reference. They just had to hope the bitek processors hadn't been glitched since they loaded them back on the island.

Shingle gave way to tacky mud. Laggard waves of the yellow slough were creeping down the beach from the land behind. Clumps of grass and small bushes were being trawled along with it.

Great, Sinon said as he waded in. **At this rate, it's going to take a week to get there.** He was aware of other squads encountering similar difficulties all along the coast.

We need to get to higher ground, Choma said. His affinity indicated a point on the guidance block image. **That should give us better terrain to traverse.**

The squad concurred, and changed direction slightly.

Any news on when this rain's going to end? Sinon queried their liaison.

No.

Not even Cochrane could be bothered to maintain the Karmic Crusader's outlandish appearance. The rain was eroding their spirits at the same rate it ate into the valley's soil. Three hours so far, without ever slackening.

Flares of lightning revealed what it was doing to their beautiful circular valley. Water cascaded over the lip, turning the orderly terraces into long curving waterfalls. At each stage it grew muckier and more glutinous as it carried the rich cultivated black soil with it. Avalanches of crops and sturdy young fruit trees were plunging down the ever-steepening slopes to sink without trace into the expanding lake. The lawn at the rear of the farmhouse was slowly submerged, bringing the water up to the ornate iron-framed patio doors.

By that time they were already loading the Karmic Crusader with their cases. Wind had ripped countless slates from the roof, letting the rain in to soak through the ceiling plaster.

'Just bear in mind, there's only one road out of this valley,' McPhee said when the first rivulet came churning down the stairs into the living room. 'And that runs above the river. If we're going to get out of here, it's got to be soon.'

Nobody had argued. They splashed their way upstairs to pack while he and Cochrane brought the bus out of the barn. Moyo was driving, keeping their speed to little more than walking pace. The dirt track along the side of the winding valley was crumbling at an alarming rate as sheets of filthy water poured down out of the trees above them, foaming round trunks and raking out the tangled undergrowth. His mind concentrated on giving the bus broader tyres in an attempt to gain some kind of traction on the quagmire surface. It was difficult; he had to get Franklin and McPhee to collaborate with him, meshing their thoughts together.

A tree crashed onto the track twenty metres ahead of them, uprooted by the relentless water. Moyo stamped down on the brakes, but the bus just kept slithering forwards. Not even the full focus of his energistic ability could affect the motion. An untimely reminder about his acute lack of omnipotence. He just managed to shout, 'Hold on to something!' before the bus's front collision buffer hit the trunk. The windscreen turned white, bulging inwards to absorb as much of the impact as it could before finally disintegrating into a hail of tiny plastic spheres. A fat bulb of twigs and spiky topaz leaves burst through the rent. Moyo tried to duck, but the seat straps held him fast. Instinct took over, and a stupendous ball of white fire engulfed the twigs. He screeched as his eyebrows smouldered and his hair shrivelled into black frazzled ash. The skin on his face went dead.

Steam belched along the interior as the Karmic Crusader juddered to a halt. Stephanie loosened her grip on the seat back in front of her, leaving deep indentations in the composite. The floor was tilted at quite an incline. What with the rain drumming on the roof, and the water from the slope pouring round them, she could only just distinguish the stressed creaking coming from the bodywork. There was no way of telling what was causing it. Even her eldritch sense was cluttered with confusing shadowforms, the rain was equivalent to strong static interference.

Then water came gurgling eagerly along the aisle, pushing a fringe of filthy scum ahead of it. It glided over her shoes. She made an effort to banish the cloying steam, trying to make out the gloomy interior.

'My eyes!' It was just a whisper, but poignant enough to carry the length of the aisle. Everyone swung round towards the front of the bus.

'Oh God, my eyes. My eyes. Help me! My *eyes*!'

Stephanie had to hang on to the overhead racks, swinging one hand in front of the other, to make her way forwards. Moyo was still sitting in the driver's seat, his body rigid. The incinerated remains of the tree's branch cluster loomed centimetres from his face like some fabulously delicate charcoal sculpture. His hands were held close to his cheeks, trembling from the fear of what he'd find if he actually touched himself.

'It's all right,' she said automatically. Her mind played traitor, fright and revulsion at what she saw surging to the surface of her thoughts. His skin had roasted away, taking most of his nose and all of his eyelids with it. Blood was dribbling out of the fissures between scabs of crisped corium layers. Both eyes had broiled, turning septic yellow as creamy fluids percolated out in a mockery of tears.

'I can't see,' he cried. 'Why can't I see?'

She reached out and grasped both his hands. 'Shush. Please, darling. It'll be all right. You just got scorched by the flame, that's all.'

'I can't see!'

'Of course you can. You've got your sixth sense until your eyes recover. You know I'm here, don't you?'

'Yes. *Don't go.*'

She put her arms round him. 'I won't.' He began shaking violently. Cold sweat was prickling his undamaged skin.

'He's in shock,' Tina said. The others were gathering round, as much as the cramped aisle would permit. Their thoughts tempered by the sight of Moyo's injuries.

'He's all right,' Stephanie insisted in a brittle tone.

'It's very common with major burns cases.'

Stephanie glared at her.

'Yo, man, give him a drag on this,' Cochrane said. He held out a fat reefer, sickly sweet smoke seeping from its glowing tip.

'Not now!' Stephanie hissed.

'Actually, yes, darling,' Tina said. 'For once the ape man's right. It's a mild sedative, which is just what he needs right now.' Stephanie frowned suspiciously at the unaccustomed authority in Tina's voice. 'I used to be a nurse,' the statuesque woman continued, gathering in her black diamanté shawl with a contemptuous dignity. 'Actually.'

Stephanie took the reefer, and eased it gently into Moyo's lips. He coughed weakly as he inhaled.

The bus groaned loudly. Its rear end shifted a couple of metres, sending them all grabbing for support. McPhee ducked his head to peer through the broken windscreen. 'We're not going anywhere in this,' he said. 'We'd better get out before we get washed away.'

'We can't move him,' Stephanie protested. 'Not for a while.'

'The river's nearly up level with this track, and we've got at least another kilometre and a half to go before we're out of the valley.'

'Level? It can't be. We were twenty metres above the valley floor.'

The Karmic Crusader's headlights were out, so she sent a slender blade of white fire arching over the track. It was as if the land had turned to water. She couldn't actually see any ground, slopes and hollows were all submerged under several centimetres of flowing yellow-brown water. Just below the flattish section which marked the track, a cavalcade of flotsam was sweeping along the valley. Mangled branches, smashed trunks, and snarled-up mats of vegetation were all cluttered together; their smooth progress was ominous, nothing stood in their way. As she watched, another of the trees from the slope above slid down past the bus, staying vertical the whole time until it reached the river.

She didn't like to think how many more trees were poised just above them. 'You're right,' she said. 'Let's get out of here.'

Cochrane retrieved his reefer. 'Feel better?' Moyo simply twitched. 'Hey, no need for the downer. Just like grow them back, man. It's easy.'

Moyo's answering laugh was hysterical. 'Imagine I can see? Oh yes, oh yes. It's easy, it's so fucking easy.' He started to sob, tapping his fingertips delicately over his ruined face. 'I'm sorry. I'm so sorry.'

'You stopped the bus,' Stephanie said. 'You saved all of us. There's nothing to be sorry for.'

'Not *you*!' he screamed. 'Him! I'm saying sorry to him. It's his body, not mine. Look what I've done to it. Not you. Oh God. Why did all this happen? Why couldn't we all just die?'

'Get me the first aid kit,' Tina told Rana. 'Now!'

Stephanie had her arm round Moyo's shoulder again, wishing there was some aspect of energistic power that could manifest raw comfort. McPhee and Franklin tried opening the door. But it was jammed solid, beyond even their enhanced physical strength's ability to shift. They looked at each other, gripped hands, and closed their eyes. A big circular section of the front bodywork spun off into the bedlam outside. Rain spat down the aisle like a damp shotgun blast. Rana struggled forwards with the first aid kit case, fiddling with the clips.

'This is no use,' Tina wailed. She plucked out a nanonic package, face wrinkled in dismay. The thick green strip dangled from her hand like so much wobbly rubber.

'Come on! There must be something in it you can use,' Stephanie said.

Tina rummaged through. The case contained several strips of nanonic package, diagnostic blocks – all useless. Even the phials of biochemicals and drugs used infuser patches, the dosage regulated by a diagnostic block. There was no non-technological method of getting the medication into his bloodstream. She shook her head weakly. 'Nothing.'

'Damn it—'

The bus groaned, shifting again. 'No more time,' McPhee said. 'This is it. Out. Now.'

Cochrane clambered out of the hole, splashing down on the track next to the fallen tree. Keeping his footing was obviously difficult. The water came halfway up his shin. Rana followed him down. Stephanie gripped the seat straps holding Moyo in, and forced them to rot in her palms. She and Franklin hauled him up, and guided him through the hole. Tina followed them through, letting out martyred squeals as she struggled to find footholds.

'Lose those bloody heels, ye moron,' McPhee yelled at her.

She glared back at him petulantly, but her scarlet stilettos faded into ordinary pumps with flat soles. 'Peasant. A girl has to look her best at all times, you know.'

'This is real, you stupid cow, not a fucking disaster movie set. You're no being filmed.'

She ignored him, and turned to help Stephanie with Moyo. 'Let's try and bandage his face, at the very least,' she said. 'I'll need some cloth.'

Stephanie tore a strip off the bottom of her saturated cardigan. When she passed it over to Tina it had become a dry, clean strip of white linen.

'I suppose that'll be all right,' Tina said dubiously. She started to wrap it round Moyo's eyes, making sure the stub remains of his nose were also covered. 'Do try and think of your face as being normal, darling. It'll all grow back, then, you'll see.'

Stephanie said nothing, she didn't doubt Moyo could repair the burns to his cheeks and forehead, but actually growing eyeballs back . . .

Franklin landed with a heavy splash; the last out of the bus. Nobody fancied trying to salvage their luggage. The boot was at the rear, and not even energistic power would help much clambering over the tree. Blasting the trunk to shreds would only send the bus spinning over the edge.

They spent a couple of minutes sorting themselves out. First priority was fending off the rain; their collective imagination produced a transparent hemisphere, like a giant glass umbrella floating in the air above them. Once that was established, they set about drying off their clothes. There wasn't anything they could do about the water coursing across the track, so they gave themselves sturdy knee-high wellingtons.

Thus protected, they set off down the track, taking turns to guide and support a shivering Moyo. A bright globe of ball lightning bobbed through the air ahead and slightly to the side of them, hissing as raindrops lashed against it, but lighting the way and hopefully giving them some warning of any more falling trees. Apart from that, their only worry was making it out of the valley before the river rose up over the track. The driving rain and roaring wind meant they never knew when another tree slithered down the slope into the dark and battered Karmic Crusader, sending it plunging into the engorged river.

*

Billesdon was a cheery little town, tucked into the lee of a large granite headland on Mortonridge's eastern coast. Sheltered from the worst of the breakers to come rolling in off the ocean, it was a natural harbour. District planners took advantage of that, quarrying the abundant rock to build a long curving quay opposite the headland, enclosing a wide deep-water basin with a modest beach at the back. The majority of boats which used it were trawlers and sandrakers, their operators earning a good living from Ombey's plentiful fish and crustacean species. Even the local seaweed was exported to restaurants across the peninsula.

It also proved a haven for pleasure boats, with several sport fishing and yachting clubs setting up shop. With so many boats to service, the marine engineering companies and supply industries were quick to seize upon the commercial opportunities available and open premises in the town. Houses, apartment blocks, shops, hotels, entertainment halls, and industrial estates were thrown up all the way back along the shallow valley behind the headland. Villas and groves began to blossom along the slopes above, next to golf courses and holiday complexes.

Billesdon became the sort of town, beautiful and economically successful, that was presented as the Kingdom's ideal, every citizen's entitlement. Sinon's squad reached the outskirts around midday. A trivial glimmer of light was penetrating the clouds, giving the world a lacklustre opacity. Visibility had risen to a few hundred yards.

Sinon wished it hadn't bothered. They were poised just outside the town, not far above the sea. Cover was ostensibly provided by a spinney of fallen fellots. None of the sturdy aboriginal trees remained standing. Their dense fan-shaped branches had cushioned the way the trunks fell, leaving them at crazy angles. Rain kept their upper sections clean from the cloying mud, giving the cerise bark a glossy sheen. Choma was pressed up against a fat trunk at the edge of the spinney, waving a sensor block slowly ahead of him. The whole squad hooked in to the block's bitek processor, examining the buildings ahead through a variety of wavelengths.

Not even the money lavished on Billesdon's infrastructure had saved it from the rain. The terraces and groves above had dissolved, sending waves of mud slithering down into the prim streets, clogging the drains within minutes. Water raced along the roads and pavements, submerging tarmac and grass alike before it poured over the quayside wall. There were no boats left in the harbour; every single craft had been used to evacuate the population before Ekelund's invasion reached the coast. In theory, that left the basin clear for the Liberation's landing boats to bring the occupation troops and support *matériel* ashore.

Seems deserted, Choma said.

Nothing moving, Sinon agreed, but infrared's useless in all this rain. There could be thousands of them tucked up nice and dry waiting for us.

Look on the bright side, the water should foul up that white fire of theirs.

Maybe, but that still leaves them with a whole load of options to use against us.

That's good, keep thinking like that. Paranoia keeps you on your toes.

Thank you.

So what do you want to do now?

Simple. We're going to have to go in and check it out one house at a time.

OK, that's what I signed up for.

They discussed it with the other squads encircling the town. Search areas were designated, tactics coordinated, blockades established on the main roads. Guyana was alerted that they were going in, and readied the low-orbit SD platforms to provide ground-strike support if called for.

The outskirts ahead of Sinon were modest houses overlooking the harbour, home to the fishing families. They had large gardens, which had been completely washed away. Long tongues of mud-slimed debris were stretched down the slope, with small streams running down their centres where the water had gouged a channel into the sandy soil. Cover between the spinney and the first house was non-existent, so the squad moved forwards with long gaps between each member. If the white fire did burst down on them, it would never be able to reach more than one at a time. Hopefully.

Sinon was third in the line. He held his machine-gun ready, crouched low to provide the smallest possible target. Ever since they came ashore, he'd been thankful that his serjeant body had an exoskeleton; the rain didn't bother him as much as it would if he had ordinary skin. Body armour had been considered and rejected, it had never been any good against the white fire before. The one concession they all made was shoes, a kind of sandal with deep-tread soles to give them traction.

Even so, it was hard to keep his feet from slipping as he hurried forward through the mud. The first house was ten metres ahead of him. A white box with long silvered windows and a large first-floor balcony at the rear. Water poured out of the sagging guttering, diluting the slow-moving sludge that percolated round the base of the walls. He kept sweeping the machine-gun nozzle across the facing wall, alert for any sign of motion from inside. Out in the open, wind was driving the rain straight at him. Even his body was aware of how cold it was; not that it was affecting his performance, not yet. Sensor blocks dangled from his belt, unused and redundant as he urged himself on. His training was his one and only defence now.

Choma had already reached the house ahead of him. Ducking down to crawl under the windows. Sinon reached the back wall, and started to follow his friend along the side of the house. It was important to keep moving, not clump together. Palm fronds and limp knots of grass wrapped themselves round his ankles, slowing him. When he reached the largest window, he took one of the sensor blocks from his belt, and gingerly pressed it to the pane. The block relayed a slightly misty image of the room inside. A lounge, cosy, with worn furniture and framed family holograms on the wall. Water was spraying out of the ceiling's central light fitting; the floor was invisible under a layer of mud which had pushed in from the hallway. An infrared scan showed no hot-spots.

Clean downstairs, he said. **And my ELINT block is clear. Looks like nobody's home.**

We need to be sure, Choma replied. **Check out the upper floor. I'll back you.**

Sinon stood up, shouldering the machine-gun. He took out a fission blade and sliced through the window frame, cutting out the lock. Raindrops sizzled on the glowing blade. The next two serjeants in his squad had already reached the house when he slipped inside. He pushed out a heavy breath from his lungs, the nearest he could get to a sigh. Actually out of the rain. Its impact was diminished to a dull drum roll on the roof. Choma splashed down into the thin mire beside him.

Hell, that's better.

Affinity made Sinon aware of the rest of the squad; two of them were in the neighbouring houses, while the rest had started to spread out along the street. **My ELINT's still clear,** he said.

Choma looked up at the ceiling, pointing his machine-gun at it cautiously. **Yes. I'm pretty sure there's nobody up there, but we've still got to check.**

Sinon made his way out into the hall, machine-gun held ready. **How can you be sure? You don't know what's up there.**

Instinct.

Crazy. He put his foot on the first step, sandal sole making a squelching sound against the sodden carpet. **We've barely got imagination operating inside these neural arrays, let alone an intuitive function.**

Then I suggest you work one up fast, you're going to need it.

Sinon turned so he could cover the landing as he ascended. Nothing moved except for the unending water, glistening as it ran down walls, curling across carpets and tile floors, dripping from furniture. He reached the main bedroom, its door ajar. His foot kicked it hard, dinting the wood. The door slammed back amid a shower of droplets. Choma was right: it was empty. In every room, the signs of panicked departure. Drawers ransacked, clothes scattered about.

Nobody here, Sinon reported to the squad when they cleared the front bedroom. Other house searches across the town were also proving negative as the squads moved in.

Ghost town, Choma said, chortling.

I think you could find a better phrase. He looked down through the window, seeing squad members scuttling along the road outside. They were going against the flow of mud, their legs churning up deep eddies. Things were trundling along the street, carried along by the relentless current. Bulges in the smooth mud; there was no way of telling if they were stones or crumpled twigs. All of them moved at the same speed.

He held up a sensor block, panning it round in search of anomalous hot spots. The image was overlapping his actual field of view, which meant he was looking straight at the house on the other side of the street when it exploded.

A serjeant had cut through the lock on a side door and crept cautiously inside, machine-gun held ready. The ground floor must have been clear, because a second serjeant followed him in. Thirty seconds later four explosions detonated simultaneously. They were carefully placed, one at each corner of the house. Long flakes of concrete and lumps of stone shot out of the billowing flame. The whole house trembled: then, its crucial support destroyed, it collapsed vertically. Windows all along the street blew out under the impact of the blast wave. Sinon just managed to twist away in time, allowing his backpack to take the brunt of the flying shards.

The affinity band boiled with hard, frantic thoughts. Both serjeants in the house were hammered by the explosions, their bodies wrecked. But the tough exoskeletons withstood the searing pressure for a few moments, long enough for the controlling personalities to instinctively begin the transfer. One of the orbiting voidhawks accepted their thoughts; then the house descended on their already weakened skulls.

'Shit!' Sinon yelled. He was curled up on the bedroom floor, aware of something wrong with his left forearm. When he brought it up to his face, the exoskeleton was cracked in a small star pattern. Blood was seeping out of the centre. Rain lashed in through the empty window, washing the crimson stain away.

Are you all right? Choma asked.

Yes . . . Yes, I think so. What happened? He stood up, peering down circumspectly onto the street. The mud and rain had swallowed almost all the immediate signs of the explosion. There was no smoke, no dust cloud. Just a pancake of rubble where the house had stood moments before. The tide of mud was already frothing round it, bubbling eagerly into cracks.

Choma pointed his machine-gun along the street, radiating satisfaction that the squad had merged with the scenery. He knew where they were, but they weren't easily visible. **Where are they? Did anyone see where the white fire came from?**

He was answered with a chorus of noes.

I don't think it was white fire, Sinon said. He ordered his block to replay the memory. The gouts of flame spearing out of each corner were orange, and they came from inside the house.

Sabotage? Choma said.

Could be. They were perfectly placed for demolition.

They were on their way down the stairs when the second house exploded. It was on the far side of town, being examined by one of the other squads. One serjeant was killed, another two were injured beyond any field medic's ability to patch up; they needed immediate evacuation. The rest of Sinon's squad stood back as he clambered up over the mound of stone and girders which had been the house. When he was clear of the mud he ran a sensor pad over the exposed rubble close to one of the corners. The rain was washing the mess clean, but the chemical analysis still had enough residual molecules to work with.

Not good, he announced. **This wasn't white fire. There's a definite trace of trinitrotoluene here.**

Sod it! Choma exclaimed. **The bastards have booby-trapped the whole town.**

Parts of it. I doubt they've got the resources to rig every building.

But you can bet they've done the critical ones, as well as picking on houses at random, he said grudgingly. **It's what I would've done.**

If you're right, we're going to have to treat each building as potentially hazardous. And we don't even know what the trigger is.

I doubt it'll be electronic. Our sensors would spot active processors, and the possessed wouldn't be able to set them up in the first place. We'll have to get some of the marine engineers in here to find out what kind of mechanism they're employing.

Sinon's response was lost amid a burst of anguish within the communal affinity band. Both of them instinctively turned to the west. The death of another two serjeants was all too clear. A warehouse in a town called Holywell had just exploded.

It's not just here, Choma said. **Ekelund's people have been busy.**

*

Confirmation that most major towns around the periphery of Mortonridge were booby-trapped came in to the Ops Room throughout the afternoon. Ralph sat in his office accessing the reports in a state of weary disbelief. Progress schematics were being revised on a fifteen-minute basis by the AI. Their original timetable was constantly rearranged, targets being pushed further and further back.

'Truly amazing,' he told Princess Kirsten during the evening's briefing. 'We're fifteen hours in, and already twenty behind schedule.'

'Conditions are pretty foul under there,' Admiral Farquar said. 'I don't see Ekelund's people having a better time of it.'

'How would we know? Fifteen hours, and we haven't had a single encounter with a live possessed. Christ, I mean I know no battle plan survives contact with the enemy, but no one ever said anything about it disintegrating before we even catch sight of them.'

'General Hiltch,' the Princess said sharply. 'I'd like you to give me some positive factors, please. Have all the possessed simply vanished into this other realm they long for?'

'We don't think so, no, ma'am. Pulling back from the coast and the firebreak is a logical move. They obviously worked it out in advance, hence the booby traps.'

'There's circumstantial evidence that they're still in the centre of Mortonridge,' Diana said. 'Our satellite sensor scans are at their worst there. Radar and UV laser is beginning to break through the fringes, but when we try to probe the centre we get the same kind of hazing effect the possessed have always generated. Ergo, they're still there.'

'That's something, I suppose.'

'I also think the worst of the rain should be over by midday tomorrow. Results from the sensors we can rely on show us the cloud is thinning out. A lot of it is simply blowing out to sea now they're no longer containing it. And of course, it's falling, big-time.'

'It certainly is,' Acacia said. She shuddered at the on-the-ground impressions affinity had delivered to him. 'You're going to have real problems with Mortonridge's vegetation when this is all over. I doubt there's a tree standing on the whole peninsula. I didn't know rain like that could exist.'

'It can't, normally,' Diana said. 'This whole meteorology situation is highly artificial. The dispersal will influence the planet's weather patterns for the rest of the year. However, it certainly isn't sustainable; as I said, the heaviest falls will be over by midday tomorrow. After that, the serjeants will be able to make decent progress.'

'Over open country, possibly,' Ralph said. 'But we're going to have to vector in these booby traps.'

'Do we know what they are, yet?' the Princess asked.

'The majority so far are good old-fashioned TNT,' Ralph told her. 'Easily produced from the kind of chemicals available in most of our urban zones. We managed to get some marine engineers in to the afflicted towns to examine what they could. There's no standard trigger mechanism, naturally enough. The possessed are using everything from trip wires to wired-up doorknobs. There's just no quick way to deal with them. The whole point of the front-line serjeants is to clear every metre of ground as they advance. Knowing you're in danger just by walking into a building is going to be very stressful for the entire army, I'm afraid. Doing the job properly is going to slow us down considerably.'

'So will the mud,' Janne said. 'We know where the roads are, but no one's actually seen a solid surface yet.'

'Progress down the M6 is slow,' Cathal confirmed. 'The major bridges are out. We expected that, of course. But the mechanoids are having a lot of trouble erecting the replacements the convoys are carrying, they're just not designed to operate in this kind of environment.'

'That situation should ease off tomorrow as well,' Diana said.

'The rain, yes; but the mud will still be there.'

'We're going to have to learn to live with that, I'm afraid. It's here for the duration.'

*

Did you know, the original ethnic Eskimos on Earth had several dozen words for snow? Sinon said.

Really? Choma answered from the other side of the winding ravine they were following.

Apparently so.

Excuse me for having my neural array assembled in too much of a hurry, but I don't quite see the relevance to our current situation.

I just thought, it might be appropriate if we had an equal number of names for mud.

Oh, right. Yes. Let's see, we could have real crappy mud, bloody awful mud, pain in the ass mud, squeezes inside your exoskeleton and squelches a lot mud, and then there's always the ultimate: drowning in mud.

You have a much higher emotional context than the rest of us, don't you? Your jest about neural array assembly might be an unintentional truism.

You are what you bring to yourself.

Quite.

Sinon stepped over yet another fallen branch. It was midafternoon of the Liberation's second day. All the serjeants had received the revised schedule from the Fort Forward Ops Room, they were expected to move across the land at about half the speed originally intended. Very optimistic, Sinon thought.

It had taken until four o'clock in the morning to secure Billesdon. Now they knew they were dealing with TNT, the sensor blocks had been programmed to sniff it out. Given TNT's relatively unstable nature, there were usually enough molecules left floating round inside the building to provide a positive detection. The damp didn't help, but by and large the blocks protected them.

Sinon himself had found two houses that were rigged. They'd learned to tie the blocks to the end of long poles, and push them through windows and doors already forced open by the mud. Each time, he'd designated the building, and it was left for the marine engineers to send mechanoids in at some later time. They'd still lost another eight serjeants before the town was cleared.

The landing boats had returned as a feeble dawn broke, carrying their supplies, more jeeps, and the first of the marine troops. The wind had calmed, although the rain was still as intense. And the big harbour basin was now clotting up with mud, hampering their manoeuvring as they docked. But by midmorning, the quayside was thick with activity. A degree of confidence returned to the serjeants. They were getting back on track. With the marines holding Billesdon, the whole battalion began to deploy back out along the coast ready for the push inland.

True to Diana Tiernan's prediction, the rain did start to slacken by midday. Or at least, they convinced themselves it had; the light perforating the clouds was noticeably brighter. It did nothing to alleviate the misery of the mud. There had never been a landscape like it on any terracompatible Confederation world. Rover reporters stood on the edge of town, starkly silent as their enhanced retinas faithfully delivered the devastation back to the millions of citizens accessing the Liberation. Only the contours of the land remained stable, the mud had claimed everything else. There were no fields, or meadows, or scrubland, just a slick shit-brown coating, undulating and gurgling as it crept inexorably along. Mortonridge had become a single quagmire, extending from the sea to the horizon. Sensors in orbit showed the stain around the coast was already ten kilometres wide, and still spreading incursive fingers hungrily into the calm turquoise ocean.

Along with the rest of his squad, Sinon trudged through the forest, scrambling over the fallen trunks and their even more troublesome roots. Nothing had been left standing upright, although the tide of mud lacked the force to carry the trees with it. Superficially, the area resembled a bayou, although here the fractured wood was razor-sharp, lacking the worn rottenness of plants growing in genuine swampland. Real bayous didn't have so many dead animals, either.

Like the vegetation, Mortonridge's indigenous creatures had taken a dreadful punishment. Birds and ground animals had drowned in their millions. Their corpses, too, were part of the loose detritus carried along by the mud as it slid downwards into the ocean. Except in the forest, where the branches and root webs acted like nets. They were clustered round each tree, anonymous lumps, distending as they started to decompose. Heavy bubbles swelled across them like clumps of inflatable fungus as body gases forced a way out.

His battalion had been arranged in a line eighty kilometres wide, centred on Billesdon. Its flanks merged with other battalions. This was the time when the army was stretched to its absolute maximum, completely encircling the entire peninsula. The AI had spaced the serjeants fifty metres apart right along the coast, planning on them yomping forwards together in a giant contracting sweep manoeuvre. If a possessed did try to hide out in the countryside they would never be more than twenty-five metres away from one of the serjeants. A combination of eyesight, infra-red, SD satellite observation (eventually), and ELINT blocks ought to be able to locate them. Jeeps, trucks and reserve squads trailed behind the front line in columns one kilometre apart, ready to reinforce any section of the line that came under heavy attack. Mustered behind them were the prisoner-handling details.

When the gigantic formation was complete, the serjeants paused, reaffirming their commitment to the Liberation, celebrating the unity and accomplishment. Mortonridge was sealed off ahead of them, and now they were physically in place after all that had befallen, success appeared tangible. Doubt was banished.

'Go,' Ralph ordered.

The pattern started to waver as soon as the serjeants left the coast behind. Mountain roads and tracks had vanished altogether. Valley floors were now deep rivers of mud. No vehicles could plough through the broken remains of the forests. The AI began to guide them round obstacles, always keeping the reserves within optimum distance of the front line, slowing some sections of the advance, directing extra serjeants to expand the line over steep terrain.

They had their first encounter with a possessed seventy-six minutes after they started. Sinon watched through another set of eyes as the serjeant up near the firebreak fired its machine-gun at a heat corona coming from behind an upturned car. Sparkling bullets ripped straight through the composite bodywork. Tendrils of enraged white fire curved over the top in retaliation. Another serjeant opened fire. The entire line halted, waiting to see what would happen.

For a moment there was no effect. Then the white fire faded, turning translucent before the rain smothered it, drops steaming as they fell through. A man staggered out from behind the wrecked car, hands waving madly as the bullets thudded into him. Ripples of purple light blazed out from every impact, swathing his body in a wondrous pyrotechnic display. The serjeant upped the fire rate.

'Stop it!' the man screamed. He crashed to his knees, hands batting feebly to ward off the machine-gun. 'Stop it, for fuck's sake. I surrender, goddam it.'

The serjeant eased off the trigger, and walked forwards. 'Lie down flat, put your hands behind your head. Do not attempt to move or apply your energistic power.'

'Fuck you,' the man snarled through clenched teeth. His body was shaking badly.

'Down. Now!'

'All right, all right.' He lowered himself into the mud. 'Mind if I don't go any further? Even we can't breathe mud.'

The serjeant took its holding stick from its belt, a dull silver cylinder half a metre long. It telescoped out to two metres, and a pincer clamp at one end opened wide.

'What the hell . . .?' the man grunted as the serjeant closed the clamp round his neck.

'This restraint has a dead-man function. If I let go, or I'm made to let go, it will fire ten thousand volts into you. If you resist or refuse to obey any instruction, I will shove a current into you and keep turning it up until your energistic ability is neutralized. Do you understand?'

'You're gonna die one day, you're going to join us.'

The serjeant switched on a two hundred volt current.

'Jesus wept,' the man squealed.

'Do you understand?'

'Yes. Yes, fuck. Turn it off. Off!'

'Very well. You will now leave this body.'

'Or what, asshole? If you zap me too hard we both die. Me and my host.'

'If you do not leave of your own volition, you will be placed in zero-tau.'

'Fuck. I can't go back there.' He started sobbing. 'Don't you understand? I can't. Not there. *Please*. Please, if you've got an ounce of humanity in you, don't do this. I'm begging you.'

'I'm sorry. That is not an option. Leave now.'

'I can't.'

The serjeant pulled on the holding stick, forcing the possessed to his feet. 'This way.'

'What now?'

'Zero-tau.'

The cheering in the Ops Room was deafening. Ralph actually grinned out at them from his office, the image of the captured possessed being led away lingering in his mind. It might work, he thought. It just might. He remembered walking out of Exnall, the girl crying limply in his arms, Ekelund's mocking laughter in the air.

'Enjoy your victory with the girl,' she'd sneered. His only personal success in that entire frightful night.

'Two down,' Ralph whispered. 'Two million to go.'

*

The fish were dying. Stephanie thought that the oddest thing. This rain should be their chance to take over the whole world. Instead the ever-thickening mud was clogging up their gills, preventing them from breathing. They lay on the surface, being pushed along by the leisurely waves of water, their bodies flapping madly.

'We should like hollow out some logs, man, use them as canoes. That's what our ancestors used to do, and those cats were like really in tune with nature,' Cochrane suggested when they cleared the end of the valley.

They'd only just made it, the sluggish river was leaking over the top of the track. At times it seemed as if the whole surface of the valley was on the move. They stood above the gurgling edge of the flow, and watched the gargantuan outpouring spread out to surge on across the lowlands.

'Fat lot of use that would be,' Franklin muttered grimly. 'Everything's heading down to the coast, and that's where *they* are. Besides,' he gestured round extravagantly at the denuded valley, 'what trees?'

'You are such a downer. I want some wheels, man. I have like totally had it with tramping through this shit.'

'I thought cars were spawned by the capitalist establishment to promote our greed and distance us from nature,' Rana said sweetly. 'I'm sure I heard somebody say that recently.'

Cochrane kicked at the fish flopping about round his feet. 'Get off my back, prickly sister. OK? I'm thinking of Moyo. He can't handle this.'

'Just . . . quiet,' Stephanie said. Even she was waspish, fed up with the pettiness they were all displaying. The ordeal of the bus and then the track had stretched everyone's nerves. 'How are you?' she asked Moyo.

His face had returned to normal, the illusion swallowing his bandage and shielding his scabbed tissue from sight. Even his eyeballs appeared to dart about naturally. But he'd taken a lot of cajoling and encouragement to walk along the track. His thoughts had contracted, gathering round a centre of sullen self-pity. 'I'll be OK,' he mumbled. 'Just get me out of this rain. I hate it.'

'Amen to that,' Cochrane chirped.

Stephanie looked round the shabby landscape. Visibility was still pretty ropy on the other side of their protective umbrella, though it was definitely lighter now. It was hard to believe this eternal featureless mire was the same vigorous green countryside they'd travelled across in the Karmic Crusader. 'Well, we can't go that way.' She gestured at the cataract of muddy water rumbling away into the distance. 'So I guess we'll have to stick to this side. Anyone remember roughly where the road is?'

'Along there, I think,' McPhee said. Neither voice nor mind-tone suggested much confidence in the claim. 'There's definitely a flat ledge. See? The carbon-concrete must have held up.'

'Till the foundation gets washed out from under it,' Franklin said.

Stephanie couldn't honestly see any difference in the mud where he was pointing. 'All right, we'll go for it.'

'How far?' Tina demanded querulously. 'And how long will it take to get there?'

'Depends where you're heading, babe,' Cochrane said.

'Well, I don't know, do I? I wouldn't ask if I did.'

'Any kind of building will do,' Stephanie said. 'We can reinforce it against the weather ourselves. I just want us out of this. We can think what to do next when we're rested up. Come on.' Stephanie gripped Moyo's hand and began to walk in the direction the road was supposed to be. Fish tails slapped pitifully at her wellingtons.

'Oh, man, it don't make no difference what we decide. We know what's like gonna happen.'

'Then stay here and let it,' Rana told the miserable hippy. She started off after Stephanie.

'I didn't say I was in a rush.' The edge of the invisible shield moved towards Cochrane, and he scrambled after them.

'There was a village called Ketton on this road,' McPhee said. 'I remember going through it before we turned off up to the farm.'

'How far?' Tina asked, her voice rising in hope.

Cochrane smiled happily. 'Miles and miles, it'll probably take us like about ten, twenty days.'

*

A ferocious jet of white fire squirted into the wall two metres above Sinon's head. He flattened himself into the mud below as paint ignited and carbon-concrete blistered.

Coming from the shops, seventy metres right. It was hard to see with all the smoke mingling with the rain, but his retinas had a long purple after image scorched across them.

Got it, Kerrial answered.

The white fire expanded into a thin circular sheet, rivulets trickled down, their tips wriggling purposefully towards Sinon. 'Shit!' If he stayed the fire would get him, if he moved he'd lose the cover which the wall provided. And there must be several of them in the shops; two other serjeants were under attack as well.

Eayres was a nothing village in the guidance block's memory, a cluster of houses clumped round a road junction, its population mostly employed by the local marble quarry. Who would expect the possessed to make a stand here? 'Expect the unexpected,' Choma had chanted happily when the white fireballs burst open amid the squad.

Sinon saw Kerrial swing himself into position, bringing his machine-gun to bear on the shops in the middle of the village. Bullet craters slammed across the brickwork in front of him. Then his body was being flung back, nerve channels shutting down. Blackness.

Kerrial's memories arose from his neural array to be absorbed by an orbiting voidhawk.

They've got guns! Sinon broadcast.

Yes, Choma said. **I saw.**

Where did they get them from?

This is the countryside, hunting is a sport here. Besides, did you think we had a monopoly?

The white fire rivulets had reached the ground. Steam roared up as they floated sinuously along the top of the mud towards Sinon. He scrambled to his feet, and jumped forward. The white fire behind him vanished. Another, brighter, spear lanced out of a shop's fractured window. He hit the mud, rolling desperately as he brought his grenade launcher to bear.

You'll kill them, Choma warned. Sinon's right leg went dead as the white fire engulfed it. He slamfired the launcher, hand pumping the mechanism with cyborg intent.

Grenades thudded into the upper floor of the shop, detonating instantly. The ceiling split open, hurling down a torrent of rubble as the roof caved in. Three radiant lines of machine-gun fire poured through the ground-floor windows and into the tumult inside. The white fire evaporated into tiny violet wisps, splattering off Sinon's leg. He scrambled up, and pushed himself hard for the buildings dead ahead, dragging his useless leg along. Crashing through the first door to land in a deserted bar.

Clever, Choma said. **I think that's got them cold.**

The white fire had gone out everywhere. Serjeants converged on the little row of prim shops, walking forwards steadily, firing their machine-guns continually. The squad had responded to the possessed like antibodies reacting to an incursive virus. Flowing in towards the village from both sides, the reserve squad racing forward. A miniature version of the noose contracting around Mortonridge. They had it encircled within minutes. Then began their advance.

Seventeen of them walked through the smoke that whirled along Main Street, impervious to the flames roaring out of the buildings all around. Their gunfire was concentrated on the shops, aiming their vivid bullets through any gap they could find. Weird lights flickered inside, as if someone had activated a night-club hologram rig. Steam fountained out through windows and cracks in the wall.

'All right. Enough. *Enough*, God damn it. We're through.'

The ring of serjeants held their places ten metres from the central shop, feet apart, juddering in time to the roaring guns.

'ENOUGH. We surrender.' The machine-guns fell silent.

Lumps of stone stirred on the mound of rubble which had been the shop's upper floor, spinning down to splash into the ubiquitous mire. Limbs began to emerge amid a welter of coughing. Six possessed squirmed free, holding up their hands and blinking uncomfortably. More serjeants moved forwards to clamp their necks with holding sticks.

*

Elena Duncan reached Eayres two hours later. The fires were out by then, extinguished by the rain. She whistled appreciatively as she climbed out of the truck, a sound violent enough to make the marines wince. 'Must have been a hell of a fight,' she said in envy. The trucks had halted in the main street. Over half of the buildings around her had been flattened into small hillocks of debris; of those that remained, few were left with roofs. Naked, heat-twisted girders skewered up into the gloomy sky. Black soot stains smeared over entire walls were already dissolving under the rain to reveal deep bullet pocks.

Marines began jumping down from the other trucks in the convoy. It was a familiar routine by now. Urban zones, whatever the size, were occupied by a garrison. They served as emergency reserves and staging posts; also a transitory field hospital a lot of the time. The possessed weren't giving up without a fight. The marine lieutenant in charge started shouting orders, and the troops fanned out to secure the perimeter. Elena and the other mercs began unloading their truck with the help of five mud-caked mechanoids.

First off was a programmable multipurpose silicon hall. An oval twenty-five metres long, with open archways along the sides, it was a standard Kulu Royal Marine Corps issue, designed for tropical climates, with an overhang in anticipation of heavy showers, and allowing a constant breeze to filter through. Ordinarily ideal for a place like Mortonridge. Now, they were having to direct the mechanoids to bulldoze up a base from soil and stone which they then sealed over with fast-set polymer. It was the only way to keep the floor above mud level.

Once that was up, they started moving the zero-tau pods in. A double file of serjeants marched down the main street, escorting three possessed. Elena splashed out to greet them. She enjoyed this part of her duty.

One of the possessed had given up, a man in his late sixties. She'd seen that before. Filthy, torn clothes. Not bothering to heal his wounds. Even the rain was allowed to soak him. The other two were more typical. Dignity intact. Clothes immaculate, not a scratch on them. The rain bounced off as if they had a frictionless coating. Elena gave one of them a long look. A woman in a prim antique blue suit, white blouse with a lace collar, and pearl necklace. Her hair was a solid bottle-blond coiffure that could have been carved from rock for all the wind affected it. She gave Elena a single distasteful glance, defiantly arrogant.

Elena nodded affably at the serjeant guarding her, whose leg was wrapped in a medical package tube. 'Hmm, she's the third one of these today. And I thought that woman was unique.'

'Excuse me?' the serjeant asked.

'They enjoy historical figures. I've been accessing my encyclopedia's history files ever since this campaign started, trying to place them. Hitlers are quite popular, so's Napoleon and Richard Saldana, then there's Cleopatra. Somebody called Ellen Ripley is a big favourite with the women, too; but none of my search programs have managed to track her down yet.'

The blue-suited woman looked dead ahead, and smiled a secret smile.

'OK,' Elena said. 'Bring them in.'

The mercenaries were hooking the zero-tau pods up to their power cells, datavising diagnostics through the management processors. Elena's ELINT block gave a warning bleep. She rounded on the three prisoners, pulling a high-voltage shock rod from her belt. Her voice boomed out from her facial grille, echoing round the hall.

'Cut that out, shitbrains. You lost, and this is the end of the line. Too late to argue about it now. The serjeants might be too honourable and decent to fry your bodies, but I'm not. And this is my part of the operation. Got that?' The ELINT block quietened. 'Good. Then we'll get along just fine in your final minutes in this universe. Any last-minute cigarettes, you can indulge yourselves. Otherwise just keep quiet.'

'I see you have found an occupation which obviously suits you.'

'Huh?' She glanced down at the serjeant with the injured leg.

'We met at Fort Forward, just after arriving. I am Sinon.'

Her three claws snapped together with a loud *click*. 'Oh, yes, the cannon-fodder guy. Sorry, you all look alike to me.'

'We are identical.'

'Glad to see you survived. Though God knows how you managed it. Trying to storm ashore through that weather was the dumbest military decision since the Trojans took a shine to that horse.'

'I think you're being unduly cynical.'

'Don't give me that crap. You must have a decent dose of it too, if you've survived this long. Remember the oldest military rule, my friend.'

'Never volunteer for anything?'

'Generals always fuck up bad.'

The first zero-tau pod opened. Elena pointed her shock rod at the blue-suited woman. 'OK, Prime Minister, you first.' Sinon kept the holding stick round her neck as she backed in. Metal manacles closed round her limbs, and Elena switched on a mild current. The woman glared out, her face drawn back with the effort of fighting the electricity.

'Just in case,' Elena told Sinon. 'We had a few try to break free once they finally realize their number's up. You can take the holding stick off now.' The clamp sprang open, and Sinon stood clear. 'You going to leave all nice and voluntarily?' Elena asked. The front of the zero-tau pod was already swinging shut. The woman spat weakly. 'Didn't think so. Not you.'

The zero-tau pod turned midnight black. Elena heard a hiss of breath from one of the waiting possessed, but didn't say anything.

'How long do you leave them in there?' Sinon asked.

'Cook them for about fifteen minutes. Then we open up to see if they're done. If not, it's just back in for progressively longer periods. I've had one hold out for about ten hours before, but that was the limit.'

'That sounds suspiciously like enjoyment to me.'

Elena waved the next possessed into his pod. 'Nothing suspicious about it. General Hiltch, God fuck him, says I'm not allowed in the front line. So this is the second-best duty as far as I'm concerned. I don't take marine discipline too good. Sitting with a bunch of those pansy-asses in a place like this counting raindrops would have me thrown offplanet inside of a day. So as I'm technologically competent, me and my friends requested this placement. It works out fine. Army's short of skilled techs who can also handle the noise if the possessed start to panic: we fit the bill. And this way I get to see the bastards booted out of their bodies. I *know* it's happening.'

The second possessed was put in a zero-tau pod. He didn't resist. Then the third zero-tau pod was activated. Elena aimed the shock rod at the last possessed, the apathetic one. 'Hey, cheer up. This is your lucky day, looks like the reserves got called out. You're on, kid.' He gave her a broken look and grimaced. His features melted, shrinking back to reveal a wizened face with anaemically pale skin.

'Catch him,' Elena yelled. The man's legs buckled. He pitched forward into her arms. 'Thought that one might quit,' she said in satisfaction.

Choma removed the holding stick's clamp from around his neck.

Elena eased him down onto the floor, calling for blankets and some pillows. 'Damn it, we haven't had time to unpack the medical gear yet,' she said. 'And we're going to need it. Those bastards.'

'What's the matter?' Sinon asked.

Elena's claw sliced through the man's raggedy shirt, exposing his chest. There were strange ridges swelling out of his skin, mimicking the lines of muscle a healthy twenty-year-old mesomorph might have. When she prodded one with the tip of a claw, it sagged like a sack of jelly.

'They always go for perfection,' she explained to Sinon and Choma. 'Assholes. I don't know what that energistic power is, but it screws up their flesh real bad under the illusion. Sometimes you get fat deposits building up, that's pretty harmless; but nine times out of ten, it's tumours.'

'All of them?' Sinon asked.

'Yep. Never satisfied with what they've got. I'm sure it's a metaphor for something, but I'm buggered if I can figure out what. We're having to ship everyone who gets de-possessed back to Xingu and into one of the major hospitals. They're overflowing already, and they don't have enough nanonic packages to go around. Another week of this, and the entire Ombey system is going to go into medical meltdown. And that's not taking you guys into account; you're not exactly emerging unscathed from the Liberation.'

'Can we help?'

'Not a thing you can do, sorry. Now if you could clear out . . . I've got to try and organize some sort of transport for this batch. Hell, I wish we had hovercraft, they're the only things that can travel properly over this swamp. That dickhead Hiltch won't allow any planes in under the cloud yet.'

Sinon and Choma left her and another couple of mercenaries running medical scanners over the unconscious man.

All of them? Sinon repeated gloomily. The prospect kindled a sensation of alarm, in itself a worrying development. He hadn't configured himself to be waylaid by impulsive emotions. *Do you know what that means?*

Trouble, Choma declared. *Real bad trouble.*

8

The vac-trains were an excellent solution to Earth's transport problem in the age of the arcologies. There were no aircraft any more. The armada storms had finished off air travel in the same way they made people abandon their cars. One of the late twenty-first century's most enduring newscable images was of a farmer's pick-up truck rammed through a nineteenth-floor window of the Sears Tower in the wake of a storm. As the planet's population flowed into cities and began strengthening them against the weather, so they turned to trains as the only practical method of transport between urban conglomerations. Heavy and solid, tornadoes couldn't fling them about so easily. Of course, they still took a battering from the wind if they were caught out in the open. So the next logical stage was to protect the tracks in the same way the domes were going up to shield the city centres. The first real example was the Channel Tunnel, which was extended to cover the whole journey between London and Paris. Once that proved viable, the global rail network was rapidly expanded. As with any macro-infrastructure project awash with government money, the technology advanced swiftly.

By the time Louise and Genevieve arrived on Earth, the vac-trains were a highly mature system, travelling at considerable speed between stations. Common wisdom had the tunnels drilled kilometres deep in the safety of the bedrock. Not so, a lot of the time they didn't even qualify as tunnels. Giant tubes were laid over the abandoned land, and buried just below the surface. It was much easier to maintain the vacuum inside that kind of factory-manufactured subway than in a rock tunnel. Tectonics played havoc with rigid lava walls that had been melted by a flame of fusion plasma; experience showed they fractured easily, and on a couple of occasions actually sheared. So tunnels were only used to thread the tubes through mountains and plunge deep under arcologies. Even trans-oceanic routes were laid in trenches and anchored in place.

With no air to create friction, the trains were free to accelerate hard; on the longer trans-Pacific runs they touched Mach fifteen. Powered by linear motors, they were quick, smooth, silent, and efficient. The trip from Mount Kenya Station to London's King's Cross took Louise and Genevieve forty-five minutes, with one stop at Gibraltar. Airlocks at both ends of their carriage matched up with platform hatches, and popped open.

'All passengers for London please disembark,' the sparkling AV pillars on the carriage ceiling announced. 'This train will depart for Oslo in four minutes.'

The girls collected their big shoulder bags and hurried out onto the platform. They emerged into a long rectangular chamber, its ornately sculpted walls harking back to long-distant imperial grandeur. The line of twenty hatches connecting to the train appeared to be made of black wrought iron, Victorian-era space technology. On the opposite side, three large archways lead to broad wave escalators that spiralled upwards with impressive curves.

Genevieve stayed close behind her big sister as she negotiated their way across the platform. At least this time they managed to avoid barging into people. Excitement was powering a smile that would not fade.

An Earth arcology. London! Where we all came from originally. Home – sort of. How utterly utterly stupendous. It was the complete opposite of the nightmare that had been Norfolk by the time they left. This world had massive defences, and its people could do whatever they wanted with lots of fabulous machines to help them. She held Louise's hand tightly as they stepped onto the wave elevator. 'Where next?'

'Don't know,' Louise said. For some reason she was completely calm. 'Let's see what's up there, shall we?'

The wave escalator brought them onto the floor of a huge hemispherical cavern. It was like the arrivals hall of Mount Kenya

Station, only larger. The base of the wall was pierced by tunnel entrances radiating out to lift shafts and platforms for the local train network, while the floor was broken by concentric rows of wave elevators to the vac-trains. Bright informational spheres formed tightly packed streamers five metres above the heads of the thronging passengers, weaving around each other with serpentine grace. Right in the centre was a single flared spire of rock that rose up to eventually merge into the roof's apex.

'It's just another station,' Genevieve said in mild disappointment. 'We're still underground.'

'Looks like it.' Louise squinted up. Black flecks were zipping through the strata of informationals, as if they were suffering from static. She smiled, pointing. 'Birds, look.'

Genevieve twirled round, following their erratic flight. There were all sorts, from pert brown sparrows to emerald and turquoise parrots.

'We'd better find a hotel, I suppose,' Louise said. She pulled her shoulder bag round to take the processor block out.

Genevieve tugged at her arm. 'Oh, please, Louise. Can't we go up to the surface first? I just want to look. I'll be good, I promise. Please?'

Louise tucked the shoulder bag back. 'I wouldn't mind a peek myself.' She studied the informationals, catching sight of one that seemed promising. 'Come on.' She caught Gen's hand. 'This way.'

They took a lift up to the surface. It brought them out in a mock-Hellenic temple at the middle of a wide plaza full of statues and fenced in by huge oaks. A small commemorative plaque on a worn pillar marked the passing of the station's old surface structures and iron rail tracks. Louise walked out from the shade of the temple, wandering aimlessly for a few yards until she simply stopped. It was as if the arcology was appearing in segments before her. Slowly. As soon as her mind acknowledged one part, another would flip up behind that, demanding recognition.

Though she didn't know it, King's Cross was the geographical heart of the tremendous Westminster Dome, which at thirty kilometres in diameter enclosed most of the original city, from Ealing in the west to Woolwich in the east. Ever since the first small protective domes went up over London (a meagre four kilometres wide to start with – the best twenty-first-century materials technology could manage), preservation orders had been slapped on every building of historical or architectural significance, which the conservationists basically defined as anything not built from concrete. By the time the Westminster Dome was constructed over that initial cluster of ageing weather shields, the outlying districts had undergone significant changes, but any Londoner from the mid-nineteenth century onwards would have been able to find their way around the central portion without too much trouble. It was essentially one of the largest lived-in museums on the planet.

The nine smaller domes circling round outside the Westminster, however, were a different matter. London didn't have the megatowers of New York, but the arcology still housed a quarter of a billion people beneath its geodesic crystal roofs. The outer domes were purpose built, four hundred square kilometres apiece of thoroughly modern arcology, with only tiny little zones of original buildings left as curios amid the gleaming condos, skyscrapers, and malls.

Louise wasn't aware of them at all. She could see on the other side of the oaks that the plaza was encircled by a wide road jammed with sleek vehicles, all driving so close together you couldn't walk between them. The vehicles merged in and out of the giant roundabout from wide streets that radiated away between the beautiful ancient grey-stone buildings surrounding the plaza. When she raised her gaze above the blue-slate roofs and their elaborate chimney stacks, she could see even grander and taller buildings behind them. Then beyond those ... It was as though she was standing at the bottom of a mighty crater whose walls were made entirely from buildings. Around the plaza they were elegant and unique, with each one somehow merging cleanly into its neighbours to form compact refined streets; but they grew from that to plainer, larger skyscrapers, spaced further apart. The towers' artistry came from the overall shape rather than detailed embellishments, moulded to suggest Gothic, Roman, Art Deco, and Alpine Bavarian influences among others.

And gathering all those disparate architectural siblings within its sheltering embrace was the external wall. A single redoubtable cliff of windows, a mosaic of panes so dense it blended into a seamless band of glass, blazing gold under the noonday sun. Out of that rose the dome itself, an artificial sky of crystal.

Louise sat down heavily on the plaza's stone slabs, and let out a whoosh of breath. Gen sat beside her, arms folded protectively round her shoulder bag. London's pedestrians flowed round them, eyes consummately averted.

'It's very big, isn't it?' Gen said quietly.

'Certainly is.' All those buildings, so many people. Despite feeling light-headed, a weight of worry was threatening to sink her again. How in Heaven's name am I going to find a single person amid this multitude? Especially when they probably don't want to be found.

'Fletcher would really love this.'

Louise looked at her sister. 'Yes. I think he would.'

'Do you suppose he'd recognize any of it?'

'There may be bits left over from his time. Some of these buildings look quite old. We'll have to look it up in the local library memory.' She broke off and smiled. That's it, everything you ever need to know is in the processor memories. Banneth will be listed somewhere, I just have to program in the right search. 'Come on. Hotel first. Then we'll get something to eat. How does that sound?'

'Jolly nice. What hotel are we going to?'

'Give me a moment.' She took her processor block out, and started querying the arcology's general information centre. Category visitors, subsection residential. Central, and civilized. They'd wind up paying more for a classy hotel, but at least they'd be safe. Louise knew there were parts of Earth's arcologies that were terribly crime-ridden. And besides, 'Kavanaghs never stay anywhere that doesn't have a four-star rating,' Daddy had said once.

Information slid down the screen. They didn't seem to have star ratings here, so she just went by price. Central London hotels, apparently, cost as much to run as starships. At least the beds would be a lot more comfortable.

'The Ritz,' she said finally.

That just left getting there. With Genevieve getting progressively more impatient, as evidenced by overloud sighs and shuffling feet, Louise requested surface transport options from King's Cross to the Ritz. After ten minutes struggling with horribly complicated maps and London Metro timetables that kept flashing up she realized she wasn't quite as adept at operating the block as she thought she was. However, the screen did tell her there were taxis available.

'We'll take a cab.'

Under Gen's ungenerously sceptical look, she picked up her

shoulder bag and started off towards the oaks at the rim of the plaza. Flocks of parakeets and budgerigars pecking at the stone slabs stampeded out of her way. Most of the subway entrances had the name of the streets they led to, but a few had the London Transport symbol on top: blue circle cut by a red line, with a crown in the middle. Louise went down one to find herself in a short passage that opened out into a narrow parking bay. Five identical silver-blue taxi cars were waiting silently, streamlined bubbles with very fat tyres.

'Now what?' Genevieve said.

Louise consulted the block. She walked up to the first taxi, and keyed the Commence Journey icon on the block's screen. The door hissed out five centimetres, then slid back along the body. 'We get in,' she told her sister smugly.

'Oh, very clever. What happens if you don't have a block to do that for you?'

'I don't know.' She couldn't see a handle anywhere. 'I suppose everyone on this world is taught how to use things like this. Most of them have neural nanonics, after all.'

There wasn't much room inside, enough for four seats with deep curving backs. Louise shoved her bag in the storage bin underneath, and studied the screen again. The block was interfacing with the taxi's control processor, which made life a lot simpler for her. The whole activation procedure was presented to her as a simple, easy-to-understand menu. She fed in their destination, and the door slid shut. The taxi told the block what their fee was (as much as the vac-train fare from Mount Kenya), and explained how to use the seat straps.

'Ready?' she asked Gen, when they'd fastened themselves in.

'Yes.' The little girl couldn't hide her enthusiasm.

Louise held her Jovian Bank credit disk up to the small panel on the taxi's central column, and transferred the money over. They started to roll forward. The taxi took them up a steep ramp, accelerating fast enough to press the sisters back into their seat cushioning. The reason was simple enough, they emerged right in the middle of the traffic racing round the King's Cross plaza, slotting in without the slightest fuss.

Genevieve laughed excitedly as they zipped across several lanes, then slowed slightly to turn off down one of the broad streets. 'Golly, this is better than the aeroambulance,' the little girl grinned.

Louise rolled her eyes. Though once she accepted the fact that the control processor did know how to drive, she began to breathe normally again. The buildings rushing past were old and sombre, which gave them a dignity all of their own. On the other side of the pavement barrier, pedestrians jostled their way along in a permanent scrum.

'I never knew there were so many people,' Gen said. 'London must have more than live on the whole of Norfolk.'

'Probably,' Louise agreed.

They turned again, curving up a ramp that looped them over the pavement with its unstoppable crush of people, and along a narrow side street. Then they were climbing fast, up onto a raised expressway that circled the Westminster Dome's central districts of low buildings. Louise could see branch roads splitting off, arching away into the network of suspended expressways that twisted round the tapering skyscrapers. Looking down, there were an astonishing number of parks, their grass and trees a vivid green invasion through the drab browns and greys of the sheltered city.

The taxi was travelling even faster now. Nearby buildings blurred together in a slipstream of brick and stone. 'This is even quicker than Daddy drives,' Gen laughed. 'Isn't it all truly wonderful, Louise?'

'Yes,' she said, finally surrendering to the inevitable, and letting the fabulous cityscape capture her. Not even her most fanciful dreams of rebellion and travel back at Cricklade had aspired to this.

The taxi took them a third of the way round the expressway, then turned off, heading back down to ground level. There were parks on both sides of the road when they started their descent, then buildings rose up to their left, and they were back on one of the ancient streets again. The pavements here didn't seem so crowded. They slowed drastically, pulling over to the right as the first building on that side appeared, a large cube of white-grey stone with tall windows lined by iron railings, and a steep state roof. An open arcade ran along the front, supported by wide arches. The taxi stopped level with a gate in the roadside barrier, which a doorman opened smartly. He was dressed in a dark blue coat and top hat, a double row of brass buttons gleamed down his chest. At last, Louise felt at home. This was something she could deal with.

If the doorman was surprised at who climbed out of the taxi he never showed it. 'Are you staying here, miss?' he asked.

'I hope so, yes.'

He nodded politely, and ushered them under the arcade towards the main entrance.

Genevieve eyed the front of the stolid building sceptically. 'It looks dreadfully gloomy.'

The lobby inside was white and gold, with chandeliers resembling frost-encrusted branches that had dazzling stars at the tip of each twig. Arches along the long central aisle opened into big rooms that were full of prim white tables where people were sitting having tea. Waiters in long black tailcoats bustled about, carrying trays with silver teapots and very tempting cakes.

Louise marched confidently over to the gleaming oak reception desk. 'A twin room, please.'

The young woman standing behind smiled professionally. 'Yes, madam. How long for?'

'Um. A week to start with.'

'Of course. I'll need your ident flek, please, to register. And there is a deposit.'

'Oh, we haven't got an ident flek.'

'We're from Norfolk,' Gen said eagerly.

The receptionist's composure flickered. 'Really?' She cleared her throat. 'If you're from offworld, your passports will be satisfactory.'

Louise handed the fleks over, thinking briefly of Endron again, and wondering how much trouble the Martian was in right now. The receptionist scanned the fleks in a block and took the deposit from Louise. A bellboy came forward and relieved the sisters of their bags before showing them into a lift.

Their room was on the fourth floor, with a large window over-looking the park. The decor was so reminiscent of the kind Norfolk landowners worshipped it gave Louise a sense of déjà vu; regal-purple wallpaper and furniture so old the wood was virtually black beneath the polish. Her feet sank into a carpet well over an inch thick.

'Where are we?' Gen asked the bellboy. She was pressed up against the window, staring out. 'I mean, what's that park called?'

'That's Green Park, miss.'

'So are we near anywhere famous?'

'Buckingham Palace is on the other side of the park.'

'Gosh.'

He showed Louise the room's processor block, which was built in to the dresser. 'Any information you need on the city for your stay should be in here; it has a comprehensive tourist section,' he said. She tipped him a couple of fuseodollars when he left. He'd been holding his own credit disk, casually visible through fingers splayed wide.

Genevieve waited until the door shut. 'What's Buckingham Palace?'

*

The AI was alert to the glitch within a hundredth of a second. Two ticket dispenser processors and an informational projector. It brought additional analysis programs on-line, and ran an immediate verification sweep of every electronic circuit in Grand Central Station.

Half a second. The response to a general acknowledgement datavise from five sets of neural nanonics was incorrect. All of them were within a seven-metre zone, which also incorporated the failing ticket dispensers.

Two seconds. Security sensors in Grand Central's concourse focused on the suspect area. The AI datavised to B7's North American supervisor the fact it had located a possessed-type glitch in New York. He had just framed his query in reply when the sensors observed Bud Johnson go cartwheeling over someone in a black robe crouched on the floor.

Three and a half seconds. There was a visual discontinuity. None of the sensor short-term memory buffers had registered the black-clad figure before. It was as if he'd just materialized out of nowhere. If he had neural nanonics they were not responding to the ident request datavise.

Four seconds. The North American supervisor took direct control of the situation in conjunction with the AI. A datavised warning went out to the rest of the supervisors.

Six seconds. The full B7 complement of supervisors was on-line, observing. The AI's visual characteristics program locked on to the shadowed face inside the black robe's hood. Quinn Dexter rose to his feet.

South Pacific: 'Nuke him. Now!'

Western Europe: 'Don't be absurd.'

Halo: 'SD platforms armed; do you want ground strike?'

North America: 'No. It's completely impractical. Grand Central Station's concourse is a hundred and fifty metres below ground, and that's spread out below three skyscrapers. There isn't an X-ray laser built that could reach it.'

South Pacific: 'Then use a real nuke. A combat wasp can be down there in two minutes.'

Asian Pacific: 'I second that.'

Western Europe: 'No! Damn it. Will you morons control yourselves.'

North America: 'Thank you. I'm not going to blast Dome One into oblivion. There are twenty million people living in there. Even Laton didn't kill that many.'

Northern Europe: 'You can't let him go. We have to exterminate him.'

Western Europe: 'How?'

Northern Europe: 'South Pacific's right. Nuke the shit. I'm sorry about the other inhabitants, but it's the only way we can resolve the situation.'

Western Europe: 'Observe, please.'

Eleven seconds. Bud Johnson's face had turned purple. He scrabbled feebly at his chest, then pitched over onto the floor. People clustered round him. Quinn Dexter became translucent and quickly faded from view. The AI reported all the processors had come back on-line.

Military Intelligence: 'Oh, shit.'

Western Europe: 'Will a nuke kill him now do you think? Wherever he is.'

South Pacific: 'One way to find out.'

Western Europe: 'I cannot permit that. We exist primarily to protect Earth. Even with our prerogatives, you cannot exterminate twenty million people in the *hope* that you kill one terrorist.'

Halo: 'The boy's right, I'm afraid. I'm standing down the SD platforms.'

South Pacific: 'Terrorist demon, more like.'

Western Europe: 'I'm not arguing definitions. All this does is confirm I was right the first time. We have got to be extremely careful how we deal with Dexter.'

North Pacific: 'Well, at least shut down New York's vac-trains.'

Central America: 'Yes. Isolate him in New York. You can creep up on him there.'

Western Europe: 'I'm going to have to say no again.'

North Pacific: 'In Allah's name, why? We know where he is, that gives us a tremendous advantage.'

Western Europe: 'It's psychology. He knows we know he's here. He's not stupid, he'll realize we'll find out about him appearing in Grand Central Station. The question is, how long does it take us to find out? If we stop the vac-trains now, it shows him we are right up to speed and deeply worried by him, and also that we'll go all out to stop him. That's not good, that puts him on guard.'

Central America: 'So, he's on guard? If he's trapped in one place, it won't do him any good. He'll still be on death row. He knows it's coming, and there's nothing he can do about it.'

Western Europe: 'First thing he'll do is mobilize New York to defend himself. And we'll be back to one option of having to nuke the place. Don't you see? Our arcologies are even more vulnerable than asteroid settlements. They are utterly dependent on technology, not just to protect us from the weather, but to feed us and condition our air. If you confine three hundred million possessed inside one, every single chunk of machinery will break down. The domes will shatter in the first storm that comes along, and the population will either starve or turn cannibal.'

Central America: 'I'm prepared to sacrifice one arcology to save the rest. If that's what it takes.'

Western Europe: 'But we don't have to sacrifice one. Certainly not yet. You're being abysmally premature. Right now, Dexter will be skipping round arcologies, establishing small groups of possessed who'll keep their heads down until he gives the word. While he's doing that, we've got a chance. There will only be small groups in each arcology, which *we* really ought to be able to find. If other worlds can track them, so can we. Dexter is our problem, not the ordinary possessed.'

Asian Pacific: 'Put it to the vote.'

Western Europe: 'How wonderfully democratic. Very well.'

Six supervisors voted for closing down New York's vac-trains right away. Ten voted to keep them open.

Western Europe: 'Thank you so much for your confidence.'

Southern Africa: 'You have the ball for now. But if you haven't dealt with Dexter in another ten days, I shall be voting to isolate him wherever he is. And then we'll see if he can hide from a nuke as well as he can from a sensor.'

*

The conference dissolved. Western Europe asked North America, Military Intelligence, and Halo to remain on-line. Natural allies in the eternal war zone of B7's internal politics, they obliged. His sensevise overlay program positioned and dressed them around his drawing room as though they were weekend guests just come in from a stroll round the grounds.

'It'll go against you eventually,' Halo warned. 'They're happy for you to take responsibility for the chase as long as Dexter hasn't caused any noticeable damage. But the minute he gets noisy, they'll revert.'

'That little crap artist, South Pacific,' North America complained. 'Telling me to nuke New York! Who the hell does she think she is?'

'She always favours the blunt approach,' Western Europe said. 'We all know that. That's why I like her so much, makes one feel constantly superior.'

'Inferior or not, she'll carry the day eventually,' Military Intelligence said.

Western Europe walked over to the tall glass-panelled door, and let his two Labradors in. 'I know. That's why I found today encouraging.'

'Encouraging?' North America asked, astonished. 'Are you kidding? I've got that Dexter bastard running round loose in New York.'

'Yes, exactly. Something went wrong for him. He was on his knees when he appeared, and he vanished within seconds. *He* was glitched. Another factor in our favour.'

'Maybe,' Halo said. He sounded very dubious.

'All right,' North America said. 'So what now?'

'You need to do two things. In forty minutes, I want you to close down all New York's vac-trains.'

'Forty minutes? He'll be long gone.'

'Yes. As I said, he knows we know he's here. We have to play along with that, but make him think we're lumbering along five steps behind him. So close the vac-trains. He won't be in New York, so it doesn't matter.'

'You hope.'

'I know. Once he'd been exposed there he had no option but to leave. New York is closed to him now, out of the equation. To do whatever he wants to do, he has to maintain his mobility. He probably took the shortest ride out there is, figuring the police would close down the vac-trains pretty fast; but that's beside the point.'

'OK. How long do you want them shut down for?'

'That's the second thing. We have to work on the assumption he was leaving. Therefore, he's more than likely left a group of possessed behind him. You have to find them, and eliminate them. Keep the arcology sealed up until you do. In fact, keeping the individual domes isolated might be a good idea if you can manage it.'

'You really think that's what he's doing?'

'Yes. He wants to inflict maximum devastation on this planet. He'll seed as many arcologies as possible with his followers. And when he gives the word, they'll hit the streets, and we'll be faced with the exponential curve again.'

'The AI is monitoring the arcology's electronics anyway.'

'Yes. I'm sure that's effective on Kulu and other modern worlds; but you and I know it can never access everything, not here, not in the old areas. There's over five hundred years' worth of electronic junk plugged together out there; we're dealing with millions of old systems, quirky one-offs, and non-standard patch-ups. The AI is a good sentry, but don't make the mistake of becoming dependent. The best source we'll have is probably the sects.'

'The sects?'

'Certainly. The one set of idiots who'll support the possessed without having to be forced. Dexter knows that, they're the ones he'll go to.'

'All right, I'll get on to it.'

'So what are you going to be doing?' Halo asked Western Europe.

'Same as before. Engineer an encounter. We have to get our people close to him while he's visible, and therefore vulnerable.'

'Vulnerable to what?'

'If he's out in the open, an SD strike. Or if our contact is through an agent, we can try for electrocution or a memory scramble.'

'Memory scramble?'

'Yes,' said Military Intelligence. 'The CNIS believes they can kill souls by firing some kind of mentallic virus at the possessed. It's the opposite of a didactic imprint. They're researching it now.'

Western Europe started making a fuss of one of the dogs, scratching its belly as it rolled around on the carpet. 'Do try and stay up to date,' he chided Halo.

'It won't be available before the end of the week,' Military Intelligence warned.

'I know. I doubt I'll manage to arrange an interception by then anyway.'

'How's that angle coming along?' Halo asked.

'The Banneth connection is just about covered. I'm not sure about the Kavanagh girls; they're a long shot, and a pretty random one at that. But I'm working on it.'

*

Louise spent an hour using the room's desktop processor block, and got nowhere. The directory provided her with enough entries under Banneth (173,364 – once she'd removed the deceased), but no matter how she tried to cross-reference that with Quinn Dexter the result was always negative. She racked her brains to remember everything Dexter had said back in the hangar at Bennett Field. Banneth was female, she remembered that for certain. And Dexter said she'd hurt him. That was about it, really.

Somewhere, somehow, those facts should link up. She was sure they did. But finding the connection was beyond her woeful programming ability. The idea that had begun back when they got in the taxi was becoming more and more attractive. If she dared.

Why not? she thought. There's nothing dangerous about neural nanonics, not physically, the rest of the Confederation uses them. Joshua has a set. It's only Norfolk which doesn't allow them. She raised her arm, and looked at the discreet medical nanonic package bracelet. Also banned on Norfolk, yet it was helping her pregnancy. That settled it. She grinned, emboldened by her decision. *I have to* take responsibility for myself now. If I need neural nanonics to help me on Earth, then I will get myself a set.

They hadn't left the room since arriving at the hotel. Lunch had been a snack delivered by room service. Genevieve had flopped on her bed in weary disgust at the inactivity, and activated her own block. She was smothered by a laser-haze of grid lines and feisty fantasy beasts which leapt about enthusiastically at every excitable shouted command.

'Gen?'

The projection shrank. Genevieve blinked up at her, trying to focus. Louise was sure that being immersed in the projection so much was bad for her little sister's eyesight.

'What?'

'We're going out. I can't get the hang of the desktop block, so I'm going to buy some neural nanonics instead.' There, she'd said it out loud. There'd be no backing down now.

Genevieve stared at her in astonishment. 'Oh, Louise, don't tease so. We're not allowed.'

'We *weren't* allowed. We're on Earth, now, remember. You can do anything you want here as long as you've got money.'

Genevieve cocked her head to one side. Then the most charming smile graced her face. It didn't fool Louise for a second. 'Please, Louise. Can I have one, too? You know I'll never be allowed once we get home.'

'I'm sorry. You're not old enough.'

'I *am!*'

'Gen, you're not. And you know you're not.'

She stamped her foot, little fists clenched in outrage. 'That's not fair! It's not. It's not. You always pick on me coz I'm the youngest. You're a bully.'

'I'm not picking on you. You just can't have one, your brain is still growing. They can't connect it. I checked. It's not legal, and it'll do a lot of damage to your brain cells. I only just scrape in if you measure my age in Earth years.'

'I hate being small.'

Louise put her arms round the girl, reflecting on how much she'd done so since leaving home. They never used to hug much before. 'You'll be bigger one day,' she whispered into her sister's fluffed-up hair. 'And things are going to be different when we get home.'

'You think so?'

'Oh, yes.'

*

The receptionist seemed rather amused at being asked, in a lofty sort of way. But she was helpful enough, telling Louise that Oxford Street and New Bond Street were probably their best bet for clothes, while Tottenham Court Road was where they would find any conceivable kind of electronics. The sisters were also assured these areas were safe for girls to walk through by themselves. 'And the hotel runs a courtesy collection service for any items that you purchase.' She handed over an authorization disk, keyed to Louise's biolectric pattern.

Louise loaded a comprehensive street map into her block, taken from the hotel's memory, and combined it with the guidance program. 'Ready?' she asked Gen. 'Let's go spend the family fortune.'

Aubry Earle had spoken the truth on the lift capsule when he told them arcology dwellers would always respect their privacy. Out on the street, Louise couldn't quite work out how people always slid to one side at the last second. She was constantly scanning bodies all round to try and find a way through the gaps, while locals moved as smoothly as the automated traffic without ever once glancing in her direction. Some of the pedestrians quite literally glided past. People their own age wearing calf-high boots with soles that seemed to flow over the pavement slabs without any resistance. Genevieve watched their effortless progress with admiration and longing. 'I want some boots like that,' she said.

A subwalk got them under Piccadilly and into New Bond Street. It turned out to be a dainty little pedestrian lane, lined with enchanting boutiques whose marble frontage was embossed with brass lettering saying when they'd been established. None of them were under three centuries old, while some claimed to be over seven. The labels on show meant nothing to either of them, but judging by the prices they must have been admiring the most exclusive designer garments on the planet.

'It's gorgeous,' Louise sighed longingly at a shimmering scarlet and turquoise evening gown, sort of like an all-over mermaid's tail – except it wasn't all-over, nowhere near. It was the kind of thing she would love to wear at a summer ball on Norfolk. The planet had never seen its like before.

'Then buy it.'

'No. We've got to be sensible. Just everyday clothes that we need to get about in the arcology. Remember, one day I'll have to explain the entire bill to Daddy.'

The evening gown was just the start of New Bond Street's provocative temptations. They trailed past window displays she could have bought en masse.

'We'll have to have supper in the hotel dining room,' Genevieve suggested artfully. 'I bet they won't let us in unless we dress up.'

It was an insidious suggestion. 'OK. One dress. That's all.'

They dashed across the threshold of the boutique in front of them. Privacy didn't apply inside the shop; three assistants swooped eagerly. Louise explained what they wanted, and then spent the next forty-five minutes ricocheting in and out of a changing room. She and Gen would look at each other, comment, and go back for the next trial.

She learned a lot in the process. The assistants were very complimentary about the sisters' hair. Except . . . on Earth, it was fashionable to have actives woven among the strands. Their one-piece suits with big pockets were current, but not that *à la mode*. Yes, Oxford Street stores were perfect for buying streetfashion clothes, and we recommend these. Louise could have sworn she heard the block's memory creaking under the load of names they entered. She used her Jovian Bank credit disk with only a momentary twinge of guilt.

Out on the street again, they laughed at each other. Gen had wound up with a scarlet dress and deep-purple jacket, while Louise had bought herself a full-length gown of deepest blue that was made from a material crossed between velvet and suede. There was also a short ginger-coloured waistcoat to go with it, which complimented its square cut neck.

'It's true,' Louise said happily. 'Retail therapy actually works.'

They didn't get directly to Oxford Street. There was a stop at a salon at the top of New Bond Street first. The beauticians made an incredible fuss over them, delighted with so much raw material to work on. The owner himself came over to direct the operation (once their credit rating had been verified).

After two hours, several cups of tea, and enthralling the staff with an edited version of their travels, Louise had the wrap taken off. She stared in the mirror, not believing she'd spent her life tolerating unmanaged hair. Norfolk's simplistic regime of washing, conditioners, and sturdy brushing was barbaric ineptitude. Under the salon's professional auspices her hair had become lustrous, individual strands conducting a little starlight shimmer of light along their length. And it flowed. Every day of her life she'd held that thick mane in place with clips and ribbons, sometimes getting the maid to braid fanciful bands. Flexitives made all that irrelevant. Of its own accord, her hair fell back over her shoulders, always keeping itself tidy and together in one large tress. It also rippled subtly, as if she was engulfed in her own permanent private breeze.

'You look beautiful, Louise,' Genevieve said, suddenly shy.

'Thank you.' Gen's hair had been straightened, darkened, and glossed, its hem curling inwards slightly. Again, it held its shape no matter what.

Stalls were lined up against the road barriers, filled with brassy, cheaper items than those in the shops. Genevieve saw one with pairs of the magical boots hanging from the awning. Slipstream boots, the cheerful owner told her as he found some her size. Popular with the under-fifteens because you didn't need neural nanonics to switch the directed frictionless soles on or off.

Louise bought them on the condition Gen waited until they got back to the hotel before she tried them out. She also got a duster bracelet. When Gen clamped the trinket round her wrist and waved it round, it sprayed out a fine powder which emitted a fiery sparkle as it fell to earth. Holding her arm up and pirouetting, a spiral of twinkling starlight spun around her.

Oxford Street at last. Bigger and brasher than New Bond Street: monolithic department stores were crushed up against each other, with tiny specialist shops and sandwich bars squeezed between them. Vivid hologram adverts roofed the pavements, brighter than the sweltering sunlight streaming down from the barren azure sky. Every store was locked in a bitter war with its rivals, promising lower prices, better quality, brighter colours, sharper cuts, manufacturers' exclusives. Claims and counterclaims blared and blazed against each other, making the girls wince, hunching their shoulders against the barrage as they would do the rain. Everyone else was immune, strolling along happily.

'Louise?' Gen tugged on her arm, pointing up, showering passers by with flaring glitter. The little girl's expression wavered between amazement and embarrassment.

Louise began to take notice of the adverts draped through the air overhead. A mild blush rose to her cheeks. There was a girl above her who had an incredibly young face and a blond elf haircut. She couldn't have been that young, though; Louise thought she had a good bust (Joshua certainly said she had) but it was nothing compared to this siren. The tiny white bikini halter proved that. Acres of bronzed skin flexed happily as the girl wrapped herself around an equally improbable boy. A sun-jewelled spray of water drenched the pair of them as they French-kissed. Louise found herself staring at the front of his jeans, which were shockingly tight, and revealing. He unhooked the girl's bikini top, and lowered his head to nuzzle the glistening breasts.

The girl smiled down at the street. 'Brooke's proactive household software leaves you more time for the kind of homemaking you really enjoy,' she cooed deafeningly, and winked. Her hand snaked down to the boy's crotch.

'Inside!' Louise grabbed Gen's hand abruptly, and tugged her towards the nearest rank of doors. A horizontal contrail of scintillating dust stretched out through the air behind them.

Gen was twisting round for a better look as Louise barged through the doors into the big store. 'They were going to do it,' the little girl giggled. 'You know. It!'

'That's not our concern. Understand?'

Gen's shoulders were quivering helplessly. 'Yes, Louise.'

Louise couldn't believe what she'd just seen – almost seen! Adverts on Norfolk nearly always involved pretty girls holding up whatever product they were selling. That was all, a nice face and a happy smile. Was that what everyone back home meant when they talked about the curse of progress? Nobody else on the pavement had been bothered by the display. Daddy always said Earth was decadent and corrupt. I just never thought it would be so out in the open. They used to have all the precepts we have, because we based ours on theirs. Now Daddy and the other landowners resist any change, because they're frightened all change leads into decay. That in five hundred years' time we'll have nude girls on our television. No matter what, she just couldn't envisage that happening on Norfolk.

'I won't tell Mummy we saw that,' Gen said, trying to appear contrite.

'It's OK. She'd never believe us anyway.'

*

Quinn sat on one of the benches along the banks of the Seine, opening his mind to the demented screeching reverberating through the beyond. It had taken him two and a half hours to reach the Paris arcology since being struck by that inexplicable wave of emotional torment that had swept through the beyond.

The first thing – obviously! – was to get the fuck out of New York. It wouldn't take the cops long to review the memories of sensors covering the concourse and identify him. He'd gone straight down to a platform and taken a vac-train to Washington. A short ride, not quite fifteen minutes. He'd kept within the ghost realm for the whole trip, apprehensive that the vac-train would be halted and returned to New York. But it arrived at Washington on time, and he switched to the first intercontinental ride available: Paris.

Even then, he'd remained invisible as it streaked along the bottom of the North Atlantic, still anxious that another of those waves would surge up and expose him. If it had done during the journey under the ocean, he knew he'd be finished. He couldn't believe God's Brother would allow that to happen. But the first time was causing all sorts of doubts.

It wasn't until he was out of the Paris terminus and walking through one of the old city's parks that he had allowed himself to fully emerge. He clothed himself in an ordinary shirt and trousers, hating the way his white skin tingled in the bright sun shining through the colossal crystal dome. But it meant he was safe, there were no processors in the middle of the park to glitch at his appearance, nobody near enough to see that he'd appeared from nowhere rather than walked round the ancient tree. He stood there for a minute, scanning the nearby minds for any sign of alarm. Only then did he relax and make his way down to the river.

Parisians strolled along behind him as they had for centuries – lovers, artists, business executives, bureaucrats – none of them paying attention to the solitary downcast youth. Nor did any of them avail themselves to the space left on his bench. Some subliminal warning steered them along past, frowning slightly at the unaccountable chill.

Slowly, Quinn started to gather the strands together. Faint images and hoarse wailing voices filling in the story. He saw clouds which surprised even him, an arcology-born. Rain cascaded down on huddled bodies, so thick it was almost solid. Terrifying blasts of lightning ripping through the darkness. The encircling forces, radiating their stern nonhuman determination, closing in.

Mortonridge was not a place where a possessed should be caught outside today; and two million of them had been. Something had struck at them, tearing away their protective covering of cloud. Some technological devilry. The signal for the Liberation to commence. A one-off; a unique act in response to a unique situation. Not some miracle wrought by the Light Bringer's great rival.

Quinn lifted his head, and smiled a contemptuous smile. Such a shock was extremely unlikely to occur again. There was no unknown threat. He was perfectly safe. Night could still dawn.

He stood up, and turned slowly, examining his surroundings properly for the first time. The celebrated Napoleonic heart of the city was encompassed by a range of splendid white, silver, and gold towers. Their burnished surfaces hurt his eyes, as their grandeur hurt his sensibility. But somewhere among all this cleanliness and vitality, the waster kids would be grubbing through dank refuse, hurting each other and unwary civilians for no reason they understood. Finding them would be as easy here as it had been in New York. Just walk in the direction everyone else was coming from. His heartland, where his words would bring its denizens purpose.

He completed his turn. Right ahead of him the Eiffel Tower stood guard at the end of a broad immaculate park, with sightseers wandering round its base. Even in Edmonton, Quinn had heard of this structure. A proud symbol of Gallic forbearance through all the centuries of Govcentral's pallid uniformity, its very endurance reflecting the strengths and determination of the people who regarded it as their own. Precious to the world. And now, so terribly fragile with age.

Quinn started to chuckle greedily.

*

Andy Behoo fell in love. It was instantaneous. *She* walked in through the door of Jude's Eworld, kicking off a cascade of datavised alarms, and he was utterly smitten.

Terminal babe. Taller than him by a good ten centimetres, with the most gorgeous cloak of hair. A face with soft features so delicate as to be way beyond anything cosmetic adapter packages could achieve – a natural beauty. She wore a white sleeveless T-shirt that showed off a hot figure without revealing anything, and a scarlet skirt that didn't reach her knees. But it was the way she carried herself that clinched it for him. Perfectly composed, yet she still looked round the shop with childlike curiosity.

The rest of the staff were all giving her clandestine glances as the doorway scanners datavised their findings. Then the smaller girl entered behind her, and the scanners gave out an almost duplicate alert. How weird. They couldn't possibly be a cop grab operation, too obvious. Besides, the manager was pretty regular when it came to slipping the shop's bung to the district station.

Andy told the customer he was dealing with, 'Look it over, and have a think about it, you won't find a better deal in London,' then left them to scoot over to the girl before any of his so-called colleagues could reach her. If the floor manager had seen, he'd probably lose his job. *Abandoning a customer before the sale is sealed – capital crime.*

'Hi, I'm Andy. I'm your sellrat. Anything you want, it's my job to push the more expensive model on you.' He grinned broadly.

'You're my what?' Louise asked, her expression was half puzzlement, half smile.

Her accent did strange things along Andy's spine, making him shiver. The ultimate in class, and foreign-exotic, too. He scanned his enhanced retinas across her face, desperate to capture her image. Even if she walked out of his life now, she would never be entirely lost. Andy had certain male-orientated software packages that could superimpose her into sensenviron recordings. He felt shabby even as he recorded her.

'Sellrat. That's what the public call customer interactivity officers round these parts.'

'Oh,' the smaller girl sighed dismissively. 'He's just a shopboy, Louise.'

Andy's neural nanonics had to reinforce his smile. Why do they always come in pairs? And why always one obnoxious one? He clicked his fingers and pointed both index fingers at the smaller girl. 'That's me. Try not to be too disappointed, I really am here to help.'

'I'd like to buy some neural nanonics,' Louise said. 'Is it very difficult?'

The request startled Andy. Her clothes alone must have cost more than twice his weekly pay, why didn't she have a set already? Beautiful and enigmatic. He smiled up at her. 'Not at all. What were you looking for?'

She sucked her lower lip. 'I'm really not very sure. The best I can afford, I suppose.'

'We don't have them on Norfolk,' Genevieve said. 'That's where we're from.'

Louise tried not to frown. 'Gen, we don't have to give our history to everyone we meet.'

Rich foreigners. Andy's conscience struggled against temptation. Conscience won out, backed up by infatuation. *I can't sell her a pirate set. Not her.* 'OK, your lucky day. We've got some top-of-the-range sets in stock. I can fix a reasonable deal for them, too, so there's no need to get sweaty about the money. This way.'

He led them over to his section of the counter, managing to get her name on the way. His neural nanonics faithfully recorded the way she walked, her body movements, even her speech pattern. Like most nineteen-year-olds who'd grown up in London's manky Islington district with its history of low-income employment, Andy Behoo fancied himself as a prospective net don. It combined the goal of fringe-legal work (also his heritage), with very little actual effort. He'd taken didactic memory courses on electronics, nanonics, and software every month since he'd passed his fourteenth birthday. His two-room flat was stocked to the ceiling with ancient processor blocks and every redundant peripheral he'd managed to scrounge or steal. Everyone in his tenement knew Andy was the guy to visit when you had a technical problem.

As to why such an embryonic datasmart prince of darkness was working as a sellrat in Jude's Eworld, he had to get the money to finance his revolutionary schemes from somewhere – or maybe even go to college. And the shop always employed technerd teenagers as their outfront salesforce, they were the only ones who kept up to date on upgrades and new marques that would work on minimum-wage weeks.

The wall behind the counter was made up entirely from boxes of consumer electronics. All of them had colourful logos and names. Louise read a few of the contents labels, not understanding a word. Genevieve was already bored; looking round at other parts of the slightly shabby shop – one of seemingly hundreds of near-identical outlets along Tottenham Court Road. The inside was a maze formed by counters and walls of boxes, with old company posters and holomorph stickers stuck up on every available surface. Holographic screens flashed out enticing pictures of products in action. The section opposite Andy Behoo had a big GAMES sign above it. And Louise had promised.

Andy began pulling boxes down and lining them up on the counter. They were rectangular, the size of his hand, wrapped in translucent foil, with the manufacturer's guarantee seal on the front. 'OK,' Andy said with familiar confidence. 'What we have here, the Presson050, is a basic neural nanonics set. Everything you need to survive daily arcology life: datavises, mid-res neuroiconic display, enhanced memory retrieval, axon block. It's preformatted to NAS2600 standard, which means it can handle just about every software package on the market. There's a company-supplied didactic operations imprint that comes with it, but we do sell alternative operations courses.'

'That sounds very . . . comprehensive,' Louise said. 'How much?'

'How are you paying?'

'Fuseodollars.' She showed him her Jovian Bank credit disk.

'OK. Good move. I can give you a favourable rate on that. So, we're looking at about three and a half thousand, for which we'll throw in five free Quantumsoft supplement packages from their BCD30 range. Your choice of functions. I can arrange finance for you if you want, better percentage than any Sol-system bank.'

'I see.'

'Then we've got . . .' His hand moved on to the next box.

'Andy. What's the top of the range, please?'

'OK, good question.' He disappeared behind the counter for a moment, returning with a fresh box and a suitably awed tone. 'Kulu Corporation ANI5000. The King himself uses this model. We've only got three left because of the starflight quarantine. These are most wanted items all over town right now. But I can still give you level retail.'

'And that's better than the first one?'

'Yes, indeed. Runs NAS2600, of course, with parallel upgrade potential for when the 2615 comes out.'

'Um. What's this NAS number you keep saying?'

'Neural Augmentation Software. It's the operating system for the whole filament network, and the number is the version. 2600 was introduced turn of the century, and boy was it a bugfeist when it came out. But it's a smooth proved system now. And the supplement packages are just about unlimited, every software house in the Confederation publishes compatible products. If you're going serious professional you can add physiological monitors, Encyclopaedia Galactica, employment waldoing, SII suit control, weapons integration, linguistic translation, news informant, starship astrogation, net search – the full monty. Then there's games applications as well, I can't even list them you have so many.' He patted the box with reverence. 'No fooling, Louise, this set gives you the full interface range: nerve overrides to control your body, sense amplification, sight-equivalent neuroiconic generation, complete reality sensenviron, implant command, total indexed memory recall.'

'I'll take it.'

'Got to warn you: not cheap. Seventeen thousand fuseodollars.' He held up his hands in placation. 'Sorry.'

Daddy will kill me, Louise thought, but it has to be done. I promised Fletcher, and that horrid Brent Roi never really believed me. 'All right.'

Andy smiled in admiration. 'Talk about power choosing. That's impressive, Louise. But, hey, I can lighten the burden. For a 5000 set, we'll throw in twenty-five software supplements, and give you twenty per cent discount on the next twenty-five you buy from us.'

'That sounds like a jolly good deal,' she said inanely, swept along by his enthusiasm. 'How long does it take to get a set?'

'For one this complex, ninety minutes. I can give you the operating didactic at the same time.'

'What's one of those?'

Andy's breezy ebullience faltered in the face of such an astonishing question. He started to access his encyclopaedia's file on Norfolk, and put a news search in primary mode for good measure. 'You don't have them on your planet?'

'No. Our constitution is pastoral, we don't have much technology. Or weapons.' Defending Norfolk, yet again.

'No weapons; hey, good policy. Didactic imprints are sort of like the instruction manual, but it gets written directly inside your brain, and you never forget it.'

'Well, if I'm going to spend this much money, I certainly need to know how to work it, don't I?'

Andy laughed heartily, then stopped quickly when he caught sight of Genevieve's expression. How come nobody ever produced a suavity program he could load? Talking to and impressing girls would be so much easier. The floor supervisor was datavising questions about his oddball customer and the door sensor alert, which he answered briefly. Then the Norfolk information started to emerge.

'We have a preparation room.' Andy gestured to the back of the shop.

'Louise, I want to look round,' Genevieve said winningly. 'There might be something for me.'

'All right. But if you see something just ask, don't touch anything. That's all right, isn't it?' she asked Andy.

'Sure thing.' Andy winked at Genevieve and gave her a thumbs-up. Her sneer could have withered an oak tree.

Louise followed Andy into the small preparation room, a cube-space whose walls were fashioned from dark panelling, with various electronic units poking out. It was furnished with just a glass cubicle, like a shower but without any visible nozzle, and a low padded bench similar to a doctor's examination table.

The attention Andy showed her was somewhat amusing. She thought possibly it wasn't entirely due to her high-spending customer status. Most of the young gentlemen (and others – slightly older) on Norfolk had shown a similar, if less blatant, interest over the last couple of years. Now, of course, she was wearing what amounted to little more than an exhibitionist's costume. Though by Earth's standards it was tame. But the top and skirt had made her look so damn good in the department store's mirror. She could hold her own against London girls in this. For the first time in her life she was *sassy*. And free to enjoy it. And loving it.

The glass door slid shut with a definitive *click* behind her. She shot Andy a suspicious glance.

*

'Bugger,' Western Europe muttered as his linkages with Louise were cut. He switched to Genevieve, which was about as useless; the little girl was investigating a Gothic fantasy, standing in a castle courtyard as a column of priestess warriors rode off to battle on their unicorns.

Western Europe had wanted Louise to discover the bugs at some stage. He just hadn't planned on it being quite so early in the operation. But then, buying neural nanonics wasn't what he expected of a girl from Norfolk, either. She was quite a remarkable little thing, really.

*

Andy Behoo scratched at his arm awkwardly. 'You do know you've been stung, don't you?' he asked.

'Stung?' Louise took a guess. 'You're not talking about insects, are you?'

'No. The door sensors spotted it as soon as you and your sister came in. There are nanonic bugs in your skin; like miniature radios, I guess you'd call them. They transmit all sorts of information about where you are, and what's going on around you. There are four on you, Genevieve has three. That we can detect, anyway.'

She drew in a shocked breath. How stupid! Of course Brent Roi wouldn't let her walk round freely. Not someone who'd tried to sneak a possessed down to Earth. He was bound to want to see what she did next. 'Oh, sweet Jesus.'

'I reckon Govcentral must be nervous about foreigners right now, especially as you come from Norfolk,' Andy said. 'What with the possessed, and all. Don't worry, this room is screened, they can't hear us now.'

His sellrat swagger had diminished as he tried to reassure her. In fact, he'd become almost sheepish, which made him actually quite pleasant, she thought. 'Thank you for telling me, Andy. Do you scan all your customers?'

'Oh, yes. Mainly for dodgy implants. There's quite a few gangs try to syphon our software fleks. Then we do sell bugs ourselves, see, so sometimes we get cops coming in and trying to find who those customers are. Jude's Eworld has a strong neutrality policy, which we enforce. We have to, or we'd never sell anything.'

'Can you get them off me?'

'All part of our customer service. I can give you a more detailed scan, too, see if there are any others.'

She followed his instructions, standing in the cubicle, which gave her a comprehensive bodyscan down to a sub-cellular level. So now someone else knows I'm pregnant, she acknowledged in resignation. No wonder Earth's population value their privacy so, they don't get very much of it. The bodyscan located another two bugs. Andy applied a small rectangular patch similar to a medical package (same technology, he said) to her arms and leg; then she pulled her T-shirt up so he could press it against her back.

'Is there any way of knowing if the police sting me again?' she asked.

'An electronic-warfare block should tell you. We had a shipment of front-line equipment in from Valisk a couple of months back. I think there's still some left. Good stuff.'

'I think you'd better put one of those removal patches on the list as well.' Louise called Genevieve into the room, and explained what'd happened. Thankfully her sister was more curious than outraged. She peered at her skin after Andy took the nanonic package away, fascinated by the removal process. 'It doesn't look any different,' she complained.

'They're too small to see,' Andy said. 'Which makes them too small to feel. They shouldn't call it getting stung, really. More like being feathered.'

When Genevieve scooted back into the shop to continue her appraisal of consumer goodies, Andy handed over the box of Kulu Corporation neural nanonics to Louise. 'You need to check the seal,' he said. 'Make sure it hasn't been broken, and see that the wrapping hasn't been tampered with as well. You can tell that by the colour. If someone tries to cut or tear it, the stress turns it red.'

She turned it over obediently. 'Why do I have to do this?'

'Neural nanonics connect directly into your brain, Louise. If someone changes the filaments or subverts the NAS codes they could get into your memories or manipulate your body like a puppet. This guarantees the set hasn't been tampered with since it left the factory;

and you have the Kulu Corporation's assurance that their design wouldn't sequestrate you.'

Louise gave the box a closer examination. The foil seemed intact and clear.

'Sorry, didn't mean to scare you,' he said quickly. 'It's a standard speech; we implant fifty of these a day. I mean, think what would happen to the shop or the manufacturer if anything like that did ever happen. We'd be lynched. It's in our interest to make sure everything's kosher for you. Another reason we have sensors at the door.'

'OK, I suppose.' She handed the box back. Andy broke the seal in front of her, and took out a small black capsule a couple of centimetres long. He slotted that into the back of a specialist medical implant package. The only other item in the box was a flek.

'This is the operating didactic, which is standard, but it also contains the first-time access code specific to this set,' he told her. 'Basically, it allows you to activate the neural nanonics. After that, you change the code by just thinking of a new one. So even if someone got hold of your flek afterwards it wouldn't do them any good. Don't worry, it's all explained in the didactic.'

She lay face down on the cushioned bench, with a pair of collar wings holding her neck steady. Andy pushed her hair to one side, ready to apply the medical package to the nape of her neck. There was already a tiny nearly healed scar on her skin. He knew exactly what it was, he'd seen it a thousand times before, every time the implant package was taken off.

'Is everything all right?' Louise asked.

'Yes. No problem. It just takes a minute to line this up right.' He datavised the bodyscan cubicle's processor. Its memory file of her scan confirmed there was absolutely no foreign matter in her brain.

Andy took the coward's way out and said nothing. Mainly because he didn't want to alarm her. But something here was desperately wrong. Either she was lying to him, which he couldn't believe. Or ... he couldn't quite decide what the other options were. He was trespassing deep in Govcentral territory. All that did was enhance her mystery up to the level of pure enchantment. A babe in distress right out of the sensevise dramas. In his shop!

'Here we go,' he said lightly, and put the package over her existing scar. Now there would never be any proof.

Louise tensed slightly. 'It's gone numb.'

'That's OK. It's supposed to.'

All the medical package did was open a passage through to the base of the skull, and ease the capsule containing the densely pleated neural nanonics into place. Then the filaments began to unwind from each other and project forward, their probing tips slowly winding their way round cells as they sought out synapses. There were millions of them, active molecular strings obeying their AI formatted protocol; instructions determined by their own structure of spiralling atoms. They formed a wondrously intricate filigree around the medulla oblongata, branching to connect with the nerve strands inside while the main filaments seeped further into the brain to complete their interface.

With the implant package in place, Andy fetched the didactic imprinter. Louise thought it looked like a pair of burnished stainless-steel ski glasses. He put the flek in a small slot at the side, and placed it carefully on her face. 'This works in pulses,' he said. 'You'll get a warning flash of green, then you'll see a violet light for about fifteen seconds. Try not to blink. It should happen eight times.'

'That's it?' The edges of the imprinter had stuck to her skin, leaving her in total blackness.

'Yep, not so bad, is it?'

'And this is the way everyone on Earth learns things?'

'Yes. The information is encoded within the light, and your optic nerve passes it straight into your brain. Simple explanation, but that's the principle.'

Louise saw a flicker of green, and held her breath. The violet light came on, an otherwise uniform sheen broken by that unique monotone sparkle which a laser leaves on the retina. She managed not to blink until it went off. 'Your children don't go to school?' she asked.

'No. Kids go to day clubs, keeps them busy and you make friends there. That's all.'

She was silent for some time, considering the implications. The hours – years! – of my life I have sat in classrooms listening to teachers and reading books. And all the time, this way of learning, of discovery, existed. One of the demonic technologies that will ruin our way of life. Banned without question. That's nothing to do with keeping Norfolk pastoral, that's denying people opportunity, stunting their lives. It's worse than cousin Gideon's arm. She clenched her teeth together, suddenly very, very angry.

'Hey, are you all right?' Andy asked timidly.

The violet light came on again. 'Yes,' she snapped primly. 'I'm fine, thank you.'

Andy didn't say anything else until the didactic imprinter finished. Too scared he'd say the wrong thing again and annoy her further. He hadn't got a clue why her mood had swung so fast. When the imprinter did come off, it revealed a very pensive expression.

'Could you do me a favour?' Louise said. A knowing smile licked along her lips. 'Keep an eye on Genevieve for me. I promised I'd buy her something from here, so if you could steer her to some kind of gadget that's relatively harmless I'd be grateful.'

'Sure, my pleasure. Consider her guarded from any possible digital grief.' Andy had to use a nerve override impulse to prevent her from seeing how crushing that request was. He'd been counting on using the time it took to implant the neural nanonics to talk to her. Yet again, Andy blows out, he raged silently. Just once, I'd like to score with a major babe. Once!

The games section wasn't nearly as exciting as Genevieve had expected. Jude's Eworld was actively promoting a thousand games through its display screen catalogues, with direct access to ten times that many over encrypted links to publishers, covering the whole genre from interactive roles to strategy general's command. But as she flipped through them she could see they were all variants of each other. Everybody promised newer, hotter graphics, unrivalled worldbuilding, tac-stim activants, ingenious puzzles, more terrifying adversaries, slicker music. Always greater than before, never different. She sampled four or five, standing inside a projection cone beamed out from a high-wattage AV lens on the ceiling. Bor-*ing*. In truth, she'd begun to tire of them back on the *Jamrana*; like spending a whole day eating chocolate cake, really.

There didn't seem to be much else in Jude's Eworld that was interesting. Their main market was neural nanonics and associated software, or else no-fun processor blocks with strange peripherals.

'Hi. How's it going, there? Are you hyping cool yet?'

Genevieve turned to see the gruesomely oiky little shopboy Andy smiling ingratiatingly at her. One of his front teeth was crooked. She'd never seen that on someone his age before. 'I'm having a lovely time, thank you so much for caring.' It was the tone that would earn her a sharp slap from her mother or Mrs Charlsworth.

'Uh huh,' Andy grunted, fully flustered. 'Er, I thought perhaps I could show you what we've got to offer for kids your . . . I mean, the kind of blocks and software you might enjoy.'

'Oh, whoopee do.'

His arms rearranged themselves chaotically, indicating the section of the shop he wanted her to move towards. 'Please?' he asked desperately.

With an overlong sigh and slouched shoulders, Genevieve shuffled along despondently. Why does Louise always attract the wrong type? she wondered. Which sparked an idea. 'She's got a fiancé, you know.'

'Huh?'

A modest smile at his horror. 'Louise. She's engaged to be married. They announced the banns at our estate's chapel.'

'Married?' Andy yelped. He flinched, looking round the shop to see if any of his colleagues were paying attention.

This was fun. 'Yes. To a starship captain. That's why we're on Earth, we're waiting for him to arrive.'

'When's he due, do you know?'

'A couple of weeks, I think. He's very rich, he owns his starship.' She glanced round in suspicion, then leaned in towards the boy. 'Don't tell anyone I said this, but I think the only reason Daddy gave his permission was because of the money. Our estate is very big, and it takes a lot to keep it running.'

'She's marrying for money?'

'Has to be. I mean he's so *old*. Louise said he's thirty years older than she is. I think she was fibbing so it didn't sound so bad. If you ask me, it's more like forty-five.'

'Oh my God. That's disgusting.'

'It looks so awful when he kisses her, I mean he's virtually bald, and hideously fat. She says she hates him to touch her, but what can she do about it? He's her future husband.'

Andy stared down at her, his face stricken. 'Why does your father allow this?'

'All marriages are arranged on Norfolk, it's just our way. If it makes you feel any better, I think he really likes Louise.' She'd have to stop now. Crying shame, but it was getting really difficult to keep a straight face. 'He keeps on saying he wants to have a big family with her. He says he expects her to bear him at least seven children.' Jackpot! Andy had started trembling with indignation – or worse.

Her day made, Genevieve gently took his hand in hers, and smiled up trustfully. 'Can we see the hyper-cool electronics now, please?'

*

Understanding arrived within Louise's mind like a solstice sunrise. Quietly irresistible, bringing with it a fresh perspective on the world. A new season of life begun.

She knew precisely how to utilize the augmented mentality opening up within her brain as the filaments connected with her neurons, controlling the expanded potential with an instinct that could have been a genetic heritage it was so deep seated. Audio discrimination, analysing the murmur of sounds resonating through the door from the shop. Visual memory indexing, saving and storing what she saw. Pattern analysis. A test datavise, requesting an update from the medical package on her wrist. And the neuroiconic display, sight without eyes, moulding raw data into colour. It left her giddy and sweating from excitement. The sense of achievement was extraordinary.

I'm equal to everybody else now. Or I will be when I've learned how to use all the applications properly.

She datavised the implant package on her neck for a status check. A procedural menu sprang up inside her skull, and she ran a comparison. It confirmed the implantation process was complete. She instructed the package to disengage, withdrawing the empty capsule from which the filaments had sprouted, and knitting the cells together behind it.

'Steady on,' Andy said. 'That's supposed to be my job.'

Louise grinned at him as she climbed off the bench, and stretched extravagantly, flexing the stiffness out of limbs held still for too long. 'Oh, come on,' she teased. 'All your clients must do that. It's the first taste of freedom we get. Having neural nanonics must be like being allowed to vote, you've become a full member of society. Aren't they wonderful gadgets?'

'Um. Yeah.' He got her to lean forwards, and peeled the implant package from her neck. 'You can actually become a full citizen, you know.'

The strangely hopeful tone earned him an inquisitive look.

'What do you mean?'

'You could apply for residential citizenship. If you wanted. I checked the Govcentral legal memory core. It's no problem; you just need a Govcentral citizen to sponsor you, and a hundred fuseo-dollars fee. You can datavise them for an application. I've got the eddress.'

'That's um . . . very kind, Andy. But I don't really plan on staying here for long.' She smiled, trying to let him down gently. 'I have a fiancé, you see. He's going to come and take me away.'

'But Norfolk laws wouldn't apply to you,' Andy blurted desperately. 'Not here. Not if you're an Earth citizen. You'd be safe.'

'I'm sure I am anyway. Thank you.' She smiled again, slightly more firmly this time, and slipped past him out into the shop.

'Louise! I want this,' Genevieve shrieked. The little girl was standing in the middle of the shop, arms held rigid at her side as she turned round and round. There was a small block clipped onto her belt with DEMONSTRATOR printed in blue on its top. Louise hadn't seen her smile like that in a long time.

'What have you got, Gen?'

'I gave her a pair of realview lenses to try,' Andy said quietly. 'Like contact lenses, but they receive a datavise from the block which overlays a fantasyscape on what you're seeing.' He datavised a code to her. 'That'll let you view direct from the block.'

Louise datavised the code, marvelling at how smoothly she did it, and closed her eyes. The world started to spin around her. A very strange world. It had the same dimensions as the inside of Jude's Eworld, but this was a cave of onyx, where every surface corresponded to walls and counters, fat stalagmites had replaced the flek sale bins. People had become hulking black and chrome cyborgs, whose limbs were clusters of yellow pistons.

'Isn't it fabulous?' Gen whooped. 'It changes whatever you look at.'

'Yes, Gen, it's good.' She saw the mouth on one of the cyborgs clank apart to speak her own words, and smiled. The cyborg's mouth froze open. Louise cancelled her reception from the realview block.

'You can get about fifty different imagery programs for it,' Andy said. 'This one's *Metalpunk Wasteland*. Quite popular. There's an audioplug peripheral to change the voices.'

'*Please*, Louise! This one.'

'All right, all right.'

Andy datavised an off code to the demonstrator block. Genevieve pouted as the cave melted back into the shop. Andy started piling boxes and small flek cases up on the counter. 'What supplements do you want?' he asked.

Louise consulted the market menu already included in the NAS2600. 'News Hound, Global Eddress Directory Search, People Tracker ... um, the pregnancy supplement for my physiological monitor, Universal Message Script. I think that's it.'

'You're entitled to another twenty.'

'I know. Do I have to collect them all today? I'm not really sure what else I'll need.'

'Take as much time as you need to choose, and drop in whenever you want. But I'd recommend NetA, that'll give you your own eddress, you've got to pay an annual fee to the link company, but nobody will be able to contact you without one. Oh, and Streetnav, too, if you're going to stay in London – shows you the short cuts and how to use public transport.'

'OK, fine, put them on.' More flek cases began to appear on the counter. 'And that electronic-warfare block we talked about earlier.'

'Sure thing.'

When he slapped it down, it didn't look much different to her ordinary processor block, same anonymous oblong of dark grey plastic.

'Who buys bugs and things like that from you?' she asked.

'Could be anyone. Girl wanting to find out if her boyfriend's cheating on her. Manager who needs to know which of his staff are ripping him off. Voyeur perverts. Mostly, though, it's private detectives. Regular spooks' convention at times, this place.'

Louise didn't approve of the notion that just anybody could come along and spy on their friends and enemies. There ought to be some restrictions on who could buy such items. But then regulation was one thing Earth didn't seem to have much of.

Andy handed over the shop's accounts block with an apologetic smile. Louise tried not to shiver as she transferred the money over from her Jovian Bank credit disk. She gave the realview block and a packet of disposable lenses to Genevieve, who promptly tore the wrapping off with a gleeful, 'Yesss.'

'I'll see you when you come back for the rest of your software?' Andy asked. 'And if you change your mind about ... the other thing. I'll be happy to sponsor your application. I'm entitled to do that. I'm an adult citizen.'

'Right,' she said gingerly. There was something very odd about the way he'd latched on to the idea. She was debating whether to quiz him further when she caught the glint of devilment in Gen's eye. The little girl spun round quickly. 'You've been very kind, Andy,' Louise said. 'Please don't worry about me.' She leant over the counter and gave him a light kiss. 'Thanks.'

Genevieve was already making for the door, giggling wildly. Louise snatched up the carrier bag full of fleks, and chased after her.

*

Louise lay back on her bed as the brilliant sun finally sank away below Green Park. Genevieve was sleeping on the bed next to her, exhausted by the very long day.

Terrible child, Louise thought fondly. I must make sure she gets a set of neural nanonics when she turns sixteen. She closed her own eyes and put the news hound program into primary mode. The room's net processor acknowledged her datavise, and she began asking for general items on the possessed. That was when she had her crash course on using News Hound's filter program accessories and designating more refined search parameters. It took an hour, but she was eventually able to slot the myriad events reported by Earth's news agencies into an overall picture. The arrival of the *Mount's Delta* was a weird one. The way its crewman had been shredded hinted strongly at Quinn Dexter to her mind.

New York's abrupt isolation was the principal current topic for the agencies, in fact it was just about their only topic. Govcentral's North American Commissioner appeared before the reporters to assure everyone that it was just a precaution, and they were investigating a 'possessed-type' incident in Dome One as a matter of procedure. No schedule was given for opening the vac-trains. Police squads, reinforced with riot-control mechanoids, were out in force on the streets as the arcology residents became highly restless.

Then there was the event which caused Louise to jerk upright on the bed, opening her eyes wide in surprise and delight. Tranquillity's arrival at Jupiter. Joshua was *here*! In this star system.

She sank back onto the pillows, shaking with excitement. The Universal Message Script was hurriedly brought into primary mode. She composed a file for him which she really hoped didn't sound too desperate and pathetic, and datavised it triumphantly into the communication net. Her neural nanonics told her that Jupiter was five hundred and fifty million miles away, so the signal would take about forty minutes to reach it. She might have a reply within two hours!

*

Western Europe, who was monitoring her net connection, instructed the AI to block the message. The last thing he needed right now was some dunderhead boyfriend charging to the rescue, especially one as famous as Lagrange Calvert.

9

The party was a good one, though the guy with only one arm was kind of weird. Liol knew he was staring, and loaded a mild protocol reminder into his neural nanonics. It was just that he'd never seen anything like that before. Didn't seem to affect the guy's balance out on the dance floor, and the girl he was with obviously didn't mind. Or perhaps she enjoyed the novelty value. Knowing the girls in this habitat, that was a strong option. Come to that, maybe the missing arm was an obscure fashion statement. Not impossible.

Liol headed for the buffet table, picking his way through the crowd. Just about everyone smiled and said hello as they jostled together. He replied to most of them, their names familiar now without having to access a memory file. Plutocrat princes and princesses, with media celebrities jumbled in for variety. They tended to work hard during the day, expanding corporate empires, starting new dynasties, never taking their wealth for granted especially in these times. Tranquillity's change of location was causing them unique problems in sustaining their traditional markets, but there were fabulous benefits to be had from being placed in the Confederation's wealthiest star system. They'd set about exploiting that as ruthlessly and gleefully as only they could. But nights were given over to a single giant funtime: parties, restaurants, shows, clubs – Tranquillity boasted the best of them all in profusion.

He wasn't even sure who his host was. The apartment was as expensively anonymous as all the others he'd been in over the last few days, a hospitality showcase. Everything selected by designers to demonstrate their talent and taste – bitched over by other designers. Just another party. No doubt he and Dominique would grace two or three more before the night was out. The social set he'd belonged to in Ayacucho had never been shy of a good time, and were wealthy enough to indulge themselves. But compared to this mob, they were jejune provincials.

They were fascinated that he was Joshua's brother. Smiled indulgently when he told them he had his own business back in Ayacucho. But he could reveal little about *Lady Mac*'s last flight. So conversation tended to dry up fast after that. He really didn't know much about Confederation politics, or the money shifts in multistellar markets, or hot entertainment items (Jezzibella was Capone's girl – oh, come *on!*); and he certainly didn't relish discussing the possessed, and how the crisis was developing.

He took a plate along the long table of canapés, deliberately picking the more bizarre-looking items. Jupiter was rising across the window behind the table, so he munched and stared, as overwhelmed by the spectacle as any hick farm boy. Not quite the reaction of a sophisticated starship crewman-about-the-galaxy. The aspiration he'd cherished for himself since first hearing *Lady Mac* was supposedly his rightful inheritance. Now he'd flown in *Lady Mac*, actually getting to pilot her. He'd seen new star systems, even fought in an orbital war and (ironically implausible) saved the Confederation – or at least alleviated some of the navy's burden. After the pinnacle, there was always the journey back down again. He would never, ever be as good a pilot as Joshua. The manoeuvres his brother had flown during the *Beezling* encounter had made that quite obvious. And the Confederation wasn't such a fun place to roam through any more. Neither was life, now the beyond waited.

A reflection in the window made him turn. Joshua and Ione were mingling among the guests. Talking with ease, laughing. A good-looking couple, Josh in a formal black jacket, she in a flowing green evening dress. He was about to go over when Joshua led Ione out onto the dance floor.

'Yoo hoo.' Dominique waved from across the room. People struggled to get out of the way as she cut a line straight for him. Liol was granted the knowledge of what it must be like for a planet to face an invading fleet. Her hand grasped his arm, and she rubbed her nose against his. 'I missed you,' she murmured with silky reproach.

'I was hungry.'

'Me too.' The resentment snapped off, replaced with bountiful mischief. She plucked one of the canapés from his plate and popped it straight into her mouth. 'Eeek. Sungwort seaweed, and they coated it in coriander.'

'It was interesting,' he apologized meekly. She was as adorable as she was terrifying. By far the most beautiful girl in the room, Dominique favoured a more natural look than her contemporaries, a gypsy girl among the glossy mannequins. Her black evening gown was full-length, but that somehow didn't stop it from displaying a huge quantity of strategic flesh. Her broad lips curved up into a delighted smile. She dabbed her finger on his nose. 'I just love your innocence.' A quality of which he had very little left. Sex with Dominique was narcotic, ruining you with pleasure.

She held his gaze for a moment, face enraptured by devotion. He wanted to turn and flee. 'Someone I'd like you to meet,' she said neutrally, as if divining his response. A finger beckoned. There was a slim girl standing behind her, completely blocked by Dominique's broad, healthy physique. She had a prim Oriental face with hair several shades fairer than Dominique's. 'This is Neomone.'

'Hi.' Neomone darted forward and kissed him. Then swayed back, blushing, looking very pleased with herself.

'Hi.' He didn't quite know what to make of her. She was in her late teens, wearing a slinky silk dress that revealed an almost androgynous figure, all ribcage and stringy muscle. Thrilled and nervous at the same time, she kept giving Dominique worshipful glances.

'Neomone is training to be a ballerina,' Dominique purred.

'I've never been to a ballet,' Liol admitted. 'We've had troupes visit Ayacucho, but I didn't think it would be quite me. Sorry.'

Neomone giggled. 'Ballet is for everyone.'

'You should dance with him,' Dominique told her. 'Let him see there's nothing to be scared of from cultural élitism.' She cocked an eye at Liol. 'Neomone's quite a fan of yours, you know.'

He grinned, slightly awkward. 'Oh. Why's that?'

'You flew in the *Lady Mac*,' the girl said breathlessly. 'Everyone knows Joshua was on a secret mission.'

'If you know, then it can't be that secret, can it.'

'Told you he was a modest hero,' Dominique said. 'In public, anyway.'

Liol managed to keep smiling valiantly. Maybe he had bragged a little. That was the nature of the starflight business. 'You know how it is,' he shrugged.

Neomone's giggles were unstoppable. 'Not yet,' she said. 'But I'm going to find out tonight.'

*

The beach glowed a pale silver under the light-tube's lunar radiance. Joshua took his shoes off to walk along it, holding Ione's hand. The sand was warm and soft, flowing over his toes like grainy liquid. Tiny fluorescent fish darted about just under the sea's surface, as if a shower of pink and azure sparks was tumbling horizontally through the water. Somebody had made a row of small melted-looking mounds just above the shoreline, meandering away into the distance.

Ione sighed contentedly, and leaned into him. 'I know it's silly, but I keep coming back. She loved playing on this beach. I suppose I'm expecting to find her here.'

'Jay?'

'Yes.' She paused. 'And Haile. I hope she's all right.'

'The Kiint say she is. They wouldn't lie about that. Many things, but not the welfare of a child.'

'She must be so lonely.' Ione sat down with her back to one of the small dunes. She slid her silk scarf from her neck. 'I don't see why they won't let us bring her back from Jobis. Starships are still going there.'

'Bloody mystics.' Joshua sat beside her. 'Probably not in their horoscopes.'

'You're starting to sound like dear old Parker Higgens.'

Joshua laughed. 'I can't believe that old duffer is coming with us. And Getchell as well.'

'They're the best I've got.'

'Thanks for asking me to go. I need to be flying. I'm no good to anybody just sitting around.'

'Joshua.' She reached over to trace the stark line of his jawbone. 'I'm pregnant again. You're the father.'

His mouth flopped open. She smiled, and kissed him gently. 'Sorry. Bad timing. Again. I'm very good at that.'

'No,' he said with weak defiance. 'No, that's, er, not bad timing at all.'

'I thought you should know before you left.' Even in the twilight she could see the shock and wonder in his eyes. There was something absolutely gorgeous about him when he looked so vulnerable. It means he cares, I suppose. She touched his face again.

'Um. When?' he asked.

'Before you went to Norfolk. Remember?'

He grinned, almost shy. 'We'll never know the exact time, then. There's an awful lot to choose from.'

'If I had a choice, I think I'd make it the one in Adul Nopal's apartment.'

'Oh, Jesus, yes. The middle of his dinner party.' He flopped down onto the sand, and grinned up. 'Yeah! That would be fitting.'

'And Joshua. It was very deliberate. I'm not in this state by accident.'

'Right. Thanks for consulting me. I mean, I thought we'd already established the next Lord of Ruin with Marcus.'

'Just say no.'

He put his hand round her head, and pulled her down, kissing her. 'I think we've already confirmed I can't.'

'You're not angry with me?'

'No. Worried, maybe. More about the future than anything. But then the kid won't have it any different to the rest of the human race when he dies. We can't fear for that, or we'd be utterly paralysed. The Kiint found a solution, the Laymil, too – for all it's inapplicable. We damn well can.'

'Thank you, Joshua.'

'I'd like to know why, though. I mean, we already have the next Lord of Ruin established.'

She closed her eyes, shutting out his gentle curiosity. 'Because you're perfect,' she whispered. 'For me. Great body, good genes.'

'Little Miss Romantic.'

'And a wonderful lover.'

'Yeah, I know that bit. I carry the burden well, though.'

She laughed spryly, then she was crying helplessly.

'Hey. No.' He cradled her, hugging lightly. 'Don't do that.'

'Sorry.' She wiped a hand across her eyes. 'Joshua. Please. I don't love you. I can't love you.'

He flinched, but didn't recoil. 'I see.'

'Oh, God damn it. Now I've gone and hurt you. And I didn't want that. I never wanted that.'

'What the hell do you want, Ione? I don't understand. Don't tell me this was convenience, that I was the male easily to hand when you happened to make your mind up. You wanted my baby. And now you've told me about it. If you hate me so much, you wouldn't have done that.'

'I don't hate you.' She gripped him tighter. 'I don't.'

'Then what?' He made an effort not to shout. Every emotion in his head was free falling. Thought was almost impossible, only instinct, blind response. 'Jesus Christ, do you have any idea what you're doing to me?'

'Well, what do you want out of this, Joshua? Do you want to be a part of this child's life?'

'Yes! Jesus, how can you question that?'

'What part?'

'A father!'

'How will you be a father?'

'In the same way you're a mother.'

She took both his hands in hers, quelling the trembling. He shook her loose angrily. 'You can't be,' she said. 'I have an affinity bond with the baby, so does Tranquillity.'

'Jesus. I can get symbionts, I can be equal to you and this bloody habitat. Why are you trying to block me out of this?'

'Joshua. Listen to me. What would you do all day? Even if you were my consort, officially my husband. What would you do? You can't run Tranquillity. That's me, that's what I do. And then it'll be the job of our first child.'

'I don't know, I'll find something. I'm versatile.'

'There is nothing. There can never be anything for you in Tranquillity, not permanently. I keep telling you this, you are a starship captain. This is your port, not your home. If you stay here, you'll become like your father.'

'Leave my father out of this.'

329

'No, Joshua, I won't. He was the same as you, a great captain; and he stayed here in Tranquillity, he never flew after you were born. That's what wrecked him.'

'Wrong.'

'I know he didn't fly again.'

Joshua looked at her. For all his instinct, his experience, that beautiful face defeated him every time. What went on inside her head could never be known. 'All right,' he said abruptly. 'I'll tell you. He had it all, and lost it. That's why he never flew again. Staying here didn't break his heart, it was broken before that.'

'Had what?'

'Everything. What all us owner-captains fly for. The big strike, a flight that kills the banks. And I had it with Norfolk. I was *this* close, Ione, and loving it. That mayope exchange deal could have earned me hundreds of millions, I would have become one of the plutocrats that infest this bloody habitat. Then I would have been your equal. I would have had my empire to run, I could have bought a fleet of ships just like Parris Vasilkovsky. That's what I'd do during the day. And we'd be able to get married, and none of this question about how *worthy* I am would ever arise.'

'It's not about being worthy, Joshua. Don't say that, don't ever. You stopped the Alchemist from being used, for Heaven's sake. You think I look down on you for that? How could some dusty desk-bound company president compare to what you are? Joshua, I am so proud of you it hurts. That's why I wanted you as the baby's father. Because there is nobody better, not just your genes or your intuition, there can be no heritage finer than yours. And if I thought for one second there was a single chance you would be happy staying here with me, as my husband, or my partner, or just fitting me in as one of your harem, then I would have *Lady Mac* flung into a recycling plant to stop you leaving. But you won't be happy, you know that. And you'd end up blaming me, or yourself; or worse, the child, for keeping you here. I couldn't stand that, knowing I was responsible for your misery. Joshua, you're twenty-two, and unta-med. And that's beautiful, that's how it should be, that's your destiny as much as ruling Tranquillity is mine. Our lives have touched, and I thank God they have. We've both been rewarded with two children by it. But that's all. That's all we can ever be. Ships that pass in the night.'

Joshua searched round for the anger that had blazed so bright just a moment ago. But it had gone. There was mostly numbness, and a little shame. I ought to fight her, make her see I'm necessary. 'I hate you for being right.'

'I wish I wasn't,' she said tenderly. 'I just hope you can forgive me for being so selfish. I suppose that's my heritage; Saldanas always get their way, and to hell with the human fall out.'

'Do you want me to come back?'

Her shoulders slumped wearily. 'Joshua, I'm going to drag you back. I'm not forbidding you anything, I'm not saying you can't be a father. And if you want to stay in Tranquillity and make a go of it, then nobody will help and support that decision more than me. But I don't believe it will work, I'm sorry, but I really don't. It might for years, but eventually you'd look round and see how much you'd lost. And that would creep into our lives, and our child would grow up in an emotional war zone. I couldn't stand that. Haven't you listened to anything I've said? You're going to be the joy of your child's life, he's going to ache for when you visit and bring presents and stories. The times you'll spend together will be magical. It's you and I that cannot be inseparable, one of history's great love affairs. That's the *convention* of fatherhood you'll be missing, nothing more.'

'Life never used to be this complicated.'

The sympathy she felt for him was close to a physical suffering. 'I don't suppose it was before I came along. Fate's a real bitch, isn't she.'

'Yeah.'

'Cheer up. You get joy without responsibility. The male dream.'

'Don't.' He held up a warning finger. 'Don't make a joke of this. You've altered my life. Fair enough, encounters always result in some kind of change. That's what makes life so wonderful, especially mine with the opportunities I have. You're quite right about my wanderlust. But encounters are chance, natural. You did this quite deliberately. So just don't try and make light of it.'

They sat with their backs resting on the dune for some time, saying nothing. Even Tranquillity was silent, sensing Ione's reluctance to discuss what had been said.

Eventually they wound up leaning against each other. Joshua put his arm around her shoulder, and she started crying again. A sharing,

if not of sorrow for what had been done, then reluctant acceptance.
'Don't leave me alone tonight,' Ione said.

'I will never understand you.'

*

Preparing to go to bed took on the quality of a religious ceremony. The bedroom's window overlooking the underwater vista was opaqued, and the lights reduced to the smallest glimmer. All they could see was each other. They undressed and walked slowly down the steps into the deep spa hand in hand. Bathing was accomplished with scented sponges, graduating into erotic massage. Their lovemaking which followed was deliberately extreme, ranging from aching tenderness to a passion that bordered brutality. Each body responding perfectly to the demands of the other, an exploitation that only their complete familiarity with one another could achieve.

The one aspect they could never recapture was the emotional connection they'd experienced in the previous few days. This sex was a reversion to their very first time, fun, physically enjoyable, but essentially meaningless. Because they didn't mean the same to each other. The attraction was almost as strong as before, but of the devotion there was little evidence. Joshua finally conceded she was right. They'd come full circle.

He wound up lying across the bed, cushions in disarray around him, and Ione sprawled over his chest. Her cheek stroked his pectoral muscles, rejoicing in the touch.

'I thought the Lords of Ruin sent their children off to be Adamists,' he said.

'Father's and Grandfather's children became Adamists, yes. I've decided mine won't. Not unless that's what they decide they want to become, anyway. I want to bring them up properly, whatever that is.'

'How about that, a revolution from the top.'

'Every other part of our lives is changing. This particular little ripple won't be noticed amid the storm. But having a family in whatever form will move me closer to my human heritage. The Lords of Ruin have been terribly isolated figures before.'

'Will you marry, then?'

'That really is stuck in your brain, isn't it? I have no idea. If I meet someone special, and we both want to, and we're in a *position* to, then of course I will. But I am going to have a great many lovers, and I'll have even more friends; and the children will have their friends to play with in the parkland. Maybe even Haile will come back and join in the fun.'

'That sounds like the kind of neverland I'd want to grow up in. Question is, now, will it ever happen? We have to survive this crisis first.'

'We will. There's a solution out there somewhere. You said it, and I agree.'

He ran his fingers along her spine, enjoying the happy sighs it incited. 'Yeah. Well, let's see if this Tyrathca god can offer any hints.'

'You're really looking forward to the flight, aren't you? I told you, this is what you are.' She snuggled up closer, one hand stroking his thigh. 'What about you? Will you marry? I'm sure Sarha would be interested.'

'No!'

'OK, strike Sarha. Oh, of course, there's always that farm girl on Norfolk, you know . . . oh, what's her name, now?'

Joshua laughed, and rolled her over, pinning her arms above her head. 'Her name, as you very well know, is Louise. And you're still jealous, aren't you?'

Ione stuck her tongue out at him. 'No.'

'If I can't hack it as a consort for you, I hardly think a life tilling the fields is going to enthral me.'

'True.' She lifted her head, and gave him a fast jocose kiss. He still didn't let go of her arms. 'Joshua?'

He groaned in dismay, and collapsed back onto the mattress beside her; which sent out slow waves to flip the cushions. 'I hate that tone. I always hear it right before I wind up in deep shit.'

'I was only going to ask, what did happen to your father that last flight? *Lady Mac* got back here with a lot of fuselage heat damage and two jump nodes fused. That couldn't be pirates, or a secret mission for the Emperor of Oshanko, or rescuing a lost ship from the Meridian fleet that was caught in a neutron star's gravity well, or any of the other explanations you've come up with over the years.'

'Ye of little faith.'

She rolled onto her side, and propped her head on one hand. 'So what was it?'

'OK, if you must know. Dad found a xenoc shipwreck with

technology inside that was worth a fortune: they had gravity generators, a direct mass–energy converter, industrial-scale molecular
synthesis extruders. Amazing stuff, centuries in advance of Confederation science. He was rich, Ione. He and the crew could have
altered the entire Confederation economy with those gadgets.'

'Why didn't they?'

'The people who'd hired *Lady Mac* to prospect for gold asteroids
turned out to be terrorists, and he had to escape down a time warp
in the centre of the xenoc wreck.'

Ione stared at him for a second, then burst out laughing. Her
hand slapped his shoulder. 'God, you're impossible.'

Joshua shifted round to give her a hurt look. 'What?'

She put her arms round him and moulded her body contentedly
to his, closing her eyes. 'Don't forget to tell that one to the children.'

Tranquillity observed Joshua's expression sink to mild exasperation. Elaborate thought routines operating within the vast neural
strata briefly examined the possibility that he was telling the truth,
but in the end decided against.

*

Harkey's Bar was having a modest resurgence in fortune. Relative to
the absolute downtime endured during the quarantine when its
space industry clientele were careful with their money, this was a
positive boom. Not back up to pre-crisis levels yet; but the ships
were returning to Tranquillity's giant counter-rotating spaceport.
Admittedly they were mundane inter-orbit vessels rather than starships, but nonetheless they brought new cargoes, and crews with
heavy credit disks, and paid the service companies for maintenance
and support. The masters of commerce and finance living in the
starscraper penthouses were already making deals with the awesome
Edenist industrial establishment in whose midst they had so fortunately materialized. It wouldn't be long before all the dormitoried
starships were powered up and started travelling to Earth, and
Saturn, and Mars, and the asteroid settlements. Best of all, the buzz
was back among the tables and booths, industry gossip was hot and
hectic. Such confidence did wonders for liberating anticipation and
credit disks.

Sarha, Ashly, Dahybi, and Beaulieu had claimed their usual booth,
as requested by Joshua, who'd told them he wanted a meeting. They

didn't have any trouble, at quarter to nine in the morning there were only a dozen other people in the place.

Dahybi sniffed at his coffee after the waitress had departed. Even their skirts were longer at this time of day. 'It's not natural, drinking coffee in here.'

'This time isn't natural,' Ashly complained. He poured some milk into his cup, and added the tea. Sarha tsked at him; she always mixed it the other way round.

'Are we flying?' Dahybi asked.

'Looks like it,' Beaulieu said. 'The Captain authorized the service engineering crew to remove the hull plates over *Lady Mac*'s damaged node. The only reason to do that is to replace it.'

'Not cheap,' Ashly muttered. He stirred his tea thoughtfully.

Joshua pulled the spare seat out and sat down. 'Who's not cheap?' he asked briskly.

'Replacement nodes,' Sarha said.

'Oh, them.' Joshua stuck up a finger, and a waitress popped up at his side. 'Tea, croissants, and orange juice,' he ordered. She gave him a friendly smile, and hurried off. Dahybi frowned. Her skirt was short.

'I'm flying *Lady Mac* tomorrow,' Joshua told them. 'Just as soon as the *Oenone* returns from the O'Neill Halo with my new nodes.'

'Does the First Admiral know?' Sarha enquired lightly.

'No, but Consensus does. This is not a cargo flight, we'll be leaving with Admiral Saldana's squadron.'

'We?'

'Yes. That's why you're here. I'm not going to press-gang you this time. You get consulted. I can promise a long and very interesting trip. Which means I need a good crew.'

'I'm in, Captain,' Beaulieu said quickly.

Dahybi sipped some coffee, and grinned. 'Yes.'

Joshua looked at Sarha and Ashly. 'Where are we going?' she asked.

'To the Tyrathca Sleeping God, so we can ask it how to solve the possession crisis. Ione and the Consensus believe it's on the other side of the Orion Nebula.'

Sarha deliberately looked away, studying Ashly's face. The pilot was lost in stupefaction. Joshua's simple words were the perfect bewitchment for a man who'd given up normal life to witness as much of eternity as he could. And Joshua knew that, Sarha thought. 'Monkey and a banana,' she muttered. 'All right, Joshua, of course we're with you.' Ashly nodded dumbly.

'Thanks,' Joshua told them all. 'I appreciate it.'

'Who's handling fusion?' Dahybi asked.

'Ah.' Joshua produced an uncomfortable expression. 'The not so good news is that our friend Dr Alkad Mzu is coming with us.' They started to protest. 'Among others,' he said loudly. 'We're carrying quite a few specialists with us this trip. She's the official exotic physics expert.'

'Exotic physics?' Sarha sounded amused.

'Nobody knows what this god thing actually is, so we're covering all the disciplines. It won't be like the Alchemist mission. We're not on our own this time.'

'OK, but who do you want as fusion officer?' Dahybi repeated.

'Well . . . Mzu's specialist field at the Laymil Project was fusion systems. I could ask her. I didn't know how you'd all feel about that.'

'Badly,' Beaulieu said. Joshua blinked. He'd never heard the cosmonik express a definite opinion before, not about people.

'Joshua,' Sarha said firmly. 'Just go and ask him, all right? If he says no, fine, we'll get someone else. If he says yes, it'll be with the understanding that you're the captain. And you know Liol's up to the job. He deserves the chance, and I don't just mean to crew.'

Joshua looked round the other three, receiving their encouragement. 'Suppose there's no harm in asking,' he admitted.

*

The crews were starting to refer to themselves as the Deathkiss squadron. On several occasions the phrase had almost slipped from Rear-Admiral Meredith Saldana's own mouth as well. Discipline had kept it from being spoken, rather than neural nanonic prohibitions, but he sympathized with his personnel.

The Sol-system news companies were hailing Tranquillity's appearance in Jupiter orbit as a huge victory over the possessed, and Capone in particular. Meredith didn't see it quite that way. It was the second time the squadron had gone up against the possessed, and the second time they'd been forced to retreat. This time they owed their lives entirely to luck . . . and his own rebel ancestor's foresight. He wasn't entirely sure if the universe was being ironic or contemptuous towards him. The only certainty in his life these days was the squadron's morale, which was close to non-existent. His day cabin's processor datavised an admission request, which he granted. Commander Kroeber and Lieutenant Rhoecus air-swam through the open hatch. They secured their feet on a stikpad and saluted.

'At ease,' Meredith told them. 'What have you got for me?'

'Our assignment orders, sir,' Rhoecus said. 'They're from the Jovian Consensus.'

Meredith gave Commander Kroeber a brief glance. They'd been waiting for new orders from the 2nd Fleet headquarters in the O'Neill Halo. 'Go ahead, Lieutenant.'

'Sir, it's a secure operation. CNIS has located an antimatter production station, they asked Jupiter to eliminate it.'

'Could have been worse,' Meredith said. For all it was rare, an assault on an antimatter station was a standard procedure. A straightforward mission like this was just what the crews needed to restore confidence in themselves. Then he noticed the reservation in Rhoecus's expression. 'Continue.'

'A supplementary order has been added by the Jovian security sub-Consensus. The station is to be captured intact.'

Meredith hardened his expression, knowing Consensus would be observing his disapproval through Rhoecus's eyes. 'I really do hope that you're not going to suggest we start arming ourselves with that *abomination*.'

If anything, Rhoecus seemed rather relieved. 'No, sir, absolutely not.'

'Then what are we capturing it for?'

'Sir, it's to be used for fuelling the *Lady Macbeth*'s antimatter drive unit. Consensus is sending a pair of ships beyond the Orion Nebula.'

The statement was so extraordinary Meredith initially didn't know what to make of it. Though that ship's name ... Oh, yes, of course, Lagrange Calvert; and there was also the matter of a ludicrously ballsy manoeuvre through Lalonde's upper atmosphere. 'Why?' he asked mildly.

'It's a contact mission with the non-Confederation Tyrathca. We believe they may have information relevant to possession.'

Meredith knew he was being judged by Consensus. An Adamist

– a Saldana – being asked by Edenists to break the very law the Confederation was formed to enforce. At the least I should query 2nd Fleet headquarters. But in the end it comes down to trust. Consensus would never initiate such a mission without a good reason. 'We live in interesting times, Lieutenant.'

'Yes, sir; unfortunately, we do.'

'Then let's hope we outlive them. Very well. Commander Kroeber, squadron to stand by for assault duties.'

'Consensus has designated fifteen voidhawks to join us, sir,' Rhoecus said. 'Weapons loading for the frigates has been given full priority.'

'When do we leave?'

'The *Lady Macbeth* is undergoing some essential maintenance. She should be ready to join the squadron in another twelve hours.'

'I hope this Lagrange Calvert character can stay in formation,' Meredith said.

'Consensus has every confidence in Captain Calvert, sir.'

*

The two of them sat at a table by the window in Harkey's Bar. Glittering stars chased a shallow arc behind them as their drinks were delivered. Two slender crystal flutes of Norfolk Tears. The waitress thought that wonderfully romantic. They were both captains, he in crumpled overalls but still with the silver star on his shoulder, she in an immaculate Edenist blue satin ship-tunic. A handsome couple.

Syrinx picked her glass up and smiled. 'We really shouldn't be drinking. We're flying in seven hours.'

'Absolutely,' Joshua agreed. He touched his glass to hers. 'Cheers.' They both sipped, relishing the drink's delectable impact.

'Norfolk was such a lovely world,' Syrinx said. 'I was planning on going back next midsummer.'

'Me too. I'd got this amazing deal lined up. And . . . there was a girl.'

She took another sip. 'Now there's a surprise.'

'You've changed. Not so uptight.'

'And you're not so irresponsible.'

'Here's to the sustainable middle ground.' They touched glasses again.

'How's the refit coming on?' Syrinx asked.

'On schedule so far. We've got the new reaction mass tanks installed in *Lady Mac*'s cargo holds. I left the engineering team plumbing them in. Dahybi is running integration protocols through the new node; there's some kind of software disparity with the rest of them. But then there always is a problem with new units, the manufacturers can never resist trying to improve something that works perfectly well already. He'll have it debugged ready for departure time.'

'Sounds like you have a good crew.'

'The best. How's *Oenone*?'

'Fine. The supplement fusion generators are standard items. We already had the attachment points for them in the cargo cradles.'

'Looks like we're running out of excuses, then.'

'Yeah. But I bet the view from that side of the nebula is quite something.'

'It will be.' He hesitated for a moment. 'Are you all right?'

Syrinx studied him over the top of the flute; her ability to read Adamist emotions was quite adroit these days, she considered. His genuine concern gladdened her. 'I am now. Bit of a basket case for a while, after Pernik, but the doctors and my friends helped put me back together again.'

'Good friends.'

'The best.'

'So why this flight?'

'Mainly *Oenone* and I are flying because we think this is how we can contribute best. If that sounds superior, I apologize, but it's what I feel.'

'It's the *only* reason I'm here. You know, you and I are pretty unique. There's not many of us who've come face to face with the possessed and survived. That does tend to focus the mind somewhat.'

'I know what you mean.'

'I've never been so scared before. Death is always so difficult for us. Most people just ignore it. Then when you start to see your last days drifting away, you content yourself that you've had a good life, that it hasn't been for nothing. And, hey, there might be an afterlife after all, which is good because deep down you've convinced yourself you did your best, so the plus column is always going to be in the black when it comes to Judgement Day. Only there isn't a Judgement Day, the universe doesn't care.'

'Laton worked it out; that's what gets me. I've retrieved that last message of his time and again, and he really believed Edenists won't be trapped in the beyond. Not even one in a billion of us, he said. Why, Joshua? We're not that different, not really.'

'What does Consensus think?'

'There's no opinion yet. We're trying to ascertain the general nature of the possessed, and compare it to our own psychological profile. Laton said that would provide us with an insight. The Mortonridge Liberation ought to generate a great deal of raw data.'

'I'm not sure how helpful that'll be. Every era has a different outlook. What's thoroughly normal behaviour for a seventeenth-century potter is going to be utterly different from yours. I always think Ashly's ridiculously old fashioned on some things; he's horrified by the way kids today can access stim programs.'

'So am I.'

'But you can't restrict access, not in a universal data culture like ours. You have to educate society about what's acceptable and what isn't. A little adolescent experimentation isn't harmful, in moderation. We have to concentrate on pushing the moderation aspect, help people come to terms with what's out there. The alternative is censorship, which the communication nets will defeat every time.'

'That's defeatism. I'm not saying people shouldn't be educated about the problems of stim programs; but if you made the effort, Adamist culture could abolish them.'

'Knowledge can't be destroyed, it has to be absorbed and accommodated.' He glanced dolefully out at Jupiter. 'As I tried to argue with the First Admiral. He wasn't terribly impressed, either.'

'I'm not surprised. The fact we're going to use antimatter on this flight is restricted information. Rightly so.'

'That's different—' Joshua began, then grunted. 'Looks like I'm not going to make it past the beyond. Don't think like an Edenist.'

'No, that's not right. This is just a difference in beliefs. We both agree stim addiction is a dreadful blight, we just differ on how to treat it. We still think the same way. I don't understand this! Damn it!'

'Let's hope the Sleeping God can show us the difference.' He gave her a tentative look. 'Can I ask a personal question?'

She rubbed the tip of her index finger round the rim of the flute, then sucked on it. 'Joshua Calvert, I have a devoted lover, thank you.'

'Er, actually, I was wondering if you had any children.'

'Oh,' she said, and promptly blushed. 'No, I don't. Not yet anyway. My sister Pomona has three; it makes me wonder what I've been doing with my time.'

'When you do have children, how do you raise them? Voidhawk captains, I mean. You don't have them on board, do you?'

'No, we don't. Shipboard life is for adults, even aboard a voidhawk.'

'So how do they grow up?'

'What do you mean?' It was a strange question, especially from him. But she could see it was important.

'They haven't got you there as a mother.'

'Oh, I see. It doesn't matter, for them anyway. Voidhawk captains tend to have fairly large extended families. I must take you to see my mother some time, then you'll see first-hand. Any children I have while I'm still flying with *Oenone* will be taken care of by my army of relatives, and the habitat as well. I'm not propagandizing, but Edenism is one giant family. There's no such thing as an orphan among us. Of course, it's hard on us captains, having to kiss goodbye to our babies for months at a time. But that's been the fate of sailors for millennia now. And of course, we do get to make up for it at the end. When *Oenone*'s eggs are birthed, I wind up at ninety years old in a house with a dozen screaming infants. Imagine that.'

'Are they happy, those other children? The ones you have to leave behind.'

'Yes. They're happy. I know you think we're terribly formal and mannered, but we're not mechanoids, Joshua, we love our children.'

She reached over and squeezed his hand. 'You OK?'

'Oh, yeah. I'm OK.' He concentrated on his flute. 'Syrinx. You can count on me during the flight.'

'I know that, Joshua. I reviewed the Murora memory a few times, and I've spoken to Samuel, too.'

He gestured out at the starfield. 'The real answer lies out there, somewhere.'

'Consensus has known that all along. And as the Kiint wouldn't tell me . . .'

'And I'm not smart enough to help the research professors . . .'

They smiled. 'Here's to the flight,' Syrinx said.

'Soaring where angels fear to fly.'

They downed the remainder of their Norfolk Tears. Syrinx blew heavily, and blinked the moisture away from her eyes. Then she frowned at the figure standing at the bar. 'Jesus, Joshua, I didn't know there was two of you.'

The enjoyable surprise of hearing an Edenist swear in such a fashion was quelled with pique when he saw who she was talking about. He stuck his hand up and waved Liol over.

'Delighted to meet you,' Liol said when Joshua introduced them. He polished up the Calvert grin for her benefit, and kissed her hand.

Syrinx laughed, and stood up. 'Sorry, Liol, I'm afraid I had my inoculation some time ago.' Joshua was chuckling.

'I'll leave the pair of you to it,' she said, and gave Joshua a light kiss. 'Don't be late.'

'Got her eddress?' Liol asked from the side of his mouth as he watched her walk away.

'Liol, that's a voidhawk ship-tunic. Syrinx doesn't have an eddress. So how are you?'

'Absolutely fine.' Liol reversed a chair, and straddled it, arms resting on the back. 'This is party city for me all right. I think I'll move Quantum Serendipity here after the crisis.'

'Right. Haven't seen much of you since we docked.'

'Well, hey, no surprise there. That Dominique, hell of a girl.' He lowered his voice to a throaty gloating growl. 'Game on, five, six times a night. Every position I know, then some that's got to be just for xenocs.'

'Wow.'

'Last night, you know what? Threesome. Neomone joined in.'

'No shit? You record a sensevise?'

Liol put both hands down on the table, and stared at his brother. 'Josh.'

'Yep.'

'For Christ's sake, take me with you.'

*

Kerry was the first planet, the test. Catholic Irish-ethnic to the bedrock, its inhabitants gave the priests of the Unified Church a very hard time. Stubbornly suspicious of technology, it took them half a century longer than the development company projected to reach full technoindustrial independence. When they did achieve it, their economic index never matched the acceleration curve of the more driven Western Christian work-ethic planets. They were comfortably off, favoured large families, traded modestly with nearby star systems, contributed grudgingly to the Confederation Assembly and Navy, and went to church regularly. There were no aspirations to become a galactic player like Kulu, Oshanko, and Edenism. Quiet people getting on with their lives. Until the possession crisis arrived.

The planet was seven light-years from New California, and worried. Their strategic-defence network was the absolute minimum for a developed world, and combat wasp stocks were never kept very high; maintenance budgets were also subject to political trimming. Since the crisis began, and especially post-Arnstadt, Kerry had been desperately trying to upgrade. Unfortunately their industrial stations weren't geared towards churning out military hardware. Nor were they closely allied to Kulu or Earth, who did produce an abundance of such items. The Edenists of the Kerry system, orbiting Rathdrum, lent what support they could; but they had their own defences to enhance first.

Still, went the hope and reasoning, that's the benefit of being galactic small fry, Capone isn't going to bother with us. When it came to the effort of mounting a full-scale invasion along the lines of Arnstadt they were absolutely right. Which is why Al's sudden change of policy caught them woefully unprepared.

Twelve hellhawks emerged five and a half thousand kilometres above Kerry's atmosphere, and fired a salvo of ten (fusion-powered) combat wasps each. The bitek craft immediately started accelerating at six gees, flying away from each other in an expanding globe formation. Their combat wasps raced on ahead of them, ejecting multiple submunitions. Space was infected by electronic-warfare impulses and thermal decoys, a rapidly growing blind spot in Kerry's sensor coverage. Submunitions began to target sensor satellites, inter-orbit ships, spaceplanes, and low-orbit SD platforms. A volley of fusion bombs detonated, creating a further maelstrom of electro-magnetic chaos.

Kerry's SD network controllers, surprised by the vehemence of the attack, and fearing an Arnstadt-style assault, did their best to counter. Platforms launched counter-salvos of combat wasps; electron beams and X-ray lasers stabbed out, slashing across the vacuum to punch submunitions into bloating haze-balls of ions. Electronic-warfare generators on the platforms began pumping out their own disruption. After four seconds spent analysing the attack mode, the network's coordinating AI determined the hellhawks were engaged in a safe-clearance operation. It was right.

Ten front-line Organization frigates emerged into the calm centre of the combat wasp deluge. Fusion drives ignited, driving them down towards the planet at eight gees. Combat wasps slid out of their launch-tubes, and their drives came on.

The AI had switched all available sensor satellites to scanning the frigates. Radars and laser radars were essentially useless in the face of New California's superior electronic-warfare technology. The network's visual pattern sensors were being pummelled by the nuclear explosions and deception impulse lasers, but they did manage to distinguish the unique super-hot energy output of antimatter drives. The ultimate horror unchained above Kerry's beautiful, vulnerable atmosphere.

Unlike ordinary combat wasps, a killstrike didn't eliminate the problem. Hit a fusion bomb with a laser or kinetic bullet and there is no nuclear explosion, it simply disintegrates into its component molecules. But knock out an antimatter combat wasp and the drive's confinement spheres will detonate into multi-megaton fury, as will the warheads.

As soon as the launch was verified, the AI's total priority was preventing the antimatter combat wasps from getting within a thousand kilometres of the stratosphere. Starships, communication platforms, port stations, and industrial stations were reclassified expendable, and left to take their chances. Every SD resource was concentrated on eliminating the antimatter drones. Weapons were realigned away from the hellhawks and frigates, and brought to bear solely on the searing lightpoints racing over the delicate continents. Defending combat wasps performed drastic realignment manoeuvres; platform-mounted rail guns pumped out a cascade of inert kinetic missiles along projected vectors. Patrolling starships accelerated down at high gees, bringing their combat wasps and energy-beam weapons in range.

The hellhawks fired another barrage of combat wasps, sending them streaking away from the nebulous clot of plasma which the initial drone battle had smeared across the sky. They were aimed at the remaining low-orbit SD platforms shielding the continent below. Apart from activating the platforms' close-defence weapons, there was little the network controllers could do. Hurtling towards the planet, the frigates began to diverge, curving away from each other. Nothing challenged their approach. The continent was completely open to whatever they chose to throw at it.

As the antimatter exploded overhead in a pattern that created an umbrella of solid incandescent radiation three thousand kilometres across, they made a strange selection. Two hundred kilometres above the atmosphere, each warship flung out a batch of inactive ovoids, measuring a mere three metres high. Their task complete, the frigates curved up, striving for altitude with an eight-gee acceleration. A second, smaller salvo of antimatter combat wasps was fired, providing the same kind of diversionary cover as they'd enjoyed during their descent.

This time, the invaders didn't have it all their own way. The number of weapons focused on, and active within, the small zone where the frigates and hellhawks were concentrated began to take effect. Even Kerry's second-rate hardware had the odds tilting in its favour. A nuclear-tipped submunition exploded against one of the frigates. Its entire stock of antimatter detonated instantaneously. The radiation blaze wiped out every chunk of hardware within a five hundred kilometre radius. Outside the killzone ships and drones spun away inertly, moulting charred flakes of nulfoam. Exposed fuselages shone like small suns under the equally intense photonic energy release. To those on the planet unlucky enough to be looking up at the silent, glorious blossoms of light during the first stage of the battle, it was as though the noon sun had suddenly quadrupled in vigour. Then their optic nerves burnt out.

Two of the hellhawks were crippled in the explosion, their polyp penetrated by lethal quantities of gamma radiation. One of the frigates was unable to handle the massive energy impact. The dissipation web beneath its hexagonal fuselage plates turned crimson and melted. The patterning nodes facing the massive explosion flash suffered catastrophic failures as the radiation smashed delicate molecular junctions into slag. The fusion drives failed. Plumes of hot vapour squirted angrily out of emergency vent nozzles. Inside, the crew charged through their contingency procedures, desperate to sustain the integrity of the antimatter-confinement spheres in their remaining combat wasps.

None of their Organization colleagues went back for them. As soon as the eight remaining frigates reached a five thousand kilometre altitude they jumped outsystem. The hellhawks followed within seconds, leaving Kerry's population wondering what the hell had happened. Behind the shrinking wormhole interstices, the black eggs thundered earthwards with total impunity. SD sensors never found them amid the electronic disorder. People on the planet couldn't see their laser-like contrails against the dazzling aftermath of the orbital explosions.

They fell fast before decelerating at excruciatingly high gees in the lower atmosphere. Sonic booms rocked across the sleepy farmland, the first indication that anything was wrong. When the rural folk started to scan the sky in mild alarm, all that was to be seen were chunks of flaming debris streaking down from the battle – to be expected, claimed those who knew something of such things. The eggs reached subsonic speed a kilometre above the land. Petals flipped out from the lower half, presenting a wider surface area to the air, doubling the drag coefficient. At four hundred metres, the drogue chute shot up. Two hundred metres saw the main chute deployment.

Two hundred and fifty of the black eggs thudded to ground at random across an area measuring over three hundred thousand square kilometres. The petals failed on eight, while a further nine suffered chute failure. The remaining two hundred and thirty-three produced a bone-rattler landing for their passengers, bouncing and rolling for several metres before they came to a halt. Their sides slit open with a loud crack, and the possessed stepped forth to admire the verdant green land they had volunteered to infiltrate.

*

The hellhawks arrived back at New California thirty hours later. They didn't even get a hero's welcome. The Organization knew the seeding flight had been a success; information from the infiltrators had already squirmed its way back through the beyond.

Al was jubilant. He ordered Emmet and Leroy to put together another five seeding flights immediately. The fleet crews and asteroids cooperated enthusiastically. The success was nothing like as momentous as the Arnstadt victory, but it kicked in a resurgence of confidence throughout the Organization. We're a power again was the shared opinion. Beefs and recalcitrance sloped away.

The *Varrad* discarded its fantasy starship image as it approached Monterey. It slid over the docking-ledge pedestal and slowly sank down, radiating a desultory relief.

You did well, Hudson Proctor told Pran Soo, the hellhawk's resident soul. Kiera says she's pleased with you.

Commence nutrient fluid pumping, Pran Soo said flatly.

Sure thing. Here it comes. Enjoy.

Hudson Proctor gave a short command, and the fluid surged along the pipes and into the hellhawk's internal reserve bladders.

Two of us were exterminated, Pran Soo announced to the other hellhawks. Linsky and Maranthis. They were irradiated when Kerry's SD network took out the *Dorbane*. It was awful. I felt their structure withering.

Price we pay for victory, Etchells said swiftly. Two of us, against an entire Confederation planet taken out.

Yeah, said Felix, who possessed the *Kerachel*. Kerry had me real worried. When it comes to drinking contests and pub brawls, they'd got us beat every time.

Keep your goddam pinko loser opinions to yourself, Etchells sneered back. This was a concept-proving mission. What the fuck do you know about overall strategy? We're the hard edge of operations, the cosmic shock troops.

Give it a rest, you boring little prat. And don't pretend you were ever in an army. Even armies have a minimum IQ requirement.

Oh yeah? What you know. I killed fifteen men when I was in combat.

Yeah, he was a nurse. Couldn't read the label on the medicine bottle.

Careful, shit-for-brains.

Or what?

I'm sure Kiera would be interested to know about this sedition you're spreading. See what a little fasting does to your attitude.

SHUT THE FUCK UP, YOU BOLLOCKBRAINED NAZI REDNECK MORON.

The general affinity band fell silent for quite some time.

Were you listening to all that? Pran Soo asked Rocio on singular engagement.

I heard, the *Mindori*'s possessor replied. I think things might be starting to slide our way.

Could be. I'm sure each of us can do simple maths. Two of us per soft-target planet. When we start hitting hard targets, Kiera's going to have a full-scale strike on her hands.

Which she'll win unless we can provide everyone with an alternative food source.

Yeah. How's it going?

I have been tracking the *Lucky Logorn*, they're almost back at Almaden.

You think this Deebank guy will go for our pitch?

He was the first to offer us a deal. At least he'll listen to what I suggest.

*

The First Admiral had stayed away from the CNIS secure laboratory ever since the incident in Court Three. Maynard Khanna had been a damn fine officer, not to mention young and personable. The boy would have gone a long way in the Confederation Navy, so Samual Aleksandrovich had always told himself. With or without my patronage. Now he was dead.

The funeral ceremony in Trafalgar's multi-denominational church had been short and simple. Dignified, as was fitting. A flag-draped coffin, the enduring image of military service for centuries, placed reverently on a pedestal before the altar by the marine dress guard. It was intended as a focus for their honour. But Samual had thought it looked more like a sacrificial offering.

Standing in the front pew, mouthing the words of a hymn, he suddenly wondered if Khanna was actually watching them. Information gleaned from captured possessed indicated those ensnared in the beyond were aware of events inside the real universe. It was a moment of profound spookiness; he even lowered his hymn book to stare at the coffin in suspicion. Was this why the whole funeral ritual had started back in prehistory times? It was one of the most common cross-cultural events, a ceremony to mark the passing of life. The deceased's friends and relatives coming to pay homage, to wish them well on their way. It would be reassuring for a soul, otherwise so naked and alone, to gain the knowledge that so many considered their life to be worthwhile.

The remnants of Maynard Khanna's body mocked the notion of a fulfilled existence. Young, tortured to death, his ending had been neither swift nor noble.

Samual Aleksandrovich had raised his hymn book again and sung with a vigour which surprised the other officers. Perhaps Khanna would witness the mark of devotion from his superior officer, and draw some comfort from the fact. If it made a difference, the effort should be made. Now Samual Aleksandrovich was having to confront the cause of his regret. Jacqueline Couteur was still possessing her stolen body. Immune from the usual laws that would deliver justice upon such a treacherous multiple murderess.

He was accompanied by Mae Ortlieb and Jeeta Anwar from the Assembly President's staff, as well as Admiral Lalwani and Maynard Khanna's replacement, Captain Amr al-Sahhaf. The presence of the two presidential aides he found mildly annoying; an indication of how his decisions and prerogatives were increasingly coming under political scrutiny. Olton Haaker had that right, Samual acknowledged, but it was being wielded with less subtlety as the crisis drew out.

For the first time he was actually thankful for the Mortonridge Liberation. Positive physical action on such a massive scale had diverted the attention of both the Assembly and the media companies from navy activities. The politicians, he conceded grimly, might have been right about the psychological impact such a campaign would create. He'd even accessed a few rover reporter sensevises himself to see how the serjeants were doing. My God, the mud!

Dr Gilmore and Euru greeted the small elite delegation with little sign of nerves. A good omen, Samual thought. His spirits lifted further when Gilmore started to lead them along to the physics and electronics laboratory section, away from the demon trap.

Bitek Laboratory Thirteen was almost the same as any standard electronic research facility. A long room lined with benches, several morguelike slabs arranged down the centre, and glass-walled clean rooms at one end. Tall stacks of experimental equipment were standing like modern megaliths on every surface, alongside ultra-high-resolution scanners and powerful desktop blocks. The only distinguishing items the First Admiral could see were the clone vats. Those you normally wouldn't find outside an Edenist establishment.

'Exactly what are you demonstrating for us?' Jeeta Anwar asked.

'The prototype anti-memory,' Euru said. 'It was surprisingly easy to assemble. Of course, we do have a great many thoughtware weapons on file, which we've studied. And the neural mechanisms behind memory retention are well understood.'

'If that's the case, I'm surprised no one has ever designed one before.'

'It's a question of application,' Gilmore said. 'As the First Admiral pointed out once, the more complex a weapon is, the more impractical it becomes, especially in the field. In order for the anti-memory to work, the brain must be subjected to quite a long sequence of imprint pulses. You couldn't just fire it at your opponent the same way you do a bullet. They have to be looking straight into the beam, and a sharp movement, or even an inappropriately timed blink, will nullify the whole process. And if it was known to be in use, retinal implants could be programmed to recognize it, and block it out. However, once you hold a captive, application becomes extremely simple.'

Mattox was waiting for them by the last clean room, looking through the glass with the air of a proud parent. 'Testing has been our greatest stalling point,' he explained. 'Ordinary bitek processors are completely useless in this respect. We had to design a system which duplicates a typical human neuron structure in its entirety.'

'You mean you cloned a brain?' Mae Ortlieb asked, a blatant note of disapproval in her voice.

'The structural array is copied from a brain,' Mattox said defensively. 'But the construct itself is made purely from bitek. There was no cloning involved.' He indicated the clean room.

The delegation moved closer. The room was almost empty, containing a single table which held a burnished metal cylinder. Slim tubes of nutrient fluid snaked out of the base to link it with a squat protein-cycler mechanism. A small box protruded from the side of the cylinder, halfway up. Made of translucent amber plastic, it contained a solitary dark sphere of some denser material, set near the surface. The First Admiral upped the magnification on his enhanced retinas. 'That's an eye,' he said.

'Yes, sir,' Mattox said. 'We're trying to make this as realistic as possible. Genuine application will require the anti-memory to be conducted down an optic nerve.'

A black electronic module was suspended centimetres from the bitek eye, held in place by a crude metal clamp. Fibre-optic cables trailed away from it, to plug into the clean room's utility data sockets.

'What sort of routines are you running inside the construct?' Mae Ortlieb asked.

'Mine,' Euru said. 'We connected the cortex to an affinity capable processor, and I transferred a copy of my personality and memories into it.'

She flinched, looking from the Edenist to the metal cylinder. 'Isn't that somewhat unusual?'

'Not relative to this situation,' he replied with a smile. 'We are attempting to create the most realistic environment we can. For that we need a human mind. If you would care to give it a simple Turing test.' He touched a processor block on the wall beside the clean room. Its AV lens sparkled.

'Who are you?' Mae Ortlieb asked, with some self-consciousness.

'I suppose I ought to call myself Euru-two,' the AV lens replied. 'But then Euru has transferred his personality into a neural simulacrum twelve times already to assist with the anti-memory evaluation.'

'Then you should be Euru-thirteen.'

'Just call me Junior, it's simpler.'

'And do you believe you've retained your human faculties?'

'I don't have affinity, of course, which I regard as distressing. However, as I won't be in existence for very long, its absence is tolerable. Apart from that, I am fully human.'

'Volunteering for a suicide isn't a very healthy human trait, and certainly not for an Edenist.'

'Nonetheless, it's what I committed myself to.'

'Your original self did. What about you, have you no independence?'

'Possibly if you left me to develop by myself for several months, I would become reluctant. At the moment, I am Euru Senior's mind twin, and as such this experiment is quite acceptable to me.'

The First Admiral frowned, troubled by what he was witnessing. He hadn't known Gilmore's team had reached quite this level. He gave Euru a sidelong glance. 'I'm given to understand that a soul is formed by impressing coherent sentient thought on the beyond-type energy which is present in this universe. Therefore, as you are a sentient entity, you will now have your own soul.'

'I would assume so, Admiral,' Euru Junior replied. 'It is logical.'

'Which means you have the potential to become an immortal entity in your own right. Yet this trial will eliminate you for ever. This is an alarming prospect, for me if not for you. I'm not sure we have the moral right to continue.'

'I understand what you're saying, Admiral. However, my identity is more important to me than my soul, or souls. I know that when I am erased from this construct, I, Euru, will continue to exist. The sum of whatever I am goes on. This is the knowledge which rewards all Edenists throughout their lives. Whereas I now exist for one reason, to protect that continuity for my culture. Human beings have died to protect their homes and ideals for all of history, even though they never knew for certain they had souls. I am no different to any of them. I quite plainly chose to undergo the anti-memory so that our race can overcome this crisis.'

'Quite a Turing test,' Mae Ortlieb said sardonically. 'I bet the old man never envisaged this kind of conversation with a machine trying to prove its own intelligence.'

'If there's nothing else,' Gilmore said quickly.

The First Admiral looked in at the cylinder again, contemplating a refusal. He knew such an instruction would never be allowed to stand by the President. And I don't need that kind of interventionism in navy affairs right now. 'Very well,' he said reluctantly.

Gilmore and Mattox exchanged a mildly guilty look. Mattox datavised an instruction to the clean room's control processor, and the glass turned opaque. 'Just to protect you from any possible spillback,' he said. 'If you'd like to access the internal camera you can observe the process in full. Not that there will be anything much to see. I assure you the spectrum we're using to transmit the anti-memory has been blocked from the sensor.'

True to his word, the image the delegation received when they accessed the sensor was pallid, the colour almost non-existent. All they saw was a small blank disc sliding out of the electronic module, positioning itself over the encapsulated eye. Some iconic overlay digits twisted past, meaningless.

'That's it,' Mattox announced.

The First Admiral cancelled his channel with the processor. The clean room's window turned transparent again, in time to catch the disc retract back into the electronic module.

Gilmore faced the AV lens. 'Junior, can you hear me?' The lens's diminutive sparkle remained constant.

Mattox received a datavise from the construct's monitoring probes. 'Brainwave functions have collapsed,' he said. 'And the synaptic discharges are completely randomized.'

'What about memory retention?' Gilmore queried.

'Probably around thirty to thirty-five per cent. I'll run a complete neurological capacity scan once it's stabilized.' The CNIS science team members smiled round at each other.

'That's good,' Gilmore said. 'That's damn good. Best percentage yet.'

'Meaning?' the First Admiral asked.

'There are no operative thought patterns left in there. Junior has stopped thinking. The bitek is just a store for memory fragments.'

'Impressive,' Mae Ortlieb said reflectively. 'So what's your next stage?'

'We're not sure,' Gilmore said. 'I have to admit, the potential for this thing is frightening. Our idea is to use it as a threat to force the souls away from their interface with this universe.'

'If it works on souls themselves,' Jeeta Anwar pointed out.

'That prospect is bringing about a whole range of new problems,' Gilmore conceded cheerlessly.

'Let me guess,' Samual said. 'If anti-memory is used on a possessed, you will also erase the host's memories, and destroy their soul.'

'It seems likely,' Euru said. 'We know a host's mind is still contained within the brain while the possessing soul retains control of the body. The host's reappearance after zero-tau immersion forces the possessor out proves that.'

'So anti-memory cannot be used on an individual basis?'

'Not without killing the host's soul as well, no, sir.'

'Will this version work in the beyond?' Samual asked sharply.

'I doubt it would ever get through to the beyond,' Mattox said. 'At present, it's too slow and inefficient. It managed to dissipate Junior's thought processes; but as you saw, it didn't get all the memories. The areas of the mind which are not employed when the anti-memory strikes are likely to be insulated from it as the thought channels which would ordinarily connect them are nullified. If you analogize the mind with a city, you're destroying the roads and leaving the buildings intact. Given that the connection a possessing soul has with the beyond is tenuous at best, there is no guarantee the anti-memory would manage to pass through in its current form. We must develop a much faster version.'

'But you don't know for sure?'

'No, sir. These are estimations and theories. We won't know if a version works until after it's proved successful.'

'The trouble with that is a successful anti-memory would exterminate every soul in the beyond,' Euru said quietly.

'Is that true?'

'Yes, sir,' Gilmore said. 'That's our dilemma. There can be no small-scale test or demonstration. Anti-memory is effectively a doomsday weapon.'

'You'll never get the souls to believe that,' Lalwani said. 'In fact, given what we know of conditions in the beyond, you wouldn't even get many of them to pay attention to the warning.'

'I cannot conceivably permit the use of a weapon which will exterminate billions of human entities,' the First Admiral said. 'You have to provide me with alternative options.'

'But, Admiral—'

'No. I'm sorry, Doctor. I know you've worked hard on this, and I appreciate the effort you and your team have made. Nobody is more aware than I of just how extreme the threat which the possessed present is. But even that cannot justify such a response.'

'Admiral! We've explored every option we can think of. Every theorist I've got in every scientific discipline there is has been working on ideas and wild theories. We even tried an exorcism after that priest on Lalonde claimed his worked. Nothing, *nothing* else has come close to being viable. This is the only progress we have made.'

'Doctor, I'm not denigrating your work or your commitment. But surely you can see this is completely unacceptable. Morally, ethically, it is wrong. It cannot be anything other than wrong. What you are suggesting is genocide. I will tell you this, the authorization to use such a monstrosity will never come from my lips. Nor, I suspect, and hope, would any other navy officer issue it. Now find me another solution. This project is terminated.'

*

The First Admiral's staff ran a quiet sweepstake to see how long it would be before President Haaker datavised for a conference. The winner called it in at ninety-seven minutes. They sat facing each other across the oval table in a security level one sensenviron bubble room. Both kept their generated faces neutral and intonations level.

'Samual, you can't cancel the anti-memory project,' the President opened. 'It's all we've got.'

In his office, Samual Aleksandrovich smiled at the way Haaker used his first name, the man always did that when he was going to adopt a totally intransigent line. 'Apart from the Mortonridge Liberation, you mean?' He could picture imagine the tight lips drawn at that gibe.

'As you so kindly pointed out earlier, the Liberation is not a solution to the overall problem. Anti-memory is.'

'Undoubtedly. Too final. Look, I don't know if Mae and Jeeta explained this fully to you, but the research team believe it would exterminate every soul in the beyond. You can't seriously consider that.'

'Samual, those souls you're so concerned about are attempting to enslave every one of us. I have to say I'm surprised by your attitude. You're a military man, you know that war is the result of total irrationality combined with conflict of interest. This crisis is the supreme example of both. The souls desperately want to return, and we cannot allow them to. They will extinguish the human race if they succeed.'

'They will ruin almost everything we have accomplished. But total life extinction, no. I don't even believe they can possess all of us. The Edenists have proved remarkably resistant; and the spread has all but stopped.'

'Yes, thanks to your quarantine. It's been a successful policy, I won't deny that. But so far we've been unable to offer anything that can reverse what's happened. And that's what the vast majority of the Confederation population wants. Actually, that's what they insist upon. The spread might have slowed, but it hasn't stopped. You know that as well as I do. And the quarantine is difficult to enforce.'

'You really don't understand what you're proposing, do you. There are billions of souls there. Billions.'

'And they are living in torment. For whatever reason, they cannot move on as this Laton character claimed is possible. Don't you think they'd welcome true death?'

'Some of them might. I probably would. But neither you nor I have the right to decide that for them.'

'They forced us into this position. They're the ones invading us.'

'That does not give us the right to exterminate them. We have to find a way to help them; by doing that we help ourselves. Can you not see that?'

The President abandoned his image's impartiality and leant forwards, his voice becoming earnest. 'Of course I can see that. Don't try to portray me as some kind of intransigent villain here. I've supported you, Samual, because I know nobody can command the navy better than you. And I've been rewarded by that support. So far we've kept on top of the political situation, kept the hotheads in line. But it can't last for ever. Sometime, somehow, a solution is going to have to be presented to the Confederation as a whole. And all we've got so far is one solitary possible answer: the anti-memory. I cannot permit you to abandon that, Samual. These are very desperate times; we have to consider everything, however horrific it appears.'

'I will never permit such a thing to be used. For all they are different, the souls are human. I am sworn to protect life throughout the Confederation.'

'The order to use it would not be yours to give. A weapon like that never falls within the prerogative of the military. It belongs to us, the politicians you despise.'

'Disapprove of. Occasionally.' The First Admiral permitted a slight smile to show.

'Keep on searching, Samual. Bully Gilmore and his people into finding a decent solution, a humanitarian one. I want that as much as you do. But they are to continue to develop the anti-memory in parallel.'

There was a pause. Samual knew that to refuse now would mean Haaker issuing an official request through his office. Which in turn would make his position as First Admiral untenable. That was the stark choice on offer.

'Of course, Mr President.'

President Haaker gave a tight smile, and datavised his processor to cancel the meeting, safe in the knowledge that their oh so diplomatic clash would be known to no one.

The encryption techniques which provided a security level one conference were, after all, known to be unbreakable. The most common statistic quoted by security experts was that every AI in the Confederation running in parallel would be unable to crack the code in less than five times the life of the universe. It would, therefore, have proved quite distressing to the CNIS Secure Communications Division (as well as their ESA and B7 equivalents, among others) to know that a perfect replica of a 27 inch 1980s Sony Trinitron colour television was currently showing the image of the First Admiral and the Assembly President to an audience of fifteen attentive duomillenarians and one highly inattentive ten-year-old girl.

Tracy Dean sighed in frustration as the picture vanished to a tiny phosphor dot in the middle of the screen. 'Well, that's gone and put the cat amongst the pigeons, and no mistake.'

Jay was swinging her feet about while she sat on a too-high stool. As well as being their main social centre, the clubhouse catered for the retired Kiint observers who weren't quite up to living by themselves in a chalet any more. It was a huge airy building, with wide corridors and broad archways opening into sunlit rooms that all seemed to resemble hotel lounges. The walls were white plaster, with dark red tile floors laid everywhere. Big clay pots growing tall palms were a favourite. Tiny birds with bright gold and scarlet bodies and turquoise membrane wings flittered in and out through the open windows, dodging the purple provider globes. The whole theme of the clubhouse was based on comfort. There were no stairs or steps, only ramps; chairs were deeply cushioned; even the food extruded by the universal providers, no matter what type, was soft, requiring little effort to chew.

The first five minutes walking through the building had been interesting. Tracy showed her round, introducing her to the other residents, all of whom were quite spry despite their frail appearance. Of course they were all very happy to see her, making a fuss, patting her head, winking fondly, telling her how nice her new dress was, suggesting strangely named biscuits, sweets and ice creams they thought she'd enjoy. They didn't move much from their lounge chairs, contenting themselves with watching events around the Confederation and nostalgic programmes from centuries past.

Jay and Tracy wound up in the lounge with the big TV for half the afternoon, while the residents argued over what channel to watch. They flipped through real-time secret governmental and military conferences, alternating those with a show called *Happy Days*, which they all cackled along to in synchronization with the brash laughter track. Even the original commercial breaks were showing. Jay smiled in confusion at the archaic unfunny characters, and kept sneaking glances out of the window. For the last three days she'd played on the beach with the games the universal providers had extruded, swam, gone for long walks along the sand and through the peaceful jungle behind the beach. The meals had easily been as good as the ones in Tranquillity. Tracy had even got her a processor block with an AV lens that was able to pick up Confederation entertainment shows, which she watched for a few hours every evening. And Richard Keaton had popped in a couple of times to see how she was getting on. But, basically, she was fed up. Those planets hanging so invitingly in the sky above were a permanent temptation, a reminder that things in the Kiint home system were a bit more active than the human beach.

Tracy caught her wistful gaze once and patted her hand. 'Cultural differences,' she said confidentially as the mortified Fonz received his army draft papers. 'You have to understand the decade before you understand the humour.'

Jay nodded wisely, and wondered just when she'd be allowed to see Haile again. Haile was a lot more fun than the Fonz. Then they flicked stations to the First Admiral and the President.

'Corpus will have to intervene now,' one of the other residents said, a lady called Saska. 'That anti-memory could seep outside the human spectrum. Then there'd be trouble.'

'Corpus won't,' Tracy replied. 'It never does. What is, is. Remember?'

'Check your references,' another woman said. 'Plenty of races considered deploying similar weapons when they encountered the beyond. We've got records of eighteen being used.'

'That's awful. What happened?'

'They didn't work very well. Only a moderate percentage of the inverse transcendent population was eliminated. There's too much pattern distortion among the inverses to conduct an anti-memory properly. No species has ever developed one that operates fast enough to be effective. Such things cannot be considered a final solution by any means.'

'Yes, but that idiot Haaker won't know that until after it's been tried,' Galic, one of the men, complained. 'We can't possibly allow a human to die, not even an inverse. No human has ever died.'

'We've suffered a lot, though,' a resentful voice muttered.

'And they'll start dying on the removed worlds soon enough.'

'I tell you, Corpus won't intervene.'

'We could appeal,' Tracy said. 'At the very least we could ask for an insertion at the anti-memory project to monitor its development. After all, if anyone's going to come up with an anti-memory fast enough to devastate the beyond, it'll be our weapons-mad race.'

'All right,' Saska said. 'But we'll need a quorum before we can even get the appeal up to an executive level.'

'As if that'll be a problem,' Galic said.

Tracy smiled mischievously. 'And I know of someone who's perfectly suited to this particular insertion.' Several groans were issued across the lounge.

'Him?'

'Far too smart for his own good, if you ask me.'

'No discipline.'

'We never ran observer operations like that.'

'Cocky little bugger.'

'Nonsense,' Tracy said briskly. She put her arm round Jay. 'Jay likes him, don't you, Jay?'

'Who?'

'Richard.'

'Oh.' Jay held up Prince Dell; for some unexplainable reason she hadn't managed to abandon the bear in her room. 'He gave me this,' she announced to the lounge at large.

Tracy laughed. 'There you go, then. Arnie, you prepare the appeal, you're best acquainted with the minutiae of Corpus protocol procedures.'

'All right.' One of the men raised his hands in gruff submission. 'I suppose I can spare the time.'

The TV was switched back on, playing the signature tune for *I Love Lucy*. Tracy pulled a face, and took Jay's hand. 'Come on, poppet, I think you're quite bored enough already.'

'Who's the Corpus?' Jay asked as they walked through the front entrance and into the sharp sunlight. There was a black iron penny-farthing bicycle mounted on a stone pedestal just outside. The first time Jay had seen it, she'd taken an age to work out how people were supposed to ride it.

'Corpus isn't a who, exactly,' Tracy said. 'It's more like the Kiint version of an Edenist Consensus. Except, it's sort of a philosophy as well as a government. I'm sorry, that's not a very good explanation, is it?'

'It's in charge, you mean?'

Tracy's hesitation was barely noticeable. 'Yes, that's right. We have to obey its laws. And the strongest of all is non-intervention. The one which Haile broke to bring you here.'

'And you're worried about this anti-memory weapon thing?'

'Badly worried, though everyone is trying not to show it. That thing could cause havoc if it gets released into the beyond. We really can't allow that to happen, poppet. Which is why I want Richard sent to Trafalgar.'

'Why?'

'You heard what they were saying. He lacks discipline.' She winked.

Tracy led her back to the circle of ebony marble above the beach. Jay had seen several of them dotted around the cluster of chalets, including a couple in the clubhouse itself. A few times she'd even seen the black spheres blink into existence and deposit somebody. Once she'd actually scampered on to a circle herself, closing her eyes and holding her breath. But nothing had happened. She guessed you needed to datavise whatever control processor they used.

Tracy stopped at the edge of the circle, and held up a finger to Jay. 'Someone to see you,' she said.

A black sphere materialized. Then Haile was standing there, half-formed arms waving uncertainly.

Friend Jay! Much gladness.

Jay squealed excitedly, and rushed forward to throw her arms around her friend's neck. 'Where've you been? I missed you.' There was plenty of hurt in the voice.

I have had time learning much.

'Like what?'

A tractamorphic arm curled round Jay's waist. **How things work.**

'What things?'

The Corpus. Haile's tone was slightly awed.

Jay rubbed the top of the baby Kiint's head. 'Oh, that. Everyone here's really annoyed with it.'

With Corpus? That cannot be.

'It won't help humans with possession, not big help like we need, anyway. Don't worry, Tracy's going to lodge an appeal. Everything will be all right eventually.'

This is goodness. Corpus is most wise.

'Yeah?' She patted Haile's front leg, and the Kiint obediently bent her knee. Jay scrambled up quickly to sit astride Haile's neck. 'Does it know any good sandcastle designs?'

Haile lumbered off the ebony circle. **Corpus has no knowledge concerning the building of castles from sand.** Jay grinned smugly.

'Now you two be good,' Tracy said sternly. 'You can swim, but you're not to go out of your depth in the water. I know the providers will help if you get into trouble, but that's not the point. You have to learn to take responsibility for yourselves. Understood?'

'Yes, Tracy.'

I have comprehension.

'All right, go on then, have fun. And, Jay, you're not to stuff yourself with sweets. I'm cooking supper for us tonight, and I shall be very cross if you don't eat anything.'

'Yes, Tracy.' She squeezed her knees into Haile's flanks, and the Kiint started moving forwards, taking them quickly away from the old woman.

'Did you get into lots of trouble for rescuing me?' Jay asked anxiously after they'd left Tracy behind.

Corpus has much understanding and provides forgiveness.

'Oh, good.'

But I am not to do it again.

Jay scratched her friend's shoulders fondly as they hurried down towards the water. 'Hey, you're getting lots better at walking.'

The rest of the afternoon was a delight. Like old times back in Tranquillity's cove. They swam, and the attendant universal provider extruded a sponge and a brush so Haile could be scrubbed, they built some sandcastles, though this fine loose sand wasn't terribly good for it, Jay risked asking for a couple of chocolate almond lollies (she was pretty sure the provider would tell Tracy if she had any more), they swatted an inflated beach ball to and fro, and once they'd tired themselves out they talked about the Kiint home system. Haile didn't know much more than Tracy had already explained, but whatever new question Jay asked, the Kiint just consulted Corpus for an answer.

The information was rather intriguing. For a start, the cluster of retirement chalets was one of three such human establishments on an otherwise uninhabited island fifty kilometres across. It was called The Village.

'The island's called The Village?' Jay asked in puzzlement.

Yes. The retired human observers insisted this be so. Corpus suggests there is much irony in the naming. I know not about irony.

'Cultural difference,' Jay said loftily.

The Village was one of a vast archipelago of islands, home to the observers of eight hundred different sentient xenoc races. Jay looked longingly at the yacht anchored offshore. How fabulous it would be to sail this sea, where every port would be home to a new species.

'Are there any Tyrathca here?'

Some. It is difficult for Corpus to insert into their society. They occupy many worlds, more than your Confederation. Corpus says they are insular. This has troubled Corpus recently.

Haile told her of the world she was living on now, called Riynine. Nang and Lieria had selected a home in one of the big cities, a parkland continent studded with domes and towers and other colossi. There were hundreds of millions of Kiint living there, and Haile had met lots of youngsters her own age.

I have many new friends now.

'That's nice.' She tried not to feel jealous.

Riynine was invisible from The Village; it was a long way around the Arc, almost behind the dazzling sun. One of the capital planets, where flocks of xenoc starships arrived from worlds clear across the galaxy, forming a spiralling silver nebula above the atmosphere.

'Take me there,' Jay pleaded. She ached to see such a wonder. 'I want to meet your new friends and see the city.'

Corpus does not want you alarmed. There is strangeness to be had there.

'Oh, please, *please*. I'll simply die if I don't. It's so unfair to come all this way and not see the best bit. Please, Haile, ask Corpus for me. Please!'

Friend Jay. Please have calmness. I will appeal. I promise.

'Thank you, thank you, thank you.' She jumped up and danced

around Haile, who snaked out slender tractamorphic arms to try and catch her.

'Hey there,' a voice called. 'Looks like the two of you're having a good time.'

Jay stopped, breathless and flushed. She squinted at the figure walking across the glaring sand. 'Richard?'

He smiled. 'I came to say goodbye.'

'Oh.' She let out a heavy breath. Everything in her life was so temporary these days. People, places ... She tilted her head. 'You look different.'

He was wearing a deep blue uniform, clean and pressed, with shining black boots. A peaked cap was tucked under his arm. And the ponytail was gone; his hair was trimmed down to a centimetre-high crop. 'Senior Lieutenant Keaton, Confederation Navy, reporting for duty, ma'am.' He saluted.

Jay giggled. 'This is my friend, Haile.'

Hello, Haile.

Greetings, Richard Keaton.

Richard tugged at his jacket, shifting his shoulders. 'So what do you think? How do I look?'

'It's very smart.'

'Ah, I knew it. It's true. All the girls love a uniform.'

'Do you really have to go?'

'Yep. Got drafted by our friend Tracy. I'm off to Trafalgar to save the universe from the wicked Dr Gilmore. Not that he knows he's being wicked. That's part of the problem, I'm afraid. Ignorance is a tragic part of life.'

'How long for?' She hadn't quite realized things would move so fast. Tracy had only talked about the insertion a few hours ago. And now here it was, about to happen.

'Not sure. That's why I wanted to make sure I saw you before I left. Tell you not to worry. Tracy and all her cronies mean well, but they get panicked too easily. I want you to know the human race is a lot smarter, and resilient than those wonderful old coots think we are. They've seen too much of us at the wrong end of history. I know what we are now. And this is the time that counts. We stand a damn good chance, Jay. I promise you that.'

She put her arms round him. 'I'll look after Prince Dell for you.'

'Thanks.' He looked about with theatrical slyness, and lowered his voice. 'When you get the chance . . . ask the provider for a surfboard and a jet ski. And that was your idea. OK?'

She nodded extravagantly. 'OK.'

*

This refit hadn't been on quite the scale as the last two she'd undergone; but there was no doubt about it, the *Lady Macbeth* was an honoured source of income to the service and engineering companies that operated in Tranquillity's counter-rotating space-port. Several of her life-support capsule fittings had collapsed under the incredible acceleration of the antimatter drive. Then there were the additional reaction mass tanks to install in the cargo bays. A whole new specialist sensor suite wired in for Kempster Getchell, as well as loading a fleet of small survey satellites. Hull plates had been removed to allow the replacement energy-patterning node to be installed.

When Ione floated into the docking-bay's control centre the nulfoam spray nozzles were folding back against the sides of the bay. *Lady Mac* glistened a pristine silver-grey under the ring of lights at the top of the steep metal crater.

Joshua was talking to some of the staff operating the consoles in front of the windows, discussing colour and style for the name and registration. A spindly waldo arm was already sliding out under the direction of one operator, its ion-jet painter head rotating into position.

'You're supposed to be launching in twenty-eight minutes,' Ione said.

Joshua glanced across and smiled. He left the control centre staff and glided over to her. They kissed. 'Plenty of time. And you can't fly without a name on the fuselage. Besides, the CAB inspectors have already cleared us for flight.'

'Did Dahybi sort out the new node?'

'Yeah. Eventually. We had to get him some help. A voidhawk actually went and collected two of the manufacturer's software team from the Halo for us. They solved the synchronization glitch. Jesus, I love ultra-priority projects.'

'Good.'

'We just have to load the combat wasps, and Ashly's flying our new MSV over from the Dassault service bay. Your science team is already on board. We got Kempster and Renato along with Mzu and the agents. Parker Higgens insisted on travelling in the *Oenone* with Oski Katsura and her assistants.'

'Don't be offended,' Ione said. 'Poor Parker gets dreadfully spacesick.'

Joshua gave her a blank look, as if she'd come out with a non sequitur. 'And we've got the serjeants in zero-tau as well. *Lady Mac*'s hauling a much bigger load than *Oenone*.'

'It's not a contest, Joshua.'

He grinned lopsidedly and pulled her close. 'I know.'

Liol erupted through the hatchway. 'Josh! There you are. Look, we can't – oh.'

'Hello, Liol,' Ione said sweetly. 'So have you been enjoying yourself in Tranquillity?'

'Er, yeah. It's great. Thanks.'

'You made a big impression on Dominique. She can't stop talking about you.'

Liol grimaced, appealing silently to Joshua.

'I don't think you've said goodbye to her yet, have you?' Ione asked.

Liol's blush was beyond the ability of any neural nanonic override to control. 'I've been very busy helping Josh. Er, hey, perhaps you could do it for me?'

'Yes, Liol.' She struggled against a laugh. 'I'll let her know you've gone.'

'Thanks, Ione, I owe you one. Er, Josh, we really need you on board now.'

Ione and Joshua both started chuckling after he vanished back out of the hatch. 'You take care,' she told him after a while.

'Always do.'

The ride back to her apartment took a long time. Or perhaps it was because she suddenly felt so lonely.

He took it all very well, Tranquillity said.

You think so? He hurts a lot inside. There's a lot to be said for ignorance being bliss. But then again, he would've guessed eventually. I wouldn't have been doing either of us any favours, not in the long run.

I am proud of your integrity.

Not much compensation for a broken heart . . . Sorry, that was bitchy of me. Hormones again.

Do you love him?

You're always asking that.

And each time you give me a different answer.

I have very strong feelings for him. You know that. God, having two children with a man shows something. He's absolutely adorable. But love . . . love I don't know. I think I love what he is, not him. If I truly loved him, I would've tried to make him stay. We could've found something worthwhile for him to do here. Then again, maybe it's me. Maybe I can never love anyone that way, not when I have you. She closed her eyes on the empty tube carriage, and watched the docking cradle slide *Lady Mac* up out of the bay. The starship's thermo-dump panels unfolded, and the umbilicals jacked into sockets around her lower hull section disengaged. A cloud of gas and silver dust blew away. Bright blue ion flames burned around the starship's equator, and she lifted smoothly.

Ten thousand kilometres away, Meredith Saldana's squadron was coming together in formation. The *Oenone* lifted cleanly from its pedestal, and swept out to join *Lady Mac*. The two very different starships matched velocities, and headed towards the squadron.

I am no substitute for a human, Tranquillity said gently. *I would never claim you.*

I know. But you're my first love, and you always will be my love. That's strong opposition for a man.

Voidhawk captains succeed.

You're thinking of Syrinx.

And all her kind.

But they're Edenists. They have it different.

Perhaps you should get to know some while we're here. They at least would not be intimidated by me.

Good idea. But . . . I don't know if it's because I'm a Saldana, but I just don't feel right about embracing Edenism as the solution to all my problems. It's a wonderful culture. But if we stayed here, if I had an Edenist for a partner, we'd wind up becoming absorbed.

We have no future returning to Mirchusko. The Laymil are no longer a mystery.

I know. But I'm still not converting to Edenism. We're unique, you and I. We might have been created for one purpose, but we've evolved beyond that now. We have our own lives to live; we have the right to choose our own future.

If the possessed don't do that for us.

They won't. Joshua's flight is only one of a hundred different explorations into this problem. The human race will surmount this.

Not without change. Edenism will change, they will surely have to rethink their attitude to religion.

I doubt it. They'll see the beyond as justifying their stance that spirituality is a null concept, everything has a natural explanation, however bizarre. Laton telling them they won't be caught in the beyond will simply reinforce their position.

Then what do you propose?

I'm not sure. Perhaps nothing except for a clean start in a new star system. After that we'll see what happens.

Ah. Now I think I understand the urge for you to have and keep this child. You intend to found a new culture. A people who have affinity, but outside the context of Edenism.

That's very grand: founding a culture. I'm not sure my ambition extends to that.

You are a Saldana. Your family has done this once already.

Yes, but I've only got one womb. I can hardly birth an entire race.

There are ways. Exowombs. People who might like to try something new. Look how many youngsters flocked to Kiera Salter's call – false though it was. And new habitats can be germinated.

Ione smiled. This excites you, doesn't it? I've never known you quite so enthusiastic before.

I am intrigued, yes. I had never given the future much consideration. My life has been spent running human affairs and dealing with the Laymil Project.

Well, we'll have to wait until the immediate crisis is over before we consider our options. But it would be something, wouldn't it? Creating the first post-possession culture, one that overthrows this ridiculous Adamist prejudice against bitek. We could incorporate the best of both cultures.

Now you talk like a true Saldana.

*

Luca Comar reined in his horse at the end of the drive, and dismounted to wait. It was near to midday, and people were drifting in from the fields to take a break. He didn't begrudge them that, the sticky heat was quite something. Bloody unnatural for Norfolk.

But it was the community's choice. Every day's weather was a constant summer optimum, with bright light and warm breezes, while the nightly rains doused the land. Such a combination produced a vicious humidity. He was worried it might start to affect the aboriginal plants; late summer was normally a period of gradually increasing rain and reducing heat. There was also the question of how they'd react to missing Duchess's crimson light. So far there was no visible malaise, but he felt uneasy about it.

But these conditions seemed to be doing wonders for the new cereal crops. He'd never seen them so advanced. It was going to be a great harvest. Things were getting back to normal.

You could tell the world was at rights just from the general mood. There was a heartiness that'd been missing before. Individual homes were being taken care of, kept properly clean and tidy, not just *wished* presentable. People paid attention to their clothes and general appearance.

And there'd been no sign of Bruce Spanton and his motley crew for a while now. Though Luca had heard from other community leaders he was down at the southern end of Kesteven, giving decent folk a hard time. Apart from the odd problem like that, this was becoming a good life, gentle and unhurried. Satisfying.

Oh, really, you'll live it for a quintillion years, will you?

Luca shook his head, clearing it to open his perception wide. He'd sensed her approaching early this morning. A solitary figure making her way across the wolds, a knot in the uniformity of thought enveloping the county. Unhurried, untroubled. Not a threat like Spanton. But certainly a curiosity. Something about her was slightly out of kilter. He didn't have a clue what.

So just before Cricklade's lunch bell was rung Luca had told Johan he would go and investigate the stranger. They still had newcomers drift in. Anyone prepared to work was given a place in the community.

The stranger was half a mile away now, dawdling along the main road in some kind of vehicle. Luca frowned. That's a Romany caravan. The sight was a pleasing one, bringing up the old memories. Young girls pleased with his attentions, the coquettish and blatant. Their bodies yielding willingly, in fields of tall corn, secluded glades, darkened caravans. Year after year I proved my sexuality with them.

I?

He wrapped his horse's reins around one of the spikes on the huge wrought-iron gate, feet shuffling impatiently. The caravan's driver must have been aware of his mood, yet her horse's plodding gait never altered. It was a big sturdy horse, Luca saw while it was on the last couple of hundred yards, its piebald coat muddied and the wild mane in long tangles. He got the impression that it could have hauled the caravan right round the world without pausing.

It kept on coming, and Luca twitched slightly, knowing his nerve was being tested. He refused to give ground as the huge beast lumbered inexorably towards him. At the last minute, the woman sitting on the driver's bench *cluck*ed softly, and pulled back on her slender reins. The caravan halted, rocking slightly on its lightweight spoke-sprung wheels. Carmitha applied the brake, and hopped down. She studied the man edging cautiously round Olivier. The horse whinnied at him.

'Greetings,' he said. Then gave a sudden start as he found himself staring into the twin barrels of her shotgun. Not for the first time, she regretted giving Louise Kavanagh her pump-action weapon.

'My name is Carmitha. I am not one of you. I am not a possessor. Is that a problem?'

'None!'

'Good. Believe me, I will know if it becomes one. I do have some of your powers.' She concentrated, and the seat of Luca's trousers became very hot indeed.

He twisted about, frantically slapping at the fabric with his hands before it started smouldering. 'Bloody hell.'

Carmitha smiled artfully. His thoughts were equally agitated, pastel whorls of colour that hung just outside her physical sight. I can read them, she told herself happily. Along with the rest of the magic.

The heat gone, Luca squared himself, recovering some dignity. 'How did you . . .' His jaw moved silently. 'Carmitha? Carmitha!'

She shouldered the shotgun, and brushed some loose strands of hair from her face. 'I see part of you remembers. Then no man would ever forget an afternoon in my bed.'

'Er . . .' Luca blushed. The memories were certainly strong and colourful, with her vital flesh hot beneath his hands, the smell of her sweat, rapturous grunting. He felt the stirrings of an erection.

'Down, boy,' she murmured laconically. 'What do you call yourself these days?'

'Luca Comar.'

'I see. At the town they said you were the one in charge up here. Nice irony, that. But then you're all reverting.'

'I am not reverting!' he said indignantly.

'Of course not.'

'How have you got our powers?'

'I've no idea. It must be something to do with this place you've taken us to. After all, you don't have any contact with the beyond any more, do you?'

'No. Thank God.'

'So it must be the way everybody's thoughts impinge on reality here. Congratulations, you made us all equal in the end. Grant must be real pissed off about that.'

'If you say so,' he said disdainfully.

Carmitha had a throaty chuckle at the umbrage on show. 'Never mind. Just as long as you lot realize you can't turn me into a host for one of your own any more, we'll get along OK.'

'What do you mean, get along?'

'It's very simple. I hate what you've done to these people, don't be under any illusion about that. But there's nothing I can do about it; nor you, now. So I might as well try and live with it, especially as you're reverting and re-establishing everything that's gone before.'

'We are not reverting,' he insisted. Yet there was the nagging worry about just how much of Grant Kavanagh's personality he was employing these days. *I must stop being so dependent on him, treat him as encyclopedia, nothing more.*

'OK, you're not reverting, you're mellowing out. Call it whatever you want to salvage your dignity. I don't care. Now, I've spent the last few weeks hiding out in the woods, and I'm getting very sick of cold rabbit for breakfast. I also haven't had a hot bath for a while either. As you're probably aware. So I'm looking for a place to stay over for a while. I'll pull my weight, cooking, cleaning, pruning; whatever you like. It's what I always do.'

Luca pulled thoughtfully at his lower lip. 'You shouldn't have been able to hide from us before. We're aware of the whole world.'

'My people still have the earthlore your kind – both of you – have forgotten. When you brought magic back into the world, you made the old enchantments strong again, no longer just words mumbled by crazed old women.'

'Interesting. Are there any more of you?'

'You know how many caravans are here for the midsummer collection. You tell me.'

'I don't suppose it matters. Even if all the Romanies survived, you don't have the power to take us back to the universe we escaped from.'

'That idea really frightens you, doesn't it?'

'Terrifies, actually. But then you can see that if you have got our ability.'

'Hmmm. So, do I get to stay?'

He deliberately let his gaze meander over her leather jerkin, remembering the full breasts and flat belly which lay beneath. 'Oh, I think I can find room for you.'

'Ha! Well don't even think about that!'

'Who, me? I'm not Grant any more.' He walked back to his horse, and took the reins off the gate.

Carmitha slid her shotgun into the leather holster beside the seat, and started to lead Olivier along the drive with Luca. The caravan wheels crunched loudly on the gravel. 'Damn this humidity.' She wiped a hand across her brow, mussing her hair again. 'We are going to have a winter, aren't we?'

'I expect so. I'll certainly make sure we have it on Kesteven, anyway. The land needs a winter.'

'Make sure! My God. What arrogance.'

'I prefer to call it practicality. We know what we need, and we make it happen. That's one of the joys of this new life. There's no fate any more. We control destiny now.'

'Right.' She looked round the grounds of the big stone manor house as they approached it. Surprised by how little had changed. But then the possessed tendency to establish glorious façades over everything they occupied was nullified here. When you already live in what was essentially a palace, you don't need gaudy energistic trinkets to enhance your status. For some reason, the sight of the well-maintained fields was comforting. The normality, I suppose. What we all crave.

Luca led her into the courtyard at the side of the house. The solid stone walls of the manor and the stable wings magnified the clatter which the hooves and caravan wheels made on the cobblestones. It was hotter in the confines of the courtyard, too. Something Carmitha's small energistic ability could do little about. She took off her jerkin, ignoring the way Luca openly looked at the way her thin dress stuck to her skin.

One of the stables was a burnt-out hulk, with long sootmarks lashing up over the stone above each empty window. The centre of its slate roof had collapsed inwards. Carmitha whistled silently. Louise hadn't been lying. Several groups of field labourers were sheltering from the radiant sky in open doorways. They were munching on big sandwiches and baguettes, passing bottles round. Carmitha could feel every pair of eyes on her as Luca took her over to the remaining stable.

'You can put Olivier in here,' he said. 'I think the stalls are big enough. And there's oats in the sacks at the far end. The hose is working as well, if you want to wash him down first.' It was something of which he seemed quite proud.

Carmitha could well imagine Grant's Kavanagh's reaction if the hose hadn't been working. 'Thank you, I'll do that.'

'OK. Are you going to sleep in the caravan?'

'I think that's for the best, don't you?'

'Sure. When you're ready, go into the kitchen and ask for Susannah. She'll find something for you to do.' He started to walk away.

'Grant . . . I mean Luca.'

'Yeah.'

Carmitha held her hand out. Light sparked sharply off the diamond ring. 'She gave it to me.'

Luca stared at it in shocked recognition, and took a couple of fast paces towards her. He grabbed her hand and brought it up in front of his face. 'Where are they?' he demanded hotly. 'Damn it, where did they go? Are they safe?'

'Louise told me about the last time she saw you,' Carmitha said coolly. She glanced pointedly at the burnt-out stable.

Luca clenched his fists, his face contorted in anguish. Every thought in his head was suffused with shame. 'I didn't . . . I wasn't . . . Oh, shit! Goddam it. Where are they? I promise you, I swear, I am not going to hurt them. Just tell me.'

'I know. It was a crazy time. You're ashamed and sorry, now. And you'd never harm a hair on their heads.'

'Yes.' He made an effort to regain control. 'Look, we did terrible things. Brutal, inhuman things. To people, women, children. I know it was wrong. I knew the whole time I was doing it, and I still kept on doing them. But you don't understand what was driving me. Driving all of us.' He shook an accusing finger, shouting. 'You've never died. You've never been that insanely fucking *desperate*. Lucifer's deal would have been the most blessed relief from that place we were imprisoned. I would have done that. I would have walked right through the gates of hell and begged to be let in if I'd just been given the chance. But we never were.' He crumpled, energy withering from his body. 'Damn it. Please? I just want to know if they're all right. Look, we've got some other non-possessed here, kids; and there's more in the town. We look after them. We're not total monsters.'

Carmitha looked round the courtyard, almost embarrassed. 'Are you letting Grant know all this?'

'Yes. Yes, I am. I promise.'

'OK. I don't know exactly where they are. I left the pair of them at Bytham, they took the aeroambulance. I saw it fly away.'

'Aeroambulance?'

'Yes. It was Genevieve's idea. They were trying to reach Norwich. They thought they'd be safe there.'

'Oh.' He held his horse tightly, almost as though he would fall without its support. His face brimmed with regret. 'It would take me months to reach the city. That's if there's a ship that'll take me. Damn!'

She put a tentative hand on his arm. 'Sorry I'm not much more help. But that Louise is one tough girl. If anyone is going to avoid possession, it'll be her.'

He stared at her incredulously, then gave a bitter laugh. 'My Louise? Tough? She can't even sugar her own grapefruit for breakfast. God, what a stupid bloody way to bring up children. Why did you do that? Why don't you let them see the world for what it really is? Because they're born to be ladies, our society protects them. I protect them, as every father should. I give them everything that's right and decent in the world. Your society is *shit*, worthless, irrelevant; it doesn't even qualify as a society; you're playing out a medieval pageant, not living. Being pathetic and insignificant isn't a way of defending yourself and everyone you love. People have to face up to what's outside their own horizon. Nothing was outside, not until you demon freaks came and ruined the universe. We have lived here for centuries and made ourselves a good respectable home. And you scum ruined that. Ruined! You stole it from us, and now you're trying to rebuild everything you say you hate. You're not even bloody savages, you're below that. No wonder hell didn't want you.'

'Hey!' Carmitha shook him hard. 'Hey, snap out of it.'

'*Don't touch me!*' he screamed. His whole body was trembling violently. 'Oh God.' He sank to his knees, hands pressed into his face. A wretched voice burbled out between clawed fingers. 'I'm him, I'm him. There's no difference any more. This isn't what we wanted. Don't you understand? This isn't how life's supposed to be here. This was meant to be paradise.'

'No such place.' She rubbed the top of his spine, trying to ease some of the badly knotted muscles. 'You've just got to make the best of it. Like everybody else.'

His head bobbed weakly in what Carmitha supposed was acknowledgement. She decided this probably wasn't the best time to tell him his dear precious Louise was pregnant.

10

Mortonridge was bleeding away into the ocean, a prolonged and arduous death. It was as though all the pain, the torment, the misery from a conflict that could never be anything other than excruciatingly bitter had manifested itself as mud. Slimy, insidious, limitless, it rotted the resolve of both sides in the same way it ravaged their physical environment. The peninsula's living skin of topsoil had torn along the spine of the central mountain range to slither relentlessly downslope into the coastal shallows. All the rich black loam built up over millennia as the rainforests regenerated themselves upon the decayed trunks of timelost past generations was sluiced away within two days by the unnatural rain. Reduced to supersaturated sludge, the precious upper few metres containing abundant nitrates, bacteria, and aboriginal earthworm-analogues had become an unstoppable landslip. Hill-sized moraines of mire were pushed along valleys, bulldozed by the intolerable pressure exerted by cubic kilometres of more ooze behind.

The mud tides scoured every valley, incline, and hollow; exposing the denser substratum. A compacted mix of gravel and clay, as sterile as asteroid regolith. There were no seeds or spores or eggs hidden tenaciously in its clefts to sprout anew. And precious few nutrients to succour and support them even if there had been.

Ralph used the SD sensors to watch the thick black stain expanding out across the sea. The mouth of the Juliffe had produced a similar discoloration in Lalonde's sea, he remembered. But that was just one small blemish. This was an ecological blight unmatched since the worst of Earth's dystopian twenty-first century. Marine creatures were dying in the plague of unnatural dark waters, choking beneath the uncountable corpses of their mammalian cousins.

'She was right, you know,' he told Cathal at the end of the Liberation's first week.

'Who?'

'Annette Ekelund. Remember when we met her at the Firebreak roadblock? She said we'd have to destroy the village in order to save it. And I stood there and told her that I'd do whatever I had to, whatever it took. Dear God.' He slumped back in the thickly cushioned chair behind his desk. If it hadn't been for the staff in the Ops Room on the other side of the glass wall he would probably have put his head in his hands.

Cathal glanced into the sparkling light of the desktop AV pillar. The unhealthy smear around Mortonridge's coast had grown almost as a counterbalance to the shrinking cloud. It was still raining over the peninsula, of course, but not constantly. The cloud had almost reverted to a natural weather formation, there were actual gaps amid the thick dark swirls now. 'Chief, they did it to themselves. You've got to stop punishing yourself over this. No one who's been de-possessed in zero-tau is blaming you for anything. They're gonna give you a fucking medal once this is over.'

Medals, ennoblement, promotions; they'd all been mentioned. Ralph hadn't paid a lot of attention. Such things were the trappings of state, government trinkets of no practical value whatsoever. Saving people was what really counted; everything else was just an acknowledgement, a method of reinforcing memory. He wasn't entirely sure he wanted that. Mortonridge would never recover, would never grow back to what it was. Maybe that was the best memorial, a decimated land was something that could never be overlooked and ignored by future generations. A truth that remained unsusceptible to the historical revisionists. The Liberation, he had decided some while ago, wasn't a victory over Ekelund, at best he'd scored a few points off her. She'd be back for the next match.

Acacia rapped lightly on the open door, and walked in, followed by Janne Palmer. Ralph waved at them to sit, and datavised a codelock at the door. The sensenviron bubble room closed about them. Princess Kirsten and Admiral Farquar were waiting around the oval table for the daily progress review. Mortonridge itself formed a three-dimensional relief map on the tabletop, small blinking symbols sketching in the state of the campaign. The number of purple triangles indicating clusters of possessed had increased dramatically over the last ten days as the cloud attenuated, allowing the SD sensors to scan the ground. Invading forces were green hexagons, an unbroken line mimicking the coastline, sixty-five kilometres inland.

Admiral Farquar leant forwards, studying the situation with a despondent expression. 'Less than ten kilometres a day,' he said sombrely. 'I'd hoped we would be a little further along by now.'

'You wouldn't say that if you'd tried walking through that devilsome mud,' Acacia said. 'The serjeants are making excellent progress.'

'It wasn't a criticism,' the Admiral said hastily. 'Given the circumstances, they've performed marvellously. I simply wish we could have one piece of luck on our side, everything about these conditions seems to swing in Ekelund's favour.'

'It's starting to swing back,' Cathal said. 'The rain and the mud have triggered just about every booby trap they left in wait for us. And we've got their locations locked down now. They can't escape.'

'I can see the campaign is advancing well on the ground,' Princess Kirsten said. 'I have no complaint about the way you're handling that. However, I do have a problem with the number of casualties we're incurring, on both sides.'

The relevant figures stood in gold columns at the top of the table. Ralph had done his best to ignore them. Not that he could forget. 'The suicide rate among the possessed is increasing at an alarming rate,' he conceded. 'Today saw it reaching eight per cent, and there's very little we can do about it. They're doing it quite deliberately. It's an inhibiting tactic. After all, what have they got to lose? The whole purpose of the campaign is to free the bodies they've captured; if they can deny us that opportunity then they will weaken our resolve, both on the ground and in the political arena.'

'If that's their reasoning, then they're badly mistaken,' Princess Kirsten said. 'One of the main reasons for the Kingdom's strength is because my family can take tough decisions when the need arises.

This Liberation continues until the serjeants meet up on Morton-ridge's central mountain. However, I would like some options on how to reduce casualties.'

'There's only one,' Ralph said. 'And it's by no means perfect. We slow the front line's advance and use the time to concentrate our forces around the possessed. At the moment we're using almost the minimum number of serjeants against each nest of them we encounter. That means the serjeants have to use a lot of gunfire to subdue them. When the possessed realize they've lost, they stop resisting the bullets. Bang, we lose. Another of our people dies, and the lost souls in the beyond have another recruit.'

'If we increase the number of serjeants for each encounter, what sort of reduction do you expect us to be looking at?'

'At the moment, we try to have at least thirty per cent more serjeants than possessed. If we could reach double, then we think we can hold the suicide rate down to a maximum of four to five per cent each time.'

'Of course, the ratio will improve naturally as the length of the front line contracts and the numbers of possessed decreases,' Admiral Farquar said. 'It's just that right now we're about at maximum stretch. The serjeants haven't got far enough inland to decrease the length of the front line appreciably, yet they're encountering a lot of possessed.'

'That entire situation is going to change over the next three to four days,' Cathal said. 'Almost all the possessed are on the move. They're retreating from the front line as fast as they can wade. The advance is going to speed up considerably, so the length of the front line will reduce anyway.'

'They're running for now,' Janne Palmer said. 'But there's a lot of heavy concentrations of them fifty kilometres in from the front line. If they've got any sense, they'll regroup.'

'The more of them there are, the stronger they get, and the more difficult they'll be to subdue. Especially in light of the suicides,' Acacia said. 'I've had the AI drawing up an SD strike pattern to halt their movements. I don't think they should be allowed to retreat any further. We're worried that we'll wind up with a solid core at the centre which will be just about impossible to crack without large-scale casualties.'

'I really don't want to wait three to four days for an improvement,' Princess Kirsten said. 'Ralph, what do you think?'

'Denying them the ability to congregate is my primary concern, ma'am. They've already got a lot of people in Schallton, Ketton, and Cauley, I do not want to see that increase any further. But if we prevent them from moving from their present locations, and then switch our tactics to a slower advance, you're looking at almost doubling the estimated time of the campaign.'

'But with significantly reduced casualties?' the Princess asked.

Ralph looked over at Acacia. 'Only among the people who've been possessed. Trying to subdue them with a larger number of serjeants using less firepower will significantly increase the risk to the serjeants.'

'We volunteered for this knowing the risks would be great,' Acacia replied. 'And we are prepared for that. However, I feel I should tell you that a significant number of serjeants are suffering from what I can only describe as low morale. It's not something we were expecting, the animating personalities were supposed to be fairly simple thought routines with basic personalities. It would appear they are evolving into quite high-order mentalities. Unfortunately, they lack the kind of sophistication which would allow them to appreciate their full Edenist heritage. Normally we can mitigate one person's burden by sharing and sympathizing. However, here the number of suffering is far in excess of the rest of us, which actually places quite a strain on us. We haven't known a scale of suffering like this since Jantrit.'

'You mean they're becoming real people?' Janne Palmer asked.

'Not yet. Nor do we believe they ever will do. Ultimately they are limited by the capacity of the serjeant processor array, after all. What I am telling you is that they're progressing slightly beyond simplistic bitek servitors. Do not expect machine levels of efficiency in future. There are human factors involved which will now need to be taken into account.'

'Such as?' the Princess asked.

'They will probably need time to recuperate between assaults. Duties will have to be rotated between platoons. I'm sorry,' she said to Ralph. 'It adds considerable complications to the planning. Especially if you want them to prevent the possessed suicides.'

'I'm sure the AI can cope,' he said.

'It looks like the campaign is going to take a lot longer whatever option we go for,' Admiral Farquar said.

'That does have one small benefit,' Janne Palmer said.

'I'd love to hear it,' the Princess told her.

'Reducing the flow of de-possessed is going to alleviate some of the pressure on our medical facilities.'

Back in her private office, Kirsten shuddered, a movement not reproduced inside the bubble room. That, out of all the other horrors revealed by the Liberation, had upset her the most. Cancers were such a rarity in this day and age that to see several bulging from a person's skin like inflated blisters was a profound shock. And there were very few de-possessed who didn't suffer from them. To inflict such an incapacitating disease for what was apparently little more than vanity was hubris at an obscene level. That it might also be simple blind ignorance was almost as bad. 'I have requested aid from the Kingdom and our allies as a matter of urgency,' she said. 'We should start to receive shipments of medical nanonic packages over the next few days. Every hospital and clinic on the planet is being used, and civilian ships are being deployed to fly people out to asteroid settlements in the system – not that they have many beds or staff, but every little helps. I just wish we could ferry people outsystem, but at the moment I can't break the quarantine for that. In any event, my Foreign Minister has cautioned me that there would be some reservation from other star systems about accepting our medical cases. They're worried about infiltration by the possessed, and I can't say I blame them.'

'Capone's new lunacy doesn't help ease the paranoia,' Admiral Farquar grunted. 'Damn that bastard.'

'So you would prefer the slow-down scenario?' Kirsten asked.

'Very much so, ma'am,' Janne Palmer said. 'It's not just a question of providing medical support, there are transport bottlenecks as well. It's improved slightly now we can land aircraft at the coastal ports, but we have to get the de-possessed there first, and they need care which my occupation forces really aren't geared up to provide.'

'General Hiltch, what do you favour?'

'I don't like slowing down the advance, ma'am. With all respect to Admiral Farquar's SD officers, I don't think they'll be able to prevent the possessed from congregating. Slow their movements, maybe, but halt them, no. And once that happens, we'll be in a real mess. The kind of firepower we're going to need to break open Ketton at the moment is way in excess of any assault so far. We have to prevent it from turning into a runaway situation. At the moment we're dictating the pace of events to them, I'd hate to abandon that level of control. It's our one big advantage.'

'I see. Very well, you'll have my decision before dawn local time.'

The sensenviron ended with its usual abruptness, and Kirsten blinked irritably, allowing her eyes to register the familiar office. Touching base with normality. Necessary, now. These nightly reviews were becoming a considerable drain. Not even the Privy Council Grand Policy Conclaves back in the Apollo Palace had quite the same impact, they implemented policies that would take decades to mature. The Liberation was all so *now*. Something the Saldanas were not accustomed to. In any modern crisis, the major decision would be whether or not to dispatch a fleet. After that, everything was down to the admiral in charge.

I make political decisions, not military ones.

But the Liberation had changed all that, blurring the distinction badly. Military decisions were political ones.

She stood up, stretching. Then went over to Allie's bust. Her hand touched his familiar, reassuringly sober features. 'What would you do?' she murmured. Not that she would ever be accused of making the wrong choice. Whatever it was, the family would support her. Her equerry, Sylvester Geray, scrambled to his feet in the reception room, the chair legs scraping loudly on the tushkwood floor as Kirsten came out of her office.

'Tired?' she asked lightly.

'No, ma'am.'

'Yes, you are. I'm going back to my quarters for a few hours. I won't need you before seven o'clock. Have a sleep, or at least a rest.'

'Thank you, ma'am.' He bowed deeply as she walked out.

There were few staff about in the private apartments, which was how she liked them. With the rooms all dark and quiet, it was almost how she imagined a normal home would be late in the evening. An assistant nanny and a maid were on duty, sitting up chatting quietly in the lounge next to the children's bedrooms.

Kirsten stood outside for a moment, listening; the nanny's fiancé was in the Royal Navy, and hadn't called her for a couple of days. The maid was sympathizing.

Everyone, Kirsten thought, this has touched and involved every one of us. And the Liberation is only the beginning. So far the Church had been noticeably unsuccessful in quelling people's fears of the beyond. Though Atherstone's bishop reported that attendance was high in every parish on the planet – greater than Christmas Eve, he'd said almost in indignation.

She opened the door to Edward's study without knocking, only realizing her mistake once she was well inside. There was a girl with him on the leather settee; his current mistress. Kirsten remembered the security file Jannike Dermot had provided: minor nobility, her father owned an estate and some kind of transport company. Pretty young thing, in her early twenties, with classic delicate bonework. Tall with very long legs, as they all invariably were with Edward. She stared at Kirsten in utter consternation, then frantically tried to adjust her evening dress to a more modest position. Not that she could achieve much modesty with so little fabric, Kirsten thought in amusement. The girl's wineglass went flying from trembling fingers.

Kirsten frowned at that. The antique carpet was Turkish, a beautiful red and blue weave; she'd given it to Edward as a birthday present fifteen years ago.

'Ma'am,' the girl squeaked. 'I . . . We . . .'

Kirsten merely gave her a mildly enquiring glance.

'Come along, my dear,' Edward said calmly. He took her arm and escorted her to the door. 'Affairs of state. I'll call you in the morning.' She managed a strangled whimper in response. A butler, responding to Edward's datavise, appeared and gestured politely to the by now thoroughly frightened and bewildered girl. Edward shut the study door behind her, and sighed.

Kirsten started laughing, then put her hand over her mouth. 'Oh, Edward, I'm sorry. I should have let you know I was coming.'

He spread his hands wide. '*C'est la vie.*'

'Poor thing looked terrified.' She knelt down and picked the wineglass up, dabbing at the carpet. 'Look what she did. I'd better get a valet mechanoid, or it'll stain.' She datavised the study's processor.

'It's a rather good Chablis, actually.' He picked the bottle out of its walnut cooler jacket. 'Shame to waste it, would you like some?'

'Lovely, thank you. It has been a very bad day at the office.'

'Ah.' He went over to the cabinet and brought her a fresh glass.

Kirsten sniffed at the bouquet after he'd poured. 'She was jolly gorgeous. Slightly young, though. Wicked of you.' She brushed at imaginary dust on his lapel. 'Then again, I can see why she's so obliging. You always did look rather splendid in uniform.'

Edward glanced down at his Royal Navy tunic. There were no royal crests, just three discreet medal ribbons – earned long ago. 'I'm just doing my bit. Though they are all depressingly young at the base. I think they regard me as some kind of mascot.'

'Oh, poor Edward, the indignity. But not to worry, Zandra and Emmeline are terribly impressed.'

He sat on the leather settee and patted the cushion. 'Come on, sit down and tell me what's wrong.'

'Thank you.' She stepped round the small mechanoid that was sniffing at the wine stain, and sat beside him, welcoming his arm around her shoulders. The secret of a successful (royal) marriage: don't have secrets. They were both intelligent people, which had allowed them to work out the grounds of a sustainable domestic arrangement a long time ago. In public and in private he was the perfect companion, a friend and confidant. All she required was loyalty, which he supplied admirably. In return he was free to gather whatever perks his position presented – and it wasn't just girls, he was an avid art collector and *bon viveur*. They even still slept together occasionally.

'The Liberation is not progressing as well as could be,' he said. 'That much is obvious. And the net is overloading with speculation.'

Kirsten sipped some of the Chablis. 'Progress is the key word, yes.' She told him about the decision she was faced with.

After she'd finished, he poured some more wine for himself before answering. 'The serjeants developing advanced personalities? Hmm. How intriguing. I wonder if they'll refuse to go back into their habitat multiplicities when the campaign is over.'

'I have no idea; Acacia never ventured an opinion. And to be honest, that part is not my problem.'

'It might be if they all start applying for citizenship afterwards.'

'Oh, God.' She snuggled up closer. 'No. I'm not even going to consider that right now.'

'Wise lady. You want my opinion?'

'That's why I'm here.'

'You can't ignore the serjeant situation. We are utterly dependent on them to liberate Mortonridge, and there's a hell of a way to go yet.'

'A hundred and eighty thousand people de-possessed, seventeen thousand dead, so far; that leaves us with one point eight million left to save.'

'Exactly. And we're about to enter the phase which will see the heaviest fighting. If they keep advancing at their current rate, the front line will reach the first areas where the possessed are concentrated the day after tomorrow. If you slow them now, the serjeants are going to start taking heavy losses just before that. Not good. I'd say, keep things as they are until the front line hits those concentrations, then shift to General Hiltch's outnumbering tactics.'

'That's a very logical solution.' She stared at the wine. 'If only all I had to consider were numbers. But they're depending on me, Edward.'

'Who?'

'The people who've been possessed. Even locked away in their own bodies, they know the Liberation is coming now; a practical salvation from this obscenity. They have faith in me, they trust me to deliver them from this evil. And I have a duty to them. That duty is one of the few true burdens placed on the family by our people. Now I know there is a way of reducing the number of my subjects killed, I cannot in all conscience ignore it for tactical convenience. That would be a betrayal of trust, not to mention an abdication of duty.'

'The two impossibles for a Saldana.'

'Yes. We have had it easy for an awful long time, haven't we?'

'Shall we say: moderately difficult.'

'Yet if I want to reduce the death rate, I'm going to have to ask the Edenists to take it on the chin for us. You know what bothers me most about that? People will expect it. I'm a Saldana, they're Edenists. What could be simpler?'

'The serjeants aren't quite Edenists.'

'We don't know what the hell they are, not any more. Acacia was hedging her bets very thoroughly. If they're worried enough to bring the problem to me, then it has to be a substantial factor. One I cannot discount from the humanist equation. Damn it, they were supposed to be automatons.'

'The Liberation is a very rushed venture. I'm sure if Jupiter's geneticists had been given enough time to design a dedicated soldier construct then this would never have arisen. But we had to borrow from the Lord of Ruin. Look, General Hiltch was given overall command of the Liberation. Let him make the decision, it's what he's paid for.'

'Get thee behind me,' she muttered. 'No, Edward, not this time. I'm the one who insisted on reducing the fatalities. It is my responsibility.'

'You'll be setting a precedent.'

'Hardly one that's likely to be repeated. All of us are sailing into new and very stormy territory; that requires proper leadership. If I cannot provide that now, then the family will ultimately have failed. We have spent four hundred years engineering ourselves into this position of statesmanship, and I will not duck the issue when it really counts. It stinks of cowardice, and that is one thing I will never allow the Saldanas to stand accused of.'

He kissed her on the side of her head. 'Well, you know you have my support. If I could make one final observation. The personalities in the serjeants are all volunteers. They came here knowing what their probable fate would be. That purpose remains at their core. In that, they are like every pre-twenty-first-century army; reluctant, frightened even, but committed. So give them the time they need to gather their nerve and resolution, and then use them for the purpose for which they were created: saving genuine human lives. If they are truly capable of emotion, then their only hope of gaining satisfaction will come from achieving that.'

*

Ralph was eating a cold snack in Fort Forward's command complex canteen when he received the datavise.

'Slow the assault,' Princess Kirsten told him. 'I want that suicide figure reduced as low as you can practically achieve.'

'Yes, ma'am. I'll see to it. And thank you.'

'This is what you wanted?'

'We're not here to recapture land, ma'am. The Liberation is about people.'

'I know that. I hope Acacia will forgive us.'

'I'm sure she will, ma'am. The Edenists understand us pretty well.'

'Good. Because I also want the serjeant platoons given as much breathing space between assaults as they require.'

'That will reduce the rate of advance even further.'

'I know, but it can't be helped. Don't worry about political and technical support, General, I'll ensure you get that right to the bitter end.'

'Yes, ma'am.' The datavise ended. He looked round at the senior staff eating with him, and gave a slow smile. 'We got it.'

*

High above the air, cold technological eyes stared downwards, unblinking. Their multi-spectrum vision could penetrate clean through Mortonridge's thinning strands of puffy white cloud to reveal the small group of warm figures trekking across the mud. But that was where the observation failed. Objects around them were perfectly clear, the dendritic tangle of roots flaring from fallen trees, a pulverized four-wheel-drive rover almost devoured by the blue-grey mud, even the shape of large stones ploughed up and rolled along by thick runnels of sludge. In contrast, the figures were hazed by shimmering air; infrared blobs no more substantial than candle flames. No matter which combination of discrimination filters it applied to the sensor image, the AI was unable to determine their exact number. Best estimate, taken from the width of the distortion and measuring the thermal imprint of the disturbed mud they left behind, was between four and nine.

Stephanie could feel the necklace of prying satellites as they slid relentlessly along their arc from horizon to horizon. Not so much their physical existence; that kind of knowledge had vanished along with the cloud and the possessed's mental unity. But their avaricious intent was forever there, intruding upon the world's intrinsic harmonies. It acted as a reminder for her to keep her guard up. The others were the same. Messing with the sight on a level which equated to waving a hand at persistent flies. Not that satellites were their problem. A far larger note of discord resonated from the serjeants, now just a couple of miles away. And coming closer, always closer. Machinelike in their determination.

At first Stephanie had ignored them, employing a kind of bravado that was almost entirely alien to her. Everybody had, once they'd reached the shelter (and *dryness*!) of the barn. The building didn't amount to much, set on a gentle hillock, with a low wall of stone acting as a base for composite-panelling walls and a shallow roof. They'd stumbled across it five horrendous hours after setting out from the end of the valley. McPhee claimed that proved they were following the road. By then, nobody was arguing with him. In fact, nobody was speaking at all. Their limbs were trembling from exertion, not even reinforcing them with energistic strength helped much. They'd long since discovered such augmentation had to be paid for by the body in the long run.

The barn had come pretty much at the end of their endurance. There'd been no discussion about using it. As soon as they saw its dark, bleak outline through the pounding rain they'd trudged grimly towards it. Inside there was little respite from the weather at first. The wind had torn innumerable panels off the carbotanium frame, and the concrete floor was lost beneath a foot of mud. That didn't matter, in their state it was pure salvation.

Their energistic power renovated it. Mud flowed up the walls, sealing over the lost panels and turning to stone. The rain was repelled, and the howl of the wind muted. Relief united them again, banishing the misery of the retreat from the valley. It was an emotion which produced an overreaction of confidence and defiance. Now, they found it possible to ignore the occasional mind-scream of anguish as another soul was wrenched from its possessed body by the peril of zero-tau. They cooperated gamely in searching round outside for food, adopting a campfire jollity as they cleaned and cooked the dead fish and mud-smeared vegetables.

Then the rain eased off, and the serjeants crunched forwards remorselessly. Food became very scarce. A week after the Liberation began, they left the barn, tramping along the melted contour line which McPhee still insisted was the road. Even living through the deluge under a flimsy roof hadn't prepared them for the scale of devastation wrought by the water. Valleys were completely impassable. Huge rivers of mud slithered along, murmuring and burbling incessantly as they sucked down and devoured anything that protruded into their course.

Progress was slow, even though they'd now fashioned themselves sturdy hiking attire (even Tina wore strong leather boots). Two days spent trying to navigate through the buckled, decrepit landscape. They kept to the high ground, where swaths of dark green aboriginal grass were the only relief from the overlapping shades of brown. Even they were sliced by deep flash gorges where the water had found a weak seam of soil. There was no map, and no recognizable features to apply one against. So many promising ridges ended in sharp dips down into the mud, forcing them to backtrack, losing hours. But they always knew which way to travel. It was simple: away from the serjeants. It was also becoming very difficult to stay ahead. The front line seemed to move at a constant pace, unfazed by the valleys and impossible terrain, while Stephanie and her group spent their whole time zigzagging about. What had begun forty-eight hours ago as a nine-mile gap was down to about two, and closing steadily.

'Oh, hey, you cats,' Cochrane called. 'You like want the good news or the bad news first?' He had taken point duty, striding out ahead of the others. Now he stood atop a dune of battered reeds, looking down the other side in excitement.

'The bad,' Stephanie said automatically.

'The legion of the black hats is speeding up, and there's like this stupendously *huge* amount of them.'

'What's the good?' Tina squealed.

'They're speeding up because there's like a road down here. A real one, with tarmac and stuff.'

The others didn't exactly increase their pace to reach the bedraggled hippy, but there was a certain eagerness in their stride that'd been missing for some time. They clambered up the incline of the dune, and halted level with him.

'What's there?' Moyo asked. His face was perfect, the scars and blisters gone; eyes solid and bright. He was even able to smile again, doing so frequently during the last few days they'd spent in the barn. That he could smile, yet still refuse to let them see what lay underneath the illusory eyeballs worried Stephanie enormously. A bad form of denial. He was acting the role of himself; and it was a very thin performance.

'It's a valley,' she told him.

He groaned. 'Oh, hell, not again.'

'No, this is different.'

The dune was actually the top of a steepish slope which swept down several hundred yards to the floor of Catmos Vale, a valley that was at least twenty miles wide. Drizzle and mist made the far side difficult to see. The floor below was a broad flat expanse whose size had actually managed to defeat the massive discharges of mud. Its width had absorbed the surges that coursed out of the narrower ravines along either side; spreading them wide and robbing them of their destructive power. The wide, boggy river channel which meandered along the centre had siphoned the bulk of the tide away, without giving it a chance to amass in dangerously unstable colloidal waves.

Vast low-lying sections of the floor had turned directly into quagmire from the rain and overspill. Entire forests had subsided, their trunks keeling over to lean against each other. Now they were slowly sinking deeper and deeper as the rapidly expanding subsurface water level gnawed away at the stability of the loam. Watched over the period of a day or two, it was almost as if they were melting away.

Small hillocks and knolls formed a vast archipelago of olive-green islands amid the ochre sea. Hundreds of distressed and emaciated aboriginal animals scurried about over each of them, herds of kolfrans (a deer-analogue) and packs of the small canine ferrangs were trampling the surviving blades of grass into a sticky pulp. Birds scuttled among them, their feathers too slick with mud for them to fly.

Many of the islands just below the foot of the slope had sections of road threaded across them. The eye could stitch them together into a single strand leading along the valley. It led towards a small town, just visible through the drizzle. Most of it had been built on raised land, leaving its buildings clear of the mud; as if the entire valley had become its moat. There was a church near the centre, its classic grey stone spire standing defiantly proud. Some kind of scarlet symbols had been painted around the middle.

'That's got to be Ketton,' Franklin said. 'Can you sense them?'

'Yes,' Stephanie said uncomfortably. 'There's a lot of us down there.' It would explain the condition of the buildings. There wasn't a tile missing from the neat houses, no sign of damage. Even the little park was devoid of puddles.

'I guess that's why these guys are like so anxious to reach it.' Cochrane jerked a thumb back down the valley.

It was the first time they'd actually seen the Liberation army. Twenty jeeps formed a convoy along the road. Whenever the carbon-concrete surface left the islands to dip under the mud, they slowed slightly, cautiously testing the way. The mud couldn't have been very deep or thick, barely coming over the wheels. A V-shaped phalanx of serjeants followed on behind the jeeps, big dark figures lumbering along quite quickly considering none of them was on the road. On one side of the carbon-concrete strip their line stretched out almost to the central river of mud; on the other it extended up the side of Catmos Vale's wall. A second train of vehicles, larger than the jeeps, was turning into the valley several miles behind the front line.

'Ho-lee shit,' Franklin groaned. 'We can't make that sort of speed, not over this terrain.'

McPhee was studying the rugged land behind them. 'I cannot see them up here.'

'They'll be there,' Rana said. 'They're on the other side of the river as well, look. That line is kept level. There's no break in it. They're scooping us up like horse shit.'

'If we stay up here we'll be nailed before sunset.'

'If we go down, we can keep ahead of them on the road,' Stephanie said. 'But we'll have to go through the town. I have a bad feeling about that. The possessed there know the serjeants are coming, yet they're staying put. And there's a lot of them.'

'They're going to make a stand,' Moyo said.

Stephanie glanced back at the ominous line moving towards them. 'They'll lose,' she said, morosely. 'Nothing can resist that.'

'We've no food left,' McPhee said.

Cochrane used an index finger to prod his purple sunglasses up along the bridge of his nose. 'Plenty of water, though, man.'

'There's nothing to eat up here,' Rana said. 'We have to go down.'

'The town will hold them off for a while at least,' Stephanie said. She resisted glancing at Moyo, though he was now her principal concern. 'We could use the time to take a break, rest up.'

'Then what?' Moyo grunted.

'Then we move on. We keep ahead of them.'

'Why bother?'

'Don't,' she said softly. 'We try and live life as we always wanted to, remember? Well, I don't want to live like this; and there might be something different up ahead, because there certainly isn't anything behind. As long as we keep going, there's hope.'

His face compressed to a melancholic expression. He held one arm out, moving his hand round to try and find her. She gripped his fingers tightly, and he hugged her against him. 'Sorry. I'm sorry.'

'It's all right,' she murmured. 'Hey, you know what? The way we're heading, it takes us right up to the central mountain range. You can show me what mountain gliding is like.'

Moyo laughed gruffly, his shoulders trembling.

'Look, guys, I hate to fuck up my karma any more by breaking up your major love-in scene here, but we have to decide where we're like going. Like *now*. This is one army that doesn't take time out, you dig?'

'It has to be down to Ketton,' Stephanie said briskly. She eyed the long slope below. It would be slippery, but with their energistic power they ought to cope. 'We can get there ahead of the army.'

'Only just ahead,' Franklin said. 'We'll be trapped in the town. If we stay up here, we can still keep ahead of them.'

'Not by much,' McPhee said.

'And you'll not have time to gather any food,' Rana said. 'I don't know about you, but I know I can't keep this pace up for much longer without eating a full meal. We must consider the practicalities of the situation. My calorie intake has been very low over the last couple of days.'

'It's a permanent downer,' Cochrane said. 'Your practical problem is that you don't eat properly anyway.'

She glared at him. 'I really hope you aren't going to suggest I should eat dead flesh.'

'Oh, brother.' He raised his arms heavenwards. 'Here we go again. Check it out: no meat, no smoking, no gambling, no sex, no loud music, no bright lights, no dancing, no fucking fun.'

'I'm going down to Ketton,' Stephanie said, overriding the pair of them. She started to walk down the slope, her hand holding on to Moyo's fingers. 'If anyone else wants to come, you'd better do it now.'

'I'm with you,' Moyo said. He moved his feet along cautiously.

Rana shrugged lightly, and started to follow. A reefer slid up out of Cochrane's fist and the tip ignited. He stuck it in his mouth and went after Rana.

'Sod it!' Franklin said wretchedly. 'I'll come. But we're giving up by going down there. There'll be no way out of that town.'

'You can't keep ahead of them up here,' McPhee said. 'Look at the bastards. It's like they can walk on mud.'

'All right, all right.'

Tina gave Rana a desperate look. 'Darling, those *things* will simply demolish the town. And we'll be in it.'

'Maybe. Who knows? The military always makes ludicrously extravagant propaganda claims about their macho prowess. Reality invariably lags behind.'

'Yo, Tina.' Cochrane proffered the reefer. 'Come with us, babe. You and me, we could like have our last night on this world together. Fucking-A way to go, huh?'

Tina shuddered at the grinning hippy. 'I'd rather be captured by those beastly things.'

'That's a no, is it?'

'No, it is not. I don't want us to split up. You're my friends.'

Stephanie had turned to watch the little scene. 'Tina, make up your mind.' She started off down the slope again, leading Moyo.

'Oh, *heavens*,' Tina said. 'You simply never give me time to decide anything. It's so unfair.'

'Bye, doll,' Cochrane said.

'Don't go so fast. I can't keep up.'

Stephanie made a deliberate effort to expel the woman's whingeing from her mind, concentrating solely on navigating her way down the slope. She had to take quite a shallow angle, constantly reinforcing the slippery soil below her boot soles with energistic power. Even then her progress was marked by long skid marks.

'I can sense a lot of possessed below us,' Moyo said when they were a hundred yards above the quagmires of the valley floor.

'Where?' Stephanie asked without thinking. She hadn't been paying attention to what waited below, traversing the tricky slope required her complete attention. Now she looked up, she could see the convoy of jeeps was barely a mile behind them. The sight gave her heart a cold squeeze.

'Not far.' His free hand pointed out across the valley. 'Over there.'

Stephanie couldn't see anyone. But now she scrutinized the mental whispers around the edge of her perception she was aware of rising anticipation in many minds.

'Hey, Moyo, man, good call.' Cochrane was scanning the valley. 'Those cats are like *low* in the mud. I can't see anyone.'

'Come on,' Stephanie said. 'Let's find out what's happening.'

The last section of the slope started to flatten out, allowing them to increase their speed. Stephanie was tempted just to keep to the undulating foothills that ran along the valley wall. They could certainly make good time on the reasonably dry ground. Except it curved gradually away from Ketton. One of the visible sections of road was about three hundred yards away across a perfectly flat expanse of slough. Stephanie stood on the edge, mud oozing round her ankles. Her boots kept her feet dry, but as a precaution she made the leather creep up her shins towards her knees. The silence down here was unnerving, it was as if the mud had some kind of anti-sound property. 'I don't think it's very deep,' she ventured.

'One way to find out,' McPhee said vigorously. He struck out for the road with confident strides. Mud sloshed away slowly from his legs as he ploughed across. 'Come on, ye great bunch of woofters. It's not like *we* can drown.' Cochrane and Rana gave each other a reluctant glance, then started in.

'It's going to be all right,' Stephanie said. She kept a tight grip on Moyo's hand, and they waded in together. Tina held on to Franklin's hand as they went in. The action drew a lecherous grin from Cochrane.

Stephanie was right about it not being particularly deep, but the mud was soon up to her knees. After a couple of attempts to clear a trench through it with her energistic power, she gave up. The mud responded so sluggishly it would have taken at least an hour for them to reach the road by such a method. This had to be crossed the hard way, and the level of exertion needed to keep going placed a terrible strain on already fatigued muscles. All of them diverted their energistic power to force recalcitrant legs forward against mud that seemed to exert an equal pressure against them. Their efforts were given an extra edge by the onward march of the army. They were travelling almost at right angles to the front line, losing precious separation distance with every minute.

Stephanie kept telling herself that as soon as they made the road they'd be able to build it back up again. But even using the road, there was a lot of mud to surmount before Ketton, and her body was already approaching its physical limit. She could hear Cochrane wheezing loudly, a sound which carried a long way over the quagmire.

'They're right ahead of us now,' Moyo said. He'd opened the front of his oilskin jacket in an attempt to cool himself. The drizzle was seeping through his energistic barrier, combining with sweat to soak his shirt. 'Two of them. And they're not happy with us.'

Stephanie glanced up, trying to distinguish the source of the animus thoughts. The slight rise carrying the road was seventy yards in front. Badly mangled grass and a few straggly bushes gleaming dully in the grizzly skin of rainwater. Dozens of ferrangs were pelting about excitedly, running together in packs of six or seven. Their cohesive motion reminded her of schools of fish, every movement enacted in unison.

'I can't see anyone,' McPhee grunted. 'Hey, shitheads,' he shouted. 'What the fuck is wrong with you?'

'Oh, groovy,' Cochrane said. 'Way to go, dude. That'll make them real friendly. I mean it's not like we're in cosmically deep shit at this point and need help, or anything.'

Tina let out a miserable gasp as she slipped. 'I hate this fucking mud!'

'You tell it as it is, babe.' Franklin helped her up, and the two of them leant against each other as they forced their way onwards. Stephanie glanced back down the length of Catmos Vale, and sucked in a fast breath. The jeeps were barely half a mile away. Fifty yards to solid ground.

'We're not going to make it.'

'What?' Moyo asked.

'We're not going to make it.' She was panting heavily now. Not bothering with clothes, appearance, any energistic frippery – even the satellites would be able to see her now. She didn't care. All that mattered was maintaining the integrity of her boots and shoving near-useless legs one in front of the other. Muscle spasms were shaking her calves and thighs.

Rana stumbled, falling to her knees. Mud squelched obscenely as it closed over her legs. She blew heavily, her face radiant, glistening with sweat. Cochrane sloshed over and put his arm under her shoulders, dragging her up. The glutinous mud was reluctant to let go. 'Hey, man, give me a hand here,' he yelled at the land ahead. 'Come on, you guys, quit fooling around. This is like big-time serious.'

The ferrang packs dodged round each other as they wheeled about aimlessly. Their footpads thundered loudly. Whoever the people were up ahead, they chose not to reveal themselves. A slight single-tone mechanical whine was becoming audible. The jeep engines.

'Get me to her,' Moyo hissed.

He and Stephanie staggered over to the faltering couple. McPhee had come to a halt twenty yards from the land, staring back at them. 'Keep going,' Stephanie yelled at him. 'Go on. Somebody's got to get out of this.'

With her help, Moyo took some of Rana's weight from Cochrane. They slung her between them, and kicked their way forward again. 'My legs,' Rana groaned miserably. 'I can't keep them going. They're like fire. God damn it, this shouldn't happen, I can move mountains with my mind.'

'No matter,' Cochrane said through gritted teeth. 'We got you now, sister.' The three of them stumbled forwards. McPhee had reached the land, standing just above the mud to urge them on. Tina and Franklin were almost there. The pair of them were plainly exhausted. Only the big Scot seemed to have any stamina left.

Stephanie brought up the rear. The jeeps were seven hundred yards away now, on a stretch of dry road. Picking up speed. 'Shit,' she whispered. 'Oh shit oh shit.' Even if McPhee started sprinting right now, he'd never make it to Ketton; they'd overhaul him easily. Perhaps if the rest of them started flinging white fire at the serjeants ... What a ridiculous thought, she told herself. And I don't have any to spare. I must focus on channelling my energistic power.

Ten yards to go.

I won't put up a fight. It wouldn't be the slightest good, and it might damage the body. I owe her that much.

At the heart of her mind she could feel the captive host stirring in anticipation. All four of them staggered up out of the mud, and simply collapsed on the soggy ground next to Tina and Franklin. And she still couldn't see the owners of the two minds impinging so strongly on her perception.

'Stephanie Ash,' a woman's voice said from the empty air. 'I see your timing is as fucking atrocious as always.'

'Any second now,' an unseen man announced.

Both of their minds were hot with eagerness. Somewhere nearby, the slow-motion wheeze of bagpipes started up, swirling to a level piercing tone. Stephanie raised her head. Halfway between her and the jeeps, a lone Scottish piper stood facing the vehicles. Dressed in a kilt of Douglas tartan, black leather boots shining, he seemed totally oblivious of the mortal foe riding towards him. His fingers moved sedately as he played 'Amazing Grace'. One of the serjeants in the front vehicle was standing up to get a clear look in over the mud-caked windscreen.

'I like it,' McPhee hooted.

'Our call to arms,' the concealed man replied. 'It has a certain *je ne sais quoi*, no?'

Stephanie glanced round urgently, trying to pin down the voice. 'Call to arms?'

An explosion sounded in the distance, rumbling fast over the quagmires and stagnant pools smothering Catmos Vale. A mine had detonated under the leading jeep, punching the front of the chassis into the air. It crashed down, spilling serjeants across the road. Blue-white smoke billowed out from the crater in the concrete. Lumps of debris rained down. The other jeeps braked sharply. Serjeants froze all along the front line, crouching down.

The piper finished, and bowed solemnly at his enemies. There was a dull, potent *thock*, loud enough to quiver Stephanie's gullet. Then another. A whole barrage started up, the individual thumps merging into a single sound wave. Tina squealed in fright.

'Ho, shit,' Cochrane growled. 'Those are mortars.'

'Well done,' said the woman. 'Now keep down.'

It was, the Liberation's coordinating AI acknowledged, a classic ambush, and executed perfectly. The jeeps were confined to one of the narrowest strips of land in the valley, unable to veer away. A sleet of mortar shells fell upon them, ranged precisely. High explosives detonated in a near constant bombardment, pulverizing the stalled vehicles, and shredding the serjeants riding them. Smoke, flame, and spumes of superfine mud belched out, obliterating the carnage from view.

The AI could do absolutely nothing to prevent it. Radar pulses from the SD sensor satellites swept the length of the valley, but they required several seconds to acquire lock-on. The first bombardment lasted for ninety seconds, then the mortar operators switched to airburst shells, and changed elevation. Dense black clouds burst open above the line of serjeants as they toiled desperately through the quagmire. Broad circles of mud erupted into cyclones of beige foam as the shrapnel slashed down, obliterating the struggling figures.

Only then did the SD radars finish backtracking the mortar trajectories. The AI launched its counterstrike. Incandescent scarlet beams stabbed down in retaliation, vaporizing the possessed and their weapons in microseconds. More than a dozen patches of dry land were targeted. Supersonic torrents of steam flared out from the base of each impact. When they gusted away, the mortar sites had been reduced to shallow craters of hard-baked clay, their centres still radiant. They chittered softly as the drizzle fell, prising open millions of tiny heat-stress fractures.

The empty silence returned. Swirls of smoke drifted over the valley floor, dissipating slowly to reveal the burning wrecks of the jeeps. Spread out across the quagmire, the ruptured bodies of the serjeants were gradually claimed by the mud's tireless embrace. Within an hour, there would be little left to hint at the conflict.

Stephanie found herself clawing into the soft soil, every muscle locked solid to resist the laser pulse. It never came. She let out a wretched sob, surrendering to the severe shaking that claimed her limbs. Two of the ferrang packs crept towards her and her friends. They dissolved into a pair of human figures dressed in dark grey and green combat fatigues. Annette Ekelund and Hoi Son looked down at them with anger and contempt.

'You idiots could have got us blown back into the beyond by blundering about like that,' Annette said. 'What if dear Ralph considered you to be part of this operation? They would have zeroed this patch of ground for sure.'

Cochrane lifted his head, mud dribbling down his face to saturate his wild beard. His dead reefer was squashed against his lips. He spat it out. 'Well, like fuck me gently with a chainsaw, sister. I'm real sorry to cause you any inconvenience.'

*

Not even Lalonde's oppressive climate prepared Ralph for the awesome humidity when he stepped out of the Royal Marine hypersonic transport plane. It prickled his skin at the same time as it siphoned away vital body energies. Just breathing it in was exhausting.

With the last strands of cloud at last gusting out to sea, the tropical sun could finally exert its full strength against poor malaised Mortonridge. Thousands of square kilometres of mud began to effervesce, thickening the air with hot cloying vapour. Looking round from the top of the airstair, Ralph could see long ribbons of tenuous white cloud flowing with oily tenacity around the hummocks and foothills of the broad valley. More mist was percolating up from the highlands on either side, with long snow-white streamers spilling out through clefts in the valley walls to slither down the slope like slow-motion waterfalls.

He sniffed at the air. Threaded through the blanket of clean moisture were the traces of corruption. The peninsula's dead bio-mass was starting to rot and ferment. In another few days the stench would be formidable, and no doubt extremely unhealthy. One more factor to consider. Though it was a long way down on the priority list.

Ralph hurried down the aluminium stairs, with Brigadier Palmer and Cathal just behind him. For once there was no marine detail waiting to guard him. They'd landed outside the staging camp established in the mouth of Catmos Vale. Hundreds of programmable silicon igloos had sprung up in rows like giant powder-blue mushrooms, a miniature recreation of Fort Forward. The only people here were serjeants, occupation troops, and medical case de-possessed. Plus a handful of rover reporters; all officially authorized Liberation correspondents, with a pair of Royal Marine information officers shepherding them.

When he looked up the valley, the loose smears of mist blurred into a single featureless white sheet carpeting the floor. His enhanced retinas zoomed in on the only visible feature, the slim greyish spire of Ketton's church rising out of the mist. Just by looking at it, Ralph could sense the possessed mustering in the town, a replay of the gentle mental pressure they'd all known in the days of the red cloud.

'She's here,' he murmured. 'The Ekelund woman. She's in Ketton.'

'Are you sure?' Cathal asked.

'I can feel her, just like before. In any case, she's one of their leaders, and this bunch are well organized.' Cathal gave the distant spire a dubious glance.

The camp's commander, Colonel Anton Longhurst, was waiting at the bottom of the airstairs. He saluted Ralph. 'Welcome to Catmos Vale, sir.'

'Thank you, Colonel. Looks like you've got yourself an interesting command here.'

'Yes, sir. I'll show you round. That's after . . .' He indicated the reporters.

'Ah yes.' Ralph kept his ire under control. They'd probably all be using audio-discrimination programs, the bastards never missed a trick.

The information officers signalled the all clear, and the rover reporters closed in. 'General Hiltch, Hugh Rosler with DataAxis; can you please tell us why the front line has stalled?'

Ralph gave a wan knowing smile to the plain-looking man in a check shirt and sleeveless jacket who'd asked the question. An in-your-face transmission of the cordial public persona he'd developed and deployed for the last few weeks. 'Oh, come on, guys. We're consolidating the ground we've already recovered. There's a lot more to the Liberation than just rushing forward at breakneck pace. We have to be sure, and I mean absolutely sure, that none of the possessed has managed to sneak through. Don't forget, it was just one possessed who got into Mortonridge that was responsible for this in the first place. You don't want a repeat of that, do you?'

'General, Tim Beard, Collins; is it true the serjeants simply can't hack it any more now that the possessed have started to put up real resistance?'

'No, it is categorically not true. And if you show me the person who said that, I'll give them a personal and private demonstration of my contempt for such a remark. I flew in here today, and you people drove in from the coast.' He waved a hand back at the mud-covered land. 'They walked the whole way from the beaches, engaged in tens of thousands of separate combat incidents. And on the way they've rescued nearly three hundred thousand people from possession. Now does that really sound as though they can't hack it to you? Because it doesn't to me.'

'So why isn't the front line continuing its advance?'

'Because we've reached a new stage of the campaign. Forgive me for not broadcasting our gameplan before, but this kind of reinforcement manoeuvre was inevitable. As you can see, we've reached Ketton, which has a large number of well-organized and hostile possessed in residence – and this is just one of several such assemblies around Mortonridge. The army is simply redeploying accordingly. When we have sufficient resources assembled, then the serjeants will take the town. But I have no intention of committing them until I'm convinced such an operation can be achieved with the minimum of loss on both sides. Thank you.' He started to walk forwards.

'General, Elizabeth Mitchell, Time Warner; one final question, please.' Her voice was authoritative and insistent, impossible to ignore. 'Have you got any comment about the defeat in the valley?'

Trust the owner of that voice to ask something he'd really rather avoid, Ralph thought. 'Yes, I have. In hindsight advancing down Catmos Vale so fast was a tactical error, a very bad one; and I take full responsibility for that. Although we knew the possessed are equipped with hunting rifles we weren't expecting them to have artillery. Mortars are about the crudest kind of artillery it's possible to build; but even so, very effective given certain situations. This was one of them. Now we know what the possessed are capable of, it won't happen again. Every time they use a new weapon or tactic against us, we can analyse it and guard against it in future. And there are only a very limited number of these moves they can play.' He moved on again, more determined this time. A fast datavise to the two information officers, and there were no more shouted questions.

'Sorry about them,' Colonel Longhurst said.

'Not a problem for me,' Ralph replied.

'You shouldn't play up to scenes like that,' Cathal said in annoyance as they made their way to the camp's headquarters. 'It's undignified. At least you could hold a proper press conference with vetted questions.'

'This is as much propaganda as it is physical war, Cathal,' Ralph said. 'Besides, you're still thinking like an ESA officer: tell nobody, and tell them nothing. The public wants to see authority in action on this campaign. We have to provide that.'

Convoys of supply trucks were still arriving at the camp, Colonel Longhurst explained as he took them on an inspection tour. The Royal Marine engineering squads had little trouble securing the programmable silicon igloos; this section of land was several metres above the mud of the valley floor. But there were logistics problems with supplying the troops.

'It's taking the trucks fifteen hours to get here from the coast,' he said. 'The engineers have virtually had to rebuild the damn road as they went along. Even now there are some sections that are just lines of marker beacons in the mud.'

'I can't do anything about the mud,' Ralph said. 'Believe me, we've tried. Solidifying chemicals, SD lasers to bake it; they're no good on the kind of scale we're dealing with here.'

'What we really need is air support. You flew out here.'

'This was the first inland flight,' Janne Palmer said. 'And your landing-field could barely accommodate the hypersonic. You'll never be able to handle cargo planes.'

'There's plenty of clear high ground nearby, we can build a link road.'

'I'll look into authorizing it,' Ralph said. 'We should certainly consider flying in the serjeants ready for the assault on the town.'

'Appreciate that,' the Colonel said. 'Things out here are a little different than the AI says they should be.'

'That's one of the reasons I'm here, to see how you're coping.'

'We are now. It was bedlam the first day. Could certainly have done with the planes to evac the injured and the de-possessed out. That ride back to the coast isn't doing them any good.'

They came to the big oval hall where Elena Duncan and her team had set up shop. The massive boosted mercenary greeted Ralph with a casual salute of her arm, clicking her claws together. 'Not much ceremony in here, General,' she said. 'We're rather too crowded for that right now. Go see whatever you want, but don't bother my people, please, they're kind of busy right now.'

Ten zero-tau pods were lined up down the centre of the hall, all of them active. The big machines with their thick power cables and compact mosaic of components looked strangely out of place. Or it could be out of era, Ralph acknowledged. The rest of the hall was given over to cots for the serjeants. A field hospital whose primitiveness dismayed him. Elena's mercenaries were carrying large plastic bottles and rolls of disposable paper towels, doing their rounds along the dark bitek constructs. There was a strong chemical smell in the air which Ralph couldn't place. He had some distant memory of it, but certainly not one indexed by his neural nanonics, nor a didactic memory – although they were notoriously inaccurate when it came to imparting smells.

Ralph went over to the first serjeant. The construct was sucking quietly at the tube of a clear polythene bag containing its nutrient syrup, a liquid like thin honey. 'Did you get hit by the mortars?'

'No, General,' Sinon said. 'I wasn't here for the Catmos Vale incident. I am, I believe, one of the lucky ones. I have participated in six assaults which resulted in a possessed being captured, and received only minor injuries during the course of those actions. Unfortunately, that means I have walked the whole way here from the coast.'

'So what happened?'

'Moisture exposure, General. Impossible to avoid, I'm afraid. As I said, I was slightly injured previously, resulting in small cracks within my exoskeleton. Although they are not in themselves dangerous, such hairline fissures are ideal anchorages for several varieties of aboriginal fungal spores.' He indicated his legs.

Now he knew what he was looking for, Ralph could see the long lead-grey blotches criss-crossing round the serjeant's lower limbs; they were slightly fuzzy, like thin velvet. When he glanced along the row of cots, he could see some serjeants where the fungus was full grown, smothering their legs in a thick furry carpet, like soggy coral.

'My God. Does that . . .'

'Hurt?' Sinon enquired. 'Oh, no. Please don't be concerned, General. I don't feel pain, as such. I am aware of the fungus's presence, of course. It does itch rather unpleasantly. The major problem is derived from its effect on my blood chemistry. If left unchecked the fungus would extrude a quantity of toxins that my organs would be unable to filter out.'

'Is there a treatment?'

'Funnily enough, yes. An alcohol rub to eradicate the bulk of the fungus, followed with iodine, appears to be effective in eliminating the growth. Of course, further exposure to these conditions will probably reintroduce the spores, especially as they appear to thrive in this current humidity.'

'Iodine,' Ralph said. 'I thought I knew that smell. Some of the Church clinics on Lalonde used the stuff.' The incongruity of the situation was starting to nag at him. He could hardly be playing the role of older officer giving comfort to a young trooper. If Sinon followed usual Edenist lines, he must have been at least a hundred and fifty when he died. Older than Ralph's grandfather.

'Ah, Lalonde. I never visited. I used to be a voidhawk crew-member.'

'You were lucky; I was posted there for years.'

Somebody started wailing, a piteous gasping cry of bitterness. Ralph looked up to see a couple of the boosted mercenaries helping a man out of a zero-tau pod. He was wrapped in tattered grey clothes, almost indistinguishable from the folds of pale vein-laced flesh drooping from his frame. It was as if his skin had started to melt off him.

'Aww, shit,' Elena Duncan snapped. 'Excuse me, General, looks like we've got another crash-course anorexic.' She hurried over to help her colleagues. 'OK, let's get some protein infusers on him pronto.' The de-possessed man was puking a thin greenish liquid on the floor, an action which was almost choking him.

'Come on,' Ralph said. 'We're just in the way here.' He led the others out of the hall, ashamed that the most helpful thing he personally could do was run away.

*

Stephanie went out on to the narrow balcony and sat in one of the cushioned deckchairs next to Moyo. From there she could look both ways along Ketton's High Street, where squads of Ekelund's guerrilla army marched about. All signs of the mud deluge had been ruthlessly eradicated from the town, producing a pristine vision of urban prosperity. Even the tall scarlet trees lining the streets and central park were in good health, sprouting a thick frost of topaz flowers.

The five of them had been billeted in a lovely mock-Georgian town house, with orange brick walls and carved white stone window lintels. The iron-railed balcony ran along the front, woven with branches of blue and white wisteria. It was one of a whole terrace of beautiful buildings just outside the central retail sector. They shared it with a couple of army squads. Not quite house arrest, but they were certainly discouraged from wandering round and *interfering*. Much to Cochrane's disgust.

But Ekelund and her ultra-loyalists controlled the town's diminishing food supply, and with that came the power to write the rules.

'I hate it here,' Moyo said. He was slumped down almost horizontally in his chair, sipping a margarita. Four empty glasses were already lined up on the low table beside him, their salt rims melting in the condensation. 'The whole place is wrong, a phoney. Can't you sense the atmosphere?'

'I know what you mean.' She watched the men and women thronging the road below. It was the same story all over Ketton. The army was gearing up to defend the town from the serjeants massing outside. Fortifications were first conceived as ghostly sketches in the air, and then made real by an application of energistic strength. Small factories around the outskirts had been placed under Devlin's command. He had his engineers working round the clock to churn out weapons. Everybody here moved with a purpose. And by doing so, they gave each other confidence in their joint cause.

'This is fascist efficiency,' she said. 'Everybody beavering away as they're told for her benefit, not their own. There's going to be so much destruction here when the serjeants come in. And it's all so pointless.'

His hand wavered in the air until he found her arm. Then he gripped tight. 'It's human nature, darling. They're afraid, and she's tapped into that. The alternative to putting up a fight is total surrender. They're not going to go for that. *We* didn't go for that.'

'But the only reason they're in this position is because of her. And we weren't going to fight. I wasn't.'

He took a large drink. 'Ah, forget about it. Another twenty-four hours, and it won't matter any more.'

Stephanie plucked the margarita from his hand and set it down on the table. 'Enough of that. We've rested here quite long enough. Time we were moving on.'

'Ha! You must be drunker than me. We're surrounded. I know that, and I'm fucking blind. There's no way out.'

'Come on.' She took his hand and pulled him up from the chair.

Muttering and complaining, Moyo allowed himself to be led inside. McPhee and Rana were in the lounge, sitting round a circular walnut table with a chess game in front of them. Cochrane was sprawled along a settee, surrounded by a haze of smoke from his reefer. A set of bulky black and gold headphones were clamped over his ears, buzzing loudly as he listened to a Grateful Dead album. Tina and Franklin came in from one of the bedrooms when they were called. Cochrane chortled delightedly at the sight of Franklin tucking his shirt in. He only stopped at that because Stephanie caught his eye.

'I'm going to try and get out,' Stephanie told them.

'Interesting objective,' Rana said. 'Unfortunately, la Ekelund is holding all the cards, not to mention the food. She's hardly given us enough to live on, let alone build our strength back to a level where we can contemplate hiking through the mud again.'

'I know that. But if we stay in the town we're going to get captured by the serjeants for sure. That's if we survive the assault. Both sides are upping their weapons hardware by an alarming degree.'

'I told you this would happen,' Tina said. 'I said we should have stayed above the valley. But none of you listened.'

'So what's the plan?' Franklin asked.

'I haven't got one,' Stephanie said. 'I just want to change the odds, that's all. The serjeants are about five miles away from the outskirts. That leaves a lot of land between us and them.'

'So?' McPhee asked.

'We can use that space. It certainly improves our chances from staying here. Maybe we can sneak through the line in all the confusion when they advance. We could try disguising ourselves as kolfrans, or we could hide out somewhere until they pass by us. It's got to be worth a try.'

'A non-aggressive evasion policy,' Rana said thoughtfully. 'I'm certainly with you on that.'

'No way,' McPhee said. 'Look, I'm sorry, Stephanie, but we've seen the way the serjeants move forwards. You couldn't slide a gnat between them. And that was before the mortar attack. They're wise to us using the ferrangs as camouflage now. If we go out there, we're just going to be the first to be de-possessed.'

'No, no, wait a minute,' Cochrane said. He swung his feet off the settee and walked over to the table. 'Our funky sister might be on to something here.'

'Thanks,' Stephanie grunted sarcastically.

'Listen, you cats. The black hats and their UFOs are like scoping the ground out with microscopes, right? So if we like cooperate with each other and dig ourselves a nice cosy bunker out in the wilderness, we could sit tight down there until they've invaded the town and moved off.'

Several surprised looks were passed round. 'It could work,' Franklin said. 'Hot damn!'

'Hey, am I like *the man*, or what?'

Tina sneered. 'Definitely a what.'

*

'I keep expecting to be asked for my ident flek,' Rana said as the seven of them walked down Ketton's High Street.

They were the only people not wearing military fatigues. Ekelund's army gave them suspicious glances as they passed by. Cochrane's tinkling bells and cheery, insulting waves didn't contribute to making them inconspicuous. When they walked out of the house, Stephanie considered junking her dress and adopting the same jungle combat gear style. Then she thought: To hell with that. I'm not hiding my true self any more. Not after what I've been through. I have a right to be me.

Near the outskirts the road led between two rows of houses. Nothing as elaborate as the Georgian town house, but comfortably middle class. The barrier between town and country was drawn by a deep vertical-walled ditch, with thick iron spikes driven into the soil along the top. Some kind of sludge trickled along the bottom of the trench, stinking of petrol. The arrangement wasn't terribly practical, it was more a statement than a physical danger.

Annette Ekelund was waiting for them, lounging casually against one of the big spikes. Several dozen of her army were ranged beside her. Stephanie was quite sure the hulking guns they had slung over their shoulders would be impossible to lift without energistic power fortifying their muscles. Three-day stubble seemed compulsory for the men, and everyone wore ragged sweatbands.

'You know, I'm getting a bad case of déjà vu here,' Annette said with ersatz pleasantry. 'Except this time you haven't got a good cause to tug my heartstrings. In fact, this is pretty close to treachery.'

'You're not a government,' Stephanie said. 'We don't have loyalties.'

'Wrong. I am the authority here. And you do have obligations. I saved your pathetic little arse, and all these sad bunch of losers you have trailing round with you. I took you in, protected you, and fed you. Now I think that entitles me to a little loyalty, don't you?'

'I'm not going to argue this with you. We don't want to fight. We won't fight. That gives you three choices: you kill us here on the spot, imprison us, which will take up valuable manpower, or let us go free. That's the only issue here.'

'Well, that's actually only two choices, then, isn't it? Because I'm not diverting anybody from their assigned duty to watch over ingrate shits like you.'

'Fine, then make your choice.'

Annette shook her head, genuinely puzzled. 'I don't get you, Stephanie, I really don't. I mean, where the fuck do you think you're going to go? They do have us surrounded, you know. An hour walking down that road and you're straight into zero-tau. Do not pass Go, do not collect two hundred dollars. And you will never, ever get out of jail again for the rest of time.'

'We might be able to dodge them in open ground.'

'That's it? That's your whole gameplan? Stephanie, that's pitiful even for you.'

Stephanie pressed closer to Moyo, unnerved by the level of animosity running free in Annette's thoughts. 'So what's your alternative?'

'We fight for our right to exist. It's what people have been doing for a very long time. If you weren't such a small-town imbecile you'd see that nothing easy ever comes free; life is cash on delivery.'

'I'm sure it is, but you haven't answered my question. You know you're going to lose, what's the point in fighting?'

'Let me explain,' Hoi Son said. Annette flashed him a look of pure anger, then nodded permission.

'The purpose of our action is to inflict unacceptable losses on the enemy,' Hoi Son said. 'The serjeants are almost unstoppable here on the ground, but the political structure behind them is susceptible to a great many forces. We might not win this battle, but our cause will ultimately triumph. That triumph will come sooner once the Confederation leadership is forced to retreat from ventures like this absurd Liberation. Their victory must be as costly as we can make it. I ask you to reconsider your decision to leave us. With your help, the time we have to spend in the beyond will be reduced by a considerable margin. Just think, the serjeant you exterminate today may well be the one that breaks the camel's back.'

'You lived before Edenism matured, didn't you?' Moyo asked.

'The habitat Eden was germinated while I was alive. I didn't survive long after that.'

'Then I have to tell you, what you're talking is total bullshit. The political ideologies you're basing your justifications on are centuries out of date – just like all of us. Edenism has a resolution which is frightening in its totality.'

'All human resolve can be broken in the end.'

Moyo turned his perfect, unseeing eyes to Stephanie, and twisted his lips in a humble grimace. 'We're doomed. You can't reason with a psychopath and a demented ideologue.'

'You should tell your boyfriend to watch his lip,' Annette said.

'Or what?' Moyo laughed. 'You said it, Psycho Mamma, you told Ralph Hiltch all those weeks ago: the possessed don't lose. It doesn't matter how many bodies of mine you blast away. I will always be back. Learn to live with me, because you can never escape. For all of eternity you have to listen to me whingeing on and on and on and on . . . How do you like that, you dumb motherfucker?'

'Enough.' Stephanie patted his shoulder in warning. He couldn't see Annette's expression, but he'd be able to sense her darkening thoughts. 'Look, we're just going to go, all right.'

Annette turned and spat into the trench. 'You know what's down there? It's something called napalm. Hoi Son told us about it, and Milne made up the formula. There's tons of the stuff, lying down there in squirt bombs, loaded into flame-throwers. So when the serjeants come over, it's going to be barbecue time. And that's just this section. We've got a shitload of grief rigged up for them around this town. Every street they walk down is going to cost them in bodies. Hell, we're even running a sweepstake, see how many we can take with us.'

'I hope you win.'

'The point is, Stephanie, if you leave now, you don't come back.

I mean that. If you desert us, your own kind, then you're our enemy just as much as the non-possessed are. You're going to be trapped out there between the serjeants and me. They'll shove you into zero-tau, I'll have you strung up on a crucifix and fried. So you see, it's not me that makes the choices. In the end, it's down to you.'

Stephanie gave her a sad smile. 'I choose to leave.'

'You stupid bitch.' For a moment, Stephanie thought the woman was going to launch a bolt of white fire straight at her. Annette was fighting very hard to control her fury.

'OK,' she snapped. 'Get out. Now.'

Praying that Cochrane would keep his mouth shut, Stephanie tugged Moyo gently. 'Use one of the spikes,' she murmured to McPhee and Rana. They both began to concentrate. The nearest spike started to droop, lowering itself like a drawbridge across a moat. When its tip touched the other side, the metal flattened out, producing a narrow walkway.

Tina was over first; shaking and subdued at the naked hostility radiating from Ekelund and imitated by her troops. Franklin guided Moyo over. Stephanie waited until the other three were on the far side before using it herself. When she turned round, Annette was already marching back down the road into Ketton. Hoi Son and a couple of others walked behind her, taking care not to come too close. The remaining troops stared hard over the trench. Several of them primed the pump-action mechanism on their guns.

'Yo, nooo problem, dudes,' Cochrane crooned anxiously. 'We're outta here. Like yesterday.'

*

It was midday, the sun blazed down on them like a visible X-ray laser, and the mist had gone long ago. Three miles ahead, the rumpled foothills of the valley wall rose up out of the sluggish quagmires. The serjeants were strung out across the slopes, forming a solid line of dark blobs standing almost shoulder to shoulder. Larger groups were arranged at intervals behind the front line, reserves ready to assist with any sign of resistance.

A couple of miles behind, the air shimmered silver, twisting light beams giddily around Ketton. Dry mud creaked and crumbled under their feet as they tramped along the gently undulating road. They weren't going particularly fast. It wasn't just hunger draining their bodies. Apathy was coming on strong.

'Oh, hell,' Stephanie said abruptly. 'Look, I'm sorry.'

'What for?' McPhee asked. There was bravado in his voice, but not his thoughts.

'Oh, come on!' She stopped and flung her arms out, turning full circle on a heel. 'I was wrong. Look at this place. We're snowflakes heading straight for hell.'

McPhee gave a grudging look around the flat, featureless valley floor. During the few days they'd rested in Ketton the mud had claimed just about every fallen tree and bush. Even the long pools between the quagmires were evaporating away. 'Not much in the way of ground cover, granted.'

She gave the big Scot an admonitory stare. 'You're very sweet, and I'm really glad that you're with me. But I goofed. There's no way we can avoid the serjeants out here. And I do think Ekelund was serious when she said we wouldn't be allowed back in.'

'Yeah,' Cochrane said. 'That's the impression I got, too. You know, that bug is shoved so far up, it's going to be flapping its way out of her mouth any day now.'

'I don't understand,' Tina said miserably. 'Why don't we just stick to Cochrane's original idea, and dig in?'

'The satellites can see us, lass,' McPhee said. 'Aye, they don't know how many of us there are, exactly, or what we're doing. But they know where we are. If we stop moving and suddenly vanish, then the serjeants will come and investigate. They'll realize what we've done and excavate us.'

'We could split up,' Franklin said. 'If we walk about at random and keep crossing each other's tracks, then one or two of us could vanish without them realizing. It'd be like a giant-sized version of the shell game.'

'But I don't want us to split up,' Tina said.

'We're not splitting up,' Stephanie told her. 'We've been through too much together for that. I say we face them together with dignity and pride. We have nothing to be ashamed of. They're the ones who have failed. That huge, wonderful society with all its resources, and all it can do is fall back on violence instead of trying to find an equitable solution for all of us. They've lost, not us.'

Tina sniffed, and dabbed at her eyes with a small handkerchief. 'You say the most beautiful things.'

'Certainly do, sister.'

'I'll face the serjeants with you, Stephanie,' McPhee said. 'But it might be a good idea to get off this road first. I'll give you good odds our friends behind have got it in their mortar sights.'

*

Ralph waited until there were twenty-three thousand serjeants deployed at Catmos Vale before giving the go-ahead to take the town. The AI estimated at least eight thousand possessed were trapped inside Ketton. He wasn't going to be responsible for unleashing a massacre. There would be enough serjeants to overcome whatever lay ahead.

As soon as the first mortar attack finished, the AI pulled the front line back. Then the flanks, up in the high ground above the valley, were directed forwards again. By the time the sun fell, Ketton was surrounded. To start with, the circle was simply there to prevent individual possessed from trying to sneak out. Any large group that tried their luck would be warned off with SD lasers in a repeat of the firebreak protocol across the neck of the peninsula.

Very few did attempt to run the gauntlet. Whatever method of discipline Ekelund was using to keep her people in check, it was impressive. The perimeter was progressively reinforced as planes and trucks brought in fresh squads. Occupation forces were also assembled and dispatched around the front line, ready to handle the captured possessed. Medical facilities were organized to cope with the predicted influx of new, unhealthy bodies (though shortages of equipment and qualified personnel were still acute). The AI had exhaustively analysed every possible weapon from history which the possessed could have constructed, and computed appropriate counter-measures.

Ralph was quietly pleased to see that the simplest policy was amongst the oldest: the best defence is a good offence. He might not be able to employ saturation bombardment against the town, or melt it down into the bedrock. But he could certainly rattle the doors of Ekelund's precious sanctum, a quite severe rattling, in fact. 'Quake them,' he datavised.

Two thousand kilometres above Ombey, a lone voidhawk began its deployment swoop.

Ralph waited beside the rectangular headquarters building with Acacia and Janne Palmer standing beside him. They all stared along Catmos Vale at the sliver of dense mangled air at the far end which marked the town. Maybe he should have been back at the Fort Forward Ops Room, but after visiting the camp he realized how restricted and isolated he was sitting in his office. Out here, at least he had the illusion of being involved.

*

It was one of the larger patches of land above the lagoons and mires that cluttered the valley floor. Plenty of aboriginal grass poked up through the solidifying cloak of mud, as yet untrampled by animals. There were even some trees surviving near the centre; they'd fallen down, their lower branches stabbing into the soft ground, but the trunks were held off the ground, and their battered leaves were slowly twisting to face the sky.

Stephanie made her way over to them, putting the road a quarter of a mile behind her. The ground around the sagging boughs was deeply wrinkled, producing dozens of small meandering pools of brackish water. She threaded her way through them, into the small dapple of shade thrown by the leaves, and sank down with a heavy sigh. The others sat down around her, equally relieved to be off their feet.

'I'm amazed we didn't step on a mine,' Moyo said. 'Ekelund must have rigged that road. It's too tempting not to.'

'Hey, guys, let's like turn her into an unperson, please,' Cochrane said. 'I don't want to spend my last remaining hours in this body talking about that bitch.'

Rana leant back against a tree trunk, closed her eyes and smiled. 'Well, well, we finally agree on something.'

'I wonder if we get a chance to talk to the reporters,' McPhee said. 'There's bound to be some covering the attack.'

'Peculiar last wish,' Rana said. 'Any particular reason?'

'I still have some family left alive on Orkney. Three kids. I'd like to ... I don't know. Tell them I'm all right, I suppose. What I'd really like to do is see them again.'

'Nice thought,' Franklin said. 'Maybe the serjeants will let you record a message, especially if we cooperate with them.'

'What about you?' Stephanie asked.

'I'd go traditional,' Franklin said. 'A meal. You see, I used to like eating, trying new stuff, but I never really had much money. So, I've done most everything else I want to. I'd have the best delicacies the universe can offer, cooked by the finest chef in the Confederation, and Norfolk Tears to go with it.'

'Mine's easy,' Cochrane said. 'That's like apart from the obvious. I wanna relive Woodstock. Only this time I'd listen to the music more. Man, I can like only remember about five hours of it. Can you dig that? What a bummer.'

'I want to be on the stage,' Tina said breathlessly. 'A classical actress, in my early twenties, while I'm so beautiful that poets swoon at the sight of me. And when my new play opens, it will be *the* event of the year, and all the society people in the world are fighting to buy tickets.'

'I'd like to walk through Elisea Woods again,' Rana said. She gave Cochrane a suspect look, but he was listening politely. 'It was on the edge of my town when I was growing up, and the slandau flowers grew there. They had chroma-tactile petals; if you touched one, it would change colour. When the breeze blew through the trees it was like standing inside a kaleidoscope. I used to spend hours walking along the paths. Then the developers came, and cleared the site to make room for a factory park. It didn't matter what I said to anyone, how many petitions I organized; the mayor, the local senator, they didn't care how beautiful the woods were and how much people enjoyed them. Money and industry won every time.'

'I think I'd just say sorry to my parents,' Moyo said. 'My life was such a waste.'

'The children,' Stephanie said. She grinned knowingly at McPhee. 'I want to see my children again.'

They fell silent then, content to daydream what could never be.

The sky suddenly brightened. Everyone apart from Moyo looked up, and he caught their agitation. Ten kinetic harpoons were descending, drawing their distinctive dazzling plasma contrails behind them. It was a conical formation, gradually expanding. A second batch of ten harpoons appeared above the first. Sunglasses automatically materialized on Stephanie's face.

'Oh, shit,' McPhee groaned. 'It's yon kinetic harpoons, again.'

'They're coming down all around Ketton.'

'Strange pattern,' Franklin said. 'Why not fire them down all at once?'

'Does it matter?' Rana said. 'It's obviously the signal to start the attack.'

McPhee was eyeing the harpoons dubiously. The first formation was still expanding, while the blazing, ruptured air around their nose-cones was growing in intensity.

'I think we'd better get down,' Stephanie said. She rolled over, and imagined a sheet of air hardening protectively above her. The others followed her example.

The harpoons Ralph had chosen to deploy against Ketton were different to the marque he'd used to smash Mortonridge's communication net at the start of the Liberation. These were considerably heavier and longer, a design which helped focus their inertia forwards. On impact, they penetrated clean through the damp, unresisting soil. Only when they struck the bedrock below did their tremendous kinetic energy release its full destructive potential. The explosive blast slammed out through the soft soil. Directly above the impact point the whole area heaved upwards as if a new volcano was trying to tear its way skywards. But the major impetus of the shock waves radiated outwards. Then the second formation of harpoons hit. They formed a ring outside the first, with exactly the same devastating effect.

Seen from above, the twenty separate shock waves spread out like ripples in a pond. But it was the one very specific interference pattern they formed as they intersected which was the goal of the bombardment. Colossal energies clashed and merged in peaks and troughs that mimicked the surface of a choppy sea, channelling the direction in which the force was expended. Outside the two strike rings, the newly formatted shock waves rushed off across the valley floor, becoming progressively weaker until they sank away to nothing more than a tremble which lapped against the foothills. Inside the rings, they merged into a single contracting undulation, which swept in towards Ketton, building in height and vigour.

Annette Ekelund and the troops manning the town's perimeter defences watched in stupefaction as the newborn hill thundered towards them from all directions. The surviving network of local roads leading away from the outskirts were ripped to shreds as the swelling slope flung them aside. Boulders went spinning through the air in long lazy arks. Mud foamed turbulently at the crest while mires and pools avalanched down the sides, engulfing the frenzied herds of kolfrans and ferrangs.

It grew higher and higher, a tsunami of soil. The leading edge reached Ketton's outlying buildings, trawling them up its precarious ever-shifting slope. Defence trenches either slammed shut or split wide as though they were geological fault lines, their napalm igniting in a third-rate imitation of lava streams. People diverted every fraction of their energistic strength to reinforcing their bodies, leaving them to bounce and roll about like human tumbleweed as the demented ground trampolined beneath them. Without the possessed to maintain them, the prim, restored houses and shops burst apart in scattergun showers of debris. Bricks, fragments of glass, vehicles, and shattered timbers took flight to clot the air above the devastation.

And still the quake raced on, hurtling into the centre of the town. Its contraction climaxed underneath the charming little church, culminating in a solid conical geyser of ground fifty metres high. A grinding vortex of soil erupted from its pinnacle, propelling the entire church into the sky. The elegant structure hung poised above the cataclysm for several seconds before gravity and sanity returned to claim it. It broke open like a ship on a reef, scattering pews and hymn books over the blitzed land below. Then as the quake's pinnacle ebbed, shrinking down, the church tumbled over, walls disintegrating into a deluge of powdered bricks. Yet still, somehow, the spire remained almost intact. Twisting through a hundred and eighty degrees, with its bell clanging madly, it plunged down to puncture the tormented crater of raw soil that now marked the quake's epicentre. Only then did its structural girders crumple, reducing it to a pile of ruined metal and fractured carbon-concrete.

Secondary tremors withdrew from the focal point, weaker than the incoming quake, but still resulting in substantial quivers amid the pulverized ruins. The quake's accompanying ultrasound retreated, only to echo back off the valley walls. In ninety seconds, Ketton had been abolished from Mortonridge, leaving a two mile wide smear of treacherously loose soil as its sole memorial. Spears made from building rafters jabbed up out of the rumpled black ground, ragged lumps of concrete were interspersed with the mashed-up remnants of furniture, every fragment embedded deep into the loam. Rivulets of flaming napalm oozed along winding furrows, belching out black smoke. A curtain of dust thick enough to blot out the sun swirled overhead.

Annette raised herself to her elbows, fighting the mud's suction, and swung her head slowly from side to side, examining the remains of her proud little empire. Her energistic strength had protected her body from broken bones and torn skin, though she knew that there was going to be heavy bruising just about everywhere. She remembered being about ten metres in the air at one point, cartwheeling slowly as a single-storey café did a neat somersault beside her to land on its flat roof, power cables and plastic water pipes trailing from a wall to lash about like bullwhips.

Strangely enough, through her numbness, she could admire the quake; there was a beautiful precision to it. Strong enough to wreck the town, yet pitched at a level that enabled the possessed to protect themselves from its effects. As dear Ralph had known they would. Self-preservation is the strongest human instinct; Ketton's buildings and fortifications would be discarded instantly in the face of such a lethal threat.

She laughed hysterically, choking on the filthy dust. 'Ralph? I told you, Ralph, you had to destroy the village first. There was no need to take it so fucking literally, *you shit!*' There was nothing left now to defend, no banner or cause around which she could rally her army. The serjeants were coming. Unopposed. Unstoppable.

Annette flopped onto her back, expelling grit from her eyes and mouth. Her mouth puffed away, eager for much-needed oxygen. She had never been so utterly terrified before. It was an emotion shining at the core of every mind littered around her in the decimated town. Thousands of them. The one aspect they had left in common.

*

The trees had stood up and danced during the quake. They left the cloying mud behind with loud sucking sounds and pirouetted about while the ground rearranged itself. It was probably an impressive sight. But only from a distance.

Stephanie had screamed constantly as she wriggled frantically underneath the carouselling boughs, ducking the smaller branches that raked the ground. She'd been struck several times, slapped through the air as if by a giant bat. Only the energistic power binding her body's cells together had saved her from being snapped in two.

Tina hadn't been so fortunate. As the ground started to calm, one of the trees had fallen straight on top of her. It pushed her deep into the soaking loam, leaving only her head and an arm sticking out. She was whimpering softly as the others gathered round. 'I can't feel anything,' she whispered. 'I can't make myself feel.'

'Just melt the wood away,' McPhee said quickly, and pointed. 'Here to here. Come on, concentrate.'

They held hands, imagining the scarlet bark parting, the hard dark wood of the trunk flowing like water. A big chunk of the trunk turned to liquid and splattered down on the mud. Franklin and McPhee hurried forward and pulled Tina out from the mud. Her hips and legs were badly crushed, blood was running out of several deep wounds, splintered bones protruded through the skin.

She looked down at her injuries, and wailed in fear. 'I'm going to die! I'm going to go back to the beyond.'

'Nonsense, babe,' Cochrane said. He knelt down beside her and passed his hand over one of the abdominal cuts. The torn flesh sealed over, melding together. 'See? Don't give me none of this loser shit.'

'There's too much damage.'

'Come on, guys.' Cochrane looked up at the rest of the group. 'Together we can do it. Each take a wound.'

Stephanie nodded quickly and sank down beside him. 'It'll be all right,' she promised Tina. The woman had lost an awful lot of blood, though.

They circled her, and laid on their hands. Power was exerted, transmuted by the wish to heal and cleanse. That was how Sinon's squad found them, kneeling as if in prayer around one of their own. Tina was smiling up placidly, her pale hand gripping Rana, their fingers entwined.

Sinon and Choma approached cautiously through the jumbled trees, and levelled their machine-guns at the devout-seeming group. 'I want all of you to lie down flat, and put your hands behind your head, now,' Sinon said. 'Do not attempt to move or apply your energistic power.'

Stephanie turned to face him. 'Tina's hurt, she can't move.'

'I will accept that claim for the moment, providing you do not try to resist. Now, the rest of you lie down.'

Moving slowly, they backed away from Tina and lowered themselves onto the mushy loam.

You can come forward, Sinon told the rest of the squad. **They appear to be compliant.**

Thirty serjeants emerged from the tangle of branches and twigs, making remarkably little sound. Their machine-guns were all trained on the prone figures.

'You will now leave your captured bodies,' Sinon said.

'We can't,' Stephanie said. She could feel the misery and fear in her friends, the same as that found in her own mind. It was turning her voice to a piteous croak. 'You should know by now not to ask that of us.'

'Very well.' Sinon took his holding stick out.

'You don't have to use those things, either,' Stephanie said. 'We'll go quietly.'

'Sorry, procedure.'

'Look, I'm Stephanie Ash. I'm the one that brought the children out. That must count for something. Check with Lieutenant Anver of the Royal Kulu Marines, he'll confirm who I am.'

Sinon paused, and used his processor block to query Fort Forward's memory core. The image of the woman certainly appeared to match, and the man with flamboyant clothes and a mass of hair was unmistakable.

We can't rely on what they look like, Choma said. **They can forge any appearance they want.**

Providing they cooperate, there is no reason to use unnecessary force. So far they have obeyed, and they know they cannot escape.

You're far too trusting.

'You will get up one at a time when instructed,' Sinon told them. 'We will escort you back to our field camp where you will be placed in zero-tau. Three machine-guns will be trained upon you at all times. If any order is refused, we use the holding sticks to neutralize your energistic ability. Do you understand?'

'That's very clear,' Stephanie said. 'Thank you.'

'Very well. You first.'

Stephanie climbed cautiously to her feet, making sure every

motion was a slow one. Choma flicked the nozzle of his machine-gun, indicating the small track through the collapsed trees. 'Let's go.' She started walking. Behind her, Sinon was telling Franklin to get up.

'Tina will need a stretcher,' Stephanie said. 'And someone will have to guide Moyo, he's damaged his eyes.'

'Don't worry,' Choma said gruffly. 'We'll make sure you all get to the camp OK.'

They emerged from the trees. Stephanie looked at where Ketton had been. A dense cloud of dark grey dust churned over the annihilated town. Small fires burned underneath it, muted orange coronas shining weakly. Twenty slender purple lines glowed faintly in the air above, linking the cloud with the top of the atmosphere. Streaks of lightning discharged along them intermittently.

'Bloody hell,' she murmured. Thousands of serjeants were walking along the valley floor towards the silent, murky ruins. The possessed cowering within knew they were coming. Raw fear was spilling out of the dust cloud like gaseous adrenalin. Stephanie's heart started to beat faster. Cold shivers ran along her legs and up her chest. She faltered.

Choma nudged her with his machine-gun. 'Keep going.'

'Can't you feel it? They're frightened.'

'Good.'

'No, I mean really frightened. Look.'

Glimmers of burgundy light were escaping through gaps in the dust cloud. Billowing tendril-like wisps around the edges were flattening out, becoming smooth and controlled. The shield against the open sky was returning.

'I didn't think you were stupid enough to try that again,' Choma said. 'General Hiltch won't permit you to hide.'

Even as he spoke an SD electron beam stabbed down through the clear air. A blue-white pillar two hundred metres wide struck the apex of the seething roof of dust. It sprayed apart with a plangent boom, sending out broad lightning forks that roamed across the boiling surface to skewer into the mud. This time, the possessed resisted. Ten thousand minds concentrated within a couple of square miles, all striving for the same effect. To be free.

The random discharges of the SD beam were slowly tamed. Jagged forks compressing into garish rivers of electrons that formed a writhing cage above the dust. Carmine light brightened underneath. Fear turned to rapture, followed swiftly by determination. Stephanie stared across at the clamorous spectacle, her mouth open in astonishment, and pride. Their old unity was back. And with it came a formidable sense of purpose: to achieve the safety that so many other possessed had obtained. To be gone.

The red light in the cloud strengthened to a lambent glare, then began to stain the ground of the valley floor. A bright circular wave spreading out through the mud and sluggish water.

'Run,' Stephanie told the confounded serjeants. 'Get clear. Please. Go!' She braced herself as the redness charged towards her. There was no physical sensation other than a near-psychosomatic tingle. Then her body was glowing along with the ground, the air, her friends, and the hulking bodies of the serjeants.

'All right!' Cochrane whooped. He punched the air. 'Let's go for it, you crazy-ass mothers.'

The earth trembled, dispatching all of them to their knees again. Sinon tried to keep his machine-gun lined up on the nearest captive, but the ground shook again, more violently this time. He abandoned that procedure, and flattened himself. All the serjeants in the Ketton assault linked their minds through general affinity, clinging to each other mentally with a determination that matched their grip on the ground.

'What is happening?' he bellowed.

'We're like outta here, man,' Cochrane shouted back. 'You're on the last bus out of this universe.'

*

Ralph watched the red light inflate out of the dust cloud. Datavises from SD sensors and local occupation forces spread around Catmos Vale relayed the image from multiple angles, granting him complete three hundred and sixty degree coverage. He knew what it looked like from the air, from the ground, even (briefly) as it engulfed marines who were following close behind the serjeants. But most of all, he just stared ahead as it poured out across the valley.

'Oh my God,' he breathed. It was going to be bad. He knew that. Very bad.

'Do you want a full SD strike?' Admiral Farquar asked.

'I don't know. It looks like it's slowing.'

'Confirmed. Roughly circular, twelve kilometres across. And they've got two-thirds of the serjeants in there.'

'Are they still alive?' Ralph asked Acacia.

'Yes, General. Their electronics have collapsed completely, but they're alive and able to use affinity.'

'Then what—' The ground shifted abruptly below his feet. He landed painfully on his side. The programmable silicon buildings of the camp were jittering about. Everywhere, people were on their knees or spreadeagled.

'Shit!' Acacia shouted.

A sheer cliff was rising up vertically right across the valley floor, corresponding to the edge of the red light. Huge cascades of mud and boulders were tumbling down its face. The red light followed them down, pervading the rock, and growing brighter.

Ralph rejected his instinct. What he was seeing was just too much, even though he knew they'd done this to entire planets. 'They can't,' he cried.

'But they are, General,' Acacia replied. 'They're leaving.'

The cliff was still ascending. Two hundred metres now, lifting with increasing confidence and speed. It was becoming difficult to look at as the light turned scarlet, casting long shadows across the valley. Three hundred metres high, and Ralph's neural nanonics had crashed in the backwash of the blossoming reality dysfunction. On the ground around him the battered blades of grass were wriggling their way back upwards again, shedding their cloak of mud to turn the camp into a verdant parkland. Fallen trees bent their trunks like the spine of an old man rising from his chair, cranking themselves upright again.

The vivid red light began to diminish. When Ralph squinted against it, he could see the cliff retreating from him. It was five hundred metres high, moving away with the majestic serenity of an iceberg. Except it wasn't moving, he realized. It was shrinking, the red light contracting in on itself, enveloping the island of rock which the possessed had uprooted from Mortonridge to sail away into another universe. As it left he could see its entire shape, a flat-topped inverted cone wrapped with massive curving stress ridges that spiralled down to its base, as if it had unscrewed itself from the peninsula.

Air was roaring hard overhead, sucked into the space the island

421

was vacating. It still hovered in the centre of the valley, but now it was becoming insubstantial as well as small. The light around it turned a dazzling monochrome white, obliterating details. Within minutes it had evaporated down to a tiny star. Then it winked out. Ralph's neural nanonics came back on-line.

'Cancel the other two assaults,' he datavised to the AI. 'And halt the front line. Now.'

He scrambled cautiously to his feet. The reinvigorated grass was withering all around him, shrivelling back to dry brown flakes that crumbled away in the howling wind. Images from the SD sensors showed him the full extent of the massive crater. Its edges had already begun to subside, mountain-sized landslides were skidding downwards, taking a very long time to reach the bottom. Waiting for them five kilometres down was a medieval orange glow that fluctuated in no comprehensible rhythm. He frowned at that, not understanding what it could be. Then the vivid area ruptured, and a vast fountain of radiant lava soared upwards.

'Whoever's left, get them back,' he shouted desperately at Acacia. 'Get them as far away from the lip as possible.'

'They're already retreating,' she said.

'What about the others? The ones on the island? Can your affinity still reach them?'

Her forlorn look was all the answer he needed.

*

Stephanie and her friends looked at the serjeants, who stared back with equal uncertainty. For the first time in what her dazed thoughts insisted must be hours, the ground had stopped oscillating beneath her. When she looked up, the sky was a starless ultra-deep blue. White light flooded down from nowhere she could see – but felt right, what she wanted. Her gaze tracked round to where the other side of the valley had been. The blank sky came right down to the ground, and the true size of their island became apparent. A tiny circle of land edged with a crinkled line of hillocks, adrift in its own eternal universe.

'Oh, no,' she murmured in despair. 'I think we screwed up.'

'Are we free?' Moyo asked.

'For now.' She started describing their new home to him.

Sinon and the other serjeants used the general affinity band to call to each other. There were over twelve thousand of them spread out around the island. Their guns worked, their electronics and medical nanonics didn't (several had been injured in the waves of quakes), affinity was unaffected, and there were new senses available. Almost a derivative of affinity, allowing him to sense the minds of the possessed. And there was also the energistic power. He picked a stone from the mud and held it in his palm. It slowly turned transparent, and began to sparkle. Not that a kilogram of diamond was a lot of use here.

'Could you dudes like give this heavy military scene a break now?' Cochrane asked.

It would appear our original purpose is invalid in this environment, Sinon told his comrades. He shouldered his machine-gun. 'Very well. What do you propose we do next?' he asked the hippy.

'Wow, man, don't look at me. Stephanie's in charge around here.'

'I'm not. And anyway, I haven't got a clue what happens now.'

'Then why did you bring us here?' Choma asked.

'Because it's not Mortonridge,' Moyo said. 'That's all. Stephanie told you, we were frightened.'

'And this is the result,' Rana said. 'You must now face the consequences of your physical aggression.'

We should regroup and pool our physical resources, Choma said. **It may even be possible for us to use the energistic power to return to the universe.**

Their minds flashed together into a mini-Consensus and agreed to the proposal. An assembly area was designated.

'We are going to join up with our comrades,' Sinon told Stephanie. 'You would be very welcome to come with us. I expect your views on the situation could prove valuable.'

That last image of Ekelund popped up annoyingly in Stephanie's mind. The woman had banished them from Ketton. But Ketton no longer existed. Surely they wouldn't be excluded now? Somehow she couldn't convince herself. And the only other alternative was staying by themselves. Without food. 'Thank you,' she said.

'Wait, wait,' Cochrane said. 'You guys have like got to be kidding. Look, the end of the world is maybe half a mile away. Aren't you even curious what's out there?'

Sinon looked to where the island's crumpled surface ended. 'That's a good suggestion.'

Cochrane grinned brightly. 'You cats'll have to get used to them if you're going to hang with me.'

The breeze picked up considerably as they approached the edge of the island. Blowing outward, which troubled the serjeants. Air had become a finite commodity. Long rivulets of mud were sliding gently to the edge and spilling over, dribbling down the cliff like ribbons of candle wax. There was nothing else to see. No break in the uniformity of the midnight-blue boundary of the universe that might indicate another object, micro or macro. The realization they were on their own percolated through all of them, growing stronger as they approached the rim.

It was only Cochrane who inched his way cautiously right up to the edge and peered down into the murky void of infinity which buoyed them along. He spread his arms wide and threw his head back, letting the breeze flowing over the island blow his hair around. 'WAAAAAHOOOO.' His feet jigged about crazily as he cried out ecstatically: 'I'm on a fucking flying island. Can you believe this? Here be dragons, Mom! And they're GROOVY.'

11

For some reason, the tangled strands of black mist which filled this dark continuum would always slide apart to allow Valisk through. Not one wisp had ever touched the polyp. The habitat personality still hadn't managed to determine the nature of movement outside its shell. Without valid reference points, there was no way of knowing if it was sailing along on some unknowable voyage, or the veils of darkness were simply gusting past. The identity, structure, and quantum signature of their new continuum remained a complete mystery. They didn't even know if the ebony nebula was made from matter. All they did know for certain was that a hard vacuum lay outside the shell.

Rubra's uncorked brigade of descendants had devoted considerable effort into modifying spaceport MSVs into automated sensor platforms. Five of the vehicles had already been launched, their chemical rockets burning steadily as they raced off into the void. Combustion, at least, remained an inter-universal constant. The same could not be said for their electronic components. Only the most basic of systems would function outside the protection of the shell. And even those decayed in proportion to the distance travelled. The power circuits themselves failed at about a hundred kilometres. By which time the amount of information transmitted had fallen to near zero. Which was information in itself. The continuum had an intrinsic damping effect on electromagnetic radiation; presumably this accounted for the funereal nature of the nebula. Physicists and the personality speculated that such an effect might be influencing electron orbits, which in turn would explain some of the electrical and biochemical problems they were encountering.

The gigantic web of ebony vapour wouldn't touch the probes, either, denying them a sample/return mission. Radar was utterly useless. Even laser radar could only just track the modified MSVs. Ten days after the axial light-tube was powered up, they were floundering badly. No experiment or observation they'd run had resulted in the acquisition of hard data. Without that, they couldn't even start to theorize how to get back.

By contrast, life inside the habitat was becoming more ordered, though not necessarily pleasant. Everybody who'd been possessed required medical treatment of some kind. Worst hit were the elderly, whose possessors had quite relentlessly twisted and moulded their flesh into the more vigorous contours sported by youthful bodies. Anyone who'd been overweight was also suffering. As were the thin, the short, anyone with different skin colour to their possessor, different hair. And without exception, everyone's features had been morphed about – that came as naturally as breathing to the possessed.

Valisk didn't have anything like the number of medical nanonic packages required to treat the population. Those packages that were available operated at a very low efficiency level. Medical staff who could program them correctly shared the same psychologically fragile demeanour as all the recently de-possessed. And Rubra's descendants were tremendously busy just trying to keep the habitat supplied with power to give much assistance to the sick. Besides, the numbers were stacked hard and high against them.

After the initial burst of optimism at the return of light, a grim resignation settled among the refugees as more and more of their circumstances were revealed to them. An exodus began. They started walking towards the caverns of the northern endcap. Long caravans of people wound their way out from the starscraper lobby parks, trampling down the dainty paths as they set off down the interior. In many cases, it took several days to walk the twenty kilometres across the scrub desert. They were searching for a haven where the medical packages would work properly, where there was some kind of organized authority and a decent meal, a place where the ghosts didn't lurk around the boundaries. That grail wasn't to be found amid the decrepit slums encircling the starscraper lobbies.

I don't know what the hell they expect me to do for them, the habitat personality complained to Dariat (among others) as the first groups set out. *There's not enough food in the caverns, for a start.*

Then you'd better work out how to get hold of some, Dariat replied. *Because they've got the right idea. The starscrapers can't support them any more.*

Power within the towers was as erratic as it had been ever since they arrived in the dark continuum. The lifts didn't work. Food-secretion organs extruded inedible sludge. Digestion organs were unable to process and flush the waste. Air circulation tubules spluttered and wheezed.

If the starscrapers can't sustain them, then the caverns certainly won't be able to, the personality replied.

Nonsense. Half the trees in your interior are fruiting varieties.

Barely a quarter. In any case, all the orchards are down at the southern end.

Then get teams organized to pick the fruit, and strip the remaining supplies from the starscrapers. You'd have to do this, anyway. You are the government here, remember. They'll do as you tell them; they always have. It'll be a comfort having the old authority figure take charge again.

All right, all right. I don't need the psychology lectures.

Order, of a kind, was established. The caverns came to resemble a blend of nomad camps and field hospital triage wards. People slumped where they found a spare patch of ground, waiting to be told what to do next. The personality resumed its accustomed role, and started issuing orders. Cancers and aggravated anorexias were assessed and prioritized, the medical packages distributed accordingly. Like the fusion generators and physics lab equipment, they worked best in the deeper caverns. Teams were formed from the healthiest, and assigned to food procurement duties. There were also teams to strip the starscrapers of equipment, clothes, blankets – a broad range of essentials. Transport had to be organized.

The ghosts followed faithfully after their old hosts, of course. Flittering across the desert during the twilight hours to skulk about in the hollows and crevices decorating the base of the northern endcap during the day. Naked hostility continued to act as an intangible buffer, preventing them from entering any of the subterranean passages.

It also expelled Dariat. The refugees didn't distinguish between ghosts. In any case, had they discovered he was the architect of their current status, their antipathy would probably have wiped him out altogether. His one consolation was that the personality was now part self. It wouldn't disregard him and his needs as an annoying irritation.

In part he was right, though the assumption of privilege was an arrogant one – the pure Dariat of old. However, in these strange, dire times, there were even useful jobs to be had for cooperative ghosts. The personality gave him Tolton as a partner, and detailed the pair of them to take an inventory of the starscrapers.

'Him!' Tolton had exclaimed in dismay when Erentz explained his new duties.

She looked from the shocked and indignant street poet to the fat ghost with his mocking smile. 'You worked well together before,' she ventured. 'I'm proof of that.'

'Yeah, but—'

'OK. Most of that row need seeing to.' She gestured at the long line of beds along the polyp wall. It was one of eight similar rows in the vaulted cavern, made up from mattresses or clustered pillows hurriedly shoved into a loose kind of order. The ailing occupants were wrapped in dirty blankets like big shivering pupae. They moaned and drooled and soiled themselves as the nanonic packages sluggishly repaired their damaged cells. Their helpless state meant they needed constant nursing. And there were few enough people left over from the teams prospecting the habitat able to do that.

'Which starscraper do we start with?' Tolton asked.

Each starscraper took at least three days to inventory properly. They'd adopted a comfortable routine by the time they started on their third, the Djerba. The tower had survived Valisk's recent calamities with minimal damage. Kiera's wrecking teams hadn't got round to 'reclaiming' it from Rubra's control. There had been few clashes between possessed and servitors inside before it was abandoned. That meant it should contain plenty of useful items. They just needed cataloguing.

To send the work teams down on a see/grab brief was inefficient, especially as there were so few of them. And the personality's thought routines had almost been banished from the habitat's extremities; its memories of room contents were unreliable at best.

'Mostly offices,' Tolton decided as he waved a light stick around. He was holding one in his hand, with another two slung across his chest on improvised straps. Together, the three units provided almost as much illumination as one working at full efficiency.

'Looks like it,' Dariat said. They were on the twenty-third-floor vestibule, where the walls were broken by anonymously identical doors. Tall potted plants in big troughs were wilting; deprived of light, their leaves were turning yellow-brown and falling onto the blue and white carpet.

They moved down the vestibule, reading names on the doors. So far offices had resulted in very few worthwhile finds; they'd learned that unless the company was a hardware or medical supplier there was little point in going in and searching. Occasionally the personality's localized memory would recall a useful item, but the neural strata was becoming more incapable with each floor they descended.

'Thirty years,' Tolton mused. 'That's a long time to hate.' There hadn't been much else to do except swap life stories.

Dariat smiled in recollection. 'You'd understand if you'd ever seen Anastasia. She was the most perfect girl ever to be born.'

'Sounds like I'll have to write about her some time. But I think your story is more interesting. Man, there's a lot of suffering in you. You died for her, you actually did it. Actually went and killed yourself. I thought that kind of thing really did only happen in poems and Russian novels.'

'Don't be too impressed. I only did it after I knew for sure souls existed. Besides – ' he gestured down at his huge frame and grubby toga – 'I wasn't losing a lot.'

'Yeah? Well, I'm no sensevise star, but I'm hanging on to what I've got for as long as I can. *Especially* now I know there are souls.'

'Don't worry about the beyond. You can leave it behind if you really want to.'

'Tell that to the ghosts upstairs. In fact, I'm even keener to hang on to my body while we're in this continuum.'

Tolton stopped outside a sensevise recording studio, and gave Dariat a shrewd look. 'You're in touch with the personality, is there any chance of us getting out of here?'

'Too early to say. We really don't know very much about the dark continuum yet.'

'Hey, this is me you're talking to. I survived the whole occupation, you know. Quit with the company line and level with me.'

'I wasn't going to hold anything back. The one conjecture all my illustrious relatives are worried about is the lobster pot.'

'Lobster pot?'

'Once you get in, you can't get out. It's the energy levels, you see. Judging by the way our energy is being absorbed by this continuum's fabric it doesn't have the same active energy state. We're louder and stronger than normal conditions here. And that strength is slowly being drained away, just by being here. It's an entropy equilibrium effect. Everything levels out in the end. So if we take height as a metaphor, we're at the bottom of a very deep hole with our universe at the top; which means it's going to take a hell of an effort to lift ourselves out again. Logically, we need to escape through some kind of wormhole. But even if we knew how to align its terminus coordinates so that it opens inside our own universe, it's going to be incredibly difficult to generate one. Back in our universe, they took a lot of very precisely focused energy to open, and the nature of this continuum works against that. With this constant debilitation effect, it may not be possible to concentrate enough energy, it'll dissipate before it reaches critical distortion point.'

'Shit. There's got to be something we can do.'

'If those rules do apply, our best bet is to try and send a message out. That's what the personality and my relatives are working towards. If they know where we are, the Confederation might be able to open a wormhole to us from their side.'

'*Might* be able?'

'All new suggestions welcome. But as it stands, getting them to lower us a rope is the best we can come up with.'

'Some rescue plan. The Confederation has its own problems right now.'

'If they can learn how to grab us back, they'll be halfway to solving them.'

'Sure.'

They reached the end of the vestibule and automatically turned round.

Nothing here, Dariat reported. *We're moving down to the twenty-fourth floor.*

All right, the personality replied. *There's a hotel, the Bringnal, a couple of floors down from where you are now. Check its main linen store, we need more blankets.*

You're going to ask one of the teams to lug blankets up twenty-five floors?

All the large hoards above that level have been used. And right now it's easier to find new ones than wash the old; nobody's got enough energy for that.

All right. Dariat faced Tolton, taking care to exaggerate his speech. 'They want us to find blankets.'

'Sounds like a real priority job we got ourselves here.' Tolton slithered through a partly open muscle membrane and into the stairwell. The quivering lips didn't bother him nearly so much now.

Dariat followed him, taking care to use the gap. He could slip through solid surfaces, he'd found, if he really wanted to. It was like sinking through ice.

One of the random power surges flowered around them. Electrophorescent cells shone brightly again, illuminating the stairs in stark blue-tinged light. A jet of foggy air streamed out of a tubule vent, sounding like a sorrowful sigh. A thin film of grey water was slicking every surface. Tolton could see the breath in front of his face. He gripped the handrail tighter, fearful of slipping.

'We're not going to be able to salvage stuff from the starscrapers for much longer,' Tolton said, wiping his hand against his leather jacket. 'They're getting worse.'

'You should see what kind of state the ducts and tubules are in.'

The street poet grunted in resentment. He was actually eating a lot better than most of the population. Inventory duties had a great many perks. The private apartments with their small stocks of quality food and fashionable clothes were his to pick over as he wished. The salvage teams were only interested in the larger stores that were in restaurants and bars. And now the endless succession of lightless floors no longer bothered him, he was glad to be away from the caverns with all their suffering – and smell.

Dariat.

The startled tone made him halt. *What?*

There's something outside.

Affinity made him aware of the consternation spreading through his relatives, most of whom were in the counter-rotating spaceport and the caverns.

Show me.

One of the slow flares of red and blue phosphorescence was shimmering through the ebony nebula, sixty kilometres away from the southern endcap. As it dwindled, several more began to bloom in the distance, sending pastel waves of light washing across the gigantic habitat's shell. The personality didn't believe the sudden increase in frequency was a coincidence. It was busy concentrating on collecting the images from its external sensitive cells. Once again, Dariat was uncomfortably aware of the effort expended in what should be a simple observation routine.

A speck of hoary grey flitted among the strands of blackness, snapping in and out of view. Following the smooth curving motions put Dariat in mind of a skier, the thing's course was very much like a slalom run. Every turn brought it closer to Valisk.

The nebula doesn't get out of its way, the personality remarked. **It's dodging the braids.**

That implies a controlling intelligence, or at least animal-level instinct. Absolutely.

The initial consternation of Rubra's descendants had given way to a slick buzz of activity. Those out in the spaceport were activating systems, aligning them on the visitor. An MSV was powered up, ready for an inspection/interception flight.

An MSV can't match that kind of manoeuvrability, Dariat said. The visitor performed a fast looping spiral around a grainy black curlicue, shooting off in a new direction parallel to Valisk's shell, fifteen kilometres distant. Visual resolution was improving. The visitor was about a hundred metres across, appearing like a disc of ragged petals. **Even a voidhawk would have trouble making rendezvous.**

The visitor darted behind another frayed column of blackness. When it re-emerged it was soaring almost at right angles to its original course. Its petals were bending and flexing.

They look like sails to me, Dariat said.

Or wings. Although I don't understand what it could be pushing against. If this continuum has such a low energy state, how come it can move so fast?

Beats me.

Several spaceport dishes started tracking the visitor. They began transmitting the standard CAB xenoc-interface communication protocol on a multi-spectrum sweep. Dariat allowed his affinity bond to decline to a background whisper. 'Come on,' he told a frowning Tolton. 'We've got to find a window.'

The visitor didn't respond to the interface protocol. Nor did it show any awareness of the radar pulses fired at it. That was perhaps understandable, given that they produced no return signal. The only noticeable change as it spun and danced ever closer was the way shadows congealed around it. Visually it actually appeared to grow smaller, as though it was flying away from the habitat.

That's like the optical distortion effect which the possessed use to protect themselves with, Dariat said. He and Tolton had found a snug bar called Horner's on the twenty-fifth floor. The two big oval windows were misted over inside, forcing Tolton to wipe them clean with one of the coarse tablecloths. His breath kept splashing against the icy glass, condensing immediately.

Well, we did choose a realm suitable for ghosts, the personality said.

I've never heard of a ghost that looked like that.

The visitor was within five kilometres of the shell now, about where the filigree of nebula stands began. There was only empty space between it and the habitat now.

Maybe it's scared to come any closer, the personality said. **I am considerably larger.**

Have you tried an affinity call?

Yes. It didn't respond.

Oh, well. Just a thought.

The visitor left the convoluted weave of the nebula and flashed towards the vast bulk of the habitat. By now its deceptive *glamour* had reduced it to a rosette of oyster ribbons twirling gracelessly in the wake of a fluctuating warp point. The image of the nebula and its strange borealis storms fluxed and bent as the visitor traversed them; oscillating between iridescent scintillations and a black boundary deeper than an event horizon. Nothing about it remained stable.

It streaked over to within fifty metres of the shell then veered round to follow the curve, wriggling wildly from side to side. The quick serpentine orbit allowed it to cover a considerable portion of the habitat's exterior.

It's searching, the personality said. **That implies a degree of organization. It has to be sentient.**

Searching for what?

A way in, I imagine. Or something it can recognize, some method of establishing communication.

Do any of the spaceport defences still work? Dariat asked.

You have to be bloody joking. We need all the allies we can get.

Before we fused, you used to be the mother of all suspicious neurotic bastards. I think that would be a preferable attitude for you right now.

Well, that's the effect of your mature calming influence for you. So you've only got yourself to blame. But don't worry, I'm not going to send the MSV after it.

Thank Tarrug for that.

Our visitor should be coming over your horizon any second now. Perhaps your eyes will do better than my sensitive cells.

'Wipe the glass again,' Dariat told Tolton.

The soaking tablecloth smeared the moisture in long streaks. Tiny flecks of frost were glistening dull white over the rest of the big oval. Tolton switched off two of his light sticks. Both of them peered forward. The visitor arched over the rim of the shell, lensing thin spires of vermilion and indigo light as it came. They wavered in the runnels of water, wobbling insubstantially before sinking back down into the visitor's core. Now all that remained was a black knot in the continuum's fabric racing over the dark rust-coloured polyp.

Tolton's weak grin was bloated with uncertainty. 'Am I being paranoid, or is that heading towards us?'

*

In the earlier time and place, long ago and far away, they had called themselves the Orgathé. Now, names had lost all meaning and relevance, or perhaps they themselves had devolved into something else, such was the way of this atrocious existence. There were many others adrift in the dark continuum, sharing their fate. Identity was no longer singular. A myriad of racial traits had blended and faded into a singleton over the aeons.

Purpose, though, purpose remained steadfast. The quest for light and strength, a return to the sweet heights from whence they had all fallen. A dream sustained even within the mélange. Few forms existed now outside the mélange. The process of diminution claimed every life to fall into these depths. But this one had risen yet again, buoyed up by the tides of chaotic chance that rioted within the mélange. Spat out to roam the murk for as long as it had strength. The free-flying state of such escapees was still that of the Orgathé, though the essence of many others rode upon its wings. Its chimerical shape was a tortured mockery of the once glorious avian lords who ruled the swift air currents of their homeworld.

Ahead of it now drifted the exotic object. Composed of a substance to be found only in the oldest of the Orgathé's memories, those that predated the dark continuum. How strange that it could barely recognize the antecedent of its own salvation.

Matter. Solid organized matter. Alive with a heat so fierce it took the Orgathé some time to acclimatize to the radiance; elevating itself to a near ecstatic level of warmth. Incredibly, just within the scorching surface, a sheet of life-energy burned bright and vigorous. The entire object was a single mighty entity. Yet passive. Vulnerable. This was a feast which would sustain a huge proportion of the mélange for a long time. It might even trigger a total dispersal.

The Orgathé slithered close to the object's surface, feeling the mind within follow its flight. Vast swirls of rich thought flowed underneath it as it basked in the warmth. But there was no way to reach the abundant life-energy through the hard surface. If the Orgathé attempted to claw its way through, it would surely incinerate itself. Contact with so much heat for so long could probably not be sustained. But the craving within itself from proximity to so much vital life-energy was overwhelming.

There must be some way in. Some orifice or chink. The Orgathé coasted along over the object, heading for the spikes radiating out from the centre. They were smaller, weaker than the rest of it. Long hollow minarets leaking their energy away into the dark continuum. The life-energy was shallower here, the heat not so intense. Each of the structures was broken by thousands of dark ovals, curtained by cooler sheets of transparent matter. Light twinkled briefly through some of them, never lasting long. Except one. A single oval burning steadily.

The Orgathé glided eagerly towards it. Two flames of life-energy gleamed behind the transparent sheet. One naked, the other clad in hot matter; both enraging the Orgathé's craving. It surged forward.

*

'FUCK!' Tolton screamed. He dived to one side, scattering tables and chairs. Dariat jumped the other way just as the Orgathé hit the window. Frost blossomed like a living thing, strands of long delicate crystals multiplying across the glass, then reaching out through the air. Shapes moved on the other side of the hoary fur, dark indistinct serpents, thicker than a human torso, that could be tentacles or tongues scrabbling furiously at the outer surface. The unmistakable grinding shriek of deep score lines being ripped into the material penetrated the bar, drowning out Tolton's terrified cries.

Do something! Dariat wailed.

You name it, I'll do it.

Tolton was scuttling backwards on his hands and legs, unable to take his eyes from the window. The serpent shapes were writhing with rabid aggression as they clawed their way through. A badly stressed *snap* sounded above the vicious squealing, corresponding to a thin dark shadow materializing across the frosted window. Furniture was rattling, shaking its way erratically across the floor. Glasses and bottles abandoned on top of the marble bar juddered vigorously and tumbled off.

It's coming through! Dariat cried. When he tried to clamber to his feet, he discovered he didn't have the strength. Fatigue was numbing every limb.

'Kill it!' Tolton bellowed.

We can try and zap it, the personality said, like we did the possessed.

Just bloody do it!

It might kill you as well; we don't know.

You're part me. Do you seriously think I want that to catch me?

Very well.

The personality began to reroute its patched-up power supply. Diverting current away from the axial light-tube and the caverns, pumping the precarious fusion generators up to their maximum output. Electricity poured back into the Djerba starscraper's organic conductor grid. The first-floor windows blazed with golden light; mechanical and electronic systems came alive in frantic chitters of movement and data emissions. Milliseconds later the second floor sprang back to life. The third, fourth . . .

Dazzling shafts of light sliced out from the Djerba's windows, piercing the gloom outside. They snapped downward storey by storey towards the beleaguered twenty-fifth floor. The personality gathered its major thought routines and plunged them down into the starscraper, a sensation like diving into a pitch-black well shaft. Bitek networks were swiftly resurrected around its descending mentality.

A dead zone was concentrated around Horner's window. The external polyp was so cold the personality could no longer calibrate it. Living cells deeper in had frozen solid. The personality could feel vibrations running through the floor as the Orgathé pounded and scraped against the window.

Junctions within the organic conductor web switched polarity, high-order subroutines cancelled the safety limiters. Every erg of power from the fusion generators was channelled into Horner's. Ceiling strips of electrophorescent cells ignited, flooding the bar with searing white light. Organic conductors behind the walls fused, burning out long lines of polyp in a cascade of amber sparks. Incandescent arcs stormed through the air as a lethal charge of electrons was fired into the external wall.

Coming on top of the heat and life-energy, the electron hammer blow was just too much. The Orgathé recoiled from the window, appendages flailing madly as the streams of alien energy churned within its body. There was a brief glimpse of sinuous chrome-black tendrils bristling with curving blades coiling back protectively around a bulbous midsection. Ragged wing petals began to flex. Then the distortion smeared it with refracted scintillations from the gleaming starscraper, and it shot away at a bruising acceleration. Within seconds it was lost inside the nebula.

Dariat took his arm away from his face. The tremendous barrage of noise and light saturating the bar had faded. A few sparks were still popping out from the deep scorch marks in the walls. The glossy electrophorescent cells had shattered and shrivelled to rain across the floor, their fragments curling up, puffing out licks of smoke.

You all right, my boy? the personality enquired.

Dariat looked down at himself. The feeble yellow glow from

Tolton's remaining light stick showed his spectral body unchanged. Though possibly more translucent than usual. He still felt terribly weak. **I think so. I'm bloody cold, though.**

Could have been worse.

Yeah. Dariat felt the personality's major routines withdrawing from the starscraper. The lights were going off again in the upper floors, autonomic bitek functions shutting down.

He struggled to his knees, shivering intensely. When he looked round he could see ice encrusted on every surface, turning the bar into an arctic grotto. The electrical discharge had melted very little of it. That was probably what had saved them; it was several centimetres thick over the window. And the fracture pattern in the glass underneath was unnervingly pronounced.

Tolton was spasming on the floor, spittle flecking his lips. His hair was rimed with frost. Each shallow panted breath was revealed in a cloud of white vapour.

'Shit.' Dariat staggered over to him. Just in time he remembered not to try and touch the tormented body. **Get a medical team down here.**

Oh yeah. I'll get right on it. They should be with you in about three hours.

Shit. He knelt down next to Tolton, and leaned right over, staring into delirious eyes. 'Hey.' Limpid fingers clicked right in front of Tolton's nose. 'Hey. Tolton. Can you hear me? Try and steady your breathing. Take a deep breath. Come on! You've got to calm your body down. Breathe.'

Tolton's teeth chittered. He gurgled, cheeks bulging.

'That's it. Come on. Breathe. Deep. Suck that air down. Please.'

The street poet's lips compressed slightly, making a whistling sound.

'Good. Good. And again. Come on.'

It took several minutes for Tolton's bucking to subside. His erratic breathing reduced to sharp gasps. 'Cold,' he grunted.

Dariat smiled down at him. 'Ho, boy. You had me worried there. We really don't need any more ghosts floating around in here right now.'

'Heart. My heart. God! I thought . . .'

'It's OK. It's over.'

Tolton nodded roughly, and tried to lever himself up.

'Stop! You just lie there for another minute longer. There's no paramedic service any more, remember? First thing we need is some proper food for you. I think there's a restaurant on this floor.'

'No way. As soon as I can get up, we're leaving. No more starscrapers.' Tolton coughed, and started to glance round. 'Jesus.' He scowled. 'Are we safe?'

'Sure. For now, anyway.'

'Did we kill it?'

Dariat grimaced. 'Not exactly, no. But we gave it a hell of a fright.'

'That lightning bolt didn't kill it?'

'No. It flew off, though.'

'Shit. I nearly died.'

'Yeah. But you didn't. Concentrate on that.'

Tolton slowly eased himself into a sitting position, wincing at each tiny movement. Once he was propped up against a table leg, he reached out and caressed the ice which was engulfing a chair, fingers stroking curiously. He gave Dariat a grim look with badly bloodshot eyes. 'This isn't going to have a happy ending, is it?'

*

The seven hellhawks glided in towards Monterey, acknowledging the query from the SD network defence as the sensors locked on.

The Sevilla SD network was a hell of a lot stronger than anything we were briefed about, they told Jull von Holger, when he asked how the mission had gone. Seven frigates were lost, and we're all that's left of our squadron.

Did the infiltration succeed?

We think over a hundred got through.

Excellent.

Neither side said anything more. Jull von Holger could sense the quiet rage of the surviving hellhawks. He chose not to mention the fact to Emmet Mordden; the hellhawks were all Kiera's problem.

Go straight to the docking-ledges, Hudson Proctor told the hell-hawks. We've already cleared the pedestals. You'll be fed as soon as you land. He focused on Kiera's face. She smiled her brightest ingénue smile, pouring as much gratitude into her thoughts as possible for her deputy to relay.

'Well done. I know it's not easy, but believe me there won't be many more of these ridiculous seeding missions.' She arched an eyebrow in query to Hudson. 'Was there a reply?'

He coloured slightly at the emotional backlash to her little speech that flooded the affinity band. 'No. They're pretty tired.'

'I understand.' Her sweet expression hardened. 'End your contact.'

Hudson Proctor nodded curtly, signalling it had been done.

'You hope there ain't going to be many more seeding flights, you mean,' Luigi said indolently.

The three of them were sitting in one of the smaller, more private lounges above the asteroid's docking-ledges, waiting for the last member of their group to arrive. Kiera's small revolution had picked up a respectable degree of momentum over the last ten days. The success of the seeding flights had bolstered Al's popularity and authority considerably. But that triumph came with a high price in terms of starships, and quite a few people were starting to acknowledge that the infiltration campaign was short-termism. Slowly, quietly, Kiera had exploited that. Being able to see the dissatisfaction and worry in people's minds gave her a handy advantage when it came to spotting potential recruits.

Silvano Richmann came in and took his seat around the coffee table. There was a cluster of bottles in the centre, he poured himself a shot of whisky.

'The Sevilla flotilla is back,' Kiera told him. 'Seven frigates and five hellhawks got zapped.'

'Fuck.' Silvano shook his head in dismay. 'Al's putting together another fifteen of these missions. He just doesn't see it.'

'He sees it the way he wants to see it,' Kiera said. 'They're successful in that they're landing infiltrators each time. The Confederation is going apeshit. We're knocking off five of their planets a day. It buys him complete respect and loyalty with the Organization down on the planet.'

'While my fleet gets chopped to shit,' Luigi snapped. 'That goddam whore Jezzibella. She's got him by the balls.'

'Not just your fleet,' Kiera said. 'I'm losing hellhawks fast. Much more of this, and they'll leave.'

'Where to?' Silvano asked. 'They've got to stick with you. That was a neat sting you pulled on them with the food.'

'The Edenists keep making offers to try and lure them away,'

Hudson said. 'Etchells keeps us informed. The latest offer is that they'll actually accept the blackhawk host personality into their habitat neural strata, leaving our guys as the only soul in there. In exchange they get all the food they want, providing they just cooperate with the Edenists, help them find out about our powers.'

'Shit,' Silvano muttered. 'We gotta stop this. I'd be mighty tempted by any offer that got rid of this body's host soul.'

'Wouldn't we all,' Kiera said. She sat back and sipped at her wine. 'OK, the question is, how far are you prepared to go?'

'Pretty goddam obvious for me,' Luigi said. 'I'll waste that shit Capone myself. Busting me down to a fucking errand boy. Nobody could have handled Tranquillity any different.'

'Silvano?'

'He's got to go. But there's one condition for me signing up with you. And it ain't negotiable.'

'What's that?' Kiera asked, though she was fairly sure she knew. Silvano was feared as Al's chief enforcer, but he did have one major difference with his boss.

'After we do this, there are no more non-possessed in the Organization. We take them all out. Understood?'

'Suits me,' Kiera said.

'No way!' Luigi shouted. 'I can't run my fucking fleet with just possessed crews. You know that. You're shitting on me here, man.'

'Yeah? Who says there's going to be a fucking fleet after this. Right, Kiera? We're doing this for our own safety. We're going to take New California out of here; out of this universe. Just like all the other possessed have done. And for that, we can't afford no non-possessed to be around. Come on, Luigi, you know that. As long as there's one of them left, they're going to be plotting and scheming how to get rid of us. For Christ's sake. We steal their bodies from them. If you was alive right now, you wouldn't give jack shit about anything else other than getting them back from us.' He slammed his tumbler back down on the table. 'We eliminate all the non-possessed, or there's no deal.'

'Then there's no fucking deal,' Luigi stormed.

Kiera held up her hands. 'Boys, boys, this is how Al wins. You ever heard of divide and rule? All of us have different interests, and the only way we can hang on to them is if we're part of the Organization. Only the Organization needs a fleet, and hellhawks, and lieutenants that have to be kept in line.' She shot Silvano a significant look. 'He's made it complicated so that we have to support him to keep our own places. What we've got to do is dismantle the Organization, but rig whatever's next so that we three come out on top.'

'Like what?' Luigi asked suspiciously.

'OK, you want the fleet back, right? Tell me why?'

'Because it's fucking mine, you dumb broad. I built that fleet up from nothing. I was here right from the start, the day Al walked into San Angeles City Hall.'

'Fair enough. But all the fleet did was make you a player. Do you really want to risk flying to Confederation planets and going up against their SD networks? They're getting wise to us now. These seeding flights are pissing them off bad. They're killing us out there, Luigi.'

'So? Like I should care. I'm the admiral. I don't have to go with them every time.'

'The whole fleet doesn't have to go anywhere, Luigi; that's the point. What you need is to exchange the fleet for something else that will keep you in the game, right?'

Luigi eyed her cautiously. 'Maybe.'

'That's what we've got to work out between the three of us. Right now, we can carry the Organization if we eliminate Capone. But the Organization's a dead end. Dishing out tokens instead of money, for Christ's sake. If we take it over, we've got to use it to establish a new type of government. One that has us at the top.'

'Like what?' Silvano asked. 'The second New California leaves this universe, nobody needs any kind of government.'

'Says who?' Kiera sneered. 'You've seen the cities down there. Unless the Organization keeps putting the squeeze on the farmers to supply food, they'll collapse overnight. If New California escapes this universe, everyone on it is going to have to turn into some kind of medieval peasant just to stay alive. And that's such bullshit. Five per cent of the population working in the fields can sustain the rest of us. Now I don't know what kind of society we can build on the other side, but I'm damned if I'm going to live in a mud hut and spend my days walking behind a horse's arse to plough a field. Especially when someone else can be made to do it for me.'

'So what are you saying here?' Silvano asked. 'That we keep the farmers working while the rest of us live it up?'

'Basically, yeah. It's just like what I've done with the hellhawks, but on a much bigger scale. We have to keep the farmers farming, and we have to be in charge of distributing the food to the urban areas. Convert the Organization into a giant supplier; and the only people who get supplied are the ones who we say.'

'You'd need a fucking army for that!' Luigi exclaimed.

Kiera gestured magnanimously. 'There you are, then. That's what you turn the fleet into. Find a portable weapon that's effective against the possessed: something like those bastard serjeants use on Mortonridge, manufacture it up here, and equip our supporters with it. Use the same chain of command network that's already in place, but with a land army to back it up instead of the SD platforms.'

'That might work,' Silvano said. 'So if Luigi's got himself an army, what do I get?'

'Communications are vital, otherwise this whole thing will just collapse. And we'd need to be more subtle with the farmers than forcing them at gunpoint. That's an enforcer's job.'

He poured himself another whisky. 'OK. Let's talk about it.'

*

Western Europe always took his dogs for a walk himself. Dog ownership was a healthy reminder of responsibility; you either do it properly or not at all. There weren't many crises which could make him skip a day. Though he suspected one of his staff was going to have to start substituting fairly soon.

The formal lawns extended for over three hundred metres from the back of the house (they were yards back in the days when he bought the estate, but even he had fallen to using that appalling modern French metric system now). A hedge of ancient yews marked the end, ten metres high, laden with their squishy dull-red berries. He pushed through the gap marked by crumbling stone pillars that used to be gateposts, making a mental note to get a gardening construct to prune the twigs. The carpet of dry needles compressed beneath his brogues as the Labradors scampered round him. It was meadowland beyond, the shaggy grass thick with daisies and butter-cups. A gentle slope led down to a long still lake eight hundred metres away (half a mile). He whistled softly, and threw his stick.

'Found them,' North America datavised.

'Who?'

'The possessed Quinn Dexter left behind in New York. Just to make you more insufferable, you were right. He went for the Light Bringer sect.'

'Ah.' The Labradors found the stick, one of them clamped it in his jaw. Western Europe slapped his hands on his thighs, and the dogs started to bound back to him. 'How bad is it?'

'Not too bad, I believe. I lost the High Magus, of course. I guess he suicided. But there are several actives left. Two of them called me before the energistic effect glitched their neural nanonics. They're taking over the covens one at a time. Eight down already, including the arcology headquarters in the Leicester skyscraper.'

'Numbers?'

'That's the good news. About ten possessed to each coven. The moron acolytes are actually welcoming them, and doing as they're told. Their new masters are just sitting tight, and holding some pretty gross orgies. They've made sure each coven's electronics are switched off, not that many of their units were ever interfaced with the net anyway.'

'I knew it. They're moving with a purpose.'

'Definite infiltration tactics. They've got their foothold, now they're waiting.'

'If they're spreading to each dome, then some of them must be on the move.'

'Yes, I know. And they've had it easy in all the confusion. With all those riots resulting from the vac-train shutdown there's been a lot of vandalism; that makes it tough for the AI to locate glitches.'

'So when are you going to hit the covens?'

'Good question. I wanted your opinion on that. If I hit them now, then whoever's moving about will be warned and go to ground. That'll leave New York vulnerable.'

Western Europe took the stick from the Labrador, and paused. 'Yes, but if you wait until every coven is taken over, you'll have a lot of the bastards to deal with. Someone will inevitably get through the police cordons, and you'll be back in the same leaky boat. How many covens can you monitor in real time?'

'All of them. That's already being done. Those I have no direct access to are being watched by agents.'

'Then you've got it covered. Wait until a group of possessed shows up at a new coven, then take them all out together.'

'And if there's more than one group moving round?'

'I'm paranoid, but am I paranoid enough. What sort of assault were you planning?'

'GISD tactical team, with shoot to kill orders. Wipe each coven out, I don't want prisoners to interrogate. Fletcher is still cooperating with Halo's science teams.'

'Given the stakes, here, I'd suggest using a gamma pulse against them first. You'll get peripheral casualties, but it'll be nothing like as bad as an SD strike. Send the tactical teams in to secure and mop up afterwards.'

'All right. I can live with that.'

'We might even get a vote of confidence from our illustrious colleagues.'

'Not even this century's geneering can make pigs fly yet. I'll get the assault organized for 0300 hours EST.'

'If you need any help, just whistle.' Western Europe smiled happily, and slung the stick high into the air.

*

Not even B7 could block news of events inside New York from spilling out across the global net. Speculation had been hot and intense ever since the arcology's vac-trains had been shut down after the Dome One 'incident'. Several riots had been captured by rover reporters; two of them had been badly injured during the coverage, adding extra spice to the sensevise. Then eleven hours later the North American Commissioner had appeared before the press once more to announce the investigation had been completed, and confirm the incident was not caused by the possessed. It was in fact a professional assassination carried out in Grand Central Station involving a sophisticated weapons implant and a chameleon suit. Business rivals of the deceased Bud Johnson were currently being sought for questioning.

The vac-trains had been reopened. The rioters and looters had cleared the streets. The police reinforcements had been stood down. Celebrity news presenters were given extended programmes to cover the paranoia raging across the planet. The arrival of the *Mount's Delta* appeared to have acted as the trigger for a multitude of small events that were blamed on the possessed, culminating in the Grand Central Station disturbance. And Capone's recent switch in tactics to flying infiltration attacks against Confederation planets served to exacerbate people's fears. The Confederation Navy and local SD networks seemed unable to prevent the Organization's strike flotillas. After the quarantine appeared to be preventing the spread, worlds were starting to fall again. Everyone, ran the feeling, was vulnerable. But the lifting of the vac-train restrictions eased the tension a little, right up until 0250 EST when they were abruptly shut again. Frustrated commuters datavised the information to the news agencies within ten seconds. New York's rover reporters, who had descended en masse into the arcology's bars after a hard day's sensationalizing, were hauled back out onto the concrete canyons by their editors. Agencies which datavised information requests to the arcology's civic authority were met with blank puzzlement. Nobody had told the graveyard shift about the vac-trains. The police precinct houses were equally baffled. Even the urgent requests to in-house sources produced a blank, at least in the ten minutes that counted.

With all of the B7 supervisors on-line and observing, North America gave the order to launch the assault.

The Internal Security Directorate tactical teams had been arriving in New York ever since the vac-trains started running again. By the time the assault was launched, there were over eight hundred personnel deployed around the various sect covens. They were all armed with projectile weapons loaded with chemical or electric rounds. Complementing them were the gamma lasers. Intended for anti-terrorist interception situations, they were powerful enough to penetrate at least five metres of carbon-concrete. Such a range would allow the teams to strike at targets holed up deep inside skyscrapers and megatowers. One would usually be sufficient to eliminate an entire room full of hostiles instantaneously.

North America had ringed each coven with nine, while the Leicester skyscraper had fifteen ranged against it. The supervisor's deepest worry was that the possessed with their extended senses would discover the preparations. To try and deny them any hint, engineering mechanoids had been used throughout the day to unpack and install the gamma lasers in surrounding buildings. Giveaway human supervision had been kept to an absolute minimum. As well as the gamma lasers, North America had the exits and service tunnels rigged to electrify anyone who scuttled down them. That was the most dangerous aspect of the work, but again mechanoids with New York's Civic Service emblem on their sides trundled along modifying wires and cables without drawing questions or interest.

The tactical teams had assembled several blocks away to avoid attention. North America started to move them forward simultaneously with closing down the vac-trains. He also closed down all road traffic and metro transit carriages inside the arcology, and sealed the domes from each other – an aspect the news agencies didn't realize until a lot later. According to every asset and functional bug infiltrated into the covens, neither the possessed nor the acolytes were aware of the preparations. They didn't even know the tactical teams were advancing.

The gamma-ray lasers fired at 0255 EST. The fifteen beams transfixing the Leicester skyscraper swept through the lower eight storeys which made up the sect's headquarters. They used a scan pattern, switching between vertical and horizontal to cover every cubic centimetre. When the beams were aimed right through the core of the skyscraper the energy was absorbed by the structure, while furnishings and composite walls ignited instantly under the intense radiation barrage. Thick, radiant orange lines were scratched across the carbon-concrete support pillars and floors as the beams traversed the building. The air was superheated, dissolving into its component atoms. Windows detonated outward from the appalling pressure, showering the street below with daggers of glass.

Fire sprinklers burst into life, only for their water to vaporize first into steam then clouds of ions. Glaring blue and violet streamers jetted out of the smashed windows, and fountained up the skyscraper's elevator shafts. Ruptured air-conditioning ducts provided secondary routes for the heatstorm to pervade the building. The entire lower floors were engulfed in a dazzling fireball.

Human bodies caught within the flexing three-dimensional mesh of beams burst apart from the terrible energy input. Their water content exploded into steam as the carbon combusted. When the beams reached the outer sections of the skyscraper, they were powerful enough to pierce clean though the walls. Surrounding skyscrapers were strafed with the radiation, resulting in vast tracts of damage. Then the sharp spires of ions exhaled by the Leicester played across their outer walls, igniting dozens of ordinary fires.

The gamma-ray lasers switched off. The night was filled with the roar of flames and the screams of those being burnt alive. There was enough light thrown out from the fires to light the entire district. Unharmed residents of the nearby buildings lucky enough to live on the lower floors rushed onto the street; those higher up could only stare out helplessly as the flames took hold. The images they relayed to the news agencies, which were distributed across the planet in real time, showed the GISD tactical teams marching down every approach road to the Leicester. Against the raging orange flames, their heat-proof flexarmour suits appeared as matt-black silhouettes. Weapons with long snouts were cradled casually on their arms as they walked into the conflagration with astounding nonchalance.

Three times, figures rushed out of the skyscraper's main entrance doors, making their bid for freedom. They were like fire monsters, flames shooting from every part of their bloated figures. The tactical team guns spat short pulses of turquoise flame with quiet efficiency, and the fiery creatures crumpled to burn unhindered on the wide sidewalk.

It was those scenes of perfunctory extermination which finally convinced the world that the possessed had somehow penetrated the titanic defences of the Halo. The political fallout was considerable. A motion of impeachment was put before the Govcentral Grand Senate, condemning the President for not informing the senatorial Defence Committee in advance. The President, who could hardly admit publicly to knowing nothing about the situation, fired the chiefs of GISD Bureaux 1 through 4, for gross insubordination and overreaching their authority. The GISD's New York chief was charged with reckless homicide, and put under immediate arrest. Such machinations went almost unnoticed by the public, who were fed a continual stream of updates of the on-the-ground aftermath by the news agencies.

Once the tactical teams had confirmed that there were no possessed left alive in any of the sect covens, they withdrew. Only then were the emergency services allowed in. It took ten hours for the fire department mechanoids to extinguish the last fires. Paramedic crews followed them through the burnt-out floors. The arcology hospitals were swamped by casualties (not helped by the domes remaining sealed from each other). Preliminary insurance damage estimates ran into hundred of millions of G-dollars. Dome One's Mayor, in conjunction with the other fourteen mayors of the arcology, instigated an official day of mourning, and opened a bereavement fund.

Officially, one thousand two hundred and thirty-three people died in the assault against the New York possessed, nearly half as a result of being hit by gamma radiation. The rest were either burned or asphyxiated. Over nine thousand needed hospital treatment for minor burns, shock, and other injuries. Double that number lost their homes, with several hundred businesses forced to try and relocate. The vac-trains in and out of New York remained closed.

*

'Well?' North Pacific asked. It was five hours after the tactical teams had finished their sweep of the covens, and B7 had reconvened to hear the genuine results.

'We got a hundred and eight possessed, that's the best estimate I can provide. There wasn't a hell of a lot left for the forensic crew to analyse after the gamma lasers finished.'

'I'm more interested in the ones you didn't eliminate.'

'Eight of the electrocution traps we rigged along possible escape routes were triggered. The teams pulled eleven corpses out of various ducts and service tunnels.'

'Quit stalling!' South America said. 'Did any of them get out?'

'Probably, yes. Forensics thinks maybe three or four people got past the electrocution traps. There's no way of telling if they were possessed or not, but it would take one inhumanly tough mother to survive what we threw at them.'

'Shit! We're right back where we started. You're going to have to initiate this kind of slaughter operation each time they regroup. Only now they don't have any convenient sects to flee back to.'

'Well, this time, I'm going to insist on keeping New York's vac-trains shut,' North Pacific said. 'We can't let them get out of New York.'

'I quite agree,' Western Europe said.

'Only because you can't risk another vote.'

'There's no need to get personal. We remain on top of the situation.'

'Really? Where's Dexter, then?'

'When the time comes, I will eliminate him.'

'You're so full of shit.'

*

The K5 star had a catalogue number, but that was all. Only three planets were in orbit around it, two of them smaller than Mars, and a gas giant fifty thousand kilometres in diameter. Undistinguished in astronomical terms, it lay forty-one light-years outside the loose boundary of space claimed by the Confederation. There had been a single scoutship visit in 2530, which quickly established its worthlessness. As far as official records were concerned, that was the first and last time humans had visited the barren system. Certainly the navy never bothered with it; their patrols were stretched thinly enough as it was searching for illegal activity within the Confederation and through the stars fringing the boundary. Although the surrounding wreath of stars was an obvious locations for black cartel operations (and several highly dubious independent colony ventures), forty-one light-years was just too far away to justify the expense of regular inspection flights.

Such a safeguard made it ideal for the black cartel. Their antimatter station orbited five million kilometres from the star's surface, a closeness which stretched human materials science to its limit. The radiation, heat, particle, and magnetic forces it encountered were appalling. An approaching ship would see it as a simple black disc sailing across the incandescent solar glare. Sixty kilometres in diameter, it cast a significant cone-shaped umbra behind it; a zone insulated from the star's heat, the one place where hell's proverbial snowflake might just have survived. The surface facing the star was a radial concertina array of solid state cells absorbing the incredible blast of heat and converting it directly into electricity. At the back they glowed a gentle pink, utilizing their own shade to radiate the immense thermal load away into space. In total, the array was capable of generating over one and a half terawatts of electricity.

The antimatter production system itself was housed in a cluster of boxy silver-white industrial modules right in the centre of the array. The mundane method of churning out antimatter was essentially unchanged since the late twentieth century, although the levels of scale and efficiency had risen considerably since the first few experimental antiprotons had been manufactured in high-energy physics laboratories. Production requires individual protons to be accelerated until their energy becomes greater than a giga-electronvolt, at which point each one has more energy in its motion than its mass. Once that state has been achieved, they are collided with heavy nuclei, resulting in a spray of elementary particles that includes antiprotons, antielectrons, and antineutrons. These are then separated, collected, cooled, and merged into antihydrogen. But it is that initial proton acceleration stage which absorbs the phenomenal amount of electricity produced by the solar array in its entirety.

The whole operation was overseen by a crew of twenty-five technicians, stationed in a large, heavily shielded rotating carbotanium wheel that floated deep inside the array's umbra. They had now been joined by eight members of the Organization to keep them in line. Taking over the station had been absurdly easy.

Because the black cartel took the elementary precaution of installing its own modified neural nanonics in everyone who knew of the station's location, there could only ever be two kinds of visitor: the Confederation Navy on a search and destroy mission, or a legitimate buyer. The arrival of Capone's lieutenants came as a severe shock to the crew. The few hand weapons available were utterly useless against the possessed; their only other option was to kamikaze. Once the Organization's terms and conditions had been laid on the line, that was postponed indefinitely. The same kind of uneasy stand-off balance between need and fear that had claimed New California settled across the station.

After supplying the first Organization convoy with every gram of antimatter held in storage, the station had been operating a full production schedule ever since, attempting to cope with Capone's desperate demands for more. Starships came from New California every five or six days for new supplies.

*

Admiral Saldana's squadron made no attempt at stealth or subtlety when it jumped into the system, emerging twenty-five million kilometres from the star. Navy starships always had a tremendous advantage against the stations they hunted. Deep inside the star's gravity field, there could be no quick escape for the station's crew. Defensive weapons were almost useless. Not even antimatter propulsion and warheads could produce their usual overwhelming advantage; in such proximity to the star, combat wasp sensors were almost blind.

Standard procedure for the navy starships was to launch a volley of kinetic projectiles in a retrograde orbit. It was a tactic that would quickly exhaust the station's stock of drones, leaving them with beam weapons alone. Against a swarm of ten thousand harpoons, their chances of vaporizing every one before it hit was effectively nil. That was assuming the station sensors were even capable of locating the incoming missiles to begin with. In most cases the hellish solar environment completely masked their approach. As the navy vessels would never issue a warning, the station might never know of their presence until the first missile struck.

All the attackers needed was a single strike against the production system. Any large explosion would inevitably set off a chain reaction within the antimatter storage chambers. The resulting blast could at times be five or six times the size of a planet-buster, depending on how much of the substance was in store.

This time it was going to have to be a little different. Meredith Saldana waited impatiently on the *Arikara*'s bridge while the void-hawks deployed around the star in small swallow manoeuvres. Each of them launched a pack of small sensor satellites to scan the huge magnetosphere in which they were all immersed.

Locating the station was easy enough, though the sheer volume of space they were searching through made it a lengthy task. The *Arikara*'s tactical situation computer started to receive datavises from the satellites, blending them into a harmonized picture of the whole near-solar environment. When the information was complete, it showed the star as a dark sphere surrounded with graded shells of pale gold translucence. The innermost seethed like a restless sea as the magnetic forces fluxed and coiled, above that they smoothed out considerably.

A tiny knot of twisted copper light was sliding along a five million kilometre circular orbit. The squadron's comparative position was fed in, and Meredith began issuing orders. Because of their vulnerability to the star's heat and radiation, the voidhawks maintained their orbits, enabling them to keep watch for any emerging starships. The Adamist starships flew inward. Eight frigates were vectored into high inclination orbits, a location from which they could launch a kinetic assault on the station. The remaining starships, including

Lady Macbeth, aligned themselves on an interception course and accelerated along it at three gees.

When they were three million kilometres away, the *Arikara* pointed her main communication dish on the station, and boosted the signal to full strength.

'This communiqué is directed to the station commander,' Meredith datavised. 'This is the Confederation Navy ship *Arikara*. Your illegal operation is now terminated. Ordinarily, you would be executed for your actions in producing antimatter, but I have been authorized to offer you transport to a Confederation penal colony planet if you cooperate with us. This offer is also applicable to any possessed who are resident at the station. I will require your answer within one hour. Failure to respond will be taken as a refusal to cooperate, and you will be destroyed.' He datavised the flight computer to repeat the message, and the squadron waited.

It took ten minutes for a static-heavy signal to emerge from the station. 'This is Renko, I'm the guy Al left in charge around here. And I'm telling you to get the fuck out of here before we smear your pansy asses across the sun. You got that clear, pal?'

Meredith glanced across the bridge's acceleration couches to where Lieutenant Grese was lying. The intelligence officer managed to grin, despite the gee-force. 'That's a break,' he said. 'We got Capone's source, no matter what the outcome.'

'I believe the navy is due a break,' Meredith said. 'Especially our section of it.'

'He'll have to stop those bloody infiltration flights now. His fleet will need all the antimatter they've got left to defend New California.'

'Indeed.' Meredith was almost cheerful when he ordered the computer to datavise a reply to the station. 'Consult your crew, Renko. You're in the losing position here. All we have to do is launch a single missile once an hour. You have to fire five each time just to make sure it doesn't get through. And we're in no hurry, we can keep shooting at you for a couple of weeks if we have to. There's just no way you can win. Now are you going to accept my offer, or do you want to go back to the beyond?'

'Nice try, but you don't mean it. Not for us, leastways. I know you guys, you'll slam us into zero-tau the second we put our hands up.'

'For what it's worth, I am Rear-Admiral Meredith Saldana, and you have my word that you will be given passage to an uninhabited world capable of supporting human life. Consider your alternatives. If we attack the station, you go back to the beyond; if I'm lying about transporting you to a planet you go back. But there is the very strong possibility that I'm not lying. Can you really reject that hope?'

Along with the rest of the squadron, Joshua had to wait another twenty minutes for the answer. Eventually, Renko agreed to surrender. 'Looks like we're on,' Joshua said. They were accelerating hard again, preventing him from smiling. But there was no hiding the rise of excitement in his labouring voice.

'Christ, the other side of the nebula,' Liol marvelled. 'What's the furthest anyone's ever been before?'

'A voidhawk scout group travelled six hundred and eighty light-years from Earth in 2570,' Samuel replied. 'Their course took them directly galactic north, not in this direction.'

'I missed that,' Ashly complained. 'Was there anything interesting out there?'

Samuel closed his eyes, questioning the voidhawks racing along their orbits millions of kilometres away. 'Nothing unusual, or dramatic. Stars with possible terracompatible planets, stars without. No sentient xenoc species.'

'The Meridian fleet went further,' Beaulieu said.

'Only according to legend,' Dahybi countered. 'Nobody knows where they vanished to. In any case, that was centuries ago.'

'Logically, then, they must have gone a long way if no one's ever found them.'

'Found the wreckage, more like.'

'Such pessimism is bad for you.'

'Really? Hey, Monica,' Dahybi lifted one hand to make an appeal before the acceleration made him lower it fast again, 'do your lot know where they went? It could be important if they're waiting out there for us.'

Monica stared stubbornly at the compartment's ceiling, a headache building behind her compressed eyeballs that no program could rid her of. She really hated high gees. 'No,' she datavised (her throat was suffering along with the rest of her), irritated she couldn't put any emphasis into her digitized speech. Not that snapping at the crew would endear her to them, but their relentless discussions of utter trivia were starting to chafe. And she'd possibly got a month or more to go. 'The ESA was in its infancy back when the Meridian fleet was launched. Even today I doubt we'd bother planting assets in with a bunch of paradise-seeking fools.'

'I don't want to know what's there,' Joshua said. 'The whole point of this mission is discovery. We're real explorers going out on a limb, first for at least a century.'

'Amen to that,' Ashly said.

'Where we are now is new for most people,' Liol said. 'Just look at that station.'

'Standard industrial modules,' Dahybi said. 'Hardly exotic or inspiring.'

Liol sighed sadly.

'OK, we're getting close to injection point,' Joshua announced. 'Systems review, please. How's our fuselage holding out?' The flight computer was datavising images from the localized sensors into his neural nanonics. *Lady Mac*'s thermo-dump panels were fully extended, constantly rotating to present their narrow edges towards the raging star. Their flat surfaces were glowing radiant pink as they expelled the ship's accumulated heat. He'd programmed a permanent spin into their vector, a fifteen-minute cycle to ensure the immense thermal input was distributed evenly across the fuselage. Fine manoeuvring was slow, given the additional reaction mass they were carrying, but the balance-compensation programs were handling it providing he kept tweaking them.

'No hot spots yet,' Sarha reported. 'That extra layer of nultherm foam is doing its job quite well. But it is picking up a lot of particle radiation, far more than we're used to. We'll have to watch that.'

'Should lose it when we get behind the shield,' Liol said. 'Won't be long now.'

'See?' Beaulieu told Dahybi. 'You are surrounded by optimists.'

The squadron's interception ships were sliding into an orbital slot three thousand kilometres behind the antimatter station. If Renko did decide to switch off the storage confinement chambers, the radiation impact from the blast would tax the shielding on the starships to an uncomfortable degree. But they should be safe. So far, he appeared to be cooperating.

Commander Kroeber was handling the negotiation on how the handover was to be accomplished. The civil starship already docked at the station was to depart with everyone on board. It would rendezvous with one of the squadron's marine cruisers. The possessed would disembark and proceed directly to the brig under heavily armed guard where they would stay for the duration of the flight. Any indication of them using their energistic power, for whatever reason, would result in a forty thousand volt current being run through the brig. The cruiser, accompanied by two frigates, would fly directly to an uninhabited terracompatible world (currently in the middle of an ice age) where the possessed would be shot down to the tropical-zone surface in one-way descent capsules, with a supply of survival equipment. There would be no further contact with that planet by the Confederation, apart from delivering any further possessed with whom similar exceptional deals had been made.

Kroeber's other offer, that they help the CNIS with its research into energistic power until such time as a solution was found for possession, was summarily rejected.

Once the possessed were safely incarcerated, another marine cruiser would rendezvous with the starship and take off the station's regular crew ready to transport them to a penal planet. Complete control of the station systems was to be handed over to the navy technical crew, who would remote test their new domain. If total access was confirmed, a third marine cruiser would dock with the station itself, and perform a boarding and securement manoeuvre.

After some haggling, mainly over the contents of the survival equipment they could take with them down to the icy planet, Renko agreed to the arrangement. *Lady Macbeth*'s crew watched the proceedings through the sensors. The handover went remarkably smoothly, taking just less than a day. A datavise from the first marine cruiser showed the possessed, dressed defiantly in double-breasted suits, laughing brashly as they were led into the brig. The station crew looked frankly relieved that they'd escaped with exile. They datavised over their access codes without a qualm.

'You may proceed to docking, Captain Calvert,' Admiral Saldana datavised. 'Lieutenant Grese informs me we are now in full command of the station. There is enough antimatter in storage for your requirements.'

'Thank you, sir,' Joshua replied. He triggered the fusion drives. The simple course over to the station had been plotted for hours. Accelerate, flip, and decelerate. They were already inside the station's umbra and commencing final rendezvous manoeuvres when the Organization's convoy arrived.

*

'Eleven of them, sir,' Lieutenant Rhoecus said. 'Confirmed emergence thirty-seven million kilometres out from the star, one hundred and forty-three million from the station.'

'Threat assessment?' the Admiral enquired. How typical, he thought, that something should come along to thwart the squadron's mission once again.

'Minimal.' The Edenist liaison officer appeared almost happy. '*Ilex* and *Oenone* report there are five hellhawks and six frigates in the enemy formation. Their hellhawks can't swallow down to us, not at this altitude. And even if we assume the frigates are armed with antimatter combat wasps, they would take hours to reach us accelerating continually. I've never heard of a combat wasp that has an hour's fuel in it.'

'They'd have to be custom built,' Grese said. 'Which is unlikely for Capone. And even if they do exist, we can evade them easily at this distance.'

'Then Calvert can carry on?' the Admiral asked.

'Yes, sir.'

'Very well. Kroeber, inform the *Lady Macbeth* to proceed as planned. I'd appreciate it if the good captain didn't dawdle.'

'Aye, sir.'

Meredith reviewed the tactical display. The *Oenone* was barely five million kilometres from the cluster of Organization ships. 'Lieutenant Rhoecus, voidhawks to group together twenty-five million kilometres directly above the antimatter station. I don't want them isolated, it might give the hellhawks ideas. Commander Kroeber, move the rest of the squadron up to rendezvous with the voidhawks, the frigates in high inclination orbits to meet us there. Two of our frigates to remain with the station until *Lady Macbeth* has completed her fuelling. Once they're at a safe distance, the station is to be destroyed.'

'Aye, sir.'

Meredith instructed the tactical computer to compile options. The resulting assessment just about matched his own opinion. The two sides were evenly matched. He had more ships, but the Organization

457

was expected to be armed with antimatter combat wasps. And if he did order the squadron up to intercept, it would take hours to reach them. The Organization ships could simply jump away, leaving only the voidhawks to pursue them – who would then be outgunned.

Effectively, it was a stand-off. Neither side could do much to affect the other.

Yet I cannot allow them to go unchallenged, Meredith thought, it sets a bad precedent. 'Lieutenant Grese? What do we know about the non-possessed crews on board Organization ships? Just how much of a hold does Capone have on them?'

'According to the debriefings we've conducted, they all have family being held captive on Monterey. Capone is very careful about who is given command authority over antimatter. So far it's a strategy that's worked for him. A number of crews on ordinary Organization starships have managed to eliminate their possessed officers and desert. But we've never had any indication of attempted mutiny on ships equipped with antimatter.'

'Pity,' Meredith grunted as the *Arikara* started to accelerate up to the rendezvous with the voidhawks. 'Nevertheless, I'll issue them with the same ultimatum the station was given. Who knows, the opportunity to capitulate might be enough to spark a small rebellion.'

*

Etchells listened to the Admiral's message as it was beamed out to the convoy. Slippery, vague promises of pardons and safe passage. None of it was relevant to him.

We repeat Edenism's offer to you, the voidhawks added. You may transfer your host's personality over to us, and we will provide your nutrient fluid. All we ask in return is your help in finding a satisfactory resolution.

Don't any of you bastards even answer, Etchells warned his fellow hellhawks. They're running scared. They wouldn't make that kind of offer unless they were absolutely desperate.

He could sense the uncertainty rumbling through their affinity bond. But none of them were brave enough to challenge him directly. Satisfied he'd kept them in line for now, Etchells asked the convoy's commander what he intended to do. Withdraw, came the answer, there's nothing else we can do.

Etchells wasn't so sure. The navy hadn't destroyed the station.

And that went against everything the Confederation stood for. There had to be a phenomenal reason for such a change of policy. We should stay, he told the convoy commander. They cannot engage us for hours yet. That gives us a chance to discover what they are doing here. If they're going to start using antimatter against us, Capone should be told. Reluctantly, the commander agreed. However, he did order the Adamist ships to accelerate towards a new jump coordinate that would take them back to New California, leaving the hellhawks to observe the station.

It was difficult to look directly into that dangerous glare. Etchells' sensor blisters began to suffer from glare spots, similar to purple afterimages which plagued human eyes. He started to roll lazily, flicking his ebony wingtips to bank against the gusts of solar particles, switching the view between the blisters. Even then, concentrating on that tiny speck millions of kilometres away was inordinately stressful. A headache began to pound away inside his stolen neuron structure.

None of the electronic sensors loaded into his cargo cradles were any use, they were mostly military systems, intended for close defence work. And his distortion field couldn't reach that far. The visual spectrum provided him with the greatest coverage. He could see the navy's Adamist ships accelerating up out of the star's enormous gravity field, little sparks of light, actually brighter than the photosphere.

After half an hour three more fusion drives ignited around the station. Two of them started to follow the navy squadron. The last one took a different course altogether; curving round the star's southern hemisphere on a very high inclination trajectory.

Etchells opened his beak wide to let out an imaginary warble of success. Whatever it was doing, the lone starship had to be the reason behind the navy's strange action. He issued a flurry of instructions to the other hellhawks. Despite his brute-boy attitude, Etchells had actually absorbed a great deal of information from his host's mentality. The façade of toughness was a deliberate ploy – always let your opponents believe you're dumber than you are. Becoming Kiera's most dependable and trusted hellhawk made sure she wouldn't risk him on those mad seeding flights, or any other dangerous actions. Convoy escort was about the safest duty to pull.

Wasted decades spent bumming round pointless mercenary

actions across the Confederation had taught him to disguise his true potential. Survival was dependent on intelligence and the lowest cunning, not worthy courage. And he knew for sure that surviving his current situation was going to take a great deal of ingenuity. Like Rocio in the *Mindori*, he had come to admire his new bitek form, finding it utterly superior to a human body. Quite how he could hang on to it was a question he'd been unable to resolve. There would be no place for hellhawks in the place where possessed took their planets to escape the universe, he was sure. And the Confederation would never rest until they'd solved the problem of how to evict souls back into the beyond permanently.

So he bided his time, keeping a giant yellowing eye open for some opportunity to save his own ass, and to hell with his comrades.

The navy's unconventional behaviour might just be the break he'd been looking for.

When the last three starships were thirty thousand kilometres from the antimatter station, it exploded with a violence which outshone the prominence arching through the chromosphere below. As if in acknowledgement of their defeat, the hellhawks swallowed away.

The voidhawks analysed the way their distortion fields applied energy against space-time to open a wormhole interstice. All five hellhawks appeared to be heading back to New California.

They have left the remaining frigates extremely vulnerable, Auster, *Ilex*'s captain, reported to Rhoecus. *What are the Admiral's orders?*

Hold your position. If you attack they will just jump clear. We could harass them all the way home, but there is no tactical advantage to be gained from that. Our objective has been accomplished.

Very well.

Syrinx.

Yes, Rhoecus.

Oenone is cleared to rendezvous with the Lady Macbeth. The Admiral wishes you both bon voyage.

Thank you.

*

Etchells didn't believe the voidhawks would follow, certainly not instantaneously. The hellhawks all swallowed ten light-years clear of the star, then swallowed again three seconds later. Unless a voidhawk had been with them to observe the second swallow, there was no way of knowing where they'd gone.

Four of them carried on back to New California. Etchells returned directly to the star, emerging twenty-two million kilometres above its south pole. With the voidhawks all clustered together in their twenty-five million kilometre equatorial orbit, there was no way they could detect his wormhole terminus opening and closing. His position was ideal to observe the navy starships flying out from their low orbit. His sensor blisters didn't have to focus against the overwhelming white blaze. Even his headache started to fade.

He did keep a cursory watch on the navy ships as they rose out of the gravity field, but it was the lone ship heading south that interested him. When it was twenty million kilometres from the star its drive cut out. Etchells projected its course, and started to check his captured spatial memories. Given its jump alignment there were twenty possible Confederation systems it could be heading for. And one other. Hesperi-LN. The Tyrathca planet.

12

Fifteen minutes Courtney sat up at the bar waiting. Four men offered to buy her a drink. Not as many as usual, but then there were very few civilians abroad these days. Even the Blue Orchid was suffering from the scare stories flashing across the net. Its numbers were well down. Normally it would be jammed at this time of night; the kind of not-quite-sleazy club where lower-middle management could hang out after work and not have to worry if someone else from the company saw them. Courtney had been in a lot worse than this. The doormen didn't give her any hassle even though her ass was virtually hanging out of her cocktail dress. Courtney liked the dress, cool black fabric with straps on the front to hold her titties up high, and more cross straps down the cut-out back. It made her look hot, without being too cheap.

Banneth said she looked good wearing it. Best thing the sect had ever done, putting her in this dress; she'd never been so fem before. And it worked. There hadn't been a night she didn't deliver for them. Sometimes twice. It was a good gig, taking the men back to one of the student rent hotels where the sect had squeezed the manager. Then as soon as the mark's pants were off, Billy-Joe, Rav, and Julie would storm in and kick the shit out of him. Then when he was unconscious Billy-Joe took a recording of his bioelectric pattern and emptied his credit disk.

She'd done much the same thing for all of the last three years since her brother introduced her to the Light Bringer. Except to start with she'd attracted paedopervs, who mostly had their own dens to take her to, or just hauled her into the dark end of a downtown alley. Those days, it had been Quinn Dexter who pimped her. In a strange way, she'd always been safer with him in charge. No matter how big a sicko the man was, Quinn had always arrived in time.

Now she was fifteen, and too big to pass for a juvenile any more. Banneth had switched the hormones she took. This new batch didn't prevent her breasts from growing; quite the opposite, they promoted development. She'd still got a skinny frame, but now she was huge with it. In the last nine months her targets had changed completely. It wasn't the pervs who wanted her now, just the losers. Courtney reckoned she'd come out of the alteration OK. Big tits was one of the mildest modifications Banneth made to sect members.

The fifth man to ask if she was all right and did her glass need freshening had what it took. Overweight, round face with perspiration on his brow, hair slicked back with gel, a good suit cleaned too often. His expression was hesitant, ready for a slapdown. Courtney drained her glass, and held it out to him, smiling. 'Thanks.'

He was too fat to dance. That was a shame, she liked to dance. So that meant having to sit and listen to about an hour of bitching – his boss, his family, his apartment; how none of it was going right for him. The drone was so she'd see he was a real genuine guy who'd had a couple of bad breaks lately, hoping for the sympathy fuck.

She made all the right sounds at the right places. After this time working the arcology's clubs she could probably have filled in his life story just by looking at him. Proof of that: she never chose wrong. They always had a loaded disk. After the hour and three drinks he had enough nerve to make his innocent suggestion. To his utter surprise the answer was a demure smile and a hurried nod.

It wasn't far to the student hall, which was good. Courtney didn't like getting into a cab with them; there was too much chance Billy-Joe might lose her. She didn't look to see if the three sect members were trailing after her down the street. They'd be there. This was a real smooth routine now.

Twice though, she thought she heard footsteps following. Real distinctive, regular thuds of someone using a lot of metal in their heels. Dumb idea, there was a whole bunch of people walking along the street. When she did snatch a look, there was no one she could see that looked like a cop. Just a bunch of civilians scurrying around, making out their stupid lives meant something.

The cops were her only worry. Even given the fact less than a quarter of the targets reported the assault and theft, it wouldn't take an AI to spot the pattern. But Banneth would know if there was any sort of operation being mounted. Banneth knew fucking everything going down in Edmonton. It was scary, sometimes. Courtney knew some of the sect's acolytes didn't really believe in God's Brother, they were just too shit-scared of Banneth to step out of line.

'This is it,' she told the man. They'd stopped outside the worn entrance of a two-century-old skyscraper. A couple of genuine students were sitting on the steps, taking charges from a power inhaler. They looked at Courtney with glazed uncaring eyes. She pulled the man past and into the foyer.

In the elevator he made his first tentative move. Going for a kiss, which she let him have. Tongue straight down her throat. He didn't have time for anything more; the room they'd hijacked for the night was on the third floor. Its real owner was lost somewhere in the arcology as the black stimulant program shorted out her neurons.

'What are you studying?' he asked once they were inside.

That caught her short. She didn't have a story in place for that – he wasn't supposed to care. Nothing to help here, either. The room was a usual student's jumble, badly lit with fleks and clothes everywhere, a decades-old desktop block on the one shabby table. Courtney didn't read too good, so she couldn't tell what the tiny print on the flek cases said.

Easy way out. She shoved the shoulder straps down, and let her tits bobble free. That shut him up. It took him about thirty seconds to push her down on the bed, then one hand was up her skirt while the other was squeezing a tit crudely. She groaned like it was good, hoping Billy-Joe and the others got a fucking move on. Sometimes the shits waited and let the man fuck her. Watching the show through some sensor or peep hole, getting off on the scene and laughing quietly. They always claimed it looked less like a set-up if they came in afterwards. Banneth laughed too if she complained.

The man's hand was tugging at her panties. Mouth all hot and slobbering over a nipple. Courtney tried not to grimace. Then she was shivering, as if the conditioning duct had suddenly dumped a shitload of ice into the air.

He gave out a single puzzled grunt, pulling his head back. They looked at each other for an instant, both equally bewildered. Then a white hand clamped over his gelled hair, yanking his head away from her. He yelled in shock and pain as he was pulled off her and flung over the room. His flabby body hit the opposite wall with a loud crash, and crumpled to the floor. A figure in a black robe was standing at the side of the bed, blank hood tipped down towards Courtney. She drew in a breath to shriek, knowing fucking well this wasn't Billy-Joe or any of the others.

'Don't,' the figure warned. The darkness inside the hood withered to reveal the face.

'Quinn!' Courtney squeaked. A smile flicked her lips. 'Quinn? God's Brother, where the fuck did you come from? I thought you got transported.'

'Long story. Tell you in a minute.' He turned and went over to the quivering man, grabbed his head and pulled back viciously. The man's throat was exposed along its entire length, skin stretched tight.

'Quinn, what are you . . . Urrgh!' Courtney watched in a kind of interested shock as a couple of sharp fangs slid out of Quinn's mouth. He winked at her as he lowered his head to bite the man's neck. She could see Quinn's Adam's apple bobbing as he sucked down the blood, several drops dribbled past his lips. The man was whimpering in high-pitched terror. 'Oh, fuck, Quinn, that's disgusting.'

Quinn stood up, grinning, and wiped the back of his hand across his mouth, smearing the blood. 'No it's not. It's the final conquest. Blood is the best food a human can have. Think on it; every nutrient you need all nicely refined and cooked ready for you. It's your right to take it from the followers of the false Lord you defeat. Use them to make you strong, Courtney, replenish your body.' He looked down at the fat man who was clutching the neck wound desperately. Blood was pouring through his fingers.

Courtney giggled at the feeble gurgling sounds the man was making. 'You've changed.'

'So have you.'

'Yeah!' She cupped her tits and lifted them. 'Grew these for a start. Good, aren't they?'

'God's Brother, Courtney, you are a total slut.'

She straightened a leg and dangled her shoe from one toe. 'I like what I am, Quinn. That's my serpent beast, remember? Dignity is a weakness, along with all the other crap on the middle-class wish list.'

'You did listen to the sermons.'

'Sure did.'

'So how's Banneth?'

'Same, I guess.'

'Not for long. I'm back now.' He held out his hands, making simple gestures. The room began to change, the walls darkening, furniture turning to matt-black cast iron. Manacles appeared on the metal railings at the head of the bed.

Courtney looked round wildly at the manifestations, and scrambled backwards over the crumpled duvet, cramming herself into a corner away from Quinn. 'Shit, you're a possessed!'

'Not me,' he said softly. 'I possess. I am the one God's Brother has chosen as his Messiah. This power the returning souls have depends on the force of their will. And nobody believes in themselves more than me. That's how I regained control of my body, through the belief He gave me in myself. Now I'm stronger than a hundred of those snivelling lost dickheads.'

Courtney unfolded her legs and peered forward. 'It is you, isn't it? I mean, like really you. You've got your own body and everything.'

'You never were very quick, were you? But then, it was never your brain the sect wanted.'

'Were you in New York?' she asked in quiet admiration. 'I saw all the fighting on the AV. The police killed skyscrapers full of people they were so scared.'

'I was there a while back. I was also in Paris, Bombay, and Johannesburg, which the police don't know about yet. Then I gave in to myself, and came home.'

'I'm glad you did.' Courtney bounded off the bed, and flung her arms round him, licking from his ear to his mouth. 'Welcome back.'

'You will follow me now, not Banneth.'

'Yes.' She slid her tongue over the tacky blood congealing on his chin, tasting its salt.

'You will obey.'

'Of course.'

Quinn focused on the thought currents in her brain, and knew she was telling the truth. Not that he'd expected anything else from

Courtney. He opened the door and let the other three in. Bobby-Joe and Rav he knew from before; it hadn't taken much to cow them. Five people standing made the little student room badly cramped, their breath helping to heat it up. Fast breathing which came from nerves and excitement. They were all eager to see what Quinn would do next.

'I came back to Earth so I could bring down the Night,' he told them. 'You'll play a big part in that, and so will the possessed. I'm going to leave a nest of you in every arcology. But Edmonton is special for me, because Banneth's here.'

'What you going to do to her?' Billy-Joe asked.

Quinn patted the slender youth's wirelike arm. 'The worst I can imagine,' he said. 'And I've spent a lot of time imagining.'

Billy-Joe's mouth split into an oafish grin. 'All right!'

Quinn looked down at the fat man. He was gasping like a fish. Blood had formed an enormous puddle on the scuffed tile floor. 'You're dying,' Quinn said cheerfully. 'Only one way to save you now.' Fields of energy shifted at his command, exerting a specific pressure against reality. The cries of the souls began to filter out of the beyond. 'Courtney, hurt him.'

She shrugged to the others, and kicked the man hard in the crotch. He shivered, eyes bugging before the lids began to flutter uncontrollably. An extra squirt of blood pumped out of the wound.

'And again,' Quinn directed mildly. In his mind, he was dictating terms to the lost souls who clustered round the weak rent between universes. Hearing the pleas of those who claimed they were worthy. Making his judgement.

Courtney did as she was told, watching in fascination as a soul (a real dead person!) took control of the wretched man. The wound closed up. He started hissing in consternation. Tiny rivulets of lightning slithered along the creases of his blood-soaked suit fabric.

'Give him something to drink,' Quinn said.

Billy-Joe and Julie ransacked the cupboards for cans of soda, popping them and handing them down to the grateful possessed.

'It'll take you a while to replace that much blood,' Quinn said. 'Just lie there and take it easy for a while. Enjoy the show.'

'Yes, Quinn,' the possessed muttered weakly. He managed to roll onto his back, the effort coming close to making him faint.

The iron manacles snapped open loudly. Courtney took one look at them, and glanced back enquiringly at Quinn. His robe was already dissolving. 'You know how to use them,' he told her.

She wriggled out of her dress and bent over the bed, placing her wrists in the manacles. They hinged shut, and locked.

*

Ilex emerged above Avon, radiating profound satisfaction (and considerable hunger). Every Edenist within Trafalgar picked up the emotional emission, and smiled simultaneously at the results Auster was declaring. Lalwani immediately declassified the strike mission against the antimatter station, and the navy press office started relaying the information to the system's news companies. Everything happened so fast that the First Admiral's staff only just managed to officially brief Jeeta Anwar before the presidential office staff received it off the communication net.

The voidhawk's easy two-gee flight to the naval base's docking-ledges was considerably more relaxed than the last time it had burst out of wormhole close to Trafalgar. General affinity hummed with a great many ironic comments pointing this out to its triumphant crew.

Two hours after *Ilex*'s arrival, Captain Auster was escorted into the First Admiral's office by Lieutenant Keaton, the newest member of the Admiral's staff. Samual Aleksandrovich greeted the Edenist captain warmly, and gestured to the sunken reception area. Lalwani and Kolhammer joined them on the leather couches, while the Lieutenant served tea and coffee. As he was moving round with their china cups, the bulky AV cylinder at the apex of the ceiling shimmered brightly, and the images of President Haaker and Jeeta Anwar materialized in the reception area.

'My congratulations to the navy, Admirals, Captain,' Haaker said. 'The destruction of an antimatter station at this time is particularly satisfying.'

'Capone's antimatter station, Mr President,' Kolhammer said significantly. 'That's a considerable bonus.'

'Essentially he will be unable to mount any more of these damnable infiltration missions against Confederation planets, let alone attempt another full-scale invasion along the lines of Arnstadt,' Samual said. 'That means he's been neutered. We shall now resume our harassment campaign, and enhance it considerably this time around. That should wear down the hellhawks, and deplete his stock of antimatter in defence. Given its unstable social base, we expect the Organization to collapse within a few weeks, two months at the most.'

'Unless he pulls another rabbit out of his capacious fedora,' Haaker said. 'I don't mean to disparage your action against the antimatter station, Samual, but in Allah's name, it was a long time coming. Possibly too long. According the latest report I have, nearly a third of Kerry's population is now possessed, and it's only a question of time until the remainder are taken over. On top of that, we know of eleven other worlds Capone has successfully managed to infiltrate. That means we'll lose them, too, you know that as well as I do. And there will no doubt be starships currently en route, telling us of more infiltrations launched before the station was destroyed. Your pardon, but this success rings hollow indeed.'

'What else would you have us do?'

'You know very well. How is Dr Gilmore's project progressing?'

'Slowly, as Mae Ortlieb has been telling you.'

'Yes, yes.' Haaker waved an irritable hand. 'Well, keep me informed of any further developments. Preferably ahead of the media.'

'Yes, Mr President.'

The image of the President and his aide vanished.

'Ungrateful old git,' Kolhammer muttered.

'It's understandable,' Lalwani said. 'The Assembly is beginning to resemble a zoo these days. The ambassadors have realized that for once their magnificent speeches alone aren't going to solve this crisis. They're shouting for action, though of course they don't name a specific.'

'The antimatter ought to relieve a lot of pressure on the navy,' Kolhammer said. 'We should be able to press individual governments to maintain the civil starflight quarantine.'

'There's still a lot of reticence there,' Lalwani said. 'The smaller, more distant asteroids are suffering badly from the economic situation. To them, the conflict is a remote one. That justifies their clandestine flights.'

'It's only remote until their selfish idiocy allows a possessed into their settlement,' Kolhammer snapped.

'We're making progress on identifying the principal offenders,' Lalwani said. 'I'm getting a lot of cooperation from other intelligence agencies. Once we've confirmed the offence, the problem then becomes a diplomatic one.'

'And everything goes pear-shaped,' Kolhammer said. 'Bloody lawyers.'

Samual put his tea cup down on the central rosewood table, and turned directly to Auster. 'You were with Meredith's squadron at Jupiter, I believe?'

'Yes, Admiral,' Auster said.

'Good. I accessed all of your report on the antimatter station mission while the *Ilex* was docking; and I'd like you to tell me directly why Consensus is sending two ships to the other side of the Orion Nebula. *Specifically* why one of them is the *Lady Macbeth*. I simply could not make it plainer that I expected Captain Calvert and that despicable Mzu woman to remain in Tranquillity, and incommunicado.'

The voidhawk captain gave a slight bow, his face respectfully grave. Despite all the mental bolstering which came from unity with other Edenists, and his link with *Ilex*, facing the displeased First Admiral was quite an ordeal. 'I assure you, Consensus regards the Alchemist problem with the utmost seriousness. However, there was some on-the-ground information available which required reassessing your proscription.'

Samual Aleksandrovich settled back in the leather upholstery, knowing he shouldn't enjoy playing the inflexible tyrant. Sometimes it was hard to resist. 'Go on.'

'The Lord of Ruin has discovered that the Tyrathca religion may have some physical basis.'

'I didn't know they had a religion,' Kolhammer said. His neural nanonics was running a search through various encyclopedia files.

'That was also something of a revelation,' Auster said. 'But they do, and their god would appear to be some kind of powerful artefact. They believe it capable of saving them from human possessed.'

'So Consensus sent a pair of starships to investigate,' Samual said.

'Yes. Given the distance involved, the only kind of Adamist ship that can get there is one that has an antimatter drive.'

'And such a flight also removes Calvert and Mzu from any possible contact with the possessed. How very convenient.'

'Consensus considered it so, Admiral.'

Samual laughed drily. 'Lagrange Calvert meeting a real live god. What a spectacle. We should be able to see that clash of egos from this side of the nebula.' Lalwani and Auster grinned in unison.

'Well, there are slimmer straws to grasp, I suppose,' Samual said. 'Thank you, Captain, and my congratulations to *Ilex* on a successful mission.'

The Edenist stood, and bowed formally. 'Admiral.'

Lieutenant Keaton went with him to the door.

Although he considered it faintly ridiculous, if not rude, Samual waited until Auster was outside before speaking to the other two admirals. Privacy was a hard concept for him to abandon; and he knew Lalwani kept their secure sessions confidential as a matter of courtesy. 'A god?' he asked Lalwani.

'I don't know anything about it,' she said. 'But Consensus wouldn't embark on such a course unless it had a degree of confidence in the result.'

'Very well,' Samual said. 'I'd like to receive a complete briefing from the Jovian Consensus, please.'

'I'll see that we're updated.'

'Until we are, we won't be including biblical salvation in our strategic planning sessions.'

'Yes, Admiral.'

'That just leaves us with our last current problem,' Samual said. 'Mortonridge.'

'Could have told you that was a waste of time,' Kolhammer retorted.

'You did. Frequently. As did I. But it is first and foremost a politically motivated campaign. However, we cannot ignore the fact it isn't going quite to plan. This latest development is unnerving to say the least. It also looks as though our marine battalions are going to be tied up there for longer than we originally estimated.'

'Longer! Ha,' Kolhammer said in disgust. 'Have you accessed any of those sensevises? God, that mud. The whole bloody Liberation is completely stalled.'

'It hasn't stalled, they're just encountering more problems than they anticipated,' Lalwani said.

Kolhammer chuckled, and raised his coffee cup in salute. 'I've always been a massive admirer of the Edenist ability to understate.

But I think defining a chunk of land fifteen kilometres across that suddenly takes flight and wanders off into another dimension as a little problem is possibly the best example yet.'

'I never said *little*.'

'Ketton's disappearance isn't my main concern,' Samual said. He received the surprised look which the others gave him with calm humour. 'I was thinking about the medical difficulties de-possession is leaving us with. So far we've been fortunate the news companies have been playing it down, but that won't last. People will eventually wake up to the implications if we're ever successful in returning planets like Lalonde and Norfolk to this universe. There's been a commendable effort by the Kingdom's allies to assist with fresh medical supplies, but the number of cancer-related deaths is still rising.' He clicked his fingers at Keaton, who was hovering near the samovar.

'Sir.' The Lieutenant stepped forward. 'Trafalgar's medical office has been examining the consequences of de-possession. Frankly, we're lucky Mortonridge doesn't have a larger population. The Kingdom and its allies should just manage to provide enough nanonic packages to cope with two million cancer patients. Though we're dubious about correct application; the number of experienced doctors is a critical factor. However, we estimate that an entire planet of de-possessed, with an average population of three-quarters of a billion, would essentially exhaust the entire Confederation's medical facilities. To our knowledge, the possessed have so far taken over eighteen planets, with several hundred additional asteroid settlements. And we expect the planets Capone has infiltrated will soon join them. Ultimately, we could be dealing with as many as thirty planetary populations, possibly more than that.'

'Shit,' Kolhammer exclaimed. He gave the youngish lieutenant a very worried frown. 'So what's going to happen if we get them all back?'

'Given the development level of cancers we've seen on the de-possessed so far, there will be a rapid and extremely high mortality rate among their respective populations if they remain untreated.'

'That's a very clinical way of putting it, Lieutenant.'

'Yes, sir. You should also consider, the possessing souls are either unaware of the damage they're inflicting on their hosts, or are unable to cure it. Their energistic power is capable of repairing physical injury, but we haven't seen them deal with this kind of illness yet. It may be they can't.'

'What are you getting at?' Lalwani asked.

'Unless the biochemical environment on the planets they've removed from this universe is radically different in some way, then the possessed will all be suffering like this no matter where they are. In which case, if they don't start to effect some kind of treatment, their host bodies might die.'

Lalwani's shock was so vehement she couldn't prevent some of it from leaking into the general affinity band. Edenists in the asteroid automatically opened their minds, proffering emotional support.

Reluctantly, Lalwani refused. 'Thirty planetary populations?' she demanded, incredulous. She glanced from the Lieutenant to the First Admiral. 'You knew?'

'I accessed the report this morning,' Samual admitted. 'And I haven't informed the President yet. Let him get on top of the Assembly again before we break news like this.'

'Dear God,' Kolhammer muttered. 'If we pull them back from wherever they've gone, we won't be able to save them. And if we leave them alone, they won't survive either.' He gave Keaton a look that was almost a plea. 'Did the medical office come up with *any* ideas?'

'Yes, sir, they had two.'

'Finally! Someone with some bloody initiative. What are they?'

'The first is fairly simple. We broadcast a warning to the possessed groups we know are still remaining in this universe. Ask them to stop trying to change the appearance of their host bodies. It should appeal to their own self-interest.'

'If they don't just ignore it as propaganda,' Lalwani said. 'By the time a tumour actually becomes noticeable, it's usually too late for primitive medical treatments.'

'Nonetheless, we will definitely proceed with that option,' Samual said.

'And the second?' Kolhammer asked.

'We formally request the Kiint Ambassador for help.'

Kolhammer let out a disgusted breath. 'Ha! Those bastards won't help us. They've already made that clear enough.'

'Um, sir?' Keaton said. He gave the First Admiral a glance, and received a nod of permission. 'They said they wouldn't provide us with a solution to possession. In this case, we're just asking them for material aid. We know they have a more sophisticated technology than ours; human companies have been buying upgrades and improvements for a variety of products ever since we made contact with them. And now with the Tranquillity incident we know they haven't abandoned their manufacturing base as thoroughly as they claimed. They may well be able to produce the kind of medical systems we require in the quantities we'll need. After all, we'll only have a use for them if we solve the possession problem for ourselves. If the Kiint are as sympathetic as they assure us they are, then there is a good chance they'll say yes.'

'Excellent analysis,' Lalwani said. 'We can't possibly ignore the option.'

'I wasn't planning to,' Samual said. 'In fact, I've already requested a personal meeting with Ambassador Roulor. I'll sound him out about the prospect.'

'Good move,' Kolhammer said. 'That's a commendable advisory team your medical office put together, Samual.'

*

It felt strange to be back. Quinn stalked through the ghost realm, observing the sect's Edmonton headquarters. His peculiar, hazy perception of the real world from this shadowed existence might account for his new interpretation of the familiar rooms and corridors. Or it could just be time and a very different attitude to when he was last here.

This had been home for many years. A place of refuge and of terror. Now it was just a cluster of gloomy chambers, devoid of any appeal or memories. The routine of the place hadn't changed, though it was slowing down. Much to the fury of the senior acolytes. He smiled as they shouted and brutalized the juniors. His fault. His word was spreading.

All of Edmonton would soon be aware of his arrival. So far he'd taken over eight covens, and was ready to visit the remainder. Those that had fallen under his thrall were now actively pursuing the will of God's Brother. Over the last few days he'd been dispatching several small groups to attack strategic sections of the arcology's infrastructure. Generators, water stations, transport junctions: they'd all been damaged to some degree. It was primitive stuff, chemical explosives concocted from formulae loaded into public databanks centuries ago by freethink anarchists, the files replicated so many times they were impossible to erase. On Quinn's orders, the possessed would only supervise the missions, never actually venturing to the target themselves. That was left to the faithful: useful, disposable imbeciles. He couldn't risk the authorities discovering a possessed in Edmonton, not yet. So for now such destruction would appear to be the work of a breakaway sect faction, fanatics who had split away from their high magus. That way they would appear as sympathizers to the anarchist groups in Paris, Bombay, and Johannesburg that were also bombing and terrorizing their fellow citizens.

The authorities would discover who was behind it eventually. But by then he would have established enough cells of possessed to bring about the Night.

Quinn arrived at the temple, and surveyed it slowly. A tall chamber, more elaborate than the smaller covens. Pictures of violent depravity alternated with runes and pentagons along the walls. A wreath of small yellow flames flickered weakly around the tarnished inverted cross on the altar. He was drawn to the big slab as the memories of this place finally returned. There was the pain of his initiation, then more pain as he was used for further ceremonies. Each time, Banneth had smiled down serenely; a dark angel ministering to his body. Drugs and packages were applied, and an obscene variety of pleasure would be combined with his agony. Banneth's laugh would wrap around him, taking on the power of an indecent caress. She/he/it, that terrible androgynous multi-sexed monster, conditioned him to respond to the torment in the way that generated the most enjoyment – for it. Eventually the two extremes of sensation merged, becoming one.

A triumph, Banneth had declared. The creation of the perfect sect mentality. Birthing the serpent beast.

Quinn gave the altar a curious look, seeing himself bound to it, skin glistening with sweat and blood as he screamed. The pain and the images were real enough, but he couldn't recall anything before then. It was as if Banneth had created his flesh at the same time as his mind.

'Quinn? Is that you, Quinn?'

Quinn turned slowly, squinting at the pale figure sitting on the front pew. A face he was sure he knew, belonging to this place but from a long time ago. The figure stood, a hunched-up adolescent in a torn leather jacket and dirty jeans. He was pitifully insubstantial. 'It is you, isn't it? You remember me, Quinn. It's me. It's Erhard.'

'Erhard?' He wasn't sure.

'Damn, we shovelled shit together for long enough. You must remember.'

'Yes. Yes, I do.' A novice acolyte who'd joined the sect around the same time as Quinn. One who lacked the strength to survive such a brotherhood. The same relentless battery of ordeals and punishments which had fortified Quinn had crushed Erhard. It had culminated in a ritual in the temple, one which Banneth had never intended Erhard to live through. There was rape and torture and drugs and burrowing parasites of Banneth's devising; atrocities performed to the hot chants and wild laughter of the entire headquarters coven. Erhard's final pleas had risen above their chorus, a thin wail of ultimate terror. Then Banneth had brought the jewelled sacrificial knife down in a fast slash.

The joy Quinn had experienced that day was almost orgasmic. He'd been the one tasked to carry the knife for Banneth.

'It's not fair, Quinn. I don't belong here. I hate this place. I hate the sect.'

'You never did feed your serpent beast,' Quinn said contemptuously. 'Now look at you. You're as much a loser now as you ever were.'

'It's not fair!' Erhard cried. 'I didn't know what the sect was like, not really. And then they killed me. You killed me, Quinn. You were one of them.'

'You deserved it.'

'Fuck you. I was nineteen. I had my life, and you took it away, you and that psycho fruit Banneth. I want to kill Banneth. I swore I would.'

'No!' Quinn stormed. Erhard quailed, cowering back from the command. 'Banneth does not die,' Quinn said. 'Not ever. Banneth belongs to me.'

The ghost edged forward, holding out a hand as though feeling the warmth thrown out by a fire. 'What are you?'

Quinn giggled quietly. 'I don't know. But God's Brother has shown me what I've got to do.' He walked out of the temple, leaving the ghost behind.

Three figures were marching along the corridor, one of them with desperate reluctance. Quinn recognized him. Acolyte Kilian. They'd met a few days ago. All three frowned as they passed their invisible watcher, puzzled by why they suddenly felt so chilly.

Quinn followed them. He knew where they were going, he'd taken this route himself enough times. Soon he would see it again: Banneth. That's all it would be, this time. Just a look, a reminder of that face. Nothing fast would happen to Banneth. It had taught Quinn well, in that respect. The most delectable punishments were the slowest ones. And when Night came, it would be in tandem with eternity.

*

Darkness has arrived. Even when the acolytes didn't whisper it, the phrase hung in the smoky air of the sect's Edmonton headquarters. A threat more menacing than any sadism the serjeant acolytes could bestow.

Banneth knew what that meant. The AV projectors were broadcasting a constant coverage of the New York situation, which the entire headquarters coven was obsessed by. The arcology's continuing isolation. Rumours of free possessed. Portents wherever you looked. And many of the coven looked very hard indeed.

Their work suffered as a consequence. Income from the scams and hustling were well down in every coven across town. Even she, the High Magus, couldn't rack up much enthusiasm. What chance did the lesser maguses have?

When she did rage at the sergeant acolytes, they just shuffled their feet and muttered dourly that there was little point continuing their old activities. Our time has come, they said, God's Brother is returning to Earth. Who cares about knocking off dumb-ass civilians? Given the creed of the Light Bringer sect, it wasn't an attitude she could effectively argue against. The irony of the situation didn't escape her.

All she could do was keep listening to the rap from the street, hunting out clues. It was a thin source of information, especially now. Like a great many of Earth's arcologies, Edmonton was slowly shutting down as it spewed out its own fear. Commercial districts were reporting increasing absenteeism. People were calling in sick, taking holidays. Parks and arcades were nearly deserted. Football, baseball, ice hockey, and other games fixtures were played to small crowds. Parents kept their kids away from day clubs. For the first time in living memory it was always possible to get a seat on metro buses and tube carriages.

The vac-trains weren't shut. Keeping the routes open was a bravado example of Govcentral confidence, intended to reassure people that Earth was still safe. Passenger numbers were under thirty per cent. Nobody wanted to do anything that brought them into contact with other people. Especially strangers. Civic utility companies had to threaten employees with lawsuits to keep essential services going. Government workers were intimidated with the prospect of disciplinary proceedings if they didn't perform their duties as normal, especially the police. The mayors were desperate to provide the image of normality in the hope the public would follow their cue. A desperation that was taking on increasingly surreal dimensions in the face of such stubborn public reticence.

Banneth kept dispatching sect members to wander through the eternal half-light gulleys that were downtown streets, hunting any sign of a score. The usual broken inhabitants shuffling along the sidewalks would huddle away from them in sealed-up doorways, sniffing suspiciously as they strutted past. Cop cars swished along silently, creating whirlpools of silvery wrapping foils; the only vehicles moving at ground level. They slowed as they drew level with the sect gangs, examining the sullen faces through misty armoured glass before tooting the siren and accelerating away. Forcing them to go out was a mostly futile exercise. But she had persevered while the world slowly choked on its own paranoia. And now it seemed as though she'd got lucky.

Acolyte Kilian was doing his level best not to shake as the sergeant acolytes hurriedly left him alone in Banneth's inner sanctum. The chamber was buried at the centre of the skyscraper which the sect used as its headquarters. As with the Light Bringer covens the world over, the original layout of rooms and corridors had been corroded and corrupted as acolytes burrowed their way through walls and ducts like human maggots. Haphazard partitions were hammered and cemented up behind them, creating a bizarre onion-layer topology of chambers and cells that protected the core. Banneth had dwelt there for nearly three and a half decades without once ever venturing out. There was no need now, everything necessary to make her life enjoyable was brought to her.

Unlike several high maguses she was aware of, Banneth didn't go in for ostentation. Her senior acolytes were permitted whatever decadent luxuries they could steal and bribe for themselves. But they lived several floors above her, decorating their apartments with expensive hedonistic amenities, and harems of beautiful youths and freakish supplicants (Banneth had created them specially). She indulged herself on somewhat different levels.

When Kilian started to look round, he found he was in a place that was way beyond the worst-case scenarios that acolytes whispered among themselves. Banneth's sanctum was an experimental surgery. Its mainstay was a broad bench desk with high-capacity processor blocks and shiny new medical equipment. Three stainless-steel tables were lined up in the middle of the floor, with discreet leather restraint straps placed strategically round the edges. Life-support canisters were arranged around the walls, like huge glass pillars. Aquarium-style lighting caps shone brightly on their contents. Kilian really wished they didn't, the things inside were enough to make him shit his pants. People, in a few of them. Suspended by a white silk web in some thick clear fluid, tubes going into their mouths and noses (those that still had mouths and noses). Always with their eyes open, looking about. Acolytes he remembered from not so long back, with new appendages grafted on, or with parts removed, their incisions raw and open to reveal the missing organs. Then there were the less than human creatures, made worse by having very human pieces attached. Clusters of organs bound together by a plexus of naked pumping veins. Animals, game cats and gorillas with the tops of their skull removed, and no brain left inside. Pride of place on the wall above the work desk was taken by an ancient oil painting of a young woman in a dress with a stiff bodice and long skirt.

Although Kilian had never been in the sanctum before, it was the place where everyone came eventually, either for boosting or punishment. Banneth performed both types of operation herself. Now he stood as still as his trembling limbs would allow as the High Magus walked briskly across the floor to him.

Banneth's face had a male jawline, a blunt protuberant blade of bone. But that was the only masculine feature, the eyes and mouth were soft, very feminine. A shaggy pelt of straw-blonde hair completed the enigma. Kilian glanced nervously at the white shirt Banneth wore. Everyone said the High Magus got aroused at the sight of fear. If her nips were jutting, then she was in the feminine stage of her cycle.

Dark circles of skin were definitely tenting the cotton. Kilian wondered if it really made a difference. Banneth was a hermaphrodite (by design, so rumour said). She looked as if she was about twenty, either as a male or a female; though age was an easy enough cosmetic adaptation. Nobody knew how old she really was, nor even how long she had been High Magus. In fact, legend and rumour were all that existed about her past. Questions were discouraged.

'Thank you for coming to see me,' Banneth said. Her hand stroked Kilian's cheek, the cool skin of her knuckles drifting gently along his cheekbone. An appraisal by a gifted sculptor, finding his exact form. He quivered at the touch. Pink eyes with feline irises blinked in amusement at his reaction.

'Nervous, Kilian?'

'I don't know what I've done, High Magus.'

'That's true. But then a barely human grunt like you doesn't know much of anything. Do you? Well, don't worry yourself too much. Actually, you've been quite useful to me.'

'I have?'

'Amazingly, yes. And as you know, I always reward the devout.'

'Yes, High Magus.'

'What can I do for you now, I wonder?' She began to circle the apprehensive acolyte, grinning boyishly. 'You're how old now? Twenty-five, isn't it? So I ask myself, what does a nice young boy your age always want? And the answer's a much bigger cock, of course. That's pretty standard. I can do that, you know. I can snip off that pitiful rat-sized cock you've got now, and replace it with something much better. A cock that's as long as your forearm and as hard as steel. You would like me to do that, wouldn't you?'

'Please, High Magus,' Kilian whimpered.

'Was that a "Yes, please", Kilian?'

'I . . . I just want to help you. However I can.'

She blew him a kiss, still prowling her circuit around him. 'Good boy. I asked to see you because I'd like to know something. Do you believe in the teachings of the Light Bringer?'

Trick question, Kilian screamed silently. If I say no, she'll do whatever she wants as punishment; if I say yes she'll ask me to prove it through endurance. 'All of it, High Magus, every word. I've found my serpent beast.'

'An excellent answer, Kilian. Now tell me this: do you welcome the coming darkness?'

'Yes, High Magus.'

'Really? And how do you know it's coming?'

Kilian risked a glance over his shoulder, trying to follow the High Magus as she circled round him. But she was directly behind him now, and the only thing he really noticed was the way the eyes of the acolytes in the life-support containers were tracking her movements. 'The possessed are here. He sent them, our Lord. They're going to bring His Night to the whole world.'

'So everyone says. The whole arcology is talking about nothing else. Indeed the whole planet has little else to say. But how do you know? You, Kilian?'

Banneth stopped in front of him, lips curved in a sympathetic, expectant smile.

I'll have to tell the truth, Kilian realized in horror. But I don't know if that's what she wants to hear. Fuck! Oh God's Brother, what'll she do to me if it's wrong? What will she turn me into?

'Cat got your tongue?' Banneth asked coyly. The smile hardened slightly, becoming less playful. Her glance flicked to one of the life-support canisters containing a puma. 'Of course, I can give the cat your tongue, Kilian. But what would I fit in its place? What would be appropriate, do you think? I have so much material I don't really need any more. Some of it is long past its sell-by date. Ever felt flesh that's started to decay, Kilian? Necromorphology is a somewhat acquired taste. You never know, though, you might get to like it in time.'

'I saw one!' Kilian shouted. 'Oh fuck, I saw one. I'm sorry, High Magus, I didn't tell my sergeant acolyte, I—'

She kissed his ear lobe, shocking him into silence. 'I understand,' she whispered. 'Really I do. To understand the way people think, you must first understand the way they work. And I've made the workings of the human body my special area of study for a long time. Physiology begets psychology, you might say. Mightn't you, Kilian?'

Kilian *hated* it when the High Magus talked all this weird big-word shit. He never knew how to answer. None of the acolytes did, not even the seniors.

'It— I saw him in the Vegreville dome coven's chapel,' Kilian said. He knew for sure now that the High Magus wanted to hear about the possessed. Maybe this would get him off the hook.

Banneth stopped her pacing, standing directly in front of the woeful acolyte. There were no more smiles left on her androgynous face. 'You didn't tell your sergeant acolyte because you thought you'd wind up in deep shit. Because if the possessed are real, then the sect hierarchy that you've so devoutly been kissing ass to for the last six years will be replaced by them. By telling everyone what you'd seen you would in effect be spreading sedition; though I doubt you would be able to rationalize it quite like that. To you it was simple instinct. Your serpent beast looks after you, it puts you first. As indeed it should, in that respect you've been loyal to yourself and God's Brother. Of course, you couldn't resist telling a few people, could you? You should have known better, Kilian. You know I reward acolytes who betray their friends to me.'

'Yes, High Magus,' Kilian mumbled.

'Well, I'm glad that's settled, then. Unfortunately the golden rule of the sect is that I am to be told everything. I and I alone decide what is important, and what is not.' Banneth walked over to one of the stainless-steel tables, and tapped a finger on it. 'Come over here, Kilian. Lie down for me.'

'*Please*, High Magus.'

'Now.'

If he'd thought running would have done him the slightest good, he would have run. Actually, he even had the wild thought that he could attack Banneth. The High Magus was physically weaker. But that idea was resolved in a second by a simple clash of wills. He was foolish enough to glance at her pink eyes.

'That's a very bad thought,' Banneth said. 'I don't like that at all.'

Kilian walked over to the table, taking the smallest steps possible. In the faintly violet light thrown out by the life-support containers, he could see the scuffed silvery surface was sprinkled with small black flecks of dried blood.

'Remove your clothes first,' Banneth told him. 'They get in the way of what I want to do.'

The initiation ceremonies, the punishments, the degradations he'd undergone for the sect – none of them prepared him for this. Simple pain he could endure. It was soon over, making him all the meaner, stronger for it. Each time his serpent beast would come away slightly larger, more dominant. None of that helped him now. Each garment he took off was another portion of himself sacrificed to her.

'In times gone by, they used to say the punishment should fit the crime,' Banneth said. Kilian removed his jeans, and she smiled thinly at his flabby legs. 'An appropriate sentiment, I always thought. But now I believe it's more fitting that the body part should fit the crime.'

'Yes,' Kilian said thickly. That, he needed no explanation for. He had spent hour after hour mucking out the pigs as part of his duty. All the acolytes had to do it. All of them detested the filthy squealing animals. It was an insidious reminder of what fate ultimately greeted Edmonton sect members, no matter you were being disciplined or rewarded.

Banneth's herd were special, developed centuries ago when geneering was in its infancy. They were originally designed to provide organs for human transplants. A worthy project, to help people with worn-out hearts or failed kidneys. Pig organs were the same size as human ones, and it was the first practical success of the geneticists to modify porcine cells so they didn't trigger a rejection by their new host's immune system. For a few brief years at the start of the twenty-first century the concept had flourished. Then medical science, genetics, and prosthetic technology had raced on ahead. Humanized pigs were abandoned and forgotten by everyone except medical historians and a few curious zoologists. Then Banneth had come across the obscure file in some long-outdated medical text.

She had identified and traced descendants of the original pigs, and began breeding them anew. Modern genetic improvements had been sequenced in, strengthening the bloodline. It was the raw primitiveness of the concept which appealed to her. The sect's use of modern technology was so much at odds with its basic gospel. Pigs and old-fashioned surgery were an ideal alternative.

When an acolyte needed boosting, it wasn't AT muscle she implanted to enhance the original human ones. Like the rest of the porcine organs, the muscles wouldn't cause rejection. Pig skin, too, was thicker, sturdier, than its human counterpart. Lately, she had begun to experiment with other animals. Grafted monkey feet turned an acolyte into an efficient acrobat, useful for gaining entry to upper storeys. Lighter leg bones allowed them to outrun police mechanoids. Given time and research subjects, she knew she could match any modification used by cosmoniks and the combat-boosted mercenaries so prevalent out there among the Confederation worlds.

The surgical techniques could also be used to rectify behaviour. For example, an attempt to run away from the sect would be easily curtailed by replacing legs with trotters. In Kilian's case, Banneth hadn't finalized on an effective lesson. Though she did favour extending and re-routing his colon into the back of his throat, so that every time he wanted to shit he'd have to do it through his mouth. The extra tubing would give him a very thick neck. A nice irony, that. It would match his thick head.

When he was naked, she made him lie face down on the table, then used the straps to secure him in place. Creative punishment would have to wait. Since he blurted confirmation about a possessed, only one thing had mattered to her. She smeared a big dollop of depilatory cream on the back of his neck, and squirted it off with a cold water hose. It left his skin clean and bare, ready to receive the nanonic implant package.

Kilian wasn't permitted an anaesthetic or sedative. He groaned and whimpered continually as the personality debrief filaments pierced his brain, their brutal intrusion sparking cascades of aberrant nerve impulses that sent spasms rippling along his limbs. Banneth sat on one of the desk bench stools, sipping a chilled, hand-mixed martini as she supervised the procedure, occasionally datavising new instructions into the package. After nearly two hours, the first erratic impulses started to flood back along the invading filaments. Banneth brought her AI on-line to analyse and interpret the confusing deluge of impulses. Visualizations that were nothing more than randomized detonations of colour slowly calmed as the AI began to marshal Kilian's synaptic discharges into ordered patterns. Once his thought patterns had been catalogued and correlated with his neural structure, his entire consciousness became controllable. The filaments could simply inject new impulses into the synaptic clefts they'd penetrated, superseding any natural thoughts he had.

Kilian was thinking about his family, such as it was. Mother and two younger half-brothers, living in a couple of dingy rooms in a downtown skyscraper over in the Edson dome. Years ago, now. Mother surviving on a Govcentral parent work-pay scheme; never there during the day. All he had was the constant noise, the shouted arguments, fights, music, footsteps, metroline traffic. At the time he'd wanted nothing more than to escape. A bad decision.

'Why?' Banneth asked.

Kilian flinched. He was sprawled on the sagging bed-settee by the window, looking fondly at all the familiar old objects that had occupied his brief childhood.

Now Banneth stood by the doorway, regarding him contemptuously. She was brighter than anything else in the room, more colourful.

'Why?' she repeated.

A spherical wave of pressure contracted through Kilian's skull, squeezing his thoughts out through his mouth in an unstoppable stream. 'Because I left this to join the sect. And I wish I hadn't. I hate my life, I fucking hate it. And now I'm on your table and you're gonna turn me into a dog, or chop my dick off and give it to someone else to fuck me with. Some kind of crap like that. And it's not fair. I didn't do anything wrong. I've always done whatever the sect asked. You can't do this to me. You can't, please God. You're not human. Everybody knows that. You're a fucking weirdo freak cannibal.'

'Now there's gratitude. But who gives a fuck about this pathetic little comfort regression you're in? I want when you saw the possessed.'

The pressure wave found another part of Kilian's mind to crush. He screamed out loud as memories erupted like fountains of acid behind his eyes. Home was coldly scorched out of existence, huge great sections of it peeling away like rotten flesh to reveal the Vegreville chapel's temple. Kilian had been there three days back, sent by his sergeant acolyte to pick up some package. He didn't know what was in it, just that 'Banneth wants it fast.'

The coven was different than before. There was a new atmosphere percolating through the dark nest of rooms: the night before the big game. And they regarded him as a joke. His urgency to complete the assignment, to get the package and leave, made them snigger and scoff. Every time he asked them to be quicker they delighted in delaying. They were like frisky kids at a day club who'd found a new boy to taunt and bully.

Eventually he'd been taken to the temple where the senior acolyte told him the package was waiting. The chamber walls were made from thousands of slim metal reinforcement rods welded together, the inside of a bird's nest woven out of iron twigs. Its altar was a tight-packed mound of rusty spikes, their tips all shaved down to the same length. Twin flames rose out of the bristling metal at each end, long yellow tongues dancing in the gloom. Pews were composite roof planks nailed to a variety of pedestals. The sect's usual runes were still on the walls, but they were barely visible now. A single new slogan had been sprayed everywhere: Night is coming. On the walls, on the ceiling, even on the floor.

Kilian was made to enter alone, his little escort clustering round the thick doors behind him, giggling wildly. His annoyance dropped away as he walked quietly towards the altar, replaced by growing nervousness. Three figures waited silently for him behind the altar, clad in black robes. These garments had none of the embellishments or pentagons usually favoured by senior sect members. If anything it made them appear even more menacing than usual. Their faces were almost lost inside the large hoods. Flickering yellow beams from the candles would occasionally reveal a feature within two of the hoods: bloodshot eyes, hooked nose, wide mouth. The third hood could have been empty, for all that Kilian saw. Even when he reached the altar, he could see nothing inside that night-like cavity of fabric.

'The High Magus sent me,' he stammered. 'You've got a package for me, yeah?'

'We certainly have,' a voice said from somewhere inside that veiled hood.

Alert now, Banneth ran the voice through an analysis program, though ordinary memories of voices were a notoriously unreliable source for such verification programs. Nonetheless, it showed remarkable similarities to recordings of Dexter's voice. Kilian trembled as the hidden figure slowly held out an arm. He was almost expecting a pistol nozzle to poke out at him. But it was just a snow-white hand that emerged from the voluminous sleeve. A small plastic container was dropped carelessly on the altar.

'Our gift to Banneth. I hope it is useful.'

Kilian scooped it up hurriedly. 'Right. Thanks.' All he wanted now was to get the fuck out of here. These guys were almost as creepy as Banneth.

'I am interested that the High Magus is carrying on as though nothing is happening.'

Kilian didn't know how to answer. He cast a glance over his shoulder, wondering if he should make a dash for it. Not that he could ever get out of the chapel unless he was allowed to. 'Well, you know how it is,' he shrugged lamely.

'I certainly do.'

'Sure. I'd better get this back to her, then.'

'The Night will fall.'

'I know.'

'Excellent. Then you will join us when the time comes.'

'My serpent beast is strong.'

A head emerged from the hood, the darkness slowly washing backwards to expose more and more features. 'You'll need to be,' Quinn said.

Banneth froze the image. No doubt about it. Skin as white as snow, eyes infinite pools of black – though that could have just been emotion-aggravated exaggeration. But it was Quinn.

The High Magus smiled thinly as the image hung in her mind. The fierceness which had once so animated him, and fascinated her, was gone. If anything, he looked rather stressed out. Crinkled lines radiated away from the corner of his eyes, while those sweet cheeks were rather sadly sunken.

She concentrated her thoughts, focusing on the personality traits of one individual. **Dexter's in Edmonton. One of my acolytes encountered him three days ago.**

Ah. Thank you, Western Europe replied.

*

The ten ships in the convoy emerged above New California, immediately confirming who they were to Monterey's SD Command. For once the hellhawks accompanying the frigates hadn't raced on ahead.

They were quite content to let the convoy commander break the bad news they were carrying.

Where's Etchells? Hudson Proctor asked once the four remaining hellhawks had checked in.

We don't know, Pran Soo said. **He left us to scout round the antimatter station. He will probably emerge soon.**

You're sure the Confederation destroyed it?

The frigates were still there. They saw it explode.

A fact which the convoy commander was very reluctantly confirming to Monterey. The news was all around the asteroid within thirty minutes, and down to New California's cities in roughly the same timescale. Word spread across the countryside within a couple of days. The more remote Organization asteroid settlements lagged behind by anything up to a week, the last ones actually got to hear about it from Confederation propaganda broadcasts – who damn well weren't going to miss that opportunity.

This time Emmet Mordden refused point-blank to be the one who had to tell Al. So the senior lieutenants decided that Leroy Octavius should be awarded the honour. Their unspoken thought (no matter which faction they belonged to) as they watched him waddle out of the asteroid's command centre was that he too would chicken out and simply tell Jezzibella.

A lifetime juggling temperamental personalities in the entertainment industry had left Leroy wise to that option. Knowing that Jezzibella was the only guarantee his own precious body and soul remained intact, he simply couldn't permit her position to be weakened. He did toy with the notion of passing the buck to poor Avram Harwood, but that might just be one demand too many for the fragile ex-Mayor. Instead, Leroy gathered his courage up and went down to the Nixon Suite. Walking along the last few metres to the doors his legs had more than a little wobble of apprehension. The two gangsters on guard outside picked up on his emotions, and studiously avoided eye contact as they opened the big doors for him.

Al and Jezzibella were having breakfast in the conservatory, a long, narrow room with one wall made entirely of curving enhanced sapphire, which gave a slightly bluish tint to the view of the planet and stars outside. The opposite wall had vanished beneath a trellis of flowering vines. Pillars running the length of the conservatory were transparent tubes, aquariums filled with the strange and beautiful fish from a dozen worlds.

There was only one table, a broad wrought-iron oval, with a vase of orange lilies in the middle. Al and Jezzibella sat next to each other, dressed in identical aquamarine towelling robes, and casually munching toast. Libby was limping round the table, pouring coffee.

Al looked up as Leroy came in. His welcoming smile faded when he caught the anxiety in the obese manager's mind. 'You don't look too happy, Leroy, my boy. What's eating you?' Jezzibella glanced up from her history book.

Leroy took a breath and plunged in. 'I have some news. It's not good.'

'OK, Leroy, I ain't gonna bite you because those wiseasses dumped a shitty job on you. What the fuck's happened?'

'That last convoy we sent to the antimatter station just made it back. Thing is, the navy was there waiting for them. They blew it up, Al. We're not going to get any more antimatter, not ever.'

'Jesus H. Christ!' Al's fist thumped the table, bouncing the crockery. Three slim scars throbbed white on his cheek. 'How the hell did they find out? Ain't *nothing* we do more careful than sending the convoy to the station. Did the last lot get followed?'

'I don't know, Al. The frigates'll dock in another ninety minutes; maybe the captains'll tell us more.'

'They'd fucking better.' Al's fists clenched. He stared at the starfield outside the conservatory.

Leroy hesitated, glancing at Jezzibella. She inclined her head silently to the door. It was all the permission Leroy needed; he ducked his head at Al, and shifted himself the hell out of there as fast as his thick legs would allow. Jezzibella waited patiently, not saying anything. By now she was well used to the cycle of Al's moods.

After a minute in which he could have been frozen, Al roared: 'Fuck it!' and smashed a fist down on the table again. This time it had his energistic power behind the blow. The iron bent alarmingly. Plates, jam pots, cups, and the vase went sliding down the new valley to crash together along the fold. He stood up fast as the boiling coffee splashed onto the floor with the lilies. His chair legs caught on the tiling. 'FUCK!' Al spun round and kicked the chair, sending it flying into the curving sapphire window. Libby whimpered in fright, cradling the milk jug as if it alone could protect her. Jezzibella sat back, holding on to the coffee cup she'd saved. Her expression was strictly neutral.

'Goddam motherfucking shit-eating bastards! That was *my* goddam station. *Mine.*' He put both hands under the buckled table and shoved it upwards. The entire thing went somersaulting along the conservatory. Crockery tumbled away to smash against the floor. Libby cowered as one of the heavy metal legs flashed centimetres above the bun of her grey hair. 'Nobody takes my property away from me. *No*body! Don't they know who the fuck they're dealing with here? I'm not some chickenshit small-time loser pirate! I am Al goddam Capone. I've got a fleet that kicks the shit out of whole planets, for Christ's sake. Are they fucking insane? I'll blow that whole stinking pennyass navy of theirs out of the goddam water. That knucklehead Russki Admiral is gonna get a baseball rammed so far up his ass he'll be pitching it out of his mouth.'

'Space,' Jezzibella said firmly.

'*What?*' Al whirled round and bellowed at her. 'What did you fucking say to me?'

'You'll blow them out of space. Not water. We're not on Earth now, Al.'

He pulled a fist back. It shook violently as he held it over her. Then he swung round and punched one of the tall aquariums. The glass shattered. Water and a shoal of long purple fish poured out of the big hole, splattering the hem of his robe.

'Shit. Goddam.' He danced backwards, trying to keep his house slippers out of the water.

Jezzibella calmly lifted her feet off the tiles as the tide swirled round her chair. Fish started wriggling frantically over the mosaic, their movements skidding them against the plant troughs. 'Did you have antimatter when you started?'

Al was watching the fish in mild perplexity; as if he couldn't quite understand where they'd come from. 'What?' he demanded.

'You heard.' She deliberately looked away from him, and gave Libby a gracious smile. 'Go and fetch a bucket, or something, there's a dear.'

'Yes, poppet,' Libby said nervously. She scurried away.

'You frightened her,' Jezzibella accused.

'Fuck her,' Al said irritably. 'What did you say about antimatter?'

'First off, we've still got tonnes of the stuff. Think how many convoys got through.'

'Tons?'

'All right, not tonnes, but certainly kilograms. Work it out if you don't believe me: one kilogram equals two and a fifth pounds. So the fleet and the SD network still has more than enough to wipe the floor with any Confederation Navy task force stupid enough to try its luck against New California. Then there's Kingsley Pryor. You haven't forgotten him, have you?'

Al stopped his mental arithmetic. He was actually very good at it, a hangover from the days when he was working as an accountant in Baltimore. Jez was right again, they had got a healthy stash of the superbomb material. And no he hadn't forgotten Kingsley, exactly, it was just a long time since they set him loose on his clandestine assignment. 'That flaky asshole? I've written him off. Chrissake, it's been too long.'

'No, it hasn't. He's a courier, not a missile. He'll get there eventually.'

'Could be.'

'Will be, and then you've won. Once the Confederation's been broken, you don't have to worry about New California being hauled back here.'

'Could be,' he sighed. 'But we ain't going to get any more antimatter. Hell, Jez, if they send two task forces, we're up shit creek.'

'They won't. Believe me. It's a political impossibility. So we're back to my original question. You didn't have antimatter when you started out, and you still managed to take over this planet. Antimatter was a beautiful bonus, Al. And you used it perfectly. You've not only got the Confederation public terrified of you, but with those infiltration flights you've weakened them physically. Twenty-five planets seeded. That's *crippled* their economies and leadership. They can't challenge you on your home ground. No way. And that's what really counts.' She extended her legs, and rested her heels on one of the two remaining chairs. 'We're never going to see navy warships outside this window. Not now. You're secure, Al. You've made it clean. You've dug the moat to keep those bastards out, now concentrate on cementing what you've conquered. Don't let those moaning weaklings who claim to be your friends chip away at the Organization.'

'God damn, you're beautiful.' He splashed through the thin runnels of water to kiss her. She smiled up at him, and used a forefinger to tickle under his chin.

'The guys are going to go apeshit about losing the station.'

'They're going to be frightened, that's all,' she said. 'Just show them they don't have to be, that you're in charge of the situation. They need that reassurance. They need you, Al, no one else can hold things together.'

'You're right. I'll call the senior lieutenants in. Spin them some bullshit, and kick ass.'

Her hand curled round the back of his neck. 'It can wait an hour.'

*

Al buckled down on his disapproval when he arrived at the Chiefs of Staff office. No point in biting people's balls off before they'd even started the meeting. It was just – he couldn't help remembering what the plush office had looked like the first time they'd used it. Tidy and gleaming, with coffee served from a silver pot into elegant china. Now, it was suffering from the general tide of crap washing through Monterey. Without mechanoids, nothing was being cleaned, let alone polished. There were plates and crumpled sachets on the table, dating back three or four meetings; cups with mould growing in the bottom. No one could be bothered to take them back to the nearest canteen.

It wasn't good. Not at all. Jez was right. He had to consolidate what he'd got. Make things function smoothly again. Like it all had at the start.

Kiera was last to arrive. That was getting to be a habit. Al couldn't work out if she was doing it to annoy him, or make everyone take notice of her. She took her place halfway down the side of the table, between Patricia and Leroy. Al performed his own theatre by getting up again and refilling his coffee cup from the wheezing espresso machine.

'Hey, Leroy, where's Webster?' Al asked suddenly. 'He should be dishing this stuff out.'

The manager broke off his murmured conversation with Patricia and glanced round the office in surprise. 'Kid's probably skiving off.'

'Yeah? I ain't seen him about for a while. How come?' Now he thought about it, Al couldn't remember the last time the boy had been in attendance. It was goddam typical of the sloppy way things were being run these days. No hostage was more important than Webster Pryor; he was the only person who could make Kingsley Pryor go through with the assignment.

Leroy took out his pocket block and typed quickly, summoning up staff rotas. The results made him uneasy, which everyone was very aware of. 'He's down in the kitchens, I think. That was his last assignment, helping the chef. His supervisor hasn't reported back since.'

Al sat down and stirred his coffee. 'Silvano, where's the kid?'

The morose lieutenant's scowl deepened. 'I don't fucking know.'

'It's your job to fucking know. Je-zus, I put you in charge of keeping people in order, and you can't even look after a brat. You know what's riding on keeping Webster in line. He's more important than all the other hostages put together.'

'Sure, Al. I'll find him.'

'You'd better. Fuck me, this is goddam typical of how slack things are getting up here.' He took a sip of coffee, making sure his temper sank back. 'OK, are you guys all up to speed on what's happened with the antimatter station?' By the way everyone mumbled and avoided his eye he guessed they had. 'Well, don't all make out like it's the end of the world. It ain't. We just about achieved what we set out to do. Dwight, how many planets have we screwed now?'

The Fleet Commander flushed as everyone concentrated on him. 'Seventeen confirmed infiltrations, Al. We're waiting for another two flights to get back.'

'Nineteen planets.' Al grinned round the lieutenants. 'Plus Arnstadt. Not bad. Not bad at all. We've kicked so much shit into the navy's face they can't even see us now. And if they do try a raid ... What'll happen, Emmet? We still got what it takes to see them off?'

'No problem, Al. The SD platforms are all armed with antimatter, along with half the fleet. The only navy ships that'll visit New California for a rumble are the ones on a suicide mission.'

'Glad to hear it. You all hear that, too?' He searched round, trying to spot any major-league dissenters with his ethereal senses as they all swore they heard and approved. There was the obvious one – Kiera, with her cool contempt: the rest were just jittery, or, like

493

Silvano, sullen and resentful. But so far he was carrying it. 'OK, so we've done what we set out to when we walked into City Hall. We got us an entire planet, along with a haul of space factories. And the important thing is, we took out the nearest opposition. This planet is a fucking fortress now. That means we can ease up on watching our backs, and get on with running this shebang properly. Leroy, how's the food situation down on the surface?'

'Nobody's starving, Al. The farms aren't producing as much as they did before. But they are producing. I think we can get them back up to the old levels if the lieutenants on the ground apply some pressure. We need to motivate them.'

'OK. So food is something we can improve if we have the time. Mickey, your boys jiving you, or are they marching round like a bunch of Krauts whenever you give the word?'

Mickey Pileggi licked at the beads of sweat that had suddenly erupted on his upper lip. 'I got them under control, Al. Yeah. Sure thing.'

'Mickey, you're full of crap. This whole fucking joint is going down the pan. We've been humping away at the Confederation so bad, we ain't noticed the rain coming in.'

'That's what you wanted.'

Al stopped in full flow, hauling back on his anger. He'd just been getting nicely into his spiel. 'Kiera, stop being such a ballbuster. I did what I had to to protect us. Ain't nobody here gonna argue with that.'

'I'm not arguing, Al. I'm saying the same thing as you. We are where we are, because this is where you've brought us.'

'You want to be somewhere else right now?'

'No.'

'Then shut the fuck up. I'm telling you, all of you; now is when we start getting things working properly again. You gotta start keeping tabs on the soldiers under your command, else everyone's gonna finish up going AWOL like Webster. And that way, we wind up in deep shit. We gotta have things working smoothly around here again. If you don't start exerting some proper discipline then the whole Organization's gonna fall apart. And if it goes down, then we go down with it.'

'Al, the Organization is set up to keep the fleet working,' Kiera said.

'Hey, fucking lady Einstein, you just worked that out for yourself, or did one of the kids from the gym explain it when he was banging you?' Al chuckled loudly, encouraging the others to join in.

'I've always known it. I just wondered if you did.'

Al's humour faded out. 'What are you getting at?'

'The only reason we need the fleet is if New California remains in this universe.'

'Aw, shit, not this crap again. Don't you get it? If we leave, then the Confederation longhairs are going to be free to dream up some way of snatching us back. We have to stay here, it's the only way we can see what's coming.'

'And if you see something like that coming at you, Al, what are you going to do about it? A technology powerful enough to pull a planet back from the other side of the beyond! Launch a combat wasp at it? Believe me, if the Confederation ever gets to be that powerful, then we don't stand a chance. But I don't think they'll ever learn how to do anything like that. We can do it because we've got the Devil's own power charging us up. No chunk of machinery can challenge that. If we leave, then I say we're going to be a hell of a lot safer there than we are here.'

There was an itch in Al's palm, running across his skin exactly where he gripped the handle of his baseball bat. He held off from making it real. Her talk about the Devil being behind them made him uncomfortable. A Catholic by birth, he didn't like examining the implications of what he was now, nor why. 'We ain't pinning our future on what you *think* might be right, sister,' he growled. 'If we want a certainty, then we stay right here.'

'The Organization can be transported down to the planet,' Kiera said, as if Al hadn't even spoken. 'We can use the SD network to keep our power base secure until we assume control of the cities. After that, we use ground troops to enforce order. Al was right about that. There's been too much slippage allowed recently. We know we have to keep the farms and a lot of the industries going if we want any kind of decent life on the other side. It'll take a strong, positive government to achieve that. And that's us.'

'We can do all that crap, and still stay here,' Al said. His voice had become little more than a whisper. That worried those who had been with him the longest, though Kiera didn't seem to notice the barely concealed danger. 'When I want someone else to tell me how

495

to run my Organization, I'll let you know. Got that, baby doll? Or do I need to make it real plain for you?'

'I hear what you say, Al.' The tone was amused indolence.

'That's smart of you. Now I want the rest of you guys to start doing like I've said. We need a crackdown like God's foot is stomping through the clouds. I want things up and jumping around here. Put the word out to your soldiers, as of now you shape up or ship out. And out is where you don't want to be.'

*

Al told Emmet and Silvano to stay behind after the others trooped out. He flicked a switch to turn the wall clear, and waited impatiently as transparent waves skidded about in front of him. With his mind all het up, it was hard to cool down his energistic power. Eventually, the wall stabilized, giving him a view across the SD Tactical Operations Centre. Five people were sitting behind the long ranks of consoles, two of them playing cards.

'The bitch is good,' Al said. He was surprised more than anything.

'She used to be married to a politician,' Silvano said. 'Knows how to sound plausible.'

'Certainly convinced me scooting our asses out of here is a good idea,' Al muttered. He turned back to his two senior lieutenants. 'Emmet, is what she said right? Can we take the planet out of their reach? I mean, right away?'

Emmet wiped a hand across his forehead. 'Al, I can make the machines we've got work for you. Do a few repairs, make sure everything's plugged in where it oughta be. But, shit, questions like that . . . That's out of my league, Al, way out. You need a theoretical physicist, or a priest. But even if they can learn how to do that, it's not gonna be tomorrow. We'd be safe there a long time. And could be we'd learn how to keep ourselves there. Shit, I just don't know, Al.'

'Ha.' Al sat himself down, annoyed by how badly he'd come out of the clash. 'And we don't get to find out, neither. God damn that bitch. Now she's declared for the running away option, I've gotta make my stand to stay here. And you can be certain she'll start shouting her idea about.'

'Leaving this universe has a strong appeal to the possessed,'

Silvano said. 'It's intrinsic. Perhaps you should bow to the inevitable, boss.'

'You think I'm gonna knuckle under to that whore?'

'Not to her, no. But she's backing a winning idea.'

'I still need the hellhawks awhile,' Al said. 'Emmet, you done anything more about building another feeding trough for them?'

'Sorry, Al, haven't had time.'

'You've got it now.'

*

Banneth was making her preliminary preparations to Kilian when one of the senior acolytes pounded on the door of her sanctum. Kilian gurgled weakly as she eased the slim tube deeper inside him.

'I'll be back in a minute,' Banneth promised him cheerfully, and fastened a clamp around the incision to stop the bleeding. She stripped the thin isolation gloves from her hands as she walked over to the door.

'A body, High Magus,' the acolyte panted. 'There's a body in the temple.'

She frowned. 'Who?'

'Acolyte Tilkea, High Magus. He was butchered. We didn't authorize it. Tilkea is one of the better ones.'

'I see.' Banneth datavised a codelock at her sanctum door, and strode off towards the temple. 'How awful, a corpse we didn't authorize.'

'Yes, High Magus,' the acolyte agreed nervously. Like everyone in the headquarters, he never knew if she was joking or not.

Even by the standards of the sect, the killing was fairly extreme. The remains of acolyte Tilkea were suspended from strands of carbon wire above the altar, arms and legs extended wide. Large hooks punctured the skin above his shoulder blades, as well as his buttocks, wrists, and ankles, fastening him to the wires. His chest had been split open from throat to crotch, ribs levered apart to allow the internal organs to spill out. They'd splattered down on the altar, along with a small lake of blood. Banneth circled the corpse carefully, while a gaggle of acolytes stood at a respectful distance. It was ironic, she thought, that a death in the temple where they themselves had killed hundreds over the last few decades should invoke such trepidation. A sign of the times.

The blood was still warm. Banneth took a small medical block from her pocket, and pressed its sensor pad against Tilkea's glistening liver. 'This happened within the last half-hour,' she announced. 'Was he on duty in here?'

'Yes, High Magus.'

She datavised the headquarters network processor, and instructed it to review the security systems. Nobody had left the building within the last hour. 'I want every door guarded by a team of five acolytes. You can issue the hand weapons, chemical projectiles only.'

The senior acolytes hurried to obey. When she stood up, Banneth saw the writing on the wall behind the altar. Someone had used Tilkea's heart as a sponge, scrawling in blood: *Darkness has arrived.* Her gaze switched from that to the wires disappearing into the shadows cloaking the ceiling. 'Who fixed them up there?' she asked quietly. Not a difficult job, but hardly one that could be done unnoticed. The acolytes simply shrugged helplessly.

This is a very elaborate death, Banneth told Western Europe. It obviously took some time to prepare. And getting in and out of the building would be hard even for the possessed. My AI is running a constant glitch scan.

It wouldn't be difficult for Dexter, Western Europe replied. From what we've seen so far he can circumvent all your electronics. I'd suggest he's starting a war of nerves. If he's as fixated on you as we believe, then a quick death will hardly suffice.

I expect you're right.

Cheer up, it confirms that he's still in Edmonton. And if Tilkea was killed only half an hour ago, he can't have left yet. I'll have the vac-trains shut down immediately.

If Dexter can make himself invisible, he's probably still inside this temple right now. Banneth resisted the urge to stare round into the many dark recesses. I imagine he'll want to see my reaction.

You could make him happy. Scream, faint; that kind of thing.

I'll consider it for the future.

Perhaps you ought to trigger your gender cycle early, Western Europe suggested. Shift into a man.

I fail to see the relevance.

A male's aggression would probably be a more appropriate response to this situation. Dexter is a raging psychotic, after all.

Banneth dispatched a dry laugh down the affinity bond. That's one of my more treasured privileges, an intimate knowledge of both psychological profiles owned by the human race. I can exploit the relevant weaknesses to perfection. Men have less of a conscience, I'll grant you; but your claim that you're rougher and tougher is a rather sad ego-enhancing lie you tell yourselves.

Charmed, I'm sure. Well, if you don't want to do that, is there anything else you need?

I can't think of anything. This place is so heavily booby-trapped I'm more worried about one of these bumpkin acolytes setting off a charge than I am an invasion of possessed.

Very well.

Are you watching the other sects?

Yes. North America and I have them all covered. Eight of Edmonton's chapels have been taken over by possessed. It's only a matter of time before the remainder follow. Quinn has also started to sabotage Edmonton's infrastructure. The acolytes have been sent out several times to damage fusion generators and water-pumping stations. They actually got through in three or four instances.

I haven't noticed any reduction in services.

Because there haven't been any. Not yet. But the margins are being cut, which raises a considerable question mark over Dexter's ultimate goal. However, it's proved an interesting footprint for us. There have been similar acts in Paris and Bombay.

You think that's where he's been?

Yes. I'm investigating Paris myself, of course. The East Asian supervisor is giving the Bombay sect his personal attention.

Your observers here should keep watch for Courtney and Billy-Joe. Banneth concentrated on their images. They've been missing for a couple of days now. Dexter used to pimp Courtney for me when he was an acolyte. You couldn't classify her as a friend, but she'll be loyal to him. If he keeps anyone close, it'll be her.

Thank you. We'll keep an eye out.

*

The program's visualization took the form of a three-dimensional spider's web that filled the entire universe. Strands were all primary colours, crossing and recrossing against each other, a weave that

... away to an infinity where they blurred into null-grey ...nity. Louise's mind hung in the centre, looking in every ...tion at once.

What her neural nanonics were showing her was Earth's communication net. Or at least, part of London's informational structure. Then again, it might have been just the Ritz's internal house network. She wasn't entirely sure, only that this was what surrounded her room's net processor ... when she ran this particular symbology protocol, anyway. There were some interpretations which were like cybernetic coral, others that had cartoon roads, looping gas giant rings, even one that was an intertexture of glowing liquids. But this, she felt, was the most real.

Information taxis were flooding back towards her, silent sparkles of light riding the strands down to the centre, condensing around her like a new galaxy. A response to the latest questor she'd fired into the digital ether; the fiftieth variant on that one basic enquiry: find a connection between Quinn Dexter and Banneth, any category. She'd tried multiple combinations of the most preposterous phonetic spellings, removed time restrictions so that the questors could search centuries-old memories, allowed fictional works (every media type from books onwards) to be incorporated. If she could just get that first connection, discover a single positive reference, then the questors and news hounds and directory extractors and credit profilers and a hundred other search programs installed in her neural nanonics could be unleashed on Banneth like dogs after a hax.

The information taxis loaded their passenger files into the analysis program she was running in primary mode. 'Oh, hell,' she groaned. The neuroiconic display vanished, and she propped herself up on her elbows.

Genevieve was sitting at the room's desk, running an English geo-historical tutorial through her processor block. She gave her big sister a sympathetic look. 'Zeroed out again?'

'Yep.' Louise leaned over the side of the bed, and hunted round for her shoes. 'Not a single file entry, not that combines them.'

'You've just got to keep asking.' Genevieve indicated the pile of flek cases on the desk. 'Computers aren't smart, just fast. Garbage in, garbage out.'

'Is that so?' Louise wasn't going to quibble about Gen's new-found interest of boning up on educational texts. It was better than games. Trouble was, the knowledge was superficial.

Like mine.

'I don't know enough,' she confessed. 'Even with the program tutors to help me format the questor.' It wasn't just her inability to get a lead on Banneth that bothered her. There was still no response from Joshua. She'd sent half a dozen messages now without so much as an acknowledgement from Tranquillity. 'I need professional help.'

*

She was back. Andy Behoo sighed helplessly as soon as he saw her walk in. The magic was only slightly soiled by Genevieve trailing after her. This time he didn't even bother to say anything to the customer he was serving before he abandoned them. Louise was standing in the middle of the shop, looking round with that same slightly befuddled expression as the first time. She smiled lightly when she saw him approaching (not too fast, don't run – you'll look pathetic).

'Back for some more?' he asked. God, what a stupid thing to say. Why not just yell out: I don't have a life.

'I'd like to choose some programs, yes,' Louise said.

'Excellent.' His eyes tracked up and down in a fast sweep, feeding the image into a memory cell. Today she wore a lemon-yellow dress made from a sparkly fabric that was tight around her bottom, and a pair of antique wire-rimmed sunglasses. An odd combination, but very stylish. You just had to have considerable poise to carry off the effect. 'What can we get you?'

'I need a very powerful questor. You see, I'm trying to find someone, and I've got very little information about them. The NAS2600 questor can't locate them for me.'

Interest in what she was saying actually diverted Andy's eyes from her cleavage. 'Really? It's usually pretty good. Your friend must be very well hidden.' And pray it's her loathsome fiancé.

'Could be. Can you help?'

'What I'm here for.' Andy walked back to his counter, working out in his mind what he could do to use the situation. He plain didn't have the nerve to ask her outright if she'd like to come for a drink with him after work. Especially not with Genevieve at her side.

had to be some way he could get to see her again, outside
world.

was very conscious of Liscard, the general manager, tracking
rogress. Liscard had been on edge ever since a couple of Special
Branch cops had paid Jude's Eworld a visit. They'd taken the
manager back into her office, and spoken to her for over an hour.
Whatever they said, her suppressor programs couldn't get a grip on
her subsequent nerves. She'd certainly given Andy a hard time all
day, snarling at him for little or no reason.

Andy had a horrible feeling it might all be connected with Louise.
Specifically de-stinging her and Genevieve. If they had been Govcen-
tral bugs, then Jude's Eworld had probably broken the law removing
them. But there'd been no real reprimand. The sellrats had been
nibbling on curiosity and rumour ever since. Each of them bragged
about their own special shady customer who was the probable cause.

The shop's inventory flashed up in Andy's head, and he ran
through the specs for questors. 'I expect half of your trouble is that
the 2600 questor only reviews current file indexes,' he told Louise.
'What we need to do is get you one that'll review entire files and
disregard data status, that should help with obscure references.'
Andy ducked down below the counter top, and looked at the clutter
of fleks stacked up on the shelves below. 'Here we go.' He surfaced,
holding up a flek case. 'Killabyte. It's almost an AI in its own right.
A one-shot request that operates on fuzzy breeder intuition, which
means it can utilize whatever references it finds to build new
associations which you haven't loaded in, and search through them.
It won't taxi back until it's found the answer, no matter how long it
takes. Tenacious little bugger.'

'That's good. Thank you, Andy.'

'What I'd really like to give you is the Hyperpaedia, but we haven't
got any fleks of it in stock right now. If it's used in tandem with
Killabyte I'd guarantee you'll find your friend. They're the two
market leaders right now.'

'I'm sure Killabyte will be fine.'

'I'll put in an order for Hyperpaedia. The software collective won't
datavise it to us, they're worried about bootlegs.' He put his elbows
on the counter and leaned towards her in a confidential fashion.
'Course, the encryption has already been cracked. You can get a
pirate clone at any stall in Chelsea Market, but it'll probably have

transcription degradation. Best you have an original. It'll be here tomorrow morning. I can have it delivered straight to wherever you're staying.'

'I'm at the Ritz.' Louise fished round in her shoulder bag and produced the hotel's courtesy collection disk.

'Ah.' Andy held up the counter's delivery log block to accept the Ritz's code. 'Your fiancé hasn't arrived yet, then?' Genevieve had to bend over and hide her face in her hands to stop the giggles.

'No, not yet,' Louise answered levelly. 'But I'm expecting him any day now. He's already in the solar system. I was wondering if you could help me with something else?'

'Sure. Anything!'

Louise smiled demurely at his enthusiasm. I ought to be firmer with him. But somehow being firm with Andy Behoo would be like drowning kittens. 'It's just in case the questors can't find what I want. You said some private detectives use the store. Could you recommend one?'

'I can ask,' he said thoughtfully. 'Hang on a minute.'

Liscard gave him an alarmed look as he walked over to her. 'A private dick?' she mumbled when Andy asked which one he should recommend.

'Yeah,' Andy said. 'One that's good at finding people. Do you know if any of them are?'

'I think so,' Liscard stammered. She waited apprehensively. As soon as the Kavanagh girls had come back into the store, she'd established a sensevise link to the eddress which the Special Branch officers had given her. Her retinas and audio-discrimination program had been capturing the scene for whoever was at the other end of the link. She didn't have the nerve to load any of the tracer programs available to employees of Jude's Eworld. The software houses who produced them guaranteed they would be completely undetectable, but she wasn't about to take the risk. Not with the people who claimed they were from Special Branch. When she asked her fixer in the local police about them he'd abruptly told her never to contact him again, and cut the datavise.

'What do you want me to say?' she datavised to the anonymous receiver.

'There's someone I know who can help the girl,' came the answer. Liscard datavised the information directly into Andy's neural nanonics. He took his time walking back across the shop, a measured approach allowed him to savour her shape. The images he'd snatched before were fine as far as they went, but they amounted to little more than photonic dolls in his sensenviron. After conjuring them up he was left craving for more substantial replicants. Now, with his retinas switched to infrared, and feeding through discrimination program, he could trace her abdominal muscle pattern and ribcage through the fabric of her dress. A scan grid overlay revealed the precise three-dimensional measurements of those wonderful breasts. And her skin tone spectrum was already on file; that would be a simple continuation for the sculptor program, extending up from the legs, and down from her bare shoulders. That just left the taste of her as he ran his tongue along her belly and down between her thighs. The correct pitch as she cried out in gratitude, the praise she would moan to him, her greatest ever lover.

Andy hated himself for resorting to sensenviron sprites. It was the final humiliating proof that he was a complete loser. But she was so fantastic. Better to have loved and lost than never loved at all. Even if that love was purely digital.

'What's the matter with him?' Genevieve asked loudly. 'Why's he looking at you all funny?'

Andy's smile was a thin mask over his horror as her piping voice broke through his distracted thoughts. Cool sweat was beading across his flushed skin. His neural nanonics couldn't help dispel the blush, they were too busy fighting down his erection.

Louise gave him a vaguely suspicious look. 'Are you all right?'

'Fine,' Andy mumbled. He scurried back behind the counter, ignoring Genevieve's frown. 'I think the person you want is Ivanov Robson. He specializes in missing persons, both kinds.'

'Both kinds?'

'Yeah. Some people are genuinely missing: they drop out of life, or haven't updated their directory entries – like your friend. Then there's the kind who're deliberately trying to vanish: debtors, unfaithful partners, criminals. You know.'

'I see. Well, thank you, this Mr Robson sounds about right.'

Andy datavised the detective's address and eddress over. Louise smiled and gave him an uncertain wave as she walked out. Breath whistled out between Andy's crooked teeth. His hands were shaking again, forcing him to grip the edge of the counter. Idiot. Idiot. *Idiot!*

But she hadn't stormed out, or made an issue of his stupid erotic daydreaming. There was still a chance.

Yeah, about the same as me getting crowned King of Kulu.

He looked down to double-check. The counter's middle shelf held a stack of fifteen Hyperpaedia fleks, all with their wrapping intact. His one and only excuse to see her again.

*

The taxi pulled up at the end of Fernshaw Road, where it intersected with Edith Terrace. Louise and Geneviève stepped out, and the door slid shut behind them. The vehicle accelerated away silently down the road. It had deposited them in a quiet residential street, where the pavements were actually made from slabs of stone rather than a simple band of carbon-concrete. Silver birch and sycamore trees that must have been a couple of centuries old lined both sides of the road, their giant boughs merging together to provide a gentle emerald shield against the fierce sunlight. The houses were all ancient two- or three-storey affairs, painted white or cream. Bricks and slate roofs were betraying their age by sagging and bulging; centuries of subsidence and environmental decline had distorted every wall and support timber. Window frames were tilted at the oddest angles. There wasn't a straight line to be seen anywhere in the street. Each house had a tiny front garden, though they'd all been paved over; the massive trees absorbed so much light they prevented any shrubs or vines from growing underneath.

'This must be it,' Louise said dubiously. She faced a high wall with a single golden oak door in it, heavily tarnished with age. There was a brass panel with a grille on one side. It looked far too primitive to datavise at. She pressed the ivory button on top.

'Yes?' the grille squealed.

'I'm here to see Mr Robson,' she said. 'I called before. I'm Louise Kavanagh.'

The door buzzed loudly, and she pushed it open. There was a rectangular patio beyond, running along the front of the building, home to a set of wrought-iron furniture and a couple of dead conifer bushes in cracked pots. The front door, a duplicate of the one behind, was open. Louise peered cautiously into the small hallway. A blonde girl, barely older than her, was standing behind a reception desk whose surface was smothered with folders, flek cases, and china coffee mugs. She was staring into a small AV pillar that protruded from the top of a very expensive-looking stack of processor blocks. Pale turquoise light from the sparkling pillar was reflected in her narrow, brown eyes. Her frozen posture was one of shock.

Her only acknowledgement of the sisters' entry was to ask: 'Have you accessed it?' in a hoarse voice.

'What?' Genevieve asked.

The receptionist gestured at the pillar. 'The news.'

Both sisters stared straight into the pillar's haze of light. They were looking out across a broad park under a typical arcology dome. Right across the centre of their view, a big tapering tower of metal girders had collapsed to lie in a lengthy sprawl of contorted wreckage across the immaculate emerald grass. Several of the tall, cheerfully shaggy trees that surrounded it had been smashed and buried beneath the splinters of rusty metal. A vast crowd encircled the wreckage, with thousands more making their way along the paths to swell their numbers. They were people in profound mourning, as if the tower had been some precious relative. Louise could see they all had their heads bowed, most were weeping. Thin cries of grief wove together through the air.

'Bastards,' the receptionist said. 'Those utter bastards.'

'What is that thing?' Genevieve asked. The receptionist gave her a startled look.

'We're from Norfolk,' Louise explained.

'That's the Eiffel Tower,' the receptionist said. 'In Paris. And the Nightfall anarchists blew it up. They're a bunch of crazies who're going round wrecking things over there. It's their mission, they say, preparing the world for the fall of Night. But everyone knows they're just a front for the possessed. Bastards.'

'Was the tower really important?' Genevieve asked.

'The Eiffel Tower was over seven hundred years old. What do you think?'

The little girl looked into the projection. 'How horrid of them.'

'Yes. I think that's why there is a beyond. So that people who do things like that can suffer in it until the end of time.'

A glassed-in spiral stair took Louise up to the first floor. Ivanov Robson was waiting for the sisters on the landing. Travelling in the *Far Realm* had accustomed Louise to people who didn't share the bodyform template she'd grown up with. And of course, London had an astonishing variety of people. Even so, she nearly jumped when she first saw Robson. He was the biggest man she'd ever seen. Easily over seven foot tall, and a body that seemed bulky even for that height. Not that any of it was fat, she noticed. He was frighteningly powerful, with arms thicker than her legs. His skin was the deepest ebony, glossy from a health club's spar treatment. With thick gold-tinted auburn hair twirled into a tiny ponytail, and wearing a stylish yellow silk business suit, he looked amazingly dapper.

'Miss Kavanagh, welcome.' From the confident humour in his smooth voice, it was obvious he knew the effect he had on people.

Floorboards creaked under his feet as he showed them into his office. The bookcases reminded Louise of her father's study, although there were very few leather-bound volumes here. Ivanov Robson eased himself into a wide chair behind a smoked-glass desk. The surface was empty apart from a slimline processor block and a peculiar chrome-topped glass tube, eighteen inches high, that was full of clear liquid and illuminated from underneath. Orange blobs glided slowly up and down inside it, oscillating as they went.

'Are they xenoc fish?' Genevieve asked. It was the first time she'd spoken. The huge man had even managed to quash her usual bravado. She'd kept well behind Louise the whole time.

'Nothing as spectacular,' Ivanov said. 'It's an antique, a genuine twentieth-century lava lamp. Cost me a fortune, but I love it. Now, what can I do for you?' he tented his fingers, and looked directly at Louise.

'I have to find somebody,' she said. 'Um, if you don't want to take the case when I've told you who, I'll understand. I think she's called Banneth.' Louise launched into a recital of her journey since leaving Cricklade, not quite as heavily edited as usual.

'I'm impressed,' Ivanov said softly when she'd finished. 'You've come face to face with the possessed, and survived. That's quite a feat. If you ever need money, I know a few people in the news media.'

'I don't want money, Mr Robson. I just want to find Banneth. None of the questors seem to be able to do that for me.'

'I'm almost embarrassed to take your money, but I will, of course.' He grinned broadly, revealing teeth that had been plated entirely in gold. 'My retainer will be two thousand fuseodollars, payable in advance. If I locate Banneth, that will be another five thousand. Plus any expenses. I will provide receipts where possible.'

'Very well.' Louise held out her Jovian Bank credit disk.

'A couple of questions first,' Ivanov said after the money had been transferred. He tilted his chair back, and closed his eyes in thought. 'The only thing you know for certain about Banneth is that she hurt Quinn Dexter. Correct?'

'Yes. He said so.'

'And Banneth definitely lives on Earth? Interesting. Whatever happened between the two of them sounds very ugly, which implies they were involved in some kind of criminal activity. I think that should provide my investigation with an adequate starting point.'

'Oh.' Louise didn't quite look at him. It was so obvious, laid out like that. She should have sent a questor into criminal archives.

'I am a professional, Louise,' he said kindly. 'You do know the possessed have reached Earth, don't you?'

'Yes. I accessed the news from New York. The Mayor said they'd been eliminated, though.'

'He would. But Govcentral still hasn't opened the vac-train lines to New York. That should tell you something. And now we've had the Eiffel Tower blown up for no reason other than to demoralize and anger people. That probably means they're in Paris as well. A feat like that is beyond the ability of some stimbrained street gang. What I'm trying to say, Louise, in my dear bumbling way, is that if Quinn Dexter is here, then he'll be heading for Banneth as well. Now do you really want to bump into him again?'

'No!' Genevieve squeaked.

'Then bear in mind that's where your current path is taking you.'

'All I need is Banneth's eddress,' Louise said. 'Nothing else.'

'Then I will do my best to ensure you receive it. I'll be in touch.'

Ivanov waited until the sisters were circling down the spiral stair before asking: Do you want me to give her Banneth's eddress?

I'm afraid it's a bit pointless right now, Western Europe answered. Edmonton has been sealed up, with Quinn inside. I can't get her in to meet him; she'll just have to sit this out on the substitutes' bench for a while.

13

The prospect of interstellar flight had always been real to certain sections of the human race for a long time before Sputnik One thundered into orbit. A notion which began with visionaries like Tsiolkovskii, Goddard, and somewhat more whimsical science fiction writers of that age was quickly taken up and promoted by obsessive space activists when the first microgee factories came on-line, proving that orbital manufacturing was a profitable venture. With the development of the O'Neill Halo and the Jupiter mining operation in the twenty-first century the concept finally began to seem practical. Asteroids were already being hollowed out and made habitable. Now it was only an engineering and finance problem to propel them out of Earth orbit and across the gulf to Proxima Centauri. There were no theoretical show stoppers; fusion or antimatter engines could be built to accelerate the giant rocks up to speeds of anything between five and twenty per cent of lightspeed, depending on which physicist you asked. Generations of crew would live, tend their machinery, and die within the rock as they crawled across the emptiness, with the anticipation that their descendants would inherit a fresh world.

Sadly, human nature being what it is, century-duration flights were just too long, the ideal of colonization too abstract to motivate the governments and large institutions of the time into building these proposed space arks. The real clincher, inevitably, was cost. There could never be any return on the investment. So it seemed as though the fresh start idealists would just have to go on dreaming.

One such thwarted dreamer was Julian Wan, who, more resourceful than his colleagues, persuaded the board of the New Kong corporation to research faster than light travel. His pitch was that it would be a small, cheap project testing the more dubious equations of Quantum Unification Theory. Essentially a few wild theoretical physicists with plenty of computer time; but if it could be made to work the commercial opportunities would be phenomenal. Noble concern for human destiny and the search for pure knowledge never got a look in.

New Kong successfully tested the ZTT drive in 2115, and the arkship concept was quickly and quietly discarded. Beautifully detailed plans and proposals drawn up by a multitude of starflight societies and associations were downloaded into university library memories to join the ranks of other never-made-it technologies like the nuclear-powered bomber, the English Channel Bridge, geostationary solar power stations, and continent birthing (the so-called Raising Atlantis project, where fusion bombs were proposed to modify tectonic activity). Then the Tyrathca world of Hesperi-LN was discovered in 2395, along with the news that it was actually a colony founded by an arkship. The old human plans were briefly revisited by history of engineering students, interested to see how they stood up to comparison with a proven arkship. A period of academic interest which faded away inside of a decade.

Joshua, who fancied himself as something of a spaceflight buff, was fascinated by the dull blip of light which *Lady Mac*'s sensors were focused on. It was in a wildly elliptical orbit around Hesperi-LN: a twelve thousand kilometre perigee, and four hundred thousand kilometre apogee. Fortunately for their mission, it was just under three hundred thousand kilometres away from the Tyrathca planet, and climbing.

They'd emerged two million kilometres out from Hesperi-LN, a distance which put them safely beyond the planet's known SD sensor coverage. The Tyrathca world was not a cradle for the kind of space activity found above industrialized human worlds. There were a few low-orbit docking stations, industrial module clusters, communication and sensor satellite networks, and twenty-five SD platforms supplied and operated by the Confederation Navy. Not that there was a lot of worry about pirate activity, the Tyrathca simply didn't manufacture the kind of goods which could be sold on any human market, let alone the underground one. The Confederation was far more concerned by the prospect of blackmail by a rogue starship captain armed with ground-assault weapons. Although they didn't have consumer products, the Tyrathca did mine gold, platinum, and diamonds among other precious commodities for their indigenous industries. And the colony had been established in AD 1300; rumours of vast stockpiles accumulated over millennia persisted on every human world. Any bar or dinner party would have someone who knew somebody else who had been told of a first-hand witness who'd walked through the endless underground caverns filled with their glittering dragon hoards.

So the navy maintained a small cost-ineffective outpost to guard against the possibility of any inter-species *incident*. It had been abandoned, along with all the other human-maintained systems, when the Tyrathca broke off contact. According to the briefing Monica and Samuel had given to the *Lady Mac*'s crew, the Tyrathca would find it difficult to keep the SD systems functional for very long.

'But we have to expect them to try,' Monica said. 'Their Ambassador was pretty damn insistent that we don't intrude on them again.'

Joshua and Syrinx assumed the SD network was on-line and fully functional, and planned their tactics accordingly. The goal was to land an explorer team on Tanjuntic-RI, which would attempt to locate a reference to the Sleeping God in the arkship's ancient electronics. Getting it inside unnoticed was the big problem.

Both craft were in full stealth mode when they emerged. Jumping into the system, Joshua had aligned *Lady Mac* so that her vector would carry her in a rough trajectory from the emergence coordinate towards the arkship. As long as he didn't have to use the fusion (or antimatter) drive, the starship would probably remain undetected. At this stage, they were back-up; there to rush in and provide covering fire in case things got noisy and *Oenone* had to rescue their team. They were using passive sensors only, with just the chemical verniers firing occasionally to hold them stable; every non-essential system was in stand-by mode, reducing the power consumption and with it their thermal emission. Internal heat stores were soaking up the fusion generator output, although they could only last for a couple of days before the thermo-dump panels would have to be extended to dissipate the heat. Even that wasn't too much of a problem, the radiation could be directed away from the SD network sensors. They'd have to be extremely unlucky to be discovered by anything that guarded Hesperi-LN.

'Picking up some radar pulses from the SD network,' Beaulieu reported. 'But it's very weak. They're not scanning for us. Our hull coating can absorb this level easily.'

'Good,' Joshua said. 'Liol, what about spacecraft activity?'

'Infra-red's showing twenty-three ships using their drives above the planet. The majority are travelling between low orbit and the SD platforms. Four seem to be heading up for high polar orbits. I'd say they're complementing the platforms. But none of them are moving very fast, half a gee maximum. They are big ships, though.'

'That's how the Tyrathca like them,' Ashly said. 'Plenty of room to move round in the life-support sections. It's like being inside a bloody cathedral.'

'Offensive potential?'

'If they're armed with human-made combat wasps, considerable,' Liol said. 'With that drive signature I'm assuming they're Tyrathca interplanetary ships; they have got a dozen asteroid settlements to provide the planetary industries with several kinds of bulk microgee compounds. Which means their payload is considerably larger than ours. They're like highly manoeuvrable weapons platforms.'

'Wonderful.' Joshua datavised the new bitek processor array they'd installed during the last refit. '*Oenone*, what's your situation?'

'I remain on schedule, Joshua. We should be rendezvousing with Tanjuntic-RI in another forty-two minutes. The exploration team is suiting up now.'

Unlike the *Lady Macbeth*, *Oenone* had been able to accelerate and manoeuvre after emerging above the planet. By reducing its distortion field to a minimum, the voidhawk could accelerate at half a gee towards the arkship. Given the distance involved, the network satellites were unable to pick up such a small ripple in space-time. The disadvantage was, with such a reduced field the voidhawk couldn't perceive a fraction of the local environment it usually did. If for some unaccountable reason the Tyrathca had surrounded

Tanjuntic-RI with proximity mines, they wouldn't know until they were very close indeed.

Syrinx always hated being dependent on just the sensor blisters and passive electronic arrays. The voidhawks' ability to pervade a huge spherical volume of space around the hull was intrinsic to their flight.

We managed like this in our navy days, *Oenone* said, unperturbed.

Syrinx grinned in the half-light of the bridge. The crew toroid's internal power consumption was minimal as well. **You mean back when we were young and foolish?**

This is not a foolish venture, the voidhawk chided. **Wing-Tsit Chong considers it of the utmost importance.**

Me too. But this part just brings back memories. Of Thetis, though she didn't mention him. Lately she'd started to wonder if her brother had managed to elude the beyond as that ever-damned Laton had promised. Mild feelings of guilt had kept her away from his strange stunted existence within the Romulus multiplicity before they left. Really, what was the point in preserving him when his soul was free?

What is our best landing point, do you think, *Oenone* asked.

As always, the voidhawk knew when she needed distracting. **I'm not sure. Show me what we can see.** She accessed the all too scant files on Tanjuntic-RI stored in the on-board processors, and attempted to match them up with the image the voidhawk was seeing.

Tanjuntic-RI had been completely abandoned less than fifty years after it arrived in the Hesperi-LN star system. An unduly harsh treatment by human standards, but it had fulfilled every duty its long-dead builders had required of it, and the Tyrathca were not a sentimental species. Fifteen thousand years old, it had travelled one thousand six hundred light-years to ensure the Tyrathca race didn't die along with their exploding home star. Five separate successful colonies had been established along its route. Each time the arkship had stopped inside a star system to create a new colony, the Tyrathca had virtually rebuilt it, refuelled it, then carried on with their crusade of racial survival. Even so, there are limits to the most sturdy machinery. After Hesperi-LN was founded, Tanjuntic-RI was left to circle ceaselessly above the planet.

Borrowing *Oenone*'s sensor blisters, Syrinx could see the details becoming clear as they glided in for a rendezvous. Tanjuntic-RI was a dark cylindrical rock six kilometres long, two and a half in diameter. Its surface was a gentle mottle of flattened craters, resembling a wind-sculpted ice field. Remnants of vast machines sketched out a random topology of tarnished metal lines along the floors of the meandering valleys. These appurtenances had succumbed to millennia of particle impacts and vacuum ablation. What had once been a surface bristling with elaborate towers and radiator panels the size of lakes was left with little more than their stubby mounting fixtures as a reminder of past grandeur. The forward end was the most heavily speckled, due mainly to the extensive remnants of a coppery hexagonal grid.

With Tanjuntic-RI capable of travelling at over fifteen per cent of lightspeed, a collision with a single pebble could result in catastrophic damage. So in flight the arkship was protected by a plasma buffer, a cloud of electrically charged gas that broke up and absorbed any mass smaller than a boulder. It rode ahead of the arkship, a luminous mushroom-shape held in place by a magnetic field generated by the superconductor grid.

Right in the centre of the grid, aligned along the rotation axis, was the arkship's spaceport. Although the concept was the same as the counter-rotating spaceports on Edenist habitats, the Tyrathca had fashioned an elaborate conical structure made up from tiers of discs. Its peak disappeared below the surface of the rock, as if it were a kind of giant arrow tip which had impaled itself in some forgotten era. The larger discs at the top end had broken off centuries ago, probably when the magnetic bearing seized up. Those that remained were vacuum ablating, their edges fraying like worn cloth, while their flat surfaces slowly dissolved, reducing their overall thickness. With the last maintenance crew departing thirteen centuries previously, the vast sheets of metal were down to a few centimetres' thickness, and perforated by thousands of micrometeorite holes.

Oenone was also relaying the image of the arkship to the little exploration team suiting up in the crew toroid's airlock prep chamber. Given the clandestine nature of their mission, Monica Foulkes and Samuel were leading the team. There were only two technical staff coming with them; Renato Vella, who was Kempster Getchell's chief assistant, and Oski Katsura, head of the Laymil Project's Electronics Division. Their job would be to reactivate Tanjuntic-RI's electronic library and extract whatever files concerning the Sleeping God that they could locate. Tactical support was supplied by four serjeants, loaded with Ione's personality.

Kempster Getchell and Parker Higgens were also in the prep chamber; helping with the suits when they were asked, but mainly rehearsing mission goals with Renato and Oski. The formless black silicon of the SII suits had enveloped each of the team, and now they were busy clipping their rigid exoskeleton suits on top. They were using standard issue Confederation Navy Marine armour, generator-reinforced monobonded carbon with power augmentation. As sleek and featureless as the SII suits, they were designed for both asteroid and ship assault roles, capable of supporting and keeping the wearer active in high-gee environments, and with built-in manoeuvring packs.

The team started to run integration diagnostics. Arm joints bent and twisted, sensor inputs flicked through the spectrum. Monica, Samuel, and the serjeants ran their weapons interface programs, and stowed the various items of lethal hardware on their belts and racks once the suit processor confirmed the connection. Oski and Renato started picking up their blocks and equipment kits; there were too many to hang on their belts, so they were both using small chest packs.

Kempster held Renato's pack steady as it adhered to the armour suit. 'I can't feel the weight,' the young astronomer datavised. 'I just have to balance right. And I've even got a program for that.'

'The wonders of science,' Kempster muttered. 'Mind you, I ought to be flattered. Commando raids to acquire astronomical data. I suppose that's a sign of how important my profession has become.'

'The Sleeping God isn't an astronomical event,' Parker chided irritably. 'We're sure of that now.'

Kempster smiled at the blank neutral-grey back of his assistant. Now he was ready, Renato datavised *Oenone*'s processor array for an update on their approach. Tanjuntic-RI's dilapidated spaceport was a hundred and fifty kilometres away, and the voidhawk's sensor blisters had it in perfect focus. The large discs were separated by a single central column that appeared to be made up from hundreds of braided pipes. They were spaced far enough apart, a hundred metres at least, to admit ships between them. Tyrathca craft had used them as hangar floors, anchoring themselves to docking pins and plugging into the utility sockets. Now, the discs were essentially flat sheets of decaying metal; their thin lattice of ancillary systems had evaporated away along with the rim.

'We're not going to land on those, are we?' Renato Vella asked. 'They don't look very reliable.'

Samuel used his suit's bitek processor to datavise a reply. '*Oenone* will take us in under the bottom disc. We'll go EVA and try and find a way in along the spaceport's support column.'

'It shouldn't be a problem,' Monica datavised. 'The archaeology team from the O'Neil Halo got in easily.'

'A hundred and thirty years ago,' Kempster said. 'The decay rate Tanjuntic-RI is suffering from could well make things difficult for you. The original route may be blocked.'

'This isn't an archaeology project, Doc,' Monica datavised. 'We'll just cut our way in if we have to. Decay should help us there. The structure won't put up much resistance.'

Kempster caught Parker's eye, the two of them registering their disapproval in unison. Cut it open, indeed!

'At least we have a basic layout file of the internal chambers,' Oski datavised. 'If we really did have to explore, I doubt we'd achieve anything.'

'Yeah,' Monica agreed. 'How come the Tyrathca allowed that university team in?'

'Wrong question,' Parker said. 'Why shouldn't they? The Tyrathca couldn't understand our interest in the arkship at all. You know they seal up and abandon a house once the breeders have died? Well, Tanjuntic-RI is a similar case. Once something of theirs has ended its natural life, it becomes . . . *invalid*, is about the nearest definition we have. They just don't use it, or visit it again. And it's not due to the kind of respect we have for graves; they don't consider their relics or burial houses to be sacred.'

'Weird species,' Monica datavised.

'That's what they think of us, too,' Parker said. 'The various Lords of Ruin have asked them on several occasions if they would join the Laymil research project, another viewpoint would always be valuable. It was the same answer each time. They're simply not interested in examining obsolete artefacts.'

Oenone folded its distortion field to almost nothing as it crept across the last kilometre to Tanjuntic-RI. The arkship was rotating around its long axis once every four minutes, with only a small wobble picked up over the centuries. Which said a lot for how well they'd managed the internal mass distribution, Syrinx thought. As a result of the minute instability, the spaceport was pursuing a small loop which the voidhawk could match easily.

They slid in under the bottom disc, which was only seventy metres in diameter. The short length of the support column which emerged from the disc's centre to burrow into the rock was twenty-five metres wide.

That lower disc must have been used to dock the Tyrathca analogue of our MSVs, Syrinx suggested. With the big interplanetary ships on the top deck.

That would be logical, *Oenone* agreed. I wonder what they looked like?

Very similar to those the Tyrathca use today, Ruben said. They don't innovate much. Once a system is finalized they never change it.

That doesn't make a lot of sense, Serina said. How can you know when something is as good as possible unless you keep analysing and tinkering with the design? A bicycle is a good, efficient method of getting from one place to another, but the car came along because we weren't satisfied with it.

I hadn't really thought about it, Ruben admitted. Now you mention it, thirteen hundred years is a long time to stick with one design, an awful lot more if you add their voyage time to that. We're still improving our fusion drives, and we've only had them six hundred years.

And they're a lot better than Tyrathca fusion drives, Oxley said. We've been selling them improvements ever since we made contact.

You're applying human psychology to them, Ruben said. It's a mistake. They don't have our intuition or imagination. If it works, they really don't try to fix it.

They must have some imagination, Cacus protested. You can hardly design an arkship without it.

Ask Parker Higgens, Ruben said. A slight tinge of defensiveness was leaking into his affinity voice. Maybe he can explain it. I guess being slow and methodical gets you there in the end.

Syrinx examined the twisted braid of pipes and girders that made up the spaceport's support column. Following her silent urging, *Oenone* expanded its distortion field enough to pervade the dilapidated structure. A picture of entwined translucent tubes filled her mind. The number of black-crack flaws in the metal and composite was alarming, as was the thinness of individual tubes. That really is very fragile, she declared. **Samuel, please be careful when you egress. It won't take much to snap the spaceport clean off.**

Thanks for the warning.

Oenone rotated gently, turning its crew toroid airlock towards the lead-grey shaft. Standing in the open hatch, Samuel's suit sensors showed him the stars slip past until he was facing the wrinkled mesh of metal. Even though it was basically just a frayed mechanical structure, it had a quality that told him it wasn't human. Neatness, he decided, it lacked neatness, the kind of confident elegance that was the signature of human astroengineering. Where humans would use failsofts and multiple redundancy, the Tyrathca built tough simple devices in tandem. If one was taken out of service for repair or maintenance they trusted the second to remain functional. And it was obviously a philosophy which worked. Tanjuntic-RI's existence and triumph was evidence of that. It was just ... reality at one degree from human sensibilities.

The voidhawk's movement halted. Shadows plagued the hull, turning the marbled polyp a dingy walnut. Gravity in the airlock faded away as the distortion field flowed away from it.

This is as close as we can get, Syrinx said. **The archaeology team went in just above the bearing ring.**

The spaceport support column appeared to be holding steady just past the lip of the hull. Stars waved about behind it. Samuel triggered the cold-gas jets in his armour, and drifted out from the airlock. Gaps in the column were easy enough to find. The original close weave of pipes and structural girders had been loosened when the bearings seized up, opening a multitude of chinks. Though it was impossible to guess which one had been used by the archaeology team all those years ago. He selected one ten metres above the huge bearing ring set in the rock.

Nitrogen puffed out from tiny nozzles around his slimline manoeuvring backpack, edging him closer to the gap. It was lined with a buckled pipe on one side, and a tattered conduit casing on the other. He reached out with his left gauntlet, and made a tentative grab for one of the flaky cables inside the conduit. Dust squirted out around his fingers, and tactile receptors in his palm told him the cable had compressed slightly in his grip. But it held. His main worry had been that everything they touched along the column would disintegrate like so much brittle porcelain.

'OK, there's a degree of integrity left in the material,' he datavised back to the rest of the team. 'You can come over. I'm going in.'

Helmet and wrist lights came on, and he shone the beams into the black cavity ahead. When the column bearings seized up, the torque stress exerted by the spaceport's inertia had splintered hundreds of structural girders, ripping apart the multitude of pipes and cables they carried. If it had happened abruptly, the whole cone of discs would have sheered away. But it must have been a long drawn-out process, friction-braking the rotation to zero over several weeks – even then the large upper discs had broken free.

The result was to fill the inside of the column with a forbidding tangle of wreckage. Samuel activated his inertial-guidance block. Bright green directional graphics flicked up over the monochrome sensor image, and he eased himself forward. According to his suit sensors, the spaces between the interlocking struts contained a thin molecular haze from the slowly ablating metal.

The chinks were becoming smaller, with fragments scraping against his armour as he hauled himself in the direction the graphics indicated. He pulled a ten-centimetre fission knife from his belt. The blade's yellow light shone brightly, shimmering off the strands of ash-grey metal. It cut through without the slightest resistance.

I feel like some kind of Victorian soldier aristocrat hacking through a jungle, he confided to *Oenone*'s crew.

Scraps of crumbling metal were whirling round him, bouncing and twirling off the corners and angles of the shambolic maze. The second armour-suited figure had reached the gap: Renato Vella, who was quickly wriggling along after him. One of the serjeants was next, followed by Monica, another serjeant, then Oski Katsura. Syrinx and the crew used the sensor blisters to watch them vanish inside one after the other.

Looking good, she said, sharing a quiet confidence with her crew.

Parker Higgens and Kempster Getchell walked into the bridge, and took the chairs Syrinx indicated. 'They're making progress,' Edwin told the two elderly science advisers. 'At this rate, Samuel will have reached the main airlock chamber in another ten minutes. They could be at their target level in a couple of hours.'

'I hope so,' Tyla said. 'The quicker we're away from here, the better. This place gives me the creeps. Do you suppose the Tyrathca souls are watching us?'

'An interesting point,' Parker said. 'We've not had any reports of our returning souls encountering a xenoc soul in the beyond.'

'So where do they go?' Oxley asked.

'We'll put that on the list of questions for the Sleeping God,' Kempster said jovially. 'I'm sure that's quite trivial compared to—' He broke off as all the Edenists froze, closing their eyes in unison. 'What?'

'A starship,' Syrinx hissed. '*Oenone* can sense its distortion field. Which means the Tyrathca detectors will pick it up, too. Oh . . . bloody hell.'

I see you, the *Stryla* gloated.

*

Etchells hadn't realized that there was a voidhawk accompanying the rogue Adamist starship. Not until he swallowed in above Hesperi-LN, and started scanning round for the ship he'd pursued from the antimatter station. There was plenty of activity above the xenoc planet, big sedate ships powering their way into high inclination orbits, complementing the protective sphere thrown up by the SD platforms. The twin moons were sending out constant gravitational perturbations as they orbited round each other, half a million kilometres above Hesperi-LN itself. A network of sensor satellites. An unusually thick band of dust slithering above the upper Van Allen belt. He had to move around cislunar space in small swallows so that his distortion field could complete a clean sweep above the planet.

The Adamist starship was easy to locate, a tight curve in the uniformity of space-time. He focused on it, prying and probing at its composition by creating a multitude of tiny ripples within his distortion field, seeing how they reacted to the encounter, the defraction pattern created as they washed across the hull and internal machinery. One thing was clear, it wasn't a navy ship. The layout was all wrong for that. And navy ships didn't have an antimatter drive. Its main fusion generators were shut down, leaving just a couple of ancillary tokamaks to power the life-support capsules; and the biggest give-away of all: its thermo-dump panels were retracted. It was in stealth mode.

A Confederation Navy sanctioned starship on a clandestine mission in the Tyrathca system. It would have to be a very important mission to risk an inter-species clash at this delicate time. Etchells knew damn well it had to be connected to the issue of possession somehow. Nothing else would warrant approval. When he extrapolated its trajectory, he saw it was going to fly past a moonlet. He ran through a batch of his stolen almanac memories, discovering that the moonlet was actually an arkship, abandoned over a thousand years ago after a flight from an exploding star. His knowledge of Tyrathca history was almost zero, although the fundamentals were there. But he certainly couldn't imagine any connection with their ancient ship and the possession crisis.

A quick swallow manoeuvre put him a thousand kilometres from Tanjuntic-RI, hours ahead of the Adamist starship, and he began to examine it. That was when he found the stealthed voidhawk lurking so close to the surface it was almost touching.

His flush of achievement was tempered by continuing worry. What the hell were they doing here? It had to be important. Critical, even. Which meant it was a threat to him. Among all his possible options, one thing was very clear. They had to be prevented from achieving their goal, whatever it was.

This is Captain Syrinx of the voidhawk *Oenone*. Who am I addressing?

The name's Etchells, and I'm one of Capone's hellhawks.

Leave this star system immediately. We will not hesitate to use force to make you comply.

Tough bitch, huh? Well, give me a reason to leave, bitch. In fact, I'd like you to tell me what you two are doing here.

Our task is not your concern. Leave, now.

Wrong. I think it has a lot to do with me. Etchells launched a combat wasp at the arkship, then immediately swallowed away. The wormhole terminus opened a hundred kilometres from the Adamist starship. He loaded a hunter program into another combat wasp, and launched it as he emerged into real space.

*

As soon as Syrinx warned him a hellhawk had arrived, Joshua initiated combat status. He knew damn well their cover either had been, or was about to be, blown. *Lady Mac*'s main fusion generators powered up, the full suite of combat sensors rose out of their recesses, combat-wasp launch-tubes opened. Alkad Mzu and Peter Adul hurriedly secured themselves on the large, zero-tau capable acceleration couches in the lounge. Up in the bridge, webbing tightened around the crew.

'Wormhole terminus opening,' Beaulieu warned. 'One hundred kilometres.'

Joshua triggered the *Lady Mac*'s triple fusion drives. That close wasn't an accident, the hellhawk had their exact coordinate. 'Liol, maser the bastard.'

'On it, Josh.' A targeting program went primary in his neural nanonics. Three of the starship's eight maser cannons aligned themselves on the terminus, and fired. The beams caught the hellhawk as it slid out, and tracked it perfectly. At a hundred kilometres, the inverse square law meant they couldn't kill the hellhawk immediately. Joshua didn't care about that. He just wanted to force it away. *Lady Mac* could take a lot more radiation punishment than any bitek construct if the hellhawk wanted an energy-beam duel.

It didn't. A single combat wasp shot out of its launch cradle, curving round to intercept *Lady Mac*. The hellhawk's harpy shape wavered and imploded into a narrow polyp ovoid pimpled by steel-grey mechanical modules. It rolled frantically, trying to dodge the beams. After three seconds of futile manoeuvring, its distortion field applied a near-infinite force against space, and an interstice blossomed open. Joshua fired four combat wasps to intercept the incoming drone, and changed course again. His crew groaned in dismay as they accelerated at ten gees. Space behind *Lady Mac*'s triad of dazzling fusion drive plumes ruptured into a gale of plasma as the combat wasps ejected their submunitions. A curtain of nuclear explosions erected an impenetrable barrier while particle beams and X-ray lasers lashed out.

'I think we're clear,' Beaulieu datavised. 'Our combat wasps knocked out their combat wasp.'

Joshua reviewed the sensor data, which was calming as the expanding plasma wreaths from the explosions turned to purple then began to decay through the spectrum. Stars began to shine through the squall of enraged ions again. He reduced their acceleration to four gees, and switched course once more.

'We just ditched our softly, softly policy,' Sarha grunted.

'Yeah,' Dahybi said. 'Whoever possesses that hellhawk knows their tactics. One combat wasp was never going to hurt us. But it made us expose ourselves to the SD network.'

'Not just us,' Beaulieu said.

The sensors were showing them another combat-wasp clash developing several hundred kilometres away from Tanjuntic-RI. 'Syrinx, where the hell did it go?' Joshua datavised. 'Could you get a fix?'

'It swallowed over to the moons,' Syrinx said.

Joshua already had the star system's almanac file open. He reviewed the data on the twin moons. Airless rocks, three thousand kilometres in diameter. If they hadn't been orbiting Hesperi-LN they'd be categorized as exceptionally large asteroids. 'There's nothing there for it,' he protested. 'The Tyrathca don't even bother mining them, the ore's so poor.'

'I know. We think it's just a good location for a tactical withdrawal at this point in time. And it'll be at least partially shielded from the SD sensors. The Tyrathca probably don't know it's here.'

'Great. Did you manage to get the team in?'

'Yes, they're in. But *Oenone* is now holding station a hundred kilometres out from Tanjuntic-RI in case the hellhawk tries to swallow in and launch some more combat wasps. The arkship is very fragile, Joshua, it couldn't withstand a nuclear assault. That leaves us totally exposed. The SD sensors have already locked on to us.'

The flight computer reported that three radars were already focused on *Lady Mac*'s hull. 'Shit.' Joshua shut down the fusion drives, and let the starship coast along. Their trajectory wasn't taking them anywhere near Tanjuntic-RI any more. 'They're watching us, too,' he told Syrinx. 'Now what?'

'It's their move. We wait.'

The message came eight minutes later, beamed at both *Lady Macbeth* and *Oenone* from one of the low orbit docking stations. 'Human craft, you are not permitted here. You have fired weapons above our planet. This is an act of war. Leave now. Do not return.'

'Brief, but not open to much misinterpretation,' Ashly said as the message began to repeat. 'I'm surprised they didn't put in an *or else.*'

'They just have,' Beaulieu said. 'Three ships on their way to intercept us. One point two gee acceleration.'

'For them, that's really racing along,' Liol said. 'The Tyrathca hate high gees.'

'Another three fusion drive ignitions,' Beaulieu said. 'One heading for us. Two aligning on Tanjuntic-RI.'

'At least we're out of range from the platforms' combat wasps,' Liol said. 'That could have been nasty.'

'What's your assessment?' Joshua asked Syrinx. He started to run the Tyrathca ship trajectories through some tactical analysis programs. While he was doing it, another two ships ignited their fusion drives and started to fly up on a course for the arkship.

'I think the situation's still manageable,' she replied. 'Providing it doesn't escalate any further.'

'Yeah. I'm working on that aspect. We've got to make sure the team can continue. You're going to have to stop that hellhawk from coming back to Tanjuntic-RI.'

'We can swallow out to the moons and keep it very busy. But that leaves the team without protection. One of those Tyrathca ships is bound to investigate the arkship. Even with their phlegmatism, they'll want to know what we're doing here.'

'Leave it to me. I'll divert them. You get over to the moons.'

'Acknowledged.' Joshua lifted his head, and smiled round at his crew.

'Oh, God,' Sarha moaned with unfeigned consternation. 'I hate it when you smile like that!'

'Cheer up. We're going to invade Hesperi-LN.'

*

The rotating airlock chamber had survived the spaceport bearing seizure almost intact. Samuel cut through the wall and floated into the big empty space. His helmet lights automatically defocused, throwing their radiance all around him. It was a cylindrical chamber, fifteen metres in diameter and fifty long, stark even by Tyrathca standards. The walls were lined with a petrified sponge material resembling pumice stone, with thousands of regularly spaced indentations. Each one was just big enough to accept a Tyrathca breeder's hoof.

There were three airlock hatches at each end, large circular affairs with chunky electromechanical locking rims. Precisely halfway down the chamber was a bulging hoop, the rotating seal to provide the Tyrathca with a pressurized transfer from the arkship to the spaceport. Now, its working fluid had evacuated, internal components were reduced to granular sculptures of their former selves; a technological cave etching.

Renato Vella squirmed into the chamber with jerky motions, knocking large chips of the wall material from the edge of the hole Samuel had cut. 'Oh, great, late era gloomy,' he pronounced. 'They didn't exactly go in for frills, did they?'

'I doubt a translator could even find an equivalent word,' Samuel datavised back.

The first serjeant was emerging from the hole, fracturing even more wall material as it came. There was an almost identical hole a third of the way round the wall, slightly larger. A matching opening had been made next to one of the airlocks at the ship end of the chamber. Samuel's gauntlets gripped the indentations in the desiccated sponge fabric, and he moved cautiously hand over hand towards it.

'This must be where the archaeology team cut their way in,' he datavised. 'Wait. Yes.' The suit sensors showed him a small plastic box fixed close to the jagged rim by a blob of epoxy, narrow lines of red human lettering covered a third of its dark blue surface. 'Some kind of communication block. There are several cables running through the hole.' He ordered his suit communicator to transmit a standard interrogation signal. 'No response. I guess the power's drained by now.'

'Shame,' Renato datavised. 'It would have been convenient to have some kind of communication net in there.'

'We could probably power it up again,' Oski replied. 'It's only a century old, the processors will be fully functional.'

'Forget it,' Monica told them. 'The bitek processors can keep us in touch with each other, and *Oenone*. We're not going to be inside long enough to justify getting cosy.'

'We hope,' Samuel said. With the whole team now in the airlock chamber, his helmet lights refocused into wide beams. He grasped the edge of the old hole, and pulled himself through.

The archaeology team had cut their way into a broad corridor that served one of the large jammed-up airlocks. It was a simple square-section shaft sliced straight through the rock, with the spongy hoof-grab fabric along the floor, and pipes fastened to both walls. He barely did more than look round when Syrinx announced the presence of a hellhawk. She gave them a running commentary as the other team members emerged into the corridor.

'The *Oenone* is swallowing over to the moons to tag the hellhawk,' Syrinx told them. '*Lady Macbeth* will distract the Tyrathca.'

'For how long?' Monica asked.

'As long as possible,' Joshua replied. 'Worst case, we fail completely. Their first ship should reach Tanjuntic-RI in fifty-three minutes – mark.'

'That's no good. We won't even have reached the second level by then.'

'I'll swap with you any time.'

'Sorry, Joshua; that wasn't a complaint. How did that hellhawk know we were here?'

'Probably followed us from the antimatter station,' Syrinx said. 'It wouldn't be too difficult.'

'Thank you, Captains,' Samuel datavised. 'We'll try to be as quick as we can.'

'If things get too hot, let us know,' Joshua replied.

'We'd better get on,' Samuel told the team. 'Every minute of lead time could be indispensable later.' He ordered his backpack to fire the cold-gas jets, and slid easily along the corridor to the first big airlock. Monica triggered her own backpack, and glided after him.

The corridor flared out around the airlock, which was a typical example of Tyrathca engineering: a square of titanium four metres in diameter with rounded corners, edged with locking seals, thick, sturdy, and reliable. And vacuum-welded into place. The archaeology team had solved the egress problem by cutting out a metre-wide circle of metal from the Tyrathca slab, and installing their own airlock. It was a simple mechanical hatch with frictionless hinges and seals. A chrome purple handle was half recessed in the middle, with standard operating instructions stencilled beside it.

Samuel secured himself, and pulled the handle. His armour's power augmentation barely kicked in to help. The handle slid up, and rotated ninety degrees.

'One up to human engineering,' Renato datavised as Samuel pushed the hatch inwards.

'Not really,' Oski datavised. 'It's our materials science that makes the difference. The hatch was designed for long-term vacuum exposure. Their airlock was built with regular maintenance services in mind.'

There was another corridor identical to the first on the far side of the airlock. One of the serjeants shut the small hatch after them. This corridor also ended in a big titanium airlock, with an identical human hatch inserted. Samuel pulled the lever up. Before he could attempt to push the hatch open, his suit sensors advised him of an environment change. 'It's venting,' he datavised. 'Very small nitrogen release, minute contamination. Pressure must be equalizing.'

'Open it,' Monica datavised. 'There can't be any real atmosphere in there. We're wasting time.'

Samuel gripped one of the titanium spars with one gauntlet, and pushed with the other. The suit's power augmentation whined on the threshold of audibility. A whirl of silvery dust scooted around Samuel's armour as the hatch flipped back.

'Just how many of these corridors are there?' Renato asked as he air-swam through, only to be faced with yet another blank rock shaft. His inertial guidance display showed him it was inclined slightly, heading away from the rotation axis, though there was still no appreciable gravity.

'This is the last one, according to our file,' Samuel said.

The airlock at the far end had a human hatch in it; there was also a small plaque.

HIGH YORK UNIVERSITY ARCHAEOLOGY EXPEDITION OF 2487
We respectfully offer our tribute to the generations of Tyrathca
who ventured forth in this vessel.
In this place we have stumbled through the remnants of greatness,
eternally thankful for the glimpse of nobility they reveal.
Though the Tyrathca have no god, they are clearly not devoid
of miracles.

Renato floated over to the silvered plaque after Monica moved aside. 'Well, that's a nice way to start,' he datavised. 'The arcology expedition never found any reference to a Tyrathca god.'

'We knew that already,' Oski datavised. 'Besides, I doubt they were looking. The only memory files they accessed were in the systems management architecture. We've got to go a lot deeper than that to find anything useful.'

Samuel shifted his sensors from the plaque to the hatch. 'I don't think I've ever felt more like a grave robber.'

'There have been worse assignments,' Monica datavised. 'For you as well as me, I suspect.'

Samuel didn't reply. He grasped the hatch's handle, and pulled up. This time there was a significant gas vent.

'This is it,' Oski datavised. 'We're in. Terracompatible nitrogen–oxygen mix, several trace gases. Three per cent standard atmospheric pressure. No water vapour content. Guess it's too cold. Registering thirty degrees below zero.'

'Checks with the file,' Monica confirmed. Samuel pushed the hatch open, and glided through.

The archaeology expedition had spent six weeks exploring the interior of Tanjuntic-RI. Given the timescale, it could hardly be thorough. But the main sections were all mapped, allowing the nature of the arkship's engines and environmental maintenance mechanisms to be inspected. Tanjuntic-RI was arranged in three principal levels. Along the rotation axis were three long cylindrical chambers six hundred metres wide. Each contained a shallow lake which served as the principal biological recycling system. The water was a combination fish-tank/algal air regenerator, powered by a thermal lighting array strung along the axis. Surrounding that was an extensive warren of hemispherical caverns linked by kilometre after kilometre of broad corridors. This level was devoted to engineering and flight mainten-ance; the caverns were filled with machinery, everything from fusion generators to chemical filtration plants, cybernetic factories to mineral storage silos. The rear quarter of the caverns were all used to house support systems and fuel for the fusion engines.

Encircling the second level were the eight principal life-support rings. Tunnelled out of the rock and lined with metal, like giant binding bands, they had a rectangular cross-section, five hundred metres wide, a hundred metres high. Their floor was a single looped strip of Tyrathca tower houses threaded by narrow roads of greenery, a computer design program's notion of urban pleasantries.

'We need the third level, ring five,' Oski datavised as soon as they were through the last airlock. 'That's where the archaeologists found the control offices.' A three-dimensional map of the interior expanded into her mind. Her guidance block extended a glowing green line through the tunnels, linking her present location to ring five.

The last airlock had brought the team into a standard-sized corridor that circled the forward end of the arkship. Over a hundred other corridors branched off from it. Gravity was barely noticeable, taking several minutes to pull objects towards the floor. Monica used her gas jets to take her over to a clump of human crates stacked against the wall. The thin, freezing atmosphere had turned the white plastic a faint cream. She read some of their labels. 'Nothing we can use,' she datavised. 'It's their camp equipment. Programmable silicon shelters, life-support units, microfusion generators, that kind of thing.'

'What about lighting?' a serjeant asked.

'Good question.' Monica shifted position, scanning more labels. 'Yes, here we go. Monochrome projectors, three hundred metre illumination radius. I don't think they're self-powered, though.'

'Leave it,' Samuel datavised. 'We don't have the time.' He fired his manoeuvring pack, and started drifting along the corridor. The wall opposite the airlocks had archways leading away into the interior, their depth defeating his suit sensors and lights. 'There should be a lift here somewhere. Ah.' The fifth archway had a palm-sized plastic disc stuck on the wall beside it, a small lifelong beacon light in the centre. Samuel couldn't resist flicking it with a gauntlet finger as he went past. There was no spark of light from the beacon, its tritium-decay power source had been exhausted decades ago.

His gas jets squirted strongly, steering him through the archway. Fifteen metres down the corridor was a lift door. A single panel of metal ten metres long, and three high. The team didn't even pause by it. There was a smaller door on either side, each heading a ramp that spiralled, DNA-fashion, around the entire length of the lift shaft. One of them was open; it had a dead light beacon just inside.

'This should take us nearly a kilometre straight down,' Samuel datavised.

'At least it'll be a smooth ride once the gravity kicks in,' Renato datavised. 'Thank God the Tyrathca don't use steps. Can you image the size and spacing?'

Monica halted in midair beside the doorway, and focused her suit beams through the gap. The downward slope was barely noticeable, though the curve was pronounced. She took a tube dispenser from her belt, and thumbed out the first disc. Jupiter had supplied the little bitek sensors, completely transparent discs a centimetre wide. Their affinity range was only a few kilometres – enough for this mission. She pressed it against on the door rim. It stuck instantly.

When she requested an affinity bond with it from her suit's bitek processor, the disc revealed a fish-eye view of the corridor, with the suits floating before the ramp doorway.

'Pity we don't have a swarm of bitek insects covering the interior,' she datavised. Samuel didn't rise to the gibe. 'But this'll give us plenty of warning. There's a motion trigger if anything starts moving around behind us.'

'Onward, then,' Samuel datavised. His gas jets flared, pushing him along the ramp.

Everyone's bitek processor received Joshua's troubled hail. 'I'm afraid you're going to have company,' he announced.

*

Lady Mac was accelerating at six gees, a quarter of a million kilometres above Hesperi-LN and heading in a shallow curve around the planet's north pole. Two five-strong formations of Tyrathca ships were heading out to intercept, rising from their hundred thousand kilometre orbits at one and a half gees. He wasn't worried about them, nor the three ships that were on course for the twin moons to investigate the antics of the two bitek starships. Another group of four ships were flying straight for Tanjuntic-RI, seventy-five thousand kilometres from *Lady Mac*.

'Definite interception course,' Beaulieu confirmed. 'Looks like they want to know what was going on there.'

'Wonderful,' Joshua grunted. 'The only way to stop them is if they think we're hostile.'

'I think they know that already,' Sarha said with as much irony as five gees allowed.

As soon as they'd accelerated along their present course, Joshua had launched three combat wasps. There was no real target designation, just the planet; and they were programmed to detonate ten thousand kilometres above the atmosphere if they managed to get that far. But the Tyrathca didn't know that. All they'd seen was three nuclear missiles charging in towards their planet at twenty-seven gees. An unprovoked attack from a human starship that was continuing to manoeuvre in a hostile manner.

Joshua changed course again, flying along a vector which would take him below the ships heading for Tanjuntic-RI. Logically, a position he could bombard the planet from. Another two combat wasps flew out of their tubes, searing fusion drives thrusting them towards the four ships.

It was a good tactical move, which almost paid off. Three of the Tyrathca ships changed course to defend themselves against the combat wasps, and pursue *Lady Mac*. The fourth remained on course for the arkship.

'Thirteen ships heading right at us,' Beaulieu confirmed. 'Twelve SD platforms have also acquired lock-on. No combat-wasp launch yet.'

Joshua reviewed the tactical situation display again, purple and orange vector lines flipping round inside his skull. *Lady Mac* was now heading in almost the opposite direction to the last Tyrathca ship. There was nothing left he could do to distract it. The only option left was an attack, which wasn't an option at all. First he would have to reverse his current vector, which would take up a vast amount of time and delta-V, then he would have to fight his way past the three other ships with their potentially large stock of combat wasps. And even if he achieved that, he'd have to kill the ship to stop it rendezvousing.

It was a bad deal. The Tyrathca crewing the ship were innocent – just trying to defend themselves and their world against aggressive xenocs. Although, if you looked at it in an abstract way, they could well be all that stood between the exploration team and salvation from the possessed. Can you really allow a dozen Tyrathca to bring about the end of an entire race because of what was essentially a communication breakdown on a multitude of levels?

Joshua used the bitek array to call the exploration team and warn them of the approaching ship. 'We estimate it'll dock in another forty minutes,' he said. 'Just how long do you need?'

'If everything goes without a hitch, a couple of hours,' Oski said. 'But I would think a day would be more realistic.'

'A day is out of the question,' Joshua said. 'If I get seriously noisy out here I might be able to buy you an hour or so.'

'That's not necessary, Joshua,' a serjeant said. 'This is a very big ship. If they do come on board, they'll have to find us.'

'Not too difficult with infra-red sensors.'

'That's assuming a straightforward pursuit scenario. Now we know the Tyrathca are coming, we can make that pursuit extremely difficult for them. And there is also the Horatius option to consider. We four are expendable, after all.'

'Our weapons are superior, as well,' Monica said. 'Now we haven't got to worry about the hardware glitching on us, we can deploy some real firepower.'

'What about getting out afterwards?' Dahybi asked.

'Advance planning for a situation this fluid is a waste of time,' Samuel said. 'Let's wait until we have the relevant data before we consider how to achieve extraction.'

'OK,' Joshua said reluctantly. 'Your call. But we're here if you need us.' He returned to the tactical situation. Although they were a potential threat to Hesperi-LN, *Lady Mac* herself wasn't in any real danger from the planet's defences. They were too far away from the Tyrathca ships and SD platforms. At this separation distance, any combat wasp would take a minimum of fifteen minutes to reach them. The starship could jump out of trouble long before that.

'Right, let's keep these bastards busy,' Joshua said. He instructed the flight computer to fire another combat wasp at the planet.

*

Halfway down the giant spiral ramp, and the easiest way to descend was to sit and slide. Black frost had coated the floor, sending broad tendrils scurrying up the wall like frigid creepers. Along with the others Monica was bumping along on her bum as if she was on an après-ski glissade, gradually picking up speed, and ignoring the total lack of dignity. Clouds of filthy ice motes were spraying up from where the suit was making its grinding contact with the ramp. Every now and then she'd hit an uneven patch and glide through the air for a metre. Though the length of each arc was shortening as the gravity grew.

'Getting near the bottom,' Samuel datavised.

He was two people down the line from Monica, nearly obscured by the black particle haze. Suit beams were jouncing about chaotically, throwing discordant shadows across the walls.

Monica put her gauntlets down to try and brake her speed. They just skipped and skidded about. 'Just how do we slow down?' she asked.

'Manoeuvring pack.' Samuel triggered the jets at full throttle, feeling the gentle thrust slow him. The serjeant directly behind bumped into his back. 'Everybody at once, please.'

The ramp shaft was suddenly full of whirling pearly-white fog as ice granules and nitrogen blended together, boosting the air pressure. Suit lights fluoresced it to a uniform opacity.

Monica shifted to micro-radar as her speed slowed drastically. This time when she put her hands down she pressed hard enough to activate the augmentation. It allowed her to dig her fingertips into the sheet of ice, producing a loud wince-inducing screech as they gouged out ten straight furrows. She halted on a relatively flat section. Radar showed her the end of the ramp fifteen metres ahead, and the other armour suits skating elegantly to a halt around her. The white fog vanished as quickly as it'd emerged, sucked away back up the ramp, and out through the archway ahead.

They picked themselves up and scanned round. The ramp had come out at an intersection of eight corridors. Beacons had been stuck on each archway. The ice along the floor of every corridor was slightly rumpled, like stone paving slabs worn by centuries of feet. Nothing else showed the archaeology expedition had once passed this way.

'This is where we should split up,' one of the serjeants datavised. 'Two of us will lay heat trails, while you head for ring five.'

Monica accessed the archaeology expedition's map file, and integrated it with her inertial-guidance block. Orange graphics overlaid her sensor vision, indicating the corridor they should take. She took another sensor disc from the tube, and stuck it on the wall. 'OK. You two take care, they'll be here in another twenty minutes. Oski, Renato, let's go.' The four humans and two remaining serjeants started off down the corridor, bouncing along in low glides in the one-third gravity field.

Ione's quad mind started to melt away into four more individual, independent identities as the serjeants separated from each other. One of her chose a corridor which the map file showed would lead towards a chemical plant of some kind. She drew a laser pistol and datavised it to a very low power setting, with an intermittent discharge varying over three seconds. As she walked forwards in long loping steps she began sweeping it in a short arc, keeping the muzzle pointed at the ground. Speckle points of warmth blossomed around her feet – never enough to thaw the ice, just to make an imprint. To an infrared sensor it would appear as if several people had walked along beside her.

The darkness which contracted around the bubble of light from her suit lights was absolute, isolating her to an unnerving degree. A fact only slightly alleviated by affinity contact with her other three selves, and Samuel.

My third experience of life outside Tranquillity, and it's just rock tunnels not much different from Ayacucho. But a lot more oppressive, and that's without the possessed after me.

The others in the team were feeling the same low harmonic of unease. Monica was leading now, locomotion auto-balance programs keeping her movements smooth and steady in the low gravity. Despite the depressing surroundings, their easy progress was confidence-enhancing. She'd had a lot of misgivings about the whole mission, and this part most of all. In her mind during the flight here, Tanjuntic-RI had taken on the appearance of a large chunk of debris, just like the fragments that made up the Ruin Ring. Reality was considerably better. Nothing was broken inside the arkship. Merely neglected and cold. She could even imagine revitalizing the old wanderer. If the fusion generators could be started up again, and power fed through the distribution net, it would be a simple matter for light and heat to return.

'How come they abandoned this?' she asked. 'Why not rendezvous with an asteroid and use it as a ready-made base for their microgee industry?'

'Because of the upkeep,' Oski datavised back. 'The whole thing is interdependent, you can't just keep a life-support ring going and dump the rest. And it's big. Keeping it functioning would take too much effort for the level of return. They were much better off building smaller-scale asteroid habitation caverns from scratch.'

'Shame. At the very least the Tyrathca could have made a fortune selling it as a human tourist destination.'

'That'll be that famous phlegmatism of theirs. They just don't care about it.'

After five minutes they came to the first second-level cavern, a hemisphere two hundred metres high, the walls ribbed by bands of tubes. There was a single huge machine in the centre, supported by ten three metre thick pipes that rose out of the ground to act as its legs. Another ten pipes emerged from the top of the machine to vanish into the chamber's apex. The team stood just inside the entrance, playing their suit beams over the metal beast. Its sides were fluted with long glass columns, tarnished on the inside with heat-blackened chrome. Valves, coils, relays, motors, intake grids, high-voltage transformers, and pumps protruded from the rest of the edifice like metallic warts.

'What in Christ's name is that?' Renato asked.

'Access your file,' Oski told him. 'It's some kind of biological reactor. They bred a lot of organic compounds inside it.'

Renato walked over to one of the big pipes and took a look directly underneath the reactor's formidable bulk. The casing had cracked as the arkship lost its heat, allowing ragged strings of some blue-green compound to ooze out all over the base. They'd clotted in hanging webs before freezing solid. Smears and stains of other liquids were splattered across the floor.

'There's something wrong with all of this,' Renato datavised.

'What do you mean?' Samuel asked.

'Just look at this thing.' The young astronomer slapped his hand against the pipe. Even in the rarefied atmosphere, the suit audio sensors could pick up a faint clang. 'It's, like . . . immortal. I can't imagine anything else occupying this chamber since the day they left their star. I know they'll have rebuilt it a hundred times during the voyage. And I know they go for the brute-strength engineering solutions. But I don't understand how nothing can have changed in fifteen thousand years. Nothing, for Christ's sake. How can you draw a line across your technology and say we will never develop anything that goes beyond this?'

'You'll be able to ask them soon,' Monica datavised. 'Their ship will reach us in another ten minutes. Look, Renato, I know this is all fascinating, but we really don't have the time. OK?'

'Sure, I'm sorry. I just hate unsolved puzzles.'

'That's what makes you a good scientist. And I'm glad you're here to help us. Now, this is the corridor we want.' Monica left another sensor disc on one of the stolid pipes, and started walking again. Renato took a last glance at the ancient reactor, and followed her. The two serjeants brought up the rear.

*

'The Tyrathca ship is definitely docking,' Beaulieu said. 'They've matched velocities with Tanjuntic-RI.'

'Bugger,' Joshua grunted. They were enjoying a slight lull in the three-dimensional chess game that was the high-orbit diversion. *Lady Mac* was accelerating at one gee, sliding over Hesperi-LN's pole at a hundred and seventy-five thousand kilometres' altitude. Eighteen combat wasps were arrowing in towards her from every direction, a classic englobing manoeuvre. The closest one would reach them in another four minutes. At least the hellhawk wasn't a current factor. Syrinx confirmed they were still chasing the *Stryla* round the two moons.

'Liol, break the bad news to the team, will you?' Joshua concentrated on the starship's systems schematic, ordering the flight computer to configure the hull for a jump. Somewhere near the back of his mind, almost in the subconscious, was a smiling astonishment that he could now be so confident about taking part in a space battle. Contrast his, and the crew's, calm responses and performance today to the frantic shouting and adrenalin-powered high-gee desperation above Lalonde, and it was as though they used to belong in an alternative universe. The major difference, of course, was that he'd initiated this, he was calling the shots.

'Dahybi?'

'Nodes charged and on-line. Ready to jump, Captain.'

'Great. Let's see how accurate we can be.' He cut the fusion drives, and initiated the jump.

The watching Tyrathca saw the dangerous invader vanish from the middle of their combat wasp swarm. SD sensors picked up its emergence point simultaneously. Fifty thousand kilometres from where it had jumped. Its fusion drive came on again, powering it back down towards the planet, presenting fresh danger to the population. The pursuing craft all changed course to resume their chase.

*

A crackling smog of hot ions splashed across the front of Tanjuntic-RI as the Tyrathca ship finished its approach manoeuvre. Electrical discharges flashed along the remnants of the superconductor grid, burning off the fragile surface molecules in scintillating spectral fountains. The pilot hadn't bothered to rendezvous at a distance and nudge in towards the spaceport cone using secondary drives. Their flight vector was projected to bring them to a halt less than a kilometre from the arkship, completely disregarding the damage the fusion drives would inflict on the ancient vessel.

The ship was a typical Tyrathca interplanetary craft (there was only one model), a simple cylinder a hundred and fifty metres wide, three hundred long. Unlike human designs, which were built round a load-carrying gantry to which modules and capsules were attached as required, this had everything encased inside an aluminium hull. A basic, ugly workhorse of a ship, discoloured by years of exposure to the thermal and ultraviolet emissions of the Hesperi-LN's star. Four big rectangular hatches were spaced equidistantly round its front end, while five stumpy fusion rocket nozzles protruded from the rear.

When it finished its deceleration burn it was floating parallel to Tanjuntic-RI's spaceport, two kilometres out. Small chemical rockets flared around its edges, brilliant sulphur-yellow flames pushing the ship in towards the rotation axis. It started to turn at the same time, aligning its base towards the spaceport. The chemical rockets around its front end throttled up to maximum, and two fusion rockets ignited briefly. Their plasma plumes stabbed out, twin incandescent spears transfixing the centre of the spaceport. The burn didn't last for more than a couple of seconds, nor was it particularly powerful. But the damage caused was immense. Metal and composite detonated into vapour, roaring out from the impact point.

It was too much for the enfeebled spaceport structure to withstand. The entire cone of stacked discs snapped off close to the base, tumbling away. Individual discs tore loose, spinning off in every direction, spewing fragments as they went. One disc actually collided with Tanjuntic-RI, crumpling as if it were made from paper before it started to rebound. All that was left of the spaceport's support column was a shattered ten metre stub sticking out from the rock. It was rapidly eclipsed as the massive Tyrathca ship positioned itself directly overhead. Two hatches hinged open, and several dozen pale ovoid shapes were ejected. At first they drifted as aimlessly as thistledown in a zephyr, then puffs of gas erupted from small spouts around their crests, and they started to fly in towards the broken end of the support column.

*

Hesperi-LN's twin moons were not a hospitable location for spacecraft. Their clashing gravity fields had drawn in a great deal of cosmic debris since their formation, and continued to do so. Dust, sand, and smaller motes were eventually liberated by the solar wind, light-pressure and high-energy elementary particles blowing them back out towards the stars. But the larger chunks remained. Pebbles, boulders, entire asteroids; once they'd fallen into a looping orbit, they were slowly hauled in over the millennia as the ever-changing gravity perturbed their new orbit. Ultimately, they wound up at the central Lagrange point, poised equidistantly between the moons. It was a cluttered zone over a hundred kilometres across, visible from the surface of Hesperi-LN as a fuzzy grey patch. In composition, it mimicked a galaxy, with the largest asteroids clumped together at the centre, surrounded by a whirl of smaller boulders and stony nuggets.

A place, then, where the use of combat wasps and energy beams was essentially impossible. You could stay within its fringes and observe your enemy waiting outside with impunity. Providing you could ward off the clouds of dark, high-velocity gravel swirling endlessly around the periphery of the Lagrange cluster.

Oenone's attempts to pursue the hellhawk inside the cluster had come to nothing. After twenty minutes of dangerous slaloming and weaving, during which it gained barely a hundred metres on the contemptuous hellhawk, Syrinx had decided enough was enough. They were draining the energy cells at an alarming rate to maintain the distortion field, essential to deflect the hail of stone from the hull. And they would need that power later, no matter what the outcome at Tanjuntic-RI. She told *Oenone* to halt and match the orbital vector of the surrounding particles.

Once Etchells realized he was no longer being actively pursued, he also eased back, and simply held his position. They were no more than fifteen kilometres apart. Though the only way they knew that was by sensing each other with their distortion fields, visual or radar observation was impossible.

This is not a valid status quo, Syrinx told the hellhawk. **There are three**

Tyrathca ships on their way to us. You cannot stay inside the cluster for ever. Leave this system.

Not a chance, Etchells said. You've got to stay here with me, now. That means I've won. You can't achieve whatever the fuck you came here to do. And your Adamist pals are in deep shit. They're neutered, too.

With reservations, I will accept that observation, she told him, careful not to let any emotional context slip into the affinity contact. He obviously wasn't aware they'd landed the team in Tanjuntic-RI. All they had to do was keep him here until Oski and Renato had accessed the files.

String him along, she told the crew. I want to monitor the spacecraft situation. We may have to move in a hurry.

Of course, Cacus said.

Ruben, get our new fusion generators on-line. I'd like *Oenone*'s energy cells recharged as fast as possible. When we leave here, I want to be able to leave this hellhawk far behind.

Understood. Ruben ordered the processor array to begin the generator power-up sequence.

*

The links between the second and third levels on Tanjuntic-RI were mainly cargo lifts. Again, each was wrapped by the ubiquitous spiralling ramps. The exploration team had to engage their boot spikes as they made their way down one which led to ring five. Icy floors combined with the strengthening gravity provided a treacherous environment.

There was a large airlock chamber at the bottom, with doors more suited to bank vaults than spaceships. But this had been the Tyrathca's first line of defence against a breach in the upper levels, and their design philosophy had come into its own here. As tribute to that efficiency, Tanjuntic-RI's caverns and rings still retained a tiny atmosphere after thirteen centuries of disuse.

A cache of human machinery was spread out before the door at the end of the ramp: a couple of microfusion generators, mobile cherry-picker platforms, industrial thermal-inducer plates, hydraulic rams, and electromechanical actuators, all hooked together with loosely bundled cables and flexible hoses. The archaeology expedition had used them to reactivate the massive airlock. It was a quarter open, allowing them access to ring five. Four small jeeps were parked just inside, standard airless-planet mobility vehicles, with large low-pressure tyres and a composite latticework chassis. Ridiculously dainty in comparison to the engineering on display around them.

Samuel went over and inspected them, flicking switches on the dashboard. 'I'm getting a response from the control processor,' he datavised. 'There's some power left in the standby circuits, but that's about all. The main energy cells are dead.'

'Irrelevant,' Monica datavised. She ordered her suit lamps to emit a high-wattage pulse, and readied the sensors. Her neural nanonics memory froze the image when the lights flared. Buffer programs isolated the image for her to examine.

Not even the suit's lights could penetrate the gloom right across the ring. As a result, the curvature effect was completely lost. She was standing in a metal cave, walls, floor, and ceiling made up from millions of aluminium alloy panels, heat sealed to the naked rock underneath and welded together. Plants had been grown up the walls while the arkship was occupied, vigorous creepers clawing their way along metal trellises. Their leaves were black and wizened now, dead from lack of water and light long before the heat seeped away into space. But the cold had arrived before they'd fallen in their final autumn, sprinkling them with frost then freezing them into place against the dull metal tiling.

The ring's ceiling had an analogue in human warehouse roofs; criss-crossed with thick pipes and sturdy gantry crane rails, it gave the vast chamber an overtly industrial feel. Its illumination had been provided by thousands of large circular discs of smoked glass, which peered out of the gaps.

'A winter wonderland palace,' Monica datavised. 'Even if it was built by the Devil's own elves.'

'How could they live in this, for Christ's sake?' Renato asked. 'It's just a machine. There's no attempt to make it pleasing or hospitable. You couldn't stay inside all of your life, it would drive you insane.'

'Us,' Oski datavised. 'Not them. They don't have our psychological profile.'

'Nor our artistic sensibilities, by the look of things,' Samuel said. 'I expect they would find one of our habitats equally disenchanting.'

'The Tyrathca have arrived,' one of the serjeants datavised.

Everyone saw it through the sensor disc Monica had left up in level one. A flash of light from the airlock which led up to the spaceport support column. Large jagged sections of the square titanium hatch flew into the corridor, rebounding from the walls amid cascades of ice chips to twirl away in both directions. The Tyrathca emerged, and began moving in a slow canter towards the entrance to the spiral ramp. They were in spacesuits, which made it hard to tell breeders from soldiers. Although the SII had tried many times to sell them programmable silicon suits modified to their physiology, they'd resolutely stuck to their own original design.

The bodies of Tyrathca spacesuits were made from a tough flexible plastic, a silvery blue in colour, like metallic silk. They formed overalls that were loose and baggy enough for the big creatures to slip into easily, with concertina-like tubes for legs and arms. After that, instead of inflating them with oxygen, they were pumped full with a thick gel, expelling all the air. Given how many limbs (and therefore joints) a Tyrathca body had, such a concept neatly did away with the problem of providing multiple pressurized joints on every suit. In order to breathe, they wore simple tight-fitting masks inside the suits. Oxygen tanks, a regulator mechanism, and a heat exchanger were worn in a pack along their backs, with two black radiator fins running along their spine. Additional equipment was carried on a harness around their necks.

'Looks like subtlety is another trait we don't share,' Monica datavised. 'They must have blown out every airlock along that first corridor to get inside. The sensor disc is registering a lot of gas motion in that corridor. They just don't care that Tanjuntic-RI is going to vent its remaining atmosphere.'

'If they don't, we shouldn't,' Renato datavised. 'It won't affect our mission.'

'They're all armed,' Samuel datavised. 'Even the breeders.'

The Tyrathca were each carrying a pair of long matt-black rifles, with coiled leads plugged into power packs on their harnesses. Monica put an armaments library file into primary mode, and let it run through the catalogue for a match. 'Masers,' she datavised. 'Fairly basic medium-output projectors. Our armour should withstand an energy strike from them. But if we get caught in a saturation situation we'll be in trouble. And they're carrying other ordnance as well. I think I can make out some guided rockets, and EE grenades on those harnesses. Human-built.'

'I wonder who sold those to them,' Oski datavised. 'I thought the Confederation didn't permit armaments sales to the Tyrathca.'

'Not relevant,' Samuel datavised. 'Come on, let's locate the control offices that archaeology expedition found.'

Monica bled in her suit sensor's infra-red visualization as they moved off. The Tyrathca buildings materialized around her, tapering towers of a pale blue luminescence, like flame frozen against the empty blackness which stretched out along the ring. A cold necropolis with every street and building identical, as if each section had been stamped from the same die and laid out end to end. Gardens of tangled plants besieged each of the towers, their entwined stalks caught in the act of sagging. Unrelenting cold had turned the vegetation as hard and black as cast iron. Fanciful leaves, strangely shaped flowers and bloated seed pods had all been reduced to the same sombre shade of charcoal.

'Damn, those Tyrathca can move fast in low-gee,' Samuel datavised. They hadn't been walking ten minutes, and already the Tyrathca had reached the bottom of the first spiral ramp. A sensor disc showed one of them sweeping a portable electronic scanner over the floor while the others waited behind. The group split into three, following the various thermal trails.

'I make that eighteen coming our way,' Monica datavised. 'I think we've got four breeders. They're slightly larger.'

'I will return to the entrance,' one of the serjeants datavised. 'I will have time to lay several false heat trails before they reach this ring. That should split them again. And I may manage to close the airlock door. Either way, it will reduce the force that will ultimately pursue you.'

'Thank you,' Monica datavised.

The serjeant turned round, and walked back down the road.

'And then there were five,' Renato muttered uneasily round his respirator tube.

*

Ione wanted to know as soon as possible what the Tyrathca intended. The knowledge would certainly help her plan the kind of tactics needed to keep them away from the team. The two diversion serjeants had busily laid their heat trails, meandering between several of the big machinery chambers on the second level. That was when she found that the map made by the archaeologists was not perfect. Several times she'd had to use her inertial guidance to work out where she was when corridors didn't correspond to the indicated layout. It was a factor to consider when she sketched in her possible escape routes. The Tyrathca wouldn't suffer from such misinformation. Tanjuntic-RI's exact topology would be known to them, passed down from generation to generation via their chemical program glands.

One of the diversion serjeants was now hanging back from the archway that opened into a hemispherical chamber. It was a big space, occupied by what appeared to be a refinery constructed entirely out of glass. Colonnades, spheres, bulbs, and minarets formed their own miniature city, bound together with a tangled lattice of tubes. Individual containers were full of coloured liquids that had turned to ice. Cracks were visible everywhere. If heat ever did return to this chamber, the whole edifice would probably collapse.

There were three other entrances to the glass refinery, the one opposite the serjeant was where the heat trail from the ramp led. Sensor discs on the corridor wall showed Ione the Tyrathca advancing steadily along it. Ione waited. She knew her suit's heat signature would be visible to the Tyrathca as soon as they entered the refinery chamber, shining with the tenacity of a red dwarf star against the arctic corridor.

The first Tyrathca came in. Stopped. Raised the scanner it was holding, pointed it directly at her. Her suit communication block picked up a burst of encrypted data. The whole column of Tyrathca came to a halt. Then two of them moved up to support the first. They immediately fanned out on either side of the chamber, reducing her target opportunity.

Damn, she said. I think we can kiss the entrapment goodbye. The rest are waiting to see what happens.

It was to be expected, Samuel replied. They are soldier caste, after all. Bred for conflict. The breeders don't need to impart chemical programs of tactics among them; such knowledge is instinctive.

The serjeant moved out of the shallow alcove which had been masking it. Ione was ordering the communication block to open a channel on the frequency the Tyrathca were using when both the soldiers fired their maser rifles. The beams struck the serjeant's armour, almost overloading its energy dissipation web. She jumped, a movement enhanced considerably by low gravity and the suit's augmentation. At the same time she triggered the EE charges she'd placed above each of the chamber's entrances. Tonnes of rock descended in four separate avalanches, sealing the three Tyrathca in.

Ione climbed to her feet, and focused the suit sensors back. The jump had sent her soaring fifty metres down the corridor, barely avoiding hitting the roof. Small lumps of rock were spinning and bouncing towards her in lazy motions. The sensor discs in the refinery chamber showed nothing but a swirling cloud of dust, while the others showed the remaining Tyrathca retreating swiftly. They started to split up, vanishing down side corridors where there were no sensors to follow them.

The bad news is they're operating a shoot to kill policy, she said. **I guess they're not curious why we're here.**

That's to be expected, Samuel said. **You don't evolve an entire caste devoted to aggression unless you have a great need for them. The Tyrathca social structure is based around a clan hierarchy, they are extremely territorial. And we're violating their oldest piece of territory in defiance of their explicit instructions.**

Yes. Well, at least you know what to expect when they reach ring five. Now I'd better get out of here before they pop up from some secret passage and shoot me.

*

The control offices were a series of rooms bored into the wall of ring five, fourteen hundred metres from the spiral ramp. Simple open rectangles, plated in aluminium alloy, with the floor covered in composite. Each room was lined by bulky computer terminals, with twin rosette keyboards for Tyrathca fingers. The walls above them were covered by long display screens to project the arkship's engineering schematics and navigational plot. To all intents and purposes, this was Tanjuntic-RI's bridge.

According to the archaeology expedition there was less frost and ice inside, which had permitted them to reactivate several of the electronic systems without much trouble. The control offices were on an independent environmental circuit with much reduced humidity levels, and the airlocks were shut prior to the arkship's final evacuation so there was no contamination from ring five's damper atmosphere.

The archaeology expedition had known the sealed rooms were important; they'd traced the arkship's internal communication network, and discovered the principal node was inside. With due respect, they'd installed their own hatches in the Tyrathca airlocks, as they had up in level one. There was no worry about atmospheric contamination any more, not with all the water frozen out, but they wanted to maintain the environmental integrity. This was the first human exploration through an artefact belonging to a sentient xenoc species; ethics were a paramount concern – even though the Tyrathca were indifferent to such matters.

So, Monica and the others discovered, was someone else.

The large titanium rectangles leading to the control offices had been reactivated and opened, swinging back against the chamber wall. Not only that, the safety interlocks had somehow been circumvented, allowing all three to be opened at once. The five suited figures stood in front of the opening, scanning round with their sensors.

'This has got to be it,' Monica datavised. 'The human hatches are still here. The archaeologists didn't install them anywhere else.'

'Has there been another expedition since the first?' Renato asked.

'If there was, then neither Earth, Jupiter, nor Kulu knew anything about it,' Samuel datavised. 'I have to say that's extremely unlikely.'

'In any case, why not just use the arcology team's hatches?' Renato asked. 'We know they work. It must have taken a lot of effort to get these brutes open again.'

Oski stepped forward gingerly, using a hand-held sensor pad to scan around the airlock rim. 'I can't pick up any electrical impulses. But this was opened very recently. There's still some very faint thermal traces in the surrounding structure. They probably had to warm the airlocks back up to their operating temperature to get them to function again.'

Monica resisted the instinct to whirl round and check the streets of the necropolis behind. Her suit's micro-radar was scanning constantly for any sign of local movement. But the arkship's chill had somehow managed to stroke her skin through the armour. 'How recent?' she asked.

'Within the last five days.'

'And not human,' Renato datavised.

'Why do you say that?'

'Obvious. If it was our species, they would have used the hatches the archaeologists installed. Whoever it was, they were too big to fit through them.'

'It has to be the Kiint,' Samuel datavised. 'After all, they are partly the reason we're here. Ione and Kelly were right, Lieria was interested in the Sleeping God. And this is the obvious place where information on it would be stored. They must have teleported in here not long after they left Tranquillity. And simply opening the original airlock is the kind of elegance I'd expect from them. We've seen what the Tyrathca do to doors that won't budge for them.'

'Why not just teleport directly inside the control offices?' Monica asked.

'They're extremely small on a cosmic scale. I'm guessing such an action would require impossible accuracy, especially over three hundred light-years from Jobis.'

'Could be. Do you think they're still here?'

Oski pointed her sensor pad along the short airlock tunnel. 'It's inert, as far as I can tell.'

'And our time is running out,' Monica datavised. 'Let's get in there.'

The control offices were noticeably warmer. Suit sensors detected thermal concentrations around three of the computer terminals in the second room. 'This is the astrogration centre,' Oski datavised. 'One of our information targets. If we're to get a fix on the Sleeping God's location, we ought to find it stored in here.'

'Get started,' Monica datavised. The sensor discs were showing her the Tyrathca moving through the second level chamber with the biological reactor. They'd slowed their advance slightly since the diversion serjeant's attempted entrapment, treating each chamber with suspicion, never allowing more than three soldiers inside together. Even so, they'd be at the spiral ramp leading to ring five in another fifteen minutes.

Oski and Renato knelt down beside one of the terminals, and spread out their equipment. Monica, Samuel, and the last serjeant quickly searched the remaining rooms, then went back out into ring five.

'We should backtrack a bit and lay some false heat trails,' Monica datavised. 'That will give us a few minutes more.'

'I don't think it will,' Samuel replied. 'By the time they get here, it will be obvious to them that we came for the control offices. Diversions won't work. We shall have to defend our position.'

'Shit, I hope not, because this is a tactical lost cause. They can come at us from all sides, and we don't have a way out.'

'But we do have superior weaponry. Let's just hope we don't have to use it.'

'Fine. And now we've actually reached the mission target, why don't we start thinking of a way out of here.'

*

The second diversion serjeant had rigged a hundred and fifty metre length of corridor. A simple enough entrapment. Wait until the lead Tyrathca reached the EE charge, then trigger both of them. The length of corridor should trap all twelve of the pursuing xenocs between the rockfalls. But when the lead Tyrathca approached the first EE charge, it slowed, and the others stopped. Ione cursed as it moved forwards carefully, waving its scanner round. She must have left an abnormal thermal trace in the corridor when she was placing the EE charges.

The Tyrathca consulted the scanner display a final time, and pointed its maser rifle at the corridor roof. If the beam did wash over the EE charge's trigger electronics, the radiation would destroy them.

Annoyed, Ione set off the EE charge, bringing down a five metre section of roof. It didn't harm any of the Tyrathca. They cantered back down the corridor, and split up. Presumably to bypass the blockage and pick up the diversion serjeant's heat trail again, although without any sensor disc coverage, she couldn't be sure where they were. She started to move again, heading deeper into the arkship's interior, certain they weren't ahead of her, at least.

*

Oski was in her element. Worry about her physical predicament had vanished completely as she and Renato removed the computer terminal panels, exposing the circuitry inside. Tyrathca electronics lagged behind current human systems by several generations – if not centuries. She hadn't dealt with anything this crude since her compulsory History of Electronics semester while she was studying for her degree.

Renato followed her datavised instructions efficiently. Tracing the terminal's main power cable, and splicing in one of the energy matrices they'd brought with them. Small coloured symbols ringing the rosette keyboard lit up.

'Thank heavens they don't have any imagination,' Oski datavised. 'I'd hate to try and do this kind of thing on non-standard systems in the timescale we've got. But that's a null concept for the Tyrathca.'

'Which I still think is a paradox,' Renato datavised. 'Imagination is the root cause of all fresh ideas. You can't design a starship without it. It's the Siamese twin of curiosity.'

'Which they also don't seem to have much of.'

'But probing your environment is a basic survival trait. You have to know if there's any kind of threat out there if you want to keep on living. Then you have to work out how to overcome it.'

'I'm not arguing. Let's just save it for another time, OK?' Oski began attaching the processor blocks she'd brought to the databuses inside the terminus; unspooling long ribbons of fibre-optic cable with custom-built interface plugs on the end. The Laymil Project had the specifications of known Tyrathca electronic systems on file in Tranquillity, of course, but she'd referenced the archaeology expedition's records to be sure. Tanjuntic-RI's systems were identical to those used today, even down to the size and configuration of the sockets. Fifteen thousand years of standardization! Renato was right, that wasn't merely odd, it was downright eerie.

The interface plugs clicked smoothly into their sockets, and the block datavised that the high-density photonic link had been established. Which was ridiculous. She'd been waiting to apply a chemical spray that would have eased the plugs into place. They had been invented by her division to clean up optical contacts that had been exposed to the vacuum, dust, and general degradation of the Ruin Ring; they used a lot of it on the scant remnants of Laymil electronics they acquired.

She put the spray canister down and picked up a micro scanner. 'I can accept that their electronics are in a much better condition than the Laymil modules we have,' she datavised. 'The environment here is so much more benign, and they haven't been abandoned as long. But *this* lucky is absolutely impossible.' The blocks finished assembling an iconographic display of the terminal's architecture. 'The entire terminal is on-line, there isn't a single element not functioning. The Kiint didn't just access this, they repaired the damn thing to full operational status. Some of these components are brand new, for Heaven's sake.'

'How much of it is new?'

'According to my scanner, it's just processors and some support circuitry. The memory crystals are original. Which makes sense. They want the data stored inside them, just like us.'

'Can you get it?'

'No problem.' They already knew the Tyrathca program language, and there was certainly no such thing as security protocols or codes to guard against unauthorized access. Before leaving Tranquillity, the division's software experts had written customized questors that could examine all the information contained within Tyrathca memory crystals. Oski datavised the first batch of pre-formatted programs into the terminus architecture. Some of them were hunting for distinct references, while the others were classifying the information according to file type. The pair of them accessed the questor results as they returned.

'Well, it would have been too much to expect a direct reference to the Sleeping God,' Renato datavised.

'No mention of an unusual cosmological event, either,' Oski observed. She studied the file index, seeing what kind of database they'd activated, and shaping the next batch of questors accordingly. 'We have plenty of navigational fixes.'

'I'm going to see if the questors can find a list of star fixes they used to align their communication laser during the flight. At least that'll give us an idea of their contact protocol with the other arkships.'

'Good idea. I'll see if any other arkship flight paths are stored in here. That should tell us what kind of spatial volume we're dealing with.'

The questors revealed several tens of thousands of star fixes performed to align the interstellar communication laser. Eighty-five per cent of them were performed during the first six thousand years of the flight, after that the number of communiqués transmitted and received by the arkship dropped off considerably. During the later stages of the flight, the star fixes were performed almost exclusively to align the laser on the five colony planets which Tanjuntic-RI had established.

With the fixes established, Oski began to search for associated files. 'The messages aren't stored in here,' she datavised eventually. 'I keep getting a link code with all the laser alignment files. But it's to a different system altogether.'

'Do you know where it is?' Renato asked.

'Not yet.' She composed a new batch of questors, and sent them probing through the terminal's basic management routines. 'How are you doing?'

'Unpleasantly successful. The Tyrathca built over a thousand arkships.'

'Good God.'

'Yeah, quite. If they all travelled as far as this one, that gives us a phenomenal area to search through for their Sleeping God. We're talking about a percentage of the entire galaxy. Small, admittedly. But everything is relative. Parker and Kempster will love this.'

The questors started to display their answers to Oski. 'Ah, here we go. The files we want are stored in some kind of principal archive. I've got the identification code.'

'But it could be anywhere. We can't access anything from here.'

'Yes. Come on. We want the office which dealt with the arkship's general systems. We'll see if we can activate one of the terminals in there, and call up a general schematic.'

*

The maser beam caught the diversion serjeant on its thigh as it was crossing one of the hemispherical chambers. Ione's response was automatic, a fast powered dive behind a huge clump of machinery. The beam cut off as she fell behind it. Her armour's electronic-warfare block had pinpointed the origin. The Tyrathca was shooting from just inside one of the corridors.

She loaded the coordinate into her weapons hardware. A homing grenade shot out of her belt dispenser, curving over the top of the sheltering machinery. An EE explosion obliterated the corridor entrance. Another maser slashed across the serjeant's armour. Ione rolled quickly, swinging the launcher round. A second homing grenade eliminated the corridor the Tyrathca soldier was charging out of.

They're moving bloody fast, she told her other selves and Samuel. **It was a good pincer manoeuvre.** She used the suit's sensors to scan down the corridor ahead. No motion or anomalous infra-red source was detectable.

You can't go back, the serjeant with Monica and Samuel down in ring five told her. **You know they're behind you.**

Yes. She unclipped a magazine from her belt and slotted it into her multi-barrelled launcher as she walked over to the one remaining corridor entrance. Three slender missiles were fired at two second intervals, streaking away down the lightless tunnel. The serjeant flattened itself against the wall.

Each of the three missiles was tipped with a neutron-pulse warhead. They detonated simultaneously, soaking a five hundred metre length of the corridor with a lethal cascade of radiation. If there had been any Tyrathca lurking down there, the neutron bombardment would have killed them almost instantaneously. Holding the fat missile launcher in one hand, and an X-ray laser in the other, the diversion serjeant started to creep down the radioactive corridor.

*

'Oski, progress report, please,' Monica datavised. A sensor disc showed her the Tyrathca massing at the top of the spiral ramp which led down to ring five. 'We're getting a little critical out here.'

'I'm in the general systems layout. Should have the archive location any second now. This is another terminal the Kiint have refurbished. That must mean we're on the right track.'

'Oski,' Samuel datavised, 'please store as much of the layout as possible. It might help us to get out of here.'

'To get out?' Monica queried.

'Yes. I have an idea.'

'I'd love to hear it.'

'One moment.' **Syrinx?**

Yes, Samuel. Are you making progress?

Not as much as I'd like, but yes. Oski will start to datavise the information we have acquired so far to you and the *Lady Macbeth* in case we do not get out.

There's still only one Tyrathca ship at Tanjuntic-RI. They'll be no match for *Oenone*. As long as you can get back up to what's left of the spaceport support column, you'll be fine.

That may prove difficult. The Tyrathca soldier caste are very capable, as the serjeants are discovering. And they know where we have to return to. An ambush would be easy for them.

What do you propose?

Monica and I were both present when Dr Mzu escaped from Tranquillity.

Now wait a minute— Syrinx protested.

I could do that, *Oenone* said. If the *Udat* can, I can. There was considerable eagerness in the voidhawk's mental tone.

No, Syrinx said, instinctively protective. Tanjuntic-RI is a hell of a lot smaller than Tranquillity. You'd never fit into one of the rings.

But I would fit into the level one chambers.

That was what I was going to suggest, Samuel said. We ought to be able to reach one of them. And I doubt the hellhawk could swallow in to harass you. Whereas if you came back here to fight your way past the Tyrathca ship, it could certainly complicate the situation for you.

I can do it, *Oenone* insisted.

Are you sure? This isn't just bravado, is it?

You know I can. And we would honour *Udat*'s memory by doing so.

· All right. Syrinx couldn't hide the pride and simmering excitement in her mind. Samuel, we'll attempt to pick you out from one of the axial chambers.

Thank you, Samuel said emphatically.

*

Oski and Renato were almost running as they emerged from the control offices airlock. Their suit programs were having to limit the augmentation to stop them from hitting their heads on the airlock chamber ceiling.

'I've found the archive.' Renato datavised the layout file over to Monica, Samuel, and the serjeants. 'It's on the other side of the ring, a kilometre away.'

'Move out,' Monica datavised. Her guidance block was analysing the new data, incorporating it into existing files.

'According to this file, there's a ramp up to the second level just past the archive,' Samuel datavised. 'I'll blow the airlock hatch, and we'll evacuate through there as soon as you've got the information.'

'Sounds good,' Renato datavised.

The five of them were skating along the lightless streets in long low bounds, utterly reliant on their guidance programs. Nothing changed around them. At every turn, the wintered towers were the same ahead and behind, their infra-red signatures identical.

'The Tyrathca are on their way down the ramp to this ring,' datavised the serjeant who was guarding the entrance. 'I've rigged the airlock. Do you want me to blow it?'

'No,' Monica datavised. 'Wait until they're all inside the ring, then blow it.'

'You want to trap them in here?' Renato datavised. 'With us?'

'Good tactics,' Samuel confirmed. 'If we block them now, we won't know where they are, nor how they gain entry. But once they're in, they can't get out easily, and we can monitor them via the sensor discs. It gives us the strategic high ground.'

*

A glimmer of infra-red started to shine down the corridor ahead of the diversion serjeant, like an autumnal dawn. Ione stopped, and slapped a magazine of smart-seeker missiles in the launcher, datavising the Tyrathca profile into their processors. Suit sensors showed a similar infra-red glow expanding behind her.

Surrounded, she informed her other selves. **Be warned. They really are making good use of their knowledge.**

A couple of neutron-pulse tipped missiles were fired at the group behind her. She dropped a grenade, and started to run forwards. Smart-seeker missiles sliced out of the big launcher ahead of her. The neutron pulses went off. She triggered the grenade, bringing down the corridor roof. Small EE detonations were flaring up ahead as the missiles punctured the Tyrathca spacesuit fabric, burying themselves deep in the xenoc bodies before detonating.

Infra-red vision was wiped out in splashes of brilliant crimson. Still firing missiles. Something like a medium-sized cannonball hit her right leg. Exploding. She was flung violently against the ceiling, bouncing down against the floor. Internal bones snapped. Cracks multiplied across her exoskeleton. But the armour held, reinforced by the molecular-binding-force generators.

The diversion serjeant raised its head, dislodging various rocks which were lodged on its helmet. It moved its arms, actuators pushing hard against the weight of rocks holding its torso down. More rocks slithered off the armour. Two soldier-caste Tyrathca were bounding towards it. Ione waited until they were fifteen metres away, and fired a couple of homing grenades.

*

The sensor disc by the spiral ramp up in level one noted a rise in the thermal environment beyond its pre-set parameters, and broadcast an alert. Visual observation showed twenty new Tyrathca marching into the interior.

*

'Oh, God,' Monica datavised. 'Just what we need.'

'It will take them forty minutes to reach ring five,' Samuel datavised. 'If Oski hasn't retrieved what we need by then I doubt it will matter.'

They were fifty metres short of the ring wall, passing the last of the towers. Five sets of suit lights slithered erratically over the wall, kindling small refractive auras from the curtain of frosted creeper leaves.

'There,' Renato datavised. Rather uselessly, he raised an arm and pointed. But the others saw where his suit lights had come to rest, and focused their own beams on the spot. The airlock door to the archive was very similar to those of the control offices. And like them, open.

'It's recent,' Oski datavised. 'Several faint infra-red footprints, very similar to those at the control offices.'

'Monica, you go in with them,' Samuel datavised. 'I'll set the charges ready to open that ramp for us.'

Monica drew an X-ray laser rifle from her belt, and switched her homing grenades to active mode. Feeling slightly more confident, she stepped through the open airlock. Oski and Renato had been issued with the same weapons suite as her, but not even full field combat programs could turn a pair of academics into decent troops. She didn't have surprise on her side. Instead she went for speed, flashing through the final doorway with sensor gain on maximum. Radar and infra-red covered the whole interior of the archive chamber in milliseconds. The results filtered through her tactical location program, which declared there was noting active inside.

'You can come in,' she datavised.

The archive was substantially different from the control offices. A lot larger, a long hall tunnelled out of naked rock, with an arching ceiling thirty metres high. Despite having Tyrathca-sized computer terminals and display cases, it was the most human place they'd seen in Tanjuntic-RI.

Principally, Monica decided, because it was instantly recognizable: a museum. Five-metre glass cube display cabinets were standing in regimented rows the whole length of the hall. The glass was fogged by grime and ice. When they shone their suit beams on the cabinets, the contents were visible only as intriguing dark shadows. From what they could discern, it was machinery inside; the outlines had too many flat sides and regular angles to be anything biological.

Each line of cubes was divided into sections by broad areas given over to computer terminals clustered round a central hexagonal pedestal of giant display screens. Oski walked over to the nearest one. 'These zones must be the archive's operating stations,' she datavised. Her light beams fanned up and down the casings then settled on the screens. 'There's a plaque here.' Neural nanonics put her Tyrathca translation program into primary mode. 'Atmospheric engineering,' she read out. 'They must cover different disciplines at each station. Try and find anything relating to navigation or communications.'

'Can you see if the Kiint repaired any of the terminals?' Renato asked. 'That would save a minute or two.'

'Nothing like that showing yet,' Monica datavised.

Renato walked along a row of the big cubes, annoyed they were all so opaque. The first station of terminals was mineral distillation, followed by thermal maintenance, then distillation mining. On impulse he wiped a gauntlet against the ice on one cube, upping the brightness on his suit lights. It was a chunk of machinery inside. 'These gizmos look like they're brand new,' he datavised. 'I'm not sure this is a museum. Could be they archived actual physical components, the ultimate template back-up in case something screwed up their electronics.'

'Any kind of disaster big enough to eradicate their crystal memories would wreck these machines first,' Oski datavised. 'Besides, think how many different components there are to make Tanjuntic-RI work. A hell of a lot more than we can see in here.'

'OK, so it's just the really critical ones.'

'I think I've found it,' Monica datavised. 'This terminal has been spruced up, and it's still a couple of degrees warmer than the rest.'

Oski scanned her suit sensors round to locate the ESA operative. 'What's the station?'

'Planetary habitation.'

'That doesn't sound quite right.' She hurried over to where Monica was standing, suit lights converging on one of the terminals.

'The Tyrathca are now in ring five,' the serjeant guarding the ramp entrance datavised. 'I am blowing the airlock behind them.'

Despite her high suit-sensor resolution, Monica could receive no indication of the explosion. 'Oski, we really don't have any more time to hunt round,' she datavised. 'Just get what you can from this terminal, and pray the Kiint knew what they were doing.'

'Confirmed.' The electronics specialist knelt down beside the terminal, and started working on the front panel.

*

Ione was tracking the Tyrathca through multiple observation points as they spread out through the streets of ring five. As soon as the airlock detonated and collapsed behind them (trapping the last two in the rubble), they had deployed in a wide sweep formation. The sensor discs were picking up microwave radar pulses from several of the soldiers. Their emissions helped to target the first batch of homing grenades which she launched, eliminating a further three. Then they wised up to that and switched the radars off. She launched a swarm of smart-seeker missiles, programming them to flit above the tops of the towers. Arrowing down as soon as they located a suit.

The launch betrayed her general direction. Ultimately, another plus point. She was on the other side of the airlock from the control offices and archive, drawing them away from the exploration team.

One of the sensor discs showed a soldier raise a rifle the size of a small human cannon. Ione started running, not caring about the lack of cover. A tower disintegrated behind her; the blast strong enough to create a rumble in the ring's near-non-existent atmosphere. Big nodules of debris crashed into neighbouring towers, shattering the brittle concrete. Three of them toppled over, throwing up thick clouds of black dust which surged along the streets in every direction, blocking vision in all spectrums.

*

Monica followed what she could of the fight via the sensor discs. Nervous energy created a nasty itch along her spine and ribs. Impossible to scratch through the suit. Even twisting round inside the armour was useless. There was nothing she could do to assist Oski and Renato. The pair of them had exposed the terminal's electronics, and were busy attaching their own blocks to the primitive components inside. Their fluid motions were bringing effective results. Little lights were flashing around the rosette keyboard, and the monitor screen was producing a snowstorm of green and scarlet graphics.

She started walking round the outlying display cubes, alert for any other signs of Kiint activity. The one contribution she could still make. Not that it would be a lot of use at this point. It wasn't until after she'd started on her second circuit of the planetary habitation station that her subconscious alarm grew strong enough to make her stop and take a proper look at what she was seeing. The shapes inside the opaque cubes were no longer nice and regular.

With real unease replacing her anxiety now, Monica swiped her gauntlet over the crinkled, sparkling ice, rubbing a patch clear. Her suit lights brightened, converging on the cube. Visual sensors altered their focus. Monica took a half step back, breath catching in her throat. Her medical monitor program warned her of a sudden fast heart rhythm. 'Samuel?' she datavised.

'What is it?'

'They've got xenocs in here. Xenocs I've never seen before.' She scanned her sensors across the creature inside the cube, building up a pixel file image for the Edenist. It was bipedal, shorter than a human, with four symmetrically arranged arms emerging from midtorso. No elbow or knee joints were apparent, the limbs moved as a single unit. Bulbous shoulder/hip joints hinted at a considerable articulation. All four arms ended in stumpy hands with four clawfingers, while the legs finished in rounded pads. The head was a fat cone, with deep folds of skin ringing a thick neck, which would permit a great deal of rotation. There was a vertical gash, which could be either a nose or mouth, and deep sockets that could have held eyes.

'My God, Samuel, it's sentient. It's wearing things, look.' She focused on an arm, where a silver bracelet was wrapped around the wizened caramel skin. 'That could be a watch, I think. Its certainly technological. They caught a sentient xenoc and stuffed the poor bastard for their kids to look at in this freak show. Oh, for Christ's sake, what are we dealing with here?'

'You're jumping to some very wild assumptions, Monica.'

'Then you explain what the fucking hell it's doing in here. I'm telling you, they put it on show. It must have come from one of the planets they stopped at.'

'You're in an archive, not a circus zoo.'

'Is that supposed to make me happy? So this is scientific not entertainment. What were they doing studying it? It's sentient. It's not a laboratory creature.'

'Monica, I know it's shocking, but it isn't relevant to our current situation. I'm sorry, but you'll just have to ignore it for the moment.'

'Jesus fucking wept.' She spun round, and marched back towards the terminal where Oski and Renato were working. Heat and anger kept her going for several paces. Then she stopped and scanned the cube again. Her suit lights refracted off the gritty ice with its dark adumbrate core of sorrow and suffering.

When they'd come on board, she'd wondered about Tyrathca souls watching them. Now all she could think about was the soul of the unknown xenoc; lost and alone, crying out desperately for others of its kind. Could it see her now? Was it shouting its pleas for salvation from some obscure corner of the dreadful beyond? Unheard even by its own deities.

The medical monitor warned Monica she wasn't breathing properly. She made an effort to inhale in a regular motion. 'Oski? How are you doing?'

'I'm not sure. There are some files in here that look like communiqués. I've just reverted to our fall-back option. We're copying every memory to analyse later.'

'How long?'

'Programming is almost complete. It'll take half an hour to datavise all their files over to our processors.'

'We can't afford that.'

'I know. The bitek processors can shunt the information directly over to *Oenone* and *Lady Mac* in real time. We just have to hope the Tyrathca don't come in here and find out what we're doing until it's finished.'

'That's a safe enough bet. I expect they'll be too busy chasing us.'

*

How the hell did they get up there? Ione asked.

At least three Tyrathca soldiers were cantering along ring five's ceiling gantries. The narrow metal walkways threaded amongst the crane rails and irrigation pipes were shaking alarmingly as the heavy bodies thundered down them. But they were holding. And they provided the Tyrathca with a dangerously effective vantage point.

There were now six separate smears of billowing dust blotting out entire sections of the ring, evidence of shattered towers caught in the increasingly brutal crossfire. Tyrathca bodies lay everywhere, bleeding fluid and heat onto the cold alloy floor. One of the two remaining serjeants was limping badly, its suit leg crushed almost flat around the knee, caught by a huge chunk of debris whose inertia defeated the binding generators. Several processors and hardware units on its belt were dead, ruined by maser fire.

Worse, from a tactical viewpoint, only one Tyrathca was currently stalking it. The remainder had moved away from the mayhem it'd unleashed to chase down the remaining heat trails. Four of them, including one breeder, were congregating round the open airlock into the control offices.

'They know we went in there now,' Samuel datavised.

'The ones on the gantries will be looking for us,' Ione datavised. 'And they'll see us soon enough.'

'We've finished programming the file extraction,' Oski said. 'The data is being received by the starships.'

'Excellent. Get out of the archive, I'm about to blow the airlock. Ione, can you take out the soldiers on the gantries?'

'I'll try.'

'At this point, you're not expendable to us, OK? We're going to need back-up to get out of here.'

'Understood. But only one of me will be able to keep up with you on the ramp.'

The injured serjeant raised its missile launcher, and fired the two remaining smart-seeker missiles. They soared off into the gloom, twin spikes of intense amber light, seemingly rising out of sight around the ring's curvature. It began to limp into the seething dust, heading back towards the archive. Searching round on its belt, Ione found a magazine containing neutron-pulse missiles. Only four of the twelve responded to a datavise. She slipped the magazine into the launcher anyway.

When the others made it to the shelter of the ramp, she could then make life seriously unpleasant for the Tyrathca left in ring five.

*

Samuel and the last serjeant were waiting for Monica, Oski, and Renato right outside the archive. Monica's thoughts were still in such turmoil after finding the xenoc that she didn't trust herself to say anything to him.

'There's still one soldier caste left up on the gantry,' Samuel datavised. 'Not that it matters much now.' He triggered the charges he'd laid around the airlock.

They were close enough to see the flash. A dazzling ripple of pure white light that burst across the ring, fading fast.

Samuel started running straight at it. They only had a hundred and fifty metres to go. He datavised instructions to the others, who activated their rocket launchers. A semicircle of towers fell in unison as the missiles pulverized their ground floors. Dust strangled the thin plumes of potent flame, sending out a curtain of impenetrable darkness that fountained straight upwards.

The airlock leading to the ramp had been wrenched to one side by the charges Samuel had laid around its rim, buckling the thick slab of titanium like so much plastic sheeting. A tide of rock had spewed out of the gap, narrowing it still further. His boots dislodged small loose fragments as he scrambled up. There was enough space to pass through, providing he turned sideways. As soon as he was on the other side, he started slapping EE charges on the walls. Monica and the others wriggled through the gap, with the serjeant bringing up the rear.

*

Eighteen combat wasps were closing on *Lady Mac*. The third time in an hour Hesperi-LN's defences had launched such a salvo at them. Each time, *Lady Mac* had simply jumped away before any of them were in range, leaving the drones to search round helplessly for their target.

'Good job the Tyrathca never met anything hostile when they were on their voyage here,' Joshua remarked. 'I mean, Jesus, they are absolutely crap at space warfare. Why do they keep firing salvos when we're far enough above the planet to jump?'

'They're lulling us into complacency,' Ashly said cheerfully. 'They've worked out roughly where we've got to emerge next time, and they've flown their superweapon there ready to zap us.'

'Nope. Keeping the jump emergence coordinate as a random variable is file one in the combat manual.'

'They wouldn't have a superweapon anyway,' Liol said. 'Building stuff like that takes inventive flare. And they just ain't got it.'

'They do seem to be very dogmatic,' Dahybi said. 'As they haven't got a combat-capable starship to field against us, their options are limited.'

'Limited, yes,' Joshua agreed. 'But not to one.' He studied the tactical display. The nearest combat wasp would be close enough to start deploying submunitions in another two minutes. 'Stand by for jump. Sarha, how's the memory dump coming on?'

'No problems, Joshua. The bitek array is accepting the load.'

'Great, let's hope there's something useful in there.' He cut the fusion drives, holding the starship stable with ion thrusters. The flight computer showed him the energy-patterning node status as the combat sensors retracted. 'Here we go.' They emerged forty thousand kilometres from the combat wasp swarm. Hesperi-LN's SD network took nearly three minutes to acquire lock-on.

'Are you launching another combat wasp?' Liol asked.

'Not yet,' Joshua said. He datavised the bitek array for a link to the exploration team. 'Where are you?'

'Coming up to level two,' Monica replied. 'The ramp is sealed behind us, so if we don't get ambushed, we'll be at level one in another twelve minutes.'

'OK, thanks, Monica. Syrinx, we'd better start finalizing our next move.'

'Agreed. We must assume the blackhawk will try and follow us again.'

'I can throw it off with multiple consecutive jumps. Can you do something similar?'

'No problem. Designate a rendezvous coordinate.'

'That's trickier. This bloody diversionary battle has screwed around with our vector. I can get a rough alignment on the second planet with a small burn. We'll slingshot around it, and realign on the Orion Nebula. After that, we can lose the hellhawk.'

'Very well. *Oenone* will swallow out to the second planet as soon as we've picked the team up. See you there.'

*

The second level cavern housed a gigantic fusion generator, three pale metal spheres standing one on top of the other, eighty metres high. Arching buttresses of pipes and cables were wrapped around the main section like mechanized viaducts, sinking away into the walls and floor. A quintet of heat exchangers surrounded it. Fluids had leaked from their valves and feed tube junctions, dribbling down the casings to solidify in colourful multi-layered ribbons. The cavern's irradiated rock kicked off datavised Geiger warnings as soon as the exploration team bounded in from one of the corridors.

'This is it,' Samuel datavised. 'Our shortcut.'

'It will be very short with this radiation level if we're not careful,' Monica datavised. 'This is as bad as a fission core meltdown. What kind of fuel did they use?'

'Heaven only knows.' Samuel scanned his sensors across the pipes that disappeared into the curving apex overhead. 'Any of those three.' His suit's tactical program datavised the designation icon to the others, highlighting the pipe he'd chosen. 'According to the file Oski pulled from the control offices it's a thermal gas duct. The exchangers transferred some of their heat along it to keep the level one lakes warm. It's an express route straight there. All we have to do is slice it open.'

Monica didn't argue with him, despite the sudden doubts. She'd stayed with Oski and Renato in the archive, leaving details of their withdrawal to Samuel. That was teamwork. And it was as though he'd been her partner for ever. They knew they could rely on each other now. She took the stumpy laser rifle from her belt, datavised its control processor for a continual burn, and lined it up on the pipe he'd designated.

Five ruby red beams stabbed out, puncturing the pipe. Bright molten metal droplets drizzled down slowly, losing their radiance before they reached the ground. Monica's radar caught the movement just before the maser beam hit her suit. A couple of homing grenades fired immediately from her dispenser, looping through the three-dimensional maze of pipes to smash the corridor entrance where the Tyrathca soldier was lurking.

Backwash from the EE blast rolled her across the ground to clang against the base of a heat exchanger. Her infra-red sensor caught a blur of motion away on the other side of the chamber. Radar was useless, there was too much machinery in the way.

'They're in,' she warned.

'Oski, Renato, finish cutting the pipe open,' Samuel ordered. 'We'll take care of them.'

One of the Tyrathca cannon fired, blowing a hole in the side of the fusion generator. Monica grabbed her missile launcher, and fired off a pair of smart seekers. Samuel was kangaroo-jumping up the side of a heat exchanger. Homing grenades spat out of his dispenser, zipping away to pummel the corridor entrances. Maser beams slashed at him. Monica's sensors triangulated their origin, and she launched more smart seekers in retaliation. Explosions ripped round the chamber as the corridor entrances were closed.

'Pipe's open,' Oski datavised.

'Go straight in,' Samuel datavised. 'We'll cover you.'

Monica dived under a buttress, scanning at ground level. The lower section of four hot Tyrathca spacesuit legs were visible ahead of her, below a coil-wound beam. She chopped them with the laser, slashing straight through the fabric. Large globs of weird purple gel burped out, oscillating wildly as they bounced off the floor and machinery. The Tyrathca stumbled and fell. Monica slid the laser along its flank. A tidal wave of gel blobs erupted. Then the body went into explosive decompression.

Oski's manoeuvring pack fired at full power, lifting her towards the apex of the cavern. Every suppressor program she had that could squash down on her fear was in primary mode. They must have worked, she was quietly delighted at how calmly she was reacting to being shot at. Guidance programs bent her flight around the clutter of arching pipes as she rose higher and higher. She actually passed a two metre section of the pipe on her way up, its edges still glowing pink as it tumbled end over end.

A maser beam struck her legs. The suit's tactical program shot a homing grenade down in response. Then she was concentrating solely on her flight, arrowing for the gaping hole they'd sliced in the pipe. Its rim flashed past her, catching her shoulder, and scraping along her arms. Then she was completely inside. Radar was the only sense which functioned in here, showing a rigid, featureless tube stretching out above her for nearly three hundred metres. Her manoeuvring pack thrusters throttled down, slowing her to a less reckless speed as the gravity dropped off. A second armour suit slid into the pipe below her.

'Hell of an escape route,' Renato datavised.

*

Etchells had no warning that the *Oenone* was going to swallow away from the twin moons. The crew were still boring him crazy with their promises and propaganda when it happened. But he felt it go, a massive tear in the uniformity of his distortion field.

What are you doing? he asked. The Tyrathca ships were still hours away.

We're leaving now, Ruben said. Why don't you go home? Think about what we've been saying.

There was a momentary lapse in the affinity contact. Etchells observed the amount of energy *Oenone* applied to open the wormhole interstice, determining the terminus location. They had returned to that damn arkship!

Why are you here? he demanded. What's so special about that ship?

If you join our efforts to solve this crisis, then such questions will be answered for you, Serina said.

Fuck your psychobabble bullshit. He sent the energy flashing through his patterning cells, uncomfortably aware of how much he had expended in warding off impacts from the Lagrange point particles. A wormhole opened, and he dived down it, emerging into real space again, barely twenty kilometres from the arkship.

The *Oenone* was probing the ancient vessel very thoroughly with its distortion field (an act which Etchells didn't understand). And the large Tyrathca ship was firing its secondary drive, moving up from its holding position at the front of Tanjuntic-RI. Etchells didn't really want to go into combat against the xenocs at this point, especially not with uncertain allies like the Edenists.

Oenone was performing another swallow manoeuvre.

You can't elude me, Etchells said.

Fine, Syrinx replied with icy superiority. **Follow us in, then.**

Etchells derived the voidhawk's wormhole terminus. Which was impossible. They were swallowing *inside* the arkship. There were cavities in there, he could feel them. Tenuous bubbles within the hard rock. So very small.

He didn't dare. That kind of accuracy was staggering.

The Tyrathca ship had risen above the arkship's horizon. It launched fifteen combat wasps straight at him. He swallowed away fast.

*

The level one cavern was quickly and silently saturated with light, revealing the cyclorama of frozen water. Ripples and wavelets were caught in mid-swell, drained of colour as they had been of heat. The endocarps were different. Flat cliffs of rock, rimmed with ledges of metal just above the ice. One of them boasted a tiny pinprick of warmth. Five armour-suited figures hovered in front of it, watching the light source expand; twisted fragments of starlight threaded through length of the wormhole to spray out at random. There was no other indication of the terminus opening.

As the light dimmed it shone across *Oenone*'s marbled blue hull, glinting off the crew toroid. The huge voidhawk swept round the lake's curvature towards the exploration team, skirting the rickety old axial gantry with simple grace.

You've no idea how good it is to see you, Samuel said, accompanying the statement with a wash of gratitude and relief.

You too, *Oenone* replied. **I knew I could do this.**

*

Etchells conceded defeat. He wasn't going to find out why the two starships had come here, not now. *Oenone* was inside the arkship for less than five minutes before swallowing away again. Its wormhole terminus opened out above the star system's second planet. The Adamist ship jumped there as well.

Etchells joined them, at a non-threatening distance, observing the Adamist ship fly round the planet on a tight slingshot trajectory. When it jumped, Etchells tried to follow. But it must have used multiple consecutive jumps, because he couldn't find it anywhere near the emergence coordinate. With his energy patterning cells badly depleted, and his nutrient reserve getting low, he began the long, lonely trip back to New California. It was time to hand the whole problem over to Kiera and Capone.

14

Candles shaped like dark lily pads bobbed about over the bathwater, never managing to touch the two bodies resting in the middle. Several of them had become mired in the apple-scented bubbles, their wicks sizzling as the flames struggled to stay alight. More candles were flickering gamely along the marbled rim. Half a metre tall, they were cemented into place by thick rivulets of wax. As the only source of light in the suite's dilapidated bathroom, their weak yellow flickers bestowed an appropriately dingy appearance.

For years the Chatsworth had been one of central Edmonton's most renowned five-star hotels, attracting the wealthy and the famous. But successive changes of management and ownership had seen it decay badly over the last two decades as too much of its cash flow had been diverted from maintaining standards to inflating shareholder dividends. Eventually it was trading solely on its name, and that could never last. Now it was closed for a much needed refurbishment and relaunch. But the work crews and their mechanoids hadn't even started stripping the old fittings out when New York's problems with the possessed hit the AV news. After that, most of Earth's long-term commercial investment projects were put on hold while the financiers and entrepreneurs waited to see what the outcome would be. The Chatsworth included.

Quinn had taken it over with quiet efficiency to use as his home base in the arcology. The three-man caretaker team left inside were possessed, and every last connection to the outside world was severed: power, water, data, air-conditioning. He knew that police and government security forces tracked the possessed by the glitches they caused, but they could only do that when there was working processor-governed machinery nearby. So he and his loyal followers made do with the water left in the hotel tanks, cooked on camping gear in one of the ritzy function rooms, and used candles. Bathwater was heated purely by energistic power. The soaps and oils were stolen from a local mall. Along with booze.

Quinn reached for the bottle of Norfolk Tears chilling in an ice bucket among the candles, and poured the pale liquid over Courtney's glistening breasts. She giggled as her nipples hardened from the cold, and arched herself further out of the water. There were bruises and teeth marks on her gold-tanned skin, evidence of Quinn's recent predilections. She didn't mind the kind of sex he wanted; it was kind of interesting, the physical things he could do with his new black magic. That kind of misused power really turned her on, further proof of his omnipotence. He didn't have to worry about censure, or being caught. He wrote the rules now. And there was never much pain, nor did it last long. He didn't have to hurt her to confirm their relationship; he knew she had submitted herself completely to him and the cause. Joyfully, too. By embracing the serpent beast in its dark lair, Courtney's life had changed, becoming so much better. Hotter. Brighter. She got all the stuff like clothes and AV fleks she wanted now; and she didn't have to take shit from anyone any more, either. Not bad going for a sect whore.

Quinn threw away the bottle, and started to lick the luxurious drink off her skin. 'This is the fucking max,' he said. 'You know, it really is true; the bad guys get the best of everything. Best clothes. Best drugs. Best babes. Best parties. Best sex. It's fucking *great*.'

'We're the bad guys?' Courtney asked, puzzled. 'I thought we were doing the right thing smashing up the world?'

Quinn stood up, sending the floating candles surfing into the bubbles. His erection grew to a thick flesh sword hanging over Courtney's upturned face. 'We're both; we're bad and we're right. Believe it.'

Her confusion vanished, and she was smiling with simple contentment again. 'I believe in you.' She cupped his balls, squeezing like he'd taught, and started to lick the length of his dick.

'After I've finished fucking you, I'm going to go over and kill another one of Banneth's people,' Quinn said. 'This time, I'm going to do it right in front of her. Force her to see how impotent she is.'

'I don't get it.' Courtney sat back, glancing up enquiringly. 'Why don't you just march in there and start torturing her? It's not like she can stop you, or anything.'

'Because this is exactly what she did to me. To us. All of us. She frightens people. It's her bang. What she can do to you up in that sanctum of hers is so fucking freaky and scary it hammers into your brain like some monster prick. All you can think of is how to stop her doing anything bad to you. Everybody in the coven knows they're gonna be strapped down on one of her tables some day. All you can do is ask God's Brother that when it's your turn she does something that boosts you. Nothing you can do about the pain. That's fucking standard issue with Banneth.'

'I see what you're doing,' Courtney said, pleased with herself. 'You're stalking her.'

'That's a part of it, yeah. Each time I go over there and kill one of her people, it ruins a little more of what she is. The Banneth they all fear is growing smaller and smaller every day. Even dickheads that dumb are going to realize that the one person who can defeat anything is utterly helpless against the coming Night. I want her sitting there while the entire headquarters coven freaks out and deserts her. I'm going to make that he-bitch feel what we all did. That she's a total nothing; all that power she's spent fuck knows how many decades building up isn't worth shit any more. She used to make people piss themselves just by being sarcastic. *Sarcastic*, for shit's sake! Can you believe that? But that's how strong she was. Well, now she's going to *know* what I'll do to her, and she's going to *know* there's no way out when I come for her. That puts me in control, and me on top. It switches her whole life around; screws with the way her brain's wired. I love that almost as much as I love the pain I'm going to inflict.'

Courtney rubbed her cheek along his dick, eyes closed in dreamy admiration. 'I want to watch.'

'You can.' He beckoned. She was taken up against the wall, hands pinned above her head. A loutish violation of hard thrusts, energistically strengthened muscles overcoming any hindrance to pummel his body against hers. In his mind he let it be Banneth, enhancing the pleasure.

Halfway through, when Quinn's orgasm was building, Billy-Joe knocked tentatively on the door. 'Get in here, you little shit,' Quinn yelled. 'Wait. Watch us.'

Billy-Joe did as he was told. Standing well out of the way. Keeping still, but with inflamed eyes following every aspect of Courtney's contortions. Quinn finished with her, and let go. She sank to the floor, propped up clumsily against the wall, shivering heavily. Her hands stroked gingerly over her body, touching the fresh bruises.

'What do you want?' Quinn asked.

'It's one of the possessed come to see you,' Billy-Joe said. 'He's one of the new ones. Come from the Lacombe sect. Says he's got to see you. It's like real urgent, he says.'

'Shit.' Quinn's skin dried; his robe materialized around him. 'Hey! You want any of those healing up?'

'It's all right, Quinn,' Courtney said thickly. 'I've got some cream and stuff to rub on. I'm fine.'

*

'This better be fucking important,' Quinn said. 'I told you dickheads not to move around the arcology. The police are going to be watching for you.'

'I was careful,' the possessed man said. His name was Duffy. He'd taken over the Lacombe coven's Magus. Unlike the Magus, Quinn judged him devout enough to God's Brother. Duffy had been left in charge of the coven, organizing several successful strikes against Edmonton's infrastructure.

Quinn sat down in one of the lounge's fraying leather armchairs, and let his mind wander through the Chatsworth and its neighbouring buildings. They were only a couple of blocks away from Banneth's headquarters, a location perfect in every respect.

There were no suspicious minds anywhere near. If Duffy had been spotted and followed, then the police were keeping well back. Quinn resisted the impulse to go over to the window and pull back one of the tatty curtains to peer down onto the street. 'OK, you haven't completely fucked up. What is it?'

'This Magus, Vientus, I been squeezing him. He ain't a Magus, not a real one. Doesn't believe in God's Brother.'

'Big deal. None of those shits ever did, not really.'

Duffy played with his hands, wretchedly nervous. Nobody liked the idea of telling Quinn what to do – like shut up and *listen* – but this was vital.

'All right,' Quinn grunted. 'Go on.'

'He's some kind of secret police informer. Has been for years. Every night he makes a report to some kind of supervisor about what the coven's been doing and what's going down on the street.'

'That's impossible,' Quinn said automatically. 'If the police had that kind of information they would have raided the coven.'

'I don't think the supervisor's that kind of police, Quinn. Not like you get in the local precinct house. Vientus never met them, he just datavised the information to some eddress each night. There was other stuff going on, too. Vientus sometimes got told to target people for this supervisor, local business people, buildings that needed to be firebombed. And they'd talk about what other gangs were doing, and if they needed to be chopped back. Real detailed shit like that. It was almost like the supervisor was running the coven, not Vientus.'

'Anything else?' Quinn was listening, but not really paying attention. He was too involved thinking through the implication, and with that came a growing sense of alarm.

'This supervisor must have had some influence with the cops. Quite a bit, I guess. There were times when Vientus got useful sect members released from custody. All he had to do was ask the supervisor for them, and the cops would let them go. Easy bail, or community work sentence, some shit like that.'

'Yeah,' Quinn said quietly. That recollection was one of the most bitter he owned. Waiting in Edmonton's Justice Hall for days with the dwindling prospect that Banneth would get him released. Banneth could make the whole legal system do tricks for her, like every judge owed her a favour. Murder suspects out on parole within an hour. Stim suppliers given house arrest sentences.

'Er.' Duffy was sweating badly now. 'And, er . . . the supervisor had told Vientus to look out for you.'

'Me? The supervisor used my name?'

'Yes. There was a visual file on you and everything. The supervisor said you were using the possessed to take over sect covens, and they thought you'd try to kill Banneth.'

'Shit!' Quinn stood up, and sprinted for the door. Halfway across the lounge he shifted into the ghost realm, running through the closed door without breaking stride.

*

Half-past two Edmonton local time, and the arcology was at its quietest. Solaris tubes suspended underneath the elevated roads between the uptown skyscrapers shone down on deserted streets. Hologram adverts swarmed up the frontage of the ground-level shops, bright fantasy worlds and beautiful people shining enticingly. An army of municipal mechanoids crawled along the pavements in front of them, spraying their solvents on tacky patches and guzzling down fast-food wrappers. The only pedestrians left to avoid were a few late-night stimheads thrown out of clubs by the bouncers, and romantic youthful couples slowly strolling the long route home.

Quinn adopted Erhard's image as he hustled along the street. Not an exact replicant, but a reasonable facsimile of the pathetic ghost. Good enough to deceive any characteristics-recognition program scanning pedestrian faces through the street monitor sensors for a glimpse of Quinn Dexter. He stopped by the taxi rank a full block from the Chatsworth, and the barrier slid down. One of the sleek silver Perseus cabs glided up out of the subway garage, opening its door for him.

Quinn pulled the seatbelt on with one hand, keying in his destination on the central control column with the other. He transferred the displayed fee from his bank disk (keeping his energistic power reined in), and the little vehicle sped off along the street.

It all made a frightening amount of sense. He remembered the High Magus in New York, who obviously knew too much to risk being possessed. And back in Edmonton when he'd been a junior acolyte; the way everyone on a sect gig had to tell their sergeant acolyte all the crap that was going down on the street. It happened every single day. The sergeants would report to the senior acolytes, who in turn reported to Banneth. An uncompromising routine, drilled in to Quinn along with all the others right from their initiation. Information is the weapon which wins all wars. We need to know what the gangs are doing, what the police patrols are doing, what the locals are doing. Every coven was the same, in every arcology. The sect knew the moves of every downtown illegal on the whole planet.

'Perfect!' Quinn shouted. He thumped his fist into the seat cushion. 'Fucking perfect.' The taxi was starting to rise up a ramp to the elevated express-road. Vertical lines of blanked windows zipped past as they increased speed, then curved round to a horizontal blur. Thousands of slumbering minds slipstreamed through his consciousness. Restful and content. Just as they were supposed to be. As they had to be.

Arcologies were the social equivalent of nukes. Half a billion people crammed into a couple of hundred square kilometres; an impossibility of human nature. The only society which could conceivably hang together in those circumstances was a total-control dictatorship. Everything licensed and regulated with no tolerance of dissent or rebellion. Anarchy and libertarian freedoms didn't work here, because arcologies were machines. They had to keep working smoothly, and the same way. Everything interlocked. If one unit fucked up, then every other unit would suffer. That couldn't be allowed. Which was a paradox, because you couldn't keep the jackboot stamping down for ever. However benign a dictatorship, some generation down the line will rebel. So somebody, centuries ago, had worked out how to keep the lid screwed down tight. An old enough idea, never quite managed in practice. Before now. A government department that quietly and secretly takes control of society's lowest stratum. Criminals and radical insurgents actually working for the very people whose existence they threaten.

Quinn could feel his energistic power starting to boil up. His thoughts were so hot with fury he could barely contain the power. 'Gotta keep it in,' he spat through clenched teeth. One mistake now, and they'd have him. 'Got to.' He pummelled his hands against his head, the shock of the craziness helping to bring himself back under control. Deep breath, and he glanced out of the cab's window. Uptown's layout was second nature, though he'd rarely experienced it from an elevated road before, much less a cab. They'd be taking the down ramp soon, angling in to Macmillan Station. Minutes only.

His breathing evened out, though he was still outraged. The sect, the awesome gospel he'd given his very life to, was being used as the front of some ultra-spook department. No wonder Banneth and Vientus could fix for an acolyte's bail with the cops; they were the fucking cops. Anyone with the slightest potential for danger was sucked in by the sect. And if they couldn't be cowed into dumb obedience and neutralized that way, then they were thrown to the cops and given an Involuntary Transportee sentence.

'That was me,' he whispered in pride. 'Banneth couldn't subdue me. Not even with all that shit she can do to bodies. Not *me*!' So the cops had been told about the persona-sequestrator nanonics (though there probably never had been any in the carton) he was bringing into the arcology. He'd always wondered who'd tipped them off, who the traitor was amongst his fellow devout.

Banneth. Always fucking Banneth.

The taxi drew up in front of one of the hundreds of vehicle entrance bays to Macmillan Station. Quinn knew there and then that he was in the deepest shit imaginable. He climbed out of the cab, and walked slowly into the main concourse.

The giant arena of corporate urban architecture was almost as empty as the streets outside. There were no arrivals. No streams of frantic passengers racing away from the tops of the escalators. Icons had evaporated from the informationals, which were hanging motionless in the air. Stalls had been folded up and abandoned by their sellrats. A few clumps of listless people stood under holo-screens, cases clutched tightly, staring up at the single red message that was repeated like a parallel mirror image everywhere you looked across the station: ALL VAC-TRAIN SERVICES TEMPORARILY SUS-PENDED. Even the scattering of ghosts Quinn could see were wandering aimlessly about their haunt, their expressions even more glum and bewildered than usual.

A group of cops were standing together outside a closed Burrow Burger outlet, drinking from plastic cups, talking quietly among themselves. The loud echo of his footsteps as he walked towards them stirred way too many memories inside Quinn's skull. It was the same concourse, same dark cop uniform. Then, there had been pounding feet, heart thudding hard in his chest. Screams as people dived out of his way, shouted warnings. Alarms blaring. Brilliant lightbursts. The pain of the nervejam shot.

'Excuse me, officer; could you tell me what's happening here? I have a connection to San Antonio in half an hour.' Quinn smiled

Erhard's twitchy smile at the cops. It must have been a good copy; most of them sneered. Finally, the failed acolyte had performed a useful service for God's Brother.

'Check the station bulletin,' one of them said. 'Christ's sake.'

'I, ah ha, I don't have a set of neural nanonics. I qualify for the company loan scheme next year.'

'OK . . . sir; what we have here is a vacuum breach. The tunnels were pressurizing, so the transit company had to activate the emergency seals. There's a repair crew down there now. Should be fixed in a day or so. Nothing to worry about.'

'Thank you.' Quinn walked back to the taxis.

I can't get out, he realized. God's Brother! The bastards have snared me here. Unless I can get to the other arcologies, His work will remain incomplete. The Night may be held off. And that cannot be allowed. They are thwarting the Light Bringer Himself!

It was frightening, the way he'd been lulled into a false sense of security. He, of all people. Ever suspicious, ever mistrustful. And he'd fallen into their trap. Yet they must be frightened of him to go to such elaborate lengths. Whoever they were.

He stood outside a taxi for a long time, working out where he should go. In the end, there wasn't a lot of choice. He was in Edmonton for one person. And only one person would be able to tell him who his real enemy was.

*

This was the part Billy-Joe didn't like. He was holding a laser pistol in one hand, there was a heavy-calibre magnetic carbine hanging on a strap round his left shoulder, fitted with a magazine of EE-tipped projectiles, a bag full of EE demolition charges on his right shoulder, codebuster and ELINT blocks on his belt, and a slim omniview band worn like a tiara on his forehead to boost his sight. It was enough hardware to start a war. Kicking the shit out of Courtney's punters was Billy-Joe's usual gig. Fast, nasty, and personal. None of this commando shit, where security systems would shoot back at him if anybody in the group screwed up.

But Quinn had wanted to stir things up in Edmonton, keep the cops busy and away from uptown. So Billy-Joe was sneaking down a lightless alley at half-past four in the morning with ten other acolytes from Duffy's coven.

'This is the place,' said the possessed man who was leading them, and stopped at a blank section of the alley wall.

He gave Billy-Joe the creeps, maybe even more than Quinn. One of the five possessed which Duffy had let into the bodies of snatched civilians. They all lived at the coven headquarters, treating the acolytes like shit and lording it up. The core of what Quinn promised was to be the army of the Night. Billy-Joe wasn't so sure about all that dark destiny stuff now, despite all he'd seen Quinn do. From where he was, it was just replacing one bunch of turds for another. The sect never changed; he always got dumped on no matter who was in charge.

The possessed rested his hands on the wall, tensing as if he was trying to push it over. He probably could, Billy-Joe acknowledged. And that was without energistic power. He was at least thirty centimetres taller than Billy-Joe, and must have weighed half as much again.

A door materialized in the wall. Made of wooden planks with big black iron bolts, and a sturdy circular handle. It opened silently, letting a wedge of bright light spill out into the foetid alley. There was a long hall of machinery on the other side; bulky turbine casings half submerged in the carbon-concrete floor. Billy-Joe was looking down on them from at least sixty metres; the door had opened onto a high metal gantry running round the inside.

'In you go,' the possessed man ordered. His bass voice rumbled along the alley, agitating the rats.

'I thought you weren't supposed to use your power,' Billy-Joe said. 'The cops know how to look for it now.'

'They can only detect those fireballs we use,' the possessed said glibly. 'Listen, kid; Quinn wants you to bugger up this water station, he was real keen for you to do that. That's why I'm here with you, so I can let you guys in quietly. Now, unless you'd like to go in by the front gate, this is the way to do it.'

Three of the water station's perimeter sensors perched along the top of the alley wall picked up the blasé assurance, relaying it to the intrigued supervisors of North America and Western Europe. The big possessed man had been leaving a trail of glitched processors ever since the little sabotage group emerged from the coven headquarters.

The ever-vigilant AI had datavised North America as soon as the first two were confirmed. A GISD covert tactical team had been dispatched to shadow them within seconds. But the trail had been so ridiculously blatant that North America had alerted Western Europe, and kept the tactical team a block away. Both of the B7 supervisors waited to see exactly where Billy-Joe and the others were heading.

'I can't let them damage the water station,' North America said. 'Edmonton's operating margins are becoming critical as it is, thanks to Quinn's vandalism.'

'I know,' Western Europe said. 'And our big friend has to know that as well. Use the snipers to target the waster scum, but don't let them shoot this new possessed. I've become very curious about his attitude.'

'Haven't we all.' North America issued his orders to the tactical team, who started to take up position inside the water station hall.

Internal sensors showed the sabotage group sneaking in through the new door, glancing from side to side to make sure no one was watching them, then stalking along the catwalk in an almost theatrical mime of caution. Nine of them went inside. Then the possessed man grabbed Billy-Joe's shoulder with a meaty hand, and pulled him back just as he was about to slip through. White fire spat from the fingertips of his free hand, soaring into the hall. A couple of balls struck an electrical junction panel, detonating loudly.

'What the fuck?' Billy-Joe gasped. He struggled uselessly in that implacable grip as his colleagues shouted in panic. The door slammed shut with a vociferous *bang*, and vanished. 'You bastard!' Billy-Joe screamed. He swung his laser pistol round, and fired at the chuckling possessed at point-blank range. Nothing happened. The weapon's electronics had crashed.

Several explosions sounded inside the hall, reverberating through the solid wall. Both supervisors watched with little interest as the tactical team eliminated the saboteurs. Their attention was focused almost entirely on the small, intense drama unravelling outside in the alley.

'Traitor!' Billy-Joe yelled recklessly. 'You killed them, they're dying in there.'

The possessed man's grip tightened, lifting Billy-Joe off the floor, and bringing their faces close together. 'Quinn's gonna chop you into rat bait,' Billy-Joe hissed in defiance.

'I spared you so you can deliver a message to him.'

'What? What . . . I—'

A palm slapped into Billy-Joe's cheek. It was hard enough to make bones rattle. A red veil flashed up over Billy-Joe's vision, like someone had shot the omniview band with a targeting laser. He groaned, tasting blood. 'Are you listening to me?' the possessed purred.

'Yeah,' Billy-Joe whimpered miserably.

'You tell Quinn Dexter that the friends of Carter McBride are coming for him. We're going to piss all over his crazy little schemes, then we're going to make him pay for what he's done. Understand? The friends of Carter McBride.'

'Who are you?'

'I just told you, dickhead.'

Billy-Joe was dropped to stumble among the slippery bags of trash and fleeing rats. A boot kicked his ass with terrible force, sending him flying. He hit the wall and rebounded, crying out at the pain stabbing through his buttocks.

'Now start running,' the possessed said. 'I want you out of here before the cops start hunting us.'

'Keep the tactical team away from them,' Western Europe said. A shout had almost escaped from his lips, the revelation was so astounding.

'Thank you for your insight,' North America said caustically. 'They'll stay clear.'

'My God, we've got an ally. A bona fide ally. A possessed at war with Quinn Dexter.'

'We won't have him for very long, I suspect.'

The big possessed man was almost chasing a terrified Billy-Joe along the alley. They emerged onto a broad patch of wasteland, cracked sheets of carbon-concrete with rows of severed metal support pillars sticking up all along the edges. Typical of that area on the edge of dome, dominated by warehouses and shabby industrial buildings.

'What are you talking about?' Western Europe demanded.

'Smart boy, this friend of Carter McBride. He's heading for the utility labyrinth.' North America datavised the file over.

Neural icons flowed together, producing a horrendously complex three-dimensional maze for Western Europe to examine. Pipes, tunnels, subway tracks, underground cargo roads, power conduits, they all seemed to interlock under that one section of the dome. A nexus where utility providers and transport industries joined together to supply Edmonton with the essentials its inhabitants expected; the busy powerhouse behind the public stations, efficient suppliers, and immaculate malls. The ground for kilometres around the water station was riddled with concrete warrens and bunkers, with a thousand entrances and ten thousand junctions.

'And those are just the ones marked on the file,' North America said bitterly. 'Christ knows what's actually down there.'

The possessed man and Billy-Joe stopped beside a giant metal trapdoor whose rectangular rim was marked out by thin lines of thistles. It hinged upwards, tearing the tangle of yellow tap roots with a loud ripping sound. Crumbs of soil dribbled down into the chasm revealed underneath. The top rungs of a rusty ladder were just visible. Billy-Joe started to climb down. The possessed man followed. As soon as his head was level with the ground, the trapdoor closed over him. For a second, the rim glowed purple, as if it had been haloed by neon tubes.

'I bet he just sealed it up,' North America said.

'Get the tactical team over there fast,' Western Europe said. 'Welding the edges isn't going to stop them cutting it open, not with their firepower.'

'They're on their way.'

'Can the AI track him down there?'

'It's already accessed all sensors and processors in the labyrinth. But that shaft they went down was an inspection and maintenance access for an old industrial heat-exchange coolant-fluid pipe. There's no active electronics in there, it hasn't been used for fifty years. They could come out anywhere.'

'Damn it. Flood the place with your bitek insects. Use every operative you have to physically cover the exits. We cannot let him escape.'

'Please. Don't tell me how to manage my assets. I have some experience in these matters.'

'I apologize,' Western Europe said. 'Damn, this is so frustrating. That possessed could be the real break we're looking for. He might manage to neutralize Dexter for us. We have to make contact.'

The tactical team reached the metal trapdoor, and promptly carved a circle out of it. One by one they hurried down the ladder.

'Billy-Joe would probably lead us direct to Dexter,' Western Europe said. 'If we could just find him when he comes out.'

'Maybe,' North America said. 'I'm not making any promises.'

*

Searching the labyrinth was a huge operation, though subtle enough to avoid the attention of the media. Police were diverted from their usual patrol routes to cover every entrance. Swarms of bitek spiders, bees, earwigs, and roaches were released into the maze of tunnels and passageways, their examination coordinated by North America's sub-sentient bitek processor array. Every employee working in the labyrinth was stopped and questioned as they came on and off shift. The AI assumed direct control of every mechanoid the labyrinth companies used, reassigning them to assist the search.

North America discovered several stim dens, enough deadbeats to populate a couple of condos, caches of weapons dating back decades, and enough illegally dumped toxic-waste canisters to warrant urgent official attention. There were also a large number of bodies, ranging from the freshly dumped to skeletons picked clean by the rats.

Of Billy-Joe and the friend of Carter McBride there was no sign.

*

'Carter McBride?' Incredulity swept all Quinn's anger away as the name finally registered. 'God's Brother! This possessed definitely said Carter McBride? You're sure?' Quinn could barely remember Carter's face, just one of the little brats running loose round Aberdale. Then, as he found out later, Laton had the boy murdered, making it look as though the Ivets had done it. The villagers had systematically set out to kill Quinn and his colleagues in revenge.

'Yes,' Billy-Joe said. His limbs wouldn't stop trembling. He expected Quinn to blast him into a lump of smoking meat when he returned to the Chatsworth. In fact, he'd been wondering if he should even bother returning to the old hotel at all. Five hours of shitting himself about the consequences as he slunk round diseased tunnels full of those fucking rats and worse. Expecting the cops to burst out of the walls any second. Getting mugged. Fucking mugged! Some bunch of deadbeats clubbing him over the head and making off with most of his gear. Not daring to shoot them in case the cops detected his weapon.

It had taken a long time before he trudged back to the Chatsworth. In the end he did it because he believed Quinn would ultimately win. Edmonton would fall into a state of demonic anarchy, ruled over by sect possessed. And when that happened, the dark Messiah would catch up with Billy-Joe. Explanations would have to be made. Punishment would follow that. So he came back. This way only one failure had to be accounted for.

'Shit,' Quinn breathed. 'Him! It's got to be him again.'

'Who?' Courtney asked.

'I don't know. He keeps . . . pissing me off. He's appeared a few times now, screwing with what I do. What else did he say?' he asked Billy-Joe.

'That he was going to wreck whatever you were doing.'

'Figures. Anything else?' The tone was unnervingly mild.

'You'll pay for what you've done. He said it, Quinn, not me. I swear.'

'I believe you, Billy-Joe. You've been obedient to Our Lord. I don't punish loyalty. So he said he'd make me pay, did he? How?'

'Just that he'd catch up with you. Didn't say nothing else.'

Quinn's robe changed, the fabric hardening around his limbs. 'I shall enjoy that encounter.'

'What are you going to do, Quinn?' Courtney asked.

'Shut up.' He stalked over to the window, and peered down through a gap in the heavy curtains. Cars and trucks flashed along the ramp five storeys below, curving down to street level. Fewer vehicles than usual, and the crowds on the sidewalk were noticeably thinner. But then Edmonton had been in a mild panic for most of the day, since the early morning commuters discovered the vac-trains were closed. Every Govcentral spokesperson in the arcology assured the reporters that there were no possessed loose. Nobody believed them. Things were falling apart across the domes. But not in the way Quinn intended.

I don't fucking believe this, he raged silently. Some kind of supercops know I'm here. I can't bring about the fall of true Night without the vac-trains. And now Heaven's own bastard vigilante is gunning for me. God's Brother, how could everything go so *wrong*? Even Banneth is diminished.

It's another of His tests. It must be. He is showing me the true path to Armageddon lies elsewhere. That as His Messiah I must not rest, not even to gorge my own serpent beast. But who the fuck is Carter's friend? If he knew Carter, then he must be someone from Lalonde, Aberdale itself. One of the men.

Although that conclusion hardly reduced the field of suspects. All the men at that sewer of a village hated him. He forced himself to be calm, to remember the few words the bastard had spoken back on Jesup asteroid when he fucked up the sacrifice ceremony.

'Remember this part?' Quinn's own mimicked face had taunted. So whoever it was had witnessed the sect ceremony before, then. And was from Aberdale.

The realization was so pleasurable it blessed Quinn's face with the kind of smile usually bought by orgasm. He turned from the window. 'Call everyone,' he told one of the nervous acolytes. 'We're going to tool up and march against Banneth. I want every one of my followers to accompany me.'

'Shit, we're going for her?' Courtney's eyes were shining with greed.

'Of course.'

'You promised I could watch.'

'You will.' It was the only way. The cops would only allow the vac-trains to run again if they thought they'd eliminated all the possessed in the arcology.

Quinn would bring them together, and do to them what Carter McBride's friend had done to the sabotage group. After that, time would become his most powerful weapon. Not even the supercops could keep the vac-trains closed for months when there were no further signs of possession.

'But first, I have something else which needs taking care of.'

Courtney did as she was told, and switched on a processor block, establishing a link with Edmonton's net. Quinn stood a couple of metres away, watching the little screen over her shoulder as the questor was launched into Govcentral's main citizens directory. It took eight minutes before the requested file expanded into the block's memory. He read down the information, and smiled victoriously. 'Her!' he said, and thrust the block towards Courtney and Billy-Joe, showing them the picture he'd found. 'I want her. You two go down to the vac-train station and wait. I don't give a fuck how long you have to stay there for, but the first vac-train out of here, you take it and you get over to Frankfurt. Find her, and bring her to me. Understand? I want her alive.'

*

A call from reception informed Louise that she had a delivery to accept. The house telephone was almost identical to the chunky black instruments back on Norfolk, except it had a bell rather than a shrill chime. Now she had neural nanonics, the whole thing seemed absurdly primitive. Presumably, for people who didn't have them as their sole planetary communication system, they were endearingly quaint. Part of the Ritz's old-world elegance.

Louise looked around the lobby as soon as the lift doors opened. Curious about what could have been sent to her. She was sure all the department stores had delivered. Andy Behoo was slouching against the reception desk under the suspicious gaze of the concierge. He jerked to attention when he saw Louise, his elbow nearly knocking over a vase of white freesias. She smiled politely. 'Hello, Andy.'

'Uh.' He stuck his hand out, holding a flek case. 'The Hyperpaedia questor's arrived. I thought I'd better bring it round myself to make sure you got it OK. I know it was important to you.'

The concierge was watching with considerable interest. He didn't get to see such naked adoration very often. Louise gestured towards the other end of the vaulted chamber. 'Thank you,' she said when Andy pressed the flek into her hand. 'That's very kind.'

'Part of the service.' He smiled broadly, crooked teeth on show.

Louise was rather stuck for what to say after that. 'How are you?'

'You know. The usual. Overworked, underpaid.'

'Well, you do a very good job at the shop. I'm grateful for the way you looked after me.'

'Ah.' Andy's world was suddenly very short on oxygen. But she'd come down by herself. That must mean her fiancé hadn't arrived yet. 'Um, Louise.'

'Yes?'

Her soft smile was wired directly into his brain's pleasure centre, shorting out his coordination. He knew he was making a right old balls-up of this. 'I was wondering. If you haven't got anything planned, that is. I mean, I'll understand if you have and all that. But

I thought, you know, you haven't been in London long and had a chance to see much of it. So if you like, I could take you out to dinner. This evening. Please.'

'Oh. That's really sweet of you. Where?'

She hadn't said no. Andy stared, his smile numbed into place. The most beautiful, classy, sexy girl in existence hadn't said no when he asked her for a date. 'Huh?'

'Where do you want to go for dinner?'

'Um, I thought the Lake Isle. It's not far, over in Covent Garden.' He'd asked Liscard for a two week advance on his pay, just in case Louise said yes (Liscard granted it on a four per cent interest rate). That way he could actually afford the Lake Isle. Probably. It had cost a lot more than he'd expected to reserve the table; and that deposit was non-refundable. But the other sellrats all said it was the right kind of place to take a girl like Louise.

'That sounds nice,' Louise said. 'What time?'

'Seven o'clock. If that's OK?'

'That's fine.' She gave him a light kiss on his cheek. 'I'll be here.'

Andy walked back with her to the waiting lift. There had been something about a dress code in the datavise when he reserved the table. He now had two and a quarter hours to find a dinner jacket. A clean one, that fitted. It didn't matter. A man who'd got himself a date with Louise Kavanagh could do anything. Louise pressed the button for her floor. 'You don't mind if I bring Genevieve, do you? I really can't leave her here by herself, I'm afraid.'

'Uh.' From nirvana to hell in half a second. 'No. That'll be lovely.'

*

'I don't want to spend an evening with *him*. He's all peculiar. And he fancies you. It's creepy.'

'Of course he fancies me,' Louise said with a grin. 'He wouldn't have asked me out otherwise.'

'You don't fancy him, do you?' a thoroughly shocked Genevieve asked. 'That would just be too hideous, Louise.'

Louise opened the wardrobe, and started to rifle through the dresses they'd managed to acquire on their shopping trips. 'No, I don't fancy him. And he's not peculiar. He's quite harmless.'

'I don't understand. If you don't fancy him, why did you say yes? We can go out by ourselves. Please, Louise. London isn't nearly as dangerous as Daddy thinks it is. I like it here. There's so much to do. We could go to one of the West End shows. They sell tickets at reception. I checked.'

Louise sighed and sat down on the bed. She patted the mattress, and Gen made a show of being reluctant to sit beside her. 'If you really, really don't want to go out with Andy for the evening, I'll cancel.'

'You're not going to kiss him or anything, are you?'

'No!' Louise laughed. 'Devil child. What a dreadful thing to say.'

'Then *why*?'

Louise stroked the dark hair from Gen's face, letting the flexitives ripple it over her ears. 'Because,' she said softly, 'I've never been asked out to dinner with a boy before. Not to a fancy restaurant where I can dress to kill. I don't suppose it'll ever happen again. Not even Joshua asked me out. Not that he could, of course. Not when we were at Cricklade.'

'Is he the baby's father?'

'Yes. Joshua's the father.'

Gen brightened. 'That means he's going to be my brother-in-law.'

'Yes. I suppose it does.'

'I like Joshua. It'll be stupendous having him living at Cricklade. He's such jolly fun.'

'Oh yeah. He's fun all right.' She closed her eyes, remembering the way his hands had caressed. Warm and skilful. It had been so long since she'd seen him. But he did promise . . . 'So, what do I tell Andy Behoo, then? Do we go, or do we stay here all night?'

'Can I wear my party dress, too?' Gen asked.

*

The scene playing out above the B7 sensenviron conference room table was the one involving the failed sabotage attempt against Edmonton's water station. It wasn't a particularly good image, the station's perimeter sensors were hardly commercial quality; but the two humanoid figures shouting at each other had enough colour and resolution to sketch in their individual features. Billy-Joe was being suspended several centimetres off the floor of the alley by the large possessed man. Their noses were almost touching. Then Billy-Joe was slapped hard, more words were exchanged. The two of them ran off down the squalid alley.

'We think we know who Carter McBride is,' Western Europe told the other supervisors as the recording ended. 'The AI found several references. He was the child of a colonist family on the same starship that took Quinn Dexter to Lalonde. According to the Lalonde Development Company files I accessed, the McBrides were also in the same village that Dexter was assigned to for his work-time.'

'A friend of Carter McBride,' Southern Africa mused. 'You mean this new possessed was on Lalonde?'

'Yes,' Western Europe said. 'And the whole Quallheim Counties trouble was originally thought to be an Ivet rebellion over the killing of some boy. The obvious conclusion is that it was Carter. That implies the possessed who blew the sabotage group in Edmonton has to be someone killed on Lalonde at around the same time.'

'So you're saying that this possessed person is out for revenge against Quinn Dexter?'

'Exactly,' North America said. 'We have a new ally.'

'Bullshit,' South Pacific said sharply. 'Just because the possessed have internal disputes, that doesn't make one faction friendly towards us. Suppose this new possessed does manage to eliminate Dexter? Do you really think he'll just conveniently vanish for us afterwards? I certainly don't. In any case, we're not exactly communicating with him, are we? You lost him, and this waster boy. What kind of amateurism is that?'

'I'd like to see you do better in that goddam labyrinth,' North America snapped.

'Given the speed at which this new development broke, I think the situation was handled as adroitly as possible,' Western Europe said. 'However, it does introduce some new factors which I believe warrant our consideration.'

'Such as?' North Pacific asked suspiciously.

'I believe it will force Dexter to abandon all his activities for a while. Unfortunately, this wretched little oik Billy-Joe couldn't be intercepted, so we must assume he returned to Dexter and passed on the message he was given. As a consequence, Dexter will know he has a possessed stalking him; and that after the sabotage mission was exposed, the authorities have confirmed there are possessed in Edmonton. If we're right about his reasons for being here, to wreck as much of the planet as possible; he'll have no choice but to ignore Banneth and either abandon or betray the remaining possessed in the arcology. Then he'll lie low until political pressure forces the North American Senate to reopen the vac-train lines again. Face it, we can't keep them shut for months unless there is a visible threat to rattle the public with. Time is on his side. We're already compromising ourselves with the actions we've taken to date.'

'Not a chance,' South Pacific blurted. She pointed a hostile finger at Western Europe. 'Very smooth. But I can see what you're angling for, and I say no. No way.'

'Angling for what?' Central America asked.

'He wants us to open Edmonton's vac-train routes.'

'Count me out,' Asian Pacific said quickly.

'Absolutely not,' East Asia agreed. 'We've got Dexter bottled up in one place. Keep him there. You'll just have to improve your surveillance techniques and track him down.'

'He's goddam invisible!' North America stormed. 'You saw what happened in Grand Central Station. There aren't any techniques to improve that can catch up with that kind of ability.'

'If we don't reopen the vac-train routes, then we'll be condemning Edmonton and everyone in it to possession,' Western Europe said. 'And very probably removal from this universe. Remember what happened to Ketton on Mortonridge. That's what they'll do to it. They can't survive here.'

'That outcome is certainly acceptable to me,' North Pacific said. 'We've discussed this before. Better to lose one arcology if that means saving the rest.'

'But we don't have to,' Western Europe insisted. 'Dexter becomes visible to us when he's moving. That's when he vulnerable.'

'He's not visible,' South Pacific said. 'We know he's moved simply by the destruction he leaves behind. I mean, shit, blowing up the Eiffel Tower! Face it, we can't catch him.'

'We have to make the attempt. It's the reason we exist, the only reason. If we cannot protect Earth from a single possessed when we have the opportunity, especially because of political cowardice, then we have failed.'

'I'm not buying into any of this *noblesse oblige* crap, I never did. That might be your heritage, but it certainly isn't mine. We formed B7 out of sheer bloody-minded self-interest. And you were a big part of that, don't forget. We exist to protect our own interests. Ninety-nine times out of a hundred, that means protecting Earth and looking out for its citizens. Well, bravo us. I don't begrudge them that expenditure. But this is not one of those benevolent times. This time we safeguard ourselves against possession, and especially against Quinn bloody Dexter. I'm sorry about the inhabitants, but Edmonton falls to this Night of his. Probably Paris and the others as well. Tough. We'll be safe, though.'

'I was wrong,' Western Europe said coldly. 'It's not political cowardice. You're frightened of him.'

'That's beneath contempt,' South Pacific sneered. 'I'm not going to open the vac-trains simply because you insult me.'

'I know that. I was just insulting you anyway. You deserve it.'

'Big deal. Don't tell me you're not making preparations to desert the sinking ship.'

'All of us are, as we all know. It would be foolish not to. But for me it's a last resort. To be perfectly honest, starting afresh on some new world holds little appeal. I suspect the same applies to the rest of you.'

The representations around the table remained silent.

'Exactly,' Western Europe said. 'We have to defeat Dexter on the ground. Our ground.'

'By letting Edmonton fall, we are defeating him,' Central America said. 'He'll vanish from the whole planet along with the arcology.'

'He won't. He's too smart to fall into that trap, and his agenda is different from the ordinary possessed. The vac-trains will be opened again no matter how determined you all are. It's only a matter of time. I say we should lure him out into a target ground of our own choosing.'

'He's already exterminated four of Banneth's acolytes in her own headquarters,' Military Intelligence said. 'We know he keeps going back there, yet we still haven't managed to kill the little bastard. I don't see how taking him to another arcology helps.'

'We can't change Banneth's environment now, that would be too blatant. Dexter would be warned off. But we can take her to a more suitable location for a strike.'

'You just said he'll sacrifice his vendetta against Banneth to achieve his greater objective,' Asian Pacific said. 'Do try to present a consistent argument, please.'

'I can get him out of Edmonton,' Western Europe insisted. 'The Kavanagh girls appearing at this stage will be an irresistible enigma to him. He'll have to follow them to find out what's happening. And they will be manoeuvred wherever I choose.'

'Well, you needn't try choosing my territory,' South Pacific said.

'I wouldn't dream of it. This requires efficiency and total cooperation. Qualities apparently beyond your ability to provide.'

'Lead him into your territory, then.'

'I intend to.'

'Then what are you whingeing about?'

'I don't want any interference. This requires finesse. If I initiate this operation, you stay out of it. No surprise presidential decrees wrecking my preparations. No media novas. We all know what we're capable of if we want to screw each other over. We've been at it long enough in our other arenas, but this is not the time for those sort of games.'

South Pacific looked from Western Europe to North America. 'You two do whatever you like. But you do it between yourselves. Your territories are now embargoed, along with Bombay and Johannesburg. Would you like to put a counter motion to the vote?'

'No,' Western Europe said. 'I have what I want.'

*

In the end Andy had to go back to Liscard and ask for a further advance. Four weeks' pay at seven and a half per cent interest! He deliberately didn't put a calculator program in primary mode, didn't want to know how long he was going to be shackled to Jude's Eworld to finance one date. But he could hardly ask Louise to pay for Genevieve. That would be cheap.

This time when he walked into the lobby of the Ritz, the concierge smiled pleasantly. Andy's dinner jacket had been loaned from someone he'd done repair work for a couple of months back; midnight black with a reasonably fashionable cut. The white dress shirt he'd borrowed from a fellow sellrat, along with the scarlet bow tie. His black shoes came from a neighbour. Even the silk handkerchief in his top pocket was his mother's. In fact the only thing he wore of his own were his boxer shorts. He could risk that, somehow he was pretty sure Louise wouldn't get to see them tonight.

Seven o'clock and she wasn't there. Six minutes past and he was debating if he should ask reception to call her room. Eight minutes, and he knew he'd been stood up. Hardly surprising.

The lift doors opened. Louise was wearing a full-length gown of deep-blue fabric, accessorized by a small rust-coloured waistcoat. No longer the breezy teenager who'd sauntered into Jude's Eworld needing assistance, her demeanour had gained twenty years. Andy didn't bother recording her image into a memory cell. No program could ever capture that combination of beauty and sophistication. His own recollection of this moment would stay with him throughout his entire life, he knew.

When he smiled at her, it was almost in sadness. 'Thank you for coming.'

Her answering expression was uncertain, sensing somehow just how important this had become for him. 'I'm flattered to be asked, Andy.' She prodded Genevieve.

'Thank you very much for letting me come along,' the little girl said. There was nothing in the voice that gave hint of duplicity.

'That's OK,' Andy said. 'Hey, you look great. Give us a twirl.'

Genevieve smiled in appreciation, and put her arms out to turn a complete circle. Her scarlet dress flapped about. A slim chain was fastened round her throat, its tarnished pendant bobbing against her neckline. Andy looked straight at Louise. 'Another five years and the boys won't know what hit them.'

'What do you mean?' Genevieve asked.

'He means you're very pretty,' Louise told her.

'Oh.' Genevieve blushed, but still managed to grin up at Andy.

Having her along wasn't so bad, after all, Andy found. In fact, she removed a lot of the tension that would probably have come from being alone with Louise for the whole evening. It wasn't boy–girl, one on one, with him desperate to impress with every word. That, he acknowledged, would have been an utter disaster.

He paid for the short taxi ride round to Covent Garden. The Lake Isle was one of a hundred restaurants in the area. An antique frontage enclosing a small bar, with a seating area at the back which was inexplicably large given the size of the neighbouring buildings, and too shiny to be genuinely old. As they stepped inside, Louise tapped Andy's shoulder. 'We're going Dutch tonight. No arguments. I brought Gen along, after all. It wouldn't be fair.'

The head waiter handed them over to an assistant waiter, who showed them to a table. Glancing round, Louise thought that they were possibly overdressed. But she couldn't turn down the chance to wear the blue dress, and Andy certainly didn't complain. If eyes had been hands, he would've crushed her.

'Did you find your friend?' he asked once they were seated.

'Not yet. That detective you recommended seemed quite good, though. Thank you.'

The wine list appeared. Louise looked wistfully at the Norfolk Tears, not quite believing the price. She let Andy choose; a dry white wine from the Jovian habitats, and sparkling mineral water for Gen.

'You can have one glass of wine,' Louise said when her sister started to look mutinous.

'Yes, Louise. Thank you, Louise.'

She stared the little girl down. Gen had been threatened with dire retribution if she stepped out of line during the meal.

It was a strange evening. Louise enjoyed it for the knowledge it gave her. What it would really be like to live in a vibrant arcology, and be asked out by boys. Dressing up. The taste of exotic food. Conversation that wasn't just about crops, relatives, and local events; but of the momentous things facing the Confederation, and how the navy was coping, and the latest news from the Mortonridge Liberation campaign. She had the freedom to say what she thought, based on her personal experience. To have an astonishing tale to tell, and be listened to.

While it was happening, she could actually forget how phoney it all was. That she could never actually be that girl about town, because she was due to be a mother. That Joshua had never seen her dressed like this. How life could never be lived without a care any more now the human race knew the beyond awaited. And Quinn Dexter, who stalked Earth's beautiful, awesome arcologies, ready to smash them into a trillion pieces.

Over dessert she found herself looking at Andy in what was near to envy. He could still have that life: chase girls, go out partying with his friends, attend university, earn his degree, write his programs, travel. Possibly. If the possessed didn't win.

'Are you OK?' Andy asked. He'd been in the middle of telling her about his plans to set up his own software house when he'd raised enough money. This month's dream.

'I'm sorry.' She put her hand on top of his, and squeezed softly. 'You probably won't believe the cliché, but this has been one of the nicest evenings of my whole life. I'm very grateful you asked me out.' The look of utter longing he gave her in reply nearly made her cry for what could never be. She caught their waiter's attention. 'Three glasses of Norfolk Tears, please.'

Genevieve stopped attacking her dessert bowl with a spoon in an attempt to scrape out the very last morsels of chocolate orange soufflé. She smiled in hopeful astonishment.

'Yes, you, too,' Louise laughed. To Andy she said: 'My treat. If you've never had it, you should. It's the only way to end an evening as perfect as this.'

The drinks arrived in slim crystal glasses on a silver tray. Louise sniffed gently at the bouquet. 'Wessex County, probably the Clayton estate.'

'Yes, miss,' the startled waiter said. 'That's right.'

The three of them raised their glasses. 'To living life, not wasting it,' Louise said.

They drank to that.

*

Louise received the datavise when they were in the taxi heading back to the Ritz; a purple telephone handset icon blinking silently at the corner of her vision (NAS2600 had thousands of symbols and sounds to choose from – but this was the most familiar). The sense of cosiness which the evening had engendered immediately shrank away. It couldn't be anything other than business.

Her neural nanonics acknowledged the call, and Ivanov Robson's icon tag replaced the purple telephone.

'I've got some good news for you,' the detective datavised. 'I've found Banneth.'

'Where?' Louise datavised back.

'She's currently in Edmonton.'

'Thank you.' That was one of the arcologies which the news had said was isolated. 'Do you have an eddress for her?'

'Certainly.' He datavised the file over. 'Louise, you may have a problem selling this story of yours to her. If that happens, please call me. I might be able to help.'

'Of course, and thank you again.'

The doorman gave Andy a dubious stare when they got back to the hotel. Louise saw him hesitate, full of his old uncertainties, and felt an uncomfortably strong stab of sympathy. 'Wait for me inside the lobby,' she told Genevieve.

Her sister smiled mischievously up at Andy, winked, then skipped inside.

Thankful no giggles had been audible, Louise took a deep breath. 'I have to go now, Andy.'

'Can I see you again?'

The amount of hope in his voice was awful. I should never have agreed to come out tonight, she thought, he was always going to misinterpret it. Yet for all his faults, he has a good heart. 'No, Andy, I'm sorry. I have this person I need to find, and I also have my fiancé. I shall be leaving Earth as soon as I can. It wouldn't be right, not for either of us. I don't want you to think this is something it isn't.'

'I see.' His head drooped down.

'You can kiss me goodnight, though,' she said shyly.

More in fear than joy, he pressed himself against her, touching his lips to hers. When they parted, her mouth crinkled up in compassion. 'I really did enjoy tonight, Andy. Thank you.'

'If it doesn't work with your fiancé, and you come back . . .' he began optimistically.

'You'll be top of my list. Promise.'

He watched her disappear through the doors, standing with his arms hanging limply at his side. The finality of it was appalling. For one mad moment he wanted to rush after her.

'You'll get over it, son,' the doorman said. 'Plenty more of them out there.'

'Not like her!' Andy shouted back.

The doorman shrugged, and smiled with infuriating smugness.

Andy turned fast, and walked away through the night-time crowds that were clogging the pavement. 'I kissed her, though,' he whispered. 'I really did.' He gave an incredulous little guffaw as the enormity of the contact finally registered. 'I kissed Louise Kavanagh.' Laughing broadly he set off towards Islington; he was far too broke to pay for a metro trip.

*

Louise waited until Genevieve was tucked up in bed before she called Banneth.

'Hello. You don't know me, but I'm Louise Kavanagh. I'm calling to warn you about someone called Quinn Dexter. Do you know him?'

'Fuck off.' The contact was cancelled.

Louise datavised Banneth's eddress to the room's net processor again. 'Look, this is important. I met Quinn Dexter on Norfolk, and he's going to—'

A red cross icon flashed persistently as the contact was cancelled again. The next time Louise datavised Banneth's eddress she got a filter program which requested her icon tag. She loaded it in, only to be told she wasn't on the receiver's approved reception list. 'Damnation!'

'What's the matter?' Genevieve peered over at her from the bed, duvet clutched round her shoulders.

'Banneth won't talk to me. I don't believe this, after everything we've been through to warn her. How . . . How *stupid*.'

'What are you going to do now?'

'Call Robson, I suppose.' She datavised the detective's eddress into the processor, wondering if the man was psychic. Not a bad thing for a private eye.

'Don't worry,' he told her. 'I'll come right over.'

*

The cocktail lounge was a mistake. Louise sat at a table by herself and ordered an orange juice while she waited for Ivanov Robson to arrive. The decor was as polished as the rest of the hotel, with honey-brown wooden panels and gold-framed mirrors covering the walls. Chandeliers kept it well lit, although it seemed shady, like a woodland glade. There were enough different bottles behind the rosewood bar to make the shelving look like an art exhibition.

Whether it was the wine and Norfolk Tears finally catching up with her, or just the superb cushioning of the deep leather chair, Louise suddenly started to feel warm and drowsy. It didn't help that she had to deflect seemingly dozens of offers from young (and not so young) men to buy her a drink and keep her company. She was worried that she was being too sharp when she turned them down. Whatever would Mother say?

One of the tailcoated waiters eventually came over. An ancient man with large white sidebums, who put her in mind of Mr

Butterworth. 'Are you sure you want to stay here, miss?' he asked kindly. 'There are quieter rooms available for residents.'

'I'll take care of her,' Ivanov Robson said.

'Of course, sir.' The waiter bowed, and backed away.

The giant detective's gaze slid along the line of men sitting up at the bar. All of them suddenly found something else of interest.

'No offence, Louise, but if you're going to wear that kind of dress, you really shouldn't be in a bar by yourself. Not even here. It sends out some seriously strong signals.' He sat down in the chair beside her, his bulk making the leather creak.

'Oh.' She looked down, only just realizing she was still in the blue dress she'd worn as a treat for Andy. 'I think I may have had too much to drink. I went out for a meal with a friend earlier on.'

'Indeed? I didn't think you were wearing it for my benefit. Though I would have been highly flattered. You look quite gorgeous.'

Louise blushed. 'Um . . . thank you.'

'You do know your neural nanonics have a suppression program to deal with a wee bit too much mouth–alcohol interaction, don't you?'

'No.'

'Well, they do. Perhaps if you were to put it into primary mode, this would be a more productive meeting.'

'Right.' She called up the control architecture, and hunted round for the suppressor program. It took a couple of minutes, but eventually the bar wasn't so warm. Deep breaths conjured up the kind of alertness she employed during difficult school exams.

A cut-crystal tumbler of whisky had appeared on the small table at Ivanov's side. He took a sip, watching her intently. 'Better now?'

'Yes. Thank you.' Though she was unhappy about the dress; people were still giving her the kind of looks Andy had, but without his endearing reticence.

'What happened with Banneth?' Ivanov asked.

'She cut me off. I couldn't tell her anything.'

'Hmm. Not entirely surprising. I accessed several facts about her during my investigation that indicate she's not an average citizen. The Edmonton police have amassed a rather large file on her activities. They believe she's involved with some kind of criminal organization, supplying illegal hormones and bitek products. Any mention of her former colleagues is bound to make her prickly. And you were right about this Dexter character, he was deported; the charge was aggravated resistance of arrest. The cops suspected he was a courier for Banneth.'

'Now what do I do?'

'You have two options. One, you can forget it and stay in London. We're safe for now. I keep my ear close to the ground, the possessed haven't appeared here yet.'

'I can't. Please don't ask why, but I have to give Banneth a proper warning. I didn't come all this way to be thwarted by the last mile.'

'I understand. In that case, I reluctantly advise you to visit Edmonton. If you meet Banneth face to face she'll see you are neither a police entrapment agent, nor a nutcase. She'll take your warning seriously.'

'But Edmonton has been isolated.'

'Not any more.' He took a sip of whisky, watching her closely. 'The vac-trains have started running again. I guess the authorities have eliminated the possessed, or think they have.'

'Quinn Dexter will be there,' she said softly.

'I know. That's why I advised you to stay away before. However, if you're set on this, I'll accompany you and provide what protection I can. If he's as bad as you say he is, it won't amount to much. But it's better than nothing.'

'You'd do that?'

'You'll have to pay for it. But I include bodyguard services in my job description.'

It still wasn't over. Louise fought to hold back the fear she felt at the prospect of walking into an arcology where she was sure Quinn would visit. But dear Fletcher had been so adamant, and she'd promised. 'Do you know where Banneth is?'

'Yes. I have a contact in the Edmonton police who's keeping me informed. If you decide you want to do this, we can go straight to her. You deliver your message, and we walk out. I doubt that'll take more than ten minutes. We could be back here in London in less than five hours.'

'I can't leave Gen. Not even for that.'

'I'm sure the hotel can arrange for someone to look after her tonight.'

'You don't understand. She's my responsibility; Gen and I are all that's left of our home, our family, maybe even our whole planet. I can't put her in any more danger. She's only twelve years old.'

'The danger is the same here as it is in Edmonton,' he said levelly.

'No, it isn't. Just being in the same arcology as Banneth is dangerous. Govcentral should never have opened the vac-trains to Edmonton again.'

'I can get my hands on the kind of weapon which the Liberation army is using on Mortonridge. They're proven against the possessed. That puts the odds back in our favour.'

She gave him a long look, puzzled by his attitude. 'It's like you want me to go.'

'All I'm doing is explaining the options to you, Louise. We agreed before that I know most of the ground rules in this arena, didn't we. This kind of mission is well inside my expertise.'

Maybe it was his sheer presence, or just his intimidating size, but Louise certainly felt a lot safer with the detective around. And everything he said did sound plausible.

She propped her forehead up against a hand, surprised to find she was perspiring. 'If we go, and I don't like what we find at Banneth's home, then I'm not going in to meet her.'

Ivanov smiled gently. 'If it's so bad that even you can see it's wrong, I won't let you go in.'

Louise nodded slowly. 'All right. I'll go and fetch Gen. Can you book us some tickets?'

'Sure. There's a vac-train in thirty minutes. We can be at King's Cross by then.'

She climbed to her feet, dismayed at how tired she'd become.

'Oh, and Louise? Appropriate clothing, please.'

*

The AI picked up the deluge of tell-tale glitches a few seconds before frantic citizens started to bombard Edmonton's police with emergency datavises about the army of the dead that had risen to march through the centre of the dome. It was mid-afternoon, and the sun shone down brightly from an admirable storm-free sky, illuminating the scene perfectly. Cars and metro buses performed emergency braking manoeuvres as their motors jammed and power cells failed. Their occupants spilled out, sprinting away from the advancing possessed and sect acolytes. Pedestrians hammered against closed doors, desperate for admission.

Quinn had spent most of the afternoon carefully positioning his minions along the four main roads leading to the sect's headquarters. Ordinary acolytes were easy, dividing them into pairs or threes, designating cafés and shops where they should wait, keeping their weapons out of sight in bags or backpacks. The possessed were more difficult; he had to identify deserted offices or empty ground-floor apartments for them. A couple of non-possessed acolytes who'd been given basic didactic electronics courses would break in and deactivate any processors they found, leaving it safe for the possessed to wait inside. It had taken two hours to get everyone into position. None of them complained, at least not to his face. They all accepted that it was part of some grand strategy to bring about his Night. The only thing standing in their way, he told them, was the sect headquarters and the traitors inside.

With every possessed in Edmonton (except one, Quinn thought glumly) assembled, Quinn had given the order to advance. If the supercops were as good as he suspected, then the response would be swift and effective. None of the possessed, and few acolytes, would survive.

Quinn walked the first few paces with his small doomed army as they flooded out into the streets, pulling out their weapons and taking on a variety of gruesome appearances. Once everyone was committed, he discreetly slipped away into the ghost realm.

Those civilians lucky enough to be behind the possessed when they emerged slowed their retreat and glanced nervously over their shoulders. The more commercially minded among them contacted local media offices, and began to relay sensevises. Anyone receiving the show was presented with an astonishing display of defiance; the deliberate flaunting of a prowess which even the possessed could never truly own. A magnificent final charade, blowing their cover in a single grand *fuck you* gesture. Entire offices of editorial staff froze in slack-jawed amazement at what they were witnessing.

The marchers closed swiftly on the unexceptional fifty-storey skyscraper. There were over a hundred in each of the groups, spearheaded by the possessed. Elaborate, archaic warrior costumes sparked and flashed, ripe with energistic power. Whenever they passed the pillars supporting elevated roads the air seethed with wrestling coils of miniature lightning bolts, grounding out through the metal amid spumes of molten droplets. Following close behind their silent deadly leaders, the bulk of each group was made up by the non-possessed acolytes; striding along blithely, weighed down by the largest pieces of weapons hardware the covens had stashed away in their secret armouries.

None of them paid any attention to the whimpering civilians scampering out of their way, they were focused on the skyscraper alone. Vehicles littering the street ahead of them flared electric-blue before bursting apart into a sleet of black granules. The army of the damned walked through the smouldering wreckage. Again, it was all panache. Show time.

To the majority of Edmonton's citizens, the skyscraper that was the centre of their wrath was just a modest, ordinary building divided into standard commercial and residential sections. The police knew different, as did most of the locals. Rumours of the sect presence inside began to filter back to the media anchors. But by then professional rover reporters were on the scene, watching the police seal off the area, and armed squads take up position.

Sixty per cent of Earth's population were now on-line, waiting for the shoot-out. The greatest audience in history.

Inside the sect headquarters, the senior acolytes broke open the armoury, and began handing out heavy-calibre chemical-projectile rifles and machine-guns to the acolytes. There was little panic, the beleaguered sect members were almost glad they had a tangible enemy at last. Banneth herself supervised setting up their defences, first establishing a ring of snipers peeking through the skyscraper's windows then consolidating their heavier firepower around the convoluted barriers inside.

She hurried round all of them, issuing orders and offering encouragement – never threats, not now. Quinn and the possessed had become the new fear-figures. It was interesting that they had returned to her. After all Quinn had done to fill them with doubt and mistrust, the random tortures and deaths he had silently enacted throughout the headquarters had come to nothing in the end. They still believed that she was the stronger of the two.

You realize this is probably a diversion, don't you? she asked. **He's most likely planning to snatch me or kill me in the battle.**

Possibly, Western Europe replied equably. **Personally, I believe this**

pathetic conflict he's staging is purely a case of collateral slaughter while he achieves his real goal: escaping from our grasp.

Thanks. That makes me feel a lot better.

Frightened? You?

Wouldn't you be?

If I was physically in your position, no doubt I would, yes. But I'm not, am I?

Don't give me that natural superiority crap.

I apologize.

Very magnanimous. Does that mean you've got the SD platforms zeroed in on me?

I'm afraid so, yes. Again, I doubt if we'll have to use them. Quinn won't reveal himself, not today.

Banneth took a look along the familiar darkened corridors of the headquarters as she made her way back to her own rooms. On her orders, they were lit with candles and crude chemical batteries powering low-voltage halogen bulbs – technology the possessed would be unable to glitch without considerable effort. Not that it particularly matters, she thought, we're not protecting anything we can salvage. After this, the headquarters would be no more. All her acolytes were doing was fighting a delaying action until the police and B7 eliminated Quinn's ersatz invasion. But then, the sect was nothing more than a B7 creation anyway. A convenient umbrella for them and her.

She walked through the temple, giving it a nostalgic look. The first rocket hit the skyscraper; a light EE-tipped anti-armour missile. Duffy fired it – Quinn had given him the honour of opening the fighting as a reward for unswerving loyalty to the cause of Night. The explosion sent shock waves yammering through the skyscraper's structure, blowing out a huge crater on the northern corner and shattering hundreds of surrounding windows. Huge lumps of rubble cascaded down onto the street to smash apart in front of the possessed. The surviving snipers inside picked themselves up, and opened fire.

*

The vac-train carriage had seating for a hundred. Louise, Genevieve, and Ivanov Robson were the only people using it. In fact, Louise had only seen a dozen or so people milling about on the platform at

King's Cross when they got on. She wasn't sure if they were passengers or station staff.

Despite her growing uncertainty, and Gen's sulky resentment, she'd followed the private detective in through the airlock door. Even now there was something about him that reassured her. More than just his physical size, he had a self-confidence greater than Joshua's. Which was saying a lot. She settled back with dreamy thoughts of her fiancé filling her mind. Although the seats were worn, they were comfortable; and her alcohol-suppressor program was off. Joshua had such a warm smile, she remembered. It would be so nice to have it shine on her again.

'I love you, and I'm coming back for you.' His words. Spoken to her when they were naked and alone, their bodies clinging together. A promise that could be nothing but totally honest.

I *will* find him again, despite all this horrid mess.

Her news hound program alerted her to the situation developing in Edmonton. She went through Time Universe to access a sensevise of the fight. And there she was, crouched behind one of the abandoned buses, peering cautiously round the front at the crazy army marching along the street. Dazzling white fireballs were pumping up from a dozen upstretched hands, smacking into the skyscraper. Flames were roaring out of windows and missile craters all the way up the first eight or nine storeys. Heavy-calibre guns were firing down in retaliation, pummelling the carbon-concrete sidewalk with small intense topaz explosions. Several bodies were scattered along the street, clothes still smouldering from beam-weapon scorches.

Figures began to race past the bus. Police in dark-grey armour suits, hauling even larger automatic guns than those in use up ahead. Their movements were arachnid, scuttling from cover to cover. They began to fire, the discharge from their weapons a continuous howl ripping into the delicate tissue of her inner ear. She started, hands halfway to her ears before the reporter's audio-limiter program cut in. Then she was ducking down as multiple explosions ploughed up the street. White fireballs flew directly overhead.

Louise reduced the sensevise to monitor function, bundling it away until it became a vivid real-time memory. She looked at Ivanov. 'Now what?' she asked. 'They won't let this train into Edmonton now, will they? Surely?'

'They ought to. Access the overview commentary. The possessed are concentrated in one area, and the police have them contained. They've got enough firepower concentrated on them to exterminate ten times as many as there are on the ground. Besides, if we were being diverted the train company would have told us immediately.'

Louise accessed the carriage's processor and requested a schedule update. It reported that they were going to arrive in Edmonton in forty-one minutes. 'That doesn't make any sense. The authorities were paranoid about outbreaks before.'

'It's politics. Edmonton is trying to prove they don't have a problem with the possessed; that they're on top of the situation.'

'But—'

'I know. They should have waited until after this fight is over before any grand announcements. Being premature with the good news is hardly new for Govcentral. As soon as the Edmonton isolation was announced, a lot of highly connected lobbyists will have been called in to pressure the President's office and sympathetic senators to have the vac-train lines reopened. If Edmonton is taken out of the global economic loop, all the companies in the arcology will start to fall behind their competitors; and an entire arcology is a huge market for outside companies to sell into – that's a factor, too.'

'They're endangering people because of money?' Louise asked in astonishment. 'That's awful.'

'Welcome to Earth.'

'Don't they understand what'll happen if the possessed get into other arcologies?'

'Of course they do. Now the possessed have been exposed in Edmonton, there'll be an equal amount of pressure applied to close the vac-trains down again. Action and reaction, Louise.'

'You mean we might not get out after we arrive?'

'We will. There'll be enough time. I promised you: back home again in five hours. Remember?'

She glanced over at Gen, who was sleeping, curled up in the seat, her small face scowling even as she dreamed. 'I remember.' Not that there was much she could do about her worries now. The train was going to stop in the arcology. She hadn't felt this out of control since that first mad ride away from Cricklade the day Quinn Dexter appeared.

*

That the fight around the skyscraper would be uneven was never in doubt. Even so, the effectiveness of the police tactical team was impressive. Heavy-calibre portable weapons deployed by the front line were backed up by X-ray lasers from the rear support groups, far enough back to resist glitching by the possessed. As a consequence, very few possessed actually made it into the skyscraper; and judging by the amount of gunfire coming from inside, the sect members weren't exactly a pushover. That was where the commercial sensevise coverage ended. B7 immediately switched to the surviving sensors in the headquarters, watching nervous, indistinct figures creeping along dark smoke-filled corridors. One of them walked over a grid with twenty thousand volts running through it. Their body ignited into a pillar of flame hot enough to melt the concrete corridor around it.

'Well, that's a neat trick,' Northern Europe said. 'What kind of energy level is that, do you think?'

'Could be total chemical conversion,' Central America suggested. 'It can't be a direct mass–energy reaction. That would eliminate the entire arcology.'

'Hardly relevant,' South Pacific said.

'On the contrary,' Central America said. 'The more we learn of their ability, the closer we come to defeating them.'

'You can hardly classify their death throes as part of their ability.'

'All information is useful,' Western Europe said, deliberately bleeding a note of snobbery into his representation's voice. 'We wouldn't have had this kind of success without it.'

'Success?' South Pacific pointed at the image above the conference table. The possessed had burnt out, leaving a human sculpture of ash standing amid the drizzle of molten carbon-concrete. It pitched over, disintegrating into a slush of grey flakes. 'That's a success, Edmonton under siege from the possessed? May we please be preserved from your failures.'

'By studying the data on Dexter we determined his likely course of action. I told you he'd betray the remaining possessed to us. This merely proves I was right all along.'

'And Edmonton is not under siege,' North America said. 'The police tactical teams have the possessed surrounded.'

'Wrong,' South Pacific said. 'That friend of Carter McBride won't be among this group. You haven't got him surrounded.'

'He is not a threat to anyone other than Dexter,' Western Europe said.

'Only in your book. As far as I'm concerned, nothing has changed. One invisible possessed and one elusive possessed are running round loose. Your territories remain embargoed.'

'Thank Heaven for that. We all know what would happen to Edmonton if you had any say in events over here.'

'At least with my way only one arcology suffers. I can't believe you're willing to expose another to Dexter.'

'You can't win at this level without taking risks. And I do intend to win. Dexter is the epitome of all we have fought against these last five hundred years. He is the yobbish anarchy that B7 has successfully banished from this world. I'll not have him return. The investment in blood and money it has cost us must be honoured.'

'You sound like a third-rate Shakespearean king the night before battle. Damn, and you accuse me of arrogance.'

*

Banneth walked back into her sanctum as the police tactical team searched through the rest of the sect headquarters for any possessed that might have survived the assault. She knew none had, but it wasn't her place to interfere. The North American supervisor had given the police commissioner instructions that she was to be left alone, along with her suite of rooms. Senior officers had taken up position outside the doors to enforce the order in case any of the tactical team turned bolshie. People hyped high on adrenalin after a fight were liable to have a healthy disregard for authority, especially where the possessed were concerned.

The rest of the sect, those that had survived, weren't so fortunate. Police officers, while sympathetic to their erstwhile allies, were disarming and cuffing them. The temple was proving a popular viewing point for awed, angry officers. Quinn's last two victims were still in there on show. And when the forensic crew got to work they'd find an awful lot of DNA samples around the altar and in the drains. It was going to be a busy night down at Edmonton's Justice Hall.

The sanctum was a wreck. A couple of lights had survived when the ceiling cracked open, hanging on their cables, spinning slowly round and round. Clear fluid from the life-support canisters sloshed over Banneth's shoes, several centimetres deep and tinged with blood. Most of the canisters had been smashed, spilling their bizarre occupants onto the floor. Their tubules had invariably torn out, depriving them of the vital chemicals she was feeding into them, leaving the poor creatures to flop their limbs (those that had any) feebly until death overcame them. The organs and appendages that were simply being suspended until she found a use for them were ruined.

Banneth picked up the oil painting of Mary Shelley, and tipped the broken glass out of its frame. Life-support fluid had discoloured the canvas quite badly. She stared at the author's drawn face for a moment, then sighed and cast the painting aside. 'How poetic,' she said quietly. Her suspicions about the sanctum were strengthening. There was an awful lot of damage considering it hadn't taken a direct hit. If the structural quakes and blast waves from the explosions had been this powerful they ought to have brought down the entire skyscraper.

Louise Kavanagh has arrived, Western Europe said. **Please stick to the scenario we worked out.**

Sure. She knew her rebelliousness was coming through. Not that it mattered. She certainly couldn't evade the supervisors. That was the bargain she'd shaken on all those years ago. Not that she'd ever suspected it would come to this: a suicide bait. But when you sign in blood, you must expect the Devil to write the small print in his favour.

Go down to one of the lower floors, Western Europe said. **I don't want Louise to see your little dungeon of horrors. It's important she isn't upset by you.**

Banneth hesitated. Her legs quivered. A pointed reminder of what this particular affinity bond was capable of. If she refused, they would simply take her over and puppet her body.

OK, God's Brother, I'm doing it. Just don't expect me to smile and say thanks. She turned slowly, gazing carefully round the ruins. One last nostalgic look. A cool breeze drifted against her cheek, causing the dangling lights to sway as they spun. The door was shut.

Is something the matter? North America asked.

No, she said, then relented. They could pick up on her emotional state easily enough through affinity. **Possibly. I think he might be in here with me right now. I have the feeling I'm being watched. It's the spookiest thing.** She projected a starched ironic smile.

Call out, Western Europe said excitedly. **Challenge him. Provoke him. Something. See if you can get him to materialize. We only need a second.**

'Quinn? Is that you, my little darling? Are you here at last?' Banneth put out a hand and stroked the central table, fingers lingering on the straps. 'Have you come home to me? You're not afraid, are you, my darling? I made you better than that. Remember that beautiful pain that birthed you. I cleansed you of fear amid that pain so you could serve God's Brother properly. And you have, haven't you? How you've grown since I banished you. The very Messiah of darkness, now. That's what you claim, isn't it? But can you do what you claim, or have you become flawed? I can correct that, Quinn, I can make you whole again. Submit to me. Return to me, and I'll love you in that very special way. Our way. Just like before.' She held up the strap invitingly.

Quinn trembled in fury. He wanted to take her there and then. Every word she spoke, each mocking syllable teased out the memories of what she'd done to him. This room had been the place where the real violations had been performed. His screaming and her silken laughter mingling long into the nights. The urge to reverse those acts made his serpent beast howl in torment as he denied himself. *She* should be the one bound by those straps. He should be the one standing over the table.

His hands reached out to her, ready to caress and crush.

An annoyed frown creased her face, verging on petulance. 'It's no good,' she muttered. 'The little prick can't hear me.'

Quinn leaned closer, puzzled. It was as though she was talking to someone.

Banneth came to a decision, and strode out of the door. Anger evident in every tense muscle and furious grimace. Her mind tone was sullen, and extremely fearful. It was similar to those Quinn had perceived in his sacrificial victims. He followed her as she stomped through the headquarters. Two police officers fell in beside her, escorting her down the stairs. More proof of the treachery she had indulged in at the expense of God's Brother. As if he needed more.

They came to an office below the headquarters edifice itself. The place belonged to an alcohol wholesaler, one of the sect's commercial fronts. And Quinn received the biggest shock of all since he'd returned to Earth. The Kavanagh sisters were there, waiting for Banneth.

*

Louise was amazed to find they'd arrived at the skyscraper featured on the news sensevise. It did make her wonder about Ivanov Robson, though. For a start, there was something very odd about the way he was always right about things. And then there was this 'contact' he had inside the Edmonton police division. She could believe that he'd worked with police departments before, and no doubt a few favours were owed on both sides. But to pass so effortlessly through the cordon of armed police around the skyscraper was hard to credit.

Nonetheless, the major in charge of the tactical squad had been waiting to greet them when their taxi pulled up fifty metres short from the rear of the buzzing crowd. Now it was safe, thousands of Edmonton's ordinary citizens had flocked in to soak up whatever was left of the drama. Rover reporters and several district councillors formed the inner wall, pressing against the barriers, shouting and datavising the line of implacable police for snatches of information, or pleading to be allowed just that fraction closer than their rivals.

Six tactical team officers fell in around Louise's party and cleared their way through the tightly packed crowd. Inside the barriers, the fire department was doing most of the work. Hoses snaked away from large tenders, trailing down from mechanoids that were scampering across the vertical walls of the skyscraper, extinguishing the last of the fires. The police were concerned only in bundling the surviving combatants from both sides into secure trucks so they could be driven away to the Justice Hall. One of them, a girl younger than Louise, was sobbing hysterically, kicking and bucking violently as four officers carried her to a waiting truck. She screamed, 'The Messiah lives! His Night will claim you all!' as they flung her unceremoniously inside.

Just as they were going in through the main entrance, three fully grown pigs rampaged out, squealing and grunting as they raced down the broken stairs towards the street. Sweating, angry officers chased after them. Louise simply stood aside and let them go past; it was one of today's milder insanities.

The Major led them inside. Fire and explosions had wrecked the lobby. Water and foam from the fire mechanoids was pooling underfoot. Lighting came from temporary rigs set up at strategic corners. None of the lifts or escalators were working. They went up four flights of stairs before being shown into some kind of office that had escaped any serious damage. Despite the fires, Louise felt chilly. The Major left them, and a strange-looking woman walked in.

At first Louise wasn't entirely sure she was a woman. Her jaw was strong enough to be male, although her feminine figure countered the argument. And the way she walked, straightforward easy strides, that was masculine, too. The oddest feature were her eyes with their pink irises. When she looked at Louise, there was no hint of what she was thinking.

'I don't know who you people are,' Banneth said. 'But you must have a lot of clout to get in here right now.' She stared at Genevieve. For the first time her face betrayed an emotion. 'Very strange,' she muttered in puzzlement.

'I have contacts,' Ivanov said modestly.

'I'm sure you do.'

'My name is Louise Kavanagh. I called you earlier, about Quinn Dexter. Do you remember?'

'Yes. I remember.'

'I think he may have done all this, or at least sent people to do it. He told me he was coming back to Earth to get you. I did try and warn you.'

Banneth's gaze remained on Genevieve, who was fingering her pendant. 'So you did. My mistake for not listening. Although, as you can imagine, I have good reason to be sceptical. Quinn was deported. I didn't expect to see him again.'

'He really hated you. What did you do to him?'

'We had several disagreements. As you might have guessed, my occupation is outside the mainstream. I earn a living by supplying certain items to people, which cannot be bought through normal commercial channels. It's an activity which has brought me into conflict with the police on several occasions. Dear Quinn was one of my couriers. And he rather stupidly got caught. That was the reason he was deported, in fact. I expect he blames me for his sentence. I didn't contribute to his defence; at the time I was using my contacts to protect myself. His incompetence landed me in a very difficult legal situation. So you see, the antipathy is mutual.'

'I'm sure of it,' Louise said. 'But he's a possessed now, one of the strongest. That makes him very dangerous, especially to you.'

Banneth gestured round. 'I'm beginning to appreciate that. Though I'm curious, why are you, someone I've never met before, interested in saving me? I guarantee, I really am someone a nice girl like you wouldn't want to meet.'

Louise was beginning to ask herself the same thing. Banneth was nothing like the image in her mind; she'd been expecting a slightly older version of herself: innocent and bewildered. Not this cold, criminal woman, whose every gesture and syllable was rich with disdain. 'He was obsessed with you, and people need to be warned what he's capable of. I'm frightened that once he's murdered you, he'll do to Earth what he did to Norfolk. That was my home planet, you see.'

'How very noble and unselfish of you, Louise. Behaviour no one on this planet is remotely accustomed to. Not in this day and age.' She arched an eyebrow at Ivanov. 'So what do you suggest I do now?'

'I'm not sure,' Louise said. 'I just had to deliver the warning, I promised myself that. I didn't really think about afterwards. Can you convince the police to give you a twenty-four-hour guard?'

'I expect that if I told them a possessed was hunting me, they'd probably show Quinn where I was, and laugh a lot while they were doing it. I've used up every contact and legal resource I had merely to avoid getting arrested for the crime of being in the same building he attacked.'

'Then you'll have to leave.'

'I can see this means a lot to you. But the police have killed every possessed involved in the attack. I wouldn't worry. Quinn Dexter's soul is back where it belongs, suffering badly in the beyond.'

'You don't know that,' Louise insisted. 'If any of them survived, it'll be him. At least leave here until the police confirm there are no more possessed left in Edmonton. If they didn't get him, he'll come after you again. I know he will. He told me. Killing you is a filthy obsession with him.'

Banneth nodded. Reluctantly, Louise considered, as if there was something demeaning in taking advice from her. What horrible snobbery. To think of everything I risked in coming to her aid, not to mention the money it's cost. Not even Fletcher would have bothered if he'd known how awful she is.

'I suppose there's no harm in playing it safe,' Banneth said. 'Unfortunately, Quinn knows all my associates and safe houses here in the arcology.' She paused. 'The vac-trains are open to half of Europe and most of North America; though the rest of the world seems more sceptical about Edmonton's assurances. Good for them.'

'We're going back to London this evening,' Ivanov Robson said. 'Do you know anyone there you can stay with?'

'Like you, I have contacts.'

'OK, I can arrange for a police tactical team to escort us back to the station. But once we get to London, you're on your own.'

Banneth gave an indifferent shrug.

*

Quinn watched the entire scene play out, resisting the impulse to interfere at Banneth's petty lies. He was captivated, not just by what was said, but the emotional content behind the words. Louise backed every word she spoke with intense fervour. Banneth was her usual serene, egotistical self, a state she shared with the husky private detective (which made Quinn highly suspicious of him). It was pure theatre. It had to be. Yet it must be a paradox. Louise Kavanagh had no script, no coaching; she believed what she was saying, that she had some higher mission to save Banneth from him. That couldn't be forged. The entire thing must have been orchestrated by the supercops.

For whose benefit? That was the really unnerving part.

There was no possible way Louise could have found Banneth unless the High Magus wanted her to. The girl must have been steered here by the supercops for one reason, to get Banneth out of Edmonton. Yet Banneth was part of the supercop set-up, she didn't need Louise to tell her where to go. It didn't make any sense.

One thing he couldn't ignore, the vac-trains were running again. Though that might be the trap, the reason for this charade. To snare him on the ocean bed halfway between continents; even he couldn't get out of that. But how would they know if he was on board a specific train?

He followed the group out of the office and down the stairs, not really paying much attention. His mind was savaging the possibilities. If they could detect me when I'm in this realm, they would have done everything they could to destroy me. That means they can't. So this must be a ploy to lure me out. The supercops know I want Banneth, so they're using her as bait. The vac-train isn't the trap, wherever she goes in London is their kill arena. And that's where they'll be; this planet's strongest, most subtle line of defence against His Night.

Quinn smiled lustily, and increased the speed of his gliding walk through the ghost realm, determined not to let Louise and her party out of his sight. After so many false starts, the true Armageddon was beginning.

15

It was a foul job, but better than scouting round the starscrapers. Tolton and Dariat were driving a truck slowly over Valisk's grass plains in search of servitor bodies. Food was becoming a critical commodity within the enfeebled habitat. During Kiera's reign the possessed had simply helped themselves to existing supplies with little thought devoted to replenishing them. Then after plunging into the dark continuum the survivors had turned to butchering the wild terrestrial animals that had fallen into unconsciousness. Large cooking pits had been dug outside the northern endcap caverns, where the Starbridge tribes took charge of trussing the beasts on long poles to be roasted over the flames as if for a medieval banquet. It was a predictably monotonous diet of goat, sheep, and rabbits; but it was nourishing enough. None of the other lethargic survivors complained.

Now that operation was being accelerated. The animals were gradually slipping from their strange comas into death. Their carcasses had to be recovered and cooked before they started to decay. If it was hung in the coolest caverns, properly cured meat could be stored for several weeks and still remain eatable. Building up a stockpile of food was also a logical precaution to be undertaken in times of war. Rubra's regiment of descendants all knew about the visitor, and had been surreptitiously supplementing their armaments ever since. The remaining survivors hadn't been told.

Tolton wondered if that was why he and Dariat had been given this particular task, so he wouldn't have much contact with the refugees occupying the caverns.

'Why should the personality distrust you?' Dariat asked as the street poet drove them along the side of a stream in one of the shallow valleys meandering through the southern grasslands. 'You're one of the real survivors of the possessed occupation. You've proved yourself as an asset as far as it's concerned.'

'Because of what I am; you know I'm on the side of the underclass, that's my nature. I might warn them.'

'Do you think warning them is helping them? They're in no fit state to put up any resistance if that thing comes back. You know damn well my illustrious relatives are the only ones who stand a chance of stopping it. Go ahead and tell the sick there's some kind of homicidal ice dragon stalking us, see how much you improve their morale. I don't want to preach homilies, but class distinction has been suspended for the duration. We're divided into effectives and dependants, now. That's all.'

'All right, damn it. But you can't keep them in ignorance for ever.'

'They won't be. If that thing ever gets inside, everyone's going to know about it.'

Tolton gripped the top of the steering-wheel with both hands, and slowed so he could watch Dariat's answer. 'You think it will come back?'

'The opinion is a resounding yes. It wanted something the first time, and all we did was make it mad at us. Even assuming it has the wackiest psychology possible, it'll come back. The only questions are: when? And: will it be alone?'

'Bloody hell.' Tolton twisted the throttle again, and sent the truck splashing through a shallow section of the stream. 'What about the signalling project? Can we call the Confederation yet?'

'No. There's still a team working on it, but most of my relatives are doing what they can to beef up the habitat defences.'

'We still have some?'

'Not many,' Dariat admitted.

Tolton saw a suspicious avocado-green lump amid the wispy tips of pink xenoc grass, and slowed the truck to a halt. The body of a large servitor lizard was lying curled up on the ground. A tegu, geneered for agronomy maintenance, it measured one and a half metres from nose to tail, with long rake-like fingers on its hands. There were hundreds of them in Valisk, patrolling the streams where they were employed to clear jams of dead grass and twigs that built up along rocky snags.

Dariat stood and watched as his friend bent over and gingerly touched the creature's flanks.

'I can't make out if it's alive or not,' Tolton complained.

'It's dead,' Dariat told him. 'There is no life-energy left in the body.'

'You can tell that?'

'Yeah. It's like a little internal glow; all living things have it.'

'Hell. You can see that?'

'It's similar to seeing, yes. I guess my brain just interprets it as light.'

'You haven't got a brain. You're just a ghost. A whole bunch of thoughts strung together.'

'There's more to me than that, if you don't mind. I'm a naked soul.'

'OK, there's no need to get touchy about it.' Tolton grinned. 'Touchy. Get it? A ghost, touchy.'

'I hope your poetry is better than your humour. After all, you're the one that's got to pick it up.' His translucent foot nudged the dead lizard.

Tolton's grin crumpled. 'Bugger.' He went round to the back of the truck and lowered the tailgate. There were already three dead servitor chimps lying on the metal floor. 'I didn't mind the goats so much, but this is like cannibalism,' he grumbled.

'Monkeys were a delicacy in several pre-industrial societies back on Earth.'

'No wonder they all died out, then; their kids ran off to the city and lived happily ever after on Chinese takeaways.' He put his hands under the lizard's body, disgruntled by the dry-slippery feel of the scales and the way they shifted so easily over protuberant bones. Muttering about the truck's lack of a winch, he started to drag the body over to the tailgate. The lizard was quite a weight, needing several stages to haul it up the steep ramp. Tolton was flushed by the time he finally skewed it over the chimps. He jumped down, and lifted the tailgate back up, shoving the latches home.

'Good job,' Dariat said.

'Just as long as I don't have to butcher them, I don't care.'

'We should get back. That's a big load already.'

Tolton grunted in agreement. The trucks had been stripped down to the minimum number of systems: there were no governing processors, no power steering, no collision-alert radar, no impact-triggered seat webs. A power cell was wired directly to the wheel hub motors, with the throttle as the only control. Such an arrangement gave the vehicles a modicum of reliability, though even that was far from a hundred per cent. Switching them on was always a lottery. And if they had too much weight in the back they wouldn't work at all.

Dariat, the personality called. **The visitor is back, and it's not alone.**

Oh, Thoale. How many?

A couple of dozen, I think. Maybe more.

Once again, Dariat knew how much mental effort it took for the personality to focus on the approaching specks. Even then, he wasn't sure it was observing all of them. As before, pale streaks of turquoise and burgundy were fluxing within the strands of the dusky nebula outside. A scattering of wan grey dots swished between the ragged strands, curving sharply at each turn, but always coming closer. Their movements were confusing, but even so the personality should have been able to track them.

Dariat looked through the truck's grimed windscreen. The northern endcap was thirty kilometres away, suddenly a huge distance across the rolling grasslands and scrub desert. It would take them at least forty minutes to get there, assuming the cloying blades of pink grass didn't get any thicker before they reached one of the rough tracks. And that was a long time to be alone in this continuum. Not that the caverns would offer much sanctuary.

It was ironic, Dariat thought, he who had managed to isolate himself for thirty years now wanted to surround himself with people. He could never forget that debilitating cold the visitor had inflicted on him last time. His soul was unprotected in this realm. If he was going to truly die, he preferred to do it in the company of his own kind. He turned to Tolton, making sure his lips were exaggerating his words. 'Does this thing go any faster?'

The street poet gave him a panicked glance. 'Why?'

'Because now would be a good time to find out.'

'The bastard's come back?'

'More than one.'

Tolton twisted the throttle urgently, nudging the speed up to over forty kilometres an hour. The wheel hub motors started making erratic buzzing sounds – normally they were completely silent. Dariat used affinity to watch the visitors' approach. The personality had activated the seven lasers and two masers emplaced around the rim of the counter-rotating spaceport. As before, there was no radar return from any of the visitors.

The first ones began their final dash from the shifting fringe of the nebula through the clear space to the habitat's shell. They were condensing the darkness around themselves now, twirling sharp horns of light in kaleidoscopic arcs. Optical sensors locked on, aligning the energy weapons on one of the giveaway distortion swirls. Nine intense energy beams pinioned the visitor. Its sole response was to spin faster, wriggling wildly along its trajectory as it plummeted in towards the shell. The radial spires of distorted luminescence flared brighter and higher. Then it was falling behind the tips of the starscrapers, beyond the weapons' elevation. They slid back to find another target. It, too, was unaffected by the energy strike.

The personality stopped firing. Anxiety spread like a mental virus among Rubra's descendants as they waited to see what the visitors would do next. The personal weapons they'd prepared were distributed and primed. Not that anyone held out much hope. If the spaceport lasers couldn't harm them, then rifles (however large the calibre) were going to be completely useless. Not that anybody refused them. Having a hefty chunk of destructive hardware you could grip in your hands was always a nice psychological boost.

*

The Orgathé led a swarm of its eager kith towards the giant living object, soaking up the blaze of heat which it threw away so casually. They had come to pre-empt the absorption that was the fate of all beings in the dark continuum, gorging on as much of its life-energy as they could before it reached the mélange. Once that happened, so many of the entities entombed within would be empowered to resurrection and individuality that the whole mélange would be loosened, possibly even breaking apart for a short while. But there would never be enough energy to return them all to the place from which they'd fallen. That privilege could only be granted to those who empowered themselves before the dispersal.

That was why it had called upon the others, the strongest of their kind, able to fly far and long from the mélange. Together they might successfully storm the object where one had failed. To be rewarded with enough energy to elevate themselves out of the dark continuum was worth any risk.

The Orgathé swooped closer. Huge waves of thought rippled through the layer of life-energy below the object's surface, focusing on it. Pillars of energy lashed out from the dead section at the far end; a kind unusable by the Orgathé. It closed its boundary against the flow, letting the power splash apart harmlessly. The pillars of energy vanished when it dived down close to the surface. Its kith were following it down, hungered by the abundant energy, crying victoriously among themselves.

Ahead now were the hollow spindles protruding from the object's midsection. The Orgathé increased its speed, hardening itself with a reckless expenditure of energy. It remembered the sheet of transparent matter it had landed on before. Easy to identify amid the thousands of other identical sheets inlaid along the length of the spindle, a dead section, drained of life-energy and heat. This time the Orgathé didn't slow down.

The window of Horner's Bar detonated inwards with a terrifyingly violent explosion. Craggy shards of crystal blasted into the bar, scything through the furniture. Frozen, ice-cloaked tables and chairs disintegrated into billowing clouds of glossy silvery fragments. Then the entire maelstrom reversed its flow, and howled out through the shattered window. The badly shredded main door into the vestibule buckled and collapsed, allowing the air to rush through.

Emergency pressure locks all across the twenty-fifth storey started to slide shut. They were mechanical systems, self-powered, activated by simple failsafe pressure sensors. The majority of them were unaffected by the malaise inflicted by the dark continuum. Only a minority of the starscraper's muscle membranes reacted to the potentially lethal development.

The personality concentrated hard, ensuring that the muscle membranes around the Djerba's lobby were shut, then tried to reach the floors immediately below that. Its thought routines encountered a tide of exhaustion that grew worse the further it inserted itself into the starscraper. Only the vaguest images from the twenty-fifth floor were available.

The Orgathé gripped the rim of the bar's window with several appendages, waiting until the gale subsided. Bottles detonated in mid-flight as they were swept across the room, their exotic liquor solidifying in weird bulbous shapes the instant they broke free of the glass. Anything which struck the Orgathé simply bounced off, gyrating away into the void outside. As soon as the roar of air began to ebb, it moved into the starscraper. The wall around the empty door simply burst apart as it went through.

Still there was no clear image of it as it moved along the vestibule, all the sensitive cells could discern before they died was a tumour of darker shadow within the lightless chamber. And now the habitat personality was having to divert its attention to the rest of the Orgathé swarm that were slamming their way through other starscraper windows. Emergency pressure locks and muscle membranes were closing throughout the deserted structures, desperately trying to contain the atmospheric breaches.

The Orgathé continued to surge forward into the starscraper, hunting round for concentrations of life-energy to consume. It was spread thinly here, nothing like as rich as the layer beneath the object's outer surface. Instinctively, the Orgathé barged upwards towards that mammoth source. Flat planes of matter splintered as it hammered through them. Further harsh gusts of gas whistled past. Then it found what it wanted, a solid stream of liquid suffused with life-energy pouring along the core of the starscraper. It moved as close as it could, siphoning the heat out of the thick wall of matter surrounding the stream until the outside began to crack. Then it bored through with a couple of appendages, and immersed their tips in the current. Sweet, vital life-energy flowed back into the Orgathé, replenishing it after its considerable exertions. It settled down and began consuming the apparently infinite torrent, growing in a way impossible before.

*

Three trucks approached the ring of dilapidated hovels encircling the Djerba's lobby. Each vehicle had two people inside, a nervous driver and an even more nervous lookout armed with a heavy-calibre rifle. They began to nudge along the muddy tracks between the precarious walls, heavy wheels squelching cans and empty sachet wrappers into the ground.

Past the hovels, they pulled up short of the lobby. As with all Valisk's internal buildings, it was an elaborate edifice, a dome shaped from gradually inclined tiers of long white polyp window arches with a circular apex of amber-tinted crystal. Inside, it had the kind of furniture nests and large marble floors endemic to any human travel station. A few cracked windows along the bottom tier and smashed furniture smeared across the floor were the only evidence of past battles between Kiera and Rubra.

Tolton gave it all a jaundiced look. 'God, I really didn't expect to be coming back here,' he grumbled.

'You're not alone,' Dariat told him.

Erentz climbed down out of the passenger seat, keeping her rifle trained squarely on the lobby. The visitors had been in Valisk for thirty hours now. In all that time, not one of them had emerged from a starscraper, nor made any hostile move. If it hadn't been for the broken windows and closed emergency locks there would be no evidence of their incursion at all. After their desperate efforts to gain entry, such inactivity had everyone troubled and confused. The personality was determined to discover what nefarious activity they were cooking up in the starscrapers.

The lifts were clumped together in the centre of the lobby, a broad column of grey polyp reaching halfway to the amber crystal above. Its curving wall was inset with silvery mechanical doors. One of them slid open as the group approached. Erentz put down the large case of equipment she was carrying, and inched over to the rim so she could snatch a look down. The top of the lift was out of sight, leaving a dark circular shaft with vertical rails that faded from sight after a few metres. She shone a torch into the gulf. All that did was show her more of the rails, and another set of emergency fire-control doors on the inside. If she leaned right over, she could just make out the door below.

From what I can discern, the visitor is now on the twenty-second floor, the personality said. I have managed to seal off the floors below, so the twenty-second remains fully pressurized. The twenty-third is the same. Twenty-four is partially pressurized. Twenty-five is now in a vacuum. Your only escape route, Erentz, is up. Dariat, I imagine you can use the lower floors. A vacuum really shouldn't bother you.

Dariat nodded thoughtfully. **Let's try not to put that theory to the test, OK? Besides, where would I go once I reached the bottom?**

It took twenty minutes to prepare. Three of the group started to rig up a winch they'd brought, securing it on the lobby floor with large bolts. The rest helped Erentz into the silver-grey suit which she was going to wear for the reconnaissance. They'd chosen a thermal emission suit, capable of protecting its wearer from extreme temperatures. It had a thick layer of insulation with a molecular structure similar to the nultherm foam used by starships. The one drawback to that particular property was that the heat generated by a living body's organs and muscles couldn't escape. Any wearer would cook themselves to death inside thirty minutes. So before getting into it, Erentz had to put on a tight-fitting regulator overall made from heat-absorber fabric. It was capable of soaking up and storing her body's entire output for seven hours before having to be drained.

'Are you sure this is going to work?' Tolton asked as he sealed the outer gauntlets to her sleeves. The suit's puffy appearance was making her look like an Arctic skier.

'You were down there with it before,' she answered. 'It has some kind of active heat-sink ability. I've got to have something to shield me from that if I get too close. And I can't risk wearing an SII suit, not in this continuum; there's no guarantee it'll even work below the first floor.'

'All right. If you're happy . . .'

'I'm not.' She slipped the suit's breathing mask on, fiddling with it until it was comfortable. The suit wasn't pressurized, but the mask maintained her air supply at a constant temperature.

Tolton handed her the electron rod. Its spiked tip was capable of giving off a ten thousand volt shock. 'This should stop it getting too close. Electricity seems to be our one constant these days. It can blast the possessed back into the beyond, and it certainly scared the visitor.'

She held up the rod, then slipped it into her belt next to a laser pistol and a fission blade. 'I feel like I'm off to poke the tiger,' she mumbled round the mask.

I'm sorry, said the personality. **But we really do need to know what these things are up to.**

Yeah, yeah. She pulled the helmet visor down, a transparent material thick enough to give the world a gentle turquoise shade. **You ready?** she asked Dariat.

Yes. His affinity voice might have said it, but his mind didn't.

The winch cable had been looped round a pulley at the top of the lift shaft. It ended in a couple of simple straps which Erentz clipped onto a harness around her torso. Above the straps, there was a simple control box on a flexible stalk, with four buttons to govern the winch. She tugged at the thin cable, testing its strength.

It's a linked molecule silicon fibre, explained one of the engineers who'd rigged it up. **Totally reliable; it can support a hundred times your bodyweight.** He indicated a small toggle-like handle nesting in the junction between the two straps. **This is your fast retrieval handle. The winch drum is recoil-wound, like a spring. The further you go down, the tighter the tension. So if you need to get back up here in a hurry, forget the control box, simply twist and pull. It'll reel you in fast. And the whole mechanism is mechanical, so no demon spook can mess with it.**

Thanks. Erentz touched the little toggle reverently, the way she'd seen Christians stroking a crucifix. She walked over to the rim of the lift shaft, switching on her helmet and wrist lights. **We're on.**

Dariat nodded and came over to stand behind her. He put his arms round her chest. His legs he bent so they were wrapped round hers, his feet hooking together between her ankles. It felt like a solid hold. **I think I'm secure.**

Erentz stepped off into space, and swung out into the shaft. She dangled over black emptiness, rotating very slowly. Dariat weighed nothing at all. The only way she knew he was still there was the faintest glow coming from his arms as they clung to her. **All right, let's go see what it's up to.** She pressed the descent button, and the cable started to play out, lowering her. The last she saw of the lobby was three people crowded shoulder to shoulder in the bright doorway, craning down to watch her. Twenty-two floors is a long way to go when you're hanging on the end of an invisible cable in absolute darkness.

The shaft's horizontal pressure seal on the thirtieth storey is closed, the personality said. **The drop is not as fearsome as you imagine it.**

I'm really trying not to imagine it at all, she shot back waspishly.

Dariat didn't say anything. He was too busy fighting the fatigue trembles in his legs. The awkward position he was in made his muscles prone to cramps. Stupid for a ghost, he told himself repeatedly.

The lift doors kept sliding by, buff silver panels affixed to the polyp by a web of support rails and actuator cabinets. Dariat kept trying to use the sensitive cells on each floor to survey the vestibule as they dropped past, but the neural strata was badly affected by the dark continuum's enervation. The thought routines inside were confused and slow, providing meagre pictures of the darkened corridors. Even those had vanished by the twenty-first storey. Real worry began to seep into Dariat's thoughts. It was the visitor who was causing this part of the affliction. Almost an anti-presence, soaking up life and heat like some hazy event horizon. This was *alien* at its extreme.

Here we are, Erentz said. She slowed their descent until they were level with the doors to the twenty-second floor vestibule.

I don't think I can hold on for much longer, Dariat said. **My arms are starting to ache.**

Erentz's mind was moderately incredulous, but she spared him a direct comment. She started to sway, building up pendulum momentum, carrying them closer to the shaft wall each time. Catching hold of the struts and conduits beside the door was easy, and she steadied them against the polyp, feet resting on a latch motor casing. There was an emergency release handle on the top rail, which she turned through ninety degrees. The door slid open with a quiet hiss of compressed air.

With one hand poised ready on the retrieval toggle, she shuffled along the lower rail and swung round the edge of the door. **OK so far,** she told the personality and all her relatives who were monitoring her progress. The vestibule was as dark as the lift shaft. Even the emergency lights had failed. Frost glinted everywhere her lights touched. The suit's environment sensor reported the air was fifty degrees below freezing. So far the electronic systems here were functioning close to their operational parameters.

Erentz slowly unclipped the winch cable, and secured it to a strut just inside the rim of the door; easily available in a hurry. She and Dariat shared an affinity layout of the floor, with the visitor's approximate position indicated by a black blob. It wasn't very precise, and they both knew that since the floor's bitek and electronics had failed it could have moved without the personality knowing.

That was one of the reasons the personality had wanted Dariat along on the reconnaissance. They knew he was affected by the visitor, implying he might just be able to sense it while Erentz in her insulated suit would remain unaware. As theories went, it wasn't the most inspiring. In the end, Dariat only agreed to accompany Erentz because he knew more than most just how grim their position was. The personality held nothing from him, treating him almost as an adjunct of itself, like an exceptionally mobile observation subroutine (or favourite pet, he thought on occasion). They desperately needed quantifiable data on the dark continuum if they were going to get a message out to the Confederation. So far the probes and quantum analysis sensors had returned next to zero information. The visitor was the only source of new facts they'd encountered. Its apparent ability to manipulate energy states could prove valuable.

'Earth's recipe for omelettes,' Dariat murmured silently. 'First steal some eggs.'

Let's go, Erentz said.

Try as he might, Dariat couldn't find true fear in her mind. Apprehension aplenty, but she genuinely believed they would be successful.

They set off along the gently curving vestibule, heading for the visitor. Fifteen metres from the lift, a massive hole had been punched through the floor. It was as if a bomb had detonated, smashing the neat layers of polyp into a jumble of large slabs and pulverized gravel. Nutrient fluid, water, and sludge had leaked out from various severed tubules, oozing down the piles of detritus before turning to rucked tongues of dull grey ice. They stood at the broken rim, and looked down.

We won't stand a chance against this thing, Dariat said. Holy Anstid, look at what it can do; the strength of the fucking thing! That polyp's over two metres thick, look. We've got to get out of here.

Calm down, the personality replied. Whoever heard of a ghost being frightened?

Well, hear it and weep. This is suicidal.

Physical strength alone didn't do this, Erentz said. It was helped by the cold. If you lower the polyp's temperature far enough it becomes as brittle as glass.

That's a real comfort to know, Dariat retorted scathingly.

The personality is right, we shouldn't balk just because of this. It demonstrates that the visitor uses cold the same way we use heat, that's all. If we'd wanted to break through a wall, we'd heat it with lasers or an induction field until it weakened. This is an example of how logic progresses in this continuum; concentrating enough energy to heat something is fantastically difficult here, so the visitors simply apply the inverse.

But we don't know how they apply it, Dariat said. *So we can't defend ourselves against it.*

Then we need to find out, Erentz said simply. *And you have to admit, if this is how it moves about, we'll definitely hear it coming.*

Dariat cursed as she started to pick her way over the loose debris bordering the hole. He knew now why the personality had picked her. She had more gung-ho optimism than a whole squadron of test pilots. Reluctantly, he started to follow.

There were deep gouge marks in the floor that had torn the scarlet and lemon carpet into crumpled waves. The naked polyp underneath was pocked with small craters in a triangular pattern every couple of metres. Dariat had no trouble picturing them as talon marks. The visitor had bulldozed its way along the vestibule, cracking the walls and shredding the furniture and fittings. Then it had veered off deeper into the interior of the starscraper. According to the personality, it was resting right against the core. The door to a large apartment suite was missing, along with a considerable chunk of the surrounding wall. Erentz halted several of metres short, and ran her suit's wrist beams around the big aperture.

The vestibule on the other side is undamaged, she said. *It has to be in there.*

I agree.

Can you tell for certain?

I'm a ghost, not a psychic.

You know what I mean.

Yeah. But I feel OK so far.

She knelt down and began unhooking sensors from her belt, screwing them onto a telescopic pole. *I'll just run a visual and infra-red scan first, with spectral and particle interpretation programs hooked in, no active sweeps.*

Try a magnetic scan as well, the personality suggested.

Right. Erentz added one last sensor to the small clump, then looked round at Dariat. **OK?**

He nodded. She extended the pole cautiously. Dariat used affinity to receive the results directly from the bitek processor governing the sensors, seeing a pale image of the frosted wall sliding past. It was superimposed with translucent sheets of colour that shimmered with defraction patterns, the results of the analysis programs which Dariat fully failed to understand. He shifted the focus, cancelling everything but the raw visual and infra-red image.

He watched the edge of the smashed wall go past. Then there was nothing. **Is it still working?** he asked.

Yes. There's absolutely no light in there. No electromagnetic emissions at all. That's odd, the walls should register on the infra-red no matter how cold they are. It's like the visitor has thrown some kind of energy barricade across the hole.

So go for an active scan, Dariat said. **Laser radar, perhaps.**

Simpler if you just go and take a peek, the personality said.

No bloody way! You don't know it's an energy barricade; that might be the visitor itself hiding round the corner.

If it was that close, you really would sense it.

We don't know that for sure.

Stop farting about like an old woman, and go stick your head round the edge.

Erentz had already pulled the telescopic pole back. She wasn't going to give him any support at all.

OK, I'll look. The whole notion was even worse than when he'd taken that suicide pill back in Bospoort's apartment. At least then he'd had a pretty good idea what he was letting himself in for. **Shine as much light over here as you can,** he told Erentz.

She put the last sensor back on her belt, then pulled out the laser pistol and a small tubular flare launcher. **Ready.**

They both moved over to the other side of the vestibule, giving Dariat a better angle. Erentz focused her helmet beams on the gap as he crept towards it. There was nothing to see. The beams could have been trying to illuminate a cold neutron star for all the effect they had.

Dariat was standing opposite the gap now. **Shit. Maybe it is an event horizon. I can't see a bloody thing in there.** It was as if the universe ended inside the apartment. An uncomfortable analogy, given their circumstances.

Stage two, then, Erentz said. She brought her flare launcher up, aiming it at the gap. **Let's see if this exposes anything.**

We shouldn't rush into this, Dariat said quickly.

Fine, the personality interjected. **As you can't see anything from outside, and you don't want to use the flare, why don't you just go in there and take a look around.**

It might think the flare is some kind of weapon, Dariat said.

Then what do you suggest?

I'm just saying, that's all. It doesn't hurt to be prudent.

We've taken every precaution we can. Erentz, use the flare.

Wait! Right out on the very edge of visibility there was a perturbation in the curtain of darkness. Faint shadow-shapes moved sinuously, the surface distortion of something stirring deep inside. The blackness started to recede from him with the leisurely speed of an outgoing tide, uncovering the edges of the apartment.

His mind was aware of Erentz's finger tightening on the launcher's release trigger. Determination in her mind not to come back without some useful information on the visitor.

No. Don't . . .

The flare streaked across the vestibule, a searing-white magnesium blaze that punctured the pseudoveil across the gap. Dariat looked directly into the shattered apartment.

*

Paradoxically, the new strength it had gained was weakening the Orgathé as a whole. As it absorbed the life-energy contained within the stream of liquid, its once-quiescent riders began to rise out of their unity. It was no longer a singleton. The collective which had originally formed the Orgathé was separating. Before, they had bound their meagre scraps of life-energy together, a synergistic combination which had allowed them to fly free of the mélange. Together, they had been strong. Now there was more than enough life-energy to make them strong individually. They had no real need for each other any more.

Physically, they remained in the same place. There was no reason to move. Quite the opposite. They needed to stay and consume the life-energy which would finally allow them their independence. That ultimate condition hadn't yet been achieved, though it was very close now. Already the Orgathé's physical composition was changing in anticipation of the splendid moment. Internally, it had begun to compartmentalize; dividing in a mockery of biological cell multiplication, with each section attaining a unique shape. The Orgathé had become a womb for a dozen different species.

Then it sensed the two entities approaching. Their flames of life-energy were too small and weak to be worthy of any active intervention. The liquid supply of life-energy was far more enriching than any it would gain by devouring individuals. The Orgathé simply coiled the darkness protectively around itself and carried on consuming.

And Erentz fired the flare into the apartment. Dariat saw the vast bulk of the Orgathé clinging to the far wall, a sagging glossy-black membrane with flabby protuberances that pulsed in discordant rhythms, as if something was scrabbling round underneath. Tentacle-like bands of raw muscle were wound round it so tightly they quivered with tension.

The flare smacked into a wall, bounced, dropped to the frost-sprinkled carpet where it started to burn through into the polyp. Heat and light drenched the apartment in equal proportions. The Orgathé could ward off the light, but not the heat. That penetrated right through its fractions, bringing a wave of pain with it.

Dariat watched the Orgathé peel apart like segments of rotting fruit as it fell off the wall. A torrent of ice-frothed sludge poured out of two puncture holes it had been suckling from. The thick bubbling tide swept a grotesque menagerie of malleable creatures across the floor before it. They tottered and rolled chaotically in the dimming light, churning up the slough. Multi-jointed legs scrabbled round in the same fashion as a newborn deer attempting to stand. Damp wings fluttered ineffectually, flinging off fantails of sticky droplets. Mouths, beaks, and gullets pumped and gasped in silence.

Oh fuck, Dariat moaned. The habitat's affinity band was stunned into mortified silence as he shared his vision with everybody.

Erentz started to back down the vestibule, fear sending cold shivers along her limbs. The flare sputtered and died, sending up a final spiral wisp of smoke. Just before the light vanished, Dariat thought the creatures were solidifying, their skin hardening. In the darkness, he heard a *clack* as might be made by the teeth in an excessively large jaw snapping shut. Dizziness struck him like a rubber truncheon. He staggered away from the apartment, almost unaware of Erentz's suit lights bobbing about wildly as she started running.

Move, Dariat! The level of worry in the personality's plea goaded him into taking a few shaky steps. **Come on, boy. Get the fuck out of there.** He took a few more steps, sobbing in frustration at the weakness that had infected his spectral limbs. Lodging in his mind, though not through the gateway of affinity, was an awareness of the visitor's stupendous hunger.

Dariat had stumbled on for several metres before he even realized he was going the wrong way. Wretched despair produced a pitiful growl in his throat. 'Anastasia, help me.'

Come on, boy. She wouldn't want you to give up, not now.

Angry at the injustice of her memory being used against him, he glanced over his shoulder. Erentz's lights were almost out of sight as she raced away. He saw a halo of darkness eclipse the thin slices of fading light behind him. His legs almost gave out at the sight.

Keep going. I've got you a way out.

He took a couple more fumbling steps before the personality's words even registered. **Where?**

Next lift shaft. The door is jammed open.

Dariat could see very little now. It wasn't just the lack of light, his vision was misted with grey. Only his memory placed the lift shaft for him, and that was being reinforced by the personality. Four or five metres ahead, and on his left.

How's that going to help? he asked.

Simple, the lift is stalled ten storeys down. You just jump. Land on top, and walk through the door. You can do that, you're a ghost.

I can't, he wailed. **You don't understand. Solid matter is hideous.**

While the visitor right behind you is . . . what?

Sobbing he ran his hand along the wall, and found the open lift door. The visitor was sliding smoothly and silently towards him; chilling him further. He sank to his knees, perched right on the edge as if in prayer.

Not ten storeys. That'll kill me.

Exactly which of those solid bones in your transparent body do you think you'll break? Listen to us, you little shithead, if you had any scarp of decent imagination at all you'd just float up to the lobby. Now JUMP!

Dariat could actually sense the polyp dying all around him as the visitor swept towards him. **Lady Chi-ri, help me.** He topped over the lip and into the eternal lift shaft.

Erentz sprinted as hard as she could back down the vestibule. Something was stopping her frantic muscles from delivering their best. She felt feeble. She felt nauseous. The rucked carpet did its devious best to trip her.

Keep going, the personality implored passionately.

She didn't actually look round. Didn't need to. She knew something was coming after her. The floor was vibrating as a heavy body pounded along. Strident screeches were repeated again and again as some claw or fang ripped across the polyp. And cold was penetrating her suit as if there was no insulation at all. Without ever looking back, she waved the laser pistol behind her and fired off a series of wild shots. They had no apparent effect on her pursuer.

Affinity showed her the group up in the lobby. Her relatives were snatching up their weapons, thumbing the safeties. Tolton, in ignorance from his lack of affinity, was becoming frantic, shouting: 'What? What?'

You are approaching the hole in the floor, the personality warned.

'Shit!' She intended it as a defiant bellow. It came out as a whimper. Her body was twice its proper weight. The weakness seemed to amplify her fear, clotting her mind with dread.

An easy jump, the personality promised. **Don't stop running. It's just a question of timing and sure footing.**

Where's Dariat? she asked suddenly.

Four more paces. Concentrate.

It was as though she was already losing her balance, leaning too far forward and having to windmill her arms to keep upright. The edge wobbled towards her. Her knees were bending and she didn't know why.

Now!

The personality's command fired her muscles. Erentz leapt across the hole, flinging her arms forward. She hit the floor on the other side, and collapsed, tumbling painfully. Elbows and knees managed to hit every jutting chunk of rubble.

Get up. You're almost there. Come on!

Groaning in anguish, she staggered to her feet. As she turned, her wrist beams shone back across the hole. Erentz screamed. The Orgathé itself had come after her. Still the largest and strongest of

629

all the dissociated collective, it clawed its way along the vestibule after the small fleeing entity. There was no way it could fly in here. Even though it was diminished in physical size by the separation of the others, the vestibule was too narrow for its wings to be extended. As it was, the Orgathé had to hunch in on itself to avoid the ceiling.

Fury powered it now. Fury at being ripped from the nourishment. It had been *so* close to achieving the energy level it wanted. To have that triumph burned away was excruciating. It didn't care about feeding again, it didn't even care about breaking out of the dark continuum. It wanted vengeance.

Erentz jerked into motion again. Pure adrenalin-rush terror overrode her recalcitrant leg muscles. She sprinted for the open lift door. A gust of buffeting air told her the Orgathé had sprung across the hole behind her. There wasn't going to be enough time to fasten the cable straps to her harness.

She slammed into the wall at the side of the lift doors, spinning round to face the Orgathé. It had obscured itself in folds of darkness again. Only the purposeful ripples slithering across the nebulous surface hinted at the terrible menace contained within. She fired the laser pistol, simply to see the darkness stiffen around the beam's impact point. A wavering dawn of pink light bloomed behind the Orgathé, making a mockery of the weapon.

The flare, the personality urged. **Fire the flare at the bugger.**

Erentz had nothing else left. All there could be now was to jump into the shaft, and hope the fall killed her before the Orgathé caught her. She brought the slim launcher tube up, pointing it at the centre of the ethereal darkness, and pulled the trigger.

A pathetically small spark of incandescence plunged into the vast Orgathé. It spasmed uncontrollably, appendages writhing to thrash against the walls and ceiling. Huge splinters of polyp were sent whirling in dangerous cascades from the force of the blows. Erentz stared at the monster as it bucked about, incredulous that a tiny flare could induce such an awesome result. The whole vestibule was shaking violently.

Yeah, fascinating, said the personality. **Now get out of there while it's distracted.**

She snatched the straps from the strut where she'd secured them. Only one was attached to the harness when she yanked down on the toggle. The power of the rewind made her yipe in shock as she went hurtling upwards. Unexpected gee forces tore the laser pistol and the flare launcher from her hands. The narrow band of the shaft wall illuminated by her lights was a continuous blur of grey.

Brace yourself, the personality said.

Abruptly she was in free fall, still rocketing up. Coils of cable floated sedately around her. The lobby door was visible above: blank white rectangle. It expanded at a frightening rate. Then she was slowing, reaching the top of her arc, level with the door. The slack loops of cable sped through the pulley just as she started to fall, and she was wrenched to a halt. Hands reached out to haul her in through the door. She sank down on the black and white marble tiles of the lobby floor, taking fast gulps of air. Her helmet was removed. Annoying voices buzzed querulously in her ears.

'Where is he?' Tolton demanded. 'Where's Dariat?'

'Down there,' she panted miserably. 'He's still down there.' Her mind sent out a desperate affinity call to the ghost. All she could perceive in return was a faint incoherent cry of consternation.

A brutal howl of tearing metal and disintegrating polyp reverberated out of the lift shaft's open doors. The whole group froze, then looked at the gap as one.

'It's coming up,' Erentz stammered. 'Oh, shit, it's coming after me.'

They scattered, racing for the lobby doors and the trucks outside. Erentz's exhaustion and bulky suit slowed her to little more than a hobble. Tolton grabbed her arm and pulled her along.

The Orgathé exploded out of the top of the lift shaft at near-sonic velocity, a comet of anti-light. It punched through the lobby roof without even slowing down. Big lethal shards of amber crystal slashed down, shattering on the marble tiles. Erentz and Tolton both dived for cover under one of the upturned couches as a surf of crystal fragments skittered around them.

The personality watched the visitor curve round and flatten out; perceptive cells strained to keep it in focus. It was a roughly triangular patch of slippery air, surrounded by black diffraction rainbows similar to a magnified heat shimmer effect. Big iron-hard hailstones pattered onto the grass below it. A kilometre above the parkland, it started to curve round, heading back for the Djerba's lobby. Tolton and Erentz had reached his truck. Both of them were squinting up against the reddish glare of the axial light-tube, trying to spot the visitor. He squeezed the throttle round as far as it would go, and the wheels grumbled into life. They trundled towards the wall of shanty huts at less than ten kilometres per hour.

'Faster!' Erentz yelled frantically.

Tolton reset the throttle. It made no difference to their speed. Another of the trucks was rocking lazily over the ground twenty metres away, going even slower than they were. 'This is all the juice we've got,' Tolton barked.

Erentz was staring at a thin line of wavering silver-black air that was sliding through the sky towards them. Pellucid streamers were unfurling below it, like long coiling jellyfish tendrils. She knew what they were intended for, and what they were going to grab. 'This is it. Endgame.'

No, it's not, the personality said. **Get in amongst the shacks. Forget the trucks, and make sure you take all your lasers and flares with you.**

With the rest of the personality's plan expanding into her mind, she shouted, 'Come on,' to Tolton.

He braked the truck just short of the first rickety hut of plastic sheeting and lashed-up composite poles. They started running down the muddy alley between precarious walls. High above them, the Orgathé had started its approach run, a cascade of hail falling all around it.

Erentz and her relatives started firing their lasers round wildly. 'Incinerate it!' she bellowed at Tolton. 'Burn it all.' Bright scarlet beams slashed at walls and roofs, scorching long lines in the plastic. Edges smouldered and started to burn, curling and dripping. Flames spat along junctions, pumping out jets of black smoke.

The group had congregated in one of the larger open yards between the flimsy buildings. Tolton was shrinking back from the apparent madness, shielding his face from the heat that the eager, leaping flames were throwing out. 'What are you doing?' he cried.

Erentz started firing her flare launcher at piles of rubbish. There were several spectacular bursts of flame as bundles of packaging and abandoned containers ignited. Sooty flakes wafted round in the microthermals. 'It can't stand the heat,' she shouted at the bewildered street poet. 'The flames can beat it back. Come on, help us!' Tolton aimed his own laser, adding to the mêlée.

The Orgathé was just visible, a lenticular patch of shaded, rippling air, itself distorted by the heat gushing upwards from the tips of the flames. It held its course, arrowing down towards them, until the last possible moment. The long scrabbling tendrils hanging from its underbelly it parted furiously as they skimmed the flames.

Tolton couldn't see it any more. His eyes were smarting from the bitter chemical smog billowing out from the roaring plastic. Lush ebony smoke was swirling round his legs, obscuring the ground. Heat seared the skin over the back of his hands as he held them up to defend his face. He could smell singeing hair. A blast of air sent him staggering to his knees, whipping the smoke round into a blinding cyclone. For a second the heat vanished, replaced by its absolute opposite. Glistening sweat transmuted into frost right across his body. He thought his blood was going to turn solid inside his veins, the cold was so frighteningly intense. Then it was gone.

Smoke was rolling itself into vortex spirals as hail stung his face.

'Yes!' Erentz shouted up at the retreating Orgathé. 'We beat the bastard. It's frightened.'

It's repelled, the personality chided. There's a big difference.

Sensitive cells showed her the airborne monster coming round back to the shanty village in a long curve. The flames from the first buildings they'd fired were shrinking.

Move to a new section, the personality said. Let's hope the bugger gives up before you run out of things to burn.

The Orgathé made another five attempts to assail Erentz and her group before it finally withdrew and flew deeper into the habitat interior. Over half of the shanty village had been razed by then. Tolton and the others were caked in grime, and retching badly from the smoke and fumes. Their exposed skin was cracked and bleeding from the heat. Only Erentz, with her suit and mask, was unaffected.

You'd better start walking towards the caverns, the personality said. We'll have a couple of trucks sent to pick you up.

Erentz slowly surveyed the blackened ruins with their slowly solidifying lakes of molten plastic. Couldn't we just wait here? These guys have been through hell.

Sorry, more bad news. We think the other sections of the visitor are coming up from the Djerba. The last few functioning systems we've got in there are being extinguished floor by floor. It can't be anything else.

Shit. She gave the lobby an apprehensive look. What about Dariat?

Nothing.

Damn it.

We are he. In us he lives on.

He'd argue that.

Yes.

There must have been fifty of those brutes down there.

No, the personality said. The glimpse we were given of the visitor without its visual shield was a brief one, but detailed memory analysis of the scene indicates twelve, at most fifteen, were birthed from the mother creature. We don't believe they are anything like the size of the one which has pursued you.

Well, that's a real big relief.

They started picking their way through the sulphurous, carbonized wreckage of the buildings, heading for the track that wound its way across the scrub desert to the northern endcap. Tolton balked until Erentz started explaining the reason for urgency. 'So we can't get down there to find what happened to him?' he asked.

'Not until we know it's clear. And then ... what do the remnants of a ghost look like? It's not as if there are going to be any bones.'

'Yeah,' Tolton gave the lobby a final, remorseful look over his shoulder. 'I suppose not.'

*

The Orgathé cruised through the air, scanning the inside of the object for the nearest source of life-energy. The interior was even worse than the external shell. Here the living layers were protected by many metres of dead matter with just the thinnest sprinkling of cells smeared on top. Plants that had a pitiful content of life-energy. No use to the Orgathé, it needed to regain the true richness which lay beneath. There were several entrances back down to the protruding spindles, which it ignored. This time it wanted a more secure feeding place.

For a while it scouted round over the pink grasslands before eventually turning towards the strip of liquid. Just above the beaches and coves of the far side the surface was riddled with large cave entrances, leading deep into the solid mantle of matter. In there, large currents of the life-energy burned brightly, flowing through vast layers of living cells stacked one on top of the other. Tunnels of living fluids formed complex warrens, thousands of tributary channels connecting to the town-sized organs encased within the endcap.

The Orgathé landed on a broad expanse of platinum sand that

formed one of the trim little coves. Elaborate filigrees of glacial frost sprang out from its feet as it clawed its way up to the nearest cave. As soon as it reached the bluff, grass and bushes perished instantly, their leaves turning a rancid brown and freezing into shape. It barely scraped through the cave entrance. Mock-stalactites snapped off as its hardened carapace brushed against them, shattering as they clattered to the floor. The Orgathé's appendages were modified then hardened by further expenditures of energy to help it bulldoze its way past constrictions and awkward bends. Contact with the hot matter bruised its body, but it was slowly acclimatizing to the heat endemic within the habitat. Pain from each collision was reducing progressively.

After a while it came up against a huge tunnel conveying the living fluid. It broke through the thick wall and eased its entire body into the driving torrent. For the first time since it had slipped into the dark continuum it knew contentment. With that came the shiver of expectation.

*

The trucks still hadn't reached Erentz and the others, though she could just see a small dark speck moving somewhere out there on the scrub desert ahead of them. Walking had become an automatic trudge while her mind followed the flight of the visitor. Valisk's general affinity band was filled with speculation and comment as the personality and Erentz's relatives discussed what was to be done next.

Coverage once the Orgathé moved into the cave wasn't so easy. Tracking its movement was a question of following the null-zone surrounding it by the trail of dead polyp left in its wake.

The damn thing has definitely broken into the nutrient artery feeding my mineral digestion tract, the personality said. It's creating severe pressure-flow problems.

What's it actually doing to the nutrient fluid? Erentz asked. Can you sense any change?

The fluid has been chilled down considerably, which is understandable given what we know of the visitor's intrinsic capability. And over ninety per cent of the corpuscles are dead. A strange outcome, the fluid temperature alone is not sufficient to kill them.

When Dariat and I disturbed it down in the Djerba, it'd broken into one of the starscraper's nutrient fluid tubules. That must be what it's after. It's feeding on your nutrient fluid.

An excellent hypothesis. However, it is not digesting the fluid, we would have been alerted to the loss of volume. And we strongly doubt we have a compatible biochemistry.

It must need something the nutrients contain. Can you run an analysis on the fluid in the Djerba and the other starscrapers where you have visitors squatting?

One moment.

Erentz felt the personality's principal thought routines focusing on the vast network of tubules and conduits that wormed through Valisk's gigantic mitosis layer, probing for aberrations. A big part of the problem in locating any interference was the way the nutrient fluid was pumped into and around the starscrapers. For a start there were many different types. Some just fed the mitosis layer and the muscle membranes, others fed the environmental filter organs down in the basement floors. Specialist fluids supplied the food synthesis organs in each apartment. And all of them underwent a long cycle from the digestive and treatment organs of the southern endcap to the starscrapers and back again, taking several days to complete the circuit. The entire process was autonomic, with the governing subroutines and specialist monitoring cells inside the tubule walls watching for known toxins seeping into the fluid. They weren't looking for whatever kind of corruption was being inflicted by the visitor.

With the bitek systems inside the starscrapers currently functioning erratically at best, the return flow was sluggish. Some of the corpuscles had been naturally depleted by the organs they were intended to replenish, while a fair quantity returned still carrying the fresh molecules and oxygen they were originally bound with. It made a review of the fluid that was emerging from the starscrapers inordinately difficult. Eventually, though, the personality said: We concur that the visitors are all somehow consuming the nutrient fluids. The proportion of dead corpuscles is approaching ninety per cent in some tubules. The nature of the consumption is unclear. We can only conclude it is somehow connected with their heat-sink ability, certainly there is no detectable physical digestion involved.

They're ghouls, she said. Dinosaur-sized parasites. We've got to find some way of stopping them.

Fire is the only effective method we've discovered so far. It will take time to manufacture flame-throwers.

It'll have to be done. They'll eat you alive otherwise.

Yes. Until we can build the appropriate weapons hardware, we're shutting down the supply of nutrient fluid to the starscrapers.

Good idea. She could see the trucks growing out of the scrub desert, trundling along the hard-packed dirt track. **Maybe that'll stop them multiplying. If we can't, the bastards will evolve into a plague.**

*

Fifty light-years from Hesperi-LN, *Lady Mac* and *Oenone* moved tentatively towards each other. Joshua had to use radar for the manoeuvre, while Syrinx utilized the voidhawk's distortion field. This deep in interstellar space there wasn't enough starlight to illuminate a white gas giant. Two small technological artefacts coated in non-reflective foam were simply zones of greater darkness. The only clue to their existence an observer might have had was when they occasionally eclipsed a distant star.

When Joshua did fire *Lady Mac*'s ion thrusters to lock attitude, Syrinx had to blink water from her eyes in reflex. The blue flames were completely dazzling to *Oenone*'s deep space acclimatized optical sensor blisters. Both ships extended their airlock tubes and docked. Joshua led Alkad, Peter, Liol, and Ashly into the voidhawk's crew toroid. They'd come for a conference to review the data from Tanjuntic-RI and determine the next stage of the flight. The two physicists were obviously required. Joshua had brought Ashly because of his wide experience (and delight) in new and strange cultures, which might be useful. Liol's presence was a little harder to justify. Out of all of them, he'd seen the least of the universe. It was just that . . . Joshua was getting used to having him around, someone he didn't have to explain everything to. They thought the same way about the same things. That made Liol useful back-up if he wanted to argue a point of contention.

Syrinx was waiting for them at the inner airlock hatch, a sly reminiscence in her mind at the last time Joshua had come aboard when the two ships were docked. If she'd ever had any lingering doubts about him, they'd ended at Hesperi-LN. Now she was glad it was him accompanying *Oenone* rather than some gruesomely efficient Confederation Navy captain from Meredith Saldana's Deathkiss squadron.

She led the party into *Oenone*'s main lounge. The long compartment was furnished with plain autumn-red couches which matched the gentle curvature of the walls. Glass-fronted shelves displayed a large, varied collection of objects the crew had collected during their flights, ranging from simple pebbles to antique carvings, even examples of unusual consumer products.

Monica was sitting with Samuel in one of the couches. Joshua took the one next to theirs, which put him opposite Renato, Oski, and Kempster. Alkad and Peter sat with Parker, who gave his former colleague a simple polite greeting, as if he had no feelings about her activities and motives. Joshua didn't believe that for a second.

Syrinx claimed a seat next to Ruben, and smiled round. 'Now we're all here: Oski, did we retrieve everything from the arkship?'

The electronics specialist glanced at the slim processor block on the rosewood table in front of her. 'Yes. We managed to datavise all the files stored in the Planetary Habitation terminal into our processors. They're all translated now. There's a lot of information on the five planets they colonized prior to Hesperi-LN.'

'And I've been accessing some of the files,' Monica said. 'I was right, one of those planets was inhabited by a sentient species. They were at an early industrial age.' She datavised the lounge's processor. An AV lens on the ceiling came alive, projecting a laser-like cone of light down into the compartment. A series of two-dimensional pictures materialized at the base, just above the decking. Aerial reconnaissance shots of grey, dirty towns, their brick and stone buildings sprawled across a landscape of blue-green vegetation. They all had rows of factories clustering around the outskirts, tall drab chimneys squirting thick smoke into the azure sky. Small vehicles moved along narrow stone roads, puffing out exhaust fumes. Cultivation was extensive, with human-style checkerboard squares of fields cutting into forests and lapping against the steeper hills.

Tyrathca spaceplanes started to feature in the pictures, landing in the fields and meadows outside towns. Crowds of the four-armed bipeds Monica had found in the archive display cube were shown running from armed soldier-caste Tyrathca. Close-ups of the quirky alien buildings with their arched roofs. They didn't have windows in the outer walls, instead a funnel-like light well delivered illumination to the interior. The architectural arrangement was obvious, many of them had been struck by Tyrathca missiles, exposing the burnt-out structure.

At some time, what passed as the xenocs' army had rallied. Crude artillery pulled by lumbering eight-legged horse-analogue beasts had been deployed against the spaceplanes. Masers reduced them to smouldering ruin.

'Jesus,' Joshua muttered when the file had finished. 'A genuine invasion by bug-eyed space aliens. The whole thing looked like snatches from a low-budget adaptation of *War of the Worlds*.'

'I'm afraid it was inevitable,' Parker said in regretful tones. 'I'm beginning to learn the hard way just how rigidly individual species stick to their own philosophies and laws, and how different that philosophy can be to ours.'

'They committed genocide,' Monica said, glaring at the old project director. 'If there's any of those xenocs left alive, they've probably been enslaved. And you're calling it a philosophy? For fuck's sake!'

'We regard genocide as one of the worse crimes a person or government can commit,' Parker said. 'The massive extermination not only of life, but an entire way of living. Such an act repels us, and rightly so, because that's the way we are. We have emotion and empathy, some would say they govern us. I remind you the Tyrathca do not have these traits. The nearest they come to emotion is the protectiveness they extend to their children and their clan. If you put a breeder caste into a human war crimes court to answer for this atrocity it would never be able to understand what it was doing there. They cannot be judged by our laws, because our laws are the embodiment of our civilization. We cannot condemn the Tyrathca, however much we despise what they do. Human rights are precisely that: human.'

'They took over an entire planet, and you don't think they've done anything wrong?'

'Of course they have done wrong. By our standards. And by our standards, so have the Kiint in continually refusing to give us the solution to possession which we know they have. What are you proposing, that we file charges against Jobis as well?'

'I'm not talking about filing charges, I'm talking about the whole Tyrathca situation. We have to reconsider our mission in view of what we've uncovered.'

'What do you mean, reconsider?' Joshua asked. 'The original circumstances haven't changed, and our goal certainly hasn't. OK, the Tyrathca committed a terrible crime thousands of years ago. We personally, these two ships, can't do anything about that. But we do know to treat them more cautiously than before. When we get back, the Confederation Assembly can work out what to do about the genocide.'

'If they're allowed to take that initiative,' Monica said quietly. 'I admit I'm angry about the genocide. But I'm more worried about the present day implications.'

'How can that affect us?' Alkad asked. 'And I speak of someone with direct experience of a genocide. What we've seen is awful, yes. But it was a long time ago, and a long way off.'

'It affects us,' Monica said, 'because it shows us the Tyrathca in their true light. Consider, we've now established that there were a thousand arkships.'

'One thousand two hundred and eight,' Renato said. 'I rechecked the flight path files.'

'Great, even worse,' Monica said. 'Even assuming each of them was less successful than Tanjuntic-RI, say they only founded a couple of colonies apiece, that gives them a population at least two to three times greater than the Confederation.'

'Spread over a huge volume of space,' Kempster said. 'And not a cohesive political entity like our civilization.'

'Only because there's been no need for them to achieve unity,' Monica said. 'So far. Look, I'm in intelligence; Samuel and I both spend our time assessing potential risk, it's what we're trained for. We catch problems in their embryonic stage. And that's the situation we have here. We've discovered a massive threat to the Confederation, in my opinion at least as dangerous as possession.'

'Physically dangerous,' Samuel interjected. He smiled for the interruption. 'I do concur with Monica that the Tyrathca present us with an unexpected problem.'

'Crap,' Joshua said. 'Look at what we did to them back at Hesperi-LN. You and the serjeants defeated an entire regiment of the soldier caste. And Lady Mac flew circles round their ships. Confederation technology means we outclass them by an order of magnitude.'

'Not quite, Joshua,' Ashly said. The pilot was still gazing at the last picture projected by the AV lens, an apprehensive expression on his face. 'What Monica is saying is that we've stirred up the proverbial hornets' nest. The potential of the Tyrathca threat is a serious one. If all those thousands of colony worlds joined together, sheer numbers would present us with a huge problem. And they do have Confederation technology, we sold them enough weapons in the past. They could retro-engineer combat wasps if they had to.'

'You saw how they used them against *Lady Mac*,' Joshua said. 'The Tyrathca can't handle space warfare, they don't have the right kind of neural wiring for that kind of activity.'

'They could learn. Trial and error would improve them. Granted, they'll probably never be as good as us. But that's where their superior numbers come in, and it works against us. In the very long haul they could wear us down.'

'Why should they?' Liol asked. He spread his arms wide in appeal. 'I mean, Christ, you're sitting here talking like we're at war with them. Sure they're narked we jumped into their system and raised a little hell. But this flight is totally deniable, right? Nobody's going to admit to sending us. You don't commit your entire race to a conflict that will kill billions because we beat up a chunk of wreckage they'd already abandoned.'

'We tend to overlook what they are so that we can maintain our preferred policy of diplomatic tolerance,' Samuel said. 'We like to see them as slightly simple, and stubborn; the ultimate big lummox. A species we can feel superior to, without them ever being aware of our complacent condescension. While in fact, they are a species so aggressive and territorial that they have evolved a soldier caste. *Evolved* one. We can barely comprehend the drive behind such a phenomenon. Such a thing requires tens of millennia to achieve. Throughout all that time on their homeworld the social climate maintained the pressures necessitating such a development. Their history is a solid monoculture of conflict.'

'I still don't see how that makes them a danger,' Liol persisted. 'If anything it works in our favour. We provided the Hesperi-LN Tyrathca with the ZTT drive over two hundred years ago. And what do they do with it? Do they rush off to contact their long-lost relatives on the first five colony worlds? Do they bollocks. They've founded more colony worlds for themselves, so their immediate relatives could benefit. They didn't want to share that little technological gem with anybody else.'

'You're right,' the Edenist said. 'Providing you add one qualifier: to date. As Monica said, we are dealing with the concept of potential here. In one respect, the Tyrathca are like us; an external threat will unite them. The arkships themselves are proof of that.'

'We're not a threat to them!' Liol was almost shouting.

'We haven't been until now,' Monica said. 'Until now they didn't know we could become *elemental*. They were so disturbed by the prospect of human possessed they immediately opted for isolation. We have become a danger. Possessed humans have attacked Tyrathca settlements. Our already superior military strength has been multiplied by an unknown amount. Remember they do not see humanity divided between possessed and non-possessed. We are one species, which has suddenly and dramatically changed for the worse.' She pointed to the projection. 'And now we've seen what happens to xenoc species which come into dispute with the Tyrathca.'

Liol lapsed back into silence. Scowling, worried now rather than angered by losing the argument.

'All right,' Joshua said. 'There's a potential for conflict between the Tyrathca and the Confederation, assuming we survive possession intact. It still doesn't affect our mission.'

'The Confederation should be warned of this development,' Monica said. 'We have learned more about Tyrathcan nature than anyone has before. And with their isolation policy, nobody else is likely to find out. That knowledge is now of considerable strategic importance.'

'You're not seriously suggesting we turn back already?' Joshua asked.

'I have to concur with Monica, that's now a factor we should consider,' Samuel said.

'No, no,' Joshua said. 'You're blowing this out of all proportion. Look, we're forty-two light-years from Yaroslav, which is the nearest Confederation star system. *Lady Mac* would have to expend a lot of delta-V to match velocities. We'd take over a day to get there, and the same to get back here. And right now, time is the biggest critical factor we have. Who knows what the possessed are cooking up behind us? They might even have taken over the Yaroslav system.'

'Not the Edenist habitats,' Monica said. 'Voidhawks could distribute our warning.'

'The *Oenone* would only need a day to get to Yaroslav and back,'

Ruben said. 'That's not so much of a delay.' He gave Syrinx an encouraging smile.

She didn't return it. 'I really don't want us to separate at this point,' she said. 'Besides, we haven't even established how the search for the Sleeping God is progressing. I think we should at least hear the status review from Parker's team before we go making that kind of decision.'

'Agreed,' Joshua said quickly. Monica glanced at Samuel, then shrugged. 'OK.'

Parker leaned forward, permitting himself a small smile. 'At least I have one piece of good news for us, we have confirmed the Sleeping God does exist. There's a reference in one of the Tyrathca files.'

There were smiles all round the lounge. Ashly clapped his hands together, and let out an exhilarated: 'Yes!' He and Liol grinned broadly at each other.

'The file didn't tell us what the bloody thing was,' Kempster said gruffly. 'Just what it did. And that's really weird.'

'Assuming it's true,' Renato said.

'Don't be such a depressive, my boy. We've already been through that aspect. The Tyrathca don't invent stories, they can't.'

'So what can it do?' Joshua asked.

'From what we can determine, it transported one of their arkships a hundred and fifty light-years. Instantaneously.'

'It's a stardrive?' Joshua asked in disappointment.

'I don't think so. Oski, would you put this in perspective for us, please.'

'Certainly.' She datavised the processor block on her table, clearing the final picture of the Tyrathca invasion from the AV projection. 'This is a simulation of Tanjuntic-RI's flight path from Mastrit-PJ to Hesperi-LN, based on what we've discovered in the files from the arkship.' The AV lens projected a complex starchart centred on the colourful smear of the Orion Nebula. A red star on the opposite side of the nebula from the Confederation was surrounded by a swarm of informational icons. 'Mastrit-PJ is now either a red giant or a supergiant, and it has to be quite close to the far side of the nebula, which is why we've never seen it before. Now, Tanjuntic-RI flew right round the nebula. We don't know which way round, the Tyrathca have never revealed the location of their other colonies to us, and we didn't extract enough information from their terminals to determine them. However, we know for certain that it stopped eleven times en route, eventually finishing up at Hesperi-LN. Five of those stops were to found colonies; the others were in star systems without a biocompatible planet, so they just refuelled and repaired Tanjuntic-RI, and carried on.' A thin blue line extended out from Mastrit-PJ, linking eleven stars in a rough curve going around on the galactic south side of the luminescent nebula. 'This course is important, because it actually cut the arkship off from direct line of sight to Mastrit-PJ. Their communication laser simply wasn't powerful enough to penetrate the dust and gas that makes up the nebula. So after the fourth star they visited, all messages to and from Mastrit-PJ had to be relayed through the colonies. Which is also why the latter communiqué files were stored in the Planetary Habitation terminal.'

'We think Mastrit-PJ's stellar expansion must account for the eventual fall-off in message traffic,' Renato said eagerly. 'Towards the end of the flight, Tanjuntic-RI was communicating with the colonies alone. Some messages were also forwarded from colonies established by other arkships, but there was nothing coming from Mastrit-PJ at all.'

'I'm surprised there ever was,' Alkad said. 'If it detonated into a red giant, nothing should have survived. The star's planets would have been consumed.'

'They must have set up some kind of redoubt in the cometary halo,' Renato said. 'Their astroengineering resources were quite considerable by that time, after all. The Tyrathca who didn't get to leave on arkships would have made some kind of survival attempt.'

'Fair assumption,' Alkad acknowledged.

'But that civilization would be finite,' Renato said. 'They have no new resources to exploit, they can't replenish themselves like the arkships do at every new star system. So eventually, they died off. Hence the lack of messages in the last five thousand years.'

'But one of the last communiqués from Mastrit-PJ was the one concerning the Sleeping God,' Parker said. 'A century later, they finally went off air. Tanjuntic-RI had beamed a message back, asking for further details, but by then they were eight hundred light-years away. The Mastrit-PJ civilization was probably extinct before the first colony world received the original communiqué.'

'Can we see it, please?' Ruben asked.

'Of course,' Oski said. 'We isolated the relevant text from the message, there's a lot of softbloat garbage about source and compression. And they repeat each message thousands of times over about a fortnight to ensure the entire chunk is eventually received intact.' She gave them a file code. When they accessed it, the processor showed a simple text sheet.

INCOMING SIGNAL RECEIVED
DATE 75572–094–648
SOURCE FALINDI-TY RELAY
MASTRIT-PJ REPORTS
FLIGHTSHIP SWANTIC-LI SIGNAL RE-ACQUIRED DATE
38647–046–831. LAST SIGNAL RECEIVED DATE
23867–032–749.

INCLUDED
TRANSMISSION DETAILS
SWANTIC-LI REPORTS
DATE 29321–072–491. PLASMA BUFFER FAILURE WHILE
DECELERATING INTO STAR SYSTEM **********.
MULTIPLE IMPACT DAMAGE. 1 HABITATION RING
DEPRESSURIZED. 27 INDUSTRIAL SUPPORT CHAMBERS
DEPRESSURIZED WITH ASSOCIATED EQUIPMENT LOSS.
32% POPULATION KILLED. LIFE-SUPPORT FUNCTIONS
UNSUSTAINABLE. TOTAL LIFE-SUPPORT CESSATION
EXPECTED WITHIN 7 WEEKS. NO INHABITABLE PLANETS IN
STAR SYSTEM. SENSORS LOCATED AN EXTENSIVE SPATIAL
DISTURBANCE ORBITING THE STAR. IT IS A DORMANT
SOURCE OF GODPOWER. IT SEES THE UNIVERSE. IT
CONTROLS EVERY ASPECT OF PHYSICAL EXISTENCE. ITS
REASON IS TO ASSIST PROGRESS OF BIOLOGICAL
ENTITIES. OUR ARRIVAL WOKE IT. WHEN WE ASKED FOR
ITS HELP IT TRANSPORTED SWANTIC-LI TO THIS STAR
SYSTEM 160 LIGHT-YEARS AWAY, WHERE THERE IS A
HABITABLE PLANET. TO ANY WHO COME AFTER US, WE
DEEM IT AN ALLY OF ALL TYRATHCA.

DATE 29385–040–175. SWANTIC-LI POPULATION
TRANSFERRED TO HABITABLE PLANET. COLONY
GOERTHT-WN ESTABLISHED.

Tagged on to the end of the file were three pictures. The quality was uniformly low, even after passing through discrimination and amplification filter programs. All of them showed a silver-grey smear against a stellar background. Whatever the object was, the Tyrathca of Coastuc-RT had reproduced its shape almost exactly: a broad disc with conical spires rising from each side. Its surface was smooth, without any visible markings or structures, a constant metallic sheen.

'How big is it?' Joshua asked.

'Unknown,' Renato said. 'And unknowable. We don't have any references. There was no focal length given for any of the pictures, so there's no way we can put a number on the beast. It could be gas giant sized, or a couple of kilometres across. The only clue I have to go on is their claim that it comes complete with an extensive spatial disturbance, which I'm assuming is some kind of intense gravity field. That would tend to prohibit anything too small. The one object that can qualify as coming near to filling the parameters we've got so far is a small neutron star, but that couldn't have this shape.'

Joshua gave Alkad a long look. 'Neutron stars of whatever size don't have the properties described by the Tyrathca in that communiqué,' she said. 'Nor do they look like that. I think we have to conclude it's an artefact.'

'I'm not going to quibble with anyone's theories,' Kempster said. 'Plain and simple, we don't have enough information to determine its nature. Sitting here trying to second-guess what five fuzzy pictures are showing us is completely pointless. What we have established is the existence of something with some very strange properties.'

'The term godpower is fascinating,' Parker said. 'Especially as we're not dealing with spoken nuances. Plain text gives our translation a much higher level of accuracy.'

'Ha!' Kempster waved a dismissive hand at the director. 'Come off it, we don't even have an accurate definition of god in our own language. Every culture assigns different values to god. Humanity has used the term to mean everything from creator of the universe to a group of big angry men who have nothing better to do than mess about with the weather. It's a concept, not a description.'

'However you want to squabble over semantics, god implies an extraordinary amount of power in any language.'

'Godpower, not god,' Ruben corrected pointedly. 'That has to be significant, too. It's definitely an artefact of some kind. And as the

Tyrathca didn't build it, we've probably got as much chance as anyone of switching it back on.'

'It was dormant, and their approach woke it up,' Oski said. 'Sounds like you don't even have to press the button to activate it.'

'I say it still sounds like a stardrive to me,' Liol said, with a nod to Joshua. 'The communiqué said it assists the progress of biological entities, and it shunted that arkship a hundred and sixty light-years. That seems pretty clear cut. No wonder the Tyrathca thought it was bloody miraculous. They don't have FTL technology. And a stardrive big enough to transport an arkship is going to be built on one hell of an impressive scale. It was bound to astonish them, even with their fatalistic phlegmatism.'

'They said a lot of things about it,' Joshua said. 'None of which quite match up. What I mean is, none of the qualities they've given it are aspects of a single machine. Stardrives don't observe the universe, nor do they control physical existence.'

'I could add several questions,' Syrinx said. 'Like what is it doing in a star system with no biocompatible planet? It would also appear that there's some kind of controlling sentience. Remember the Tyrathca asked it for help, they didn't just switch it to stardrive function and fly away.'

'They couldn't have anyway,' Samuel said. 'It sent Swantic-LI to a system with an inhabitable planet. In other words, it knew there was one there, the Tyrathca didn't.'

'That makes it benign, as well,' Kempster said. 'Or at least, friendly; presumably to biological entities. And I'm just arrogant enough to believe that if it was cooperative with the Tyrathca it really ought to extend the same courtesy to us.'

Joshua looked round the group. 'If no one has anything to add about its abilities or nature, I think we've learned enough to confirm we should continue with this mission. Monica, you want to say no?'

The ESA agent pressed her hand into her hands and stared at the decking. 'I agree this thing sounds pretty impressive, but I wasn't just drawing attention to the Tyrathca to be a pain. They do worry me.'

'Not on any timescale we have to worry about,' Oski said. 'Even assuming you're one hundred per cent right, and they now see the human race as a dangerous plague to be wiped out, it would be decades before they could even contemplate such an action. Take the worst case, and assume they've already travelled from Hesperi-LN to the other colonies Tanjuntic-RI founded. They still won't be able to build ZTT starships for years to come, not in any quantity. Frankly, I have my doubts they would ever manage it. Retro-engineering our systems would be extremely difficult for them, given their lack of intuition. Even if they did crack it, they'd have to build production stations. So even if this flight takes us a couple of years, we'll still be back well in time to warn the First Admiral.'

Monica consulted Samuel. 'I think that's reasonable,' he said.

'All right,' she said reluctantly. 'I admit I'm curious about this Sleeping God.'

'Good,' Joshua said. 'Next question, where the hell is it? You left the star system location blank.'

'It's a ten digit coordinate,' Kempster said. 'I can give you a direct translation if you really want. Unfortunately, it's a total nonsense, because we don't have the Tyrathca almanac from which it was taken.'

'Oh, bollocks!' Liol slumped back into the couch, slapping the cushion fabric in frustration. 'You mean we've got to go back into Tanjuntic-RI?'

'Unwise,' Samuel said. 'I believe the hornets' nest analogy applies. We really did stir them up.'

'Can't the *Oenone* work it out?' Liol asked. 'I thought voidhawks have a real good spatial awareness.'

'They do,' Syrinx said. 'If we had a Tyrathca almanac, we could take you straight to the star with the Sleeping God. But first we need that almanac, and there's only one place to get it from. We have to go back.'

'Not so,' Kempster said cheerily. 'There is a second star system where we know it exists: Mastrit-PJ itself. Even better, they received Swantic-LI's messages direct; there may be others which were never relayed to Tanjuntic-RI. All we have to do is fly around the Orion Nebula, any red giant star will shine at us like a damn great beacon. As soon as the sensors see it, we can work out a valid approach vector.'

'More promising, from our point of view, Mastrit-PJ is now uninhabited,' Parker said. 'This time we'll be able to undertake a more leisurely, and thorough, retrieval of the files we want from the ruins.'

'We don't know how long this redoubt civilization has been dead for,' Oski said, a note of worry in her voice. 'The condition of the Laymil relics are bad enough, and they're only two and a half thousand years old. I can't promise I can recover anything from electronics that have been exposed to space for twice that long.'

'If necessary, we can just scout round the stars closest to Mastrit-PJ for other Tyrathca colonies. There must be a lot of them in that area. They won't have been warned about us devious humans yet. The point is, we can find copies of that almanac on the other side of the nebula.'

'I wasn't disputing that,' Oski said. 'I'm just saying, for the record, there may be problems.'

'You're all overlooking one thing,' Joshua said. He almost smiled when he received their indignant looks. 'Is there even going to be a Sleeping God waiting for us if the Kiint get there first? And what the hell do they want with it anyway?'

'We can't not continue because of the Kiint,' Syrinx said. 'In any case, we don't have real proof that . . .' She trailed off under Joshua's mocking gaze. 'All right, they were at Tanjuntic-RI. But we knew they were interested before we set out. It's because of them we're here now. To my mind, this just proves the Sleeping God is a big deal.'

'All right,' Joshua said. 'The other side of the nebula it is.'

16

Fifty years ago, Sinon had visited the Welsh-ethnic planet Llandilo, where he'd spent a cold three hours straddling sunrise to watch a clan of New Druids welcome the first day of spring. As pagan ceremonies went, it was a fairly boring affair for an outsider, with off-key singing and interminable Gaelic invocations to the planet's mother goddess. Only the setting made it worthwhile. They'd gathered on the headland of some eastward-facing coastal cliffs, where a line of tremendous granite pillars marched out to sea. God's colonnade, the locals called it.

When the sun rose, pink and gold out of the swaddling sea mist, its crescent was aligned perfectly along the line of pillars. One by one, their tops blazed with rose-gold coronas as the shadows flowed away. Gladdened by nature's poignancy, the congregation of white-clad New Druids finally managed to achieve a decent harmony and their voices rang out across the shore.

It was a strange recollection for Sinon to bring to his new serjeant body with its restricted memory capacity. He certainly couldn't remember his reason for retaining it. An overdose of sentiment, presumably. Whatever the motive, the Llandilo memory was currently providing a useful acclimatization bridge to the present. Nine thousand of the serjeants trapped on Ketton Island had gathered together near the edge of the plateau to exert their will, with the remainder joining their endeavours via affinity as they walked resolutely over the mud towards the rendezvous point. They weren't praying, exactly, but the visual similarity with the New Druids was an amusing comfort. The beleaguered Edenists needed whatever solace they could garner from the dire situation.

Their first, and urgent, priority had been to stem the gush of atmosphere away from the flying island before everybody suffocated. A simple enough task for their assembled minds now they had acquired some degree of energistic power; the unified wish bent whatever passed for local reality into obedience. Even Stephanie Ash and her raggedy little group of followers had aided them in that. Now it was as though the air layer around the outside of the island had become an impregnable vertical shield.

Encouraged and relieved, they stated their second wish loud and clear: to return. In theory, it should have been easy. If a massive concentration of energistic power had brought them here to this realm, then an equally insistent concentration should be able to get them back. So far, this argument of logical symmetry had failed them utterly.

'You dudes should give it a rest,' Cochrane said irritably. 'It's real spooky with all of you standing still like some zombie army.'

Along with the others of Stephanie's group, the redoubtable hippy had spent a quarter of an hour trying to help the serjeants open some kind of link back to the old universe. When it became obvious (to them) that such a connection was going to be inordinately difficult, if not impossible, he'd let his attention drift. They'd ended up sitting in a circle round Tina, giving her what support and comfort they could.

She was still very weak, sweating and shivering as she lay inside a heavily insulated field sleeping bag. One of the serjeants with medical knowledge who'd examined her said that loss of blood was the biggest problem. Their direct infusion equipment didn't work in this realm, so it had rigged up a primitive intravenous plasma drip feed for her.

Stephanie's unvoiced worry was that Tina had suffered the kind of internal injuries they could never repair properly with their energistic power however much they willed her to be better. As with Moyo's eyes, the subtleties of the flesh had defeated them. They needed fully-functional medical nanonic packages. Which wasn't going to happen here.

Her other concern was exactly what would happen to the souls of anyone whose body died in this realm. Their connection with the beyond had been irrevocably severed. It wasn't a prospect she wanted to explore. Though looking at Tina's poorly acted cheer, she thought they might all find out before too long.

Sinon broke out of his trance state, and looked down at Cochrane. 'Our attempt to manipulate the energistic power is not a physically draining exercise. As there is nothing else for us to do here, we consider it appropriate to continue with our efforts to return home.'

'You do, huh? Yeah, well, I can dig that. I purge myself with yoga. It's righteous. But, you know, us cats, we've got to like *eat* at some time.'

'I'm sorry, you should have said.' Sinon walked over to one of the large piles of backpacks and weapons which the serjeants had discarded. He found his own, and unfastened the top. 'We don't ingest solid food, I'm afraid, but our nutrient soup will sustain you. It contains all the proteins and vitamins required by a normal human digestion system.' He pulled out several silvery sachets and distributed them round the dubious group. 'You should supplement the meal with water.'

Cochrane flipped the cap off the sachet's small valve, and sniffed suspiciously. With everyone watching intently, he squeezed a couple of drops of the pale amber liquid onto his finger, and licked at them. 'Holy shit! It tastes like seawater. Man, I can't eat raw plankton, I'm not a whale.'

'Big enough to qualify,' Rana muttered under her breath.

'We have no other source of nourishment available,' Sinon said in mild rebuke.

'It's fine, thank you,' Stephanie told the big serjeant. She concentrated for a moment, and her sachet solidified into a bar of chocolate. 'Don't pay any attention to Cochrane. We can imagine it to be whatever taste we like.'

'Bad karma'll get you,' the hippy sniffed. 'Yo there, Sinon. You got a glass going spare? I figure I can still remember what a shot of decent bourbon tastes like.'

The serjeant rummaged round in his pack, and found a plastic cup.

'Hey, thanks, man.' Cochrane took it from him, and transformed it into a crystal tumbler. He poured a measure of the nutrient soup out, watching happily as it thinned into his favourite familiar golden liquor. 'More like it.'

Stephanie peeled the wrapper from her chocolate, and bit off a corner. It tasted every bit as good as the imported Swiss-ethnic delicacy she remembered from her childhood. But then, in this case the memory is the taste, she told herself wryly. 'How much of this nutrient soup have you got left?' she asked.

'We each carry a week's supply in our pack,' Sinon said. 'That period is calculated on the assumption we will be physically active for most of the time. With careful rationing it should last between two and three weeks.'

Stephanie gazed out across the rumpled grey-brown mud which made up the surface of the flying island. Occasional pools of water glinted in the uniform blue-tinted glare that surrounded them. A few scattered ferrangs and kolfrans nosed around the edges of drying mires, nibbling at the fronds of smothered vegetation. Not enough to provide the combined human and serjeant inhabitants with a single meal. 'I guess that's all the time we've got, then. Even if we had warehouses full of seed grain, three weeks isn't enough time to produce a crop.'

'It is debatable if the air will sustain us for that long anyway,' Sinon said. 'Our estimate for the human and serjeant population on this island is twenty-thousand-plus individuals. We won't run out of oxygen, but the increase in carbon dioxide caused by that many people breathing will reach a potentially dangerous level in ten days' time unless that air is recycled. As you can see, no vegetation survives to do this. Hence our determination to explore the potential of our energistic power.'

'We really ought to be helping you,' Stephanie said. 'Except I don't see how we can. None of us have affinity.'

'The time might come when we need your instinct,' Sinon said. 'Your collective will brought us here. It is possible that you can find a way back. Part of our problem is that we don't understand where we are. We have no reference points. If we knew where we were in relation to our own universe, we might be able to fashion a link back to it. But as we played no part in bringing the island here, we don't know how to begin the search.'

'I don't think we do either,' Moyo said. 'This is just a haven for us, a place where the Liberation isn't.'

'Interesting,' Sinon said. More serjeants started to listen to the conversation, eager for any clue that might be scattered amid the injured man's words. 'You weren't aware of this realm before, then?'

'No. Not specifically. Although I suppose we were aware that such a place existed, or could exist. The desire to reach it is endemic among us, the possessors, that is. We want to live where we don't have any connection to the beyond, and where there's no night to remind us of empty space.'

'And you believe this is it?'

'It would seem to fill the criteria,' Moyo said. 'Not that I can vouch for the lack of night,' he added bitterly.

'Are the other planets here?' Sinon asked. 'Norfolk and all the others? Were you aware of them at any time?'

'No. I never heard or felt anything like that when we moved here.'

'Thank you.' **Instinct appears to be the governing factor**, he said to the others. **I don't believe we can rely on it for answers.**

I don't understand why we can't simply wish ourselves back, Choma said. **We have a power equal to theirs, we also have a commensurate desire to return.**

The united minds in their mini-Consensus decided there were two options. That the possessed had spontaneously created a sealed continuum for themselves. An improbable event. While that would account for several properties of this realm – the failure of their electronic hardware, the cutting-off of the beyond – the creation of an entirely new continuum by manipulating existing space-time with energy would be an inordinately complex process. Coming here was achieved by sheer fright, which discounted such a procedure.

More likely, this continuum already existed, secluded among the limitless dimensions of space-time. The beyond was such a place, though with very different parameters. They must have been thrown deep inside the multitude of parallel realms conjunctive within the universe. In such circumstances, home would be no distance at all away from where they were now. At the same time, it was on the other side of infinity.

There was also the failure to open even a microscopic wormhole, despite a formidable concentration of their energistic strength. That did not bode well at all. Before, ten thousand possessed had opened a portal wide enough to embrace a lump of rock twelve kilometres in diameter. Now, twelve thousand serjeants couldn't generate a fissure wide enough to carry a photon out.

The explanation had to be that energy states were different here. And in ten days' time, that simple difference was going to kill them when the clean air ran out.

Stephanie watched Sinon for a couple of minutes, until it became apparent that he wasn't going to say anything else. She could sense the minds of the serjeants all around her, just. There were none of the emotional surges which betrayed normal human thoughts, just a small, even glow of rationality, which occasionally fluttered with a hint of passion, a candle flame burning a speck of dust. She didn't know if that was indicative of Edenist psyches, or normal serjeant mentality.

The swarthy bitek constructs remained unnervingly motionless as they stood in a loosely circular formation. Every new platoon which arrived after yomping across the sodden loam immediately discarded their backpacks and joined their fellows in stationary contemplation of their predicament. As far as Stephanie could tell, they were the only humans among them. The newly arrived serjeants had all given the remnants of Ketton a wide berth. Yet she could sense a stir of minds amid the ruined town. At first puzzled why not one of them had ventured out to talk to the serjeants, she'd now assigned a certain resignation to the fact.

'We should go over and talk to the others,' she said. 'Having this kind of division is ridiculous in these circumstances. If we're going to survive, we have to cooperate and work together.'

McPhee sighed, and wriggled his large frame comfortably over the sleeping bag he was lying on. 'Oh, lass, you only see good in everyone. Open your eyes. Remember what yon bastards did to us, and let them stew.'

'I'd like to open my eyes,' Moyo said harshly. 'Stephanie's right. We should at least make an attempt. Setting up different camps is stupid.'

'I didn't mean to offend. I'm just pointing out that they've made no attempt to talk to us or the serjeants.'

'They're probably too nervous of the serjeants,' Stephanie said. 'It's only been half a day, after all. I doubt they even know how much trouble we're in. They're not as disciplined as the Edenists.'

'They'll find out eventually,' Rana said. 'Let them come to us when they're ready. They won't be so dangerous then.'

'They're not dangerous now. And we're in a perfect position to make the first move.'

'Woah there, sister,' Cochrane said. He struggled up into a sitting position, which sent a lot of bourbon slopping out of his tumbler. 'Not dangerous? Like funky! What about the Ekelund chick? She put up some mighty fine barricades last time we waved goodbye.'

'That situation hardly applies any more. You heard Sinon. We're going to die if we don't find a way out of here. Now I don't know if their help will make any difference, but it certainly won't reduce our chances.'

'Urrgh. I like hate it when you're reasonable, it's the ultimate bad trip. I know it's big-time wrong, and I can never escape.'

'Good. You'll come with us, then.'

'Oww, shit.'

'I'll stay here with Tina,' Rana said quietly, and gave her friend's hand a small squeeze. 'Someone has to keep her comfortable.'

Tina smiled with hollow defiance. 'I'm such a nuisance.' There was a chorus of indignant reassuring noes from the group. They all hurriedly smiled at her or made encouraging gestures. Moyo's face wore a forlorn expression as he fumbled round for Stephanie's guiding hand.

'We won't be long,' she told the pair of them positively. 'Sinon?' She tapped the serjeant lightly on its shoulder. 'Would you like to come with us?'

The serjeant stirred. 'I will. Making contact is a good idea. Choma will accompany us, also.'

Stephanie couldn't quite sort out the reason she was doing this. There was none of the automatic protectiveness which had driven her to help the children back on Mortonridge. Not even the sense of paternalism which had kept them all together in the weeks before the Liberation. She supposed it could have been simple self-preservation. She wanted the two sides working together to salvage this situation. Anything else than their wholehearted effort might not be enough.

The ground outside Ketton had suffered few changes following the quake. There was the shallowest of curves across the width of the island, betraying the original shape of the valley from which it had been snatched. Long hummocks bordered the slowly drying mires, rambling gently across the slope like the sand-ripples of a tidal estuary. All that remained of the forests which had smothered the foothills were denuded black branches poking resolutely skywards. There was no sign of the roads which had survived the deluge, the quake had swept them away. Twice they found craggy sheets of carbon-concrete jutting up from the mud, leaning over at acute angles. Neither of them corresponded to their memory of where the road had been.

With the loam all churned up again, Stephanie found her feet sinking a couple of inches at every step. It wasn't as bad as when they'd raced to keep ahead of the jeeps, but walking was an effort. And they still hadn't fully regained their strength. Half a mile from the outskirts of the town, she stopped for a rest, disappointed at how hard she was breathing. Each inhalation made her feel guilty at the way she was poisoning the air.

From a distance, Ketton was at least different to the surrounding land. Individual, tightly packed zones of colour supported the theory that although most of the buildings were damaged, they at least remained loosely intact. Now she could see what a fallacy that was. She should have been warned by the complete absence of trees.

Cochrane prodded his narrow purple sunglasses up to his forehead, and peered ahead. 'Man, oh, man, what were you cats thinking of? I mean, this is like *wasted*, with the world's biggest capital W.'

'The harpoon assault against Ketton was intended to deprive the occupying possessed of any tactical cover,' Sinon said. 'We have suffered considerable attrition due to your booby traps and ambushes. As you were determined to make a stand here, General Hiltch was equally resolved to deny you any advantage the town itself could offer. I believe the quake was also supposed to be a psychological blow as well.'

'Yeah?' the hippy scoffed. 'Well, that backfired on you, didn't it? Look where scaring us shitless got you.'

'You consider yourself better off here?' McPhee laughed snidely at Cochrane's chagrin.

'Is it bad?' Moyo asked.

'There's nothing left,' Stephanie told him. 'Nothing at all.' Up close the patches of colour were actually just dull variations of grime, low mounds of rubble that fused into the mud. Even with their energistic power almost undimmed, the possessed had made no attempt to resurrect the buildings. Instead, people were picking their way among the ruins, a constant swarm of movement.

As they drew closer, she realized there was nothing aimless and disorientated in the actions of the survivors. They were methodically excavating the mounds, scooping out quantities of bricks and shattered concrete with a combination of physical and energistic force. It was all very purposeful and efficient. In other words, organized.

'Maybe this wasn't such a good idea,' she said in a low voice as they reached the outer knolls of rubble. 'I think Ekelund might still be in charge here.'

'In charge of what?' Cochrane asked. 'This is like a municipal landfill site. And they've only got ten days to live.'

A team of two women and one man, barely out of his teens, were working away on one of the piles, shifting large metal frames as if they were made of plastic. They'd already dug several short tunnels into the pile. Battered composite boxes of sachets had been stacked neatly just above the mud. The three of them stopped what they were doing as Stephanie and Sinon walked over. Stephanie's spirits fell even further when she saw they were wearing army fatigues.

'We thought we ought to see if there was anything we could do to help,' she said. 'If there's somebody trapped in the wreckage, or anything.'

The young man scowled, looking between her and her companions. 'Nobody trapped. What you doing with those Kingdom monster things? You some kind of spy?'

'No, I'm not a spy,' she said carefully. 'There is nothing for anyone to spy on here. We're on this island together. Nobody has anything to hide any more. There's nothing to fight for, not amongst ourselves.'

'Oh yeah? How much food have you got? Not much, I'll bet. Is that why you're here?' His anxious glance slipped to the small stack of boxes they'd uncovered.

'The serjeants have enough food to last us, thank you. Who's actually in charge here?'

The man was opening his mouth to answer when an incredible stab of hot pain punctured Stephanie's hip. It was so intense she couldn't even cry out in shock. She was flung back by the force of the impact, the world spinning madly about her. Landing on her back, she saw her limbs splayed out in the air. Gore and blood splattered onto the mud around her as she went limp.

I've been shot!

Everyone was shouting wildly. Dashing about in total confusion. The air hazed over with bright scintillations, thickening protectively around her. Stephanie raised her head, looking along her body with numb interest. Her trousers and blouse were glistening crimson with blood. There was a long rent in the fabric over her hip, showing the torn flesh and splinters of bone underneath. Shock gave her vision a perfect clarity. Then her head suddenly became very warm, and the hideous pain returned. She screamed, her vision turning grey as her muscles relaxed, dropping her head down into the mud again.

'Stephanie! Fuck, oh fuck, what's happened?'

That was Moyo, his anguish and fright making her frown.

'Ho-lee shit! Those dudes shot her. Yo, Stephanie, babe, you hear me? You hang on. It's like a scratch. It's nothing. We'll fix it for you.'

A dark demon was kneeling beside her, its carapace alive with wriggling sparks.

'I'm applying pressure. It should stop the bleeding. Focus your thoughts on repairing the bone first.'

Stephanie was receding from them, only vaguely aware of a dry liquid spilling all across her torso. It was deepest over her hips, exerting a cool weight. A beautiful opalescent cloud twinkled languidly in front of her eyes. Soothing to watch. She could feel her yammering heart slowing to a more pedestrian rhythm. Which brought her frantic gasps back under control. That was good. She still harboured a lot of guilt about using all that air.

'It's sealing up.'

'God, the blood.'

'She's all right. She's alive.'

'Stephanie, can you hear me?'

Long shivers were rippling up and down her body. Her skin had turned to ice. But she could blink her eyes into focus. The faces of her dear friends were staring down, paralysed with grief.

Her lips flicked into a tiny smile. 'That hurt,' she whispered.

'Just take it easy,' Franklin grunted. 'You're in shock.'

'Certainly am.' Moyo's hand was clutching her upper arm so tightly it was painful. She tried to reach for him, offer some reassurance.

'The wound has been repaired,' Sinon said. 'You have lost a considerable amount of blood, however. We'll need to take you back to our camp, and get some plasma into you.'

Something familiar was creeping into her sphere of consciousness. Familiar and unwelcome. Cold, hard thoughts, reeking of callous satisfaction.

'I told you so, Stephanie Ash. I told you not to come back here.'

'You piece of fascist shit!' McPhee bellowed. 'We're no armed.'

Stephanie struggled to lift her head. Annette Ekelund was standing at the head of some thirty or so soldiers. She was wearing an immaculately pressed pale khaki field commander's uniform, complete with forage cap. Three stars glinted unnaturally on her epaulettes. A powerful hunting rifle was cradled casually in her hands. Holding Stephanie's gaze, she worked the bolt slowly and deliberately. A spent cartridge case was ejected.

Stephanie groaned, her shoulders sagging with dismay. 'You're insane.'

'You bring the enemy into our camp, and you expect to go unpunished? Come, come, Stephanie, that's not how it works.'

'What enemy? We came to see if you needed help. Don't you understand?' She wanted to retreat back into the numb oblivion of pain and shock. It was preferable to this.

'Nothing has changed simply because we've won. They are still the enemy. And you and your loony bin refugee friends are traitors.'

'Excuse me,' Sinon said. 'But you have not won. This island has no food. The air will run out in ten days' time. All of us have to find a way back before then.'

'What do you mean, the air's running out?' Devlin asked.

Sinon's voice became louder. 'There is no fresh air in this realm, only what we brought with us. At the current rate, our breathing will exhaust it in ten days, a fortnight at the most.'

Several soldiers in the ranks behind Ekelund exchanged solicitous glances with each other.

'Simple disinformation,' Annette said dismissively. 'It sounds very plausible. If we were back in our old universe I'd even believe it myself. But we're not. We're in the place of our choosing. And we chose an existence that would carry us safely down through eternity. This is as close to classical heaven as the human race will ever get.'

'You specified the boundary qualifications,' Sinon said. 'A realm where you were cut off from the beyond, and night is a null concept. But that's all you did. This realm isn't going to safeguard you from folly. It's not some actively benign environment that will happily provide every need. You are responsible for what you bring here, and all you brought was a lump of lifeless rock with a thin smear of air on top. Tell me, I'm interested, how do you think this island is going to sustain you for tens of thousands of years?'

'You are a machine. A machine designed with one purpose, to kill. That is all you understand. You have no soul. If you had, you would feel as one with this place. You would know its glory. This is where we longed to be. Where we are safe, and at peace. You have lost, machine.'

'Yo there.' Cochrane had raised his hand. He smiled broadly, radiating enthusiasm like an eager schoolboy. 'Um, lady, I'm normally like *organic* I'm so in touch with the music of the land. And I gotta tell you, I don't feel shit for this lump of mud. There's no karmic vibes here, babe. Believe me.'

'Believe a seditious junkie? I think not.'

'What do you want?' Stephanie asked. She could see Cochrane losing his cool if he kept on arguing with Ekelund. That would turn out bad for everybody. Ekelund needed very little justification to exterminate all of them. In fact, Stephanie was wondering what was holding her back. Probably just enjoying her gloat.

'I don't want anything, Stephanie. You broke our arrangement and came here to me, remember?'

'In peace. Wanting to help.'

'We don't need help. Not from you. Not here. I have everything under control.'

'Stop this.'

'Stop what, Stephanie?'

'Let them go. Give these people back their liberty. For pity's sake, we'll die here if we can't find a way out, and you've got them fenced in by your authoritarian regime. This isn't heaven. This is a huge mistake we got panicked into making. The serjeants are trying to help us. Why can't you cooperate with that?'

'Ten hours ago, these *things* you've befriended were trying to kill us. No, worse than kill. Any of us they capture, they throw back into the beyond. I didn't see you rushing to hand back your nice new body, Stephanie. You went crawling out of Ketton hoping to hide in the dirt until they passed over.'

'Look, if it's some kind of revenge trip you want, then just shoot me in the head and get it over with. But let the others go. You can't condemn everyone on this island just because you have so much fear and hatred inside.'

'I abhor your assumed nobility.' Annette walked past Cochrane and Sinon to stand over Stephanie. The barrel of the rifle hung inches above her clammy forehead. 'I find it utterly repellent. You can never accept that you might be wrong. You perpetually claim the moral high ground as if it's some kind of natural inheritance. You use your own sweetness-and-light nature as a shield to ignore what you've done to the body you've stolen. That disgusts me. I would never try to deny what I am, nor what I've done. So, just for once, admit the truth. I did what was right. I organized the defence of two million souls, including yours, and prevented you from being cast back into that horror. Tell me, Stephanie, was that the right thing to do?'

Stephanie closed her eyes, squeezing small trickles of moisture out onto her cheeks. *Maybe Ekelund is right, maybe I am trying to ignore this monstrous crime. Who wouldn't?* 'I know what I've done is wrong. I've always known. But I haven't got a choice.'

'Thank you, Stephanie.' She turned to Sinon. 'And you, death machine, if you believe what you say, then you should switch yourself off and allow real humans to live longer. You're wasting our air.'

'I am human. More so than you, I suspect.'

'The time will come when we will throw the serpent back out into the emptiness.' She smiled without humour. 'Enjoy the fall. It looks like being a long one.'

*

Sylvester Geray opened the doors to Princess Kirsten's private office, and gestured Ralph to go through. The Princess was sitting at her desk, with the French doors open behind her, allowing a slight breeze to ruffle her dress. Ralph stood to attention in front of her, saluted, then put his flek down on the desk. He'd worked on the single file stored inside during the flight over from Xingu.

Kirsten looked at it with pursed lips, making no attempt to pick it up. 'And that is . . .?' She said it with the air of someone who knew very well what it contained.

'My resignation, ma'am.'

'Rejected.'

'Ma'am, we lost twelve thousand serjeants at Ketton, and God knows how many possessed civilians went with them. I gave the order. It is my responsibility.'

'It certainly is, yes. You assumed that responsibility when Alastair placed you in charge of the Liberation. And you will continue to bear that responsibility until the last possessed on Mortonridge is placed in zero-tau.'

'I can't do it.'

Kristen gave him a sympathetic look. 'Sit down, Ralph.' She indicated one of the chairs in front of the desk. For a second it appeared as though Ralph might refuse, but he gave a subdued nod and eased himself down.

'Now you know what being a Saldana is like,' she told him. 'Admittedly, we're not faced with quite such momentous decisions every day, but they still pass across this desk here. My brother has authorized fleet deployments which have resulted in a far higher cost of life than Ketton. And as you of all people know, we indirectly license the elimination of people who would one day cause trouble for the Kingdom. Not very many, and not very often, perhaps, but it mounts up over the course of a decade. Those decisions have to be made, Ralph. So I grit my teeth, and give the necessary orders, the really tough ones that the Cabinet would have a collective fit over if they were ever made to take them. That's genuine political power. Making the decisions which affect other people's lives. The overall daily running of the Kingdom is our domain, us Saldanas. Now call us what you like, ruthless dictators, heartless capitalists, or benign guardians appointed by God. The point is, what we do, we do very well indeed. That's because we take those decisions without hesitation.'

'You're trained to, ma'am.'

'True. But so are you. I admit the scale here is vastly different to

663

what an ESA head of station is accustomed to. But in the end, you've been deciding who lives and who dies for some time now.'

'I got it wrong!' Ralph wanted to shout at her, make her see reason. Something in his subconscious held him back. Not out of respect, or even fear. *Perhaps I just want to know I did the right thing.* Nobody else in the Kingdom, except perhaps Alastair II himself, could provide that assurance and have it mean anything.

'Yes, Ralph, you did. You got it very badly wrong. Squeezing the possessed into Ketton was a bad move, even worse than using electron beams against the red cloud.'

He looked up in surprise, meeting the Princess's uncompromising stare.

'Were you looking for compassion, Ralph? Because you won't get it in here, not from me. I want you back on Xingu revising the advance across Mortonridge. Not just because you're there to stop me and the family from taking the blame. I remember you the night we discovered Ekelund and the others had landed on this planet. You were driven, Ralph. It was mighty impressive to watch. You didn't compromise a single decision to Jannike or Leonard. I enjoyed that. People of their rank don't often get publicly stonewalled.'

'I didn't realize you were paying me that much attention,' Ralph grunted.

'Of course you didn't. You had one job to do, and nothing else mattered. Now you have another job. And I expect you to see it through.'

'I'm not the right man. That drive you saw, that's what landed us with the Ketton fiasco. The AI gave me several options. I chose the brute force approach because I was too fired up for a rational alternative. Hammer them with overwhelming firepower and battalions of troops until they capitulate. Well, now you know what that policy leaves us with. A damn great hole in the ground.'

'It was a painful lesson, wasn't it?' She leant forward, determined to convince rather than alienate. 'That just makes you better qualified to carry on.'

'Nobody will trust me.'

'Snap out of that self-pitying bullshit routine right now.'

Ralph almost smiled. Sworn at by a Saldana princess.

'This is what war is about, Ralph. The Edenists aren't going to carry grudges, they were part of the decision making process to storm Ketton. As for the others, the marines and occupation forces, they all hate you anyway. One more cock-up by the chief isn't going to make any difference to their opinion. They'll get their orders for the next stage, and the lieutenants and NCOs will make sure they're carried out to the letter. I want you to issue those orders. I've asked you twice, now.' Her finger pushed the flek back over the desk, a chess master going for checkmate.

'Yes, ma'am.' He picked up the flek. Somehow he'd known all along it would never be that easy.

'Right,' Kirsten said briskly. 'What's your next move?'

'I was going to recommend my successor change our assault policy again. One of our principal concerns over the Ketton incident is how the inhabitants and serjeants are going to survive. Even if the possessed were stockpiling all the town's supplies, there can't be much food left wherever they've gone.'

'You're guessing.'

'Yes, ma'am. But unless we have totally misread the situation, it is a logical one. Prior to this, the possessed have removed entire planets to this hidden sanctuary dimension of theirs. A planet gives them a viable biosphere capable of feeding them. Ketton is different, it's just rock with a layer of mud on top. It's just a question which they run out of first, air or food.'

'Unless they find one of the other planets where they can take refuge.'

'I hope they can do that, ma'am, I really do. I don't know what kind of conditions exist wherever they are, but they would have to be very weird indeed if they enabled them to land that section of rock on a planet. In fact, we believe the strongest possibility is that they'll return once they realize how much trouble they're in. The geologists say that'll cause all kinds of trouble, but we're preparing for the eventuality.'

'Good grief.' Kirsten tried to imagine that vast section of country-side coming down to land in its own crater, and failed. 'You realize, if they do come back, it will have a profound implication for the other planets? That would be proof that they can be returned as well.'

'Yes, ma'am.'

'All right, this is all interesting theorizing, but what was the change of policy?'

'After we reviewed Ketton's problems, we started to consider the supply situation on Mortonridge itself. Thanks to the deluge, there is no fresh food left at all; the satellites haven't managed to find a single field of crops left intact on the whole peninsula. Some animals managed to survive, but they're going to die soon because there's nothing left for them to feed on. We know the possessed cannot use their energistic power to create any food, not out of inorganic matter. So it's only a matter of time until they run out of commercially packaged food.'

'You can starve them out.'

'Yes. But it's going to take time. Mortonridge had an agricultural economy. Most towns have some kind of food industry, either a processing factory or warehouse. If the possessed organize properly and ration what they've got, they can hold out for a while yet. What I'd suggest we do is continue the front line's advance, but modify the direction they're taking. The serjeants can still engage small groupings of possessed in the countryside without too much worry. Larger concentrations in the towns should be left alone. Set up a firebreak around them, leave a garrison to watch, and then just wait until the food runs out.'

'Or they pull another disappearing act.'

'We believe Ketton happened because the possessed we'd trapped there were pressured into reacting by the assault. There's a big psychological difference between seeing ten thousand serjeants marching towards you, and simply squabbling among yourselves over the last sachets of spaghetti bolognese.'

'The longer we leave them possessed, the worse condition the bodies will be in. And that's before malnutrition.'

'Yes, ma'am. I know that. There's also the problem that if we just simply contract the front line the way we have been doing we'll push a lot of possessed into one giant concentration in the middle. We'll have to split Mortonridge into sections. That'll mean redeploying the serjeants to drive inland in columns and link up. And if we're leaving serjeants behind as garrisons, the numbers available for front-line duties will be depleted just when we need them most.'

'More decisions, Ralph. What I said to you the other day about providing political cover still stands. Do what you have to on the ground, leave the rest to me.'

'Can I expect any improvement in the medical back-up situation? We're really going to need it if we start sieges.'

'The Edenist Ambassador has indicated that their habitats will take the worst cancer cases from us, but their voidhawks are badly stretched. Admiral Farquar is looking into making troop transports available, at least they have zero-tau pods in them. In fact, I've asked Alastair for some Kulu Corporation colony transport ships. We can start storing patients until the pressure on facilities eases off.'

'That's something, I suppose.'

Kirsten stood, and datavised Sylvester Geray that the audience was over. 'The most fundamental rule of modern society: everything costs more and takes longer. It always has done, and always will do. And there's nothing you or I can do about it, General.'

Ralph managed a small bow as the doors opened. 'I'll bear it in mind, ma'am.'

*

'I think I can manage to walk now,' Stephanie said.

Choma and Franklin had carried her back to the serjeants' camp on an improvised stretcher. She'd lain on the muddy ground beside Tina, a sleeping bag wrapped round her legs and torso, and a plasma drip in her arm. Too weak to move, she'd dozed on and off for hours, falling victim to vague anxiety-drenched dreams. Moyo had stayed at her side the whole time, holding her hand and mopping her brow. Her body was reacting to the wound as if she'd come down with a fever.

Eventually the cold shivers passed, and she lay passively on her back gathering her woozy thoughts back together. Nothing much had changed, the serjeants were still standing motionless all around. Occasionally, a circular patch of air high above them would inflate with white light, and pulse briefly before extinguishing. If she closed her eyes, she could sense the flow of energistic power into the zone they designated; an intense focal point that was attempting to tear a gap in the fabric of this realm. The pattern which they applied the energy changed subtly every time, but the result was always the same: dissipation. This realm's reality remained stubbornly intact.

Choma looked over from where he was examining Tina's lower spine. 'I would rather you did not exert yourself for a while longer,' he said to Stephanie. 'You did lose a lot of blood.'

'Just like me,' Tina said. It was little more than a whisper. Her arm lifted a couple of inches off the ground, hand feeling round through the air.

Stephanie touched her, and they twined fingers. Tina's skin was alarmingly cold.

'Yes, I ought to take things easy, I suppose,' Stephanie said. 'We won't get better if we stress ourselves.'

Tina smiled and closed her eyes, a contented hum stealing away from her lips. 'We are getting better, aren't we.'

'That's right.' Stephanie kept her voice level, hoping the discipline would also keep her thoughts from fluttering. 'Us girls together.'

'Just like always. Everybody's been so kind, even Cochrane.'

'He wants you back on your feet, so he can carry on trying to get you on your back again.'

Tina grinned, then slowly dropped back into a semi-slumber.

Stephanie raised herself onto her elbows, imagining the sleeping bag fluffing up into a large pillow. The fabric rose up to support her spine. Her friends were all there, watching her with kind or mildly embarrassed expressions. But all of them were concerned. 'I'm such an idiot,' she said bitterly to them. 'I should never have gone back to Ketton.'

'No way!' Cochrane boomed.

McPhee spat in the direction of the ruined town. 'We did the right thing, the human thing.'

'It's not you who is to blame,' Rana said primly. 'That woman is utterly deranged.'

'Nobody knew that more than me,' Stephanie said. 'We should have taken some elementary precautions, at least. She could have shot all of us.'

'If showing compassion and trust is a flaw, then I'm proud to say I share it with you,' Franklin said.

'I should have guarded myself,' Stephanie said, almost to herself. 'It was stupid. A bullet would never have done any damage before, we were careful back on Ombey. I just thought we would all pull together now we're in the same predicament.'

'That was a big mistake.' Moyo patted her hand warmly. 'First you've made since we met, so I'll overlook it.'

She took his hand, and brought it up to her face, kissing his palm lightly. 'Thank you.'

'I don't think being prepared and paranoid would have been much use to us anyway,' Franklin said.

'Why not?'

He held up one of the nutrient soup sachets. The silver coating gradually turned blue and white as the shape rounded out. He was left holding a can of baked beans. 'We're not as strong here. Changing that sachet would have taken an eyeblink back in the old universe. And that's why they can't get back.' He indicated the serjeants just as another white blaze of air above them broke apart into expanding rivulets of blue ions. 'There isn't enough power available here to do what we did. Don't ask me why. Presumably it's got something to do with being blocked from the beyond. I expect those rifles Ekelund has could cause quite a bit of harm no matter how hard we made the air around ourselves.'

'Any more good news for the patients?' Moyo asked, scathingly.

'No, he's right,' Stephanie said. 'Besides, hiding from the facts now isn't going to help anyone.'

'How can you be so calm about it? We're stuck here.'

'Not exactly,' she said. 'Being an invalid has had one benefit. Sinon?'

Since the unfortunate trip to Ketton, the serjeants had been keeping a cautionary watch on the town in case Ekelund made any hostile move. Sinon and Choma had taken the duty, combining it with helping the two patients. It wasn't particularly difficult, from their slightly raised elevation they could see anything moving across the bland stretch of ochre mud between them and the desolated town. There would be plenty of warning if anyone came.

Sinon was checking over a batch of the sniper rifles which the serjeants were equipped with. Not that he expected they would be used. If Ekelund did send her people, the serjeants would simply establish a barrier around their camp similar to the one holding in the air around the island, offering passive yet insurmountable resistance.

He put down the sight he was cleaning. 'Yes?'

'Are you and the others aware we're actually moving?' Stephanie asked him. For some time, she'd been watching what passed for a sky in this realm. When they'd first arrived, it had appeared to be a uniform glare being emitted from some indefinable distance all around them. But as she'd lain there looking at it, she became aware of subtle variants. There were different shades arching above the flying island, arranged like flaccid waves, or streamers of thin mist. And they were moving, sliding slowly in one direction.

As Stephanie started to describe them, more and more serjeants broke away from their mental union to look upwards. A mild emotion of self-censure washed through the assembled minds. **We should have noticed this. Direct observation is the most basic method to gather data on an environment.**

By using affinity to link their vision together, the serjeants could scan the sky like some multi-segment telescope. Thousand of irises tracked the same faint wavering irregularity as it passed gently overhead. Parallel minds performed basic mental arithmetic to derive the parallax, putting the aberration roughly fifty kilometres away.

'As the bands of dimmer light seem to be fluctuating slightly in width, we conclude there is some kind of extremely tenuous nebula-like structure enveloping us,' Sinon told the fascinated humans. 'However, the source of the light remains indeterminable, so we cannot say for certain if it is the nebula or the island which is moving. But given that the speed appears to be close to a hundred and fifty kilometres an hour, we are tentatively assigning movement to the island.'

'Why?' Rana asked.

'Because it would take a great deal of force to move the nebula at that speed. It's not impossible, but as the environment outside the island is essentially a vacuum the problem of what force could be acting on the nebula is multiplied by an order of magnitude. We cannot detect any physical or energy impacting against the island, ergo there is no "wind" to push it along. We concede that it could still be expanding from its origin point, but as the fluctuations within it indicate a reasonably passive composition, such a possibility is unlikely.'

'So we really are flying,' McPhee said.

'It would appear so.'

'I don't want to like piss all over your parade or anything,' Cochrane said. 'But have you cats ever considered we might be like *falling*?'

'The direction of flow we can see in the nebula makes that unlikely,' Sinon said. 'It appears to be a horizontal movement. The most probable explanation is that we emerged at a different relative velocity to this nebula. Besides, if we had been falling since we arrived, then whatever we are falling towards would surely be visible by now. To exert such a powerful gravitational field, it would be massive indeed; several times the size of a super-Jovian gas giant.'

'You don't know what kind of mass or gravity are natural in this realm,' McPhee said.

'True. This island is proof of that.'

'What do you mean?'

'Our gravity hasn't changed since we arrived. Yet we are no longer part of Ombey. We assumed it has remained normal because the subconscious will of everyone here required that it do so.'

'Holy shit.' Cochrane jumped up, giving the bottom of his wide velvet flares a startled glance. 'You mean, we're like only dreaming there's gravity?'

'Essentially, yes.'

The hippy clenched his hands, and pressed them hard against his forehead. 'Oh man, that is a total bummer. I want my gravity to be the real stuff. Listen, you don't fool around with something as basic as this. You just don't.'

'Reality is now essentially contained in your mind. If you perceive gravity acting on you, then it is real,' the serjeant said imperturbably.

A large lighted reefer appeared in Cochrane's hand, and he took a deep drag. 'I am heavy,' he chanted. 'Heavy, heavy, heavy. And don't no one forget that. You listening to me, people? Keep thinking it.'

'In any event,' Sinon told McPhee, 'if we were in the grip of a gravity field, the nebula would be falling with us. It isn't.'

'Some good news,' McPhee grunted. 'Which is also no natural here.'

'Forget the academics of the situation,' Moyo said. 'Is there any way we can use it?'

'We intend to set up an observation detail,' Sinon said. 'A headland watch, if you like, to see if there is anything out there in front of us. It could be that all the other planets the possessed removed from the universe are here in this realm with us. We will also start using our affinity to call for help; it's the only method of communication we have that works here.'

'Oh, man, no way! Who's going to hear that? Come on, you guys, get real.'

'Obviously we don't know who, if anyone, will hear. And even if there is a planet out there, we doubt we'd be able to reach its surface intact.'

'You mean alive,' Moyo said.

'Correct. However, there is one strong possibility for rescue.'

'What?' Cochrane yelled.

'If this is the realm where all the possessed yearn to go, then it is conceivable Valisk is here. It might hear our call, and its biosphere would be able to support us. Transferring ourselves inside would be a simple matter.'

Cochrane let out a long sigh, blowing long trails of sweet-smelling green smoke from his nostrils. 'Hey, yeah, more like it, dude. Good positive thinking. I could dig living in Valisk.'

*

Watching was one thing the humans could do almost as well as the serjeants, so Stephanie and her friends hiked across the final kilometre to the edge of the island to help establish the headland lookout camp. It took them over an hour to get there. The terrain wasn't particularly rough – crusted mud cracked and squelched under their feet, and they had to go around several pools of stagnant water – but Tina had to be carried the whole way on a stretcher, along with her small array of primitive medical equipment. And even with energistic strength reinforcing her body, Stephanie had to stop for a rest every few minutes.

Eventually they reached the top of the cliff, and settled themselves down fifty metres short of the precipice. They'd chosen the brow of a mound, which gave them an excellent uninterrupted view out across the glaring emptiness ahead. Tina was placed so she could look outward by just raising her head, making her feel a part of their enterprise. She smiled a painful tired thanks as they rigged her plasma container up on an old branch beside her. The ten serjeants accompanying them clumped their backpacks together, and sat down in a broad semicircle like a collection of lotus-position Buddhas.

Stephanie eased herself down on a sleeping bag, quietly content the journey had ended. She promptly turned a sachet of nutrient soup into a ham sandwich, and bit in hungrily. Moyo sat beside her, allowing his shoulder to rest against hers. They exchanged a brief kiss.

'Groovy,' Cochrane hooted. 'Hey, if love is blind, how come lingerie is so popular?'

Rana regarded him in despair. 'Oh, very tactful.'

'It's a joke,' the hippy protested. 'Moyo doesn't mind, do you, man?'

'No.' He and Stephanie put their heads together and started giggling.

Giving them a slightly suspicious look, Cochrane settled down on his own sleeping bag. He'd changed the fabric to scarlet and emerald crushed velvet. 'So how about a sweepstake, you dudes? What's going to come sailing over the horizon first?'

'Flying saucers,' McPhee said.

'No, no,' Rana said primly. 'Winged unicorns ridden by virgins wearing Cochrane's frilly white lingerie.'

'Hey, come on, this is serious, you guys. I mean, like our lives depend on it.'

'Funny,' Stephanie mused. 'Not so long ago I was wishing death was permanent. Now it could well be, and I'd like to keep on living just that little bit longer.'

'I would like to ask, why do you believe you will actually die?' Sinon enquired. 'You have all indicated that is what will happen in this realm.'

'It's like the gravity, I suppose,' Stephanie said. 'Death is such a fundamental. That's what we expect at the end of life.'

'You mean you are willing your own extinction?'

'Not exactly. Being free of the beyond was only a part of what we wanted. This realm was supposed to be marvellously benign. It probably is if we were on a planet. We wanted to come here and live for ever, just like the legends of heaven. And if not for ever, certainly thousands of years. A proper life, like we used to think we had. Life ends in death.'

'In heaven, death would not return you to the beyond,' Choma ventured.

'Exactly. This life would be better than before. Energistic power gives us the potential to fulfil our dreams. We don't need a manufacturing base, or money. We can make whatever we want just by wishing it into being. If that can't make people happy, nothing can.'

'You would never know a sense of accomplishment,' Sinon said. 'There would be no frontier to challenge you. Electricity is virtually non-existent, denying you any kind of machinery more advanced than a steam engine. You expect to live for a good portion of eternity. And nobody can ever leave. Forgive me, I do not see that as paradise.'

'Always the downside,' Cochrane muttered.

'You might be right. But even a jail planet trapped in the eighteenth century followed by genuine death is better than the beyond.'

'Then your energies would surely be better directed in solving the problem of human souls becoming trapped in the beyond.'

'Fine words,' Moyo said. 'How?'

'I don't know. But if some of you would cooperate with us, then avenues of possibility would be opened.'

'We are cooperating.'

'Not here. Back in the universe where the Confederation's scientific resources could be marshalled.'

'All you ever did when we were on Ombey was assault us,' Rana said. 'And we know the military captured several possessed to vivisect. We could hear their torment echoing through the beyond.'

'If they had cooperated, we wouldn't have to use force,' Choma said. 'And it was not vivisection. We are not barbarians. Do you really think I wish to consign my family to the beyond? We want to help. Self-interest dictates that if nothing else.'

'Another wasted opportunity,' Stephanie said sadly. 'They do mount up, don't they.'

'Someone is coming from the town,' Choma announced. 'They are walking towards our encampment.'

Stephanie automatically turned to look back over the mud prairie behind them. She couldn't see anything moving.

'It is only five people,' Choma said. 'They don't appear hostile.' The serjeant continued to give them a commentary. A squad was dispatched to intercept the newcomers who claimed they were leaving Ekelund, disillusioned by the way things were in the ruined town. The serjeants directed them to the headland group.

Stephanie watched them approach. She wasn't surprised to see Devlin was with them. He was dressed in his full nineteen-hundreds army officer regalia, a dark uniform of thick wool with plenty of scarlet, gold, and imperial purple ribbons.

'Phallocentric military.' Rana sniffed disdainfully, and made a show of turning round to gaze out over the precipice.

Stephanie gestured to the newcomers to sit down. They all seemed apprehensive about the kind of reception they'd receive.

'You dudes had enough of her, huh?'

'Admirably put,' Devlin conceded. He turned a sleeping bag into a tartan-pattern blanket, and lounged across it. 'She's gone completely batty. Mad with power, of course. Saw it enough times back in the Great War. Any spark of dissension is classed as mutiny. I expect she'll have us shot if she ever sees us again. Quite literally.'

'So you deserted.'

'I'm sure she'll see it that way, yes.'

'We believe we can keep her forces away,' Sinon said.

'Glad to hear it, old chap. Things were getting pretty dire back there. Ekelund and Hoi Son are still preparing for some kind of conflict. She's got the power, you see. Now there's no beyond for souls to flee back into, the threat of discipline is jolly effective. And of course she's in charge of dishing the food out. A whole bunch of silly asses still believe in what she's doing. That's all it ever takes, you know, one leader with a bunch of loyalists to enforce orders. Damn stupid.'

'What does she think is going to happen?' Stephanie asked.

'Not too sure about that. I don't think she is, either. Hoi Son keeps spouting on about how we are as one with the land, and how you serjeant chaps are ruining our harmony. They're egging each other on. Trying to convince the rest of those poor sods over there that everything will be dandy once you've been thrown over the edge. Utter bilge. Any idiot can see this chunk of land isn't going to be the slightest use to anyone, no matter who's on it.'

'Only Annette could think that this island is worth fighting over.'

'I agree,' Devlin said. 'Sheerest bloody folly. Seen it before. People become obsessed with one idea and can't let go. Don't care how many die in the process. Well, I'm not going to help her. I made that mistake before. Never again.'

'Yo, man, welcome to Decentville.' Cochrane held out a silver flask.

Devlin took a small nip, and smiled appreciatively. 'Not bad.' He took a larger drink, and passed it on. 'What exactly are you all looking for out there?'

'We don't know,' Sinon said. 'But we'll recognize it when we see it.'

*

Jay spent twenty minutes correcting and castigating the universal provider after breakfast that morning. It kept reabsorbing the dress and extruding a new one for her. The variations were small, but Jay was determined to get it right. Tracy had sat in on the session for the first five minutes, then patted Jay lightly and said: 'I think I'll leave the pair of you to it, sweetie.'

The design she wanted was simple enough. She'd seen it back in the arcology one day: a loose, pleated reddish skirt that came down to the knee, and blended smoothly up into a square-cut neck top that was bright canary-yellow, the two colours interlocking like opposing flames. It had looked wonderful on the shop mannequin two years ago, expensive and attractive. But when she asked, her mother said no, they couldn't afford it. After that, the dress had come to symbolize everything wrong with Earth. She always knew what she wanted in life, but she could never get to it.

Tracy knocked on the bedroom door. 'Haile will be here in a minute, poppet,' she called.

'Coming,' Jay yelled back. She glared at the globe floating over the wicker chair. 'Go on, spit it out.'

The dress glided out through the purple surface. It still wasn't right! Jay put her hands on her hips, and sighed in disgust at the provider. 'The skirt is still too long. I told you! You can't have the hem level with the knee. That's awful.'

'Sorry,' the provider murmured meekly.

'Well, I'll just have to wear it now. But you're going to get it right when I come back this evening.'

She hurriedly pulled the dress on, wincing as it went over the bruise on her ribs (the edge of the surfboard had whacked her hard when she fell off). Her shoes were totally wrong as well. White plimsolls with a tread that was thick enough to belong on a jungle boot. Blue socks, too. Sighing at her martyrdom one last time, she picked up the straw boater (at least the provider had got that right) and perched it on her head. A quick check in the mirror above the sink to see just how bad the damage was. That was when she saw Prince Dell lying on the bed. She screwed her face up, riddled with guilt. But she couldn't take him with her to Haile's home planet. Just couldn't. The whole flap over the dress was because she was the first human to go there. She felt very strongly that she ought to look presentable. After all, she was kind of like an ambassador for her whole race. She could imagine what her mother would say; carrying a scruffy old toy about with her simply wasn't on.

'Jay!' Tracy called.

'Coming.' She burst through the door and scampered out onto the chalet's little veranda. Tracy was standing beside the steps, using a small brass can with a long spout to water one of the trailing geraniums. She gave the little girl a long look.

'Very nice, poppet. Well done, that was a good choice.'

'Thank you, Tracy.'

'Now just remember, you're going to see lots of new things. Some of them are going to be quite astonishing, I'm sure. Please try not to get too excitable.'

'I'll be good. Really.'

'I'm sure you will.' Tracy kissed her lightly. 'Now run along.'

Jay started down the steps, then stopped. 'Tracy?'

'What is it?'

'How come you've never been to Riynine? Haile said it's really important, one of their capital planets.'

'Oh, I don't know. Too busy when that kind of sightseeing would have excited me. Now I've got the time, I can't really be bothered. Seen one technological miracle, seen them all.'

'It's not too late,' Jay said generously.

'Maybe another day. Now run along, you'll be late. And Jay, remember, if you want the toilet, just ask a provider. No one's going to be embarrassed or offended.'

'Yes, Tracy. Bye.' She pressed a hand on the top of her boater, and raced off across the sand to the ebony circle.

The old woman watched her go, overlarge knuckles gripping the handle of the watering can too tightly. Bright sunlight caught the moisture poised at the corner of her eyes. 'Damn,' she whispered.

Haile materialized when Jay was still ten metres away from the circle. She whooped, and ran harder.

Friend Jay. It is a good morning.

'It's a wonderful morning!' She came to a halt beside Haile, and flung an arm round the baby Kiint's neck. 'Haile! You grow every day.'

Very much.

'How long till you get to adult size?'

Eight years. I will itch all that time.

'I'll scratch you.'

You are my true friend. Shall we go?

'Yes!' She did a little jump, smiling delightedly. 'Come on, come on!'

Blackness plucked both of them away.

The falling sensation didn't bother Jay at all now. She just shut her eyes and held her breath. One of Haile's appendages was coiled comfortingly round her wrist.

Weight returned quickly. Her soles touched a solid floor, and her knees bent slightly to absorb the impact. Light was shining on her closed eyelids.

We are here.

'I know.' She was suddenly nervous about opening her eyes.

I live there.

Haile's tone was so eager Jay just had to look. The sun was low in the sky, still casting off its daybreak tint. Long shadows flowed out behind them across the large ebony circle they'd arrived on. It was out in the open air, with the rumpled landscape sweeping away for what seemed like a hundred kilometres or more to the horizon. Flat-cone mountains of pale rock, crinkled with pale-purple gorges, rose regally out from the lavish mantle of blue-green vegetation; not strung out in a range as normal, but spread out across the whole expanse of steppe. Large serpentine rivers and tributary streams threading through the vales glinted silver in the fresh sunlight, while tissue-fine sheets of pearl-white mist wound around the lower slopes of the mountains. The vista was nature at its most striking. Yet it wasn't natural; this was what she imagined the inside of an Edenist habitat would be like, but on an infinitely larger canvas. There was nothing ugly permitted here; designed geology ensured this world would have bayous rather than dark, stagnant marshes, languid downs instead of lifeless lava fields.

That didn't stop it from being truly lovely, though.

There were buildings nestled amid the contours, mainly Kiint domes of different sizes, but with some startlingly human-like skyscraper towers mingled among them. There were also structures that looked more like sculptures than buildings: a bronze spiral leading nowhere, emerald spheres clinging together like a cluster of soap bubbles. Each of the buildings was set by itself; there were no roads, or even dirt tracks as far as she could see. Nevertheless, undeniably, she was in a city: one that was conceived on a vaster, grander scale than anything the Confederation could ever achieve. A post-urban conquest of the land.

'So where do you live?' she asked.

Haile's tractamorphic arm uncoiled from her wrist, and straightened out to point. The ebony circle was surrounded by a broad meadow of glossy aquamarine grass-analogue bordered by clumps of trees. They at least looked like natural forests rather than carefully composed parkland. Several different species were growing together, black octagonal leaves and yellow parasols competing for light and space; long smooth boles, capped with a fuzzy ball of pink fern-fronds, had stabbed up from the tops of more bushy varieties, resembling giant willow reeds.

A steel-blue dome was visible through the gaps in the trees half a kilometre away. It didn't look much bigger than the ones back in Tranquillity.

'That's nice,' Jay said politely.

It has difference to my first home in the all-around. The universal providers have eased life greatly here.

'I'm sure. So where are all your friends?'

Come. Vyano has been told about you. He would like to initiate greetings.

Jay gasped as she turned to follow the baby Kiint. There was a huge lake behind her, with what she assumed could only be the castle of some magical elf lord. Dozens of featureless, tapering white towers rose from its centre; the tallest spires were those right at the centre of the clump, easily measuring over a kilometre high. Delicate single-span bridges wove their way through the gaps between the towers, curving around each other without ever touching. As far as she could understand it, they followed no pattern or logic; sometimes a tower would have as many as ten, all at different levels, while others had only a couple. The whole edifice scintillated with brilliant red and gold flashes as the strengthening sunlight slithered slowly across its quartz-like surface. It was as dignified as it was beautiful.

'What is that?' she asked as she hurried after Haile.

This is a Corpus locus, a place for knowledge to grow and ripen.

'You mean like a school?'

The baby Kiint hesitated. Corpus says yes.

'Do you go to it?'

No. I am still receiving many primary educationals from the Corpus and my parents. First I must understand them fully. That is a hardness. When I have understanding I can begin to expand my own thoughts.

'Oh, I get it. That's like the way we do it, too. I have to receive a lot of didactic courses before I can go on to university.'

You will go to university?

'I suppose so. I don't know how on Lalonde, though. There might be one in Durringham. Mummy will tell me when she comes back and things get better.'

I hope for you.

They had reached the lake's shore. Its water was very dark, even when Jay stood on the shaggy grass-analogue right at the edge and peered over cautiously she couldn't see the bottom. The surface reflected her image back at her. Then it started to ripple slightly.

Haile was walking out towards the white towers. Jay paused for a moment to watch her friend. There was something not quite right about the scene, something obvious which her mind couldn't quite catch.

Haile was about ten metres from the shore when she realized Jay wasn't following. She swung her head round to look at the girl. Vyano is in here. Do you not want to meet him?

Very slowly, Jay cleared her throat. 'Haile, you're walking on the water.'

The baby Kiint looked down at where her feet-pads were dinting the surface of the lake. Yes. Query puzzlement. Why do you find wrongness?

'Because it's water!' Jay shouted.

There is stability for those wishing to attend the locus. You will not fall in.

Jay glared at her friend, though intense curiosity was a strong temptation. Tracy's warning rang clear in her mind. And Haile would never trick her. She put a toe cautiously on the water. The dark surface bent ever so slightly as she began to apply pressure, but her shoe couldn't actually break the surface tension and get wet. She put even more weight on her foot, allowing her whole sole to rest on the water. It supported her without any apparent strain.

A couple of tentative steps, and Jay glanced from side to side, giggling. 'This is brilliant. You don't need to build bridges and stuff.'

You have happiness now?

'You bet.' She started to walk towards Haile. Slow ripples expanded out from under her shoes, clashing and shimmering away. Jay couldn't stop the giggles. 'We should have had this in Tranquillity. We could have got out to that island, then.'

Rightness.

Smiling happily, Jay let Haile's arm tip wrap round her fingers, and together they walked over the lake. After a couple of minutes the towers of the locus seemed no closer. Jay began to wonder just how big they were.

'Where's Vyano, then?'

He comes.

Jay scanned the base of the towers. 'I can't see anybody.'

Haile stopped, and looked down at her feet, head swaying from side to side. **I have sight.**

Promising herself she wouldn't yelp or anything, Jay looked down. There was movement beneath her feet. A small pale-grey mountain was sliding through the water, twenty metres beneath the surface. Her heart did sort of go thud, but she clamped her jaw shut and stared in amazement. The creature must have been bigger than any of the whales in her didactic zoology memories. There were more flippers and fins than Earth's old behemoths, too. A smaller version of the creature was swimming along beside it, a child. It curved away from its parent's flank, and started to race upwards, its fins wriggling enthusiastically. The big parent rolled slowly, and dived off into the depths.

'Is this Vyano?' Jay exclaimed.

Yes. He is a cousin.

'What do you mean, cousin? He's nothing like you.'

Humans have many subspecies.

'No we don't!'

There are Adamists and Edenists, white skin, dark skin; more shades of hair than colours in the rainbow. This I have seen for myself.

'Well, yes, but ... Look here, there's none of us live underwater. That's just totally different.'

Corpus says human scientists have experimented with lungs that can extract oxygen from water.

Jay recognized that particular mental tone of pure stubbornness. 'They probably have,' she conceded.

The aquatic Kiint child was over fifteen metres long, and flatter than a terrestrial whale, with a thick tractamorphic tail that was contracting into a bulb as it neared the surface. Its other appendages, six buds of tractamorphic flesh, were spaced along its flanks. To help propel it through the water, they were currently compressed into semicircular fans that undulated with slow power. Perhaps the most obvious pointer to a shared heritage with landbound Kiint was the head, which was simply a more streamlined version that had six gills replacing the breathing vents. The same large semi-mournful eyes were shielded with a milky membrane.

Vyano broke surface with a burst of spray and energetic waves, which churned outward. Jay was suddenly trying to keep her balance as the lake's surface bounced about underneath her like some hyperlastic trampoline. Haile was bobbing up and down beside her, in almost as much trouble, which was slightly reassuring. When the swell had eased off, a mound of glistening leaden flesh was floating a couple of metres away. The aquatic Kiint formshifted one of its flank appendages into an arm, tip spreading out into the shape of a human hand.

Jay touched palms.

Welcome to Riynine, Jay Hilton.

'Thank you. You have a lovely world.'

It has much goodness. Haile has shared her memories of your Confederation worlds. They are interesting also. I would like to visit after I am released from parental proscription.

'I'd like to go back, too.'

Your plight has been spoken of. I grieve with you for all that has been lost.

'Richard says we'll pull through. I suppose we will.'

Richard Keaton is attuned to Corpus, Haile said. **He would not tell untruths.**

'How could you visit the Confederation? Does that jump machinery of yours work underwater as well?'

Yes.

'But there wouldn't be much for you to see, I'm afraid. Everything interesting happens on land. Oh, except for Atlantis, of course.'

Land is always small and clotted with identical plants. I would see the life that teems below the waves where nothing remains the same. Every day is joyfully different. You should modify yourself and come to dwell among us.

'No, thank you very much,' she said primly.

That is a sadness.

'I suppose what I mean is, you wouldn't be able to see what humans have achieved. Everything we've built and done is on the land or in space.'

Your machinery is old to us. It holds little attraction. That is why my family returned to the water.

'You mean you're like our pastorals?'

I apologize. My understanding of human references is not complete.

'Pastorals are people who turned away from technology, and lived life as simply as they can. It's a very primitive existence, but they don't have modern worries, either.'

All races of Kiint embrace technology, Haile said. **The providers cannot fail now, they give us everything and leave us free.**

'This is the bit about you which I don't really get. Free to do what?'

To live.

'All right, try this. What are you two going to be when you grow up?'

I shall be me.

'No, no.' Jay would have liked to stamp her foot for emphasis. Given what she was standing on, she thought better of it. 'I mean, what profession? What do Kiints spend all day doing?'

You know my parentals were helping with the Laymil Project.

All activity has one purpose, Vyano said. **We enrich ourselves with knowledge. This can come from simply interpreting the observed universe or extrapolating thoughts to their conclusion. These are complementary.**

Enrichment is the result life is dedicated to. Only then can we transcend with confidence.

'Transcend? You mean die?'

Body lifeloss, yes.

'I'm sure doing nothing but thinking is all really good for you. But it seems really boring to me. People need things to keep them occupied.'

Difference is beauty, Vyano said. There is more difference in the water than on land. Our domain is where nature excels, it is the womb of every planet. Now do you see why we chose it over the land?

'Yes. I suppose so. But you can't all spend the whole time admiring new things. Somebody has to make sure things work smoothly.'

That is what the providers do. We could not ascend to this cultural level until after our civilization's machinery had evolved to its current state. Providers provide, under the wisdom of Corpus.

'I see, I guess. You have Corpus like Edenists have Consensus.'

Consensus is an early version of Corpus. You will evolve to our state one day.

'Really?' Jay said. Arguing philosophy with a Kiint wasn't really what she had in mind when she wanted to visit Riynine. She gestured round, trying to indicate the locus and all the other extravagant buildings. An act of human body language which was probably wasted on the young aquatic Kiint. 'You mean humans are going to wind up living like this?'

I cannot speak for you. Do you wish to live as we do?

'It'd be nice not having to worry about money and stuff.' She thought of the Aberdale villagers, their enthusiasm for what they were building. 'But we need concrete things to do. That's the way we are.'

Your nature will guide you to your destiny. It is always so.

'I suppose.'

I sense we are kindred, Jay Hilton. You wish to see newness every day. That is why you are here on Riynine, query?

'Yes.'

You should visit the Congressions. That is the best place for a view of the physical achievement which you value so.

She looked at Haile. 'Can we?'

It will have much enjoyment, Haile said.

'Thanks, Vyano.'

The aquatic Kiint began to sink back below the water. **Your visit is a newness which has enriched me. I am honoured, Jay Hilton.**

*

When Haile had told Jay that Riynine was a capital world, the little girl had imagined a cosmopolitan metropolis playing host to a multitude of Kiint and thousands of exciting xenocs. The Corpus locus was certainly grandiose, but hardly kicking.

Her impression changed when she popped out of the black teleport bubble onto one of Riynine's Congressions. Although the physical concept was hardly extravagant for a race which had such extraordinary resources, there was something both anachronistic and prideful in the gigantic cities which floated serenely through the planet's atmosphere. Splendidly intricate colossi of crystal and shining metal proclaimed the true nature of the Kiint to any visitor, more so than the ring of manufactured planets. No race which had the slightest doubt about its own abilities would dare to construct such a marvel.

The one in which Jay found herself was over twenty kilometres broad. Its nucleus was a dense aggregation of towers and circuitous columns of light like warped rainbows; from that, eight solid crenated peninsulas radiated outwards, themselves bristling with short flat spines. The bloated tufts of cloud it encountered parted smoothly to flow around its extremities, leaving it at the centre of a doldrum zone whose clarity seemed to magnify the landscape ten kilometres below. Shoals of flying craft spun around it, their geometries and technologies as varied as the species they carried; starships equipped with atmospheric drives cavorted along the same flight paths as tiny ground-to-orbit planes. All of them were landing or taking off from the spines on the peninsulas.

Jay had arrived at one end of an avenue which ran along the upper reaches of a peninsula. It was made from a smooth sheet of some burgundy mineral, host to a web of glowing opalescent threads that flowed just below the surface. Every junction in the web sprouted a tall jade triangle, like the sculpture of a pine tree. A roof of crystal arched overhead, heartbreakingly similar to an arcology dome.

Jay held on to Haile's arm with a tight grip. The avenue thronged with xenocs, hundreds of species walking, sliding, and in several cases flying along together in a huge multi-coloured river of life.

All her pent-up breath was exhaled in a single overwhelmed: 'Wow!' They hurried off the teleport circle, allowing a family of tall, feathered octopeds to use it. Globes similar to providers, but in many different colours, glided sedately overhead. She sniffed at the air, which contained so many shifting scents all she could really smell was something like dry spice. Slow bass grumbles, quick chittering, whistles, and human(ish) speech gurgled loudly about her, blurring together into a single background clamour.

'Where do they all come from? Are they all your observers?'

None of them are observers. These are the species who live in this galaxy, and some others. All are friends of Kiint.

'Oh. Right.' Jay walked over to the edge of the avenue. It was guarded by a tall rail, as if it was nothing more than an exceptionally big balcony. She stood on her toes, and peeked over. They were above a compact city, or possibly a district of industrial structures. There didn't appear to be any movement in the lanes between the buildings. Right in front of her, spacecraft swished along parallel to the peninsula's crystal roof as they vectored in on their landing sites. Several times she caught sight of small scarlet cones with narrow fins flitting among the darker, more utilitarian vehicles; like sports marque spaceplanes, she imagined. They would be fun to fly.

The Congression was high enough above the land to lose fine details amid the broader colour swaths of mountains and savannahs. But as though to compensate the curvature of the horizon could be seen, a splinter of purple neon separating the land and the sky. A coastline was visible far ahead. Or behind. Jay wasn't sure which way they were travelling. If they were.

She contented herself with watching the spacecraft flying past. 'So what are they all doing here, then?'

Different species come here to perform exchanges. Some have ideas to give, some require knowledge to make ideas work. Corpus facilitates this. The Congressions act as junctions for those who seek and those who wish to give. Here they can find each other.

'That all sounds terribly noble.'

We have opened our worlds to this act for a long time. Some races we have known since the beginning of our history, others are new. All are welcome.

'Apart from humans.'

You are free to visit.

'But nobody knows about Riynine. The Confederation thinks Jobis is your homeworld.'

I have sadness. If you can come here, you are welcome.

Jay eyed a quartet of adult Kiint walking along the avenue. They were accompanied by what looked suspiciously like spectres of some slender reptilians dressed in one-piece coveralls. They were certainly translucent, she could see things through them. 'I get it. It's sort of like a qualifying test. If you're smart enough to get here, you're smart enough to take part.'

Confirm.

'That'd be really helpful for us, learning new stuff. But I still don't think people want to spend their life philosophizing. Well . . . one or two like Father Horst, but not many.'

Some come to the Congressions asking for our aid, and to improve their technology.

'You give them that, machines and things?'

Corpus responds to everyone at a relative level.

'That's why the provider wouldn't give me a starship.'

You are lonely. I brought you here. I have sorrow.

'Hey . . .' She put her arm round the baby Kiint's neck, and stroked her breathing vents. 'I'm not sorry you brought me here. This is something not even Joshua has seen, and he's been everywhere in the Confederation. I'll be able to impress him when I get back. Won't that be something?' She gazed out at the fanciful craft again. 'Come on, let's find a provider. I could do with some ice cream.'

17

Rocio waited a day after the Organization's convoy returned from the antimatter station before he abandoned his routine high-orbit patrol above New California and swallowed out to Almaden. Radar pulses from the asteroid's proximity radar washed across *Mindori*, returning an odd fuzzy blob on the display screens. It fluctuated in time with the human heart. The visual-spectrum sensors showed the huge dark harpy with its wings folded, hovering two kilometres out from the counter-rotating spaceport. A glitter of red light could just been seen through eyelids that weren't completely shut.

In turn, Rocio focused his own senses on Almaden's docking-ledge. Each of the pedestals had been struck by laser fire, spilling a sludge of metal and plastic out across the rock where it had solidified into a grey clinker-like puddle with a surface badly pocked by burst gas bubble craters. As well as the pedestals, the nutrient fluid refinery and its three storage tanks had also been targeted.

Rocio shared his view with Pran Soo, who was back at Monterey. What do you think? he asked his fellow hellhawk.

The refinery isn't as badly damaged as it looks. It's only the outer layers of machinery that have been struck. Etchells just ripped his laser backwards and forwards over it, which no doubt looked spectacular. Lots of molten metal spraying everywhere, and tubes detonating under the pressure. But the core remains intact, and that's where the actual chemical synthesis mechanism is.

Typical.

Yes. Fortunately. There's no practical reason why this can't be returned to operational status. Providing you can get the natives to agree.

They'll agree, Rocio said. **We have something they want: ourselves.**

Good luck.

Rocio shifted his senses to the counter-rotating spaceport, a small disc whose appearance suggested it was still under construction. It was mostly naked girders containing tanks and fat tubes, with none of the protective plating that spaceports usually boasted. Three ships were docked, a pair of cargo tugs, and the *Lucky Logorn*. The inter-orbit craft had returned ten hours earlier. If the Organization lieutenants in the asteroid were going to discipline the crew, they would have done it by now.

Rocio opened a short-range channel. 'Deebank?'

'Good to see you.'

'Likewise. I'm glad you haven't been thrown out of your new body.'

'Let's just say, there are more people sympathetic to my cause than there are to the Organization.'

'What happened to the lieutenants?'

'Complaining to Capone direct from the beyond.'

'That was risky. He doesn't take rebellion kindly. You may find several frigates arriving to make the point.'

'We figure he's got enough problems with the antimatter right now. In any case, the only real option he's got left against this asteroid is to nuke us. If that looks likely, we'll shift out of this universe and take our chances. We don't want to do that.'

'I understand perfectly. I don't want you to do that, either.'

'Fair enough, you and I both have our own problems. How can we help each other?'

'If we're going to break free from the Organization we require an independent source of nutrient fluid. In return for you repairing your refinery, we are prepared to transport your entire population to a planet.'

'New California won't take us.'

'We can use one which the Organization has already infiltrated. Myself and my friends have enough spaceplanes to make the transfer work. But it will have to be soon. Without the antimatter station there will be no new infiltrations, and those that have been seeded will not remain in this universe for much longer.'

'We can start repairing the refinery right away. But if we all leave, how are you going to maintain it?'

'Spare parts must be manufactured in sufficient quantity to keep the refinery functional for a decade. You will also have to adapt your mechanoids for remote waldo operation.'

'You're not asking for much.'

'I believe it's an equal trade.'

'OK, cards on the table. My people here say the components shouldn't be any problem, our industrial stations can handle that. But we can't produce the kind of electronics which the refinery needs. Can you get hold of them for us?'

'Datavise a list over. I will make enquiries.'

*

Jed and Beth had listened to the exchange in the stateroom cabin they'd moved into. They were spending a lot of time in the neatly furnished compartment by themselves. In bed. There wasn't a lot else to do since Jed's mission to resupply their food stocks. And despite Rocio's assurances that his plans were progressing smoothly, they couldn't shake off their sense of impending disaster. Such conditions had completely suppressed their inhibitions.

They were lying together on top of the bunk in post-coital languor, stroking each other in cosy admiration. Sunlight streaming in through the wooden slats that covered the porthole was painting warm stripes across them, helping to dry damp skin.

'Hey, Rocio, you really think you can make this deal swing?' she asked.

The mirror above the teak dresser shimmered to reveal Rocio's face. 'I think so. Both of us want something from the other. That is the usual basis for trade.'

'How many hellhawks want in?'

'A sufficient number.'

'Oh, yeah? If a whole load of you bugger off, Kiera's gonna do her best to cripple you. You'll have to defend Almaden for a start. You'll need combat wasps for that.'

'Good heavens, do you really think so?'

Beth glared at him.

'There are no suitable asteroid settlements available in other star

690

systems,' Rocio continued. 'This is our one chance to secure an independent future for ourselves, despite its proximity to the Organization. We will make quite sure we're capable of defending that future, never fear.'

Jed sat up, making sure the blanket was covering his groin when he faced the mirror (Beth never did understand that brand of shyness). 'So where do we fit in?'

'I don't know yet. I may not need you, after all.'

'You gonna turn us in to Capone?' Beth asked, hoping her voice didn't waver.

'That would be difficult. How would I explain your presence on board?'

'So you just let Deebank and his mates in here to take care of us, huh?'

'Please, we are not all like Kiera. I had hoped you'd realize that by now. I have no desire to see the children possessed.'

'So where are you going to let us off?' Beth asked.

'I have no idea. Although I'm sure the Edenists will be happy enough to retrieve you from my corrupt clutches. Details can be worked out when we have locked down our own position. And I have to say that I'm disappointed by your attitude, given what I saved you from.'

'Sorry, Rocio,' Jed said immediately.

'Yeah, didn't mean no offence for sure,' Beth said, one degree above sarcasm.

The image faded, and they looked at each other. 'You shouldn't annoy him so much,' Jed protested. 'Jeeze, babe, we're like totally dependent on him. Air, water, heat, even bloody gravity. Stop pushing!'

'I was just asking.'

'Well, don't!'

'Yes, sir. Forgot for a moment that you were in charge of everything.'

'Don't,' Jed said remorsefully. He reached out and stroked her cheek tenderly. 'I never said I was in charge, I'm just worried.'

Beth knew full well that when he looked at her body the way he was doing now, what he actually saw was the memory of Kiera's fabulous figure. It didn't bother her any more, for reasons she didn't question too closely. Need overcoming dignity, most likely. 'I know. Me too. Good job we've found something to keep our minds off it the whole time, huh?'

His grin was sheepish. 'Too right.'

'I'd better get going. The kids'll be wanting their supper.'

Navar squealed and pointed when they walked into the galley. 'You've been at it again!'

Jet tried to bat her hand away, but she dodged back, laughing and sneering. He could hardly rebuke her; he and Beth hadn't exactly been secretive about what they were doing.

'Can we eat now?' Gari asked plaintively. 'I've got everything ready.'

Beth gave the preparations a quick inspection. The girls and Webster had prepared six trays for the induction oven, mixing food packets together. Potato cakes with rehydrated egg mash and cubes of carrot. 'Well done.' She keyed in the quantity on the oven's control panel, and activated it. 'Where's Gerald?'

'Doing his nut in the main lounge. What else?'

Beth gave the girl a sharp glance.

Navar refused to give ground. 'He is,' she insisted.

'You dish the food out,' Beth told Jed. 'I'll go see what the problem is.'

Gerald was standing in front of the lounge's large viewport, palms pressed against it, as though he was trying to push the glass out of its frame.

'Hey there, Gerald, mate. Supper's ready.'

'Is that where she is?'

'Where, mate?'

'The asteroid.'

Beth stood behind him, looking over his shoulder. Almaden was centred in the viewport. A dark lump of rock, rotating slowly against the starscape.

'No, mate, sorry. That's Almaden, not Monterey. Marie isn't in there.'

'I thought it was the other one. Monterey, where she is.'

Beth gave his hands a close inspection. The knuckles were lightly grazed from pounding on something. Fortunately, they weren't bleeding. She gently put her hand on his forearm. Every muscle was locked rigid beneath her fingers, trembling. His forehead was beaded in sweat.

'Come on, mate,' she said quietly. 'Let's get some tucker down you. Do you good.'

'You don't understand!' He was near to tears. 'I have to get back to her. I don't even remember when I saw her last. My head is so full of darkness now. I hurt.'

'I know, mate.'

'Know!' he screamed. 'What do you know? She's my baby, my beautiful little Marie. And she makes her do things, all the time.' He shuddered violently, his eyelids fluttering. For a moment, Beth thought he was going to fall over. She tightened her grip as he swayed unsteadily.

'Gerald? Jeeze . . .'

His eyes abruptly sprang open, hunting frantically round the room. 'Where are we?'

'This is the *Mindori*,' she said calmly. 'We're on board, and we're trying to find a way to get back to Monterey.'

'Yes.' He nodded quickly. 'Yes, that's right. We have to go there. She's there, you know. Marie's there. I have to find her. I can free her, I know how to. Loren told me before she left. I can help her escape.'

'That's good.'

'I'm going to talk to the captain. Explain. We have to fly back there right away. He'll do it, he'll understand. She's my baby.'

Beth stood completely still as he turned round sharply, and hurried out. She let out a long despondent breath. 'Oh, shit.'

Jed and the three kids were sitting round the small bar in the galley, spooning up the pinkish mush from their trays. They all gave Beth an apprehensive glance as she came in. She tilted her head at Jed, and retreated back into the corridor. He followed her out.

'We've got to get him to a doctor, or something,' she said in a low voice.

'Told you that the day we first saw him, doll. The feller's a genuine braincrash.'

'No, it's not just that, not just in his head. He's really ill. His skin's all hot, burning, like he's got a fever, or a virus.'

'Oh, *Jeeze*, Beth.' Jed pressed his forehead against the cool metal wall. 'Think, will you. What the hell can we do? We're inside a bleeding hellhawk fifty trillion light-years from anyone who'd give a toss about us. There's nothing we can do. I'm real sorry about him catching some xenoc disease. But all I'm worried about now is that he doesn't infect us with it.'

She hated him for being right. Being completely impotent, not to mention dependent on Rocio, was tough. 'Come on.' With a final check on the kids to make sure they were eating, she hauled Jed into the lounge. 'Rocio.'

A translucent image of his face materialized in the viewport. 'Now what?'

'We've got a real problem with Gerald. Reckon he's sick with something. It's not good.'

'He's here on your insistence. What do you want me to do about it?'

'I dunno for sure. Have you got a zero-tau pod? We could shove him in there until we leave. The Edenist doctors can give him a proper going over then.'

'No. There's no working zero-tau pod any more. The possessed are understandably nervous about such items; the first ones to come on board broke it up.'

'Bugger! What do we do?'

'You'll have to nurse him along as best you can.'

'Terrific,' Jed muttered.

Almaden began to slide across the viewport.

'Hey, where are we going now?' Jed asked. The asteroid vanished below the rim, leaving only stars which were slicing thin arcs across the blackness as the hellhawk accelerated in a tight curve.

'Back to my patrol route,' Rocio said, 'and hope no one has noticed my absence. Deebank has datavised the list of electronic components they need to get the nutrient refinery functioning again. They're all available at Monterey.'

'Well, glad to hear it, mate,' Jed said automatically. A cold thought ran clean through his brain. 'Wait a minute. How are you going to get the Organization to hand them over?'

Rocio's translucent image winked, then vanished.

'Oh, Jeeze. Not again!'

*

In peacetime, Avon's starship emergence zones were positioned round the planet and its necklace of high-orbit asteroids at convenient distances to the stations and ports which they served. The one exception was Trafalgar, which, of necessity, was always on alert for suspicious arrivals. Following the official outbreak of war, or as the diplomats in Regina preferred, crisis situation, all the emergence zones were automatically shifted further away from their port. Every Confederation almanac carried the alternative coordinates, and the onus was on captains to ensure they were aware of any official declaration.

Emergence zone DR45Y was situated three hundred thousand kilometres away from Trafalgar, designated for use by civil starships flying with government authorization. The sensor satellites which scanned it were no less proficient than those covering the zones designated for various types of warships, there was after all no telling what vessels an enemy might employ. So when the gravitonic distortion scanners began to pick up the familiar signature of a ship starting to emerge, additional sensor batteries were brought on-line within milliseconds. The rapidly expanding warp in space-time was the focus of five SD weapons platforms. Trafalgar's SD control also vectored four patrol voidhawks towards it and put another ten on rapid-response alert status.

The event horizon expanded out to thirty-eight metres and vanished, revealing the starship's hull. Visual-spectrum sensors showed the SD controllers a standard globe coated with dull nultherm foam. All perfectly normal, except for a single missing hexagonal hull plate. And the ship was impressively close to the centre of the zone; the captain must have taken a great deal of care aligning his last jump coordinate. Such a manoeuvre indicated someone anxious to please.

Radar pulses triggered the starship's transponder. Trafalgar's AI took under a millisecond to identify the response code as the *Villeneuve's Revenge*, captained by André Duchamp.

Following the standard transponder code, the *Villeneuve's Revenge* promptly transmitted its official flight authorization code issued by the Ethenthian government.

Both codes were linked to grade two security protocols. The CNIS duty officer in Trafalgar's SD command centre took immediate charge of the situation.

Another, altogether quieter alert was initiated within the asteroid's secure communication net, of which the CNIS knew nothing. The televisions, radios, and holographic windows inside The Village's clubhouse abandoned their nostalgiafest to warn the observers of this latest development.

Tracy sat up to stare at the screen. The large lounge had fallen very quiet. Colourful SD sensor imagery was scrolling down the big Sony television set as various weapons locked on to the starship's fuselage. She backed up that somewhat poor supply of data with a more comprehensive summary from Corpus as it gathered information from a variety of sources in and around Trafalgar.

'They won't let the ship get near them,' Saska said in a hopeful voice. 'They're far too paranoid right now, thank the saints.'

'I hope you're right,' Tracy muttered. A quick check with Corpus showed her Jay was still in the Congression with Haile. Best place for her right now; Tracy definitely didn't want her to pick up on all their doubts and worries. 'Hell alone knows how Pryor managed to worm his way off Ethenthia.'

'Ethenthia's possessed could probably be cowed with Capone's name,' Galic said. 'Blagging your way into the headquarters of the Confederation Navy is a very different matter.'

The CNIS duty officer appeared to share the thought. She immediately declared a C4 condition, prohibiting the suspected hostile starship from moving, and requesting the patrol voidhawks to interdict. Warnings were datavised directly to the *Villeneuve's Revenge*, making very clear what action would be taken if SD Command's orders were not obeyed. They were then prohibited from using any propulsion system, not even the RCS thrusters to lock attitude, nor were they permitted to extend their thermo-dump panels, no more sensor booms were to be extended, or any other fuselage hatch activated. Non-propulsive vapour dumps were allowed, but prior warning should be given. Once a grudging Captain Duchamp had confirmed his compliance, the four patrol voidhawks accelerated in towards the inert ship at a respectable five gees.

Kingsley Pryor datavised his personal code to the CNIS duty officer, identifying himself as a Confederation Navy officer. 'I've managed to elude New California to get here,' he told her. 'I secured a lot of tactical data on the Organization fleet before I left. It should be delivered to Admiral Lalwani as soon as possible.'

'We are already aware of your period with Capone,' the duty officer said. 'Our undercover operative Erick Thakrar's report of his time crewing with the *Villeneuve's Revenge* was very thorough.'

'Erick is here? That's good, we thought he'd been caught.'

'He's filed charges of desertion and collaboration against you.'

'Well, even if I have to undergo a court martial to prove my innocence, it doesn't change the fact that I'm carrying a great deal of useful information. The Admiral will want me debriefed properly.'

'You will be. The patrol voidhawks will escort you to a secure dock once we have confirmed your ship's status.'

'I assure you, there are no possessed on board. Nor is this ship a military threat. I'm amazed we even managed to get here at all given the state some of our systems are in. Captain Duchamp is not the most proficient of officers.'

'We know that, too.'

'Very well. You should also be aware there is a nuclear device embedded in hull plate 4–36–M, it has a point three kiloton yield. I have the control timer's reset code, and it's currently seven hours from detonation.'

'Yes, that's Capone's standard method of ensuring compliance. We'll confirm its location with a remote probe from one of the voidhawks.'

'Fine; what do you want me to do?'

'Nothing at all. The hull plate will be removed before you can proceed to dock. Duchamp must open the flight computer to us, and remove all access restrictions. You will be given further instructions as we proceed with our analysis.'

On the bridge, Kingsley removed the straps securing him to his acceleration couch, and gave the seething Captain a detached glance. 'Do as she requests. Now.'

'But of course,' André growled. A thousand times during the flight he had considered simply refusing to go any further, calling Pryor's bluff. Arriving at Trafalgar was going to put an end to his life, permanently. The *anglo* navy knew too much about him now, thanks to Thakrar. They would take his ship and probably his liberty away from him, no matter how much money he spent on villainous lawyers. This was one port where he had no favours to call in at all. But each time the option popped up into his head, one nasty little aspect of cowardice prevented him from actually putting thoughts into deeds. Refusal meant certain death from the nuke in the hull plate, and André Duchamp could no longer face that fate as confidently as he once had. He had stared the possessed in the eye, and defeated them (not that the Confederation Navy had ever thanked him for that – oh, no), more than most he knew how real they were. With that came the cold knowledge of what awaited his soul. Any fate, however humiliating, had suddenly become more attractive than death.

André datavised a set of instructions into the flight computer, enabling the SD command centre to take control. The procedure was well established now. All internal sensors were activated, verifying the number of crew on board, establishing their identities. They were then required to datavise files and physiological data to SD Command, stage one in corroborating that they weren't possessed. Stage two would be an intensive sensor examination once they had docked.

Once SD Command had provisionally classified the five people on board as non-possessed, diagnostic routines were run through every processor in the starship. In the case of the *Villeneuve's Revenge* this procedure wasn't quite as smooth as would be in a ship that adhered closer to CAB maintenance requirements. Several legally required systems remained stubbornly off-line. However, SD Command confirmed that there were no tell-tale glitches in those processors which were working. This, coupled with an analysis of the (admittedly incomplete) environmental system logs, allowed them to assign a ninety-five per cent probability that the starship wasn't smuggling any possessed.

André was allowed to deploy the thermo-dump panels, relieving the heat sinks. Thrusters fired, stabilizing their attitude. An MSV from one of the voidhawks slid out of its hangar, and manoeuvred itself over hull plate 4–36-M. Waldo arms reached out, ready to detach the section.

Tracy watched the camera feed on the big Sony television screen as the anti-torque keys engaged around the panel's rim. 'I don't believe this!' she exclaimed. 'They think it's safe!'

'Be reasonable,' Arnie said. 'Those precautions are good enough to locate any possessed skulking on board.'

'Except Quinn Dexter,' Saska grumbled.

'Let's not complicate matters. The fact is, the navy is being very prudent.'

'Rubbish,' Tracy snapped. 'That CNIS officer is criminally incompetent. She must know Capone had exerted some kind of coercive hold over Pryor, yet she's not taken that into account. They'll let that bloody ship dock once they've unscrewed the hull plate.'

'We can't stop them,' Saska warned. 'You know the rules.'

'Capone and his influence is waning,' Tracy said. 'No matter what delusory victory he inflicts he cannot regain what he's lost, not now. I say we cannot permit him this gesture. The overall psychological dynamic of the situation has to be taken into account. The Confederation must survive; not only that, it must be the entity which brings this crisis to a successful resolution. And the navy is the embodiment of the Confederation, especially now. It must not be damaged. Not to the extent Pryor's mission is capable of.'

'You're being as arrogant as Capone,' Galic said. 'Your thoughts, your opinions, are the ones which must prevail.'

'We all know very well what has to prevail,' she replied. 'There has to be a valid species-wide government mechanism to implement the kind of policies which are going to be needed afterwards, and oversee the transition phase. For all its faults, the Confederation can be made to work properly. If it fails the human race will fragment, socially, politically, economically, religiously, and ideologically. We'll be right back where we were in the pre-starflight age. It'll take centuries to recover, to get us back to where we are today. By that time we should have joined the transcendent-active population of this universe.'

'*We?*'

'Yes. We. We privileged few. Just because we were engineered here doesn't mean we're not human. Two thousand years spent walking amongst our own people makes this the alien world.'

'Now you're being melodramatic.'

'Call it what you like. But I know what I am.'

*

The internal sensors on the *Villeneuve's Revenge* revealed Kingsley Pryor to be alone in his own small cabin. He'd adopted the same unnerving posture which André and his three crew had witnessed throughout the tortuous flight. He hung centimetres from the decking, legs folded in lotus position, with eyes granted a vision of some terribly personal hell. Even over the link from the starship, the CNIS duty officer could see he was suffering.

With the remote electronic survey complete, and hull plate 4–36-M now detached and held in the MSV's waldo, André was given a vector taking them in towards Trafalgar at a tenth of a gee. SD Command observed the flight computer responding to the crew's instructions, coaxing the fusion tube to life. They were following the security protocols to the last byte.

Kingsley drifted the last few centimetres down onto the decking, and suppressed a whimper at what that meant. During the flight he'd elevated his dilemma to a near physical pain, every thought he had concerning his destination burning from within. There simply was no way out of the box Capone and his whore had trapped him in. Death surrounded him, making him more compliant than any set of sequestration nanonics could ever achieve. Death and love. He couldn't allow little Webster and Clarissa to vanish into the beyond. Not now. Nor could he let them be possessed. And the only way to prevent that from happening also could not be permitted.

Like men in his position throughout history, Kingsley Pryor did nothing as events swept him to their conclusion; simply waited and prayed that a magical third option would spring from nowhere. Now with the fusion drive pushing the starship towards Trafalgar, hope had cast him aside. The power he had been given to inflict suffering was insane in its size, yet he could *feel* Webster and Clarissa. The two balanced, as Capone knew they would. And now Kingsley Pryor had to make that impossible choice between the intimate and the abstract.

The cabin sensor had enough resolution to observe his lips contracting into a bitter smile. It looked as though a scream was about to burst loose. The CNIS duty officer shook her head at the way he was acting. Looks as though his brain's cracked, she thought. Though he was keeping passive enough.

What the sensor never showed her was a patch of air beside

Kingsley's bunk thicken silently into the shape of Richard Keaton. He smiled sadly down at the stricken navy officer.

'Who are you?' Kingsley asked hoarsely. 'How did you hide on board?'

'I didn't,' Richard Keaton said. 'I'm not a possessed here to check up on you. I'm an observer, that's all. Please don't ask for who, or why. I won't tell you that. But I will tell you that Webster has escaped from Capone, he's no longer on Monterey.'

'Webster?' Kingsley cried. 'Where is he?'

'As safe as anyone can be right now. He's on a rogue ship that takes orders from no one.'

'How do you know this?'

'I'm not the only person observing the Confederation.'

'I don't understand. Why tell me this?'

'You know exactly why, Kingsley. Because you have a decision to make. You are in a unique position to affect the course of human events. It's not often an individual is put in this position, even though you don't appreciate all the implications stretching out ahead of you. Now, I can't make that decision for you, much as I'd like to. Even I can't break the restrictions I work under. But I can at least bend them enough to make sure you have all the facts before you pass your judgement. You must choose when and where you die, and who dies with you.'

'I can't.'

'I know. It's not easy. You just want the status quo to carry on for so long that you become irrelevant. I don't blame you for that, but it isn't going to happen. You must choose.'

'Do you know what Capone did to me, what I'm carrying?'

'I know.'

'So what would you do?'

'I know too much to tell you that.'

'Then you haven't told me everything I need to know. Please!'

'Now you're just looking for absolution. I don't provide that, either. Consider this, I have told you what I believe you should know. Your son will not suffer directly from any action you take. Not now, nor in the time which follows.'

'How do I know you're telling the truth? *Who are you?*'

'I am telling you the truth, because I know exactly what to tell you. If I wasn't what I say I am, how would I know about you and Webster?'

'What should I do? Tell me.'

'I just have done.' Richard Keaton started to raise his hand in what could have been a gesture of sympathetic compassion. Kingsley Pryor never found out, his visitor faded away as beguilingly as he'd arrived.

He managed a small high-pitched snigger. People (or xenocs, or maybe even angels) were watching the human race; and were very good at it. It wouldn't take much to see what was going on among the Confederation – a few carefully placed scanners could pick up the appropriate datavises, the CNIS and its counterparts did that as a matter of routine. But to secrete observers among the possessed cultures was an ability far beyond any ordinary intelligence agency. That kind of ability was unnerving. Despite that, he felt a small amount of relief. Whoever they were, they cared. Enough to intervene. Not by much, but just enough.

They knew the devastation he would cause. And they'd given him an excuse not to.

Kingsley looked straight at the cabin sensor. 'I'm sorry. Really. I've been very weak to come this far. I'm ending it now.' He datavised an instruction into the flight computer.

On the bridge, André twitched in reaction as red neuroiconic symbols shrilled their warnings inside his skull. One by one, the starship's primary functions were withdrawn from his control.

'Duchamp, what are you doing?' SD Command queried. 'Return our access to the flight computer immediately or we will open fire.'

'I can't,' the terrified Captain datavised back. 'The command authority codes have been nullified. Madeleine! Can you stop them?'

'Not a chance. Someone's installing their own control routines through the Management Operations Program.'

'Don't shoot,' André begged. 'It's not us.'

'It must be someone who had direct MOP access. That's your crew, Duchamp.'

André gave Madeleine, Desmond, and Shane a frightened glance. 'But we're not . . . *merde*, Pryor! It's Pryor! He's doing this. He was the one who wanted to come here.'

'We're powering down!' Desmond shouted. 'Fusion drive off.

Tokamak plasma cooling. Damn, he's opened the emergency vent valves. All of them. What's he doing?'

'Get down there and stop him. Use the hand weapons if you have to,' André shouted. 'We're cooperating,' he datavised at SD Command. 'We'll regain control. Just give us a few minutes.'

'Captain!' Shane pointed. The hatch in the decking was sliding shut. Orange strobes started to flash with near-blinding pulses in time to a piercing whistle.

'*Mon dieu, non!*'

SD sensors relayed a perfectly clear image of the *Villeneuve's Revenge* to the CNIS duty officer. The ship was well into its deceleration phase when the emergency started. It was less than two hundred kilometres away from Trafalgar's counter-rotating spaceport, which was grave cause for concern. The crew's apparent dismay could just be one massive diversion. If a salvo of combat wasps were fired at the asteroid from this distance it would be almost impossible to intercept all of them.

Had it just been Duchamp and his crew on board, she would have vaporized the starship there and then. But Pryor's actions and enigmatic statement just before his cabin sensor had gone off-line stayed her hand. She was sure he was doing this; and the one routine which the starship had left open to Trafalgar's scrutiny was fire control to the combat wasps. Pryor must be trying to reassure SD Command. None of the lethal drones had been armed.

'Keep tracking it with a full weapons lock,' she datavised to her fellow officers in the SD Command centre. 'Tell the voidhawk escort to stand by.'

Long jets of snowy vapour were squirting out from the *Villeneuve's Revenge* as the emergency vent emptied every tank on board. Hydrogen, helium, oxygen, coolant fluid, water, reaction mass; they all emerged under high pressure to shake the ship about as if a dozen thrusters were firing in conflicting directions. None of them were powerful enough to affect its orbital trajectory. With its deceleration burn interrupted, it continued to fly towards Trafalgar at nearly two kilometres per second.

'They're not going to have any fuel even if they do regain control of the propulsion systems,' the SD guidance officer said. 'The ship will impact in another two minutes.'

'If it gets within ten kilometres of Trafalgar, destroy it,' the CNIS duty officer ordered.

The multiple vent continued unabated for another fifteen seconds, giving the ship a highly erratic tumble. Explosive bolts detonated across the fuselage, punching out dry plumes of grey dust as they severed the outer stress structure. Huge segments of the hull peeled free like dusky silver petals opening wide, exposing the tight-packed metallic viscera. Sharp bursts of blue light flashed beneath the surface, visible only through the slimmest of fissures; more explosive bolts, detaching equipment from the internal stress grid. The starship began to break apart, its tanks, drive tubes, tokamak toroids, energy-patterning nodes, heat exchangers, and a swarm of subsidiary mechanisms forming a slowly expanding clump.

Three high-thrust solid rocket motors were clustered around the base of the life-support capsule which contained the bridge; they ignited with only the briefest warning, thrusting the sphere clear of the cloud of technological detritus. Duchamp and the others were flung back into their acceleration couches, bodies straining against the fifteen-gee acceleration.

'My ship!' André screamed against the punishing force. The *Villeneuve's Revenge*, the one last minuscule glint of hope for a post-crisis existence he had left, was unravelling around him, its million-fuseodollar components spinning off into the depths of the galaxy, transforming themselves into unsalvageable junk. Loving it more deeply than any woman, he forgave the eternal demands which it made for his money, its temperamental functions, its thirst for fuel and consumables; for in return it gave him a life above the ordinary. But it wasn't quite fully paid for, and years ago he'd forsaken a comprehensive insurance policy with those legalized thieving *anglo* insurance companies in favour of trusting his own skill, and financial acumen. His scream ended in a wretched juddering sob. This universe had just become worse than anything which the beyond promised.

Kingsley Pryor didn't ignite the rockets on his own life-support capsule. There was nowhere for him to escape to. The debris of the *Villeneuve's Revenge* was churning heatedly now, agitated by the bridge's life-support capsule erupting from its centre. But it was still all sweeping towards Trafalgar, and carrying Kingsley along with it. He didn't know exactly where he was, he couldn't be bothered to access the rudimentary sensors surmounting the capsule. All he knew was that he'd done his best by the crew, and he wasn't in Trafalgar where Capone wanted him to be. Nothing else mattered any more. The decision had been taken.

Floating alone in a cabin illuminated only by tiny yellow emergency lights, Kingsley datavised the off code to an implant in his abdomen. The little containment field generator represented the peak of Confederation technology, even so it pushed way beyond the kind of safety specifications normally used for handling antimatter. The ultra-specialist military lab in New California which manufactured it had neglected to include the standard (not to mention common sense) failsoft capacity which even the most cheapskate black syndicates employed. Capone had simply decreed that he wanted a container defined by size alone. That's what he got.

When the confinement field shut down, the globe of frozen antihydrogen touched the side of the container. Protons, electrons, anti-protons, and anti-electrons annihilated each other in a reaction that very, very briefly recreated the energy density conditions which used to exist inside the Big Bang. This time, it didn't result in creation.

SD platform lasers were already picking off the gyrating chunks of equipment around the fringe of the debris cloud that had once been the *Villeneuve's Revenge*. The bulk of the swarm was less than twenty-five kilometres from Trafalgar, on a course that would collide with one of the spherical counter-rotating spaceports. Ionized vapour from the disintegrating components fluoresced a pale blue from the energy beams stabbing through them, forming a seething bow-wave around the remaining pieces. It was as if a particularly insubstantial comet was shooting across space.

Kingsley Pryor's life-support capsule was twenty-three kilometres, and eight seconds, away from the spaceport when it happened. Another three seconds and the SD lasers would have targeted it, not that it would have made much difference. Capone had intended to do to Trafalgar what Quinn Dexter had done to Jesup; with the antimatter detonating in one of the biosphere caverns the asteroid would have been blown apart. Even if Kingsley hadn't cheated his way past the inevitable security checks, and had had to kamikaze in the spaceport, the damage would have been considerable, destroying the counter-rotating sphere and any ships docked, and possibly dislodging the asteroid from its orbit.

By switching off the confinement chamber outside Trafalgar, Kingsley would be reducing the damage considerably. Enough to salvage his conscience, and allow him to return to New California claiming a successful mission. However, in physical terms, he wasn't doing the Confederation Navy much of a favour. Unlike a fusion bomb, the antimatter explosion produced no relativistic plasma sphere, no particle blast wave; but the energy point which sprang into life had the strength to illuminate the planet's nightside a hundred thousand kilometres below. The visible and infra-red spectrum it emitted contained only a small percentage of the overall energy output. Its real power was concentrated in the gamma and X-ray spectrums.

The surrounding shoal of metal trash which had been the *Villeneuve's Revenge* twinkled for a picosecond before evaporating into its sub-atomic constituents. Trafalgar proved somewhat more resilient. Its mottled grey and black rock gleamed brighter than the sun as the energy tsunami hammered against it. As the white light faded, the surface facing the blast continued to glow a deep crimson. Centrifugal force stirred the sluggish molten rock, sending it flowing out along the humps and crater ridges where it swelled into bulbous fast-growing stalactites. Town-sized heat exchangers crumpled with their ancillary equipment anchored to the rock, their composite components shattering like antique glass while the metal structures turned to liquid and dribbled away, scattering scarlet droplets across the stars.

Hundreds of starships were caught by the micro-nova burst. Adamist vessels were luckier, in that their bulky structure shielded the crews from the worst of the radiation. Their mechanical systems underwent catastrophic failure as the X-rays penetrated them, instantly turning them into flying wrecks, coughing out vapour like the *Villeneuve's Revenge*. Scores of life-support capsules hurtled clear of the dangerously radioactive hulks.

Exposed voidhawks suffered badly. The ships themselves died wretchedly as their cells' integrity was decimated. The further they were from the detonation, the longer their misery was dragged out. Their crews in the thin-walled, exposed toroids were killed almost instantly.

Trafalgar's spherical counter-rotating spaceport buckled like a beachside shack in a hurricane. The nultherm foam coating its girders and tanks crisped to black and moulted away. Air in the pressurized sections was superheated by the radiation, expanding with explosive force, ripping every habitable section to shreds. Tanks ruptured. Fusion generators destabilized and flash vaporized.

The concussion was totally outside the load capacity of the spindle. With fusion generator plasma roaring out of the collapsing sphere, the slender gridwork started to bend. It snapped off just above the bearing and took flight, deflating into a flaccid carcass beneath the short-lived fireballs puffing open across its superficies.

A dozen datavised emergency situation alerts vibrated urgently inside Samual Aleksandrovich's skull. He looked up at the staff officers conducting the daily strategy review. More worrying than the initial crop of alerts was three of them immediately failing as their processors crashed. Then the lights flickered.

Samual stared at the ceiling. 'Bloody hell.' Information pouring into his mind confirmed there'd been an explosion outside the asteroid. But big enough to affect internal systems? Outside his panoramic window, the central biosphere's axial light gantry was darkening as the civil generators powered down in response to loosing their cooling conduits. Whole sections of the asteroid's ultra-hardened communications net had gone off-line. Not a single external sensor remained active.

The office lighting and environmental systems switched to their back-up power cells. High-pitched whines, the daily background sound pervading the entire asteroid, began to deepen as pumps and fans shut down.

Seven fully armed marines in body armour rushed into the office, a detachment of the First Admiral's bodyguard. The captain in charge didn't even bother to salute. 'Sir, we are now in a C10 situation, please egress to your secure command facility.'

A circular section of floor beside the desk was sinking down to reveal a chute that curved away out of sight. Flashing lights and sirens had begun to echo the datavised alarms. Thick metal shields were closing across the window. More marines were running along the corridor just outside the office, shouting instructions. Samual almost laughed at how close such dramatics came to being counter-productive. People needed to remain calm in such events, not have their fears accentuated. He considered refusing the earnest young captain's directive; gut instinct, acting out the role of gruff lead-from-the-front commander. Trouble was, that kind of gesture was so totally impractical at his level. Preserving the authority of the command structure was essential in a crisis of this magnitude. Threats had to be countered swiftly, which only an uninterrupted chain of command could achieve.

Even as he hesitated, the floor trembled. They really were under attack! The concept was incredible. He stared at the cups on the table in astonishment as they started to jitter about, spilling tea.

'Of course,' he told the equally apprehensive marine captain.

Two of the marines jumped down the chute first, their magpulse rifles drawn ready. Samual followed them. As he skidded his way down along the broad spiral an assessment and correlation program went primary in his neural nanonics, sorting through the incoming datastreams to discover exactly what had happened. SD Command confirmed the *Villeneuve's Revenge* had detonated a quantity of antimatter. The damage to Trafalgar was considerable. But it was the thought of what had happened to the ships of the 1st Fleet which chilled him. Twenty were docked at the time of the explosion, three further squadrons holding station a hundred kilometres away. Two dozen voidhawks were on their docking-ledge pedestals. Over fifty civil utility and government craft were in close proximity.

The secure command facility was a series of chambers dug deep into Trafalgar's rock. Self-sufficient and self-powered, it was designed to hold the First Admiral's staff officers during an attack. Any weapon powerful enough to damage it would split the asteroid into fragments.

In view of what had just happened, it wasn't the most comforting thought Samual had with him as he came off the end of the chute. He strode into the coordination centre, drawing nervous glances from the skeleton crew on duty. The long rectangular room with its complex curving consoles and inset holographic windows always put him in mind of a warship's bridge – with the one advantage that he'd never have to endure high-gee manoeuvres in here.

'Status, please,' he asked the lieutenant-commander in charge.

'Only one explosion so far, sir,' she reported. 'SD Command is trying to re-establish contact with its sensor satellites. But there were no other unauthorized ships within the planetary defence perimeter when we lost contact.'

'Don't we have *any* linkages?'

'There are some sensors functional on the remaining spaceport, sir. But they're not showing us much. The antimatter's EM pulse crashed a lot of our electronics, even the hardened processors are susceptible to that power level. None of the working antennas can acquire an SD platform signal. It could be processor failure, or actual physical destruction. We don't know which yet.'

'Get me a GDOS satellite, then. Link us to a starship. I want to talk to somebody who can see what's going on outside.'

'Yes, sir. Combat back-up systems are deploying now.'

More of the coordination centre crew were hurrying in and taking their places. His own staff officers were coming in to stand behind him. He caught sight of Lalwani and beckoned urgently.

'Can you talk to any voidhawks?' he asked in a low voice when she reached him.

'Several.' Deep pain was woven across her face. 'I feel them dying still. We've lost over fifty already.'

'Jesus Christ,' he hissed. 'I'm sorry. What the hell's happening out there?'

'Nothing else. There are no Organization ships emerging, as far as the survivors are aware.'

'Sir!' the Lieutenant-Commander called. 'We're re-establishing communications with the SD network. Three GDOS satellites are out, they must have been irradiated by the explosion. Five are still functional.'

One of the holographic windows flickered with orange and green streaks, then stabilized. The image was coming from an SD sensor satellite positioned on the perimeter of Trafalgar's defence network, ten thousand kilometres away. None of the inner cordon of satellites had survived.

'Hell,' the First Admiral muttered. The rest of the coordination centre was silent.

Half of Trafalgar's lengthy peanut-shape glimmered a deep claret against the starscape. They could see sluggish waves of rock crawling across the ridges, boulder-sized globules sprinkling from the crests, cast away by the asteroid's rotation. The ruined spaceport was retreating from its fractured spindle, turning slowly and scattering blistered fragments in its wake. Igneous spheres drifted without purpose around the stricken rock, squirting out sooty vapour like cold comets: the ships too close to the antimatter blast for their crews to survive the radiation blaze.

'All right, we're intact and functional,' the First Admiral said sombrely. 'Our first priority has to be re-establishing the SD network. If they have any sense of tactics, the Organization will try to hit us while our weapons platforms are disabled. Commander, bring in two squadrons of 1st Fleet ships to substitute for the SD platforms, and reassign the planetary network to provide us with as much cover as it can. Tell them to watch for an infiltration mission, as well; I wouldn't put that past Capone at this point. Once that's done, we can start initiating rescue flights for the survivors.'

The coordination centre crew spent an hour orchestrating the surviving 1st Fleet squadrons into a shield around Trafalgar. With more and more back-up communication links coming on-line, information began pouring in. Three-quarters of the asteroid's SD network had been wiped out in the blast. Over a hundred and fifty ships had been completely destroyed, with a further eighty so radioactive they were beyond rescue. Of the spaceport facing the *Villeneuve's Revenge* nothing had survived; once the bodies had been retrieved it would have to be nudged into a sun-intercept orbit. Initial casualty figures were estimated at eight thousand, though the coordination centre crew felt that was optimistic.

Once his orders were being implemented, the First Admiral reviewed the SD command centre files on the *Villeneuve's Revenge*. He convened a preliminary inquiry team of six from his staff officers, briefing them to assemble a probable chain of events. The last moments of the angst-laden Kingsley Pryor replayed a dozen times through his neural nanonics. 'We'll need a full psychological profile,' he told Lieutenant Keaton. 'I want to know what they did to him. I don't like the idea that they can turn my officers against the navy.'

'The possessed are only limited by their imagination, Admiral,' the medical liaison officer said politely. 'They could apply a great deal of pressure to individuals. And Lieutenant-Commander Pryor had his family stationed with him on New California, a wife and son.'

'"I pledge to place myself and my actions above all personal considerations",' Samual quoted quietly. 'Do you have family, Lieutenant?'

'No, sir, no direct family. Though there is a second cousin I'm quite fond of; she's about the same age as Webster Pryor.'

'I suppose academy oaths and good intentions don't always survive the kind of horror real life throws at us. But it looks like Pryor was having second thoughts at the end. We should be grateful for that. God alone knows what kind of carnage he would have unleashed if he'd got inside Trafalgar.'

'Yes, sir. I'm sure he did his best.'

'All right, Lieutenant, carry on.' Samual Aleksandrovich returned to the situation display swarming through his mind. With the strategic defence redeployment under way and ships assigned to rescue duties, he could concentrate on Trafalgar itself. The asteroid was in bad shape. Essentially, all of its surface equipment had been vaporized; and that was ninety per cent heat-dump mechanisms. The asteroid was generating almost no power, its environmental systems were operating on their reserve supplies alone. None of the biosphere caverns or habitation sections could get rid of their heat into space, the emergency thermal stores had ten days' capacity at most. When the habitat was designed no one had envisaged this kind of absolute damage, it had been assumed that the heat-dump panels wrecked by a combat wasp could be replaced in the ten-day time scale. Now, though, even if Avon's industrial stations could manufacture enough hardware fast enough, it couldn't be attached. Half of the rock surface was so radioactive it would have to be cut off to a depth of several metres. And that same half was also extremely hot. Most of that heat would radiate outwards over the next couple of months, but a considerable fraction would also seep inwards. Left unchecked, the temperature in the biosphere caverns would rise high enough to sterilize them. The only way to prevent that from happening was with heat-dump mechanisms, which couldn't be replaced because of the heat and radiation.

Samual cursed as the civil engineering teams datavised their various assessments and recommendations. Cost aside, he couldn't possibly begin a program like that in the middle of this crisis.

He was going to have to evacuate the asteroid. There were contingency plans for dispersing the navy institutions and forces around Avon's moons and asteroid settlements. That wasn't the problem. Capone had won a profound propaganda victory. The headquarters of the Confederation Navy bombed into extinction, whole squadrons lost, voidhawks dead. It would completely negate the entire Mortonridge Liberation campaign in the opinion of the general public.

Samual Aleksandrovich sank back into his chair. The only reason he didn't bury his head in his hands was because of all the eyes watching him, needing him to remain confident.

'Sir?'

He looked up to see Captain Amr al-Sahhaf's normally calm face contaminated with apprehension. Now what? 'Yes, Captain.'

'Sir, Dr Gilmore reported that Jacqueline Couteur has escaped.'

A cold fury that Samual hadn't experienced for a long time pushed its way through his rational thoughts. The damned woman was becoming his *bête noire*, a ghoul feeding off the navy's misfortune. Lethal, and contemptuously smug . . . 'Has she broken out of the laboratory?'

'No, sir. The demon trap's integrity has been maintained throughout the assault.'

'Very well, assign a squad of marines, and whatever else Dr Gilmore says he needs to find her. Full priority.' He ran a search program through several files. 'I want Lieutenant Hewlett placed in charge of the search mission. My orders to him are very simple. Once she has been recaptured, she is to be put directly into zero-tau. And I do mean directly. In future, Dr Gilmore can use someone less troublesome for his research.'

*

By the third doorway, it was noticeably warmer than usual in the broad corridor leading towards the CNIS secure weapons laboratory. The heat given off by the armour of thirty-five marines was accumulating in the air. Conditioning vents running along the ceiling were operating on reduced cycle mode; only a third of the light panels were on.

Murphy Hewlett took point duty himself, leading his squad along. They were each armed with static-bullet machine-pistols modelled on Ombey's design, with five of the team carrying Bradfields just in case. Murphy had taken time to brief them personally while they suited up; laying down simple procedures for engaging the possessed, hoping he was coming on confident.

As they arrived at the third door he signalled their technical sergeant forward. The man walked over to the door's control processor, and studied his own block.

'I can't find any time log discrepancies, sir,' he reported. 'It hasn't been opened.'

'OK. Front line ready,' Murphy ordered.

Eight marines spread out across the corridor, lining their machineguns up on the door. Murphy datavised Dr Gilmore that they were in position and ready. The door swung up, hissing from the pressure difference. Tendrils of pale white vapour licked around the edges as hot and cold air intermingled. Dr Gilmore, five other researchers, and three armed marines were standing just inside. No one else was visible.

Murphy switched on his suit's audio circuit. 'In!' he ordered.

The marine squad surged forward, forcing the scientists to bunch together as they bustled past. Murphy datavised a close order at the door's processor, and entered his own codelock. The big slab of metal swung down again, sealing into place.

'Jacqueline isn't in this section,' Dr Gilmore said, bemused by their military professionalism.

In answer, Murphy beckoned him forwards and touched a static sensor against his arm. The result was negative. He told his squad to check the others. 'If you say so, Doctor. What exactly happened?'

'We think the EMP interrupted the electricity supply we were using to neutralize her energistic power. It shouldn't have done, we're exceptionally well shielded in here, and our systems are all independent apart from the heat-exchange mechanisms. But somehow she was able to overcome the marine guards and break out of the isolation laboratory.'

'Overcame, how, exactly?'

Pierce Gilmore gave a humourless smile. 'She killed them, and two of my staff. This escapade is a futile gesture of defiance. Not even Jacqueline can walk through two kilometres of solid rock. She knows this, of course. But causing us the maximum amount of disruption is part of her tiresome little game.'

'The whistle has just been blown, Doctor. My orders are that upon capture she is to be placed in zero-tau. They came right from the First Admiral, so please don't query them.'

'We are on the same side, Lieutenant Hewlett.'

'Sure thing, Doc. I was in the courtroom. Remember that.'

'I am on record as objecting to that adventure. Couteur is extremely duplicitous, and intelligent. It is a bad combination.'

'We'll bear that in mind. Now how many of the lab staff have you accounted for?'

Gilmore glanced along the main corridor running round the laboratory complex. Several of the silvery doors were open, with people peering out nervously. 'Nine have not responded to my general datavise.'

'Shit!' Murphy accessed the floor plan file in his neural nanonics. The laboratory complex covered two levels, essentially a ring of research labs on top of the environmental and power systems, with storage and engineering facilities included. 'OK, everyone is to return to their office or lab, wherever they are now. The existing marine detail is to stay with them and guard against intrusion. I don't want anyone moving round except for my squad, and that includes you, Doctor. Then I want an AI brought on-line to monitor the complex's processors for glitches.'

'We're doing that already,' Gilmore said.

'And it can't find her?'

'Not yet. Jacqueline knows how we track possessed, of course. She will be concealing her power. Which means she will be vulnerable during the first few seconds after you locate her.'

'Yeah. Tell you, it's all good news, this assignment, Doc.'

The procedure Murphy initiated was a simple enough one; five marines were left behind to cover the door in case Couteur made a break for it. Unlikely, Murphy admitted to himself, but with her there was always the prospect of double bluff. The remainder of the squad, he split into two groups, going in opposite directions to work their way round the ring. Each laboratory was examined in turn, using electronic-warfare blocks and infra-red (in case Couture was disguising herself as a piece of equipment). All the staff were tested and verified; they then had to leave their neural nanonics open to the CNIS office overseeing the mission, to confirm they weren't being possessed after the marines left. One room at a time, and even scanning the corridor walls as they progressed. Murphy was leaving absolutely nothing to chance.

He led the group going anticlockwise from the door. The laboratory corridor might have been a much simpler geometry than

Lalonde's jungle, denying her any real ambush opportunity, but he couldn't get rid of the old feeling that the enemy was right behind him. Several times he caught himself turning to stare past the marines following along behind. That wasn't good, because it made them jumpy, distracted. He concentrated hard on the curving space ahead, securing each empty room. Taking it a stage at a time, setting a proper example.

Despite the jumble of equipment in most labs, it was a simple enough task to scan their sensors round. The scientists and technicians inside were profoundly relieved to see them, although each welcome was subdued. Every time, they were checked out then sealed in.

The biological isolation facility, where Couteur had been held, was the ninth room Murphy visited. Its door had been forced halfway open, buckled metal runners preventing it from moving further. Murphy signalled the technical sergeant forward. He flattened himself against the wall, and gingerly extended a sensor block around the edge of the door.

'Clean sweep,' the sergeant reported. 'If she's in there, she's not in range.'

It was a perfect double cover advance into the room. The marines deployed inside, scanning every centimetre as they went. A glass wall divided the room in half, with a large oval hole smashed through it. That, Murphy was expecting, along with the bodies torn by unpleasantly familiar deep char marks. There was a surgical table on the other side of the glass, surrounded by equipment stacks. Tubes and wires were strewn around it, a complement to the limb restraint straps which hung limply over the edges where they'd been severed.

Who could really blame the occupant for breaking free? Murphy didn't appreciate being made to ask that question.

They left two sensor blocks behind to cover the broken door as they filed out, in case she returned. The next room, an office, had one of Couteur's other victims sprawled on the carpet. They scanned the corpse first, and applied the static sensor. Murphy wasn't going to be caught out that way.

But it was a genuine corpse, with a large number of small burns and several broken bones. A characteristics scan confirmed it was Eithne Cramley, one of the Physics Department technicians. Murphy was sure Couteur had tried to make Cramley submit to possession, but wouldn't have had enough time to make a success of the process. The rest of the room was empty. They sealed it and moved on.

It took ninety minutes for the two marine groups to meet up. All they'd found was six of the staff who didn't respond to Gilmore's datavise.

'Looks like she's lurking in the basement,' he told them. He ordered ten marines to stand guard at the top of the stairs, and took the remainder down with him. This, he thought, was more her territory. The construction crew hadn't lavished the same kind of care down here as they had up in the ring of laboratories. They'd made it spacious enough, and well lit; but in the end it was just six caverns drilled in a line to house utility systems.

Again the marines deployed in perfect formation when they reached the bottom of the stairs. Murphy supervised them with growing unease. His heart rate now had to be regulated by his neural nanonics; he was wired so tight, even the regenerated flesh on the fingers of his left hand was tingling with phantom sensation. He just wished it was a reliable way of warning him a possessed was coming close. With each metre they advanced he was expecting Couteur to launch some vicious attack. He just couldn't understand what she was doing. Most likely scenario was that the three staff they hadn't located yet were now possessed, but she would know he'd be working on that assumption. There was nothing in this for her. Except being free of her bondage for a few hours. A reasonable enough impetus for most people. Murphy couldn't forget that voyage back to Trafalgar on the *Ilex*, the wearisome power struggle she'd waged against her captors the whole time. It hadn't taken him long to realize she'd allowed herself to be captured, making a mockery of poor old Regehr's terrible burns.

Advantage, that was her sole ambition, gaining the upper hand. This escape couldn't provide that for her. Not unless there was some enormity he'd overlooked. He felt as though his brain was being fossilized by the pressure of worry.

'Sir,' the marine on point duty shouted. 'Infra-red signature.'

They'd reached the environmental processing machinery. A hall of naked rock with seven big boxy air filter/regenerator units in a row down the centre. Pipes and ducts rose out from them in conical webs, leading away into glare of the overhead lighting panels.

The marines were advancing along both sides of the bulky grey casings.

Someone was crouching down on top of the third, secreted amid a twist of metre-wide pipes. When Murphy switched his retinas to infra-red, a distinctive thermal emission hazed around the edge of the pipes like a pink mist. Neural nanonics computed the output as consistent with a single person.

'Wrong,' he muttered. His suit audio speaker boosted the word, sending it rumbling round the hall. OK, she'd made an effort to hide, but it was a pitiful one. Going through the motions. *Why?*

'Dr Gilmore?' Murphy datavised. 'Is there any kind of super-weapon she could have stolen from one of your laboratories?'

'Absolutely not,' Gilmore datavised back. 'Only three portable weapons are undergoing examination in the laboratory. I verified their locations as soon as we knew Couteur had escaped.'

Another explanation gone, Murphy acknowledged miserably. 'Encirclement,' he datavised to the squad. They began to fan out along the hall, keeping behind the pipes and machinery. When they had her surrounded he cranked the volume up further. 'Come along, Jacqueline. You know we're here, and we know where you are. Game over.' There was no visible response.

'Sir,' the technical sergeant said, 'I'm picking up activity on the electronic-warfare block. She's increasing her energistic power.'

'Jacqueline, stop that right now. I have full shoot to kill authorization on this mission. You really have pissed off our top brass with these stunts of yours. Now take a good look at what you're sitting on. That casing is all metal. We don't even have to use our machine-guns, I'll just order someone to lob an EE grenade in your direction. You ought to know what electricity does to you by now.'

He waited a few seconds, then fired three rounds at the pipes just above the thermal emission. The bullets sliced a dim violet streak across his vision that vanished as soon as it began.

Jacqueline Couteur slowly stood up, hands raised high. She glanced round with supreme disdain at the marines crouched beneath her, their weapons gripped purposefully.

'Down on the ground, now,' Murphy ordered.

She did as she was told with insultingly measured slowness; descending the rungs welded on to the side of the conditioner. When she reached the ground five marines advanced on her.

'On the ground,' Murphy repeated.

Sighing at how she'd been wronged she lowered herself to her knees, and slowly bent forward. 'I trust this makes you feel safe?' she enquired archly.

The first marine to reach her shouldered his machine-gun and took a holding stick from his belt. It telescoped out to two metres, and he closed the pincer clamp around Couteur's neck.

'Scan and secure the rest of the hall,' Murphy instructed. 'We're still missing three bodies.'

He walked over to where Jacqueline Couteur was being held fast. The pincer was riding high on her neck, tilting her jaw back. It was an uncomfortable position, but she never showed any ire.

'What are you doing?' Murphy asked.

'I believe you're in charge.' The tone was calculated to annoy, superior and amused. 'You tell me.'

'You mean this is all you've achieved? Two hours' liberty and you're sulking about down here? That's pathetic, Couteur.'

'Two hours tying up your resources, frightening your squad. And you, I can see the fear clouding your mind. Then I also eliminated several key CNIS science personnel. Possibly I engendered some more possessed to run loose in your precious asteroid. You'll have to find that out for yourself. Do you really regard that as insignificant, Lieutenant?'

'No, but it's beneath you.'

'I'm flattered.'

'Don't be. I'll find out whatever scam you're pulling, and I'll blow it out the fucking airlock. You don't fool me, Couteur.' Murphy pushed up his visor, and shoved his face centimetres from hers. 'Zero-tau for you. You've abused our decency for way too long. I should have shot you back on Lalonde.'

'No, you wouldn't,' she sneered. 'As you said, you're too decent.'

'Get her up to the lab,' Murphy snarled.

Gilmore was waiting for them at the top of the stairs; he directed them to Professor Nowak's laboratory, where a couple of technicians had prepared a zero-tau pod. Jacqueline Couteur hesitated slightly when she saw it. Two machine-guns prodded into the small of her back, urging her forwards.

'I ought to say sorry for any suffering you've undergone,' Gilmore said awkwardly. 'But after the courtroom, I feel completely vindicated.'

'You would,' Jacqueline said. 'I shall be watching you from the beyond. When your time comes to join us, I'll be there.'

Gilmore gestured at the zero-tau pod, as if getting in was voluntary. 'Empty threats, I'm afraid. By that time, we shall have solved the problem of the beyond.'

Couteur gave him a final withering glance, and climbed into the pod.

'Any final message?' Murphy asked. 'Children or grandchildren you want to say something to? I'll see it's passed on.'

'Go fuck yourself.'

He grunted and nodded to the technician operating the pod. Couteur was immediately smothered beneath the jet-black field.

'How long?' Murphy asked tensely. He still couldn't believe this was all there was to it.

'Leave her in for at least an hour,' Gilmore said with bitter respect. 'She's tough.'

'Very well.' Murphy refused to allow the door connecting the secure laboratory with the rest of the asteroid to be reopened, not with three people still unaccounted for. The marines continued their sweep of the utility caverns. As well as people, Murphy had them examine the fusion generators. Since the loss of the external heat exchangers, they'd been operating in break-even mode, shunting their small thermal output into the emergency heat storage silo. Couteur couldn't rig them to explode, but the plasma could do a lot of damage if the confinement field had been tampered with.

The technicians reported back that they were untouched. After another forty minutes one of the missing bodies was found, dead, and stuffed behind an air-conditioning vent. Murphy ordered the squad to go back through the rooms they'd covered and open all the remaining grilles, no matter what size. A possessed could easily hollow out a small nest for themselves in the rock.

He waited seventy minutes before ordering the zero-tau pod to be switched off. The woman inside was wearing a tattered and burnt laboratory tunic with the CNIS insignia on her shoulder. She was weeping fervently as she tottered out, clutching at a bloody wound across her abdomen. Murphy's characteristics recognition program identified her as Toshi Numour, one of the weapons section's biophysics researchers.

'Shit,' Murphy groaned. 'Dr Gilmore,' he datavised. There was no reply. 'Doctor?' The communications processors in the secure laboratory complex reported they couldn't acquire Dr Gilmore's neural nanonics.

Murphy burst out into the main corridor, and shouted at his squad to follow. With ten suited figures clattering along at his heels, he sprinted for Gilmore's office.

*

As soon as the black shell of the zero-tau field had snapped up around Jacqueline Couteur, Pierce Gilmore headed back for his office. He didn't protest at Hewlett's continuing restrictions in preventing them from leaving the secure laboratory complex. In fact, he rather approved. He'd received a nasty shock when Couteur escaped, on top of the asteroid physically shaking in the wake of the antimatter blast. Under the circumstances, such precautions were both logical and sensible.

The office door slid shut behind him, and some of the lighting came on. Current power rationing permitted him only four of the ceiling panels, the kind of light provided by a cold winter afternoon. None of the holographic windows were active.

He walked over to the percolator jug, which was still bubbling away contentedly, and poured himself a cup. After a moment of regret, he switched it off. There probably wouldn't be enough space in his evacuation allocation to take it or any of the bone china cups with him. Assuming there would be any allocation for personal effects. With over three hundred thousand people to evacuate in a week, the amount of baggage they could take with them would be minimal to zero.

The small solaris tube running above his orchids was also off. Several of the rare pure-genotype plants were due to flower, their fleshy buds had almost burst. They never would now. There would be no light and fresh air, and the heat would arrive soon. The secure laboratory was closer to the surface than most of the asteroid's habitable sections, it would receive the worst of the inward seepage. Furniture, equipment, it would all be lost. The only thing to survive would be their files.

Pierce sat behind his desk. In fact, he really ought to be drawing up procedures to safeguard the information ready for when they transferred to their secondary facility. He put his cup down on the leather surface, next to an empty cup. That hadn't been there before.

'Hello, Doctor,' Jacqueline Couteur said.

He did flinch, but at least he didn't jump or yelp. She didn't have the satisfaction of witnessing any disconcertion, which in the game they played was a big points winner. His eyes locked on an empty section of wall directly ahead, refusing to turn round and look for her. 'Jacqueline. You have no feelings. Poor Lieutenant Hewlett really won't enjoy being outsmarted in this manner.'

'You can stop trying to datavise for help now, Doctor. I disabled the room's net processors. Not with my energistic power, either, there was no glitch to alert the AI. Kate Morley had some knowledge of electronics, a couple of old didactic courses.'

Pierce Gilmore datavised the comprehensive processor array installed in his desk. It reported that its link with Trafalgar's communication's net had been removed.

Jacqueline chuckled softly as she walked round the desk into his line of sight. She was carrying a processor block, its small screen alive with graphics that monitored his datavises. 'Anything else you'd like to try?' she enquired lightly.

'The AI will notice the processors have gone off-line. Even if it isn't caused by a glitch, a marine squad will be sent to investigate.'

'Really, Doctor? A lot of systems were damaged by the EM pulse. I've apparently been caught and shoved into zero-tau, and the marines have already cleared this level. I think that gives us time enough.'

'For what?'

'Oh, dear me. Is that finally a spike of fear I sense in your mind, Doctor? That has got to be the first arousal of any kind you've had for many a year. Perhaps it's even a hint of remorse? Remorse for what you put me through.'

'You put yourself through it, Jacqueline. We asked you to co-operate; you were the one who chose to refuse. Very bluntly, as I recall.'

'Not guilty. You tortured me.'

'Kate Morley. Maynard Khanna. Should I go on?'

She stood directly in front of the desk, staring at him. 'Ah. Two wrongs making a right? Is that what I've reduced you to, Doctor? Fear does things to the most brilliant of minds. It makes them desperate. It makes them pitiful. Is there any other excuse you'd like to offer?'

'If I was facing a jury, good and true, I could offer several justifications. Such arguments would be wasted on a bigot.'

'Petty, even for you.'

'Cooperate with us. It's not too late.'

'Not even clichés change in five hundred years. That says quite a lot about the human race, don't you think? Certainly everything I need to know.'

'You're transferring onto an abstract concept. Self-hatred is a common aspect of a diseased mind.'

'If I'm the one that's ill and incapable, how come you're the one in terminal trouble?'

'Then stop being the problem, and help us with a solution.'

'We are not *problems*.' Her hand slammed down on the front of the desk, making the two coffee cups jump. 'We are people. If that simple fact could ever register in that fascist bitek brain of yours then you might be able to look in a different direction, one that would help bring an end to our suffering. But that is beyond you. To think along those lines you have to be human. And after all these weeks of study, the one definite conclusion I have come to is that you are not human. Nor can you ever become human. You have nothing, no moral foundation from which to grow out of. Laton and Hitler were saints compared to you.'

'You're taking your situation far too personally. Understandably, after all, you can hardly retreat from it. You lack the courage for that.'

'No.' She straightened up. 'But I can make my last noble stand. And depriving the Confederation Navy of your so-called talent will be a satisfactory achievement for me. Nothing personal, you understand.'

'I can put an end to this, Jacqueline. We're so very close to an answer now.'

'Let's see how your rationality endures the reality of the beyond. You will now experience every facet of it. Being possessed by one of its inhabitants; living within it, and if you're really fortunate, as a possessor, forever terrified that some lucky living bastard is going to rip you out of your precious new prize and send you back screaming. What will your answer be then, I wonder?'

'Unchanged.' He gave her a sad defeated smile. 'It's called resolution, the ability and determination to see things through to the end. However unexpected or disappointing that end turns out to be. Not that anyone will ever know now. But I held true to myself.'

Alarmed by his mind tone, Jacqueline started to point her right arm. Slivers of white fire licked up from her wrist.

In Gilmore's mind the alternatives were stark. That she would torture him was inevitable. He would be possessed, or more likely damaged so badly that his body died, banishing his soul to the beyond. That was where logic broke down. He believed, or thought he did, that there was a way out of the beyond. Doubt undermined him, though. Factious, unclean human emotion, the type he hated so. If a way through the beyond existed, why did the souls remain trapped? There was no certainty any more. Not for him, not there. And he couldn't stand that. Facts and rationality were more than the building blocks of his mind, they were his existence. If the beyond was truly a place without logic, then Pierce Gilmore had no wish to exist there. And his own sacrifice would advance human understanding by a fraction. Such knowledge was a fitting last thought.

He datavised the processor array for the latest version of the antimemory. Jacqueline's hand was already lining up desperately on him when the desktop AV projection pillar silently pumped a blindingly pervasive red light across the office.

*

Sixty minutes later Murphy Hewlett and his squad blew the office door out with an EE charge, and rushed in to the rescue. They found Gilmore slumped over his desk, and Kate Morley lying on the floor in front of it. Both of them were alive, but completely unresponsive to any kind of stimulus the squad medic could apply. As Murphy said later during his debriefing, they were nothing but a pair of wide-awake corpses.

18

From the safety of the little plateau, a quarter of the way up the northern endcap, Tolton trained his telescope on the lobby of the Djerba starscraper. Another swirl of darkness was pushing up through the dome of white archways. Pieces of the structure tumbled across the crumpled lawn circling the forlorn building. He kept expecting to hear the sound of breaking glass reach across the distance. The telescope provided a good, sharp image, as if he was just a few metres away. He shivered at that errant thought, still able to feel the wave of coldness that had swept through him every time the flying monster passed overhead.

'This one's a walker.' He moved aside and let Erentz use the telescope's eyepiece.

She studied it for a minute. 'You're right. It's picking up speed, too.' The visitor had shoved its way through the smouldering ruins of the shanties, leaving a deep furrow in its wake. Now it was traversing the meadows beyond. The wispy pink grass stalks around it turned black, as if they'd been singed. 'Moving smoothly enough; fast, too. It should reach the southern endcap in five or six hours at that rate.'

Just what we need, the personality groused. Another of the buggers leeching off us. We'll just have to reduce nutrient fluid production to survival minimum, keep the neural strata alive. That'll play hell with our main mitosis layer. It'll take us years to regenerate the damage.

Eight of the dire visitors had now emerged from the Djerba, three of them taking flight. Without fail, they had headed for the southern endcap, just as the first and largest had done. Those that moved over the land had left a contrail of dead vegetation behind them. When they reached the endcap, they bored their way through the polyp and into the arteries which fed the giant organs, suckling the nutrient fluid.

'We should be able to burn them out soon,' she said. 'The flame-throwers and incendiary torpedoes are coming on fine. You'll be OK.'

The look Tolton gave her made his lack of affinity irrelevant. He bent over the telescope again. The visitor was crunching its way through a small forest. Trees swayed and toppled, broken off at the base. It seemed incapable of going round anything. 'That thing is goddam strong.'

'Yeah.' Her worry was pronounced.

'How's the signal project coming?' He asked the question several times every day, frightened he might miss out on some amazing breakthrough.

'Most of us are working on developing and producing our weapons right now.'

'You can't give up on that. You can't!' He said it loud for the benefit of the personality.

'Nobody's giving up. The physics core team is still active.' She didn't tell him it was down to five theorists who spent most of their time arguing about how to proceed.

'OK, then.'

Two more are approaching, the personality warned.

Erentz gave the street poet a swift glance. He was engrossed with the telescope again, tracking the movements of the visitors still loose on the grass plains. **No need to panic the others.**

Quite.

The creatures had been arriving at the rate of nearly one every half-hour ever since Erentz's disastrous foray into the Djerba. The personality was now worried about its ability to maintain the habitat's environmental integrity. Each new arrival invariably smashed its way into a starscraper, then proceeded to hammer the tower's internal structure. So far the emergency inter-floor pressure seals had held. But if the invasion continued at this rate a breach was inevitable.

We believe some of the incumbents are now starting to move, the personality said. **It's slow, which makes it hard to tell, but they could start to emerge into the parkland within the next day or so.**

Do you think they're multiplying like the first one did?

Impossible to tell. Our perception routines close to them are almost completely inviolable now. We suspect a great deal of the polyp is dead. However, if one did, then it is logical to assume the others will follow that pattern.

Oh, great. Oh, shit. We're going to have to tackle each one separately. I'm not even sure we can win. The numbers are starting to stack up against us.

We will have to review our tactics after the first few encounters. If the expenditure is too great then we may adopt Tolton's wishes and deploy everyone on the signal project.

Right. She let out a beaten sigh. **You know, I don't even consider that defeatist. Anything which gets us out of this is fine by me.**

A healthy attitude.

Tolton straightened up. 'What next?'

'We'd better get back down to the others. The visitors aren't immediately threatening.'

'That can change.'

'If it does, I'm sure we'll know about it real soon.'

They walked into the small cave at the back of the plateau. It housed a tunnel which spiralled down through several chambers to the caverns at the base of the endcap. Wave escalators and stairs were arranged in parallel down each level. Most of the wave escalators had stopped, so the descent took them quite a while.

The caverns had taken on the aspect of a fort under siege. Tens of thousands of people lay ill on whatever scraps of bedding was available. There was no order to the way they were arranged. Nursing the bedridden was left entirely to those slightly less ill, and consisted mainly of taking care of their sanitary needs. Those qualified (or with basic how-to didactic memories) to operate medical packages circulated constantly, perpetually exhausted.

Erentz's relatives had formed an inner coterie in the deepest caverns, where the light manufacturing tools and research equipment were concentrated. They'd also taken care to stockpile their own food supply, which could last them for well over a month. Here at least, a semblance of normality remained. Electrophorescent strips shone brightly in the corridors. Mechanical doors whirred open and shut. The clatter of industrial cybernetics vibrated along the polyp. Even Tolton's processor block let out a few modest bleeps as basic functions returned to life.

Erentz let him into a chamber serving as an armoury. Her relatives had been busy since the reconnaissance in the Djerba, designing and producing a personal flame-thrower. The basic principle hadn't changed much in six hundred years, a chemical tank carried on the user's back, with a flexible hose leading to a slim rifle-like nozzle. Modern materials and fabrication techniques allowed for a high-pressure system, giving a narrow flame that could reach over twenty metres or be switched to a wide short-range cone. Scalpel or blunderbuss, Erentz commented. There were also incendiary torpedo launchers – essentially scaled-up versions of an emergency flare.

She started into discussions with several of her relatives, mostly using affinity. Only a few exclamations were actually voiced. Tolton felt like a child left out of abstruse adult conversation. His attention wandered off. Surely the personality wouldn't expect him to join the combatants fighting the dark creatures? He lacked the kind of driven intensity Erentz and her relatives flaunted, their birthright. He was afraid to ask in case they said yes. Worse, they could say no and kick him out of their caverns to rejoin the rest of the population.

There must be some important noncombatant post he could fill. He raised his processor block to type an unobtrusive question for the personality. The Rubra of old would sympathize with that, and the Dariat section was his friend. Then he realized Erentz and her cousins had stopped talking.

'What?' he asked nervously.

'We can sense something in the rail tube approaching one of the endcap stations,' the block said. It was essentially the same voice Rubra had used to speak with him the whole time he was in hiding; though something about it had changed. A stiffness in the inflexion? Minor yet significant.

'One of them's coming here?'

'We don't believe so. They rampage about without any attempt to disguise themselves. This is more like a mouse sneaking along. None of the surrounding polyp is suffering the usual heat-loss death. But our perceptive cells are unable to obtain a clear image.'

'The bastards have changed tactics,' Erentz snarled. She snatched one of the flame-throwers from a rack. 'They know we're here!'

'We are uncertain on that point,' the personality said. 'However, this new incursion will have to be investigated.'

Several more people ran into the armoury, and began picking up weapons. Tolton watched the abrupt whirr of activity with bewildered alarm.

'Here.' Erentz thrust an incendiary torpedo launcher at him.

He grabbed it in reflex. 'I don't know how to use this.'

'Aim it and shoot. Effective range two hundred metres. Any questions?'

She didn't sound in forgiving mood.

'Oh, crap,' he grunted. He rocked his head from side to side, attempting to force the stiffness out of his neck muscles, then joined them in the hurried exodus.

There were nine of them in the group which marched down the stairs to the endcap tube station. Eight of Rubra's heavily armed, grim-faced descendants; and Tolton, hanging as close to the back of the pack as possible while trying not to make it too obvious.

The main lighting strips were dark and cold. Emergency panels flickered with sapphire phosphorescence as if stirred into guilty life by the clumping footsteps. Not that they were of much use. Helmet projectors encased each member of the group in a sphere of bright white light. So far their power cells were unaffected.

'Any change?' Tolton whispered.

'No,' the block whispered back. 'The creature is still moving along the tube tunnel.'

Rubra hadn't damaged this particular station during the brief active phase of his conflict with the possessed. Tolton kept expecting everything to return to life in a blast of light and noise and motion. It was *Marie Celeste* territory. A carriage was standing abandoned at one of the twin platforms, its door open. A couple of fast-food packets lay on the marble floor outside, their contents dissolved into a pellicle of grey mould.

Erentz and her cousins fanned out along the platform, and edged cautiously towards the blank circle of the tunnel mouth behind the carriage. Three of them dropped down onto the rail, and crossed swiftly to the far wall. They slunk back into various crannies, crouched down, and aimed their weapons forward.

Along with those remaining on the platform, Tolton secured himself behind one of the central pillars, and brought his launcher up. Nine helmet projectors focused their illumination on the tunnel entrance, banishing the shadows for several metres along its length.

'This isn't exactly an ambush,' he observed. 'It can see we're here.'

'Then we find out just how determined they are to get at us,' Erentz said. 'I tried the subtle approach back in the Djerba. Believe me, it's a bunch of shit.'

Wondering just how much their definitions of subtle were at variance, Tolton tightened his grip on the launcher. Once again, he checked the safety catch.

'Getting close now,' the personality cautioned.

A speck of grey materialized at the furthest extreme of the tunnel's shadows. It rippled as it moved steadily forwards towards the station.

'Different,' Erentz muttered. 'It's not concealing itself this time.' Then she gasped as the habitat's sensitive cells finally managed to focus.

Tolton squinted at the slowly resolving shape, pointing his launcher to the vertical so he could strain ahead. 'Holy shit,' he said quietly.

Dariat emerged from the tunnel mouth, and smiled softly at the semicircle of lethal nozzles pointing at him out of the blazing light. 'Something I said?' he asked innocently.

You should have identified yourself to us, the personality said in censure.

I have been busy thinking, discovering what I am.

And that is?

I'm not quite sure yet.

Tolton whooped happily, and emerged from behind his pillar.

'Careful!' Erentz warned.

'Dariat? Hey, is that you?' Tolton hurried along the platform, grinning madly.

'It's me.' There was only a slightly sardonic tone colouring his voice.

Tolton frowned. He'd heard his friend's voice loud and clear, never even needing to concentrate on the lip movement. He came to a confused halt. 'Dariat?'

Dariat put his hands flat on the platform edge, and heaved himself up like a swimmer emerging from a pool. It looked like a lot of effort to lift so much weight. His toga stretched tight over his shoulders. 'What's up, Tolton? You look like you've seen a ghost.' He chuckled as he walked forward. The frayed hem of his toga brushed against one of the fast-food packets, and sent it spinning.

Tolton stared at the rectangle of plastic as it skidded to a halt. The others were bringing their weapons to bear again.

'You're real,' Tolton stammered. 'Solid!' The obese grinning man standing in front of him was no longer translucent.

'Damn right. The Lady Chi-Ri smiled on me. A warped kind of smile, I guess, but definitely a smile.'

Tolton reached out gingerly and touched Dariat's arm. Cold bit into his questing fingers like razor fangs. He snatched his hand back. But there had definitely been a physical surface; he'd even felt the crude weave of the toga cloth. 'Shit! What happened to you, man?'

'Ah, now there's a story.'

*

'I fell,' Dariat told them. 'Ten bloody storeys down that lift shaft, screaming all the way. Thoale alone knows why suicides are so fond of jumping off cliffs and bridges – they wouldn't if they knew what that trip's like. I'm not even sure I did it on purpose. The personality was bullying me to do it, but that thing was getting closer, which made me weaker. I probably lost control of my legs, I was so debilitated. Whatever . . . I went over the edge and landed smack on top of the lift. I even penetrated it a few centimetres, I was falling so hard. Shit, I hate that. You've no idea how bad solid matter feels to a ghost. Anyway, I was just forcing my legs through the roof to get out of there when the bloody bogeyman lands right bang beside me. I could even feel it coming, like a gust of liquid helium blowing down the shaft. But the thing is, it didn't break when it hit. It splashed.'

'Splashed?' Tolton queried.

'Absolutely. It was like a goo bomb detonated on top of the lift. The whole shaft was splattered in this thick fluid. Everything got coated, including me. But the fluid reacted to me, I could feel the droplets. It was like getting caught in a spray of ice.'

'How do you mean, reacted?'

'They changed while they were going through me. Their shape and colour tried to match the section of my body they were in. I figured it's like my thoughts have a big influence over them. I'm imagining my shape, right. So that imagination interacts with the fluid and formats it.'

'Mind over matter,' Erentz said sceptically.

'You got it. Those creatures are no different from any human ghost, except they're made up of this fluid; a solid visualization. They're souls, just like us.'

'So how come you became solid?' Tolton asked.

'We fought for it, me and the other entity's soul. The impact made it lose concentration for a moment, that's why the stuff went flying off. Both of us started scrambling round to suck up as much as we could. And I was a hell of a lot stronger that it was. I won. Must have got seventy per cent of what was there before I made a run for it. Then I hid in the bottom floors until the rest of them had gone.' He looked round the circle of faintly suspicious faces. 'That's why they've come here. Valisk is saturated with energy that they can use. It's the kind of energy that makes up our souls, life-energy. The attraction is like a bee for pollen. This is what they crave; they're sentient just like us, they've come from the same universe as us, but blind instinct rules them now. They've been here so long they're severely diminished, not to mention totally irrational. All they know is that they have to feed on life-energy, and Valisk is the biggest single source to emerge here that they can remember.'

'That's what they were doing to the nutrient fluid,' the personality said. 'Absorbing the life-energy from it.'

'Yeah. Which is what trashes it. And once it's gone, you'll never be able to produce any more. This dark continuum is like a damned version of the beyond.'

Tolton slumped onto the bottom stair. 'Just fucking great. This is worse than the beyond?'

'I'm afraid so. This must be the sixth realm, the nameless void. Entropy is the only lord here. We will all bow down before him in the end.'

'This is not a Starbridge realm,' the personality retorted sharply. 'It's an aspect of physical reality, and once we understand and tabulate its properties we will know how to open a wormhole interstice and escape. We've already put a stop to these creatures consuming any more of us.'

Dariat glanced suspiciously round the empty station. 'How?'

'The habitat's nutrient fluid arteries have been shut down.'

'Uh oh,' Dariat said. 'Bad move.'

*

With their nourishment denied them, the Orgathé began to search round for further sources of raw life-energy, crying out in their own strange intangible voices. Their kith who had infested the southern endcap organs shrilled in reply. Even there, the rich fluids were drying up, but the organs themselves were suffused with a furnace glow of life-energy. Enough for thousands.

The Orgathé pummelled their way up through the starscrapers one by one, and took flight.

Dariat, Tolton, Erentz, and several others stood outside one of the endcap caverns they were using as a garage for the rentcop trucks. They shielded their eyes from the bruised tangerine nimbus of the light-tube to watch one of the dark colossi soar upwards from a collapsing lobby. With its tattered wing sails extended, it was bigger than a cargo spaceplane. A small pearl-white twister of hail and snow fell from its warty underbelly.

Erentz puffed a relieved breath out through her teeth. 'At least they're still heading for the southern endcap.'

There are over thirty of them gnawing their way through our organs now, the personality said. The damage they are inflicting is reaching dangerous levels. And there's only a single pressure door in the Igan starscraper preventing an atmosphere breach. You will have to go on the offensive. Dariat, will the flame-throwers kill them?

No. Souls cannot be killed, even here. They just fade away to wraiths, maybe shadows not even that strong.

You know what we mean, boy!

Yeah, sure. OK, the fire will fuck with their constituent fluid. They're taking a long time to acclimatize to the heat levels in the habitat. We're Thoale alone knows how many thousands of degrees above the continuum's ambient.

You mean hundreds.

I don't think so. Anyway, they can't take a direct blast of physical heat. Lasers and masers they can simply deflect, but flame should dissipate the fluid, and leave their souls naked. It'll turn them into another just bunch of ghosts skulking round the parkland.

Excellent.

'If they can't die, what do they want with all that life-energy?' Erentz asked.

'It boosts them above the rest,' Dariat said. 'Once they're strong, they'll stay free for a long time before the life-energy leaks away again.'

'Free of what?' Tolton asked uneasily. He had to stand several paces away from his friend. Not out of rudeness. Dariat was *cold*. Moisture condensed across his toga as it would on a beer bottle fresh from the fridge. None of the droplets stained the cloth, though, Tolton noticed. And that was only one of the oddities this reincarnation displayed. There were differences in behaviour, too, little quirks which had come to the fore. He'd watched Dariat quietly as they'd all walked up out of the tube station. There was a confidence about him that had been missing before; as if he was merely indulging his relatives rather than helping them. That deep anger had been expelled, too. Replaced by sadness. Tolton wondered about that combination, sadness and confidence was a strange driving force. Probably quite volatile, too. But then given what poor old Dariat had been through in the last few weeks, that was eminently forgivable. Worthy of a verse or two, in fact. It had been a long time since Tolton had composed anything.

'We didn't have a real long conversation on top of the lift,' Dariat said. 'It was the kind of pressurized memory exchange I experienced in the beyond. The creature's thoughts weren't very stable.'

'You mean it knows about us?'

'I expect so. But don't confuse knowing with being interested. Absorbing life-energy is all they exist for now.'

Erentz squinted after the receding Orgathé as it headed over the circumfluous sea. 'We'd better get organized, I suppose.' She couldn't have sounded less enthusiastic.

Dariat gave up on the dark invader, and looked around. A crowd of ghosts was hanging back from the cavern entrance, keeping among the larger boulders littering the desert. They regarded the little band of tenacious corporeal humans with grudging respect, avoiding direct eye contact like a shoplifter eluding the store detective.

'You!' Dariat barked suddenly. He started to march over the powdery sand. 'Yes, you, shithead. Remember me, huh?'

Tolton and Erentz trailed after him, curious at this latest behaviour.

Dariat was closing on a ghost dressed in baggy overalls. It was the mechanic he'd encountered when he went searching for Tolton just after the habitat arrived in the dark continuum.

Recognition was mutual. The mechanic turned and ran. Ghosts parted to let him through their midst. Dariat chased after him, surprisingly fast for his bulk. As he passed through the huddle of ghosts they shivered and shuffled further away, gasping in shock at the cold he exuded.

Dariat caught hold of the mechanic's arm, dragging him to a halt. The man screeched in pain and fear, flailing about, unable to escape Dariat's grip. He started to grow more transparent.

'Dariat,' Tolton called. 'Hey, come on, man, you're hurting him.'

The mechanic had fallen to his knees, shaking violently as his colouring bled away. Dariat by contrast was almost glowing. He glowered down at his victim. 'Remember? Remember what you did, shithead?'

Tolton drew up short, unwilling to touch his erstwhile friend. The memory of the cold he'd experienced back in the station was too strong.

'Dariat!' he shouted.

Dariat looked down at the mechanic's withering face. Remorse opened his fingers, allowing the incorporeal arm to slip away. What would Anastasia say about such behaviour? 'Sorry,' he muttered shamefully.

'What did you do to him?' Tolton demanded. The mechanic was barely visible. He'd curled up into a foetal position, half of his body had sunk into the sand.

'Nothing,' Dariat blurted, ashamed of his action. The fluid which brought him solidity apparently came with an ugly price. He'd known it all along, simply refused to acknowledge it. Hatred had been an excuse, not a motivator. As with the Orgathé, instinct was supplanting rationality.

'Oh, come on.' Tolton bent down and moved his hand through the whimpering ghost. The air felt slightly cooler, otherwise there was no trace that he existed. 'What have you done?'

'It's the fluid,' Dariat said. 'It takes a lot to maintain myself now.'

'A lot of what?' Rhetorical question, Tolton knew without needing an answer.

'Life-energy. Just keeping going uses it up. I need to replenish. I don't have a biology, I can't breathe or eat a meal; I have to take it neat. And souls are a strong concentration.'

'What about him?' A tiny patina of silver frost was forming on the ground within the ghost's vague outline. 'What about this particular *concentration*?'

'He'll recover. There's plants and stuff he can recoup the loss from. He did a lot worse to me, once.' No matter how much Dariat wanted, he couldn't look away from the drained ghost. This is what we're all going to end up like, he acknowledged. Pathetic emancipated remnants of what we are, clinging to our identity while the dark continuum depletes us until we're a single silent voice weeping in the night. There's no way out. Entropy is too strong here, drowning us away from the light.

And I was instrumental in bringing us here.

'Let's get back inside,' Erentz said. 'It's about time we put you under the microscope, see if the physics gang can make any sense of you.'

Dariat thought about protesting. Eventually he just nodded meekly. 'Sure.'

They walked back towards the cavern entrance, through the clutter of subdued ghosts. Two more Orgathé hatched from the Gonchraov starscraper lobby, tumbling up into the wan twilight sky.

*

There were vigilantes at King's Cross Station, hard young gang members drafted in from the low-cost residential estates scattered around the outer districts of Westminster Dome. Their uniforms went from pseudo-military to expensive business suits, denoting their differing membership. Ordinarily such a mixture was hypergolic. See/kill. And if civilians got caught in the line of fire, tough. In some cases, feuds between boroughs and individual gangs went back centuries. Today, they all wore a simple white ribbon prominently on their various lapels. It stood for Pure Soul, and united them in commitment. They were here to make sure all of London stayed pure.

Louise stepped off the vac-train carriage, yawning heavily. Gen leaned against her side, nearly sleepwalking as they moved away from the big airlock door. It was almost three in the morning, local time. She didn't like to think how long she'd been up for now.

'What are you creeps doing getting off here?'

She hadn't even noticed them until they stood in front of her. Two dark-skinned girls with shaved heads; the taller one had replaced her eyeballs with blank silver globes. Both of them wore identical plain black two-piece suits of some satin fabric. They didn't have blouses, the jackets were fastened by a single button, exposing stomachs as muscular as any Norfolk field labourer. Their cleavage was the only way to tell they were female. Even then Louise wasn't entirely sure, they might just be butched-up pectorals.

'Uh?' she managed.

'That train's from Edmonton, babe. That's where the possessed are. Is that why you left? Or are you here for some other reason, some kind of freako nightclub?'

Louise began to wake up fast. There were a lot of young people on the platform; some dressed in suits identical to the girls (the voice finally convinced her about gender), others in less formal clothes. None of them showed any inclination to embark on the newly arrived train. Several armour-suited police were clumped round the exit archway, with their shell-helmet visors raised. They were looking in her direction with some interest.

Ivanov Robson moved smoothly to stand at Louise's side, his movement hinting at the same kind of inertia carried by an iceberg. He smiled with refined politeness. The gang girls didn't flinch, exactly, but they were smaller now, somehow, less menacing.

'Is there a problem?' he asked quietly.

'Not for us,' the one with the silver eyes said.

'Good, then please stop hassling these young ladies.'

'Yeah? So what are you, their dad? Or maybe just their great big friend out for some fun tonight?'

'If that's the best you can do, stop trying.'

'You didn't answer my question, bigfoot man.'

'I'm a London resident. We all are. Not that it's any of your concern.'

'Like fuck it isn't, brother.'

'I'm not your brother.'

'Is your soul pure?'

'What are you all of a sudden, my confessor?'

'We're guardians, not priests. Religion is fucked; it doesn't know how to fight the possessed. We do.' She patted her white ribbon. 'We keep the arcology pure. No shitty little demon gets in past us.'

Louise glanced across at the police. There were a couple more of them now, but they showed no sign of intervening. 'I'm not possessed,' she said indignantly. 'None of us are.'

'Prove it, babe.'

'How?'

The gang girls both took small sensors from their pockets. 'Show us you contain only one soul, that you're pure.'

Ivanov turned to Louise. 'Humour them,' he said in a clear voice. 'I can't be bothered to shoot them; I'd have to pay the judge far too much to bounce us out of jail before breakfast.'

'Fuck you,' the second gang girl shouted.

'Just get on with it,' Louise said wearily. She held out her left arm, the right was curled protectively round Gen. The gang girl slapped the sensor on the top of her hand.

'No static,' she barked. 'This is a pure babe.' Her follow-up grin was weird, showing teeth that were too long to be natural.

'Check the sprog.'

'Come on, Gen,' Louise coaxed. 'Hold out your hand.' A scowling Genevieve did as she was told.

'Clean,' the gang girl reported.

'Then you must be what I can smell,' Genevieve scoffed.

The gang girl drew her hand back for a slap.

'Don't even dream it,' Ivanov purred.

Genevieve's face slowly broke into a wide smirk. She looked straight at the girl with the silver eyes. 'Are they lesbians, Louise?'

The gang girl had trouble controlling her temper. 'Come with us, little girl. Find out what we do to fresh meat like you.'

'That's enough.' Ivanov stepped forward and proffered his hand. 'Genevieve, behave, or I'll smack you.' The gang girl put her sensor to his skin, taking care to do it softly.

'I've met a possessed,' Genevieve said. 'The nastiest one there's ever been.'

Both gang girls gave her an uncertain look.

'If a possessed does ever comes out of a train, you know what you should do? Just run. Nothing you can do will stop them.'

'Wrong, titchy bitch.' The gang girl patted a pocket; there was something heavy bulging the fabric. 'We just pump them with ten thousand volts and watch the firework display. I've heard it's real pretty. Be good to me, I'll let you watch, too.'

'Seen it already.'

'Huh!' The girl turned her silver eyes on Banneth. 'You too. I want to know you're pure.'

Banneth laughed gently. 'Let's hope your sensor can't probe my heart.'

'What the hell are you all doing here?' Ivanov asked. 'The only time I've seen the Blairs and the Benns in the same place before was a morgue. And I can see a couple of MoHawks over there as well.'

'Looking after our turf, brother. These possessed, they're part of the sect. You don't see none of those bastards down here, do you? We're not going to let them crunch us like they done New York and Edmonton.'

'I think the police will do that, don't you?'

'No fucking way. They're Govcentral. And those shits let the possessed down here in the first place. This planet's got the greatest defences in the galaxy, and the possessed just breezed through them like they weren't even there. You want to tell me how come that happened?'

'Good point,' Banneth drawled. 'I'm still waiting to hear on that one myself.'

'And why haven't they shut down the vac-trains properly?' the girl continued. 'They're still running to Edmonton where we know the possessed are. I accessed that sensevise of the fight, it was only a couple of hours ago, for Christ's sake.'

'Criminal,' Banneth agreed. 'They were probably bribed by big business.'

'You taking the piss, bitch?'

'Who, me?'

The gang girl gave her a disgusted stare, not knowing what to make of her attitude. She jerked thumb over her shoulder. 'Go on, get the fuck out of here, all of you. I hate you rich kinks.' She watched them walk through the exit archway with a vague sense of unease scratching away at her mind. There was something badly wrong about the group, the four of them were a complete mismatch. But screw that, as long as they weren't possessed who cared what kind of orgy they were heading off to. She shivered suddenly as a cold breeze swept along the platform. It must have been caused by the carriage airlocks swinging shut.

*

'That was awful,' Genevieve exclaimed when they reached the big sub-level hall above the station's platforms. 'Why didn't the police stop them doing that to people?'

'Because it's way too much trouble at three o'clock in the morning,' Ivanov said. 'Besides, I expect most of the officers down there are quite happy to let the vigilantes take the heat if a possessed did step out of a train. They act as a buffer.'

'Is Govcentral being stupid allowing the vac-trains to continue?' Louise asked.

'Not stupid, just slow. It is the universe's largest bureaucracy, after all.' He waved a hand at the informationals flittering overhead. 'See? They've shut a few routes down already. And public pressure will close a lot more before long. It'll snowball once everyone's had time to access the Edmonton fight. This time tomorrow you'll have trouble getting a taxi to take you further than a couple of streets.'

'Do you think we'll be able to leave London again?'

'Probably not.'

The way he said it sounded so final, a pronouncement rather than an opinion. As always, an authority in knowledge he had no business knowing.

'All right,' Louise said. 'I suppose we'd better go back to the hotel, then.'

'I'll come with you,' Ivanov said. 'There might be a few more of these nutters around. It wouldn't do for the natives to learn you're from Norfolk right now. These are paranoid times.'

For some reason, Andy Behoo popped into Louise's mind; his offer to sponsor her for Govcentral citizenship. 'Thank you.'

'What about you?' Ivanov asked Banneth. 'Do you need to share a cab?'

'No, thank you. I know where I'm going.' She walked off towards the lifts around the rim of the hemispherical cavern.

'Don't mention it,' Louise muttered grumpily at her back.

'I expect she's grateful, really,' Ivanov said. 'Probably just doesn't know how to express it.'

'She could try harder.'

'Come along, let's get you two home to bed. It's been a long day.'

*

Quinn watched the lift doors close on Banneth. He didn't bother to rush after her. Finding her again would be relatively simple. Bait was never hidden. Oh, it wouldn't be obvious. He would need time, and resources, and have to make an effort. But her location would be filtered through the arcology's downtowners, the sect covens and gangs would be informed. That was why he'd been lured here, after all. London was the largest, most elaborate trap ever assembled for one man. In a strange way, he felt rather flattered. That the supercops were prepared to sacrifice the whole arcology just to nail him was a mark of extreme respect. They feared God's Brother exactly as He should be feared.

He trailed after Louise as she walked over to the lifts with her brat sister and the huge private eye. She was very drowsy, which relaxed her face. It left her delicate features unguarded and natural; a state which served only to amplify her beauty. He wanted to put out a hand and stroke her exquisite cheeks, to see her smile gently at his touch. Welcome him.

She frowned, and rubbed her arms. 'It's cold down here.' The moment broke.

Quinn rode up to the surface with the trio, then left them as they went off to the taxi garage. He took a subwalk under the busy road, and hurried along one of the main streets radiating out from the station. There would only be a limited amount of time until the supercops closed down the vac-trains.

The second alley leading off from the main street contained what he wanted. The Black Bull, a small, cheap pub, filled with hard-drinking men. He moved among them, unseen as his expanded senses examined their clothing and skulls. None of them were fitted with neural nanonics, but several were carrying processor blocks.

He followed one into the toilets, where the only electrical circuit was for the light panel.

Jack McGovern was peeing blissfully into the cracked urinal when an icy hand clamped round the back of his neck and slammed his face into the wall. His nose broke from the impact, sending a torrent of blood to splash into the porcelain.

'You will take your processor block from your coat pocket,' a voice said. 'Use your activation code, and make a call for me. Do it now, or die, dickhead.'

Rat-arsed he might have been, but overdosing on self-preservation allowed Jack's mind to focus with remarkable clarity on his options. 'OK,' he mumbled, a lip movement which sent more blood dribbling down the wall. He fumbled for his processor block. There was an emergency police-hail program which was activated by feeding in the wrong code.

The terrible pressure on his neck eased off, allowing him to turn. When he saw who his assailant was, the thought of deviously calling for help vanished faster than hell's solitary snowflake.

*

Quinn returned to King's Cross, sharing a lift down to the underground chamber with a cluster of vigilantes. He wandered through the vaulting hall, ambling round the closed kiosks and steering clear of industrious cleaning mechanoids. The lifts kept disgorging gang members, who immediately took the wave escalators down to the platforms. He kept watching the informationals, paying particular attention to the arrivals screens. In the two hours which followed, five vac-trains arrived from Edmonton. All departures slowed down to zero.

The Frankfurt train pulled in at five minutes past five. Quinn went and stood at the top of its platform's wave escalator. They were the last to come up, Courtney and Billy-Joe gently guiding the drugged woman between them. The two acolytes had smartened up, looking closer to a pair of grungy university students than downtown barbarians now. Their snatch victim, a middle-aged woman wearing a crumpled dress with an unbuttoned cardigan, had the vacant eyes typical of a triathozine dose; her body fully functional, brain in an advanced hypnoreception state. There and then, if she'd been told to jump off the top of an arcology dome, she'd do it.

They moved at a brisk pace across the floor, and hopped into a lift. Quinn wanted to materialize, just so he could cheer at the top of his voice. The tide was turning now. God's Brother had given His chosen Messiah another sign that he remained on the path.

At five thirty, the sixth train from Edmonton arrived. A notice slithered over the holograms announcing that the routes to North

America had now been shut by order of Govcentral. Five minutes later, all departures were cancelled. Vac-trains already en route to the arcology were being diverted to Birmingham and Glasgow. London was now physically isolated from the rest of the planet.

It was just a little scary how his prediction had come so true. But then he was bound to be right, with God's Brother gifting him understanding.

People were coming up from the platforms; the last straggle of passengers, the vigilante gangs (already eyeing each other now the reason for their truce was over), the police duty teams, station crews. Informationals floating overhead vanished like pricked bubbles. Display boards blanked out. The twenty-four-hour stalls closed up, their staff gossiping hotly together at they rode the lifts up to the surface. The wave escalators halted. All the solaris lights overhead dimmed down, sinking the cavern into a gloomy dusk. Even the conditioning fans slowed, their whining dropping several octaves.

It was the paranoiac moment every solipsist fears. The world was a stage constructed around him, and this chunk of it was shutting down as it was no longer part of the act. For a second, Quinn worried that if he went to the dome wall and looked out there would be nothing there to see.

'Not yet,' he said. 'Soon, though.'

He took a last look round, then went over to one of the emergency fire stairs and started the long trek to the surface and the rendezvous point.

*

Louise was surprised at how much she associated the hotel room with home. But it was reassuring to be back after the ordeal of Edmonton. Partly it was because she now considered her obligation over, she'd done what she promised dear Fletcher, and warned Banneth. A small blow struck against that monster Dexter (even though he'd never know). The fact that the Ritz was so comfortable helped a lot, too.

After Ivanov Robson dropped them off, both girls slept well into the morning. When they finally went downstairs for breakfast, reception informed Louise there was a small package for her. It was a single dark-red rose in a white box, with a silver bow tied round. The card that came with it was signed from Andy Behoo.

'Let me see,' Gen said, bouncing on her bed in excitement.

Louise smelt the rose, which to be honest was rather a weak scent. 'No,' she said, and held the card aloft. 'It's private. You can put this in water, though.'

Gen regarded the rose suspiciously, sniffing it cautiously. 'OK. But at least tell me what he says.'

'Just thank you for last night. That's all.' She didn't mention the second half of the message, where he said how lovely she was, and how he'd do anything to see her again. The card was put into her new snakeskin bag, and the little pocket codelocked against small prying fingers.

Gen took one of the vases from the ancient oak dresser, and went off to the bathroom for some water. Louise datavised her net connection server and enquired if there were any messages for her. The six-hourly ritual. Pointless, as the server would automatically deliver any communiqué as soon as it received one.

There were no messages. Specifically, no messages from Tranquillity. Louise flopped back on the bed, staring at the ceiling as she tried to puzzle it out. She knew she'd got the message protocol right, that was part of the NAS2600 communication program. Something had to be wrong at the other end; but when she put the news hound into primary mode, there was no report of anything untoward happening to Tranquillity. Perhaps Joshua simply wasn't there, and her messages were piling up in his net server memory.

She thought about it for a while, then composed a brief message to Ione Saldana herself. Joshua said he knew her, they'd grown up together. If anybody knew where he was, she would.

After that, she launched a quick directory search and datavised detective Brent Roi.

'Kavanagh?' he replied. 'God, you mean you bought yourself a set of neural nanonics?'

'Yes, you didn't say I couldn't.'

'No, but I thought your planet didn't allow you that kind of technology.'

'I'm not on Norfolk, now.'

'Yeah, right. So what the hell do you want?' he asked.

'I'd like to go to Tranquillity, please. I don't know who I have to get permission from.'

'From me, I'm your case officer. And you can't.'

'Why not? I thought you wanted us to leave Earth. If we got to Tranquillity, you wouldn't have to worry about us any more.'

'Frankly, I don't worry about you now, Miss Kavanagh. You seem to be behaving yourself – at least, you haven't tripped any of our monitor programs.'

Louise wondered if he knew about the bugs Andy had removed at Jude's Eworld. She wasn't going to volunteer the information. 'So why can't I go?'

'I gather you haven't got the hang of your news hound program yet.'

'I have.'

'Really. Then you ought know that as of oh-five-seventeen hours GMT, the global vac-train network was shut down by an emergency presidential executive decree. Every arcology is on its own. The President's office says they want to prevent the possessed in Paris and Edmonton from sneaking into more arcologies. Myself, I think it's a load of crap, but the President is scared of public opinion more than he is of the possessed. So like I told you before, you're on Earth for the duration.'

'Already?' she whispered aloud. So much for Govcentral moving slowly. But Robson had been right again. 'There must be a way out of London to the tower,' she datavised.

'Only the vac-trains.'

'But how long will this go on for?'

'Ask the President. He forgot to tell me.'

'I see. Well, thank you.'

'Don't mention it. You want some advice? You have finite funds, right? You might consider shunting along to a different hotel. And if this goes on for much longer, which I suspect it will, you'll need a job.'

'A job?'

'Yeah, that's one of those nasty little things ordinary people do, and in return they get given money by their employer.'

'There's no need to be rude.'

'Eat it. When you apply to the local Burrow Burger as a waitress, or whatever, they'll want your citizenship number. Refer them to me, I'll grant you temporary immigrant status.'

'Thank you.' That much sarcasm couldn't be carried along a datavise, but he'd know.

744

'Hey, if you don't fancy that, at least you've got an alternative. A girl like you won't have any trouble finding a man to look after her.'

'Detective Roi, can I ask what happened to Fletcher?'

'No, you can't.' The link ended.

Louise looked out of the window across Green Park. Dark clouds swirled over the dome, hiding the sun. She wondered who'd sent them.

*

It was a forty-storey octagonal tower in the Dalston district, one of eight similar structures that made up the Parsonage Heights development. They were supposed to raise the general tone of the neighbourhood, encumbered as it was by low-cost housing, bargain centre market halls, and a benefits-reliant population. A partnership between Dalston Council and Voynow Finance, a Halo property investment company, intended as a tax-relief hothouse for local entrepreneurs and small businesses. The towers were supposed to rest on a huge underground warren of factory and light-manufacturing units. Above that buzzing industrial core, the first seven floors would be given over to retail outlets, followed by five floors of leisure industry premises, three more floors of professional and commercial offices, and the remaining floors residential apartments. The whole entity would be an economic heart transplant for Dalston, creating opportunity, and invigorating the maze of shabby ancient streets outside with rivers of commerce and new money.

But Dalston's underlying clay had a water-table problem which would have tripled the cost of the underground factory warren in order to prevent it from flooding, so it was downgraded to a couple of levels of storage warehousing. The local market halls cut their rock bottom prices still further, leaving half of the retail units unrented; franchise chains took over a meagre eight per cent of the designated leisure floorspace. In order to recoup their investment, Voynow hurriedly converted the thirty upper floors into comfortable apartments with a reasonable view across the Westminster Dome, which market research indicated they could sell to junior and middle management executive types.

The rushed compromise worked, after a fashion. Certainly, sixty years on from its construction, Parsonage Heights was home to a slightly more affluent class than Dalston's average. There were even some reasonable shops and cafés established on the lower floors. Though what activities went on in the dilapidated, damp, and crumbling warehouses hidden beneath was something the top-floor residents declined to investigate.

The local police station knew there was a Light Bringer coven down there; but for whatever reason (usually given as budgetary) the chief constable had never instituted a raid. So when Banneth's tube train pulled in at Dalston Kingsland Station, the Magus and a fifteen-strong bodyguard were waiting with impunity on the platform to greet her. She took one look at the blank-faced young toughs carrying their pathetic assortment of inferior weapons, and had trouble preventing herself laughing.

Did you arrange this? she asked Western Europe.

I simply told the Magus how important you are to God's Brother. He reacted appropriately, don't you think?

Too appropriately. This is becoming a farce.

The Dalston coven Magus stepped forwards, and bowed slightly. 'High Magus, it's an honour to have you here. We have your safe house ready.'

'It better be a good one, or I'll have you strapped down on your own altar and demonstrate how we deal with people who fail God's Brother in Edmonton.'

The Magus's vaguely hopeful air wafted away, leaving behind a belligerent expression. 'You won't be able to fault us. *Our* position hasn't been compromised.'

She ignored the crude reference. 'Lead on.'

The bodyguard clumped their way noisily up the carbon-concrete stairs and out onto Kingston High Street. The first four out of the station's automatic door levelled their TIP carbines along the road, which startled the few late-night pedestrians heading home from the district's grotty clubs. They swept their muzzles round in what they thought was a professional scanning manoeuvre.

'Clear!' the leader barked.

Banneth rolled her eyes as the rest of the bodyguard hurried out around her. Cars had been halted in the street to let them cross. They hurried into the ground-floor mall of the Parsonage Heights tower opposite the station. Three more sect members were waiting inside, standing guard beside an open lift. The Magus and eight bodyguards crowded in around Banneth. They rode it to the top floor, where it opened out directly into the penthouse vestibule. More sect members were inside, toting their weapons, and finishing off the new security sensor array.

'No fucker's going to sneak up on you while you're here,' the Magus said confidently. 'We've got every approach covered. There'll be guards outside, and in all the stairwells. Nobody gets in or out without a secure access code, which you have command authority over.'

Banneth walked into the penthouse. It occupied the whole fortieth floor, arranged around a big open-plan lounge and dining area. The absent owner had chosen its decor straight out of a thirty-year-old catalogue file specializing in unashamed chintz; green leather furniture, Turkish rugs over polished marble tiles, glowing primary-colour sketches hanging on the walls, and a red marble fireplace complete with holographic flames. A glass wall had swing-up slab doors which led out to a roof garden with a swimming pool and hot spa; the sun loungers were sculpted blue plastic frogs.

'The fridge is full,' the Magus said. 'If you take a fancy to anything, just let us know and we'll have it sent up. I can get anything you need. My grip on this town is total.'

'I'm sure,' Banneth said. 'You, you, and you – ' her finger singled out two attractive girls and a teenage boy – 'stay. The rest of you, fuck off. Now.'

The Magus blushed heavily. Treating him like a piece of street shit in front of his acolytes would be a serious blow to his authority. She stared right at him, a silent direct challenge.

He snapped his fingers, gesturing everyone out, then stomped through the big blackwood doors without looking back.

'Dump the guns,' Banneth told the three remaining acolytes. 'You won't be needing them in here.'

After a moment's hesitation they left them beside the kitchen bar. Banneth walked out into the small paved garden. Night fuchsias spilled their sweetness into the air. It had a balcony of high, one-way glass, allowing her to look over the glimmering crater of lights which defined the city. Nobody could see in. A reasonable protection against snipers, she acknowledged.

Did I cause a big enough splash? she asked Western Europe.

Oh, yes. The dear Magus is currently screaming at London's High Magus about how big a shit you are. All the covens will be talking about your arrival by this evening.

Evening. She shook her head irritably. I hate train lag.

Not relevant. I'll have the little traffic-stopping scene downstairs logged on the police intelligence bulletin as well. The patrol constables will ask their informants for further information about the coven's new activities. We'll have the whole arcology covered. Dexter will find you.

'Shit,' Banneth mumbled. She beckoned the nervous acolytes out onto the roof garden. 'One, find me a decent glass of Crown whisky; then take your clothes off. I want to watch you swimming.'

'Um, High Magus,' one of the girls said anxiously, 'I can't swim.'

'Then you'd better learn fast. Hadn't you?'

Banneth ignored their whispering behind her, and looked upwards. Long strips of faintly luminescent cloud curved round the dome, breaking into agitated foam as they hit the surface flow boundary. Patches of night sky were visible through the choppy fringes. Stars and spacecraft shone bright against the blackness. There was the hint of a hazy ark above the northern horizon.

This penthouse is difficult to reach from the ground, but wide open to the sky, she observed. That means an SD strike.

Correct. I have no intention of using a nuke inside the dome. But an X-ray laser can penetrate the crystal with minimal damage. If he can survive that, then frankly there is no hope for us.

There certainly isn't for me.

You created him.

B7 created me.

We permitted you, there's a difference. You were convenient for us. Under our patronage you fulfilled most of your ambitions. Without us, you would now either be dead or an Ivet.

If I can take him out ...

No. I don't want you fighting back. He must not be made to turn invisible again. I only have one chance at this. It's quite poetic, really; the whole world's future depending on an individual.

Poetic. Fuck, what the hell are you people?

I believe our original agreement was that B7's patronage would be provided on a no-questions-asked basis. Despite your predicament, you still don't qualify to ask that question, and I have no intention of indulging you. When you are dead, then you can observe me from the beyond.

Some people make it past the beyond. That's what the Edenists claim.
Then I wish you bon voyage.

Banneth glanced out over the preserved city again. The first pale grey photons of dawn were slipping up from the eastern horizon to lap against the bottom of the giant crystal dome. She wondered how many more dawns she was going to see.

Truthful estimate, knowing the way she'd put Dexter together, no more than a week.

The acolytes were splashing about in the pool now, including the non-swimming girl clinging resolutely to the shallow end. Banneth didn't care, the whole point was just to see their great young bodies glistening wet. Indulging herself with them was definitely one up on the customary last meal. However, there were files stored in her neural nanonics which had to be edited and prepared. Her lifetime's work. She could hardly allow it to go to waste, though finding an institution that would accept it might prove difficult. It wasn't just that she wanted it preserved, she wanted it studied, utilized. An important body of knowledge: human behaviour under the kind of extreme conditions that would for ever remain closed to academic medical circles. It was unique, which made it all the more valuable. Perhaps some day it might become a classic reference for psychology students.

She went back into the lounge and settled into one of the dreadful green leather couches, ready to start indexing the files. It would be amusing to see how long the acolytes stayed in the water.

*

The Lancini had been built at the start of the twenty-first century, a huge department store intended to rival London's best; set on Millbank overlooking the Thames, it had a *très* chic view which along with its retro-thirties decor was calculated to bring in the affluent and curious alike. As with all outsize endeavours, its decline was never going to be swift. It had limped along for decades with falling customer numbers and negative profits. The image it attempted to foster right from the start was dignity without snobbishness. According to the market survey programs worshipped by its executives, such a policy would attract older shoppers, with their correspondingly larger credit funds. Floor managers, left with no margin for innovation, kept ordering established, unhip, brands to serve their loyal, ageing shoppers. Every year, fewer of them returned.

The execs really should have known that. If they'd just cross-linked their market surveys with the store's own funeral service department, they would have seen just how far their customer loyalty extended. Unfortunately, it didn't quite extend to after-burial purchasing. So 2589 saw the very last traditional January sale ending with an undignified auction to dispose of the store's fittings. Now only the shell of the building remained; the long sales halls, gutted of their counters and carpets, became a haven for moths and mice. Every day thick pillars of sunlight streamed in through the tall arching windows, tracing the same parabola across the walls and floorboards. Time had bleached their route in the paint and varnish as firmly as any chisel.

Nothing changed, because nothing was allowed to change. The London Historical Buildings Continuity Council made quite sure of that in its rigorous defence of heritage. Anyone was free to purchase the Lancini and start a commercial business up in it, providing it was refurbished to match the original interior plans, and that business was retail shopping. Another setback to refurbishment was the price the receivers were demanding to satisfy the store's creditors.

Then news of possession and the beyond reached Earth. And, quite paradoxically, age suddenly became a highly motivating factor in change. It was old people who sat on the Historical Buildings Continuity Council. London's most venerated (and richest) banks and financial institutions were mostly governed by centenarians. These were the people who were going to be the first generation of humans who would enter the horror of the beyond knowing it was waiting for them. Unless of course, a method of salvation was found. So far the Churches (any/every denomination), Govcentral's science councils, and the Confederation Navy had been unable to provide that salvation.

That just left one possible refuge: zero-tau.

Several companies were quickly formed to supply demand. Obviously, long-term facilities would ultimately be needed to carry these customers of oblivion through the millennia; mausoleums more enduring than the pyramids. But they'd take time to design and build, meanwhile the hospital chaplains remained in business. Temporary storage facilities were urgently required.

By a near unanimous vote, the Historical Buildings Continuity Council quickly approved a change of use of premises certificate for the Lancini. Zero-tau pods were shipped in from the Halo and taken in via delivery gates more used to household furnishings and haute couture. The ancient cage lifts had the load capacity to take them up to every floor. Oak floorboards, seasoned by five centuries of dehumidified conditioning, were strong enough to hold the new weight distribution pattern. Heavy duty cabling laid in for the floor displays carried sufficient electricity to feed the pods' power-hungry systems. In fact, if it hadn't been for the building's projected three hundred year lifespan, the Lancini would have made a good eternity crypt.

Certainly, Paul Jerrold thought it appropriate enough when he was shown to his pod. It was on the fourth floor, one of a long row in the old Horticultural section, lined up opposite the windows. Over half of the big sarcophagi were active, their black surfaces absorbing the dust-choked sunbeams as if they were spatial chasms. The two nurses helped him in over the rim, then fussed round, smoothing down his loose fitting track-suit. He kept quiet through the nannying; at a hundred and twelve he was becoming used to the attitude of medical staff. Always exaggerating the attention they gave their patients, as if the care would go unnoticed if they didn't.

'Are you ready?' one asked.

Paul smiled. 'Oh, yes.' The last couple of weeks had been busy ones, itself a blessing at his age. First the devastating news of possession. Then the slow response, the determination by himself and the others at his elite West End club that they should not become victims of the beyond. The web of discreet contacts put out, offering an alternative for those who could pay for it. His solicitors and accountants had been tasked with shifting his substantial holdings into a long-term trust that would pay for maintaining his stasis. It didn't cost much: maintenance, rent, and power. Even if the trust was badly bungled, he had enough money in the bank to keep himself secure for ten thousand years. Assuming there was still money after that time. Then once it had been arranged, there had been the arguments with his children and their swarm of offspring, all of whom had adopted a quiet waiting policy to obtain his wealth. A brief legal battle (he could afford much better lawyers than them), and that was it, and here he was: a new breed of chrononaut.

His habitual dread of the future had faded, replaced by a keen interest in what awaited. When the zero-tau field switched off, there would be a full solution to the beyond, society would have evolved radically to take knowledge of the afterlife into account. There might even be a decent rejuvenation treatment available. Possibly, humans would have finally achieved physical immortality. He would become as a god.

A flicker of greyness, shorter than an eyeblink . . .

The pod cover lifted, and Paul Jerrold was slightly surprised to see he was still in the Lancini. He'd expected to be in some huge technological vault, or perhaps a tasteful recovery room. Not right back where his voyage through eternity had started. Unless these new, magnificently advanced humans had re-created the Lancini to provide their ancestors with the psychological comfort of familiar territory, a considerate way to ease their introduction to this fabulous new civilization built in his absence.

He glanced eagerly through the big, dirty window opposite. Dusk had fallen across the Westminster Dome. The thriving lights of the south bank glimmered brightly in front of the steel grey clouds smothering the vast arc of the dome. A projection of some kind?

The pair of medical staff attending him were somewhat unconventional. A girl leaned over the pod, very young, with amazingly large breasts squeezed up by a tight leather waistcoat. The adolescent boy standing beside her wore an expensive pure-wool sweater that was somehow wrong on him; his face was stubbly, with animal-mad eyes. He held a loop of power cable in one hand, plug dangling loosely.

Paul took one look at the plug, and datavised an emergency code. He couldn't get a response from any net processor; then his neural nanonics crashed. A third figure clad in a jet-black robe slipped out of the gloom to stand at the foot of the pod.

'Who are you?' Paul croaked in fright. He levered himself up into a sitting position, skinny hands with their bulging veins gripping the edge of the pod.

'You know exactly who we are,' Quinn said.

'Have you won? Did you defeat us?'

'We're going to, yes.'

'Oww shit, Quinn,' Billy-Joe protested. 'Look at these old farts, they ain't good for nothing. No soul's gonna make them last, not even with your kind of black magic.'

'They'll last long enough. That's all that matters.'

'I told you, you want decent possessed you gotta go to the sects for bodies. Fuck, they worship you. All you've gotta do it tell them to bend over, they ain't gonna put up no fight.'

'God's Brother,' Quinn growled. 'Don't you ever think, shithead? The sects are a lie. I've told you, they're controlled by the supercops. I can't go to them for anything, we'd just give ourselves away. This place is fucking perfect. Nobody's going to notice people going missing from here, as far as this world's concerned they stopped existing as soon as they walked through the door.' His face jutted out of the hood to grin down at Paul. 'Right?'

'I have money.' It was Paul's last gambit, the one thing everyone desired.

'That's good,' Quinn said. 'You're almost one of us already. You don't have far to go.' He pointed a finger, and Paul's world howled into pain.

*

Western Europe had hooked eight AIs into London's communication net, which gave him enough processing capacity to review each chunk of electronic circuitry in the arcology on a ten-second cycle, providing it had a net connection. All processor blocks, no matter what their function, were datavised on a fifteen-second rota and examined for suspect glitches.

He wasn't the only worried citizen. Several commercial software houses had gripped the marketing opportunity and offered possession-monitoring packages. They consisted of a neural nanonics program which sent a continual capacity diagnostic and location datavise to the company security centre, who would alert the police if the user suffered an unexplained glitch or drop-out. Bracelets were also spilling into the shops which did the same thing for kids too young for neural nanonics.

Communication bandwidth was becoming a serious problem. Western Europe had used GISD authority to prioritize the AI scanning programs, leaving them unimpeded while civil data traffic suffered unheard-of capacity reductions and switching delays.

*

The visualization of the arcology's electronic structure was a theatrical gesture, impressing no one. It stood on the table of the sensenviron secure conference chamber like an elaborate glass model of the ten domes. Fans of coloured light rotated through the miniature translucent structures with strobe-like repetition.

South Pacific studied their movement as the other B7 supervisor representations came on-line around the oval table. When all sixteen were there, she asked: 'So where is he, then?'

'Not in Edmonton,' North America said. 'We kicked their asses out of the universe. The whole goddam nest of them. There's none of the bastards left.'

'Really?' Asian Pacific said. 'So you've accounted for the friend of Carter McBride as well, have you?'

'He's not a threat to the arcology, he only wants Dexter.'

'Crap. You can't find him, and he's just an ordinary possessed.' Asian Pacific waved an arm at the simulacrum of London. 'All they have to do is steer clear of electronics, and they're safe.'

'Got to eat sometime,' Southern Africa said. 'It's not like they've got friends to take care of them.'

'The Light Bringer sect loves them,' East Asia grumbled.

'The sects are ours,' Western Europe said. 'We have no worries in that direction.'

'OK,' South Pacific said. 'So tell us how you're doing in New York? We all thought the police had got them that time as well.'

'Ah yes,' Military Intelligence said. 'What's the phrase the news anchors keep using? Hydra syndrome. Shove one possessed into zero-tau, and while you're doing that five more come forth. Emotive figures, but true.'

'New York got out of hand,' North America said. 'I wasn't prepared for that.'

'Obviously. How many domes have been taken over now?'

'Figures of that magnitude are unnecessarily emotive,' Western Europe said. 'Once the possessed base population climbs above two thousand, there's nothing anyone can do. The exponential curve takes over and the arcology is lost. New York is going to be this planet's Mortonridge. It's not our concern.'

'Not our concern!' North Pacific said. 'This is bullshit. Of course it's our concern. If they spread through the arcologies this whole planet will be lost.'

'Large numbers are not our concern. The military will have to deal with New York later.'

'If it's still here, and if they don't turn cannibal. The food vats won't work around possessed, you know, and the weather shields won't hold, either.'

'They're reinforcing the domes they've captured with their energistic power,' North America said. 'The arcology caught the tail end of an armada storm last night. The domes all held.'

'Only until they complete their takeover,' South Pacific said. 'The remaining domes can't barricade themselves in for ever.'

'New York's inevitable fall is regrettable, I'm sure,' Western Europe said. 'But not relevant. We have to accept it as a defeat and move forward. B7 is about prevention, not cure. And in order to prevent Earth itself from falling, we have to eliminate Quinn Dexter.'

'So like I asked, where is he?'

'Undetermined at this moment.'

'You lost him, didn't you? You blew it. He was a sitting duck in Edmonton, but you thought you were smarter. You thought your dandy little psychology game would triumph. Your arrogance could have enslaved us all.'

'Interesting tense, there,' Western Europe snapped. 'Could have. You mean, until you saved the day by closing down the vac-trains, after we agreed not to screw each other over.'

'The President had a very strong public mandate for closing them down. After Edmonton's High Noon firefight, the whole world was clamouring for a shut-down.'

'Led by your news companies,' Southern Africa said.

Western Europe leaned over the table towards a smiling South Pacific, his head centimetres short of the simulacrum. 'I got them back, you moronic bitch. Banneth and Louise Kavanagh returned to London safely. Dexter will do everything in his power to follow them there. But he can't bloody well do that if he's trapped in Edmonton. Six trains, that's all that got out before your stupid shut-down order. Six! It's not enough to be certain.'

'If he's as good as you seem to think, he would have got on one of them.'

'You'd better hope he has, because if he was left behind you can kiss goodbye to Edmonton. We have nothing in place there which could confirm his existence.'

'So we lose two arcologies. The rest are now guaranteed safe.'

'I lose two arcologies,' North America said. 'Thanks to you. Do you realize how much territory that is for me?'

'Paris,' South Pacific said. 'Bombay, Johannesburg. Everyone's taking losses today.'

'You're not. And the possessed are on the run in those arcologies. We have them locked down, thanks to the sects. None of those will escalate into a repetition of New York.'

'We hope,' said India. 'I'm managing parity at the moment, that's all. But panic is going to be a factor in the very near future. And that works to their advantage.'

'You're quibbling over details,' South Pacific said. 'The point is, there are methods of solving this problem other than obsessing over Dexter. My policy is the correct one. Confine them while we engineer a permanent solution. If that had been adopted at the start, we would have lost the Brazilian tower ground station at most.'

'We didn't know what we were dealing with when Dexter arrived,' South America said. 'We were always going to lose one arcology to him.'

'Dear me, I had no idea this was a policy forum,' Western Europe said. 'I thought we were conducting a progress review.'

'Well, as you've made no progress . . .' South Pacific said sweetly.

'If he's in London, he won't be found by conventional means. I thought we'd established that. And for your information, total inactivity isn't a policy, it's just the wishful thinking of small minds.'

'I've stopped the spread of possession. Remind us what you've achieved?'

'You're fiddling while Rome burns. The cause of the fire is our paramount concern.'

'Eliminating Dexter will not remove the possessed in New York or anywhere else. I vote we devote a higher percentage of our scientific resources to finding a permanent solution.'

'I find it hard to credit that even you are playing politics with this. Percentages aren't going to make the slightest difference to the beyond at this stage. Anyone who can provide a relevant input to the problem had been doing just that since the very beginning. We don't need to call in the auditors to verify our compassion credentials; they're hardly quantifiable, in any case.'

'If you don't want to be a part of the project, fine. Be sure you don't endanger us any further by your irresponsibility.'

Western Europe cancelled his representation, withdrawing from the conference. The simulacrum of London vanished with him.

*

The cave was at the lowest level of the endcap caverns, protected on all sides by hundreds of metres of solid polyp. Tolton felt quite secure inside it; first time in a long time.

Originally a servitor veterinary centre, it had been pressed into use as a physics lab. Dr Patan headed up the team which the Valisk personality had charged with making sense of the dark continuum. He'd greeted Dariat's arrival with the joy of a long-lost son. There had been dozens of experiments, starting with simple measurements, temperature (Dariat's ersatz body was eight degrees warmer than liquid nitrogen, and almost perfectly heat resistant) and electrical resistivity (abandoned quickly when Dariat protested at the pain), then energy spectrum and quantum signature analysis. The most interesting part for a layman observer like Tolton was when Dariat gave a sample of himself. Patan's team quickly decided an in-depth study was impossible when the fluid was being animated by Dariat's thoughts. Attempts to stick a needle into him and draw some away proved impossible, the tip wouldn't penetrate his skin. In the end it was down to Dariat himself, holding his hand over a glass dish and pricking himself with a pin which he'd conjured into existence by imagination. Red blood dripped out, changing as it fell away from him. Slightly sticky grey-white fluid splattered into the bowl. It was carried away triumphantly by the physicists. Dariat and Tolton exchanged a bemused look, and went to sit at the back of the lab.

'Wouldn't it have been easier to tear off a bit of cloth from your toga?' Tolton asked. 'I mean, it's all the same stuff, right?'

Dariat gave him a flabbergasted look. 'Bugger. I never thought of that.'

They spent the next couple of hours talking quietly, with Dariat filling in the details of his ordeal. The conversation stopped a couple of hours later when he fell silent, and gave the physicists a cheerless glance. They'd been quiet for several minutes, five of them and Erentz studying the results of a gamma-spike microscope. Their expressions were even more worried than Dariat's.

'What have you found?' Tolton asked.

757

'Dariat might be right,' Erentz said. 'Entropy here in the dark continuum appears to be stronger than in our universe.'

'For once I wish I hadn't said I told you so,' Dariat said.

'How do you know?' Tolton asked.

'We have contended this state for some time,' Dr Patan said. 'This substance seems to confirm that. Although I can't give you an absolute yet.'

'What the hell is it, then?'

'Best description?' Dr Patan smiled thinly. 'It's nothing.'

'Nothing? But he's solid.'

'Yes. The fluid is a perfect neutral substance, the end product of total decay. That's the best definition I can give you based on our results. A gamma-spike microscope allows us to probe sub-atomic particles. A most useful device for us physicists. Unfortunately, this fluid has no sub-atomic particles. There are no atoms as such, it appears to be made up from a single particle, one with a neutral charge.'

Tolton summoned up his first grade physics didactic memories. 'You mean neutrons?'

'No. This particle's rest mass is much lower than that. It has a small attractive force, which gives it its fluidic structure. But that's its only quantifiable property. I doubt it would ever form a solid, not even if you were to assemble a supergiant star mass of the stuff. In our own universe, that much cold matter will collapse under its own gravity to form neutronium. Here, we believe there's another stage of decay before that happens. Energy is constantly evaporating out of electrons and protons, breaking down their elementary particle cohesion. In the dark continuum dissipation rather than contraction would appear to be the norm.'

'*Is* evaporating? You mean we're leaking energy out of our atoms right now?'

'Yes. It would certainly explain why our electronic systems are suffering so much degradation.'

'How long till we dissolve into that stuff?' Tolton yelped.

'We haven't determined that yet. Now we know what we're looking for, we will begin calibrating the loss rate.'

'Oh, shit.' He whirled round to face Dariat. 'The lobster pot, that's what you called this place. We're not going to get out, are we?'

'With a little help from the Confederation, we can still make it back, atoms intact.'

Tolton's mind was racing ahead with the concept now. 'If I just fall apart into that fluid, my soul will be able to pull it back together. I'll be like you.'

'If your soul contains enough life-energy, yes.'

'But that fades away as well . . . Yours does, you had to steal more from that ghost. And those entities outside, they're all battling for life-energy. That's all they do. Ever.'

Dariat smiled with sad sympathy. 'That's the way it goes here.' He broke off, and stared at a high corner of the cave. The physicists did the same, their expressions all showing concern.

'Now what?' Tolton demanded. He couldn't see anything up there.

'Looks like our visitors have got tired with the southern endcap,' Dariat told him. 'They're coming here.'

*

The first of three Confederation Navy Marines flyers soared across Regina just as twilight fell. Sitting in the mid-fuselage passenger lounge, Samual Aleksandrovich accessed the craft's sensor suite to see the city below. Street lighting, adverts, and skyscrapers were responding to the vanishing sun by throwing their own iridescent corona across the urban landscape. He'd seen the sight many times before, but tonight the traffic along the freeways was thinner than usual.

It corresponded to the mood reported by the few news shows he'd grazed over the last couple of days. The Organization's attack had left the population badly shaken. Of all the Confederation worlds, they had supposed Avon to be second only to Earth in terms of safety. But now Earth's arcologies had been infested, and Trafalgar was so badly damaged it was being evacuated. There wasn't a countryside hotel room to be had anywhere on the planet as people claimed their outstanding vacation days or called in sick.

The flyer shot over the lake bordering the eastern side of the city, and swiftly curved back, losing height as it approached the navy barracks in the shadow of the Assembly Building. It touched down on a circular metal pad, which immediately sank down into the underground hangar. Blast-proof doors rumbled shut above it.

Jeeta Anwar was waiting to greet the First Admiral as he emerged from the flyer. He exchanged a couple of perfunctory words with her, then beckoned the captain of the marine guard detail.

'Aren't you supposed to check new arrivals, Captain?' he asked.

The Captain's face remained blank, though he was strangely incapable of focusing on the First Admiral. 'Yes, sir.'

'Then kindly do so. There are to be no exceptions. Understand?' A sensor was applied to the First Admiral's bare hand; he was also asked to datavise his physiological file into a block.

'Clear, sir,' the Captain reported, and snapped a salute.

'Good. Admirals Kolhammer and Lalwani will be arriving shortly. Pass the word.'

The marine guard squad emerging from the flyer, and the two staff officers, Amr al-Sahhaf and Keaton, were also quickly vetted for signs of possession. Once they were cleared, they fell in around the First Admiral.

The incident put Samual Aleksandrovich in a bad frame of mind. On the one hand the Captain's behaviour was excusable; that the First Admiral would be a possessed infiltrator was inconceivable. Yet possession was still spreading precisely because no one believed their friend/spouse/child could have been taken over. That was why the navy was leading by example, the three most senior admirals all taking different flyers to the same destination in case one of them was targeted by a rogue weapon. Enforced routine procedures might just succeed where personal familiarity invited disaster.

He met President Haaker in the barracks commander's conference room. This was one discussion both of them had agreed shouldn't be taken to the Polity Council just yet.

The President had Mae Ortlieb with him, which gave them two aides each. All very balanced and neutral, Samual thought as he shook hands with the President. Judging by Haaker's unconstrained welcome, he must have thought the same.

'So the anti-memory does actually work,' Haaker said as they sat round the table.

'Yes and no, sir,' Captain Keaton said. 'It eradicated Jacqueline Couteur and her host along with Dr Gilmore. However, it didn't propagate through the beyond. The souls are still there.'

'Can it be made to work?'

'The principle is sound. How long it will take, I don't know.

Estimates from the development team range from a couple of days to years.'

'You are still giving it priority, aren't you?' Jeeta Anwar asked.

'Work will be resumed as soon as our research team is established in its back-up facility,' Captain Amr al-Sahhaf said. 'We're hoping that will be inside a week.'

Mae turned to the President. 'One team,' she said pointedly.

'That doesn't seem to be much of a priority,' the President said. 'And Dr Gilmore is dead. I understand he was providing a lot of input.'

'He was,' the First Admiral said. 'But he's hardly irreplaceable. The basic concept of anti-memory has been established, developing it further's a multi-disciplinary operation.'

'Exactly,' Mae said. 'Once a concept has been proved, the quickest way to develop it is give the results to several teams; the more people, the more fresh ideas focused on this, the faster we will have a usable weapon.'

'You'd have to assemble the teams, then bring them up to date on our results,' Captain Keaton said. 'By the time you've done that, we will have moved on.'

'You hope,' she retorted.

'Do you have some reason to think the navy researchers are incompetent?'

'None at all. I'm simply pointing out a method which ensures our chances of success are significantly multiplied. A standard approach to R&D, in fact.'

'Who would you suggest assists us? I doubt astroengineering company weapons divisions have the necessary specialists.'

'The larger industrialized star systems would be able to assemble the requisite professionals. Kulu, New Washington, Oshanko, Nanjing, Petersburg, for starters, and I'm sure the Edenists would be able to provide considerable assistance, they know more about thought routines than any Adamist culture. Earth's GISD has already offered to help.'

'I'll bet they have,' Samual Aleksandrovich grunted. By virtue of his position he had an idea of just how widespread Earth's security agency was across the Confederation stars. They had at least three times the assets of the ESA, though even Lalwani was uncertain just how far their networks actually reached. One of the reasons it was so difficult to discover their size was the network's essentially passive nature. In the last ten years there had only been three active operations that CNIS had discovered, and all of those were mounted against black syndicates. Quite what they did with all the information their operatives gathered was a mystery, which made him cautious about trusting them. But they always cooperated with Lalwani's official requests for information.

'It's a reasonable suggestion,' the President said.

'It would also remove exclusivity from the Polity Council,' the First Admiral said. 'If sovereign states acquired a viable anti-memory weapon they could well use it without consultation, especially if one of them was facing an incursion. After all, that kind of supra-racial genocide would not leave any bodies as evidence. Anti-memory is a doomsday weapon, our primary negotiating tactic. As I have always maintained, it is not a solution to this problem. We must face this collectively.'

The President gave a reluctant sigh. 'Very well, Samual. Keep it confined to the navy for now. But I shall review the situation in a fortnight. If your team isn't making the kind of progress we need, I'll act on Mae's suggestion and bring in outside help.'

'Of course, Mr President.'

'That's good, then. Let's go face the Polity Council and hear the real bad news, shall we.' Olton Haaker rose with a pleasant smile in place. Content another problem had been smoothly dealt with in the traditional consensus compromise. Mae Ortlieb appeared equally sanguine. Her professional expression didn't fool Samual Aleksandrovich for a second.

*

For its private sessions the Confederation's Polity Council eschewed secure sensenvirons, and met in person in a discrete annex of the Assembly Building. Given that this was where the most crucial decisions affecting the human race would be taken, the designers had seen fit to spend a great deal of taxpayers' money on the interior. It was the amalgam of all government Cabinet rooms, infected with a quiet classicism. Twelve native granite pillars supported a domed roof painted in Renaissance style, with a gold and platinum chandelier hanging from the centre, while swan-white frescos of woodland mythology roamed across powder blue walls. The central round table was a single slice of ancient sequoia wood, taken from the last of the giant trees to fall before the armada storms. Its fifteen chairs were made from oak and leather to a nineteenth-century Plymouth design, and new (each delegate was allowed to take theirs home with them after their term was over). Glass-fronted marbled alcoves displayed exactly eight hundred and sixty-two sculptures and statuettes, one donated by each planet in the Confederation. The Tyrathca had contributed a crude hexagonal slab of slate with faint green scratches on the surface, a plaque of some kind from Tanjuntic-RI (worthless to them, but they knew how much humans valued antiquity). The Kiint had presented an enigmatic kinetic sculpture of silvery foil, composed of twenty-five concentric circular strips that rotated around each other without any bearings between them, each strip suspended in air and apparently powered by perpetual motion (it was suspected they were pieces of metallic hydrogen).

Lalwani and Kolhammer joined the First Admiral outside the council chamber, and the three of them followed the President in. Twelve chairs were already filled by the Ambassadors currently appointed to the Polity Council. Haaker and Samual took their places, leaving the fifteenth empty. Although Ambassador Roulor was entitled to take the seat vacated by Rittagu-FUH, the Assembly had delayed formally voting to confirm his appointment. The Kiint hadn't complained.

Samual sat down with minimum fuss, acknowledging the other Ambassadors. He didn't enjoy the irony of being called here in the same way he'd called them to request the starflight quarantine. It indicated events were now controlling him.

The President called the meeting to order. 'Admiral, if you could brief us on the Trafalgar situation, please.'

'The evacuation will be complete in another three days,' Samual told them. 'Active navy personnel were given priority, and are being flown to their secondary locations. We should be back up to full operational capability in another two days. The civilian workers are being ferried down to Avon. All decisions about refurbishing the asteroid will be postponed until the crisis is over. We'll have to wait until it's physically cooled down anyway.'

'What about the ships?' the President enquired. 'How many were damaged?'

'One hundred and seventy-three Adamist ships were destroyed, a further eighty-six are damaged beyond repair. Fifty-two voidhawks were killed. Human deaths so far stand at nine thousand two hundred and thirty-two. Seven hundred and eighty-seven people have been hospitalized, most of them with radiation burns. We haven't released those figures to the media yet. They just know it's bad.'

The Ambassadors were silent for a long moment.

'How many starships belonged to the 1st Fleet?' Earth's Ambassador asked.

'Ninety-seven front-line warships were lost.'

'Dear God.' Samual didn't see who muttered that.

'Capone cannot be allowed to get away with an atrocity of this magnitude,' the President said. 'He simply cannot.'

'It was an unusual set of circumstances,' Samual said. 'Our new security procedures should prevent it happening again.' Even as he spoke the words, he knew how pathetic it sounded.

'Those circumstances, possibly,' Abeche's Ambassador said bitterly. 'What if he dreams up some new course of action? We'll be left with another bloody great disaster on our hands.'

'We'll stop him.'

'You should have expected this, made some provision. We know Capone had antimatter, and he has nothing to lose. That combination was bound to result in a reckless strike of some kind. Jesus Christ, don't your strategy planners consider these scenarios?'

'We're aware of them, Mr Ambassador. And we do take them seriously.'

'Mortonridge hasn't delivered anything like the victory we were expecting,' Miyag's Ambassador said. 'Capone's infiltration flights have got everybody petrified. Now this.'

'We have eliminated Capone's source of antimatter,' the First Admiral said levelly. 'The infiltration flights have stopped because of that. He does not have the resources to conquer another planet. Capone is a public relations problem, he is not the true threat.'

'Don't tell me we should just ignore him,' Earth's Ambassador said. 'There's a difference between confining your enemy and not doing anything in the hope he'll go away, and the navy has done precious little to convince me it's got Capone under control.'

The President held a hand up to prevent the First Admiral from replying. 'What we're saying, Samual, is that we have decided to change our current policy. We can no longer afford the holding tactics of the starflight quarantine.'

Samual looked around the hard, determined faces. It was almost a vote of no confidence in his leadership. Not quite, though. It would take another setback before that happened. 'What do you propose to replace it with?'

'An active policy,' Abeche's Ambassador said hotly. 'Something that will show people we're using our military resources to protect them. Something positive.'

'Trafalgar should not be used as a *casus belli*,' the First Admiral insisted.

'It won't be,' the President said. 'I want the navy to eliminate Capone's fleet. A tactical mission, not a war. Wipe him out, Samual. Eliminate the antimatter threat completely. As long as he still has some, he can send one Pryor after another sneaking through our defences.'

'Capone's fleet is all that keeps him in charge of the Organization. If you take that away, we'll loose Arnstadt and New California. The possessed will take them out of the universe.'

'We know. That's the decision. We have to get rid of the possessed before we can start to deal with them properly.'

'An attack on the scale necessary to destroy his fleet, and New California's SD network will also kill thousands of people. And I'd remind you that the majority of crews in the Organization ships are non-possessed.'

'Traitors, you mean,' Mendina's Ambassador said.

'No,' the First Admiral said steadily. 'They are blackmail victims, working under the threat of torture to themselves and their families. Capone is quite ruthless in his application of terror.'

'This is exactly the problem we must address head on,' the President said. 'We are in a war situation. We must retaliate, and swiftly, or we will lose what little initiative we have. Capone must be shown we are not paralysed by this diabolical hostage scenario. We can still implement our decisions with force and resolution when required.'

'Killing people will not help us.'

'On the contrary, First Admiral,' Miyag's Ambassador said. 'Although we must deeply regret the sacrifice, eradicating the Organization will give us a much needed breathing space. No other group of possessed has managed to command ships with the same proficiency as Capone. We will have returned to the small risk of the possessed spreading through quarantine-busting flights, which the navy should be able to contain as you originally envisaged. Eventually, the possessed will simply remove themselves from this universe entirely. That is when we can begin our true fight back. And do so under a great deal less stress than our current conditions.'

'Is that the decision of this Council?' Samual asked formally.

'It is,' the President said. 'With one abstention.' He glanced at Cayeaux. The Edenist Ambassador returned the look unflinchingly. Edenism and Earth held the two other permanent seats on the Polity Council (awarded because of their population size), and formed a powerful voting block; they were rarely in disagreement over general policy. Ethics, of course, nearly always set the Edenists apart.

'They're inflicting too much damage on us,' Earth's Ambassador said, adopting a measured tone. 'Physically and economically. Not to mention the disintegration of morale propagated by events like Trafalgar, and unfortunately our arcologies. It has to be stopped. We cannot show any weakness in dealing with this.'

'I understand,' the First Admiral said. 'We still have the bulk of Admiral Kolhammer's task force available in the Avon system. Motela, how long would it take to deploy it?'

'We can rendezvous the Adamist warships above Kotcho in eight hours,' Kolhammer replied. 'It will take a little longer for affiliated voidhawk squadrons to gather. Most could join us en route.'

'That will mean we can hit Capone in three days' time,' Samual said. 'I would like some extra time to augment those forces. The tactical simulations we've run indicate we need at least a thousand warships to challenge Capone successfully in a direct confrontation. We'll need to call in reserve squadrons from national navies.'

'You have one week,' the President said.

19

The news of Trafalgar was whispered through the beyond until it reached Monterey, whereupon it sparked jubilation in some quarters.

'We beat the bastards,' Al whooped. He and Jez were fooling around in the Hilton's swimming pool when Patricia rushed in with the news.

'Sure did, boss,' Patricia said. 'There was thousands of the navy ship crews joined the beyond.' She was smiling brightly. Al couldn't remember seeing her do that before.

Jezzibella flung herself at Al's back, wrapping her arms round his neck and her legs round his hips. 'Told you Kingsley would make it!' she laughed. She was in her carefree adolescent persona, clad in a gold micro-bikini.

'OK, yeah.'

She splashed him. 'Told you so.'

He tipped her under the water. She shot up again laughing gleefully, a mermaid Venus.

'What about the asteroid?' Al asked. 'Did we get the First Admiral?'

'Don't think so,' Patricia said. 'Seems like the antimatter went off outside. The asteroid is still intact, but it's completely screwed.'

Al cocked his head to one side, listening to the multitude of voices murmuring at him, each one suffused with a plea. Rummaging through the nonsense which made up most of it took awhile, but eventually he built up a picture of the disaster.

'So what happened?' Jezzibella asked.

'Kingsley didn't get inside. Guess the security nazis were on to him. But he came through all right, Jee-ze did he ever. Wiped out a whole spaceport full of their warships, and a shitload of hardware got busted up with it.'

Jezzibella circled round in front of him, and embraced him passionately. 'That's good. Smart propaganda.'

'How do you figure that?'

'Blew up all their machines, but didn't kill too many people. Looks like you're the good guy.'

'Yeah.' He rubbed his nose against hers, hands moving round to cup her ass. 'Guess I am.'

Jezzibella shot Patricia a sly look. 'Has anyone broken the good news to Kiera, yet?'

'No. I don't think so.' Patricia was smiling again. 'You know, I think I'll go tell her.'

'She won't let you into her little ghetto,' Al said. 'Just invite her to the celebrations.'

'We're having a celebration?' Jezzibella asked.

'Hey, girl, if this ain't worth one, I don't know what the fuck is. Give Leroy a call, tell him to break out the good booze in the ballroom. Tonight, we are gonna party!'

*

Kiera stood in front of the lounge's window, staring down at the hellhawks on their docking pedestals. The yammering, pitiful voices of the beyond were intent on explaining the magnitude of the Trafalgar disaster to her. The Organization's triumph infuriated her. Capone was turning out to be a lot harder to crack than she'd envisioned at the start of her little rebellion. It wasn't just the mystique of his name, or his cleverly insidious hold on the Organization's power structure. Those two facets she could have worn down eventually. He was getting more than his fair share of luck. Far more. For a while the elimination of the antimatter station had tilted events in her favour. With the cancellation of the seeding flights the fleet had been getting edgy again. Now this. And Capone was well aware of her less than loyal actions, even though nothing was out in the open. Yet.

She couldn't see it from this window, but a third of the way round the docking-ledge, that little nerd Emmet Mordden was trying to rebuild one of the nutrient fluid refineries that she'd disabled. If he succeeded, then she was going to lose, and lose badly. One voice, pathetically eager to please, told her that at least one squadron of voidhawks had perished in the awesome explosion.

'Fuck it!' Kiera stormed. She refused to acknowledge any more of the insidious incorporeal babble. 'I didn't know he was cooking this up.'

Her two senior co-conspirators, Luigi Balsamo and Hudson Proctor, gave each other a look. They knew how dangerous life became when she was in this kind of mood.

'Me neither,' Luigi said. He was sitting on one of the long settees, drinking some excellent coffee and watching her carefully. 'Al used a quantity of antimatter for a secret project a while back. I never guessed it was for anything like this. Gotta give him credit, this is going to skyrocket his credibility among the crews.'

'That barbarian wouldn't have the intelligence to plan this out by himself,' she snapped. 'I bet I know who put the idea in his head. Little whore!'

'Smart for a whore,' Hudson Proctor said.

'Too smart,' Kiera said, 'for her own good. I shall enjoy telling her that some day soon.'

'It's going to make life difficult for us, though,' Luigi said. 'We've been getting through to a lot of people recently. There was plenty of support for all of us heading down to the planet.'

'There still is,' Kiera said. 'How long is this triumph going to last for him? A week? Two? Ultimately, it changes nothing. He has nothing else to offer. I'll take the Organization with me to New California, and Capone and his whore can freeze their asses off up here until the remainder of the Confederation Navy comes knocking. See how he likes that.'

'We'll keep plugging away,' Luigi promised.

'I might be able to turn this to our favour,' Kiera said thoughtfully, 'if the crews can be made to see that it's mainly a propaganda stroke, one that's got the remaining ninety-nine per cent of the Confederation Navy badly pissed off with us.'

'And are likely to come and settle the score,' Hudson finished excitedly.

'Exactly. And there's only one place we'll be truly safe from that retaliation.'

A bleep escaped from an AV pillar on the glass table in front of the settee. Kiera walked over to it in annoyance, and keyed an acknowledgement. It was Patricia Mangano, calling to tell them, if they hadn't already heard, the fabulous news about Trafalgar. And they were all invited to the victory party Al was throwing that evening.

'We'll be there,' Kiera replied sweetly, and switched off.

'We're going?' a startled Hudson Proctor asked.

'Oh, yes,' Kiera said. Her smile upgraded to pure malice. 'This is the perfect alibi.'

*

Mindori swooped in round the counter-rotating spindle and dropped on the pedestal which Hudson Proctor had assigned it. Rocio didn't fold in the hellhawk's distortion field immediately, there was some activity further up around the rocky ledge that he found interesting. Several non-possessed were in spacesuits, concentrated round a section of machinery that was pinned to the vertical cliff.

How long has that been going on for? he asked Pran Soo in singular-engagement mode.

Two days now.

Anyone know what they're doing?

No. But it's nothing to do with Kiera.

Really? The only systems on the ledge are connected with voidhawk and blackhawk maintenance and service.

Gaining the ability to provide us with nutrients is an obvious move for Capone, Pran Soo said. It would appear our options are finally starting to open up.

Not for me, Rocio said. Capone only wants us to complement the Organization fleet. No doubt he will offer better terms than Kiera's ever done, but we will still be drawn into the conflict. My goal remains achieving complete autonomy for all of us.

There are now fifteen of us who will provide whatever covert assistance we can. If the Almaden equipment can be made to function, we believe most of the others will join us. With a few noticeable exceptions.

Ah yes, where is Etchells?

I don't know. He still hasn't returned.

We can't have gotten that lucky. Did you check with Monterey's net to see if the electronics we require are in stock?

Yes. Everything is there. But I don't understand how we can get them out. We'll have to ask the Organization direct. Are you going to negotiate with the Organization? The fleet still needs us to patrol local space around the planet; it is not a combat duty.

No. Capone won't take kindly to my deal with Almaden; we'll be depriving him of their industrial capability. I believe I can obtain the electronics without the assistance of outside groups.

Rocio used the bitek processors in *Mindori*'s life-support cabin to establish a link with Monterey's communication net. Last time he had just accessed visual sensors to locate the food storage facilities for Jed. That had been simple enough, this task had an altogether different level of complexity. With Pran Soo's help he gained access to the maintenance files, and tracked down the physical location of the components they wanted. That information wasn't restricted, although they used a false log-on code to make sure there were no incriminating bytes that could ever link them to the components in question. After that, Rocio loaded in a requisition for the items. The spares allocation procedure which Emmet Mordden had erected around Monterey's stock of components had several integral security protocols. Rocio had to bring the hellhawk's on-board processor array into the loop to circumvent the safeguards with a powerful codebuster program. Once they were in the system, he ordered the electronics to be delivered to a maintenance shop outside the section of the spaceport which was under Kiera's physical jurisdiction.

Very good, Pran Soo said. Now what?

Simple. Just walk in and collect them.

Jed studied the route Rocio had devised, trying to spot any flaws. So far, he'd found the depressing number of zero. The hellhawk's possessor was using the big screen in the lounge to display it, though it would also be loaded into the spacesuit's processor. Jed could call it up on the visor's graphics overlay so that this time he wouldn't be reliant on Rocio calling out a stream of directions. He would have to walk about a kilometre along the ledge to reach the designated airlock. No complaints about that, despite having to wear a ball-crusher again. The possessed couldn't use spacesuits, so as long as he was outside there wouldn't be any of the buggers near him. It was inside when his troubles would begin. Again!

'There is a large celebration party due to begin in another fifty minutes,' Rocio said, his own face taking up a small square on the top right corner of the screen. 'That is when you should perform this mission. Most of the possessed will be there, it will minimize the chance of discovery.'

'Fine,' Jed mumbled. It was hard to concentrate; as well as sitting next to Beth on the couch, Gerald was pacing up and down behind him, muttering gibberish to himself.

'Half of the components have been delivered to the maintenance shop already,' Rocio said. 'That's the beauty of a heavily automated system like Monterey. The freight mechanoids don't start asking questions when there's no one there in the shop to receive them. They just dump them and go back for the next batch.'

'Yeah, we know,' Beth said. 'You're a bloody genius.'

'Not everyone could pull this off so stylishly.'

Jed and Beth shared a look; her hand went across his thigh and squeezed. 'Fifty minutes,' she murmured.

Gerald walked round the settee and up to the big screen. He held a hand out, and traced a green dotted route from *Mindori* to the asteroid's airlock, fingers stroking the glass gently. 'Show her,' he asked quietly. 'Show me Marie.'

'I can't, I'm sorry,' Rocio said. 'There's no general net access to the section of the asteroid where Kiera has barricaded herself in.'

'Barricaded?' Gerald's face flashed with alarm. 'Is she all right? Is Capone shooting at her?'

'No, no. Nothing like that. It's all politics. There's a big tussle going on for control of the Organization right now. Kiera's making sure she's safe from any kind of digital prying, that's all.'

'OK. All right.' Gerald nodded slowly. He gripped his hands together, kneading them until his knuckles cracked.

Jed and Beth waited anxiously. This kind of behaviour usually preceded an announcement.

'I'll go with Jed,' Gerald said. 'He'll need help.'

Rocio gave a deep chuckle. 'No way. Sorry, Gerald, but if I let you out, we'll never see you again. And that just won't do, now will it?'

'I'll help him, really I will. I won't cause any trouble.'

Beth hunched down small in the couch, not meeting anyone's eye. The pitiful way Gerald kept beseeching them was acutely embarrassing. And physically he was in a bad way, with sweaty skin and dark baggy skin accumulating under his eyes.

'You don't understand!' Gerald backed away from the screen.

'This is my last chance. I've heard what you're saying. You're not coming back. Marie is here! I have to go to her. She's only a baby. My little baby. I have to help, have to.' His whole body was shaking, as if he was about to cry.

'I will help you, Gerald,' Rocio said. 'Truly I will. But not now. This is critical to us. Jed has to get those components. Just be patient.'

'Patient?' It came out as a strangled gasp. Gerald turned round, his hands ready to claw at the air. 'No! No more.' He drew a laser pistol from his pocket.

'Christ,' Jed groaned. His hands went automatically to pat at his jacket. Pointless, he knew it was his pistol all right.

Beth was struggling to her feet, hampered by her arms being caught up with Jed's panicked movements. 'Gerald, mate, don't,' she cried.

'She's asking, I'm telling you,' Rocio said sternly.

'Take me to Marie! I'm not kidding.' Gerald aimed the laser at the two entangled youngsters, walking fast towards the couch until the muzzle lens was centimetres from Jed's forehead. 'Don't use your energistic power on me. It won't work.' His free hand tugged at the hem of his sweatshirt, revealing several power cells and a processor block taped to his stomach. They were connected together by various wires. The block's small screen had an emerald spiral cone that turned slowly. 'If this glitches, we all go up. I know how to bypass the cells' safety locks. I learned that a long time ago. When I was on Earth. Before all this happened. This life I brought them all to. It was supposed to be good. But it isn't. It isn't! I want my baby back. I want to make things right again. You're going to help me. All of you.'

Jed looked directly at Gerald, seeing the way he kept blinking as if in pain. Very slowly, he started to push Beth away from him. 'Go on,' he urged when she started to protest, 'Gerald isn't going to shoot you, are you, Gerald? I'm your hostage.'

The hand holding the laser pistol wobbled alarmingly. But not by enough for Jed to dodge free. Not that he would, he decided, the power cells saw to that.

'I'll kill you,' Gerald hissed.

'Sure you will. But not Beth.' Jed kept on pushing at her, until she started to stand.

'I want Marie.'

'We'll give you Marie, if you let Beth go.'

'Jed!' Beth protested.

'Go on, doll, walk out now.'

'Not bloody likely. Gerald, put that bloody gun down. Switch off the block.'

'*Give me Marie!*' Gerald screamed. Beth and Jed both flinched.

Gerald pressed the pistol against Jed's skin. 'Now! You'll have to help. I know you're frightened of the beyond. See, I know what I'm doing.'

'Gerald, mate, with all respect, you haven't got a fucking clue w—'

'Shut up!' He started panting, as if there wasn't enough oxygen in the compartment. 'Captain, are you hurting my head? I warned you not to use your power on me.'

'I'm not, Gerald,' Rocio said hurriedly. 'Check the block, there's no glitch, is there?'

'Oh, Jesus, Gerald!' Beth wanted to sit down again; the strength was flowing out of her legs.

'There's enough power in the cells to blow a hole in the capsule hull if they detonate.'

'I'm sure there is, Gerald,' Rocio said. 'You've been very clever. You outsmarted me. I'm not going to fight you.'

'You think that if I go in there they'll catch me, don't you?'

'It's a pretty good probability, yes.'

'But you're flying away after this is all over, aren't you? So it doesn't matter if they catch me, does it?'

'Not if we get the components.'

'There you go, then.' Gerald gave a semi-hysterical giggle. 'I'll help Jed load up the components, and then I'll go and look for her. It's easy. You should have thought about it first.'

'Rocio?' Beth said desperately. She looked imploringly at the little portion of the screen containing his face.

Rocio considered his options. It was unlikely he could negotiate with the madman. And stalling was useless. Time was the critical factor. He only had another four hours at the most before he finished ingesting his nutrient fluid; he'd been feeding slowly as it was. This opportunity would never be repeated.

'All right, Gerald, you win; you leave with Jed,' Rocio said. 'But remember, I will not let you back on board, under any circumstances. Do you understand that, Gerald? You are absolutely on your own.'

'Yes.' It was as if the laser pistol's weight had abruptly increased twentyfold; Gerald's arm drooped to hang at his side. 'But you'll let me go? To Marie?' His voice became an incredulous squeak. 'Really?'

*

Beth said nothing while Jed and Gerald suited up. She helped them with their helmet seals, and checked the backpack systems. Their suits contracted around them; Gerald's outlined the power cells around his torso. She'd had a couple of opportunities to snatch the laser pistol from him while he was struggling into the bulky fabric sack. It was the thought of what he might do which had restrained her. This wasn't the bewildered, hurt eccentric she'd been looking out for since Koblat. Gerald's illness had elevated itself to a level that was potentially lethal. She honestly thought he would blow himself up if anyone got in his way now.

Just before Jed closed his visor she kissed him. 'Come back,' she whispered.

He gave an anxious, brave smile.

The airlock closed, and started cycling.

'Rocio!' she yelled at the nearest AV lens. 'What the hell are you doing? They'll be caught for sure. Oh, Jeeze, you should have stopped him!'

'Name an alternative. Gerald might be dangerously unbalanced, but that trick with the power cells was clever.'

'How come you never saw him putting them together? I mean, why aren't you watching us?'

'You want me to watch everything you do?'

Beth blushed. 'No, but I thought at least you'd keep an eye on us, make sure we're not messing with you.'

'You and Jed can't mess with me. I admit I made a mistake with Gerald. A bad one. However, if Jed does manage to obtain the components, it won't matter.'

'It will to Gerald! They'll catch him. You know they will. He won't be able to take that again, not what they'll do to him.'

'Yes. I know that. There is nothing I can do. Nor can you. Accept it. Learn how to deal with it. This won't be the last time you experience tragedy in your life. We all do. I'm sorry. But at least with Gerald out of the way we can get back on track. I am grateful to you for your efforts, and your physical assistance. And I will turn you over to the Edenists. You have my word, for what it's worth. I can give you nothing else, after all.'

Beth made her way into the bridge. Sensor and camera images filled most of the console screens. She didn't touch any of the controls, just sat in one of the big acceleration chairs and tried to scope as much as she could all at once. One screen was centred on a pair of spacesuited figures waddling across the smooth rock of the docking-ledge. Others were focused on various airlock doors, windows, and walls of machinery. A group of five were relaying pictures from inside the asteroid, a couple of deserted corridors, the maintenance shop with Rocio's precious stack of pilfered components, and two views of the Hilton lobby where Capone's guests were arriving for the party.

One girl, barely older than Beth, swept in through the lobby, escorted by two handsome young men. Most people turned to look, nudging each other.

The girl's exquisite face made Beth scowl. 'That's her, isn't it? That's Kiera?'

'Yes,' Rocio said. 'The man on her right is Hudson Proctor, I don't know who the other is. Some poor stud she's wearing out in bed. The bitch is a complete whore.'

'Well, don't tell Gerald, for Christ's sake.'

'I wasn't planning on it. Mind you, most of the possessed go sex mad to begin with. Kiera's behaviour is nothing exceptional.'

Beth shuddered. 'How much further has Jed got to go?'

'He's only just started. Look, don't worry, he's got a clear route, the components are waiting. He'll be in and out in less than ten minutes.'

'If Gerald doesn't foul it up.'

*

Bernhard Allsop didn't mind missing the big party. He didn't get on with too many of Al's bigshots. They all sneered and laughed at him behind his back. The possessed ones, that is; the non-possessed treated him with respect, the kind of respect you gave a pissed rattler. It didn't bother him none. Here he was, at the centre of things. And Al trusted him. He hadn't been demoted or sent down to the planet like a lot of lieutenants who didn't measure up. Al's trust meant a hell of a lot more than everyone else's sniggering.

So Bernhard didn't complain when he drew this duty. He wasn't afraid of hard work to get ahead. No, sir. And this was one of Al's top projects. Emmet Mordden himself had said so. Second only to the hit against Trafalgar. That was why work wasn't stopping even during the party. Al wanted a whole bunch of machinery fixing. It was stuff connected with the hellhawks. Bernard wasn't so hot on the technical details. He'd tuned and overhauled auto engines when he was back home in Tennessee, but anything more complex than a turbine was best left to rocket scientists.

He didn't even mind that. It meant he didn't have to get his hands dirty, all he had to do was supervise the guys Emmett had assigned to this detail. Watch for any treachery in the minds of the non-possessed and make sure they pulled the whole shift. Easy. And when it was over, Al would know that Bernhard Allsop had come through with the goods again.

It was a long way through the corridors from Monterey's main habitation quarters to the section of the docking-ledge where the refurbishment was being carried out. He didn't have a clue what went on behind all the doors he walked past. This part of the rock was principally engineering shops and storage rooms. Most of it had fallen into disuse since the Organization had taken over from the New California Navy. Which just left miles of well-lit, warm corridors all laid out in a three-dimensional grid, unused except for the occasional mechanoid and maintenance crew. There were big emergency pressure-seal doors every couple of hundred yards, which was how Bernhard got to learn his way around. They all had a number and a letter which told you where you were. Once you'd done it a couple of times, it was kind of like Manhattan, obvious.

Pressure door 78D4, another ten minutes' walk from the nutrient refinery chamber. He stepped over the thick metal rim and started walking along the corridor. It ran parallel to the docking-ledge, though he could never make out a curve along the floor, even though he knew it had to be there. The doors on his left led to a couple of maintenance offices with long windows overlooking the ledge, a lounge, an airlock chamber, and two EVA prep rooms. There were only two doors on his right, a mechanoid service department and an electronics repair shop.

A quiet metallic whine made him look up. Pressure door 78D5, sixty yards ahead of him, was sliding across the corridor. Bernhard felt his borrowed heart thump. They only closed if there was a pressure loss. He whirled round to see 78D4 sliding into place behind him.

'Hey,' he called. 'What's happening?' There were no flashing red lights and shrill alarms like there had been in all the drills. Just unnerving silence. He realized the conditioning fans had stopped; the ducts must have sealed up as well.

Bernhard hurried along towards 78D5, pulling his processor block from his pocket. When he pressed the keys to call the control centre, the screen printed NO NET ACCESS AVAILABLE. He gave it a puzzled, annoyed look. Then he heard a hissing sound start up, growing very loud very quickly. He stood still and looked round again. Halfway down the corridor, an airlock door was sliding open. It was the one leading out onto the docking-ledge. One thing Emmet had emphasized time and again to reassure Organization members from earlier centuries: it was impossible for both airlock doors to open at once.

Bernhard howled in terrified anger, and started sprinting for 78D5. He shoved a hand out, and fired a bolt of white fire. It struck the stolid pressure door and evaporated into violet twinkles. Someone was on the other side, deflecting his energistic power.

Air was surging past him, building to hurricane force and producing short-lived streamers of white mist that curved sinuously round his body. He hammered another bolt of white fire at the pressure door. This time it didn't even reach the dull metal surface before it was negated.

They were trying to murder him!

He reached the slab-like pressure door and pounded against the small transparent port in the centre while the wind clawed at his clothes. Its roar was growing fainter. Someone was moving on the other side of the port. He could sense two minds; one he thought he recognized. Their gratification was horribly conspicuous.

Bernhard opened his mouth and found there was hardly anything left to inhale. He concentrated his energistic power around himself, making his body strong, fighting the sharp tingling sensation sweeping over his skin. His heart was yammering loudly in his chest.

He punched the pressure door, making a tiny dint in the surface rim. Another punch. The first dint straightened out amid a shimmer of red light.

'Help me!' he shrilled. The puff of air was ripped from his throat, but the cry had been directed at the infinity of souls surrounding him. Tell Capone, he implored them silently. It's Kiera!

He was having trouble focusing on the stubborn pressure door. He punched it again. The metal was smeared with red. It was a fluid this time, not the backspill from energistic power warping physical reality. Bernhard dropped to his knees, fingers scraping down the metal, desperate for a grip. The souls all around him were becoming a lot clearer.

*

'What's that?' Jed asked. He hadn't spoken to Gerald since they walked down the *Mindori*'s stairs, and even then it had only been to tell him the direction they were to take. They'd walked along together ever since, trudging past the feeding hellhawks. Now they were on a section of ledge unused by either Kiera or Capone. No man's land. The purple physiology icons projected against his visor told their usual sorry tale; his heart-rate was too high, and his body was hotter than it should be. This time he'd steered clear of snorting an infusion to calm his jabbering thoughts. So far.

'Is there a problem?' Rocio asked.

'You tell me, mate.' Jed pointed at the cliff wall, fifty metres ahead. A horizontal fountain of white vapour was gushing out of an open airlock hatch. 'Looks like some kind of blow-out.'

'Marie,' Gerald wheezed. 'Is she there? Is she in danger?'

'No, Gerald,' Rocio said, an edge of exasperation in his voice. 'She's nowhere near you. She's at Capone's party, drinking and making merry.'

'That's a lot of air escaping,' Jed said. 'The chamber must have breached. Rocio, can you see what's going on in there?'

'I can't access any of the sensors in the corridor behind the airlock. That section of the net has been isolated. There isn't even a pressure-drop alert getting out to the asteroid's environmental control centre. The corridor has been sealed. Someone's gone to a lot of trouble concealing whatever the hell they're up to.'

Jed watched the spurt of gas die away. 'Shall we keep going?'

'Absolutely,' Rocio said. 'Don't get involved. Don't draw attention to yourselves.'

Jed glanced along the line of blank windows above the open airlock. They were all dim, unlit. 'Sure thing.'

'Why?' Gerald asked. 'What's in there? Why don't you want us to see? It's Marie, isn't it? My baby's in there.'

'No, Gerald.'

Gerald took a few paces towards the open airlock.

'Gerald?' Beth's voice was high, strained and excitable. 'Listen to me, Gerald, she's not in there. OK? Marie's not there. I can see her, mate, there are cameras in the big hotel lobby. I'm looking at her right now. I swear it, mate. She's in a black and pink dress. I couldn't make that up, now could I?'

'No!' Gerald started to run, a laboured half-bouncing motion. 'You're lying to me.'

Jed stared after him in mounting dismay. Short of letting off a flare, there was nothing more he could do to attract attention to them.

'Jed,' Rocio said, 'I'm using your private suit band, Gerald can't hear this. You have to stop him. Whoever opened that airlock isn't going to want him blundering in. And they have to be a major faction player. This could ruin our whole scheme.'

'Stop him how? He'll either shoot me or blow both of us into the bloody beyond.'

'If Gerald triggers an alarm, none of us will ever get off this rock.'

'Oh, *Jeeze*.' He shook his fist helplessly at Gerald's crazy lurching run. The loon was fifteen metres from the open airlock.

'Take a hit,' Beth said. 'Chill down before you go after him.'

'Fuck off.' Jed started to run after Gerald, convinced the whole world was now watching. And worse, laughing.

Gerald reached the open airlock, and ducked inside. By the time Jed arrived half a minute later, he was nowhere to be seen. The chamber was standard, like the one Jed had come though last time he'd gone inside this bloody awful maggot-nest of rock. He moved along it cautiously. 'Gerald?'

The inner door was open. Which was deeply wrong. Jed knew all about asteroid airlocks, and one thing you could positively not ever do was open an internal corridor to the vacuum. Not by accident. He glanced at the rectangular hatch as he passed, seeing how the swing rods had been sheered, the melted cables around the rim seal interlock control.

'Gerald?'

'I'm losing your signal.' Rocio said. 'I still can't access the net around you. Whoever did it is still there.'

Gerald was slumped against the corridor wall, legs splayed wide in front of him. Not moving. Jed approached him cautiously. 'Gerald?'

The suit band transmitted a shallow, frightened whimper.

'Gerald, come on. We've got to get out of here. And no more of this crazy shit. I can't take it any more, OK? I mean really can't. You're cracking my head apart.'

One of Gerald's gauntleted hands waved limply. Jed stared past him, down to the end of the corridor. A dangerous geyser of vomit threatened to surge up his throat.

Bernhard Allsop's stolen body had ruptured in a spectacular fashion as the energistic power reinforcing his flesh had vanished. Lungs, the softest and most vulnerable tissue, had burst immediately, sending litres of blood pouring out of his mouth. Thousands of heavily pressurized capillaries just beneath his skin had split, weeping beads of blood into the fabric of his clothes. It looked as though his double-breasted suit was made from brilliant scarlet cloth. Cloth that seethed as if alive. The fluid was boiling away into the vacuum, surrounding him with a hazy pink mist.

Jed attacked his suit wrist pad as if it was burning him. Dry air scented with peppermint and pine blew into his face. He clamped his jaw shut against the rising vomit, turning bands of muscle to hot steel as he forced himself not to throw up. This spacesuit wasn't sophisticated enough to cope with him spewing.

Something loosened inside him. He coughed and spluttered, sending disgustingly tacky white bile spraying over the inside of his visor. But his nausea was subsiding. 'Oh God, oh Jeeze, he's just pulped.'

The pine scent was strong now, thick in his helmet, draining feeling away from his limbs. His arms moved sluggishly, yet they were as light as hydrogen. Good sensation.

Jed let out a snicker. 'Guess the guy couldn't hold it together, you know?'

'That's not Marie.'

The processor governing Jed's spacesuit cancelled the emergency medical suppressor infusion. The dosage had exceeded CAB limits by a considerable margin. It automatically administered the antidote. Winter fell across Jed, chilling him so badly he held a gauntlet up to his visor, expecting to see frost glittering on the rubbery fabric. The coloured lights flashing annoyingly into his eyes gradually resolved into icons and digits. Someone kept chanting: 'Marie, Marie, Marie . . .'

Jed looked at the corpse again. It was pretty hideous but it didn't make him feel sick this time. The infusion seemed to have switched off his internal organs. It also implanted a strong sensation of confidence, he could tackle the rest of the mission without any trouble now.

He shook Gerald's shoulder, which at least put an end to the dreary chanting. Gerald squirmed from the touch. 'Come on, mate, we're leaving,' Jed said. 'Got a job to do.'

A motion caught Jed's attention. There was a face pressed up against the port in the pressure door. As he watched, the blood smearing the little circle of glass began to flow apart. The man on the other side stared straight at Jed.

'Oh, bloody hell,' Jed choked. The balmy feeling imparted by the infusion was gusting away fast. He turned frantically to see the airlock's inner hatch starting to close.

'That's it, mate, we're outta here.' He pulled Gerald up, propping him against the wall. Their visors pressed together, allowing Jed to look into the old loon's helmet past the winking icons. Gerald was oblivious to anything, lost in a dream-state trance. The laser pistol slid from lifeless fingers to fall onto the floor. Jed glanced longingly at it, but decided against. If it came to a shoot-out with the possessed, he wasn't going to win. And it would only piss them off. Not a good idea.

The face at the port had vanished. 'Come on.' He tugged at Gerald, forcing him to take some steps along the corridor. Thin jets of grey gas started to shoot out of the conditioning vents overhead. Green and yellow icons appeared on his visor, reporting oxygen and nitrogen thickening around him. One thing Jed clung to was that the possessed were no good in a vacuum; suits didn't work, their power couldn't protect them. As soon as he got back out on the ledge he was safe. Relatively.

They reached the airlock hatch, and Jed slapped the cycle control. The control panel remained dark. Digits were flickering fast across his visor; the pressure was already twenty-five per cent standard. Jed let go of Gerald, and pulled the manual lever out. It seemed to move effortlessly as he spun it round and round. Then it jarred his arms. He frowned at it, cross that something as simple as a lock should try to hurt him. But at least the hatch swung open when he pulled on it.

Gerald stumbled into the chamber, as obedient as a mechanoid. Jed laughed and cheered as he pulled the hatch shut behind him.

'Are you all right?' Rocio asked. 'What happened?'

'Jed?' Beth cried. 'Jed, can you hear me?'

'No sweat, doll. The bad guys haven't got what it takes to spin me.'

'He's still high,' Rocio said. 'But he's coming down. Jed, why did you use the infuser?'

'Just quit bugging me, man. Jeeze, I came through for you, didn't I?' He pressed the outer hatch's cycle control. Amazingly, a line of green lights on the panel turned amber. 'You'd have snorted a megawatt floater too if you saw what I did.'

'What was that?' Rocio's voice had softened down to the kind of tone Mrs Yandell used when she talked to the day-club juniors. 'What did you see, Jed?'

'Body.' His irritation at the insulting tone was lost under a memory of wriggling scarlet cloth. 'Some bloke got caught in the vacuum.'

'Do you know who he was?'

'No!' Now he was sobering up, Jed desperately wanted to avoid thinking about it. He checked the control panel, relieved to see the atmosphere cycle was proceeding normally. The electronics at this end of the airlock were undamaged. Not sabotaged, he corrected himself.

'Jed, I'm getting some strange readings from Gerald's suit telemetry,' Rocio said. 'Is he OK?'

Jed felt like saying, 'Was he ever?' 'I think the body upset him. Once he realized it wasn't Marie, he just shut up.' And who's complaining about that?

The control panel lights turned red, and the hatch swung open.

'You'd better get out of there,' Rocio said. 'There's no alert in the net yet, but someone will discover the murder eventually.'

'Sure.' He took Gerald's hand in his, and pulled gently. Gerald followed obediently.

Rocio told them to stop outside a series of horseshoe-shaped garage bays at the base of the rock cliff, a hundred metres from the entrance they were supposed to use to get into the asteroid. Three trucks were parked in the bays, simple four-wheel-drive vehicles with seating for six and a flatbed rear.

'Check their systems,' Rocio said. 'You'll need one to drive the components back to me.'

Jed went along them, activating their management processors and initiating basic diagnostic routines. The first one was suffering from some kind of power cell drop-out, but the second was clean, and fully charged. He sat Gerald in one of the passenger seats, and drove it round to the airlock.

When the chamber's inner hatch swung open, Jed checked his sensor reading before he cracked his visor up. A lifetime of emergency procedure drills back on Koblat made him perpetually cautious about his environment. The icons showed him the atmosphere mix was good, but the humidity was up on the (Koblat) norm. It got that way in an asteroid's outlying sectors if the duct filters weren't cleaned regularly. Engineers were always cursing moisture contamination.

'There's nobody even close to you,' Rocio said. 'Go get them.'

Jed hurried along the corridor, took a right turn, and saw the broad door to the maintenance shop, three down on the right. It opened for him as he touched the lock panel. The lights sprang up to full intensity, revealing a basic rectangular room with pale-blue wall-panelling. Cybernetic tool modules stood in a row down the centre, encased in crystal cylinders to protect their delicate waldos. A grid of shelving covered the rear wall, intended to hold a stock of spares used regularly by the shop. Now there were just a few cartons and packages left scattered around; apart for the large pile in the middle which the mechanoid had delivered.

'Oh, Jeeze, Rocio,' Jed complained. 'There's got to be a hundred here. I'm never going to muscle that lot out, it'll take for ever.' The components were all packed in plastic boxes.

'I'm getting a sense of déjà vu here,' Rocio said smoothly. 'Just pile them onto the freight trolley, and dump them in the airlock chamber. It'll be three trips at the most. Ten minutes.'

'Oh, brother.' Jed grabbed a trolley and shoved it over to the shelving. He started to throw the boxes on. 'Why didn't you get the mechanoids to dump them at the airlock for me?'

'It's not a designated storage area. I would have had to reprogram the management routines. Not difficult, but it might have been detected. This method reduces the risk.'

'For some,' Jed muttered.

Gerald walked in. Jed had almost forgotten him. 'Gerald, you can take your helmet off, mate.' There was no response.

Jed went up to him and flipped the helmet seals. Gerald blinked as the visor was raised.

'Can't stay in that spacesuit here, mate, you'll get noticed. And you'll suffocate eventually.'

He thought Gerald was about to start crying, the bloke looked so wretched. To cover his own guilt, Jed went back to loading the boxes. When he had as many as the trolley could handle, he said: 'I'm going to get rid of this bundle. Do me a favour, mate, start loading the next lot.'

Gerald nodded. Even though he wasn't convinced, Jed hurried out back to the airlock. When he got back, Gerald had put two boxes on the second trolley.

'Ignore him,' Rocio said. 'Just do it yourself.'

It took a further three trips to carry all the boxes to the airlock. Jed finished loading the trolley for the last time, and paused. 'Gerald, mate, look, you've got to get a grip, OK?'

'Leave him,' Rocio said curtly.

'He's gone,' Jed said sadly. 'Total brainwipe this time. That corpse did for him. We can't leave him here.'

'I will not permit him back on board. You know what a danger he has become. We cannot treat him.'

'You think this gang are going to help him?'

'Jed, he did not come here looking for their help. Don't forget he has a home-made bomb strapped to his waist. If Capone does become unpleasant with Gerald, he's going to be in for a nasty surprise himself. Now get back to the airlock. Beth and your sister are the people you should be concentrating on now.'

More than anything, Jed wanted another dose out of the suit's medical kit. Something to take away the hurt at abandoning the crazy old man. 'I'm real sorry, mate. I hope you find Marie. I wish she wasn't, well ... what she is now. She gave a lot of us hope, you know. I guess I owe both of you.'

'Jed, leave now,' Rocio ordered.

'Screw you.' Jed steered the trolley at the wide door. 'Good luck,' he called back.

He forced himself not to go fast on the drive back to the *Mindori*. There was too much at stake now to risk drawing attention to himself by a last-minute error. So he resisted twisting the throttle as he passed the fateful airlock with the corpse behind it. Rocio said the net in that section had returned to full operation and the corridor's emergency doors had opened, but no one had found the body yet.

Jed drove under the big hellhawk, and parked directly below one of its cargo holds. Rocio opened the clamshell doors, and Jed set about transferring the boxes over onto the loading platform which telescoped down. At the back of his mind he knew that when the last box was on board, then he and Beth and the kids were no longer necessary. And probably a liability to boot.

He was quite surprised to be allowed back up the ladder into *Mindori*'s airlock. Shame finally overwhelmed him when he took his helmet off. Beth was standing in front of him, ready to help with his suit; face composed so she didn't show any weakness. The enormity of everything he'd done snatched the strength from his legs. He slid down the bulkhead, and burst into tears.

Beth's arms went round him. 'You couldn't help him,' she crooned. 'You couldn't.'

'I never tried. I just left him there.'

'He couldn't come back on board. Not now. He was going to blow us up.'

'He didn't know what the hell he was doing. He's mad.'

'Not really. Just very sick. But he's where he wanted to be, near Marie.'

*

Jack McGovern drifted back into consciousness aware of a sharp, deep stinging coming from his nose. His eyes fluttered open to see dark-brown wood crushed against his cheek. He was lying on floorboards in near darkness in the most uncomfortable position possible, with his legs bent so his feet were pressing into his arse and his arms twisted behind his back. Blood was pounding painfully in his forearms. His hangover was the greatest yet. When he tried to stir, he couldn't. His wrists and ankles were all bound up together by what felt like a ball of red-hot insulating tape. An attempt to groan revealed his mouth was also covered with tape. One nostril was clogged with dry blood.

That frightened him badly, sending pulse and breathing wild. Air hissed and thrummed through his one small vulnerable air passage. It was like reinforcement feedback, making him even more aware of how dependent he was. Attempting to hyperventilate and half-suffocating because of it made his head pound worse than ever. His vision vanished under a red sparkle.

Insensate panic dragged on for an indeterminable time. All he knew was that when his sight finally returned along with his sluggish thoughts, his breathing was slowing. His attempted thrashing had shifted him several centimetres across the floorboards. He calmed a lot then, still wishing his hangover would fuck off and leave him alone. The memory of what had happened in the Black Bull's toilet trickled back into his mind. He found that the tape across his mouth didn't stop him from whimpering at the back of his throat.

A possessed! He'd been mugged by a possessed. Yet . . . he wasn't possessed himself, which is what they always did to people – everyone knew that. Unless this was the beyond?

Jack managed to roll round onto his side and take a look round. Definitely not the beyond. He was in some kind of ancient cube of a room, a half-moon window set high up on one wall. Old store display placards were stacked opposite him, fading holophorescent print advertising brands of bathroom accessories he could dimly remember from his childhood. A heavy chain led from his ankles to a set of metal pipes that ran straight up from the floor to the ceiling.

He shuffled along the floor for all of half a metre, until the chain was tight. Nothing he did after that even scratched the pipes, let alone weakened them or made them bend away from the wall. He was still three metres from the door. Bracing and clenching his arm and shoulder muscles had the solitary effect of making his wrists hurt more. That was it then. No escape.

His hangover had long abated when the door finally opened. He didn't know when; only that hours and hours had passed. Cold arcology night light slithered in through the high window, painting the bare plaster walls a grubby sodium yellow. It was the possessed man who came in first, moving without sound, his black monk's robe swirling round him like orderly mist. Two others followed him in, a young teenage girl and a sulky, adolescent boy. They were hauling a woman along between them; middle-aged, her shoulders slumped in defeat. Her chestnut hair was arranged in a pleated crown, as if she'd put it up ready for a shower; wisps had escaped to dangle in front of her eyes. It hid most of her face, though Jack could make out the broken, lonely expression.

The boy bent down and yanked the tape over Jack's mouth as hard as he could. Jack grunted at the pulse of pain as it ripped free. He gulped down air.

'Please,' he panted. 'Please don't torture me. I'll surrender, OK. Just fucking don't.'

'Wouldn't dream of it,' Quinn said. 'I want you to help me.'

'I'm yours. Hundred per cent! Anything.'

'How old are you, Jack?'

'Hu . . . uh, twenty-eight.'

'I'd have put you older, myself. But that's fine. And you're about the right height.'

'What for?'

'Well, see, Jack, you got lucky. We're gonna smarten you up a bit, give you a makeover. You're gonna be a whole new man by the time we're finished. And I won't even charge you for it. How about that?'

'You mean different clothes and stuff?' Jack asked cautiously.

'Not exactly. You see, I found out that Greta here is a fully qualified nurse. Course, some assholes would call that synchronicity. But you and I know that's total bullshit, don't we, Jack.'

Jack grinned round wildly. 'Yeah! Absolutely. No fucking way.'

'Right. It's all part of His plan. God's Brother makes sure everything comes together for me. I am the chosen one, after all. Both of you are His gifts to me.'

'You tell him, Quinn,' Courtney said.

Jack's grin had been frozen into place by the aching realization of how deep into their shared insanity he'd fallen. 'A nurse?'

'Yep.' Quinn signalled Greta forwards.

Jack saw she held a medical nanonic package. 'Oh Jesus fuck, what are you going to do?'

'Hey, asshole, Jesus is dead,' Courtney shouted. 'Don't you go calling his name around us, he can't help you. He's the false Lord. Quinn is Earth's new Messiah.'

'Help me!' Jack yelled. 'Somebody help.'

'Mouthy little turd, ain't he,' Billy-Joe said. 'Ain't nobody gonna hear you, boy. They didn't hear any of the others, and Quinn hurt them a fuck of a lot more.'

'Look, I said I'd help you,' Jack said desperately. 'I will. Really. I'm not bullshitting. But you gotta keep your end of the bargain. You said no torture.'

Quinn walked back to the door, putting as much distance as he could between himself and Jack in the small room. 'Is it working now?' he asked Greta.

She looked at the small display on her processor block. 'Yes.'

'OK. Start by getting rid of his vocal cords. Billy-Joe's right, he talks too much. And I need him to be quiet when I use him. That's important.'

'No!' Jack yelled. He started to squirm round on the floor.

Billy-Joe laughed and sat down hard on his chest, forcing the air out of his lungs. It fluted weakly as it escaped through his nostril.

'The package can't remove his vocal cords,' Greta said in an uninterested monotone. 'I'll have to disengage the nerves.'

'Fine,' Quinn said. 'Whatever.'

Jack stared right at her as she leaned over and applied the glossy green package to his throat. Direct eye to eye contact, the most personal human communication there was. Pleading, imploring. *Don't do this.* He could have been looking into a mechanoid's sensor lens for the effect it had on her. The package adhered to his skin, soft and warm. He clenched his throat muscles against the invasion. But after a minute or so they began to relax as he lost all feeling between his jaw and his shoulders.

Silencing him was just the beginning. He was left alone as the package did its work, then the four of them returned. This time

Greta was carrying a different type of nanonic package, a face-mask with several sac-like blisters on the outer surface, inflated by some glutinous fluid. There were no slits for him to see out through when she placed it over his face.

That was when the routine started. Every few hours they would return and remove the mask. Greta would refill the sacs. His face would be examined, and Quinn would issue a few instructions before the mask was replaced. Occasionally they'd give him cold soup and a cup of water.

He was left alone in a darkness that was frightening in its totality. His face was numbed by the package, and whatever it was doing prevented even the red strain blotches that usually appeared behind closed eyelids. That just left him with hearing. He learned how to tell the difference between night and day. The half-moon window let in a variety of sounds, mostly traffic flowing along the big elevated motorway running down the middle of the Thames. There was also the sound of boats, swans and ducks squabbling. He began to get a feel for the building, too. Big and old, he was sure of that; the floorboards and pipes conducted faint vibrations. In the day there was some activity. Whirring sounds that must be lifts, clumping as heavy objects were moved around. None of it close to his room.

At night there was screaming. A woman, starting with a pitiful wail which was eventually reduced to miserable sobbing. Each time the same, and not far away. It took a while for him to realize it was Greta. Obviously, there were worse things than having your features modified by a nanonics package. The knowledge didn't act as much of a comfort.

*

The ghosts knew the Orgathé were approaching Valisk's northern endcap, their new awareness perceiving black knots of menacing hunger sliding through the air. It was enough to overcome their apprehension towards the humans that hated them, sending them fleeing into the caverns harbouring their ex-hosts.

Their presence was one more complication for the defenders. Although the personality could watch the Orgathé flying along the habitat, it certainly didn't know where they'd land. That left Erentz and her relatives with the entire circumference to guard. They'd already decided that it would be impossible to move the thousands of sick and emaciated humans from the front line of the outer caverns. Flight time down the length of the habitat was barely fifteen minutes, and the Orgathé emerging from the southern endcap were joined by several of the new arrivals who had just entered through the starscrapers. There simply wasn't time to prepare, all they could do was snatch up their weapons and assemble in teams ready to respond to the nearest incursion; even the way they were spaced round the endcap was less than ideal.

Wait until they get inside, the personality said. **If you fire while they're still in the air, they'll just swoop away. Once they're in the caverns they can't escape.**

The Orgathé hesitated as they glided down towards the scrub desert, in turn sensing the hatred and fear of the entities below. For several minutes they circled above the cavern entrances as the last ghosts fled inside, then the flock descended.

Thirty-eight of the buggers. Stand by.

Tolton shifted his grip on the incendiary torpedo launcher as Erentz told him to get ready. His sweat was making its casing slippery. He was standing behind Dariat, who in turn was at the tail end of a group of his relatives waiting in a passage at the back of one of the hospital caverns. What he thought of as his special status hadn't exempted him from this brand of lethal madness.

He heard a lot of groaning start up in the cavern. It quickly degenerated into weak screams and shouted curses. The ghosts were flooding in, ignoring the bedridden humans to plunge deeper into the cavern network. They started to run past him, mouths open to yell silent warnings. Their movements sketched short-lived smears of washed-out colour through the air.

Then one of the Orgathé hit the entrance outside. Its body elongated, the front section pressing forward eagerly through the curving passageway, while the bulbous rear quarter squirmed violently, adding to its impetus. Those ghosts that had only just made it inside were engulfed by writhing appendages as the huge creature surged along. Their savage cries of suffering penetrated the entire endcap as their life-energy was torn away from them. The other ghosts and Dariat could actually hear them, while the humans experienced their torment as a profound wave of chilling unease. Tolton looked down at the launcher for reassurance, only to find his hands were trembling badly.

'We're on!' Erentz barked.

The Orgathé charged into the cavern, preceded by a hail of freezing polyp pebbles and a technicolour ripple of terrified ghosts. Ahead of it, three rows of grubby bedding were laid out across the polyp floor, home to over three hundred lethargic patients, already disturbed by the ghosts. They did their best to retreat, staggering or crawling back against the wall; some of the nurses managing to lug their charges towards the passageways. The Orgathé lunged forwards greedily, turning the cavern into a riot of hysterical bodies and slashing appendages. Each time it coiled a tentacle around someone their body turned to solid ice and shattered, releasing a ghost that sank to its knees and waited for the devastating follow-up blow.

Through it all, Erentz and her relatives attempted to spread out and encircle the Orgathé. Every metre of ground had to be fought over, elbowing through the throng of terrified people. Blankets, plastic cartons, and chunks of rock-hard frosted flesh were kicked about underfoot, making every step treacherous. The pincer movement was never going to work properly, the best they could hope for was positioning themselves close to the passageways, blocking the Orgathé's escape.

When they had five of the possible seven exit routes covered, they opened fire. A cowering Tolton saw slivers of dazzling light pulse through the air to be absorbed by the Orgathé's nebulous form, and assumed that was the signal to start firing. He pushed a couple of elderly, enfeebled men aside, and brought his own launcher up. His mind was so battered by the sight of panic and devastation across the cavern floor he barely aimed it. He just pulled the trigger and watched numbly as the incendiary torpedoes pummelled the dark mass.

The flame-throwers opened fire with a raucous howl, adding their particular brand of carnage to the onslaught. Eight lines of bright yellow fire jetted over the heads of the cowering crowd to flower open against the Orgathé. The beast jerked frenziedly, buffeted from all sides by the terrible flame. Its constituent fluid boiled furiously, sending clouds of choking mist to saturate the beleaguered cavern.

Tolton clamped a hand over his mouth as his eyes smarted. The vapour was colder than ice, condensing over his skin and clothes to form a slick mucus-like film. He had trouble standing as it built up underfoot. All around him people were falling over and skating across the floor. He couldn't aim the launcher with any accuracy now, the recoil from each shot sent him slithering back wildly. In any case, he wasn't entirely sure where the creature was any more. The mist was fluorescing strongly as the jets of flame continued to sear through it, turning the whole cavern into a uniform topaz haze.

Without any visible target, Tolton stopped firing. People were everywhere, shrieking and crying as they skidded about, a racket which fused with the roar of the flame-throwers to create total sonic bedlam. Any random shot would probably hit someone. He dropped to all fours, and tried to find the cavern wall, a way out.

Erentz and the others kept on firing. The personality's perception of the cavern through its sensitive cells was less than perfect, but it could keep them informed of the Orgathé's approximate location. She twisted about continually, keeping the flame playing on the creature's flanks. With the billowing mist, running figures, and the target continually shrinking, she had a lot of trouble keeping aligned. But it was working, that mattered above all else, helping to blank the knowledge of what a misapplied jet would strike.

Dariat finally perceived the Orgathé's denuded ghost flying back out into the habitat. He shared his enhanced cognition with his relatives and the personality, showing them the wraith flashing past. The light and sound of the flame-throwers swiftly died away.

As the disgustingly clammy mist descended out of the air to congeal over people and polyp alike, it revealed a floor littered with bodies. Those who hadn't been too badly burnt, or had escaped the Orgathé's slashing appendages, were wriggling mutely beneath the slick membraneous muck. Nearly a third remained motionless; whether they were too exhausted or wounded to make an effort was impossible to tell. The grungy fluid concealed details.

Tolton watched with numb incredulity as ghosts started to rise up out of the floor like humanoid mushrooms, stretching elastic fronds of the fluid with them. They were harvesting the material as Dariat had done, cloaking their form with substance.

Erentz and her team were striding through the slaughter and misery as if it didn't exist, whooping out greetings to each other as they congregated by one of the side passageways. Dr Patan was among them, wiping sloppy goo from his face and grinning with the same vivacity as the others as he checked his launcher.

Tolton stared after them as they hurried off down the passageway, totally immune to the suffering throughout the cavern. The personality had informed them of another visitor raising hell in a cavern close by, and they were eager to resume the fight. It wasn't just entropy which was stronger in this continuum, he reflected, inhumanity was equally pervasive.

Eventually he stirred himself, though he was uncertain what to do next. Dariat came over to stand at his side, and they surveyed the cavern with its dead, its wounded, and its enervated ghosts. Together they moved out to offer what comfort they could.

*

The mask came away cleanly from Jack's McGovern's face. He blinked against the gentle light coming through the storeroom's high window. Without the package, his bare skin was host to a peculiar sensation, somewhere between numb and sore. What he wanted to do was dab at it with his hands, trace his fingertips over his cheeks and jaw to find out what they'd done to him. But he was still bound up with the tape and chain.

'Not bad,' Courtney said. She gave Greta an affectionate slap on the arm. The woman flinched badly; muscles on her neck and limbs twitched in a cascade reaction.

'Even got the eye colour right.'

'Show him,' Quinn said.

A giggling Courtney bent down and thrust a small mirror at Jack. He stared at the image. It was the last thing he expected; they'd given him Quinn's face. He frowned the question.

'You'll see,' Quinn said. 'Get him ready.' A single gesture, and the chain fell from Jack's ankles. The tape wasn't so simple. Billy-Joe produced a vicious-looking combat knife, and started sawing.

Returning blood brought pain roaring into Jack's feet and hands as the tape was prised away. He couldn't stand. Courtney and Billy-Joe had to drag him out between them. First stop was a staff washroom. They dumped him in a shower cubicle and turned the nozzle on full. Cold water sluiced down, making him gag, batting feebly at the spray. Dark stains seeped out of his trousers. Never once had they let him use a toilet.

'Take your clothes off,' Quinn ordered. He chucked a tube of soap gel down onto the cracked tiles. 'Wash thoroughly. That stink is a giveaway.'

They stood round, watching as he slowly opened the seals on his shirt and trousers. Feeling and movement were slow to return to his extremities. He had a lot of trouble keeping hold of the tube as he applied the gel. Standing was also very painful, it felt like he was tearing tendons as his knees straightened out. But it was Quinn who'd told him to stand, and he didn't dare not.

Quinn snapped his fingers, and Jack was abruptly dry. Courtney handed him a black robe. Its cut was identical to Quinn's, voluminous arms and deep hood, but it was just ordinary cloth, not the patch of empty space which clung to the dark Messiah.

Courtney and Billy-Joe inspected them as they stood side by side. Height was almost the same, within three centimetres. A slight weight difference was obscured by the robe.

'God's Brother must be laughing His ass off,' Billy-Joe said. 'Shit, it's like you's twins.'

'It'll do,' Quinn decided. 'Any updates on her position?'

'No way, man,' Billy-Joe said, suddenly serious. 'Those dudes from the Lambeth coven swore on it. It's a big fucking deal for them having another high magus visiting the arcology, especially now. They's all taking about how this is His time. But she's staying put in her tower, won't move, won't see anyone, not even London's High Magus. And she's a real pain in the ass, they all say that. Who else is it gonna be?'

'You've done good, Billy-Joe,' Quinn said. 'I won't forget that, and neither will He. When I bring Night to this arcology I'll let you loose inside a model agency. You can keep yourself a harem of the hottest babes there are.'

'All right!' Billy-Joe punched the air. 'Rich bitches, Quinn. I want me some rich bitches, all dressed up real fine in silk and stuff. They always wear that for their own kind, don't even look at the likes of me. But I'm gonna show them what it's like to fuck with a real man.'

Quinn laughed. 'Shit, you don't ever change.' He took another look at Jack, and nodded in satisfaction. The man was eerily similar to himself. It ought to be enough. 'Do it,' he told Courtney.

She pushed Jack's hood aside, and pressed a medical spray to his neck.

'Just to keep you calm,' Quinn said. 'You've handled this all right so far, I'd hate for you to blow it now.'

Jack didn't know what the drug was, only that it buzzed warmly in his ears. The fear of what was going to happen to him set sail and drifted away. Just standing still and admiring the glistening droplets form around the shower nozzle was fascinating entertainment. Their fall was an epic voyage.

'Come here,' Quinn said.

It was a very loud voice, Jack thought. But he had nothing else to do, so he slowly walked over to where Quinn was standing. Then his skin grew cold, as if a winter breeze was flowing through his robe. The room began to change, its drab colours melting away. The walls and floor became simple planes of thick shadow. Billy-Joe, Courtney, and Greta were blank statues, frothing with iridescence. Other people became visible, everything about them was clearly defined, their features, clothes (odd, ancient styles), hair. Yet they lacked colour to the point of translucency. And they were all so sad, mournful faces with anguished eyes.

'Ignore them,' Quinn said. 'Bunch of assholes.' By contrast to the others, Quinn was vibrant with life and power.

'Yes.'

Quinn gave him a sharp look, then shrugged. 'Yeah, well, I suppose we're not really talking. After all, you're not actually alive in here.'

Jack contemplated that. His thoughts were losing their sluggishness. 'What do you mean?' He realized he couldn't hear his heart beating any more. Nor was his mouth moving when he spoke.

'Shit.' Quinn's exasperation manifested itself as a tide of warmth flooding from his shining body. 'The hypnogenic doesn't work here, either. Should have figured that. OK, let's put it real simple for you. Do as I say, or I'll hurt you real bad; and in this realm that can be very bad indeed. Understand?'

They started to slide through the room. Jack didn't know how, his legs weren't moving. The wall came at him, and passed by with a stinging sensation that made his thoughts quake.

'It'll get worse,' Quinn said. 'Going through thick chunks of matter is painful. Ignore it, just you sit back and enjoy the view.' They started to pick up speed.

*

Banneth had tired of the acolytes. Even watching them fucking each other senseless was a bore. It was all so ordinary. She kept thinking of the improvements and modifications she could make to their thrashing bodies to spice up the sex and make it potentially a great deal more interesting. There were definitely attributes she could bestow upon the boy to make him more ruthless, both in bed and in life, the first arena acting as a training ground for the second. After critical deliberation, she concluded the girls would probably both benefit from a more feline nature.

Not that any of it mattered now. She'd acquired the same kind of fatalism as the rest of the planet's population. Since the vac-train shutdown, absenteeism and petty crime had increased considerably in every arcology. After an initial flurry of concern, the authorities had decided such actions were not in fact precursors to wholesale possession. Basically, it was people taking the news badly. Apathy had risen to rule with all the intangible force of a dominant star sign.

Banneth pulled on her robe and walked out of the penthouse's master bedroom, not even glancing back at the fresh outburst of moaning from the tangle of bodies on the mattress behind her. She went over to the lounge area's cocktail bar and poured herself a decent measure of Crown whisky. Four days' inactivity floating round the apartment had reduced the bottle's contents down to the last couple of centimetres.

She settled back into one of the atrocious leather chairs and datavised the room's management processor. Tasselled curtains swished shut across the glass wall, cutting off the sight of the night-time arcology. A holographic screen above the gross fireplace bar flared with colour, giving her a feed from the local news station.

Another two of New York's domes had succumbed to the possessed. Rover reporters relayed the images from the vantage point of a megatower, revealing a faint red glow emanating from the buildings inside the geodesic crystal roof. Police in Paris claimed they had captured nineteen more possessed and thrown them into zero-tau pods. There were interviews with dazed ex-hosts: one claimed to have been taken over by Napoleon; another swore she'd been used by Eva Perón. From Bombay a terse official statement assured residents that local disturbances were under control.

Several times the station switched back to that morning's address by the President, who had asserted that there were no new incidents of suspected possession. He said his decision to shut down the vac-trains was now fully justified. Local law-enforcement agencies were successfully keeping the possessed confined, in the regrettable cases where they'd managed to establish themselves in arcologies. He called on all people to pray for New York.

Banneth took another sip of the Crown, enjoying the all too rare sensation of alcohol seeping through her synapses. **No mention of London, then.**

None at all, Western Europe confirmed. **I'm not even suppressing any. He's being remarkably restrained.**

If he's here.

He is.

You shut down the vac-trains awful quick.

I didn't.

Really? Banneth perked up at that. Any information she could gather on B7 always fascinated her. In all the years she'd been working for them, she'd learned so little about how they operated. **Who did?**

A flash of pique escaped along the affinity link. **An idiotic colleague panicked. Sadly not all of us are completely focused on the problem.**

How many are there?

No. Old habits die hard, and the habit of secrecy is very old indeed in my case. You should appreciate that, with your obsession in behavioural psychology.

Come on. You can indulge me. I can't even fart without your consent. And I am about to be vaporized.

A pat on the head for a faithful old servant?

Whatever you want to call it.

Very well, I suppose I do have some small obligation. You have behaved yourself admirably. I will reveal one aspect of myself, on the condition that you don't pester me any further.

Done deal.

The habit. It has formed over six hundred years.

Shit! You're six hundred years old?

Six hundred and fifty-two, actually.

What the fuck are you?

Done deal, remember.

Xenoc, is that it?

The affinity link carried a mental chuckle. I'm fully human, thank you. Now stop asking questions.

'Six hundred years old,' Banneth muttered in awe. It was an astonishing disclosure. If it was true. But the supervisor had no reason to lie. You keep going into zero-tau; stay in for fifty years, come out for a couple every century. I've heard of people doing that.

Dear me, I'm disappointed. It must be all that whisky you're guzzling down, it's fogging your brain. I don't consider myself to be that mundane. Zero-tau, indeed.

What then?

Work it out. You should be grateful. I've given you something to keep your mind active in your last days. You were becoming morbid and withdrawn. Now your files are all edited and catalogued, you need a fresh mental challenge.

What's going to happen to my files? You will publish them, won't you?

Ah, sweet vanity. It's been the downfall of egomaniacs greater than you.

Won't you? she repeated, annoyed.

It will make an excellent archive resource for my people.

Your people? What do they want with... The holoscreen image wobbled; a story from Edmonton, a reporter touring round a sabotaged power plant, detailing the repairs. Did you see that?

The AI is picking up microfluctuations in the penthouse's electrical circuits. He's there. Western Europe's excitement was crackling down the affinity link like a static slap to the brain.

'Shit!' Banneth downed the whisky in one swift gulp. *Nothing I can do.* The phrase was locked in her mind, repeating and repeating. Now the moment was swooping down on her, bitter resentment surged up. She struggled to her feet. Quinn was never going to see her slumped in defeat. He was also damn well going to know she was the principal factor in outsmarting him.

She datavised the lights up to full strength, and turned a circle, scanning the penthouse. Moisture was smearing her vision. The holoscreen wobbled again, its sound jolting.

Slowly, and with a taunting smile on her face, she said: 'Where are you, Quinn?'

It was like a poorly focused AV projection coming to life. A dark shadow wavering in front of the door to the bedroom, blocking out the motion of the oblivious acolytes. It was translucent at first, but thickened quickly. The overhead lights flickered and the holoscreen image imploded into a soiled rainbow. Banneth's neural nanonics crashed.

Quinn Dexter stood on the marble tiles, clad in his ebony robe, looking right at her. Fully materialized.

Gotcha, you bastard!

The supervisor's victorious cry rang out in Banneth's skull. For a whole second she stared at her beautiful creation, every gorgeous feature; remembering the angry power locked up beneath the smooth pale skin. He stared right back. Rather, his eyes were unmoving. Wrong. Wrong! WRONG. **Wait, it's not—**

The SD X-ray laser fired. Kilometres above Banneth, the beam penetrated the arcology's crystal dome. It struck the top of the Parsonage Heights tower, transmuting the carbon-concrete structure and dubious decor into a blast of ions. A twister of near-solid blue light flared up towards the dome from the skyscraper's ruined crown.

Quinn floated down lightly through the heart of the explosion, intrigued by the level of violence storming through the physical universe outside. He'd been wondering exactly what weapon they'd use once they found him. Only an SD platform could produce such spectacular savagery.

He observed Banneth's soul disconnect from the dispersing atoms of her body. She howled in rage as she became aware of him; the real him. Jack McGovern's desolated soul was already slithering into the beyond.

'Nice try,' Quinn mocked. 'So what are you going to do for an encore?' He extended his perception as she dwindled away, savouring her anguish and useless fury. And also ... Out there, trembling weakly on the furthest edge of awareness, was a ragged chorus of more tenuous cries. Resonant with misery and terrible pain. Far, far away.

That was interesting.

20

The uniform sheet of light which appeared above Norfolk to signify daytime wasn't quite as glaring now. Although still several weeks away, the onset of autumn was plain to see for those who knew their weather lore.

Luca Comar stood at his bedroom window, looking out over the wolds as he'd done every morning at daybreak since . . . Well, every morning. There was a particularly thick mist covering the estate today. Beyond the lawns (un-mown for weeks now, damn it), all he could see were the old cedars, great grey shadows guarding Cricklade's orchards and pastures. Gravely reassuring in their size and familiarity.

It was completely still outside. A morning so insipid it couldn't even coax native animals out of their burrows. Dewdrops cloaked every leaf, their weight bending branches out of alignment, making it seem as though every bush and tree was sagging from apathy.

'For Heaven's sake come back to bed,' Susannah grunted. 'I'm cold.'

She was lying in the middle of their huge four-poster bed, eyes closed, sleepily trawling the duvet back around her shoulders. Her dark hair fanned out across the rumpled pillows like a broken bird's nest. Not as long as it used to be, he thought wistfully. The two of them getting together had been inevitable. Back together, in one respect. However you wanted to look at it, they were suited for each other. And there had been one argument too many with Lucy.

Luca went back and sat on the edge of the bed, looking down at his love. Her hand crept out from under the duvet, feeling round for him. He held it gently, and bent over to kiss her knuckles. A gesture that had carried over from their courting days. She smiled lazily.

'That's better,' she purred. 'I hate it when you leap out of bed every bloody morning.'

'I have to. The estate doesn't run itself. Especially not now. Honestly, some of the buggers are more idle and stupid now than they were before.'

'Doesn't matter.'

'Yes, it does. We still have a crop to get in. Who knows how long this winter is going to last.'

She lifted her head and peered up at him in modest confusion. 'It'll last the same time as it always does. That's what's right for this world, and that's what we all feel. So that's the way it will be. Stop worrying.'

'Yeah.' He looked back at the window again. Tempted.

She sat up and gave him a proper look. 'What is it? I can sense how troubled you are. It's not just the crops.'

'It is, partly. You and I both know that I have to be here to make sure it's done right. Not just because they're a bunch of slackers. They need the kind of guidance Grant can give them. Which silos are used for what, how much drying the grain should be given first.'

'Mr Butterworth can tell them that.'

'Johan, you mean.'

They managed to avoid each other's eye. But the mild guilt was the same in both of them. Identity was a taboo topic on Norfolk these days.

'He can tell them,' Luca said. 'Whether they'll listen and actually do the work is another matter. We've still got a way to go before we're one big harmonious family working for the common good.'

She grinned. 'Arses need to be kicked.'

'Damn right!'

'So what's with all the angst?'

'Days like this give me time to think. They're so slow. There's no urgent farm work to do at the moment, only the pruning. And Johan can supervise that OK.'

'Ah.' She drew her knees up under her chin, and hugged them. 'The girls.'

'Yeah,' he admitted sheepishly. 'The girls. I hate it, you know. It means I'm more of Grant than I am of me. That I'm losing control. That can't be right. I'm Luca; and they're nothing to me, they're nothing to do with me.'

'Me neither,' she said miserably. 'But I think we're fighting an instinct we can never beat. They're the daughters of this body, Luca. And the more I settle into this body, the more it belongs to me, then the more I have to accept what comes with it. What Marjorie Kavanagh is. If I don't, she'll haunt me for ever; and rightly so. This is supposed to be our haven. How can it be if we reject them? We will never be given peace.'

'Grant hates me. If he could put a gun to my head right now, he'd do it. Sometimes, when I'm more him than me, I think I'm going to do it. The only reason I'm still here is because he's not ready to commit suicide yet. He desperately wants to know what's happened to Louise and Genevieve. He wants that so bad that I do too, now. That's why today is so tempting. I could take a horse and ride over to Knossington, there's another aeroambulance stationed there. If it still works I could be in Norwich by evening.'

'I doubt any kind of plane would work, not here.'

'I know. Getting to Norwich by boat is going to be a hell of a lot more difficult. And then winter will make it damn near impossible. So I ought to start now.'

'But Cricklade won't let you.'

'No. I don't think so. I'm not sure any more. He's getting stronger, wearing me down.' He gave a short bitter laugh. 'Taste the irony in that. The person I possess, possessing me in return. No more than I deserve, I suppose. And you know what? I do want to see that the girls are OK. Me, my own thoughts. I don't know where that comes from. If it's the guilt from what I tried to do to Louise, or if it is him, his first victory. Carmitha says we're reverting. I think she could be right.'

'No, she's not, we will always be ourselves.'

'Will we?'

'Yes,' she said emphatically.

'I wish I could believe that. So much of this place isn't what we expected. All I ever truly wanted was to be free of the beyond. Now I am, and I'm still being persecuted. Dear God, why can't death be real? What kind of universe is this?'

'Luca, if you do go looking for the girls, I'm going with you.'

He kissed her, searching to immerse himself in normality. 'Good.'

Her arms went round his neck. 'Come here. Let's celebrate being us. I know quite a few things Marjorie never did for Grant.'

*

Carmitha spent the morning working in the rosegrove, one of a thirty-strong team gainfully employed to return Norfolk's legendary plants to order. Because of the delay, it was harder work than usual. The flower stems had toughened, and new late-summer shoots had flourished, tangling their way through the neat wire trellises. It all had to be trimmed away, returning the plants to their original broad fan shape. She started by deadheading each plant, then used a stepladder to reach the topmost shoots, snipping through them with a pair of heavy-duty secateurs. Long whiplike shoots fell from her snapping blades to form a considerable criss-cross pile around the foot of the steps.

She also considered that the grass between the rows had been allowed to grow too long. But held her tongue. It was enough that they were keeping the basics of her world ticking over. When the end came, and the Confederation descended out of the strange blank sky to banish the possessing souls, enough would remain for the genuine inhabitants to carry on. Never *as before*, but there would be a degree of continuity. The next generation would be able to build their lives over the ruins of the horror.

It was the thought she remained faithful to throughout every day. The prospect that this wouldn't end was a weakness she could not permit herself. Somewhere on the other side of this realm's boundary the Confederation was still intact, its leadership pouring every ounce of effort into finding them, and with that an answer.

Her belief faltered at what that answer might be. Simply expelling the souls back into the dark emptiness of the hereafter solved nothing. Some place devoid of suffering must be found for them. They, of course, thought they'd already found it by coming here. Fools. Poor blighted, tragic fools.

Similarly, her imagination failed to embrace exactly what life on Norfolk, and the other possessed worlds, would be like afterwards. She'd always respected the mild culture of spirituality in which she'd been raised, just as the house-dwellers worshipped their Christian God. Neither gave the slightest clue how to live once you truly knew you had an immortal soul. How could anyone take physical existence seriously now they knew that? Why do anything, why achieve anything when so much more awaited? She'd always resented this world's artificial restrictions, while admitting she could never have an alternative. A butterfly without wings, her grandmother used to call her. Now the doorway into an awesome, infinite freedom had been flung wide open.

And what had she done at the sight of it? Clung to this small life with a tenacity and forcefulness few others on this world had contrived. Perhaps that was going to be the way of it. A future of perpetual schizophrenia as the inner struggle between yin and yang went nuclear.

Far easier not to think about it. Yet even that was unwelcome. Implying she had no mastery over her destiny. Instead, being content to await whatever fate was generously awarded by the Confederation, a charity dependant. Something else contrary to her nature. These were not the easiest of times.

She finished levelling the top of the bush, and pulled a couple of recalcitrant shoots out of the thick lower branches where they'd stuck, letting them fall. The secateurs moved down, slicing into some of the older branches. Apart from the five main forks, a bush should be encouraged with fresh outgrowth every six years. Judging by the wizened bark, and bluish algae streaks starting to bubble out of the hairline cracks, this one had been left long enough. She quickly fastened the new shoots she'd left into place, using metal ties. Her wrist moved automatically, twisting them tight, not even having to look what she was doing. Every Norfolk child could do this in their sleep. Others in the team were attending their bushes in the same way. Instinct and tradition were still the rulers here.

Carmitha went down four rungs on the stepladder, and started cutting at the next level of branches. A little knot of foreign anxiety registered in her mind. It was gliding towards her. She hung on to a sturdy trellis upright, and leaned out to look along the row to spot the source. Lucy was running along the grass, dodging the piles of shoots, waving her arms frantically. She stopped at the foot of Carmitha's ladder, panting heavily.

'Can you come, please,' she gasped. 'Johan's collapsed. God knows what's the matter with him.'

'Collapsed? How?'

'I don't know. He was in the carpentry shop for something, and the lads said he just keeled over. They couldn't get him to stand, no matter what they did, so they made him comfortable and sent me to fetch you. Damn it, I've ridden the whole way out here on a bloody horse. What I wouldn't give for a decent mobile phone.'

Carmitha climbed down the stepladder. 'Did you see him?'

'Yes. He looks fine,' Lucy said a shade too quickly. 'Still conscious. Just a bit weak. Been overdoing it, I expect. That bloody Luca thinks we're all still his servants. We're going to have to do something about that, you know.'

'Sure you are,' Carmitha said. She hurried along the row towards the thatched barn where her own horse was tethered.

*

When Carmitha rode into the stable she dismounted and handed the reins over to one of the (unpossessed) boys Butterworth/Johan had promoted to stable hand. He smiled in welcome, and quietly muttered: 'This has got them all shook up.'

She winked. 'Too bad.'

'You gonna help him?'

'Depends what it is.' Since she'd arrived at Cricklade, a surprising number of its residents had popped over to her caravan to ask for her help with various ailments. Colds, headaches, aching limbs, sore throat, indigestion; little niggling things which their powers found hard to banish. Broken bones and cuts they could heal up, but anything internal, less immediately physical, was more troublesome. So Carmitha started dispensing her grandmother's old herbal potions and teas. As a result, she'd taken over tending the manor's herb garden. Many evenings were spent pounding the dried leaves with her pestle, mixing them up and pouring the resulting powders into her ancient glass jars.

More than anything, it eased her acceptance into the manor's community. They'd rather turn to naturalistic Romany cures than consult the few qualified doctors available in the town. Properly prepared ginseng (sadly geneered for Norfolk's unique climate, so probably with its original properties diluted) and its botanical cousins remained preferable to the kind of medicines which Norfolk's restricted pharmaceutical industry was licensed to produce. Not that their stocks were very large; and Luca had given up trying to negotiate more from Boston. The townies hadn't got the factory working.

She found it strange that the simple knowledge of plants and land which was her heritage, and which had hidden her from them, had earned her their respect and thanks.

The carpentry shop was a tall single-storey stone building at the back of the manor, in amid a nest of bewilderingly similar buildings that were tacked together like some titan's maze. They all looked like oversized barns to her, with high wooden shutters and steep solar-cell roofs; but they housed a wheelwright's, a dairy, a smithy, a stone mason's, innumerable stores, even a mushroom house. The Kavanaghs had made sure they had every craft the manor needed to be virtually independent for its basic needs.

When she arrived several people were milling around the entrance of the carpentry shop with the embarrassed air of someone who's been forced to endure a family row. Not wanting to be there, yet unwilling to miss out. She was greeted with relieved smiles and ushered through. The electric saws and lathes and tenoning machines were silent. The carpenters had cleared their tools and lengths of wood from one of the benches, and laid Johan out on top, his head propped up on spongy cushions, body wrapped in a tartan blanket. Susannah was holding a glass of ice water to his lips prompting him to drink, while Luca stood at the end of the bench, frowning down in thoughtful concern.

There was a permanent grimace on Johan's rounded adolescent face, turning his usual lines into deep creases. Sweat glistened on his skin, sticking his thin sandy hair to his forehead. Every few seconds a big shiver ran down his body. Carmitha put a hand on his brow. Even though she was prepared for it, she was surprised by how hot his skin was. His thoughts were a bundle of worry and determination.

'Want to tell me what happened?' she asked.

'I just felt a bit faint, that's all. I'll be all right in a while. Just need to rest up. Food poisoning, I expect.'

'You never eat any,' Luca muttered.

Carmitha turned round to face the audience. 'OK, that's it. Take your lunch break or something. I want some clear air in here.'

They backed out obediently. She motioned Susannah aside, then pulled the blanket off Johan. The flannel shirt under his tweed jacket was soaked with sweat, and his plus-fours seemed to be adhering to his legs. He shuddered at the exposure to the air.

'Johan,' she said firmly. 'Show yourself to me.'

His lips tweaked into a brave smile. 'This is it.'

'No, it isn't. I want you to end this illusion right now. I have to see what's wrong with you.' She wouldn't let him look away from her eyes, conducting a silent power struggle with his ego.

'OK,' Johan said eventually. His head dropped back onto the cushion in exhaustion after the small clash. It was as though a ripple of water swept down him from head to toe; a line of twisted magnification that left a wholly different image in its wake. He expanded slightly in all directions. His flesh colour lightened, revealing the veins underneath. Patchy grey stubble sprouted from his chin and jowls as he aged forty years. Both eyes seemed to sink down into his skull.

Carmitha drew in a startled breath. It was the sagging jowls which clued her in. To confirm it, she unbuttoned his shirt. Johan wasn't quite a classic famine victim; their skin was stretched tight over the skeleton, with muscles reduced to thin strings wound round their limbs. He had plenty of loose flesh, so much it hung off him in drooping folds. It was as if his skeleton had shrunk, leaving a sack of skin that was three sizes too big.

There were big hints that this wasn't just caused by lack of eating. The folds of flesh were strangely stiff, arranged in patterns that mocked the muscle pattern belonging to an exceptionally toned twenty-five-year-old. Some of the ridges were pink, as if rubbed sore; in several places they were so red she suspected they were long blood blisters.

Shame welled up in Johan's mind, responding to the dismay and tinges of disgust in the three people surrounding him. The emotional oscillation was so powerful Carmitha had to sit on the edge of the bench beside him. What she wanted to do was turn and leave.

'You wanted to be young again,' she said quietly. 'Didn't you?'

'We're building paradise,' he told her in desperation. 'We can be whatever we want to be. It only takes a thought.'

'No,' Carmitha said. 'It takes a lot more than that. You haven't even got a society that functions as well as Norfolk's old one.'

'This is different,' Johan insisted. 'We're changing our lives and this world together.'

Carmitha bent over the trembling man until her face was a couple of inches from his. 'You're changing nothing. You are killing yourself.'

'There's no death here,' Susannah said sharply.

'Really?' Carmitha asked. 'How do you know?'

'We don't want death here, so there is none.'

'We're in a different place. Not a different existence. This is a giant step back from reality. It won't last, it's built on a wish not a fact.'

'We're here for eternity,' Susannah said gruffly. 'Get used to it.'

'You think Johan is going to survive eternity? I'm not even sure I can get him through another week. Look at him, take a bloody good look. This is what your ridiculous powers have reduced him to, this . . . wreck. You haven't been granted the power to work miracles, all you can do is corrupt nature.'

'I'm not going to die,' Johan wheezed. 'Please.' His hand gripped Carmitha's arm, a hot, damp pressure. 'You have to stop this. Make me better.'

Carmitha gently pulled herself free. She started to study his self-inflicted impairments properly, trying to work out what the hell she could realistically achieve. 'Most of the healing will be down to you. Even so, this convalescence will stretch the concept of holistic medicine to its limit.'

'I'll do anything. Anything!'

'Hmm.' She ran her hand over his chest, tracing the creases in the flesh, testing them for firmness as she would ripe fruit. 'OK. How old are you?'

'What?' he asked, bewildered.

'Tell me how old you are. You see, I know already. I've been coming to this estate for the rose season for over fifteen years now. My earliest recollection is of Mr Butterworth supervising the grove teams. He was the estate manager even back then. He was a good one, too; never shouted, always knew what to say to get people going, never treated the Romanies different to anyone else. I always remember him dressed in his tweeds and yellow waistcoat; when I was five I thought he was King of the World, he looked so fine and jolly. And he knew the way Cricklade worked better than anyone other than the Kavanaghs. None of that happens overnight. So now you tell me, Johan, I want to hear it from your own mouth; how old are you?'

'Sixty-eight,' he whispered. 'I'm sixty-eight Earth years old.'

'And how much do you weigh when you're healthy?'

'Fifteen and a half stone.' He was silent for a moment. 'My hair's grey, too, not blond. I don't have much of it anyway.' The confession relaxed him slightly.

'That's good. You're beginning to understand. You must accept what you are, and rejoice in it. You were a soul tormented by emptiness, now you have a body again. One that can provide you with every sensation that was taken from you in the beyond. What it looks like is a supreme irrelevance. Allow the flesh to be what it is. Hide from nothing. I know, it's tough. You thought this place was the solution to everything. Admitting it isn't to yourself will be difficult, coming to believe it even more so. But you must learn to accept your new self, and the limitations Butterworth's body imposes. He had a good life before, there's no reason why that can't continue.'

Johan was trying to appear reasonable. 'But how long for?' he asked.

'His ancestors were geneered, I expect. Most colonists were. So he'll last decades more at least, providing you don't pull a stunt like this again.'

'Decades.' His voice was bitter with defeat.

'Or days if you don't start to believe in yourself again. You have to help me help you, Johan. I'm not joking. I won't even waste my time with you if you don't stop dreaming that you're destined for immortality.'

'I'll do it,' he said. 'I really will.'

She patted him comfortingly, and drew the blanket back up.

'Very well, you lie here for now. Luca will arrange for some of the lads to carry you back to your room. I'm going to go over to the kitchen and have a word with Cook about what sort of foods she's got available. We'll start off giving you plenty of small meals each day. I want to avoid putting any sudden stress on your digestive system. But it's important we get some decent nutrition back into you.'

'Thank you.'

'There are some treatments I can use which will make this easier for you. They'll need preparing. We'll make a start this afternoon.'

She left the carpentry shop, and walked back to the manor's rear courtyard. Cricklade's kitchen was a long rectangular room, bridging the gap between the west wing's storerooms and the main hall. Tiled with plain black and white marble, one wall was lined with a ten-oven Aga radiating a fierce heat that the open windows couldn't eradicate. Two of Cook's assistants were taking loaves from the baking ovens and knocking them out of their tins onto wire racks below a window. Three more assistants were busy by the row of Belfast sinks, chopping vegetables ready for the evening meal. Cook herself was supervising a butcher who was cutting up a sheep carcass on the central island. Copper-bottomed pots and pans of every size and shape dangled from a large suspended rack overhead like segments of a polished halo. Carmitha had hung bunches of her herbs between the pots along the side facing the Aga, helping them to dry faster.

She waved at Cook and went over to Véronique, who was sitting at the last Belfast sink, scraping carrots on the wooden chopping board. 'How's it going?' Carmitha asked.

Véronique smiled, and put a hand worshipfully on her heavily pregnant stomach. 'I can't believe he hasn't started yet. I need to take a pee every ten minutes. Are you sure it wasn't twins?'

'You can sense him for yourself now.' Carmitha slid her hand over the baby, experiencing only warm contentment. Véronique was possessing Olive Fenchurch's body, a nineteen-year-old maid who had married her estate-worker love about two hundred days ago. A short engagement, followed by an equally short, if biologically improbable, pregnancy. For here she was about to give birth with nearly seventy days' gestation misplaced. A common occurrence on Norfolk.

'I don't like to,' Véronique said shyly. 'It's like bad luck, or something.'

'Well, take it from me, he's just fine. When he wants to make a move, he'll let us all know.'

'I hope it's soon.' The girl shifted uncomfortably on the wooden chair. 'My back's killing me, and my legs ache.'

Carmitha smiled in sympathy. 'I'll come and rub some peppermint oil into your feet this evening. That should perk you up.'

'Ooh, thank you. You have the most cleverest hands.'

It was almost as if the possession hadn't taken. Véronique had such a quiet, gentle nature, nervously trying to please, so very similar to Olive. She'd once confessed to Carmitha that she'd died in some kind of accident. She wouldn't say how old she'd been, but Carmitha suspected early to mid-teens; there had been occasional mention of bullies at her day club.

Now her French accent was blending with a raw Norfolk dialect. An unusual combination, although mellow enough to the ear. The rich Norfolk vowels became more pronounced each day, rising as the turmoil endemic to possessed minds shrank away inside her. Carmitha had a strong suspicion about that as well.

'Did you hear about Mr Butterworth?' she asked.

'Why, yes,' Véronique said. 'Is he all right?'

Interesting that she doesn't think of him as Johan, Carmitha thought; then felt shabby at such a feeble trick. 'Just a bit wonky, that all. Mostly because he hasn't been eating properly. I'll fix him up all right, which is why I'm here. I need you to make up some oils for me.'

'I'd love to.'

'Thanks. I want some crab apple; there are plenty of those in store so it shouldn't be a problem. Some bergamot, remember that's to be made mainly from the rind. And we'll need angelica, too; that can help to rouse his appetite, so I'll need a fresh batch each day. Then when he's recovering we can apply avocado to improve his skin tone, help his self-esteem that way.'

'I'll get right on to it.' Véronique glanced at the door and blushed.

Carmitha saw Luca standing in the doorway, watching them. 'I'll be back for them in a little while,' she told the girl.

'You think all that's going to help?' Luca asked as she brushed past him into the utility corridor running the length of the west wing.

'Careful,' she said. 'You nearly said: that rubbish.'

'But I didn't, though, did I?'

'No. Not this time.'

'Three of the lads took him upstairs. Doesn't look very good, does it? I mean, the state of him!'

'Depends on your attitude.' She went out into the courtyard with Luca trailing behind. Her caravan was standing close to the gates, curtains drawn and door shut. Still her small fortress against this realm. It was more her world than the planet was now.

'All right, I'm sorry,' Luca called. 'You should know by now what I'm like.'

She leant against the front wheel and grinned wickedly. 'Which one of you, my lord, sir?'

'That's got to be quits.'

'Maybe.'

'So, please, what are the oils for?'

'Mainly aromatherapy massage, though I'll use some in his bath as well; probably a lavender.'

'Massage?' The doubt was back.

'Look, even if we had Confederation medical technology, that's not the whole story, not in this case. There's more to curing people than slamming their biochemistry back into gear, you know. That's always been scientific medicine's problem, it's only interested in the physical. Johan must fight this affliction both within and without. That's not his original body, and the instinct to shape it into what he remembers as his own form must be broken. Powerful physical contact, exemplified by massage, can put him in touch with this body. I can make him acknowledge it, end this resentment and subconscious rejection. That's where the oils come in; a crab-apple base is an excellent relaxant. The two combined should ease his acceptance of his true existence.'

'Amazing. You sound like an expert on the subject of possessed body rejection.'

'I'm adapting several old methods. There are some strong precedents here. This is not too dissimilar from classic anorexia.'

'Oh, come on!'

'I'm speaking the truth. In a lot of cases, young girls simply couldn't come to terms with their developing sexuality. They tried to regain the body they'd lost by slimming themselves back down to what they were, with disastrous consequences. Now here on this planet, you all firmly believe you've become angels or godlings or crap like that. You think this is a real garden of Eden, and you're the immortal youths frolicking around the fountain. Like a politician believing her own bullshit, you've convinced yourselves your illusions are as strong as reality. They're not.'

His smile was devoid of conviction. 'We can create. You know that. You've done it yourself.'

'I've carved matter, that's all. Taken a magic invisible blade held firmly in my mind, and whittled away until I'm left with the shape I want. The nature of that matter always remains the same.' She glanced around the courtyard at the usual midday loungers taking their break in the small pools of shade close to the walls. Several sets of eyes were watching them idly. 'Come inside,' she said.

Even with all that time sitting quiet in the forest, and her new powers, she hadn't quite got round to tidying the caravan. Luca looked round politely as she cleared some clothes off her chair, and gestured him to sit. She took the bed. 'I didn't say anything in front of Susannah, but I suppose I've got to tell someone.'

'What?' he enquired charily.

'I don't think it was entirely malnutrition. I could feel hard lumps of flesh under his skin. If he wasn't so obviously wasting away, I'd say new muscle was growing. Except, it didn't feel like muscle tissue, either.' She bit her lip. 'That doesn't leave a lot of choices.'

It took Luca a long time to link up what she was saying. Mostly because he was desperate to avoid the conclusion. 'Tumours?' he said softly.

'I'll give him a proper examination when I give him his first massage. But I don't know what else it can be. And, Luca, there's a fuck of a lot of it.'

'Oh, Jesus H. Christ. You can cure it, right? The Confederation doesn't have cancer like we did in my day.'

'The Confederation can deal with it, yes. But there's no single solution, no twenty-seventh-century pill I can whip up a formula for and crank out in a chemistry lab. It needs working medical nanonics, and people who know how to use them. Norfolk never had any of that to start with. I think you'll have to start calling in qualified doctors. This is all way outside my league.'

'Oh, shit.' He held his hands up in front of his face, fingers held wide. They were shaking. 'We can't go back. We just can't.'

'Luca, you've been changing your body as well. Nothing like as bad as Johan. But you've been doing it. Smoothing out the wrinkles, tucking in the old gut. If you'd like me to examine you, I'll do it now. No one has to know.'

'No.'

For the first time, she felt sorry for him. 'OK. If you change your mind . . .' She started opening the caravan's little wooden cupboards, preparing the items she wanted to take up to Johan's room.

'Carmitha?' Luca asked softly. 'What the hell were you doing, going to bed with Grant for money?'

'What the fuck kind of question is that?'

'You know exactly what I mean. A girl like you. You're smart, young, you're bloody attractive. You could take your pick of any young man you wanted, even from landowner families. That's been known. Why that?'

Her arm shot out, and she caught his chin in a tight grip, making it impossible for him to look away from her furious expression. 'This day's been a long time coming, Grant.'

'I'm not—'

'Shut up. You are him, or at least you're listening. And this time you can't close your mind. You're too desperate for any sight of outside. Isn't that right?'

He could only grunt as her fingers squeezed tighter.

'He made you think, didn't he? That Luca. Made you stop and take a look around your precious world. Well, he's right to ask, why did I have to whore myself with you? The reason I did it is easy enough. You admire my independence, my free spirit. Well, that independence costs. It would take me an entire season tending the groves to earn enough money to replace a single wheel on this caravan. One broken wheel, one half-hidden rock in the mud, and my freedom is taken away from me. The rim is made from tythorn, I can saw and plane a new section for myself if I have a mishap. But the bearings and spring-spokes are made in your factories. And we need sprung wheels because there aren't any proper roads. You don't build them, do you, because you want everyone to use the trains. If people had cars, that would skew the whole economy away from you, your ideal. And I'm not even going to go into how much a horse like Olivier costs to buy and feed. So there's your answer, plain to see. I do it for the money, because I have no choice. I was born your whore. You've made everybody on this planet your whores. Your landowner freedoms are bought at our expense. I let you have me, because you would pay well, that *gratuity* you so kindly leave behind means I don't have to do it often. You're a commodity, Grant, you and the other landowners. You're valuable currency, nothing more.' She shoved him away hard. The back of his head cracked into the curving planks of the caravan, making him yelp and wince. When he put his hand round to dab at his skull, it came away with a smear of blood. He gave her a frightened look.

'Heal yourself,' she told him. 'Then get out.'

*

For a city which banned all commercial overflights, there was a surprising number of skywatchers in Nova Kong. Their attention was inevitably directed at the Apollo Palace, charting the movements of the ion flyers, planes, and spaceplanes which came and went from the building's landing pads and courtyards. The volume, arrival time, and marque of vehicles was a good indicator of the kind of diplomatic and crisis management activity being dealt with by the Saldana family staff. Kulu's communication net even had a couple of very unofficial bulletin sites devoted to the topic – carefully monitored by the ISA to make sure no active sensors were being used.

With the onset of the possession crisis, the skywatch enthusiasts gave the Palace airspace the kind of coverage matched only by the city's defence array sensors. Civilian craft such as those used by junior ministers and waggish royal cousins had vanished. Now it was only military vehicles darting in and out among the ornate rotundas and stone chimney stacks. Even so, their squadron insignias gave some clues away about their passengers and cargo. The gossip bulletins were well served by the skywatchers (with a few contributions of ISA disinformation).

This particular morning when the city was overcast with grey clouds sprinkling sleet across the boulevards and parks, they faithfully recorded the arrival of four flyers from the Royal Marines 585

Squadron in amongst the twenty other landings. 585's dedicated role was logistics, a description broad enough to cover many sins. As a consequence its presence went unremarked.

Also unremarked was the arrival over the previous thirty-hour period of warships from (among other planets) Oshanko, New Washington, Petersburg, and Nanjing, which were now parked in low equatorial orbit. They had brought, respectively, Prince Tokama, Vice-President Jim Sanderson, Prime Minister Korzhenev, and Deputy Speaker Ku Rongi. Such was the secrecy surrounding the high-power guests that not even the Kulu Foreign Ministry had been notified, certainly the embassies of the planets concerned knew nothing.

It was left to the Prime Minister, Lady Phillipa Oshin, to greet them as their flyers touched down in an inner quadrangle one after the other. She smiled with polite firmness as a Royal Marine tested each guest for static, which they accepted with equal aplomb. The palace cloisters were unusually empty as she escorted them to the King's private study. Alastair II rose from the deep chair behind his desk to give them a more cordial welcome. There was a fierce log fire burning in the grate, repelling the chill which washed off the frozen quadrangle outside the French windows. The chestnut trees around the prim lawn were denuded of leaves, leaving the branches glinting under encrustations of ice like clustered quartz.

Lady Phillipa sat at the side of the desk next to the Duke of Salion; the guests were in green leather chairs facing Alastair.

'Thank you all for coming,' the King said.

'Your Ambassador said it was important,' Jim Sanderson said. 'And our diplomatic relationship is old and valuable enough to get you my ass over here. Though I have to say I should be back home where I'm visible to the voters. This crisis is about appearing confident more than anything.'

'I understand,' Alastair said. 'If I might make an observation, the crisis is now developing outside the arena of public confidence.'

'Yeah, we heard Mortonridge is in trouble.'

'The rate of advance has slowed down after Ketton,' the Duke of Salion admitted. 'But we are still gaining ground and de-possessing the inhabitants.'

'Good for you. What's that got to do with us? You've already had as much help as we can reasonably provide.'

'We believe the time has come to make some positive decisions on the policies we adopt to defeat the possessed.'

Korzhenev grunted in amusement. 'So you called us here in secret to discuss this action rather than take it to the Assembly? I feel as if I am a member of some old cabal plotting revolution.'

'You are,' the King said. Korzhenev's smile faded.

'The Confederation is failing,' the Duke of Salion told the surprised guests. 'The economies of the developed worlds like ours are suffering badly from the civil-starflight quarantine. Stage two planets are paralysed. Capone has acted with singular brilliance with his infiltration flights and the strike against Trafalgar. Our populations are in a state of physical and emotional siege. Quarantine-busting flights continue to spread possession slowly but surely. And now Earth, the industrial and military core of the entire Confederation, has been infected. Without Earth on our side, the whole equation is changed. We must take its loss into account if we are to survive.'

'Just hold on there a minute,' Jim Sanderson said. 'The possessed have got a toehold in a couple of arcologies, is all. You can't sign Earth off that easily. GISD is one tough mother of an agency, they'll crack whatever heads they have to in order to clear the possessed out.'

Alastair looked at the Duke, and nodded permission.

'According to our GISD contact, there are now at least five arcologies host to the possessed.'

Prince Tokama raised an eyebrow. 'You are well informed, sir. I had not been told of this development before I left Oshanko.'

'Half of the Royal Navy's auxiliary vessels are doing nothing but running round on courier duty for us,' the Duke said. 'We're keeping as current as we can, but even that information is a couple of days old now. According to the report, the worst situation is in New York, but the other four arcologies will fall within weeks at the most. Govcentral has been commendably quick in closing down the vac-train routes, but we believe that ultimately the possessed will spread to the remaining arcologies as well. If anyone is capable of surviving Earth's climate without technological protection, it is a possessed.'

'And that isn't even the big problem,' Alastair said. 'Lalonde's population was roughly twenty million, of which we can assume a minimum of eighty-five per cent were possessed. Between them, they had enough energistic power to snatch the planet from this universe. New York's official population is three hundred million. By themselves they have more than enough power to remove Earth. They won't even have to wait until the other arcologies are taken over.'

'A valid observation; however, the Halo will surely remain,' Ku Rongi said. 'That is the main source of commerce with the Confederation. Trade with the Sol system will be diminished, not erased.'

'Hopefully, yes,' the Duke said. 'Our GISD contact says they don't yet understand how the possessed penetrated Earth's defences. So the possibility exists that they may be able to spread among the Halo asteroids as well. The other problem facing the Halo is that when the Earth is removed to some other realm, its gravity field will go with it. The Halo asteroids will physically disperse.'

'Very well,' Prince Tokama said. 'I am sure your analyists have produced a definitive report on the outcome of these events. So assuming we are deprived of Earth, and at least some of the Halo's resources, what do you see as the most effective policy to proceed with?'

'Olton Haaker and the Polity Council have just ordered a full scale Confederation Navy attack against Capone's fleet,' the Duke said. 'It should close down the Organization's rule, and allow the possessed on New California to do what comes naturally. They'll shunt it away, thus eliminating the threat of any further infiltration flights and antimatter terrorism. What we propose is taking that policy to its conclusion.'

'The industrialized star systems should align themselves into a core-Confederation,' Lady Phillipa said. 'At the moment we're dangerously overstretched trying to enforce the quarantine and supporting actions like Mortonridge. The cost simply cannot be sustained, not with the economic slowdown we're all suffering from. If we contract our spheres of influence, the cost is considerably reduced, and the effectiveness of our military forces in maintaining security over a smaller volume of space is correspondingly improved. Given that increased security, we could begin trading among ourselves again.'

'You mean no one else would be allowed to fly in?'

'Essentially, yes. We would extend the government authorization process we have in place today to cover commercial starships. Any vessel registered in one of the secured star systems would be allowed to resume flying between systems, subject to a reasonable security inspection. Ships which came from unsecured systems would not be permitted to dock. In other words, we stake out our perimeter and guard it very well indeed.'

'And the other planets,' Korzhenev enquired, 'the ones we leave out in the cold? What do you foresee for them?'

'They're the principal source of our trouble in the first place,' the Duke said. 'They do not police their asteroid settlements effectively, which encourages quarantine-busting flights, and with it the prospect of possessed getting loose inside another star system.'

'So we just abandon them?'

'By withdrawing our present unconditional military support, they will be forced to take the responsibility they've so far avoided. With the present quarantine in force, their marginal industrial asteroid settlements are inviolable anyway. In effect, we have been subsidizing their suspended status for the owners. Once that situation is ended, the asteroids will be mothballed and their populations returned to the home star system's terracompatible planet. In itself that will considerably reduce the number of routes by which the possessed can continue to spread. We may even rid ourselves of their incursion into this universe entirely. If they see they cannot reach fresh planets, then those who remain will take themselves away to this new realm of theirs.'

'Then what?' Jim Sanderson asked. 'OK, we regain most of what we've lost in financial terms. I'm in favour of that. But it doesn't solve anything long-term. Even if the possessed clear out and leave us alone, we still have to consider the bodies, the *people*, they've stolen and enslaved. There's hundreds of millions of them depending on us to rescue them, billions probably by now. That's a healthy percentage of our whole species. We can't ignore that. The whole issue of souls and what happens to us after death has got to be thoroughly addressed. That's what I was hoping for when I came here today, something new.'

'If there was an easy solution we would have found it by now,' the King said. 'The amount of research and effort focused on this is like no other endeavour in our history. Every university, every company and military laboratory, every fertile mind in eight hundred inhabited star systems has been working on it. The best anybody has come up with is the possibility of a doomsday anti-memory for the souls in the beyond. One can hardly consider such mass slaughter as a valid answer, even if it can ever be made to work. We have to start looking at this from a different angle altogether. In order to do that, we must have stability and a reasonable degree of prosperity as an umbrella to work under. Society will have to change in many ways; most of which will be profoundly unsettling. One doesn't even know if it will ultimately reinforce or obliterate our faith in God.'

'I can see the logic in what you're saying,' Korzhenev said. 'But what about the Assembly and the Confederation Navy itself? They exist to protect all planets equally.'

'Bottom line,' Lady Phillipa said, 'is that he who pays the piper ... And those of us in this room do pay a considerable amount. We're not abandoning anybody, we're restructuring policy to a more realistic response towards this crisis. If it could be solved quickly, then all we'd need is the quarantine and a few interdiction flights. As that quite obviously hasn't happened, we are going to have to take the tough decision and settle in for the long haul. This is the only way we can offer those already possessed with any prospect of regaining their own identity one day.'

'How many other star systems do you envisage joining this core-Confederation?' Prince Tokama asked.

'We believe ninety-three systems have the kind of fully developed technoindustrial infrastructure to qualify for admission. We don't envisage this as being a small elite. Our fiscal analysis shows that many stars would be able to sustain a modest but steady economic growth pattern between themselves.'

'Do you envisage asking the Edenists to join?' Ku Rongi asked.

'Of course,' the King replied. 'In fact we took inspiration from them. After Pernik they have demonstrated an admirable resolution in safeguarding their habitats from infiltration. That's precisely the kind of determination we wish to institute among ourselves. If the stage two planets and developing asteroids had done the same right from the start, we wouldn't even be in this appalling position.'

Jim Sanderson looked round the three other guests, then turned back to the King. 'OK, I'll brief the President, and tell him it gets my vote. It ain't what I wanted, but at least it's something practical.'

'My honourable father will be informed,' Prince Tokama said. 'He will need to bring your proposal to the attention of the Imperial Court, but I can see no problem if enough planets can be convinced.'

Korzhenev and Ku Rongi gave their assent, promising to take the proposal to their governments. The King shook hands and had a few personal words of thanks with each as they were ushered out. He didn't hurry them, but time was important; the next four senior representatives were due in an hour. 585 Squadron had a busy three days scheduled.

*

A hundred and eighty-seven wormhole termini opened with impressive synchronization a quarter of a million kilometres away from Arnstadt, directly between the planet and its sun. Voidhawks emerged from the gaps and immediately established a defence sphere formation five thousand kilometres in diameter, scanning space with their distortion fields and electronic sensors for any sign of nearby technological activity. They detected the planet's SD platforms, of course; a much depleted network in the aftermath of the Organization's successful invasion. Nonetheless, local sensor satellites had already discovered them, and the remaining high-orbit platforms were locking on. The SD network was reinforced by Organization fleet warships, of which there were a hundred and eighteen currently in orbit, along with twenty-three hellhawks, and a token half-dozen new low-orbit platforms ferried in from New California (which were principally used to enforce Organization rule on the ground). Their presence, especially in conjunction with the antimatter combat wasps which some of them carried, had effectively upgraded the planetary defence shield to the same level as it had been with a full SD network.

Capone and Emmet Mordden were satisfied the Organization could defeat any task force of warships the Confederation sent in an attempt to reclaim space above the Arnstadt. In any case, it was only the Organization's dominance of that space which prevented the planet from being taken out of the universe by the possessed on the surface, effectively stymieing the First Admiral.

True, there had been an considerable increase in lightning raids recently, with voidhawks swallowing in to shoot off combat wasps and stealth munitions, but few of the missiles had ever hit a target – interception rate was over ninety-five per cent. The state of constant alert had given the crews operating the sensor satellites a high proficiency rating; complemented by the hellhawks' distortion fields, they were confident nothing could get close enough to the orbiting asteroid settlements or industrial stations to inflict any kind of serious damage.

Nothing happened for the first two minutes after the voidhawks emerged. Both sides were searching for clues of what the other was going to do. The Organization chief didn't know what to make of it. A voidhawk force in this formation was normally a securement operation, enabling a larger fleet of Adamist warships to jump in with impunity. But a hundred and eighty-seven was a colossal number for a beachhead detachment, more likely to be the task force in its entirety. The distance was also puzzling: at the moment they were outside effective combat wasp engagement range. But antimatter combat wasps would give the Organization an advantage, allowing them to engage the attackers first as they flew in towards the planet.

The voidhawks confirmed the Organization was unable to reach them – unless the hellhawks chose to swallow up for a confrontation. None of them did. More wormhole termini started to open. Then the first Adamist ship emerged in the middle of the defence sphere formation.

Admiral Kolhammer was using the battleship *Illustrious* as his flagship. Its size permitted him to carry a full complement of tactical staff, and provided them with a fully fledged C&C compartment independent of the bridge. No ship in the Confederation Navy was better suited to coordinating an attacking force of this magnitude, though even with the number of antenna which *Illustrious* boasted the tactical staff were hard pressed to establish and maintain communication with all the thousand-plus ships under his command.

Emphasizing the monumental strength they represented, it took the task force over thirty-five minutes to complete their emergence manoeuvre. To the officers and crew of the Organization fleet it seemed as though the torrent of ships would never end.

Kolhammer's staff began datavising ships with new vectors as soon as they established contact. Fusion drives blinked on, powering the task force into a giant disc formation. So many plasma exhausts concentrated in one place produced a blazing purple-white haze brighter than the sun. People on the surface of the planet could see the attackers as a coin-sized patch flowering open against the centre of the dazzling photosphere. An unnerving portent of what was to come.

Eight hundred Adamist warships formed the nucleus of the new attack formation, while five hundred voidhawks flocked around their periphery. Once their relative positions were locked, the main drives burst into life, accelerating the ships in towards the planet at eight gees. Voidhawks expanded their distortion fields, and matched the acceleration of their technological comrades.

The gigantic neuroiconic display wheeled slowly inside Motela Kolhammer's mind, each ship a pinprick of golden light trailing a purple vector tag. A headlong rush to the solid bulk of the planet ahead, represented by a blank ebony sphere. The strength of the planetary defence layers were illustrated by translucent coloured shells wrapped around the blackness. The ships still had some way to go before the outermost, yellow shell. And still neither side had fired a shot.

The simulation put him in mind of a hammer descending on an egg, rendered with impossibly delicate artistry for what it actually portrayed. Even he was dismayed at the level of violence to be unleashed when those two forces collided in the physical world. Something he never expected. But the tradition of the Confederation Navy was to prevent exactly this kind of monstrosity from happening, not to instigate it. He couldn't help the guilt which came from knowing this was happening because politicians considered the navy had failed in its principal duty.

Stranger than that, the knowledge and its burden were bearable because of those politicians. The very people who had declared the attack must be made had made it possible to do so with minimal casualties – on the navy's side. By insisting on total success, the Polity Council had given Kolhammer the one thing all military commanders crave before battle is joined: overwhelming firepower.

Kolhammer's task force accelerated towards Arnstadt at a constant eight gees for thirty minutes. When he gave the order for the starships to switch off their drives, they were still a hundred and ten thousand kilometres out, just on the fringes of the outer SD network, and travelling at over a hundred and fifty kilometres per second. Frigates, battleships, and voidhawks fired a salvo of twenty-five combat wasps each. Every drone was pre-programmed to operate in an autonomous seek-and-destroy mode. A perfect engagement scenario: any chunk of matter above Arnstadt, from pebble-sized interplanetary meteorites to kilometre-long industrial stations, MSVs to asteroids, was classified as hostile. The Confederation Navy ships didn't have to stay to supervise the attack over encrypted communications links; there would be no salvos of Organization antimatter combat wasps fired at their ships to counter, no twelve-gee evasive manoeuvres. No risk.

Adamist warships began to jump away. Wormhole interstices were prised open, carrying some of the voidhawks to their rendezvous coordinate. Only the *Illustrious*, ten escort frigates, and three hundred accompanying voidhawks remained to observe the outcome. All of them now decelerating at ten gees as the armada of thirty-two thousand combat wasps swept on ahead, accelerating at a full twenty-five gees.

It was a clash which had one outcome from the moment it was instigated. Even with over five hundred antimatter combat wasps available, the Organization could do nothing to stop the incoming weapons. Not only did the Confederation have an incredible weight of numbers on its side, the ever-increasing velocity at which they were approaching gave them an overwhelming kinetic advantage. Kills could only be achieved by a first-time direct hit; no defending submunition would ever have a second chance.

The hellhawks swallowed out en masse without even bothering to consult Arnstadt's SD Command. Organization frigates began to retract their sensor booms and communication dishes down into their hull recesses prior to jumping clear. Those of them assigned to low-orbit enforcement duty began to accelerate at high gees, striving for an altitude where they could use their patterning nodes successfully.

Voidhawk distortion fields examined the pressure which the Organization frigates applied against space-time in order to escape. Each combination of energy compression and trajectory was unique, allowing for only one possible emergence coordinate. Three voidhawks swallowed away in pursuit of each Organization ship, with orders to interdict and destroy. With the Adamist warships needing several seconds after emergence to extend their sensors, the voidhawks would have a small window when their target was utterly defenceless. Kolhammer was determined none of them should return to New California to bolster Capone's strength, and add their antimatter to his stockpile.

The combat wasps in the attacking swarm began to dispense their submunitions, stretching a dense filigree of white fire across space for tens of thousands of kilometres. Brief, tiny pulses of glowing violet gas spewed out at random as the SD network's outer sensor satellites detonated. Then the explosions began to multiply as more and more of Arnstadt's hardware was obliterated. The swarm swept across the first of the planet's four asteroid settlements circling above geosynchronous orbit, overwhelming its short-range defences. Kinetic spears and nuclear-tipped submunitions pummelled the rock, biting out hundreds of irradiated craters. Vast cataracts of ions and magma flared away into space from each impact, the asteroid's rotation curving them sharply to wrap itself in a thick psychedelic chromosphere. Second-tier SD platforms and inter-orbit shuttles were caught next. They were followed by another of the asteroids. For a moment it looked as though the pure savagery of the weapons had somehow ignited a fission reaction within the rock's atomic structure. The lush stipple of explosions melded into a single radiative discharge of stellar intensity. Then the light's uniformity cracked. At its core, the asteroid had shattered, releasing a deluge of molten debris, kicking off a wave of cascade explosions as each fresh target was intercepted by the submunitions.

Pressed deep into his acceleration couch by air molecules heavier than lead, Motela Kolhammer watched the results through a combination of optical sensor datavises and tactical graphic overlays. The two were becoming indistinguishable as reality began to imitate the electronic displays. Distinct shells of light were enveloping the planet as clouds of plasma cooled and expanded. It was low orbit, inevitably, where the largest number of vehicles, stations, and SD hardware was emplaced. Consequently, when the submunitions tore through them, the resultant blast waves became a mantle of solid light that sealed the entire planet away from outside observation.

Beneath it, wreckage fell to earth in bewitchingly attractive pyrotechnic storms. Streaks of ionic flame tore through the upper atmosphere, a sleet of malignant shooting stars heating the stratosphere to furnace temperatures. A potent crimson glow rose up from the clouds to greet them.

Illustrious raced eighty thousand kilometres over the south pole as the possessed on the ground chanted their spell. First warning came when the planetary gravity field quaked, warping the battleship's trajectory by several metres. The shroud of light around Arnstadt never faded, it merely changed colour; rippling through the spectrum towards resplendent violet as it contracted. Optical-spectrum sensors had to bring several shield filters on-line during the last few minutes as the source shrank towards its vanishing point.

Motela Kolhammer kept one optical sensor aligned on the accusingly empty zone as the battleship's radar and gravitonic sensors scanned space for any sign of the planet's mass. Every result came in negative. 'Tell our escort to jump to the task force rendezvous coordinate,' he told the tactical staff. 'Then plot a course for New California.'

*

Sarha fell through the open hatchway into the captain's cabin, ignoring the dark composite ladder, and allowing the half-gee acceleration to pull her down neatly onto the decking. She landed, flexing her knees gracefully.

'Ballet really missed out when you chose astroengineering at university,' Joshua said. He was standing in the middle of the room, dressed in his shorts, and towelling off a liberal smearing of lemon-scented gel.

She gave him a hoydenish grin. 'I know how to exploit low-gee to my advantage.'

'I hope Ashly appreciates it.'

'I don't know what you're talking about.'

'Hmm. So how are we doing?'

'Official end of duty watch report, sir. We're doing the same as yesterday.' Her salute lacked efficiency.

'Which was the same as the day before.'

'Damn right. Oh, I tracked down the leak in that reaction-mass feed pipe. Somebody slacked off when the tanks were installed in the cargo holds, a junction was misaligned. Beaulieu says she'll get on it later today. In the meantime I isolated the pipe; we have enough redundancy to keep the flow at optimum.'

'Yeah, right, fascinating.' He balled the towel and chucked it in a low arc across the cabin. It landed dead centre on the hopper's open throat, and slithered down.

She watched it vanish. 'I want to keep the fluid volume up. We might wind up needing it.'

'Sure. How were Liol's jumps?' He already knew of course, *Lady Mac*'s log was the first thing he'd checked when he woke up. Liol had completed five jumps on the last watch, each essentially flawless according to the flight computer. That wasn't quite the point.

'Fine.'

'Hmm.'

'All right, what's the matter? I thought the two of you were getting on OK these days. You can hardly fault his performance.'

'I'm not.' He fished a clean sweatshirt out of a locker. 'It's just that I'm asking a lot of people for advice and opinions these days. Not a good development for a captain. I'm supposed to make perfect snap judgements.'

'If you ask me a question about guiding *Lady Mac* I'll be worried. Anything else . . .' Her hand waved limply, wafting air about. 'You and I bounced around in that zero-gee cage enough to start with. I know you don't connect the same way most people do. So if you want help with that, I'm your girl.'

'What do you mean: don't connect?'

'Joshua, you were scavenging the Ruin Ring when you were eighteen. That's not natural. You should have been out partying.'

'I partied.'

'No, you screwed a lot of girls between flights.'

'That's what eighteen-year-olds do.'

'That's what eighteen-year-old boys dream of doing. Adamist ones, anyway. Everyone else is busy falling helter-skelter into the adult world and desperately trying to find out how the hell it works, and why it's all so difficult and painful. How you handle friendships, relationships, break-ups; that kind of thing.'

'You make it sound like we have to pass some kind of exam.'

'We do, though sitting it lasts for most of your life. You haven't even started revising yet.'

'Jesus. This is all very profound, especially at this time of the morning. What are you trying to tell me?'

'Nothing. You're the one that's troubled. I damn well know it'll be nothing to do with our mission. So I guess I'm trying to coax you into telling me what's on your mind, and convince you it's OK to talk about it. People do that when they're close. It's normal.'

'Ballet and psychology, huh?'

'You signed me up for my multi-tasking.'

'All right,' Joshua said. She was right, it was hard for him to talk about this. 'It's Louise.'

'Ah! The Norfolk babe. The very young one.'

'She's not . . .' he began automatically. Sarha's lack of expression stopped him. 'Well, she is bit young. I think I sort of took advantage.'

'Oh, wow. I never thought the day would come when I heard you say that. Exactly why is it bothering you this time? You use your status like a stun gun.'

'I do not!'

'Please. When was the last time you went planetside or even into port without your little captain's star bright on your shoulder?' She gave him a sympathetic smile. 'You really fell for her, didn't you?'

'No more than usual. It's just that none of my other girlfriends wound up being possessed. Jesus, I had a hint of what that was like. I can't stop thinking what it must have been like for her, how fucking ugly. She was so sweet, she didn't belong in a world where those kind of things happen to people.'

'Do any of us?'

'You know what I mean. You've done stims you shouldn't have, you've accessed real news sensevises. We know this is a badass universe. It helps, a bit. As much as anything can. But Louise – damn, her brat sister, too. We flew off and left them, just like we always do.'

'They spare children, you know. That Stephanie Ash woman on Ombey brought a whole bunch of kids out. I accessed the report.'

'Louise wasn't a child. It happened to her.'

'You don't know that for certain. If she was smart enough, she might have eluded them.'

'I doubt it. She doesn't have that sort of ability.'

'She must have had some pretty amazing quality features to have this effect on you.'

He thought back to the carriage journey to Cricklade after they'd just met, her observations on Norfolk and its nature. He'd agreed with just about everything she'd said. 'She wasn't street-smart. And that's the kind of dirty selfishness you need to elude the possessed.'

'You really don't believe she made it, do you?'

'No.'

'Do you think you're responsible for her?'

'Not responsible, exactly. But I think she was sort of looking at me as the person who was going to take her away from Cricklade Manor.'

'Dear me, whatever could have given her that impression, I wonder?'

Joshua didn't hear. 'I let her down, just by being me. It's not a nice feeling, Sarha. She really was a lovely girl, even though she'd been brought up on Norfolk. If she'd been born anywhere else, I'd probably . . .' He fell silent, shifting his sweatshirt round, not meeting Sarha's astonished stare.

'Say it,' she said.

'Say what?'

'Probably marry her.'

'I would not marry her. All I'm saying is that if she'd been given a proper childhood instead of growing up in that ridiculous medieval pageant there might've been a chance that we could have had something slightly longer term than usual.'

'Well, that's a relief,' Sarha drawled.

'Now what have I done?' he exclaimed.

'You've been Joshua. For a moment there I thought you were actually evolving. Didn't you hear yourself? She hasn't had the education to become a crew-member on *Lady Mac*, therefore it can't possibly work between you. There was never a thought that you might give up your life to join her.'

'I can't!'

'Because the *Lady Mac* is far more important than the Cricklade estate, which is her life. Right? So do you love her, Joshua? Or do you just feel guilty because one of the girls you shagged and dumped happened to get captured and possessed?'

'Jesus! What are you trying to do to me?'

'I'm trying to understand you, Joshua. And help if I can. This matters to you. It's important. You have to know why.'

'I don't know why. I just know I'm worried about her. Maybe I'm guilty. Maybe I'm angry at the way the universe has crapped all over us.'

'Fair enough. All of us are feeling that way right now. At least we're doing something about it. You can't fly *Lady Mac* to Norfolk and rescue her; not any more. As far as anyone knows, this is the next best thing.'

He gave her a sad grin. 'Yeah. I guess that's me being selfish, too. I have to be doing something. Me.'

'It's the kind of selfishness the Confederation needs right now.'

'That still doesn't make it fair what happened to her. She's suffering through no fault of her own. If this Sleeping God is as powerful as the Tyrathca believe, then it's got some explaining to do.'

'We've been saying that about our deities ever since we dreamt them up. It's a fallacy to assume it shares our morals and ethics. In fact it's quite obvious it doesn't. If it did, none of this would have happened. We'd all be living in Paradise.'

'You mean the argument against divine intervention is for ever unbreakable?'

'Yep, free will means we have to make our own choices. Without that, life is meaningless; we'd be insects grubbing along the way our instincts tell us. Sentience has to count for something.'

Joshua leant over and placed a grateful kiss on her forehead. 'Getting us into trouble, usually. I mean, Jesus, look at me. I'm a wreck. Sentience hurts.'

They went out into the bridge together. Liol and Dahybi were lying on their acceleration couches, looking bored. Samuel was emerging from the hatchway.

'That was a long handover,' Liol remarked waspishly.

'Can't you manage those yourself?' Joshua asked.

'You might have a Calvert body, but don't forget which of us has more experience.'

'Not in all the relevant fields, you don't.'

'I'm off watch,' Dahybi announced loudly. His couch webbing peeled back, allowing him to swing his feet down onto the decking. 'Sarha, you coming?'

Joshua and Liol grinned at each other. Joshua made a polite gesture towards the floor hatch, which Liol acknowledged with a gracious bow. 'Thank you, Captain.'

'While you're in the galley I could do with some breakfast,' Joshua shouted after them. There was no reply. He and Samuel settled down on their acceleration couches. The Edenist was becoming a proficient systems officer, helping the crew with their shifts, as had the other science team specialists travelling on board. Even Monica was chipping in.

Joshua accessed the flight computer. Trajectory graphics and status schematics overlaid the external sensor images. Space had become awesome.

Three light-years ahead, Mastrit-PJ poured a strong crimson light across the dull foam which coated the starship's fuselage. The Orion Nebula veiled half of the starscape to galactic north of *Lady Mac*: a glorious three-dimensional tapestry of luminescent gas with a furiously turbulent surface, composed from scarlet, green, and turquoise clouds clashing as rival oceans, their million-year antagonism throwing out energetic, chaotic spumes in all directions. Inside, it was knotted with proplyds, the glowing protoplanetary discs condensing out of the maelstrom. Right at the heart lay the Trapezium, the four hottest, massive stars, whose phenomenal ultraviolet output illuminated and energized the whole colossal expanse of interstellar gas.

Joshua had come to adore the infinitely varied topology of the nebula as they'd slowly flown out of Confederation space to soar around it. It was alive in a way no physical biology could match, its currents and molecular shoals a trillion times as complex as anything found in a hydrocarbon-based cell. Ebbing and flowing in geological time; yet fast as well. The young, frantic stars which cluttered the interior were venting tremendous storms of ultra-hot gas, propagating shock waves that travelled over a hundred and fifty thousand kilometres an hour. They took the form of loops which curled and twisted sinuously, their frayed ends shimmering brightly as they fanned away the wild energy surging along their length.

For the crews in both *Lady Mac* and *Oenone*, watching the nebula had replaced all forms of recorded entertainment. Its majesty had lightened their mood considerably: theirs was now a true flight into history, no matter what the outcome.

Joshua and Syrinx had decided on flying around the galactic south of the nebula, an approximation of Tanjuntic-RI's flight path. During the first stages they'd utilized observations from Confederation observatories to navigate around the quirky folds of cloud and glimmering prominences visible from human space, even though the images were over one and a half thousand years out of date. But after the first few days they were traversing space never glimpsed by human telescopes. Their speed slowed as they had to start scanning ahead for stars and dust clouds and parsec-wide cyclones of iridescent gas.

Long before Mastrit-PJ itself was visible, its light coloured the cooler outer strands of the nebula like a two-day sunrise. The ships flew onwards with its thick red glow deepening around them. As soon as the star rose into full view seven hundred light-years ahead, parallax measurements enabled *Oenone* to calculate her position, enabling them to plot an accurate trajectory straight for it.

Now Joshua was piloting *Lady Mac* to her penultimate jump coordinate. Radar showed him *Oenone* a thousand kilometres away, matching their half-gee acceleration. The burn was stronger than Adamist ships usually employed, but they hadn't been altering their delta-V much during the flight round the nebula, choosing to wait until they got a fix on Mastrit-PJ before matching velocity with the red giant.

'Burn rate is holding constant,' Samuel said, after they'd run their diagnostic programs. 'You have some quality drive tubes, here, Joshua. We should have just under sixty per cent of our fusion fuel left when we jump in.'

'Good enough for me. Let's hope we don't soak up too much delta-V searching for the redoubt. I want to hold all the antimatter in reserve for the Sleeping God.'

'You are positive about the outcome, then?'

Joshua thought about the answer for a moment, mildly surprised by his own confidence. It was a pleasant contrast to the disquiet he felt over Louise. Intuition, a tonic against conscience. 'Yeah. Guess I am. That part of it, anyway.'

The orange vector plot which the flight computer was datavising into his neural nanonics showed him the jump coordinate was approaching. He started reducing their acceleration, datavising a warning to the crew. Samuel began retracting the sensor booms and thermo-dump panels.

Lady Mac jumped first, covering two and a half light-years. *Oenone* shot out of her wormhole terminus six seconds later, a healthy hundred and fifty kilometres away. Mastrit-PJ wasn't quite a disc, though its brilliant glare would make it hard for the naked eye to tell. From a mere half light-year distance its red light was sufficient to wash out the nebula and most of the stars.

'I've been hit by lasers with less power,' Joshua muttered as the sensor filters cut in to deflect the rush of photons.

'It's only recently ended its expansion phase,' Samuel said. 'In astrological terms, this has only just happened.'

'Stellar explosions are fast events. This happened fifteen thousand years ago, at least.'

'Once the initial expansion occurs, there is a long period of adjustment within the photosphere as it stabilizes. Either way, the overall energy output is most impressive. As far as this side of the galaxy is concerned, it outshines the nebula.'

Joshua checked the neuroiconic displays. 'No heat, and precious little radiation. Particle density is up on the norm, but then it's been fluctuating the whole time we've chased round the nebula.' He datavised the flight computer to establish a communication link with *Oenone*. 'How are we doing with the final coordinate?'

'I was pleasingly correct with my earlier estimates,' the voidhawk replied. 'I should have the final figure ready for you in another five minutes.'

'Fine.' After their first sighting of Mastrit-PJ, Joshua had checked the figures which *Oenone* had supplied a couple of times, out of interest rather than distrust. Each time they'd been better than any reading *Lady Mac*'s technological sensors could provide. He didn't bother after that.

'We should be able to measure the photosphere boundary to within a thousand kilometres,' Syrinx datavised. 'Defining exactly where it ends and space begins is problematical. Theory has an effervescence zone measuring up to anything between five hundred and half a million kilometres thick.'

'We'll stick to Plan A, then,' Joshua datavised back.

'I think so. Everything's checked out as we expected so far. Kempster has activated every sensor we're carrying, recording it like flek memories are infinite. I expect he'll let us know if he and Renato spot any anomalies.'

'OK. In the meantime I'll plot an initial vector to leave *Lady Mac* with a neutral relative velocity. I can refine it when you've finished working out the coordinate.' He suspected *Oenone* could supply him with the appropriate vector within milliseconds. But damn it, he had some pride.

Lady Mac's star trackers locked on to the new constellations they'd mapped. He brought his navigation programs into primary mode, and began feeding in the raw data.

*

Joshua and Syrinx had decided on an interval of several hours before making the final jump to Mastrit-PJ. Partly it was due to their lack of knowledge on its real position and actual size. Once that was determined, they intended to emerge in the ecliptic plane, a safe distance above the top of the photosphere, with their velocity matched perfectly to the star. It meant the only force acting on them would be the star's gravity, a tiny tidelike pull inwards. From that vantage point they would be able to scan space for a considerable distance. Logically, the remnants of the Tyrathca's redoubt civilization should be orbiting the star's equator. Possibly on a Pluto-type planet that had survived the explosion, or a large Oort ring asteroid. Although the volume of space was admittedly huge, by jumping in steady increments round Mastrit-PJ's equator they should eventually be able to find it.

Oenone would also spend the time to completely recharge its energy patterning cells from cosmic radiation (saving its fusion fuel). Not only would that prepare the voidhawk to carry out the search, it would then have the ability to withdraw across a considerable distance, matching *Lady Mac*'s sequential jump facility, should they unwittingly enter a hostile armed xenoc environment. That was an imaginative worst-case scenario dreamt up by Joshua, Ashly, Monica, Samuel, and (surprisingly) Ruben; which everyone else cheerfully told them verged on outright paranoia. As it turned out, they'd done quite a good job.

*

A star is a perpetual battleground of primal forces, principally those of heat and gravity which manifest themselves as expansion and contraction. At its core, a main-sequence star is a giant hydrogen fusion reaction, heating the rest of the mass sufficiently to counter gravitational contraction. However, fusion is only as finite as its fuel supply, while gravity is eternal.

After billions of years of steady luminescence, Mastrit-PJ exhausted the hydrogen atoms of its core, burning them into inert helium. Fusion energy production continued within a small envelope of hydrogen wrapped around the central region, yielding more helium which slowly sank inward. Temperature, pressure, and density all began to change as the envelope took over from the core as the principal source of heat. All stars come to this turning point eventually, and what happens next depends on their size. Mastrit-PJ was one and a half times the size of Earth's sun, too big to suffer a decline into electron degeneracy, too small to become a supernova. As such, its fate was inevitable.

As the transformation of its internal structure progressed, so Mastrit-PJ left its original stable luminous sequence behind at an ever-increasing rate. Its outer layers began to expand, heated by convection currents surging up from the growing fusion envelope, while on the inside of the envelope the core continued its gravitational contraction as a snow of helium atoms drifted downwards adding to its mass. As the core shrank, its heat and density increased until its temperature passed the magic hundred and twenty million Kelvin mark, at which point helium fusion occurred.

Mastrit-PJ divided into two distinct and very different entities: the centre burning with renewed vigour as it continued its contraction, and the outer layers bloating out and cooling through the spectrum from white through yellow and into red. The star was now radiating the phenomenal heat output of its core via convection currents the size of planetary orbits, resulting in the high luminosity unique to red giants, although at the same time that it was producing its deluge of light the temperature of the surface layers fell to around a chilly twelve thousand degrees K, they were so far from the core.

That was the epoch of stellar evolution from which the Tyrathca had fled. The expanding star inflated out to over four hundred times its original radius, eventually settling down with a diameter of one thousand six hundred and seventy million kilometres. It swept across the three inner planets, including the Tyrathca homeworld, and quickly devoured the two outer gas giants. For a few glorious millennia, the frozen comets in the Oort belt flared into life as their volatiles erupted, encircling the blazing new titan with an exquisitely fragile sparkling scarlet necklace, as if a billion primitive rockets were all migrating inwards. But even they were soon depleted, their flimsy chemical vents boiled dry, leaving only darkened clinker-like rocks circling supinely in their four-century orbit.

There was no exact line to show where the star ended and space began, instead the inflamed hydrogen thinned out into a thick solar wind which blew steadily out into the galaxy. However, for catalogue and navigational purposes, *Oenone* had defined Mastrit-PJ's periphery at seven hundred and eighty million kilometres from its invisible core.

*

Lady Macbeth was the first to emerge, a respectable fifty million kilometres above the wispy radiant sea of dissolving particles. Normal space had ceased to exist, leaving the starship coasting between two parallel universes of light. On one side, the spectral eddies of the nebula jewelled with young stars; on the other, a flat, featureless desert of golden-hot photons.

Oenone emerged twenty kilometres from the dark Adamist ship.

'Contact locked,' Joshua datavised in confirmation to Syrinx as their dish acquired *Oenone*'s short-range beacon. *Lady Mac*'s full complement of survey sensors were rising out of their fuselage recesses, along with the new systems which Kempster had requested. He could actually see a similar suite deploying from the pods riding in the voidhawk's lower fuselage cargo cradles.

'I see you,' she replied. 'Confirming no rocks or dust clouds in our immediate vicinity. We're starting the sensor sweep.'

'Us too.'

'How's your thermal profile?'

'Holding fine,' Sarha replied when he consulted her. 'It's hot out there, but not as bad as the approach to the antimatter station. Our dump panels can radiate it away faster than we're absorbing it. Wouldn't want you to fly us too much closer, though. And if you can give us a slow continuing roll manoeuvre, I'd be happy. It'll avoid any hot spots building on the fuselage.'

'Do my best,' he told her. 'Syrinx, we can cope. How about you?'

'Not a problem at this distance. The foam insulation is intact.'

'OK.' He fired the starship's equatorial ion thrusters, initiating the slow barbecue mode roll Sarha wanted.

The crew were all at their bridge stations, ready to cope with any contingency the red giant threw at them. Samuel and Monica were down in the main lounge in capsule B, sharing it with Alkad, Peter, and Oski, who were accessing the sensor data. *Oenone*'s results were being delivered directly to Parker, Kempster, and Renato. The ships were exchanging their data in real time, allowing the experts to review it simultaneously.

The image of local space built up quickly, charting the strong riot of particles flowing past the hull. Outside didn't quite qualify as a vacuum.

'Calmer than Jupiter's environment,' Syrinx commentated. 'But just as dangerous.'

'Not as much hard radiation as we predicted,' Alkad said.

'The hydrogen bulk must be absorbing it before it reaches the surface.'

Their optical and infra-red sensors were performing slow scans of space away from the red giant's surface. Analysis programs searched for shifting light-points which would indicate asteroids or moonlet-sized bodies, even a planet. *Oenone*'s distortion field could find little local mass bending space-time's uniformity. The brawny solar wind seemed to have blown everything away. Of course, they were looking at less than one per cent of the equatorial orbit track.

The first result came from a simple microwave-frequency sensor that picked up an unidentified pulse lasting less than a second. It was coming from somewhere closer to the surface.

'Kempster?' Oski datavised. 'Is there any way a red giant could emit microwaves?'

'Not with any of our current theories,' the surprised astronomer replied.

'Captain, can we take a closer look at the source, please?'

On the bridge, Joshua gave Dahybi a warning look. Intuition fluttered his heart. 'Node status?

'We can jump clear, Captain,' Dahybi said quietly.

'Liol, keep monitoring our electronic-warfare detectors, please. I want to play this very safe indeed.'

The flight computer reported the sensors had picked up another microwave pulse.

'That's very similar to radar,' Beaulieu said. 'But not a recognizable Confederation signature. It's nothing like the Tyrathca ships used, either.'

'Oski, I'm switching our sensor focus area for you now,' Joshua said.

Both passive and active sensor clusters rotated on the end of their booms to study the direction the pulse had come from. The flight computer assembled their results into a generalized neuroiconic image in accordance with its governing graphic-generation programs, approximating the physical structure which the image-enhancement subroutine was delivering, and combining it with a thermal and electromagnetic profile.

'Remind me again,' Sarha said in a subdued breath. 'In our expert team's professional opinion, we're here for an aeons-dead civilization whose relics are going to be extremely difficult to find. That's what you sold us, wasn't it?'

The most powerful telescopes *Oenone* and *Lady Mac* carried were quickly aligned on the structure which the sensor clusters had located, amplifying and clarifying the first low-resolution image. Orbiting twenty million kilometres ahead of the starships, a city was flying unperturbedly above the slow-churning blooms of the convection currents which contoured the red giant's surface. Spectrography confirmed the presence of silicates, carbon compounds, light metals, and water. Microwaves buzzed across its turrets. Butterfly wing magnetic fields flapped in a steady heartbeat. A forest of rapier spines rose from its darkside, gleaming at the top of the infra-red spectrum as they radiated away its colossal thermal load.

It was five thousand kilometres in diameter.

21

Quinn used simple timing rather than risk sending his orders out through London's communication net. No matter how innocuous the message, there was always a chance the supercops would pick up the chain. Even though they thought they'd eliminated him in the Parsonage Heights strike, they would be watching for signs of other possessed in the arcology. Standard procedure. Quinn would have done the same in their place. However, their paranoia had been quenched amid the flames and death engulfing the tower's penthouse. With that would be a slight relaxation of effort, falling back to established routine rather than determined proactive searches. It gave him the interlude he desired.

By necessity, London was now destined to be the capital of His empire on Earth. Such honour would only be visited upon the ancient city and its outlying domes by using possessed as disciples to deliver His doctrine. But there were inherent problems recruiting them. Even they were reluctant to follow the gospel of God's Brother to its exacting, painful letter. As he'd learned on Jesup, apart from people like Billy-Joe and Dwyer violent coercion was often required to obtain the wholehearted cooperation of non-sect members. Even Quinn was limited in the number of people he could intimidate at once. And without that strict adherence to His cause, the possessed would do what they always did, and snatch this world from the universe. Quinn couldn't allow that, so he'd adopted a more tactical strategy, borrowing heavily from Capone's example, exploiting the hostility and avarice most possessed exhibited on their return to the universe.

The possessed from the Lancini had been carefully and stealthily scattered throughout the arcology, and provided with very detailed instructions. Speed was the key. Come the appointed hour, each one would enter a preselected building and open the night staff to possession. When the day workers arrived they would be possessed one by one, jumping the numbers up considerably, but stopping short of exponential expansion. Quinn wanted about fifteen thousand by ten o'clock in the morning.

After that had been achieved, they would surge out of their buildings and physically disperse across the arcology. By then, there would be little the authorities could do. It took an average of five to ten well-armed police officers to eliminate one possessed. Even if they could track them via electronic glitches, they simply didn't have the manpower available to deal with them. Quinn was gambling that Govcentral wouldn't use fifteen thousand SD strikes against London. The rest of the population would be his hostages.

While that was going on, Quinn himself would be establishing a core of loyalists who would venture forth to exert a little discipline. Again, a hierarchy based on the Organization. The newly emerged possessed would be taught that they had to maintain the status quo, and encouraged to target the police and local government personnel – anyone who could organize resistance. A second stage would see them shutting down the transport routes, then going on to seize power, water, and food production centres. A hundred new fiefdoms would emerge, whose only obligation was obedience and tribute to the new Messiah.

With his empire founded, Quinn intended to put the non-possessed technicians to work on secure methods of transport that would enable him to carry the crusade of God's Brother to fresh arcologies. Eventually, they would gain access to the O'Neill Halo. From there, it was only a matter of time until His Night fell across this whole section of the galaxy.

*

The night after the Parsonage Heights incident, patrol constables Appleton and Moyles were cruising their usual route in central

Westminster. It was quiet at two o'clock in the morning when their car passed the old Houses of Parliament and turned down Victoria Street. There were few pedestrians to be seen walking along outside the blank glass façades of the government agency office buildings which transformed the start of the street into a deep canyon. The constables were used to that; this was a bureaucrat district, after all, with few residents or nightlife to attract anyone after the shops and offices closed. Though in recent days, even the small trickle of late-nighters had died back to almost nothing.

A body fell silently out of the black sky above the lighting arches to smash into the road thirty metres ahead of Appleton and Moyles. The controlling processor automatically reversed power to the wheel-hub motors, and turned the vehicle sharply to the right. They braked to a halt almost directly beside the battered body. Blood was flowing out of the jump suit's sleeves and trouser legs to spread in big puddles across the carbon-concrete surface.

Appleton datavised a priority alert to his precinct station, requesting back-up, while Moyles ordered Victoria Street's route and flow processors to divert all traffic away from them. They emerged from the patrol car with their static-bullet carbines held ready, holding position behind the armoured doors. Retinal implants scanned round in all spectrums, motion-detector programs in primary mode. There was nobody on the pavements within a hundred metres. No immediate ambush potential.

Cautiously, they started scanning the sheer cliffs of glass and concrete on either side, hunting for the open window which the body had come from. There wasn't one.

'The roof?' Appleton asked nervously. His carbine was swinging about in a wide arc as he tried to cover half the arcology.

The precinct station duty officers were already accessing the Westminster Dome's sensor grid, looking down from the geodesic structure to see the two officers crouched down beside their car. Nobody was on the roofs of the buildings flanking the road.

'Is he dead?' Moyles yelled.

Appleton licked his lips as he weighed up the risks of leaving the cover of the door to dash over to the body. 'I think so.' Assessing severely battered and bloody flesh, it was an old bloke, really old. There was no movement, no breathing. His enhanced senses couldn't detect a heartbeat, either. Then he saw the deep scorch marks branding the corpse's chest. 'Oh, bloody hell!'

*

The civil engineering crew repaired the hole in the Westminster Dome with commendable speed. A small fleet of crawler pods traversed the vast crystal edifice, winching a replacement segment along with them. Removing the old hexagon and sealing the new segment into place took twelve hours. Molecular-bonding-generator tests were initiated, making sure it was now firmly integrated with the rest of the dome's powered weather defences.

Checking the superstrength carbon-lattice girders and beefing up suspect strands of the geodesic structure was still going on as darkness fell; work continued under the pods' floodlights.

Far below them, the clearing up of Parsonage Heights tower was an altogether messier affair. Fire service mechanoids had extinguished the flames in the shattered stub of the octagonal tower. Paramedic crews hauled the injured out of the remaining seven towers of the development project that had been bombarded with a blizzard of shattered glass and lethal debris. Smaller fires had broken out on the two skyscrapers next to the one hit by the SD strike. Council surveyors had spent most of the day examining the damaged buildings to see if they could be salvaged.

There was no doubt that the remnants of the tower struck by the X-ray laser would have to be demolished. The remaining eight floors were dangerously weak, with metal reinforcement rods melting to run out of the carbon-concrete slabs like jam from a doughnut. It was the local coroner's staff who went in there after the fire mechanoids were pulled back and the walls had cooled down. The bodies they recovered were completely baked by the X-ray blast.

It was London's biggest spectator event, drawing huge crowds which spilled over into the open market and surrounding streets. Civilians mingled with rover reporters, gawping at the destruction, and the knot of activity on the dome high above. It was the crawler pods which proved that some kind of SD weapon had been used, despite the original denials of the local police chief. By early morning a grudging admission had come from the Mayor's office that the police had suspected a possessed to be holed up in the Parsonage

Heights tower. When pressed how a possessed had infiltrated London, the aide pointed out that a sect chapel was established in the warehouse below the tower. The acolytes, she assured reporters, were now all under arrest. Those that had survived.

Londoners grew jittery as more facts were prised out of various Govcentral offices over the long morning and afternoon, a lot of the information contradictory. Several lawyers acting for relatives of the tower's vaporized residents lodged writs against the police for the use of extremely excessive force and accused the police commissioner of negligence in not attempting an evacuation first. Absenteeism all over the arcology grew steadily worse during the day. Productivity and retail sales hit an all-time low, with the exception of food stores. Managers reported people were stocking up on sachets and frozen meat bricks.

All the while, images of the broken tower with its blackened, distended, mildly radioactive fangs of carbon-concrete were pushed out by the news companies. Bodybags being carried over the rubble remained the grim background for everybody's day, talked over by news anchors and their specialist comment guests.

A police forensic team was sent in with the coroner's staff. Their orders weren't terribly precise, just to search for anomalies. They were backed up by three experts from the local GISD office, who managed to remain anonymous amid everyone else poking round the restricted area.

The crowd went home before nightfall, leaving just a simple police cordon, patrolled by officers who fervently wished they'd drawn a different duty that evening.

A preliminary forensic report was compiled before midnight by the GISD experts, who had been following their police colleagues' tests and analyses. It contained nothing of the remotest relevance to Banneth or Quinn Dexter.

'One was just going through the motions anyway,' Western Europe told Halo and North America after he'd accessed the report. 'Although I'd dearly like to know how Dexter pulled that invisibility stunt.'

'I think we should just count ourselves fortunate that none of the other possessed seem capable of it,' Halo said.

'That SD strike has caused quite a stir,' North America said. 'The honourable senators are demanding to know who gave SD Command the authority to fire on Earth. Trouble is, this time the

President's office is screaming for the same answer. They may try to launch a commission of inquiry. If the executive and the representatives both want it, we might have trouble blocking them.'

'Then don't,' Western Europe said. 'I'm sure we can appoint someone appropriate to chair it. Come on, I shouldn't have to explain basic cover-your-arses procedure. That strike request is logged from the Mayor's Civil Defence Bureau to SD Command. It was a legitimate request. Senior Govcentral officers have the right to call for back-up from Earth's military forces in emergency. It's in the constitution.'

'SD Command should have requested fire authority from the President,' Halo said bluntly. 'The fact they can actually fire on Earth without the appropriate political authorization has raised a few eyebrows.'

'South Pacific isn't stirring this, is she?' Western Europe asked sharply.

'No. Frankly, she has as much to lose as the rest of us. The current presidential defence adviser is hers; he's doing a good job in damage limitation.'

'Let's hope it's sufficient. I'd hate to pull the plug on the President right now. People are looking for leadership stability to get them through this.'

'We'll ensure the news agencies will mute the story, however loud the senators shout,' Halo said. 'Shouldn't be a problem.'

'Jolly good,' Western Europe said. 'That just leaves us with the problem of the ordinary possessed.'

'New York's a mess,' North America admitted glumly. 'The remaining non-possessed citizens are defending themselves, but I expect they'll lose eventually.'

'We'll have to call another full B7 meeting,' Western Europe concluded without enthusiasm. 'Decide what we're going to do in that eventuality. I for one have no intention of being carried off to this realm the other planets have vanished to.'

'I'm not sure we'll get a full turnout,' Halo said. 'South Pacific and her allies are pretty pissed with you.'

'They'll come round,' Western Europe said confidently. He never did get a chance to find out if he was right. London's Deputy Police Commissioner datavised him at quarter past two with the news of the body in Victoria Street.

'There was no identification on the old boy,' the Deputy Commissioner reported. 'So the constables took a DNA sample. According to our files, it's Paul Jerrold.'

'I know the name,' Western Europe said. 'He was quite wealthy. You're sure the burn marks were caused by white fire?'

'They match the configuration. We'll know for sure when the forensic team get there.'

'OK, thank you for informing me.'

'There's something else. Paul Jerrold was a zero-tau refugee. He transferred his holdings to a long-term trust and went into stasis last week.'

'Shit.' Western Europe sent a fast enquiry into his AI, which ran an immediate search. Paul Jerrold had entrusted himself to Perpetuity Inc., one of many recently formed companies specializing in providing zero-tau for the elderly wealthy. The AI's review of the company's memory core established Jerrold had been sent to an old department store called Lancini which Perpetuity Inc. was renting until more suitable premises could be built.

Under Western Europe's direction, the AI shifted its attention to the department store, reactivating ancient security sensors on every floor. Hall after hall filled with bulky zero-tau pods jumped into blue-haze focus. The AI switched to the only scene of activity. Perpetuity Inc. had set up a monitor centre in the manager's old office; a couple of night-shift technicians were sitting by their desks, drinking tea and keeping an eye on an AV projector squirting out a news show.

'Datavise them,' Western Europe ordered the Deputy Commissioner. 'Tell them to switch off Paul Jerrold's pod and see who's in there.'

It took a short argument before the technicians agreed to do as they were asked. Western Europe waited impatiently as the ancient cage lift creaked it way up to the fourth floor and they walked over to the Horticulture section. One of them switched the pod off. There was no one inside.

Thoroughly unnerved, they now did exactly as they were told, and went along the row of zero-tau pods switching them off. All of them were empty.

'Clever,' Western Europe acknowledged bitterly. 'Who's going to notice they were missing?'

'What do you want to do?' the Deputy Commissioner asked.

'We have to assume the zero-tau refugees have been possessed. There are four hundred pods in the Lancini, so get some of your officers in there immediately, find out exactly how many people have been taken. Next, seal off London's domes and shut down all the internal transport systems. I'll have the Mayor's office declare an official civil curfew. We might have got lucky, it's two thirty, ninety-five per cent of the population will be at home, especially after today's frights. If we can keep them there, then we can prevent the possessed from spreading.'

'Patrol cars are on their way.'

'I also want every duty forensic team in the arcology shifted over there now, you've got thirty minutes to get them inside. Have them examine every room which looks like someone's been inside recently. Staff rooms, storerooms, the kind of locations where there aren't any security sensors. They're to search for human traces. Every piece they find is to be DNA tested.'

There were other orders. Tactical preparation. All police and security personnel were woken and called in, ready to be deployed against the possessed. Hospitals were put on amber status three, preparing for heavy casualties. The arcology's utility stations were put under guard, their technicians billeted in nearby police stations. GISD members were put on standby.

As soon as the administration was underway, orchestrated by the mayor's Civil Defence Bureau, but actually run by B7's AI, Western Europe called his colleagues. They appeared slowly, and grudgingly, in the sensenviron conference room. North and South Pacific were the last to show.

'Trouble,' Western Europe told them. 'It looks like Dexter managed to take over nearly four hundred people while he was here.'

'Without you knowing?' an incredulous Central America asked. 'What about the AI search programs?'

'He snatched them from zero-tau pods,' Western Europe said. 'You should check the companies offering people stasis in your own arcologies. It was a blind spot.'

'Obvious with hindsight,' North America said.

'Trust Dexter to find it,' Asian Pacific said. 'He does seem to have an unnervingly direct talent to find our weaknesses.'

'Not any more,' Halo said.

'I really hope so,' Western Europe said. It was the first sign of hesitancy he'd ever shown. The others were actually shocked into silence.

'You hit him with a strategic defence X-ray laser!' Eastern Europe said. 'He couldn't survive that.'

'I'm hoping the forensic tests at the Lancini will confirm that. In the meantime, we've reactivated his psychological profile simulation to determine what he was hoping to achieve with these new possessed. The fact that they've been dispersed indicates some kind of attempted coup. Letting the possessed run wild doesn't help him. Remember, Dexter wants to conquer humanity on behalf of his Light Bringer. It's likely he wanted control over a functioning arcology, which he could then use as a base to further his ambitions.'

'Question,' Southern Africa said. 'You said Paul Jerrold was a victim of white fire. That indicates he wasn't a possessed.'

'This is where it gets interesting,' Western Europe said. 'Assume Jerrold was possessed, and Dexter sent him out with all the others from the Lancini. They spread out over London, and start possessing new recruits for the cause. One of those new arrivals is our ally from Edmonton, the friend of Carter McBride.'

'Shit, you think so?'

'Absolutely. He overpowers Paul Jerrold's possessor, and gives us a warning impossible to ignore. Apparently those two constables nearly had a heart attack when the corpse landed in front of their patrol car. Do you see? He's telling us that the possessed are active, and letting us know where they came from. Dexter's entire operation was exposed by that single act.'

'Can you stop them?'

'I think so. We were given enough advance notice. If we can prevent the arcology's population from congregating, then the possessed will have to move themselves. Movement exposes them, makes them vulnerable.'

'I don't know,' East Asia said. 'Put one possessed into a residential block, and they don't have to move about much to possess everybody in there with them.'

'We'll see it happening,' Western Europe said. 'If they bunch together in that kind of density they won't be able to disguise their glitch-effect from the AI.'

'So you see it happening,' South Pacific said. 'So what? No police team will be able to pacify a block filled with two or three thousand possessed. And it won't be just one block, you said there were hundreds of people missing from the Lancini. If you have a hundred residential blocks taken over, you will not be able to contain them. B7 certainly cannot independently order a hundred SD strikes, not after Parsonage Heights.'

'We're right back to our original problem,' South America said. 'Do we exterminate an entire arcology to prevent the Earth being stolen from us?'

'No,' Western Europe said. 'We do not. That's not what we exist for. We are a police and security force, not megalomaniacs. If it looks like there is a runaway possession effect in one of the arcologies, then we have lost. We accept that loss with as much grace as we can muster, and retreat from this world. I will not be a party to genocidal slaughter. I thought you all realized that by now.'

'Dexter beat you,' South Pacific said. 'And the prize was our planet.'

'I can contain four hundred possessed in London,' Western Europe said. 'I can contain four thousand. I might even manage fifteen thousand, though it will be bloody. Without Dexter they are just a rabble. If he's still alive, he will assume control, and Earth will not be lost. He will not permit that to happen. It's not London we have to worry about.'

'You don't know anything,' South Pacific said. 'You can't do anything. All any of us can do now is watch. And pray that the Confederation Navy anti-memory can be made to work. That's what you've reduced us to. You think I'm stubborn and cold-blooded. Well, I choose that over your monstrous arrogance every time.' Her image vanished.

The other supervisors followed her until only North America and Halo were left.

'The bitch has got a point,' North America said. 'There's not an awful lot left for us to do here. Even if you're successful with London, it'll be Paris, New York, and the others which drag us down. They're a lot further along the road to total possession. God damn, I'm going to hate leaving.'

'I didn't tell our fraternal colleagues everything,' Western Europe said calmly. 'Thirty-eight of the people missing from the Lancini only arrived there yesterday, after the Parsonage Heights strike. In other words, the plot to snatch and possess them was still operating up until about nine hours ago. And we know it's Dexter's operation; the friend of Carter McBride made that quite clear when he delivered Jerrold.'

'Holy shit – he's still alive!' Halo exclaimed. 'Good God, you hit him with an SD weapon, absolute ground zero. And he survived. What the hell is he?'

'Smart and tough.'

'Now what do we do?' North America asked.

'I play my ace,' Western Europe said.

'You have one?'

'I always have one.'

*

The terrible, tragic cries were still faint. Quinn pushed himself deeper into the ghost realm than he had ever done before, so much so he had reduced himself to little more than the existence-impoverished ghosts themselves. He flung his mind open, listening to the ephemeral wailing that came from somewhere still further away from the real universe. The first ones he'd sensed were human, but now he was closer he thought there were others. A kind he didn't recognize.

These were nothing like the woeful pleas that issued forth from the beyond. These were different. A torment more refined, so much graver.

Strange to think that somewhere could be worse than the beyond. But then the beyond was only purgatory. God's Brother lived in an altogether darker place. Quinn's heart lifted to think he might be hearing the first stirrings of the true Lord as He rose to lead His army of the damned against the bright angels. A thousand times that long night, Quinn called out in welcome to the entities whose cries he experienced, flinging all his power behind the silent voice. Yearning for an answer.

None was granted.

It didn't matter. He had been shown what was. Dreams laid siege to the furthest limits of his mind while he floated within the ghost realm. Darkling shapes locked together in anguish, a war which had lasted since the time of creation. He couldn't see what they were, like all dreams they danced away from memory's focus. Not human. He was sure of that now.

Warriors of the Night. Demons.

Elusive. For this moment.

Quinn gathered his thoughts, and returned to the real world. Courtney yawned and blinked rapidly as Quinn's toe nudged her awake. She smiled up at her dark master, uncurling off the cold flagstones.

'It's time,' he said.

The possessed disciples he had chosen stood in a silent rank, waiting obediently for their instructions. All around them, the ghosts of this place howled their anger at Quinn's desecration, bolder than any he had encountered before. But still helpless before his might.

Billy-Joe came ambling along the aisle, scratching himself with primate proficiency. 'It's fucking quiet outside, Quinn. Some kind of weird shit going down.'

'Let's go and see, shall we?'

Quinn went out into the hated dawn.

*

The curfew announcement was glowing on the desktop block's screen when Louise and Genevieve woke. Louise read it twice, then datavised the room's net processor for confirmation. A long file of restrictions was waiting for her, officially informing her that the mayor had temporarily suspended her rights of travel and free association.

Gen pressed into her side. 'Are they here, Louise?' she asked mournfully.

'I don't know.' She cuddled her little sister. 'That Parsonage Heights explosion was very suspicious. I suppose the authorities are worried some of them escaped.'

'It's not Dexter, is it?'

'No, of course not. The police got him in Edmonton.'

'You don't know that!'

'No, not for certain. But I do think it's very unlikely he's here.'

Breakfast was one of the few things the curfew didn't prohibit. When they arrived at the restaurant, the hotel's assistant manager greeted them in person at the door and apologized profusely for the reduction in service, but assured them that the remaining staff would do their utmost to carry on as normal. He also said that, regrettably, the doors onto the street had been locked to comply with the curfew edict, and told them the police were being very strict with anyone they found outside.

Only a dozen tables were occupied. In fearful exaggeration of the curfew order, none of the residents were talking to each other. Louise and Genevieve ate their corn chips and scrambled eggs in a subdued silence, then went back upstairs. They put a news show on the holographic screen, listening to the anchor woman's sombre comments as they looked out over Green Park. Flocks of brightly coloured birds were walking along the paths, pecking at the stone slabs as if in puzzlement as to where all the humans had gone. Every now and then, the girls saw a police car flash silently along Piccadilly and travel up the ramp onto the raised expressway circling the heart of the old city.

Genevieve got bored very quickly. Louise sat on the bed watching the news show. Rover reporters were stationed at various vantage-point windows across the arcology, relaying similar views of the deserted streets and squares. The mayor's office, ever mindful of its public relations dependency, had granted some reporters a licence to accompany constables in patrol cars. They faithfully delivered scenes of constables chasing groups of louche youths off the streets where they were hanging in spirited defiance of authority. An unending number of senior Govcentral spokespersons offered themselves up for interview, reassuring the audience that the curfew was a precaution indicative of the mayor's strong leadership, and his determination that London should not become another New York. So please, just cooperate and we'll have this all sorted out by the end of the week.

Louise turned it off in disgust. There was still no message from Joshua.

Genevieve laced on her slipstream boots and went down to the lobby to practise her slalom techniques. Louise went with her, helping to set up a line of Coke cartons along the polished marble.

The little girl was halfway down her run, and pumping her legs hard, when the main revolving door started moving, allowing Ivanov Robson into the lobby. She squeaked in surprise, losing all concentration. Her legs shot from under her, sending her on another painful tumble against the marble. Momentum kept skidding her right up to Robson's shoes. She bumped up against him.

'Ouch.' She rubbed her knee and her shoulder.

'If you're going to do that, you should at least wear the right protective sports kit,' Robson said. He put a big hand down, and pulled her upright.

Genevieve's feet began to slide apart; she hurriedly double-clicked her right heel before she made another undignified tumble.

'What are you doing here?' she gasped.

He glanced at the receptionist. 'I've been asked to collect the pair of you.'

Louise glanced through the glass panes of the revolving door. There was a police car parked outside, its windows opaqued. Private detectives couldn't acquire official transport during a curfew, no matter how well placed the contacts they claimed to have. 'By whom?' she enquired lightly.

'Someone in authority.'

She didn't feel in the least bit perturbed by this development. Quite the contrary, this was probably the first time he was being completely honest with them. 'Are we under arrest?'

'Absolutely not.'

'And if we refuse?'

'Please don't.'

Louise put an arm round Gen. 'All right. Where are we going exactly?'

Ivanov Robson grinned spryly. 'I have absolutely no idea. I'm rather looking forward to finding out myself.' He accompanied them back up to their room, urging them to pack everything as quickly as possible. The doorman and a couple of night porters picked up all their bags and struggled downstairs with them.

Robson settled their account with the receptionist, brushing aside Louise's half-hearted protests. Then they were out through the revolving door and into the back of the police car, their bags being placed in the boot.

'This is very comfy,' Louise said as Robson climbed in and took a seat opposite them. The interior was more like a luxury limousine, with thick leather seats, air-conditioning, and one-way glass. She half expected a cocktail bar.

'Not quite your standard arrest wagon, no,' he agreed.

They accelerated along Piccadilly, and curved smoothly up onto the circular express route. Louise could see all the hologram adverts glimmering over the empty streets below, the only visible movement in the arcology. Their intense colours and childish enthusiasm to delight giving their irrelevance a forlorn poignancy amid the silent buildings.

The car shot along the web of elevated roads threaded round the skyscrapers, and she imagined millions of pairs of eyes behind the blank glass façades looking out to see them flash past. People would wonder what they were doing, if they were rushing to contain an outbreak of possession. There was no other reason for the police to be active. Not even the mayor himself was allowed out of 10 Downing Street, as his press office had been keen to point out a hundred times that morning.

Curiosity was becoming a very strong force in Louise's head. She was keen to meet the person who had summoned them. There had obviously been so much going on around her of which she was totally ignorant. It would be nice to have an explanation. Even so, she couldn't for the life of her work out why anyone so powerful would want to see her and Gen.

Her hope that all would be quickly revealed was doused as the police car took a ramp down to the base of the rim, and drove straight into an eight-lane motorway tunnel. A huge set of doors rumbled shut behind the car, sealing them in. Then there was nothing but the carbon-concrete walls lit by glareless blue-white lights. More than the arcology, the broad deserted motorway gave her the greatest impression of the curfew and the sense of fear powering London's residents into obedience.

Some unknown distance later, they turned off the motorway into a smaller tunnel road, leading down to the subterranean industrial precincts. The car delivered them to a huge underground garage with the style of arching roof more suited to a train station in the age of steam. Long rows of grubby heavy-duty surface vehicles stood unattended in their parking bays. The police car drove along until they came to the end bay, containing a Volkswagen Trooperbus. Two technicians and three mechanoids were fussing round the big vehicle, getting it ready for its trip.

The car door slid open, sending in a wave of hot humid air that reeked of fungal growth. Holding her nose in exaggerated disdain, Genevieve followed Robson and her sister out to look at the vehicle. The Trooperbus had six double wheels along each side, one and a half metres in diameter with tread cracks deep enough to hold

Genevieve's hand. A heavy retractable track bogie was folded up against its rear, capable of pushing it out of quagmires which came up over the wheel axles. Its dirty olive-green body resembled a flat-bottomed boat hull, with small oblong windows set along the side, and two large angled windscreens at the front. All the thick glass was tinted a deep purple. With its steel and titanium armour bodywork it weighed thirty-six tonnes, making it virtually impossible for an armada storm to flip it over. Just to make sure, there were six ground-securement cannon, which could fire long tethered harpoons into the earth for added stability in case it was ever caught outside in rough weather.

Genevieve slowly looked along the length of the brutish mud-splattered machine. 'We're going outside?' she asked in surprise.

'Looks that way,' Robson replied cheerfully.

One of the mechanoids was directed to unload the sisters' department store bags, transferring them to a locker on the side of the Trooperbus. A technician showed them the hatchway.

The main cabin of the Trooperbus was designed to hold forty passengers; this one was fitted with ten very comfortable leather-upholstered swivel chairs. There was a toilet and small galley at the back, and a three-seat cab at the front. Their driver introduced himself as Yves Gaynes.

'No stewardess on this trip,' he said, 'so just have a rummage round in the lockers if you need anything to eat or drink. We're well stocked.'

'How long is this going to take?' Louise asked.

'Should be there for afternoon tea.'

'Where exactly?'

He winked. 'Classified.'

'Can we watch out of the front?' Genevieve asked. 'I'd love to see what Earth's really like.'

'Sure you can.' He gestured her forward, and she scrambled up into the cab.

Louise glanced at Robson. 'Go ahead,' he told her. 'I've been outside before.' She joined Gen in the spare seat.

Yves Gaynes sat in front of his own console, and initiated the start-up routine. The hatch closed, and the air filters cycled up. Louise let out a sigh as the air cooled, draining out the moisture and smell. The Trooperbus rolled forwards. At the far end of the garage, a slab of wall began to slide upwards, revealing a long carbon-concrete ramp saturated in sunlight bright enough to make Louise squint despite the heavily shielded glass.

*

London didn't end along the perimeter of its nine outer domes. The arcology itself was principally devoted to residential and commercial zones, while the industries sited inside were focused chiefly on software, design, and light manufacturing. Heavy industry was spread around outside the domes in underground shelters ten kilometres long, with their own foundries, chemical refineries, and recycling plants. Also infesting the dome walls like concrete molluscs were environmental stations, providing power, water, and cool filtered air to the inhabitants. But dominating the area directly outside were the food factories. Hundreds of square kilometres were given over to the synthesis machinery capable of producing proteins and carbohydrates and vitamins, blending them together in a million different textural combinations that somehow never quite managed to taste the same as natural crops. They supplied the food for the entire arcology, siphoning in the raw chemicals from the sea and the sewage and the air to manipulate and process into neat sachets and cartons. Rich people could afford imported delicacies, but even their staple diet was produced right alongside the burger paste and potato granules of the *hoi polloi*.

It took the Trooperbus forty minutes to clear the last of the vast, half-buried carbon-concrete buildings full of organic synthesizers and meat clone vats. Strictly rectangular mounds, sprouting fat heat-exchange towers, gave way to the natural rolling topology of the land. The sisters stared out eagerly at the emerald expanse unfurling around them. Louise was struck by growing disappointment, she'd expected something more dynamic. Even Norfolk had more impressive scenery. The only activity here came from the long streaks of bruised cloud fleeing across the brilliant cobalt sky. Occasional large raindrops detonated on the windscreen with a dull *pap*.

They drove along a road made from some kind of dark mesh which blades of grass had risen through to weave together. The same vivid-green plant covered every square inch of land.

'Aren't there any trees?' Louise asked. It looked as though they were driving through a bright verdant desert. Even small irregular lumps she took to be boulders were covered by the plant.

'No, not any more,' Yves Gaynes said. 'This is just about the only vegetation left on the planet, the old green, green grass of home. It's tapegrass, kind of a cross between grass and moss, geneered with a root network that's the toughest, thickest tangle of fronds you'll ever see. I've broken a spade before now trying to dig through the stuff. It goes down over sixty centimetres. But we've got to grow it. Nothing else can stop soil erosion on the same scale. You should see the floods we get after a storm, every crease in the ground turns into a stream. If they'd had this on Mortonridge it would have been a different story, I'll tell you.'

'Can you eat it?' Genevieve asked.

'No. The people who sequenced it were in too big a rush to produce something that would just do the job to build in refinements like that, they just concentrated on making it incredibly tough, biologically speaking. It can withstand as much ultraviolet as the sun can throw at it, and there's not a disease which can touch it. So now it's too late to change. You can't replace it with a new variety, because it's every-where. Half a centimetre of soil is enough to support it. Only rock cliffs defeat it, and we've got limpet fungi for them.'

Genevieve puckered her lips up, and pressed herself up against the windscreen. 'What about animals? Are there any left?'

'Nobody's really sure. I've seen things moving round out there, but not close, so it could just be knots of dead tapegrass blowing about. There's supposed to be families of rabbits living in big warrens along some of the flood-free valleys. Friends of mine say they've seen them, other drivers. I don't know how, the ultraviolet ought to burn their eyes out and give them cancer. Maybe there's some species that developed resistance, they certainly breed fast enough for it to evolve, and they always were tough buggers. Then there's people say pumas and foxes are still about, feeding on the rabbits. And I'll bet rats survived outside the domes if anything has.'

'Why do you come out here at all?' Louise asked.

'Maintenance crews do plenty of work on the vac-train tubes. Then there's the ecology teams, they come out to repair the worst aspects of erosion; replant tapegrass and restore river banks that get washed away, that kind of thing.'

'Why bother?'

'The arcologies are still expanding, even with all the emigration. There's talk of building two more domes for London this century. And Birmingham and Glasgow are getting crowded again. We've got to look after our land, especially the soil; if we didn't, it would just wash away into the sea and we'd be left with continents that were nothing more than plateaux of rock. This world's suffered enough damage already, imagine what the oceans would be like if you allowed all that soil to pollute them. It's only the oceans which keep us alive now. So I suppose it boils down to self-interest, really. At least that means we'll never stop guarding the land. That's got to be a good result.'

'You like it out here, don't you?' Louise asked.

Yves Gaynes gave her a happy smile. 'I love it.'

They drove on through the wrecked land, sealed under its single precious, protective living cloak. Louise found it almost depressingly barren. The tapegrass, she imagined, was like a vast sheet of sterile packaging, preserving the pristine fields and spinneys which slept below. She longed for something to break its uniformity, some sign of the old foliage bursting out from hibernation and filling the land with colour and variety once more. What she wouldn't give for the sight of a single cedar standing proud: one sign of resistance offered against this passive surrender to the unnatural elements. Earth with all its miracles and its wealth ought to be able to do better than this.

They drove steadily northwards, rising out of the Thames valley. Yves Gaynes pointed out old towns and villages. The walls of their buildings were now nothing more than stiff lumps drowned under tapegrass, names decaying to waypoints loaded into the Trooperbus's guidance block. The Trooperbus had left the simple mesh road behind a long time ago when Louise went back into the main cabin to heat some sachets for lunch. They were driving directly across the tapegrass now, big wheels crushing it to pulp, leaving two dark green tracks behind them. Outside, the land was becoming progressively more rugged, with deepening valleys, and hills sporting bare rock crowns clawed by talons of grey-green lichen and ochre fungus. Gulleys carried silver streams of gently steaming water, while lakes rested in every depression.

'Here we are,' Yves Gaynes sang out, four hours after they left London.

Ivanov Robson squeezed his bulk into the cab behind the sisters, staring ahead with an eagerness to match theirs. A plain geodesic crystal dome rose out of the land, about five miles wide, Louise guessed; its rim contoured around the slopes and vales it straddled. The dome itself was grey, as if it was filled with thick fog.

'What's it called?' Genevieve asked.

'Agronomy Research Facility Seven,' Yves Gaynes replied, straight faced.

Genevieve responded with a sharp look, but didn't challenge him.

A door swung open at the base of the dome to admit the Trooperbus. Once the door closed, a red fungicide spray shot out from all sides to wash away mud and possible spores from the vehicle's body and wheels. They rolled forward into a small garage, and the hatch popped open.

'Time to meet the boss,' Ivanov Robson said. He led the two girls out into the garage. The air was cooler than inside the Trooperbus, and the Westminster Dome, Louise thought. She was only wearing a simple navy-blue dress with short sleeves. Not that it was cold, more like a fresh spring day.

Ivanov beckoned them forwards. Genevieve double-clicked her heel, and glided along at his side. There was a small four-seater jeep waiting, with a red and white striped awning, and a steering-wheel. The first one Louise had seen on this planet. It made her feel more comfortable when Ivanov sat behind it. She and Gen took the rear seats, and they started off.

'I thought you didn't know this place,' Louise said.

'I don't. I'm being guided.'

Louise datavised a net processor access request, but got no response. Ivanov drove them into a curving concrete tunnel a couple of hundred yards long, then they were abruptly out in full sunlight. Gen gasped in delight. The agronomy research dome covered a patch of countryside which was the England they knew from history books: green meadows flecked with buttercups and daisies, rambling hawthorn hedges enclosing shaggy paddocks, small woods of ash, pine, and silver birch lying along gentle valleys, giant horse chestnuts and beeches dotted across acres of parkland. Horses were grazing contentedly in the paddocks, while ducks and pink flamingos amused themselves in a lake with a skirt of mauve and white water lilies. In the centre was a sprawling country house that made Cricklade seem gaudy and pretentious in comparison. Three-storey orange-brick walls were held together by thick black oak beams in traditional Tudor diagonals, though they were hard to see under the mass of topaz and scarlet climbing roses. Windows of tiny leaded-glass diamonds were thrown wide to let the lazy air circulate through the rooms. Stone paths wound through a trim lawn that was surrounded by borders of neatly pruned shrubs. A line of ancient yews marked the end of the formal garden. There was a tennis court on the other side, with two people swatting a ball between them in an impressively long rally.

The jeep took them along a rough track over the meadows round to the front of the house. They turned in through some wrought-iron gates, and trundled along a mossy cobbled drive. Swallows swooped mischievously low over the grass on either side, before arrowing back up to the eaves where their ochre mud nests were hidden. A wooden porch around the front door was completely smothered by honeysuckle; Louise could just see someone waiting amid the shadows underneath.

'We've come home,' Genevieve murmured in delight.

Ivanov stopped the jeep in front of the porch. 'You're on your own now,' he told them.

When Louise shot him a look, he was staring ahead, hands gripped tightly on the steering-wheel. She was just about to tap him on the shoulder, when the person waiting in the porch stepped forwards. He was a young man, about the same age as Joshua, she thought. But where Joshua's face was lean and flat, his was round. Quite handsome, though, with chestnut hair and wide green eyes. Lips that were curved somewhere between a smile and a sneer. He was wearing a white cricket jumper and tennis shorts; his bare feet were shoved into shabby plimsolls with a broken lace.

He put a hand out, smiling warmly. 'Louise, Genevieve. We meet at last, to coin a cliché yet again. Welcome to my home.' A black Labrador padded out from the house, and sniffled round his feet.

'Who are you?' Louise asked.

'Charles Montgomery David Filton-Asquith, at your service. But I'd really prefer you to call me Charlie. Everybody here does. As in Right, one expects.'

Louise frowned, still not shaking his hand, though he hardly seemed threatening. Exactly the kind of young landowner she'd grown up with, though with a good deal more panache, admittedly. 'But who are you? I don't understand. Are you the one that summoned us here?'

''Fraid so. Hope you'll forgive me, but I thought this would be an improvement on London for you. Not very jolly there right now.'

'But how? How did you get us out through the curfew? Are you a policeman?'

'Not exactly.' He pulled a remorseful face. 'Actually, I suppose you could say I rule the world. Pity I'm not making a better job of it right now. Still, such is life.'

*

There was a swimming pool on the other side of the ancient house, a long teardrop shape with walls of tiny white and green marble tiles. It had a mosaic of the *Mona Lisa* on the floor of the deep end. Louise recognized that, though she couldn't remember the woman flashing her left breast in the original painting. A group of young people were using the pool, splashing about enthusiastically as they played some private-rules version of water polo with a big pink beach ball.

She sat on the York stone slab patio with Charlie and Gen, relaxing at a long oak table which gave her an excellent view out over the pool and the lawns. A butler in a white coat had brought her a glass of Pimm's in a tall tumbler, with plenty of ice and fruit bobbing round. Gen was given an extravagant chocolate milkshake clotted with strawberries and ice cream, while Charlie sipped at a gin and tonic. It was, she had to admit, all beautifully civilized.

'So you're not the President, or anything?' she enquired. Charlie had been telling them about the GISD, and its bureau hierarchy.

'Nothing like. I simply supervise serious security matters across Western Europe, and liaise with my colleagues to combat global threats. Nobody elected us, we had the ability to dictate the structure and nature of the GISD back when continental governments and the UN were merging into Govcentral. So we incorporated ourselves into it.'

'That was a long time ago,' Louise said.

'Start of the twenty-second century. Interesting times to live through. We were a lot more active in those days.'

'You're not that old, though.'

Charlie smiled, and pointed across at the rose garden. A neat, sunken square, divided up into segments, each one planted with different coloured rose bushes. Several tortoise-like creatures were moving slowly among the tough plants, their long prehensile necks standing proud, allowing them to munch the dead flowers, nibbling the stem right back to the woody branch. 'That's a bitek construct. I employ twelve separate species to take care of the estate's horticulture for me. There's a couple of thousand of them here altogether.'

'But Adamists have banned bitek from all their worlds,' Gen said. 'And Earth was the first.'

'The public can't use it,' Charlie said. 'But I can. Bitek and affinity are very powerful technologies, they give B7 quite an advantage over would-be enemies of the republic. It's a combination which also allows me to live for six hundred years in an unbroken lineage.' He waved a hand over himself in a proud gesture. 'This is the thirty-first body I've lived in. They're all clones, you see; parthenogenetic, so I retain the temperament for the job. I'm affinity capable, I had the ability long before Edenism began. I used neuron symbionts at first, then the affinity sequence was vectored into my DNA. In a way, the immortality method B7 uses is a variant on Edenism's end of life memory transfer. They use it to transfer themselves into their habitat neural strata. I, on the other hand, use it to transfer myself into a new, vigorous young body. The clone is grown in sensory isolation for eighteen years, preventing any thought patterns from developing. In effect, it's an empty brain waiting to be filled. When the time comes, I simply edit the memories I wish to take with me, and move my personality over to the new body. The old one is immediately destroyed, giving the process a direct continuity. I even store the discarded memories in a bitek neural construct, so no aspect of my life is ever truly lost.'

'Thirty-one bodies is a lot for only six hundred years,' Louise said. 'A Saldana lives for nearly two centuries these days. And even us Kavanaghs will last for about a hundred and twenty.'

'Yes,' Charlie said with an apologetic shrug. 'But you spend the last third of that time suffering from the restrictions and indignity of age. An illness which only ever gets worse. Whereas as soon as I reach forty I immediately transfer myself again. Immortality and perpetual youth. Not a bad little arrangement.'

'Until now,' Louise took a drink of Pimm's, 'those previous bodies all had their own souls. That's quite different from memories. I saw it on a news show. The Kiint said they're separate.'

'Quite. Something B7 has collectively ignored. Hardly surprising given our level of conservatism. I suppose our past bodies will have to be stored in zero-tau from now on; at least until we've solved the overall problem of the beyond.'

'So you were really alive in the twenty-first century?' Gen asked.

'Yes. That's what I remember, anyway. As your sister says, the definitions of life have changed a lot recently. But I've always considered myself to be the one person for all those centuries. That's not a conviction you can break in a couple of weeks.'

'How did you get to be so powerful in the first place?' Louise asked.

'The usual reason: wealth. All of us owned or ran vast corporate empires during the twenty-first century. We weren't merely multi-nationals, we were the first interplanetaries, and we made profits that outgrossed national incomes. It was a time when new frontiers were opening again, which always generates vast new revenues. It was also a time of great civil unrest; what we'd called the Third World was industrializing rapidly thanks to fusion power, and the ecology was destabilizing at equal speed. National and regional governments were committing vast resources into combating the biosphere break-down. Social welfare, infrastructure administration, health care, and security, the fields government used to devote its efforts to, were all slowly being starved of tax money and sold off to private industry. It wasn't much of a jump for us. Private security forces had guarded company property ever since the twentieth century; jails were being built and run by private firms; private police forces patrolled closed housing estates, paid for out of their rates. In some countries you actually had to take out insurance in order to pay the state police to investigate a crime if you were a victim. So you see, evolving to an all private police force was an intrinsic progression for an industrialized society. Between the sixteen of us, we controlled ninety per cent of the world's security forces, so naturally we collaborated and cooperated on intelligence matters. We even began to invest in equipment and training at a level that would never bring us a fiscal return. It paid us, though, nobody else was going to protect our factories and institutions from crime lords and regional mafias. The crime rate actually started to fall for the first time in decades.

'After that, we made the decision to bring about Govcentral, along with its centralized tax laws, which were slanted in our favour. Our lawyers were parachuted into senior advisory positions to Cabinet ministers and state executives, our lobbyists helped steer parliaments and congresses through controversial legislation. B7 was just the formalization and consolidation of our position.'

'That's monstrous,' Louise said. 'You're dictators.'

'As is the landowner class on Norfolk,' Charlie replied. 'Your family is the same as me, Louise, except you're not quite so honest about it.'

'People came to Norfolk after the constitution was written, they didn't have it imposed on them.'

'I might argue that with you, but I completely understand your sense of outrage, probably better than you do yourself. I've encountered it enough times down the centuries. All I can ask is that you judge the means by what it achieved. Earth has a stable, comfortably middle-class population free to live their lives more or less as they want. We survived the climate collapse, and we've spread out to colonize the stars. None of that would have been accomplished without a degree of strong leadership, the lack of which is the curse of modern media-accountable democracy. I'd say that was a pretty impressive achievement.'

'The Edenists are democratic, and they've prospered.'

'Ah yes, the Edenists. Our greatest accidental triumph.'

'What do you mean, accidental?' Louise couldn't help her interest. For the first time she was getting to know the truth about the way the world was structured, and its history. The kind of real history that was never filed and indexed. Everything she was denied at home.

'Because we wanted to keep bitek for ourselves we attempted to have the entire technology prohibited,' Charlie said. 'We knew we could never do it with a political declaration, our control over the legislative and legal establishment wasn't total at that time. So we went with a religious condemnation, building up to it with a decade of negative publicity. We were almost there. Pope Eleanor was ready to declare affinity an unholy desecration, and the Ayatollahs were falling into line. We only needed a few more years of pressure, and the independent companies would be forced to abandon further development. Bitek and affinity would have withered away, another dead-end technology. History is littered with them. Then Wing-Tsit Chong went and transferred his personality into Eden's neural strata. Ironically, we hadn't realized the potential of the habitats, even though we were experimenting along similar lines to achieve our own immortality. It forced the Pope's hand; her declaration came just too early. There was still too much bitek and affinity in general use on Earth for her to be obeyed unquestioningly. Its supporters emigrated to Eden, which by then had seceded from our control. We had absolutely nothing to do with shaping their society; after all, it's not one our operatives could infiltrate.'

'But you laid down the law for everyone else.'

'Absolutely. We control the principal policy aspects of Govcentral, our companies dominate Earth's industry, and in turn its economic power dominates the Confederation. We're the ones who make the majority investment in every new colony world development company, because we live long enough to reap the rewards which come from share dividends that take two centuries to mature. Between us, our financial institutions own a healthy percentage of the human race.'

'What for? Nobody can possibly want that much money.'

'You'd be amazed. Proper policing and defence consumes trillions of fuseodollars, the Govcentral Navy is like a financial event horizon. We still fund our own security, just as we always have. And in doing so, we safeguard everyone else. I own up to being a dictator, but plead that I am as benign as it's possible to be.'

Louise shook her head in sorrow. 'And for all that power and strength, you still couldn't stop Quinn Dexter.'

'No,' Charlie admitted. 'He is our greatest failure. We may well lose this planet, and all of its forty billion souls with it. All because I wasn't good enough to outsmart him. History will brand us as the ultimate sinners, after all. Rightly so.'

'He really has won?' Louise asked in dismay.

'We hit him with an SD weapon at Parsonage Heights. Somehow he eluded that. Now he's free to do whatever he wants.'

'So he followed us to London.'

'Yes.'

'You manipulated me and Gen the whole time, didn't you? Ivanov Robson is one of your agents.'

'Yes, I manipulated you. And I have no regrets or remorse about that. Given what was at stake, it was wholly justified.'

'I suppose so,' she said meekly. 'I quite liked Robson, though he was always a little too good to be true. He never made a mistake. People aren't like that in real life.'

'Don't concern yourself about him. He's not an agent; I'm afraid I commandeered him after his trial. Such people are always useful to me. But dear old Ivanov is not a nice man. Not as unpleasant as Banneth, I admit. She was just a human-sized virus, even managed to spook me with her deranged obsessions, and that's not easy after all the atrocity I've witnessed in my life.'

'And Andy? What about him? Was he one of yours as well?'

Charlie brightened. 'Oh, yes, the romantic sellrat. No. He's a real person. I never expected you to go and buy a set of neural nanonics, Louise. You are a constant surprise and delight to me.'

She scowled at him over the Pimm's. 'What now? Why did you bring us here? I don't believe it was just so you could explain all this to us first-hand. It's not like you're going to apologize, is it?'

'You were my last throw of the dice, Louise. I had hoped Dexter might try and follow you here. I have one final weapon available which could work. It's called anti-memory, and it destroys souls. The Confederation Navy developed it, although it's only in the prototype stage. Which means it has to be used at very close range. If he'd come with you, we might have had a chance to deploy it against him. It would have been my last noble stand. I was quite prepared to face him.'

Louise looked round quickly, her eyes sweeping the garden for any sign of the Devil whose face she could never forget. A foolish reaction. But the prospect of Quinn Dexter doggedly pursuing her across the desolated countryside was chilling. 'But he didn't follow us.'

'Not this time, no. So I'll be happy to take the pair of you along with me when I leave. I'll make sure you get a flight to Jupiter now.'

'You stopped all my messages to Joshua!'

'Yes.'

'I want to talk to him. Now.'

'That's another piece of unfortunate news, I'm afraid. He's no longer at Tranquillity. He left with a Confederation Navy squadron on some kind of strike against the possessed; even I wasn't able to discover exactly what their mission was. You're quite free to send a message to the Lord of Ruin for confirmation if you want.'

'I will,' Louise said crossly. She stood up, and put her hand out to Gen. 'I want to go for a walk, unless that's against your rules, too. I need to think about everything you've said.'

'Of course. You're my guests. Go wherever you wish, there's nothing that can harm you in the dome – oh, apart from some giant hogweed, there's a clump growing by one of the streams. It stings rather badly.'

'Fine. Whatever.'

'I hope you'll join me for supper. We normally meet for drinks on the terrace beforehand, around half-past seven.'

Louise didn't trust herself to say anything. With Gen's hand clasped tightly in her own, she walked off across the lawn, angling away from the swimming pool and its happy crowd.

'That was all ultra-stupendously incredible,' Gen gushed.

'Yes. Unless, of course, he's the biggest liar in the Confederation. I've been so stupid. I did everything he wanted me to, just like some dumb clockwork doll set in motion. How could I ever have thought you and I would be let off with a police caution for trying to smuggle a possessed down to Earth? They execute people for less than that.'

Gen's expression was puppyishly mournful. 'You didn't know, Louise. We're from Norfolk, we're never told *anything* about how things are on other worlds. And we escaped from Dexter twice, by ourselves. That's more than Charlie ever managed to do.'

'Yes.' The trouble with her anger was that all its considerable heat was focused inwards, against herself. The B7 people had done everything they should have to protect Earth. Charlie was right, she was completely expendable. She hadn't understood how big a danger Dexter was to the universe. Even so, not to have realized anything untoward was happening, other than a vague disquiet about Robson ... Stupid!

They walked across the lawn and through one of the magnolia hedges, finding themselves in an apple orchard. The short trees were showing their considerable age through twisted trunks and gnarled grey bark. Great clumps of mistletoe hung from their boughs, the parasite's roots swelling the wood in lopsided bulges. Bitek constructs like miniature sheep with a golden-brown fur were grazing round the trunks, trimming the grass to a neat level.

Gen watched their placid movements for a while, fascinated by how cute they looked. Not exactly the Devil's spawn that Colsterworth's vicar had condemned every Sunday from his pulpit. 'Do you think he will take us to Tranquillity? I'd like to see it. And Joshua,' she added hurriedly.

'I expect so. He's finished using us now.'

'But how are we going to get up to the Halo? The vac-trains and the towers are shut down, and people aren't allowed to use spacecraft in Earth's atmosphere any more.'

'Didn't you listen to anything? Charlie *is* the government. He can do whatever he wants to.' She grinned and pulled Gen closer. 'Knowing B7, this whole dome can probably blast off into orbit by itself.'

'*Really?*'

'We'll find out soon enough.'

They slowly circled the house, comforted by the familiarity of it all. On the other side of the orchard they came across a large dilapidated timber-framed greenhouse, whose shelves were packed with clay pots of cacti and pelargonium cuttings. A servitor chimp shuffled along the aisle, dragging a hosepipe and sprinkling the pots of small green shoots.

'Looks like they have winter in this dome,' Louise said to Gen as they peered round the door.

There was an avenue of cherry trees after the greenhouse. A pair of big peacocks strutted around underneath them, their shrill cries ringing through the heavy air. The sisters stood to watch as one of them spread his green and gold tail wide, neck cranked back imperiously. The gaggle of diminutive peahens loose in the avenue continued to peck away at the wiry grass, ignoring the display.

When they crossed the driveway there was no sign of the four-seat jeep, nor Ivanov Robson. They emerged through a gap in a hedge of white fuchsia bushes to find themselves back at the swimming pool. Charlie had vanished from the patio.

One of the girls playing by the pool caught sight of them and waved, shouting as she jogged over. She was a couple of years older than Louise, wearing a purple string bikini.

Louise waited politely, a neutral expression masking a slight sense of discomfort. The bikini was very small. She tried to banish the thought that no Norfolk shop would ever stock it on grounds of decency. Gen seemed perfectly at ease.

'Hi!' the girl said brightly. 'I'm Divinia, one of Charlie's friends. He told us you were coming.' She pursed her lips at Genevieve. 'Fancy a dip? You look hot and bored.'

Gen glanced longingly at the group of laughing young people sporting in the pool, some of them were close to her own age. 'Can I?' she asked Louise.

'Well . . . we don't have costumes.'

'No probs,' Divinia said. 'There's plenty spare in the changing room.'

'Go on, then,' Louise smiled. Genevieve flashed a grin, and bounded off towards the house.

'I don't want to be rude,' Louise said, 'but who are you?'

'I told you, darling, Charlie's friend. A very good friend.' Divinia followed the line of Louise's gaze, and chortled. She pushed her breasts out further. 'When you've got 'em, flaunt 'em, darling. They don't last for ever, not even with geneering and cosmetic packages. Gravity always beats us in the end. Honestly, it's worse than taxes.'

Louise blushed so hard she had to combat it with a program from her neural nanonics.

'Sorry,' Divinia said, smilingly contrite. 'Me and my big mouth. I'm not used to people with strong body taboos.'

'I don't have taboos. I'm just getting used to things here, that's all.'

'Pooey, you poor thing, this world must be dreadfully loud and brash for you. And I don't exactly help make it quiet.' She took hold of Louise's fingers, and tugged her towards the pool. 'Come on, let's introduce you to the gang. Don't be shy. You'll have fun, promise.'

After a second of resistance, Louise allowed herself to be pulled along. You couldn't hold a grudge against someone with such a sunny nature.

'Do you know what Charlie does?' she enquired cautiously.

'Oh, God, yes, darling. Lord of all he bloody surveys. That's why I'm with him.'

'With . . .?'

'We shag each other senseless. That kind of with. Mind you, I have to share him with half the girls here.'

'Oh.'

'I'm quite appalling, aren't I? Dearie me. Not a lady at all.'

'Depends on whose terms,' Louise said pertly.

Divinia's smile produced huge dimples among her mass of freckles. 'Wowie, a genuine Norfolk rebel. Good for you. Give those macho medieval pillocks hell when you get back.'

Louise was introduced to everyone at the pool. There were over twenty of them, six children, and the rest in their teens and twenties, two-thirds were girls. All of them quite gorgeous, she couldn't help noticing. Afterwards, she wound up with her shoes off, sitting on the edge of the pool, dangling her bare feet in the shallow end. Divinia sat down beside her, handing her another glass of Pimm's.

'Cheers.'

'Cheers.' Louise took a sip. 'How did you meet him?'

'Charlie? Oh, Daddy's done business with him for simply decades. We're not as rich as him, of course. Who is? But I've got the right pedigree, darling. Not to mention the body.' She swizzled her stick round the glass, her smile taunting. Louise smiled right back.

'It's a class thing,' Divinia went on. 'You don't qualify for entry in this particular magic circle without a bankload of money, and even that's not enough by itself. Outlook counts almost as much. You need the arrogance and contempt for the ordinary so that the whole notion of B7 doesn't shock you. I've got that in bucketfuls, too. I was brought up utterly spoiled, tons more money than brains. And I've got plenty of brain, too, the best neurons money can sequence. That's what saved me from the vacuous life of a trust-fund babe. I'm too smart for it.'

'So what do you do?'

'At the moment, nothing at all, darling; I'm just here because I'm good company for Charlie. It means I can have fun, and lots of it. Plenty of sex, party with Charlie and Co., have some more sex, access stims, sex again, hit the London clubs, sex, do mountains of gratuitous shopping, sex, see shows and gigs, sex, tour the Halo – free fall sex! That's where I am in life right now, and I'm doing it to the max. Like I said, everything sags badly and sadly as you get older, so enjoy youth while you've got it. That's the way I turned out, you see, I know myself very well indeed. I know there's no point living life like this for a hundred years solid. It's a waste, a total, pitiful waste. I've seen the idle rich at sixty, they make me sick. I've got money, and I've got brains, and I've got no scruples; that adds up to a hell of a lot of potential. So when I hit thirty-five or forty, I strike out for myself. I don't know what I'll do yet, fly a starship to the core of the galaxy, build a business empire that rivals the Kulu Corporation, start a culture more beautiful than Edenism. Who knows? But I'm going to do it superbly.'

'I always wanted to travel,' Louise said. 'Right back as far as I can remember.'

'Excellent.' Divinia knocked her glass to Louise's with a loud chink. 'See, you did it. You've seen more of the galaxy than I have. Congratulations, you're one of us.'

'I had to leave home, the possessed were after me.'

'They were after everybody. But you were the one who escaped. That takes balls, especially for someone with your background.'

'Thank you.'

'Don't worry.' She stroked Louise's long hair, directing the waving flexitives to slide it back gently over her shoulders. 'Somebody will find a solution. We'll get Norfolk back for you, and blast Dexter's mind into oblivion along with his soul.'

'Nice,' Louise purred. Sunlight and Pimm's were making her deliciously drowsy. She held up her glass for a refill.

Of all the strange days since she'd waved goodbye to her father, this one was undoubtedly the most mentally liberating. Conversing and mixing with Charlie's friends and children left her faintly envious of them. They weren't less moral than her, just different. Fewer cares and hangups, for a start. She wondered if true aristocracy meant having the gene for guilt removed. A nice life.

When the appallingly energetic swimmers finally tired, and the sun was edging down the side of the dome, Divinia insisted on taking her for a massage, dismayed by the fact Louise had never had one before. A couple of the other girls joined them in one of the house's original stable blocks which had been converted to a sauna and health spa.

Lying face down on a bench with just a towel over her rump,

Louise experienced the painful glory of the masseur's hands pummelling then kneading her muscles. Her shoulders became so loose she thought they'd fall off.

'Who are all the staff here?' she asked at one point. It was hard to believe that everyone in on the secret of B7 could be kept quiet.

'They're sequestrated,' Divinia said. 'Criminals that got caught by GISD.'

'Oh.' Louise twisted to look at the burly woman who was digging stiff fingers into her calf muscles. She seemed completely unperturbed by having her enslavement discussed openly. The idea bothered Louise, although it wasn't that much different to turning them into Ivets. Either way saw them sentenced to work for others. This method was just more severe. But then she didn't know how bad the original crime had been. Don't think about it. It's not as if I can change anything.

Divinia and the other girls gossiped their way through the massage, twittering and laughing over boys, parties, games. Though it began to take on the tone of a farewell reminiscence, places they'd never visit again, friends left out of reach. They talked as though Earth had already been lost.

Louise left the spa tingling everywhere, feeling thoroughly energized. Divinia walked with her back to the house to show her the guest room she'd been given. It was on the first floor, overlooking the orchard. The oak-beamed ceiling was low, barely a foot above Louise's head, giving the room a snug atmosphere. A four-poster bed contributed generously to the theme, as did the rich gold and claret fabrics used for its canopies and the curtains.

All Louise's bags and cases were stacked neatly on the pine blanket-box at the foot of the bed. Divinia spied them greedily, and started to go through the dresses. The long blue gown was taken out and admired, as were a number of others. None of them were quite right, Divinia declared, but she had something which might just suit the evening.

It turned out to be a quite disgraceful little black cocktail dress that Louise balked at on first sight. Divinia spent a full ten minutes coaxing her into it, outrageously flattering and encouraging. When it was on, Louise suffered a whole new plague of misgivings; you needed supreme confidence to wear anything like this in front of other people.

Genevieve came in just before they were due to go downstairs. 'Blimey, Louise,' she said, wide eyed at the dress.

'I'm treating myself,' Louise told her. 'It's just for tonight.'

'That's what you said last time.'

The admiration she received from Charlie and his friends when she emerged out onto the terrace was reward enough. Charlie and the men wore dinner jackets, while the girls were all in cocktail dresses, some even more alluring than Louise's borrowed number.

Outside the dome, the sun had finally reached the horizon. Light spilled out symmetrically from the brilliant orange disc to spread in waves along the crest of the verdant land. Charlie guided Louise over to the end of the terrace so they could watch it. He handed her a slim crystal flute.

'A champagne sunset shared with a beautiful girl. Not a bad last memory of the old planet, if somewhat laboured. How very considerate of the weather to stay clear for us. Its first favour in five centuries.'

Louise sipped her champagne as she admired the clean elegance of the shimmering orange star. She could remember the air as clear as this above Bytham, how it had been infiltrated by insidious wisps of red cloud. Her last memory of home.

'It's lovely,' she told him.

She sat next to Charlie for dinner. Inevitably, it was a sumptuous affair; the food exquisite, the wine over a century old. She remembered being enthralled by the topics of conversation, and laughing at stories of mistakes and social catastrophes that could only ever happen to an elite such as this. Even though they knew they would have to abandon their world within days, they had an assurance like no other. After an age exposed to depression and anxiety it was wonderful to experience such unabashed optimism.

Charlie, of course, made her laugh most of the time. She knew why, and no longer cared. Her clever, persistent seduction, and the effort he put into it, gave her a strong sense of belonging. It was classically played, and hauntingly refined. For a planetary oppressor, he was terribly charming.

He even helped Divinia guide her upstairs at the end of the evening. Not that she was drunk and needed help, she just didn't want to spoil the mood by putting that nasty little detox program into primary mode. Their hands let go of her just outside her door, allowing her to lean against the frame, happy at the support it offered.

'My bedroom is just down there,' Charlie murmured. His lips kissed Louise gently on her brow. 'If you want to.' He put his arm round Divinia, and they moved off down the landing.

Louise closed her eyes, pressing her lips together. She rolled against the wall to face her own bedroom door, and stumbled inside.

Her breathing still wasn't under control, and her skin was flushed. She pushed the door shut firmly behind her. A white silk negligée had been laid out on the bed, it made the little black dress demure by comparison.

Oh, sweet Jesus, now what the hell do I do?

She picked up the negligée.

It's not as if anybody here will think less of me for having sex with them. The fact that it was even an option actually made her smile in amazement. There was no order in the universe any more, nothing familiar.

So do I, or don't I? The only guilt I'll carry is what I manufacture for myself. And that's the product of heritage. So for all my bravado, just how independent from Norfolk have I become?

She stood in front of the mirror. Her hair was unbound, the flexitives inert, turning it back into a dark unruly cloak. The negligée clung to her body, showing it off provocatively. Just how aroused she'd become was blatantly obvious. A sultry grin was widening on her face as she acknowledged how sexually formidable she looked.

Joshua had always adored her naked body, almost delirious with praise as she gave herself up to him. Which was the answer, really.

*

Louise was woken by Genevieve bouncing onto her bed, and shaking her enthusiastically. Her head rose up, face curtained by wild hair. She had a headache and a revoltingly dry mouth.

For future reference, put the detox program into primary mode *before* you fall asleep. Please!

'What?' she croaked.

'Oh, come on, Louise, I've been up simply hours.'

'Oh, God.' Sluggish thoughts designated too-bright neuroiconic symbols, and her neural nanonics datavised a string of instructions to her medical package. It began to adjust her blood chemistry, filtering out the residue of toxicants. 'I need the loo,' she mumbled.

'When did you get that nightie?' Gen shouted after her as she tottered towards the en suite bathroom. Fortunately there was a big towelling robe hanging up on the inside of the door. She was able to cover up the first-night-of-the-honeymoon garment before she went back to confront Gen. Her head was a lot clearer thanks to the package's ministrations, though her body hadn't caught up yet.

'Divinia loaned it to me,' she said quickly, forestalling any more questions.

Gen's smile was wretchedly smug; she fell back on the bed, hands behind her head. 'You've got a hangover, haven't you?'

'Devil child.'

The breakfast room had a long table of big silver warmers containing a considerable variety of food. Louise went along lifting up each lid. She didn't recognize half of the items. In the end she settled for her usual of corn chips followed by scrambled eggs. One of the maids fetched her a pot of fresh tea.

Divinia and Charlie arrived just after Louise started to eat. He gave Louise a modest little smile, conveying a tinge of regret. That was the only reference ever made to the invitation.

He ruffled Genevieve's hair as he sat with them, earning himself a disapproving look.

'So when do we leave?' Louise asked.

'I'm not sure,' Charlie said. 'I'm keeping an eye on developments. New York and London are the critical places to watch right now. It looks like New York is going to fall within a week. The inhabitants can only keep resisting the possessed for so long. And they're losing ground.'

'What'll happen if the possessed take over?'

'That's when life becomes really unpleasant. I'm afraid our dear President has woken up to what that many possessed are capable of. He's scared they'll try to take the Earth out of this universe. That gives him two options. He can fire the SD electron beams in a circle around the arcology, and hope they'll do a Ketton, and just take themselves and a big chunk of landscape out of here. If not, it's a very stark choice; we either go with them, or the SD weapons are focused on the arcology itself.'

'Kill them?' Gen asked in fright.

'I'm afraid so.'

'Will he really do that? A whole arcology . . .'

'I doubt he has the courage to make that kind of decision. He'll consult the Senate in an attempt to get them to take the blame, but they'll just give him the authority and pass the buck right back at him without committing themselves. If he does give the order to hit the arcology, then obviously B7 will stop the SD network from actually firing. I'm of the opinion we should let the possessed remove Earth. It's a cold equation, but that outcome causes the least harm in the long term. One day we'll learn how to bring it back.'

'You really think that's possible?' Louise asked.

'If a planet can be moved out of the universe, it can be returned. Don't ask me for a timetable.'

'So what about London?'

'That's more difficult. As I told my colleagues, if Dexter gains control of enough possessed he'll be able to dictate his own agenda to everyone, possessed and non-possessed alike. If that becomes the case, we might have to use the SD weapons to kill the possessed he commands to take that power away from him.'

Louise lost all interest in her food. 'How many people?'

'SD weapons have a large target footprint. There's going to be a lot of innocent bystanders caught. An awful lot,' he said significantly. 'There are thousands of possessed that have to be targeted.'

'You can't. Charlie, you can't.'

'I know. B7 is actually considering if we should actively help the New York possessed to take over that arcology. If they do so before Quinn expands his power base, then Earth will be taken out of this universe before he can menace it.'

'Oh, sweet Jesus. That's just as bad.'

'Yeah,' he said bitterly. 'Who wants to rule the world when it means making those kind of choices. And they do have to be made, unfortunately, we can't jump ship now.'

*

After the mild euphoria of yesterday, when they'd finally reached a genuine safe haven, however unorthodox, Charlie's news left the sisters despondent again. They spent the morning in the drawing room, watching a big AV projection pillar to find out what was happening.

At first they switched between London's news shows, then Louise found the house's processors allowed her to access the security sensors studding the Westminster Dome's geodesic framework. She was also able to superimpose the police tactical display grid over their peerless view of the streets and parks. They could follow events in real time, without the intrusive commentary and speculation from reporters. Not that there was much to see. An occasional running figure. Pulses of bright white light flaring behind closed windows. Police cars converging on a building, heavily armed officers moving inside. Sometimes they came out, hauling possessed off to zero-tau pods. Sometimes they didn't, leaving a circle of empty cars blocking off the surrounding streets, their strobe lights flashing red and blue in futile distress. Local council offices and precinct stations would burst into flames without warning. No fire appliances came to their rescue. When the government facility concerned had been consumed, the flames mysteriously died away, leaving a blackened husk of crumbling masonry trapped between two unblemished buildings.

Reports from dwindling police patrols and the AI's monitor programs indicated that small bands of the possessed were moving round by using the tube lines and utility service tunnels. As they infiltrated themselves across the arcology, electrical supplies failed in several districts. Then corresponding sections of the communication net went dead. More and more street-level cameras were targeted, showing a snatched glance of impacting white fire before dying. Rover reporters began to go off-air in mid-sensevise. Police datavises also fell, faster than possessed assaults against them could statistically account for. GISD estimated the desertion rate to be reaching forty per cent.

There was still a curfew operating across London, but Govcentral was no longer enforcing it.

Servitor chimps ambled into the drawing room around mid-morning, and began packing away the ancient silverware and vases. Their preparations emphasized how desperate the situation was becoming, despite the physical distance between the house and London.

Louise caught sight of Charlie through one of the open patio doors; he was taking his two Labradors for a walk across the lawn. She and Gen hurried out after him.

He stopped at a gate in the row of yew trees, waiting for them to catch up. 'I just wanted to give the dogs one last walk,' he said. 'We'll probably leave tomorrow morning. You'll have to start packing again, I'm afraid.'

Gen knelt down and stroked the yellow Labrador. 'You're not leaving them here, are you?'

'No. They'll be put in zero-tau, I'm definitely taking them with me. And a great deal more, of course. I've spent centuries building up my little collection of knick-knacks. One does become dreadfully sentimental about the stupidest things. I own four domes like this in various parts of the world, each with a different climate. There's a lot of occupation invested in them. Still, look on the bright side, I can literally take the memories with me.'

'Where are you going to go?' Louise asked.

'I'm not sure, to be honest,' Charlie said. 'I'll need a developed world as a base if I want to retain control of my industrial assets. Kulu is hardly going to welcome me, the Saldanas are very territorial. New Washington, possibly, I have influence there. Or I might germinate an independent habitat somewhere.'

'But it's only going to be temporary, isn't it?' Louise urged. 'Just until we find an answer to all this.'

'Yes. Assuming Dexter doesn't come gunning for all of us. He's quite a remarkable person in his own repellent way, at least as competent as Capone. I didn't expect him to consolidate his hold over London quite so quickly. One more mistake added to a depressingly long list.'

'What will you do? The President isn't going to order the SD strike, is he? The news said the Senate has gone into closed session.'

'No, he won't fire today. London's safe from him, at least. Unless he sees red clouds hovering over the domes, he doesn't consider the possessed capable of endangering the rest of the world.'

'That's it, then, we just leave?'

'I am doing my best, Louise. I'm still trying to locate Dexter's actual position. There's still a chance I can use the anti-memory against him. I'm convinced he's somewhere in the centre of the old city, that's where he's concentrated his blackout procedures. If I can just get someone close enough to him he can be eliminated.

We've built a projector that uses bitek processors, it should work long enough even with the possessed ability to glitch electronics.'

'The possessed can sense the thoughts of anyone hostile to them. Nobody dangerous would get near to him.'

'Ordinarily, yes. But we do have one ally. Calls himself the friend of Carter McBride. A possessed who hates Dexter, and has the courage to oppose him. And I know he's in London; he could probably get close enough. The problem is, he's as elusive as Dexter.'

'Fletcher could have helped,' Gen said. 'He really hated Dexter. And he wasn't afraid of him, either.'

'I know,' Charlie said. 'I'm considering if I should ask him.'

Louise gave him a blank look, sure she'd misheard. 'You mean Fletcher is still here?'

'Well, yes,' Charlie said, as if surprised at her surprise. 'He's been kept in GISD's secure holding facility up in the Halo, helping our science team research the physics of possession. They haven't made much progress, I'm afraid.'

'Why didn't you tell me?' Louise asked weakly. It was the most wonderful news, even though it was accompanied by guilt for the man whose body Fletcher was possessing. There was also the knowledge she'd have to mourn all over again eventually. But . . . he was still with them. That made all the complications bearable.

'I thought it best not to. You'd both managed to put him behind you. I'm sorry.'

'Then why tell us now?' she asked, angry and suspicious.

'Desperate times,' Charlie replied levelly.

'Oh.' Louise slumped as understanding arrived. She began to wonder just how deep his manipulation went. 'I'll ask him for you.'

'Thank you, Louise.'

'On one condition. Genevieve is taken to Tranquillity. Today.'

'Louise!' Gen yelped.

'Not negotiable,' Louise said.

'Of course,' Charlie said. 'It will be done.'

Gen put her hands on her hips. 'I won't go.'

'You have to, darling. You'll be safe there. Really safe, not like this planet.'

'Good. Then you come, too.'

'I can't.'

'Why not?' The little girl was fighting tears. 'Fletcher wants you to be safe. You know he does.'

'I know. But I'm the guarantee that he'll do as he's asked.'

'*Of course* he'll kill Dexter. He hates him, you know he does. How can you even think anything else! That's awful of you, Louise.'

'I don't think badly of Fletcher. But other people do.'

'Charlie doesn't. Do you, Charlie?'

'I certainly don't. But the other members of B7 will need assurances.'

'I hate you!' Gen screamed. 'I hate all of you. And I won't go to Tranquillity.' She ran off back over the lawns towards the house.

'Dear me,' Charlie said. 'I do hope she'll be all right.'

'Oh, shut up,' Louise snapped. 'At least have the courage to acknowledge what you are. Or is that something else you've lost along with the rest of your humanity?'

Just for an instant, she caught sight of his true self in a flickering expression of annoyance. A centuries-old consciousness regarding her dispassionately through its youthful doll. His body was an illusion more skilful than any reality dysfunction the possessed had achieved. Everything he did, every emotion shown, was simply a mental state he switched on when it became appropriate. Five hundred years of life had reduced him to a bundle of near-automatic responses to his environment. Very clever responses, but they weren't rooted in anything she could recognize as human. Wisdom had evolved him far beyond his origin.

She hurried off after Gen.

*

The link to the Halo was organized to go through a big holoscreen in one of the house's lounges. Louise sat on a sofa opposite, with Gen cuddled up at her side. The younger girl was all cried out, and the battle of wills had been won. After this, she'd be packed off to Tranquillity. That didn't make Louise feel much better.

Blue lines rippled away from the front of the holoscreen, then a picture swivelled into focus. Fletcher was sitting at some metallic desk, dressed in his full British navy uniform. He blinked, peering forwards, then smiled.

'My dear ladies. I cannot tell you how gladdened I am to see you safe.'

'Hello, Fletcher,' Louise said. 'Are you all right?' Gen was all sunny smiles, waving furiously at his image.

'It would appear so, my lady Louise. The scholars of this age have kept me busy indeed, testing and prodding my poor bones with their machines. Much good it has done them. They freely admit Our Lord guards the mysteries of His universe jealously.'

'I know,' Louise said. 'Nobody down here has a clue what to do.'

'And you, lady Louise. How are you and the little one faring?'

'I'm OK,' Genevieve blurted spryly. 'We've met a policeman called Charlie, who's a dictator. I don't like him much, but he did get us out of London before things got too bad.'

Louise laid a hand on Gen's arm, silencing her. 'Fletcher, Quinn Dexter is down here. He's running loose in London. I'm supposed to ask, will you help track him down?'

'My lady, that fiend has bested me before. We escaped by God's grace and a fortuitous quantity of luck. I fear I would be of little use against him.'

'Charlie has a weapon that might work if we can get it close enough to him. It has to be a possessed carrying it, no one else stands a chance. Fletcher, it's going to get really bad down here if he isn't stopped. The only alternative the authorities have is to kill lots of people. Millions, possibly.'

'Aye, lady, I already hear the souls stirring in anticipation of what is to come. Many, many bodies are being made available for their occupation, with promises of more. I fear the time of reckoning draws nigh. All men will soon have to choose where their hearts lie.'

'Will you come down, then?'

'Of course, my dear lady. How could I ever refuse your request?'

'I'll meet you in London, then. Charlie has made all the arrangements. Genevieve won't be there, she's going to Tranquillity.'

'Ah. I believe I understand. Treachery lurks under every stone along the path we tread.'

'He's doing what he thinks he has to.'

'The excuse of many a tyrant,' he said sadly. 'Little one? I want you to promise me you will cause your sister no distress as you leave for this magical flying castle. She loves you dearly and wishes no harm to befall you.'

Genevieve clutched at Louise's arm, trying hard not to blub. 'I won't. But I don't want to leave either of you. I don't want to be left alone.'

'I know, little one, but Our Lord tells us that only the virtuous can be brave. Show courage for me, be safe even if it means forgoing those who love you. We will be reunited after victory.'

Right from the start, Al knew it was going to be a bad day.

First it was the body. Al was hardly a stranger to blood, he'd seen and been responsible for enough slaughter in his time, but this was turning his stomach. It had been a while before anyone noticed poor old Bernhard Allsop was missing. Who was going to care that the little weasel wasn't getting underfoot like usual? It was only when he skipped a couple of duty details that Leroy finally got round to asking where he was. Even then, it wasn't an urgent request. Bernhard's processor block didn't respond to datavises, so everyone assumed he was goofing off. A couple of guys were asked to keep an eye out. After another day, Leroy was concerned enough to bring it up at a meeting of senior lieutenants. A search was organized.

The security cameras found him eventually. At least, they located the mess. Confirming first what, then who it was had to be done in person.

There was a quite extraordinary amount of blood smearing the floor, walls, and ceiling. So much so, Al figured that more than one person had been whacked. But Emmet Mordden said the quantity was about right for a single adult male.

Al lit a cigar, puffing heavily. Not for pleasure; the smoke covered the smell of decaying flesh. Patricia's face was creased up in dismay as they stood around the corpse. Emmet held a handkerchief over his nose as he examined the remains.

The face was recognizably Bernhard. Though even now Al

remained slightly doubtful. It was as though the skin had been roughly rearranged into Bernhard's features. A caricature rather than a natural face. Al had seen doctored photos before, this was the body equivalent.

'You're sure?' Al asked Emmet, who was prodding the blood-drenched clothing with a long stylus.

'Pretty much, Al. These are his clothes. That's his processor block. And you can't expect his face to be a close match, we only see illusions of each other, remember. His body's face was becoming him, but it takes time.'

Al grunted, and took another look. The skin had shrunk to wrap tightly round the skull and jaw; a lot of capillaries had ruptured, and the eyeballs had burst. He turned away. 'Yeah, OK.'

Emmet plucked the processor block from Bernhard's rigid, clawed fingers, and gestured a couple of non-possessed medical orderlies to take over. They manoeuvred the desiccated corpse into a body bag. Both of them were sweating badly, struggling against nausea.

'So what happened?' Al asked.

'He was trapped in here by the pressure doors, then someone opened the airlock.'

'I thought that was impossible.'

'This airlock's been tricked out,' Patricia said. 'I checked. The electronic safeties were blown to shit, and someone sliced through the swing rods.'

'You mean it was a proper professional hit,' Al said.

Emmet was keying commands into Bernhard's block. There were few coherent responses: small blue spirals of light drifted through the holographic screen, fracturing any icons which did emerge from the management program. 'I think somebody datavised a virus into this. I'll have to link it up to a desktop and run a diagnostic to be sure. But he wasn't able to call for help.'

'Kiera,' Al said. 'She did this. Nothing tripped the alarms. They knew he'd be using this corridor, and when. It takes organization to set up a hit this smart. She's the only one up here who could pull it off.'

Emmet scraped at the bloody wall with the tip of his stylus. By now, the blood had dried to a fragile black film. Tiny dark flakes snowed away from the composite instrument. 'Several days old, even taking vacuum boiling into account,' Emmet said. 'Bernhard never turned up for his assignment during the victory party, so I guess that's when it was done.'

'Gives Kiera an alibi,' Patricia said, sullen with resentment.

'Hey!' Al spat. 'There ain't no goddam federal courts up here. She doesn't get no fancy lawyer to smartmouth her out of this by screwing the jury's mind. If I say she did it, then that's it. Period. The bitch is guilty.'

'She won't give herself up easily,' Patricia said. 'The way she's been stirring things over Trafalgar, the fleet is starting to get jittery about the navy retaliating. She's got a lot of support, Al.'

'Shit!' Al glared at the body bag, cursing Bernhard. Why couldn't the little asshole be stronger? Fight back against the bastards who whacked him, at least take a couple of them back to the beyond with him. Save me all this grief.

He relented. Bernhard had been loyal right from the moment he swung by in his make-believe Oldsmobile and picked Al up back in San Angeles. In fact that loyalty was probably what got him whacked. Chew away at the middle ranks, the really valuable ones, and you erode the power base of the guy at the top.

That motherfucking *bitch*.

'This is interesting.' Emmet was bending down to examine part of the corridor floor at one end of the bloodstain. 'These marks here. Could be footprints.'

Suddenly interested, Al went over to take a look. The splotches of dried blood were roughly the right shape and size of someone's boot sole. There were eight of them, becoming progressively smaller as they led towards the airlock.

He laughed abruptly. Goddam. I'm doing fucking detective work! Me, a cop.

'I get it,' he said. 'If they made prints, then the blood was still wet, right? That means it happened around the time Bernhard was killed.'

Emmet grinned. 'You don't need me.'

'Sure I do.' Al clapped him on the shoulder. 'Emmet, my boy, you just made Chief of Police for this whole crummy rock. I want to know who did this, Emmet. I really want to know.'

Emmet scratched the back of his head, looking round the grisly murder scene, thinking out what needed to be done. These days, getting put on the spot by Al hardly affected his bladder at all. 'A forensic team would be useful. I'll check with Avram, see if we've got any police lab people that I can use up here.'

'If there ain't, get them sent up from the planet,' Al said.

'Right.' Emmet was looking at the pressure door. 'The guys doing the hit must have been close; that's the only way to stop him from getting out. Breaking through a door like this would be no problem to a possessed, even Bernhard.' His stylus tapped the glass port in the middle of the door. 'See? There's no blood on this, even though it's sprayed across the rest of the surface. They probably took a look at him, make sure he was dead.'

'If they stayed on the other side of the door, where did the footprints come from?'

'Dunno.' Emmet shrugged.

'This corridor got any of those police spy cameras fitted?'

'Yeah. I'll review all their memories, but it's pretty doubtful, Al. These guys are pros.'

'See what you can find for me, my boy. And in the meantime, pass the word, I want you guys taking a few precautions. Bernhard's only the start. She's gunning for all of us. And I can't afford to lose any more of you. Capeesh?'

'I hear you, Al.'

'That's good. Patricia, I think maybe we should return the compliment.'

Patricia's thoughts swelled with dark delight. 'Sure thing, boss.'

'Hit the bitch hard, someone she relies on. What's that rat-face SOB always following her round? Got the psychic shit with the hellhawks?'

'Hudson Proctor.'

'That's the guy. Bust his ass back to the beyond. But make sure he suffers some first, OK?'

*

There was a bunch of people waiting for Al when he got back to the Nixon Suite. Leroy and Silvano were talking in low tones with Jez, worry hovering round them like a persistent fog. One guy (possessed) that Al didn't recognize was being covered by a couple of his soldiers. The stranger had a head filled with the strongest thoughts

Al had ever come across. His mind burned on pure anger alone. It deepened a shade when Al came in.

'Je-zus, what is going down here? Silvano?'

'Don't you remember me, Al?' the stranger asked. The tone was dangerously mocking. His clothes began to change, flowing into the full-dress uniform for a lieutenant-commander in the Confederation Navy. His face changed as well, stirring Al's memory.

Jezzibella gave Al a nervous flicker of a smile. 'Kingsley Pryor's back,' she said.

'Hey, Kingsley!' Al smiled broadly. 'Man, is it good to see you. Shit, goddamit, you're a fucking hero around these parts. You did it, man, you actually fucking did it. You wiped out the whole Confederation Navy single-handed. Can you believe this shit?'

Kingsley Pryor produced the kind of wide-eyed smile that even troubled Al. He wondered if the two soldiers were enough to keep the navy man down.

'You just go right ahead believing that shit,' Kingsley said. 'That's fine by me. In the meantime, I killed fifteen thousand people for you. Now it's time for you to keep your end of the bargain. I want my wife, my child, and I've decided I want a starship, too. That's a little bonus you're going to award me for completing my mission.'

Al spread his arms wide, his thoughts the epitome of reasonableness. 'Well, hell, Kingsley, the agreement was you blow up Trafalgar from the inside.'

'GIVE ME CLARISSA AND WEBSTER.'

Al swayed back a pace. Kingsley was actually glowing, a light deep inside his body had flicked on, illuminating his face and uniform. Except for the eyes, they sucked light down. Both soldiers nervously tightened their grip on the Thompson sub-machine-guns they were holding.

'All right,' Al said, attempting to calm things down. 'Je-zus, Kingsley, we're all on the same side here.' He conjured up a Havana, and held it out, smiling.

'Wrong.' Kingsley stuck a rigid finger in the air, preacher-style, and slowly levelled it at Al. 'Don't talk to me about taking sides, you piece of shit. I have died because of you. I have slaughtered my comrades because of you. So don't you ever, *ever* think you can tell me anything about faith, or trust, or loyalty. Now you either give me my wife and my son, or we settle this right here and now.'

'Hey, I ain't holding nothing back. What you want, you got. Al Capone don't break his word. You understand that? We had an agreement. That's like solid greenback currency around here these days. And I don't never welsh. Never! You understand? All I got here is my name, that is all I am worth. So you don't go questioning that. I appreciate how fucked off you are. OK, you got that right after what's happened. But you don't ever say to no one I went back on my promise.'

'Give me my wife and son.'

Al couldn't understand how Kingsley's teeth didn't shatter, the man was crunching his jaw so hard. 'No problem. Silvano, take Lieutenant-Commander Pryor here to his wife and kid.'

Silvano nodded, and gestured Pryor to the door.

'And nobody laid a finger on them while you were gone,' Al said. 'You remember that.'

Pryor turned at the door. 'Don't worry, Mr Capone, I won't forget anything that's happened here.'

Al sank down into the nearest chair when he'd gone. His arm curved round Jez for comfort, only to find she was trembling. 'Jezus H. Christ fucking wept,' Al wheezed.

'Al,' Jez said firmly. 'You have got to get rid of him. He frightened the bejezus out of me. Maybe sending him to Trafalgar wasn't one of my better ideas.'

'Too fucking true. Leroy, for Christ's sake tell me you found that kid of his.'

Leroy was running a finger round his collar. He looked scared. 'We didn't, Al. I don't know where the little brat's gone. We looked everywhere. He just vanished.'

'Fuck-a-doodle. Kingsley's going to blow when he finds out. It'll be a bloodbath. Leroy, you'd better start calling in some of the guys. And no fucking marshmallows, either. It's going to take a lot of us to pound him.'

'And then he can come straight back into another body,' Jez said. 'It just starts over again.'

'I'll start another search for Webster,' Leroy said. 'The kid's got to be somewhere, for Heaven's sake.'

'Kiera,' Jezzibella said. 'If you really did look everywhere for him before, then he's got to be with Kiera.'

Al shook his head in amazed admiration. 'Goddam, I can't believe I was dumb enough to let that woman into this rock. She doesn't miss a single trick.'

*

Etchells emerged from his wormhole terminus ten thousand kilometres out from Monterey. The asteroid was a small grey disc traversing one of New California's sunlit turquoise oceans. Drab, but enormously welcoming. He could almost hear his stomach growling from hunger.

New California's defence network locked on to his hull, and he identified himself to the control centre in Monterey. They cleared him for a five-gee approach. His energy patterning cells couldn't quite manage that.

Clear a pedestal for me, he told the hellhawks on the docking-ledge. **I need nutrient fluid.**

We all do, Pran Soo replied tartly. **There's a rota, remember?**

Don't fuck with me, bitch. I've been away longer than I expected. I'm exhausted.

And I'm heartbroken.

Pran Soo's attitude surprised him. Sure, the hellhawks grumbled and quarrelled; and none of them liked him. But this casual superior taunting was something new. He'd have to get to the reason eventually. But that would have to wait. He was genuinely concerned for his condition.

Where the hell have you been? Hudson Proctor asked.

Hesperi-LN, if you must know.

Where? There was a good deal of puzzlement in Hudson's mind.

Never mind. Just get a pedestal ready for me. And tell Kiera I'm back. There's a lot she needs to hear.

One of the feeding hellhawks was ordered to disengage from the pedestal it was using, freeing the metal mushroom for Etchells. He swung in over the ledge with little grace as the affinity band filled with gibes and derision about his flight path. Service crews stood well back as the big bitek starship wobbled uncertainly over the docking pedestal. It settled after a laboured descent, and the feed tubules rose up to insert themselves into its reception orifices. He started to gulp down the nutrient fluid as fast as it could be pumped in.

His on-board bitek processors datavised the section of the habitat Kiera had claimed as her own. She was in a lounge overlooking the docking-ledge, sitting on one of its long sofas. Her dress was bright scarlet with a tight bodice fastened by cloth buttons. The skirt was loose enough for her to fold her legs up on the sofa, presenting a feline posture to the camera.

Etchells hesitated for a second, enjoying the small sexual thrill that came from so much young, beautifully shaped female skin on show for his benefit. It was a rare thing for him to wish he hadn't possessed a blackhawk. Kiera could do that. Not many others.

'I was worried about you,' she said. 'You are my principal hellhawk, after all. So what happened at the antimatter station?'

'Something odd. I think we've got real trouble. This goes way beyond everyone's little power plays. We're going to need help.'

*

Rocio accessed Almaden's net to watch the repair operation. Deebank had kept his part of the bargain, co-opting all the non-possessed technicians left in the asteroid to work on the nutrient fluid refinery. They had replaced the damaged heat exchanger out on the ledge, resealed the chamber Etchells's laser had breached, stripped down the machinery and rebuilt it using new components manufactured in their own industrial stations. That just left the electronics.

As soon as the *Mindori*'s bulk had settled on one of the asteroid's three docking pedestals, a team had unloaded the packages from its cargo bay. Integrating the new processors and circuits into the refurbished refinery had taken over a day. Operating programs had to be modified. Then start-up proved an arduous task. There were synthesis tests, integral analysis calibration runs, mechanical inspections, performance examinations, fluid quality reviews. Eventually, the first batch was pumped along the pipes to *Mindori*'s pedestal. The hellhawk's internal bitek taste filters took a sample, evaluating the protein structures suspended within the fluid.

'Tastes good,' Rocio told the asteroid's expectant population. Their cheers at his verdict reverberated out from the synthesis refinery chamber, spreading like a high-frequency quake throughout the lonely rock.

'Do we have a deal?' a smiling Deebank asked.

'Absolutely. My colleagues will start lifting your people off. Possessed to the nearest world which Capone has seeded; non-possessed to the Edenists.'

The haggard non-possessed nearest to the AV pillar broadcasting the link up heaved a huge sigh of relief. The news was passed on back to their hostage families.

Deebank and Rocio carried on their negotiations. The evacuation would be staged. First the refinery had to be checked out thoroughly for long-term continuous operation, and any modifications to be made before the crews left. Mechanoids had to be adapted for specialized maintenance work. Technicians would stay on to train the disappointingly few hellhawk possessors who laid claim to a scientific background. The asteroid's fusion generators were to be overhauled for similar long-term duties. Vast quantities of raw hydrocarbon chemicals for the refinery were to be prepared and stored in tanks which had yet to be fabricated. Fuel supply reserves of deuterium and He_3 were to be established so they could feed the remaining generators (not a problem now the settlement's biosphere cavern was to be powered down).

We can begin, Rocio told Pran Soo. Get our core sympathizers on high-orbit patrol out here. They've just pulled transport duties. We can start ferrying the population to a possessed world.

Do you want a general exodus to Almaden?

Not yet. We'll keep this development to our group alone for now. It would be nice if more of us received a full weapons load before the Organization realizes we're deserting. Kiera is bound to try some kind of attack when she finds out.

There aren't many of us who'll follow her.

I know, but we play it safe. There's no telling what that bitch is capable of.

Jed and Beth stood behind the lounge's curving window, watching the hellhawks arrive. The creatures swooped down out of the stars to land on the two remaining pedestals. Blunt cylindrical crew buses trundled over the ledge, airlock tubes extending eagerly to mate with the life-support capsule hatches.

A small square in the corner of the window shimmered with grey light, and turned into Rocio's smiling face. 'Looks like we've done it,' he said. 'I want to thank you; especially you, Jed. I know this hasn't been easy.'

'Are they coming on board?' Beth asked.

'No. I'm swallowing back to Monterey in a couple of hours. I'll be missed if I don't report back at the end of my patrol orbit.'

Jed's arm went round Beth, instinctively protective. 'You said you'd take us to one of the Edenist habitats,' he said.

'I will. All the non-possessed from Almaden will be handed over to them once our preparations here are finished. You'll go with them.'

'Why can't we go first? We're the ones who helped you. You just said.'

'Because I haven't even spoken to the Edenists about this, yet. I don't want their voidhawks showing up here and wrecking every-thing. Just be patient. You have my word I'll get you out of this.'

Rocio cancelled his link to the lounge, and began to alter the shape of his distortion field. It pushed him up off the docking pedestal, and he slipped away from the ledge. One of the hellhawks that had just swallowed in from New California passed him as it swooped down towards the vacated pedestal. They exchanged excited smile images across the affinity band.

Rocio's mood lifted further as he accelerated away from the asteroid. It was all coming together beautifully. His next priority was gathering as many fully armed hellhawks as possible, and deploying them to guard Almaden. Then in another couple of days he and Pran Soo would inform the remaining hellhawks about Almaden. Everyone would have to make their choice. He didn't expect many to stay with Kiera; Etchells, of course, probably Lopex; others who hadn't come to terms with their new form, or didn't fully understand its potential. Not enough to ruin the plan.

He swallowed back to New California, resuming his high-altitude patrol orbit. The planet turned peacefully two million kilometres below him. His distortion field swept out, carefully propagated ripples testing and probing the fabric of space-time. No voidhawks within a hundred thousand kilometres. Nor was there any sign of stealthed weapons or sensor globes heading in towards the Organiz-ation ships and stations. Nobody asked him where he'd been.

An internal sensor check showed him the young kids playing

some kind of tag game along the main corridor. Jed and Beth were in their cabin, screwing again. Rocio sighed fondly. What it was to be a teenager.

Two hours later, Hudson Proctor ordered him to report to the docking-ledge.

What for? Rocio asked. **I have enough nutrient fluid for now.** In fact, he had filled every fluid reserve bladder at Almaden. If they were calling him in ahead of schedule for a feed, he'd have to vent it all before he got to Monterey.

We're going to install some auxiliary fusion generators in your cargo bays, Hudson Proctor said. **You've got the connections to receive power directly from them, haven't you?**

Yes. But why?

There's a long-range mission being planned. You fit the parameters.

What mission?

Kiera will tell you when you've been prepped.

Will I be using combat wasps as well?

Yes, we'll give you a full complement. They'll be loaded at the same time as the fusion generators. Your lasers need checking, too.

I'm on my way.

*

Al stared at Kiera, not quite believing she had the balls to turn up in his suite like this. Jez was at his side, arm tucked through his, while Mickey, Silvano, and Patricia were bunched up behind him, along with half a dozen soldiers. Kiera was backed up by Hudson Proctor and eight of her goons on bodyguard duty. Animosity seeped out from both groups, thickening the air.

'You said it was urgent,' Al said.

Kiera nodded. 'It is. Etchells has just returned.'

'That's the hellhawk who ran from the antimatter station when things looked tough?'

'He didn't run. He found out the navy was up to something strange there. He thinks one of their ships was loaded with anti-matter before the station was destroyed. Afterwards, it rendezvoused with a voidhawk, and the two of them flew to Hesperi-LN. That's the Tyrathca world.'

'I heard of them. They're like Martians, or something.'

'Xenocs, yes.'

'So what's this got to do with us?'

'The voidhawk and the other ship were very interested in an old Tyrathca spaceship that's orbiting Hesperi-LN. Etchells thinks they put a team on board. After that, they took off for the Orion Nebula. That's where the Tyrathca came from originally. And it's a long way away.'

'One thousand six hundred light-years,' Jezzibella said.

'So?' Al asked. He couldn't work out her angle. 'So what's this got to do with us?'

'Think about it,' Kiera said. 'We're in the middle of the biggest crisis the human race has ever known. And the Confederation Navy breaks the one law it enforces above all others. It actually helps fill a starship up with antimatter. Then that ship and another fly somewhere no other human has ever been before. And they're looking for something. What?'

'Fuck's sake,' Al muttered. 'How do I know?'

'It has to be something very, very important to them. Something the Tyrathca have got and the navy wants. Bad enough to risk a war. Etchells said they actually fired on the Tyrathca ships when they were orbiting Hesperi-LN. Whatever it is, they are desperate to get their hands on it.'

'You trying to jerk me around here?' Al asked Kiera. He was losing his cool about the whole phoney meeting, but then he always did when the talk turned to that space and machines stuff he couldn't quite follow. 'We've been through all this superweapon shit before. I sent Oscar Kern and some guys after that Mzu broad and an Alchemist bomb. Fuck lot of good that did me.'

'This is different,' Kiera insisted. 'I don't know exactly what the navy's after, but it has to be something they can use against us. If it is a weapon, then it must be an extremely powerful one. Ordinary weapons are useless against us. If the navy does put together enough force to harm us, we just leave this universe behind. They know that, especially after Ketton. We automatically protect ourselves; nothing can reach us on the other side. Nothing human, that is.'

'Ho, boy! Lady, have you ever changed your tune. Yesterday you were telling me how nothing the longhairs dream up could ever touch us if we take New California out of here.'

'This is xenoc technology. We don't know what it's capable of.'

'This is bullshit,' Al said in exasperation. 'Maybe. If. Perhaps. Might be. You got zip and you know it. Know what? I heard this speech once before. The prosecution lawyer at my last trial used it. Everyone knew it was a bunch of crap then, and there ain't nothing changed since. And let me tell you, dark sister, you ain't even as convincing as he was.'

'If the Confederation has something that can reach the planets we've removed, then we've already lost.'

'Yeah? What's the matter, Kiera, running scared?'

'I can see I'm wasting my time. I should have known this was going to fly straight over your head.' She turned to go.

Al got a hold on his temper. 'OK. Hit me.'

'We send some ships after them,' Kiera said. 'I'm already preparing three hellhawks for pursuit duty. Just forget about our beef for one hour, and assign some of your frigates to go with them.'

'You mean frigates armed with antimatter,' Al said.

'Of course. We have to have superior firepower. If possible, we capture the Tyrathca weapon. If not, we destroy it along with the navy ships.'

Al chewed the idea over for a minute, enjoying the way Kiera got all antsy at the delay. 'You want to cut a deal?' he asked. 'OK, I'll tell you what I'll do for you, and this is only because you've come over all noble about our future. I'll let you have a couple of frigates; I'll even arm them with half a dozen antimatter combat wasps each for you. How's that?'

Kiera gave a relieved smile. 'That's good for me.'

'Glad to hear it,' Al's grin shrank to nothing. 'In return, all you gotta do is give me Webster.'

'What?'

'Webster fucking Pryor. That's what.'

Kiera gave Hudson Proctor a confused look. The General shrugged with equal bewilderment. 'Never heard of him,' he said.

'Then until you remember, it's no deal,' Al said.

Kiera glared at him. For a moment, Al thought she was going to go for it.

'Fuckhead!' Kiera yelled. She spun round and stormed out.

'She's sure got a way with words,' Al chuckled. 'Real lady.'

Jezzibella couldn't share his humour. She had a troubled expression on her face as she regarded the big doors that had closed behind Kiera. 'Maybe we should have a talk with Etchells ourselves,' she said. 'Find out what the hell is going on.'

*

Everyone around Kiera kept very quiet as they took the lift up to the Hilton's lobby. Her fury at Capone's stupidity gradually cooled to an iron-hard determination. Capone would have to be disposed of, and quickly. No question about it.

After that, there were new questions.

Etchells's story bothered her badly. She simply couldn't believe the navy would send ships to the Orion Nebula without a very good reason. It had to be connected to possession somehow. With a weapon as the obvious choice. Infuriatingly, if that was the case, then Capone had been right all along about staying here and making a stand.

If she stuck with the original plan, to transfer the Organization down to New California and leave the universe, then there'd be no way to counter any future developments which the Confederation might make. Always a factor, but now requiring more urgent consideration.

And of course, once she gained control of the Organization fleet, she could dispatch a whole squadron of antimatter-armed frigates to the Orion Nebula. But then she'd have to go with them. A quick glance at Hudson Proctor confirmed that. He was loyal, but only because she was the ride he'd chosen to get himself to the top. Give him the chance to intercept a Tyrathca superweapon by himself, and he'd do to her what she was about to do to Capone. It was a bad corner to be backed into.

The lift door opened, and she strode out into the lobby. This section of the Hilton was actually embedded into the asteroid's rock, connecting the external tower structure with the rest of the habitation zone via a warren of corridors. Several Organization gangsters were lounging around in the couches, drinking and talking as they were served by a non-possessed barkeeper. Three more gangsters were leaning against the long reception desk as a team of non-possessed cleaners worked to clear up the last of the trash left over from the Trafalgar victory party.

Kiera took it all in with a quick scan, trying not to let her tension

896

show. She knew Capone's people wouldn't hassle her on the way in. Getting out was something different altogether. All the gangsters had fallen silent, staring at her.

One of the exits led to a station serving Monterey's small metro tube network. It would be the quickest way of returning to the docking-ledge territory she'd marked out as her own. But the carriages could be tampered with. Especially likely now they'd found Bernhard Allsop.

'We'll walk,' she announced to her entourage.

They pushed through the tall glass doors and went out into the wide public hall outside. Nobody tried to interfere with them or block them. The few pedestrians in the hall gave them a wide berth as they marched along determinedly.

'How long until the hellhawks are refitted?' Kiera asked.

'Another couple of hours,' Hudson Proctor said. He frowned. 'Jull von Holger says the SD sensors have lost track of the *Tamaran*. It was on high-orbit patrol.'

'Did the voidhawks kill it?'

'I never heard a death cry, neither did any of the other hellhawks. And ambushing our ships would be a big change of policy for the Edenists.'

'Run an SD sensor check on the other patrol hellhawks, make sure they're still with us.' Kiera let out a disgusted breath. Another complication. She didn't like to think about the hellhawks defecting to the Edenists. Their offers of refuge were still pretty constant from what Hudson, Jull, and the other affinity-capable told her. The only other alternative, that Capone had finally repaired a nutrient fluid refinery, was even worse.

A few metres in front of her, a non-possessed shambling along behind a trolley loaded with food suddenly veered across the hall. Annoyed, she stepped sideways to avoid the wayward trolley. The man pushing it was a wreck, unshaven, his grey jump suit crumpled and dirty, oily hair smeared across his brow. A haggard face was screwed up in an expression of total anguish. She'd paid him no attention, just like all the other non-possessed she encountered in Monterey, because his mind was a standard jumble of misery and fear.

He opened his arms wide, and grabbed her in a fierce bear hug that turned into a rugby tackle. 'Mine!' he howled. 'You're mine.' They crashed painfully to the floor, Kiera's knee cracking against the carbon-concrete. 'Darling, baby, Marie, I'm here. I'm here.'

'Daddy!' She didn't say it. The voice came from within, rising irresistibly from Marie Skibbow's imprisoned mind. Incredulity poured through Kiera's thoughts, smothering her own responses. Marie was sweeping back towards full control.

'I'm going to get her out of you, I promise,' Gerald shouted. 'I know how. Loren told me.'

Hudson Proctor finally recovered from his shock, and leant over the squirming couple to grab Gerald's sleeve. He pulled hard, muscles reinforced by energistic strength, attempting to tear the deranged man free from Kiera. Gerald stabbed a small power cell against Hudson's hand, its naked electrodes digging deep. Hudson screamed as the excruciating bolt of electricity flowed across his skin. He lurched back in terror and pain, a bud of flame sizzling bright from his hand. Two of the bodyguards pounced on Gerald, trapping his legs and one arm. He bucked about frantically.

Kiera went skidding over the floor, barely aware of the disorderly scrum tumbling around her. Her limbs were starting to move in the way which Marie commanded, as the girl's thoughts expanded rapidly back along their old pathways. She concentrated on fighting the girl's re-emergence.

Gerald jabbed the power cell towards Marie's face, the electrodes halting millimetres from her eyes. 'Get out of her,' he raged. 'Out! Out! She's mine. My baby!'

One of the bodyguards grabbed his wrist and twisted hard. Gerald's bone shattered. The power cell dropped to the floor. Gerald screamed in fury. He slammed his elbow back with berserker strength. It caught the bodyguard in his stomach, doubling him up.

'Daddy!'

'Marie?' Gerald gasped, fearful with hope.

'Daddy.' Marie's voice was dwindling. 'Daddy, help.'

Gerald scrabbled round desperately for the power cell. His cold fingers closed around it. Hudson Proctor landed on his back, and the two of them rolled over together.

'Marie!' He could see her beautiful face in front of him. Shaking like a dog coming out of deep water, hair fanning round.

'Not any more,' she snarled. Her fist smashed dead into Gerald's nose.

Kiera slowly climbed to her feet, swaying slightly as long tremors clattered along her body. The bitch girl was back where she belonged, weeping at the centre of her brain. One of the bodyguards was curled up on the floor, clutching his abdomen, cheek resting in a small puddle of vomit. Hudson Proctor was hopping about, shaking his hand violently as if it was still on fire. A deep pock of blackened flesh above his knuckles was trailing smoke, filling the air with a disgusting smell. His eyes were shedding tears of pain. The remaining bodyguards were standing round Gerald, spoiling for trouble.

'I'm going to kill the bastard!' Hudson shouted. He kicked Gerald hard in the ribs.

'Enough,' Kiera said. She wiped a shaking hand across her forehead. Her tangle of hair stirred itself, straightening out and flowing back to its usual dark glossy arrangement. She looked down at Gerald. He was groaning faintly, fingers pawing weakly at his side where Hudson had kicked him. Blood was pumping out from his flattened nose. His thoughts and emotions were a discordant nonsense. 'How the fuck did he get here?' she grumbled.

'You know him?' Hudson asked in surprise.

'Oh, yes. This is Marie Skibbow's father. Last seen on Lalonde. Which was last seen departing this universe.'

Hudson gave an uncomfortable flinch. 'You don't think they're coming back, do you?'

'No.' Kiera glanced along the hall. Three of Al's gangsters had emerged from the Hilton's lobby to look at what was going on.

'We have to move. Get him up,' she told her bodyguards.

They grabbed Gerald under his shoulders, and hauled him upright. His dazed eyes peered at Kiera. 'Marie,' he pleaded.

'I don't know how you got here, Gerald, but we'll find that out eventually. You must really love your daughter to have attempted this.'

'Marie, baby, Daddy's here. Can you hear me? I'm here. Please, Marie.'

Kiera bent her bruised knee, wincing at the lick of pain the movement brought. She focused her energistic power around the joint, feeling it ease up. 'Ordinarily, just working you over ready to receive a soul from the beyond would be punishment enough. But after all you've done, you deserve better.' She smiled, leaning in closer. Her voice became husky. 'You're going to be possessed, Gerald. And the lucky boy who wins your body is going to get me as well. I'm going to take him to bed, and let him fuck me any way he wants, as much as he wants. And you're going to feel it happening the whole time, Gerald. You're going to feel yourself fucking your darling daughter.'

'Noooo!' Gerald howled, shuddering in his captor's grip. 'No, you can't. You can't!'

Kiera slowly licked Gerald's cheek, holding his head fast as he tried to squirm away. Her mouth arrived at his ear. 'It won't be Marie's first perversion, Gerald,' she whispered smoothly. 'I enjoy how hot this body gets when I use it to perform my deviances. And I have a lot of them, as you'll find out.'

Gerald began a tormented wailing; his knees buckled. 'It hurts again,' he burbled. 'My head hurts. I can't see anything. Marie? Where are you, Marie?'

'You'll see her, Gerald, I promise I'll open your eyes for you.' Kiera jerked her head at the bodyguards holding the wretched madman. 'Bring him.'

*

The office Emmet Mordden had claimed for himself was on the same corridor as the Tactical Operations Centre. Its previous occupant, the Admiral commanding New California's SD network, had favoured striking colours for his furniture. The easy chairs were purple, scarlet, lemon, and emerald, while his curving desk was a perfect mirror. A continual holographic screen formed a narrow band circling the room halfway up the wall, showing a view out over a coral reef colonized by some xenoc species of aquatic termites. Emmet didn't mind, like all possessed he enjoyed the impact of strong colours, and found the ocean relaxing. Besides, there was a very powerful desktop processor which allowed him to track down most of the problems he was given, and he was close to the Organization's communication centre when a crisis hit – like five times a day. The Admiral also had an excellent stash of booze.

When Al came in he gave the easy chairs a disapproving grunt. 'I gotta sit in one of those? Je-zus, Emmet, don't you tell no one. I got an image around here.' Al sat in the one nearest the desk and rested his fedora on its wide arm. He took a longer look round. Same as everywhere else in the asteroid. Trash piling up, food wrappers and cups, along with a pile of clothes in one corner waiting for the laundry. If anyone should have room service sorted, he expected it to be Emmet. Bad sign that he hadn't. But the brain boy had been busy in other ways. His desk was covered in those electric calculation machines, all stitched together with glass wire. Picture screens lined the edge of the desk, standing on things like sheet music racks; the whole set up was hurried, just out of the workshop. 'You been busy by the looks of things.'

'I have.' Emmet gave him a pensive look. 'Al, I gotta tell you, I've wound up with more questions than when we started.'

'Figures.'

'First off, I checked the corridor cameras, and all the ones round about that area. They came to a big zero. I don't know who killed Bernhard, but they definitely messed with the camera processors. The memories were deleted, someone used a codebuster against our protocols.'

'Emmet . . . come on, man, you know I don't grab any of that shit.'

'Sorry, Al. OK, it's like the photos the cameras take are automatically locked inside a safe. Well, somebody cracked it, took the photos out, then locked it up again behind them.'

'Shit. So no pictures, huh?'

'Not in the corridor, no. So I widened the search, and hunted through the cameras outside, the ones covering the ledge.' He tapped one of the makeshift screens. 'Watch.'

A picture of the docking-ledge sprang up. They were looking down on the airlock as it jetted air out to the stars. Two spacesuited figures stood watching it. One of them started bounding towards the open hatch. After a short interval, the other one followed him.

'Nothing happens for a couple of minutes,' Emmet said.

The image zipped with static, then the two spacesuits emerged from the airlock and carried on walking down the ledge.

'The footprint guys?' Al suggested.

'I think so. But I don't think they're part of Bernhard's hit.'

'Sure they are. They didn't holler about what happened.'

'They're in spacesuits, so they're not possessed. Look at it from their angle. They've just stumbled over the newly dead corpse of one of your senior lieutenants, and they've even got his blood on their boots. There's no one else around they can point the finger at. What would you do?'

'Keep my mouth shut,' Al agreed. 'Do you know who they are?'

'This is where it gets odd. I backtracked them; they came out of a hellhawk called *Mindori*.'

'Goddam! Kiera's people.'

'I don't think so.' The camera memory played on, showing the two spacesuited figures getting into a small truck and driving it round to another airlock. 'I couldn't get a record off the cameras in this section either. So I don't know what they got up to inside. But it was a different program which erased their memories, not the same one used in Bernhard's hit.' One of the spacesuited figures re-emerged onto the docking-ledge and loaded several trays of small packages onto the truck. It was then driven back to the *Mindori*. The figure eventually climbed back up into the hellhawk's life-support module.

'Kiera doesn't use non-possessed to crew her hellhawks,' Emmet said. 'And that guy was still on board when it took off. The other one must still be inside the habitat.'

'Je-zus. He's walking around in here?'

'Looks that way. All we know for sure is that they're nothing to do with Kiera.'

'But he could be the goddam Confederation Navy. Some kind of assassin. Their version of Kingsley Pryor.'

'I'm not so sure, Al. Those boxes in the truck. I ran a search through our stores inventory. It's not exactly tight at the best of times, but there's a lot of electronics I can't account for. I can't see the Confederation Navy breaking in here to steal a truck full of spare parts. That doesn't make any sense.'

Al stared at the screen, which had frozen on the last image of the spacesuited guy stepping into *Mindori*'s airlock. 'All right, so we've got two separate things going on here. Kiera hits Bernhard, and a hellhawk helps someone steal our electrical stuff. The first one I can understand. But the hellhawk . . . Can you figure what it's doing?'

'No. But it's back here right now. We can just ask it straight out. *Mindori* docked on the ledge this morning. Kiera's got her engineering teams out there fitting it ready for a long-duration flight.

Something else to consider, our defence network says another hellhawk has gone missing from its patrol. They're running a check on the rest to see how many are still there.'

Al leaned back into the chair, and grinned happily. 'They could be trying to break free. How long till that food factory they need is fixed?'

'Another week. Five days if we really hustle.'

'Then hustle, Emmet. Meantime I'm going out to take a ride in Cameron, he can talk to the other hellhawks for me, without Kiera listening in.'

*

Gerald's fractured thoughts slithered through a universe of darkness and pain. He didn't know where he was, what he was doing. He didn't really care. Flashes erupted from time to time as neurons made erratic connections, releasing bright images of Marie. His thoughts clustered round them like worshipful congregations. The reason for such adulation was slipping from him.

Voices began to impinge on his miserable existence. A chorus of whispers. Insistent. Relentless. Growing louder, stronger. They began to intrude on his vague consciousness.

A blast of white-hot pain put him in sudden, frightening contact with his body again.

Let us in. End the torment. We can help.

The pain changed position and texture. Burning.

We can stop it.

I. I can stop it. Let me in. I want to help.

No, me. I'm the one you need.

Me.

I have the secret to end the torture.

There was sound. Real sound, rattling through the air. His own thin screams. And laughter. Cruel, cruel laughter.

Gerald.

No, he told them. No, I won't. Not again. I'd rather die.

Gerald, let me in. Don't fight.

I'll die for Marie. Rather that . . .

Gerald, it's me. Feel me. Know me. Taste my memories.

She said . . . She said she'd . . . Oh, no. Not that. Don't make me, not with her. No.

I know. I was there. Now let me come through. It's difficult, I know. But we have to help her. We have to help Marie. This is the only way now.

Astonishment at the soul's identity crumbled his mental barriers. The soul roared through from the beyond, permeating his body, the energy it brought seething along his limbs, sparkling down his spinal column. Invigorating. New memories invaded his synapses, colliding with the emplaced recollections in cascades of sights, sounds, tastes, and sensation. It wasn't like before. Before he'd been confined, shoved down to the very edge of awareness, knowing of the outside by the tiniest trickle of nerve impulses. A passive, near-insensate passenger/prisoner in his own body. This time it was a more equal partnership, though the newcomer was dominant.

Gerald's eyes opened, a flush of energistic power helping them to focus. Another application finally banished the terrible headache that had raged for so long.

Two of Kiera's bodyguards were smirking down at him. 'Who's a lucky boy, then,' one chortled. 'Man, you are in for the shag of a lifetime tonight.'

Gerald raised a hand. Two searing spears of white fire flashed from his fingertips, drilling straight through the craniums of both bodyguards. Four souls gibbered their fury as they plunged back into the beyond.

'I have other plans for this evening, thank you,' said Loren Skibbow.

*

It had been a while since Al took a ride in his rocketship. Sitting in the fat green-leather couch on the hellhawk's promenade deck made him realize just how long. He stretched out, putting his feet up.

'Where can I take you, Al?' Cameron's voice asked from the silver tannoy grille on the wall.

'Just off Monterey, you know.' He needed a break, just a short time alone to get his head around what was happening. In the old days he would have just gone for a drive, maybe take a fishing rod with him. Golf, too, he'd played golf a few times; though not to any rules the Royal and Ancient had ever heard about. Just buddies fooling around on a fine day.

The view through the big forward window showed him the

asteroid's counter-rotating spaceport slipping away overhead as they leapt off the docking-ledge. Gravity inside the cabin was rock steady. New California tracked in from the riveted steel rim around the window, a silvery half-crescent, like the moon had looked on clear summer nights above Brooklyn. He never could get used to how much cloud planets had. It was amazing anyone on the surface ever saw the sun.

Cameron was curving out from the big asteroid, rolling continually like a playful dolphin. If Al looked back through the portholes down the side of the promenade deck he could see brilliant sunlight sweeping over the yellow fins and scarlet fuselage.

'Hey, Cameron, can you show me the Orion Nebula?'

The hellhawk's antics slowed. Its nose swung across the starscape, hunting like a compass needle. 'There we go. Should be dead centre in the window now.'

Al saw it then, a delicate haze of light, like God had wet his thumb and smeared a star across the canvas of space. He sat back in the couch, and drank cappuccino from a tiny cup as he looked at it. Weird little thing. A fog in space, Emmet said. Where stars are born. The Martians and their death rays lived on the other side.

There was no way he could get his head round that. The idea of the navy ships going there had frightened Kiera, and even Jez was concerned. But it didn't connect for him. He was going to have to ask for advice again. He sighed, acknowledging the inevitable. But there were some things he could still take care of by himself. Chicago had more territories, factions and gangs than the whole Confederation put together. He knew how to manipulate them. Make new friends, lose old ones. Apply some heat. Bribe, blackmail, extort. Nobody today, living or dead, had his kind of political experience. Prince of the city. Then, now, and always.

'Cameron, I want to talk to a hellhawk called *Mindori*, and I want it confidential.'

The sharply pointed scarlet nose began to turn, sending the nebula sliding from view. Monterey reappeared, a grubby ochre splodge with pinpricks of light shimmering around its spaceport.

'The guy's name is Rocio, Al,' Cameron said.

A square in the corner of the window turned grey, then swirled into a face. 'Mr Capone,' Rocio said politely. 'I'm honoured. What can I do for you?'

'I don't like Kiera,' Al told him.

'Who does? But we're both stuck with her.'

'You're hurting me, Rocio. You know that's bullshit. She's got you by the short and curlies because she blew up all your food factories. What if I told you I might be able to rebuild one?'

'OK, I'm interested.'

'I know you are. You're trying to set one up yourself. That's why you grabbed those electric gadgets the other day, right?'

'I don't know what you're talking about.'

'We got it all on film, Rocio; your guys breaking in to Monterey and driving a truckload of stuff back to you.'

'I was docked for a routine maintenance overhaul, some replacement components were fitted, so what?'

'Want me to check on that with Kiera?'

'I thought you didn't like her.'

'I don't, that's why I came to you first.'

'What do you want, Mr Capone?'

'Two things. If your factory doesn't work out, come and talk to me, OK? We can arrange much better terms than Kiera's giving you. No rumbles for a start. You hellhawks just keep a lookout for us around New California. That long-range sight of yours is a valuable commodity. I respect that, and I'm prepared to pay you the top dollar price for it.'

'I'll consider the offer. What's the other thing?'

'I want to talk to the guy who saw the murder. That was a good friend of mine got whacked. I got some questions about it for your guy.'

'Not in person. He's useful to me, I don't want him taken away.'

'Hell, no. I know he ain't a possessed. I just wanna talk, is all.'

'Very well.'

Al sat drinking the rest of his coffee for a minute, trying to display patience. When Jed's sullen suspicious face finally appeared he laughed softly. 'I'll be goddamned. How old are you, kid?'

'What do you care?'

'I'm impressed, that's why. You got balls, I'll say that for you, kid. Waltzing straight into my headquarters and stinging me for a hundred grand's worth of electrical garbage. That's the kind of style I like. Ain't many in this universe would have done that.'

'Didn't have any choice,' Jed grunted.

'Hell, I know that. I grew up in a tough neighbourhood myself. I know how it works when you're on the bottom of the pile. You gotta show the boss you can take the heat, right? If you can't take it, you ain't no use to him. You get kicked out, because there's always some other wiseass who thinks he can do better.'

'Are you really Al Capone?'

Al ran his hands down his jacket lapel. 'Check out the threads, sonny. Nobody else got my class.'

'So what do you want to talk to me for?'

'I need to know things. Now I can't offer you much in return. I mean, you ain't too keen to come visit me in person. I can appreciate that, so I can't give you no reward; dames, booze, that kind of thing. What I got plenty of is local currency. You heard about that?'

'Some kind of tokens?'

'Yeah. Tokens, backed up by my word. If I say you owe somebody something, then you have to pay. So I'll owe you three favours. Me, Al Capone, I will personally go into debt to you. That's bankable on any possessed planet. Now you can't ask for stuff like world peace, or crap like that. But any service or help you need, it's yours. Think of it as the ultimate insurance. I mean, us possessed, we're spreading through this universe. So, you game?'

It wasn't a smile, but the sullen scowl had gone. 'OK, what do you want to know?'

'First off, that other guy with you, the one you left behind. Is he here to kill me?'

'Gerald? Christ, no. He's ill, real bad.' Jed brightened. 'Hey, that's my first favour. His name is Gerald Skibbow, and if you find him, I want you to bung him in a proper hospital with real doctors and stuff.'

'OK. This is more like it, we got a dialogue here, you and me. OK, Gerald Skibbow. If we find him, he gets good medical care. Now the other thing is, I want to know if you saw anyone else hanging around in that corridor when you found the corpse.'

'There was one bloke, yeah. I saw him through the glass in the door. Didn't see much of him. Got a long nose. Oh, and really thick eyebrows. You know, the kind that meet over your nose.'

'Luigi,' Al growled. I should have known he'd side with Kiera.

Disciplining people always sparks off a shitload of resentment. He's going to have contacts among the fleet officers, too, a lot of contacts. She'll love that. 'Thanks, kid, I still owe you a couple of favours.'

Jed gave an exaggerated nod. 'Right.' His image faded out.

Al let out an infuriated breath. Partly angry at himself. He should have kept an eye on Luigi. It was this whole return set up. You couldn't have a wiseguy whacked no more, because there was a good chance he'd come back somewhere on New California, and madder at you than when the beef started.

A wave of surprise and consternation flowed through the souls in the beyond, for once drawing Al's attention. Something momentous was happening. Terror and awe at the event were the dominant sensations spiralling off from the relayed impression.

'What?' Al asked them. 'What is it?'

Nothing like that first agonizing blow against Mortonridge, thank Christ. When he concentrated on the slippery grey images fluttering from soul to soul he saw a sun with another sun erupting out of it. Space was filled with flame, and death flooded inexorably across the sky like a stormfront.

Arnstadt!

'Holy Christ,' Al gasped. 'Cameron? You seeing this?'

'Loud and clear. I think the hellhawks swallowed out.'

'Don't blame them.' Organization warships were vanishing inside blossoming shells of dazzling white light.

The Confederation Navy had answered Trafalgar in a way he had never dreamed they would. Brute force on an irresistible level. His warships were helpless. Their precious antimatter useless. 'Don't they understand?' he asked the desperate souls. 'Arnstadt will go.'

Already flashes of joy were cutting through the beyond as a multitude of bodies were proffered for possession. The reality dysfunction around Arnstadt began to strengthen as more and more possessed added themselves to its gestalt. With the Organization's orbital weapons falling to earth in a rain of smoke there was nothing left to prevent them.

'Cameron, get me home. Fast.'

He knew what would happen. The Confederation Navy was going to come visiting New California next, its imminent arrival presenting Kiera with her main chance. This time the lieutenants and soldiers would most likely listen when she told them they should return to the planet.

A bad day getting worse.

*

The hostage families of the starship crew-members were held on several floors of a hotel overlooking Monterey's biosphere. During the day, they gathered together in the building's lounges and public areas to provide each other with whatever comfort they could muster. It wasn't much. They had become a weary crowd surviving each day on shattered nerves; barely fed, denied information, ignored and despised in equal measure by their Organization guards.

Silvano and the two gangsters ushered Kingsley into the hotel's conference suite. He saw Clarissa immediately, helping serve the morning meal. She caught sight of him and cried out, dropping her serving spatula into the pan of beans. Everybody watched as they embraced.

She was overjoyed to see him. For the first minute. Then Kingsley could stand the dishonesty no longer, and confessed what he had become. She stiffened, backing away in anguish. Wanting to block out the words, for them never to have been spoken.

'How did it happen?' she asked. 'How did you die?'

'I was in a starship. There was an antimatter explosion.'

'Trafalgar?' she whispered. 'Was it Trafalgar, Kingsley?'

'Yes.'

'Oh dear God. Not you. Not that.'

'I have to know something. I'm sorry I'm not asking about you, I should be, I guess, but this is the most important thing in the universe right now. Do you know where Webster is?'

She shook her head. 'They keep us apart. He was assigned to the kitchen staff by that fat collaborator bastard Octavius. I used to see him every week. But it's been over a fortnight since they brought him last. None of them will tell me anything.' She broke off at the strange smile rising on Kingsley's face. 'What is it?'

'He was telling the truth.'

'Who?'

'I was told that Webster had gotten away from the Organization, that he was on a starship. Now you tell me you haven't seen him, and Capone can't find him.'

'He's free?' The knowledge overcame her reluctance, and she reached out to touch him again.

'It looks that way.'

'Who told you?'

'I don't know. Someone very strange. Clarissa, believe me, there's a lot more going on in this universe than we realized.'

Her smile was tragic. 'I can hardly doubt my dead husband.'

'Time to go,' he said abruptly.

'Go where?'

'For you, anywhere but here. Capone owes me that, but I suspect I might have trouble trying to collect. So we'll just take this one stage at a time.'

He walked over to the conference suite's door, Clarissa following timidly behind him. The two gangsters lounging by the door straightened up as he approached; Silvano had disappeared, and they didn't know what they were supposed to do.

'I'm leaving now,' Kingsley said in a smoothly reasonable tone. 'Be sensible. Move aside.'

'Silvano won't like this,' one said.

'Then he should tell me in person. It's not your job.' He concentrated on the door, visualizing it swinging open.

They tried to prevent it, focusing their own power on keeping it shut. A black-magic version of arm wrestling.

Kingsley laughed as the door crashed open. He looked from one gangster to the other, eyebrow arched in mocking challenge. Unopposed, he stepped through, and took Clarissa's hand.

Behind him, one of the gangsters picked up an ivory telephone, and dialled furiously.

*

Gerald walked cautiously along the corridor, pausing by each door to discover if anyone was inside. It took a lot of Loren's attention just to make sure his legs moved in a regular motion. The state of his mind had horrified her; thoughts disjointed, personality retarded to a childlike confusion, memories becoming fainter and difficult to recall. Only his emotions remained at their adult strength, unmollified by reason and consideration. They pummelled what was left of his rationality with the sharp peaks of extreme states. He experienced fear, never mild anxiety; shame, not embarrassment.

She was constantly having to calm and soothe, offering the kind of persistent encouragement longed for by every child. Her presence was a comfort to him, he kept talking to her, a stream of consciousness drivel she found highly distracting.

He was in bad physical shape, too. The crude injuries Kiera's goons had inflicted were easy enough to heal with energistic power. But his body remained perpetually cold, and there was a nasty sharp ache behind his temples which even energistic power couldn't banish entirely. What he needed was a week of proper sleep, a month of good meals, and a year on a psychiatrist's couch. It would have to wait.

They were somewhere inside the docking-ledge spaceport which Kiera had taken over for herself and her fraternity. Cabal Centre. Except it was virtually deserted. Apart from the two goons she'd killed, she'd only seen three other possessed. None of them had paid her any attention, hurrying along with fraught minds to obey whatever orders they'd received. The lounges and halls were all empty.

Loren entered the main lounge, almost familiar with the bland decorations and subdued furniture. She'd seen this place often enough from the beyond. Kiera's haunt.

Gerald's hand ran over the woolly fabric of the couch. Marie had sat on it for hours, talking to her fellow conspirators. The coffee machine; she'd had that brought in along with fine china. It was bubbling away, filling the lounge with its aromatic scent. His eyes moved fast across the door to her bedroom. The men she'd taken in there.

Loren tried asking the souls of the beyond where she was. But the agitation and unrest created by Arnstadt was snarling up their bitter cacophony even more than usual. There were some glimpses of a female shape. Possibly her. Running with a group of people along an unknown corridor.

The face was less like Marie's than it used to be.

Loren swore viciously. To have come this far. She and Gerald enduring horrors greater than anyone knew existed. To have prevailed through all that. To be *so* close. Whatever omnipotent entity had designed the beyond must surely have come up with the concept of fate as well.

She could feel Gerald starting to crumple in utter dismay as the prospect of reclaiming their daughter started to recede once again. It will not happen, she promised him.

As she moved across the lounge she saw a hellhawk on its pedestal outside. Gerald's surprise halted her as he recognized the *Mindori*'s naked form. Platforms and mobile gantries were ranged up against its cargo holds, each one surrounded by bright floodlights. Maintenance crews in sleek black SII spacesuits were installing bulky equipment modules, mating their power and coolant lines to the spacecraft's existing utility points. Though she couldn't understand any of the activity, Loren was confident they now had an escape route when the time came. Providing that time was soon.

She left the lounge and descended one level. This was the engineering section, though none of its workforce had spent much time on internal upkeep recently. Lightpanels along the corridor roof were a feeble yellow; a few of the air ducts buzzed irritably as they blew out erratic streams of air, but most were still. The only clue it wasn't entirely abandoned came from a near-subliminal humming thrown out by heavy machinery. Loren swivelled round trying to guess the direction, curious about what could be functioning at such a pace when nobody else was around.

When she finally located the guilty door and opened it, she emerged into a vast maintenance shop that had been converted into a cybernetic factory. Rows of industrial machinery were pounding away with furious intent, hammering, drilling, and cutting components out of raw metal. Crude conveyor belts had been set up between them, carrying the freshly minted chunks of meal to assembly tables at one end. Over two dozen non-possessed workers were employed building machine-guns. They were stripped to the waist, their skin gleaming with sweat from the unfiltered heat given off by the machinery.

None of it really registered with Gerald, while Loren looked round in complete confusion. She walked over to one of the non-possessed workers.

'Hey! You. What the hell are these for?'

The man looked up in shock, then bowed his head. 'They're guns,' he grunted sullenly.

'I can see that, but what are they for?'

'Kiera.'

It was all the answer she was going to get from him. Loren picked up one of the guns, her hands slipping on the fine spray of protective oil. Neither she nor Gerald knew much about weapons outside of a didactic course they'd both taken to handle the laser hunting rifle they were allowed on the homestead. Even so, this looked strange. She watched one being put together. Its firing mechanism was too large, and the barrel was lined with some kind of composite.

Memories which belonged to neither of them foamed away behind Gerald's eyes. Memories of mud and pain. Of dark humanoid monsters armed with blazing machine-guns, advancing with deadly inexorability out of the grey rain.

Mortonridge. Kiera was building the kind of weapons the Confederation had used at Mortonridge. Against the possessed!

Loren looked round the factory again, thoroughly unnerved by what she was seeing. The production rate must run into hundreds a day. She was surrounded by non-possessed churning out the one weapon that could blast her back to the beyond in a second. If they had any ammunition.

She checked over the gun she was holding, wiping off the surplus oil with a tissue. Satisfied it was fully functional, she left the factory and started hunting for the second one. It wouldn't be too far away.

*

Monterey was twenty kilometres away; Cameron's approach made it look as though the asteroid was moving to eclipse New California. Sliding across the crescent as it expanded in the promenade deck's big window. The flight path, coming in at ninety degrees to the rotation axis, made it look as though the rock was sprouting a glittery metallic mushroom straight up. That changed as Cameron curved round above the counter-rotating spaceport, and started to slide in parallel to the spindle. The docking-ledge was directly ahead, a deep circular gully chiselled into the rock, with tiny brilliant lights on one side producing wide circles of illumination on the other. Orientation shifted again as the hellhawk chased the asteroid's rotation, turning the gully sides to a floor and ceiling. And Al finally began to understand the way centrifugal force worked.

An explosion bloomed out of the cliff-face rear of the ledge, a quarter of the way round from Cameron's position. It came from a section of rock that was clad in a big mosaic of metal and composite equipment. A broad fountain of brilliant white gas, moving sluggishly enough to be a liquid, spitting out from a jagged hole at the centre of the machinery. Tiny chunks of solid matter spun through the plume.

Al took the Havana from his mouth and crossed over to the window, pressing against it for a better look. 'Holy shit. Cameron, what the hell was that? Is the navy here already?'

'No, Al. There's been a breach in the rock. I'm monitoring the radio, nobody's quite sure what happened.'

'Where did it happen?' Al was straining to see if there were any hellhawks or people on the ledge near the plume.

'It's in an industrial sector, where you were repairing that nutrient fluid refinery.'

Al slammed the palm of his hand into the window. 'That *bitch*!' His three small scars were snow-white against a burning cheek. He stared at the plume as it slowly died down, exposing the crumpled wreckage that was peeling away from the vertical rock. 'OK, a straight fight is what she wants, that's what she gets.'

'Al, I'm picking up a broadband message to the fleet. It's Kiera.'

One of the small circular ports along the side of the observation deck shimmered over and began showing Kiera's face. '. . . after Arnstadt there can be no alternative. The Confederation Navy is coming, and with the numbers to defeat us. Unless you want to be banished back to the beyond we have to transfer ourselves down to the planet. I have the means to do this, and the ability to maintain our authority on the surface without relying on the SD platforms and antimatter. Everything you have now, your status and position, can be continued under my patronage. And this time around you don't have to risk yourselves on those dangerous war missions of Capone's. His day is over. For those of you who chose to have a privileged future, get in touch with Luigi, he will be joining you in the *Swabia*. If you follow him to low orbit, I will provide the means to establish yourselves on the surface. Anyone who wants to stay and wait for the navy, feel free.'

'Damn it.' Al picked up the black telephone. 'Cameron, get me Silvano.'

'He's there, boss.'

'Silvano?' Al yelled. 'You hearing Kiera?'

'I hear her, boss,' the lieutenant's voice crackled.

'Tell Emmet he's to stop any ship that doesn't stay where it is any way he goddam can. I'll talk to the fleet myself later. And I want that fucking message closed down. Now! Send a bunch of our soldiers to surround her headquarters, don't let anybody out. I'm gonna come and deal with her personally. Tonight she starts sleeping with the fish.'

'You got it.'

'I'll be docking any minute. I want you and some of the guys there to meet me. Loyal ones, Silvano.'

'We'll be waiting.'

*

Luigi arrived at the base of the docking spindle feeling pretty damn good. The waiting and plotting had been getting to him, too much like sneaking around in the dark. He was an out in the open kind of guy. Kiera had insisted he keep a low profile, he was still running round after that nobody Malone down in the gym, shovelling shit for non-possessed. The times when he got out to meet his old friends flying the Organization warships were few and far between, and at the meetings all he did was drop a few words of sedition, plant the seeds of doubt.

Every time he'd go back to Kiera and assure her the fleet was losing patience with Capone. Which was so. But he hyped the figures a little, carving himself a bigger slice.

Now that didn't matter any more. He'd walked out of Malone's cruddy basement as soon as Arnstadt registered, not even waiting for Kiera's call. This was it, their chance. Once he was back out there with the fleet, all those numbers wouldn't mean shit. They'd follow him again, he knew it. He'd always been good with his lieutenants, they respected him.

The big transfer chamber at the axial hub was almost deserted when he came out of the tube. He air-swam over to the doors for the commuter cabs.

A man and a woman glided across to him. It annoyed him, but this wasn't the place to make a scene. Ten minutes, *ten*, and he'd be back inside a starship again, in command.

'I remember you,' Kingsley Pryor said. 'You were one of Capone's lieutenants.'

'What's it to you, pal?' Luigi snapped back. He'd never been able to live with the nudges and whispers which followed him everywhere, like he was some kind of child molester on the run.

'Nothing. Are you going out to a ship?'

'Yeah. That's right.' Luigi looked away, maybe the dumbass would catch on.

'That's nice,' said Kingsley. 'So are we.'

The doors opened, revealing the commuter cab's empty interior. Kingsley gestured politely. 'Please, you first.'

*

After she showered, Jezzibella marched along the side of the bed, inspecting each of the dresses Libby had laid out. The problem was, none of them were new. She'd gone through her whole wardrobe since she hooked up with Al. I need new clothes. It had never been a problem when she was touring. Clothes were such a minuscule part of the tour budget that the company would never quibble if she bought a new range on every planet – not that she had to. Each fresh star system was colonized by hot young designers who'd kill for her to be seen just looking at their labels.

She sighed and reviewed the line-up again. It would have to be the blue and green summer dress with its wide shoulder straps and micro-skirt. Worn over the girlishly sympathetic persona.

The tiny dermal scales began to contract and expand in response to the sequence she keyed in, performing their minute adjustments to her baseline facial expression so that she appeared perpetually intrigued and trusting. Skin texture softened to a young, healthy glow. Twenty-one all over again.

Jezzibella went over to the angled mirrors on the dressing table to check herself over. The eyes weren't right, they were too rigid, insufficiently awed and excited by the beautiful mysterious world they explored. A little piece of the tough executive persona hanging on past its sell-by date. She scowled at the offending patches; another expression which didn't belong on this face. The dermal scales were degenerating again. It was always the areas around the eyes which wore out first. Her supply of replacements was none too high, either. Not even a planet could make up that shortfall; her stocks had always come straight from Tropicana, the one Adamist world with relaxed bitek laws.

'Libby,' she shouted. 'Libby, get in here, and bring that package with you.'

The old dear had worked wonders recently, patiently reapplying the scales with a true artisan's touch to gloss over the reduced coverage. But even her magic couldn't last for ever without new scales. Jezzibella didn't want to consider that.

'Libby, get your arthritic ass in here right now!'

Kiera, Hudson Proctor, and three goons stepped into the bedroom; passing straight through the door without opening it, as if the clanwood panels were nothing more than coloured air. All five of them were cradling static-bullet machine-guns.

'Showing our age, are we?' Kiera asked silkily.

Jezzibella clamped down on her shock and budding fear. Kiera would be able to see that, and she wouldn't give her the satisfaction. Her mind slipped directly into the cool empress persona without any help from her crashed neural nanonics. 'Here for some beauty tips, Kiera?'

'This body doesn't need any. It's a natural. Unlike yours.'

'Pity you don't know how to use it properly. With breasts like those I could have ruled the galaxy. All you have is twenty male morons whose hard-ons have drained the blood from their brains. You can't inspire them, you're just their whore. What a force not to be reckoned with that makes.'

Kiera took a step forward, her serenity cooling rapidly. 'That mouth of yours has always been a problem for me.'

'Wrong again, it's the smarter brain behind it which beats you every time.'

'Kill the slut,' Hudson Proctor barked. 'We don't have the time for this. We've got to find him.'

Kiera lifted her machine-gun up, and touched the tip of the barrel lightly against the base of Jezzibella's neck. Watching closely for a reaction, she slid the barrel down, teasing open the thick white robe. 'Oh, no,' she murmured. 'If we kill her, she'll just come back as our equal. Won't you?'

'I'd have to lower myself a long way before I reached that point.'

Kiera had to put an arm out to restrain Hudson Proctor. 'Now look what you've done,' she chided Jezzibella. 'These are my friends you're upsetting.'

Jezzibella's expression was of complete amusement. She didn't even have to speak.

Kiera nodded a reluctant submission to the private sparring. She gently shifted the towelling robe back to its original state. 'Where is he?'

'Oh, please. At least threaten me.'

'Very well. I will not allow you to die. And I do have that power. How's that?'

'For fuck's sake,' Hudson Proctor said. 'Give her to me. I'll find out where he's gone.'

Kiera gave him a pitying glance. 'Really? Will you gang-bang her into capitulation, or simply keep on hitting her until she tells you?'

'Whatever it takes.'

'Tell him,' Kiera said.

'If I thought you could win, I would have joined you at the start,' Jezzibella said simply. 'You can't, so I didn't.'

'The game has changed,' Kiera said. 'The Confederation Navy has destroyed our ships at Arnstadt. They're coming here. New California has to leave, with us on it. And the only thing stopping that is Capone.'

'Life's a bitch, death's a tragedy, then you meet me.'

'One of your better lyrics. Too bad you won't be remembered for it.'

The processor block Jezzibella had left on the dressing table began to shrill an alarm.

'Right on time,' Kiera said. 'That'll be my team dealing with Capone's refinery. I'm covering my back in case he subverts any of my hellhawks. Not that I actually have to blast him back into the beyond in person. One of my sympathizers has already been given that job. But I was so looking forward to being there. So once again, you've spoilt my fun.' She held a finger up. A long yellow flame flared from the tip, dancing in front of Jezzibella's stoic face. 'Let's see if I was wrong about being unable to force you, shall we? After all this effort I think I deserve some kind of payoff.' The flame turned blue, shrinking until it was a small fiercely hot jet.

*

Life in Emmet Mordden's office had suddenly become very hectic. One set of screens was covering the explosion in the nutrient fluid refinery, providing images from surviving cameras and sensors, along with a general schematic of the section. Whoever placed the bomb knew what they were doing. It had taken out a huge segment of the outer wall, crumpling the internal machinery and cutting power and data cables. Depressurization had damaged the refinery still further, rupturing pipes and synthesizer modules. At least there were no fires, the vacuum made sure of that.

Emmet was busy coordinating with the project manager, trying to ensure that everyone who'd withstood the blast was safe behind pressure doors or in emergency igloos, as well as doing a body count. Medical teams were on their way.

The SD sensor grid was splashed across the largest screen, with a full tactical overlay. It showed the long-range sensor focus sweeping the high-orbit vectors which the hellhawks were supposed to be patrolling. Six were missing. The scans had also revealed two voidhawks swallowing in to take advantage of the gaps.

His analysis of the virus in Bernhard's block was still running, filling one holographic screen with cubist alphanumerics. He didn't even have time to suspend that.

Several questors from his desktop block were running through the asteroid's memory cores, hunting down references on Tyrathca military history and the Orion Nebula. Al had wanted to read up on them. So far they'd produced very few files. All of them on the soldier caste. None of which he'd accessed.

Kiera's face was smiling complacently out of another, her re-fined voice booming round the room, telling the fleet that they should turn their backs on Capone and emigrate down to the planet with her. The screen next to her was flipping through the asteroid's communication circuits, running a program to track down which antenna she was using and where her input entered the network.

The SD sensor network flashed up a priority one alert. The *Swabia* had disengaged from its docking-bay cradle, and initiated a jump immediately. The assholes hadn't even cleared the rim!

His desktop block bleeped urgently. 'What?' Emmet yelled.

'Emmet, this is Silvano. I've got a message from the boss.'

'I'm a little busy right now.' He squinted at the display of the communication circuits. Sections were dropping out. Viral warnings started to appear.

'Get into the control centre and make sure the fleet stays on duty. Anyone starts heading for the surface, nuke the fuckers with the SD weapons. Got that?'

'But—'

'Now, you pissant little mother.' The block went dead. Emmet snarled at it, the closest he'd ever come to showing disrespect to Al's chilling enforcer. He took the time to load a couple of orders in the desktop to run a virus scan through the office hardware, and went out at a run.

The thick door to the control centre slid open. Jagged lines of white fire ripped through the air centimetres in front of him. Alarms were screaming as red strobes burned down his optic nerves. Layers of smoke lashed out down the corridor. He squealed in panic, and dived behind one of the consoles as he hardened a bubble of air around himself. Two fireballs burst open against its boundary. Instinctively he sent white fire of his own back along the direction they'd come from. It sizzled sharply in the torrent of purple retardant foam spraying out of the ceiling nozzles.

'What the fuck is going on?' he yelled. He could sense two distinct groupings of minds in the control centre, clustered at opposite ends of the chamber. Most of the consoles between them were smothered with foam that seethed and writhed as it absorbed the flames licking up from smoking puncture holes.

'Emmet, that you? Kiera's bastards tried to shut down the SD network. We stopped them. Snuffed one.'

Despite the lethal environment, Emmet lifted one arm away from his head to glance round again. Stopped what? he thought incredulously. The centre was a total wreck.

'Emmet!' Jull von Holger called. 'Emmet, tell your guys to pack it in. We've won and you know it. The navy's coming and it's not taking prisoners. We have to get down to the planet.'

'Oh, shit,' Emmet whispered.

'Emmet, help us,' Capone's faction called. 'We can whip their asses.'

'Put a stop to it, Emmet,' Jull called. 'Come with us. Be safe.'

The white fire was slashing faster, its brightness building. Emmet curled up tighter, trying to shut it all out.

*

The gleaming scarlet rocketship edged slowly over the docking-ledge, creeping up to the pedestal positioned only sixty metres from the vertical wall of rock. It settled smoothly, and a metallic airlock tube telescoped away from the cliff face to search out the hellhawk's hatch. They engaged and sealed.

Al Capone stomped along the tube into the reception lounge, a baseball bat gripped firmly in his right hand. His lieutenants were waiting for him. Silvano and Patricia, grim-faced but obviously spoiling for a fight. Leroy at their side, anxious and desperate to prove his loyalty. A semicircle of over a dozen more behind them, equally committed, dressed in their best pinstripe suits, Thompson sub-machine-guns gleaming and ready.

Al nodded round, pleased with what he saw. He would have preferred old friends, but these would do. 'OK, we all know what Kiera wants. The dame's running scared of the navy and that Russki Admiral. Well, now we've seen what those bastards will do when their back's to the wall, I say that makes it more important than ever to stay here and cover our asses. We've still got antimatter, and lots of it. That means we got clout where it hurts, we can make them the offer. Unless the Feds agree to stop dicking around with us, every planet they got's gonna live in fear from now on. That's the only way to be sure. I've lived with being wanted all my life, and I know how to deal with that kind of bullshit. You never, fucking *ever*, let your guard down. You gotta make like you're the meanest SOB on the street to stop them messing with you. If they don't respect you, they don't fear you.' He slapped the top of the baseball bat against his left palm. 'Kiera needs to be told that in person.'

'We're with you, Al,' someone called.

The semicircle of gangsters parted, and Al strode forward. 'Silvano, we know where she is?'

'I think she went to the hotel, Al. We can't get them on the phone. Mickey's gone back there to take a look. He'll call if he finds her.'

'What about Jez?'

Silvano shot Leroy a glance. 'We think she's still there, Al. Couple of the guys are there with her. She'll be fine.'

'Better be,' Al muttered. He looked ahead to see Avram Harwood III standing in the lounge's doorway. The man was a total tow-truck job. Breathing badly, his unhealed wounds leaking cheesy fluid down pale damp skin; he could barely stand.

'I am the mayor,' Avram wheezed. 'I am entitled to respect. That's your big thing, isn't it, respect.' He giggled.

'Avvy, get the fuck out of my way,' Al snapped.

'Kiera showed me respect.' Avram raised his static-bullet machine-gun. 'Now it's your turn.' The weapon's fire rate control was set at maximum. He pulled the trigger.

Al was already jumping out of the way. Silvano was raising his own Thompson. Leroy brought his arms up, yelling a frantic 'No!' at the top of his lungs. The other gangsters were diving to the floor or aiming at Avram.

Electrically charged bullets tore across the lounge. A devastating line of throbbing blue-white light complemented the dragon's roar. Al hit the floor just as the first possessed body ignited in its unique spectacular fashion. The searing glare wiped out everyone's vision. A shockwave of heat washed over them, blistering exposed skin, singeing hair. Another body ignited.

Al screamed in raw fury, flinging a white firebolt as strong as the internecine furnace of flesh. Eight identical streamers of white fire smashed into Avram Harwood's body, vaporizing his torso instantly amid a bloom of ash and blood steam. Arms that had been held outstretched dropped to the melting carpet next to his collapsing legs. Heat detonated every chemical bullet left in the machine-gun's magazine as it fell, sending out a lethal volley of shrapnel to slash walls and flesh.

When the light, heat, and noise shrank away, Al swayed to his feet. All he could see at first was a giant purple afterimage which his energistic power was incapable of ridding. His weird psychic sense couldn't track down Avram Harwood's thoughts anywhere. As he blinked the blotches away from his eyes, he realized how badly parts of him were hurting. His suit and hands were running with blood from half a dozen wounds where the shrapnel had sliced into him. One by one he made the slivers of hot metal slide up out of his body, and closed the lips on each cut, bonding the skin back together. The pain dwindled away.

Leroy was lying on the floor at Al's feet. Bullets had torn their way across him, the last one removing half of his throat. Dead eyes stared upwards. Al switched his gaze to the two piles of charcoal scattered over the molten composite floor tiling. 'Who?' he demanded.

The gangsters were picking themselves up, healing and sealing their shrapnel wounds. A head count told Al that Silvano had been among the victims of the static bullets. Nobody dared say anything as Al stood over the small black pile of cooling ash that used to be his chief enforcer. His head was bowed as if in prayer. After a minute he walked over to the four battered limbs that remained of Avram Harwood. 'Bastard!' Al screamed. He brought his baseball bat crashing down on an arm. 'Motherfucking!' The bat slammed into the arm again. 'Shit eating!' This time he hit a leg. 'Psycho Bastard!' The other leg. 'I'll kill your family. I'll burn your house to the ground. I'll dig up your mother's coffin and shit on her. You wanted respect? That what you wanted? This is the kind of respect I got for a cornholing son of a bitch like you.' The bat pounded and pounded on the limbs, pulping them to roadkill smears.

Patricia stepped forward from the rank of badly alarmed gangsters. 'Al. Al, that's enough.'

The bat was brought up, ready to fly at her head. Al met her level gaze. Stood for a moment with the bat poised. A long breath shuddered out of him. 'OK,' he said. 'Let's go find Kiera.'

*

The floor under Emmet was melting, transmuting into a puddle of cold liquid rock. It would soon be deep enough to swallow him whole. Somebody was becoming very anxious to turn him into a fossil. He strove hard to turn the rock solid again as the air above him raged with white fire and profanities. The two factions were evenly matched, and both of them kept shouting at him to throw his strength in on their side.

He wanted to help Al's guys. His own side. Really wanted to. Except the idea of going with New California into a place of safety was hugely appealing. No more of this shit, for a start.

A voracious spout of white fire hit the console he was crouched behind, and started chewing its way through the composite casing and tightly packed circuitry cubes inside. Kiera's people, who had obviously decided he wasn't joining them.

Retardant foam gushed downwards, only to be catalysed into boiling green treacle by the unnatural blaze. It poured off the top of the console and splattered over Emmet, stinging his exposed skin.

He drew a deep breath, praying his bladder would hold out, and conjured up a spear of white fire. It flashed across the chamber towards Jull von Holger and his cohorts. The immediate result wasn't quite what he expected.

A thunderous roar swamped the control centre. A possessed body ignited, forcing Emmet to clamp his hand over his eyes. The mental and vocal shriek of the vanquished soul grated down his skin like needles of ice. A second body erupted, then another. The air was clogged with stifling heat and a vomitous stench of incinerated meat as they belched out thick fumes.

After a long time the bodies burnt out, returning the light level to normal. The awful fetor remained. The roaring had stopped.

A loud metallic *snick* sounded across the chamber. To Emmet's ears it sounded mechanical, and very weapons orientated. Footsteps squelched through the foam.

'You've pissed yourself,' a voice told him.

Emmet twisted his head out of the foetal position. A gaunt man in a grubby one-piece suit was looking down at him, holding a peculiar machine-gun, its warm barrel pointing directly at Emmet's forehead. A canvas satchel was slung over his shoulder, packed full of magazines.

'I was scared,' Emmet said. 'I'm not part of the Organization's muscle.'

The man's features vanished for a second, replaced by a woman's. If anything, her expression was even more forbidding. Emmet could sense the energistic power circulating through the body. It rivalled Al's strength.

Survivors from the Organization faction were peering nervously over the top of their trashed consoles.

'Who are you?' Emmet stammered.

'We are the Skibbows.'

'Uh, right. Are you on Kiera's side?'

'No. But we'd really like to know where she is.' The machine-gun's safety catch was released. 'Now, please.'

*

Mickey Pileggi had learned the hard way not to try and storm Kiera and her goons. Three of his soldiers had wound up burning like miniature suns when they all charged into the Nixon Suite. Mickey had entertained visions of lavish praise and unlimited privileges heaped upon him by Al for rescuing Jezzibella from Kiera's hands. That dream had quickly turned into a crock of shit. The guns she was armed with had caused havoc amongst the gangsters. Those screams would echo through the air around Mickey for eternity.

He'd ordered them to fall back to the hallway outside, taking up shielded positions in the twin stairwells and disabling the elevators with strategic blasts of white fire. They were at the bottom of the tower. She wasn't going anywhere. Now he just had to explain to Al how he'd fouled up.

Another spray of static bullets hammered out from the splintered doors of the Nixon Suite. All the gangsters ducked, thickening the local air.

'We should seal this floor off,' one of them said. 'Blow the windows out and see how she likes eating vacuum.'

'Great idea,' Mickey grumbled. 'Are you gonna tell Al we did to Jezzibella what they did to Brown-nose Bernhard?'

'Guess not.'

'OK. Now come on, guys. Let's concentrate on making those doors evaporate. Keep them occupied defending themselves while our reinforcements arrive.'

'If any do.'

Mickey shot the man a furious glare. 'Nobody's deserting Al, not after what he's done for us.'

'For you.'

Mickey didn't see who said that, but let the sharp anger show amid his thoughts as a warning. He focused on the door, and punched it with the force of his mind. Bullets pulverized a line in the marble wall above his head. Tiny tendrils of electricity scrabbled across the surface. Everyone flinched down fast.

His processor block bleeped. He dusted hot marble chips from his hair and pulled it out of his pocket, amazed the thing was working with so much machismo energistic power buzzing about.

'Mickey?' Emmet implored. 'Mickey, you got any idea where Kiera is?'

'Pretty sure, yeah. She's like ten yards away from me.' Mickey gave the block an infuriated look as Emmet abruptly cut the call.

'OK, guys, let's hit the doors together this time. On three. One. Two—'

*

The office door shut behind Skibbow, and Emmet let out a *huge* gasp of relief. There was a real monster of a problem torturing that wacko possessed, and Emmet was enormously glad he didn't share any part of it. He let his body calm for a few precious moments more, then called Al.

'Whatcha got for me, Emmet?'

'We had a problem in the SD control centre, Al. Kiera's people tried to knock out the orbital platforms.'

'And?'

'They're sleeping with the fish.' He held his breath, worried Al could sense half-truths along the communication circuit.

'I owe you one, Emmet. I won't forget what you did.'

Emmet's fingers were skidding fast over his desktop keyboard, rerouting the SD network's main command channels. Symbols blinked up on the tactical display, showing him what he was in charge of. He smiled uneasily at the power he'd assumed. Lord of the sky, admiral of the fleet, enforcer of order across a whole planet. 'The place is pretty much a bombsite, Al, but I've still got control of the major hardware.'

'What's the fleet doing, Emmet? Are the guys staying put?'

'Pretty much. Eight frigates are heading down to low orbit, I guess the rest are waiting to hear what you've got to say. But, Al, I count seventeen hellhawks missing.'

'Je-zus, Emmet, first chunk of good news I've had today. You keep watching everybody, make sure they don't move. I got some business to clear up, then I'll be right back with you.'

'Sure thing, Al.' He blinked, and squinted at the tactical display. It wasn't supposed to be shown on such a small scale; this was a format designed to showcase across a hundred-metre screen in front of admirals and defence chiefs. From what he could make out, two miniaturized symbols were moving very close to Monterey itself.

*

The *Varrad* skimmed above the wrinkled rock, keeping a constant fifty-metre separation from the pumice-like terrain, lifting and sinking in perfect curving parallels with the craters and ridges beneath its metallic lower hull. Pran Soo was pursuing the Hilton tower as it slid across the stars, closing on it like an atmospheric fighter on a low-visibility strike run. Along with all the other hellhawks, she'd been monitoring what communications she could access since Kiera's revolt had started. And Mickey Pileggi had spent fifteen minutes yelling across the net at his fellow Organization lieutenants for help to deal with Kiera and her dangerous weapons.

Are you sure about this? Rocio asked.

Absolutely. We know a possessed body is incapable of defending itself against a starship weapon. The power level is simply too great, even if they know they're being targeted. I can eliminate Kiera with one shot, and this time there will be no comeback from the Organization. We will truly be free.

Capone's girlfriend is in that hotel suite.

He will find another. We will never have an opportunity like this again.

Very well, but try to keep the destruction to a minimum. We may yet have to cut a deal with the Organization.

Not if the Confederation Navy gets here first.

Let me see what's happening. The rock is blocking my distortion field.

Pran Soo opened her affinity, allowing him to borrow the sights revealed to her bitek sensor blisters, showing him the rock rushing past her hull. Her other principal sense, the *Varrad*'s distortion field, was reduced to a hemispherical shape, its usual bloated coverage curtailed by the giant asteroid.

The Monterey Hilton swung towards her, sticking out proud from the rock. Visually, a pillar of tough carbon-reinforced titanium riddled with thick, multi-layered windows. Inside the distortion field it emerged as a coagulation of thin sheets of matter, threaded with a filigree of minute power cables whose electrons were imbued with a delicate spectral sheen.

She matched her vector with the asteroid's rotation. Electronic pods on her hull flowered, thrusting out sensors. They swept across the lower floors of the tower.

I can't distinguish individual people, she told Rocio. *The window's radiation shielding is an effective block against precision scanning. I am aware of their emotions, but from this distance they've blurred together. All I know is, several people are definitely in there.*

And Mickey Pileggi is still calling for assistance. Kiera must be one of those you sense.

Pran Soo activated a microwave laser, and aligned it on the base of the Hilton. The beam would slice along the side of the tower, filleting the structural girders so the entire bottom floor would just tumble away into interplanetary space. Targeting systems designated the requisite cutting pattern.

A hellhawk rose above the asteroid's flat horizon behind Pran Soo, its hull crawling with vivid lines of electrical energy feeding a comprehensive armament of beam weapons.

Etchells, Pran Soo exclaimed in surprise.

Two masers punctured her thick polyp hull, penetrating right into the central core of organs.

*

Emmet finally managed to shift the tactical display's magnification, enhancing the zone around Monterey itself. He was just in time to watch one of the symbols drift away inertly from the Hilton tower. The other symbol moved in closer to the hotel. Its data tag identified it as the *Stryla*, which he knew was possessed by Etchells. But he didn't have a clue whose side it was on, that's even if the hellhawks were taking sides.

He activated the close-range defence systems, and ordered them to target the hellhawk. The only option, given SD's hellhawk liaison guy was now a mound of ash in the ruined control centre. Etchells was an unknown factor, capable of killing possessed humans. And Al was heading down into the Hilton.

Stryla's symbol sprouted a small batch of alphanumerics, telling Emmet it was datavising directly to the asteroid's SD Command. He hunted round his program menus, desperately trying to route the message through to his office.

'Disengage your targeting lock,' Etchells said.

'No way,' Emmet told him. 'I want you a thousand kilometres away from this asteroid; you have thirty seconds to begin accelerating or I'll fire.'

'Listen, bollockbrain. I have fifty combat wasps in my launch cradles, all with innumerable submunitions, all fitted with fusion warheads. Right now, they are all armed, and activated by a deadman code. You cannot train enough beam weapons on me to vaporize me and the missiles instantaneously. If you fire, they will detonate. I'm not sure if that much megatonnage will crack Monterey open or not. Would you like to find out?'

Emmet's hands clamped round his head in an agony of frustration. I am not cut out for any of this shit. I want to go home.

What would Al do? It wasn't such a good question. He had the horrible feeling that if you put Al in a Mexican stand-off he would shoot.

'You know, I might just,' he said stubbornly. 'I've had a real shitty time today, and the Confederation Navy is on the way to make it worse.'

'I know the feeling,' Etchells said. 'But I'm really not a threat to you.'

'Then what the hell are you doing there?'

'I have to ask someone a question. Once I've done that, I'll leave. Give me five minutes, then you can start acting tough again. Deal?'

*

The expensive designer gloss had departed from the lounge in the Nixon Suite. Mickey's ill-judged attempt to beachhead the place had resulted in streamers of white fire slashing round in chaotic violence, Kiera's counterattack had only made it worse. The lights were out, a tangle of broken pipes and cables hung down out of the mashed-up ceiling, the furniture had burned enthusiastically and was now reduced to smoking embers. Torrents of energistic power poured upon the doors by both sides had turned them and the surrounding walls into a fantastic tract of heterogeneous crystal; long encrustations of quartz sprouted in jumbled antagonism, each branch fighting its neighbour like a forest of avaricious jewels. They writhed fluidly each time another burst of power doused them, growing slightly longer and more entwined.

Kiera worried that the continual assaults on the door were a diversion. She had two of her goons patrolling the other rooms, searching for the Organization gangsters grouping together on the other side of the suite's walls, and especially the ceiling. So far they hadn't tried to break through, but it would only be a matter of time. Nobody was stupid enough to keep on trying the same route in when they were so thoroughly blocked. There was also the ammunition question. She was going to run out eventually.

One thing she'd made quite sure of was keeping in contact with her deputies. Hudson Proctor could use his affinity to talk to the remaining Valisk survivors positioned through the asteroid, who in turn kept in touch with their recruits through the net. Communications remained the key to any revolution.

Unfortunately, it didn't guarantee success.

'Just how many people have declared for us?' Kiera asked.

Hudson Proctor took the figures he knew of, and added quite a few. No way was he about to deliver that much bad news by himself. 'About a thousand in the asteroid.'

'What about the fleet?' she demanded. 'How many ships?'

'Jull reported several dozen were heading for low orbit before Emmet's crew wiped him out. But they wrecked the SD centre. Capone can't use the platforms to intimidate anybody, in space or on the planet.'

'Where the hell is Luigi?'

'I don't know, he hasn't checked in.'

'Damn it, didn't anyone listen to me? Luigi's part was crucial, the fleet must follow us down to the planet. Capone is going to get us all slung back into the beyond.'

Hudson had heard the speech countless times already. He said nothing.

'I should have gone for the control centre, not Capone,' Kiera said. She looked at the crystalline bulwark, which undulated rapidly, twinkling with emerald light. One of her goons fired his machine-gun through a gap where the doors used to be. 'Maybe we should try and get up to the defence section, there's bound to be an auxiliary control room.'

'We'll never get past Pileggi,' Hudson said. 'There's too many of them.'

'Only if we make a break for it through the front.' Kiera tilted her head up to stare boringly at the ceiling. 'I'll bet we can . . .' She trailed off as a silver-white starship with glowing engine nacelles rose ponderously into view outside the big window wall.

'Oh, shit,' Hudson murmured. 'That's the *Varrad*. And Pran Soo is not your biggest fan.'

'Talk to her, find out what she wants.'

He licked his lips, and began a frown which never really had time to form. 'I can't – oh.'

The hellhawk's fantasy image burst. It dropped out of sight, rolling as it went. Another one glided up to replace it, a dark bird-shape with red-flecked reptile scales. Hudson grinned in relief. 'Etchells.'

'Ask him if he can hit Pileggi with his lasers.'

'Right.' Hudson concentrated. 'Uh, he says he has a question for you.'

Kiera's processor block bleeped. Not taking her eyes off Hudson, she slipped it out of her jacket pocket. 'Yes?'

'I need to know something,' Etchells said. 'Do you believe the navy mission to the Orion Nebula is a danger to us?'

'Of course I do, that's why you and the others have been refitted with auxiliary fusion generators. It has to be investigated.'

'We agree on that, then.'

'Good. Now target the Organization grunts holding me in here, and I'll eliminate Capone. With him out of the way I can assign antimatter warships to the flight. The threat can be dealt with properly.'

'Twenty-seven voidhawks have swallowed away from their patrol orbits without clearance. That means they have found an alternative source of nutrient fluid. Even if you gain control of the Organization, you will lose them.'

'But gain control of the antimatter.'

'The Confederation Navy is coming. Every orbital facility the planet has will be obliterated in their attack. Your strategy was to take New California out of the universe to a place of safety.'

'Yes?' she asked irritably. 'So?'

'How do you propose to maintain the blackmail threat over the crews of the ships you dispatch to the nebula?'

Kiera turned from Hudson Proctor to look directly at the hellhawk on the other side of the window. 'We'll come up with something.'

'Your rebellion has failed. Capone is on his way with enough gangsters to overwhelm you.'

'Fuck you.'

'I sincerely believe the navy mission is a threat to my continued existence in this form. That must be prevented. I intend to fly to Mastrit-PJ, and I'm offering you the chance to escape with me.'

'Why?'

'You have the arming codes for the combat wasps I have been

loaded with. Admittedly they are only fusion warheads, but I will take you off the asteroid if you make those codes available to me.'

Kiera scanned round the ruined lounge. The machine-guns opened fire again with a thunderclap tattoo. Sapphire light flexed hungrily within the crystals, causing them to expand further into the lounge. 'Very well.'

The hellhawk surged forwards, its neck flattening out. Energistic power cloaked its hooked beak with a lambent red glow. The lounge's window rippled as the tip pressed against it, then parted like water to allow the vast creature's head into the lounge. A huge iris swivelled round to fix on Kiera. The beak parted to reveal an airlock hatch inside.

'Welcome aboard,' Etchells said.

*

Al ran down the last flight of stairs to find Mickey standing at the bottom. The lieutenant took a terrified step backwards.

'Al, please, I did everything I could. I swear it.' He crossed himself elaborately. 'On my mother's life, we tried to get Jez out of there. Three of the guys got whacked just stepping through the door. Those bullets are too much. They kill you, Al, kill you dead.'

'Shut the fuck up, Mickey.'

'Sure, Al, sure thing. Absolutely. I'm dumb. From now on. Definitely.'

Al peered across the hallway. Bullets had shredded the composite wall panelling, even hacking their way into the metal behind. Opposite him, the Nixon Suite's doors glinted prismatically in the light emerging from the two surviving ceiling panels.

'Where's Kiera, Mickey?'

'She was in there, Al. I swear.'

'Was?'

'They stopped firing a couple of minutes ago. We can sense some of them still.'

Al tapped his baseball bat on the floor, contemplating the Nixon Suite. 'Hey,' he shouted. 'You in there. I brought a whole truckload of my guys with me, and any minute now we're gonna march right in and beat seven types of crap out of you. Your shooters ain't gonna be no good against this many of us. But if you come out right now, then you got my word that you don't get your balls screwed into the nearest light socket. This is between me and Kiera now. Walk away.'

The baseball bat tapped out a metronome beat on the ground. A figure moved behind the crystalline sheet with slow caution.

'Mickey?' Al asked. 'Why didn't you just jump the bastards through the ceiling?'

Mickey's shoulders wriggled awkwardly under his double-breasted suit. 'The ceiling?'

'Never mind.'

'I'm coming out,' Hudson Proctor called. He stepped through the gap in the crystal; his arm was outstretched, holding the machine-gun by its strap.

Thirty Thompson sub-machine-guns were lined up on him, most of them silver-plated. He closed his eyes and waited for the shots, Adam's apple bobbing quickly.

Al couldn't quite figure the spark of outrage glimmering in the man's mind. Fear, yes, plenty of it. But Hudson Proctor was indignant about something.

'Where is she?' Al asked.

Hudson tilted over from his waist, allowing the machine-gun to rest on the floor before letting go of the strap. 'Gone,' he said. 'A hellhawk took her off.' He paused, real anger heating his expression. 'Just her. I was climbing in behind her and she shoved a fucking gun in my face. That bitch; there was room for all of us on board – she just left us behind. Didn't give a fuck about us. I made everything happen for her, you know. Without me she would never have kept control of the hellhawks. I was the one who kept them in line.'

'Why did a hellhawk take her off?' Al asked. 'She ain't got nothing over them any more.'

'It's Etchells, the *Stryla*, he's obsessed about what kind of weapon the Tyrathca have on the other side of the Orion Nebula. He took her with him so she could fire the combat wasps. They'll probably start the first inter-species war. Both of them are crazy enough.'

'Women, huh?' Al gave him a friendly grin.

Hudson's face twitched. 'Yeah. Women. Fuck 'em.'

'All they're good for.' Al laughed.

'Yeah, right.'

The baseball bat caught Hudson square on the crown of his head, smashing through the bone to cleave the brain in two. Blood splashed down the front of Al's sharply cut suit, splattering on his patent leather shoes. 'And just look at the shit they get you into,' he told the collapsing corpse.

Thirty streamers of white fire stabbed out in unison, vaporizing the crystal wall and decimating the possessed cowering behind it.

Libby's cries brought them to the bedroom. Everyone hung back as Al went through the door into the darkened room. Libby was kneeling on the floor, cradling a figure in a stained towelling robe. Her thin voice was a constant piteous wail, like some animal braying for its dead mate. She rocked softly backwards and forwards, dabbing at Jezzibella's face. Al moved forwards, fearing the worst. But Jezzibella's thoughts were still present, still flowing through her own brain.

Libby turned her head to face him, tears glinting down her cheeks. 'Look what they did,' she whimpered. 'Look at my poppet, my beautiful, beautiful poppet. Devils, Devils all of you. That's why you were sent to the beyond. You're Devils.' Her shoulders trembled as she slowly curled herself around Jezzibella, cuddling her fiercely.

'It's OK,' Al said. His mouth was dry and he bent down beside the stricken old woman. In his whole life he'd never been so scared for what he would see.

'Al?' Jezzibella gasped. 'Al, is that you?'

Scorched, empty eye sockets searched round for him. He gripped her hand, feeling the black skin crack open under his fingers. 'Sure, baby, I'm here.' His faint voice faded as his throat closed up. He wanted to join Libby and put his head back and scream.

'I didn't tell her,' Jezzibella said. 'She wanted to know where you were, but I never said.'

Al was sobbing. Like it *mattered* if Kiera had found out, everyone who counted had stayed loyal in the end. But Jez hadn't known that. Had done what she thought was needed. For him.

'You're an angel,' he bawled. 'A goddam fucking angel sent down from heaven to show me what a worthless piece of shit I am.'

'No,' she cooed. 'No, Al.'

He traced his fingers over the remnants of her precious face. 'I'll make you better,' he promised. 'You'll see. Every doctor on this crappy little world is gonna come up here and cure you. I'm gonna make them. And you'll get well again. I'll be here right beside you the whole time. And I'm gonna take care of you from now on. Good care. You'll see. No more of this hurting and fighting. Never again. You're all that matters to me. You're everything, Jez. Everything.'

*

Mickey hung around at the back of the crowd shuffling about in the Nixon Suite when the two terrified-looking non-possessed doctors arrived. He reckoned that was the smart thing. Be there, show off your loyalty like a medal, but don't get into direct line of sight. Not at a time like this. He knew the boss well enough by now. Somebody was going to pay very hard for what was going down. Very hard indeed. The asteroid was rotten with rumours about how the Confederation had learned how to torture a possessed for months. If anybody could improve on that, it would be the Organization, with Patricia as chief researcher.

A hand clamped down on his shoulder. Mickey's nerves were so shot they fired his leg muscles to jump. The hand prevented any actual movement, holding him fast with abnormal strength. 'What is this?' he squawked with fake indignation. 'Don't you know who I am?'

'I don't care who you are,' Gerald Skibbow said. 'Tell me where Kiera is.'

Mickey tried to size up his ... well, not assailant, exactly – questioner. Unnervingly powerful, and zero sense of humour. Not a good combination. 'The bitch showed us a clean pair of heels. A hellhawk took her off. Now let me have my shoulder back, man. Jesus!'

'Where did it take her?'

'Where did ... Oh, like you're going after them?' Mickey sneered. 'Yes.'

Mickey didn't like the way this was speedballing downhill. He dropped the sarcasm approach. 'The Orion Nebula, OK. Can I go now, thank you.'

'Why would she go there?'

'What is it to you, pal?' a voice asked.

Gerald let go of Mickey and turned to face Al Capone. 'Kiera is possessing our daughter. We want her back.'

Al nodded thoughtfully. 'You and I need to talk.'

*

Rocio watched the taxi roll across the docking-ledge towards him. Its elephant trunk airlock tube lifted up and fastened onto his hatch.

'We've got a visitor,' he announced to Beth and Jed.

Both of them hurried along the main corridor to the airlock. The hatch was already open, framing a familiar figure. 'Bugger me,' she grunted. 'Gerald!'

He smiled wearily at her. 'Hello. I brought some decent grub. Figured I owe you that much.' There was a huge pile of boxes on the floor of the taxi behind him.

'What happened, mate?' Jed asked. He was peering round the old loon, trying to read the labels.

'I rescued my husband.' Loren manifested her own face over Gerald's, and smiled at the two youngsters. 'I must thank you for taking care of him. God knows it's not easy at the best of times.'

'Rocio!' Beth yelled.

A shocked Jed was stumbling backwards. 'He's possessed! Run!'

Rocio's face appeared in one of the brass-rimmed portholes. 'It's all right,' he assured them. 'I cut a deal with Al Capone. We're taking the Skibbows with us, and tracking down my murderous old friend Etchells. In return, the Organization supplies the hellhawks with every technical assistance they need securing Almaden, and then leaves them alone.'

Beth gave Gerald a nervous glance, not at all trustful, no matter who was possessing him. 'Where are we going?' she asked Rocio.

'The Orion Nebula. To start with.'

23

The STNI-986M was a basic VTOL utility jet (unimaginatively nicknamed Stony); subsonic, with a blunt tube fuselage which could carry either twenty tonnes of cargo or a hundred passengers. Seven New Washington Navy (NWN) Transport Command squadrons of the durable little vehicles had been flown to Ombey when the President answered their ally's call for military assistance to liberate Mortonridge. Ever since General Hiltch authorized aircraft to fly over secured areas of Mortonridge, they'd become a familiar sight to the occupation troops. After Ketton, they'd been invaluable in supporting the new front-line advance policy which had spread the serjeants dangerously thin over the ground as they divided the peninsula into confinement zones. Outbound from Fort Forward they would deliver food, equipment, and ammunition to the upcountry stations; on the return they invariably evacuated the most serious body-abuse cases of ex-possessed for medical treatment.

Even on airframes intended for rugged duty, full-time usage was producing maintenance problems. Spare parts were also scarce; Ombey's indigenous industries were already struggling to keep front-line equipment and the Royal Marine engineering corps going. All the Stony squadrons had experienced mid-flight emergency landings and unexplained powerdowns. The rover reporters covering the Liberation knew all about the STNI-986M's recent shortcomings, though it was never mentioned in their official reports. Not good for civilian morale. There was no outright censorship, but they all knew they were part of the Liberation campaign, helping to convince people that the possessed could be beaten. Standard wartime compromise, reporting what was in the army's interest in order to get the maximum amount of information.

So Tim Beard cut back on his physiological input when the Stony carrying him and Hugh Rosler lifted from Fort Forward at dawn. He wanted to give the accessors back home a small feeling of excitement as the plane swept low across the endless steppes of dried mud, which meant toning down his body's instinctive unease. It helped that he was sitting so close to Hugh, the pair of them wedged in a gap between a couple of composite drums full of nutrient soup for the serjeants. Hugh always seemed perfectly at ease; even when Ketton ripped itself free of the planet he'd stood up squarely, regarding the spectacle with a kind of amused awe while the rest of the rovers were crouched down on the quaking ground, heads buried between their legs. He also had a neat eye for trouble. There were a couple of occasions when the rover corps had been clambering over ruins when he'd spotted booby traps missed by the serjeants and marine engineers. Not the greatest conversationalist, but Tim felt safe around him.

It was one of the reasons he'd asked Hugh to come along. This wasn't a flight organized by the army for them, but the story was too good to wait for the liaison officer to get round to it. And good stories about the Liberation were becoming hard to find. But Tim had been covering military stories for twenty years now, he knew how to find his way round the archaic chain of command, which people to cultivate. Pilots were good material, and useful, almost as much as serjeants. Finding a ride on the early flight among the crates and pods was easy enough.

The Stony curved away from Fort Forward and headed south, following the remnants of the M6. Once they'd settled into their two hundred metre operational altitude, Tim eased the buckle back on what was laughably called his safety strap, and crouched down by the door port. Enhanced retinas zoomed in on the road below. He'd dispatched a hundred fleks back to the studio with the same view; by now the start of the M6 around the old firebreak was as familiar to the average Confederation citizen as the road outside their own home. But with each trip he progressed a little further along the road, deeper into the final enclaves of the possessed. In the first couple of weeks, it was astounding progress indeed. None of the rovers had to manufacture the optimistic buzz that pervaded their recordings. It was different today, there was progress, still, but it was difficult to capture the essence just by panning a shot from horizon to horizon.

The tactical maps urged on them by the army liaison officers had changed considerably from the original swath of incriminating pink stretching across Mortonridge which delineated the possessed territory. At first the borders had contracted noose-style, then geographical contours showed up along the rim of pinkness, interfering with the rate of advance. After Ketton it had changed again. The serjeants had been deployed in spearhead thrusts, carving corridors through the possessed territories. Separation and isolation, General Hiltch's plan to prevent the possessed from collecting in the kind of density which would kick off another Ketton incident. The current tactical map showed Mortonridge covered in slowly shrinking pink blotches separating from each other like evaporating puddles. Of course, no one actually knew what that critical number was which had to be avoided at all costs. So the serjeants toiled on relentlessly, guided by numerical simulations based on someone's best guess. And there were no more harpoon deluges to make the job easier, nor even SD laser fire to soften up a strongly defended position. The front line was back to clearing the land in the hardest way possible.

Tim's retinas tracked keenly along the carbon-concrete ribbon which the Stony was following. Royal Marine mechanoids had bulldozed entire swamps of saturated soil from the road as the army swept down the spine of the peninsula. At times the single cleared carriageway was twenty metres below the tops of the new banks, as if it was some kind of cooled lava river confined to steep heat-erosion valleys. The side walls were solidified by chemical cement, bonding the slush together in artificial molecular clusters that traded their initial strength with a limited lifespan. Sunlight shimmered off them in vast sapphire and emerald defraction patterns as the Stony whisked by overhead. All the original bridges had been swept away, leaving destitute towers protruding from the mud at precarious angles. Of their replacements, no two were the same. Small gulleys had simple scaffolding archways of monobonded silicon curving over their sluggish streams. Beautiful single-span suspension bridges leapt across gaps half a kilometre wide, their gossamer cables glinting like thin icicles in the clear dawn air. Programmable silicon pontoons carried the mesh-carpet road across broad valley floors in heroic relay.

'The financial cost of this recaptured motorway is roughly ten million Kulu pounds per kilometre,' Tim said. 'Thirty times the price of the original, and it hasn't even got electronic traffic control. It will probably be the Liberation's most enduring physical memorial, even though thirty-eight per cent of it is classed as a temporary structure. Ground troops know it as the road to the other side of hell.'

'You could always take the optimistic view,' Hugh Rosler said.

Tim put the narrative track memory on pause. 'If I could find one, I would. It's not as if I'm rooting for the possessed. Being positive after all this time is flat out impossible. We have to tell the truth occasionally.'

Hugh nodded through the rectangular port. 'Gimmie convoy, look.'

A long snake of trucks and buses was winding its way north along the reclaimed road. The buses meant it would be mostly civilians, ex-possessed being carried away to safety. 'Gimmies' was the term which the rovers had privately evolved for them. Every interview when they came staggering out of the zero-tau pods was the same litany of demands: give me medical treatment, give me clothes, give me food, give me the rest of my family, give me somewhere safe to live, give me my life back. And why did it take you so long to save me?

They'd actually stopped recording interviews with the newly reprieved. Ombey's population was becoming increasingly antagonized by their fellow citizens' lack of gratitude.

Two hundred and fifty kilometres south of the old firebreak line a big staging area had been laid out at the side of the M6, as if a batch of liquid carbon-concrete had squirted out from the edge of the motorway to stain the mud before solidifying. A single small road broke away from it to head out across the open country. There could have been an original feed road down below the hardening mires, but the Royal Marine engineers had chosen to ignore it in favour of running their own route directly over newly surveyed ground, sticking to the most stable regions. Similar staging areas were strung along the whole length of the M6, flinging off side roads which mimicked the original branch roads. They were the supply lines for the army as it overran the towns, for the benefit not so much of the front-line serjeants but the support teams and occupation forces which came in their wake.

This staging area was empty, though covered in mud tracks showing just how many vehicles had been assembled here at one time. The Stony banked sharply above it, and swept away to chase along the supply road. A couple of minutes later they were circling the remnants of Exnall.

The occupation station's landing-field was a broad sheet of micromesh composite spread out across a flat patch of land on the (official) edge of town, with chemical concrete injected into the soil underneath. Mud still percolated through in patches where the chemicals hadn't reached.

None of the cargo crew were surprised when Tim and Hugh jumped down out of the Stony's open hatch. They just grinned as the two rovers strained to lift their feet from the sticky mud.

Tim opened a new memory cell file for his report, and quickly reduced his olfactory sensitivity. Most of the dead plant and animal life had been swallowed by the mud, but the peninsula's constant natural showers kept uncovering them. Fortunately, the smell wasn't anything like as bad as it had been to start with.

They hitched a lift on the back of a jeep into the occupation station which had been set up in the square at the end of Maingreen.

'Where was the DataAxis office?' Tim asked.

Hugh stared around, trying to make sense of the alien territory. 'Not sure; I'd have to check with a guidance block. This is as bad as Pompeii the morning after.'

Tim kept recording as they splashed along the deep ruts in the mire, preserving Hugh's comments about the few landmarks of his old town which he could recognize. The deluge had hit arboreal Exnall hard. Mud had toppled the big harandrid trees onto the buildings they'd once overhung so gracefully, crumpling the shops and houses even before the foundations were undermined. Sloping roofs constructed out of carbon hyperfilament beams had sheered off to twirl away across the currents of mud, momentum snapping them through the surviving pickets of tree stumps. A whole cluster of them had come to rest at the end of Maingreen, making it look as though half of the town's buildings had been buried together up to their rafters. Façades had drifted about freely like architectural rafts until the gradually hardening mud began to anchor them fast. Where they lay across the roads, jeeps and trucks had driven straight over them, crunching parallel tyre tracks of bricks and planking deeper into the dehydrating marsh. Only the foundations and stubby, splintered remnants of ground-floor walls indicated the town's outline, along with slumbering humps of mud-smothered harandrid.

Programmable silicon halls and igloos had been set up in the central civic district to serve as the occupation station; neither the Town Hall nor the police station remained intact. Army traffic sped along the narrow lanes through the new structures, while squads of serjeants and occupation troops marched between them. Tim and Hugh left the jeep to look around.

Hugh eyed the various slopes rumpling the landscape, and consulted his guidance block. 'This is about where it happened,' he said. 'The crowd gathered here after Finnuala's blanket datavise.'

Tim panned round the gloomy panorama. 'What price victory?' he said softly. 'This isn't even the eye of the storm.' He zoomed in on several stagnant pools, examining the bent grass and weeds struggling at the edge. If vegetation was to return to this peninsula, it would spread out from fresh water, he reasoned. But these filthy, sodden blades served only to play host for a variety of brown fungal blooms which thrived in the humidity. He doubted they would last much longer.

They wandered through the occupation station, capturing random images of the army reorganizing itself. Serjeant casualties lying in rows of cots in a field hospital. Engineers and mechanoids working on all types of equipment. The unending flow of trucks that trundled past, their hub engines humming angrily as they fought for traction in the mud.

'Hey, you two!' Elena Duncan shouted from across the road. 'What the hell are you doing?'

They crossed over to her, dodging a pair of jeeps. 'We're rovers,' Tim told her. 'Just looking round.'

Claws closed around his upper arm, preventing him from moving. He was pretty sure that if she wanted to she could have snipped clean through the bone. She touched a sensor block to his chest. Not gently, either.

'OK, now you.' Hugh submitted to the procedure without complaint.

'There aren't any rover reporters scheduled to come out here today,' Elena said. 'The Colonel hasn't even cleared Exnall yet.'

'I know,' Tim said. 'I just wanted to get ahead of the pack.'

'Typical,' Elena grunted. She retreated back into the hall where twenty bulky zero-tau pods had been set up. All of them had active infinite-black surfaces.

Tim followed her. 'This your department?'

'You got it, sonny. I get to perform the final act of liberation on these great people we're here to rescue. That's why I wanted to know who you were. You're not army, and you're too healthy to be ex-possessed. I got to recognize that, it's like second nature now.'

'Glad someone's alert.'

'Knock it off.' Her head rocked up and down as she examined them. 'If you want to ask questions, ask. I'm bored enough that I'll probably answer. You're here because this is Exnall, right?'

Tim grinned. 'Well, this is where it all started. That gives me a legitimate interest. Showing the accessors that it's been retaken and sanitized makes for a good piece.'

'Typical rover, put the story before anything else, like mundane security and common sense safety. I should have just shot you.'

'But you didn't. That means you've got confidence in the serjeants?'

'Could be. I know I couldn't do what they're doing. *Still* doing. Thought I could when I came here, but this whole Liberation is one big learning curve, for all of us, right? We just don't do war like this any more, if we ever did. Even if a conflict goes on for a couple of years, individual battles are supposed to be brutal and fast. Soldiers take a break from the front, have some R & R, grab some stims and some ass before they go back. One side makes a few gains, the other knocks them back. That's the way it goes, but this – it never stops, not for one second. Have you ever captured that in your sensevises? The real essence of what this is about? One serjeant loses concentration for one second, and one of those bastards will slip through. It'll start up all over again on another continent. One mistake. *One.* This isn't a human war. The weapon which is going to win this is perfection. The possessed? They have to commit to being a hundred per cent treacherous devious sons of bitches, never let up trying to sneak one of their kind past us. Our serjeants, now they have to be eternally vigilant, never ever walk along the wrong side of the road because the mud isn't so deep and vile there. You've got no idea what that takes.'

'Determination,' Tim ventured.

'Not even close. That's an emotion. That's a way in to your heart, weakening you. That can't be allowed here. Human motivations have to be abandoned. Machines are what we need.'

'I thought that's what the serjeants are.'

'Oh, yeah, they're good. Not bad at all for a first-generation weapon. But the Edenists have got to improve on them, build some real mean mothers for the next Liberation. Something like us boosted, and with even less personality than the serjeants. I've got to know a few of them, and they're still too human for this.'

'You think there's going to be another Liberation?'

'Sure. Nobody's come up with another method of kicking the bastards out of the bodies they've stolen. Until that happens, we've got to keep them on the run. I told you, show no weakness. Pick another planet, maybe one of those Capone infiltrated, and start rescuing it before they take it away. Let them know we'll never let up chasing their asses out of our universe.'

'Would you join that next Liberation?'

'Not a chance. I've done my bit, and learned my lesson. This is too long. You wanted a story about what Exnall was like, you came a day too late. We still had some of the possessed around yesterday, waiting for zero-tau. They're the ones you should have talked to.'

'What did they tell you?'

'That they hate the Liberation the same way we do. It's wearing them down, they haven't got enough food, the rain doesn't stop, the mud climbs into bed with them each night. And ever since Ketton took that Ekelund bitch away, their organized resistance folded in. Now it's just gone back to instinct, that's why they fight. They're losing it, because they're human. They came back here because they were determined to end their suffering, right? That's the ultimate human motivator. Anything to escape the beyond. But now they're here, where they thought they wanted to be, they've got all their old flaws back. As soon as they become human again, it becomes possible to beat them.'

944

'Until they take their whole planet out of the universe,' Tim protested.

'Fine by me. That removes them from interfering with us any more. A stalemate in this war means we have won. Our purpose is to prevent them from spreading.'

'But even the war isn't an end to this,' Hugh said. 'Have you forgotten you have a soul? That you will die one day?'

Elena's claws clacked irritably. 'No, I haven't forgotten. But right now I have a job to do. That's what matters, that's what's important. When I die, I'll confront the beyond fair and square. All this philosophizing and moralizing and agonizing we're doing, it's all bullshit. When it comes down to it, you're on your own.'

'Just like life,' Hugh said with a gentle smile.

Tim frowned at him. It was most unlike Hugh to offer any comment on death and the beyond; the one subject he (strangely) always avoided.

'You got it,' Elena boomed approvingly.

Tim said goodbye, and left her monitoring the zero-tau pods. 'Live death like you live life, huh?' he chided Hugh when they were far enough away to be outside the range of the mercenary's enhanced auditory senses.

'Something like that,' Hugh responded solemnly.

'Interesting person, our Elena,' Tim said. 'The interview will need some tight editing, though. She'll depress the hell out of anyone who hears her ranting on like that.'

'Perhaps you should let her speak. She's been exposed to the possessed for a long time. Whether she admits it or not, that's influenced her thinking. Don't slant that.'

'I do not slant my reports.'

'I've accessed your pieces, you dumb everything down for your audience. They're just a compilation of highlights.'

'Keeps them accessed, doesn't it? Have you seen our ratings?'

'There's more to news than marketing points. You have to include substance occasionally. It balances and emphasizes those highlights you worship.'

'Shit, how did you ever wind up in this business?'

'I was made for it,' Hugh said, which he apparently found hilarious.

Tim gave him a bewildered glance. Then his neural nanonics reported his communications block was receiving a priority call from the Fort Forward studio chief. It was the news that the Confederation Navy had attacked Arnstadt.

'Holy shit,' Tim muttered. All around him, marines and mercenaries were cheering and calling out to each other. Trucks and jeeps sounded their horns in continual blasts.

'That's not good,' Hugh said. 'They knew what the effect would be.'

'Damn it, yes,' Tim said. 'We've lost the story.'

'An entire planet snatched away to another realm, and all that concerns you is the story?'

'Don't you see?' Tim swept his arms round extravagantly, encompassing the occupation station in one gesture. 'This was *the* story, the only one, we were on the front line against the possessed. What we saw and said mattered. Now it doesn't. Just like that.' His neural nanonics astronomy program found him the section of dark azure sky where Avon's star shone unseen. He glared at it in frustration. 'Someone up there is changing Confederation policy, and I'm stuck down here. I can't find out why.'

*

Cochrane saw it first. Naturally, he called it Tinkerbell.

Not quite limber enough to stay in a full lotus position for hours on end, the hippy was sprawled bonelessly on a leather beanbag, facing the direction Ketton Island was flying in. With a Jack Daniel's in one hand and his purple sunglasses in place he possibly wasn't as alert as he should have been. But then, none of the other ten people sharing the top of the headland with him saw it.

They were, as McPhee complained later, looking out for something massive, a planet or a moon, or perhaps even Valisk. An object that would appear as a small dark patch amid the vanishing point glare, and slowly swell in size as the island drew closer.

The last thing anyone expected was a pebble-sized crystal with a splinter of sunlight entombed at its centre arrowing in out of the bright void ahead. But that's what they got.

'Holy mamma! Hey, you cats, look at this,' Cochrane whooped. He tried to point, sending Jack Daniel's sloshing across his flares.

The crystal was sliding over the cliff edge, its multifaceted surface stabbing out thin beams of pure white light in every direction. It swooped in towards Cochrane and his fellow watchers, keeping a level four metres off the ground. By then Cochrane was on his feet dancing and waving at it. 'Over here, man. We're here. Here, boy, come on, come to your big old buddy.'

The crystal curved tightly, circling over their heads to their gasps and excited shouts.

'*Yes!*' Cochrane yelled. 'It knows we're here. It's alive, gotta be, man; look at the way it's buzzing about, like some kind of inter-cosmic fairy.' Slivers of light from the crystal flashed across his sunglasses. 'Yoww, that's bright. Hey, Tinkerbell, tone it down, baby.'

Devlin stared at their visitor in absolute awe, a hand held in front of his face to shield him from the dazzling light. 'Is it an angel?'

'Naw,' Cochrane chortled. 'Too small. Angels are huge great mothers with flaming swords. Tinkerbell, that's who we've got here.' He cupped his hands round his mouth. 'Yo, Tinks, how's it hanging?'

Choma's dark, weighty hand tapped Cochrane's shoulder. The hippy flinched.

'I don't wish to be churlish,' the serjeant said. 'But I believe there are more appropriate methods with which to open communications with an unknown xenoc species.'

'Oh, yeah?' Cochrane sneered. 'Then how come you're already boring her away?'

The crystal changed direction, speeding away to fly over the main headland camp. Cochrane started running after it, yelling and waving.

Sinon, like every other serjeant on the island, had turned to look at the strange pursuit as soon as Choma informed them of the crystal's arrival. 'We have an encounter situation,' he announced to the humans around him.

Stephanie stared at the brilliant grain of crystal leading Cochrane a merry chase, and let out a small groan of dismay. They really shouldn't have let the old hippy join the forward watching group.

'What's happening?' Moyo asked.

'Some kind of flying xenoc,' she explained.

'Or probe,' Sinon said. 'We are attempting to communicate with affinity.'

The serjeants combined their mental voice into a collective hail. As well as clear ringing words of greeting, mathematical symbols, and pictographics, they produced a spectrum of pure emotional tones. None of it provoked any kind of discernible answer.

The crystal slowed again, drifting over the headland group. There were over sixty humans camping out together now; Stephanie's initial group had been joined by a steady stream of deserters from Ekelund's army. They'd broken away over the past week, sometimes in groups, sometimes individually, all of them rejecting her authority and growing intolerance. The word they brought from the old town wasn't good. Martial law was strictly enforced, turning the whole place into a virtual prison. At the moment, her efforts were focused on recovering as many rifles as possible from the ruins and mounds of loose soil. Apparently she still hadn't abandoned her plan to rid the island of serjeants and disloyal possessed.

Stephanie stood looking up at the twinkling crystal as it traced a meandering course overhead. Cochrane was still lumbering along thirty metres behind. His annoyed cries carried faintly through the air. 'Any reply yet?' she asked.

'None,' the serjeant told them.

People had risen to their feet, gawping at the tiny point of light. It seemed oblivious to all of them. Stephanie concentrated on the folds of iridescent shadow which her mind's senses were revealing. Human and serjeant minds glowed within it, easily recognizable; the crystal existed as a sharply defined teardrop-filigree of sapphire. It was almost like a computer graphic, a total contrast to everything else she could perceive this way. As it grew closer its composition jumped up to perfect clarity: in a dimension-defying twist the inner threads of sapphire were longer than its diameter.

She'd stopped being amazed by wonders since Ketton left Mortonridge. Now she was simply curious.

'That can't be natural,' she insisted.

Sinon spoke for the mini-Consensus of serjeants. 'We concur. Its behaviour and structure is indicative of a high-order entity.'

'I can't make out any kind of thoughts.'

'Not like ours. That is inevitable. It seems well adjusted to this realm. Commonality would therefore be unlikely.'

'You think it's a native?'

'If not an actual aboriginal, then something equivalent to their AI. It does seem to be self-determining, a good indicator of independence.'

'Or good programming,' Moyo said. 'Our reconnaissance drones would have this much awareness.'

'Another possibility,' Sinon agreed.

'None of that matters,' Stephanie said. 'It proves there's some kind of sentience here. We have to make contact and ask for help.'

'That's if they understand the concept,' Franklin said.

This speculation is irrelevant, Choma said. What it is does not matter, what it is capable of does. Communication has to be established.

It will not respond to any of our attempts, Sinon said. If it does not sense affinity or atmospheric compression then we have little chance of initiating contact.

Mimic it, Choma said. The mini-Consensus queried him.

It can obviously sense us, he explained. Therefore we must demonstrate we are equally aware of it. Once it knows this, it will logically begin seeking communication channels. The surest demonstration possible is to use our energistic power to assemble a simulacrum.

They focused their minds on a stone lying at Sinon's feet, fourteen thousand serjeants conceiving it as a small clear diamond with a flame of cold light burning bright at its centre. It rose into the air, shedding crumbs of mud as it went.

The original crystal swerved round and approached the illusion, orbiting it slowly. In response, the serjeants moved their crystal in a similar motion, the two of them describing an elaborate spiral over Sinon's head.

That attracted its attention, Choma said confidently.

Cochrane arrived, panting heavily. 'Hey, Tinks, slow down, babe.' He rested his hands on his upper thighs, glancing up with a crooked expression. 'What's going on here, man? Is she breeding?'

'We are attempting to open communications,' Sinon said.

'Yeah?' Cochrane reached up, his hand open. 'Easy, dude.'

'Don't . . .' Sinon and Stephanie said it simultaneously.

Cochrane's hand closed round Tinkerbell. And kept closing. His fingers and palm elongated as though the air had become a distorting mirror. They were drawn down into the crystal. He squawked in panicked astonishment as his wrist stretched out fluidly and began to follow his hand into the interior. 'Ho, shiiiiit—' His body was abruptly tugged along, feet leaving the ground.

Stephanie exerted her energistic power, trying to pull him back.

Insisting he return. She felt the serjeants adding their ability to hers. None of them could apply their desperate thoughts around the wailing hippy. His body's physical mass had become elusive, it was like trying to grip a rope of water.

The frantic yelling cut off as his head was sucked within the crystal's boundary. The torso and legs followed quickly.

'Cochrane!' Franklin yelled.

A pair of gold-rimmed sunglasses with purple lenses fell to the ground.

Stephanie couldn't even sense the hippy's thoughts any more. She waited numbly to see who would be devoured next. It was only a couple of metres from her.

The crystal sparkled with red and gold light for a moment, then reverted to pure white. It shot off at high velocity across the rumpled mudlands towards the town.

'It killed him,' she grunted in horror.

'Ate him,' Rana said.

Alternatively, it took a sample, Sinon said to his fellow serjeants. The shocked humans probably wouldn't want to hear quite such a clinical analysis.

It didn't select Cochrane, Choma said. He selected it. Or more likely, it was a simple defence mechanism.

I hope not. That would imply we have come to a hostile environment. I would prefer to consider it a sampling process.

The method of capture was extraordinary, Choma said. Is it some kind of crystalline neutronium, perhaps? Nothing else could suck him in like that.

We don't even know if gravity or solid matter exist in this realm, Sinon said. Besides, there was no energy emission. If his mass was being compressed by gravity, we would all have been obliterated by the radiation burst.

Then let us hope it was a sampling method.

Yes. Sinon conveyed a slight uncertainty with his thought. Shame it was Cochrane.

It could have been Ekelund.

Sinon watched the crystal slicing freely across the land. It had become a cometary streak. That may yet happen.

*

Annette Ekelund had established her new headquarters on top of the steep mound which used to be Ketton's Town Hall. Rectangular sections of various buildings had been salvaged from the ruins all around, and propped up against each other; energistic power modified them into heavy canvas tents printed with green and black jungle camouflage. Three of them contained the last remaining stocks of food. One served as an armoury and makeshift engineering shop where Milne and his team worked repairing the rifles which had been dug from the wet soil. The last, sitting right on the brow, was Annette's personal quarters and command post. She had the netting rolled up at both ends, giving her a good view out across the island's blotchy grey-brown land right to the scabrous edges. Maps and clipboards were strewn across the trestle table in the centre. Coloured pencils had marked out the army's defensive fortifications around Ketton, along with possible lines of attack based on scout reports of the terrain outside. Serjeant positions and estimated strengths were all indicated.

The information had taken days to compile. Right now Annette was paying it no heed; she was glaring at the captain who stood to attention in front of her. Hoi Son lounged back in his canvas chair at the side of the table, watching the scene with no attempt to hide his amusement.

'Five of the patrol refused to come back,' the captain said. 'They just kept on walking, said they were going to pitch in with the serjeants.'

'The enemy,' Annette corrected.

'Yes. The enemy. There were only three of us left after that. We couldn't force them back.'

'You are pathetic,' Annette told him angrily. 'How you were ever considered officer material I don't know. You don't just go with your men on walks around the perimeter, you're their leader, for Christ's sake. That means you know their vulnerabilities as well as their strengths. You should have seen this coming, especially now you can sense their raw emotional state. They should never have been allowed out to betray us like this. Your fault.'

The captain gave her a look of incredulous dismay. 'This is ridiculous. Everyone here is worried shitless. I could see that in them clear enough. There's no way of telling what they were going to do about it.'

'You should have known. You're on null rations for thirty-six hours, and demoted to corporal. Now get back to your division, you're a disgrace.'

'I dug up that food. I was in the shit up to my elbows for two days working for it. You can't do this. It's mine.'

'It will be in thirty-six hours. Not before.'

They stared at each other across the table. Sheets of paper stirred silently.

'Fine,' the ex-captain snapped. He stormed out.

Annette glared after him, furious at how slack everyone was becoming. Didn't any of them understand how critical these times were?

'Well handled,' Hoi Son said, his voice verging on a sneer.

'You think he should go unpunished? You wouldn't believe how fast things would unravel if I didn't enforce order.'

'Your society would unravel. Not individual lives.'

'You think another kind of society can survive here?'

'Let go, and see what evolves.'

'That's major bullshit, even by your standards.'

Hoi Son shrugged, unconcerned. 'I'd love to know where you think we're actually heading if not oblivion.'

'This realm offers us sanctuary.'

'Will you cut my ration if I make an observation?'

'It wouldn't make any difference. I know you. You have your own little stash somewhere, I'm sure.'

'I have learned prudence, I don't deny. What I suggest you consider is the possibility that the serjeants might be correct. This realm might offer us sanctuary if we were on a planet. However, this island does appear to be terribly finite.'

'It is, but the realm is not. We came here *instinctively*; we knew this was the one place where we would be safe. It can be Paradise, if we just believe in it. You've seen how our energistic power operates here. The effects take longer to form, but when they do the change is more profound.'

'Pity they can't slowly grow us some food, or even air. I'd probably settle for a little more land.'

'If that's what you think, why stay with me? Why not run away like all those weak fools?'

'You have the food secure, and there is no bush for me to hide in. Not even a single bush, in fact. Which pains me. This land is . . . not good. It has no spirit.'

'We can have what we want.' Annette was looking directly out of the open end of the tent at the sharp, close horizon. 'We can give the land its spirit back.'

'How?'

'By finishing what we started. By escaping. They're holding us back, you see.'

'The serjeants?'

'Yes.' She gave him a smile, content that he understood. 'This is the realm where our dreams come true. But their dreams are of rationality and physics, the old order. They are machines, soulless, they cannot understand what we can become here. They hold our winged thoughts back in cages of steel. Imagine it, Hoi, if we rid ourselves of their restraints. This island expanding, new land growing out from the cliff edges. Land that's covered in rich green life. We are a seed here, we can germinate into something wonderful. Heaven is what you make it, that's such a precious destiny, every human's entitlement. And we can see it. Out there, waiting for us. We've come so far, they cannot be allowed to contaminate our minds with their dark yearning to remain in the past.'

Hoi Son raised an eyebrow. 'A seed? That's how you see this island?'

'Yes. One that can bloom into whatever kingdom we want.'

'I doubt that. I really do. We are humans in stolen bodies, not embryonic godlings.'

'And yet we've already taken the first step.' She lifted her hands up in a theatrical offering to the sky. 'After all, we said there was to be light, didn't we?'

'I've read that book, but not many of my people did. How typically Euro-Christian, you think your origins and mythology populated the world. All you actually gave us was pollution, war, and disease.'

Annette grinned wolfishly. 'Come on, Hoi, show a little levity. Get radical again. This place can be made to work. Once we eliminate the serjeants we'll have a chance.' Her smile faded as she sensed the babble of confusion and surprise emanating from within the communal mind of the serjeants. Ever-present, it sat on the edge of her consciousness, a dawn refusing to rise. Now their cool thoughts were changing, coming as close to panic as she'd known. 'What's upset them?'

She and Hoi walked over to the end of the tent, and looked over at the dark mass of serjeants clustering in the foothills of Catmos Vale's lost walls.

'Well, they're not charging at us,' Hoi said. 'That's gratifying.'

'Something's wrong.' She brought up her field binoculars, and searched the serjeants' encampment, trying to spot any abnormality amid the large dark bodies. They were sitting calmly together as always. Then she realized every head was turned to face her. The binoculars came down, allowing her to frown back at them. 'I don't get this.'

'There, look.' Hoi was pointing at a bright spark rushing over the town's perimeter fortifications. The soldiers below it were shouting and gesticulating wildly as it soared imperviously overhead.

It hurtled towards the mound at the centre of town.

'Mine,' Annette said warmly. With her feet apart, she brought her hands together in a pistol grip. A squat black maser carbine materialized, blunt barrel lining up on the approaching crystal.

'I don't think that's a weapon,' Hoi said. He started to back away from Annette. 'It didn't come from the serjeants, they're as puzzled as us.'

'It doesn't have permission to enter my town.'

Hoi started to run. A slim flare of intense white fire spewed out of Annette's gun, darting towards the approaching crystal. It veered effortlessly aside, arcing over Hoi. He stumbled as the spires of light pirouetted around him.

Smoothly and methodically, Annette turned to follow the invader. She pulled back on the trigger again, flinging the most potent bolt of white fire she could muster. It had no effect. The crystal whipped round in a tight parabola above Hoi, and accelerated back the way it came.

The serjeants watched it return. This time it never even slowed down as it tore through the air above them. Once it was over the cliff it began to curve downwards. Devlin rushed up to the very edge and flung himself flat on the crusted mud, head just peeping over. The last he saw of it was a glimmer of light descending parallel to the crinkled cliff-face before disappearing underneath the antagonistic planes of fractured rock.

*

The traders hooted and clanked their way along Cricklade's drive in seven big lorries. Steam hissed energetically out of the iron stacks behind their cabs, while gleaming brass pistons spun the front wheels. They growled to a halt in front of the manor's broad steps, dripping oil on the gravel and wheezing steam from leaky couplings.

Luca came forward to greet them. As far as he could tell, the thoughts of the people riding in the cabs were amicable enough. He wasn't expecting trouble. Traders had visited Cricklade before, but never in a convoy this size; a group of ten estate workers were on close call, just in case.

The traders' leader climbed down out of the lead lorry, and introduced himself as Lionel. A short man with flowing blond hair tied back with a leather lace, wearing worn blue denim jeans and a round-neck sweater. Working clothes which were almost an extension of his forthright attitude. After a couple of minutes' conversation, sizing each other up, Luca invited him indoors.

Lionel settled appreciatively into the study's leather armchair, sipping at the Norfolk Tears Luca offered him. If he was concerned about the restrained, moody atmosphere grumbling around the manor, it never showed. 'Our main commodity this trip is fish,' he said. 'Mostly smoked, but we have some on ice as well. Apart from that, we're carrying vegetable and fruit seeds, fertilized chicken eggs, some fancy perfumes, a few power tools. We're trying to build a reputation for reliability, so if there's something you want we haven't got, we'll try to get hold of it for our next visit.'

'What are you looking for?' Luca asked as he sat down behind the broad desk.

'Flour, meat, some new tractor bearings, a power socket to recharge the lorries.' He raised his glass. 'A decent drink.' They grinned, and touched their glasses. Lionel's gaze lingered on Luca's hand for a moment. The contrast between their skin was subtle, but noticeable. Luca's was darker, thicker, with hair on top of his palm, a true guide to Grant's age; Lionel maintained an altogether more youthful sheen.

'What sort of exchange rate were you thinking of for the fish?' Luca asked.

'For flour, five to one, direct weight.'

'Don't bugger about wasting my time.'

'I'm not. Fish is meat, valuable protein. There's also carriage; Cricklade's a long way inland.'

'That's why we have sheep and cattle; we're exporting meat. But I can pay your carriage costs in electricity, we have our own heat shaft.'

'Our power cells are seventy per cent charged.'

The haggling went on for a good forty minutes. When Susannah came in she found them on their third round of Norfolk Tears. She sat on the side of Luca's chair, his arm around her waist. 'How's it going?' she asked.

'I hope you like fish,' Luca told her. 'We've just bought three tons of it.'

'Oh bloody hell.' She plucked the glass of Tears from his hand, and sipped thoughtfully. 'I suppose there's room in the freezer room. I'll have to have a word with Cook.'

'Lionel has some interesting news, as well.'

'Oh?' She gave the trader a pleasant, enquiring look.

Lionel smiled, covering a mild curiosity. Like Luca, Susannah was letting her host body's age show. The first middle-aged people he'd seen since Norfolk came to this realm. 'We got our fish from a ship in Holbeach, the *Cranborne*. They were docked there a week ago, trading their cargo for an engine repair. Should still be there.'

'Yes?' she asked.

'The *Cranborne* is a merchant multitramp,' Luca said. 'She just sails between islands picking up cargo and passengers, whatever pays; she can fish, dredge, harvest mintweed, icebreak, you name it.'

'Her current crew have rigged her with nets,' Lionel said. 'There's not much charter work going at the moment, so trawling has become their livelihood. They're also talking about trading between islands. Once things have settled down, they'll have a better idea of who produces what, and the kind of goods they can carry to exchange.'

'I'm happy for them,' Susannah said. 'Why tell me?'

'It's a way of getting to Norwich,' Luca said. 'A start, anyway.'

Susannah looked hard into his face, now falling back into Grant's familiar features. The relapse had been accelerating ever since he returned from his trip to Knossington with the news that the aeroambulance didn't work, its electronics simply couldn't operate in this realm. 'A voyage that far would be expensive,' she said quietly.

'Cricklade could afford it.'

'Yes,' she said carefully. 'It could. But it's not ours any more. If we take that much food or Tears or horses the others will claim we stole it. We wouldn't be able to come back, not to Kesteven.'

'We?'

'Yes, we. They're our children, and this is our home.'

'One means nothing without the other.'

'I don't know,' she said, deeply troubled. 'What's to make the *Cranborne* crew stick to the agreement once we cast off?'

'What's to stop us stealing their whole ship?' Luca replied wearily. 'We have a civilization again, darling. It's not the best, I know that. But it's here, and it works. At least we can see treachery and dishonesty coming a long way off.'

'All right. So do you want to go? It's not as if we haven't got enough troubles,' she said guiltily, flicking a glance at the diplomatically quiet Lionel.

'I don't know. I want to fight this; going means Grant has won.'

'It's not a battle, it's a matter of the heart.'

'Whose heart?' he whispered painfully.

'Excuse me,' Lionel said. 'Have you considered that the people possessing your daughters might not be exactly welcoming? What were you planning on doing anyway? It's not as if you can exorcize them and go walking off into a sunset. They'll be as alien to you as you are to them.'

'They're not alien to me,' Luca said. He sprang up from the chair, his whole body twitchy. '*Damn* it, I cannot stop worrying about them.'

'We're all succumbing to our hosts,' Lionel said. 'The easiest course is to acknowledge that, at least you'll have some peace then. Are you prepared to do that?'

'I don't know,' Luca ground out. 'I just don't.'

*

Carmitha ran her fingers along the woman's arm, probing the structure of bone and muscle and tendon. Her eyes were closed as she performed the examination, her mind concentrating on the swirl of foggy radiance that was the flesh. It wasn't just tactile feeling she relied on, cells formed distinct bands of shade, as if she was viewing a very out-of-focus medical text of the human body. Fingertips moved on two centimetres, she pushed each one in carefully, as if she were stroking piano keys. Searching an entire body this way took over an hour, and even then it was hardly a hundred per cent effective. Only the surface was inspected. There were a great many cancers which could affect the organs, glands, and marrow; subtle monsters that would go unnoticed until it was far, far too late.

Something moved sideways under her forefinger. She played with it, testing its motion. A hard node, as if a small stone was embedded below the skin. Her mind's vision perceived it as a white blur, sprouting a fringe of wispy tendrils that swam out into the surrounding tissue. 'Another one,' she said.

The woman's gasp was almost a sob. Carmitha had learned the hard way not to hide anything from her patients. Invariably, they knew of the spike of alarm in her own thoughts.

'I'm going to die,' the woman whimpered. 'All of us are dying, rotting away. It's our punishment for escaping the beyond.'

'Nonsense, these bodies are geneered, which makes them highly resistant to cancer. Once you stop aggravating it with energistic power it should sink into remission.' Her stock verbal placebo, repeated so many times in the days since Butterworth's collapse that she'd begun to believe it herself.

Carmitha continued the examination, moving past the elbow. It was just a formality now. The woman's thighs had been the worst; lumps like a cluster of walnuts where she'd driven away flab to give herself an adolescent glamour-queen's rump. Fear had broken the instinct and desire for sublime youthful splendour. The unnatural punishment of her cells would end. Maybe the tumours really would go into remission.

Luca came knocking on the side of the caravan just as Carmitha was finishing. She told him to stay outside, and waited until the woman had put her clothes back on.

'It'll be all right,' she said, and hugged her. 'You just have to be you now, and be strong.'

'Yes,' came the dismal answer.

It wasn't a time for lectures, Carmitha decided. Let her get over the shock first. Afterwards she could learn how to express her inner strength, fortifying herself. Carmitha's grandmother used to place a lot of emphasis on thinking yourself well. 'A weak mind lets in the germs.'

Luca carefully avoided meeting the woman's tearful eyes as she came down out of the caravan, standing sheepishly to one side.

'Another one?' he asked after she went into the manor.

'Yep,' Carmitha said. 'Mild case, this time.'

'Jolly good.'

'Not really. So far we've just seen the initial tumours develop. I'm just praying that your natural high resistance can keep them in check. If not, the next stage is metastasis, when the cancer cells start spreading through the body. Once that happens, it's over.' She just managed to keep her resentment in check; the landowners and town dwellers were descended from geneered colonists, the Romanies had shunned such things.

He shook his head, too stubborn to argue. 'How's Johan?'

'His weight's creeping back up, which is good. I've got him walking again, and given him some muscle-building exercises – also good. And he's abandoned his body illusions completely. But the tumours are still there. At the moment his body is still too weak to fight them. I'm hoping that if we can get his general health level up, then his natural defences will kick in.'

'Is he fit enough to help run the estate?'

'Don't even consider it. In a couple of weeks, I'll probably ask him to help in my herb garden. That's the most strenuous work therapy I'll allow.'

Nothing he did could hide the disappointment in his mind.

'Why?' she asked in suspicion. 'What did you want him to do that for? I thought the old estate was working smoothly. I can hardly notice the difference.'

'Just an option I'm considering, that's all.'

'An option? You're leaving?' The notion startled her.

'Thinking of it,' he said gruffly. 'Don't tell anyone.'

'I won't. But I don't understand, where will you go?'

'To find the girls.'

'Oh, Grant,' she laid her hand on his arm, instantly sympathetic. 'They'll be all right. Even if Louise got possessed, no soul is going to alter her appearance, she's too gorgeous.'

'I'm not Grant.' He glanced round the courtyard, twitchy and suspicious. 'Talk about having an inner demon, though. God, you must be loving this.'

'Oh, yeah, having a ball, me.'

'Sorry.'

'How many have you got?' she asked quietly.

There was a long pause before he answered. 'Some down my chest. Arms. Feet, for Christ's sake.' He grunted in disgust. 'I never imagined my feet to be anything different. Why are they there?'

Carmitha hated his genuine puzzlement; Grant's possessor was making her feel far too sympathetic towards him. 'There's no logic to these things.'

'Not many people know what's happening, not outside Cricklade. That trader fellow, Lionel: hasn't got a clue. I envy him that. But it won't last, people like Johan must be dropping like flies all across the planet. When everyone realizes, things are going to fall apart real fast. That's why I wanted to start the voyage soon. If we have a second wave of anarchy, I might never find where the girls are.'

'We should get some real doctors in to take a look at you. That white fire could be used to burn the tumours away. We've all got X-ray sight now. No reason why it couldn't. Maybe we don't even need to be that drastic, you can just wish the cells dead.'

'I don't know.'

'That's not like you, either of you. Don't just sit around on your arse, find out. Get a doctor in. Massage and tea won't help much in the long run, and that's all I can provide. You can't leave now, Luca, people accept you as the boss. Use what influence you've got to try and salvage this situation. Get them through this cancer scare.'

He let out a long reluctant sigh, then tilted his head, looking at her out of one eye. 'You still think the Confederation's coming to save you, don't you?'

'Absolutely.'

'They'll never find us. They've got two universes to search through.'

'Believe what you have to. I know what's going to happen.'

'Friendly enemies, huh? You and me?'

'Some things never change, no matter what.'

He was saved from trying to get in a cutting reply by a stable hand running out into the courtyard, yelling that a messenger was coming from the town. He and Carmitha went through the kitchen and out through the manor's main entrance.

A woman was riding a white horse up the drive. The pattern of thoughts locked inside her skull was familiar enough to both of them: Marcella Rye. Her horse's gallop was matched by the excitement and trepidation in her mind.

She came to a halt in front of the broad stone stairs leading up to the marble portico, and dismounted. Luca took the reins, doing his best to soothe the agitated beast.

'We've just had word from the villages along the railway,' she said. 'There's a bunch of marauders heading this way. Colsterworth Council respectfully requests, and all that bullshit. Luca, we need some help to see the bastards off. Apparently they're armed. Raided an old militia depot on the outskirts of Boston, got away with rifles and a dozen machine-guns.'

'Oh, this is fucking brilliant,' Luca said. 'Life here just keeps getting better and better.'

*

Luca studied the train through his binoculars (genuine ones, handed down to Grant by his father). He was sure it was the same one as before, but there had been changes. Four extra carriages had been added, not that anyone travelled in comfort. This was a dark iron battle wagon whose armour plates (genuine, Luca thought) ran along its entire length, riveted crudely around ordinary carriages. It clanked along the rail track towards Colsterworth at an unrelenting thirty miles an hour. Bruce Spanton had finally managed to turn the concept of an irresistible force into a physical entity, putting it down straight into Norfolk's Tureresque countryside where it didn't belong.

'There's more of them this time,' Luca said. 'I suppose we could roll the rails up again.'

'That monstrosity isn't built for reversing,' Marcella said grimly. 'You have to turn the minds around, their tails will follow.'

'Between their legs.'

'You got it.'

'Ten minutes till they get here. We'd better get people into position and dream up a strategy.' He'd brought nearly seventy estate workers with him from Cricklade. The announcement by

Colsterworth Council had resulted in over five hundred townsfolk volunteering to fight off the marauders. Another thirty or so had gathered from outlying farms, determined to protect the food they'd worked hard to gather. All of them had brought shotguns or hunting rifles from their adopted homes.

Luca and Marcella organized them into four groups. The largest, three hundred strong, were formed up in a horseshoe formation surrounding Colsterworth Station. Two outlying parties were hanging back from the cusps, ready to swarm across the rail and encircle the marauders. The remainder, three dozen on horseback (mostly from Cricklade), made up a cavalry force ready to chase down anyone who escaped from the attack.

They spent the last few minutes walking along the ranks, getting them into order, and making sure they had all hardened their clothes into bullet-proof armour. Real gunshots were harder to ward off in this realm. Carbosilicon-reinforced flak jackets were the popular solution, making the front line take on the appearance of a police riot brigade from the mid-twenty-first century.

'It's our right to exist as we choose that we're standing for,' Luca told them repeatedly as he walked along, inspecting his troops. 'We're the ones who've made something of these circumstances, built a decent life for ourselves. I'll be buggered if I'm going to let this rabble wreck that. They cannot be allowed to live off us, that makes us nothing more than chattels.'

Everywhere he went, he received murmurs and nods of agreement. The defenders' resolution and confidence expanded, building into a physical aura which began to tint the air with a hearty red translucence. When he took up position with Marcella they simply grinned at each other, relishing the fight. The train was only a mile out of town now, coming round the last bend onto the straight leading to the station. It tooted its whistle in an angry defiant blast. The red haze over the station glowed brighter. A crack split open along the middle of the wooden sleepers, starting five yards from Luca's feet and extending out past the end of the platforms. It opened barely six inches, and halted, quivering in anticipation. Granite chippings trickled over the edges, to be swallowed silently by the abyssal darkness which had been uncovered.

Luca stared directly at the front of the train, facing down its protruding cannon barrels. 'Just keep coming, arsehole,' he said quietly.

Subtlety simply wasn't an option. Each side knew roughly the strengths and position of the other. It could never be anything other than a direct head-to-head confrontation. A contest of energistic strength and imagination, with the real guns an unwelcome sideshow.

Half a mile from the station, and the train slowed slightly. The rear two carriages detached, and braked to a halt amid fantails of orange sparks from their locked wheels. Their sides hinged down to form ramps, and jeeps raced down onto the ground. They'd been configured into armour-plated dune buggies with thick roll bars; huge deep-tread tyres were powered from four-litre petrol engines that spurted filthy exhaust fumes out into the air with a brazen roar. Each one had a machine-gun mounted above the driver, operated by a gunner dressed in a leather jacket with flying goggles and helmet.

They sped away from the carriages in an attempt to outflank the townie defenders. Luca gave a signal to his own cavalry. They charged out into the fields, heading to intercept the jeeps. The train kept thundering onwards.

'Get ready,' Marcella shouted.

Puffs of white smoke shot out from the train's cannon. Luca ducked down in reflex, hardening the air around himself. Shells started to explode at the end of the station, thick plumes of earth smearing the blank skyline amid bursts of orange light. Two struck the fringe of red air, detonating harmlessly twenty yards above the ground. Shrapnel flew away from the protective boundary. A cheer rang out from the defenders.

'We got 'em,' Luca growled triumphantly.

Machine-gun fire rattled across the fields as the jeeps raced round in tight curves, churning up furrows of mud. They drove straight through gates, bursting the timber bars apart with a flash of white light. Horses cantered after them, jumping the hedges and walls effortlessly. Their riders were shooting from the saddle, as well as flinging bolts of white fire. The jeep engines started to cough and stutter as fluxes of energistic power played hell with the power cells encased deep within the semisolid illusion.

The train was only a quarter of a mile away now. Its cannon were still firing continuously. The land beyond the end of the station was taking the full brunt of the impact: craters erupted continuously, sending soil, grass, trees, and stone walls ploughing through the air. Luca was surprised at the diminutive size of the craters, he'd expected the shells to be more powerful. They did produce a lot of smoke, though, thick grey-blue clouds churning frenetically against the sheltering bubble of redness. They almost obscured the train from view.

Luca frowned suspiciously at that. 'They could be a cover,' he shouted at Marcella above the bass thunder of exploding shells.

'No way,' she yelled back. 'We can sense them, remember. Smoke screens don't work here.'

Something was wrong, and Luca knew it. When he switched his attention back to the train, he could sense the note of triumph emanating from it, just as strong as his own. Yet nothing the marauders had done assured them of victory. Nothing he could perceive.

Layers of smoke from the shells were creeping sluggishly towards the station. As they slithered through the edge of the red light they gleamed with a dark claret phosphorescence. People in the reserve groups clustered outside the platforms were reacting strangely as the first wisps curled and flexed around them. Waving their hands in front of their faces as if warding off a mulish wasp, they began to stagger around. Ripples of panic raced out from their minds, impinging against those close by.

'What's happening to them?' Marcella demanded.

'Not sure.' Luca watched the slow spread of the crimson smoke. Its behaviour was perfectly natural, fronds undulating and twisting about on the currents of air. Nothing directed it, no malicious energistic pressure, yet wherever it spread chaos ensued. He took time to make the appalling connection; even telling himself Spanton would delve as low as it was possible to go, he found it hard to credit such depravity.

'Gas,' he said, dumbfounded. 'That's not smoke. The bastard's using gas!'

Machine-guns and rifles opened fire from every slot cut into the train's armoured sides. With the defenders distracted, bullets were able to slice nonchalantly through the rosy air. The front rank of townsfolk were punched backwards as bullets hammered into their flak jackets. Abruptly, there was no more pink air. The human survival instinct was too strong, everyone concentrated on saving themselves.

'Blow it back at them!' Luca bellowed across the commotion. The train was only a few hundred yards away now, pistons growling furiously as it slid remorselessly along the track towards him. He flung his hands out, and shoved at the air.

Marcella followed suit. 'Do it,' she shouted at the closest townsfolk. 'Push!'

They began to imitate her, sending out a stream of energistic power to repel the air and with it the deadly gas. The idea spread fast among the defenders, becoming real as soon as it was thought of. They didn't need to act, only to think.

Air began to move, groaning over the station walls as it sped above the rails, its speed increasing steadily. The pillars of smoke began to bend away from their craters, breaking into tufts which slid away towards the approaching train. Leaves and twigs from the hedges were picked up and carried along by the wind. They broke harmlessly against the black iron prow of the train, fluffing round it in an agitated slipstream.

Luca yelled in wordless exultation, adding the air from his lungs to the torrent surging past his body. It had risen to gale force, pushing at him. He linked arms with his neighbours, and together they rooted themselves in the ground. Unity of purpose had returned, bringing them an unchallenged mastery of the air. Now the flow had begun, they started to shape it, narrowing its force to howl vengefully against the train. Hanging baskets along the platforms swung up parallel to the ground, tugging frantically at their brackets.

The train slowed, braked by the awesome force of the horizontal tornado hurled against it. Steam from its stack and leaky junctions was ripped away to join the hurtling streamers of lethal gas. The marauders couldn't keep their rifles steady; the wind tore at them, twisting and shaking until they threatened to wrench free. Cannon barrels were pushed out of alignment. They'd already stopped firing.

All of the defenders were contributing their will to the raging wind now; directing it square against the train and bringing it to a shuddering halt a hundred yards from the station. Then they upped the force, adrenalin glee providing further inspiration. The iron beast rocked, the weight of its thick cladding counting for nothing.

'We can do it,' Luca cried, his words ripped away by the supernatural wind. 'Keep going.' It was a prospect shared by all, encouraged by the first creaking motion of the great engine's frame.

The marauders inside turned their own energistic power to anchoring themselves. They didn't have the numbers to win any trial of strength.

Lumps of granite from the rail track collided against the train. The rails themselves were torn up to smash against the engine, wrapping themselves around the boiler. Sleepers impaled themselves through the sides of the carriages.

One set of wheels along the side of the engine left the ground. For a moment the machine hung poised on the remaining wheels as those inside strove to counter the toppling motion. But the defending townsfolk refused to forgo the maelstrom they'd created, and the metal bogies buckled. The engine crashed onto its side, twisting the carriage directly behind it through ninety degrees.

If it had been a natural derailment, that would have been the end of it. In this case, the townsfolk kept on pushing. The engine flipped again, pointing its crushed bogies directly into the sky. Vicious jets of steam poured out of the broken pistons, only to be dissolved by the gale. Again the engine turned as the hurricane clawed at its black flanks, trawling the remaining carriages along. Its momentum was picking up now, turning the motion into a continuous roll. The links between the carriages snapped apart. They scattered across the fields, bulldozing through any trees that got in their way, and skidding down into ditches where they came to a jarring halt.

The engine just kept on rolling, impelled by the wind and thoughts of its intended victims. Eventually, the boiler broke open, severing the big machine's spine. A cloud of steam exploded out from the huge rent, vanishing quickly into the caterwauling sky to be replaced by an avalanche of debris. Fragments of very modern-looking machinery tumbled down over the ruined land. All illusion of the steam-powered colossus had expired, leaving one of the Norfolk Railway Company's ordinary eight-wheel tractor units buried in the soil.

With the wind stilled, Luca left Marcella to organize medic parties for the defenders who'd succumbed to the gas. Even now, a dangerous chemical stink prowled around the shell craters. Those who claimed knowledge of such matters said it could be a type of phosphor, or possibly chlorine, maybe something even worse. The names they gave it didn't bother Luca, only the intent behind it. He walked along the row of casualties, grimacing at the protruding eyes that wept tears of salty water and blood in equal quantities; tried to speak reassuring words over the terrible hacking coughs.

After that, there could be no doubt what had to be done.

He gathered a small band of estate workers to accompany him. Remembering his first encounter with Spanton, he headed over the fields to the wrecked engine.

Metal sheets of some kind had indeed been welded over the tractor unit's body. Not iron after all, just some lightweight construction material; a framework easily moulded into thick armour in the mind of the beholder. They'd suffered considerably from the sheer brutality of the wind. Some of the cannon barrels had broken off, while the remainder were mangled. The main body of the unit had bent itself into a lazy V, with the forward end wedged down into the ground.

Luca walked round to the cab. It had crumpled badly, sides bowing inwards and roof concave, reducing the space inside to less than that of a wardrobe. He crouched down, and peered through the crooked window slit.

Bruce Spanton stared back at him. His body was trapped between various chunks of metal and warped piping that had sprung from the walls. Blood from his crushed legs and arm mingled with oil and muddy soil. His face was the pale grey of shock victims, with different features than before. The wraparound sunglasses had been discarded along with the swept-back hair; no illusion remained.

'Thank Christ,' he gasped. 'Get me outta here, man. It's all I can do to stop my fucking legs from dropping off.'

'I thought I'd find you in here,' Luca replied equitably.

'So you found me. So I'll give you a fucking medal. Just get me out. These walls all got smashed to shit in the rumble. It hurts so bad I can't even switch off the pain like usual.'

'A rumble? Is that what this was?'

'What are you trying to pull!' Spanton screamed. He stopped, grimacing wildly from the pain which his outburst triggered. 'All right, OK. You won. You're the king of the hill. Now bend some of this metal away.'

'That's it?'

'That's *what*?'

'We won, you lose. It's over?'

'What do you fucking think, dickhead?'

'Ah. I get it. You walk off into the sunset and never come back. That's it. The end. No hard feelings. Everything turned out OK, and you'll just slaughter some other bunch of people with poison gas. Maybe a smaller town, who won't be able to fight back. Well, great. Absolutely fabulous. That's why I came out to help this town. So you could have your rumble and turn your back on us.'

'What do you fucking want?'

'I want to live. I want to be able to look out at the end of the day and see what I've accomplished. I want my family to benefit from that. I want them to be safe. I don't want to have them worry about insane megalomaniacs who think being tough entitles them to live off the backs of ordinary decent working people.' He smiled down at Spanton's stricken face. 'Am I ringing any bells here? Do you see yourself in any of that?'

'I'll go. OK? We'll get off this island. You can put us on a ship, make sure we really leave.'

'It's not where you are that's the problem. It's what you are.' Luca straightened up.

'What? That's it? Get me out of here, you shit.' He started thumping the walls with a fist.

'I don't think so.'

'You think I'm a problem now, you don't even know what a problem is, asshole. I'll show you what a real goddam motherfucking problem is.'

'That's what I thought.' Luca swung his pump-action shotgun round until the muzzle was six inches from Spanton's forehead. He kept firing until the man's head was blown off.

Bruce Spanton's soul slithered up out of his bloody corpse along with the body's true soul; an insubstantial wraith rising like lethargic smoke out of the train's wreckage. Luca looked straight into translucent eyes that suddenly realized actual death was occurring after centuries of wasted half-existence. He held that gaze, acknowledging his own guilt as the writhing spectre slowly faded from sight and being. It took mere seconds; a period which compressed a lifetime of bitter fear and aching resentment into its length.

Luca stood shivering from the profound impact of knowledge and emotion. I did what I had to do, he told himself. Spanton had to be stopped. To do nothing would be to destroy myself.

The estate workers were watching him cautiously, their thoughts subdued as they waited to see what he did next.

'Let's go round up the rest of them,' Luca said. 'Especially that bastard chemist.' He started walking towards the nearest carriage, thumbing new cartridges into the pump-action's empty magazine.

The others began to trail after him, holding their weapons tighter than before.

*

Cricklade hadn't known screams like it since the day Quinn Dexter arrived. A high-pitched note of uniquely female agony coming from an open window overlooking the courtyard. The becalmed air of a bright early autumn day helped carry the sound a long way over the manor's steep rooftops, agitating the stabled horses, and causing men to flinch guiltily.

Véronique's waters had broken in the early hours the day after Luca had led his band of estate workers away to help fight the marauders. Carmitha had been with her since daybreak, closeted away in one of the west wing's fancy bedroom suites. She suspected the room might even have belonged to Louise; it was grand enough, with a large bed as the central feature, though not big enough to qualify as a double (that would never do for a single landowner girl). Not that Louise would want it now.

Véronique was propped up on the middle of the mattress, with Cook dabbing away at her straining face with a small towel. Other than that, it was all down to Véronique and Carmitha. And the baby, who was reluctant to put in a fast appearance.

At least Carmitha's new-found sense allowed her to see that it was the right way round for the birth, and the umbilical cord hadn't got wrapped round its neck. Nor were there any other obvious complications. Basically, that just left her to look, sound, and radiate assured confidence. She had after all assisted with a dozen natural childbirths, which was a great comfort to everyone else involved.

Somehow, what with the way Véronique looked up to her as a cross between her long-lost mother and a fully qualified gynaecologist, she'd never actually mentioned that assistance involved handing over towels when told and mopping up for the real midwife.

'I can see the head,' Carmitha said excitedly. 'Just trust me now.'

Véronique screamed again, trailing off into an angry whimper. Carmitha placed her hands over the girl's swollen belly, and exerted her energistic power, pushing with the contractions. Véronique kept on screaming as the baby emerged. Then she broke into tears.

It happened a lot quicker than usual thanks to the energistic pressure. Carmitha caught hold of the infant and eased gently, making the last moments more bearable for the exhausted girl. Then it was the usual fast panic routine of getting the umbilical cut and tied. Véronique sobbing delightedly. People moving in with towels and smiles of congratulations. Having to wipe the baby off. Delivering the placenta. Endless mopping up.

New to this was applying some energistic power to repair the small tears in Véronique's vaginal walls. Not too much, Carmitha was still worried about the long-term effects which even mild healing might trigger. But it did abolish the need for stitches.

By the time Carmitha finally finished tidying up, Véronique was lying on clean sheets, cradling her baby daughter with a classic aura of exhausted happiness. And a smooth mind.

Carmitha studied her silently for a moment. There was none of the internal anguish caused by a possessing soul riding roughshod over the host. Sometime during the pain and blood and joy, two had become one, merging at every level in celebration of new life.

Véronique smiled shyly upwards at Carmitha. 'Isn't she wonderful?' she entreated of the drowsy baby. 'Thank you so much.'

Carmitha sat on the edge of the bed. It was impossible not to smile down at the wrinkled-up face, so innocent of its brand new surroundings. 'She's lovely. What are you going to call her?'

'Jeanette. Both our families have had that name in it.'

'I see. That's good.' Carmitha kissed the baby's brow. 'You two get some rest now. I'll pop by in an hour or so to check up on you.'

She walked through the manor out into the courtyard. Dozens of people stopped her on the way; asking how it had gone, were mother and child all right? She felt happy to be dispensing good news for once, helping to lift some of the worry and tension that was stifling Cricklade.

Luca found her sitting in the open doorway at the back of her caravan, taking long drags from a reefer. He leant against the rear wheel and folded his arms to look at her. She offered him the joint.

'No thanks,' he said. 'I didn't know you did that.'

'Just for the occasional celebration. There's not much weed about on Norfolk. We have to be careful where we plant it. You landowners get very uptight about other people's vices.'

'I'm not going to argue with you. I hear the baby arrived.'

'She did, yes, she's gorgeous. And so is Véronique, now.'

'Now?'

'She and Olive kissed and made up. They're one now. One person. I guess that's the way the future's going for all of you.'

'Ha!' Luca grunted bitterly. 'You're wrong there, girl. I killed people today. Butterworth's right to fear his health. Once your body goes in this realm, you go with it. There's no ghosts, no spirits, no immortality. Just death. We screwed up – lost our one chance to go where we wanted, and we didn't go there.'

Carmitha exhaled a long stream of sweet smoke. 'I think you did.'

'Don't talk crap, my girl.'

'You're back where we thought the human race started from. What exists here is all we had before people began inventing things and making electricity. It's the kind of finite world humans feel safe in. Magic exists here, though it's not good for much. Very few machines work, nothing complicated, and certainly no electronics. And death ... death is real. Hell, we've even got gods on the other side of the sky again; gods with powers beyond anything possible here, made in our own image. In a couple of generations, we'll only have rumours of gods. Legends that tell how this world was made, racing out of the black emptiness in a blaze of red fire. What's that if it's not a new beginning in a land of innocence? This place isn't for you, it never was. You've reinvented the biological imperative, and made it mean something this time. All that you are must carry on through your children. Every moment has to be lived to the full, for you'll get no more.' She took another drag, the end of the joint glowing bright tangerine. Small sparks were reflected in her gleeful eyes. 'I rather like that, don't you?'

*

Stephanie's bullet wound had healed enough to let her walk round the headland camp; she and Moyo and Sinon made the circuit twice a day. Their small secluded refuge had grown in a chaotic manner as the deserters from Ekelund's army dribbled in. Now, it sprawled like an avalanche of sleeping bags away from the cliff edge. The new people tended to stay in small groups, huddling together round the pile of whatever items they'd brought with them. The only rule the serjeants had about extending sanctuary from Ekelund was that they hand over their real weapons once they arrived. Nobody had objected enough to return.

As she circled round the knots of subdued people, Stephanie picked up enough fragments of conversation to guess what awaited any deserter foolish enough to venture back. Ekelund's paranoia was growing at a worrying rate. And Tinkerbell's appearance hadn't helped. Apparently, the crystal entity had been shot at. That was the reason for it fleeing away into the empty glare.

As if they didn't have enough to worry about with their current predicament, there was now the prospect Ekelund had started a war.

'I miss him, too,' Moyo said sympathetically. He squeezed Stephanie's hand in an attempt at reassurance.

She smiled faintly, thankful he'd picked up on her melancholic thoughts. 'A couple of days without him, and we're all going to pieces.' She paused to take a breath. Perhaps her recovery wasn't as advanced as she liked to imagine. 'Let's go back,' she said. These little walks had started out to give the newcomers some sense of identity, that they were all part of a big new family. She was the one they'd come to, and she wanted to show she was available to them if they needed it. Most of them recognized her as she walked past. But there were so many now that they had their own identity, and it was the serjeants who guaranteed their safety. Her role had diminished to nothing. *And God forbid I should try to manufacture my own importance like Ekelund.*

The three of them turned and headed back to the little encampment where their friends kept a vigil over Tina. A little way beyond it, the serjeants formed a line of watchers strung out along the top of the cliff, searching for any sign of Tinkerbell. They covered almost a fifth of the rim now, and Sinon told her their mini-Consensus was considering stationing them all the way round the island. When she'd asked if Ekelund might consider that a threatening move, the big bitek construct merely shrugged. 'Some things are considerably more important than placating her neuroses,' he'd said.

'Quick inspection tour,' Franklin remarked as they returned.

Stephanie guided Moyo to a comfortable sitting position a couple of metres from Tina's makeshift bed, and sprawled on a blanket beside him. 'I'm not exactly an inspiring sight any more.'

'Of course you are, darling,' Tina said.

Everyone had to strain to hear her. She was in a bad way now. The serjeants, Stephanie knew, had basically given up and were just making what they considered her last days as comfortable as possible. Even though Rana rarely even let go of her friend's hand, she didn't exert any energistic power other than a general wish for Tina to mend. Active interference with the woman's crushed organs would probably only make things worse. Tina didn't have the will-power to maintain any form of body illusion any more. Her dangerously pale skin was visible for anyone to see as she laboured for air. The stopgap intravenous tube was still feeding fluid into her arm, though her body seemed determined to sweat it out at a faster rate.

They all knew it wouldn't be long now.

Stephanie was furious with herself for wondering what would happen. Whether Tina's soul would migrate back to the beyond, or be trapped here; or whether she'd simply and finally die. A legitimate enough interest given their situation. But Stephanie was sure Tina would pick up the pulse of guilt in her mind.

'We're still attracting Ekelund's discards,' she said. 'At this rate everyone will be camping here with us in another week.'

'What week?' McPhee grumbled softly. 'Can you no feel the air fouling?'

'The carbon dioxide level is not detectable at this moment,' Choma said.

'Oh? And what are you lot doing to help right now?' McPhee indicated the line of stationary serjeants standing along the cliff. 'Other than making that madwoman more paranoid?'

'Our efforts continue,' Sinon said. 'We are still trying to formulate a method of opening a wormhole, and our observation role has been increased.'

'Putting our hopes on a bloody fairy! This place must be making us all soft in the head.'

'That term is a misnomer, though a perfectly understandable one for Cochrane to make.'

'I guess that means you still haven't figured out what it was,' Moyo said.

'Unfortunately not. Though the fact that some kind of intelligence exists here is an encouraging development.'

'If you say so.' He turned away.

Stephanie snuggled up closer to Moyo, enjoying the reflex way his arm went round her shoulders. Being together made the awful wait a tiny bit more tolerable. She just couldn't work out what she wanted to happen first. Though they'd not spoken of it, the serjeants would probably try to open a wormhole back to Mortonridge. As a possessed, it would hardly be a rescue for her. Perhaps staying here until the carbon dioxide built to a lethal level was preferable.

She flicked another guilty glance at Tina.

Three hours later, the wait ended. This time the serjeants saw it coming. A riot of tiny dazzling crystals swooped out around the base of the flying island to rush up vertically. They erupted over the top of the cliff like a silent white firestorm. Thousands of them curved in midair and cascaded downwards to spread out above the headland camp, slowing to hover just over the heads of the astounded humans and serjeants.

The light level was quadrupled, forcing Stephanie to shield her hand with her eyes. Not that it did much to protect her from the vivid scintillations. Even the drab ground was sparkling.

'Now what?' she asked Sinon.

The serjeant watched the swirl of crystals drifting idly, sharing what he saw with the others. There was no real pattern to their movement. 'I have no idea.'

They are watching us as we watch them, Choma said. **They have to be probes of some kind.**

It is likely, Sinon said.

Something is coming, the serjeants along the cliff warned. A disc of raw light was expanding out from underneath the island. Not that it could have been hidden there, it was well over a hundred kilometres in diameter. The emergence effect was similar to an Adamist starship's ZTT jump, but much, much slower.

Once it had finished distending, it began to rise up parallel to the cliff. A cold, brilliant sun sliding over the horizon to fill a third of the sky. It wasn't a solid sphere, snowflake geometries fluctuated behind the overpowering glare.

The small crystals parted smoothly, racing away over the landscape, leaving nothing between the headland camp and the massive visitor. Fountains of iridescence erupted deep inside it, mushrooming open against the prismatic surface. Streaks and speckles shimmered and danced around each other, striving for order within the huge blemish.

It was the sheer size of the image they melded into which defeated Stephanie for some time. Her eyes simply couldn't accept what she was seeing.

Cochrane's face, thirty kilometres high, smiled down at them.

'Hi, guys,' he said. 'Guess what I found.'

Stephanie started laughing. She used the back of her hand to smear tears across her cheeks.

The crystal sphere drifted in towards Ketton Island, dimming slightly as it came. When it was a few metres from the cliff, a tiny circular section darkened completely and receded inside in a swift fluid motion.

At Cochrane's urging, Stephanie and her friends, along with Sinon and Choma, stepped through the opening. The tubular tunnel had smooth walls of clear crystal, with thin green planes bisecting the bulk of the material around it. After a hundred metres it opened out into a broad lenticular cavern a kilometre wide. Here, the long fractures of light beneath their feet glimmered crimson, copper, and azure, intersecting in a continual filigree that melted away into the interior. There was no sign of the fearsome light emitted by the outer shell, yet they could see out. Ketton Island was clearly visible behind them, distorted by the compacted facets of crystal.

One of the red sheets of light fissuring the cavern wall began to enlarge, the crystal conducting it withdrawing silently. Cochrane walked out of the opening, grinning wildly. He whooped, and rushed over to his friends. Stephanie was crushed in his embrace.

'Man! It is good to see you again, babe.'

'You, too,' she whispered back.

He went round the rest of the group, greeting them exuberantly; even the serjeants got high-fives.

'Cochrane, what the hell is this thing?' Moyo asked.

'Don't you recognize her?' the hippy asked in mock surprise. 'This is Tinkerbell, dude. Mind you, she inverted, or something like that, since you saw us last.'

'Inverted?' Sinon asked. He was gazing round the chamber, sharing his sight with the serjeants outside.

'Her physical dimension, yeah. There's a whole load of real groovy aspects to her which I don't really dig. I think, if she wants, she can get a lot bigger than this. Cosmic thought, right?'

'But what is she?' Moyo asked impatiently.

'Ah.' Cochrane gestured round uncertainly. 'The information has been kinda flowing mostly one way. But she can help us. I think.'

'Tina's dying,' Stephanie said abruptly. 'Can anything be done to heal her?'

Cochrane's bells tinkled quietly as he shuffled about. 'Well, sure, man, no need to shout. I'm awake to what's going down.'

'The smaller crystals are gathering around Tina,' Sinon reported, looking at what he could see through the serjeants tending the invalid. 'They appear to be encasing her.'

'Can we talk to this Tinkerbell directly?' Choma asked.

'You may,' a clear directionless female voice said.

'Thank you,' the serjeant said sombrely. 'What are you called?'

'I have been named Tinkerbell, in your language.'

Cochrane twisted under the stares directed at him. 'What?'

'Very well,' Choma said. 'Tinkerbell, we'd like to know what you are, please.'

'The closest analogy would be that I have a personality like an Edenist habitat multiplicity. I have many divisions; I am singular as I am manifold.'

'Are the small crystals outside segments of yourself?'

'No. They are other members of my race. Their physical dynamic is in a different phase from mine, as Cochrane explained.'

'Did Cochrane explain to you how we got here?'

'I assimilated his memories. It has been a long time since I encountered an organic being, but no damage was incurred to his neural structure during the reading procedure.'

'How could you tell?' Rana muttered. Cochrane gave her a thumbs-up.

'Then you understand our predicament,' Stephanie said. 'Is there a way back to our universe?'

'I can open a gateway back to it for you, yes.'

'Oh, God.' She sagged against Moyo, overwhelmed with relief.

'However, I believe you should resolve your conflict first. Before we began our existence in this realm, we were biological. Our race began as yours; it is a commonality which permits me to appreciate the ethics and jurisprudence that you observe at your current level of evolution. The dominant consciousness have stolen these bodies. That is wrong.'

'So's the beyond,' McPhee shouted. 'You'll no make me go back there without a fight.'

'That will not be necessary,' Tinkerbell said. 'I can provide you with several options.'

'You said you used to be biological beings,' Sinon said. 'Will we all evolve into your current form in this realm?'

'No. There is no evolution here. We chose to transfer ourselves here a long time ago. This form was specifically engineered to sustain our consciousness in conjunction with the energy pattern which is the soul. We are complete and essentially immortal now.'

'Then we were right,' Moyo said. 'This realm is a kind of heaven.'

'Not in the human classical religious sense,' Tinkerbell said. 'There are no city kingdoms with divine creatures tending them, nor even levels of ecstasy and awareness for your souls to rise through. In fact, this realm is quite hostile to naked souls. The energy pattern dissipates rapidly. You are capable of dying here.'

'But we wanted a refuge,' McPhee insisted. 'That's what we imagined when we forced the way open to come here.'

'A wish granted in essence if not substance. Had you arrived with an entire planet to live on, then its atmosphere and biosphere would sustain you for thousands of generations; at least as long as it would orbiting a star. This realm is about stability and longevity. That's why we came here. But we were prepared for our new life. Unfortunately, you came here on a barren lump of rock.'

'You speak of change,' Sinon said. 'And you know of souls. Is your kind of existence the answer to our problem? Should our race learn how to transform itself into an entity like you?'

'It is an answer, certainly. Whether you would be ready to sacrifice what you have to achieve our actuality, I would doubt. You are a young species, with a great deal of potential ahead of you. We were not. We were old and stagnant; we still are. The universe of our birth holds no mysteries to us. We know its origin and its destination. That is why we came here. This realm is harmonious to us, it has our tempo. We will wait out our existence here, observing what comes our way. That is our nature. Other races and cultures would take the path to decadence or transcendence. I wonder which you will select when it is your time?'

'I like to think transcendence,' Sinon said. 'But as you say, we are a younger, less mature race than you. Dreaming of such a destiny is inevitable for us, I suggest.'

'I concede the point.'

'Can you tell us of a valid answer to the problem of possession we currently face, how do we send our souls safely through the beyond?'

'Unfortunately, the Kiint were correct to tell you such a resolution must come from within.'

'Do all races who have resolved the question of souls apply this kind of moral superiority in their dealings with inferior species?'

'You are not inferior, merely different.'

'Then what are our options?' Stephanie asked.

'You can die,' Tinkerbell said. 'I know you have all expressed a wish for that. I can make it happen. I can remove your soul from the body it possesses, which will allow this realm's nature to take its course. Your host will be restored, and can return to Mortonridge.'

'Not too appealing,' she said shakily. 'Anything else?'

'Your soul would be welcome to join me in this vessel. You would become part of my multiplicity.'

'If you can do that, then just give each of us our own vessel.'

'While we are effectively omnipotent within this realm, that ability is beyond us. The instrument which brought us here, and assembled our current vessels, was left behind in your universe long ago. We had no further use for it, so we thought.'

'Can't you go back?'

'Theoretically, yes. But intent is another thing. And we don't know if the instrument still exists. Moreover, you would probably be unable to adapt to such a vessel by yourself, our psychology is different.'

'None of those are very attractive,' she said.

'To you,' Choma interjected quickly. 'To most of the serjeants, transferring ourselves into a new style of multiplicity is very attractive.'

'Which opens up a further option,' Tinkerbell said. 'I can also transfer your souls into the empty serjeant bodies.'

'That's better,' Stephanie said. 'But if we go back, even in serjeant bodies, we'll still wind up in the beyond at some later time.'

'That depends. Your race may decide how to deal with souls that become trapped in the beyond before that happens.'

'You're giving us a lot of credit. Judging by our current record, I'm not sure we deserve it. If you can't shoot it, people aren't interested.'

'You are being unfair,' Sinon said.

'But honest. The military mind infiltrated government for centuries until they became one,' Rana said.

'Don't start,' Cochrane grunted. 'This is like important, you dig?'

'I don't pretend to predict what will come,' Tinkerbell said. 'We abandoned that arrogance when we came here. You seem to be determined. That usually suffices.'

'Did you come here purely to circumvent the beyond?' Sinon asked. 'Was this your racial solution?'

'Not at all. As I said, we are an old species, and while we were still in our biological form we evolved into a collective of collectives. We gathered knowledge for millennia, explored galaxies, examined different dimensional realms coexisting with our own universe. Everything a new race does as fresh insights and understanding open up. Eventually there was nothing original for us, only variations on a theme that had been played a million times before. Our technology was perfect, our intellects complete. We stopped reproducing, for there was no longer any reason to introduce new minds to the universe; they could only ever have heritage, never discovery. At such a point some races die out contentedly, releasing their souls to the beyond. We chose this transference, the final accomplishment for our technological mastery. An instrument capable of moving the consciousness from a biological seat to this state was a challenge even for us. You can only sense the physical aspects of this vessel, and even those can be at variance with what you understand. As I think you realize.'

'Why bother with an instrument? We came here by will-power alone.'

'The energistic power you have is extremely crude. Our vessels cannot even exist fully in the universe, the energy patterns they support have no analogue there. Their construction requires a great deal of finesse.'

'What about others? Have you discovered any life forms here?'

'Many. Some like us, who have abandoned the universe. Some like you, thrown here by chance and accident. Others which are different again. There are visitors, too, entities more accomplished than us, who are charting many realms.'

'I think I would like to see them,' Choma said. 'To know what you do. I will join you if I may.'

'You will be welcome,' Tinkerbell said. 'What of the rest?'

Stephanie glanced round her friends, trying to gauge their reaction to the offers Tinkerbell had made. Apprehension persisted in all of them, they were waiting for her lead. Again.

'Are there any other humans here?' she asked. 'Any planets?'

'It is possible,' Tinkerbell said. 'Though I have not encountered any yet. This realm is one of many which have the parameters you desired.'

'So we can't seek refuge anywhere else?'

'No.'

Stephanie took Moyo's hand in hers, and pulled him close. 'Very well, time to face the music, I suppose.'

'I love you,' he said. 'I just want to be with you. That's my paradise.'

'I won't choose for you,' she told the others. 'You must do that for yourselves. For myself, if a serjeant body is available I will take it and return to Mortonridge. If not, then I'll accept death here in this realm. My host can have her body and freedom back.'

24

To a civilization innocent of regularized interstellar travel, the arrival of a single starship could never be viewed as a threat in itself. What it represents, the potential behind it, however, is another matter. A paranoid species could react very badly indeed to such an event.

It was a factor Joshua kept firmly in mind when *Lady Mac* emerged from her jump a hundred thousand kilometres above the diskcity. The crew did nothing for the first minute other than running a passive sensor sweep. No particle or artefact was drifting nearby, and no detectable xenoc sensor locked on to the hull.

'That original radar pulse is all I'm picking up,' Beaulieu reported. 'They haven't seen us.'

'We're in clear,' Joshua told Syrinx. All communication between the two starships was now conducted via affinity, the bitek processor array installed in *Lady Mac*'s electronics suite relaying information to *Oenone* with an efficiency equal to a standard datavise. The bitek starship had searched through the affinity band, its sensitivity stretched to the maximum. It was completely silent. As far as they could tell, the diskcity Tyrathca didn't have affinity technology.

'We're ready to swallow in,' Syrinx replied. 'Shout if you need us.'

'OK, people,' Joshua announced. 'Let's go with the plan.'

The crew brought the ship up to normal operational status.

Thermo-dump panels deployed, radiating the starship's accumulated heat away from the gleaming photosphere; sensor booms telescoped up. Joshua used the high-resolution systems to make an accurate fix on the diskcity, not using the active sensors yet. Once he'd confirmed their position to within a few metres, he transferred the navigational data over to a dozen stealthed ELINT satellites stored on board. They were fired out of a launch-tube, travelling half a kilometre from the fuselage before their ion drives came on, pushing them in towards the diskcity on a pulse of thin blue flame. It would take them the better part of a day to fly within an operational distance when they could start returning useful data on the artefact's darkside. Joshua and Syrinx considered it unlikely the diskcity could detect them in flight, even if its sensors were focused on space around *Lady Mac*. It was one of the mission's more acceptable risks.

With the satellites launched, he brought the starship's active sensors on-line and conducted a sweep of local space. 'We're now officially here,' he told them.

'Aligning main dish,' Sarha said. She followed the grid image, waiting until the coordinates matched the diskcity.

Joshua datavised the flight computer to broadcast their message. It was a simple enough greeting, a text in the Tyrathca language, spread across a broad frequency range. It said who they were, where they came from, that humans had cordial relations with the Tyrathca from Tanjuntic-RI, and asked the diskcity to return the hail. No mention was made of the *Oenone* being present.

There were bets on how long a reply would take, even of what it would say, if all they'd get back was a salvo of missiles. Nobody had put money on getting eight completely separate responses beamed at them from different sections of the diskcity.

'Understandable, though,' Dahybi said. 'The Tyrathca are a clan species, after all.'

'They must have a single administration structure to run an artefact like that,' Ashly protested. 'It wouldn't work any other way.'

'Depends what's tying them together,' Sarha said. 'Something that size can hardly be the most efficient arrangement.'

'Then why build it?' Ashly wondered.

Oski ran the messages through their translator program. 'Some deviation in vocabulary, syntax and symbology from our Tyrathca,' she said. 'It has been fifteen thousand years, after all. But we have a recognizable baseline we can proceed from.'

'Glad to see some sort of change,' Liol muttered. 'The way everything stays the same with these guys was getting kind of spooky.'

'That's drift, not change,' Oski told him. 'And take a good look at the diskcity. We could build something like that easily; in fact we could probably do a much better job of it, like Sarha says. All it demonstrates is expansion, not development. There's been no real technological progress here, just like their colonies and arkships.'

'What do the messages say?' Joshua asked.

'One is almost completely unintelligible, some kind of image, I think. The computer's running pattern analysis now. The rest are text only. Two have returned our greeting, and want to know what we're doing here. Two are asking for proof that we're xenocs. Three say welcome, and please rendezvous with the diskcity. Uh, they call it Tojolt-HI.'

'Give me a position on the three major friendlies,' Joshua said.

Three blue stars blinked over his neuroiconic image of Tojolt-HI. Two were located in the bulk of the disc, while the other was at the edge. 'That settles it,' he said. 'We concentrate on the rim source. I don't want to try and manoeuvre *Lady Mac* anywhere near the interior until we know for sure what's there. Do we know what that section's called?'

'The dominion of Anthi-CL,' Oski said.

'Sarha, focus our com beam on them, please, narrow band.'

Joshua ran through the message from the rim to get a feel for the format, and composed a reply.

> STARSHIP LADY MACBETH
> COMMUNICATION DIRECTED AT TOJOLT-HI
> DOMINION OF ANTHI-CL
> MESSAGE
> THANK YOU FOR YOUR ACKNOWLEDGEMENT. WE HAVE
> TRAVELLED HERE IN THE ANTICIPATION OF EXCHANGE OF
> MATERIALS AND KNOWLEDGE BENEFICIAL TO BOTH
> SPECIES. WE REQUEST PERMISSION TO DOCK AND BEGIN
> THIS PROCESS. IF THIS IS ACCEPTABLE TO YOU, PLEASE
> PROVIDE AN APPROACH VECTOR.
> CAPTAIN JOSHUA CALVERT

YOU ARE WELCOME TO MASTRIT-PJ. IGNORE ALL
MESSAGES FROM OTHER TOJOLT-HI DOMINIONS. WE
RETAIN THE LARGEST DEPOSITS OF MATERIAL AND
KNOWLEDGE WITHIN OUR BOUNDARIES. YOU WILL GAIN
THE MOST BENEFIT BY EXCHANGING WITH US. CONFIRM
THIS REQUEST.
QUANTOOK-LOU
DISTRIBUTOR OF DOMINION RESOURCES

'What do you think?' Joshua asked.

'Not quite the kind of response you'd get from our Tyrathca,'
Samuel said. 'It could be their attitude has changed to adapt to their
circumstances. They seem to be tinged with avarice.'

'Resources would be scarce here,' Kempster said. 'There can be no
new sources of solid matter for them to exploit. A kilo of your waste
may well be more valuable to them than a thousand fuseodollars.'

'We'll bear it in mind when we start negotiating,' Joshua said. 'For
now, we have an invitation. I think we'll accept.'

STARSHIP LADY MACBETH
COMMUNICATION DIRECTED AT DOMINION OF ANTHI-CL
MESSAGE
WE THANK YOU FOR YOUR INVITATION, AND CONFIRM
THAT WE WISH TO EXCHANGE EXCLUSIVELY WITH YOU.
PLEASE SEND APPROACH FLIGHT VECTOR.
CAPTAIN JOSHUA CALVERT.

DOMINION OF ANTHI-CL
COMMUNICATION TO STARSHIP LADY MACBETH
MESSAGE
ARE YOU UNABLE TO COMPUTE APPROACH VECTOR?
ARE YOU DAMAGED?
QUANTOOK-LOU
DISTRIBUTOR OF DOMINION RESOURCES

'Could be they don't have traffic control here,' Joshua said. He ran
a search through his neural nanonics encyclopedia file on Hesperi-

LN. 'The Hesperi-LN Tyrathca didn't have any formal control system before they started receiving Confederation ships.'

'You also need to have a lot of ships flying before that kind of arrangement becomes essential,' Ashley said. 'We haven't even detected one ship around Tojolt-HI yet. I've been running a constant scan.'

'They're certainly scanning us in return,' Beaulieu said. 'I'm registering seventeen different radar beams focused on us now. And I think there's some laser radar directed our way, too.'

'No ships at all?' Joshua asked.

'I can't find any drive emissions down there,' Sarha said. 'With our optical sensor resolution we ought to be able to see even a chemical reaction thruster flame inside that umbra.'

'Maybe they've use something like the voidhawk distortion field,' Dahybi suggested. 'After all, Kempster said mass was precious to them. Maybe they can't afford reaction drives.'

'Gravitonic detectors say you're wrong,' Liol said. 'I'm not picking up any kind of distortion pattern in this neck of the woods.'

'They're not going to tip their hand this early in the game,' Monica said. 'They won't show us what they've got, especially if it's combat capable.'

Sarha shifted under her restraint webbing to frown at the ESA agent. 'That's absurd. You can't suddenly shut down all your spacecraft traffic the instant you detect a xenoc. You'd leave ships in transit. Besides, they don't know how long we've been watching them.'

'You hope.'

Sarha gave an exasperated sigh. 'They don't have ZTT technology, so the only interstellar ships they can conceive of are arkships. And if one of those used its fusion drive to decelerate into this system, they'd be able to track it from half a light-year out. They must be curious about us and how the hell we got here, that's all.'

'Never mind,' Joshua grumbled.

STARSHIP LADY MACBETH
COMMUNICATION DIRECTED AT DOMINION OF ANTHI-CL
MESSAGE
WE ARE NOT DAMAGED. WE HAVE CAPABILITY TO COMPUTE
AN APPROACH VECTOR TO YOUR LOCATION ON TOJOLT-HI.
WE DID NOT WANT TO BREAK ANY LAW YOU HAVE

CONCERNING APPROACHING VEHICLES. ARE THERE ANY
RESTRICTIONS COVERING APPROACH SPEED AND
SEPARATION DISTANCE FROM YOUR PHYSICAL STRUCTURE?
CAPTAIN JOSHUA CALVERT

DOMINION OF ANTHI-CL
COMMUNICATION TO STARSHIP LADY MACBETH
MESSAGE
NO RESTRICTIONS CONCERNING YOUR APPROACH. WE WILL
PROVIDE FINAL HOLDING POSITION COORDINATE WHEN
YOU ARE WITHIN ONE THOUSAND KILOMETRES OF
DOMINION TERRITORY.
QUANTOOK-LOU
DISTRIBUTOR OF DOMINION RESOURCES

STARSHIP LADY MACBETH
COMMUNICATION DIRECTED TO DOMINION OF ANTHI-CL
MESSAGE
UNDERSTOOD. EXPECTED RENDEZVOUS TIME 45 MINUTES.
CAPTAIN JOSHUA CALVERT

Joshua datavised the flight computer to ignite the fusion drives. *Lady Mac* headed in towards the diskcity at a half-gee acceleration. He refined the vector so they'd finish the main burn a hundred kilometres out from the rim. If fusion drives weren't in common use in this system, *Lady Mac*'s exhaust might prove disconcerting. A smile touched his lips at what they'd think of the antimatter drive.

'Joshua,' Syrinx called. 'We've found another diskcity.'

'Where?' he asked. Everyone on *Lady Mac*'s bridge perked up with interest.

'It's trailing Tojolt-HI by forty-five million kilometres, inclined two degrees to the ecliptic. Kempster and Renato were right. The odds of us emerging so close to the only inhabited structure are non-existent.'

'Jesus, you mean this redoubt civilization is strung out all around the star's equatorial orbit?'

'Looks that way. We're scanning probable locations for more of them. Assuming the separation distance is constant, and they're not in wildly high inclination orbits, that would mean there's well over a hundred of the things.'

'Acknowledged.'

'Over a hundred,' Ashly said. 'That makes quite a civilization all told. How many Tyrathca do you think one of those diskcities could support?'

'With a surface area of twenty million square kilometres, I should think anything up to a hundred billion,' Sarha said. 'Even with their level of technology, that's a lot of area. Think how many people we cram into an arcology.'

'Look at it from the population perspective, and no wonder the Anthi-CL dominion wanted exclusivity,' Liol said. 'The demand on resources must be phenomenal. I'm astonished they managed to survive this long. By rights they should have drowned in their own waste products a long time ago.'

'Societies only have waste products while acquiring fresh raw material remains a cheaper option than recycling,' Samuel said. 'This close to the star, the diskcities are extremely rich in energy. There can be few waste molecules that cannot be reprocessed into something useful.'

'Even so, they must have strong prohibitions on reproducing. I see a circle of life like this, and all I can think about is a culture growing in a dish.'

'That analogy doesn't hold for sentient life. The Tyrathca nature is inclined to logically empowered restrictive behaviour. After all, they regulated themselves perfectly on a ten thousand year arkship voyage. This situation is no different for them.'

'Don't assume their dominions are uniform,' Sarha said. 'I'm detecting some areas on the disc with a much higher temperature than the others, their thermal regulation has completely broken down. Heat from the star is flowing straight through. They're dead.'

'Maybe so,' Beaulieu said. 'But there's still a lot of activity down there. We're being bombarded with radar signals from every section. A lot of dominions are very interested in us.'

'Still no ship launch,' Joshua said. 'No one's trying to intercept us before we reach Anthi-CL.' He accessed the sensors to watch Tojolt-HI growing against the radiant crimson expanse of the giant star. Apart from the scale involved, it was similar to their approach to the antimatter station. A jet-black, two-dimensional circle cutting right into the photosphere. The cold light of the nebula behind them was unable to illuminate a single feature on the back of the diskcity.

Only *Lady Mac*'s sensors could reveal the topography of mountainous towers pointing blindly away from the disc's median level. The flight computer's cartography program was having trouble compiling an accurate chart; the glare of electromagnetic emissions aimed at them was interfering with their radar return.

'What are they all saying?' he asked Oski.

'I'm running a keyword discrimination program on the data traffic. From the samples so far, it's all pretty much the same. They all want us to dock at their own section of the diskcity, and each claims to have the greatest resources, as well as unique information.'

'Any threats?'

'Not yet.'

'Keep reviewing it.'

Lady Mac flipped over and began decelerating.

Sensor data on Tojolt-HI built up slowly during the approach phase, giving the crews on *Lady Mac* and *Oenone* a good idea how the massive diskcity was constructed. The median sheet which formed the actual disc itself was an amalgamation of dense webs made up out of tubular structures, varying from twenty to three hundred metres in diameter. Though closely packed, they didn't touch except at end junctions; the gaps between them were sealed over with foil sheets, preventing any of the red giant's light from penetrating and diluting the umbra. Individual web patterns were principally circular, also varying enormously in size, and overlapping in contorted tangles. Spectrographic analysis found the constituent tubes were mostly metallic, with some silicon and carbon composites stretching across large areas; over five per cent were crystalline, radiating a wan phosphorescence out towards the nebula. There were regions, spread at random over the darkside, where the tangle of pipes swelled out into complex abstract knots several kilometres wide. It was as if the tubes had been subjected to severe lateral buckling, though the radar image couldn't determine any fractures.

The dense shade of the darkside was inevitably dominated by the thermal-transfer machinery. Radiator panels stacked in kilometre-high cones stood next to circular fan towers of faint glowing fins, minarets of spiralling glass tubes with hot gases rushing through them competed for root space with encrustations of black pillars like a spiky crystal growth, whose sheer ends fluoresced coral pink. Their meandering ranks formed mountain ranges to rival anything thrown up by planetary geology, running for hundreds of kilometres along the webs. Straddling the valleys between them on long stilt-like gantries were giant industrial modules. Dark metal ovoids and trapezohedrons of machinery, their exterior surfaces a solid lacework of pipes and conduits, rose to a crown of heat-dissipation fins or panels (a direct ancestry could be traced to the machinery on Tanjuntic-RI). Although the diskcity had an overall uniformity bestowed by its basic web design, no region or structure was the same, technologies were as heterogeneous as shapes. The standardization and compatibility synonymous with the Tyrathca had clearly broken down between the dominions millennia ago.

As they drew closer, more movement became visible across the darkside. Trains, made up from hundreds of tanker carriages, and kilometres in length, slid slowly along the valleys and embankments between the thermal-transfer systems. Their rails were an open framework of girders; suspended above the tubes and foil sheets of the disc, undulating like a rollercoaster track, dipping down to merge with the larger tubes, allowing the trains to run inside them, then rising up the stilt legs of industrial modules to pass straight through the middle.

'Who the hell built this place?' Ashly asked in bemusement as the grey pixels built up into a comprehensive image in his neural nanonics. 'Isambard Kingdom Brunel?'

'If it works, don't try and fix it,' Joshua said.

'There is more to it than that,' Samuel said. 'Tojolt-HI is not a declining technology. They have selected the simplest engineering technology which can sustain them. Whilst humans would no doubt progress to developing a full Dyson sphere over fifteen thousand years, the Tyrathca have refined something that requires the minimum of effort to maintain. It does have a kind of elegance.'

'But it still fails repeatedly,' Beaulieu said. 'There are dozens of dead sections across the disc. And each failure would cost them millions of lives. Any sentient creature should try to refine its living environment to something less prone to accident, surely?'

Samuel shrugged.

The Anthi-CL dominion began issuing instructions for *Lady Mac*'s final rendezvous coordinate. A blueprint they transmitted identified a specific section of the rim, which the flight computer matched up to the sensor image. The Anthi-CL dominion wanted them to keep station two kilometres out from a pier-like structure protruding from the edge.

'How is the translation program update coming on?' Joshua asked Oski. 'Do we know enough to communicate directly now?'

'It's integrated all the new terms we've encountered so far; the analysis comparison subroutine response time is down to an acceptable level. I'd say it's OK to try and talk to them.'

Lady Mac's drive thrust was reducing steadily as she drew level with the plane of the disc. In comparison to the desolate solidity of the darkside, the rim appeared to be unfinished. It bristled with slender spires and protruding gantry platforms wrapped in cables. Clumps of tanks and pods were attached to various open frame grids.

'At last,' Sarha said. 'That's got to be a ship.'

The vessel was docked to the rim a hundred kilometres along from their rendezvous coordinate. It had a simple profile, a pentagon of five huge globes scintillating with a soft gold and scarlet iridescence under the gas giant's illumination, each one at least two kilometres in diameter. They surrounded the throat of an elongated funnel made from a broad mesh of jet-black material; its open mouth was eight kilometres across. There was no recognizable life-support section visible from *Lady Mac*'s current position.

'Picking up a lot of very complex magnetic fluctuations from that thing,' Liol said. 'Whatever it does, there's a lot of energy involved.'

'If I didn't know better, I'd say it was a Bussard ramscoop,' Joshua said. 'It was a neat idea, pre-ZTT era interstellar propulsion. Use a magnetic scoop to collect interstellar hydrogen, and feed it direct into a fusion drive. A cheap and easy way to travel between stars, you haven't got to worry about carrying any on-board fuel. Unfortunately it turns out the hydrogen density isn't high enough to make it work.'

'In our part of the galaxy, maybe,' Liol said. 'What's the hydrogen density in space between a red giant and a nebula?'

'Good point. That could mean they're in contact with the closest colony stars.' He didn't believe it, there was some missing factor here. What would be the reason to travel to a nearby star? You couldn't trade over interstellar distances, not with slower than light ships. And given your destination would have the same technology and society as your departure point, what could be traded anyway?

Any differences or technological improvements that sprung up over the millennia could be shared by communication laser. 'Hey,' he exclaimed. 'Parker?'

'Yes, Joshua?' the old director responded.

'We thought the reason for Tanjuntic-RI losing contact with Mastrit-PJ was because civilization failed here. It hasn't. So why did they go off-air?'

'I have no idea. Perhaps one of the colony worlds relaying the messages round the nebula collapsed.'

'A Tyrathca society failed? Isn't that a bit unlikely?'

'Or it was killed off,' Monica said. 'I'd like to think the enslaved xenocs finally rebelled and wiped them out.'

'Possible.' Joshua wasn't convinced. I'm missing something obvious.

Lady Mac fell through the plane of the disc. It was a deliberate overshoot, allowing them to see Tojolt-HI's sunside. Here, at last, they found the invariable conformity they'd grown to expect from the Tyrathca.

On this half of the disc, every tube section was made from glass; a trillion corrugations held together by black reinforcement hoops like the roof of God's greenhouse. Light evaporating from the photosphere below was thick enough to qualify as a crimson haze; it gusted against the diskcity, only to be rebuffed by the burnished surface in copper ripples longer than planetary crescents. This was a hint of how sunset over eternity's ocean would appear.

'Jesus,' Joshua crooned. 'I guess this makes up for Tanjuntic-RI.'

They held position for several minutes with every sensor boom extended to gather in the scene, then Joshua reluctantly fired the secondary drive rockets to bring them back into the disc plane and back towards the rim. He locked *Lady Mac*'s position in the coordinate Anthi-CL had given them, and initiated a barbecue roll. The starship's thermo-dump panels were spread out to their full extent, glimmering cherry red whenever they turned into shadow.

As soon as Sarha confirmed their on-board heat exchangers could handle the sun's heat, Joshua opened a direct communication channel to the Anthi-CL dominion.

'I would like to speak with Quantook-LOU,' he said.

The reply came back almost immediately. 'I speak.'

'Again, I thank the Anthi-CL dominion for receiving us. We look forward to beginning a prosperous exchange, and hope that it will be the first of many between our respective species.' Make them believe that others will be coming, he thought, that implies any forceful action on their part would ultimately have to be accounted for. Pretty unlikely given the scale of things around here, but they don't know that.

'We too have that anticipation,' Quantook-LOU said. 'That is an interesting ship you fly, Captain Calvert. We have not seen its like before. Those of us who disputed your claimed origin no longer do so. Is it a subsidiary vessel of your starship, or did you cross interstellar space in it?'

Joshua gave his brother a disconcerted look. 'Even if this translation program is getting creative on me, they're not responding like any Tyrathca I know about.'

'That's a leading question, too,' Samuel cautioned. 'If you confirm we travelled round the nebula in *Lady Macbeth* they'll know we have faster than light travel.'

'And they'll want it,' Beaulieu said. 'If we're right about the pressure on local resources it's their escape route out past the surrounding colony worlds.'

'No, it's not,' Ashly said. 'I lived through the Great Dispersal, remember. We couldn't even shift five per cent of Earth's population when we really needed to. ZTT isn't an escape route, not even with the industrial capacity of a diskcity. Everything is relative. They could build enough ships in a year to transport billions of breeder pairs away from Mastrit-PJ, but they'd still be left with thousands of billions living in the diskcities. All of whom would be busy laying more eggs.'

'It might not solve their problem, but it would certainly give star systems where they propose to settle one hell of a headache,' Liol said. 'We've seen what they'll do to aboriginal species occupying real estate they want.'

Joshua held up a hand. 'I get the picture, thank you. Though I think we have to consider ZTT technology as our ultimate purchasing power to get the Sleeping God's location. The Hesperi-LN Tyrathca already have ZTT, it might take decades to reach Mastrit-PJ, but it will spread here eventually.'

'*Try* not to,' Monica said forcefully. 'Try very hard.'

Joshua held her stare as he reopened the channel to Quantook-LOU. 'The nature of our ship is one of the items of knowledge we can discuss as part of the exchange. Perhaps you would like to list the areas of science and technology you have the most interest in acquiring.'

'What areas do you excel in?'

Joshua frowned. 'Wrong,' he mouthed to his crew. 'This is not a Tyratcha.'

'I agree, this is not a response I would expect from one,' Samuel said.

'Then what?' Sarha asked.

'Let's find out,' Joshua said. 'Quantook-LOU, I think we should start slowly. As a gesture of good faith, I would like to give you a gift. We might then start to exchange our histories. Once we understand each other's background we should have a better idea where useful exchanges can be made. Are you agreeable to this?'

'In principle, yes. What is your gift?'

'An electronic processor. It is a standard work tool among humans; the design and composition may be of interest to you. If so, duplication would be a simple matter.'

'I accept your gift.'

'I will bring it to you. I am eager to see the inside of Tojolt-HI. It is an astonishing achievement.'

'Thank you. Can you dock your starship to one of our ports? We do not have a suitable ship to collect you from your present position.'

'Curiouser and curiouser,' Liol said. 'They can build habitats the size of continents, but not commuter taxis.'

'We have a small shuttle craft we can use to reach the port,' Joshua said. 'We will remain in spacesuits while we are inside Anthi-CL to avoid biological contamination.'

'Is a direct physical encounter between our species dangerous?'

'Not if adequate precautions are taken. Our species is very experienced in this field. Please don't be alarmed.'

*

Joshua piloted the MSV himself, ignoring Ashly's snide remarks about union rules. It was cramped in the little cabin; Samuel and

Oski came with him, as well as a serjeant (just in case). He had to promise the others a rota for visiting the diskcity, everyone had wanted to come.

The port which Quantook-LOU had designated was a fat bulb of grey-white metal four hundred metres across, which flared out from the end of a web tube. Its apex was taken up by a circular hatch seventy-five metres in diameter, open to show a dimly lit interior.

'Looks like one big empty chamber in there,' Joshua said. He fired the thrusters carefully, edging the little craft inside. Gentle red light shone from long strips that curved round the walls like fluorescent ribs. Between them were rows of almost-human machinery. It put him in mind of the docking craters in Tranquillity's spaceport.

Directly opposite the main outer hatch was a stubby cylindrical grid, with much smaller airlock hatches at the far end. Joshua steered the MSV towards it.

'Your datavise carrier is starting to break up,' Sarha reported.

'That's to be expected, though a good host would offer us a constant link. We'll start to worry if they actually shut that hatch.'

The MSV reached the top of the cylindrical grid. Joshua extended one of the vehicle's waldo arms to grip it in the clamp. 'We're secure,' he reported, using the band they talked to Quantook-LOU.

'Please proceed to the airlock ahead of you. I await on the other side.'

Joshua and the others fastened their space armour helmets into place. They assumed the Tyrathca didn't have programmable silicon, so they wouldn't know about SII suits. The armour would appear to be their actual spacesuit, reducing the risk of offending their hosts at the same time providing a degree of protection. The MSV's cabin atmosphere cycled and the four of them slid out.

There were three airlock hatches at the end of the grid. Only one of them, the largest, was open. The chamber behind was a sphere six metres across.

'Those other hatches were too small for the breeders,' Samuel said. 'I wonder if one of the vassal caste has been bred for a higher IQ; they certainly weren't capable of useful engineering work before.'

Joshua didn't reply. He stuck his boots to what could have been the chamber floor just as the atmospheric gas started to hiss in. Suit sensors told him it was a composition of oxygen, nitrogen, carbon dioxide, argon, and various hydrocarbon compounds, the humidity level was very high, and there were several classes of organic particulate in circulation. He made a strong effort to keep his hand away from the innocuous looking cylinder on his belt which was actually a laser.

Strangely, he felt no excitement at this moment. It was almost as if there was too much riding on it for him to take anything other than an objective view. A good thing, he supposed.

The inner hatch opened, revealing one of Tojolt-HI's wider habitation tubes dwindling away to a flat metal bulkhead a kilometre away. Two colours dominated the interior: red and brown. Joshua smiled round his suit's respirator tube as he saw the cluster of xenocs waiting for him. They weren't Tyrathca.

First impression was a shoal of human-size seahorses floating cautiously in the air. They had that same kind of flowing twitch along the length of their body, as if forever poised at the start of a race. Their colouring was almost black, though Joshua suspected that was due to the unvarying red light; sensor spectral analysis showed their scales were actually a shade of dark grey-brown very close to the Tyrathca, suggesting a common Mastrit-PJ ancestry. The head was pointed, dragon-like, with a long beak-mouth and two small semi-recessed eyes. It was held almost at a right angle to the body by a heavily wrinkled neck, suggesting considerable flexibility. The rest of the body had an ovoid cross-section that gradually tapered away towards the base, though there was no sign of any tail. It curved slightly, producing an overall S-shape (as seen from the side). Three pairs of limbs were spaced equidistantly along it, all sharing the same basic profile; a long first section extending away from a shoulder-analogue socket, and ending in a wrist joint. The hand appendage was elongated with nine twin-knuckle digits. On the highest set of limbs they were thin and highly dextrous; the middle set were smaller and thicker; while the hind set were stumpy, toes rather than fingers. On most of the xenocs the hind feet appeared to be withered, becoming simple paddles of flesh, as though they were borrowed from aquatic creatures.

It was an appropriate classification. Every surface inside the tube sprouted lengthy ribbon fronds of rubbery vegetation, all of them reaching up for the geometric centre. Even those planted in the glass were growing directly away from the light, something Joshua had never seen on any terracompatible world he'd visited, no matter how bizarre some of its aboriginal botany and biochemistry.

The constant tangle of vegetation along the inside of the tube did however make movement very easy for the xenocs. They seemed to glide along effortlessly through the topmost fringe, with the lower half of their bodies immersed in the brown fronds, their limbs wriggling gently to control their motion. It was a wonderfully graceful action resulting from what was essentially a mad combination of the smooth flick of a dolphin flipper and a human hand slapping at grab hoops.

Joshua admired it with mild envy, at the same time wondering just how long evolution would take to produce that kind of arrangement. It was almost a case of symbiosis, which meant the fronds of vegetation would have to be *very* prevalent.

He couldn't doubt these xenocs were intelligent beyond any Tyrathca vassal caste the Confederation had encountered. They wore electronic systems like clothes. Mostly it was the upper half of their bodies which were covered in a garment that combined a string vest with bandolier straps to which various modules were clipped, interspersed with tools and small canisters. They also went in for exoaugmentation; lenses jutted out of eye sockets, while plenty of them had replaced upper-limb hands with cybernetic claws.

Joshua switched his sensor focus around them until he found one whose electronics seemed slightly better quality than the others. Their styling was more slimline, with elegant keypads and displays. Some of the modules were actually embossed with marmoreal patterns. A fast spectrographic scan said the metal was iron. Curious choice, he thought.

'I am Captain Joshua Calvert, and I apologize to Quantook-LOU,' he said. The communication block relayed his words into the hooting whistles of Tyrathca-style speech, which he could just make out through the muffling of the SII suit's silicon. 'We assumed the Tyrathca occupied this place.'

The creature his sensors were focused on opened its gnarled beak and chittered loudly. 'Do you wish to leave now you have found it is otherwise?'

'Not at all. We are delighted to have gained the knowledge of your existence. Could you tell me what you call yourselves?'

'My race is the Mosdva. For all of Tyrathca history we were their subjects. Their history has ended. Mastrit-PJ is our star now.'

'Way to go,' Monica said over the general communication band.

'Let's not jump to conclusions,' Syrinx admonished. 'They're clearly from the same evolutionary chain.'

'Relevant observations only,' Joshua told them. 'I mean, do we even need to carry on? We can be diplomatic here for a couple of hours, then fly off to the nearest probable Tyrathca colony star to get what we need.'

'They have the same language and origin planet,' Parker said. 'It's highly probable they share the same stellar almanac. We need to know a lot more before we even consider moving on.'

'OK.' Joshua datavised his communication block back to its translation function. 'You have achieved much here. My race has never built any structure on such a scale as Tojolt-HI.'

'But you have built a most interesting ship.'

'Thank you.' He took a processor block from his belt. Slowly and carefully. It was one that he'd found in *Lady Mac*'s engineering workshop, a quarter of a century out of date and loaded with obsolete maintenance programs (they'd erased any reference to starflight). The general management routine might be of some interest to the xenocs, especially from what he could see of their own electronics. In fact, it might be a slightly too generous gift; half of their modules would have been archaic back in the twenty-third century. 'For you,' he told Quantook-LOU.

One of the other Mosdva slithered forwards through the foliage, and gingerly took the block before hurrying back to Quantook-LOU. The distributor of resources examined it before putting it in a pouch near the bottom of his torso garment.

'I thank you, Captain Joshua Calvert. In return, I would show you this section of Anthi-CL, in which you have expressed such interest.'

'Was that cynicism?' Joshua asked his people.

'I don't think so,' Oski said. 'The Tyrathca language as we know it doesn't have the carrier mechanism for that kind of nuance. It can't, because they don't have cynicism.'

'Might be a good idea to keep the analysis program watching for those kind of patterns emerging.'

'I'll second that,' Samuel said. 'They've been bombarding us with sensor probes from the second that hatch opened. They're clearly looking for an advantage. This kind of mercantile behaviour is thankfully easy to appreciate. It almost makes them human.'

'Wonderful. Sixteen thousand light-years, and all we get to meet is the local equivalent of the Kulu Traders' Association.'

'Joshua, your first priority is to understand exactly what position Quantook-LOU has within their social structure,' Parker said. 'Once that is known, we'll be able to proceed quickly to a resolution. Their culture is plainly developed along different lines from the Tyrathca, though I'm happy to say the basics of trade apparently remain a fundamental.'

'Yes, thank you, Mr Director.' And I wonder if he understands cynicism. 'I would be honoured to see your dominion,' Joshua told the Mosdva.

'Accompany us, then. I will enlighten you.'

The whole Mosdva group turned, virtually in unison, and began their sliding glide along the vegetation. Joshua, who considered himself highly proficient in free fall conditions, was fascinated by the manoeuvre. There was a lot of torque and inertia involved with such a move, their midlimbs must apply a lot of pressure to the fronds. And the fronds themselves must be stronger than they looked; try tugging a terrestrial palm like that and you'd rip it in half.

He cancelled the takpad application on his boot soles, and kicked off after them. Ultimately, he cheated, using the cold-gas jets of his armour's manoeuvring pack as well as climbing a frond like a rope. When he reached the upper fringes, the fronds now did their best to impede his progress; where they parted for any Mosdva, they formed elastic nets for him. The best method, he found, was to stay above their tips altogether, and reach down as necessary to swing himself along. Gauntlet tactile sensors reported the vegetation was spongy, but with a solid spine.

Out of the four of them, he was the most agile, though he struggled to keep up with Quantook-LOU. And the serjeant's motions were plain painful to watch; Ione had never ventured into Tranquillity's zero-gee sections very often.

The Mosdva had slowed to observe the progress of the humans, allowing them to catch up.

'You do not fly as fast as your ship, Captain Joshua Calvert,' Quantook-LOU said.

'Our species lives on planets. We're accustomed to high-gravity environments.'

'We know of planets. The Mosdva have many stories of Mastrit-PJ's worlds before the expansion devoured them all. But there are no pictures on file in Tojolt-HI, not after such a time. They are as legend, now.'

'I have many pictures of planets in my ship. I would welcome exchanging them for any pictures you do have of Mastrit-PJ's history.'

'A good first exchange. We are fortunate to have made contact with you, Captain Joshua Calvert.'

Joshua had been hanging on to a frond tip as he waited for the serjeant to catch up; now he realized the plant was wriggling slightly. There certainly wasn't enough of a breeze to do that.

'The fronds stir the air for us,' Quantook-LOU explained when he mentioned it. All plants on Tojolt-HI flexed gently; that was why they'd originally been selected, careful breeding had enhanced the trait. Air had to be moved in free fall, or stagnant pockets of gas would build up, unpleasant, and potentially lethal for animals and plants alike. The Mosdva still had mechanical fans and ducts, but they were very much secondary systems.

'Not quite up to Edenist levels,' Sarha said.

'They're edging towards biological solutions,' Ruben replied. 'Leaving the mechanical behind.'

'You can't use wholly biological systems here, not in this environment, it's too hostile.'

'And there is precious little sign of genetic engineering techniques being employed,' Samuel said. 'Quantook-LOU told us the plants were bred. Cross-pollination is almost a lost art in human society, Adamist and Edenist alike. We shall have to be more careful here than we originally expected, both in what we say and what we exchange with them. This society is static, and it survives perfectly by being so. To introduce change, even in the form of concepts, could be disastrous to it.'

'Or save it,' Sarha said.

'From what? We are the only conceivable threat it faces.'

They progressed further along the tube, gradually encountering more Mosdva as they went. All of the xenocs stopped to watch as the humans went past, slow and clumsy in comparison to their entourage (Joshua preferred not to call it an escort). Mosdva children flashed about through the fronds, incredibly agile. They burrowed deep below the tips in smooth dives, and popped out everywhere, making sure they got a look at the humans from all angles. Like the adults, they wore torso harnesses that contained a multitude of electronic modules – but none of them had cybernetic implants.

Looking down past his gauntlets, Joshua could see straight through the corkscrew fronds. They weren't as dense as he'd first thought, a plantation rather than a jungle, which allowed him to piece together how the tube was constructed. There was an outer casing, the ribbed section with glass on the sunside, and an opaque composite or metal on the darkside. Lining that on the inside was a tightly packed spiral of transparent piping, studded with small copper-coloured annular apertures from which the plants grew. Their roots were visible inside the pipe, just. The spiral was filled with an opaque and somewhat glutinous fluid which cut down the sun's intense red glare. It was also flecked with dark granules and a swirl of tiny bubbles, which showed him how fast it was being pumped along.

The spirals contained either water or hydrocarbon compounds, Quantook-LOU said when Joshua asked what it was; its circulation formed the basis for their whole recycling philosophy. Heat from the red giant was swiftly carried round to the darkside, where it was disposed of via the thermal-exchange mechanisms, generating electricity in the process. A range of algal species flourished inside the various fluid types, absorbing Mosdva faecal waste and transforming it into nutrients for the plants, which in turn maintained the atmosphere. The thickness of the spiral pipes (none under two and a half metres in diameter) meant the fluid bulk also acted as an excellent protection from stellar radiation.

They were shown web tubes which specialized in high-yield arable plants. Living tubes, which were sectioned off by thin sheets of silvery-white fabric. Industrial tubes, whose manufacturing machinery was strung out along the axis, just above the plant tips. ('Condensation must be hell for them,' Oski said at that.) Huge public tubes thronging with Mosdva.

After two hours, they were in a section dedicated to what the translator program termed the Anthi-CL dominion's *administrative class*. Joshua began to suspect a society structured along strictly aristocratic hierarchy lines. The vegetation was lusher here, the technology less obtrusive. Personal tubes radiated away from the main branches, far more substantial than the living sections they'd seen earlier, and with a lower population density. Two-thirds of their entourage dropped away once they entered. Those that were left were heavily augmented with cybernetic prosthetics. No overt weapons, but the humans agreed they were police/military.

Quantook-LOU stopped in a large bubble of transparent material, the junction for three small tubes. The surface was still a spiral of pipe dotted with chunks of hardware, but there were no plants; and apart from the bubbles, the fluid was almost clear. It gave a peerless view out over both darkside and sunside.

'My personal space,' Quantook-LOU said.

Joshua could just make out the misty smears of the nebula through the curving walls. Sharp-edged dissipator cones formed a strange, close horizon. Sunside was a simple uniform mantle of red light. 'It is matched with everything else we have seen here,' he said.

'What of your world, Captain Joshua Calvert? Does it have sights to match this?'

The exchange of history began. Under the Mosdva's urging, Joshua, Samuel, and Oski started off describing continents and oceans (concepts which had to be clearly defined for the Mosdva – they'd even lost the words for them in their language), and moved on to explain how humans had emerged from Africa to spread across Earth after the Ice Age glaciers retreated. How a technoindustrial society had developed. The rampant pollution which had altered the planetary ecology for the worse, creating an era where ships flew between the stars to found new colonies. How the Confederation now embraced hundreds of star systems, and traders prospered among them. A colourful generalized summary, devoid of any real detail and timescale.

In return, the Mosdva told them Mastrit-PJ's long story: how neither they nor the Tyrathca were the original sentient species on the one planet which supported biological life. The Ridbat were the first, with a society that had flourished over a million years ago. Little was known of them now, Quantook-LOU said, other than whispers that trickled from generation to generation becoming wilder with each telling. They were Mastrit-PJ's true monsters, ravenous beasts with evil minds. Wars had been constant while they were alive, two of which escalated into the exchange of nuclear weapons on the planetary surface. Their civilization was knocked back from an advanced technological culture to primitive barbarian on at least three separate occasions. It wasn't known if they ever had spaceflight, there was no evidence of offplanet activity. The fourth and last Ridbat industrial era was brought to an end by thermo-nuclear conflict, concurrent with the release of biological weapons which wiped them out along with seventy per cent of the planet's animal life.

The Mosdva had risen to a rudimentary state of intelligence while the Ridbat ruled the planet. That made them useful slave creatures, who were bred for dexterity and strength and passivity, while any traits such as curiosity or stubbornness were ruthlessly culled. By the time the Ridbat exterminated themselves, the Mosdva had become fully sentient. Although their population was severely reduced by the diseases raging across the land, they did at least survive as a species.

With the Ridbat gone, Mosdva evolution reverted to more traditional lines. As normal as life could become on such a ruined planet. Their own civilization was extremely slow to emerge as a coherent whole. Mastrit-PJ, with its exhausted mineral resources, devastated biosphere, and extensive radioactive deadlands was not an environment conductive to sophisticated or high-technology based cultures, and the cautious Mosdva psychology fitted this well. They became nomadic during the period of nuclear winter which followed the demise of the Ridbat, roaming between habitable areas. It was only after the glaciers withdrew, half a million years later, that the Mosdva began to advance again.

They achieved a modest level of industrialization. Because there were no underground petrochemical deposits left, nor coal or natural gas, their technology was based around the concept of sustainability; benign and in harmony with the ecosystem. Although not opposed to change, change generated from within was extremely slow to manifest itself. Steady advances in the theoretical fields of science such as physics, astronomy and mathematics were not grasped upon for technological extrapolation. They already lived in what they considered to be a golden age. After their terrible heritage, stability was the one icon they craved above all else. Such a desire could have led to a society whose timescale rivalled geological epochs.

Fate dealt that prospect two bitter blows. Once the glaciers were gone, the Tyrathca, until then simple bovine herd animals, began to share in Mastrit-PJ's evolutionary renaissance. Their sentience was a long time emerging, but their progress towards it reflected their physical stamina, plodding forwards imperturbably. On any other world, their total lack of imagination would have been a serious flaw, but not here. Sharing the planet with a species as benevolent and (by now) advanced as the Mosdva meant that they had access to machinery and concepts they themselves could never originate.

Unfortunately for the Mosdva, the Tyrathca were more aggressive, a trait which came from their herd ancestry and its consequent territorial disputes, which in turn led to the breeding of the vassal castes, especially the soldiers. With their copied technology, greater size and larger numbers, they swiftly became the dominant of the two species.

This situation could well have spelt extinction for the Mosdva. Their settlements were being put under considerable pressure by the Tyrathca expansion. Then Mosdva astronomers discovered their star was about to expand into a red giant.

For a race whose thoughts operated on an abstract level the knowledge of certain extinction in thirteen hundred years' time would be devastating enough; for the Tyrathca, to whom a fact was immediate, it was intolerable. Racial survival provided a unifying motivator which enabled them to swiftly consolidate their domination of the planet. For the second time in their existence, the Mosdva were effectively enslaved. First they were used to devise a scheme whereby some if not all the Tyrathca could survive the star's expansion. They came up with the arkship concept which would guarantee ultimate racial survival, with habitable asteroids sheltering the remainder of the population which couldn't be evacuated. Secondly, they were made to implement it.

With their smaller bodies, greater dexterity, and higher intelligence, they made excellent astronauts – unlike the Tyrathca themselves. Mosdva technical expertise was adapted and utilized to capture asteroids and shunt them into orbit around Mastrit-PJ, where they were hollowed out and converted into arkships. The arkship building phase lasted for seven centuries, in which time 1,037 were built and launched.

After this, with the star's growing instability wrecking the planet's fragile ecology, Mastrit-PJ's massive space manufacturing capability was switched to adapting asteroids into habitats. The asteroids chosen were orbiting more than a quarter of a billion kilometres from the star, putting them outside the predicted expansion photosphere. As this operation was far simpler than changing asteroids into giant starships, over seven thousand were created in just two centuries. Unlike the arkships, which were immediately lost to the Tyrathca upon completion, building the asteroid habitats was a near-exponential growth process, as new habitats used their industrial capacity to prepare further asteroids.

A thousand years after the project began, the planet had become uninhabitable, and was completely abandoned.

No Mosdva were ever carried on an arkship, the vessels were used exclusively by the Tyrathca. As soon as they had finished building one, the Mosdva were moved on to the next.

However, they couldn't be excluded from the asteroid habitats without a policy of complete genocide. The Tyrathca tolerated them, knowing that their own numbers were constantly rising, necessitating an ongoing construction programme. And with the exact conditions of the star's expansion unknowable, they would need Mosdva technical ability to adapt the asteroid habitats to the environment of the swollen photosphere.

When Mastrit-PJ's star expanded, its diameter was larger than predicted, as was its radiant heat output. New, larger thermal-dissipation systems had to be constructed for the asteroid habitats, and quickly. As a consequence, the habitats became even more engineering-dependent, which began the gradual shift of political power. Only Tyrathca breeders were capable of any meaningful technological activity, making all but the builder, housekeeper, and farmer vassal castes redundant. Their soldier caste was now bred purely to keep the Mosdva in line.

The revolution didn't happen all at once, but rather over a thousand-year period, starting ten thousand years earlier. The asteroid habitats initially formed a cohesive one-nation grouping after the expansion. But the scarcity of mass in the form of unused asteroids to mine forced the Tyrathca to revert to their original clannish state of competition. As the number of unused asteroids declined, wars were fought over the remainder. Each asteroid habitat reverted to complete autonomy.

After that, the rise of the Mosdva to supremacy was inevitable. They controlled the habitat machinery, and industrial facilities, a power they discovered which enabled them to dictate their terms to the Tyrathca.

Under this new order, the asteroid habitats gradually banded together politically and physically. As they did, new design concepts were enacted, bringing the old Mosdva dictum of sustainability to the fore, enabling them to maximize their use of dwindling mass resources. Life-support sections outside the spun-gravity biospheres were constructed. First they were little more than adjuncts to the gridwork which held the clustered asteroid habitats together, transport and transfer tubes, eliminating the wasteful need for airlocks and vessels. But the Mosdva, with their climbing-adept limb arrangement and natural agility, found they adapted well to the free fall environment inside them. Only the Tyrathca needed gravity, and the associated complex engineering to maintain the rotating biospheres. More free fall segments were constructed and added to the clusters, hydroponics and industrial sections first, which led to their technicians spending more and more time in free fall. Living sections followed quickly. The era of the diskcities began.

'And the Tyrathca?' Joshua asked. 'Are they still here?'

'We do not keep them any more,' Quantook-LOU said. 'They are no longer our masters.'

'I congratulate you on ridding yourselves of them. The Confederation has always found them difficult to deal with.'

'But we are not difficult, I hope. And the dominion of Anthi-CL is on the edge of Tojolt-HI. That makes us rich in mass, more than any other, we are good trading partners for you, Captain Joshua Calvert.'

'How does being on the edge of Tojolt-HI make you richer than other dominions?'

'Is that not obvious? All ships have to dock at the edge. All mass flows through us.'

'Oh, classic,' Ruben said. 'The rim dominions are the diskcity harbour masters, they can charge what they like to allow cargo through. They've probably got some kind of political alliance between themselves to put the squeeze on the central dominions.'

'A minimum fee?' Joshua asked.

'Most likely. It puts us in a good position. Everything travels through them; ergo, they must have good communications with all the other dominions. They should be able to find us a copy of the almanac file if it still exists.'

'OK.' Joshua checked his neural nanonics time function. They'd been in the diskcity for nine hours. 'I thank you for your hospitality, Quantook-LOU. My crew and I would like to return to our ship now. We have gathered enough information to see where our respective interests lie, so we'll start reviewing what items and information we've brought with us which will bring about the most beneficial exchange for both of us.'

'As you wish. How long will this review process take?'

'Only a few hours. I look forward to returning, and the start of true negotiations between us.'

'As do I. Our resources will be marshalled to cope with your demands. Perhaps then I could visit your ship?'

'You would be an honoured guest, Quantook-LOU.'

Ten Mosdva formed the entourage to see them back to the MSV. It had been left untouched, though Ashly and Sarha, who'd been monitoring its status, reported it had been bombarded by every conceivable active sensor sweep.

As soon as they were back through *Lady Mac*'s decontam procedure, Joshua ordered the SII suit to withdraw, giving a huge sigh as his skin was exposed to air again. 'Jesus, I thought that Quantook character would go on for ever about how wonderful his people are. Don't they ever sleep?'

'Probably not,' Parker said. 'As a general rule, sleep evolves from a planetary day–night cycle; they don't have that here any more. I suspect they have slow periods, but no actual sleep.'

'Ah well, that's one weakness we'll have to concede to them. I need a meal, a gel wipe, and some time in the cocoon. It's been a long day.'

'I concur,' Syrinx said. 'The ELINT satellites are approaching operational range, which may or may not give us useful information on the dominions. We also need to evaluate what we've heard today, and I'd like us all fresh for that. We'll reconvene in six hours to see what the satellites have found and discuss the next stage.'

Joshua managed three hours in the cocoon before he woke. He stared at the cabin wall for fifteen minutes before acknowledging he'd need to put a somnolence program into primary if he wanted to sleep again. He hated doing that.

Liol, Monica, Alkad, and Dahybi were already in the small galley when he air-swam through the hatch. They gave him varying sympathetic looks which he acknowledged ruefully.

'We've been talking to Syrinx and Cacus,' Monica said. She shrugged at Joshua; he'd paused in the act of filling his tea sachet from the water nozzle to raise an eyebrow. 'Not just us that's restless. Anyway, they've located another seven diskcities.'

Joshua datavised the flight computer for a general communication link, and said good morning to the *Oenone*'s crew.

'The Mosdva empire appears to be quite extensive,' Syrinx told him. 'Judging by the distribution of diskcities we've seen so far, that early estimate needs to be revised upwards. Fair enough if we believe there were seven thousand asteroid habitats to begin with. Kempster and Renato have also been scanning further out from the photosphere. So far they haven't located a single lump of rock within twenty degrees of the ecliptic. Quantook-LOU was telling the truth when he said there was a desperate struggle for mass after the stellar expansion. Every spare gram must have been incorporated into the diskcities.'

'Quantook-LOU didn't say struggle,' Joshua said. 'He said wars, plural.'

'Which he blamed squarely on the Tyrathca,' Alkad said.

Joshua gave the physicist a bleak look. She didn't say much, but her comments were normally pretty valid. 'You think the Mosdva took control earlier than that?'

'We can never know exactly what this star system's history is, but I would think it likely that the Mosdva started their revolt right after the star's expansion phase. That would be when the Tyrathca were most dependent on them. Everything else we've been told does tend to paint them in an unusually generous light. An oppressed people struggle to regain their long-lost freedom? Please. History is always written by the good guys.'

'I did gloss over some of our less endearing traits,' Joshua said. 'That's human nature.'

'You should have stung Quantook-LOU's office space with some nanonic bugs,' Liol said. 'I'd love to hear what's being said in there right now.'

'Too big a risk,' Monica said. 'If they found them, at worst they could interpret it as a hostile act; and even if they were diplomatic about it, we would have handed them a whole new technology.'

'I don't think that leaves us much to worry about,' Liol said. 'The Confederation isn't about to be invaded by Mosdva, it's the Tyrathca we have to worry about.'

'Enough,' Joshua said. He shifted round to make room for a sleepy unshaven Ashly, who was drifting into the galley. 'Look, we've just about got everyone up now anyway, we'd best convene and thrash out what we're going to do next.'

There was one more discovery before the meeting started. Joshua was finishing his breakfast when Beaulieu datavised a curt message requesting him to access *Lady Mac*'s sensor suite. 'I've located a Mosdva ship,' the cosmonik said.

'At last,' Liol said eagerly. He closed his eyes and accessed the image.

Beaulieu hadn't activated any visual enhancement programs to counter the redness. All Joshua could make out was a big brilliant-white shape gliding up towards a rendezvous with Tojolt-HI – the same configuration as the ship already docked to the rim. Five huge globes clumped round a drive unit and scoop. Except these globes were glowing a vivid purple-white, brighter than the photosphere.

'It surfaced twenty minutes ago,' Beaulieu datavised.

The cosmonik replayed the recording. *Lady Mac*'s sensors had detected a magnetic anomaly within the photosphere, hundreds of kilometres wide, the flux lines twisting into a dense wood-knot pattern. But it was moving faster than orbital velocity, and growing larger. Visual sensors started tracking it, showing the endless scarlet haze. At first it was as unruffled as a sea mist at dawn, then the impossible happened and long streaks of shadow rippled across the picture. They were actually folds in the gas, something underneath was stirring the igneous hydrogen atoms, creating swirling currents in the calm envelope. A bright patch of white light started to shine up through the red plasma. The ship rose up smooth and clean through the outer layers of the photosphere, scoop first, pushing a vast bow wave of glowing ions ahead of it. Each of its five globes was shining as bright as a white-dwarf star, radiating away enormous quantities of electromagnetic and thermal energy. Thick scarlet coronas avalanched from the lip of the scoop, purling gently all the way back down into the body of the red giant. The remainder of the nimbus was sucked down into the ship's funnel, growing steadily brighter as it progressed, until it was consumed by a dazzling white flame burning brightly at the throat.

'The globes have been dimming since it surfaced,' Beaulieu said. 'Their external temperature is dropping in concert.'

'Looks like you were right about it being a ramscoop, Josh,' Liol said cheerfully. 'It's got to be where they get their mass from, now the asteroids have been consumed. Fancy that, mining the sun.'

'That thermal-dump technology is damn impressive,' Sarha said. 'It's got to be superior to anything we have. Shedding heat while you're inside a star. God!'

'Simply compressing and condensing photosphere hydrogen into a stable gaseous state wouldn't generate that much heat,' Alkad said. 'They must be fusing it, burning it down into helium, perhaps even all the way to carbon.'

'Christ, they must be desperate for mass.'

'The iron limit,' Joshua mused. 'You can't fuse atoms past iron without having to input energy. Every other reaction until that element generates energy.'

'Is that relevant?' Liol asked.

'Not sure. But it makes iron their gold equivalent. It can't hurt knowing what they value most. It's the trans-iron elements that they'll be running out of.'

'The fact that they've resorted to this extraordinary method gives us some considerable leverage,' Samuel said. 'We've seen little evidence of molecular engineering compounds in the diskcity structure. Our materials science will allow them to exploit mass far more efficiently than they do currently. Every innovation we bring has the potential for inflicting vast change upon them.'

'This is what we have to decide,' Syrinx said. 'Liol, have the ELINT satellites revealed anything that might help us?'

'Not really. They're holding station a thousand kilometres above the darkside now, which gives us excellent coverage. It's pretty much what we observed as we flew in. Trains moving about and very little else. Oh, we picked up a couple of nasty-looking atmospheric vents. The tubes must have ruptured. There were bodies in the gas stream.'

'They must fight a constant maintenance battle against structural fatigue,' Oxley said. 'That's a lot of surface area to cover.'

'Everything's relative,' Sarha said. 'There's a lot of Mosdva to cover it.'

'I wonder how interdependent the dominions are,' Parker said. 'For all Quantook-LOU says about driving a hard bargain on the cargo and mass which Anthi-CL sends to the inner dominions, they have to ensure supplies are preserved. Without fresh material, the tubes would decay. The inner dominions would react strongly to such a threat, I imagine.'

'We've confirmed eighty dead areas across Tojolt-HI,' Beaulieu said. 'They amount to just under thirteen per cent of the total.'

'So much? That would tend to indicate a society in decline, possibly even a decadent one.'

'Individual dominions might fall,' Ruben said. 'But overall their society remains intact. Face it, the Confederation has inhabited worlds that don't exactly thrive, yet some of our cultures are positively vibrant. And I find it significant that none of the rim sections are dead.'

'The other major source of external activity is based around those dead sections,' Liol said. 'It looks like major repair and reconstruction work. Those dominions certainly aren't decadent, they're busy expanding into their old neighbours' territory.'

'I can accept they're socially comparable to us,' Syrinx said. 'So based on that assumption, do we offer them ZTT technology?'

'In exchange for a ten thousand year old almanac?' Joshua said. 'You've got to be kidding. Quantook-LOU is smart, he'll know there's something very wrong about that. I'd suggest we build in an exchange of astronometrical data and records along with whatever commercial trade deal we can put together. After all, they've never seen what lies on the other side of the nebula. If we offer them the ability to break free of Tyrathca-dominated space they'll need to know what's out there.'

'I've told you,' Ashly said. 'ZTT isn't a way out.'

'Not for the proles,' Liol said. 'But the leadership might take it for their families, or clans, or members of whatever cause they rally round. And it's the leadership we have to deal with.'

'Is that the kind of legacy we really want to leave behind us?' Peter Adul asked quietly. 'The opportunity for interstellar conflict, and internal strife?'

'Don't get all moral on me,' Liol said. 'Not you. We can't afford those kind of ethics. It's our goddam species on the brink here. I'm prepared to do whatever it takes.'

'If, as intended, we're going to ask a god for its help, perhaps you should consider how worthy we're going to appear before it should you follow that course.'

'What if it considers obliterating your foes to be a worthy act? You're assigning it very human traits. The Tyrathca never did that.'

'That's a point,' Dahybi said. 'Now we know why the Tyrathca managed to get where they are with zero imagination, how does that reflect on our analysis of the Sleeping God?'

'Very little, I'm afraid,' Kempster said. 'From what we've learned about them, I'd say that unless the Sleeping God explained itself to the Tyrathca of Swantic-LI, they simply wouldn't know what the hell it was. By calling it a god, they were being as truthful as only they can be. The simplest translation equates to our own: something so powerful we do not comprehend it.'

'Just how much will ZTT change the diskcity society?' Syrinx asked.

'Considerably,' Parker said. 'As Samuel points out, just by being here, we have changed it. We have shown Tojolt-HI that it is possible to circumvent Tyrathca space. As this is a species with an intellect not dissimilar to our own, we must assume they will ultimately pursue that method. In effect, that gives us control over the timing, nothing more. And allowing them access to ZTT now may generate a portion of goodwill among at least one faction of a very long lived and versatile race. I say we should pursue every effort to make the Mosdva our friends. After all, we now know that ZTT or the voidhawk distortion field ability are hardly the last word in interstellar travel, the Kiint teleport ability has taught us that lesson.'

'Any other options?' Syrinx asked.

'As I see it, we have four in total,' Samuel said. 'We can try and get the almanac through a trade exchange. We can use force.' He paused to smile apologetically as his fellow Edenists registered their disapproval. 'I'm sorry,' he said. 'But we have that ability, therefore it should be examined. Our weaponry is likely to be superior, and our electronic and software capability would definitely be able to extract information from their memory cores.'

'That's an absolute last resort,' Syrinx said.

'Totally,' Joshua agreed firmly. 'This is a culture which wages war over any spare mass on a scale we've never seen before. They might not have sophisticated weapons compared to ours, but they'll have one hell of a lot of them, and *Lady Mac* is in the front line. What are the other two?'

'If Quantook-LOU proves uncooperative, we simply find a dominion which will help us. We're not exactly short of choice. The last option is a variant of that, we leave straight away, and find a Tyrathca colony.'

'We've established a reasonable level of contact with Quantook-LOU and the Anthi-CL dominion,' Sarha said. 'I think we should build on that. Don't forget time is a factor as well, and we came here so we wouldn't have to deal with the Tyrathca.'

'Very well,' Syrinx said. 'We'll follow Joshua's tactic for now. Set up a major commercial trade, and tack on the almanac data as a subsidiary deal.'

*

Joshua kept the same team with him when he returned to the diskcity. This time they were shown directly to Quantook-LOU's private glass bubble.

'Have you found trade items within your ship, Captain Joshua Calvert?' the Mosdva asked.

'I believe so,' Joshua said. He glanced round the translucent chamber with its barnacles of alien machinery, vaguely disquieted. Something had changed. His neural nanonics ran a comparison check with his visual memory file. 'I'm not sure if it's relevant,' he told his crew through the affinity link, 'but several chunks of hardware bolted onto the piping are different now.'

'We see them, Josh,' Liol answered.

'Anybody got any ideas what they could be?'

'I'm not picking up any sensor emissions,' Oski said. 'But they've got strong magnetic fields, definitely active electronics inside.'

'Beam weapons?'

'I'm not sure. I can't see anything that equates to a nozzle on any of them, and the magnetic field doesn't correspond to a power cell. My best guess is that they've rebuilt this whole chamber as a magnetic resonance scanner: if they've got quantum interface detectors sensitive enough they probably think it will allow them to look inside our armour.'

'Will it?'

'No. Our suit shielding will block that. Nice try, though.'

'Did you examine the processor I gave you?' Joshua asked Quantook-LOU.

'It has been tested. Your design is a radical one. We believe we can duplicate it.'

'I can offer more advanced processors than that. As well, we have power storage cells that operate at very high density levels. The formula for superstrength molecular chains; which should be very useful to you, given your shortage of mass.'

'Interesting. And what would you like in return?'

'We saw your ship returning from the sun. Your thermal dissipation technology would be extremely useful to us.'

The negotiation took off well, Joshua and Quantook-LOU reeling out lists of technology and fabrication methods. The trick was in trying to balance them: was optical memory crystal worth more or less than a membrane layer that could guard metal surfaces against vacuum ablation? Did a low-energy carbon-filtration process have parity with ultrastrong magnets?

As they talked, Oski kept monitoring the new hardware modules. The magnetic fields they put out were constantly changing, sweeping across the translucent bubble in waves. None of them were able to penetrate their suits. In return, her own sensors could pick up the resonance patterns they generated inside the Mosdva. She slowly built up a three-dimensional image of their internal structure, the triangular plates of bone and mysterious organs. It was an enjoyable irony, she felt. After forty minutes, the magnetic fields were abruptly switched off.

Liol was paying scant attention to the negotiations. He and Beaulieu were occupied reviewing the data coming in from their ELINT satellites. Now they had the observation subroutines customized properly, there was a lot of activity to see on the darkside.

Trains moved everywhere, following a simple generalized pattern. Large full tankers made their way inwards from the rim, offloading cargo at the industrial modules, then once they were empty, they turned and went directly back to the rim. Goods trains, those loaded with items produced inside industrial modules, ran in every direction. Liol and Beaulieu were beginning to think they might even be independent trading caravans, forever touring round the dominions. Something Joshua hadn't asked was if the Mosdva had currency, or if everything was bartered.

'Another vent,' Beaulieu commented. 'It's only seventy kilometres from the captain's location.'

'Christ, that's the third this morning.' Liol ordered the closest satellite to focus on the plume. Baubles of liquid were oscillating amid the gas squirting out towards the nebula. Ebony shapes, radiating brightly in the infra-red, thrashed around inside it, their motions grinding down the further away they got from the darkside. 'You'd think they'd have better structural integrity after all this time. Everything else they do seems to work pretty well. I know I wouldn't like to live with that kind of threat looming over me, it's worse than building a house on the side of a volcano.' His subconscious wouldn't leave the notion alone; there was something wrong about the frequency of the tube breaches. He ran a quick projection through his neural nanonics. 'Uh, guys, if they suffer structural failure at this rate, the whole diskcity will fail inside of seven years. And I've included some pretty generous rebuilding allowances in that.'

'Then you must have got it wrong,' Kempster said.

'Either that, or this isn't a normal event we're witnessing.'

'Venting again,' Beaulieu called out. 'Same web as the last, barely a hundred metres apart.'

In the *Oenone*'s bridge, Syrinx gave Ruben an alarmed look. 'Access all the visual records from the ELINT satellites,' she said. 'See what kind of activity there is in the vent areas prior to the actual event.'

Ruben, Oxley, and Serina nodded in unison. Their minds merged with the bitek memory processors governing the satellites.

'Do we tell Joshua?' Ashly asked.

'Not yet,' Syrinx said. 'I don't want him alarmed. Let's see if we can confirm the cause first.'

An hour after they began negotiating, Joshua and Quantook-LOU had finalized a list of twenty items to exchange. It was to be mainly information, formatted to the digital standard used by the Mosdva, with one physical sample of each item to prove the concept wasn't merely a boastful lie.

'I'd like to move on to pure data now,' Joshua said. 'We're interested in as much of your history as you're prepared to release; astronomical observations, particularly those dealing with the sun's expansion; any significant cultural works; mathematics; the biochemical structure of your plant life. More if you're willing.'

'Is this why you have come?' Quantook-LOU asked.

'I don't understand.'

'You have ventured around the nebula, sixteen thousand light-years by your own telling. You believed the Tyrathca were all that lived here. You say you came purely to trade, which I do not believe. There can be no meaningful trade between us, the distance is too great. At most it would take two or three visits by ships such as yours to level all differences between us. Your technology is so superior we cannot even scan through your spacesuits to verify you are what you say you are; which means that any machinery you see here you will be able to understand and duplicate without our assistance. In effect, you are giving us a multitude of gifts. Yet you are not driven by altruism, you pretend you are here to trade. You persevere in the task of gaining information from us. Therefore, we ask, what is your true reason for coming to this star?'

'Oh, Jesus,' Joshua moaned over their secure communication link. 'I'm not half as smart as I thought I was.'

'None of us are, it would seem,' Syrinx said. 'Damn, he saw right through our strategy.'

'In itself a useful piece of information,' Ruben said.

'How so?'

'Everything in Anthi-CL is valued in terms of resources. Quantook-LOU controls their distribution, which makes him leader of the dominion, and he's also a tough negotiator and diplomat. If those are the traits which make him a good leader, then that confirms the level of competition which exists among the dominions. We may still have leverage. I would suggest that now the cat's out of the bag you play it straight, Joshua. Tell him what we want. Frankly, what have we got to lose at this point?'

Joshua took a breath. Even with Ruben's unarguable summary, he couldn't bring himself to gamble the outcome of their mission on a xenoc's generosity. Especially when they had confirmed virtually nothing the Mosdva had told them about Mastrit-PJ's history, nor even their own nature. 'I congratulate you, Quantook-LOU,' he said. 'That is an admirable deduction from such a small amount of information. Although not entirely correct. I will profit considerably from introducing some of your technology to the Confederation.'

'Why are you here?'

'Because of the Tyrathca. We want to know where they are, how far their influence extends, how many there are of them.'

'Why?'

'At the moment our Confederation co-exists alongside them. Our leadership believes this situation cannot last for ever. We know they have conquered entire sentient species as they spread from star to star, either enslaving them as they did you, or exterminating them. We were fortunate that our technology is superior, they did not threaten us when we first encountered them. But they already have our propulsion systems. Conflict is inevitable if they continue to expand. And any further expansion must be outward, through our worlds. If we know their extent while our starships remain superior, we may be able to terminate that threat.'

'What is your propulsion system? How fast do your ships travel?'

'They can jump instantaneously between star systems.'

Quantook-LOU's reaction was enough for Joshua to class him as human, or as near as made no difference. The xenoc emitted a piping squeal, the fore and midlimbs clapping urgently against his front torso.

'I am glad I have no eggs in my pouch,' Quantook-LOU said when he had quietened. 'I would surely have cracked them.' Marsupial? Joshua wondered idly.

'Do you realize what you have in your ship, Captain Joshua Calvert? You are our salvation. We considered ourselves trapped here orbiting this dying star, encircled by our enemies, never to escape as they did. No more.'

'I take it you'd like to acquire our propulsion technology?'

'Yes. Above all things. We will join your Confederation. You have seen our numbers, our ability. Even with our limited resources, we are vast and powerful. We can build a million warships, a hundred million, and equip them with your propulsion system. The Tyrathca are slow and stupid, they will never match us in time. Together we can embark on a crusade to rid the galaxy of their evil.'

'Oh, Jesus wept,' Joshua exclaimed over the communication link. 'It just keeps getting better. We're going to let loose a cosmic genocide if the Mosdva ever get ZTT technology. And I've a feeling the four of us might not be allowed back to *Lady Mac* until Quantook-LOU has the relevant data.'

'We can shoot our way through the bubble,' Samuel said. 'Get outside and wait in the structure until *Lady Mac* can pick us up.'

'It's not that stressful,' Liol said. 'We can give Quantook-LOU any old file full of shit. Hand over the schematics for a deluxe, ten-flavour ice-cream making machine if you want. He's not going to know the difference until we're long gone.'

'That's my brother.'

'Right now, you've got more immediate troubles. We think the dominions are having some kind of armed conflict. The number of tube breaches is reaching epidemic proportions out here.'

'Fucking wonderful.' Joshua scanned round the bubble again. It wouldn't be too much trouble to break out. And he hadn't seen a Mosdva in a spacesuit. Yet. 'I am prepared to offer you our propulsion system,' he told Quantook-LOU. 'In return, I must have all your information concerning the Tyrathca flightships and the stars they colonized. This is not negotiable. They were sending messages back to this star for thousands of years. I want them, and the stellar coordinate system they used. Provide that for me, and you can have your freedom to roam the galaxy.'

'Obtaining that information will be difficult. The dominion of Anthi-CL does not keep many Tyrathca files of such antiquity.'

'Perhaps other dominions will have what I require.'

Joshua's suit sensors picked up the agitated movements of the seven other Mosdva in the bubble with them.

'You will not deal with another dominion,' Quantook-LOU said.

'Then find out where that information is kept, and trade for it.'

'I will examine the possibility.' Quantook-LOU used a midlimb to grasp a pipe rim on the surface of the bubble. Five of the electronic modules worn on his harness sprouted slim silver cables. Their ends swung round blindly, and they began to wind through the air with a serpentine wriggle, heading for one of the electronic units bolted to the piping. They plugged themselves into various sockets, and the pattern of lights on the unit's surface changed rapidly.

'Crude, but effective,' Ruben commented. 'I wonder how far their neural interface technology extends.'

'Captain,' Beaulieu called. 'We're seeing what looks like troop movements around the Anthi-CL dominion.'

'You've got to be shitting me.'

'Mosdva in spacesuits are crawling along the darkside structure. There is no fabrication or maintenance equipment accompanying them. They are most agile.'

Joshua didn't even want to ask what kind of numbers were involved. 'Sarha, go to flight readiness status, please. If we need you, we'll need you fast.'

'Acknowledged.'

'How long do we wait?' Oski asked.

'Give Quantook-LOU another fifteen minutes. After that, we're out of here.'

But the Mosdva stirred after only a couple of minutes. Three of his five cables unplugged themselves, and wound back into their harness modules. 'The dominion of Anthi-CL has five files relating to the information you want.'

Joshua held up a communication block. 'Transmit them over, we'll see if that's enough.'

'I will release the index only. If this is what you require, we must discuss how to complete the exchange.'

'Agreed.' His neural nanonics monitored the short dataflow from the bubble's electronics into his block. Syrinx and *Oenone* examined the data eagerly.

'Sorry, Joshua,' she said. 'These are just records of messages transmitted by the arkships. Standard updates on how the voyages are progressing. There's nothing of any relevance here.'

'Any messages sent from Swantic-LI?'

'No, we didn't even get that lucky.'

'This information is no good,' Joshua told Quantook-LOU.

'There is no more.'

'Five files, in the whole of Tojolt-HI? There must be more.'

'No.'

'Perhaps the other dominions won't allow you access to their databases. Is that why you're all at war?'

'You have brought this upon us. It is for you we die. Give me the propulsion system. End all our suffering. Does your species have no compassion?'

'I have got to have the information.'

'Where the Tyrathca live, what planets they have colonized, is irrelevant now. If we have your propulsion system, they will never threaten you again. You will have accomplished your aim.'

'I will not give you the propulsion system without receiving the information in exchange. If you cannot provide it, I will find a dominion that will.'

'You may not deal with another dominion.'

'I do not wish our association to end in threats, Quantook-LOU. Please find the information for me. Surely an alliance with another dominion is a small price to pay for the freedom of all Mosdva.'

'There is a place on Tojolt-HI,' Quantook-LOU said. 'The information you want might still be stored there.'

'Excellent. Then plug in, and make the deal. Anthi-CL has obtained enough new technology from us to buy another dominion.'

'This place has no link to the dominions any more. We expelled it long ago.'

'All right, time to say hello again. We'll go there and access the files direct.'

'I cannot take you beyond our borders. I no longer know which of our allies remain trustworthy. Our train may not be allowed to pass.'

'You forget. I've already invited you to visit my starship. We'll fly. It's quicker.'

*

Valisk continued to fall through the dark continuum. The ebony nebula outside flickered with faint bolts of phosphorescence, illuminating the giant habitat's exterior with a feeble glimmer of luminescence as it passed through. Had there been anyone out there who cared, they would have been saddened by how dilapidated it had become. The girders and panels of the counter-rotating spaceport appeared to be fraying with age; around the port's periphery solid matter was decaying into sluggish liquids. Large dank droplets dripped away from the eroded, tapering ends of titanium support struts, gusting away into the depths of the nebula.

Intense cold was punishing the polyp shell badly, devouring the internal heat faster than it could be replenished. Slim cracks were opening up everywhere across the surface, some of them deep enough to reach the outer mitosis layer. Thick tar-like liquids bubbled up through them in places, staining the outer surface an insalubrious sable. Occasionally a chip of polyp would flake away from the edge of a new fissure, drifting away listlessly, as though velocity too was subject to increased entropy. Worst of all, twelve jets of air were fountaining undiminished out of broken starscraper windows, spraying the icy gas in long wavering arcs. They'd been there for days, acting like a beacon for any new Orgathé who glided out of the nebula's labyrinthine nucleus. The big creatures would squirm their way through to the interior, blocking the blast for a few seconds as they crammed in through the empty rim.

Erentz and her relatives all knew about the shrinking atmosphere, but there was nothing they could do to halt it. The darkling habitat cavern belonged to the Orgathé and all the other creatures they'd brought with them. In theory the humans could have made their way to the starscrapers via the tube lines and water ducts. But even if they managed to seal up some of the breaches, the arriving Orgathé would simply smash through new windows.

Five caverns deep in the northern endcap had become the last refuge of the surviving humans, chosen because each one only had a couple of entrances. The defenders had adopted a Horatius strategy. A few people armed with flame-throwers and incendiary torpedo launchers stood shoulder to shoulder and saturated the passageway with fire whenever one of the creatures tried to get through. Human ghosts hung back during each battle, waiting until the creature retreated before they scampered forward to absorb the sticky fluid it had shed, giving themselves substance again. They formed a strange alliance with the living humans, warning them when one of the dark continuum creatures was approaching. Though none of them could be persuaded to do anything else.

'Can't say I blame them,' Dariat told Tolton. 'We're as much a target to the creatures as anyone.' He was one of the very few solid ghosts allowed in the refuge caverns, and even he preferred to skulk about in the small chamber Dr Patan and his team used rather than face the ailing, strung-out bulk of the population.

The habitat personality and Rubra's remaining relatives had consolidated their survival policy around the single goal of protecting the physics team. A cry for help to the Confederation was their only hope now. And given the state of the habitat, time was short.

Tolton had become afraid to ask for progress reports. The answer was always the same. So he hung around with Dariat, unrolling his sleeping bag in the corridor outside the physicists' chamber. As close to their last chance as he could be without actually getting in the way. The personality or Erentz would give him the odd task to do, where he had to go out into the big cavern again. Usually it was moving some bulky piece of equipment about, or assisting with their small stock of rations. He also stripped and cleaned torpedo launchers ready for the defenders, surprised by how good he was at something so mechanical. At the same time, it meant he knew how low their ammunition was.

'Not that it matters,' he complained to Dariat as he flopped down on his sleeping bag after a session cleaning the weaponry, 'we'll suffocate long before then.'

'The pressure is down by nearly twenty per cent now. If we could just find some way of sealing the starscrapers, we'd stand a better chance.'

Tolton took a deep breath, exhaling slowly. 'I don't know if I can tell yet, or if I'm just imagining the air's thinner because I know that's what I should be feeling. Mind you, with that smell coming from next door, who knows.'

'Smell is one sense I haven't regained.'

'Take my word for it, in this case that's a blessing. Ten thousand sick people who haven't had a bath for a month. I'm amazed the Orgathé don't turn tail and run screaming.'

'They won't.'

'Is there any way we can fight back?'

Dariat squatted down. 'The personality has considered pumping the light-tube.'

'Pumping?'

'Divert every last watt of electricity into heating the plasma, then switch off the confinement field. We did it before on a small scale. In theory, it should vaporize every fluid-formed creature in the habitat cavern.'

'Then do it,' Tolton hissed back.

'Firstly, there's not much power left. Secondly, we're worried about the cold.'

'Cold?'

'Valisk has been radiating heat out into this Thoale-cursed realm ever since we got here. The shell is becoming very brittle. Pumping the light-tube is like letting off a bomb inside; it might shatter.'

'Great,' Tolton griped. 'Just fucking great.' He had to pull his feet in as three people staggered past, carrying a not-so-small micro-fusion generator between them. 'Is that for the pumping?' he asked once they'd passed.

Dariat was frowning, watching the triad. **What are they doing?** he asked the personality.

They're going to install the generator back in the *Hainan Thunder*.

Why?

I'd thought that was obvious. Thirty of them are going to fly it the hell away from here.

Which thirty? he asked angrily.

Does it matter?

To the others it will. And me.

Survival of the fittest. You shouldn't complain, you've had a damn good run.

What's the point? The starships are damn near wrecks. And even if they do get a drive tube running, where are they going to go?

As far as they can. The *Hainan Thunder*'s hull is still intact, it's only the protective foam which is peeling off.

So far. Entropy will eat through it. The whole ship will rot away around them. You know that.

We also know it has functional patterning nodes. Maybe the pattern can be formatted to get a signal out to the Confederation. Some kind of energy burst that can punch through.

Holly Anstid, is that what we're reduced to?

Yes. Happy now?

'They need the generator over in the armoury,' Dariat said. 'Their power supply packed in.' He couldn't look the street poet in the eyes.

Tolton grunted indifferently, and pulled the sleeping bag round his shoulders. When he breathed out, he could see his breath as a white mist. 'Damn, you were right about the cold.'

Can Tolton go with them? Dariat asked.

We're sorry.

Come on, you are me. Part of you, anyway. You owe me that much out of sentiment. And he was the one who got our relatives out of zero-tau.

Do you imagine he will want to go? There are thousands of children cowering in the caverns. Would he walk past them to the airlock without offering to exchange places?

Oh, shit!

If there is to be a token civilian on board, it won't be him.

All right, all right. You win. Happy now?

Lady Chi-Ri wouldn't approve of bitterness.

Dariat scowled, but didn't answer. He went into the neural strata's administrative thought routines to examine the ships which were still docked at the spaceport. Most of the spaceport's net had failed, leaving only seven visual sensors operational. He used them to scan round, locating four starships and seven inter-orbit vessels. Of all of them, *Hainan Thunder* was the most flightworthy.

Wait now, the personality said.

The sheer surprise in the thought was so unusual that all the affinity capable stopped what they were doing to find out what had happened. They shared the image collected by the few external sensitive cells that were still alive.

Valisk had reached the end of the nebula, and was slowly sliding out. Its boundary was as clearly defined as an atmospheric cloud bank. A plane of slow-shifting grainy swirls stretching away in every direction as far as the sensitive cells could discern. Slivers of pale light trickled among the dull gibbous braids, an infestation of torpid static.

There was a gap of perfectly clear space extending for about a hundred kilometres from the end of the nebula.

What is that? a badly subdued personality asked.

Another flat plane surface ended the gap, running parallel to the nebula, and extending just as far. This one was hoary-grey, and looked very solid.

Visual interpretation subroutines concentrated on the sight. The entire surface appeared to be moving, seething with tiny persistent undulations.

The mélange, Dariat said. Dread made his counterfeit body tremble as memory fragments from the creature in the lift shaft surfaced to torment him. **This is where everything finishes in this realm. The end. For ever.**

Get the *Hainan Thunder* launched, the personality ordered frantically. **Patan, you and your people evacuate now. Send a message to the Confederation.**

'What's happening?' a puzzled Tolton asked. He looked along the corridor as semi-hysterical shouting broke out in the physicists' chamber. A stack of glass tubing crashed to the ground.

'We're in trouble,' Dariat said.

'As opposed to what we're in now?' Tolton was trying to make light of it, but the ghost's conspicuous fear was a strong inhibitor.

'So far our time here has been paradise. This is when the dark continuum becomes personal and eternal.'

The street poet shuddered. **Help us,** Dariat pleaded. **For pity's sake. I am you. If there's a single chance to survive, make it happen.**

A fast surge of information came pouring through the affinity bond, running through his mind with painful intensity. He felt as if his own thoughts were being forced to examine every cubic centimetre of the giant habitat, stretching out to such a thinness they would surely tear. The flow stopped as fast as it began, and his attention was twinned with the personality's. They looked at the spindle which connected the habitat to the counter-rotating spaceport. Like most of the composite and metal components of the habitat it was decaying badly. But near the base, just above the huge magnetic bearing buried in the polyp, five emergency escape pods were nesting in their covered berths.

Go, the personality said.

'Follow me,' Dariat barked at Tolton. He began to jog along the passage towards the main cavern, moving as fast as his bulk would allow. Tolton never hesitated, he jumped to his feet and ran after the solid ghost.

The main cavern was in turmoil. The refugees knew something was wrong, but not what. Assuming another attack from the Orgathé, they were shuffling back as far as they could get from the two entrances. Electrophorescent strips on the ceiling were dimming rapidly.

Dariat headed for the alcove which served as an armoury. 'Get a weapon,' he said. 'We might need it.'

Tolton snatched up an incendiary torpedo launcher, and a belt of ammunition for it. The pair of them headed for the nearest entrance. None of the nervous defenders questioned them as they raced past. Behind them, they could hear Dr Patan's team shouting and cursing as they ran across the cavern.

'Where are we going?' Tolton asked.

'The spindle. There's some emergency escape pods left that didn't get launched last time I left in a hurry.'

'The spindle? That's in free fall. I always throw up in free fall.'

'Listen—'

'Yes, yes, I know. Free fall is a paradise compared with what's about to happen.'

Dariat ran straight into a group of ghosts waiting at a large oval junction in the passage. They couldn't see the mélange, none of them were affinity capable, but they could sense it. The ether was filling with the misery and torment of the diminished souls it had claimed.

'Out of my way!' Dariat bellowed. He clamped his hand over the face of the first ghost, pulling energy out of her. She screamed and stumbled away from him. Her outline rippled, sagging downwards with a soft squelching sound. The others backed off fast, staring in wounded accusation with pale forlorn faces.

Dariat turned off down one of the junction's side passages. Light from the overhead strips was fading rapidly now. 'You got a torch?' he asked.

'Sure.' Tolton patted the light stick hanging from his belt.

'Save it till you really need it. I should be able to help.' He held up a hand, and concentrated. The palm lit up with a cold blue radiance.

They came out into a wider section of the passage. There'd been some kind of firefight here; the polyp walls were charred, the electrophorescent strip shattered and blackened with soot. Tolton felt his world constricting, and took the safety off the launcher. Dariat stood in front of a closed muscle membrane, barely his own height, that was set into the wall. He focused his thoughts, and the rubbery stone parted with great reluctance, the lips puckering with trembling motions. Air whistled out, turning into a strong gust as the membrane opened further.

There was no light at all inside.

'What is this?' Dariat asked.

'Secondary air duct. It should take us right up to the hub.'

Tolton shuddered reluctantly, and stepped inside.

Valisk had cleared the nebula, its great length taking several minutes to complete the transfer into clear space. The spaceport was the last section to leave it behind. Four lights gleamed brightly around the rim of the docking-bay which held the *Hainan Thunder*, four in a ring of at least a hundred. Nonetheless, they were extraordinarily bright in this dour environment. Their tight beams fell on the hull, revealing patches of bright silver-grey metal shining through the scabby mush of thermal-protection foam that was moulting away in a glutinous drizzle.

The windows looking out onto the bay flickered with light as the desperate crew hauled themselves past the maintenance team offices, oxygen masks clamped to their faces, torches shining ahead of them. A couple of minutes later the starship began to show some signs of activity. Thin gases flooded out of nozzles around the lower quarter of the hull. One of the thermo-dump panels slid out of its recess, and started to glow a faint pink at the centre. The airlock tube disengaged, withdrawing several metres before lurching to a halt. Clamps around the docking cradle flicked back, releasing the hull.

Chemical thrusters around the starship's equator fired, sending out shimmering plumes of hot yellow gas. They tore straight through the bay's structural panels, creating a vicious blowback of atmospheric gas from the life-support sections. The *Hainan Thunder* rose out of the bay atop a thick geyser of churning white vapour.

More powerful chemical rockets ignited, propelling the starship away from the spaceport. One of them exploded, its combustion chamber weakened by exposure to the dark continuum. The starship pitched to one side, then recovered. It began to climb steadily towards the nebula.

An Orgathé swooped out from the percolating gunge, and descended on the starship. Its talons tore through the hull plates, shredding the equipment underneath. The rockets died amid a shower of sapphire sparks. Fluids and vapour streamed out from deep clefts.

A second Orgathé joined the first, the huge creatures tugging the starship violently between them. Big chunks of metal and composite were ripped free, twirling off into the void. The creatures were eagerly clawing their way through the tanks and machinery to reach the life-support capsules and the kernels of life-energy cowering inside.

There was a final spew of gas as the capsules were punctured, then the Orgathé were still as they consumed their ephemeral meal.

The habitat personality had little time for remorse, or even anger. It was watching the surface of the mélange as it grew closer. The incessant motion was becoming clearer, an agitated ocean of thick fluid. Closer, and a billion different species of xenocs were drowning in that ocean, their appendages, tentacles, and limbs writhing against each other as they strove to keep afloat. Closer still, and the bodies were actually forming themselves from the fluid and clawing madly to lift themselves into the void above, a brief existence of useless strife and wasted energy before they collapsed and dissipated back into the mélange. If they were lucky, peaks would arise as souls merged together, combining their strength as they sacrificed identity. Those at the pinnacle stretched themselves further and urther, quivering to break free. Only once did the personality see an Orgathé, or something similar, sweep upwards, newborn and victorious.

When we hit that, the amount of energy we contain is going to blow a hole clean through to the other side, the personality said shakily.

There is no other side, Dariat said. **Just as there is no hope.** Every part of his body ached from the climb up through the air duct. He had forced himself to keep going, at first hiking up the slope, then as the gravity fell off, pulling himself along a near-vertical shaft with his arms.

Then why do you keep going?

Instinct and stupidity, I suppose. If I can delay entry into the mélange by a day, then that's a day less suffering.

A day out of eternity? Does that matter?

To me, now. Yes. It matters. I'm human enough to be terrified.

Then you'd better hurry.

The southern endcap was within twenty kilometres of the mélange. Ahead of it, the surface was churning with activity. Huge peaks were jabbing up as melting bodies climbed on top of each other so they could be the first to touch the shell and feast on the life-energy within. Entire mountains of cupidity heaved passionately.

Dariat reached the end of the duct, and commanded the muscle membrane to open. They air-swam out into one of the main corridors leading to the hub chamber.

Tolton had fastened his light stick to the launcher, as he'd seen Erentz do. He swept the beam round the black corridor in an alert fashion. 'Any bad guys around here?'

'No. In any case, they're all waiting for the impact. Nothing's moving in the habitat.'

'I'm not surprised. I can taste the horror; it's physical, like I've overloaded on downer activants. Shit – ' he smiled brokenly at Dariat – 'I'm frightened, man. Really frightened. Is there any way a soul can die here, die completely? I don't want to join the mélange. Not that.'

'I'm sorry. It can't be done. You have to live.'

'Fuck! What kind of a universe is this anyway?'

Dariat led Tolton into the darkened hub chamber and held his hand high, letting the energy pulse recklessly. The resulting burst of light revealed the geometry; silent doors leading to the spindle commuter cabs, hoop avenues down to the tube train stations. He aimed himself at a door leading to the engineering section, and kicked off.

The corridors on the other side were metal, lined with grab hoops. They slithered along them quickly, using the manual controls to get past airlock hatches. The air was freezing, but breathable. Tolton's teeth started chattering.

'Here we go,' Dariat said. The escape pod's circular hatch was open. He somersaulted in, vaguely unnerved by the familiar layout. Twelve acceleration couches were laid out around him. He chose the one under the solitary instrument panel, and started flicking switches. Same sequence as last time. The hatch hinged shut automatically. Lights came on with reluctance, and the environment pumps started to whine.

Tolton held his hands up in front of the grille, catching the warm air. 'God, it was *cold* out there.'

'Strap in, we're about to leave.'

The personality watched the tip of the southern endcap touch the surface of the mélange. **I am proud of all of you**, it told Rubra's descendants.

Fluid cratered away from the impact, then rushed back to slam against the shell. Hundreds of thousands of berserk souls surfed it inwards, and penetrated the polyp to immerse themselves in the magnificent tide of life-energy coursing within, absorbing it directly. The temperature difference between fluid and polyp was too great for the habitat's weakened shell to withstand. The existing fissures flexed wildly as thermal stresses tightened their grip.

Dariat activated the pod's jettison sequence. Explosive bolts cut away the berth's outer shielding, and five of the solid rockets fired. They were flung clear of the spindle, racing out level with the surface of the mélange.

Goodbye, the personality said. The accompanying sorrow brought tears to Dariat's eyes.

Valisk burst apart as if a fusion bomb had detonated inside. Thousands of human souls came fluttering out of the billowing core of hot gas and crumbling polyp slabs, indestructible phantoms naked in the darkness. As with all life in the dark continuum, they sank into the mélange and began their suffering.

The solid rocket burn ended, leaving the escape pod in free fall. Dariat looked out of the small port, seeing very little. He twisted the joystick, firing the cold-gas thrusters to roll the pod. Grey smears slashed past outside.

'I can see the mélange, I think,' he reported faithfully. In his mind he was aware of the wailing and torment gushing from the awesome conglomeration of pitiful souls. It chilled his own resolution. There could only ever be one fate here.

Amid the misery were several steely strands of more purposeful and malignant thought. One of them was growing stronger. Nearer, Dariat realized. 'Something's out there.' He tilted the joystick again, spinning the pod quickly. Pale blooms of light emerged deep inside the nebula, silhouetting a speck that whirled and shook as it arrowed towards them.

'Shit, it's one of the Orgathé.' He and Tolton stared mutely at each other.

The street poet twitched feebly. 'I can't even say it's been fun.'

'There are five solid rockets left. We can fire them and fly back into the nebula.'

'Won't we just wind up here again?'

'Yes. Eventually. But it'll be another day or two out of the mélange.'

'I'm not sure it makes that much difference to me now.'

'Then again, we could fire them when the Orgathé reaches us, fry the bastard.'

'It's only doing what we'd do.'

'Last choice, we can fire the rockets to take us into the mélange.'

'Into! What use will that be?'

'None whatsoever. Even if we don't break apart on impact we'll melt away into the fluid over a few days.'

'Or fly straight through to the other side.'

'There isn't one.'

'You never know unless you try. Besides, this way has the most style.'

'Style, huh.'

They both grinned.

Dariat rolled the pod again, getting a rough alignment on the mélange. He fired two of the solid rockets. Any more, and they really would crack open when they reached it.

The cold will probably do it anyway, he thought.

There was three seconds of five-gee acceleration, then they hit. The deceleration jolt was fearsome, flinging Tolton against the couch's straps. He groaned at the pain, bracing himself for the worst.

But the pod's thermal coating held, defying the devastating sub-cryonic temperature of the mélange. The pod juddered sluggishly as its rocket motors continued to fire, thrusting them deeper and deeper below the surface. Both of them could hear the cacophony of souls outside, their shock and dismay as the rocket exhaust vaporized the fluid in which they were suspended. The cries grew fainter the further in they went. After fifteen seconds the rockets burnt out.

Tolton's laugh had an unstable timbre. 'We made it.'

The port had frosted over as soon as they struck the fluid. He reached over and tried to wipe the beads of ice clear. His hand stuck to the glass. 'Bugger!' He lost some skin pulling it free. 'Now what do we do?'

'Absolutely nothing.'

25

The Volkswagen Trooperbus carried Louise and Ivanov Robson back to London. During most of the four-hour trip she sat curled up on one of the big leather chairs in the cabin, accessing news reports from the arcology. The landscape held little interest for her now.

There were few rover reporters left in the Westminster Dome to provide an impression of what was happening. Those that insisted on toughing it out were releasing their sensevises on a long delay, allowing them to get well clear of the area where they'd been recording. The possessed didn't take kindly to having their activities exposed to the planet's accessing public. Rovers who'd been caught on the first day had never accessed the net again.

What was shown by reporters still on the ground, and more comprehensively by the dome sensors, was a rough kind of order establishing itself among the ancient buildings. The possessed were organized in small bands, walking quite openly along the main roads. It was a defiant gesture at Govcentral. They could have been targeted easily by SD weapons, had the political will existed to do so. But as there was only ever a couple of hundred exposed at any one time, the remainder would be free to extract an atrocious retribution on the rest of the non-possessed population. Government forces within the arcology had been effectively eliminated. Highly specific fires had continued to rage throughout the night, disposing of all the dome's police stations and eighty per cent of the local council offices. Significantly, although power grids and the communication net had also been targeted, the possessed hadn't damaged any of the primary civic utility stations. There was still water, and fresh air, and the dome remained capable of warding off an armada storm. Somebody was controlling the possessed, and ordering their activities with a great deal of precision.

The media speculated on who.

Charlie was only interested in why. If anything, the possessed were now enforcing the original curfew with a greater efficiency than the police ever had. The AI's analysis of their movements indicated there were between seven and ten thousand of them, each with their own area to control. Enough to make sure everyone stayed indoors. Very few new possessed were being created, and there were barely a few hundred in the nine outer domes.

The only significant excursion they'd attempted was to a garage of surface vehicles. Each time they'd driven one of the lumbering machines out up the ramp, it had been targeted by SD fire. The President himself had ordered the strikes without any urging from B7 assets among his advisers and Cabinet. The possessed had made eight attempts to leave London before giving up.

'Dexter's preparing for something,' Charlie told Louise just before she left his dome. 'There's no way he'll be satisfied with just London. That's why he's holding back on possessing the rest of the population. The way he's put things together in there, he could do it in less than a week if he wanted. He's far better organized than New York.'

Louise didn't understand why Dexter was holding back any more than Charlie. The devilsome man she'd encountered back on Norfolk didn't seem capable of any restraint.

The only other information she received on the trip was progress reports on Genevieve. Her sister was being driven to Birmingham in another Volkswagen, along with Divinia and the first batch of Charlie's family. From there Charlie had arranged a vac-train to take them to the Kenya Station. Gen had been quite disappointed when it turned out that Charlie's dome couldn't fly.

It was a much shorter drive to Birmingham. Genevieve was already on the African Tower ascending to Skyhigh Kijabe while Louise was still making her way across the Thames valley.

'Coming into view now if you want to see it,' Yves Gaynes called out from the cab.

Louise stirred herself, and went forward to sit next to him. When they'd left London she'd had a poor view of the domes, the direction they were travelling in was all wrong. Now the Trooperbus was pointing straight at them as it lumbered over the last few miles.

She stared at the domes that sliced up out of the rolling horizon. Only the outer nine were visible, gathered protectively around the ancient city at the centre. The sinking sun reflected vivid pillars of copper light off the vast arcades of geodesic crystal; other than that, they were completely black. For the first time, she could appreciate just how artificial they were. How alien.

Yves was looking at her. 'Didn't expect to be coming back this way quite so soon, myself.'

'No.'

'The boss does look after his people, you know.'

'I'm sure he does.' Not that she was convinced she really qualified as a B7 staff member. Then again, it could just be Charlie remote-controlling the driver, trying to reassure her. To make her more compliant. She wasn't certain of anything any more.

The Trooperbus drove steadily past the half-buried factory halls surrounding the arcology, and dipped down a ramp into one of the huge underground garages. There were few lights on up among the vaulting ceiling, and no activity at all among the ranks of parked vehicles. They drew up in a bay near the ramp. As the external door slid down, a navy blue car sped towards them out of the gloom. Ivanov Robson stood up and popped the cabin's hatch.

'Are you ready?' he asked politely.

'Yes.' Louise made her voice cool. She hadn't spoken to him since the journey started. It was an issue dominated by anger; although she wasn't sure who she was directing it against. Him for being what he was, or herself for liking him at the start. Maybe he was just too strong a reminder that she'd been so thoroughly manipulated.

She climbed down the short ladder. It was humid in the garage, but colder than she expected. She was dressed for the arcology, in a short skirt over black leggings, with a long-sleeved emerald T-shirt (to cover the medical nanonic bracelet) and thin leather waistcoat. Her hair had been battened down into a single ponytail.

Ivanov followed as she hurried over to the car, carrying the slim alligator-skin weapons case Charlie had given him. A policewoman ushered them into the car, her face devoid of curiosity. How many people have B7 sequestrated? Louise wondered. This time the car's interior was quite ordinary. She settled back in the rear seat, with Ivanov beside her, the fateful case resting on his knees.

'I am me most of the time, you know,' he said quietly. 'B7 can't control my every waking second.'

'Oh.' Louise didn't want to talk about it.

'I regard it as a penance, not a punishment. And I get to see some interesting things. I also know how the world works, a rare privilege for anyone these days. As you now know.'

'What did you do?'

'Something very foolish, and unpleasant. Not that I had a lot of choice at the time. It was them or me. I think that's why B7 gave me this deal. I'm not what you'd call a standard career criminal. I even had a family. Haven't seen them for a couple of decades, but I'm allowed to know how they're getting on.'

'But you were still told how to treat me.'

'I was ordered what information to supply to you, and when. Everything else I ever said or did was the real me.'

'Including coming back to London now?'

Ivanov chuckled quietly. 'Oh, no. Natural altruism doesn't run to this insanity. I'm here under orders.' He paused. 'But now I'm here, I will do my best to protect you if the need arises.'

'You think coming back was stupid?'

'Completely idiotic. B7 should toughen up and nuke London. It's the only way we'll ever be rid of these possessed.'

'That kind of weapon won't work against Quinn Dexter.'

'Is that so?' A long finger stroked the alligator-skin case slowly. 'Do you trust this Fletcher guy we're going to meet?'

'Of course. Fletcher is a decent and kind man. He looked after Gen and me all the way from Norfolk.'

'Should be interesting,' Ivanov mumbled. He turned to watch the concrete wall of the tunnel slip past outside the car.

They arrived at a small vac-train freight station somewhere in one of the arcology's underground industrial zones. Charlie had selected it because there was a direct road from the garage, and the net was still functioning in that sector.

The platform was a lot narrower than those at King's Cross, with large units of heavy-duty cargo-handling machinery standing by every airlock. When Louise and Ivanov emerged out of a service lift, eight GISD field agents were waiting for them, each equipped with a static-bullet machine-gun.

The train arrived five minutes later. Only one airlock door opened. Detective Brent Roi stepped out first, looking round suspiciously. When his gaze found Louise his expression told her he was officially the unhappiest person on the planet.

'Out,' he snapped over his shoulder.

Fletcher Christian emerged from the airlock, dressed in his immaculate naval uniform. Two guards were right behind him, and there was a thick metal collar clamped round his throat. Louise didn't care, under the stiff gaze of the field agents she ran over and flung her arms round him.

'Oh, God, I missed you,' she blurted. 'Are you all right?'

'Hardy enough, my dearest lady Louise. And you? How have you fared since we parted last? More unsuitable adventures, I'll warrant.'

She was wiping tears off against his lapels, the buttons on his jacket pressing into her skin. 'Something like that.' She clutched him tighter, amazed by how glad she was to see him, the one person she really trusted on the whole planet. His hand stroked the back of her head.

'Jesus wept,' Brent Roi exclaimed in disgust.

Louise let go, and took a timid step back. Fletcher's mournful eyes showed he understood.

'You two finished?'

Ivanov stepped forwards. 'Try picking on me,' he said to the Halo detective.

'Who the hell are you?'

'Put it this way, we share the same supervisor. And if you had a high enough security rating to be told what Louise has done for us, you'd display some respect there as well.'

Fletcher was looking at the hulking private detective with some interest. Ivanov thrust his hand out. 'Pleased to meet you, Fletcher. I'm the guy who's been looking out for Louise down here.' He winked at her. 'When circumstances allow me to.'

Fletcher bowed. 'Then you do us all a service, sir. I would be sorely grieved if any harm befell such a treasured flower.'

Brent Roi sighed in disbelief. 'You want to get on with this?'

'Sure,' Ivanov said. 'We'll take over from you. I doubt I have to sign for him, right?'

'Take over? As in my part's finished? It's not that goddam easy. I haven't got any way of getting back to the Halo. I'm fucking stuck here escorting this jerk.'

Louise was about to tell him B7 could get him back up the orbital tower, then she saw Ivanov's face go blank momentarily. Charlie must be telling him something.

'OK,' Ivanov said sadly. 'But just so you know, it wasn't my idea.'

'That makes me feel a whole lot better.'

Louise sat next to Fletcher when they got back to the car. Ivanov and Brent took the jump seats opposite.

'It's your show,' Ivanov told Fletcher. 'How do you want to play this?'

'Wait a minute,' Louise said. 'Fletcher, what's that collar?'

'Pacifier,' Brent grunted. 'If he gets fruity, I can slam a thousand-volt charge through him. Believe me, that makes these possessed bastards sit up and take notice.'

'Take it off,' she demanded.

'Lady Louise—'

'No. Take it off. I wouldn't treat an animal like that. It's monstrous.'

'While I'm near him, it stays on,' Brent said. 'You can't trust them.'

'Charlie,' Louise datavised. 'Tell them to take it off. I'm not joking. I won't cooperate any further until you stop treating Fletcher like this.'

'Sorry, Louise,' Charlie replied. 'The Halo police were jumpy. It was only supposed to be while he was in transit.'

She watched Brent's expression darken as he received a datavise from Charlie. 'Fuck it all,' he spat. There was a click from Fletcher's collar, and the locking mechanism rotated ninety degrees. Fletcher reached up, and tugged at it experimentally. It came away in his hands.

'Hey.' Brent slid the front of his jacket to one side, revealing a shoulder holster containing a very large automatic pistol. Three reserve clips had small red lightning emblems on them. He stared at Fletcher. 'I'm watching you.'

Fletcher placed the collar disdainfully on the floor between them. 'Thank you.'

'No problem,' Ivanov said. 'We want you comfortable.'

'You mentioned a weapon, lady Louise.'

'Yes, the Confederation Navy has designed something that destroys souls. They want you to try and get close enough to Dexter to shoot him with it.'

'True death,' Fletcher said in wonder. 'There are many who would welcome that now. Are you certain such a device works?'

'That's confirmed,' Ivanov said. 'It's been tested.'

'If I might be so bold as to ask, upon whom?'

'The project director used it on himself and a possessed who was threatening him.'

'I am uncertain if that is heroism or tragedy. Did they suffer?'

'Not a thing. It's completely painless.'

'Another example of your much vaunted progress. May I see this fearsome instrument?'

Ivanov put the alligator-skin case on his knees, and datavised the entry code. The lock bleeped, and he opened it. Five matt-black cylinders, thirty centimetres long, were nesting on the grey foam inside. He picked one out. One end had a glass lens, and there was a single flat red button on the side.

'The majority of its components are bitek, so it should be able to resist a possessed glitching it for a while. Simple operation. Push the button forward, so – ' he worked it with his thumb – 'to activate. Then press to fire. It will shine a narrow beam of red light, which has to strike your target's eyes to work. Estimated effective range is fifty metres.'

'Yards,' Louise murmured with a smile.

Fletcher inclined his head in thanks.

'Whatever,' Ivanov said. He handed the weapon to Fletcher. Brent tensed up. But Fletcher simply examined the gadget with mild curiosity.

'It seems naught but a harmless stick,' he said.

'There's plenty goes on inside that you can't see.'

'Nor understand, I'll warrant. However, its use is plain enough to me. Tell me, what happens to the original soul of a body when this is fired at a possessing soul?'

Ivanov cleared his throat carefully. 'They die as well.'

'That is murder.'

'One death is a small price to pay for ridding the universe of Quinn Dexter.'

'Aye, the affairs of kings are not to be questioned by their subjects. For that is what makes them kings. Judged only by Our Lord.'

'Can I have one as well, please?' Louise asked.

Ivanov handed her one of the tubes without comment. She checked the trigger button briefly, then put it in an inside pocket on her waistcoat.

Ivanov took one for himself, and offered Brent Roi one. The Halo detective shook his head.

'Now all we have to do is find Quinn Dexter,' Ivanov said. He looked at Fletcher. 'Any ideas?'

'Do you have any notion where he might be?'

'Only a general assumption that he's in the Westminster Dome – that's where he seems to have consolidated his grip on the other possessed. Logically he can't be too far away from them.'

'I know of Westminster, but not of its dome.'

'Basically, the whole of the London you knew got put under a protective glass bubble. That's the dome. He could be anywhere inside the city.'

'Then I would suggest you take me to a suitable vantage point. I may be able to determine where large groups of the possessed fester. It would be a start.'

*

It was the sign of a good leader that he could adapt quickly to changing circumstances. After the last couple of days, Quinn now considered himself to be ranked among history's greatest. The curfew had come as a considerable shock, not least because it meant the supercops were on to him once more. He had a good idea who'd told them – a knowledge which was almost pleasing.

Of course, the curfew had completely screwed up his earlier plans. The possessed from the Lancini had done as they were ordered, and used the night to take over a quantity of people in the designated buildings. But then the day workers hadn't arrived, and the game changed.

Quinn had sent runners out through the maze of tunnels and service shafts below the arcology, contacting the groups and telling them what to do next. They were to take out the police as he'd originally intended, luring them into ambushes and incinerating the precinct stations. Given their smaller numbers, it would take longer, but with the curfew conveniently shutting down the rest of the arcology the police would have little backup or support available. He also told his followers to target the net and power substations, further isolating the beleaguered police.

By late afternoon, deprived of police or emergency services, power and communications, the arcology's population had effectively been imprisoned in their own homes. Quinn had achieved his goal without any need to smash the transport network, utilities, and food factories.

It was almost what he'd originally intended, and achieved with fewer possessed than he'd originally estimated. That weighed heavily in his favour; it was easier to exert discipline over a smaller number. And the arcology, with all its prized resources, remained intact for him to use as he wished. His tightest control was imposed over the Westminster Dome; fear, paralysing the nine outer domes, rendered them useless as possible sources of resistance.

With London secure, Quinn had made one attempt to send disciples to Birmingham in overland vehicles. A venture which had resulted in SD strikes, and the total destruction of the commandeered vehicles.

He knew it was never going to be that easy.

As the first night wore on, and his possessed battalions continued their mopping-up operation against the civic authorities, he had several technical and engineering experts brought to his headquarters. They were put to work on methods of travel unsusceptible to the SD platforms. A token gesture. He knew the coming war of Night would not be fought with science and machines. It would be personal and glorious, as war was meant to be.

As darkness fell, the bedlam of the demons had grown louder. Quinn supplicated himself across the desecrated altar of St Paul's Cathedral, and delved deep into the ghost realm once more. This time he was rewarded with the greatest knowledge there could be, so beautiful he whimpered at its impact. God's Brother Himself was awaking from His banishment at some unimaginable distance past the end of the universe. Cries of glory and rapture rose from the demons as they welcomed their vast Lord among them, His ominous presence bringing a vigour and strength they had never known before.

Their cold dreaming thoughts infiltrated Quinn's mind. He could know them in all their astounding multitude, bound together in an enchanted torment. God's Brother arose before them, hot and dark, radiant with malevolence. They reached out for him, to be gifted with His power. And He freed them, His energy banishing their chains so they could soar again, as they once had so long ago. An entire army of apocalyptic angels, enraptured by their new state, and hungry. Hungry for so many things they had been denied for all this terrible time. They swirled in adulation around the Light Bringer in a cyclone larger than the world, screaming their malignant pleasure at His coming.

Quinn left his ghostdreaming behind, his body solidifying to wake upon the altar just as dawn brought a grey light to the stained-glass windows around him. There were tears in his eyes as he started to laugh. 'Oh, Banneth, you piece of shit, where are you now, unbeliever. This truth is when you'd finally despair.'

'Quinn?' Courtney asked anxiously. 'Quinn, you OK?'

'He's coming.'

Courtney cast a glance towards the huge blackened oak doors at the far end of the cathedral. 'Who?'

'God's Brother, you dumb bitch.' Quinn stood on the altar, and held his arms wide as he looked down on the congregation of possessed milling across the nave. 'I have seen Our Lord. Seen Him! He lives. He has risen to lead us to the final victory. He brings an army that will tear down the bright metal angels guarding the sky. Night will fall!' He was shaking with conviction. Courtney watched in a kind of dread awe as he slowly looked down at her. 'Don't you believe me?'

'I believe, Quinn. I always believe you.'

'Yeah. You really do, don't you.' He jumped lightly to the stone and marble floor, a wild grin visible before the blackness exuded by his robe eclipsed his flesh. His hood swung round to face the subdued congregation. Over five hundred of them had been mustered now, waiting obediently for the dark Messiah to tell them what he wanted from them. Their numbers were added to slowly, as further non-possessed captives were brought to the cathedral via underground service tunnels. The immediate vicinity around St Paul's had been cleared of commercial and office buildings several centuries ago, extending its gardens and moating them with a pedestrian plaza. Quinn knew damn well that if too many people crossed all that open space to enter by any of the regular doors the satellites and dome sensors would see them. The pattern would be recorded, and the supercops would become curious at why none of them ever left. So the accumulation of his power base had to proceed slowly and cautiously.

Those who were brought to him were taken down into the crypt and broken open for possession by a handful of committed followers, loyal to His gospel. Quinn no longer cared whether those who struggled out from the beyond into the waiting bodies believed in the word of God's Brother or not. As long as he was physically close by, they could be coerced.

Studying the assembled possessed, Quinn thought he might have about a third of the numbers he actually wanted for the summoning ceremony. Just reaching the ghost realm took so much energistic strength. He would never be able to smash open the gates into hell by himself.

'Where's Billy-Joe?' he asked.

Courtney gave a sullen shrug. 'Downstairs again. He likes to watch.'

'Go and fetch him for me. What I've seen makes it fucking important that we get more warm bodies in here for possession. I want him to get word out to the shitheads on the street, make sure they keep sending them. Nobody can afford to screw up today. This is His time now.'

'Right.' Courtney started to walk towards the door at the base of the central dome which had stairs down to the crypt. She stopped and turned back. 'Quinn, what happens after?'

'After what?'

'After the Light Bringer comes, and, you know, we kill everyone that doesn't do as we say.'

'We'll live in His Kingdom, under His light, and our serpent beasts will run free and wild for the rest of time. He will have saved us from enslavement inside the false Lord's prison city; that *heaven* the dumb-ass religions keep singing about.'

'Oh. OK, that sounds pretty cool.'

Quinn watched her go, sensing the dull acceptance of her thoughts. Strange how her unquestioning compliance had begun to annoy him lately.

He spent the rest of the morning supervising the groups he had out on the streets, directing them to new targets. It consisted mainly of intimidating the shit out of their representatives when they turned up at the cathedral. A couple of times he slipped into the ghost realm and travelled through the arcology himself. The original Lancini possessed tried to keep the newer ones in line, sticking to their orders, but nothing they could say about him and what would happen if they didn't play ball was as effective as when he actually materialized without warning in the middle of them. Three times he had to make examples out of dissenters. He couldn't visit every group, but word spread fast enough, even without the benefit of the net.

When he returned to St Paul's after midday, a couple of orgies had broken out on the nave floor. Freshly arrived possessed, desperate for strong sensation. He didn't stop them, the defilement of such a sacrosanct place was enjoyable; it was one of the reasons he'd chosen it for the summoning. But he did limit future numbers of participants. When the possessed got carried away, they were apt to give off their glitching effect over quite a distance, and there were still some power circuits operating around the cathedral. He couldn't risk a giveaway impulse being tracked by an AI. Souls that possessed the bodies of police officers had reported how the net was exploited by Govcentral to hunt down possessed.

Until he had enough people to perform the summoning, he was going to practise restraint.

*

Quinn was watching the ghosts when Billy-Joe hurried up with a possessed called Frenkel. There were many tombs in St Paul's, dating back well over a millennium, including those lost when the original cathedral building burnt down in the Great Fire of 1666. All the incumbents were supposedly men of distinction or nobility, the old nation's finest. Or at least they might have been so considered while they were alive, Quinn thought they were just a total pain in the ass now. Oh, they had their pride, which came over in the form of resentment and hatred, but basically they were no better than all the other pathetic desolates inhabiting their insipid realm. The warriors who had fallen in defence of their king and country seemed to be in the majority of those who had lingered after death to haunt the land. They despised Quinn with a passion, knowing enough of his power to fear him. To start with they had done their best to disconcert his cohorts, especially Billy-Joe and Courtney, exerting themselves to their limit. Their chill presence made the walls bead with condensation, while the corner-of-the-eye visibility as they swooped around made the chancel's rich gold-braided fabrics flutter with anaemic life. They keened as well, like dogs tormented by a full moon, spilling their morbid depression into the air for all to perceive.

Twice Quinn had to shunt himself into the ghost realm to deal with them. His touch alone burnt them, sending them reeling away, weakened and cowed from the contact.

Their antics withered away, leaving them slinking round to view the gathering of possessed with mute disapproval, emitting a sullen rancour which percolated through the cathedral. Then they began to stir, as if they themselves were the victims of an unnatural incursion. They gathered together under the central dome, twittering fearfully.

The demons were growing louder.

'Something you should hear, Quinn,' Billy-Joe said. He froze at the look of displeasure Quinn gave him for interrupting. Even Billy-Joe could see the ghosts in the nave's energistically charged environment, shivering flames of colour that skidded uncertainly over the tiled floor. 'It's important, I swear.'

'Go on,' Quinn sighed.

Frenkel was breathing hard, and trying hard not to peer into the black gulf that was Quinn's hood. 'I'm from the Hampstead group. We saw something we thought you should know about. I got here as fast as I could, rode a maintenance cab through the tube.'

'Shit,' Quinn murmured. 'Yeah yeah, very good. Get on with it.'

'There was this bunch of people sneaking round the road tunnel interchange at Dartmouth Park. They'd driven a car there, which is weird, because we haven't got round to crapping over the route and flow processors yet. Their car must have some kind of police override code, because the curfew restrictions are still in primary mode. They got up onto the street through an inspection accessway, then they started moving through the buildings. We figured they must be locals, they know the building layouts pretty good. No one can scope them from outside; our guys were having a hard time keeping up with them when I left. We didn't take them out, because the thing is there's six of them; and two are really like the people you told us all to look out for.'

'Which two?' Quinn asked sharply.

'There's the chick with long hair, and that humping great black dude. The others are just soldiers, real hard nuts. Except one, which is where things get strange. He's possessed. And he's not from our group, we've never seen him before.'

'Is he controlling the others?'

'No. They're like a team.'

'Where were they going? What direction?'

'They were creeping along Junction Road when I left. Our guys are keeping tabs on them.'

'Take me there,' Quinn snarled. He started to glide swiftly towards the door leading to the connecting subways. 'Billy-Joe, bring your hardware.'

*

Louise was thankful that the two GISD field agents accompanying them were equipped with communications blocks. They provided her neural nanonics a direct, secure satellite circuit to Charlie and GISD's civil databank, circumventing the patchy net coverage in this section of the arcology. The only other reliable link they had was Ivanov's affinity bond. This way she got to see the route to Archway Tower the B7 AI had mapped out for them.

It had been scary coming up through the accessway from the underground road tunnel, especially the thirty seconds out in the open when she had to scurry to the cover of the first building. After that, she could see not only where they were but where they were going. It was surprising how reassuring that knowledge was.

Most of the buildings had some kind of route through them, interconnecting doors (all locked) or basement service corridors. Those that didn't, the GISD agents were planning on simply cutting through walls with their fission blades. Even that wasn't necessary, Fletcher conjured a door into existence each time. It didn't seem to matter what the wall was, ancient brick or modern reinforced carbon-concrete, nor how thick it was. The trick made Brent Roi very uncomfortable, but it saved a lot of time. Fletcher could also tell if there were people ahead of them, as well.

They wormed their way from building to building, staying away from the front rooms overlooking the road whenever possible. Going through pub lounges, shop storerooms, offices, even kitchens and one-room flats. Those people they did intrude upon greeted them with astonishment and fear. Then when they found out the little party was official in nature, they just wanted to know what the hell was going on outside. And rescue. Everybody wanted out.

That part was the worst, Louise found. The tension from being caught was survivable; tension was a state she was growing increasingly used to. But the pitiful pleas of the residents were relentless, their eyes accusing as they clutched small children to them.

'Isn't there another route?' she datavised Charlie after they left a woman and her three-year-old boy sobbing miserably. 'It's awful having to refuse these people.'

Brent Roi waved her through a small triangular door into a narrow disused hallway. The only light was coming through a filthy smoked-glass window above a bricked-up door.

'Sorry, Louise,' Charlie datavised back. 'The AI says this way is the most likely to get you there undetected by the possessed. It didn't take emotional stress into account. Just try and tough it out. Not much further.'

'Where's Genevieve?'

'They reached Skyhigh Kijabe seven minutes ago. I've chartered a blackhawk to take her to Tranquillity. She'll be there within the hour.'

Louise tapped Fletcher on the shoulder. 'Genevieve's safe. She's about to depart for Tranquillity.'

'I'm gladdened to hear that, my lady. Hope survives.'

Ivanov reached the end of the hallway and held his hand up. 'Outside road.'

The two GISD field agents moved forward to the metal door. One glanced at Fletcher.

'No one is near,' he said.

The agent pressed a small block to the damp wall beside the door. It fired a narrow electron beam through the plaster and brick, then extended a microfilament with a sensor on the end. The image it relayed showed them a narrow street, deserted except for a couple of cats. With the sensor switched to infra-red, the agent focused it on each visible window along the street in turn, searching for hot silhouettes. The AI had been using the overhead dome sensors to scan their immediate area the whole way, but the angle was all wrong to examine windows.

Their caution every time they had to cross a side street was adding considerably to the journey time.

'Two possibles,' the agent reported, datavising the coordinates to his colleague. The door was opened and he ran fast across the street to the building directly opposite. Their entry point was a window covered by a security grille. Cutting the restraint bolts with a fission blade took fifteen seconds, the window catch was a mere two. The agent vanished inside with a neat roll. Brent Roi was next. Louise followed, sprinting hard across the street. According to her neural nanonics it was Vorley Road, the last open space they had to cross.

Getting in, she reminded herself. It was a long, long way back to any vac-train station.

This conglomeration of buildings was gathered around the base of the Archway skyscraper itself, a monolithic twenty-five-storey tower that stood halfway up a sloping ridge of land that was topped by Highgate Hill. If it hadn't been for the buildings along the street blocking the view they would already be able to look out over the rooftops of the old city.

Once they were inside, a service corridor took them straight to the lobby. A lift was already waiting for them, door open.

'The tower's net and power are still connected,' Charlie datavised. 'The AI is hooked into every circuit in there. I can give you plenty of early warning if there are any glitches.'

They all crammed into the lift, which rose smoothly to the upper utility level. It opened out onto a world of artificial lighting, thick metal pipes, black storage tanks, and big primitive air-conditioning machines. Ivanov led them along a metal walkway to a spiral stair. The door at the top let them out on the flat roof. A flock of scarlet parakeets took flight as they emerged, startlingly loud in the warm air.

Louise glanced round cautiously. The first rank of tall, modern skyscrapers encircling the old city were only a mile or so away to the north, their glassy faces shimmering rose gold in the last of the twilight sun. To the south, the embargoed city swept away down the slope towards the distant Thames, a dusky mass of rooftops and intersecting walls. Patches of twinkling silvery light clung to some of the larger roads where the power hadn't yet been cut to the hologram adverts. Not a single window was illuminated, the residents preferring to stay in the dark, fearful of drawing attention to themselves.

Louise heard Fletcher laughing. He was leaning on the crumbling concrete parapet that ran round the edge of the roof, looking out towards the south.

'What is it?' she asked.

'I laugh at my own humility, lady. I look at this city which is supposed to be the closest to home I will ever come, only to find that it is the strangest vista I have encountered since my return. The word city no longer encompasses the meaning it had in my time. You have the power and artifice to build such a colossus, yet it is I who has been asked to perform this scant task of finding one man.'

'He's not a man. He's a monster.'

'Aye, lady Louise.' The humour faded from his handsome face, and he faced the ancient city. 'They're here, but of course you knew that.'

'Are there many?'

'Fewer than I had supposed, but enough. I feel their presence everywhere.' He closed his eyes and leant out a little further, sniffing the air. His hands gripped the top of the parapet. 'There is a gathering. I feel them. Their thoughts are quietened, deliberately so. They wait for something.'

'Waiting?' Ivanov asked quickly. 'How do you know?'

'There is an aura of anticipation about them. And unease. They are troubled, yet unable to walk away from their predicament.'

'It's him! It has to be. No one else could make a whole bunch of possessed do as they're told. Where are they?'

Fletcher took one of his hands off the parapet, leaving behind a dark sweat print. He pointed along the Holloway Road. 'Over yonder. I am uncertain as to how many leagues. Though they remain inside the dome. On that I would wager my hat.'

Ivanov moved over to stand behind Fletcher, squinting along the direction he was pointing. 'You're sure?'

'I am, sir. There.'

'OK. I've got a fix. We just need to triangulate.'

'A splendid notion.'

'I'll take you over to Crouch Hill. That ought to be far enough. Then once we get a rough idea where the bastard's hiding out, we can work out a route to get you close.'

'If I may suggest, I simply walk. No man would accost me in this guise, and fewer will suspect my intent.'

'Walk off into the goddam sunset,' Brent said. 'No fucking way.'

'We can talk about it,' Ivanov said. 'Fletcher, you got any idea how many there are in this group?'

'I would suggest several hundred. Possibly even a thousand.'

'What the hell does he want with that many in one place?'

'I can advance no rationale to elucidate Quinn Dexter's behaviour. He is, sir, quite mad.'

'All right.' Ivanov took a final look across the city, fixing the line Fletcher had indicated. 'Let's move out.'

They had just got into the lift when the AI reported an electronics glitch close to the Archway Tower. It immediately datavised a search update to Charlie. The glitch was occurring beside the electricity substation which distributed power to the Archway Tower among other consumers. A security camera revealed two people approaching the substation along a dark corridor.

Trouble, he warned Ivanov.

The substation door crumpled from a blast of white fire. Three more glitches appeared around the base of the Archway Tower. Sensors showed possessed moving purposefully through the subway, freight tunnel, and utilities passageway. The substation transformers exploded as a barrage of white fire pummelled into their casings.

Ivanov saw the lights in the lift flicker as the Tower's emergency power cells took over. They were just passing the nineteenth floor.

Down in the basement, the possessed were smashing every communications conduit they could find, searing the cables out of the wall. The AI watched the Tower's net connections fail one after the other. Independent power cells kept the internal processors running, but it could now only access them through the communications blocks carried by the GISD field agents, cutting down on the bandwidth available for surveillance and initiating possible countermoves.

Security sensors on the ground floor showed fifteen possessed running up the stairs into the lobby. They immediately started slinging small bolts of white fire at the sensors and any other electronic system. Just before the last camera failed, Charlie saw a lift door being broken down with considerable force.

Out, he ordered. **Get out of the lift.**

The AI had already established a link to the lift's controlling processor. It applied the failsafe brakes, and slammed it to a halt on the thirteenth floor.

Louise yelped in shock as the lift floor abruptly tried to shunt its way upwards, accompanied by a strident alarm siren. She grasped at the handrail as she lurched against the wall.

The doors flashed open. Charlie was datavising orders to her as Ivanov was shouting: 'Move it! The possessed are coming.' Everyone charged out into the corridor. Black apartment doors lined both walls. Smoked glass windows at either end let in a murky glow from the setting sun. Emergency lights shone brightly above both of the stairwell doors.

Charlie told one of the GISD agents to leave his communication block in the corridor, tucking it away unobtrusively in a doorway, enabling the AI to maintain contact with the tower's net. 'The possessed are now heading up both stairwells,' Charlie datavised. 'Five in one, four in the other. The remainder are waiting downstairs. You'll have to shoot your way through them. I suggest you use the anti-memory where possible.'

'Gets my vote,' Ivanov said. He drew the small weapon, holding it in his left hand. His right held a compact automatic pistol.

Fletcher and Louise drew their own weapons. The agents and Brent were checking their machine-guns.

Ivanov opened the stairwell door cautiously. Concrete steps with metal rails wound down the shaft in a rectangular corkscrew. The sound of running boots echoed upwards.

'They know we're here,' Fletcher said curtly.

The AI tracked glitches rising up the stairwell, and computed the approximate distance. Both GISD field agents entered the time into the trigger mechanism on their grenades, and dropped them down the shaft.

Louise hunched down next to the wall, her hands pressed against her ears. Explosions roared below as the chemical shrapnel grenades detonated. Then the agents tossed their gas incendiaries over the rail. Billows of flame scoured the battered stairs, searing against the groggy possessed. Screams trilled along the length of the stairwell.

'Let's go,' Ivanov said. He took off down the stairs.

Louise was third in line, behind one of the agents, with Brent pounding along behind her. She'd put a host of programs in primary mode, an auto-locomotion so she could tear round the stairwell corners without slipping, adrenalin suppressor working through the medical nanonic to keep her calm, weapons control so she'd be able to aim the anti-memory tube properly, peripheral motion analysis, heart-rate control as a counter to the adrenalin suppressor, making sure her straining muscles received enough blood, tactical analysis, which was synchronized with the AI. It informed her that possessed from the lobby were starting to invade the bottom of the stairwell in support of their injured comrades. After descending another two floors, the agents would drop more grenades, and they'd all switch stairwells.

A thick streamer of white fire plunged up the centre of the stairwell, its tip swelling rapidly.

Louise flung herself back from the rail. Brent and one of the agents stuck their machine-guns over the edge, shooting off a suppressing deluge of static bullets.

The plume of white fire burst open, spitting out a shower of incandescent sparks. Several of them landed on Louise's legs, stinging hard as they burnt their way through her leggings. She batted at them with her free hand, putting an axon block in primary to dull the pain. Her tactical program was urging her up. Neuroiconic icons began to flash warnings about capacity reduction in her neural nanonics.

A bolt of white fire flashed like lightning. It hit the GISD field agent who was covering the rear of the group, penetrating straight through the back of his skull to char the brain. He crumpled instantly.

Ivanov and the remaining agent whirled round, their weapons trying to find a target.

'Where the fuck did that come from?' Brent yelled.

Charlie knew there was only one answer. Instinctively, his affinity bond made Ivanov turn to face Fletcher. 'Well?' the detective demanded.

'He is here,' Fletcher said with trepidation. 'I feel him even though he hides beyond sight.'

The possessed were clattering up the stairwell again. Neural nanonics and blocks were beginning to glitch.

Charlie tightened Ivanov's grip around the anti-memory weapon. 'Through here,' he ordered. Ivanov went through the door to the tenth floor, arm swinging in wide arcs to cover the corridor. It was deserted, a copy of the thirteenth floor. Louise and Brent followed him while the last agent dropped a couple of grenades over the rail. They all started to run for the second stairwell. The grenades didn't go off.

'Is he still here?' Ivanov asked.

'Close,' Fletcher said. Fury and frustration boiled into his voice. 'I cannot see him. The Devil!'

'Shoot it where you think he is. It might work anyway.'

Fletcher stopped running and lifted the anti-memory weapon, his thumb pushing the trigger button forwards. He glanced about the sombre corridor as though trying to make his mind up. The trigger was suddenly pressed, sending a cone of bright ruby laser light stabbing out.

'It is useless,' Fletcher cried. 'Useless.'

The energistic glitch had crashed just about all of Ivanov's neural nanonics. He certainly couldn't receive any datavises. That meant the possessed were very close now.

The AI has lost all contact with the communication blocks, Charlie said. I can't track the possessed for you any more.

Up is no good, Ivanov said. He looked round wildly. We'll have to make a stand.

Very well. There's a chance Dexter will become visible during the fight. If that happens, you must fire the anti-memory no matter what the cost.

You won't even have to compel me. Finishing the shit will be my pleasure.

Fletcher had put his arm protectively around a trembling Louise. He suddenly fired the anti-memory again, sending the beam over Brent's head.

'Careful with that thing,' Brent shouted.

Fletcher ignored him. 'The others are almost here.'

Three machine-guns lined up on the stairwell door.

'Get away,' Ivanov told Louise, he waved her towards the window at the end of the corridor. Then he saw what was behind her, and let out a fast yell of delight. 'Yes! Oldest trick in the book. Fletcher, cover for me. We can get her out.' You should have thought of this, he accused Charlie.

There was a fire evacuation chute beside the window, a big doughnut of composite on thick swivel pinions. Ivanov grabbed Louise and hurried her along. He pulled the release leaver at the side of the chute, shoving it through a hundred and eighty degrees. The window fell out, an alarm sounded, and water rained down out of the ceiling sprinklers all along the corridor. The doughnut swung round to lock into place in front of the open window. A fabric stocking concertinaed out, the pressure it had been stored under making it pour outwards like a liquid. It fluttered away from the side of the tower as it kept on expanding, the free end sinking towards the black ground far below.

It's a manual system, Charlie protested. **The AI has no control over it.**

Louise was staring at the top of the chute in bewilderment as the cold water soaked her to the skin.

'In you go,' Ivanov shouted above the alarm. 'Feet first.' His laugh was manic.

'No,' Louise stammered. She took a frightened step backward.

A twin of the stairwell door materialized in the wall next to the original. Brent fired his machine-gun straight at it. Skeletal hands with long red nails slithered up through the solid floor at his feet, and clamped around his ankles. He got out one panicked shout before they tugged him down. Then all he could manage was a grunt of disbelief as his shins sank into the carpeting as though it was nothing more than quicksand.

Fletcher grabbed hold of the flailing Halo detective, and exerted his own energistic power to counter the destabilizing floor. Two possessed walked out of the stairwell at the far end of the corridor. They were dressed as Roman legionaries, but armed with stainless-steel crossbows. The GISD agent crouched down and opened fire with his machine-gun. Bursts of lightning followed the bullets through the downpour of water. The legionaries stumbled as the bullets struck them, twanging against their bronze breastplates. But they managed to stay upright, limbs moving in jerking motions. One raised his crossbow and fired. The bolt struck the agent on his knee, severing his lower leg. Blood foamed out of the severed limb, and he toppled to one side, stunned into stupor by the pain.

Ivanov turned to Louise. '*Go!*' he bellowed. 'Get out of here.' He shoved her roughly with one hand, and pointed the anti-memory weapon down the corridor with the other. The beam flared brightly at the advancing legionaries.

Louise gripped the rim of the doughnut, looking directly at the funnel of slippery fabric around its throat. The whole idea of jumping into it was terrifying. Another scream rang out behind her. She took hold of the handle at the top of the doughnut, and swung her legs up, pushing them through the gap. And let go.

Fletcher had got one of Brent's legs free when three possessed rushed him out of the duplicate stairwell door. He instinctively flung his arms towards them, white fire streaming from his fingertips. They thrashed about in the slithering flame, focusing their own power to send it skidding harmlessly over their own skin.

A streamer coiled round Fletcher's torso. He had to drop his own attack to counter it. The red slash of the anti-memory beam fluoresced the water droplets barely an inch from his nose as Ivanov tried to provide covering fire. One of the possessed collapsed.

Ivanov was switching targets when a crossbow bolt ripped into his forearm, tearing out a chillingly long strip of flesh, exposing the bone. Without muscles or tendons, the elbow joint flopped uselessly, hand opening to drop his compact machine-gun. Blood gushed down to splatter the weapon's dull metal.

When he glanced upwards, shaking the water and pain out of his eyes, he saw Fletcher writhing at the centre of five lightning forks being hurled at him by several possessed. At his feet, a badly scorched Brent heaved down a painful breath and raised his machine-gun, firing round wildly, heedless of who the bullets struck. There was no sign of Dexter. None.

He might just try and follow Louise, Charlie decided.

Ivanov was never certain who was in charge of his body at that moment. But he took two faltering steps backwards until the doughnut rim hit him just below his kidneys. Then he performed a fabulously well-coordinated back flip, and vanished head first down the chute.

Fletcher staggered to one side as Brent started shooting again. The possessed scrambled for cover, two diving through walls. Out of nowhere, a skilfully aimed ball of white fire plunged into Brent's left eye socket, and the gun fell silent. Two spears of white fire immediately resumed their strike against Fletcher. He twisted painfully under the impact, waving his hand in the general direction one of them was coming from, about to retaliate with his own fire. A thin metal band clamped tight around his throat, and an electric current punched into him. It took every reserve of strength to prevent the excruciating energy from pouring like hot acid into his brain.

Thought was impossible, instinct was all he had left. He slumped to his knees, the smell of frying skin thick in his nostrils. The anti-memory weapon fell from numb fingers.

'Enough.'

The current was switched off. Fletcher's muscles lost their rigour, dropping him into a twitching heap. Breath was hard to find with the unyielding circle of metal digging against his Adam's apple. His fingers scrabbled weakly against the collar.

'You just leave that alone, motherfucker, or I'll zap you again.'

Fletcher blinked against the shower of water still gushing from the sprinklers, focusing a long pole that extended away from the collar. At the other end was a young man, not possessed, whose tongue lolled out of the corner of his mouth. 'Hands down, come on, boy, down they go.'

Fletcher removed his hands from the collar.

'*Gooood* boy,' the young man sneered. 'Hey, Quinn, I got him for you. He been whupped but good.'

Quinn Dexter materialized next to Billy-Joe. The deluge of water never even touched his robe. 'Well done. I owe you at least a countess and a classical actress for this one.'

Billy-Joe put his head back and howled in joy. 'Yes, sir. Gonna die from too much fucking.'

'Shame my old friend Louise got away.'

'No, she ain't,' Billy-Joe shouted excitably. He shoved the restraint collar's pole into the hands of a startled Frenkel, who gripped it in reflex. 'I'll get her for you, Quinn. You see.'

'No,' Quinn said.

But Billy-Joe was already running for the evacuation chute.

'Billy-Joe!' The tone was ominous. Billy-Joe responded with a doltish grin, and dived clean through the doughnut.

'Shit!' Quinn exclaimed. He'd emphasized how much he wanted Louise Kavanagh as he led the possessed into the tower. And for all his loyalty, Billy-Joe was far to dumb to appreciate simple strategy.

Quinn couldn't chase after the girl himself. Fletcher was regarding him with calculating ferocity. Captured, but hardly subdued. And there were too many questions he had concerning the soulless bodies now sprawled inertly along the corridor. He snapped his fingers at a couple of the possessed from the Hampstead group. 'You two, get down there and help him out.'

If she'd just had the time to read the instructions and pictographs on the side of the doughnut, Louise might not have been so frightened. The chute was an old idea, improved by the use of modern flextailored fabric so it could be used from almost any height. She slid down the first four storeys with little resistance, then the fabric began to constrict around her, gently braking her fall. It was designed to be elastic in one direction only, making sure its length remained constant. The end would continue to dangle one metre above the pavement no matter how many people were inside the chute.

Louise was deposited gently from the end, not even having to bend her knees when her feet touched the ground. Her neural nanonics were back on-line, with the adrenalin-suppression program quickly damping down her shakes. She took a few unsteady steps from the tower, then looked up. Faint sounds of conflict were drifting out of the open window far above. A bulge was descending down the chute, putting her in mind of a guinea pig swallowed by a snake.

There was no time for her to reach cover before the person in the chute arrived. Louise gave the anti-memory weapon she was holding a blank look, then aimed it at the end of the chute.

A head cleared the rim, which surprised her. She'd been expecting feet.

Ivanov had gritted his teeth against the shocking pain from his arm while his neural nanonics slowly recovered on the ride down. When he slid out of the chute the axon block was established, cutting off all the impulses from the mangled wound. Physiological shock was more difficult to counter.

With only one arm to flail around with, he tumbled awkwardly from the chute as the hem released him. Louise rushed forward to help, only to gasp when she saw the state of his bloody arm.

'No,' Ivanov groaned. He rolled onto his knees, gripping the long wound tightly, trying to staunch the blood. 'Go,' he said earnestly.

'But you're hurt.'

'Doesn't matter. You go. Now.'

'I . . .' She stared round in despair at the dark deserted streets. 'There's nowhere to go.'

Ivanov's expression altered, a subtle but definite change. 'This is

Charlie. Run, Louise. Run now. And keep on running. Go down the Holloway Road to start, there aren't many of them in that direction. Shoot anyone you see. I mean it, don't ask questions, just shoot. Once you're clear, find somewhere deserted to hole up. I promise I'll do what I can to save London. You know that, Louise.' He looked up. A bulge was sliding down the chute, already halfway down. 'Now go! Please. Go on, leave. I'll take care of them here. They won't be following you for quite a while.'

Ivanov winked. Louise knew that was him, not Charlie. She nodded and backed off. 'Thank you.' Then she was gone, running hard down the Holloway Road.

Behind her, Ivanov swung round to face the chute. He let go of his injured arm, allowing the blood to flow freely again. His good arm brought the anti-memory weapon up to point at the chute hem, just as Billy-Joe's head popped out.

*

A fluorescent yellow Frisbee soared high above the white sand. Haile had to formshift her tractamorphic flesh into a long tentacle to catch it. Jay clapped excitedly, hopping about. 'Throw it back, throw it back,' she squealed.

Haile's tentacle curled round the rim, and released the Frisbee with a fast flick. It flew back, travelling twice as quickly as when Jay threw it, tracing a perfectly flat trajectory.

The little girl had to jump to have any chance of making a catch. It hit her hand with a sharp smack, and she tumbled over onto the sand.

'Ouch!'

You feel painfulness?

'Not half.' Jay scrambled up, shaking the tingling out of her hand. She gave the clubhouse along the beach a guilty glance. Tracy had started to warn her about the number of times she was using the provider for medical aid when she went surfing, threatening to confiscate the board. Asking for something to ease her stinging palm would probably result in more scolding.

'Rest time,' she announced, and flopped on her towel.

Haile lumbered over and used her tractamorphic flesh to scoop out a shallow depression in the warm dry sand. She settled into it, emitting strong thoughts of grateful satisfaction.

Jay eyed the cooler box again, then looked back to the clubhouse. 'What are they watching now?'

Corpus is displaying pictures from sensors on Earth for them.

'Really? Where from?'

London. Fletcher Christian has arrived to help the police locate Quinn Dexter. Tracy is concerned that the security services have acquired the life-pattern disrupter weapon.

Jay sighed with impatience. Tracy kept telling her how momentous events were back in the Confederation. Though privately Jay thought the way the old observers got into such a tizz over all the political shenanigans was stupid. All she really wanted to know was when it was all going to be over and she could see her mother again. Loads of politicians arguing about who they should ally their planets with wasn't going to bring any sort of end to the crisis.

Friend Jay, what is wrong?

'I want to go home.' She hated how miserable and whiney she sounded.

Corpus asks that you be patient.

'Huh!' Suffering quickly turned to a spike of anger. 'As if it cares.'

It does care, a distressed Haile said. **All Kiint care.**

'Right.' She wasn't going to argue with Haile, it always upset both of them.

Tracy comes, Haile said with a note of hope.

Jay saw the old woman riding a chrome-blue air scooter towards them. Several of the Village residents used the little vehicles to get about on, each one as individual as its owner. Tracy's was a fat ellipsoid shape with a recessed saddle in the middle. Stubby triangular fins with red tail lights protruded from the rear third; for show Jay assumed. There were also some positively anachronistic circular headlights on the front, like glass jewels. Tracy called it her T-bird.

Another thing Jay was banned from using by herself. She was convinced the sleek-looking vehicle could go a lot faster than Tracy's maximum speed.

It glided silently through the air at about twenty kilometres an hour, keeping a good two metres above the ground.

Jay stood up, brushing sand from her swimsuit as the T-bird landed beside her.

'Sorry I'm late, poppet,' Tracy said. 'Haile, my dear, you'll have to look after yourself this afternoon. I'm going to take Jay to Agarn.'

'What's Agarn?'

Tracy explained as they walked back to the chalet, the T-bird following faithfully behind. Agarn was another planet in the Arc, inhabited by a small number of Kiint. They didn't involve themselves in the kind of life practised by the majority of the Arc, preferring more philosophical pursuits. 'So mind your manners,' Tracy warned. 'They're a very dignified group.'

'Why are we going there?'

'The Agarn Kiint are slightly different from the others. I'm hoping they'll intervene in our favour. It's a bit of a last resort, but things are turning ugly in the Confederation. I'm worried the situation will result in a squalid kind of stalemate. Nothing will be resolved, which is one of the worst outcomes there can be.'

She inspected Jay's clothes, a pair of khaki shorts and a blue T-shirt, with sturdy hiking boots. 'You'll do, quite the little explorer.'

'Why am I going with you?'

'So they can get a look at a true human.'

'Oh.' Jay didn't like that idea at all. 'Can't they look at the pictures from the Confederation like you do?'

'In a way they already have. They haven't turned their back on Corpus. If they had there wouldn't be any point to visiting them.'

Jay just smiled. She still really didn't understand Corpus.

Agarn didn't have any buildings within sight of the teleport circle they arrived on. They were on the rolling foothills of a wide valley. It was kind of like the parkland of Riynine, but left untended for a couple of centuries. Lush emerald grass-analogue swamped the ground. Trees were twisting towers of clustered magenta bubbles. A dozen waterfalls poured over tall rock cliffs lining the valley, while every crevice was home to a stream, emptying into crater lakes that were stepped down the slopes.

Tracy looked round, dabbing at her forehead with a lace hanky. 'I'd forgotten how hot it is here,' she murmured.

Jay put her sunglasses on, and they walked down to one of the crater lakes. Two Kiint were bathing just off the shore.

Hello, Fowin, Tracy said.

The Kiint raised a blunt length of tractamorphic flesh, and began to wade ashore. **Greetings to you, Tracy Dean. You are Jay Hilton, query?**

'Yes, thank you very much. Hello.' Jay pushed her sunglasses up as the Kiint reach the shore and walked out onto the thick grass-analogue. It was very similar to Haile's parents, though she thought the breathing vents were angled steeper, and the legs were flatter.

I thank you for this visit, Tracy said. I wish to ask you to consider intervention.

I know this. Why else do observers visit me. Following the Gebal stabilization, every time a new species encounters a problem I am asked to be favourable towards them.

Your enlightenment is renowned among Corpus.

Corpus is a constant reminder of the Gebal, so much so that I doubt my wisdom in agreeing to help. Such a notion features heavily in my contemplation. It distracts me from higher thought.

The Gebal faced a unique situation. So do humans.

Humans face an unfortunate situation.

Nonetheless, we can reach full transcendence amity. The inverse population is negligible. Our progress towards social maturity, though admittedly slow, is constant. She gestured at Jay. Please consider our potential.

Jay put on her best bright smile for the Kiint.

Your attempt to influence is crude, Tracy Dean. The child of every species is a reservoir for great potential, good and bad. I cannot judge the individual path, thus logically providing a neutral witness. However, children are inherently innocent. A positive bias.

Jay is the only human available.

Very well. The Kiint turned its big violet eyes to the little girl. What do you desire above all else, Jay Hilton?

'I want my mummy back, of course. I keep telling your Corpus that.'

So you do. I grieve with you for the loss you suffer.

'But you won't help, will you. None of your kind will. I think that's horrible of you. Everyone keeps saying how we're not perfect. But do you know what Father Horst told me once?'

I do not.

'It's very simple and very smart. If you want to know if something is fair, then turn it round. So if you know us as well as you claim, and we were the ones with a thousand planets and providers and stuff, do you think we'd help you if we could?'

A healthy argument, presented with integrity. I know this is hard, but there are more issues involved than are apparent.

'Very clever,' Jay said. She folded her arms in a huff. 'I know it's possible to take possessors out of the bodies they've stolen. I saw it done. So why don't you at least help us to do that? Then we could work out what to do afterwards by ourselves. That's what you really want, isn't it? For us to stand up for ourselves.'

The weapon your military is constructing requires no assistance from us.

'Not that. Father Horst exorcized Freya. He threw the possessing soul out of her.'

I am interested in your claim, Jay Hilton. Corpus is unaware of the incident. Could you tell me what the circumstances were?

Jay launched into a description of the events that had taken place that fateful day in a small homestead on Lalonde's savannah. Just retelling it made her realize how much had happened since, how much she'd seen and done. It also pushed her mother further into the past, making her even more remote. She finished the story, and a tear trickled down her cheek.

Tracy's arm immediately went round her shoulders. 'Hush, hush, poppet. The possessed can't reach you here.'

'It's not that,' Jay wailed. 'I can't remember what Mummy looks like any more. I'm trying, but I can't.'

This at least I can remedy, Fowin said. A provider globe appeared in the air beside Jay. It extruded a square of glossy paper. Jay took it cautiously. A picture of her mother was printed on one side. Jay smiled, tears forgotten.

'That's her passport flek image,' she said. 'I remember when we went to the registry office together. How did you get this?'

It is stored in your Govcentral memory cores. We retain access.

'Thank you very much,' Jay said contritely. She looked at her mother again, warmed by the sight. 'I thought you didn't use stuff like providers on this planet, that you'd gone back to nature or something?'

Quite the opposite, Fowin said. **We have rejected everything but our technology. Permanent physical structures are unessential. We are free to pursue thought alone.**

'Humans are never going to evolve into anything like you,' Jay said sadly. 'We'd just get too bored.'

I am glad. Your appetites are unique. Treasure them. Be yourselves.

'So will you help us expelling souls?'

I believe the circumstances that allowed Father Horst his exorcism will not be repeated on many occasions.

'How come?'

As you have demonstrated this day, human children have very strong beliefs. Freya was brought up to believe in her ethnic Christian religion. When Father Horst began the ceremony of expulsion, she believed that it would work, that the soul possessing her would be cast out. At that same time, the soul experienced doubt. It had endured a form of purgatory, implying the priests of its era enjoyed some kind of fundamental truth when they discussed spiritual matters. Now it was confronted by a priest who believed he had God's aid to perform the exorcism. Three different, extremely strong beliefs were acting upon the soul, exerting considerable pressure not only from outside, but within its own thoughts. The soul convinced itself of the validity of the ceremony. Its own faith turned against it, and it withdrew as it believed it had to.

'Then Father Horst can't do it for entire planets?'

No.

'OK,' Jay said reluctantly. She was right out of arguments and hope.

Your evaluation? Tracy asked respectfully.

I acknowledge that the breakthrough event on Lalonde was extraneous. Even so, that cannot justify total intervention.

I see.

However. Your race's potential should be safeguarded. You may initiate a separate origin.

'Thank you,' Tracy said weakly.

*

'I don't understand,' Jay complained when they returned to the chalet. 'What are you so happy about? Corpus won't intervene.'

Tracy sat in one of the deckchairs on the veranda, for once breaking her own rule and ordering a cup of tea from the provider. 'You worked an absolute miracle, poppet. Fowin's evaluation immediately becomes Corpus policy. It's going to allow us to start a brand new human colony if the Confederation falls apart.'

'Why is that good? The possessed won't spread to every colony, you said that yourself.'

'I know. But it's knowledge, you see. Humans found out about souls before they were socially advanced enough to deal with such a revelation. Now that knowledge is going to act like a mental contaminant among every culture. It'll split humanity into a thousand squabbling factions – that's already started with Kulu and its idea for a core-Confederation of wealthy worlds. Recovering from such a catastrophe will take generations, and even then the resolution will be influenced by what's gone before. What Corpus will do is begin a colony of say a million people from scratch. Observers will be authorized to purchase or acquire ova and sperm stored in zero-tau from medical and biological institutes all across the Confederation. The new colony's start-up population will be gestated in exowombs and cared for by AIs during their childhood. That way, the information they're given can be carefully edited. We can start with a high-technology society equivalent to the Confederation's level of scientific knowledge and let it develop naturally.'

'Fowin can do all that?'

'Any Kiint can do that. Too many of them have conformist thought routines, if you ask me. At least the Agarn Kiint make an effort to push the envelope. Not that it's helped them with the Sleeping God.'

'What's that?' Jay asked eagerly.

Tracy gave her a solemn smile. 'Something an old race left behind a very long time ago. It's created quite a dilemma for this civilization of so-called philosophy gurus. Not that there's anything they can do to affect the situation. I think that's what upset them the most. They've been the undisputed masters of this section of the universe for so long, finding something infinitely superior to themselves is rather shocking. Perhaps that's why Fowin was so accommodating today.' She stopped as Galic appeared at the foot of the veranda's steps.

'You did it,' he said.

'Certainly did,' Tracy grinned back.

He came up and sat in the deckchair beside her. Before long, other retired observers had dropped by to discuss the new colony. They had an enthusiasm Jay hadn't seen in them before, making them younger. Not once that whole evening did they discuss the past.

After dark the party moved into Tracy's lounge and started calling up star charts and planetary surveys. Arguments about the merits of possible locations raged good-naturedly. Most wanted to see the colony in the same galaxy as the Confederation, even if it had to be on the other side of the core.

Some time around midnight, Tracy realized Jay had fallen asleep on the settee. Galic picked her up and carried her into her bedroom. She never woke as he covered her with a blanket and put Prince Dell on the pillow beside her. He tiptoed out and closed the door before returning to the debate.

*

Louise had fled for half a mile down the Holloway Road. It was narrow at the top end, the pavements lined by tall brick buildings with crumbling window sills and gutters. Their ground floors were small shops and cafés whose drab and grimy fronts were firmly shuttered. Her footsteps rattled off the stern walls, an auditory beacon signalling to everyone where she was.

Further down, the road began to widen out. The buildings along this section were better maintained, with clean bricks, glossy paintwork, and more prosperous businesses. Narrow side roads branched off every hundred yards or so, consisting of attractive, compact terrace houses, converted into flats. Silver birches and cherry trees in their front gardens overhung the pavements, to give them the semblance of a quiet rural town.

The slope began to flatten out, revealing at least a mile of straight deserted road ahead of her. The larger commercial premises had taken over on either side, their hologram adverts swirling over the broad pavements, forming a skittering iridescent rainbow. Traffic control informationals hung in the air above road lanes at the main junctions, flashing their colour sequences down onto the empty carbon-concrete.

Louise slowed to a halt, panting heavily from the exertion. She couldn't see anything move behind her, but it was so dark behind her up the hill she'd hardly see any pursuers until they were almost on top of her. Travelling on under the illumination of the holograms would be a mistake.

Tollington Way was fifty yards ahead of her, a side road leading into the backstreet maze that proliferated behind every major London thoroughfare. Holding her sides against the ache of breathing, Louise jogged for a hundred yards down it, then stopped and hunched down in the deep shadows of a doorway.

Her soaking leggings were chafing her thighs, the T-shirt was disgustingly cold and clammy, and her feet felt as though they were shrivelling up. She was shuddering all over now from the cold. High above, small green lights flashed on the dome's geodesic structure.

'Now what?' she gasped up at it. Charlie would be watching her through the sensors, seeing her infra-red image constricted into a small ball. She datavised a general net access request. There was no response.

Escape and hide, Charlie had told her. Easy to say. But where? No one was going to open their door to a stranger on this night. She'd probably be shot just for knocking and asking.

A cat yowled, and jumped off a nearby wall to run along the street. Louise was rolling to the ground and bringing the anti-memory weapon smoothly to bear before the noise had even registered properly. The cat, a furry tabby, loped past, giving her a disdainful look.

She let out a brief sob as her muscles went limp. The weapons control program was still in primary mode. She took it off-line as she climbed painfully to her feet, swatting dirt from her knees and the front of her waistcoat.

The cat was still visible, silhouetted against the hologram haze curtaining the end of Tollington Way, its tail swishing about arrogantly. It was obvious she was still too close to the Holloway Road, her pursuers would come down it, searching every side road. Fletcher said they could sense people without even having to see them.

Louise accessed the map of central London she'd stored in a neural nanonics memory cell, and began to walk away from the light. The anti-memory weapon was slipped back into her waistcoat pocket. She couldn't work out which was the better way of avoiding search parties, staying in one place (assuming she could find a disused room or warehouse) or constantly moving round. The odds were uncomputable, principally because she didn't know what she was facing, an organized systematic hunt, or a couple of possessed ambling round in a disinterested fashion.

Studying the map was almost meaningless, it didn't relate to anything. Without any goal, any destination, one street was the same as any other. Its only use was in preventing her from crossing any of the main roads.

Maybe I should just find somewhere to hide. That's what Charlie suggested.

On an impulse she called up the Ritz's address. The map had to switch magnification factors, the hotel was so far away from her.

That was out, then. Pity, no one would think to hunt for her there.

'Andy,' she whispered in shock. The one person she knew in London. And who would never turn her away.

She retrieved his eddress and ran it through the London directory she'd loaded along with all the other junk data recommended as essential personal survival tools for the arcology. Some people didn't include their physical address with their net code. But Andy had. He lived in Islington, somewhere on Halton Road. A tiny blue star burned on the map.

Two miles away.

'Sweet Jesus, please let him be there.'

*

They chained Fletcher to the altar with manacles that had an electric current running through them, nullifying his energistic power. They ripped his clothes off, and cut obscene runes into his flesh. They shaved him. They burned a pile of Bibles and prayer books at his feet, and used the ash to smear a pentagon around his body. They hung an inverted cross above his skull, dangling by a rope that was fraying and rotting.

Ghosts slithered past, offering their desolate expressions in sympathy.

'Sorry,' was their only whisper. 'So sorry.' Past heroes, humbled and degraded by their emasculation. The possessed spat at them, jeering them out of the way.

St Paul's was illuminated with the mealy light from smoking iron braziers and racks of candles, leaving the vaulted ceiling invisible. Its new incense was the smell of sweaty bodies and fried burgerbap onions. Prayers had been supplanted by rock music coming from a ghetto blaster, with the sounds of copulation heard between tracks. With his head forced back awkwardly against the stone, Fletcher could see several young possessed scrambling monkey-fashion over the stained-glass windows, painting them over with sticky black fluid. A dark shape moved into his limited field of view.

Quinn bent over him. 'Nice to see you again.'

'Enjoy your taunts while you can, you inhuman monster. You will issue them no longer once this day is through.'

'You're good. I admire that. You got off Norfolk in time, which wasn't easy. And you got down to Earth, which is fucking impossible. Very good. What did you do? Make a deal with the supercops?'

'I know naught of what you speak.'

'Shit. OK, I'll put it in real slow retard-speak for you. Who brought you down to Earth?'

When Fletcher didn't answer Quinn ran his hand over the iron band securing the man's forehead. 'I can have them increase the voltage, you know. It can get a lot, lot worse.'

'Only while I remain in this body.'

'Not such a dumb asshole after all.' Quinn crawled sinuously onto the altar beside Fletcher, and moved his hooded head right up close. 'Before we go any further,' he whispered, 'what's she like to fuck? Come on, you can tell me. Is she hot stuff? Or does she just lie there and take it like a corpse? Just between us. I won't tell anyone. Does she give good head? Does she like it up the ass?'

'You are unfit to live, sir. I shall relish your fall, for it will be a great one from the height of your arrogance.'

'Don't tell me you never tried her out? That Louise? She was with you for weeks and weeks. All that time. You must have.' Quinn withdrew a fraction, vaguely puzzled. 'Shit, you're the one that's not human.'

'Your judgements have neither value nor relevance to me.'

'Oh, yeah? There's one judgement I might interest you in. I'm gonna find out what she's like. My people will bring her here for me, and then you can watch me and Courtney go to work on her. I'll make you watch. See how long you can keep that *assholing* superiority going then. Motherfucker!'

'You will have to find her first.'

'Oh, I will. Believe it. Even if the morons I've got out there now don't do it, His army will bring her to me. And then that last little thread of defiance you treasure will snap. You'll scream and plead and cry, and curse your shitty false Lord for his divine inaction.'

'The Lord moves in mysterious ways His wonders to perform. The age of miracles may be past, but His messengers still walk amongst us. You *will* fail. It is written.'

'Bollocks. There are no messengers. And I'm busy burning the book it's written in. It's my Lord who comes, not yours. And He doesn't move mysteriously. God's Brother is very blunt, as you're going to find out. Unless I spare you.'

'I would never be sullied by your mercy, sir.'

'No? Then how about sparing Louise? Join us. Get on the winning side. I'll give her straight back to you. Won't touch a hair on her head. Promise. And that's a lot of hair.'

Fletcher gave a short, bitter laugh.

'I mean it,' Quinn said smoothly. 'You're smart, tough. I could use people like you. You were some sort of officer, right? Half these shitbrains I've got working for me can't find their own ass with both hands. I could put you in charge of a whole bunch of them. You can make out any way you like, then. Marry Louise. Live in a palace. It can't get any better.'

'I apologize, for I am mistaken. I had thought you dangerous. I see now you are merely small. Our Lord Jesus was offered the kingdoms of the world, and refused. I believe I can resist coveting another man's wife and some fine living. Have you not yet learned that in this wretched state we can create anything we desire for ourselves? You can offer nothing of any value; you may only rain down empty threats.'

'Empty!' Quinn shouted in rage. 'He *is* coming. *My* Lord, not yours. If you don't believe me, ask the ghosts. They can hear the dark angels draw near. His Night will fall. That is the new miracle.'

'Day follows night, as it is now and always will be. Amen.'

Quinn backed off the altar and stood up. He held an anti-memory weapon in front of Fletcher's face. 'OK, funtime's over, dickhead; tell me what this is.'

'I do not know, sir.'

'You were shooting it about pretty freely before. Was it meant for me? Is that why the supercops let you down here? Were you trying to find me for them?' Quinn beckoned.

Frenkel stepped forwards, and dumped Billy-Joe's body on the altar next to Fletcher. The young man's head flopped about. His eyes were open, unfocused, and he was still breathing.

'We found him like this down at the bottom of the Archway tower. The big black dude managed to shoot him with one of these gadgets before my troops took him out. Now, I can understand a weapon that forces possessors out of their host body. Every fucking scientist in the Confederation must be working on that right now. But this is a little more powerful, isn't it? Billy-Joe wasn't a possessed, but it still kicked his soul's ass out of there.' Quinn smiled, fangs pressing up into white lips as he sensed the worry trickle into Fletcher's thoughts. 'Or did it do more than that? Huh? Those supercops play for the highest stakes there are. They know I can just come back in another body and start the whole crusade up again. Because I can't die, now can I? We're all immortal now.'

Fletcher's face became a mask of stubborn determination.

'Ah,' Quinn said softly. He held the weapon up, regarding it with a new respect. 'Let's try a little experiment, shall we?' His hand made a pass over Billy-Joe, applying energistic force to open a pathway to the beyond. A soul struggled its way up into Billy-Joe's body. He sat up, wheezing for breath, looking round avidly.

'How about that?' Quinn marvelled. 'No strain, no pain. We can speed up the whole resurrection game.' He grinned down at Fletcher. 'You know what, in the wrong hands this little toy you brought me could be really dangerous.'

*

The tenement on Halton Road consisted of three low-cost apartment towers, intended for the poor and the elderly. A third of the residents still fell into that category, the rest worked in the black cash economy or lived off the dole, spending their days stimmed out on cheap activant programs and home-synthesized drugs. There were no other amenities for them. The ground between the twenty-storey towers was a concrete yard walled in by rows of small garages. Fading white lines marked out baseball and football pitches, though the baskets and goalposts had been torn out of the ground decades ago. Despite its classical urban erosion demeanour, it was a perfect site for The Disco at the End of the World.

Andy had been dancing on the worn concrete since sundown, embracing the communal madness. Out of all London's residents, the type that lived in the tenement had the least to lose when the possessed came marching out of the darkness. So . . . sod it. If you are absolutely going to get captured by the evil dead/tortured/have your body consumed by ghouls/live the rest of eternity as a zombie slave, you might as well have one last decent party before it happens.

The underground trax jammers had set up their ageing speaker stacks as twilight fell. When the sun left the sky, out came the pounding rhythm to rattle the windows and sneer an utterly worthless defiance at the arcology's new overlords. Everyone had dressed for it. That's what Andy loved. Disco divas in their sequinned microdresses, hot funk dancers in leather and infra-white shirts, jive masters in sharp suits. All grooving and swaying in one huge dense mass of hot bodies, doing the stupid moves to stupid old songs.

Andy wriggled his hips, and waved his hands, and generally boogied on down like he'd never done before. No need to be self-conscious now, there wouldn't be a tomorrow morning for people to laugh at him and his coordination. He swigged from the bottles passed round. He snogged a couple of girls. He sang along at the top of his voice. He made up his own cool moves. He cheered and laughed and wanted to know why the hell he'd wasted his life.

And then there she was. Louise, standing in front of him. Clothes wet and dishevelled. Her beautiful face deathly serious.

She'd generated her own space among the exuberant dancers. People instinctively avoided her, knowing that whatever private hell she was in they didn't want any part of it.

Her lips parted, shouting something at him.

'What?' he yelled back. The music was incredibly loud.

She mouthed: Help.

He took her hand and led her across the yard. Through the ring of elderly people around the edge of the dancing throng, happily clapping along and doing a small shuffle. Into the brick-wall lobby, and up the stone stairs to his flat.

When the door shut behind them, Andy thought he was dreaming, because Louise was in his flat. Louise! On the last night of existence, they were together.

His window looked out over the street not the yard, so the music was muted down to a constant bass drumming. He reached for a light stick, the grid power supply had failed early that morning.

'Don't,' Louise said.

Without air-conditioning, condensation had settled thickly on the glass panes, but there was enough coloured light from the disco creeping in to reveal the outline of the small room. A bed at one end, sheets unwashed for a while now. Apart from one vinyl-top table littered with electronic tools, the furniture was cardboard boxes. The kitchen fitted into an arched alcove with a plastic curtain drawn across it.

Andy hoped she wouldn't look at it all too closely. Even in this light it was seedy. His delight at seeing her was fading as his real life began to seep back to claim him.

'Is this the bathroom?' she asked, indicating the one other door. 'I got drenched. I'm still cold.'

'Um, sorry, it's supposed to be the bedroom. I just use it to keep stuff in. Bathroom's down the hall. I'll show you.'

'No.' Louise stepped up to him and put her arms round him, nestling her head against his. He was so startled he didn't respond for a couple of seconds, then he gingerly returned the hug.

'There's been so much horror in my life today,' she said. 'So many vile things. I've been so frightened. I came here to you because I have to. There's no one else left for me now. But I want to be with you as well. Do you understand that?'

'Not really. What's happened to you?'

'It doesn't matter. I'm still me. For now.' She kissed him, urgency arousing her in a way she hadn't experienced before. The desperate need to be held, and adored, to be promised that the whole world was a fine and good place after all.

She demanded all that from Andy on his small disorderly bed. Spending the night being worshipped, listening to his ecstatic cries twist away into the disco music while the hazy dapple of iridescent light played across the ceiling. Air in the small confined room grew stifling from the heat and sweat evaporating off their skin. It made them oblivious to the Westminster Dome's giant air-circulation systems shutting down.

By the time the first tendrils of thin mist were rising from the Thames to squat listlessly above the riverside buildings, their bursts of orgasmic pleasure had become close to pain as program abuse forced already overdriven flesh to continue. Finally, with the exquisite narcotic of desperation spent, they clung to each other, too senseless to know that a thin layer of cloud had started glowing red above the heart of the ancient city outside.

26

Liol piloted *Lady Mac* right up to the big spacedock globe on the diskcity rim where the MSV was parked, locking position twenty metres outside the yawning hatch. Joshua was very insistent they didn't come inside.

Working out a procedure for bringing Quantook-LOU and five of his entourage inside the starship took up the entire trip from the transparent bubble to the rim airlock hatch. They eventually agreed that two of Joshua's crew, Quantook-LOU, and another Mosdva would ride the MSV out to the starship first. There would be three shuttle flights in all, and Joshua would be the last over. That way the distributor of resources would be satisfied that the starship wouldn't fly away as soon as its captain was on board, leaving him behind. The idea that Joshua, as commander, wouldn't desert any crew was obviously foreign to him. An interesting outlook, the humans agreed, and a good marker for future behaviour.

The xenocs were assigned the lower lounge in capsule D, which had its own bio-isolation environmental circuit. Sarha modified it to provide a mix of gas to match Tojolt-HI's atmosphere, not that they carried a great deal of argon, and she had to omit the hydrocarbons altogether.

Once Quantook-LOU was inside, and Joshua was back on the bridge, the Mosdva would provide the coordinates of their destination.

Mosdva spacesuits were made from a tight-fitting fabric, woven with heat-regulator ducts. Only the upper two sets of limbs were given sleeves, the lower legs were tucked up next to the body, making the lower section look as if it was the end of a giant stocking. The helmet was chunky, with internal mechanisms bulging up like warts, and a forward glass visor that had several protective slide-down shields. Their life-support backpack was a cone whose tip flared out into a fringe of small jet-black fins. A single thick armoured cable linked it to the helmet. An oversuit web carried electronic modules and canisters the same way as their torso jackets.

Beaulieu and Ashly watched the xenocs through a ceiling sensor as they came through the connecting airlock into the lounge. They didn't move with quite the same ease as they did back in the diskcity, lacking the fronds to give them stability, but they were adapting fast to grab hoops and the inter-deck ladders.

When the last one was inside, Ashly closed the hatch and let the new atmosphere in. Quantook-LOU waited in the middle of the lounge while the others conducted a detailed examination. Most of the fittings had been stripped out for this flight, leaving a spartan cabin. It didn't leave them much technology to probe, and there was certainly nothing critical they could damage. The Mosdva satisfied themselves that the lounge wasn't actively hostile, and confirmed the atmosphere was compatible before removing their suits. They quickly transferred the electronic modules from their oversuits to their usual jackets.

Beaulieu had used a neutrino scattering detector when they were in *Lady Mac*'s airlock to scan the hardware they'd brought with them. Alkad and Peter joined her in analysing the function of various components. They were carrying small cylinders of chemical explosive, lasers, spooled diamond wire, and a gadget which Alkad and Peter thought would give off a powerful EM pulse. The internal molecular-binding-force generators could maintain the lounge decking's integrity against any of their weapons should they get hostile.

More interesting were the number of implants each of them was loaded with. The central nervous column, running through the centre of the body, had a number of attachments spliced into it, artificial fibres spread out through the tissue to form a secondary nervous system. Biochemical devices were grafted on to glands and circulatory networks, supplementing organ functions. Compact weapons cylinders were buried in limb muscles.

'The weapons I can understand,' Ruben said when Beaulieu displayed the images over the general communication link, 'but the rest seem redundant. Perhaps their organs still haven't fully evolved to free fall conditions.'

'I disagree,' Cacus said. 'Quantook-LOU doesn't have the same degree of enhancements as the other five. I'd say his escort are the Mosdva equivalent of our boosted mercenaries. They'll be able to keep functioning even when they're badly damaged.'

'It's probably significant that Quantook-LOU's physiological condition is generally superior to the others',' Parker said. 'His bone structure is certainly thicker, and from what we can understand of his internal organs their biochemical functions have a higher degree of efficiency. That suggests to me that he was actually bred. Fifteen thousand years isn't long enough for a full genetic evolutionary adaptation to free fall, there are just too many changes from a gravity environment to incorporate.'

'If you're right, that would confirm an aristocracy-based social structure,' Cacus said. 'Their whole administration class would be an elite.'

'He does have a large amount of processors hardwired into what passes for his cortex,' Oski said. 'A lot more than the soldiers. They augment his memory and analytical abilities to a similar level as neural nanonics.'

'Physical and mental superiority,' Liol said. 'That's very fascist.'

'Only in human terms,' Ruben chided. 'Imposing our values on xenocs and then going on to judge them is the height of conceit.'

'Pardon me,' Liol mumbled. He checked round the bridge to find Ashly and Dahybi grinning at the Edenist's snobbery; Sarha gave him a thumbs up.

'An aristocracy is historically arrogant,' Syrinx said. 'If all the dominions are structured the same way, it would explain why they are so quick to escalate their disagreements into war. The administration class would regard the soldiers as expendable. Like everything else here, they are resources to be exploited to the advantage of the dominion.'

'Then where exactly do we fit into their neat little hierarchy?' Sarha asked.

'What we have is valuable to them,' Parker said. 'What we are is not. They will deal with us on that level only.'

Joshua slid through the lower deck hatch into the bridge, and settled onto his acceleration couch. He datavised the flight computer for a systems review, and took over the command functions from Liol. 'We're ready,' he told Quantook-LOU. 'Please give us the location.'

One of the Mosdva's electronic modules transmitted a stream of data.

'That's one of the tangles in the web, nine hundred kilometres away,' Beaulieu said. She datavised a string of instructions to the ELINT satellites, using the closest one to give the section a close scan. 'The knot itself is approximately four kilometres across, rising seventeen hundred metres above the disc's median level. A lot of infra-red seepage in the surrounding area. Most of the knot's web tubes are dead. But the thermal-exchange mechanism around it is still functioning, but with a reduced output.'

'Somebody's still alive there,' Sarha said.

'Looks that way.'

'We have the position,' Joshua told Quantook-LOU. 'What kind of acceleration can you withstand?'

There was a slight pause. 'Thirty per cent of the acceleration you used when you approached Anthi-CL would be acceptable to us,' Quantook-LOU said.

'Understood. Secure yourselves, please.' Joshua extended *Lady Mac*'s combat sensors, and ordered the standard booms to retract. The crew went to combat alert status. A quick check of the lounge sensors showed the six Mosdva prone on the cushion padding which Beaulieu and Dahybi had laid out for them on the decking.

It wasn't worth igniting the fusion tubes. Joshua used the secondary drive to accelerate the starship at a tenth of a gee. The vector he'd plotted took them out a hundred kilometres from the sunside, then curved across towards the knot.

'Gas plumes on this side as well,' Beaulieu warned. 'They're still fighting down there.'

Joshua called Quantook-LOU. 'We can see there's still a lot of conflict on Tojolt-HI. It would help to know if we are likely to be attacked, and by what.'

'No Tojolt-HI dominion will attack this ship unless it appears you are leaving. If I have not secured your drive technology, then our desperation will increase.'

'What form will an attack against us take? Do you have ships that can intercept us?'

'We have no ships other than the sunscoops which you have already seen. Energy-beam weapons will be used to damage you. I would speculate that many dominions will be constructing fast automated vehicles. The speed which the *Lady Macbeth* can travel at has been studied. They will be swifter.'

Joshua looked round the bridge. 'I'd say we don't need to worry about missiles. It's the lasers that trouble me. The dominions have the kind of power-generation capacity which makes our SD plat-forms look feeble.'

'But not on this side of the diskcity,' Beaulieu said. 'Sensor scans have dropped considerably since we moved across the rim. Ninety per cent of their systems are mounted on the darkside.'

'They can poke a laser through the foil quick enough,' Liol said.

'We'll be watching for it,' Sarha told him.

'I'd still like to understand the circumstances,' Joshua said. 'Quantook-LOU, can you tell me which dominions are allied with Anthi-CL?'

'Outside our main alliance quartet, there is no longer any way of knowing. Your arrival has disrupted the dominions at every level. The rim dominions search for allies among the centre. The centre dominions struggle among themselves as the old alliances fall to be replaced by lies and unkeepable promises.'

'And we did all that?'

'For all our history, resources have been finite, and our society reflects this. Now you have come, and every resource has suddenly become infinite. There can only be one dominion now.'

'How so?'

'We are in balance. The central dominions have larger areas than those of the rim, but the rim is where the new mass gathered by the sunscoop ships is distributed from. Our value is therefore equal. Each rim dominion supplies its centrist allies with mass, and the amount of mass which can be delivered is obviously dependent on the number of sunscoops. The number of sunscoop ships which can be built is dependent on the size of the alliance. Their construction absorbs a fearsome quantity of our resources. When a sunscoop fails to return, the quantity of mass available to the alliance is reduced, causing shortages and hardship among the dominions. Then the alliance grows weak as dominions struggle against each other to obtain the level of mass they require. That is when the distributors in each dominion move to forge new alliances that will allow them to regain their old level of supply.'

'I understand,' Joshua said. 'With our technology allowing you to bring new mass in from other star systems, the sunscoops will not be able to compete. Every central Tojolt-HI dominion will turn to Anthi-CL to supply it with mass, becoming your allies. Without a market, the other rim dominions will fail, and also be incorporated into the alliance.'

'And I will be the distributor of resources for all of Tojolt-HI.'

'Then why are the other dominions fighting you?'

Quantook-LOU raised his midlimbs a small distance against the gee force, slapping his torso feebly. 'Because I do not yet have your drive technology. As always they search for advantage. By reducing Anthi-CL to ruin, they will deprive me of the resources to build starships. You will be forced to make the exchange with them.'

'But you said the alliances between the central dominions are unstable.'

'They are. The other distributors are greedy fools. They would destroy us all. The damage they have already caused to Tojolt-HI is on a scale we have never endured before. It will take decades to repair everything.'

'So just tell them you have our drive. I'll back you up. We can work out the details of the exchange later. That will stop the destruction.'

'Anthi-CL's allies know I have not yet acquired your starship drive. I maintain our primary alliance with the quartet by assuring them that this venture to acquire astronomical data will result in triumph. In turn, they barter this information to gain advantage should I fail. All of Tojolt-HI knows you have not yet exchanged the data with me. They watch to see the outcome of this flight. Once I can signal Anthi-CL that I have the data to build your drive, our quartet alliance will solidify once more. The other dominions will have no choice but to join with us. Faster than light travel has made our unification inevitable. All of us know this. All that remains is the question of who shall become distributor of resources for Tojolt-HI. If it is not me, then it will be another dominion's distributor. That is why they will attack should you attempt to fly away.'

Joshua switched off the link to the lounge. 'Opinions?'

'He's very good,' Samuel said. 'I think he's realized you have a conscience, or at least some kind of ethical code. That's why our arrival is blamed as the cause of the diskcity war. We're also under threat not to try and leave, otherwise we'll be shot. Everything he says is to his advantage.'

'The economic structure of Tojolt-HI certainly made sense,' Parker said. 'That lends credibility to the rest of the situation.'

'It's certainly favourable for us,' Liol said. 'Even if Quantook-LOU is exaggerating the political instability, everyone here wants to be the one who gets ZTT from us. They're prepared to go to war in order to give us what we want.'

'Pity we can't use that to negotiate some kind of peace settlement,' Syrinx said. 'I can't help but feel very uncomfortable about this.'

'We could simply beam the information across Tojolt-HI after we get a copy of the Tyrathca almanac,' Beaulieu suggested. 'Even if Quantook-LOU does get us the almanac data, and we give him ZTT technology, the physical aspect of their conflict will probably continue as the consolidation into one dominion moves forward.'

'The irony of all this astounds me,' Ruben said.

'I fail to see how,' Syrinx replied quickly. 'You must have a very black sense of humour to find this remotely funny.'

'I never said funny. But don't you see what this discussion mirrors? This is how the Kiint must have debated our species when we asked them for the solution to the beyond. To the Mosdva, faster than light travel is obviously the answer to all their problems; they can have an infinite supply of mass, they can begin fresh colonies, and they can exterminate their old oppressors. To them it is essential we supply it, and they are willing to risk everything to gain what we have. Yet for us, with our complete understanding of ZTT, giving them the technology means releasing a genocidal crusade across this whole section of the galaxy, as well as the possibility of the Confederation going to war against them at some time in the future. Which we would probably lose, given their numbers.'

'If the Tyrathca don't get us first,' Monica muttered out loud.

'Are you saying we shouldn't give them ZTT?' Joshua asked.

'Think what will happen if we do.'

'We've been through this already. The Mosdva will probably get faster than light travel anyway now they know it's possible.'

'Just as the Kiint keep saying we have to find our own solution to the souls in the beyond now we know it exists.'

'Jesus! What do you want me to do?'

'Nothing now. We were right before, the question is one of timing. I think we got the answer wrong.'

'Maybe we did,' Syrinx said. 'Though I'm not convinced. But this has made our future actions very clear-cut. We have got to solve the problem of possession and the beyond first. Only then will we be in a position to deal with the whole Tyrathca–Mosdva issue. And the only way we can do that now is get to the Sleeping God.'

The ELINT satellites continued to show the war across Tojolt-HI's darkside. Blow-outs were occurring with increasing frequency, sending long spumes of vapour and fluid racing out into space, propelling bodies along with them. Mosdva troops in armoured spacesuits continued to scurry across the valleys and ridges of the darkside structure. Almost all train movement had ceased.

The heaviest fighting was conducted around the boundary of Anthi-CL and its neighbouring allies. As well as the blow-outs decompressing entire tubes, suited Mosdva shot at each other with beam and projectile weapons as they struggled to penetrate their enemy's territory and disable critical systems. The satellites were also picking up powerful flashes of energy among the tall thermal-dissipation towers as emplaced defensive lasers and masers swept across the ranks of advancing soldiers.

'But no nukes,' Beaulieu said. 'At least not yet. I have picked up some small short-range missiles, but they use chemical rockets and warheads. They're not very successful, the lasers usually pick them off. Hardly surprising, the maximum acceleration so far has been seven gees.'

'I wonder why they use chemical systems?' Monica asked. 'One well-placed nuke would take out a whole dominion. They must have the ability to build them. Quantook-LOU said they used to move asteroids around with them, just like we do.'

'We can ask Quantook-LOU if you like,' Joshua said.

'I'd rather not,' Samuel said. 'I'd hate to put ideas in his head. In any case, you're misrepresenting the nature of conflict here. Every-thing is resource-based, even war. The aim must always be to kill an enemy's population, but keep their web tubes intact. Explosive decompression will have exactly that result every time, giving the victorious dominion room to expand. A nuclear strike would obliterate a vast amount of the diskcity structure, while the shockwave would waken even more.'

'OK, so they use neutron bombs,' Liol said. 'Kill the population and leave the structural mass intact.'

'I definitely wouldn't mention that to Quantook-LOU.'

*

Etchells expanded his distortion field to scan around as soon as he slipped out of the wormhole terminus seventy-five million kilometres above the surface of Mastrit-PJ's photosphere. Thermo-dump panels slid out to their full length from every life-support capsule and subsidiary system to get rid of the heat. Electronic sensor pods opened their petal segments, extending antenna.

Red light flooded across the utilitarian bridge compartment, cutting through the heavy shielding of the main port. Kiera blinked away the rush of liquid it brought to her eyes as she sat on the acceleration couch facing it. She was content just to admire the genuine panorama, ignoring the various graphic displays that oscillated and scrolled across the consoles as they tabulated the results of the sensor sweeps.

'Nice view, if a little characterless,' she said. A pair of sunglasses appeared in her hands, and she placed them carefully on her nose. 'Can you sense anything nearby?'

'Nothing,' Etchells said. 'Which means nothing. Searching an entire star system is impossible for a single craft. Assuming they even came here.'

'Nonsense. They're here. It's the only place they could be. This damn star has been glaring at us ever since we rounded the nebula. This is where the Tyrathca came from, and it's where that arkship came from. They have to be here, along with whatever it is they're looking for.'

'Yes, but where, exactly?'

'That's your department. Keep your sensors extended. Find them. When you do, I'll keep my part of the bargain.'

'The odds are not in our favour.'

'The fact that any odds exist at all is in our favour. If there is anything left of the Tyrathca here, it must be on a planet or asteroid. You should start a survey.'

'Thank you. I'd never have thought of that.'

Kiera didn't even bother sighing a reprimand. He could perceive her mental tone as well as she could feel his. It wasn't that they'd been getting on each other's nerves during the voyage, just that they weren't natural allies. 'Can you withstand the temperature?'

'Provisionally, yes,' Etchells said. 'Though the particle density will have to be monitored as closely as the thermal input. The technological systems can cope with the heat, as can my hull. I estimate we can endure this environment for three days, then we will have to swallow away and cool off.'

'OK.' She stood up and stretched elaborately. There had been too many hours spent sitting uselessly on the bridge during the flight. It gave her too much time to brood over what had gone wrong back on Monterey, when what she ought to be doing was planning how to use the weapon which the Confederation was chasing. 'I'm going for a shower. Let me know when you find something.'

*

Beaulieu used a full-spectrum sweep against the sunside surface as *Lady Mac* decelerated into the coordinates Quantook-LOU had provided. The web tubes and their foil sheets matched the rest of Tojolt-HI's sunside in composition, but here they had risen out of the median in a small hemispherical mound, which matched the bulge on the darkside.

'The knot is about three kilometres across, nine hundred metres high, and I can't even begin to tell you what's inside,' Beaulieu said. 'Nearly eighty per cent of the knot and its surrounding webs are dead. Surface glass is cracked, and some structural ridges snapped. But that still leaves enough mass to shield the internal structure from all our sensors.'

'Don't like it,' Liol said. 'That's over ten cubic kilometres we don't know a damn thing about. They could be hiding anything in there.'

'Nothing that's used very regularly,' Ashly said.

'Yeah, like their biggest ever weapon.'

'Electrical and magnetic fields are normal,' Beaulieu said. 'I'm not registering any large power sources on either side of the disc.'

'Not active ones. The energy for a blast would be stored ready.'

'Ready for what?' Sarha asked.

'I don't know. We haven't explored one per cent of this star system, we don't know what else is lurking around here. Fleets of refugees from other diskcities. Xenocs that live inside the Orion Nebula. Mosdva possessed.'

'Oh, come *on*.'

'Point taken,' Joshua said. 'We need to be cautious.'

'The *Oenone* can swallow in,' Syrinx said. 'Our distortion field will be able to probe the interior of the knot.'

'No,' Joshua said. 'I still don't think we're ready to give away our biggest advantage yet. Beaulieu, I want constant monitoring of the knot. Any change in its energy state, and we jump clear. In the meantime, let's see what Quantook-LOU's prepared to tell us.' Before he asked, Joshua cleared the overlay of ship schematics from the sensor image. Tojolt-HI had been bothering him, niggling away for a while now. It wasn't worry about what they were heading into, he acknowledged, it was the size of the diskcity. He'd been appropriately amazed and impressed with it ever since the sensors had delivered their first image to him. This was different, because their little flight had suddenly put it into perspective for him. They were flying over it, an artefact which was so densely populated it made an arcology appear vacant. Human bitek habitats were fabulous huge entities, but you didn't fly *across* them in a spaceship, not for minutes at a time. And they weren't even halfway to the centre yet.

The visual spectrum sensors showed him a tiny black spot trawling over the burnished sparkle of the glass and foil which made up sunside. *Lady Mac*'s shadow, smaller than the width of most web tubes. Many times he'd seen Ganymede's shadow racing over Jupiter's dayside clouds, a black blemish smaller than the planet's cyclone swirls. A moon big enough to qualify as a planet, reduced to its true insignificance by the magnificent gas giant. This was exactly the same.

'We're going to be at your designated location in a couple of minutes,' Joshua told Quantook-LOU. 'I'd like to discuss the terms of the data exchange. After all, neither of us wants this deal to fall apart now.'

'I agree,' Quantook-LOU said. 'I will take my escort into this section of Tojolt-HI and secure the information you require. As before, you will be given the indexes of the files. If you are agreeable that it is what you want, we will perform a synchronized exchange of our respective information. You will then leave Mastrit-PJ immediately.'

'Fine by me, but won't you be in danger? This is a long way from Anthi-CL, we can return you.'

'After the exchange I will be the only member of my race to have the information. That makes me more valuable than the sun's mass in iron. Nobody will harm me. If I returned to the *Lady Macbeth*, what guarantee could you give me that you would not simply fly off back to your Confederation, thus removing the knowledge from my race?'

'I would not be able to offer a guarantee that would satisfy you, Quantook-LOU. However, I know nothing of Tojolt-HI. I do not know what is contained within this section behind the web tubes. How do I know that it is not some powerful weapon that can destroy my ship as soon as you have the information you want?'

'This is an old section, its dominion has almost collapsed. Do your sensors not show you that it poses no threat?'

'There is nothing we can see on the surface, but I must know what is inside. I propose to send two of my crew-members with you. They will only observe, they will not interfere with your activities.'

'I accept.'

Joshua ended the link. 'Ione, you're on.'

Lady Mac closed slowly on the sunside surface, using ion thrusters to manoeuvre in towards the approximate boundary of the knot. The web tubes below the starship were dead, as Quantook-LOU had requested. He had also asked that Joshua provide a method of crossing the gulf. As a result, the two suited and armoured serjeants were waiting in the open EVA airlock, ready to jet across and secure a tether to the tube surface.

Ione watched the long arched segments of glass grow larger; nothing was visible below the tarnished and pitted surface. Her armour suit sensors could just make out the faint lines of the inner spiral of piping. *Lady Mac*'s shadow was expanding and darkening over the glass and foil sheeting as the starship slid inwards. She saw a flickering motion sweep across the darkened glass. A multitude of anfractuous cracks spread out from the rim of the segment as though tendrils of frost were gripping the tube.

'It's rupturing,' she told the crew.

'Thermal stress,' Liol replied. 'It's our shadow that's causing it. Don't forget, that material has never had its heat input interrupted before.'

'Ione,' Joshua said. 'I'm locking our attitude – mark. You can go over whenever you're ready.'

The curving glass was seventy metres away from the airlock hatch. The first serjeant disconnected its safety line from the chamber socket, and activated the manoeuvring pack.

Attaching the end of the tether was no problem. The cracked glass had come out of the rim of the metal reinforcement hoop, leaving a gap she could loop it through. Once it was done, she moved aside. Joshua wanted the Mosdva to cut their own way in.

The xenocs hauled themselves along the tether using the powered gauntlets they wore on their midlimb hands. There was no subtlety in their entry. One of them simply used a laser to slice a circle through the glass and the piping underneath.

Ione was last in, both serjeants following one of the bodyguard Mosdva. She thought it must have been a long time since the tube was inhabited. The fronds had petrified then ablated away in the vacuum, leaving a cloud of granular dust clogging the tube. Even with that, it was a lot brighter than the sections they'd toured in Anthi-CL. Without the fluid to shield the interior, the light from the sun was fearsome.

The Mosdva made their way purposefully along to the end of the tube. They used the tarnished plant apertures as grips, which afforded them almost the same degree of mobility as the fronds in a pressurized tube. Ione simply used the manoeuvring packs.

When they reached the end of the tube, one of the bodyguards cut through the airlock hatch with a laser. They moved through the junction and into another tube on the other side, heading into the knot.

*

As soon as the last serjeant was inside, Joshua used the chemical vernier thrusters to back them away from the sunside surface. Beaulieu reported that nine small satellites had taken off from across Tojolt-HI. All of them were emitting low-power radar pulses, tracking *Lady Mac*.

'It looks like Quantook-LOU is heading for the apex of the knot,' Samuel said. 'So far he's staying with the surface tubes.'

'I'm analysing the signals the serjeant's electronic-warfare blocks are picking up,' Oski said. 'The Mosdva are transmitting a lot of pulses, most of it's coming from Quantook-LOU. Fairly high order encryption, as well.'

'Who's he talking to?' Joshua asked.

'I don't think he is. It's short-range stuff, and there's no electronic activity in any of the tube systems. I think it's all being received by his bodyguard. I'm correlating their movements and his signals, and it looks like he's virtually remote-controlling them. The stuff they're sending back is completely different, probably sensor feeds so he can see what they're seeing.'

'A regular little squad of drones,' Ashly said. 'I wonder if he doesn't trust them?'

'It's a bit late for us to start worrying about his status now,' Joshua said. 'Oski, see if you can work out how to freeze up those bodyguards if the need arises.'

'I'll try.'

Joshua fixed their position twenty-five kilometres away from the sunside surface. Waiting was difficult for him. He really wanted to be down there with Quantook-LOU, seeing what was happening. That would put him in control and ready to respond immediately to whatever the situation threw at them. Just like he'd done at Ayacucho and Nyvan. The front line was the only place he could be sure things would be done right.

Yet if Ayacucho and Nyvan had taught him anything, it was that there was more to command than good piloting. He trusted his crew to handle the starship's systems well enough. Deploying the experts he had with him was an extension of that principle. That second time in Anthi-CL, when Quantook-LOU had become insistent, he'd known right away he shouldn't have been there in person. So now it was guilt rather than professionalism behind the decision to send the serjeants into the knot.

At least no one had protested that they should have been sent as well. He rather suspected that the diskcity was getting to the others in the same way as it did to him.

They'd been holding station for fifteen minutes when Beaulieu's sensor-monitoring programs alerted her that the sunscoop ship had altered its orbit. The massive fusion engines were firing, propelling it at a steady fiftieth of a gee. 'It is now on an interception trajectory with us,' Beaulieu told the bridge crew.

'Jesus, how long have we got?'

'Approximately seventy minutes.'

*

Ione listened to Joshua's news about the sunscoop ship, and told him: 'All right, I'll ask Quantook-LOU.'

They were in another of the dead tubes, the fifth so far, still churning up the dust as they swept through. Apart from the lack of air and fluid, they'd all seemed in reasonable condition. She could see no physical reason for them being abandoned like this. Although at some time, they'd certainly been stripped of all their ancillary equipment. Even a couple of the tube-end bulkheads had been salvaged, leaving gaping openings into the junctions.

She switched her communication block to the frequency the Mosdva were using. 'Quantook-LOU, the captain has been in touch with me. He wants you to know that the sunscoop ship has changed direction and is now heading for the *Lady Macbeth*. Do you know anything of this?'

'I do not. The sunscoop belongs to the dominion of Danversi-YV. They are not allied to us on any level.'

'Is it likely to pose a threat to our ship?'

'It does not carry any weapons. Its strategy will be to intimidate the *Lady Macbeth* into dealing with it, and to place its own group in this location in an attempt to block my progress. Do you have weapons capable of destroying it?'

'We are not sure of the effect our weapons would have. Captain Calvert does not wish to fire upon an unarmed ship.'

'His views will change when the sunscoop's fusion drive is pointing at the *Lady Macbeth*. Tell him that the dominion of Danversi-YV has suffered the loss of two sunscoops in the last fifteen years. They have been much weakened by this, their alliance has shrunk, diminishing their influence. They will be the first rim dominion to fail once I have the faster than light drive. That makes them the most desperate to obtain it for themselves.'

'Understood.'

The Mosdva glided out into a large junction chamber that had seven tubes radiating away from it.

'This could be interesting,' Ione told the others. 'Judging by the position of two of these airlock hatches, the tubes behind them lead up into the knot. If they are tubes.'

'We have your location,' Liol replied. 'You're only a hundred and fifty metres from an inhabited surface tube.'

The Mosdva launched themselves from the bulkhead rim one after the other, heading unwaveringly for the first airlock hatch that led into the knot. They cut an oval of carbon-based composite out of the centre, and went through.

'Looks like we're avoiding the locals,' Ione said.

It was completely dark inside the tube. When the first serjeant squirmed through the hole its helmet sensors picked out six broad beams of ultraviolet light coming from the Mosdva up ahead. They were moving fast along the wall of the tube.

'I recognize this surface,' Ione said with as much excitement as her bitek neurons allowed her to generate.

The walls of the tube were made up from the same baked-sponge material that the Tyrathca had used in Tanjuntic-RI's zero-gee sections. The serjeants' armoured gauntlets could fit into the regular indentations, allowing them both to swarm up the tube after the Mosdva.

'No such thing as coincidence,' Joshua said.

'The airlock ahead is a different design,' Ione said. 'Not like those on Tanjuntic-RI, but not like the ones we've just come through, either.'

The hatch at the centre of the bulkhead was a thick titanium square, with fat rim seals and piston-like hinges. It was three metres across. Her infra-red sensors showed it was a lot warmer than the tube walls.

The Mosdva had stopped at the bulkhead to apply small sensor patches to the metal. 'The next section is in use,' Quantook-LOU said. 'I wish to avoid contact for now. We will go outside.'

A patch of the ossified sponge was scraped off the wall with a power tool, revealing the glossy inner casing. They cut through it with a laser, and slid out.

Ione switched her helmet sensors to infra-red. They were deep inside the convoluted knot. She could see no order or pattern, tubes criss-crossed through space leaving small irregular gaps which were caged by thick struts, forming a bird's nest filigree around her. Brilliant red threads revealed heat conduits running outside the tubes, while magnetic sensor imagery overlaid the translucent emerald lines of power cables.

'Plenty of activity here,' Ione said, 'but every tube is solid and opaque. Can't see in yet.'

'What about where you're going?' Joshua asked. 'Any ideas?'

'Not a chance. This is just too big a tangle to see more than a hundred metres in any direction.'

Thick strips of the sponge material had been laid lengthways along each tube, allowing them to move about easily. The Mosdva started off with little fuss. Ione's guidance blocks told her they were moving still deeper into the knot.

After two hundred metres the clutter of tubes came to an abrupt end. The centre of the knot was a cavity over two kilometres broad. A cylinder eight hundred metres in diameter filled the centre, its hubs fixed to the surrounding tubes with heavy magnetic bearings, allowing it to rotate slowly. A band of regular triangular ridges covered twenty per cent of the outer surface up at one end. Ione's infra-red sensors showed the band glowing a soft uniform pink, much warmer than the rest of the shell. A radiator disposing of the cylinder's internal heat. Which meant the systems inside were functional.

'Well, well,' she said. 'Look at this. Somebody still enjoys a gravity field to live in.' She scanned her sensors round. The cavity around the cylinder resembled a spaceport maintenance bay: gantry arms and support girders stuck out of the surrounding bulwark of tubing, threaded with conduits and hoses. They ended in sturdy clamp rings that sprouted long drill bits, inert and folded inwards like defunct sea anemones. Most were empty, though some of the clamps were gripping lumps of jet-black rock. They'd been cut like diamonds, with hundreds of small sheer facets. There was no standard shape or size. One piece was so large it needed ten gantry arms to hold it in place, its contoured surface following the curve of the central cylinder. Most required only two or three clamps, while there were scraps that had been skewered by just a single drill bit. Units of machinery were clinging to the rock, so dark and cold they could have been complicated freak outcrops. Except for one, in the middle of the largest chunk, which glowed salmon pink with internal heat.

'A refinery of some kind,' Ione guessed. 'I think most of this rock is carbonaceous condrite.' As her sensor sweep continued, she picked out several dense magnetic fields. The equipment producing them was mounted on bulky platforms that encircled the cylinder. They looked like fusion drive tubes.

'Who lives here?' she asked Quantook-LOU. 'It's the Tyrathca, isn't it?'

'This is Lalarin-MG. It is their designated location. I am displeased to find that they are still alive.'

'But you hate them, they're your old slave masters. I thought you'd killed them off. That's what you implied.'

'Those that remained at the end of the time of change grouped together in their enclaves. They became difficult to dislodge. It was not worth challenging their defences. We excluded them from contact with the new-formed dominions, and allowed them to decline in isolation. Only those that were the largest still exist.'

'That's incredible,' Samuel said. 'They're like the grain of sand in an oyster; the Mosdva simply grew around them.'

'A very big grain,' Sarha said. 'Take a close look at that cavity. I'll bet you it was all asteroid rock when the diskcity was built, probably with a biosphere cavern hollowed out in the centre. They've had to refine it away over the millennia to supply themselves with fresh minerals, and the cylinder is most likely what the biosphere evolved into. They couldn't expand like the Mosdva, so they just kept to the same size. We know they can keep that kind of society running indefinitely. Tanjuntic-RI was fully operational for the same length of time as this enclave. Except that one day they're going to run out of rock to consume.'

'That fits what I can see, except for the rocket engines,' Ione said. 'Why keep them functional when you need to expend every effort to maintain a highly artificial environment in adverse circumstances?'

'They might have been spaceship rockets originally,' Liol said. 'Not any more. I think they were adapted into the defence system Quantook-LOU mentioned. Don't forget, the Mosdva revolution happened when the diskcities were in their embryonic stage. The enclave asteroid would already be attached to the rest of the cluster at that time. If you used a fusion plume like a flame-thrower, it would have caused havoc, completely broken apart the asteroids, destroyed the new inhabited tubes and thermal-exchange mechanisms. The Tyrathca didn't have anything to lose, but the Mosdva sure did. So both sides agreed to the isolation.'

'And the Tyrathca, being unimaginative SOBs, kept their end of the threat in full working order all this time,' Ashly said. 'Fusion plumes could still do a lot of damage to a diskcity, even today.'

'Except they're not all in full working order,' Ione said. 'I can see ten, of which only three have magnetic fields.'

'Yes, but the Mosdva don't know that.'

'They do now.'

Quantook-LOU and the Mosdva bodyguard were on the move again, crawling along the tubes around the circumference of the cavity. Ione set off after them. 'Looks like we're heading for the hub of the cylinder,' she said. 'He must be planning on going in to meet them.'

'I'm beginning to respect old Quantook-LOU,' Joshua said. 'He's been pretty linear with us. Coming straight to a Tyrathca civilization is a good indication he genuinely wants to get the almanac for us.'

'I wouldn't attribute his behaviour entirely to fair play,' Syrinx said. 'Our appearance gave him a simple choice. Go for the number one position, or see Anthi-CL be absorbed by someone else's unifying alliance. He doesn't want the almanac data, he needs it desperately.'

'You never used to be this cynical.'

'Not before I met you, no.'

Joshua chuckled, wishing for the first time ever that he had an affinity bond. Not that he needed to check his own crew. Liol would be covering a grin, while Sarha would be casting a sly look his way, and Dahybi would pretend it was all going way over his head.

'Trains are moving again,' Beaulieu said. 'The ELINTs are tracking five, they all started in the last ten minutes.'

'So tell us why that's bad.'

'They are all within a hundred and fifty kilometres of the Tyrathca enclave, and are heading towards it.'

'Jesus! Wonderful. Ione, did you get that?'

'Confirmed. I'll tell Quantook-LOU, not that we can speed things along much at this point.'

The serjeants were now climbing along a tube directly underneath the end of the cylinder. An uncomfortable position. The gap was gradually narrowing as they approached the hub, and the cylinder's monstrous inertia had become terribly apparent. Ione knew if she was fully human she'd be having constant memory recall of the day when she got her hand caught in her bicycle wheel (six years old, and she'd reached down to try and move a jammed brake block before Tranquillity could stop her). As it was, she could just appreciate the associative link.

'We will enter here,' Quantook-LOU announced. The Mosdva stopped around an airlock hatch in a web junction. One of them placed an electronic module over the rosette keypad on the rim. After a moment, the module's green LEDs displayed a string of figures. They were tapped into the keypad and the hatch locks disengaged, allowing it to swing down into the airlock chamber.

'We will go first,' Quantook-LOU said.

Ione waited until the cycle had run, then both serjeants pushed down into the chamber. The inner hatch opened into the junction. Her suit sensors had to disengage filter programs to adapt to the light inside. It was white. She wondered how the Mosdva would cope with that. If they could actually see colour. Not that the question was high on her agenda.

The junction was a sphere thirty metres across, with seven hatchways set into it. Ten soldier-caste Tyrathca were standing around it at conflicting angles, their hooves wedged deep into the sponge indentations, holding them perfectly still. They were pointing thick maser rifles at the Mosdva group.

Chittering and loud agitated whistles rang through the air as Quantook-LOU talked insistently to the single Tyrathca breeder who was standing among the soldiers. The distributor of resources had taken his suit helmet off.

'What are they?' the breeder asked; its hazel eyes had locked on the serjeants.

'Proof of what I say,' Quantook-LOU replied. 'They are the creatures who have come from the other side of the nebula.'

'What Quantook-LOU says is true,' Ione said. 'We are happy to meet you. I am Ione Saldana, one of the crew from the starship *Lady Macbeth*.'

Several of the soldiers rustled their antennae when she spoke. The breeder was silent for a moment.

'You speak as us, yet your shape is wrong,' it said. 'You are not a caste we know. You are not a Mosdva either.'

'No, we are humans. We learned your language from the Tyrathca who came to our domain on the flightship Tanjuntic-RI. Do you know of it?'

'I do not. The memories of that age are no longer passed on.'

'Bloody hell!' Ione exclaimed over the general communication band. 'They've junked their records.'

'It doesn't mean that at all,' Parker said. 'The Tyrathca pass useful memories down the generations via their chemical program glands. The details from fifteen thousand years ago are hardly likely to be relevant enough to be maintained in that fashion.'

'He's right,' Joshua said. 'We're after their electronic files, not family legends.'

'I would like to mediate with the family that governs the electronics of Lalarin-MG,' Quantook-LOU said. 'That is why we are here.'

'Tyrathca and Mosdva do not mediate,' the breeder said. 'It is the separation agreement. You should not have come here. We do not come to your dominions. We maintain the separation agreement.'

'What about the humans?' Quantook-LOU said. 'Should they be here? They are not a part of the separation agreement. The universe outside Tojolt-HI has changed for Mosdva and Tyrathca. A new agreement must be mediated. I can do this. Allow me to mediate. All will benefit, Mosdva, humans and Tyrathca.'

'You may mediate with Baulona-PWM,' the breeder said. 'Two of your escort may accompany you, and the humans. Follow me.'

The tube which the breeder led them down was six metres in diameter, with a cable stretched along the centre supporting clusters of lights at regular intervals. All the Tyrathca walked along the walls as though they were in a gravity field. Their whiplike antennae were waving about with vigorous sweeping motions, like undersized wings. Ione realized the breeder's antennae were much longer than the Tyrathca she was familiar with.

'We always believed them to be balance aids,' Parker said. 'It would appear low gravity has encouraged their re-use.'

Her sensors swept over the breeder. It was about ten per cent smaller than Confederation breeders, although it appeared fatter. A smattering of the scales on its sienna-coloured hide had turned pale grey, and there were small lumps on its leg muscles. Its breathing seemed to be mildly erratic, almost as if it was wheezing. When she checked the soldiers, they had similar blemishes. Two of them were also running a temperature.

'They haven't come through the isolation as well as the Mosdva,' she said.

'Small population base,' Ashly said. 'They'll be running into inbreeding problems. Couple that with the kind of medical difficulties which you get from exposure to free fall, and they'll probably have a high number of invalid eggs. Considering they don't have a research base to examine and counter the problems, they've done well to survive this long.'

The last tube opened out into the rotating airlock. It was a layout remarkably similar to the one in Tanjuntic-RI, a long cylindrical chamber with three large airlock hatches at the far end leading into Lalarin-MG, and a pressure seal halfway along. A low rumbling sound vibrated through the atmosphere as the giant cylinder revolved.

The flightship design was carried over on the other side of the airlock. A waiting freight lift was flanked by archways leading directly onto spiral ramps.

Everyone crowded into the lift together, and it started to descend. Gravity built slowly, causing trouble for the three Mosdva. They had to remove their spacesuits entirely to free their hindlimbs, allowing them to stand on them and their midlimbs. It wasn't easy, their clublike hind feet were evolving away from dexterity, while their mid-hands were almost too delicate to carry half of their bodyweight. When the lift reached the base of the cylinder, gravity was fifteen per cent Earth standard. The Tyrathca were perfectly comfortable with it; Ione reprogrammed her suit actuators to take it into account, making sure the serjeants didn't go power leaping and compensating for the coriolis factor. Quantook-LOU staggered slowly, moving his limbs with painful unfamiliarity. His two bodyguards were a little better off, they had prosthetic midlimbs to take the weight. Servo mechanisms whined loudly with their every movement. Ione wondered what kind of strain the weight was putting on their organs and heart.

The lift doors opened, revealing the interior of the cylinder. Ione had to bring more filters on-line to compensate for the glare.

Lalarin-MG was a single open space enclosed by a cyclorama of aluminium alloy. The floors were fully occupied by rank after rank of buildings, the standard tapering towers of all Tyrathca settlements. Here, though, they were built out of some jet-black composite; thick pipes and knobbly segments of equipment protruded from the walls, as if they were machines rather than residences. Countering that impression were lush vines with broad, droopy emerald and lavender leaves that scaled the walls, sprouting rings of large hemispherical turquoise and gold flowers. Thin strata of mist drifted up from the grid of streets, merging together into an unwavering pearl-grey haze as they curved their way towards the axis. Every rooftop supported a battery of brilliant lights which shone directly upwards, their broad beams intersecting within the haze and diffusing slightly before they illuminated the section of floor directly overhead.

The cylinder's sheer endwalls were simple circles of moss, broken into an elaborate tessellation pattern by structural reinforcement ribs and interconnecting spars. A slender axial gantry ran the length of the cylinder. With one interruption.

'Oh, my God,' Ione said. 'Can everybody see that?'

'We see it,' Syrinx said.

In the absolute centre of the cylinder, suspended from its tips by the axial gantry, was the effigy of the Sleeping God. From tip to tip it measured two hundred metres, giving it a diameter of a hundred and fifty at the flared central disc. Originally the surface had been given a polished metallic sheen, now it was streaked by thick runnels of algae, with tufts of sickly brown fungi sprouting from pocks and cracks. Both spires were mottled by encrustations of lichen.

The Mosdva paid it no attention as they walked painfully along the narrow streets between the towers. Humidity was high. Every surface was beaded with condensation, horizontal ledges and pipes dripped constantly. The eternal background pattering sounded like a gentle rainfall.

Tyrathca breeders (always in pairs, Ione noticed) crowded every intersection along the street, chittering among themselves as the procession made their way into the cylinder. There were few vassal castes in evidence, and most of those were soldiers. Farmers tended the curtains of vines with slow arthritic movements, training new shoots up the trellis and picking the ripe clusters of dark-purple fruit.

As they walked slowly through the buildings, her impressions of

Lalarin-MG clarified. The interior of the cylinder had the same pattern of lethargic decay that was present across all of Tojolt-HI. Some buildings were in good repair; one or two were actually new, their siege of vines barely reaching up to the first-floor windows. But for every new one, four were disused. Even the equipment on the walls of the occupied towers was allowed to fail; magnetic and infrared sensors revealed the casings were inert, sharing the ambient temperature.

'They're on the border between stability and stagnation,' she said. 'And edging over the wrong way.'

'It's the biological aspect,' Ashly said. 'It has to be. It's the one negative factor at work here. They need to interbreed, inject some vitality back into the family bloodlines. They'll die out for sure otherwise.'

They finally came out on an annular plaza directly underneath the Sleeping God effigy. It was paved with slabs of aluminium coated with a rough layer of quartz for traction. Overhead, long ribbons of algae dangled from the effigy's rim, as if it had been given a raggedy skirt. Water showered down from the fringes, falling in a wide curve to sprinkle the whole plaza.

Tyrathca breeders were lined up along the edge of the aluminium slabs, sheltered from the drizzle. They were sitting on their hindquarters, antennae rising high from the shaggy manes running down their spines.

The soldier-caste guard all halted at a single piping command from the breeder. Quantook-LOU immediately sank down so his lower belly was resting on the slabs. His breathing was coming very fast.

A breeder rose from the row of Tyrathca and came over to stand in front of the serjeants. An old one, Ione guessed. Its hide was covered in white and grey patches, rheumy fluid leaked from its eyes, and it seemed to have some trouble focusing.

'I am Baulona-PWM, my family regulates electronics throughout Lalarin-MG. The Mosdva I know of. You I do not.'

'We are humans.'

'The Mosdva distributor of resources claims you have travelled from the other side of the nebula to visit Mastrit-PJ.'

'We have.'

'Did the Sleeping God send you?'

'It did not.'

Baulona-PWM tilted its head back against the soft warm rain, and let out a soft keening. The other Tyrathca around the plaza followed suit. A mournful chorus of dismay.

'Do humans know of the Sleeping God?'

'We do.'

'Have you seen it?'

'No.'

'We have called to the Sleeping God for its aid since before the separation agreement. We called when the Mosdva began the slaughter of our clans. We called when we were herded into our enclaves. We have called to it continuously for every moment since. There is always one of us here to call. The clan riding in Swantic-LI said it sees the universe. They said it is our ally. Why then does it not answer?'

'The Sleeping God is a long way from Mastrit-PJ. It might take a considerable time for it to arrive to help.'

'You bring us nothing new.'

Quantook-LOU straightened his midlimbs, rising off his belly to look from the serjeants to Baulona-PWM. 'What is this Sleeping God?'

The old breeder hooted loudly. 'One day you will know. The Sleeping God is our ally, not yours.'

'I am here to make new allies. Humans have changed our agreements. They have come here in a ship that travels faster than light.'

Baulona-PWM's head pushed forward to within ten centimetres of the first serjeant. 'The Sleeping God knows how to travel faster than light. How can you do this without its help?'

Ione used the general communication band to say: 'I think we should avoid anything that sounds like blasphemy at this point. Suggestions?'

'Tell them it was a gift from our god,' Syrinx said. 'They can hardly argue with that.'

'I don't want to put any pressure on,' Joshua said. 'But we haven't got much time until that sunscoop ship rendezvous. And those trains are still closing on you. If it looks like Quantook-LOU can't swing a deal, then we'll just have to deal with the Tyrathca directly.'

'Understood,' Ione said. 'The faster than light drive was given to us by our god,' she told the old Tyrathca breeder.

'You have a god?'

'Yes.'

'Where is it?'

'We don't know. It visited our world a long time ago, and hasn't yet returned.'

'The humans will give me the faster than light drive,' Quantook-LOU said. 'It will provide the Mosdva dominions with fresh resources. We will build new diskcities. We will be able to leave Mastrit-PJ as the Tyrathca did.'

'Give us the drive,' Baulona-PWM said.

'The drive is mine,' Quantook-LOU said. 'If you want it, you will mediate with me. That is why I have come to you.'

'What do you want from Lalarin-MG?'

'All data and records on the Tyrathca flightships.'

Baulona-PWM hooted sharply. The soldiers shuffled round, agitated.

'You would know where our new worlds are,' Baulona-PWM said. 'You would destroy all Tyrathca. We know the Mosdva. We never forget.'

'Neither do we,' Quantook-LOU hooted back. 'That is why we must mediate now. If not, then Mosdva and Tyrathca will wage war again. You know this. Humans say they will help neither of us unless we have a new arrangement that will prevent war.'

'Smart argument,' Ione said to the others. 'I think I can see where he's taking it.'

'What is the new arrangement?' Baulona-PWM asked.

'The humans do not want war in this part of the galaxy. If we are to have the faster than light drive, then Mosdva must not use it to fly to stars with Tyrathca worlds. We must know where they are to avoid this.'

'That's the condition we make for giving you the drive,' Ione said. 'We know of your history, and the conflict between you. We will not permit that conflict to begin again and engulf other species. There is room in this galaxy for the Mosdva and Tyrathca to exist peacefully. It will be like the separation agreement you have here, but on a much larger scale.'

'We have our weapons to make the Mosdva obey the separation

1096

agreement here,' Baulona-PWM said. 'What will make them obey after you give them the faster than light drive, and they know where our new planets are? With this drive they will leave Tojolt-HI. Our weapons will mean nothing. They will destroy all Tyrathca at Mastrit-PJ. They will destroy all Tyrathca new worlds.'

'You destroy,' Quantook-LOU said. 'We build.'

'Mosdva do not keep agreements. You send your soldiers against Lalarin-MG. They are here now. We will use our weapons against all of Tojolt-HI.'

'Can you confirm this?' Ione asked the *Lady Mac*'s crew.

'We're picking up some Mosdva movement on the darkside,' Joshua said. 'Looks like they're infiltrating the tubes around the edge of the knot.'

'How many?'

'Several hundred. It's a large infra-red signature.'

'Are these the ones from the trains?'

'No. The first train won't be there for another fifteen to twenty minutes.'

'They are not Anthi-CL soldiers,' Quantook-LOU said. 'They are from the dominions who would use the humans' drive for themselves. I will mediate with Tyrathca, I will make agreements with Tyrathca. They will not. Give me the information. Once I have the drive, they will have to retreat from Lalarin-MG.'

'Make them retreat now,' Baulona-PWM said. 'When they are gone, I will mediate with you.'

'I cannot mediate with the other dominions until I have the information.'

'I will not give you the information until you mediate.'

On the *Lady Mac*'s bridge Joshua banged a fist into his couch cushioning. 'Jesus! What is wrong with these people?'

'Twenty thousand years of hatred and strife has become hereditary in both of them,' Samuel said. 'They can't trust each other, not any more.'

'Then we're going to have to break the deadlock.'

'We're about out of time on that front,' Liol said. 'The sunscoop has just reduced its deceleration thrust.'

'Oh, shit,' Joshua mumbled. He knew what that meant. The flight computer datavised the huge ship's new trajectory into his neural nanonics. With a reduced thrust the sunscoop wouldn't have nullified its velocity in time to stop beside the *Lady Mac*, twenty kilometres above Tojolt-HI's sunside. According to the new vector, it would end up one kilometre above the darkside of the knot which contained Lalarin-MG. And as it was approaching the knot drive first, its fusion plume would slice clean through the Tyrathca enclave, vaporizing the entire structure. It was also due to pass uncomfortably close to *Lady Mac*.

'I think we're going to have to take a more active interest,' Joshua told the bridge crew. He aligned *Lady Mac*'s main dish on the sunscoop. 'Attention, sunscoop ship. Your present course will result in the destruction of Lalarin-MG. Members of my crew are currently inside this dominion. Increase your deceleration thrust immediately.'

'Josh, it's over four kilometres across,' Liol said. 'That's not a ship, it's a mountain. Even if you nuke it, the debris will still rip this section of Tojolt-HI to pieces. In fact you'll probably do more damage that way.'

'I thought I'd told you how I dealt with Neeves and Sipika in the Ruin Ring.'

'Oh,' Ashly said drily. 'You mean that was a true story?'

Joshua gave the pilot a wounded look.

'No response from the sunscoop,' Liol said. 'And no change in thrust. They're still going to burn through the knot in eight minutes.'

'OK, if that's how they want it. Combat stations, please.'

Lady Mac's thermo-dump panels folded down into their hull recesses. Joshua ignited the main fusion tubes, and closed on the sunscoop at one and a half gees.

'This is going to be one very fast flyby,' he said. 'Sarha, you have primary fire control.'

'Aye, Captain,' she acknowledged. Her neuroiconic display was already showing her the sunscoop, a cluster of incandescent globes sitting on top of an even brighter flame of plasma that stretched out over thirty kilometres before dissolving into a hazy tip of blue ions. It descended relentlessly towards the vivid copper sunside like some gigantic insect stinger.

The flight computer datavised a stream of targeting data, overlaying her image with a bright purple grid. Under her guidance, it split into five segments and wrapped each piece around one of the incandescent globes. She upped the power level from the main tokamak generators, and activated the maser cannon.

Lady Mac swept past the sunscoop in a shallow curving trajectory, keeping a constant twenty kilometres away from the fusion plume. Her masers fired at the five storage globes, each beam piercing clean through the radiant thermal-dissipation material. Fissures of darkness streaked out from the impact points. The beams began to chew round in a tight spiral, widening the holes. Whatever the casing material was, its physical resistance to the microwaves was minimal. Ninety per cent of their energy went directly into the massive reservoir of hydrocarbon fluid stored inside. It started boiling immediately, belching out clouds of hot vapour. Pressure began to build up inside the globes, sending vast jets of blue-grey gas roaring out through the gashes.

'Delta-V change,' Liol reported. 'The punctures are creating thrust. Christ, Josh, it works.'

'Thank you. Sarha, keep those lasers centred, I want to heat as much fluid as we can. Stand by, reducing thrust. Let's try and avoid coming back for a second pass.'

'Captain,' Beaulieu called. 'The sunscoop drive is switching off.'

Lady Mac's combat sensor clusters tracked the sunscoop, showing Joshua the fusion plume dwindling away. 'Shit, did we do that?'

'Negative,' Sarha said. 'My shooting's not that bad. Drive systems are intact.'

'Liol, give me a trajectory update, please.'

'They've got a smart captain. Without the fusion drive, the gas plumes aren't enough to kill their velocity. They're going to hit the knot. Impact in four minutes.'

'Damn it.' Joshua immediately began plotting a new vector, taking *Lady Mac* round for another pass. The starship began accelerating at four gees. He had to be careful their own plume didn't wash across the sunside webs.

'Sunscoop gas vents are reducing,' Ashly said. 'The fluid must be cooling again. That thermal-dissipation mechanism of theirs is bloody good, Joshua. It's worth giving them the ZTT drive in exchange for that.'

Lady Mac was racing back towards the sunscoop. Sarha fired the masers again, to be rewarded by the sight of the gas jets thickening. The glare of the storage globes fluoresced them a blazing silver-white as they emerged from the holes; then they shaded down along their length until their diffuse tails shimmered cerise.

Two lasers struck *Lady Macbeth*, fired from somewhere on the diskcity's sunside. Joshua rolled the ship fast as their thermal protection foam flash-evaporated, scoring long black lines across the fuselage.

'No penetration,' Beaulieu called. 'We can handle this energy level for eight minutes. Thermal reservoirs will be saturated after that.'

'Acknowledged.' Joshua accelerated the starship at eight gees, heading back down to the sunside surface. Everyone tensed against the crushing gravity as the sensors showed them the red and gold corrugations hurtling towards them. *Lady Mac* flattened out, flying parallel to the diskcity, sixty metres from the tops of the web tubes. Her fusion drive cut out, leaving them in free fall.

'Lasers lost us,' Beaulieu said. 'They can't track us at this altitude.'

Behind them the sunscoop continued on its approach towards the knot. The five storage globes were glaring furiously as they tried to throw off the energy imparted by *Lady Mac*'s masers during the second pass. Success was measured by the way the gas jets were slowly shrinking.

'It's going to be close,' Liol said. 'But I think we've done it.'

Joshua followed the flight computer's plot. Watching the sunscoop's relative velocity winding down, comparing the rate against the declining gas vents. Flakes of grey slush had started to clot the ever-reducing gas jets. But it was going to work, he told himself, the figures were tight, but the ship would reach zero relative velocity sixty kilometres above the diskcity.

Datavised alarms suddenly glared across his neuroiconic display. *Lady Mac* was under attack again. Energy impacts bloomed against the fuselage, ablating patches of foam in spurts of soot.

'Lasers again,' Beaulieu said. 'They can't stay on us for more than two or three seconds at a time, but there's a lot of them. They're going for a coordinated saturation. Strikes are almost constant.'

'Quantook-LOU warned us the dominions would try to stop us leaving before we handed over the data,' Samuel said. 'They must think that's what we're doing.'

Joshua checked their vector. At their current velocity they'd fly over the rim in another hundred seconds. The course was taking them a long way round from Anthi-CL. He datavised the flight computer for a tactical analysis. 'The old girl can handle this level of fire. We don't need to jump clean yet.'

Lady Mac's sensors were still tracking the sunscoop ship. It was sixty-five kilometres away from the sunside, with its approach velocity down to ten metres per second. The five jets from its storage globes were still active, though the rents weren't squirting gas any more. It was mainly liquid and slush pouring out now. At sixty-three kilometres, its velocity was two metres a second.

The vector reversed at sixty-one kilometres. For a moment the sunscoop was stationary, then it began to creep away from the diskcity again at an almost unmeasurable velocity. By now the flow from the storage globes was reduced to a splutter of mushy fluid dribbling away into space.

Its fusion drive ignited.

Joshua groaned in dismay as *Lady Mac*'s flight computer translated the sensor image into pure data, providing him with the figures for the plasma's temperature, luminosity, and flow rate. This time the sunscoop was using its full thrust. The tip of the plume seared its way downwards as the giant ship began to accelerate away. There was never going to be time for the separation distance to increase beyond the range of the plasma spear.

The drive flame hammered against the crown of the knot, instantly vaporizing every tube and foil sheet it touched. A blast wave of superheated gas roared out through the tangle of tubes inside the knot, rupturing web junctions and sending shredded tube fragments whirling deeper into the tangle. Slow structural ripples flexed their way across the sunside, radiating sinuously out from the knot. Tubes cracked open around junctions and reinforcement ribs. Hundreds of fan-shaped fountains of circulation fluid and atmospheric gas howled out into space across an area fifty kilometres across, producing a stormy pellicle of crimson mist which hung over the surface. Its centre was energized to azure blue by the fusion plume from the retreating sunscoop, expanding in a perfectly symmetrical ring, swelling and fading as it raced away across the sunside.

The devastated Mosdva dominions around the knot retaliated. Every laser that remained functional was fired at the sunscoop. Small petals of darkness opened across the glaring storage globes, distending. Sprays of molten metal drifted out from the drive nozzle, followed by boiling globules of fluid. The plasma flame began to waver as it was contaminated by streaks of impurity burning emerald and turquoise.

The thick shadows slithering over the storage globes merged together into funereal blemishes until the light was completely extinguished. They shattered in unison, belching out thick wobbling rivers of hydrocarbon fluid. It began to evaporate under the red giant's unrelenting radiance, producing a surge of oily fog. A huge patch of shade crept over the sunside, defacing its usual gleaming hue to a dusky claret.

'Christ,' Liol gasped. Did we do that?'

'No,' Dahybi said. 'But they'll blame us anyway.'

'Ione?' Joshua asked. 'Are you all right?' He concentrated on the general communication link. The view through the serjeants' sensors was shaking badly. The effect of the sunscoop's plasma strike against Lalarin-MG was the same as an earthquake. Tyrathca breeders were scattered across the plaza, struggling to regain their footing. The soldiers had closed in on the three Mosdva, prodding them with their big maser rifles.

'We're OK,' she said. The serjeants began to scan round. 'No sign of structural breakdown. The cylinder is still intact, and rotating.'

'That's something.'

Above the serjeants, the Sleeping God's effigy was moving in a circular bouncing motion, completely out of phase with the cylinder's rotation. The axial gantry securing it bent and stretched with frighteningly loud stress creaks.

Baulona-PWM walked unsteadily over to Quantook-LOU. The distributor of resources was suffering in the aftermath of the attack, unable to lift himself up from the juddering plaza.

'Mosdva break their separation agreement,' Baulona-PWM said. 'You damage Lalarin-MG. You kill our vassal castes. We will fire our weapons at Tojolt-HI. You will be exterminated.'

'Wait,' Ione said. 'You cannot exterminate Quantook-LOU. He is the only Mosdva willing to deal with you. Without him there will be war. Billions of Tyrathca will die because you exterminated him. Their deaths will be your fault.'

'They will not die if you leave Mastrit-PJ. Do not give the Mosdva your faster than light drive. The Tyrathca here will survive. The Sleeping God will come to aid us.'

'The Mosdva will be given our drive. That is why we have come, to bring balance to the galaxy. The Tyrathca from Tanjuntic-RI were given the drive.'

'Tyrathca have faster than light drive?' Baulona-PWM demanded.

'Some of your worlds have it, yes. The technology is spreading slowly. Outside Mastrit-PJ your race is becoming powerful. Humans and our xenoc allies will not permit that to happen. There must be balance and harmony between races, only then can there be peace.'

Quantook-LOU heaved down a breath, but still made no effort to rise. 'Humans are stupid,' he said. 'Why did you give Tyrathca the drive? Can you not see what they are?'

'We know what both of you are. That is why we are here. Now you must choose. Will you mediate a new agreement? Will you pursue peace?'

'What will you do if we do not mediate an agreement?' Quantook-LOU asked.

'The balance will be enforced by us,' Ione said. 'We will not tolerate war.'

'The Mosdva will mediate an agreement for peace,' Quantook-LOU said. 'If the Tyrathca of Lalarin-MG do not wish to mediate with me, I will find an enclave that will.'

'Baulona-PWM, what is your answer?' Ione asked.

'I will mediate,' the breeder said. 'But the Mosdva still attack Lalarin-MG. They must stop. There can be no agreement if we are dead.'

'Quantook-LOU, can you get the other dominions to withdraw?'

'I cannot. I must have the drive first, and the *Lady Macbeth* must leave. Only then will they be forced to ally with me.'

'You can't have the drive until we have the Tyrathca information,' Ione said. 'Baulona-PWM, how long will it take you to recover the information necessary for the agreement?'

'I am uncertain where it is stored. Our old memory centres are no longer enabled. We would have to reactivate them.'

'Wonderful,' Joshua exclaimed. 'Not even total catastrophe can loosen these bollockheads up. Beaulieu, what's happened to the trains?'

'Three of them are still en route, Captain. And the surviving Mosdva in spacesuits are still infiltrating the knot on the darkside.'

'Jesus, we have to buy Ione some time.'

'We could go back to the knot and use our firepower to defend Lalarin-MG from the Mosdva troops,' Liol suggested.

'No.' Joshua rejected it automatically. It would be messy, he knew.

Lady Mac might be the most powerful ship in the system, but she wasn't invincible. They needed some way of isolating Lalarin-MG while the Tyrathca breeders found the almanac. And maybe Quantook-LOU really could negotiate some kind of peace settlement. Nice bonus.

He let the factors stream through his mind. With that arrogant Calvert certainty that they had to act on Lalarin-MG, it was just a matter of running through options. Thinking what he had available to work with.

Joshua started chuckling wickedly.

Ashly closed his eyes in prayer. 'Oh, shit.'

'Syrinx,' Joshua called. 'I need *Oenone* down here.'

*

One of the serjeants bent down beside Quantook-LOU. The distributor of resources had rolled partially on his side, which was why he couldn't right himself. His bodyweight was trapping his midlimb. Ione pushed his flank as hard as she dared, too much pressure would snap his bones.

'I thank you,' Quantook-LOU said as his midlimb wriggled free. 'You would make an excellent Mosdva. Even I am adrift among your mediating strategies.'

'A compliment indeed. My prime requirement, however, remains unchanged.'

'I understand. I will play my part.'

'Good.'

'In the expectation of reward.'

'You will collect the drive. Humans keep their word.'

'A welcome assurance at this point.'

The other serjeant had gone to talk to Baulona-PWM. They stood in the middle of the plaza, with the dirty rain from the effigy falling around them. The drops were less frequent, but larger, as the effigy continued its slow gyrations. 'My ship tells me that the Mosdva troops are invading the area around this cylinder,' Ione said. 'Can your soldiers hold them off long enough for you to retrieve the information?'

'How do you know this? We can detect no communication with your ship.'

'It is a method you are not familiar with. Now, can you hold them off?'

'We have no soldiers left outside Lalarin-MG. All is wrecked. Our food is grown in the tubes. There is no air, no fluid. Our communication links are failing. Our fusion weapons are disabled. Does your ship have weapons which can help us?'

'Not weapons, but we can certainly help. I will need your agreement to act as the mediator between you and Quantook-LOU.'

'Why?'

'If you supply me with the information which makes the agreement between Tyrathca and Mosdva possible, I may be able to offer all the Tyrathca of Lalarin-MG passage to one of the new Tyrathca worlds. It will not be today, but after we return to our home we can send larger ships to collect you. They could be here in three to four weeks.'

'We will be dead within one hour. Mosdva will come to break open Lalarin-MG's shell.'

'My ship can move Lalarin-MG away from Tojolt-HI. The Mosdva will no longer be able to reach it. This will give you time to retrieve the information and mediate an agreement with Quantook-LOU.'

'You can move Lalarin-MG?'

'Yes.'

'Once we leave the shadow of Tojolt-HI, we will be unable to get rid of the sun's heat. Our radiator bands are only sufficient to rid us of the heat we produce inside.'

'Mediating the agreement won't take that long. You will find and supply the astronomical information to me. When I am satisfied it is correct, I will release the drive to Quantook-LOU and leave. All hostilities will then cease and the agreement will become active. You can travel back to another enclave to wait for our ships to collect you.'

'I agree to this.'

*

Joshua varied *Lady Mac*'s acceleration at random as they flew back to the wrecked knot, making targeting difficult.

'Nobody's shooting at us,' Liol said. It was almost a complaint. Heavy fire might have made Joshua rethink this whole idea. Then again, part of him was looking forward to this with disgraceful childish glee. As he suspected his younger brother was as well. The rest of the crew treated the notion with an air of tolerant amusement. And Ione was doing a good job talking rings around the xenocs.

He had to admit, everything was falling into place.

'That's because we're going the wrong way to be shot at,' Monica said. 'We're coming back to them. It's leaving they object to.'

'I wonder what they'll make of this, then,' Joshua said.

Lady Mac glided over the edge of the knot. Virtually all of the foil sheets had been torn away from its sunside slopes, letting the red sunlight illuminate the snarl of dark tubes which made up the interior. Space around the knot was heavy with particles, crystals and scraps of foil reflecting the sunlight in a blossom of crimson scintillations. The sunscoop's plasma torch had blown out a huge crater at the crest of the knot. Three hundred metres in diameter, its walls were a stipple of fractured tubes with melted ends. They were still glowing coral red from the immense thermal barrage.

'I'm taking us in,' Joshua said. 'Beaulieu, start saturating the knot.'

'Aye, Captain.'

The cosmonik switched the maser cannons to wide angle dispersal, and began hosing the microwave energy around inside the crater. It wasn't powerful enough to damage the structure any further, but it would be lethal to any of the Mosdva creeping round inside the knot.

Joshua rolled *Lady Mac*, and started to edge her down into the crater. He used the forward lasers to slice through the tubes and wreckage at the bottom of the crater. Sections began to drift free, vapour from their molten ends blowing them away gently. Chemical verniers fired around the starship's equator, moving it deeper into the crater.

*

Oenone slipped out of its wormhole terminus thirty kilometres above the knot's darkside. The Edenists in the life-support toroid were all borrowing its sensor blisters, looking out in admiration at the monumental diskcity. Syrinx shared a smile with Ruben, their minds cherishing the vista together. Little bursts of excitement wafted around the mental embrace which pervaded the bridge as new facets of the xenoc construction were noticed and cherished. None of the ELINT coverage compared to actually being here.

The tall pinnacles of thermal radiators glowed a steady orange in the voidhawk's senses. It could feel the broad fans of heat they gave off, sluicing away through space towards the distant nebula. In the visual spectrum, Tojolt-HI was almost black. The exception came from the area where the sunscoop had attacked. Foil sheets had either been torn free or disintegrated, allowing sharp beams of intense red light to steal through the cluttered webs.

If Wing-Tsit Chong and the therapists could see me now, Syrinx said contentedly.

They don't need to, Ruben said. *They know they did their job properly.*

Yes, but it still galled when they said it. Just a timid tourist, indeed!

I am glad we came, Oenone said. *Everything here is fresh, but old at the same time. I feel Tojolt-HI has a dependability about it.*

I know what you mean, she told the enchanted voidhawk. *Anything that has such a long past must surely have an equally long future ahead of it.*

It did have until we arrived, Ruben said.

You're wrong. The Mosdva can't abandon it, nor any of the others. Ashly is right, ZTT won't give them that option. But maybe we'll see change. Progress will begin again. I prefer to think of that as being our legacy. And who knows what they will achieve with fresh resources and new technologies.

Let's not get ahead of ourselves.

You're right. The briefest glimmer of regret appeared amid her thoughts.

I'm picking up considerable radar activity above this side of the diskcity, Edwin said. *I think our countermeasures are deflecting them.*

Thank you, Syrinx said. *Nothing we can do about visual acquisition, I'm afraid. And we're silhouetted against the nebula for all Tojolt-HI to see. Serina, have you acquired the trains?*

Got them.

Cut the rails.

Five lasers stabbed out from the weapons pods clamped in *Oenone*'s lower hull groove. They slashed through the rail tracks meandering across the darkside's huge thermal radiators. Serina waited until the trains had halted, then used the lasers to chop the rail behind them.

Immobilized, she said. *They can't invade Lalarin-MG now.*

They'd be pretty stupid to try, Edwin said. *Our electronic sensors are picking up the* Lady Macbeth's *microwave emissions from here. They're powerful enough to leak through the knot.*

Let's go give him a hand, Syrinx told *Oenone.*

The voidhawk darted in towards the diskcity and came to rest directly over the knot. *Oenone*'s distortion field undulated through the damaged tubes and struts, allowing the Edenists to examine its anatomy. The remaining scraps of asteroid rock in the knot's central cavern were dark zones, their mass exerting a minuscule gravity field against space-time. Next to them, the cylinder rotated slowly, its thin shell nothing more than a murky shadow to the voidhawk's perception. Power circuits formed a grid of fuzzy violet lines permeating the whole edifice as the electron flows emitted their unique signature. The greatest concentration of energy was swirling around the magnetic bearings at each hub. Small instabilities flickered within the translucent folds, tarnishing the emissions. Barely fifty metres past the far end of the cylinder, *Lady Macbeth* appeared as a bright, dense twist in space-time.

'Got it, Joshua,' Syrinx said over the general communication link. 'The cylinder masses approximately one point one three million tonnes.'

'Excellent. That's no problem. With the antimatter drive, *Lady Mac* can hit forty gees, and we mass just over five thousand tonnes. That should give us nearly a fifth of a gee thrust.'

'All right, we'll start cutting.'

Ruben, Oxley, and Serina all issued instructions to the bitek processors governing the weapons pods. Eighteen lasers fired from the voidhawk's lower fuselage, and under the crew's directions began cutting through the tubes at the top of the knot.

*

Lady Mac's sensors could now focus on Lalarin-MG itself. Her lasers had scythed their way through the tangle of tubes and struts, clearing a broad passage along which Joshua had steered the starship. Hot segments of tube twirled away into the main cavity, bouncing against the metallic cylinder shell and the black lumps of rock. Light was filtering in for the first time in a hundred centuries. Trickles of red sunlight slipped past *Lady Mac*'s fuselage, complemented by sizzling scarlet flashes of the lasers.

'How's it going in there, Ione?' Joshua asked.

'We're ready. Rotating airlocks are closed and sealed. I even got Baulona-PWM to find some padding for the Mosdva to lie on.'

'OK, stand by.' The sensors were showing him the cylinder's hub with its big circular bearing dead ahead. He cut the last tube free, exposing the airlock chamber, and fired the ion thrusters to spin *Lady Mac*, matching her rotation to the cylinder. The starship's forward fuselage section moved into the bearing, crushing the jagged remnants of the tube. 'Sarha?'

'I've got the molecular-binding-force generators on maximum.'

'Take the CAB safety limiters off-line. Pump them higher. I want all the strength we've got in the stress structure.'

'You've got it.'

'We've cut this end free,' Syrinx said. 'You're clear.'

'OK everyone, stand by.' Joshua fired the fusion drives, keeping their thrust to an easy one gee. *Lady Mac* pressed forward, compressing the remnants of the airlock chamber in towards the cylinder shell. The rim of the bearing pierced the starship's protective foam until it was touching the fuselage.

'We're solid,' Liol declared.

Joshua increased the fusion drive thrust. Three strands of blue-white plasma stabbed back out through the crater, twining together. Tubes and struts facing the ultraheated torrent of ions began to boil furiously, sending out twisters of gas.

'Stress structure's holding,' Sarha said. The sound of the drive tubes was vibrating through the life-support capsules, a muffled drone. She'd never heard that before.

'It's moving,' Beaulieu called out. 'Accelerating at four per cent of a gee.'

'OK, here we go,' Joshua said. He activated the antimatter drive.

Hydrogen and anti-hydrogen collided and obliterated each other within the engine's complex focusing field. A shaft of pure energy burst into existence behind the starship, as if a flaw in space-time had cracked open. Two hundred thousand tonnes of thrust started to push Lalarin-MG out of its rapidly dissolving chrysalis.

*

'I think we might have something,' Etchells said.

Kiera looked up from the pizza slice she was munching through.

A couple of the console displays were showing elongated stars being lassoed by turquoise nets, columns of scarlet figures scrolled past too fast to be read. So far all the hellhawk had found was some radar-type pulses coming from (presumably) stations orbiting the huge star. They gave nothing away, other than the fact they weren't Confederation. Kiera and Etchells both wanted to see if anything else existed before they started investigating.

'What have you seen?' she asked.

'Take a look for yourself.'

The gauzy iridescent clouds of the nebula slid across the bridge's main port as the hellhawk swung round. Bright crimson light shone in as it faced the red giant again.

Kiera dropped her pizza back into the therm box and squinted against the glare. Right in the middle of the port was a dazzling white spark. As she watched, it grew longer and longer.

'What is that?'

'An antimatter drive.'

She smiled grimly. 'It must be the Confederation Navy ship.'

'Possibly. If it is, there's something wrong. An antimatter drive should accelerate a ship at over thirty-five gees. Whatever's producing that drive flare is barely moving.'

'We'd better take a look, then. How far away are they?'

'Roughly a hundred million kilometres.'

'But it's so bright.'

'Nobody really appreciates how powerful antimatter actually is until they encounter it first-hand. Ask the ex-residents of Trafalgar.'

Kiera gave the apparition a respectful look, then went over to the weapons console. She started arming the combat wasps. 'Let's go.'

*

Joshua switched all the starship's drives off as soon as Lalarin-MG cleared the crest of the knot. The flight computer had to tell him where that was (actually: used to be) exactly. Tojolt-HI's structure had simply melted away from the antimatter drive, leaving a hole over eight kilometres wide where the knot had been. The fringes glowed cerise, extending bent tendrils of molten metal. Only the largest lump of asteroid rock had survived intact, although it was down to a quarter of its original size. It tumbled in towards the photosphere, its surface baked to a cauldron of bubbling tar, spewing out a guttering tail of petrochemical fog.

The red giant shone through the huge circular rent in the diskcity, illuminating the end of the cylinder and a tapering slice of the shell, as if a flame was playing up the side. *Lady Mac*'s ion thrusters fired, backing her out of the crushed bearing ring. The hub had bowed inward under the enormous force she'd exerted, but the rib spars had held. Now they were retreating from the diskcity at a leisurely thirty metres per second.

'And they're still not shooting at us,' Liol said.

'I should hope not,' Dahybi retorted. 'After that little display of power they'll think twice about antagonizing us again.'

'Look how much damage we've done,' Ashly said. 'I'm sorry, but this is one accomplishment which doesn't make me very proud.'

'This section of Tojolt-HI was mostly dead,' Liol said. 'And the sunscoop had already destroyed the tubes which still had viable life-support functions.'

'Ashly's right,' Joshua said. 'All we've done is react to events. We're in control of very little.'

'I thought that's what life was,' Liol said. 'The honour of witnessing events. You need to be a god to control them.'

'That drops us into a neat little paradox, then,' Sarha said. 'We have to control events if we want to find a god. But if we can control them, then *ipso facto* we're already gods.'

'I think you'll find it's a question of scale,' Joshua said. 'Gods determine the outcome of large events.'

'What happened here was pretty big.'

'Not compared to the destiny of an entire species.'

'You're taking this very seriously,' Liol said.

Joshua didn't even smile. 'Somebody has to. Think of the consequences.'

'I'm not a total asshole, Josh. I do appreciate just how bad it's going to get if no one can find an answer to all of this.'

'I was thinking what happens if we succeed, actually.'

Liol's laugh was more a bark of surprise. 'How can that be bad?'

'Everything changes. People don't like that. There's going to have to be sacrifices, and I don't mean just physical or financial. It's inevitable. Surely you can see that coming?'

'Maybe,' Liol said gruffly.

Joshua looked over to his brother and put on his wickedest grin. 'In the meantime, you've got to admit, it's a wild ride.'

*

One of the serjeants stayed with Baulona-PWM and Quantook-LOU to act as an arbitrator as they tried to sort out the parameters of a new agreement. A triumph of optimism, she thought, that both of them believed the ZTT drive would bring about a new era among the diskcities orbiting Mastrit-PJ. It was clear that they were both conceding the remaining Tyrathca population would be evacuated to the flightship colony worlds. Their enclaves among the diskcities would not be expanded. Such a premiss made it even more important that the two species didn't clash over who had claim on new star systems. Retrieving the flightship information really had become essential to the agreement. An intriguing irony. Now all she had to worry about was Quantook-LOU's sincerity. It made her suggest several safeguards to Baulona-PWM, such as ensuring communications were opened up to all the remaining enclaves. Not that either of them knew how many there were scattered among the diskcities. Quantook-LOU even admitted he didn't know how many diskcities there were.

The other serjeant accompanied a team of six breeders that Baulona-PWM had designated to reactivate their electronics. They escorted her to the band of fat towers around the end of the cylinder. It was Lalarin-MG's utilities district, with the towers housing water-treatment plants, air filtration, fusion generators (appallingly crude, she thought), and the heat exchangers. Fortunately each service was provided by parallel stations, giving it a failsoft capability. A third of the systems were inoperable, the machinery inert and tarnished, testifying as to how long it had been since Lalarin-MG had a full population.

She was taken to a tower which the breeders said was an electrical and communications station. The ground floor was occupied by three tokamaks, only one of which was working. A ramp spiralled up to the first floor. There were no windows, and the ceiling lights didn't work. Her infra-red sensors showed her the silent ranks of electronic consoles, very reminiscent of those in Tanjuntic-RI. The

Tyrathca had brought portable lights with them, which they set up, revealing the true state of the consoles. Humidity had succoured a fur of algae over the rosette keyboards and display screens. Access panel catches had to be drilled through to release them, exposing rubbery fungal growths over the circuitry inside. The breeders had to run cables down to the generator below to power up the consoles.

One console actually burst into flames when they switched it on. Oski's curses echoed through the general communication link.

'Ask them if we can integrate our processor blocks with their network,' she told Ione. 'If I've got access, I'll be able to load some questors in. That should speed the process up. And while we're about it, let's see if they'll accept a little advice on reactivation procedures.'

*

The wormhole terminus opened six hundred kilometres above Tojolt-HI's darkside, deep in the umbra. The *Stryla* flew out; Etchells was in his harpy form, red eyes blazing as he looked round in surprise. From his position the huge disc eclipsed most of the sun's surface, with a tide of crimson light appearing to sweep up over the rim, as if it was sinking into an ooze of photons.

His distortion field billowed out, probing the xenoc structure. It also clashed with another distortion field.

What are you doing here? *Oenone* asked.

Same thing as you. He found the voidhawk, three thousand kilometres away. It was next to a large hollow cylinder, a habitation station of some kind. There was another Confederation ship close by. When he focused his optical senses in their direction he saw a small glimmer of sunlight erupting through the disc directly behind them.

He quickly altered his distortion field, opening another wormhole interstice. This time he came out a hundred kilometres from the voidhawk. Red sunlight washed over his leathery scale-like feathers, and he looked down curiously at the tear in the disc. Its melted edges were radiating strongly in the infra-red. The mountainous heat exchanges surrounding it were operating at their upper limit, trying to radiate away the immense thermal load imposed by overheated tubes.

'I'd say the Adamist ship used its antimatter drive to push the cylinder clear of the disc,' he told Kiera. 'Nothing else could cause that kind of damage.'

'Which means they consider it important,' she said.

'I don't see why. It's inhabited, and very fragile. It can't be a weapon.' His distortion field caught flocks of small chemically fuelled missiles flitting among the sharp, hot cones bristling out of the darkside. Lasers shot at them, blowing them apart in mid-flight. Over thirty radar beams from all sections of the disc were sweeping across him. One of the missiles plunged down among the heat-exchange mountains, exploding. Atmospheric gas puffed out into space from the tube it shattered. 'And there's some kind of war being fought down there. Widespread, by the look of it.'

'They flew all the way round the Orion Nebula, and when they get here they rip that cylinder out of a war zone,' Kiera said.

'All right, it's important.'

'Which means it's bad for us. Minimize your energistic effect, please.'

The hellhawk's shape rippled back to its natural profile.

Kiera's fingers typed quickly over the weapons console. Targeting sensors locked on to the cylinder.

Disengage your weapons, now, *Oenone* ordered.

Etchells let Kiera hear the affinity voice, routing it through one of the AV pillars on the bridge.

'Why?' she asked. 'What's in there?'

Several thousand unarmed Tyrathca. You would be committing butchery.

'What do you care? In fact, why are you here?'

To help.

'Very noble. And total bollocks.'

Do not fire, *Oenone* appealed to Etchells. **We will defend the cylinder.**

'That cylinder contains the means to destroy me,' Etchells replied. 'I'm quite sure of that.'

We are not barbarians. Physical destruction solves nothing.

Kiera fired four combat wasps at the cylinder.

The response from *Oenone* and *Lady Macbeth* was instant. Fifteen combat wasps launched on interception trajectories, scattering submunitions. *Lady Macbeth*'s defence masers speared the incoming drones as their submunitions ejected. Two hundred and fifty fusion bombs detonated in the space of three seconds, some pumped gamma lasers, but most were missile warheads.

Joshua absorbed the burst of sensor data disgorged by the tactical program, desperate for an overview. Visual sensors were useless against the blaze of destruction, but none of the attacking combat wasps' electronic-warfare submunitions had targeted *Lady Mac* – strangely negligent programming. The starship's sensors stared into the heart of the mayhem, filtering out the atomic and electromagnetic interference. Three small kinetic impacts registered against the cylinder, along with several beam strikes. But the structure remained intact.

'Sarha, kill the bastard,' he ordered.

Five masers fired at the hellhawk. It rolled quickly and accelerated at seven gees, trying to break free from the energy strike.

Joshua fired another five combat wasps, programming them for defence minefield deployment. Their drives flared briefly, and submunitions swarmed out, forming a wide protective cluster around Lalarin-MG. If the hellhawk was serious about attacking a target outside a gravity field, its strategy would be to swallow in as close as possible, under a kilometre usually, and fire off a combat-wasp salvo. Unless the target had an extensive array of SD lasers, some submunitions were bound to get through. The minefield ought to act as a temporary deterrence.

The hellhawk swallowed away.

'Syrinx, where the hell did it go?' Joshua asked.

'Standing off, two thousand kilometres.'

Oenone used the link with *Lady Mac*'s flight computer to datavise the coordinate over. Sensors locked on, showing the hellhawk holding station.

'They've got very strange ideas about tactics,' Joshua said. 'Oski, how much longer?'

'Half an hour at least, Captain. I've identified probable storage areas for the almanac, none of them are active.'

'Joshua, I'm not sure the cylinder can take another attack like that,' Ione said. The serjeant mediating with Baulona-PWM and Quantook-LOU had been flung to its feet when the first chunk of shrapnel punctured the cylinder shell. A small fireball had erupted out of a tower barely a hundred yards away. The plaza shook violently as the tower disintegrated, showering the area with smoking fragments of metal and burning vegetation. When she scanned round, she saw a dozen violet contrails criss-crossing through the air, molecules fluorescing from the gamma laser shots. Two had burned holes through the Sleeping God effigy. Her sensors hurriedly tracked along the axial gantry, but it hadn't been hit.

An automated truck trundled across the plaza, heading for the wrecked tower. Air was wailing as it was sucked down through the puncture hole. Hydraulic arms unfolded from the rear of the truck, carrying a thick metal plate. It was lowered over the hole, clanging into place. Thick brown sludge was sprayed out of a nozzle, smothering the plate. It solidified quickly, completing the seal.

'The Mosdva attack again,' Baulona-PWM said.

Ione thought the breeder was going to strike Quantook-LOU.

'They didn't,' she said quickly. 'That was a human ship. It's from a dominion we are not allied with. The *Lady Macbeth* has fought it off.'

'Do humans have dominions? Quantook-LOU asked. 'You did not tell us this.'

'We didn't expect them to be here.'

'Why are they here? Why have they attacked us?'

'They do not agree that Tyrathca and Mosdva should be given the faster than light drive. We must complete this agreement and recover the data. Then they will be unable to prevent the exchange.'

'My family is working hard,' Baulona-PWM said. 'We keep our agreement with you, allowing you to mediate.'

'And we will keep the agreement that you will be unharmed. Come now, we were deciding the message that is to be sent to other diskcity dominions.' She switched back to the general communication link. 'You have to get us more time.'

'We'll see to it,' Syrinx assured her. 'Joshua, hold the fort here.'

'Acknowledged.' *Lady Mac*'s gravitonic-distortion detectors showed him the voidhawk opening a wormhole interstice.

Oenone emerged fifty kilometres from the *Stryla*. Syrinx was expecting the hellhawk to fire its lasers at them straight away. That it didn't, she took as an encouraging sign.

I'm here to talk, she said.

And I'm here to survive, Etchells replied. We know you're here to find something you can use against us. I won't let that happen.

Nothing will be used against you. We are trying to resolve this to everyone's benefit.

I lack your optimism.

The hellhawk launched two combat wasps.

Oenone immediately swallowed out, emerging from a terminus on the opposite side of the hellhawk from the combat wasps, twenty kilometres away. It fired ten lasers at the other's polyp hull.

Etchells swallowed away. He emerged a hundred metres above one of the diskcity's heat-radiator cones. *Oenone* emerged just behind him. He'd expected that. His maser cannon fired on the voidhawk. It darted down behind the silvery cone, then curved round to shoot at Etchells.

The hellhawk accelerated at eight gees, tearing along a valley of cylindrical radiator towers. Kiera let out a muted yell of surprise and pain as she was squashed back into her acceleration couch.

'Give me fire control,' Etchells told her. 'You can't program the combat wasps for this scenario. I can.'

'That would make me nothing,' she said. 'No deal. Fly us out of this.'

'Fuck you.' He abandoned the secondary manipulation of the distortion field, which countered the acceleration. Kiera groaned as the full eight gees rammed her down into the couch. She began channelling her energistic power to strengthen her body. Lasers raked across his hull, and Etchells looped round a glass spiral turret, pulling twelve gees. The radiator mechanisms were a constant leaden smear to his optical senses, he was navigating by distortion-field sense alone. And going too fast, the valley end was a sharp turn, almost a right angle. He swooped up above the peaks, decelerating madly as he turned. For a moment the two starships were in direct line of sight. Lasers and masers slashed across the gulf. Then Etchells dived back down into a deep gulley of vertical mirror-surface dissipaters.

Oenone matched the manoeuvre, and fired again. Etchells flicked from side to side, accelerating and decelerating in wild bursts. His own masers fired back. The energy beams ripped long gashes across the cliffs of dissipaters as both starships twirled and rolled. Magenta effluvium percolated out, clotting the whole valley.

Etchells shot out of the smog blizzard with cyclonic eddies rolling away from his hull. He swung round a splayed clump of black

1117

pentangular pillars, then used a mushroom-like industrial refinery to slalom again.

The way Syrinx's hands dug into the acceleration couch padding was nothing to do with the appalling gee forces washing across the bridge. The image of the craggy diskcity surface hurtling past mere metres away was shining directly into her brain. Her eyes were tight shut from reflex, and it wasn't the slightest use. There was no escape. *Oenone*'s steady determination as it pursued the hellhawk prevented any censure. To doubt her love now would be selfish betrayal. She fought her own fear to bestow trust and pride.

On the other side of the bridge, Oxley was emitting a constant low moan of dismay without ever needing to draw breath.

Its resolve weakens, *Oenone* claimed buoyantly. It is slowing to turn now. We will catch it soon.

Yes. There was absolutely nothing in the tactical programs she could use to help this situation. If they rose above the artificial valleys, the hellhawk would be able to fire combat wasps straight at them. They couldn't fire back down, one errant submunition would slaughter thousands of Mosdva. So the chase continued, which was ultimately to their advantage. It prevented the hellhawk from firing on Lalarin-MG. At a terrible cost to her nerves.

Another wormhole terminus opened a hundred kilometres above them.

Hello, Etchells, Rocio said.

You? Etchells exclaimed in shock. Shoot the shit chasing me, they've found something here that'll wipe us out.

The *Mindori* fired three lasers at a glass cone heat-exchanger a couple of kilometres ahead of Etchells. The mechanism detonated, shattering into crystalline splinters spinning inside a writhing gas cloud. Etchells screamed his fury into the affinity band, and accelerated at seventeen gees, desperately trying to rise above the lethal kinetic debris. Irradiated gas streaked over the hellhawk's polyp. Energistic power flared, warding off the crystals with a ragged shield of white fire. Etchells barrel-rolled up away from the bloating indigo nimbus.

Oenone had a few extra seconds before collision, it pulled up fast, skirting the boundary of the whirling crystals. The *Stryla* was only thirty kilometres ahead of it. *Oenone*'s targeting radar locked on to the hellhawk. Then the electronic sensors warned Syrinx that the *Mindori* was targeting their hull.

Don't shoot, Rocio warned.

Kill them, Etchells demanded.

Syrinx aimed five lasers at the *Mindori.*

Etchells also targeted the other hellhawk with three masers. **Kill them now,** he said.

I won't shoot if you don't, Rocio said to Syrinx. Two of his lasers were aligned on the *Stryla.* **At least find out why we've come here first.**

So tell us, Syrinx said.

*

Jed and Beth were pressed against the port in the bridge, gazing in veneration at the xenoc artefact spread out below the hellhawk. There weren't many details, it was so dark, but the rim was close enough to see a silhouette of enticing geometries in the backscatter of red light. Gerald Skibbow was sitting on the acceleration couch behind the weapons console. Loren Skibbow studied the tactical displays keenly, watching the voidhawk and hellhawk rising fast from the darkside.

Traitor, Etchells spat, pushing his shaky anger behind the word.

To what, exactly? Rocio asked. **What's your crusade, Etchells? What do you care about other than yourself?**

I'm trying to stop these people from flinging us all back into the beyond. Maybe you're all for that.

Don't be absurd.

Then for fuck's sake help us wipe out that cylinder. Whatever they've come here for, it's in there.

There's no weapon in there, Syrinx said. I've already told you that.

Maybe I'll take a look later, Rocio said.

Shithead, Etchells raged. I'll blow you to fucking pieces if you don't help wipe out that voidhawk.

And that's why I'm here.

What? What are you fucking talking about?

Rocio enjoyed the irritation and confusion Etchells was emitting. **Death,** he said. **You're very keen to see others die, aren't you. You never gave Pran Soo a chance.**

You've got to be shitting me. You came after me because of her?

1119

And Kiera. I've got someone on board who would like to see our ex-leader.

Kiera is on board? Syrinx asked.

Yes, Rocio said.

Listen, you half-wit dickbrain, we're on the same side, Etchells said. I know the hellhawks have found another supply of nutrient fluid. That's brilliant. We're free of doing any fighting for people like Capone and Kiera. That's what I want.

You were Kiera's number one cheerleader. You're still doing what she wants even with the blackmail removed.

I was looking out for me. Just like you were doing for yourself. We had different methods, but we want the same thing for ourselves. That's why you've got to help us. Together we can beat those Confederation ships and destroy the cylinder.

Then what?

Then whatever we want, of course.

You don't really think we'd let you share our nutrient supply, do you? After what you've done?

You're starting to piss me off.

Jed and Beth saw the monstrous bird rise into view through the port, a jet-black shadow against the ruddy darkness of the umbra. Malevolent eyes gleamed scarlet, looking straight in at them. They backed away from the port together. To one side of the bird was another shadow, an elongated oval.

'Gerald,' Jed said nervously. 'Mate, there's *things* out there.'

'Yes,' he said. 'The *Oenone* and the *Mindori*. Isn't it wonderful?' He sniffed, wiping moisture from his sunken bloodshot eyes. His voice became high again: Loren's. 'She's there. And there's nowhere for the bitch to run any more.'

Jed and Beth gave each other a defeated look. Gerald was activating a lot of systems on the console.

'What are you doing?' Rocio asked.

'Bringing the remaining generators on-line,' Gerald answered. 'You can route their power into the lasers. Kill it with one shot.'

'I'm not so sure that's a good idea.'

'YES IT IS!' Gerald cried. 'Don't you try to back out now.' He clutched the edge of the console, blinking in confusion.

'Gerald?' Beth pleaded tremulously. 'Please, Gerald, don't do anything rash.'

Loren's face flicked up over Gerald's tortured expression. 'Gerald's fine. Just fine. Don't you worry.'

Beth started sobbing, clutching at Jed. His arms went round her as he stared miserably at the mad figure hunched over the console. When Skibbow had just been bonkers Gerald it'd been bad enough. This new demented combination was hell's own gatekeeper.

Loren ignored the two kids. 'Rocio. Ask the voidhawk to help. It's to their advantage. We don't want any mistakes now.'

'Very well.' There was an edge of worry in the voice. I have a proposition, he said to Syrinx, on singular engagement.

Go ahead.

I have no quarrel with you, nor do I care about your mission. Etchells and Kiera threaten both of us.

Then why did you stop us from firing at them?

Because I need to capture Kiera alive. The father and mother of the body she possesses are on board. Unfortunately, they have fire authority over my combat wasps. My energistic power can disable the missiles, but the Skibbows would be able to detect my intent. There is no way of telling how they'd react, they are not a stable combination. They could choose to kamikaze; in which case I'm not sure if I could block their commands to the warheads in time.

I see. What do you suggest?

From this range, my lasers are quite capable of killing the *Stryla*'s central organ cluster in one shot. Etchells will be flung back into the beyond, and Kiera will be left intact. I will dock, and the Skibbows can deal with her.

So what do you want us to do?

Nothing. Do not interfere when I shoot. That's all I ask.

What about Kiera's control over the *Stryla*'s combat wasps?

A second laser strike will eliminate the combat wasps in their launch cradles. I can be fast. She will not have time to launch or detonate them.

You hope.

Can you provide an alternative?

Etchells spoke into the general affinity band: Rocio, I can see you've powered up your weapon pod generators. Know this, Kiera and I have rigged my combat wasps. Any energy beam strike against me or my life-support module will result in every warhead blowing simultaneously. Both of you are well inside the lethal blast radius.

All right, Rocio said. We've all been real smart and blocked each other. Nobody can win now, so why don't we all just back off?

No, Syrinx said. If either of you accelerate away or attempt to open a wormhole interstice, I will fire. I will not give you the freedom to return to the cylinder.

So just what the hell are we supposed to do now? Rocio demanded.

We are negotiating for the cylinder to be evacuated, Syrinx said. When all the Tyrathca have left, I will permit the three of us to retreat simultaneously. Not before. You will not slaughter innocent entities to appease your paranoia.

For fuck's sake, Etchells said. Rocio, join me, we'll blow this voidhawk to shit and stop them getting the weapon.

There is no weapon, Syrinx insisted.

I'll tell you something, Etchells, Rocio said, if it comes to a choice, I'm with Captain Syrinx.

Shithead traitor! You'd better pray their weapon works, and pray real hard, because if it doesn't I will personally track you down past the end of the universe.

You won't have to chase me anywhere.

Syrinx looked over at Ruben and pouted her lips. 'Maybe we should just let them go at it.'

'Nice thought. I wonder what the Mosdva dominions are making of all this.'

'As long as they don't start shooting at us, I don't care.'

'We're getting something,' Oski announced. 'It's not the full almanac, but I'm accessing files with colony planet locations; they're linked to star map references.'

'Can you access their star map files?' Syrinx asked.

'Loading a questor now,' Oski said. 'Stand by.'

Syrinx and *Oenone* waited eagerly as the information began to trickle across the communication link. The first maps the questors accessed showed unknown starfields, but the third had a portion of the Orion Nebula covering a quarter of the picture. *Oenone* matched the image to the navigational plot of the nebula it had made on the voyage to Mastrit-PJ, instinctively correlating the Tyrathca coordinate formula into its own astronomical reference frame. More star maps followed, allowing the voidhawk to expand and refine the coordinate grid, correlating with recognizable star patterns. After eight minutes it could visualize a globe of space five thousand light-years across, centred on Mastrit-PJ. Tyrathca designations tagged the constellations.

Syrinx's thoughts flowed through the mental construct, filled with quiet pride as she absorbed the detailed configuration.

It was easy, *Oenone* said modestly.

You handled it superbly, she said. That needs to be said.

Thank you.

Syrinx made an effort to compress her sadness. But you do realize we probably won't get to go there.

I understand. We need to keep the hellhawks at bay.

I'm so sorry. I know how much you wanted to go.

So did you. We must not be selfish, though. There is more at stake than our feelings. And we have explored further than anyone else.

Oh, yes!

Joshua will do well.

I know. Amusement lifted her spirits. A year ago I wouldn't have been saying that.

It is not just you who have changed.

You always did like him, didn't you?

He was what you feared to become. Your envy became disdain. You should never be scared of what you are, Syrinx. I will always love you.

And I you. She sighed contentedly. 'Joshua, Swantic-LI found the Sleeping God at an F-class star three hundred and twenty light-years from here. Coordinates coming over.' She ordered the bridge processors to datavise the file over to *Lady Mac*'s flight computer.

'Hey, good work, *Oenone*.'

'Thank you, Joshua.'

'OK, how do you want to break up the stand-off? If I launch a combat-wasp salvo from here, they'll be forced to swallow out. We can combine to protect the cylinder. Maybe we'll get lucky and they'll wipe each other out before they come back for it.'

'No, Joshua. We can handle the stand-off. You take off now.'

'Jesus, you're kidding.'

'We can't waste the time protecting the cylinder is going to take, it'll be days most likely. And we certainly can't take the risk that we might both get damaged or killed in a fight with the hellhawks. You have to leave. Once the stand-off's over, we'll follow.'

'That's very cold and logical.'

'It's very rational, Joshua. I am an Edenist, after all.'

'All right. If you're sure?'

'Who better?' She relaxed serenely on her acceleration couch, sharing *Oenone*'s perception of local space. Waiting. *Lady Macbeth*'s jump registered as a sharp twist in space-time, gone in a nanosecond.

Syrinx looked round at her crew, reaching out to them so their thoughts and regrets could mingle with hers. Sharing herself to achieve that cherished equipoise of their culture. It must have worked, for eventually she asked: 'Anyone bring a pack of cards?'

27

The two friends walked together along the top of Ketton Island's cliff, taking a few minutes alone together to say goodbye. Their parting would be permanent. Choma had chosen to join with Tinkerbell, sharing that entity's voyage across eternity, while Sinon, almost uniquely among the serjeants, had decided to go back to Mortonridge.

I promised my wife I would return, that I would rejoin the multiplicity once more, he said. I will keep my word to her, for we believed in Edenism together. By doing this I will strengthen our culture. Not by much, I will be the first to admit, but my conviction in us and the path we have chosen will contribute to the overall conviction of the multiplicity and Consensus. We must believe in ourselves. To doubt now would be admitting we should never have existed.

And yet what we are doing is the pinnacle of Edenism, Choma said. By transferring ourselves into Tinkerbell's version of the multiplicity we are evolving the human condition, moving on from our origin with confidence and wonder. This is evolution, a constant learning curve, there is no limit to what we can find in this realm.

But you will be alone, isolated from the rest of us. What is the point of knowledge if you cannot share it? If it cannot be used to help everyone? The beyond is something the human race must face in union, we must know and accept our answer as one. If Mortonridge taught us nothing else, it was that. Towards the end I had nothing but sympathy for the possessed.

We are both right. The universe is big enough to allow us that.

It is. Though I regret what you are doing. An unusual development. I think I have become more than I was supposed to in this body. I believed such emotions would be impossible when I volunteered to join the Liberation.

Their development was inevitable, Choma said. We carry the seeds of humanity with us no matter what vessel our minds travel in. They were bound to flourish, to find their own route forward.

Then I am no longer the Sinon who emerged from the multiplicity.

No. Any sentient entity who has lived, has changed.

I will have a soul then, now. A new soul, one that is different to the Sinon I remember.

You do. All of us do.

Then once again I will have to die before I transfer myself back to the multiplicity. What I bring to the habitat is only such wisdom as I can muster. My soul doesn't follow my memories, so the Kiint say.

Do you fear that day?

I don't believe so. The beyond is not for everyone, knowing there is a way through, or round, as Laton claims, is enough to give me confidence. Though there is some trepidation stirring within me.

You will overcome, I am sure. Never forget it is possible to succeed. That thought alone should guide you.

I will remember.

They stopped on the crest of a mound, and looked out over the island. Long lines of people were picking their way over the cracked earth, the last refugees from the buried town heading towards the clifftop where Tinkerbell was pressed against the rock. The giant crystal's opalescent light sent ripples of gentle colour slithering over the drab ground. Air had coiled into a topaz nimbus all around it.

How apt, Sinon said. It looks as though they are walking off into the sunset.

If I have a regret, it is that I won't know how their lives finish. They will make a strange group, these souls who are going to occupy serjeant bodies. Their complete humanity will always be beyond their grasp.

When they came out of the beyond, they claimed all they wanted was sensation again. They have that now.

But they are genderless. Not to mention sexless. They can never know love.

Physical love, perhaps. But that certainly isn't all the love there is. As with you and I, they will become whole in their own way.

I feel their disquiet already, and they haven't even reached Mortonridge yet.

They can learn to adapt to what lies ahead. The habitats will welcome them.

Nobody has ever become an Edenist against their will before. Now you have twelve thousand bewildered, angry strangers grumbling away into the general affinity band. Most of them with a cultural background that will act against easy acceptance.

With patience and kindness they will find themselves again. Think what they have been through.

At last we come to the true difference between ourselves. I am restless and eager for the future, a voyager. You are ruled by compassion, a healer of souls. Now you see why we have to part.

Of course, and I wish you well on your splendid voyage.

Likewise. I hope you find the peace you search for.

They turned, and walked back slowly along the rocky line of the cliff. Tiny crystalline entities whisked about overhead, never pausing in one place for more than a moment. They had covered the whole island, making sure that every possessed knew there was now a way back, and what staying here meant. It was the end of Ekelund's rule. Her troops had abandoned her, banding together defiantly to walk out of Ketton. Her threats and fury only hastened their departure.

Five long queues waited before Tinkerbell's looming surface, winding through the scattered remnants of the headland camp. Two of them were made up of serjeants. The remainder (and keeping their distance) were the possessed. They waited in a strange subdued mood, their anticipation and relief that the nightmare was about to end tempered by the uncertainty of what lay ahead.

Stephanie was waiting right at the tail end of the longest queue of possessed, along with Moyo, McPhee, Franklin, and Cochrane. Tina and Rana had been amongst the first through. The crystalline entities had stabilized Tina, apparently repairing the damage to her internal organs, but they all agreed the woman's body ought to be seen by human specialists as soon as possible. For herself, Stephanie decided she should be amongst the last. It was the responsibility thing again, she wanted to know everyone else was OK.

'But you're no responsible for them,' McPhee had said. 'They all flocked to Ekelund's banner. It's their own bloody stupid fault they're here.'

'I know, but we're the ones who tried to get Ekelund to stop, and failed miserably.' She shrugged, knowing how feeble she sounded.

'I'll wait with you,' Moyo said. 'We'll go through together.'

'Thank you.'

McPhee, Franklin, and Cochrane looked at each other, and said what the hell. They all joined the queue, standing behind Hoi Son. The old eco-guerrilla was in his trademark dark jungle fatigues, with his felt bush-ranger hat tilted back as if he'd just finished an arduous job. He eyed them with wry amusement, and bowed to Stephanie. 'I congratulate you on remaining true to your principles.'

'I don't think it really matters, but thank you anyway.' She sat on one of the many boulders, resting her wounded hip.

'Out of all of us, it was you who achieved the most.'

'You held off the serjeants.'

'Not for long, and only to further an ideal.'

'I thought you valued ideals.'

'I do. Or I used to. That is the problem with this situation. The old ideals don't have any relevance here. I applied them as did the political forces behind the Liberation. Both of us were very wrong. Look what we did to people, how many lives and homes we ruined. All that effort poured into conflict and destruction. I used to say I belonged to the land.'

'I'm sure you thought you did what was the right thing.'

'Indeed I did, Stephanie Ash. Unfortunately, I didn't think enough, for it was not the right thing to do. Not at all.'

'Well, hey, it don't matter no more, man,' Cochrane said. 'The fat babe's been singing out loud for a while now. We're like going home.' He offered Hoi Son his joint.

'No, thank you. I do not wish to introduce poisons to this body. I am simply its custodian. I may soon even be held accountable for any ills I have inflicted. After all, past the end of this queue we will be facing them again, will we not? And we will only be equals.'

Cochrane gave him a sour look and dropped his joint, grinding it into the mud under his heel. 'Yeah, right, man,' he grunted.

'What about Ekelund?' Stephanie asked. 'Where's she?'

'Back at her command post. She refused the offer to return.'

'What? She's crazy.'

'Undoubtedly, yes. But she sincerely believes that once the serjeants have gone, then this land will be free. She intends to found her paradise here.'

Stephanie looked back at the patch of scabrous land that was Ketton.

'No,' Moyo said firmly. 'She has made her own decision. And she certainly isn't going to listen to you, of all people.'

'I suppose not.'

Even at the rate of one possessed every few seconds, it took over seven hours for everyone to be repatriated. The procedure was simple enough. Where Tinkerbell touched the cliff face, several oval tunnels had opened up, leading deep into her interior. Their walls shone with a soft aquamarine light that grew progressively brighter until it eventually filled the cleft. You just walked through, vanishing into the light.

Stephanie wasn't the very last in. Moyo and McPhee had quietly and insistently stood behind her. She smiled in good-natured surrender, and passed over the threshold. The air thickened in conjunction with the light, slowing the movement of her limbs. Eventually it felt as though she was trying to walk through the crystal itself. There was an insistent pressure exerted against every part of her. She felt the force move through her flesh, enabling her to speed up again. The aquamarine glow faded away, showing that her body had become transparent, a pattern of light conducted by crystal. When she looked round she saw the body she'd possessed standing behind her. The woman was holding her hands up, an expression of revulsion and satisfaction straining her face.

'Choma?' Stephanie asked. 'Choma, can you hear me? There's something I need to do.'

'Hello, Stephanie. I thought this might happen.'

Occupying a serjeant's body was the simplest thing. One waited for her, immured in crystal, completely passive with its big head bowed. It didn't matter which direction she walked, she was always walking towards it. They merged, and it thickened around her, returning the opaque aquamarine light. The sensations were peculiar; the exoskeleton had no tactile nerves, yet it was somehow rigged to provide proof of contact. Her soles were definitely pressing down on a surface, air drifted over her as she moved forwards. The aquamarine light cleared from her eyes, allowing her to focus with remarkable clarity.

She walked out of the oval tunnel, back onto the crusty trampled-down mud of Ketton Island. The rivers of coloured light which emanated from Tinkerbell's internal coruscations meandered over the ground. Nothing else moved.

It was a long slog back across the island to its central town. Even in the serjeant's robust body it took her an hour and a quarter. Tinkerbell departed when she was a third of the way there, arching away above her in an opalescent blaze, then shrinking at an improbable speed. Stephanie began to pick her pace up. The air was stirring, slowly expanding again now the serjeants had gone, a gentle breeze gusting out over the edge of the cliff. Their wishes remained for a while, of course, impregnated on the fabric of this realm. But without their active presence to reinforce them, what was normality here began to return.

It was a lot brighter when Stephanie trotted up to the boundary of the town. The air had thinned considerably now, allowing the continuum's persistent blue-white glare to shine down with unrestrained power. Every step sent her gliding a couple of metres above the ground. Gravity had reduced by about twenty per cent, she guessed.

Ekelund's headquarters were prominent at the very centre of the razed town, the big tent perched atop a mound, faintly luminous. She came out as Stephanie bounced her way up the slope, lounging against the tent pole, smiling softly.

'It's a different body, but I'd know those thoughts anywhere. I believe we've had our last goodbye, Stephanie Ash.'

'You have to leave. Please. You'll destroy Angeline Gallagher's body and her soul if you stay here.'

'Finally! It's not my well-being you're concerned about. A small victory for me, but I consider it significant.'

'Come back to Mortonridge. There are still some serjeant bodies available to host your soul. You can live a life again, a real life.'

'As what? Trite little housewife and mother? Even you can't live your old life again, Stephanie.'

'I never believe that a baby's future is preordained. After birth, you're on your own to make what you can from life. And we are being born again in these serjeant bodies. Make what you can of it, Annette. Don't kill yourself and Gallagher out of misplaced pride.

Look around! The air's all but gone, the gravity's failing. There's nothing here any more.'

'I am here. This island will bloom again once it's free of your influences. We came here to this realm because it offered us the sanctuary we needed.'

'For God's sake, admit you are wrong. There's no shame in it. What do you think I'm going to do, stalk you and gloat?'

'Now you get to it. Which of us was right. That's what it's always been between you and me.'

'There is no right. An entire army flocked to your banner. I had a lover and five mismatched friends. You win. Now, please, come back.'

'No.'

'Why not? At least tell me that.'

Annette Ekelund's stubborn smile flickered. 'For the first time ever, I have been me. I haven't had to defer to anybody, to ask permission, to conform to what society expects. And I've lost that,' her voice shrivelled to a hoarse whisper. 'I led them here, and not one stayed. They didn't want to stay, and I didn't have the strength to force them.' A tear emerged from her left eye. 'I was wrong. I got it *wrong*, God damn you!'

'You didn't bring anybody here. You didn't order us. We came because we desperately wanted to. I was a part of it, Annette. When we lay there on the mud after the harpoon strike, and the serjeants were going to throw us into zero-tau, I helped. I was so frightened that I poured every drop of my power into leaving Mortonridge behind. And I was glad when we got here. We are all to blame. All of us.'

'I organized Mortonridge's defence. I brought about the Liberation.'

'Yes, you did, and if it hadn't been you, it would have been someone else. It could even have been me. We're not responsible for the way to the beyond being opened up. Ever since that began, the outcome was inevitable. You're not to blame for fate, for the way the universe is put together. You're not that important.'

Annette had to suck hard to fill her lungs with air. The sky had become very bright. 'I was.'

'So was I. The day we took the children over the firebreak, I'd accomplished more than Richard Saldana ever had. That was how I felt. I loved it, and I wanted more of it, the way my group looked up and respected me. Typical human failing. You're nothing special, not in that way.'

'Smug, smug, smug, God I hate you.'

Stephanie watched the dry flakes of mud lift gently from the ground, flicked up by the last wisps of air. They floated around in a lazy cloud, rebounding off each other, slowly moving higher. There was no gravity left, the only thing keeping her feet on the ground was sheer will-power. 'Come with me!' She had to shout, the air was all but gone. 'Hate me some more!'

'Would you die with me?' Annette yelled back. 'Are you that fucking worthy?'

'No.'

Annette yelled again. Stephanie couldn't hear her, the air had gone. **Choma, Tinkerbell, come and get us. Quickly, please.**

Annette was clawing at her throat, gulping wildly as her skin turned dark red. Her desperate motions pushed her away from the ground. Stephanie kicked off after her, and grabbed a thrashing ankle. Together they tumbled away from the top of the mound. The universal white light had turned the mud fields a glaring silver; crinkled clifftops ignited into magnesium splendour. Ketton Island melted away into the glaring void.

Stephanie and Annette soared ever onwards, drowning in light.

'Are they really worth it?' someone asked.

'Are we?'

Cold aquamarine light clamped around them.

*

Luca didn't have to guide the horse, it simply followed the route across the wolds he'd taken so many times before, plodding along without hesitation. A great circle round the middle of the Cricklade estate; through the upper ford in Wryde Stream, around the east side of Berrybut Spinney, over Withcote Ridge, taking the narrow humpback bridge below Saxby Farm, the fire track through Coston Wood. It gave him a good overview of his land's progress. On the surface it was as good as any previous year; the crops were later by a few weeks, but there was no harm in that. Everyone had pulled together and made up for the lost weeks following the possession.

As they bloody well ought to, by damn. I sweated blood getting Cricklade back on its feet.

And now there was enough food for everybody, the coming harvest would enable them to see the winter months out without undue hardship. Stoke County had emerged from the transition exceptionally well. There certainly wouldn't be any more marauders, not since the battle of Colsterworth Station. Good news, considering the reports and rumours trickling out of Boston these days. The island's capital hadn't been so fast to re-embrace the old ways. Food there was becoming scarce, the farms immediately round the outskirts were being abandoned as citizens roamed across the countryside in search of supplies.

The idiots weren't capitalizing on their existing industrial infrastructure and producing goods to trade with the farming communities for food. There was so much the city could provide, basic stuff like cloth and tools. That needed to happen again, and soon. But the indications he'd got from Lionel and the other traders weren't good. Some factories were up and running, but there was no real social order in the city.

It's actually worse than when the Democratic Land Union was out on the streets, agitating for their claptrap reforms.

Luca shook his head irritably. There were a lot of *his* thoughts roaming free these days. Some of them were obvious, the ones he relied on to keep Cricklade going; while others were more subtle, the comparisons, the regrets, odd mannerisms creeping back, so comfortable he could never drive them out again. Worst was that eternal junkie ache to see Louise and Genevieve again, just to know they were all right.

Are you such a monster, an anti-human, you would deny a father that? A single glimpse of my beloved girls.

Luca put his head back and yelled: 'You never loved them!' The piebald horse came to a startled halt as his voice carried across the verdant land. Anger was his last refuge of self, the one defence Grant could never penetrate. 'You treated them like cattle. They weren't even people to you, they were commodities, part of your medieval family empire, assets ready to marry off in exchange for money and power. You bastard. You don't deserve them.' He shivered, crumpling down into the saddle. 'Then why do I care?' he heard himself ask. 'My children are the most important part of me; they carry on everything I am. And you tried to rape them. A pair of little children. Love? Do you think you know anything about it? A degenerate parasite like you.'

'Leave me alone,' Luca screamed out.

Shouldn't it be me asking you that?

Luca gritted his teeth, thinking about the gas Spanton used, the way Dexter had tried to make them worship the Light Bringer. Building up a fortress of anger, so his thoughts could be his again.

He tugged on the reins, wheeling the horse round so he faced Cricklade. There was little practical point to this inspection tour. He knew the condition the estate was in.

Materially they were fine. Mentally ... the veil of contentment furled around Norfolk was souring. He recognized the particular strain of forlorn resentment accumulating over the mind's horizon. Cricklade had known it first. All across Norfolk, people were discovering what lay beneath their external perfection. The slow-maturing plague of vanity had begun to reap its victims. Hope was withering from their lives. This winter would be more than the physical cold.

Luca crossed the boundary of giant cedars, and urged the horse up over the greensward towards the manor house. Just seeing its timeless grey stone façade, inset with white-painted windows, brought a peaceful reassurance to his aching thoughts. Its history belonged to him, and so assured his future.

The girls will carry on here, will keep our home and family alive.

He bowed his head, embittered by his deteriorating will. Anger was hard to maintain over hours, let alone days. Weary, weepy dismay was no defence, and those emotions were his constant companion these days.

There was the usual scattering of activity around the manor. A circular brush ejecting a puff of soot as it rose out from the central chimney stack. Stable boys leading the horses down to graze in the east meadow. Women hanging sheets out to dry on the clothes lines. Ned Coldham (Luca couldn't remember the name of the handyman's possessor) painting the windows on the west wing, making sure the wood was protected from the coming frosts. The sound of sawing drifting out through the chapel's empty windows. Two men (claiming to be monks, though neither Luca nor Grant had ever heard of their order) slowly repairing the damage Dexter had wrought inside.

There were more people bustling about in the walled kitchen garden at the side of the manor. Cook had brought a team of her kitchen helpers out to cut the shoots of asparagus ready for freezing. It was the fifth batch they'd collected from the geneered plant this year.

Johan was sitting beside the stone arched gateway, a blanket over his knees as he soaked up the warmth of the omnidirectional sunlight. Véronique was on a chair beside him, with baby Jeanette sleeping in a cradle, a parasol protecting her from the light.

Luca dismounted and went over to see his erstwhile deputy. 'How are you feeling?' he asked.

'Not so bad, thank you, sir.' Johan smiled weakly, and nodded.

'You look a lot better.' He was putting on weight again, though the loose skin around his face remained pallid.

'Soon as they gets the glass finished, I'm going to start getting some seeds set,' Johan said. 'I always like a bit o' fresh lettuce and cucumber in me sarnies during the winter. Wouldn't mind trying to grow some avocado as well, though it'll be next year before they fruit.'

'Jolly good, man. And how's this little one, then?' Luca peered into the crib. He'd forgotten just how small newborn babies were.

'She's a dream,' Véronique sighed happily. 'I wish she'd sleep like this at night. Every two hours she wants feeding. You can set your clock by her. It's really tiring.'

'Sweet little mite,' Johan said. 'Reckon she's gonna be a proper looker when she grows up.'

Véronique beamed with easy pride.

'I'm sure she will,' Luca said. It pained him to see the way the old man was looking at the baby; there was too much desperation there. Butterworth wanted confirmation that life carried on as normal here in this realm. It was an attitude that was growing among a lot of Cricklade's residents, he'd noticed lately. The kids they were looking after had been receiving more sympathetic attention. His own resolve to stay at the estate and ignore the urge to find the girls was becoming harder to maintain. A weakness he could date back to the day Johan had collapsed, and then accelerating after the battle of

Colsterworth Station. Every step he took on the sandy gravel path around the manor seemed to press blister-sized lumps deep into the flesh of his soles, reminding him of how precarious his life had become.

Luca led his horse into the stable courtyard, guilty and glad to leave Johan behind. Carmitha was over by her caravan. She was folding up freshly washed clothes and packing them into a big brass-bound wooden trunk. Half a dozen of her old glass storage jars were standing on the cobbles, full of leaves and flowers, their green tint turning the contents a peculiar grey colour.

She nodded politely at him, and kept on putting her things away. He watched her as he took the stallion's saddle off; she moved with a steady determination that discouraged interruption. Some thought had been finalized, he decided. The trunk was eventually filled, and the lid slammed down.

'Give you a hand with that?' he offered.

'Thanks.'

They lifted the trunk in through the door at the back of the caravan. Luca whistled quietly. He'd never seen the inside so tidy before. There was no clutter, no clothes or towels slung about, all the pans she had hanging up were polished to a bright gleam, even the bed was made. Bottles were lined up on a high shelf, held in place by copper travelling rings.

She shoved the trunk into an alcove under the bed.

'You're going somewhere,' he said.

'I'm ready to go somewhere.'

'Where?'

'I've no idea. Might try Holbeach, see if any of the others made it to the caves.'

He sat on the bed, suddenly very tired. 'Why? You know how important you are to people here. God, Carmitha, you can't leave. Look, just tell me if someone's said or done something against you. I'll have their bloody nuts roasted very slowly over a furnace.'

'Nobody's done anything yet.'

'Then why?'

'I want to be ready in case this place falls apart. Because that's what'll happen if you leave.'

'Oh, Jesus.' His head sank into his hands.

'Are you going to?'

'I don't know. I took a ride round the estate this morning to try and make up my mind.'

'And?'

'I want to. I really do. I don't know if it'll make Grant back off, or if it's going to be a complete surrender. I think the only reason I haven't gone already is because he's equally torn. Cricklade means an awful lot to him. He dreads the idea of it being left unsupervised for a whole winter. But his daughters mean more. I don't suppose that leaves me with much choice.'

'Stop fishing for support. You always have choice. What you should ask yourself is, do you have the strength to make and sustain the decision.'

'I doubt it.'

'Hmm.' She sat on the antique chair at the foot of the bed, looking at the despondent silhouette in front of her. There is no border any more, she decided, they're merging. It's not as fast as Véronique and Olive, but it's happening. Another few weeks, a couple of months at the most, and they'll be one. 'Have you considered you might want to find the girls as well? That's where your problem starts.'

He gave her a sharp look. 'What do you mean?'

'All that decency Grant's wicked little mind is eroding. You haven't lost it yet, you're still feeling guilty about Louise and what you tried to do to her. You'd like to know that she's all right as well.'

'Maybe. I don't know. I can't think straight any more. Every time I speak I have to listen hard to the words to find what's me and what's him. There's still a difference. Just.'

'I'm tempted to be a fatalist. If Norfolk isn't rescued for a few decades, you're going to die here anyway, so why not give in and live those years in peace?'

'Because I want to live them,' he whispered fiercely. 'Me!'

'That's very greedy for someone who'll do that living in a stolen body.'

'You always hated us, didn't you?'

'I hate what you've done. I don't hate what you are. Luca Comar and I would have got on quite well if we'd ever met, don't you think?'

'Yeah, right.'

'You can't win, Luca. As long as you're alive he'll be there with you.'

'I won't surrender.'

'Would Luca Comar really have killed Spanton? Grant would, without hesitating.'

'You don't understand. Spanton was a savage, he was going to destroy everything we are, everything we've worked to achieve here. I saw that in his heart. You can't reason with people like that. You can't educate them.'

'Why do you want to achieve anything? It is possible to live off the land here. We can, us Romanies. Even Grant would be able to show you how. Which plants to eat. Where the sheep and the cattle huddle in winter. You can become a hunter, dependent on no one.'

'People are more than that. We're a social species. We gather in tribes or clans, we trade. It's the fundamental of civilization.'

'But you're dead, Luca. You died hundreds of years ago. This return will only ever be temporary, however it ends: in death or the Confederation rescuing us. Why do you want to build a cosy civilization under those circumstances? Why not live fast and stop worrying about tomorrow?'

'Because that's not what I am! I can't do that!'

'Who can't? Who are you that wants a future?'

'I don't know.' He started sobbing. 'I don't know who I am.'

*

There were fewer people in Fort Forward's Ops Room these days, a barometer of the Liberation's progress and nature. The massive coordination effort required for the initial assault was long gone. After that, the busiest time had been following the disastrous attack on Ketton when they had to change the front-line assault pattern, splitting Mortonridge into confinement zones. It was a strategy which had worked well enough. There certainly hadn't been any more Kettons. The possessed had been divided up then divided again as the confinement zones were broken down into smaller fractions.

From his office, Ralph could look out directly at the big status screen on the wall opposite. For days after Ketton he'd sat behind his desk watching the red icons of the front line change shape into a rough grid of squares stretched over Mortonridge. Each square had gone on to fission into a dozen smaller squares, which became rings, and stopped contracting. The sieges had begun, seven hundred and sixteen of them.

It left the Ops Room with supervising the mopping-up operation across open land. The Liberation command's main activity was now managing logistics, coordinating the supply routes to each siege camp, and evacuating the recovered victims. All of which were handled by different, secondary, departments.

'We're redundant,' Ralph told Janne Palmer. She and Acacia had stayed behind after the early morning senior staff meeting. They often did, having coffee together and bringing up points which didn't quite warrant the attention of a full staff meeting. 'There's no fighting left,' he said. 'No bad decisions that I have to take the blame for. This is all about numbers, now, statistics and averages. How long it takes the possessed to finish eating their supplies, balancing our medical resources and transport facilities. We should just turn it over to the accountants and leave.'

'I've not known many generals to be so bitter about their victory,' Janne said. 'We won, Ralph, you were so successful that the Liberation has become a smooth operation where no one is shooting at us.'

He gave Acacia a quizzical look. 'Would you describe it as smooth?'

'Progress has been smooth, General. Individuals have of course suffered considerable hardship out on the front line.'

'And on the other side as well. Have you been monitoring the state of the possessed we're capturing when those sieges fail?'

'I've seen them,' Janne said.

'The possessed don't actually surrender, you know. They just become so weak the serjeants can walk in unopposed. We broke twenty-three sieges yesterday, that produced seventy-three dead bodies. They just won't give themselves up. And the remainder, Christ, cancer and malnutrition is a bad combination. Once we'd put them through zero-tau, seven actually died on the emergency evac flight back to Fort Forward.'

'I believe there are now enough colonizer ships in orbit to cope with the casualty rate,' Acacia said.

'We can store them in the zero-tau berths,' Ralph said. 'I'm not so sure about treating them. They may wind up waiting in stasis for quite a while until there's a hospital place for them. And that's even with all the help we're getting from Edenist habitats and our allies. Dear God, can you imagine what it'll be like if we ever manage to haul an entire planet back from wherever it is they vanish them away to?'

'I believe the Assembly President had asked the Kiint Ambassador for material aid,' Acacia said. 'Roulor said that his government would look favourably to helping us with any physical event which was beyond our industrial or technical ability to cope with.'

'And Ombey's medical situation doesn't count as a crisis?' Janne asked.

'Treating the de-possessed from Mortonridge is not beyond the Confederation's overall medical capability. That would seem to be the criterion the Kiint have set.'

'It might be physically possible, but what government is going to let a ship full of ex-possessed into their star system, let alone parcel them out among civilian hospitals in the cities?'

'Human politics,' Ralph grunted. 'The envy of the galaxy.'

'That's paranoia, not politics,' Janne said.

'It translates into votes, which makes it politics.' The Ops Room computer datavised a stream of information into Ralph's neural nanonics. He glanced through the window to see one of the red rings up on the status screen turn a deep mauve. 'Another siege over. Town called Wellow.'

'Yes,' Acacia said. Her eyes were shut as she eavesdropped on the serjeants actually ringing the clutter of sodden, mashed-up buildings. 'The ELINT blocks monitoring its energistic field reported a massive decline. The serjeants are moving in.'

Ralph checked the AI's administration procedures. Transport was being readied, with a flight of Stonys being assigned to the camp. Fort Forward's medical facilities were notified. It even estimated the number of zero-tau berths they'd need on the orbiting colonizer starships, basing it on the last SD sensor satellite's infra-red sweep. 'I almost wish it was the same as the first day,' Ralph said. 'I know the possessed put up a hell of a fight, but at least they were healthy. I was ready for the horrors of war, I was even coping with sending our troops into action knowing they'd take casualties. But this isn't what I expected at all, this isn't saving them any more. It's just political expediency.'

'Have you told the Princess that?' Acacia asked.

'Yes. She even agreed. But she won't allow me to stop it. We have to clear them out, that's the only consideration. The political cost outweighs the human one.'

*

The rover reporters assigned to the Liberation were all billeted in a pair of three-storey programmable silicon barracks on the western side of Fort Forward, near the administration and headquarters section. Nobody minded that, it placed them close to an officers' mess, which at least allowed them to get a drink in the evening. But as far as providing them with an authentic experience of troops quarters went, you could take realism too far. The ground floor was a single open space that was intended as a general recreation and assembly hall, with a total furniture complement of fifty plastic chairs, three tables, a commercial-sized induction oven, and a water fountain. It did at least have a high capacity net processor installed for them to stay in touch with their studio chiefs. Beds were upstairs, in six dormitories, with a communal bathroom on each floor. For a breed used to four-star (minimum) hotels, they didn't acclimatize well.

The rain started at eight o'clock in the morning when Tim Beard was downstairs having breakfast. There were three choices for breakfast at Fort Forward, all pre-prepped; tray A, tray B, and tray C. He always tried to get down in time to grab a tray A from the pile by the door, which was the most filling, so he didn't have to eat lunch; trays D, E, and F violated all kinds of human rights declarations.

He pushed the tray into its slot in the oven, and set the timer for thirty seconds. Drizzle pattered down in the big open doorway. Tim groaned in dismay. It would make the humidity hellish for the rest of the day, and if he travelled down into Mortonridge itself he'd have to use the anti-fungal gel that evening – again. Another day in the clutches of decay, watching a decaying Liberation. The oven bleeped and ejected his tray. The wrapping had split, mixing his porridge with his tomatoes.

There were a couple of chairs left at one of the tables. He sat down next to Donrell, from News Galactic, nodding at Hugh Rosler, Elizabeth Mitchell and the others.

'Anyone know where we're cleared for today?' he asked.

'Official Stonys are taking us down to Monkscliff,' Hugh said. 'They want to show us some medical team just in from Jerusalem, got a new method of cramming protein back into the malnutrition cases. Direct blood supplement, slam protein back into your cells. Hundred per cent survival rate. It's going to be real useful when the last sieges end.'

'I want to try and get back down to Chainbridge,' Tim said. 'The army set up a big field hospital there. There's been some Gimmie suicides. They couldn't handle being saved.'

'Gimmie the winning side,' Elizabeth muttered. 'God damn typical, or what.'

'No,' Donrell said complacently; he smiled round at his colleagues. 'You don't want any of that, you want to visit Urswick.'

Tim hated the smug tone, but Donrell was one of the best at ferreting information. A neural nanonics check told him Urswick was a siege town that had been liberated yesterday afternoon. 'Any reason?'

Donrell grinned, and made a show of lowering a triangle of toast into his mouth. 'They ran out of food over a week ago. That means they had to eat something different to last out so long.' He licked his lips.

'Oh, Jesus,' Tim winced. He shoved his breakfast tray away. But it would make one fantastic story.

'Who the hell told you that?' Elizabeth asked; there was a disturbing eagerness in her voice.

Tim was preparing a disapproving look for her when he saw Hugh look up suddenly.

'One of the mercs I know,' Donrell said. 'She had a buddy in the Urswick support troop. At the start of the siege the infra-red sweep showed a hundred and five people in there. The serjeants liberated ninety-three.'

Hugh was glancing round the hall, frowning, as if his name was being called.

'Could be some of your basket cases, Tim,' Elizabeth suggested. 'They couldn't handle the memory.'

Hugh Rosler stood up and walked towards the open door. Donrell gave a rough laugh. 'Hey, Hugh, you want some of my sausage? Tastes kinda strange.'

Tim gave him an annoyed look, and hurried off after Hugh.

'Something I said?' Donrell shouted after them. The whole table was chuckling.

Tim caught up with Hugh just outside. He was ignoring the rain, walking purposefully across the mesh road.

'What is it?' Tim asked. 'You know something, don't you? One of your local contacts datavise you?'

Hugh gave Tim a slight sideways smile. 'Not quite, no.'

Tim scampered along at his side. 'Is it hot? Come on, Hugh! I pool, don't I? Your best sensevises are down to me.'

'I think you just got your story back.' Hugh slowed, then turned quickly, and started jogging along the gap between a couple of barracks.

'Christ's sake,' Tim muttered. He was soaking, but nothing would make him give up now. Hugh might be a provincial hick working for a nothing agency, but he was always on the level.

There was a four-lane motorway on the other side of the barracks, with a junction right in front of them. Two loops of mesh road led round to one of Fort Forward's hospitals. Hugh hurried out onto the motorway, right in front of an automated ten-tonne truck.

'Hugh!' Tim screamed.

Hugh Rosler didn't even look at the truck. He held up a hand and clicked his fingers.

The truck stopped.

Tim gaped, not believing. It didn't brake. It didn't skid to a halt. It just stopped. Dead. In the middle of the road. Fifty kilometres an hour to zero in an instant.

'Oh, mother of God,' Tim croaked. 'You're one of them.'

'No, I'm not,' Hugh said. 'I'm the same as you, I'm a reporter. It's just that I've been doing it a lot longer. You pick a few useful things up.'

'But . . .' Tim hung back on the edge of the motorway. All of the traffic was slowing to a halt, red hazard strobes flashing brightly.

'Come on,' Hugh said cheerfully. 'Trust me, you don't want to miss this. Start recording.'

Tim belatedly opened a neural nanonics memory cell. He stepped out onto the motorway. 'Hugh? How did you do that, Hugh?'

'Transferred the inertia through hyperspace. Don't worry about it.'

'Fine.' Tim froze. A glimmer of emerald light was shining in the air behind Hugh. He gurgled a warning, and raised his hand to point.

Hugh turned to face the light, smiling broadly. It expanded rapidly to a pillar five metres wide, twenty tall. Raindrops sparkled as they fell around it, acquiring their own verdure corona.

'What is that?' Tim asked, too fascinated to be frightened.

'Some sort of gateway. I don't actually understand its compositional dynamic, which is pretty remarkable in itself.'

Tim gathered up his reporter's discipline, and focused on the cold light in front of him. There were shadows moving deep inside. They grew larger, more distinct. A serjeant stepped out onto the glistening road. Tim upped his sensorium reception, waiting in awe.

'Urgh,' the puissant serjeant exclaimed in a shrill voice. 'What a simply awful homecoming, darling. It's absolutely weeing down.'

*

Ralph got out to one of the seven emerald gateways ninety minutes after they opened. The between time was a frantic rush to make sense of what was happening, and respond appropriately. It saw the Ops Room brought back to full strength as officers ran in from all over the building to take up their stations.

That the radiant green columns were some form of wormholes was easy enough to establish. The exact status of the people walking out of them was more problematical.

'The serjeants do not contain Edenist personalities,' Acacia exclaimed. 'General affinity is a babble of voices, they declaim without adherence to simple convention. Clarity has become impossible.'

'Then who are they?'

'I believe they are ex-possessors.'

By then several serjeants with their original Edenist personalities had come through the gateways, helping to clarify the situation, telling every Edenist in or orbiting Ombey that they were the refugees from Ketton Island. Even so, Ralph activated the incursion strategy, drawn up in the weeks preceding the liberation in case a wild foray by the possessed penetrated Fort Forward's perimeter. All ground and air traffic across the camp was shut down, all personnel confined to barracks. Duty marines were rushed to the gateways. The one thing he had to confirm was that the possessors now in serjeant bodies hadn't retained their energistic power. Once that was proven, he allowed the full alert status to drop a level. Both he and Admiral Farquar agreed that the SD platforms would continue targeting the gateways. They might be benign now, but who was to say that would last.

For all its strangeness, the situation was a problem of logistics again. The humans who came staggering out of the gateways were in the same kind of physical condition as every other ex-possessed: badly in need of medical treatment and decent food. It couldn't be coincidence that each gateway had opened just outside a hospital, but their numbers and rate of arrival were putting a severe strain on the immediate medical resources.

As to the serjeants, the one contingency Ralph and his staff had never planned for was acquiring over twelve thousand ex-possessors in non-threatening guise. Ralph initially classified them as prisoners of war, and the AI reassigned three empty blocks of barracks as their accommodation. Marines and mercenaries on leave at the camp were formed into guard squads, confining them to the buildings.

It was a stall manoeuvre; Ralph didn't know what else to do with them. They had to be guilty of more than just being in the enemy army. Other charges would have to be brought, surely? Kidnap and grievous bodily harm, at least. And yet, they were the victims of circumstance – as any lawyer would be bound to argue.

But just for once, the problem of what to do with them afterwards wouldn't be his. He didn't envy Princess Kirsten that decision.

Dean and Will reported to the Ops Room to act as Ralph's escort when he was finally ready for his inspection. The closest gateway was less than a kilometre from the headquarters building itself. Even with the marine squads orchestrated by the AI, the area around it was predictably chaotic. Huge crowds of spectators from all over the camp, including every rover reporter, milled round the gateways to snatch a byte of the action. Dean and Will had to elbow people aside to let Ralph through. At least some degree of order had been established by the time they reached the gateway. The marine captain in charge had established a hundred-metre perimeter. Inside that, marines were deployed to form two distinct passages to shepherd the returnees away. One led back to the nearby hospital entrance, the other finished up at the parking lot, where trucks waited to drive serjeants away to their detention centres. As soon as a figure walked out of the shimmering green light, an assessment team decided which passage they were destined for, a decision backed up by nervejam sticks. All protests were simply ignored.

'Even our remaining original serjeants are going to the detention barracks,' Acacia told Ralph as they shoved their way through the perimeter. 'It makes things easier. We can sort them out from the ex-possessors later on.'

'Tell them, thanks. I appreciate it. We need to keep things flowing here.'

The marine captain squelched over to Ralph's little group, and saluted. Rainwater dripped steadily off his skull helmet.

'How's it going, Captain? Ralph asked.

'Good, sir. We've got a valid supervision routine up and running here now.'

'Well done. You get back, do your job. We'll try not to get in the way.'

'Thank you, sir.'

Ralph spent a couple of minutes watching quietly as the people and serjeants came flooding out of the green light. Despite the humidity and warm rain, he felt cold trickling through his chest.

Strange, I can accept a wormhole or ZTT jump across light-years as perfectly normal, but a portal leading out of this universe is like a phobia. Is this too *divine* for me, physical proof of a realm where celestials exist? Or the opposite, proof that even the human soul and omnipotent creatures have a rational basis? I'm looking at the end of religions, the fact that we were never visited by any messenger from any creator god. A fact presented in a fashion I can never ignore. The loss of our race's spiritual innocence.

He could see that the ex-possessed humans that came through were surprised, a dim-witted confusion present on every face as the dreary rain started to soak their clothes. The serjeants lumbered out, their bewilderment less obtrusive, but none of them seemed in full control of their movements during the initial few moments.

Several members of the science investigatory team were wandering round the gateway, waving sensor blocks at it. Most of the army's scientific staff were down on the peninsula, trying to make sense of the energistic ability. Diana Tiernan was one of the few people content with the sieges, explaining how it gave the physicists a chance to study the power outside the laboratory. Ralph had left her back in the headquarters building, desperately trying to arrange for instruments and personnel to be flown back to Fort Forward.

'That's Sinon,' Acacia exclaimed. 'He's an original.'

Ralph saw a serjeant who lacked the unsteadiness of the others. The assessment team of marines and medics pointed him at the passage of armoured marine troopers. 'You sure?' Ralph queried.

'Yes.'

Ralph hurried up to the assessment team. 'OK, we'll take this one.'

The marine captain's exasperation was throttled back at the interference. 'Yes sir.'

A thoroughly chastised Ralph led Sinon away. They wound up standing between the gateway and the perimeter ring of marines. His own staff gathered round. 'This crystal entity you encountered back there, did it tell you how we could solve the overall problem?' Ralph asked.

'I'm sorry, General. It took the same attitude as the Kiint. We must generate our own solution.'

'Damn it! But it was willing to help de-possess bodies.'

'Yes. It said it judged us by our own ethics, and that such a theft was wrong.'

'OK, what kind of conditions were you facing in that realm? Did you see any of the other planets?'

'The conditions were what we made of them; the reality dysfunction ability was paramount. Unfortunately, even wishes have limits. We were cast out alone on that island, without any fresh air or food. Nothing could change that. The entity implied that our planets would be considerably more fortunate, not that we saw any. That realm is too vast for any chance encounter, the entity even hinted it may be more extensive than our own universe, though not necessarily in its physical dimensions. It is an explorer, it went there because it believed it would expand its own knowledge.'

'So it's not paradise?'

'Definitely not. The possessed are wrong about that. It's a refuge, that's all. There's nothing there which you don't bring to it yourself.'

'So it is entirely natural?'

'I believe so, yes.'

*

After the burst of confusion at the start of the exodus, the marines exerted complete control over everyone who came through the gateways. They were on top of the situation, and stayed there right up until the last four serjeants came through. The marines immediately ushered them towards the trucks waiting in the parking lot as they'd done with all the others.

'No way,' Moyo said. 'We're waiting for her.'

'Who?' the marine captain asked.

'Stephanie. She must have gone back somehow.'

'Sorry, no exceptions.'

'Yo, dude,' Cochrane said. 'She's like our righteous leader; and she's doing her last good deed. So where do you cats come off acting like Colonel Asswipe?'

The captain wanted to protest, but somehow the sight of a serjeant wearing slim purple sunglasses and a paisley patterned backpack stopped the words from coming out.

'I mean, she's like out there all alone battling the last and greatest of the hobgoblin queens, to save *your* soul. The least you can do is act thankful.'

'It's closing,' McPhee shouted.

The gateway was contracting, shrinking back to a small sliver of emerald shimmering a metre above the surface of the road. The physicists shouted excitedly, datavising fresh instructions to the considerable sensor array they'd assembled round the transplanarity rift.

'Stephanie!' Moyo yelled.

'Wait,' Cochrane said. 'It's not shutting down completely. See?'

A small remnant of green light continued to burn steadily.

'She's still there,' Moyo said desperately. 'She can still make it. Please!' he appealed to the marine captain. 'You have to let us wait for her.'

'I can't.'

'Hang on in there,' Cochrane said. 'I maybe know someone who can help here.' Ever since he'd arrived back on Ombey there had been a thousand alien voices whispering away to each other at the back of his mind. Sinon, he yelled at them. Hey, big dude, you around these parts? It's me, your ol' buddy Cochrane. We like need some high-powered help right now. Stephanie's being cosmically stupid again.

*

Acacia took the problem directly to Ralph. He might have been firm about it, but the Edenist mentioned Annette Ekelund.

'Let them wait,' Ralph datavised to the marine captain. 'We'll set up a watching brief.'

An hour and twenty minutes later the gateway expanded briefly to let three humanoid figures stagger out. Stephanie and Annette, in their serjeant bodies, supported a trembling Angeline Gallagher between them. They handed her over to the small medical team, who rushed her into the hospital.

Moyo raced over and flung his arms around Stephanie, his mind leaking a torrent of distress into the general affinity band.

'I thought I'd lost you,' he cried. 'After all that, I couldn't stand it.'

'I'm sorry,' she said. A physical embrace was almost impossible, their hard skulls clacked together loudly as they attempted to kiss.

The rover reporters who'd hung on to the bitter end dodged round the marine guard to close on the strange party.

'Hi there, you dudes, I'm Cochrane, one of the like superheroes who got the kids out across the firebreak. That's Cochrane. C-O-C-H—'

*

It was quiet in the detention barracks. Not that the serjeants slept, they didn't need to. They were lying on their bunks or walking round the hall downstairs, being interviewed by the rovers, catching up on AV news shows (mainly featuring themselves). Most of all, they were getting used to the fact they were back in genuine bodies, and owned them one hundred per cent. Apprehension and marvel at their latest turn in fortune had left them stupefied.

Ralph walked through the hall in one of the barracks, escorted by a watchful Dean and Will. The marine guard was allowing the serjeants to move around freely, all except one. There were five armed troopers standing outside the door to the office the bitek construct was secured in. Two stood to attention as Ralph approached, the others kept focused on their job.

'Open the door,' Ralph ordered.

Dean and Will came in with him, expressions informing any serjeant they'd love it to try taking them on. It was read by the room's sole occupant, who was sitting passively behind a table. Ralph sat down opposite.

'Hello, Annette.'

'Ralph Hiltch. General, sir. You are becoming a depressing recurrent feature in my life.'

'Yes. And it is a life now, isn't it? How does that feel, coming back from the dead as a real person?'

'This is what I always wanted. So I can't complain. Though I expect I'll eventually become ungrateful about the lack of this body's sexuality.'

'You'll be even more unhappy if I fail, and the possessed come marching over the horizon to capture your fine new body for a lost soul to host.'

'Don't be so modest. You won't fail here on Ombey, Ralph. You're too good at your job. You love it. How many sieges are left now?'

'Five hundred and thirty-two.'

'And falling, I believe. That was a good strategy, Ralph. A good response to Ketton. But I still would have loved to see your face when we took that chunk of landscape out from under your nose.'

'Where did that stunt get you? What did you achieve?'

'I got a body, didn't I? I'm alive again.'

'Only by chance. And you didn't help a lot from what I hear.'

'Yes, yes, St bloody Stephanie the hero of the flying isle. Is the Pope going to give her an audience? I'd like to see that, a bitek abomination with a soul that's escaped from purgatory having tea at the Vatican.'

'No. The Pope's not seeing anybody any more. Earth is falling to possession.'

'Shit! Are you serious?'

'Yes. Last I heard, there were four arcologies infested. It might even have fallen by now. So you see, I won, but you were right after all. This will never be decided here.'

The serjeant sat up straighter, its recessed eyes never moving from Ralph. 'You look tired, General. This Liberation is really wearing you down, isn't it?'

'You and I both know there is no paradise now, no immortality. The possessed can never have what they wanted. What will they do, Annette? What will happen to Earth when it arrives in that sanctuary realm and none of their food-synthesis machinery works? What then?'

'They'll die. Permanently. Their suffering will end.'

'Is that what you'd call a final settlement? Problem over.'

'No. I had that opportunity. I didn't take it.'

'The beyond is preferable to death?'

'I'm back, aren't I? Would you prefer me to be on my knees?'

'I'm not here to gloat, Annette.'

'Then what are you here for?'

'I am the supreme commander of the Liberation forces. For the moment that gives me an extraordinary degree of power, and not just in military terms. You tell me if there's any point to my being here. Can this be settled on Mortonridge, or has everything we've both endured all been for nothing?'

'You're in charge of a weary army facing a dying enemy, Ralph; that's not a platform for revolution. You're still trying to validate your glorious war by searching for a noble conclusion. There is none. We are a sideshow. An incredibly expensive, fabulously dramatic entertainment for the accessing masses. We distracted their attention while the real men and women of power decided what our fate was going to be. Political policies determine how the human race confronts this crisis. War doesn't have that ability. War has only one outcome. War is stupid, Ralph. It is the desecration of the human spirit, martyring yourself for someone else's dream. It is for people who do not believe in themselves. It is for you, Ralph.'

*

The security level one sensenviron conference room never changed. Princess Kirsten was already seated at one end of the oval table as the image of white nothingness walls formed around Ralph, seating him at the other end. Nobody else was present.

'Well, what a day,' Kirsten said. 'Not only do we get all our people back safely, we wind up with fewer lost souls to plague the living.'

'I want to stop it,' Ralph said. 'We've won. What we're doing now has become utterly pointless.'

'There are still over a quarter of a million possessed on my planet. My subjects are their victims. I don't think it's over.'

'We have them confined. As a threat they've been neutralized. Of course we'll maintain their isolation, but I'm asking that we stop the actual conflict.'

'Ralph, this was your idea. The sieges have stopped all the shooting.'

'And replaced them with Urswick. Is that what you want, your subjects eating each other?'

The image of the Princess showed no emotional response. 'The longer they remain possessed, the bigger their cancers grow. Those bodies will die unless we actively intervene and rescue them.'

'Ma'am, I am going to issue an order that food and basic medical supplies are handed over to the possessed currently under siege. I will not rescind it. If you do not want it issued, then you will have to relieve me of my duty.'

'Ralph, what the hell is this? We're winning. Forty-three sieges collapsed today. Another ten days, a fortnight at the most, and it'll all be over.'

'It is over here, ma'am. Persecuting the possessed that remain is ... disgusting. You listened to me before, God, that's how this whole thing began. Please give the same consideration to what I'm saying now.'

'You're saying nothing, Ralph. This is a media war, a propaganda exercise, that's what it always was. With your cooperation, I might add. We must have total victory.'

'We already have it. This is more. We found out today that it's possible to open a gateway to the realm where the possessed flee to. Nobody understands it, the physics behind it; but we know it's possible now. We will be able to replicate the effect ourselves some day. The possessed can't hide away from us any more. That's our victory. We can make them face up to what they are, what their limits are. That way we can go on to find a solution.'

'Expand that for me.'

'We now have the power of life and death over the possessed

under siege, especially now the Confederation Navy is working on anti-memory. By concluding the sieges with their capitulation, we're wasting our position, our tactical advantage. Ekelund said this crisis will never be decided here on Ombey, by us. I used to believe her. But today changed that. We are in a unique position to force the possessed to cooperate and help us find a solution. There is a solution, the Kiint found one, the crystal entities found one, we even think the Laymil found one – not that mass suicide would be valid for humans. So give the remaining possessed food, let them recover, and then start negotiating. We can use the Ketton Island veterans to go in and open up a dialogue for us.'

'You mean the serjeants, the ex-possessors?'

'Who better? They have first-hand experience that the sanctuary realm is nothing of the sort. If anybody can convince them, those serjeants can.'

'Good God. First you want the Kingdom to adopt bitek, now you'd have me allied with the lost souls themselves.'

'We know what being antagonistic to them brings us. A fifth of a continent devastated, thousands of deaths, hundreds of thousands of cancer victims. This has been suffering on a scale we've not had since the Garissan Genocide. Make it mean something, ma'am, make some good come out of it. If it's possible, if there is the slightest chance that this might work, you cannot ignore it.'

'Ralph, you are going to be the death of my senior advisers.'

'Then they can come back from the beyond and persecute me. Am I free to give the order?'

'If any of these possessed use this as an opportunity to try and break out, I want them in zero-tau within a day.'

'Understood.'

'Very well, General Hiltch, give your order.'

*

Al had moved to a suite a couple of floors up the Hilton where all the utilities still worked. The doctors needed a reliable electrical supply, fancy phone lines, clean air, that kind of crap. They'd turned the new suite's bedroom into a treatment room, raiding Monterey's hospital for equipment and medical packages. More stuff had been flown up from San Angeles. Stuff that gave Al the creeps, bits of other people, living organs and muscles and veins and skin. Emmet had run a planet-wide search for a pair of compatible eyes, eventually tracking them down to a storage vault in Sunset Island. A priority flight had brought them up to Monterey.

The doctors said it was going well. Jez was out of danger. They'd replaced her blood, and grafted on skin and tissue where Kiera had burned down to the bone, implanted the new eyes. Once the operations were over, they'd covered her in medical packages. Now it was just a question of time until she healed over, they'd assured him.

They didn't like Al visiting too much. Jez looked so helpless smothered in that green plastic substance he got all worked up, which screwed up the packages. So he didn't get too near, just hung out by the door and watched over her. Like a guy should do for his dame. It gave him time to think a lot.

Mickey, Emmet, and Patricia came into the suite's lounge. Al had one of the stewards hand round drinks as they sat round the low brass and marble table, then ordered everyone else out of the room.

'OK, Emmet, how long till they get here?'

'I figure some time in the next ten hours, Al.'

'Fair enough.' Al lit a Havana, and blew a long trail of smoke at the high ceiling. 'On the level, can we fight them off?'

Emmet took a sip of the bourbon, and replaced the glass on the table, studying it keenly. 'No, Al, we're going to lose. Even if they only use the same level of force as they did against Arnstadt, we'll lose. And they'll be carrying enough combat wasps to fire two or three times as many at us. Everything in orbit above New California will be wiped out. The ships can jump away. But they've got nowhere to go except for the last couple of planets we infiltrated. And I'm not too sure they'll even manage that, we think the navy's voidhawks pursued a lot of our guys from Arnstadt and blew them up after they'd jumped away. There weren't too many made it back here.'

'Thanks, Emmet, I appreciate you being straight with me. Mickey, Patricia, what's the word among the soldiers?'

'They're getting jumpy, Al,' Patricia said. 'No two ways about it. There's been enough time for what that bitch Kiera said to start registering. The Organization's put us on top, but that makes us a target. We know we can't take over another planet again, New California is all we've got. A lot of them want to go down there.'

'But we're holding them, Al,' Mickey said. His nervous tic was palpitating away. 'I don't take no shit from any of my people. They're loyal. You made us, Al, we'll stay with you.'

His blind enthusiasm made Al smile faintly. 'I ain't asking no one to commit suicide for me, Mickey. They wouldn't do it anyway; they all came out of the beyond, remember. They ain't gonna go back just because I ask nice. Party's over, guys. We had fun for a while, but we've reached the end of the road. I got a bum rap from history once, I ain't having that again. This time people are gonna say I did the best for everyone. They're gonna show me some genuine respect.'

'How?' Patricia asked.

'Because we're going out in style. It's gonna be me who stops the slaughter. I'm gonna make the navy an offer they can't refuse.'

*

The *Ilex* was one of the voidhawks who had taken up an observation position two million kilometres out from New California in the wake of the mass hellhawk defection from the Organization. The Yosemite Consensus had soon found out about Almaden. Hellhawks had been delivering non-possessed survivors to the habitats, a repatriation deal for rebuilding the asteroid's nutrient refinery, they said. Consensus hadn't finished reviewing the implications of that yet; it seemed unlikely that they could maintain the machinery for more than a few years. However, that the hellhawks so actively sought to avoid combat was a particularly welcome development. Capone's actual motives for allowing, and even assisting, such an action were highly questionable.

Whatever the true reason, it left Yosemite with an excellent opportunity to re-establish its observation of New California and the Organization fleet. *Ilex* had been assigned to review the low-orbit SD network in preparation for the arrival of Admiral Kolhammer's attack force. They deployed their spyglobes, and waited for them to complete the long fall down below geostationary orbit. There was still an hour to go before the little sensors started to return useful data when a communication beam from Monterey was aligned on them.

'I wanna talk to the captain,' Al Capone said.

Auster immediately informed the Yosemite habitats. Their Consensus came together, reviewing the situation through his eyes and ears. 'This is Captain Auster. What can I do for you, Mr Capone?'

Al grinned, and turned to someone out of view. 'Hey, you got that on the dime, they're as prissy as the Limeys. OK, Auster, we all reckon that the navy is due here any minute now. Right?'

'I can neither confirm nor deny such an event.'

'Bullshit, they're on their way.'

'What do you want, Mr Capone?'

'I need to talk to the guy in charge, the Admiral. And I need to do that before he starts shooting. Can you fix that for me?'

'What do you wish to talk to him about?'

'Hey, that's between me and him, pal. Now can you set that up, or do you wanna sit back and let a whole load of people get slaughtered? I thought that was against your religion, or something.'

'I'll see what I can do.'

*

Illustrious emerged in the centre of the voidhawk defence sphere formation, three hundred thousand kilometres above New California. Admiral Kolhammer waited impatiently for the tactical display, cursing the delay while the warship's sensors deployed.

Lieutenant-Commander Kynea, the voidhawk liaison staff leader, called out: 'Sir, local voidhawks have received a communications request. Al Capone wants to talk to you.'

It wasn't something Motela Kolhammer was expecting, but the probability was always there. Capone didn't have to be a genius to work out where the attack force was heading after Arnstadt.

The tactical display was coming on-line, supplemented by information from the Yosemite voidhawks. The news that the hellhawks had departed was extremely welcome. Though even without them New California had a prodigious defence network; its strength had determined the ultimate size of the attack force. So far, none of the platforms had fired.

'I'll listen to him,' Kolhammer said. 'But I want our deployment to continue as planned.'

'Aye, sir.'

The *Illustrious* aligned one of its communication dishes on Monterey.

'So you're the Admiral, huh?' Al Capone asked once the link was established.

'Admiral Kolhammer, Confederation Navy. Currently command-ing the attack force emerging above New California.'

'I guess I must have frightened you people, huh?'

'Guess again.'

'I don't think so. I got it right first time, pal. There's one fuck of a lot of you. That means you're running scared.'

'Interpret our emergence how you choose. It is of no relevance to me. Did you wish to surrender?'

'Blunt son of a bitch, ain't you?'

'I've been called many things, that's one of the milder observations.'

'You killed a lot of people on Arnstadt, Admiral.'

'No. You did. You backed us into a position where we had no alternative but to respond appropriately.'

Al grinned brightly. 'Like I said, I frightened you. That's a big tough decision your Assembly must have made, sacrifice an entire planet just to whack me. Taxpayers ain't gonna like that, no, sir. You're supposed to be protecting them. That's your duty.'

'I'm very aware of my duty to the Confederation, Mr Capone. I don't need you to tell me that.'

'Have it whatever way you want. Thing is, I've got an offer for you.'

'Go ahead.'

'You're gonna shoot off a shitload of artillery at us, right? I mean, it's gonna be like the fucking Alamo in here.'

'You'll discover my intentions soon enough.'

'We've got over a million people up here, more if you count all us poor lost souls; but certainly a million flesh and blood bodies. Plenty of women and children, too. I can prove that; there's stuff my technical guys can send you, lists and records and such. Do you really want to kill them all?'

'No, I do not wish to kill anybody.'

'That's good, we can talk about that.'

'Talk quickly.'

'Pretty simple; I ain't gonna jive-ass you. You've already decided you'll give up New California just to get rid of me. Well, I gotta tell you, I'm real flattered. That's one hell of a price to put on a single guy's head, you know. So in return, I'm gonna do you a favour. I'll send all my people down to the planet, all the possessed here in Monterey and the other asteroids, everyone in the fleet, the whole goddam lot of them. Then when we're all down on the ground, we'll take the planet away. This way nobody gets hurt, and you get back all the hostages I'm keeping up here. I'll even throw in the antimatter as well. How does that grab you, Admiral?'

'It grabs me as fundamentally unbelievable.'

'Hey, shit-for-brains, you want a bloodbath that bad and maybe I'll just give the order to butcher all the hostages right now, before your weapons ever reach us.'

'No. Please don't. I apologize. What I should have asked was, why? Why are you making this offer?'

Al leaned in closer to the sensor transmitting his image to the *Illustrious*. 'Look, I'm just trying to do what's right here. You're going to kill people. Maybe I pushed you into that, maybe not. But now it's here, I'm trying to stop it, I ain't no goddam maniac. So I offer you a way out that leaves both of us looking good.'

'Let me get this straight, you are proposing to ferry every possessed down to the planet, disarm your fleet and hand back the asteroids?'

'Hey, slow but smart. You got it. In return for letting us keep our bodies, we leave and don't bother you again. That's it. End of story.'

'Moving that many people down to the planet would take some time.'

'Emmet, my guy, he says about a week.'

'I see. So while my ships sit out here doing nothing, what guarantee can you make that you're not simply trying to pull another Trafalgar strike against us under cover of this withdrawal?'

Al gave him the *look*. 'That's fucking low, pal. What's to stop you shooting when we're halfway through evacuating and I got fewer ships to give my people covering fire?'

'In other words we have to trust each other.'

'Bet your ever-loving ass.'

'Very well. My ships will not launch any offensive while your evacuation is in progress. And Mr Capone.'

'Yeah?'

'Thank you.'

'No problem. You just be sure and tell everyone back home that I ain't no cracker-barrel fishball. I got me some style.'

'Of course you have. I wouldn't be here otherwise.'

Al leaned back in his chair and switched off the super telephone machine. 'No, guess you wouldn't,' he said contentedly.

Jezzibella stood in the bedroom doorway. A blue towelling gown was worn loosely over her green wrappings, helping to make her look slightly more human, and not so much like a plastic version of the Tin Man out of Oz.

He shot to his feet. 'Hey, you shouldn't be out of bed.'

'It doesn't make any difference if I'm lying down or not. The packages work either way.' She walked slowly across the lounge, barely flexing her knees. Lowering herself into the chair was difficult. Al made a real effort not to go over and help, he could see how much doing it all by herself meant. Toughest girl in the galaxy.

'So what have you been doing?' she asked. The voice was muffled through the slit in her mask package.

'Putting a stop to all this crap. My guys, they can scoot down to the planet and get home free.'

'I thought so. That's very statesmanlike of you, baby.'

'I got a reputation to keep, you know.'

'I know. But Al, what happens when the Confederation finds out how to bring planets back? I mean, that's what all this was about, wasn't it? Standing up to them on their home ground.'

He reached over the table, and gripped her hands. The fingers were sticking out from the end of the packages, allowing him some genuine contact with her skin. 'We lost, Jez. OK? We were so goddam good, we lost. Go figure. We frightened them too much. I had to make a choice. The fleet can't fight this Admiral off. No way. So letting the planet go is the smart way to deal with it. The way I see it, my guys get years more living in their bodies. At least. And the Confederation longhairs ain't gonna risk bringing them back until they've found a way of giving us new bodies, or something. They'd just start the whole thing over. Who knows, maybe New California can vanish from the next universe, too. There's a lot of things can happen. This way, nobody dies, we all win.'

'You're the best, baby. I knew it right from the start. When do we go down?'

Al squeezed her fingers a little tighter, looking into her face. He could just see her new eyes through the green package, like she was wearing swimming goggles, only they were full of liquid. 'You can't, Jez. Christ, your medical stuff only just works up here. Where New

California's headed, who knows what's going to go bust. You're healing up real good now, all the docs say so. But you need more time to get perfect. I ain't gonna allow nothing to interfere with that.'

'No, Al, I'm going with you.'

'Wrong. I'm staying here. See, we'll still be together.'

'No.'

'Yeah.' He sat back, and waved an arm round in a gesture that took in the whole asteroid. 'Done deal, Jez. Someone's got to stay here and keep the space weapons going while the guys fly down to the planet. I don't trust that motherhumping Admiral none.'

'Al, you can't operate the SD platforms. For fuck's sake, you don't even know how to work the hotel air-conditioner.'

'Yeah. But the Admiral don't know that.'

'They'll catch you. They'll expel you from that body. It'll be the beyond for the rest of time. Please, Al. I'll work the SD platforms. Be safe. I can live as long as I know you're safe.'

'You forgetting something, Jez; everyone forgets, except maybe good old brown-nose Bernhard. I'm Al Capone. I ain't scared of the beyond. Never was. Never will be.'

*

The voidhawk from New California arrived just as First Admiral Aleksandrovich's flyer touched down. It meant he could walk into the Polity Council meeting primed with some good news. Always a good negotiating position to be in.

His first surprise came at the Polity Council chamber door. Jeeta Anwar was waiting outside for the navy delegation.

'The President has asked me to inform you that no aides are required for this session,' she said.

Samual Aleksandrovich gave Keaton and al-Sahhaf a bemused glance. 'They're not that dangerous,' he said jovially.

'I'm sorry, sir,' Jeeta said.

Samual considered making a fuss, he didn't like that kind of surprise being thrown at him. If nothing else, it told him the coming meeting was going to be unusual, and probably disagreeable. Having his aides with him couldn't stop that. 'Very well.'

The second surprise was how few ambassadors were sitting around the big circle of antique sequoia in the council chamber. Three in total, representing New Washington, Oshanko, and Mazaliv. Lord Kelman Mountjoy was also present. Samual Aleksandrovich gave him a cautious nod as he sat to the left of Olton Haaker.

'I don't believe you have a quorum here,' he said mildly.

'Not of the Polity Council, no,' President Haaker said.

Samual didn't like the man's stilted voice; something was making the President very nervous. 'Then please tell me what this meeting is.'

'We are here to formulate future policy towards the possessed situation,' Kelman Mountjoy said. 'It's not something the old Confederation is capable of addressing satisfactorily.'

'The old Confederation?'

'Yes. We are proposing a restructuring.'

Samual Aleksandrovich listened in growing dismay as the Kulu Foreign Minister explained the reasoning behind the core-Confederation idea. Stopping the slow spread of possession, strengthening the defences of the key star systems. Establishing a solid, economically stable society capable of finding an overall solution.

'Do you propose including the Edenists?' Samual asked when he'd finished.

'They were not receptive to the concept,' Kelman said. 'However, since they have a reserve position along very similar lines their ultimate inclusion is highly probable. We would have no problem continuing to trade with them, as they are by and large immune to the kind of infiltration that results from quarantine-busting flights.'

'And they supply every Adamist world with energy,' Samual said scathingly.

Kelman managed not to smile. 'Not all,' he said softly.

Samual turned to the President. 'You cannot allow this to happen, it is economic apartheid. It transgresses every ethic of equality which the Confederation represents. We must protect everybody alike.'

'The navy isn't even capable of doing that now,' Olton Haaker said sadly. 'And you've seen the economic projections my office compiled. We cannot afford the current level of deployment, let alone sustain it for any reasonable length of time. Something has to give, Samual.'

'In effect, it's already given,' Kelman said. 'The attack on Arnstadt and New California was an admission that we can no longer afford to indulge the current status quo. The Polity Council chose, and you agreed, that we had to lose those planets in order to help safeguard the rest. The core-Confederation is the logical conclusion of that development. It safeguards our entire race by ensuring that there will always be a part of it free from possession, and able to search for a solution.'

'I find it interesting that your proposal safeguards only your part of the human race. The rich section.'

'Firstly, by ending the unrealistic level of subsidy our worlds extend to stage two star systems, they will also contract and therefore become safer. Secondly, there is no point in the richer star systems impoverishing and weakening themselves when to do so will not result in a solution. We have to address the real facts, and do so with resolution.'

'The quarantine works. In time, and if everyone pools their intelligence data, we can end the illegal flights. There is no more Organization, Capone has surrendered New California to Admiral Kolhammer.'

'These arguments are the ebb and flow in the tide of obsolete politics,' Kelman said. 'Yes, you've nullified Capone. But we've now lost Earth. Mortonridge has been effectively liberated, but at a shocking price. Zero-tau can de-possess someone, but the released body will be plagued with cancer and tie up our medical facilities for years. This has all got to stop. A line must be drawn under the past in order to free our future.'

'You approach this as if possession is the whole problem,' Samual said. 'It is not, it is a spin-off from the fact we have immortal souls and some of them are trapped in the beyond. The answer to this, how we learn to live with such knowledge, whatever it is, must be embraced by the entire human race; from some delinquent mugger on a stage one colony planet right up to your King. We have to face this as one. If you split us up, you cannot reach and educate the very people who are most likely to be blighted by this revelation. I cannot agree to this. I will not agree to this.'

'Samual, you have to,' the President said. 'Without funding from the core-Confederation worlds, there can be no navy.'

'Every planetary system funds the Confederation Navy.'

'Not equally, they don't,' said Verano, the New Washington Ambassador. 'Between us, the worlds proposing to form the core-Confederation provide eighty per cent of your overall funding.'

'You can't just split ... Ah! Now I understand.' Samual gave Olton Haaker a contemptuous look. 'Did they offer you the new presidency in exchange for pushing the transition? You might call this coalition the core-Confederation, but in effect you'd all be withdrawing from the actual Confederation. There is no continuation, certainly not in legal terms. Every one of my officers renounced their national citizenship upon joining; the Confederation Navy is responsible to the Assembly in its entirety, not special interest blocs.'

'A hell of a lot of your fleets are made up from national detachments,' Verano said hotly. 'They will be taken back along with fleet bases. You'd be left with ships you couldn't support in star systems you couldn't defend.'

Kelman held up a hand, raising his index finger, which silenced the Ambassador. 'The navy will do as you say, Samual, we all acknowledge that. As for legality and ownership, Ambassador Verano has a point. We have paid for those ships.'

'And the core-Confederation would become the new law,' Samual said.

'Precisely. You want to protect humanity, then become a realist. The core-Confederation will be brought into existence. You understand politics probably better than most of us, you would never have been appointed First Admiral otherwise. We have decided this is the best way our interests are served. We are doing it so that ultimately a solution will be achieved. It's in our own petty selfish interest to make sure a solution is found, God knows I have no wish to die now I know what awaits. If nothing else, you can trust us to put unlimited resources into the problem. Help us safeguard our boundaries, Admiral, bring the fleet over to the core-Confederation. We are the guarantee of ultimate success for our whole race. That is what you were sworn to protect, I believe.'

'I do not need reminding of my honour by you,' Samual said.

'I apologize.'

'I will need to think about this before I give you an answer.' He rose to his feet. 'I will also consult my senior officers.'

Kelman bowed. 'I know this is difficult. I'm sorry you were ever put in such a position.'

Samual didn't speak to his two aides until he was back on the marine flyer, and heading up to the orbiting station that was serving as his new headquarters.

'Can the remaining star systems afford to keep the navy going by themselves?' al-Sahhaf asked.

'I doubt it,' Samual said. 'God damn it, they'll be left absolutely defenceless.'

'A neat piece of applied logic,' Keaton said. 'They are going to be left defenceless anyway. If you don't bring the navy to the core-Confederation, then you will have achieved nothing for them, and weakened the core-Confederation at the same time.'

'Are you saying we should go along with this?'

'Personally, sir, no I don't believe we should. But it's the oldest political squeeze manoeuvre there is. If we're left out in the cold we can achieve nothing. If we join up, then there's the opportunity to influence policy from inside, and from a considerable position of strength.'

'Lord Mountjoy isn't stupid,' al-Sahhaf said. 'He'll be willing to negotiate with you in private. Perhaps we can maintain the CNIS throughout the class two star systems, continue to provide the governments intelligence on possessed movements.'

'Yes,' Samual said. 'Mountjoy would favour that, or something very similar. It's the ebb and flow of politics.'

'Do you want to meet him, sir?' Keaton asked.

'That almost sounds as though you're putting temptation in my way, Captain.'

'No, sir!'

'Well, I don't want to meet him. Not yet. I am not prepared to see the navy disbanded and junked through my stubbornness. It's a powerful force to counter the possessed at a physical level, and that must not be lost to the human race. I need to talk this through with Lalwani, and see if the Edenists would consider supporting the fleet. If they can't, then I'll meet Mountjoy and discuss handing it over to the core-Confederation. We must remember that military force ultimately exists to serve the civilian populace, even though we might despise their choice of leaders.'

*

The intensity of the cold was astonishing. Waves of it slithered right through every part of the escape pod, washing the heat away. The temperature sink was so profound it began to alter the colour of plastic components, bleaching them like a dose of ultra-violet light.

Tolton's breath condensed into a layer of iron-hard frost on every surface.

They'd taken the survival clothing from the supply lockers, and he'd put on as many layers as it was physically possible to do. He looked even fatter than Dariat, his face shrouded by thick bandages of cloth he'd wound round and round to protect his ears and neck. His exposed skin had acquired its own sprinkling of frost, each eyelash resembled a miniature icicle.

The pod's power cells were draining away as fast as the heat. At first the environmental circuit had chugged away merrily, heating the air, and extracting the water vapour. Then they ran a simple analysis, and realized at their current rate of use the cells would be empty in forty minutes. Dariat slowly shut down all the pod's systems, like navigation and communications, and thrusters, then when Tolton was snug in two heated suits and all his insulated clothes, he switched off everything except the carbon dioxide scrubber and a single fan. At that consumption rate, the power cells should have lasted two days.

Tolton's heated suits went through their inventory of power cells a lot quicker than they'd expected. The last one was exhausted fifteen hours after they'd entered the mélange. After that he started drinking soup out of self-heating sachets.

'How much longer is the hull going to hold out?' he asked between juddering sips. He was wearing so much clothing he couldn't bend his arms, so Dariat had to hold the sachet nipple to his lips.

'Not sure. My extra senses aren't up to that kind of work.' Dariat beat his own arms against his chest. The cold didn't affect him as badly, but even so he'd clad himself in several woolly jumpers and some thick tracksuit bottoms. 'The nultherm foam has probably gone by now. The hull will just evaporate away until it's so thin the pressure from the mélange implodes us. It'll be quick.'

'Pity. I could do with feeling something. Bit of pain would be a nice sensation right now.'

Dariat grinned over at his friend. Tolton's lips were jet black, the skin peeling away.

'What's wrong?' Tolton croaked.

'Nothing. Just thinking, we could try firing one of the rockets. Maybe that would heat the pod up a bit.'

'Yeah. It would push us out to the other side quicker, too.'

''Bout time that happened. So, if you could have anything you wanted waiting for us, what would it be?'

'Tropical island, with beaches stretching on for kilometres. Sea as warm as bathwater.'

'Any women there?'

'Oh, God yes.' He blinked, and his lashes stuck together. 'I can't see anything.'

'Lucky you. Do you know what a sight you are?'

'What about you? What do you want waiting on the other side?'

'You know that: Anastasia. I lived for her. I died for her. I sacrificed my soul for her . . . well, her sister, anyway. I thought she might be watching at the time. Wanted to make a good impression.'

'Don't worry, you already have, man. I keep telling you, a love like yours is going to make her giddy. The chicks really dig that kind of mad devotion crap.'

'You're the most insensitive poet I've ever met.'

'Street poet. I don't do the roses and chocolates routine, I'm too much of a realist.'

'I bet roses and chocolates pay more.' When there was no answer, Dariat took a close look at Tolton's face. He was still breathing, but very slowly, air whistling past the fangs of ice crusting his mouth. There were no shivers any more.

Dariat rolled back onto his own acceleration couch, and waited patiently. It took another twenty minutes before Tolton's ghost rose up out of the bloated bundle of fabric. He took one astounded look at Dariat, then put his head back and laughed.

'Oh, shit, will you grab a load of this. I'm the soul of a poet.' The laughter degenerated into sobbing. 'The soul of a poet. Get it? You're not laughing. You're not laughing and it's fucking funny. It's the last funny thing you'll ever know for the rest of all eternity. *Why aren't you laughing?*'

'Shush.' Dariat's head came up. 'Do you hear that?'

'Hear them? There's a trillion billion trillion souls out there. Of course I can fucking hear them.'

'No. Not the souls in the mélange. I thought I heard someone calling. A human voice.'

28

It had been a long night for Fletcher Christian. They'd kept him chained to the altar with electricity coursing through him while the madness whirled all around. He'd seen Dexter's followers chopping up the beautifully crafted wooden model of St Paul's which Sir Christopher Wren had built to show off his dream, throwing splintered fragments into the iron braziers which now illuminated the building. The silent slaughter as people were dragged up to the altar where Dexter waited with the anti-memory weapon. Fletcher wept as their souls were destroyed in readiness for their bodies to be replenished by those from the beyond, personalities more compliant to the dark Messiah's wishes. Salty tears leaked into the runes mutilating his cheeks, stinging like acid. Courtney's crazed shrieking laugh as Dexter ravaged her until blood flowed and skin blistered.

Sacrilege. Murder. Barbarism. It never stopped. Each act pounding away at the few senses he had remaining. He recited the Lord's Prayer over and over until Dexter heard him, and the possessed closed in, screaming some obscene chant in counter. Their cruel words slipped into him with the force of daggers, their joy in evil tormenting him into silence. He feared his mind would snap from the pressure of such depravity.

Throughout it all, the font of energistic power increased along with their numbers, spreading out to engulf mind and matter alike. This was not the shared longing he'd known on Norfolk, the genuine appetite to hide from emptiness. Here Dexter absorbed what strength his followers offered and forged its shape with his own damned desires.

As the sullied red light crept through the open door, mocking the night, Fletcher finally heard the cries of the fallen angels. On top of everything else, their diabolical poignancy nearly broke his resolve. Surely not even Dexter could think of letting such beasts loose upon the Earth.

'No,' Fletcher wailed. 'You cannot bring them forth. It is madness. Madness. They will consume us all.'

Dexter's face slid into view above him, coldly radiant with satisfaction. 'About fucking time you understood.'

*

Lady Macbeth emerged from her jump deep in interstellar space, one thousand nine hundred light-years from the Confederation. The sensation of isolation and loneliness among those on board was nothing to how small that distance made them feel.

Star-tracker sensors slid out of their recesses, gathering up the faint harvest of photons. Navigation programs correlated what was there, defining their position.

Joshua triangulated on their target, an unremarkable point of light, only thirty-two light-years away now. Their next jump coordinate sprang into his mind, blinking purple at the end of a long neuroiconic tube of orange circles. The star was slightly to one side of it, a distance that represented relative delta-V. Starship and star were still moving at very different velocities as they orbited the galactic core.

'Stand by,' he said. 'Accelerating.'

There were groans across the bridge. They dried up soon enough as he activated the antimatter drive. Four gees pushed everyone down into their couches, except for Kempster Getchell; the old astronomer had gone into a zero-tau pod after the second jump. 'Too much for my bones,' he'd complained gamely. 'Fetch me out when we get there.'

Everyone else stuck it out. Not that the crew had a choice. Seventeen jumps in twenty-three hours, each one fifteen light-years long. In itself, probably a record. Nobody was counting now; they'd devoted themselves entirely to keeping the systems functioning smoothly, a professionalism not many could match. Pride had increased to accompany an edgy anticipation as the Sleeping God star grew closer.

Joshua remained in his acceleration couch, piloting them to each coordinate with his usual sublime competence. Nothing much was said as the Orion Nebula shrank away behind them. It was smaller in every star tracker scan, dwindling down to a diminutive fuzzy patch of light, the last familiar astronomical feature left in the universe. Every fusion generator was running at maximum capacity, recharging the nodes fast. That was why Joshua used high gees between coordinates, instead of the usual one-tenth. Time. It had become the most precious commodity left to him.

Instinct drove him on. That enigmatic, bland star holding steady at the apex of the sensor lock was giving out the same siren song as those strikes in the Ruin Ring once had. So much had happened on this flight. So much of his own hope had been invested now. He couldn't, didn't, believe that it had all been for nothing. The Sleeping God existed. A xenoc artefact, powerful enough to interest the Kiint. They'd been right all along, the discoveries made throughout the flight continually emphasizing its importance.

'Nodes charged and ready, Captain,' Dahybi reported.

'Thanks,' Joshua said. He automatically ran a vector check. The old girl was performing well. Three more hours, two more jumps, and they'd be there. The flight would be over. That was the part he found hard to credit. There were so many roots elevating the *Lady Mac* to this encounter. Kelly Tirell and the mercs back on Lalonde. Jay Hilton and Haile (wherever they were now). Tranquillity escaping the Organization fleet. Further back than that, a single message being passed across one and a half thousand light-years of empty space, loyally relayed from star to star by a species that should never have escaped their sun's expansion in the first place. And Swantic-LI, finding the Sleeping God originally. Improbable chances in an event chain fifteen thousand years long linking that single unlikely meeting to the fate of an entire species.

He didn't believe in odds that long. That just left destiny, divine intervention.

Interesting, given what they were supposedly flying towards.

*

Louise awoke in some confusion. A young man was lying on top of her. Both of them were naked.

Andy, she remembered. It was his flat: small, grubby, cluttered. And so warm the air itself seemed to have thickened. Condensation had licked every surface to glisten in the dark-pink light of dawn that drizzled through the fogged window.

I will not regret what we did last night, she told herself firmly. I have no reason to feel guilty. I did what I wanted to. I am entitled to do that.

She tried to ease him to one side and slip out from underneath, but the bed simply wasn't big enough. He stirred, frowning as he focused on her. Then he flinched in shock.

'Louise!'

She gave him a brave smile. 'At least you remembered my name.'

'Louise. Oh God.' He lurched back into a kneeling position. His eyes stared down greedily at her body, and his mouth twisted into a beatific smile. 'Louise. You're real.'

'Yes. I'm real.'

His head darted forward, and he kissed her. 'I love you, Louise. Darling, my darling, I love you so much.' He lowered himself against her, kissing her face urgently; his hands cupped her breasts, fingers teasing her nipples exactly the way she'd cherished last night. 'I love you, and we're together at the end.'

'Andy.' She shifted round, wincing at how sore her breasts were. For someone so skinny, he was surprisingly strong.

'Oh God, you're so beautiful.' His tongue was licking over her lips, desperate to be inside her mouth.

'Andy, stop.'

'I love you, Louise.'

'No!' She pushed herself up. 'Listen to me. You don't love me, Andy, and I don't love you. It was just sex.' Her mouth parted in a small smile, softening the blow as much as she could. 'All right, it was *very* good sex. But nothing else.'

'You came to me.' His pleading voice came close to cracking, there was so much hurt in the words.

Louise's guilt was awful. 'I told you that everyone else I know has either left the arcology or been captured by the possessed. That's why I'm here. As for the rest . . . well, we both wanted that. There's no reason not to now.'

'Don't I mean anything to you?' he asked in desperation.

'Of course you do, Andy.' She stroked his arm, and leaned in closer, making the contact more intimate. 'You don't think I'd do that with just anyone, do you?'

'No.'

'Remember what we did?' she whispered in his ear. 'How bad we were?'

Andy blushed, unable to look at her. 'Yes.'

'Good.' She kissed him lightly. 'This is one night we'll keep with us for ever. Nobody can ever take it away from us, no matter what happens to us now.'

'I still love you. I have done ever since I saw you. That'll never change.'

'Oh, Andy.' She cradled him against her chest, rocking gently. 'I didn't want to hurt you. Believe me, please.'

'You haven't hurt me. You couldn't. Not you.'

Louise sighed. 'Funny how different life could be, so many things that make you take one route instead of another. If only we could live them all.'

'I'd live them all with you.'

She hugged him tighter. 'I think I'm going to envy the girl who winds up with you. She's going to be so lucky.'

'Won't happen now, will it?'

'No. I suppose not.' She gave the opaque window a resentful look, hating the day outside, the way time was advancing and what it would invariably bring. There was something else coming through the glass, riding the crimson light: a sense of rancour. It made her uneasy, almost fearful. And that red light was very deep for a dawn sun, it reminded her of Duchess.

She let go of Andy, and padded over to the high window. Standing on one of the boxes brought her face up level with it. She smeared the condensation away.

'Oh dear Jesus.'

'What's the matter?' Andy asked. He hurried across, and peered over her shoulder.

It wasn't dawn shining in, that was still two hours away. A large circular swirl of red cloud hung in the centre of the Westminster Dome, a few hundred yards above the ground. Its malign glow glimmered off the geodesic crystal above, turning the struts to a lattice of burnished copper. The underside shone a blood-red light down on the roofs and walls of the city, staining them all an unhealthy magenta. Its leading edge was less than a mile away from the tenement, undulating gently.

'Shit!' he hissed. 'We've got to get out of here.'

'There's nowhere to go, Andy. The possessed are all around us.'

'But ... Oh, shit. Why isn't somebody doing something? New York is still holding them off. We should organize ourselves and fight back like them.'

Louise walked back to the bed, and sat down carefully. After last night some movements were quite difficult. She used her neural nanonics to run a physiological review, making sure the baby was all right. It was, and she had nothing worse than a few tender areas. The medical nanonic package infused some biochemicals into her bloodstream, which should help. 'We did try to do something,' she said. 'But it failed last night.'

'You did?' Andy was standing in front of her, sweat pricking his skin. He rubbed his forehead, brushing damp hair from his eyes. 'You mean you're involved in this?'

'I came to Earth to warn the authorities about a possessed called Quinn Dexter. I needn't have bothered, they already knew. He's the one behind all this. I was helping them to find him, because I've seen him before.'

'I thought the Capone Organization had infiltrated us.'

'No, that's just what Govcentral told the media. They didn't want anyone to know what they were actually up against.'

'Bloody hell,' he groaned, badly downcast. 'Fine excuse for a net don I make. Can't even find that out for myself.'

'Don't worry about it. GISD is a lot smarter than people think.' She stood up, the reminder of B7 making her restless. 'I need the bathroom. You said it was at the end of the hall?'

'Yes. Er, Louise.'

'What?'

'I think you'll need something to wear.'

She looked down at herself, and grinned. Totally unselfconscious standing naked in front of a boy, not just any boy, a casual sex partner. Maybe I have lost some of my Norfolk past after all. 'I think you're right.'

Her own clothes were in the pile where she'd thrown them, still damp and badly crumpled. Andy lent her a pair of grey jeans and a smartish navy-blue Jude's Eworld sweatshirt, pulling them out of a box where they'd been partially protected against the humidity.

When she got back he'd just finished wiring a couple of power cells into his air-conditioner. The galvanized box started shuddering as the motor spun up, then sent out a clammy stream of cold air. Louise stood in front of it trying to get her hair dry.

'I've got some food stockpiled,' Andy said. 'Do you want breakfast?'

'Please.'

He pulled some pre-prepped meal trays out of a box and slid them into the oven. Louise started examining the flat in detail. He really was an electronics fanatic, just as he'd claimed at the Lake Isle restaurant. None of his wages had been spent on furnishings, or even clothes by the look of it. Gadgetry lay everywhere: tools and blocks, spools of wire and fibre, microscopic components in lens cases, delicate test rigs; one wall was a rack of fleks. When she peeked into the other room, it was jumbled high with ancient domestic units. He scavenged them for components, he said. Repair work brought in some handy cash. She smiled at the familiar dinner jacket which was hanging up on the back of the door in its own plastic sheath, so obviously out of place.

The oven ejected their meal trays. Andy pushed a flat orange juice carton into the nozzle on his water dispenser, bubbles gurgled up through the big glass bottle. The carton expanded outwards as the juice constituted itself.

'Andy?' Louise stared at the conurbation of electronics, suddenly cursing herself. 'Have you got a working communications block here, something that can reach a satellite?'

'Of course. Why?'

*

'Louise, my God, I thought we'd lost you,' Charlie datavised. 'The sensor satellite says you're at a tenement on Halton Road. Ah, I see, that's Andy Behoo's address. Are you all right?'

'I survived,' she datavised back. 'Where are you?'

'I'm up in the Halo. It was a bit of a mad dash, but I thought it expedient after last night's debacle. Do you know if Fletcher got out?'

'I've no idea. I didn't see anyone else once I started running. What about Ivanov?'

'Sorry, Louise. He didn't make it.'

'There's just me, then.'

'Looks like I underestimated you again, Louise. My one consistent error.'

'Charlie, there's a red cloud under the dome.'

'Yes, I know. Clever move on Dexter's part. It means the SD electron beams can't strike it unless they blow the dome as well. It also means I've got virtually no sensor coverage underneath now. I tried sending my affinity-bonded birds and rats through to see if they could pinpoint him for me, but I lost contact with them every time. And we all thought their energistic power didn't affect bitek.'

'Fletcher says they're aware of everything that happens under their cloud. Dexter probably kills the animals.'

'Very likely. That doesn't leave us with much, does it.'

'This red cloud is different,' she datavised. 'I thought you should know that. It's why I called, really.'

'What do you mean?'

'I was under one on Norfolk as it was gathering together, that was nothing like this. I can feel this one, it's like a really low vibration, one that you can't quite hear. It's not just here to shut away the sky, it's really evil, Charlie.'

'That'll be Dexter. He must have gathered quite a few possessed together now. Whatever he intends to do, it started with that cloud.'

'I'm frightened, Charlie. He's going to win, isn't he?'

'Can you and Andy get to one of the outer domes? I have operational agents in place there. I can get you out.'

'The cloud's growing, Charlie. I don't think we'll make it.'

'Louise, I want you to try. Please.'

'Guilty, Charlie, you?'

'Perhaps. I did get Genevieve to Tranquillity. The blackhawk captain swears he'll never accept another charter from my company.'

Louise grinned. 'That's my sister.'

'Will you leave the tenement now?'

'I don't think so. Andy and I are happy where we are. And who knows what'll happen when Earth is taken out of the universe. It might not be so bad.'

'It won't happen, Louise. That's not what Dexter's about. He wants to obliterate the universe, not leave it. And there are people on Earth who can stop him from doing anything at all.'

'What do you mean? You've never been able to stop him.'

'The red cloud's appearance has finally given our wondrous President some backbone. He's worried it means the possessed are ready to take Earth out of the universe. The Senate has now given him approval to use SD weapons against the arcologies, and eliminate the possessed. It's the new fatalism, Louise. The Confederation abandoned Arnstadt and New California so they could be rid of Capone. The President will sacrifice a minority of the republic's citizens to save the majority. Not that history will remember him kindly for it, though I expect the survivors in the other arcologies will be quietly grateful.'

'You have to stop it, Charlie. There are more people in London than there are on the whole of Norfolk. You can stop it, can't you? B7 can't let them all die. You rule Earth. That's what you said.'

'We can stall the order for a few hours, at most. Crash the command communication circuits, have SD officers refuse to carry out their orders. But ultimately, a direct order from the President will get through and be obeyed. The platforms will fire gamma-ray lasers into the arcologies. Every living cell inside the domes will be exterminated.'

'No. You have to stop them.'

'Louise, get yourself to one of the outer domes. You've got the anti-memory. You can use it against anyone who tries to stop you.'

'No!' she yelled out loud. Her hand smashed down on the table, making the meal trays and glasses bounce. 'No. No. No.' She picked up the communications block and hurled it against the wall. Its casing cracked, sending plastic splinters skittling along the floor. 'I won't.'

Andy had frozen in his chair, staring at her in consternation. She whirled round to face him. 'They're going to kill everybody. The President's going to fire SD weapons into the dome.'

He got up and put his arms round her, trying to calm her angry shaking. Even in bare feet she was half a head taller, he had to look up to see the dismay in her eyes.

'We have to stop him,' she said.

'The President?'

'No, Dexter.'

'The possessed one? The maniac?'

'Yes.'

'How?'

'I don't know. Tell him. Warn him! Get him to dispose of the red cloud. He'll understand that if he has no followers left alive then he's nothing.'

'Then what?'

'I don't know!' she shouted. 'But it will stop everyone from being killed, isn't that worth something to you?'

'Yes,' he stammered.

She went over to her pile of clothes and dug out the anti-memory weapon. 'Where are my shoes?'

Andy took one look at the neat black tube she was holding with such determination, and realized just how serious she was. His first thought was to lock the door, prevent her from leaving. He was too scared even to do that. 'Don't go out there.'

'I have to,' she snapped back. 'None of those monsters care about people.'

Andy dropped to his knees. 'Louise, I'm begging you. They'll catch you. You'll be tortured.'

'Not for long. After all, we're all going to be slaughtered.' She pushed her foot into one shoe, and fastened the side clips.

'Louise. Please!'

'Are you going to come with me?'

'That's London out there,' he said, waving an arm at the window. 'You've got a couple of hours to find one person. It's impossible. Stay here. We'll never know when it happens. Not an SD weapon, they're so powerful.'

She glared down at him. 'Andy, haven't you followed any news? You have a soul. You'll know exactly when it happens. There's a good chance you'll be stuck into the beyond.'

'I can't go out there,' he moaned. 'Not where *they* are. Don't go.'

She pulled her other shoe on. 'Well, I can't stay here.'

Andy looked up at her as she stood over him. Tall, beautiful, and resolute. Utterly glorious. He'd spent all night making love to her, punishing his body with a dangerous level of stimulant programs so she would be completely overwhelmed. And it meant nothing to her. She would never be his, for she'd seen the real him. They were further apart now than they had been before he knew she lived.

His hand wiped over his nose, an attempt to cover up his sniffling. 'I love you, Louise.' He heard the pitiful words come out of his mouth, and despised himself for everything he was, everything he could never become.

Exasperation mingled with embarrassment. Louise didn't know if she wanted to shove him aside or kiss him. 'I still enjoyed last night, Andy. I wouldn't want it any different.' A pat on his bowed, trembling head would be too awful. She moved round him, and went out of the door, closing it quietly behind her.

*

Loud voices and banging doors woke Jay. She sat up in bed and yawned extravagantly, stretching her arms wide. It was night outside, she could just hear the gentle windrush sound of waves rolling onto the beach above the noises in the chalet. People were moving through the rooms, talking in excited tones. Footsteps trundled up the creaky wooden steps to the veranda, and the front door banged again.

She found Prince Dell, and tiptoed into the short hallway. There'd never been such a commotion in the chalet before, not even when the old-timers were planning the new colony. Whatever was going on must be terribly important, which could make eavesdropping interesting.

The voices stopped.

'Come in, Jay,' Tracy called from the lounge.

Jay did as she was told. It was impossible to get away with anything when Tracy was around. Seven of the ancient adults had joined Tracy, sitting and standing round the lounge. Jay kept her head down as she hurried over to the big armchair Tracy was sitting in, too shy to say anything.

'Sorry, poppet,' Tracy said as Jay slithered up onto the cushions beside her. 'Did this noisy rabble wake you?'

'What's the matter?' Jay asked. 'Why's everyone here?'

'We're trying to decide if we should petition Corpus for intervention,' Tracy said. 'Again!'

'Something's happening on Earth,' Arnie said. 'We didn't realize it at first, but Quinn Dexter might be about to do something extremely dangerous.'

'Corpus won't intervene,' Galic said dejectedly. 'There's still no reason. You know the rules, only if another, unaware, species is endangered. Quinn Dexter, according to the textbooks, qualifies as human. Therefore this will be self-inflicted.'

'Then the textbook should be rewritten,' Arnie grumbled. 'I wouldn't classify him as anything close to human.'

'Corpus won't intervene because the President will use SD weapons, that barbarian.'

'Not in time to stop Dexter, he won't,' Tracy said. 'Especially if B7 intervenes and delays the fire command.'

Jay snuggled up closer to Tracy. 'What's Dexter going to do?'

'We're not absolutely sure. It might be nothing.'

'Ha,' Arnie grunted. 'Just you wait and see.'

'Are you watching it?' Jay asked, suddenly not at all sleepy.

Tracy glared at Arnie. There was a mental exchange, too. Jay could feel it even if she couldn't make out individual words. She'd been getting good at that lately.

'Please!' Jay begged. 'It's my world.'

'All right,' Tracy said. 'You can stay up and watch for a little while. But don't think you're getting to see any gory bits.'

Jay beamed at her.

The adults settled down on the other chairs, packing three onto the settee. Tracy's television was switched on, showing a deserted street of ancient buildings. A tight tapestry of red clouds were glowing overhead. Jay shuddered at the sight. They were just like the ones on Lalonde.

'That's London,' Tracy said. She handed Jay a mug of hot chocolate.

Jay propped Prince Dell up against her tummy so he'd have a good view, and took a contented sip of the creamy drink. Someone was walking down the middle of the street.

*

Lady Mac emerged a hundred million kilometres out from the F-class star, five degrees above the ecliptic. As it was an uncharted system, Joshua ordered the combat sensors to deploy and conduct a fast preliminary sweep. Their response time was quicker than the more comprehensive standard array; if there was anything out there on a collision course, they'd hopefully discover it soon enough to jump away.

'Clean space,' Beaulieu reported.

For the first time in thirty hours, Joshua managed to relax, sagging back into the cushioning. He hadn't realized how tight his neck and shoulder muscles had become, they were lines of hot stone under his skin.

'We did it!' Liol whooped.

Amid the noisy round of self-congratulation, Joshua ordered the flight computer to extend the standard sensor booms. They slid out of the fuselage along with the thermo-dump panels. 'Alkad,' he datavised. 'Get Kempster out of zero-tau, please. Tell him we've arrived.'

'Yes, Captain,' she replied.

'Beaulieu, Ashly, activate the survey sensors, please. The rest of you, let's get *Lady Mac* into standard orbital configuration. Dahybi, I still want to be able to jump, we'll keep the nodes charged.'

'Aye, Captain.'

'Fuel status?' Joshua asked.

'Sufficient,' Sarha told him. 'We have forty per cent of our fusion fuel left, and fifty-five per cent of the antimatter. Given we burned fifteen per cent of the antimatter to move Lalarin-MG, we've got enough to get us back to the Confederation. We can even jump around this system, providing you don't want to explore every moonlet.'

'Let's hope we don't have to,' he said. The Swantic-LI message hadn't mentioned where in the system the Sleeping God was; in orbit around a planet or orbiting the star by itself.

The crew loosened up as *Lady Mac* changed from flight mode to her less demanding orbital status. They drifted around the bridge, used the washroom. Ashly went down to the galley and fetched a meal. Prolonged exposure to high gees was severely tiring. And eating anything substantial during the acceleration was unwise. The mass put a lot of pressure on internal organs, even with artificially strengthened membranes. They devoured the spongy pasta cakes eagerly, chasing runaway squirts of hot cheese sauce round the bridge.

'So if it sees the whole universe,' Liol said, talking round a mouthful, 'do you reckon it knows we're here?'

'Every telescope sees the whole universe,' Ashly said. 'That doesn't necessarily mean they can all see us.'

'OK, it detected our gravitonic distortion when we jumped in,' Liol said, unperturbed.

'Where's your evidence?'

'If it knows about us, it's keeping quiet,' Beaulieu said. 'Sensors haven't found any electromagnetic emissions out there.'

'How did the Tyrathca find it, then?'

'Easily, I would think,' Dahybi said.

Under the direction of Kempster and Renato, Beaulieu launched their survey satellites. Sixteen of them were fired, racing away from *Lady Mac* at seven gees. They were arranged in a globular formation, keeping the starship at their centre. After two minutes their solid rockets jettisoned, leaving them flying free. The main section was an omniphase visual-spectrum sensor array, a giant technological fly's eye, looking every way at once. Between them, they formed an ever-increasing telescope baseline, capable of huge resolution. Its only real limit was imposed by the amount of processing power available to correlate and analyse the incoming photonic data.

The sweep was conducted by registering every speck of light with a negative magnitude (in standard stellar classification the brightest visible star is labelled magnitude one, while the dimmest is a six – anything brighter than a one has to be a planet and is assigned a negative value). Their position was then reviewed five times a second to see if they were moving.

Once the planets had been located, the telescope could be focused on them individually to see if the extensive spatial disturbance Swantic-LI had referred to was in orbit around them. They were assuming it was a visible phenomenon, the Tyrathca didn't have gravitonic detector technology. If nothing was found, a more comprehensive sweep of the system would have to be conducted.

'This is most unusual,' Kempster datavised after the first sweep was completed. He and Renato were using the main lounge in capsule C, along with Alkad and Peter, where their specialist electronics had been installed, transforming it into a temporary astrophysics lab.

Joshua and Liol swapped a look shading between surprise and amusement. 'In what way?' Joshua asked.

'We can only detect a single negative-magnitude source orbiting this star,' the astronomer said. 'There's simply nothing else out there. No planets, no asteroids. *Lady Macbeth*'s sensors can't even find the usual clouds of interplanetary dust. All matter has been cleared away, virtually down to a molecular level. The only normal occurrence is solar wind.'

'Cleared away, or just sucked into the spatial disturbance,' Sarha muttered.

'So what is the source?' Joshua datavised.

'A moon-sized object, orbiting three hundred million kilometres from the star.'

Joshua and the rest of the crew accessed the sensor array. It showed them a very bright point of light. Completely nondescript.

'We can't get any sort of spectral reading,' Kempster said. 'It's reflecting the sun's light at essentially a hundred per cent efficiency. It must be clad in some kind of mirror.'

'You did say, easy,' Ashly told Dahybi.

'That's not easy,' Joshua said. 'That's obvious.' He loaded the object's position into the flight computer, and plotted a vector to a jump coordinate which would bring them out one million kilometres away from the enigmatic object. 'Stand by. Accelerating in one minute.'

*

The impulsive anger which had pushed Louise out of Andy's flat had faded by the time she reached Islington High Street. Walking down the empty streets had given her far too much time to think. Mainly about how headstrong and stupid this idea was. At the same time that original reason held fast. Somebody had to do something, however futile. It was the getting captured and facing Dexter part that was making her legs all wobbly and recalcitrant.

Her neural nanonics crashed when she started off along St John Street. Not that she really needed her map file any more. He wouldn't be far from the centre of the red cloud, all she had to do was walk straight down to the Thames, it was only a couple of miles. She knew she'd never actually get that far.

The edge of the cloud, a frayed agitated boundary, was still creeping slowly out towards the skyscrapers behind her. It had already reached Finsbury, barely a quarter of a mile ahead of her now. A gruff sonorous thunder reverberated down from its quaking underside, echoing along the deserted streets. Leaves on the tall evergreen trees trembled in disharmony as erratic gusts of warm air blew out from the centre. Birds rode the thermals high overhead, she could see the tiny black flecks streaming together into huge flocks, all of them heading in the same direction: out.

They were smarter than people. She was amazed that she hadn't encountered anyone fleeing the cloud's advance. The inhabitants were all staying barricaded behind their doors. Was everyone paralysed by fear like Andy?

She passed under the cloud, the sleet of redness closing in on her like a perverted nightfall. It wasn't just the humid air blowing against her now, the feeling of dismay strengthened, slowing her pace. The rumbles of thunder above her thickened, never quite dying away. Forked slivers of blackness crackled between the roiling tufts; black lightning, draining photons out of the sky.

When they'd said goodbye, Genevieve had offered her Carmitha's silver pendant of earth. Louise had refused. Now she wished she hadn't. Any totem against the evil would be welcome. She decided to think about Joshua, her real talisman against the harsh truth of life beyond Norfolk. But that just made her slip into the memory of Andy. She still didn't regret that – quite. As if it mattered.

Louise had made it down Rosebery Avenue and turned into the Farringdon Road when the possessed walked out into the street in front of her. There were six of them, moving with unhurried indolence, dressed in austere black suits. They lined up between the pavements, and stood facing her. She walked up to the one in the middle, a tall thin man with a flop of oily brown hair.

'Girl, what the fuck are you about?' he asked.

Louise pointed the anti-memory weapon straight at him, its end barely a foot from his face. He stiffened, which meant he knew what it was. It wasn't much of a comfort to her; somebody else had one. She knew who.

'Take me to Quinn Dexter,' she told him.

They all started laughing. 'To him?' the one she was threatening said. 'Girl, are you twisted, or what?'

'I'll shoot if you don't.' Her voice was very close to cracking. They would know that, and the reason why, them and their devilish senses. She gripped the weapon tighter to stop it shaking about.

'My pleasure,' he said.

She jabbed the weapon forward. His head recoiled in synchronization.

'Don't push it, bitch.'

The possessed started walking down the road. Louise took a couple of hesitant paces.

'Follow us,' the tall one told her. 'The Messiah is waiting for you.'

She kept the weapon up, not that it would do much good, they all had their backs to her now. 'How far is it?'

'Close to the river.' He glanced back over his shoulder, lips stretched into a thin smile. 'Do you have any idea what you're doing?'

'I know Dexter.'

'No, you don't. You wouldn't be doing this if you did.'

*

The pictures transmitted from Swantic-LI had been accurate after all. From a distance of a million kilometres, the shape of the Sleeping God was quite unmistakable: two concave conical spires end to end, three and a half thousand kilometres in length. A perfectly symmetrical geometry that betrayed its artificial origin. The central rim was sharp, appearing to taper down to an edge whose thickness was measured in molecules; its tips had an equally rapier-like profile. There wasn't anyone on board *Lady Mac* who didn't have an uncomfortable vision of the starship being impaled on one of those sleek spikes.

Beaulieu launched five astrophysics survey satellites towards it, fusion-powered drones, with multi-discipline sensor arrays; they arched away from the starship on trajectories that would position them in a necklace around the Sleeping God.

Joshua led the whole crew down to the lounge in capsule C where Alkad, Peter, Renato, and Kempster were gathered to interpret the data from the satellites and *Lady Mac*'s own sensor suite. Samuel, Monica, and one of the serjeants had also joined them.

Studio-quality holographic screens sprouted from the consoles installed to process the astrophysical data. Each one carried a different image of the Sleeping God. They were tinted every shade in the rainbow, as well as providing graphic representations. Their main AV projector showed the raw visual-spectrum picture, materializing it in the middle of the compartment. The Sleeping God gleamed alone in space, sunlight bouncing off its silver surface in long shimmers. That was the first anomaly, though it took Renato a full minute of puzzled study to see the obvious.

'Hey,' he exclaimed. 'There's no darkside.'

Joshua frowned at the AV projection, then accessed the console processors directly to check. The satellites confirmed it, every part of the Sleeping God was equally bright, there were no shadows. 'Is it generating that light internally?'

'No,' Renato said. 'The spectrum matches the star. Light must be bending round it somehow. I'd say it has to be a gravitational lens, an incredibly dense mass. That ties in with the Tyrathca observation that it's a spatial disturbance.'

'Alkad?' Joshua asked. 'Is it made out of neutronium?' That would be the final irony if a god was made from the same substance as her weapon.

'A moment, Captain.' The physicist seemed troubled. 'We're getting the data from the gravitational detectors on-line.' Several hologram screens flurried with colourful icons. She and Peter read them in surprise. They turned in unison to stare at the central projection.

'What is it?' Joshua asked.

'I would suggest that this so-called God is actually a naked singularity.'

'No fucking way!' Kempster said indignantly. 'It's stable.'

'Look at the geometry,' Alkad said. 'And we're detecting a torrent of gravitational wave vacuum fluctuations, all of them at very small wavelengths.'

'The satellites are picking up regular patterns in the fluctuations,' Peter told her.

'What?' She studied one of the displays. 'Holy Mary, that's not possible. Vacuum fluctuations have to be random, that's why they exist.'

'Ha,' Kempster grunted in satisfaction.

'I know what a singularity is,' Joshua said. 'The point of infinite mass compression. It's what causes a black hole.'

'It's what causes an event horizon,' Kempster corrected. 'The universe's cosmic censor. Physics, mathematics – they all break down in the infinite, because you can't have the infinite, it's unobtainable in reality.'

'Except in some very specific cases,' Alkad said. 'Standard gravitational collapse in stars is a spherical event. Once the core has compressed to a point where its gravity overcomes thermal expansion, everything falls into the centre from all directions at once. The collapse finishes with all the matter compressing into your infinity point, the singularity. At which time its gravity becomes so strong that nothing can escape, not even light: the event horizon. However, in theory, if you spin the star before the event, the centrifugal force will distort the shape, expanding it outward along the equator. If it's spinning fast enough, the equatorial bulge will remain during the collapse.' Her finger indicated the projected image. 'It will form this shape, in fact. And right down at the very end of the collapse timescale, when the star's matter has all achieved singularity density, it will still be in this shape, and for an instant, before the collapse continues and pulls it into a sphere, some of that infinite mass will project up outside the event horizon.'

'For an instant,' Kempster insisted. 'Not fifteen thousand years.'

'It looks as though someone has learned how to freeze that instant indefinitely.'

'You mean like the alchemist?' Joshua datavised to her.

'No,' she datavised back. 'These kind of mass-densities are far outside any I achieved with the alchemist technology.'

'If its mass is infinite,' Kempster recited pedantically, 'it will be cloaked in an event horizon. Light will not escape.'

'And yet it does,' Alkad said. 'From every part of the surface.'

'The vacuum fluctuations must be carrying the photons out,' Renato said. 'That's what we're seeing here. Whoever created this has learned how to control vacuum fluctuations.' He grinned in wonder. 'Wow!'

'No wonder they called it a god,' Alkad said in veneration. 'Regulated vacuum fluctuations. If you can do that, there's no limit to what you can achieve.'

Peter gave her a private, amused look. 'Order out of chaos.'

'Kempster?' Joshua queried.

'I don't like the idea,' the old astronomer said with a weak grin. 'But I can't refute it. In fact, it might even explain Swantic-LI's jump to another star. Vacuum fluctuations can have a negative energy.'

'Of course,' Renato said. He smiled eagerly at his boss, catching the idea quickly. 'They'd be exotic, that's the state which holds a wormhole open. Just like a voidhawk's distortion field.'

Samuel had been shaking his head as the discussion ploughed onwards. 'But why?' he said. 'Why build something like this, what is it for?'

'It's a perpetual source of wormholes,' Alkad said. 'And the Tyrathca said it assists the progress of biological entities. This is the ultimate stardrive generator. You could probably use it to travel between galaxies.'

'Christ, intergalactic travel,' Liol said dreamily. 'How about that.'

'Very nice,' Monica retorted. 'But it hardly helps us to deal with possession.'

Liol gave her a pained glance.

'OK,' Joshua said, 'if you guys are right about this being an artificially maintained naked singularity, there must be some kind of control centre for the vacuum fluctuations. Have you found that yet?'

'There's nothing out there except the singularity itself,' Renato said. 'Our satellites are covering all of the surface. Nothing hiding on the other side, nothing in orbit.'

'There has to be something else. The Tyrathca got it to open a wormhole for them. How do we do that?'

His neural nanonics reported a new communication channel opening. 'You ask,' the singularity datavised.

*

The cloud's luminosity remained constant, but its shading had shifted a long way down the spectrum as Louise approached its epicentre. When she walked across the paved plaza outside St Paul's Cathedral every surface was toned a deep crimson. Stone carvings embellishing the beautiful old building cast long black shadows down the wall, ebony jail bars gripping it tightly, squeezing away the last remnants of sanctity.

Her escort pranced around her like insane Morris dancers, inviting her onward with mocking gestures. The snarls of thunder ended as she reached the large oaken doors, leaving an onerous silence. Louise walked into the cathedral.

She took a couple of steps forward, then faltered. The doors closed behind her with a ululation of cold air. Thousands of possessed were standing waiting along the nave, dressed in elaborate costumes from every era of human history and culture, each one completely black.

They were all facing her. The organ began to play, blasting out a harsh hard-rock version of Mendelssohn's 'Wedding March'. Louise put her hands over her ears, it was so loud. All the possessed turned to face the altar, leaving a narrow passage clear down the very centre of the nave. She began to walk down it. It wasn't a conscious thing, her limbs did as they were commanded by the massed will of the possessed. Her anti-memory weapon fell from numbed fingers after she'd taken the first few steps, clattering away over the cracked tiles.

Ghosts drifted towards her, hands held out to implore. They swept past her as she carried on walking, shaking their heads in sorrow.

The music ended when she reached the front row of the possessed. They were standing level with the transepts; ahead of them, the floor underneath the vaulted central dome was empty. Iron braziers with foul-smelling fires were lining the walls, their black smoke smudging the pale stonework. She couldn't actually see the apex of the dome, it was obscured by a pall of grey fug. There was a gallery high above her. Several people leaned on its rail, looking down at her with mild interest.

Her compulsion ended, and she tottered forward.

'Hello, Louise,' Quinn Dexter said. He stood in front of the defiled altar, no part of him visible within the black robe.

She took a couple of unsteady steps. Fear was tightening every muscle, turning her body stiff. She wasn't even certain she could stand for much longer. 'Dexter?'

'None other.' He moved to one side, allowing her to see a man's body spreadeagled across the altar. 'And now God's Brother has brought the three of us together again.'

'Fletcher,' she squeaked.

Quinn held out an arm towards her, and extended a swan-white hand. A claw finger beckoned, granting her permission to approach.

The lacerations and dried blood coating his skin made her afraid. But as she drew closer she saw his muscles were bunched and trembling. An unfamiliar face was contorted with distress, sucking down air in fast pain-filled gulps.

'Fletcher?'

Quinn waved his hand, and the electricity was turned off. The body slumped down onto the stone, panting in shock. Slowly, Fletcher's face emerged to replace the blooded features. The chains and metal bands securing him dropped away. All of the wounds were banished from sight as his customary naval uniform materialized. He climbed down gingerly from the altar.

'My dearest lady. You should not have come.'

'I had to.'

Quinn laughed. 'Your call, Fletch. You can walk out of here with her now if you make the right decision. If not, she's all mine.'

'My lady.' Fletcher's face was riven with anguish.

'Why can you walk out?' she asked.

'He's just got to sign up for the army of the damned,' Quinn said. 'I won't even make him do it in blood.'

'No,' she said. 'Fletcher, you mustn't do that. I came here to warn you all. This has to stop. You have to disperse the red cloud.'

'Is that a threat, Louise?' Quinn asked.

'You've frightened Govcentral with the red cloud. They think you're going to take the Earth away from the universe. The President won't let that happen. He's going to use strategic defence weapons against London. Everyone will die. Millions and millions of people.'

'I won't,' Quinn said.

'But they will.' Louise waved an arm back at the silent ranks of his disciples. 'Without them you're nothing.'

Quinn glided up to Louise. His face slipped out of the robe's shadows to show her his furious expression. 'God's Brother, I hate you!' He slammed his hand across the side of her head, using energistic power to amplify the strength of the blow.

Louise screamed at the pain, flying back to crash into the altar. She crumpled forward onto the floor, whimpering as blood pumped into her mouth.

Fletcher made a start forwards, finding the end of Quinn's anti-memory weapon pressed against his nose. 'Back off, fuckhead,' Quinn snarled. 'Back!'

Fletcher retreated, breathing heavily.

Quinn glared down at Louise. 'You came here to save people. People you've never seen. People you'll never know. Didn't you?'

Louise was sobbing from the pain, holding a hand to her face. Blood ran out of her mouth, dripping onto the floor. She looked up at him, devoid of understanding.

'Didn't you?'

'Yes,' she wept.

'I hate that *decency*. This assumption you have that you can connect with me on some level, because underneath I'm human too, that I have a heart. And in the end I'm going to be reasonable. That of course I'll back down and talk things out with the supercop fucks who've been shooting at my ass ever since I got back to this stinking garbage dump of a planet. That's why I hate you, Louise. You are the end product of a religion which has systematically set about shackling the serpent beast for over two and a half thousand years. Religions, all religions, forbid our true nature to shine through, they waken us so that we'll spend our whole lives grovelling in front of the false Lord. That's the path you embrace, Louise, that's what you are: kind-hearted. Just by existing you are the enemy of the Light Bringer. My enemy. I hate you so badly I'm in pain from it. And you'll pay for that. Nobody hurts me and goes off to laugh about it with their friends. I'll make you the army's whore. I'll make every one of my followers fuck you. They'll keep on fucking you until your mind shatters and your heart bursts. Then when there's nothing left but a lump of insane meat bleeding its life away into the gutter I'll use the soul-killer to eradicate what's left of you from the universe, because there's no way I'll ever share a single night in hell with you. You're not that worthy.'

Louise shrank away from him, crabbing across the floor until she was backed up against the altar. 'You can do all that, you can hurt me until I denounce everything I believe in. But you will never change what I am right now. And that's all that matters. I'm true to me. I've already had my victory.'

'Dumbass bitch. That's why you and your false Lord will always lose. Your victory's in your head. Mine is physical. It's as mother-fucking real as you can get.'

Louise looked defiantly at Quinn. 'When evil rules, then it will be goodness which corrupts you.'

'Total bollocks. The likes of you won't be able to corrupt the army I'm bringing onto the field. Tell her, Fletcher, be *honest* with her. Is my army going to win? Is the Night coming?'

'Fletcher?' she appealed to him.

'My lady . . . I.' His head drooped in abject despair.

'No,' Louise gasped. 'Fletcher!'

Quinn watched her, grinning in ferocious satisfaction. 'Ready to watch the bad part, now?' He reached down, and grabbed her shoulder, hauling her to her feet.

'Unhand her,' Fletcher demanded. A ball of solid air slammed into his belly, its impact firing pain down every nerve in his host body. He was thrown off the ground and sent tumbling backwards. Even when he landed hard on the tiles he kept skidding as if the surface was ice. When he stopped moving and regained his wits, he found he was directly under the apex of the dome.

'Don't move,' Quinn ordered.

A pentagon of tall white flames burst into existence around Fletcher to emphasize the point. He watched helplessly as Quinn dragged Louise along into the south transept. They went through a door.

There were stairs inside, spiralling upwards. Louise had to run to keep up with Quinn. The curving stairs went on and on, making her feel dangerously dizzy, and the pain from the side of her head was so intense she thought she was going to vomit.

They came out through a narrow archway onto the gallery ringing the dome. Quinn moved round it until he was facing down the nave. He thrust Louise towards a young girl in a leather waistcoat and pink jeans.

'Look after her,' he said.

At first Louise thought Courtney was a possessed; her hair was bright emerald, all of it standing on end and twirled into flame-like spikes. But there were scabs all over her cheeks and arms, unhealed and starting to fester, and one eye was swollen almost shut.

Courtney giggled as she held Louise tight. 'I get you first.' Her tongue licked round Louise's ear, hands closing tight on her buttocks.

Louise moaned as her legs gave out.

'Shit.' Courtney pushed her back onto the low bench which ran around the gallery.

'We won't live long enough for that,' Louise said harshly.

Courtney gave her a puzzled look.

Quinn put his hands on the rail, and looked down on his silent obedient followers packed into the nave. Fletcher Christian stood still at the centre of the flaming pentagram, head bent back so he could observe the gallery. Quinn gestured, and the prison of white flames vanished, leaving Fletcher alone on the floor.

'Before the Night dawns, there's one person missing from our gathering,' Quinn announced. 'Though I know he's here. You're always here, aren't you?' The silken tone of displeasure made his followers stir uneasily.

Quinn signalled the acolyte on the gallery, who led Greta round to him. She was pushed hard against the rail, almost going over. Quinn grabbed her by the scruff of her neck, tipping her head upright. Lank hair dangled down over her face as she drew a shaky breath.

'Say your name,' Quinn told her.

'Greta,' she mumbled.

He took the anti-memory weapon from his robe, and shoved it against her eye. 'Louder.'

'Greta. I'm Greta Manani.'

'Oh, Daddy,' Quinn called out. 'Daddy Manani, come out, come out wherever you are.'

The possessed crowded into the nave began to look round. Murmurs of confusion seeped out among them. Quinn scoured their heads for someone moving.

'Get out here, fuckhead! RIGHT NOW. Or I kill her soul. You hearing me?'

The sound of lone footsteps echoed through the cathedral. The hushed possessed parted in a smooth tide to allow Powel Manani through. The Ivet supervisor looked exactly the same as the last time Quinn had seen him back on Lalonde, a brawny man dressed in a red and green checked shirt. He walked out under the dome, put his hands on his hips, and grinned up at Quinn. 'I see you're still a total loser, Ivet.'

'I'm not a fucking Ivet!' Quinn screamed. 'I'm the Messiah of Night.'

'Whatever. If you harm my daughter, Messiah of dickheads everywhere, I'll personally finish the job Twelve-T started on Jesup.'

'I have been harming her. For a long time now.'

'Bet it isn't as bad as what we did to your friends Leslie and Kay, and all the other Ivets we caught.'

For a second Quinn contemplated vaulting over the rail and swooping down on the supervisor, feeding his serpent beast. The peak of rage subsided. That was what Manani probably wanted. Quinn could sense how strong the man's energistic power was. Using him as the sacrifice to the summoned dark angels was going to be much more satisfying.

'If you kill her,' Powel said, 'you have no protection from me. And if you blast this body to pieces, I'll just come back again like before. I'm going to keep on coming back until this is settled between us.'

'I'm not going to blast you out of your body, not after the grief you've caused me. I'm not that nice, remember. Now you stay exactly where you are, or I will kill your daughter's soul.'

Powel looked round the empty expanse of floor under the dome as if he was viewing an apartment. 'Guess you're on his shit list, too, huh,' he said to Fletcher.

'I am, sir.'

'Don't worry, he'll make a mistake. He's not smart enough to pull off something like this. And when it all goes pear-shaped, his balls are mine.'

Quinn spread his arms wide in an open embrace to the assembled possessed below. 'Now that everyone's here,' he said, 'we'll begin.'

*

Joshua managed to suppress his shock without any help from programs. He knew the importance of this moment was too great for anything other than perfect clarity. 'Are you the Tyrathca's Sleeping God?' he datavised.

'You know I am, Captain Calvert,' the singularity replied.

'If you know who I am, then the Tyrathca were correct saying that you see the universe.'

'The universe is too large for that, of course, but to reply in context, yes, I observe as much of the universe as you are aware of, and a great deal more besides. My quantum structure enables an extensive interconnection with a large volume of space-time and other realms.'

'Not one for small talk, is it,' Liol muttered.

'Then you know my species is being possessed by the souls of our own dead?' Joshua asked.

'Yes.'

'Is there a solution to this problem?'

'There are a great many solutions. As the Kiint have hinted to you, each race comes to terms with this aspect of life in its own way.'

'Please, do you know of one that's applicable to us?'

'Many are. I am not being deliberately obtuse. I can list them all, and I can and will assist you in applying them where relevant. What I will not do is make the decision for you.'

'Why?' Monica asked. 'Why are you helping us? It's not that I'm ungrateful. But I am curious.'

'The Tyrathca were also correct when they said I exist to assist the progress of biological entities. Though the particular circumstances humans are currently facing were not the reason I was created.'

'Then what were you made for?' Alkad asked.

'The race which created me had reached their evolutionary pinnacle; intellectually, physically, and in their technology. A fact which should be self-evident to you, Dr Mzu. My sentience resides within a self-contained pattern of vacuum fluctuations. This provides me with an extensive ability to manipulate mass and energy; for me thought is deed, the two are one and the same. I used that ability to open a gateway for my creators into a new realm. They knew little of it, other than it existed; its parameters are very different to this universe. So they chose to embark on a new phase of existence living within it. They left this universe a long time ago.'

'And you've been helping various species progress along evolution's track ever since?' Joshua said. 'Its your reason for existing?'

'I do not require a continuing reason to exist, a motivation. That psychology is a descendant of a biological sentience. My origins are not biological, I exist because they created me. It's that simple.'

'Then why do you help?'

'Again, the simple answer would be because I can. But there are other considerations. It is an amplification of the problem your species has encountered millions of times during its history, almost daily in fact. You were even subject to it at Mastrit-PJ. When and where not to intervene? Did you believe you did the right thing by giving the Mosdva ZTT technology? Your intentions were good, but ultimately they were governed by self-interest.'

'Did we do the wrong thing?'

'The Mosdva certainly don't think so. Such judgements are relative.'

'So you don't help everybody all the time?'

'No. Such a level of intervention, shaping the nature of biological life to conform with my wishes, however benevolent, would make me your ruler. Sentient life has free will. My creators believe that is why this universe exists. I respect that, and will not interfere with its self-determination.'

'Even when we make a mess of things?'

'That would be a judgement again.'

'But you are willing to help us if we ask?'

'Yes.'

Joshua looked at the projected image of the singularity, vaguely troubled. 'All right, we're definitely asking. Can we have the list of solutions?'

'You may. I would suggest they would be more useful if you understood what has happened. That way, you would be able to make a more informed decision on which one to apply.'

'Seems reasonable.'

'Wait,' Monica said. 'You keep mentioning we have to make a decision. How do we do that?'

'What are you talking about?' Liol asked. 'Once we've heard what's on offer, we choose.'

'We do? Are we going to put it to a vote here in the ship, do we go back to the Confederation Assembly and ask them to decide? What? We need to be certain about this first.'

Liol looked round the cabin, trying to identify the mood. 'No, we don't go back,' he said. 'This is what we came here for. The Jovian Consensus thought we were up to the job. So I say do it.'

'We're deciding the future of our whole race,' she protested. 'We can't just leap into this. And . . .' She indicated Mzu. 'Bloody hell, she's hardly qualified to be passing judgement on the rest of us. That's the way I see it. You were going to use the Alchemist against an entire planet.'

'Whereas the ESA is an organization of enviable morality,' Alkad snapped back. 'How many people did you murder just tracking me down?'

'You people have got to be fucking kidding,' Liol said. 'You can't even decide how to decide? Listen to yourselves! This kind of personal stupidity is what dumps humans into the shit every time. We just discuss it and make a decision. That's it. Finish.'

'No,' Samuel said. 'The Captain decides.'

'Me?' Joshua asked.

Monica stared at the Edenist in astonishment. 'Him!'

'Yes, I agree,' the serjeant said. 'Joshua decides.'

'He never doubted,' Samuel said. 'Did you, Joshua? You've always known this would end in success.'

'I hoped it would, sure.'

'You doubted this flight,' Samuel told Monica. 'You didn't fully believe it would end in success. If you had, you would have been prepared to make the decision. Instead, you have doubts, that disqualifies you. Whoever does this must have conviction.'

'Like yours, for instance,' Monica said. 'A subset of your famous rationality.'

'I too find myself unqualified for this. Although Edenists think as one, to make a decision of this magnitude I find myself wanting the reassurance of the Consensus. It would seem Edenism has a flaw after all.'

Joshua gazed round at his crew. 'You've all been very quiet.'

'That's because we trust you, Joshua,' Sarha said simply, and smiled. 'You're our captain.'

Strange, Joshua thought, when you got right down to the naked truth, people actually had faith in him. Who he was, what he'd achieved, meant something to them. It was quite humbling, really. 'All right,' he said slowly. He datavised the singularity: 'Is that acceptable to you?'

'I cannot take responsibility for your decisions, collective or otherwise. My only constraints are that I will not permit you to use my abilities as a weapon. Other than that, you have free access.'

'OK. Show me what happened.'

*

The possessed in the nave had dropped to their knees, concentrating hard on producing the stream of energistic power which the dark Messiah demanded from them for his summoning. Up on the gallery facing them, Quinn's robe evaporated into pure shadow, and began to flow out from his body, filling the air around him like a black spectre. At the heart, his naked body gleamed silver. He accepted the offering from his followers, and directed it as he pleased. It spilled down across the floor below the cathedral's dome, prying at the structure of reality, weakening it.

Powel Manani and Fletcher Christian looked down at their feet in consternation as the tiles around them sprouted a luminous purple haze. The soles of their shoes became enmeshed with the surface, making it hard to lift their feet up.

'I need to get near him,' Powel said.

Fletcher glanced up at the swarthy occultation looming above. 'I wish to be as far from this dread place as possible. But I will not leave without her.'

Powel exerted his own energistic power to yank his feet clear of the tiles, even then it took considerable effort to move them. He shuffled right up in front of Fletcher, the two of them almost touching. The bottom of his sweatshirt was lifted a couple of centimetres, revealing Louise's anti-memory weapon shoved into the top of his waistband.

'Very well,' Fletcher said. 'But it will be no easy endeavour. I hear the fallen angels approaching.'

The haze was thrumming, issuing a howl of lament and greed. Below that, the fabric of the universe was thinning in accordance with Quinn's desire. They could both feel pressure being exerted from the other side, a desperate scrabbling.

'Not good,' Powel said. The tiles were becoming insubstantial. He pulled his feet out again, they'd sunk several centimetres below the surface.

'I will made a stand and distract him,' Fletcher said. 'You may have time to reach the stairs.'

'I don't think so. This stuff is getting worse than quicksand.'

The purple haze vanished. Fletcher and Powel looked round wildly. A drop of ectoplasm dribbled up in a crack between two tiles, making a soft *blup*. A patch of dense white frost solidified around it.

'Now what?' Powel grunted with apprehension.

More ectoplasm was bubbling up. Sluggish rivulets began to form as it ran together. The tiles left uncovered had all turned sparkling white from frost. Fletcher could feel cold air rushing off the sludgy fluid. His breath had become hoary.

'Welcome, my brothers,' Quinn's voice boomed across the cathedral. 'Welcome to the battlefield. Together we will bring down the Night of our Lord.'

The entire area of floor underneath the dome had become a pool of burping and foaming ectoplasm. Fletcher and Powel were hopping from foot to foot, frantically trying to banish the excruciating cold from their legs. They suddenly stood still, tensing as a V-shaped ripple moved across the pool. Waves of hot lustful emotion were surging up from the dimensional rift in counter to the physical cold. A curving spike lifted up out of the floor, ectoplasm flowing along its length. It was over three metres high.

Fletcher watched it rise in horrified awe. Another one was emerging at the side of it, ectoplasm gurgling loudly as it lapped against the base.

'Lord Jesus protect Your servants,' he whispered. He and Powel backed away from the twin spikes as a third one budded.

The ectoplasm was bubbling energetically now. Smaller tendrils were writhing up, erupting all over the pool like a fur of rapacious cilia. One started to curl round Powel's leg. With a cry he managed to stumble away from it. The tip blossomed into a snapping five-talon claw. He pointed a finger at it, and flung a slim blast of white fire. The claw shuddered, and large ripples of ectoplasm surged towards it.

'Stop!' Fletcher shouted hoarsely. The ectoplasm licking its way up his legs was doing far more than freezing his flesh, he realized. His mental strength was diminishing, and with it his energistic power.

The claw's talons had almost doubled in size under the impact of the white fire. Powel snatched his hand back, watching anxiously as the claw groped round blindly.

Quinn laughed in delight as he watched the desperate antics of his sacrificial victims. There were five of the huge spikes now; they started to lean over. He wondered if they were the tips of some creature's fingers.

Moans of alarm were coming from the possessed down in the nave as they realized what they were witnessing. The first signs of panic were evident as the front rank pressed back from the edge of the ectoplasm pool.

'Hold fast!' Quinn thundered at them. The opening into darkness wasn't yet complete, it fluctuated as those below hurled themselves against it. Quinn concentrated his mind on the area where reality was distorted to breaking point.

A huge bubble of noxious fumes burst from the centre of the ectoplasm, releasing an undulating spume of smaller ones. Powel and Fletcher ducked as a spray of ectoplasm splattered outwards.

Tendrils of the stuff were wriggling against their legs now. Moving had become almost impossible, the agonizing cold was squeezing in against their limbs and chests.

A dark mass slowly shrugged its way out of the subsiding froth of bubbles. It was a metallic sphere with boxes and cylinders jutting out at odd angles. Streaks of molten nultherm insulation were running down its sides, mingling with the wreath of ectoplasm that drooled away in slippery ribbons.

'What the fuck is that?' Quinn demanded.

Explosive bolts cracked loudly, and a circular hatch flew away from the sphere. A fat man in a grubby toga jumped down, splashing into the ectoplasm pool without any noticeable discomfort.

Dariat looked round at his surroundings with considerable interest. 'Bad timing?' he asked.

Tolton walked straight through the escape pod's walls. He stood in the ectoplasm and let out a grateful sigh. Fletcher watched in fascination as the ectoplasm flowed up him, turning the ghost solid. He seemed so much more *vital* than any of the other entities struggling to fruit from the ectoplasm.

Powel Manani's deep laugh rocked the air. 'These are your terrifying warriors?' he mocked.

Quinn yelled in fury, and sent a white fireball ripping down at the derisive Ivet supervisor. A couple of centimetres from Powel it fractured into screeching webs of energy that never quite managed to touch him. The ectoplasm heaved enthusiastically as the crackling tips plunged into it.

A long frond of the stuff leapt up to whip round Powel's chest. Thicker, blunt tendrils were embracing his legs, knitting together. They began to pull him downwards. 'How do we kill this stuff?' he shouted at Dariat. It had taken a worrying amount of effort to deflect Quinn's firebolt, his strength was draining away rapidly.

'Fire,' Dariat called back. 'Real fire works against them.'

Something was lumbering up out of the pool next to Tolton, a creature five times his size, seven limbs unfolding from its flanks. He looked at Dariat, and the two of them linked hands. They sent a single bolt of white fire streaking into the base of the escape pod. The last two solid rocket motors ignited.

*

The events into which Joshua plunged had a form similar to a sensevise. They were real enough as they unravelled around him, but he witnessed them all simultaneously. At the same time, he could stand back and evaluate what was happening. That wasn't an ability the human mind could perform.

'You are using my thought-processing ability,' the singularity informed him.

'Then I'm no longer human. It will be you who makes the decision.'

'The essence of what you are remains unchanged. I have simply expanded your mental capacity. Consider this a supercompressed history didactic.'

So Joshua stood at Powel Manani's side on Lalonde as Quinn Dexter performed the sacrifice, and the Ly-cilph opened a gateway into the beyond, allowing the first souls to pour through. The possessed multiplied their numbers and spread down the Juliffe. He watched Warlow talking to Quinn Dexter at Durringham spaceport, and accept the payment for *Lady Mac* to carry him to Norfolk.

Ralph Hiltch took flight to Ombey and unleashed the possession of Mortonridge. The Liberation followed on, with Ketton Island vanishing into another realm.

'Are you the instrument that transferred the crystal entities there?' Joshua asked.

'No. That was another similar to myself. I am aware of several within this universe, though all are in superclusters very distant from here.'

Valisk and its descent into the mélange. Pernik. Nyvan. Koblat. Jesup. Kulu. Oshanko. Norfolk. Trafalgar. New California. André Duchamp. Meyer. Erick Thakrar. Jed Hinton. Other places, worlds and asteroids and ships and people; their lives wound together into a cohesive whole. Jay Hilton's unauthorized escape to the Kiint home system. Their remarkable arc of planets, housing the retired observers who gathered in front of Tracy's television, dunking chocolate biscuits into their tea as they watched the human race falling apart.

'Dick Keaton,' Joshua said with mild jubilation. 'I knew there was something odd about him.'

'The Kiint use many specially bred observers to gather data on different species,' the singularity said. 'For all their scientific prowess, they do not have my perceptive faculty. Corpus still utilizes technology to amass its information. Such methods can hardly be absolute.'

'Did they find you?'

'Yes. I could do nothing for them, and told them so. One day they will be able to build my like by themselves. Not for some time, though. There is no need. They have achieved an admirable harmony with the universe.'

'Yeah, so they keep telling us.'

'Not to taunt you. They are not a malicious species.'

'Can you show me the beyond as well?' Joshua asked. 'Can you tell me how to travel through it successfully like they do?'

'It has no distance,' the singularity said. 'It only has time. That is the direction in which you must travel.'

'I don't understand.'

'This universe and all it is connected with will come to an end. Entropy carries us towards the inevitable omega point, that is why entropy exists. What is to be born next cannot be known until then. This is the time when the pattern of that which replaces it will be created, a pattern which will emerge out of mind, the collective experience of all who have lived. That is where souls go, their transcendence brings all that they are together into a single act of creation.'

'Then why do they get stuck in the beyond?'

'Because that is where they want to be; like the ghosts wedded to the place of their anguish, they refuse to discard the part of their life which is over. They are afraid, Joshua. From the beyond they can still see the universe they have left behind. All they have known, the condition that they were, everyone they have loved, is still obtainable, so very, very close to them. They fear to leave that for the unknown future.'

'All of us are frightened of the future. That's human nature.'

'But some of you venture into it with confidence. That's why you are here today, Joshua, that's why you found me. You believed in the future. You believed in yourself. That is the most precious possession any human can ever own.'

'That's it? That's all there ever was? Faith in yourself?'

'Yes.'

'Then why in God's name didn't the Kiint tell us that? You said they weren't malicious. What possible reason can they have for denying us that? A few simple words.'

'Because you have to implement that knowledge as an entire species. How you do that is your own decision.'

'It's a bloody simple decision. You just tell them.'

'Telling someone not to be afraid is one thing. To have them believe it at an instinctive level is quite another. In order not to be afraid of the beyond you must either understand its purpose, or have the naked conviction to move on once you encounter it. How many of your race are uneducated, Joshua? I don't mean those of you alive now, I mean throughout history. How many have lived unfulfilled lives? How many have died in infancy or in profound ignorance? You don't have to tell the rich and the educated, the privileged, they are the ones who will begin the great journey through the beyond of their own accord. It is the others you must convince, the ignorant masses, yet paradoxically, they are the ones hardest for you to reach. Theirs are the minds which thanks to circumstance have set and hardened against new concepts and ideas from an early age.'

'But they can still be taught. They can learn to believe in themselves, everyone can. It's never too late for that.'

'You speak of high idealism, but still you have to implement your ideals in the real, practical world. How will you reach these people? Who will pay to provide every one of them with a personal tutor, a guru who will advance their inner spirit?'

'Jesus, I don't know. How did other races do it?'

'They developed socially.'

'The Laymil didn't, they committed suicide.'

'Yes, but by that time they understood the nature of the beyond. Every one of them took the leap forward knowing that they still had a future. Their suicide was not racial extermination, a method of simply thwarting their possessing souls; they carried what they are to the omega point as one. That is what their communal society permitted them to do.'

'I get it. The Laymil possessing souls were from a time before they reached that communal society.'

'Yes. As most of your possessed are from earlier times. But not all, not by any means. Your race has not eliminated poverty, Joshua. You have not liberated people from physical drudgery to develop their minds. If you have a flaw in your nature, then it is that. You cling to what is comfortable, the old familiar. I suspect that is why humans have a slightly higher than average percentage of souls lingering in the beyond.'

'We've done pretty well in the last thousand years,' he said, irked. 'The Confederation is one vast middle-class estate.'

'The parts you travel to are. And even there "comfortable" does not equate with "satisfactory". You are not animals, Joshua. Yet the entire population on some of your planets perform mundane agrarian tasks.'

'It costs to build automated factories. Global economies have to develop to a level where it becomes affordable.'

'You have the technology to travel between the stars, and all you do when you get to your fresh world is start the old cycle over again. Only one new type of society has emerged in the last thousand years, the Edenists; and even they participate in and perpetuate your economic structure. The nature of society is governed by economic circumstance, and for all of your vast collective wealth, for all your knowledge, you remain stagnant. Throughout your voyage here you and your crew discussed how the Tyrathca were so slow to change compared to humans. Now you have seen the Kiint home system, how far ahead of you do you think their technology lies? It is a small gap, Joshua. Molecular-level replicator technology would bring about the end of your entire economic structure. If you wanted to, how long do you think it would take the combined scientific resources of the Confederation to build a prototype replicator?'

'I don't know. Not long.'

'No. Not long. The knowledge is there, but you lack the will. Although there is one final inhibiting factor we haven't incorporated yet into your knowledge base. And it's an important one.'

'I have my suspicions about you,' Joshua said. 'You with your avowed non-interventionist policy.'

'Yes?'

'How did I get here?'

'By chance.'

'A very long chance. A Tyrathca arkship is damaged while entering a star system devoid of any mass. Thousands of years later during the possession crisis we hear about something which might be able to solve the crisis for us. Would you like to compute the odds of that happening?'

'There are no odds, there is only cause and effect. The Tyrathca didn't inform you of the Sleeping God when you first encountered them because until the human possession crisis started they had no need to pray to it. You found me because you looked, Joshua. You believed I existed. Quinn Dexter has found his army of darkness because he too has conviction. Greater than yours, I would suggest. Was he led to them by omnipotent entities playing chess with lives?'

'All right. But you've got to admit, having you this close to the Confederation is a hell of a coincidence given there's only one of you per galactic supercluster.'

'That is not a coincidence, Joshua. I am aware of everything, because I am connected to everything. When you search for me, and have sufficient faith that you will find me, then you will succeed.'

'OK. Well, if I haven't said it before: thank you. I'll do my best to see your faith isn't misplaced. Now, what was that last factor?'

The singularity showed him, delivering his awareness to the orbital tower down which he rode down to Earth, with B7, Quinn Dexter, and . . .

Joshua's eyes flicked open. His crew broke off their conversations, looking at him in anticipation.

'Louise,' he said. And vanished.

*

Thick smoke and blinding yellow flame exploded out of the escape pod rocket motors. The noise was a sheer wall of energy that sent Fletcher and Powel flailing backwards. Light punched down into Fletcher's eyes as he used the remnants of his energistic power to ward off the blast.

The escape pod wobbled upwards, gathering speed. Flame splayed out from its base, scouring the surface of the ectoplasm pool. Embryonic shapes melted away under the incendiary heat. A cloud of clammy fumes billowed out, hurtling down the nave and both transepts. Brittle, ancient stained-glass windows shattered under the tremendous pressure. Horizontal jets of smoke and ectoplasm smog roared out over the deserted plaza.

The escape pod smashed into the top of the cathedral dome and crashed through into the pre-dawn morning. Its trajectory was given a savage kick by the impact, sending it racing away in a low curve underneath the red cloud, out towards Holborn.

Down on the floor of the cathedral, it was impossible to see anything. The air was coagulated with icy particles and vile acidic smoke. Fletcher sloshed about in the raging ectoplasm pool, trying to find anything that would give him his bearings. His mind could sense the possessed in the nave, their fear-ordered discipline was starting to crumble. Apart from them, nothing was clear. Chunks of debris were whistling down from above, splattering down into the turbid fluid where they immediately cracked open from the cold.

'Anybody left standing?' Powel shouted somewhere in the murk.

A vermilion glimmer began to pervade the churning mist as the light from the red cloud shone in through the gaping windows. Folds of darkness slipped across Fletcher's vision. He stood still, not daring to move.

Powel bumped into him. Both of them jumped.

'I've got to get up to the gallery,' Powel said. 'This is our chance, he'll be as blind as us.'

'I think the door is this way,' Fletcher told him. Even using his energistic power to bolster his legs, they moved reluctantly. He could feel nothing below his knees.

The mist began to scintillate with white light. It abruptly turned heavy, sighing as it sank to the ground. The rumpled upper surface descended around Fletcher, leaving him totally exposed. A wide beam of red light shone down through the hole in the dome, illuminating the whole ectoplasm pool. On the other side, Dariat and Tolton were caught in the act of trying to reach the north transept.

'Going somewhere?' Quinn asked. 'There's nowhere to run. The warriors of the Light Bringer are here.' With a theatrical motion, he gestured at the pool, conjuring its inhabitants up.

A vast upwelling of ectoplasm sent waves of the fluid pouring lazily down the nave and transepts. The crown of an Orgathé slipped smoothly upwards, emerging into the crimson light.

Quinn laughed uproariously as the monster rose into the universe. Possessed fled screaming through the cathedral doors. Powel and

Fletcher were drowning in undead sludge that sent out eager pseudopods to smother their heads. At his feet Louise and Greta lay broken and defeated, shedding tears for the torment to come. It was Night as he'd always dreamed it would be.

Something *happened* far above him. His head jerked up. 'Fuck!'

*

Andy Behoo had spent the whole time pressed against his window, watching the ugly red cloud creeping across London. Hot air helped to magnify the incursion with awful clarity. Above the arcology's crystal dome, the stars shone down with cold beauty through a storm-free sky. It would have been a lovely dawn.

Now he knew he wouldn't even see that. His neural nanonics had crashed. The front edge of the cloud was less than a quarter of a mile away. Underneath it, the eerily pervasive red light helped to illuminate the vacant streets.

He'd clung to this window when she left, staring after her mutely; so he knew which street she'd taken. If she came back, he would be able to see her. That alone would give him the courage to leave the tenement. He would go out and fetch her home. Louise would make the end liveable.

The crimson light inside the cloud flickered and died. It was so sudden Andy thought there was something wrong with his eyes. All that remained of the frightened city were outlines so faint he could be imagining them. He scoured them for signs that the SD weapons had begun their slaughter.

Nothing moved in the dead silence. He looked up.

There were no stars any more.

*

The wormhole interstice opened a million kilometres above the sun's south pole. Its edges immediately expanded. Within three seconds it was over one and a half billion kilometres in diameter, greater than Jupiter's orbit. Fifteen seconds later it reached the size Joshua had designated: twelve billion kilometres across, just wider than the entire solar system. It moved forwards, enveloping stars, planets, asteroids, and comets alike.

The interstice contracted to nothing.

All that remained was a single human figure in a black robe, tumbling wildly through space.

*

In Tracy's lounge, Arnie got up and thumped the top of the television. The picture didn't return.

'What's happening now?' Jay asked.

'Corpus doesn't know,' Tracy said. Her hands trembled at the revelation.

*

Over seventeen million possessing souls in various arcologies were exorcized from their captive bodies as Earth moved into the wormhole. Joshua arranged its internal quantum structure in a fashion similar to the conditions Dariat and Rubra had used to expel the possessors from Valisk. There was one difference, they didn't become ghosts, this time they were torn cursing in anguish straight back into the beyond.

*

From Earth, orbiting thirty thousand light-years from the centre of the galaxy, the glorious blaze of the core stars had never been visible. There was too much dark mass spread throughout the spiral arms, interstellar gas clouds and dust storms absorbing the light spun off from the densely packed supergiants. Astronomers had to turn their telescopes outwards, studying other starpools to see what such a spectacle might be like.

You had to be a lot closer in towards the centre to see the core's corona starting to expand over the shielding plane of dark matter. Even then, it would only be an exceptionally bright crescent nebula stretched across the night sky. To witness its full glory, a planet needed to be perched right at the root of the spiral arms where the core appeared as an iridescent cloak of silver-white light across half of space, outshining the local sun. Regrettably, such a place was lethal; a fierce outpouring of intense radiation from the tightly clustered stars would immediately sterilize any unprotected biological life.

No, to gain a full appreciation of the galaxy's native beauty, it had to be observed from outside. Above the spiral arms, and away from the radiation.

Joshua chose a location twenty thousand light-years out from the core, and ten thousand to the north of the ecliptic. The solar system emerged there to be greeted with the sight of a majestic bejewelled cyclone shining fiercely against a blackness devoid of any constellations.

The Kulu system was the next to arrive. Then Oshanko. Followed by Avon. Ombey. New California. They no longer emerged one at a time. The singularity was capable of creating wormholes simultaneously. Joshua shifted his participation to the executive, selecting what was to be taken. Gateways were opened into the realms where the possessed had fled with their planets. Lalonde, Norfolk, and all the others were returned to their stars, then moved out of the galaxy.

The Confederation soon formed its own unique, isolated stellar cluster sailing serenely through intergalactic space. Eight hundred stars orchestrated into a classic lenticular formation with Sol at the centre, and the rest never more than half a light-year from each other.

Other, more subtle, astronomical modifications were made, seeds of the changes to come.

*

Quinn didn't understand why he was still alive. During the cataclysm, Edmund Rigby's pitiful soul had been wrenched from the prison he'd forged at the centre of his mind. He no longer had any contact with the beyond, no interdimensional rift to bestow his fabulous energistic power. No magical sixth sense. And he was floating through empty space, with air to breathe.

'My Lord,' he cried. 'Why? Why did You take the victory from me? Nobody has served You better.'

There was no answer.

'Let me go back. Let me prove myself. I can make Night fall. I will ride the dark angels into heaven, we will tear it down and sit You upon the throne.'

A human figure appeared in front of him, bathed in gentle starlight. Quinn drew in an excited breath as he drew closer. It was spat out in disgust as he recognized the face. 'You!'

'Hi, Quinn,' said Joshua. 'Ranting won't do you any good. I resealed the opening to the dark continuum, the fallen angels aren't coming to rescue you. Nobody is.'

'God's Brother will win. Night will fall with or without me at the head of His army.'

'I know.'

Quinn gave him a suspicious glare.

'You were right all along, though not in a way you imagined. This universe ends in darkness.'

'You believe that? You accept the gospel of God's Brother?'

'Your gospel is a load of shit, and you're the only arsehole to squirt it out, Quinn.'

'I will find your soul in the beyond. When I do I will crush your pride and—'

'Oh, shut up. I have an offer for you. In words you'll understand, I want you to lead the lost souls to your Lord.'

'Why?'

'Many reasons. You deserve to be erased from time for what you did. But I can't do that.'

Quinn started to laugh. 'You're an angel of the false Lord. That's why you have the power to snatch me away from Earth. Yet He won't let you kill me, will He? He is too compassionate. How you must hate that.'

'There are worse things than death and the beyond. I can deliver you to the fallen angels. Do you think they'll be happy to see someone who failed to free them?'

'What do you want?'

A circular opening in space expanded behind Joshua. 'This leads into Night, Quinn. It's a wormhole that takes you straight to the time of God's Brother. I'll allow you to go through it.'

'Name your price.'

'I've told you, lead the damned souls out of the beyond and into your Night. Without them, the human race will stand a chance to grow. They are a terrible burden on any species who discovers the true nature of the universe. The Kiint, for instance, cloned mindless bodies to house their lost souls. It took them thousands of years, but every one was brought back, and loved, and taught to face the beyond as it should be faced. But that's the Kiint, not us. We're going to have a big enough task helping the living over the next few decades. There's no way we can deal with all those billions of lost souls, not for centuries. And all that time, they'll be suffering and inhibiting our development.'

'My heart bleeds.'

'You don't have one.' Joshua drifted to one side. There was nothing between Quinn and the opening now. 'Now tell me, do you want to meet God's Brother?'

'Yes.' Quinn stared greedily into the absolute blackness revealed by the opening. 'Yes!'

The souls who had been cast back into the beyond brought with them a devastating tide of bitterness and fury as they raged impotently against the atrocity. Freedom existed, it was possible to regain a life. Now there was only purgatory again. No chink existed in the barrier between them and reality. They screamed their wrath, at the same time pleading with those they could dimly sense moving on the other side. Begging to be let back, for just one last taste of sensation. None of the living heard them any more.

A fissure opened. One small precious gap leaking the most gorgeous human sensations into the cursed void. They flocked around it, rejoicing in its magic. And there was enough for all to feast upon. Every lost soul knew the touch of air upon skin, saw a myriad constellations shimmering against the night sky.

Quinn screamed himself raw as he was possessed by a hundred billion lost souls. Their violation was total, devouring the import of every single cell that was him.

His body soared through the opening, carrying the burden of humanity with him. The wormhole closed behind them, cutting off the sight of the stars which humans had always known as their own.

29

Though it would never be told this way, Louise actually spent most of the summoning ceremony unaware of what was happening. After Courtney shoved her down on the bench she rolled onto her side, fighting the dreadful nausea. Little of anything Quinn said registered through the pain and misery. The backlash from the energistic power marshalled by the possessed set off concussions of fright inside her skull.

Then the solid rocket motors ignited, smothering her in choking smoke. She was on the floor retching desperately as the Orgathé drew up level with the gallery.

She lay there shivering between peaks of flame and ice, and crying wretchedly. Then all the external sensations began to die away, abandoning her in a stinking grainy grey smog that obscured everything save a few yards of the gallery.

Footsteps crunched on the powdery debris that'd showered down when the escape pod hit the cathedral's dome. They stopped beside her. She moaned, aware that the person was bending down. A hand stroked the side of her head, tenderly brushing the hair from her eyes.

'Hello, Louise. I said I'd come back for you.'

It was the wrong voice. An impossibility. But so utterly right. Louise blinked up, and tears flooded her eyes again. 'Joshua!'

His arms went round her, and he kept saying: 'Shush, it's all right, it's all right,' as he rocked her shaking body against him.

'But, Joshua—'

He kissed her gently, tapped his forefinger on her nose. 'It's OK, it's all over. I promise.'

'Quinn,' she gasped. 'Quinn, he's . . .'

'Gone. Over. Finished.'

Her head swung from side to side, seeing the tendrils of smog slowly withdrawing from the gallery. The cathedral below was shockingly quiet.

'Here,' Joshua said. 'Let's get you sorted out.' He pulled the wrapping off a medical nanonic package, and applied it gently to her face where Quinn had struck her.

She realized her neural nanonics were back on-line, and hurriedly put her medical monitor program into primary.

'It's all right,' Joshua said softly. 'Our baby's fine.'

'Huh,' Louise grunted. 'How do you know about . . .'

He kissed her hand. 'I know everything,' he said with that beautifully wicked Joshua grin. The very same one which had started all this. Louise thought she might even be blushing.

'If you could hang on to the questions for a moment,' he said. 'There's someone you have to say goodbye to.'

Louise let him help her up to her feet, glad of the assistance. Every part of her seemed to be aching and stiff. When they were standing, she just couldn't resist giving him another kiss, making sure he was real. And no way was she going to let go of his hand. Then she saw Fletcher standing behind him.

'My lady.' Fletcher bowed deeply.

She drew a sharp breath. 'The possessed.'

'Gone,' Joshua said. 'Except for Fletcher. And he's not exactly possessing anybody any more, this is a simulacrum body.' He offered his hand to the solemn naval officer. 'I wanted to thank you in person for looking after Louise through all this.'

Fletcher nodded gravely. 'I confess I have been curious as to what man might be worthy of lady Louise. I see now why she speaks of no other.'

Louise knew for sure she was blushing this time.

'Am I now to return to that purgatory, sir?'

'No,' Joshua said. 'That's something else I wanted to tell you. You were there because of your own decency. Leaving your family and your country, mutinying against your King, were all terrible crimes.

You convinced yourself of that, and imposed your own punishment. Purgatory was what you believed you deserved.'

Fletcher's eyes darkened with remembered pain. 'In my heart I knew what we were doing was wrong. But Bligh was cruel beyond any man's endurance. We could withstand no more.'

'It's over now,' Joshua said. 'It's been over for nearly a thousand years. What you have done for Louise and others this time is enough to pardon a hundred mutinies. Have courage, Fletcher, the beyond is not all there is. Sail through it. Find the shore that lies on the other side. It *is* there.'

'I could never doubt a man of your valour, sir. I will do as you say.'

Joshua stood aside.

'My lady.'

She hugged him tightly. 'I don't want you to go.'

'This is not where I belong, my dearest Louise. I am adrift here.'

'I know.'

'But still, I consider myself privileged that I have known you, however bizarre the circumstances. You will prosper, I foretell, and your child too. Your universe is a many-splendoured thing. Live your life in it to the full.'

'I will. I promise.'

He kissed her on the brow, almost a blessing. 'And tell the little one I shall think of her always.'

'*Bon voyage*, Fletcher.'

His body began to attenuate, its boundary dissolving into wisps of platinum stardust. An arm was raised in a farewell salute.

Louise stared at the empty space it left for some time. 'Now what?' she asked.

'A few explanations, I think,' Joshua said. 'I'd better take you over to Tranquillity for that. You need to clean up and rest. And Genevieve is doing truly awful things to the servitor housechimps.'

Louise began to groan. Her breath stalled as the lush parkland of the habitat quietly materialized around her.

*

Samual Aleksandrovich had spent the last ten minutes accessing the station's external sensor suite. Even so, he had to see for himself before he could truly believe. The SD control centre had been alarmed by the number of starships which kept appearing above Avon, but swiftly discovered they were all ships which had been en route to other stars. They'd been snatched from interstellar space, emerging in the designated zones above the planet. Once the First Admiral confirmed they weren't an attack force, he and Lalwani took a lift capsule to the observation lounge.

The big compartment was crowded with naval personnel. They parted reluctantly to allow both admirals through to the curving transparent wall. Samual looked out in trepidation at space without stars. The station's rotation slowly brought the galaxy into view; its core shining gold and violet, embraced by the silver shimmer whorl of satellite stars.

'Is it ours?' Samual asked quietly.

'Yes, sir,' Captain al-Sahhaf said. 'SD Command is using the sensor satellites to identify neighbouring galaxies. They correspond to the known pattern, which puts us approximately ten thousand light-years outside.'

Samual Aleksandrovich turned to Lalwani. 'Is this where the possessed come, do you think?'

'I've no idea.'

'Ten thousand light-years. What in God's name did this to us?'

'Joshua Calvert did, sir.'

Samual Aleksandrovich gave Richard Keaton a very suspicious look. 'Would you care to qualify that remark, Lieutenant?'

'Calvert and the voidhawk *Oenone* succeeded in their mission, sir. They found the Tyrathca Sleeping God. It's an artefact capable of generating wormholes on this scale.'

Samual and Lalwani traded a look.

'You seem remarkably well informed,' Lalwani said. 'I'm not aware of any communication from *Oenone* or the *Lady Macbeth* reaching us since we arrived here.'

Keaton gave an embarrassed smile. 'I apologize that you didn't know in advance. Nonetheless, Calvert transferred every Confederation world out here.'

'Why?' Samual asked.

'Moving a possessed body through the specific class of wormhole we just came through closes the rift which allows a soul to extrude from the beyond into this universe. He simply did it en masse. The lost souls have all been returned to the beyond. He also brought back all the planets which the possessed had taken away.' Keaton gestured at the empty void outside. 'The whole Confederation is here. There is no more possession crisis.'

'It's over?'

'Yes, sir.'

Samual narrowed his eyes as he contemplated his staff captain for a long moment. 'The Kiint,' he said eventually.

'Yes, sir. I'm sorry, I am one of their operatives.'

'I see. And what part did they play in all this?'

'None.' Keaton grinned. 'This surprised the hell out of them, too.'

'I'm glad to hear it.' Samual glanced out at the galaxy again as it began to slide from view. 'Is Calvert going to take us back?'

'I don't know.'

'The Kiint agreed they would help us with medical supplies if we solved this crisis. Will they honour that promise?'

'Yes, sir. Ambassador Roulour will be happy to extend the Kiint government's full cooperation with the Confederation.'

'Good. Now get your shabby arse out of my headquarters.'

*

The doors parted before Joshua could datavise his arrival.

'Welcome home,' Ione said. She dabbed a platonic kiss on his cheek.

He led Louise into the apartment, enjoying her little gasp of astonishment as she saw the glass wall looking out over the bottom of the circumfluous sea.

'You're the Lord of Ruin,' Louise said.

'And you're Louise Kavanagh, from Norfolk. Joshua talks about you all the time.'

Louise smiled as if she didn't believe. 'He does?'

'Oh, yes. And what he hasn't told me about you, Genevieve certainly has.'

'Is she all right?'

'She's fine. I've got Horst Elwes looking after her. They're on their way. Which should just give you time to freshen up.'

Louise glanced down at Andy's dilapidated clothes. 'Please.'

Joshua poured himself a hefty glass of Norfolk Tears while Ione was showing Louise the bathroom. 'Thanks,' he said when she came back.

'You did it, didn't you? That's why we're here.'

Yeah. I did it. No more possessed.

A plucked eyebrow was raised delicately. **And when did you pick up this ability?**

A little gift from the Sleeping God. He let the memories flood out directly, showing her and Tranquillity what had happened.

I was right about you, all along. Her arms circled round him, and she stood on her toes to give him a kiss.

Joshua gave the door to the bathroom a guilty glance.

Ione smiled wisely. **Don't worry. I won't mess things up.**

'I don't know what to do about her, Ione. Damn it, I ruled the universe, I was given the answers to everything, and I don't know what to do.'

'Don't be stupid, Joshua, of course you know. You've always known.'

*

Brad Lovegrove regained control of his body as if waking from a debilitating coma. Every thought, every action, was dreadfully slow and confused. The whole period of Capone's possession retained the constituency of a feverish dream, flashes of revolting clarity stitched together by slipstream blurs of sensation and colour.

He found he was sitting at a glass-topped table. It was in the lounge of a five-star hotel suite. A big picture window showed New California sliding past outside. There was a pot of hot coffee in front of him, cups, a plate with a pile of scrambled eggs. A thick pool of blood was spreading over the glass, flowing round the plate to reach the edge. Big scarlet drops splattered onto the carpet around his feet.

A woman in the chair opposite was crumpled over her half of the table. Three-quarters of her body was covered in green medical nanonic packages, with a navy-blue towelling robe worn over them. One package from her throat had been removed and placed on the table. The skin it exposed had a savagely deep cut, opening her carotid artery. There was a small fission blade knife nestling in the hand of her outstretched arm.

Brad Lovegrove fell off his chair, burbling incoherently with shock.

*

Joshua and Louise waited by the airlock hatch of docking-bay MB 0–330. They'd both accessed the sensors around the bay, watching *Lady Macbeth* settle lightly on the cradle. Her chemical verniers puffed out fast bursts of bright yellow flame around the equator as Liol brought her in. She touched the cradle in perfect alignment, and the holding latches closed. Utility hoses and cables rose up to jack in one by one. Thermo-dump panels folded down into the hull, and the whole assembly started to sink down into the bay.

He did that well, Joshua admitted to himself. **How are you doing?** he asked Syrinx.

Almost there, she told him.

Affinity showed him the big voidhawk sticking close to the *Mindori* and *Stryla* as the blackhawks curved round the spaceport spindle to chase the habitat's docking-ledge. The two blackhawks needed guiding and coaxing, their personalities were almost traumatized into catatonia by the possession. Both of them desperately wanted their lost captains. It wouldn't happen, Joshua knew, Kiera had destroyed the bodies back on Valisk, forcing the newly possessing souls into the blackhawks.

They will recover with time, *Oenone* said softly. **We will be here for them.**

I'm sure you will.

Congratulations, Joshua Calvert, the Jovian Consensus said. **And our profound thanks. Samuel has told us that it was you alone who communed with the singularity.**

I had plenty of help reaching it, he said. A smile image flashed between himself and Syrinx.

Your method of terminating the crisis was spectacular, Consensus said.

Believe me, it was one of the quiet options. Godpower is a modest understatement for the singularity's abilities.

Are you still in contact?

Yes. For the moment. There's a few loose ends I want to tie up myself. After that, it's over.

To abandon such power requires considerable strength of character. We are happy to see Samuel's faith was not misplaced.

To be honest, a life spent jumping round the Confederation righting wrongs really doesn't appeal. From now on all I carry is a message.

Joshua Calvert, missionary, Syrinx teased. **Now there's a real miracle.**

Will you be returning the Confederation stars to their original position? Consensus asked.

No. I want them to stay here. That also is my decision.

And one we will have to abide by. After all, it will not be easy for us to send a starship back to the Sleeping God from here.

It's not impossible. But then that's the whole point.

Would you explain?

Humans have been lucky in the past, expanding and colonizing our way across the galaxy. I'm not knocking it. Things were pretty bad back there on Earth for a while. As a species we needed to get away, as the old saying goes, to put our eggs in more than one basket. But it can't go on for ever. We have to face up to the future, and develop in different ways. There are eight hundred stars out here in this cluster, that's all. There can be no more physical expansion at our current social, economic, and technological level. No more running away from our problems, we're mature enough to address them now.

And our isolation will ensure that we do.

I'm hoping it will concentrate a few minds, yes.

We will live in interesting times.

All times are interesting if you know how to live them properly, Joshua said. I have the new coordinates of the other stars for you. You'll have to send out voidhawks to them and spread the information, put us all back in contact.

Of course.

Joshua let the information flow out of his mind and into the Consensus.

The airlock opened, and his crew came flooding out yelling raucous greetings.

Liol hugged him first. 'Fine bloody captain you make! You abandon us there to have fun all by yourself, and the next thing we know we've got Jupiter's SD Command screaming at us.'

'I brought you back, what more do you want?'

Sarha squealed and wrapped herself round him. 'You did it!' She kissed his ear. 'And what a view.'

Dahybi slapped his back, laughing ecstatically. There was Ashly, and Beaulieu pushing at each other to get at him. Monica said, 'Looks like you got it right,' without sounding too much of a grudge. Samuel chuckled at her obstinacy. Kempster and Renato chided him for cutting off their observations so abruptly. Mzu barely thanked him before asking about the singularity's internal quantum structure.

In the end he held up his arms and shouted at them all to shut the hell up. 'Party in Harkey's Bar, right now, and the drinks are on me.'

*

Beth and Jed were pressed up against the big port in the lounge as Tranquillity expanded outside.

'It looks just like Valisk,' he said excitedly.

'Let me see!' Navar demanded.

Jed grinned, and they stepped aside. The lounge was weird now. The outlines of the steamship fittings ran through the actual walls and equipment, solid ridges cutting through composite and alloy alike. Hints of the false colours and textures were still there if he squinted hard and remembered what had gone before.

They knew where they were and roughly what had happened, because *Mindori* had spoken to them a couple of times. But the blackhawk wasn't very communicative.

'I think we're landing,' Webster said.

'Sounds good,' Jed said. He got in a good kiss with Beth. Gari gave them one dismissive glance, and went back to watching the docking-ledge.

'We'd better check on Gerald,' Beth said.

Jed tried to be a sport. At least the old loon would finally be out of his life after they landed. 'Right, sure do's.'

Gerald hadn't moved from the bridge since the amazing xenoc diskcity vanished abruptly, and Loren's possession had ended. For hour after hour during the stand-off he had stood at the weapons console, like some old-time mariner gripping the wheel during a storm. His vigilance never wavered the whole time. When it ended, he'd slithered down and sat there, legs splayed on the floor, back propped up against the side of the console. He stared straight ahead through hazed eyes, not saying a word.

Beth crouched down beside him, and clicked her fingers in front of his face. There was no response.

'Is he dead?' Jed asked.

'Jed! No, he's not. He's breathing. I think he must have some kind of exhaustion problem.'

'We'll add it to the list,' Jed muttered, *very* quietly. 'Hey Gerald, mate, we've landed. The *Stryla* came down with us. That's the one with Marie in. Good, huh? You'll be seeing her soon, then. How about that?'

Gerald kept staring ahead, unmoving.

'Guess we'd better ask for a doc to see him,' Jed said.

Gerald turned his head. 'Marie?' he whispered.

'That's it, Gerald,' Beth said. She gripped his upper arm tightly. 'Marie's here. Just a few minutes now and you can see her again. Can you get up?' She tried to lift him, stir him into moving. 'Jed, shift yourself.'

'I dunno. Maybe we should leave him for the doc.'

'He's fine. Aren't you, Gerald, mate. Just knackered, that's what.'

'Well, OK.' Jed leant over, and tried to tug Gerald up.

Several loud clanking sounds came from the airlock.

Gari ran in. 'The bus is here,' she said breathlessly.

'It'll take us to Marie,' Beth said encouragingly. 'Come on, Gerald. You can do it.'

His legs twitched feebly.

Between them, they got him standing. With one on either side, and Gerald's arms round their shoulders, they shuffled him towards the airlock.

*

Marie sat hunched up on the corridor floor outside the bridge. She hadn't stopped crying since Kiera had been exorcized. The memories of what had happened since Lalonde were vivid, deliberately so. Kiera hadn't cared about Marie knowing what was going on, what her body was doing.

It was disgusting. Filthy.

Even though it wasn't herself performing those acts, Marie knew she would never banish what her body had done. Kiera's soul might have gone, but her haunting would never be over.

She'd been given her life back, and couldn't see a single reason for living it.

The airlock cycled, and the hatch whirred open.

'Marie.'

It was a frail, pained croak, but it sliced right into her soul. 'Daddy?' she moaned incredulously. When she looked up he was standing in the airlock, holding on to the rim. He looked dreadful, barely managing to stand. But his frail old face was suffused with all the joy of a father holding his infant child for the first time. She couldn't begin to imagine what he'd gone through to be here at this time. And he'd suffered it all because she was his daughter, and that alone entitled her to his love for ever.

She stood, and held out both hands to him. Wanting a cuddle from Daddy. Wanting him to take her home where none of this would ever happen.

Gerald smiled wondrously at his pretty little daughter. 'I love you, Marie.' His body gave way, pitching him face first onto the floor.

Marie screamed and ran forwards. His breath was juddering, eyes closed.

'Daddy! Daddy, no!' She pawed at him in hysterics. 'Daddy, talk to me!'

The steward from the bus was shouldering her aside, waving a medical block sensor along Gerald's inert body. 'Oh, shit. Give me a hand,' he yelled at Jed. 'We've got to get him into the habitat.'

Jed was staring at Marie, unable to move. 'It's you,' he said, enchanted.

Beth pushed past him, and knelt beside the steward. A life-support package had covered Gerald's face, pumping air into his lungs.

'Medical emergency,' the steward datavised. 'Get a crash team to the reception lounge.' The medical block datavised a violent alarm as Gerald's heart stopped. He tore the wrapping from a paramedic package, and slapped it across Gerald's neck. Nanonic filaments invaded his throat, seeking out the major arteries and veins, pumping in artificial blood, keeping the brain alive.

*

Rather sheepishly, the participants from The Disco at the End of the World were wandering across the concrete yard in a hungover stupor, watching dawn break over the arcology. It wasn't something any of them had expected to see.

Andy was down there with them, datavising questor after questor into the segments of the net that were coming back on-line. Satellites were providing temporary coverage as the civil authorities began to re-establish some kind of control. Nothing he did could bring an acknowledgement from her neural nanonics. Every programming trick he knew was useless.

He started to walk towards the gate out onto the road. She was out there somewhere, if he had to search the whole arcology himself, he would find her.

'What's that?' someone asked.

People were stopping and looking up at the dome. The sun had only just risen over the eastern rim; it showed a low bank of grey cloud washing in from the north. It reached the geodesic crystal structure and flowed gently round it. Not an armada storm; in fact Andy had never seen a cloud move so slowly before. Then it became curiously hard to see out through the crystal hexagons. The reason took a very long time to register, he even checked the now-fervid news shows to be absolutely certain.

For the first time in nearly five and a half centuries, snow was falling on London.

*

There was no sign now that humans had ever visited or been involved with the red dwarf star named Tunja. Joshua had moved the settled Dorado asteroids to the New Washington system along with all their industrial stations; the two Edenist habitats were to be found orbiting Jupiter. Nothing remained to tell the new inhabitants of the system's infamous history.

Quantook-LOU had spent two days recovering from the effects of the gravity he'd endured in Lalarin-MG. He remained immobile in his personal space, plugged into Anthi-CL's dataweb, supervising the initial repair work. Conflicts between the diskcity dominions had ended, from surprise rather than agreement to start with. But he had mediated a new peace with the other distributors as they all examined and shared the images which came from sensors mounted on both sides of Tojolt-HI.

The bounty they revealed was almost beyond belief. Mastrit-PJ's entire population of diskcities now orbited the tiny red star, packed together in equatorial orbit. And beyond them was a supply of raw cold matter that defied logic; a vast ring of particles over two hundred million kilometres in diameter. The Mosdva were suddenly drowning in resources.

They could leave the old worn-out diskcities, building new dominions, independent from each other. As far as the distributors could tell, every Tyrathca enclave had been emptied at the same time the diskcities were taken from Mastrit-PJ. The conflicts which had cursed the Mosdva since the dominions were established would be over for all time.

Quantook-LOU also had the data from the humans, telling him how to build their faster than light ship engines. Other distributors were already mediating for favourable alliances with Anthi-CL, wanting to share the technology. This was a new part of space, strangely empty without the nebula which had dominated half of their old orbit. Billions of stars lay open to them. It would be interesting to find the humans again, and other races of which Joshua Calvert had spoken.

*

The Ly-cilph's perception field expanded slowly outward as its active functions returned out of their dormancy within its macro-data lattice. At first it believed it had suffered memory loss. It was no longer in the jungle clearing where the human sacrifice was conducted, instead it appeared to be floating in clear space. The perception field could find nothing within range. No mass existed for a billion kilometres, not even a lone electron, which was extremely improbable. The energy waves washing through the field were of a strange composition, one it had no prior record of. An analysis of this continuum's local quantum structure revealed it was no longer in the universe of its birth.

A dense mass point emerged beside it, emitting a variety of electromagnetic wave functions. It was impervious to the Ly-cilph's probing.

'We understand you are on a voyage to comprehend the full nature of reality,' Tinkerbell said. 'So are we. Would you like to join us?'

*

Oenone's crew appeared in Harkey's Bar amid cheers and boisterous hugs, and the party looked like reaching truly epic proportions. Genevieve loved every minute of it. It was noisy, hot, and colourful; nothing like parties at Cricklade. People were nice to her, she'd managed to drink a couple of glasses of wine without Louise noticing, and cousin Gideon even partnered her on the dance floor. But nothing was funnier than watching the antics of Joshua's brother, who spent the whole time trying to avoid a very beautiful, and extremely determined, blonde lady.

Louise stuck by Joshua's side the whole time, smiling more from fright than delight as everyone crowded round him wanting to hear the tale of the naked singularity from his own mouth. Eventually he led her through the door, swearing he'd be back in a second. They took a lift directly up to the lobby, and walked out into the parkland.

'You looked unhappy in there,' he said.

'I didn't realize you had so many friends. I never really thought about it. I only ever met you and Dahybi before.'

He led her down a path lined by orange wimwillows, towards a nearby lake.

'I never met half of them before today.'

'It's so pretty here,' Louise sighed as they reached the shore of the lake. The water-plants had balloon-like flowers that hung an inch below the surface, green fish nibbled at the tuft of stamen coming from their crowns. 'This must have been a wonderful place to grow up in.'

'It was. But don't tell Ione, all I ever wanted to do was fly away.'

'She's very beautiful.'

He held her closer. 'Not as beautiful as you.'

'Don't,' she said, troubled.

'I can kiss my fiancée if I want. Even Norfolk permits that.'

'I'm not your fiancée, Joshua. I just kept saying that because of the baby. I was ashamed. Which is so stupid. Having a baby is a wonderful thing, the best thing any two people can do. Fancy being prejudiced against it. I'll always love my home, but so much of it is wrong.'

He dropped down on one knee, and held her hand. 'Marry me.'

From the expression on her face she could have been in agony. 'That's very kind, Joshua, and if you'd asked that day you left Cricklade I'd even have eloped with you. But, really, you don't know anything about me. It wouldn't work; you're a starship captain, and unutterably famous, I'm a landowner's daughter. All we ever were was a beautiful dream I had once.'

'I know everything there is to know about you – thanks to the singularity I've lived every second of your life. And don't you ever call yourself someone else's daughter again. You're Louise Kavanagh, nothing else. I had one exciting flight, which was the result of thousands of people backing me up behind the scenes. You walked right up to Quinn Dexter and tried to stop him. It is not possible to possess more courage than that, Louise. You were astonishing. Those drunken buffoons in Harkey's Bar look up at me. I stand in awe at what you did.'

'You saw everything I did?' she enquired.

'Yes,' he said firmly. 'Including last night.'

'Oh.'

He gently pulled at her hand, making her kneel beside him. 'I don't think I could marry a saint, Louise. And you already know I've never been one.'

'Do you really want to marry me?'

'Yes.'

'But we'd never be together.'

'Starship captains are a thing of the past now, just like landowner daughters. There's so much we have to do in our lives.'

'You don't mind living on Norfolk?'

'We'll change it together, Louise. You and I.'

She kissed him, then smiled demurely. 'Do we have to go back to the party?' she murmured.

'No.'

Her smile widened, and she stood up. Joshua stayed on one knee.

'I haven't had my answer yet. And this classic routine is killing my leg muscle.'

'I was taught to always keep a man waiting,' she said imperiously. 'But your answer is yes.'

*

'Anastasia, is that really you?'

'Hello, Dariat, of course it's me. I waited for you. I knew you'd come eventually.'

'I very nearly didn't. There was a spot of trouble back there.'

'Lady Chi-ri has always smiled upon you, Dariat. Right from the start.'

'You know, this isn't what I expected to find on the other side of the beyond.'

'I know. Isn't it wonderful?'

'Can we see it together?'

'I'd like that.'

*

It was the last time Joshua would use the ability, and strictly speaking it wasn't necessary, but there was absolutely no way he was going to miss out on seeing the Kiint home system in person just for the sake of virtue and dignified restraint. He materialized on the white-sand beach not far from Tracy's chalet. The coast was exquisite, of course. Then he looked up. Silvery planet crescents curved away through the deep-turquoise sky.

'Now I've seen it all,' he said quietly.

Five white spheres erupted in the air around him. The same size as providers, but with a very different function.

Joshua held his arms up. 'I am unarmed. Take me to your leader.'

The spheres winked out of existence. Joshua laughed.

Jay and Haile were racing over the sands to him.

'Joshua!'

He managed to catch her as she jumped at him. Swung her round full circle.

'Joshua!' she shrieked happily. 'What are you doing here?'

'Come to take you home.'

'Really?' Her eyes were rounded with optimism. 'Back to the Confederation?'

'Yep, go pack your bags.'

Greetings, Joshua Calvert. This day is filled with much joyfulness. I am much content.

'Hi, Haile. You've grown.'

And you have strengthened.

He put Jay down. 'Well, what do you know, there's hope for all of us.'

'It's been fab here,' Jay said. 'The providers give you everything you want, and that includes ice cream. You don't need money.'

Two adult Kiint appeared on the black teleport circle. Tracy was coming down the steps from her chalet. Joshua eyed them all cautiously.

'And I've been to loads of planets in the arc. And met hundreds

1225

and hundreds of people.' Jay paused, sucking on her lower lip. 'Is Mummy all right?'

'Uh, yeah. This is the hard part, Jay. She's going to need a day or two before she can see you. OK? So I'm going to take you back to Tranquillity, and then you can go back to Lalonde with all the others in a little while.'

She pouted. 'And Father Horst?'

'And Father Horst,' he promised.

'Right. And you're sure Mummy's fine?'

'She is. She's really looking forward to seeing you, too.'

Tracy stood behind Jay, and patted her on the head. 'I've told you to wear a hat when you play out here.'

'Yes, Tracy.' The little girl pulled a face at Joshua.

He grinned back. 'You go and pack. I just need to talk to Tracy for a moment. Then we'll be off.'

'Come on, Haile.' Jay grabbed one of the Kiint's tractamorphic limbs, and they hurried off towards the chalet.

Joshua's grin faded when the youngsters were out of hearing. 'Thanks for nothing,' he said to Tracy.

'We did what we could,' she said fiercely. 'Don't you judge us, Joshua Calvert.'

'The Corpus judges us, decides our fate.'

'None of us asked to be born. We're more sinned against than sinners. And Richard Keaton saved your arse, as I recall.'

'So he did.'

'We would have made sure something survived. Humanity would have carried on.'

'But in whose image?'

'You're proud of your current one, are you?'

'As a matter of fact, yes.'

She rubbed a white hand over her forehead. 'I keep running comparisons. What the human race is compared to so many others.'

'Well, don't, it's not your concern any more. We can find our own way now.' He turned to the adult Kiint. Hello, Nang, Lieria.

Greetings, Joshua Calvert. And congratulations.

Thank you. Though this isn't quite how I thought I'd spend my wedding night. I'd like Corpus to remove your observers, and the data acquisition systems from the Confederation, please. Our future contact should be conducted on a more honest basis.

Corpus agrees. They will be removed.

And the medical help. We need that badly, right away.

Of course. It will be provided.

You could have helped us before.

Every race has the right, and obligation, to control its own destiny. The two cannot be separated.

I know, reap what you sow. We might be too aggressive, and not progress as fast as we ought, but I want Corpus to know I am immensely proud of our compassion. No matter how fabulous your technology is, what counts is how it's used.

We acknowledge your criticism. It is one that is levelled at us constantly. Given our position it is inevitable.

He sighed and looked up at the arc again. We'll get here eventually.

Of that we are sure. After all, you have already made a start.

Imitation is the sincerest form of flattery, Joshua said. So I guess that means you're not all bad after all.

Jay appeared on the chalet veranda carrying a bulging shoulder bag. She shouted and waved, then charged down the steps.

'Is her mother all right?' Tracy asked urgently.

'She's treatable,' Joshua said. 'That's all I can say. I've stopped intervening now. It's just too damn tempting. Not that the singularity would permit much more.'

'It doesn't need any more. Corpus analysed what you've done. You made some smart moves. The current economic structure won't survive.'

'I provided the opportunity for change, plus one small active measure. What happens after . . . well, let's just say, I have faith.'

*

Jed and Beth stayed with Marie in the hospital waiting room. Beth wasn't exactly overjoyed about that, she would have loved to see Tranquillity's park. But Gari, Navar, and Webster were settled in the paediatric wing, which wasn't far away. She didn't know what was going to happen to any of them next, but then right now that applied to a lot of the human race. There were worse places to be cast ashore.

The doctor who'd met the bus came out of the emergency treatment centre. 'Marie?'

'Yes?' She looked up at him, bright with hope.

'I'm terribly sorry, there was nothing we could do.'

Marie's mouth parted silently, she covered her face with her hands and started sobbing.

'What happened to him?' Beth said.

'There was some kind of nanonic filament web in his brain,' the doctor said. 'Its molecular structure had broken down. Disintegration caused a massive amount of damage. In fact, I really don't understand how he could have survived at all. You said he's been with you for weeks?'

'Yes.'

'Ah well, we'll do a post-mortem, of course. But I doubt we'll learn much. I think it's a symptom of the times.'

'Thanks.'

The doctor smiled briskly. 'The counsellor will be along in a moment. Marie will have the best help possible to overcome this. Don't you worry.'

'Great.' She saw the way Jed was looking at Marie, as though he wanted to be crying with her, or for her, sparing her the burden.

'Jed, we're done here,' Beth said.

'What do you mean?' he asked in puzzlement.

'It's over. Are you coming?'

He looked from her to Marie. 'But we can't leave her.'

'Why, Jed? What is she to us?'

'She was Kiera, she was everything we dreamed of, Beth, a new start, somewhere decent.'

'This is Marie Skibbow, and she'll hate Kiera for the rest of her life.'

'We can't give up now. The three of us can start Deadnight again, for real this time. There were thousands of people just like us who wanted what she promised. They'll come again.'

'Right.' Beth turned and marched out of the waiting room, paying no heed to his braying calls behind her. She hurried for the lift, her heart lifting at the prospect of finally seeing the lush parkland with its sparkling circumfluous sea.

I'm young, I'm free, I'm in Tranquillity, and I'm definitely not going back to bloody Koblat.

It was a great beginning.

*

1228

The Assembly Chamber was deathly silent as the vote was taken. The ambassadors on the floor were first to register.

From his seat at the Polity Council table, Samual Aleksandrovich watched the tally rise. There were several abstentions, of course, and the names were no surprise to him: Kulu, Oshanko, New Washington, Mazaliv, several of their close allies. No more than twenty, though, which made the First Admiral smile contentedly. In diplomatic terms that was as good as a censure motion in itself, a sharp warning to the larger powers.

The ambassadors of the Polity Council entered their vote. Samual Aleksandrovich was last, pressing the button in front of him, and seeing the last digit click over on the big board. Ridiculous anachronism, he thought, though certainly dramatic enough.

The Assembly speaker got to his feet, and gave the President a nervous little bow. Olton Haaker stared straight ahead, not meeting anyone's gaze.

'The motion that this house has no confidence in the President is carried by seven hundred and ninety-eight votes, with none against.'

*

Durringham had never recovered from the devastation wrought by Chas Paske. It was the docks and warehouse sector which had borne the brunt of the water's impact. Not that they'd stopped the onrush. Debris from their disintegrating frames had formed a black speckle crest on the wave as it surged on into the town's main commercial district. The wooden buildings with their minimal foundations had crumpled instantly. Three dumpers had been knocked over and pushed along.

A kilometre inland, the resistance offered by energistically reinforced walls managed to protect the buildings, though the mud on which they lay was siphoned away, dragging them back towards the Juliffe as the waters retreated. When they'd drained away, Durringham was left with a broad semicircle of destruction eating right into the heart of the town, a swamp with a million filthy splinters sticking upwards. Bodies lay among them, caked in drying mud, and slowly decomposing in the dreadful humidity. Despite this, Durringham continued to function as an urban centre all the time Lalonde was hidden away in a realm outside the universe. Like Norfolk, its essentially low-tech nature allowed its inhabitants to carry on along virtually the same lines as before. Boats continued to sail up and down the Juliffe, crops were sown and harvested, timber cut and sawn.

Now it was back in the universe. The humidity and daily rains returned with a vengeance. And with the thick carpet of weeds chopped away from the metal grid runway, spaceplanes were arriving once again. They were complemented by Kiint craft, small blunt ovoids that flew up and down the Juliffe and its myriad tributaries collecting people from the villages and delivering them to Durringham. Over two thousand of them were performing ambulance duties, racing round at hypersonic velocity, scanning the jungle for any remaining humans.

The Kiint had set up seven fat thirty-storey towers on the edge of the city. They'd been extruded in one go from a provider, coming fully fitted with all the medical equipment necessary to treat dangerously ill humans.

Ruth Hilton was picked up on the third day after the Return, as people were calling it. When the flyer landed in front of her, its controlling AI asking her to come inside, she seriously contemplated not bothering. The memories of possession acted like damping rods on her psyche. She certainly hadn't eaten anything since the Return.

In the end it was her hope for Jay which made her climb in. For the last few weeks, her possessor had been soaking up aspects of her personality. She'd travelled between villages, asking for news of Jay and any of the other Aberdale children who might have survived that fateful night. Nobody had heard much from that district after the bomb went off somewhere on the savannah.

For two days she lay in the hospital while the Kiint examined her and made her eat. The big xenocs smeared a bluish jelly on the areas of her skin around her cancers, which sank into her flesh as if she'd suddenly become porous. They told her it would flush her tumour cells away, a less invasive technique than human medical packages. One and a half days peeing a very strange fluid.

By the end of the second day she was fit enough to walk around the ward. Like a lot of her fellow patients, she sat in front of the big picture window overlooking Durringham, saying very little. Civil engineering crews were arriving hourly, fat bright-yellow jeeps crawling down the muddy streets. Programmable silicon buildings were mushrooming in the ruined semicircle of mud. Power cables were strung up; once again electric lights began to shine in several districts during the night.

As far as she was concerned it was wasted effort. There were too many memories, too many dead children out in the jungle. This could never be her home again, not any more. She kept asking the Kiint and the hospital AI if anyone had found Jay. Always the same answer.

Then on the sixth day, Horst and Jay walked into the ward, happy and healthy. She clutched Jay to her, not letting her daughter say anything for a long time while she reaffirmed her will to live by the contact.

Horst pulled a couple of chairs over, and the three of them stared down at the city with its industrious invaders.

'This is going to be a very busy place for the next century,' Horst said, his voice a mixture of surprise and admiration. 'Do you remember our first night? The old transient dormitory's gone now, but I think that's the harbour where it was.' He pointed vaguely. The circular basins of polyp had survived.

'Will they rebuild them?' Jay asked. She thought all the activity was tremendously exciting.

'I doubt it,' Horst said. 'The people who'll be emigrating here from now on will be wanting five-star hotels.'

Ruth raised her gaze to look across the sky. The morning rain-clouds had just departed eastwards, heading inland to soak the villages upriver. They'd left a patch of pristine sky above the town and its boundary of gently steaming jungle. Five brilliant stars shone through the glaring azure atmosphere, the closest one showing a definite crescent. She thought one of them might be Earth itself, though she didn't know which one.

There were forty-seven terracompatible planets sharing its orbit now. All of them stage one colony worlds, ready to absorb the population from the arcologies.

'Are we going back to Aberdale?' Jay asked.

'No, darling.' Ruth stroked her daughter's sun-bleached hair. 'I'm afraid we lost this world. People from Earth will come here and make it very different to what it was. They don't have the kind of past to overcome here which we do. It belongs to them now. We need to move on again.'

*

The bus rolled smoothly across the docking-ledge, and linked its airlock with the reception lounge. Athene was waiting for the pair of them. Standing proud in a silky blue ceremonial ship-tunic, the star of captaincy absent from her collar.

I came back, Sinon said. *I told you I would.*

I never doubted you. But I would have understood if you'd gone on with the crystal entity. It was a fabulous opportunity.

Others took that opportunity. It doesn't cease to exist because I refuse it.

Stubborn to the very end.

One day humans, or what we become, may make a similar journey by themselves. I would like to think I played my part in the culture which will set us upon such a road.

You are different to the Sinon who left.

I have a soul of my own now. I will not return to the multiplicity, I mean to live out my life in this form.

I'm glad you have found yourself again. I need someone around the house who can keep my appalling grandchildren in line.

He laughed, a harsh brazen clacking. *Every day, all I wished for was to return. I was afraid you didn't want me to.*

I would never think that thought. Not of you, no matter what you'd done.

I have brought someone with me who suffers far more than either of us.

So I see. She moved forward, and gave a slight bow. 'Welcome to Romulus, General Hiltch.'

It was the moment Ralph had dreaded most of all, passing over the threshold. If there was no forgiveness here he would never find any within this universe. He couldn't even bring himself to smile at the stately old woman whose face contained so much genuine concern. 'I have no army to command any more, Athene. I resigned my commission.'

'Tell me why you have come, Ralph.'

'I came out of guilt. I ordered so many Edenists to their death. The Liberation ruined what it was supposed to save. It existed for vanity and pride, not honour. And it was all my idea. I need to say I'm sorry.'

'We'd like to hear you, Ralph. Take as long as you want.'

'Will you accept me as one of you?'

She gave him a compassionate smile. 'You wish to become an Edenist?'

'Yes, though it's a selfish wish. I was told an Edenist can relieve his burden by sharing it with every other Edenist. My guilt has turned to pure grief.'

'That's not selfish, Ralph. You're offering to share yourself, to contribute.'

'Will it end? Will I be able to live with what I've done?'

'I've brought up a great many Edenist children in my house, Ralph.' She put her arm in his, and started walking him towards the exit. 'And I've never had a serpent yet.'

*

It took several weeks for all the mundane functions of government to return to normal after the Confederation was transferred out of the galaxy. People realized that their circumstances would change, in many ways quite profoundly. Religions strove to incorporate or explain away the singularity's gospel of the universe. Joshua didn't mind that; as he told Louise, conviction in one's god nearly always equated to a conviction in self. Time might well see an end to the undue influence religion had on the way people approached life. Then again, knowing the perversity of humans, maybe not.

Starflight was also altering. Travel between stars never more than half a light-year apart was incredibly quick, and cheap.

Every reporter who interviewed Joshua asked why he hadn't taken the Confederation stars back again. Quite infuriatingly, he just smiled and said he liked the view from out here.

Governments weren't so fond of it. There could never be any outward expansion again, unless new propulsion methods were developed. Funds for wormhole research were quietly increased.

There would be no more antimatter to terrorize planetary populations. The stars where the production stations orbited were all left behind in the galaxy (though Joshua had teleported their crews out). Politicians turned their eyes to the defence budget, seeing how funds could be shifted towards more voter-friendly spending sprees.

The Kiint provider technology was regarded with fascination by the general public as it worked its miracles on the Returned worlds. Everybody wanted one of those for Christmas.

Earth's population was almost schizophrenic over the new stage one planets available. On the one hand, their own climate had been reset to normal, making the arcology domes redundant. But Earth's surface would take a generation to restore. And if it was restored with forests, meadows, jungles, and prairies, there would be a Diaspora from the arcologies, which would ruin everything. However, if the population was spread around the new planets (less than a billion each), all of them would have a natural environment, allowing them to keep their present level of consumerist industrialization, and not totally screw up the atmospheres with waste heat. Assuming that many people could be moved economically – say if you used those nifty little Kiint craft, or something came out of all that new superdrive research.

Small, subtle changes were manifesting in all aspects of Confederation life. They would merge, and build on each other. And eventually, Joshua hoped, transformation would become irresistible.

But in the meantime, the methods of governance remained the same. Income had to be earned. Taxes still had to be paid. And laws had to be enforced. Backlogs of court cases worked through.

Traslov was one world where changes would be a long time coming. A terracompatible planet in the last stages of an ice age, it was one of five Confederation penal colonies. Joshua had included them, too. Much to the relief of various governments, Avon included. Traslov was where the criminals which the Confederation Navy brought in were sent.

Prison ship flights resumed after three weeks.

André Duchamp was led into the drop capsule by one of the guards, who fastened him in one of the eight acceleration couches. Once the straps were in place, holding André's arms and legs against the thin padding, his restraint collar was taken off.

'Behave yourself,' the guard said curtly, and air-swam out through the hatch to fetch the next prisoner.

With supreme self-control, André sat quiet. His flesh was still slightly tender where the medical nanonics had been removed. And he was sure those bastard *anglo* quack doctors hadn't fully cured his intestinal tract; he kept getting raging indigestion after meals. If you could call what he'd been fed, meals. But his indigestion was nothing to the suffering inflicted by the awesome injustice brought down upon his poor head. The navy blamed him for the antimatter attack against Trafalgar. Him! An innocent, persecuted blackmail victim. It was diabolical.

'Hello, there.'

André glared at the badly overweight, balding, middle-aged man in the couch next to him.

'Guess we ought to introduce ourselves, seeing as how we're going to spend the rest of our lives together. I'm Mixi Penrice, and this is my wife, Imelda.'

André's face cracked in mortification as a timid woman, also fat and middle aged, waved at him hopefully from the couch beside her husband.

'So pleased to meet you,' she said.

'Guard!' André yelled frantically. '*Guard!*'

There was never any contact between the Confederation at large and Traslov, in that every flight was strictly one way: down. The theory was simple enough. Prisoners, voluntarily accompanied by their family, were shot down into the equatorial band of continent not covered by glaciers. Sociologists, hired by participating governments to reassure civil rights organizations, claimed that if enough people were brought together then they'd inevitably form a stable community. After a hundred years, or a million people, whichever came first, the flights would be stopped. The communities would expand in the wake of the retreating glaciers. And in another hundred years a self-sustaining agrarian civilization would emerge, with a modest industrial capacity. At which point they'd be allowed to join the Confederation and develop like a normal colony. As yet, no one had ever found out if an ex-penal colony would want to join a society which had exiled every one of their ancestors.

André's drop capsule fired down through the atmosphere, hitting seven gees at the top of its deceleration peak. It plummeted through the low cloud layer, and deployed its parachute five hundred metres from the ground. Two metres from the ground, retrorockets fired in a half-second burst, killing the capsule's final velocity as the chute jettisoned.

The capsule crashed into the scorched earth with a bone-numbing impact. André gasped in shock at the pain transmitted along his spine. Even so, he was the first to recover, and flipped his strap catches open. The hatch was a crude affair, like everything else in the capsule. A wonder they ever got down alive. He pulled the release handle.

They'd landed in a broad valley with gently sloping sides, and a fast stone-bed stream running along the bottom. The local grass-analogue was an insipid grey-green, its monotony broken by a few wizened dwarf bushes. A cold wind blew against the capsule, carrying tiny grains of white ice. André shivered violently, the chill factor took it well below freezing. He had thought to simply collect his share of the survival equipment from the baggage lockers ringing the base of the capsule, and hike away from his fellow exiles. That action would have to be reconsidered now.

When he looked along the other end of the valley, he was amazed to see the distinct globular shape of starship life-support capsules embedded in the soil. He could see at least forty of them. A definitive count would have shown André that a total of sixteen starships had been involved in the incident which had seen them cast away here.

A lone figure was striding vigorously over the frozen ground towards the drop capsule. A young man in a black fur coat, with a crossbow slung over his shoulder. He stopped just below the hatch and put his hands on his hips to grin up at André.

'And a very good morning to you, sir; Charles Montgomery David Filton-Asquith at your service,' he said. 'Welcome to Happy Valley.'

*

The bath water was imbued with the scent of tangerines; bubbles covered its surface to a thickness of ten centimetres. Ione sank into the blood-warm water with a contented moan, sliding down the marble until only her head was visible.

Ooh, that feels good.

You should relax more, Tranquillity said. I am capable of supervising most activities.

I know, but everyone wants the personal touch; I'm starting to feel like a nursemaid rather than a dictator. And I still haven't decided what to do about the Laymil Project centre.

Most of its staff are on sabbatical from their university. Downsizing will be a simple matter.

Yes. But I feel we should make more use of its resources, turn it to something new. After all, you and I are technically out of a job these days.

A curious viewpoint.

Face it, we've got to find something else to do. I really don't want to stay here. She allowed the images from the shell's external sensitive cells shimmer up into her mind. Jupiter orbit was alive with starship flights, both Adamist and voidhawk. Two large industrial stations specializing in organic synthesis were being manoeuvred over to Aethra, where they could start repairing the damage to the young habitat's shell. Joshua had transferred all forty-odd young habitats from the stage one systems into orbit above the glorious orange gas giant.

This star system is going to be the heart of the revolution, Tranquillity said.

All the more reason we should go somewhere else. What's our status right now? Her consciousness drifted through the habitat, perceiving the state of the induction cables, the parkland, the light-tube, the vast ring of energy patterning cells. Fusion generators out on the docking-ledge were still supplying seventy per cent of Tranquillity's power. How do you feel about making another jump?

Where to? Tranquillity asked.

I think it's time you and I went home.

Home?

Kulu.

Is this some obscure bid to succeed the throne? Your Royal cousins will have a collective heart attack.

But they can hardly refuse me, not after our contribution to the Liberation. Technically, we are a Dukedom of the Kulu Kingdom. And there's a lot of He$_3$ mining activity around Tarron, I'm sure the cloudscoop crews would prefer to be billeted here. And we are an extremely valuable economic asset to any star system.

Why?

Carrying the revolution forwards. We are bitek, they are one of the most anti-bitek cultures in the Confederation. Yet they employed bitek at the first sign of trouble. That's a chink, one we can prise open with our presence. This ridiculous technological segregation has to stop. It helps no one. This is the chance for that new beginning I spoke of. Another little change to add to the momentum for overall cultural reform.

It will not be easy.

I know that. But you have to admit, it's been awfully quiet around here since Joshua left.

I still find that hardest to believe. Handing over the *Lady Macbeth* to his brother and giving up flying. Will he be happy living on Norfolk? It's very peaceful there.

Ione laughed, and reached for a cut-crystal glass of Norfolk Tears. She eyed the fabulous drink as if it was the last drop left in the universe. I think it's about to become a whole lot noisier.

*

Syrinx and Ruben stood patiently in the hospital waiting room as the psychology team assembled. Some of them she knew from her own therapy sessions, and exchanged warm greetings.

This is exciting, *Oenone* said. The last act we will perform in this saga.

You just want to go fly, she teased.

Of course. With the Confederation stars so close, there will be many more flights now.

I wonder what sort of flights, though. Now we've glimpsed Kiint technology, I doubt He_3 fusion will last much longer. Perhaps we'll go into the pleasure cruise business.

I will still love you.

She laughed. And I you, my love. Her hand closed a little tighter around Ruben's. I think I might start having children now. We've faced the worst danger there is, flown to the other side of the nebula, and now life is changing. I want to be a part of it, to embrace what's happening in the most human way possible.

I like you being truly happy. You are complete.

Only when we're together.

The chief psychologist beckoned. We're ready for you.

Syrinx walked over to the zero-tau pod in the middle of the room, standing by its head. The black field vanished, and the lid swung open. She smiled down. 'Hello, Erick.'

*

It only took a day for the Kiint to cure Grant of his tumours. He submitted to the treatment of blue jelly with passive grace, meekly doing all that was requested of him. The massive xenocs were so *overwhelming*. Any sort of protest seemed appallingly churlish. They were only here to help, coming to Norfolk's aid out of the kindness of their mighty hearts.

An enormous hospital had been built just outside Colsterworth.

In less than an hour, according to those who saw it extruded. Little flying craft zipped across the wolds, stopping next to anyone they found and asking politely if they needed assistance, then conveying them back to the hospital for the ubiquitous treatment. Apparently Colsterworth's hospital was the one dealing with all the cases on this half of Kesteven Island. Another had been built at Boston to handle the city's casualties.

Grant returned to Cricklade once his tumours had been flushed away, wandering round the big manor in a daze. The staff trickled back as they were discharged by the Kiint, looking to him to tell them what to do. That part of his reclaimed existence was easy, he knew exactly what they were supposed to be doing.

It was the reason for them doing it which had left him. He'd got his body back, not his life.

Marjorie returned on the second day, and they clung to each other in miserable desperation. There was still no sign of the girls.

Flying craft started to deliver the men from the militia who had remained in Boston after their possession, dropping down out of the sky at individual cottages and farmhouses. The weeping and fragile laughter which came from each reunion was everywhere Grant went.

He and Marjorie drove back to Colsterworth to ask if the Kiint had found the girls. The computer at the hospital said no, but that they were still cataloguing Norfolk's surviving residents. Tens of thousands were being added every hour, it told him, he would be notified immediately (the Kiint had already repaired the entire planet's telephone network). When he asked for a flying craft to take him to Norwich the computer apologized, saying they couldn't accommodate private flights, all the craft were needed for patients.

They went back to the farm rover, debating what to do next. A Kiint was walking sedately down the broad cobbled street outside, crazily incongruous amid the stone-walled cottages with their slate roofs and climbing roses. A gang of laughing children were running round it, totally unafraid. It kept holding thin tentacles of tracta-morphic flesh just above their heads, flicking them away when the children jumped to catch one. Playing with them.

'It's over, isn't it?' Grant said. 'We can't go back to how it was, not now.'

'That's not like you,' Marjorie said. 'The man I married would never allow our way of life to be cast aside.'

'The man you married hadn't been possessed. Damn that Luca to hell.'

'They'll always be with us, just as we were always with them.'

Provider globes were drifting round the manor, ejecting replacements for items which had never been repaired or replaced. The staff followed them, fitting lengths of guttering, hammering new trellis sections onto the walls, mending fence posts, plumbing in sections of central-heating pipe. Grant felt like shouting at the globes to go away, but Cricklade needed fixing up, for all Luca's attention its overall maintenance had been pretty shabby during the possession. And providers were doing the same thing for every household in Stoke County. People were entitled to some charity and good fortune after what they'd been through.

He examined that thought, wondering who it had come from. Was it too kind for Grant, not liberal enough for Luca? In the end it didn't matter, because it was right.

When he walked into the courtyard, another provider was repairing the burnt-out stable all by itself. Its purple surface flowed through buckled soot-clad walls and blackened timbers, leaving a broad line of clean straight stone and tiled roof in its wake. The process was like a brush painting detail over a preliminary sketch.

'Now that's what I call a corrupting influence,' Carmitha said. 'No one's going to forget just how green the grass is on the other side of the technological divide. Did you know they can make food as well?'

'No,' Grant said.

'I've been working my way down an impressive little menu. Very tasty. You should try it.'

'Why are you still here?'

'Are you asking me to leave?'

'No. Of course not.'

'They'll come back, Grant. You might have loosened up, but you still don't give your own daughters the credit they deserve.'

He shook his head and walked away.

Lady Macbeth's brand new ion-field flyer landed on the greensward in front of the manor the next day. Its bubble of golden haze evaporated and the hatch opened. Genevieve ran down the airstairs as they slid out, jumping the last couple of feet to the ground.

Grant and Marjorie were already coming down the portico's broad stone steps to find out what the flyer was doing. The both froze when they saw the familiar little figure emerge. Then Genevieve streaked over and cannoned into her mother so hard she nearly knocked both of them over.

Marjorie wouldn't let go of her daughter. She had trouble speaking, her throat was so choked up with crying. 'Did . . . did it happen to you?' she asked in trepidation.

'Oh, no,' Genevieve said breezily. 'Louise got us off the planet. I've been to Mars, and Earth, and Tranquillity. I was scared a lot, but it was really exciting.'

Louise put her arms around both her parents, and kissed them.

'You're all right,' Grant said.

'Yes, Daddy, I'm just fine.'

He stepped back to look at her, so wonderfully self-confident and poised in her smart-cut travel suit with a skirt that finished well above her knees. This little Louise would never meekly do as she was told, no matter how much he shouted.

Bloody good thing too, as Luca might have said.

Louise gave both her parents an impish grin, and took a deep breath. Genevieve started giggling wildly.

'I'm sure you both remember my husband,' Louise said in a rush.

Grant stared at Joshua with complete disbelief.

'I was bridesmaid!' Genevieve shouted.

Joshua put his hand out.

'Daddy,' Louise scolded firmly.

Grant did as he was told, and shook Joshua's hand.

'You're married?' Marjorie said faintly.

'Yes.' Joshua gave her a level stare, and planted a small kiss on her cheek. 'Two days ago.'

Louise held up her hand, showing off the ring.

'Oh, look,' Genevieve said, 'our stuff. I've got so much to show you.' Beaulieu, Liol, and Dahybi were struggling down the flyer's airstairs, laden with cases and department store boxes. Genevieve gallivanted back to help them, her duster bracelet spilling a shiny cometary tail through the air behind her.

'Bloody hell,' Grant murmured. He smiled, knowing resistance was useless, and being rather glad of it, too. 'Ah well, congratulations, my boy. Make damn sure you look after my daughter properly, she means everything to us.'

'Thank you, sir,' Joshua grinned his grin. 'I'll do my best.'

*

Space was different now. A hint at what was to befall in a few billion years.

Galactic superclusters no longer expanded away from each other, they were returning, drifting back to their place of origin. The quantum structure of space-time altered as the dimensional realms began to press in, flowing back towards the centre of the universe.

The wormhole terminus opened, and Quinn Dexter emerged to look out upon the multitude of forces gathering at end of time. His body dissolved painlessly, freeing his possessors. They fled away from him, free to move as they chose amid the dense energy strands flooding the cosmos. Life pervaded space all around them, the ether ringing with the song of mind. Liberated, they joined the throng, sailing in towards the omega point.

Quinn watched galaxies being torn apart a million light-years ahead of him, their arms streaming out behind the core as they accelerated into the irresistible black mass. Star clusters flared white then purple as they sank below the event horizon, vanishing for ever into this universe's final Night.

His serpent beast howled for joy as he saw his Lord's expansion into the dying universe, absorbing every atom, every thought. Triumphant at the very end, the Light Bringer was growing at the heart of darkness, ensuring all which was to follow would be different to everything that had gone before.

Epilogue

Jay Hilton

Gatekeeper's Cottage

Cricklade Estate

Stoke County

Kesteven Island

Norfolk

My Dearest Haile,

Mother is making me write this with a pen, which is a real bore. She says I have to practise my formal writing skills. As soon as I get neural nanonics I'm never going to touch a pen again.

I hope you're well. Don't forget to thank Richard Keaton for bringing you this letter.

The cottage we're renting is really pretty, far better than anything I ever saw on Lalonde. It's got thick stone walls and a thatched roof, and there's a real fireplace that burns logs. The snow is up to the ground-floor windows. It's great stuff, you'd love it. Snowmen are much more fun than sandcastles. I can't get out much, but that's OK.

There's lots of interactives to play with, and Genevieve is teaching me how to ski. We're good friends now.

We all stayed up last night to see New California appear.

It was due a couple of hours after Duke set, and happened really quickly. It's very bright in the sky, and you can just see it during Duchess-night if you know where to look. That makes five stars visible now. Can you believe that in another fifteen years I'll be able to see all the stars of the Confederation cluster? Isn't that just fab?

Mother is working at the school in Colsterworth, introducing didactic memories. Kesteven council voted to allow them. Joshua Calvert proposed it. He was elected to the council two months ago, and is already the deputy chairman. People here are really proud that he has chosen to come and live at Cricklade when he could have gone anywhere in the Confederation. He has lots of plans for things he wants to see happen, which the council are drawing up. Everyone's really excited about them. Marjorie Kavanagh says it won't last, and he'll be lynched before spring.

Louise had their baby last month. It was a boy, and they're calling him Fletcher. Father Horst is rushing round to get the family chapel ready for the christening.

I hope you'll visit soon (hint!). Genevieve says the butterflies here are quite wonderful in the summer.

Love and hugs,

Jay

Timeline

Power Corporation) begins mining Jupiter's atmosphere for He₃ using aerostat factories.

2064   Islamic secular unification.

2067   Fusion stations begin to use He₃ as fuel.

2069   Affinity bond gene spliced into human DNA.

2075   JSKP germinates Eden, a bitek habitat in orbit around Jupiter, with UN Protectorate status.

2077   New Kong asteroid begins FTL stardrive research project.

2085   Eden opened for habitation.

2086   Habitat Pallas germinated in Jupiter orbit.

2090   Wing-Tsit Chong dies, and transfers memories to Eden's neural strata. Start of Edenist culture. Eden and Pallas declare independence from UN. Launch buyout of JSKP shares. Pope Eleanor excommunicates all Christians with affinity gene. Exodus of affinity capable humans to Eden. Effective end of bitek industry on Earth.

2091   Lunar referendum to terraform Mars.

2094   Edenists begin exowomb breeding programme coupled with extensive geneering improvement to embryos, tripling their population over a decade.

2103   Earth's national governments consolidate into Govcentral.

2103   Thoth base established on Mars.

2107   Govcentral jurisdiction extended to cover O'Neill Halo.

2115   First instantaneous translation by New Kong spaceship, Earth to Mars.

2118   Mission to Proxima Centauri.

2123   Terracompatible planet found at Ross 154.

2125   Ross 154 planet named Felicity, first multiethnic colonists arrive.

2125–2130   Four new terracompatible planets discovered. Multiethnic colonies founded.

2131   Edenists germinate Perseus in orbit around Ross 154 gas giant, begin He₃ mining.

2131–2205   One hundred and thirty terracompatible planets discovered. Massive starship building programme initiated in O'Neill Halo. Govcentral begins large-scale enforced outshipment of surplus population, rising to two million a week in 2160: Great Dispersal. Civil conflict on some early multiethnic colonies. Individual Govcentral states sponsor ethnic-streaming colonies. Edenists expand their He₃ mining enterprise to every inhabited star system with a gas giant.

2139   Asteroid Braun impacts on Mars.

2180   First orbital tower built on Earth.

2205   Antimatter production station built in orbit around sun by Govcentral in an attempt to break the Edenist energy monopoly.

2208   First antimatter drive starships operational.

2210   Richard Saldana transports all of New Kong's industrial facilities from the O'Neill Halo to an asteroid orbiting Kulu. He claims independence for the Kulu star system, founds Christian-only colony, and begins to mine He₃ from the system's gas giant.

2218   First voidhawk gestated, a bitek starship designed by Edenists.

2225   Establishment of a hundred voidhawk families. Habitats Romulus and Remus germinated in Saturn orbit to serve as voidhawk bases.

2232   Conflict at Jupiter's trailing Trojan asteroid cluster between belt alliance ships and an O'Neill Halo company hydrocarbon refinery. Antimatter used as a weapon; twenty-seven thousand people killed.

2238	Treaty of Deimos outlaws production and use of antimatter in the Sol system: signed by Govcentral, Lunar nation, asteroid alliance, and Edenists. Antimatter stations abandoned and dismantled.
2240	Coronation of Gerrald Saldana as King of Kulu. Foundation of Saldana dynasty.
2267–2270	Eight separate skirmishes involving use of antimatter among colony worlds. Thirteen million killed.
2271	Avon summit between all planetary leaders. Treaty of Avon, banning the manufacture and use of antimatter throughout inhabited space. Formation of Human Confederation to police agreement. Construction of Confederation Navy begins.
2300	Confederation expanded to include Edenists.
2301	First Contact. Jiciro race discovered, a pre-technology civilization. System quarantined by Confederation to avoid cultural contamination.
2310	First ice asteroid impact on Mars.
2330	First blackhawks gestated at Valisk, independent habitat.
2350	War between Novska and Hilversum. Novska bombed with antimatter. Confederation Navy prevents retaliatory strike against Hilversum.
2356	Kiint homeworld discovered.
2357	Kiint join Confederation as 'observers'.
2360	A voidhawk scout discovers Atlantis.
2371	Edenists colonize Atlantis.
2395	Tyrathca colony world discovered.
2402	Tyrathca join Confederation.
2420	Kulu scoutship discovers Ruin Ring.
2428	Bitek habitat Tranquillity germinated by Crown Prince Michael Saldana, orbiting above Ruin Ring.

2432 Prince Michael's son, Maurice, geneered with affinity. Kulu abdication crisis. Coronation of Lukas Saldana. Prince Michael exiled.

2550 Mars declared habitable by Terraforming office.

2580 Dorado asteroids discovered around Tunja, claimed by both Garissa and Omuta.

2581 Omutan mercenary fleet drops twelve antimatter planet-busters on Garissa, planet rendered uninhabitable. Confederation imposes thirty-year sanction against Omuta, prohibiting any interstellar trade or transport. Blockade enforced by Confederation Navy.

2582 Colony established on Lalonde.

Cast of Characters

SHIPS

Lady Macbeth

Joshua Calvert *Captain*
Liol Calvert *Fusion specialist*
Ashly Hanson *Pilot*
Sarha Mitcham *Systems specialist*
Dahybi Yadev *Node specialist*
Beaulieu *Cosmonik*
Peter Adul *Mission specialist*
Alkad Mzu *Mission specialist*
Oski Katsura *Mission specialist*
Samuel *Edenist Intelligence agent*

Oenone

Syrinx *Captain*
Ruben *Fusion systems*
Oxley *Pilot*
Cacus *Life support*
Edwin *Toroid systems*
Serina *Toroid systems*
Tyla *Cargo officer*

Kempster Getchell *Mission specialist*
Renato Vella *Mission specialist*
Parker Higgens *Mission specialist*
Monica Foulkes *ESA agent*

Villeneuve's Revenge

André Duchamp *Captain*
Kingsley Pryor *Capone's agent*

Mindori

Rocio Condra *Hellhawk possessor*
Jed Hinton *Deadnight disciple*
Beth *Deadnight disciple*
Gerald Skibbow *Refugee*
Gari Hinton *Jed's sister*
Navar *Jed's half-sister*

Arikara

Rear-Admiral Meredith Saldana *Squadron commander*
Lieutenant Grese *Squadron Intelligence Officer*
Lieutenant Rhoecus *Voidhawk Liaison Officer*
Kroeber *Commander*

HABITATS

Tranquillity

Ione Saldana *Lord of Ruin*
Dominique Vasilkovsky *Socialite*
Father Horst Elwes *Priest, refugee*

Valisk

Dariat *Ghost*
Tolton *Street poet*

Erentz *Rubra's descendant*
Dr Patan *Physicist*

ASTEROIDS

Trafalgar

Samual Aleksandrovich *First Admiral, Confederation Navy*
Admiral Lalwani *CNIS Chief*
Admiral Motela Kolhammer *1st Fleet Commander*
Dr Gilmore *CNIS Research Division Director*
Jacqueline Couteur *Possessor*
Lieutenant Murphy Hewlett *Confederation Marine*
Captain Amr al-Sahhaf *Staff officer*

Monterey

Jezzibella *Mood Fantasy artist*
Al Capone *Possessor*
Kiera Salter *Possessor of Marie Skibbow*
Leroy Octavius *Jezzibella's manager*
Libby *Jezzibella's dermal technologist*
Avram Harwood III *Mayor of San Angeles*
Emmet Mordden *Organization lieutenant*
Silvano Richmann *Organization lieutenant*
Mickey Pileggi *Organization lieutenant*
Patricia Mangano *Organization lieutenant*
Webster Pryor *Hostage*
Luigi Balsamo *ex-Commander, Organization fleet*
Cameron Leung *Hellhawk Zahan*
Bernhard Allsop *Possessor*
Hudson Proctor *Possessor, Kiera's deputy*
Soi Yin *Hellhawk*
Etchells *Hellhawk 'Stryla'*

PLANETS

Norfolk

Luca Comar *Grant Kavanagh's possessor*
Susannah *Marjorie Kavanagh's possessor*
Carmitha *Romany*
Bruce Spanton *Marauder*
Johan *Mr Butterworth's possessor*
Marcella Rye *Colsterworth council officer*
Véronique *Olive Fenchurch's possessor*

Ombey

Ralph Hiltch *General, Liberation army*
Cathal Fitzgerald *Ralph's deputy*
Dean Folan *ESA G66 division*
Will Danza *ESA G66 division*
Kirsten Saldana *Princess of Ombey*
Diana Tiernan *Police Technology Division Chief*
Admiral Farquar *Commander, Royal Navy, Ombey*
Hugh Rosler *DataAxis reporter*
Tim Beard *Rover reporter*
Sinon *Liberation army serjeant*
Choma *Liberation army serjeant*
Elena Duncan *Liberation army mercenary*
Janne Palmer *Royal Marine*
Annette Ekelund *Possessor*
Hoi Son *Possessor, ex-guerrilla*
Devlin *Possessor*
Milne *Possessor*
Moyo *Possessor*
Stephanie Ash *Possessor*
Cochrane *Possessor*
Rana *Possessor*
Tina Sudol *Possessor*
McPhee *Possessor*
Franklin *Possessor*

Kulu

Alastair II *The King*
Simon Blake, Duke of Salion *Chairman, Security Commission*
Lord Kelman Mountjoy *Foreign Office Minister*
Lady Phillipa Oshin *Prime Minister*

Kiint Homeworld

Richard Keaton *Observer*
Tracy *Observer*
Jay Hilton *Refugee, Haile's friend*
Haile *Juvenile Kiint*
Nang *Haile's parent*
Lieria *Haile's parent*

Earth

Louise Kavanagh *Refugee*
Genevieve Kavanagh *Refugee*
Fletcher Christian *Possessor*
Quinn Dexter *Messiah of the Light Bringer*
Banneth *High Magus, Edmonton sect*
Andy Behoo *Sellrat*
Ivanov Robson *Private detective*
Brent Roi *Detective, Halo Police*
Courtney *Edmonton sect acolyte*
Billy-Joe *Edmonton sect acolyte*

OTHERS

Confederation

Olton Haaker *Assembly President*
Jeeta Anwar *Chief presidential aide*
Mae Ortlieb *Presidential science aide*

Cayeaux *Edenist Ambassador*
Sir Maurice Hall *Kulu Kingdom Ambassador*

Edenists

Wing-Tsit Chong *Edenism's Founder*
Athene *Syrinx's mother*

Mosdva

Quantook-LOU *Distributor of resources*

Tyrathca

Baulona-PWM *Breeder, electronics regulator*